AT THE FEET OF THE SUN

At the Feet of the Sun

Lays of the Hearth-Fire

Book Two

Victoria Goddard

This one is for all the fine folks on the HOTE Support Group Discord server (especially the moderators and everyone who kept me company through all those sprints writing and editing this book), for those who wrote to tell me how much The Hands of the Emperor meant to them, and for my ever-supportive family.

CONTENTS

I. The Man From the Proverb

CHAPTER ONE
THE COMET HE'EANKA

The bells of the Palace of Stars were barely audible outside its walls. Cliopher Mdang, Viceroy of Zunidh, listened to the faint, falling tones of the midnight bell until the echoes faded, then turned away from the looming bulk of stone behind him to walk through the dark, empty gardens.

His sandals crunched lightly on the gravel, echoed a moment later by the feet of his two guards and the soft thump of the butts of their spears. Ato and Pikabe both thought he should be in bed, but they had said nothing when he'd left his rooms and descended the back stairs to the outside door.

They passed by several patches of glimmering pale blossoms, sweetly fragrant in the still, warm air. It was deep into the dry season, this part of the world: someone must be watering them, for there to be so many flowers in bloom. A handful of pale green lunar moths the size of his hand dipped from blossom to blossom.

He ducked under the arch made by the lower branches and aerial roots of a cascading bearded fig. Roosting birds, disturbed by his passing, shifted and muttered to each other before settling down again. He scuffed at the dead leaves in the hollow below the branches, the earthy scent masking the earlier flowers. He breathed deeply in, out, releasing the tensions of the day. It had been a productive day, but a long one.

It was, he knew even without hearing the bells, rather too late for him to still be out here and not in his bed. He had the Council of Princes the next day, and that was always fatiguing. But he had not been able to resist the lure of the comet he'd been told was visible.

On the other side of the great fig was a little outpost of the Imperial Botanical Gardens, which mostly curved around to the south of the Palace. The gardens stepped down the ancient volcanic plug upon which the Palace was built to the River Dwahaii at its feet. In a bight of the river were well-managed floodplains and a system of dykes and pools where the collection of moisture-loving plants was kept. Cliopher kept meaning to go down and see the waterlilies again—they did not wait upon the wet season or the dry in equatorial Solaara—but somehow never found the time.

There were too many days like today, where it was only now, in the quiet midnight, that he managed to get out-of-doors at all.

He walked through the curving beds, a few lights set low down guiding his steps. He did not like to think he was so inattentive to his surroundings that he would wander unwittingly off the gravel paths, but it had to be said he had, once, stepped on a very rare orchid just about to bloom.

(The curator in chief of the Botanical Gardens had not been very impressed by his defence that there had been a spectacular meteor shower that particular occasion: the little magic lights had been placed well before his next night-time excursion, a week or so later.)

At the very edge of the cliff was planted a tui tree. It was, he believed, the only one to grow east of Nijan and west of the Isolates: their presence was a marker that Wide Sea Islanders lived or had lived in a place. The flowers were used in certain ceremonies, and cuttings had been taken from island to island all across the Wide Seas in the great voyages of settlement.

Cliopher did not pretend, even to himself, that there was any great universal symbolism in the fact that this particular tree had only started blooming in the past few years, when he had finally found his way to claiming himself and his culture even here in the Palace and bureaucracy of which he was so much a part.

The flowering was due to the fact that he had finally thought to ask an Islander botanist what she thought might be the problem. On her recommendation he had brought soil from under a thriving, blossoming grove of the trees at home, in case there was some crucial microbial lifeforms that his tree was missing. The tree had perked up noticeably within a week.

Nevertheless—it had been such a wonderful surprise, last year, to come out one evening when he was particularly missing home, and discover the first few shy blossoms. Microbiota or not, he rejoiced.

He was missing home tonight.

A tui tree starting its bloom was the signal to look out for the kula canoes coming across the Bay for the great festival of the Singing of the Waters. The story was that the trees blossomed each year when the trade winds across the Wide Seas shifted direction, to show they were waiting patiently for the *He'eanka*, the ship of Elonoa'a, to return home.

So many of his ancestors must have done the same, waiting for a wandering relative or lover or friend to return from an expedition of trade or discovery.

Cliopher had no reason to expect anyone to come. His family back home were waiting, not exactly patiently, for *his* boat to come home.

He leaned forward to breathe in the fragrance of one half-unfurled flower. The glimmering white petals seemed to chide him. He bit his lip as the rich chocolate scent made homesickness nearly overwhelm him.

He did not *expect* anyone, it was true. But like the tui trees, blooming every year regardless of who came or did not come, Cliopher was waiting for someone.

His lord and friend, the Last Emperor and Lord of Zunidh whose Viceroy he was, was away. Travelling.

Looking for an heir according to an ancient custom that had let him escape the confines of his Palace, his role and his rank and all that went with them.

Questing.

Cliopher had stayed behind, of course. (Of course.) His Radiancy had entrusted the government of the world to him. Someone had to ensure that the preparations for the transition of government to his Radiancy's successor went smoothly, and that someone was Cliopher, who had dedicated the majority of his life to the reconstruction and reformation of the government.

Like the tui tree, therefore, he waited.

He was finding it hard to be patient.

Many years ago, someone had placed a bench under the tree. Cliopher sat down on it, glancing once to see that Ato and Pikabe had settled themselves at parade rest behind him—even after several years of being guarded, he could not quite ignore them—and regarded the prospect before him with a certain degree of satisfaction.

The land fell steeply away below his feet, grey shadows with a few sparkling fireflies garlanding the rocks. At the bottom of the cliff was the run of water gardens, barely illuminated this time of night, and beyond them the thronging, busy neighbourhood of the Levels, lit with magic and torches of many colours. A few great red eyes suggested bonfires.

Bonfires always, to his eyes, meant a feast, a festival, a party.

He felt a stab of envy.

Sometimes he badly missed casual fun. He hated this life as a great lord, guarded and cosseted and kept well away from whatever drunken shenanigans were happening down there in the Levels.

Beyond the city were the inky meanders of the River Dwahaii, and beyond that the cultivated plains, and beyond that the great glimmering line of the sea.

He put his elbows on the backrest of the bench and tilted his head up to look at the sky. The young moon was already hidden behind the Palace to his rear.

The stars were not what they had been when he crossed the Wide Seas in the years after the Fall, when it was just him and his little boat in the entire compass of the horizon; nor as he had seen them on quiet nights camping out on the Outer Ring islands on holidays back home; but they were as brilliant as any others he had seen since.

Solaara was farther north than the Vangavaye-ve, a little above the equator. The northern pole star, Le'aia, was visible, a handbreadth above the horizon. A handbreadth was a ziva'a, he thought, putting out his hand for a moment to measure its altitude as he had been taught.

He glanced at Ato and Pikabe, smiling sheepishly. Ato was looking away, into the gardens behind them, but Pikabe caught his eye and smiled in return. "Do you see the comet, sir?"

It was hard to miss: four ziva'a above the horizon, a little south of east, in the heart of the square forming the body of the Fisherman. The tail pointed east and down, and the nose was into the great band of bright stars called Lulai'aviyë, the Wake.

"There, in the Fisherman," he said, pointing.

"We call that the Hunter," Pikabe said. "Different cultures, I suppose."

Cliopher chuckled. "I suppose so, yes."

"What other constellations do you have, sir?"

He looked up. There, just barely visible over the southern horizon, was Nua-Nui. "That one is the Great Bird—his beak points the way to the southern pole. Between him and the Fisherman—your Hunter—is one called the Shell."

"What kind of shell?" Ato asked.

"It's the general word for shell," Cliopher replied, his eyes catching the familiar doubled arc, though the lower half was very faint. "A common, ordinary white shell —the kind you find on the beach by the thousands. Clam-shells, usually, though it doesn't matter. Could be a cowrie."

"We call that one the Water-Witch—there's her staff," Pikabe said, pointing to another star that Cliopher's reckoning did not include in the constellation.

"We have a water-witch in our stories, too—Urumë, the Sea-Witch, we call her— but she doesn't have a constellation named after her." Cliopher found the tight ring of stars over the Emperor's Tower in the middle of the Palace. "There, that's Tisaluikaye—'the Island that Swallowed the Sea'. It's the full name for a tisalë, an atoll, you see, which is a ring of coral around a lagoon. The story goes that the first atoll was created by the Sea-Witch when she had a fight with the sea."

"The Island that Swallowed the Sea. I like it," Pikabe said, laughing.

"There's also the Island the Sea Spat Back—Moakiliye—moakili is the word for an uplifted coral island, one where an old reef, turned to stone, emerges back out of the sea from tectonic upheaval."

"It's not really called the Island the Sea Spat Back," Pikabe objected. "Not *really*."

"Moa'a is a word for the sea," Cliopher explained. "Kilito is the word for spitting back or rejecting something, and *ye* is a suffix that means island. So: Moa'akilito-ye is the original one. It's one of the Agirilis."

"We call that ring of stars the Ring," Ato said, and winked so quickly Cliopher was not sure he'd seen the gesture. Perhaps the stolid guard had just twitched...?

"We call it the Turtle," Pikabe said. "In the beginning, the old men say, Turtle dove down into the muck at the bottom of the sea and brought up mud to be made into land, and as a reward the Creator put him up in the sky as a constellation. It's always a good idea to be polite to turtles, the old men say."

"I shall bear that in mind," Cliopher promised gravely. "What do you call the River of Stars?"

The name for the wide band of stars was one of the few Shaian astronomical terms he knew. There had never been any reason, and little apparent point, in studying star lore after he left home. In Astandalas the stars were of another world, and anyhow masked by the lights and smoke of that great city, and in Solaara he had never felt the need.

As he looked at the sky the old Islander names stirred in his mind, teasing at the tip of his tongue. There was the long, undulating constellation of Au'aua, the Great Whale, her eye the brightest star in the northern sky. There was Jiano, one of the Sixteen Bright Guides, riding high above the shoulder of the Fisherman, the star for whom the current Paramount Chief of the Vangavaye-ve was named. And there, rising in the south of east (*remāraraka*, his great-uncle's voice said in his ear, *the direc-*

tion from which the long-tailed cuckoos come), Furai'fa, the ke'e of Loaloa, Cliopher's own ancestral island in the Western Ring.

"We call it the Path of Straw," Pikabe said. "The story goes that Turig, the god of beer, was cold one night so he went to the house of his brother Ardol, the god of farming, and borrowed a bundle of straw to take back to his home. But he was so drunk he spilled half the straw along the way home, and that's what we see. Ardol lives in the east and Turig in the west, because Ardol has to wake up early with his animals and that way Turig always knows to follow the Sun home. The path curves because he was so drunk."

Cliopher laughed, as did, surprisingly enough, the usually-taciturn Ato. "We call it the Path of the Cranes," Ato volunteered. "That's the way they migrate, where I'm from, way up north."

"What about your people, sir?" Pikabe asked. "Do you say the River of Stars, too?"

The Sea of Stars or Sky Ocean was the name for the sky, and though he had heard that Isolate Islanders called the Wake 'the Great Current', Cliopher's great-uncle, his teacher of the ways, had taught him Western Ring names and knowledge.

Cliopher's heart warmed at the inevitable thought of his Buru Tovo, who had gotten on the sea train at age ninety and come halfway around the world to see what people were saying about his wayward great-nephew. He smiled up at the stars.

"Our name for it is Lulai'aviyë. *Lulai* is the word for 'the light in the wake of a canoe'—there's a kind of phosphorescence that you see in the ocean at night, which glows when you disturb it—and *Aviyë* are the Ancestors, the first of the wayfinders. So it means 'the Light in the Wake of the Ancestors' Canoes.'"

He traced out the line of the Wake until it disappeared behind the dome of the Palace. It had been so long since he thought about these names, these stories. Cliopher's voice went a little quieter as he went on.

"The old name for the Wide Sea Islanders is Ke'e Lulai'aviyë, or just Ke'e Lulai. The people who live Under the Wake. Most of our islands lie under its path."

No one had used that name for the Wide Sea Islanders in centuries; he had never heard anyone at home say it besides the elders, when the *Lays* were sung. They were Islanders now, not the voyagers, the wayfinders, the great seafarers of legend. They still sailed the Wide Seas, but in Astandalan-style ships, not the great double-hulled parahë of the ancient past.

Traditional canoes, vaha, were used inside the Ring, from island to island within the Vangavaye-ve itself. Even the boat Cliopher had made according to the ancient pattern an old woman had taught him, which had taken him more or less safely across the Wide Seas, was intended for a local fishing canoe, not a deep-water oceangoing vessel. He had seen parahë in paintings and in carefully reconstructed models at the University of the Wide Seas museum, and once sunk fathoms deep off the coast of sunken Kavanor, but never under sail.

He had not been down to the Imperial Museum of Comparative Anthropology for ages, either. At one point the curator of what would *eventually* be renamed the Western Galleries had asked him for advice regarding that sunken parahë, with some vague indication there would eventually be an exhibit containing it.

At some point he should find the time to go and see what had been done.

"Do you have a story about comets, sir?" Pikabe asked.

In the east, the comet hung apparently motionless in the sky. Its wake was almost as luminescent a green as the lulai around a reef, if fainter. The Ouranatha—the priest-wizards of Solaara, who counted astronomy as one of their arts—had said that it would be visible at night for nearly a full month.

If Cliopher were home, and the tui trees had started to bloom today, the month that followed would be the time taken by the lead-up to the extravagant feasts and dances of the Singing of the Waters.

It would have been a likely occasion for the greater festival, when the full dances were performed by the lore-keepers. A year when the Wandering Star was seen? Assuredly a sign for the greater festival.

The trouble was, for the greater festival to be held, each and every lineage and their lore-keepers had to be prepared for the full dances. And the Mdangs were not.

Because the tana-tai, Cliopher's Buru Tovo, was in his nineties, and the tanà, Cliopher's Uncle Lazo, had a lame knee, and Cliopher himself, the rising tanà, was not there.

He breathed in, out, tasting the tui blossoms, the warm, still air, his eyes on the comet.

In years past he had not gone home because the most important of the annual court sessions started very soon. This year, with his Radiancy away and the court in recess, Cliopher was nevertheless obliged to be present as acting head of state.

"The soothsayers say a comet means change is coming," Ato supplied from behind him.

Cliopher was once again surprised Ato spoke. "That's obvious enough this year," he said, though not unkindly. It was the last year before the Great Jubilee of his Radiancy's reign, when he would be stepping down as Lord of Zunidh in favour of whatever successor he managed to find on his current quest.

This was something Cliopher tried very hard not to worry about. He could do nothing but wait for his Radiancy's return with his chosen successor.

Wait, and prepare Protocols for every possible eventuality he could think of.

Wait, and...work. There was always work.

Even if his *job* was to ensure that the government ran properly. And who knew what sort of experience said successor would have? His Radiancy's primary criterion concerned magic, not governance.

Pikabe chuckled. "We call them bearded stars, though one story is that they're lost cattle from Ardol's herds, which Turig let out one day and they haven't been able to capture again. Shooting stars are his chickens, coming home to roost."

"Turig sounds like a great troublemaker," Cliopher observed.

"He's the god of beer, what can you expect? We hold many festivals in his honour."

Cliopher stared at the comet. He wasn't sure if he had ever actually seen one before.

There had been great excitement about the expected appearance of one, at some point, but he seemed to recall it had been cloudy every time he'd tried to go see it. He had always wanted to see a comet: he had always loved the stories told of them in the *Lays* and by his father's mother, the great storyteller of Cliopher's family.

He couldn't tell if the picture he had in his mind was from some painting he had seen, somewhere in the Palace or some museum, or of a real event.

It was a truly beautiful evening, the air cool and for once lacking the humidity that usually plagued Solaara even in the dry season. The last few weeks before the rains came was Cliopher's favourite time of the year here, despite everything.

The comet, the Wandering Star, the He'eanka, hung in the air like something painted onto the firmament of the heavens, as the Ouranatha astronomers said. They held the stars were fixed in their circuits, not the variable Sky Ocean of Cliopher's people.

"There's a story," he said eventually, fishing out the Shaian words with some effort. "It's said that the comet, which we call the Wandering Star, He'eanka—in the story there is only one, which we see at different times and at different angles—is the ship of Elonoa'a. He was a real person, the last of the great Paramount Chiefs at the time when the Empire came to the Vangavaye-ve."

"The Seafarer King," said Pikabe.

Elonoa'a was probably the greatest of all the Islanders, and certainly the best-known. There was a famous classical play called *Aurelius Magnus and the Seafarer King*, and their adventures had been an increasingly popular subject for various more contemporary plays and novels. No doubt it was a kind of compliment to Cliopher and his Radiancy.

Not that Cliopher was all that much like Elonoa'a, the greatest navigator and explorer of his people.

The Islanders would still have been the Ke'e Lulai, then, for this period was the end of the voyages and the beginning of the settled years, when the Islanders became one people among many of the Empire of Astandalas, and by no means the greatest.

Elonoa'a was the last of the Paramount Chiefs, and the one who led the last Gathering of the Ships—a meeting that in later years was re-enacted as part of the Singing of the Waters—to decide to join in alliance with Astandalas.

"Elonoa'a became a great friend and companion of the Emperor Aurelius Magnus. After the emperor went to the House of the Sun, as we say in our stories, Elonoa'a took a parahë, a voyaging canoe, with a crew of thirty-two, and set sail to go find him."

That was what it said in the *Lays of the Wide Seas*. Astandalan histories said that Aurelius Magnus simply disappeared one day, never to be seen again, and did not mention anything further of the Wide Sea Islanders who had been his allies except in subsequent tax records.

Aurelius's brother Haultan became the next emperor of Astandalas, and brutally forced an end to the wars Aurelius Magnus had been fighting. Haultan's idea of rule afterwards had been hard for everyone, and shaped the nature of governance for the next thousand or so years, until the Empress Dangora V's reforms.

There were parts of Haultan's philosophy and practice of government that Cliopher was still fighting against, even now.

Shaian folktales said that Aurelius had been stolen away by the Sun on account of his magical prowess and physical beauty, and occasionally mentioned his great friend the Seafarer King who had been said to dance through flames.

Cliopher was a Mdang, and knew better: the Mdangs Held the Fire, and Elonoa'a had been Kindraa and therefore one who Knew the Wind. Kindraa dances were not over the burning coals, but used ribbons of plaited feathers to delineate their knowledge. It was as hard to dance properly, but not nearly as visually spectacular as the Fire Dance. Though perhaps Cliopher was a trifle biased on the subject.

"You can see the wake of his ship, the *He'eanka*, which he named after the Wandering Star," Cliopher said, indicating the comet's tail.

(And did the tui trees know, somehow, that their beloved He'eanka was close enough to see, though never close enough to touch?)

"It's said that when you can see the comet it is because Elonoa'a is searching our portion of Sky Ocean, and that wherever his ship is pointing will have good fortune come to it."

"A good story," Pikabe said approvingly. "Especially as it's pointing towards us!"

Indeed it was: the arc of the comet passed right over the Palace towards the distant southwestern point where the Vangavaye've lay in sunlight on the other side of the world.

Cliopher was glad he'd told that story. He had always been very private about his culture, after so many years unable to share it in the strict culture of the court without courting social ruin, and ... and it had been *private*. These stories were far too close to his heart to be put on vulgar display.

But oh, it hurt that he had always had to go to his rooms and read over the *Lays* by himself, when it should have been an occasion for everyone around him to sing and dance and cry forth the same songs that were echoing in his heart and mind, his blood and bones and soul.

Elonoa'a had followed Aurelius Magnus as friend and guide and counsellor.

It gave him heart that he followed in that most illustrious Islander's wake, even here in this Palace so apparently remote from anything truly Vangavayen.

It had been easier when he stood beside his own lord and emperor. Cliopher was not a chief or a paramount chief at heart: he had much preferred standing to the side to this sitting on the throne.

It was good to be reminded by the comet that when Elonoa'a had been parted from his friend he—being Kindraa and the superlative navigator—had taken his ship and called up a wind that could blow him quite out of the world and into Sky Ocean.

Cliopher could not call up such a wind. There was no parahë left in all the Wide Seas that could sail even the mortal ocean, nor thirty-two sailors who could crew it. And his Radiancy, Cliopher's Radiancy, was not lost in the House of the Sun, but questing under his own power and his heart's calling. Any rescuing he had needed from Cliopher had already been accomplished through his efforts at friendship and guidance and counsel, and the long, grinding work of bureaucracy and systemic change.

And Cliopher was not actually Elonoa'a, living in the time of legends.

Cliopher was a Mdang, and he Held the Fire. He could hold this fire he had been given to hold, tend this hearth-fire at the heart of the world, and when his lord, his emperor, his Aurelius Magnus, came home, Cliopher would be waiting for him.

He looked up again, at the comet and the Wake. Even so far from home, here on the other side of the world, he still laid his head below Lulai'aviyë.

Speaking of which—

"I suppose it's time for bed," he said, and stood up.

"Council tomorrow," Pikabe agreed, as he and Ato smartly fell into place.

Cliopher *did* take some small advantage of his rank, however, by carefully plucking a flowering branch from the tui tree to take inside with him. It was good to have a reminder of what it meant to be patient. It was not his natural state.

CHAPTER TWO
'GALAROO GOYGILLARRAH FOH'

The morning after the comet, Cliopher had an unexpected appointment requested by Aioru.

He agreed to it, of course—Aioru was formerly Cliopher's deputy Kiri's chief assistant, currently the Minister of the Public Weal, and, of those Cliopher informally considered his apprentices in the way of governance and bureaucracy, the one he planned to succeed him—but he was puzzled that Aioru had given no reason for the request.

Tully, Cliopher's appointments secretary, could give no further explanation either. "I'm sorry, sir," she said. "It didn't occur to me that *he* needed to give a reason."

"He doesn't," Cliopher assured her, frowning at the terse "S. Aioru" on his schedule. "Did he say how long he thought the meeting would be?"

"No, sir."

It was Cliopher's practice to give a quarter-hour to meetings with no explicit purpose. If someone couldn't say their piece in that time—if they couldn't state their problem, at the very least—then it was unlikely the problem was ready to be resolved, and Cliopher could do best by helping them speak out some of their concerns and suggest ways to figure out what they really wanted.

A quarter-hour usually sufficed for this, whether it was at the open courts where anyone could come petition him for something, to a meeting with one of the princes who governed the world's provinces.

Aioru knew that.

Cliopher felt, obscurely, that Aioru's request for a meeting (not, he noted, an *audience*) was something of a puzzle.

A challenge, even.

Challenge-songs were threaded through his culture. He wasn't sure about Aioru's —the younger man was from inland Jilkano, and Cliopher did not know very much about his customs bar a handful of ideas Aioru had brought forth to the great work of restructuring the government—but then, did he need to be?

There was something here. Either Aioru wanted to resign, or—

Or.

It wasn't as if Cliopher had kept it a secret that he considered Aioru a worthy potential successor.

"Clear the rest of my morning," Cliopher said to Tully, setting down the appointments calendar. The other scheduled appointments were none of them urgent, and indeed most could probably be dealt with by his underlings in the Private Offices of the Lords of State.

"There's the Ouranatha at noon," Tully pointed out. "They insisted, sir."

Cliopher carefully did not make a face. "Yes, and the Council of Princes after."

Neither of *those* could be handed off, alas.

"I'll move the rest," Tully promised him, and he left her in the reception room and made his way through the warren of rooms that comprised the suite of the Lord of Zunidh, which was somehow Cliopher's home.

House, anyway. *Home* was on the other side of the world.

Cliopher dealt with the morning's reports, and then sat at his desk in his study and cleaned out his writing case. It had been a gift from his Radiancy, and held more than it should have been able to.

His Radiancy was a great mage, and the subtle magic of space and organization—nothing near as flashy as the infamous poet Fitzroy Angursell's splendid and storied Bag of Unusual Capacity—had never failed.

Cliopher sorted through pens and brushes, inks and inkstand, rosewood-handled penknife (a gift from Ludvic) and perfectly-fitting inset folders (a gift from Rhodin). He refilled papers, envelopes, sealing wax, seals. Quills and metal nibs ... all the tools of his trade.

There was a secret compartment on the back side of the case, where he kept a handful of notes from his Radiancy. Cliopher pulled them out, a little embarrassed at keeping them—it was not as if even the most informal were truly *personal*—and was surprised for a moment when his hand touched on a book.

He drew it out, wrinkling his nose when a waft of dust made him sneeze. Not all of Fitzroy Angursell's poetry was banned—and Cliopher personally did not think any of it should be; even the most seditious was a truer commentary on the mechanisms and failures of government than practically any academic monograph—but it would not have been appropriate for *him* to display this particular book.

He flipped through the small volume, smiling at the familiar verses, the sketches of music, and imagined being no longer head of the government, and free to ... well.

He'd already long since memorized all these songs and poems. They'd been welcome companions on long nights of hard work, cordial fuel to keep the embers of reform burning through the long years of dispiritingly incremental change.

Perhaps one day he'd be free to write his own monograph explaining just how invaluable these banned poems and songs had been for his most-lauded reforms.

He slid the small volume back into place, or tried to: it caught on what turned out to be the only letter his Radiancy had so far sent after leaving on his quest.

Or at least, the only one that had so far arrived. From the witness of this letter, his

Radiancy had crossed over to Alinor, and the postal system there was nowhere near as refined or effective as the one on Zunidh.

Cliopher pulled out the letter and carefully smoothed out the rumpled pages. It was a strange letter, evidently written in haste, and though informal, almost casual, it was not ... it was still not *personal*.

My Lord Mdang, it began, and continued with an injunction to share the contents with Ludvic and Rhodin, the Commander of the Imperial Guard and deputy commander (and Imperial Spymaster), who were also two of the senior members of his Radiancy's household, and Cliopher's friends.

Cliopher had been glad to receive the letter from his Radiancy, glad at the sense of heady freedom in the swiftly written letters, the elliptical comments, the fleeting reference to a lead on a potential heir ...

That was the purpose of his Radiancy's quest, after all. And Cliopher was his Viceroy, the person he'd left in charge: he needed to know the progress of the search for an heir. So did Ludvic and Rhodin, and indeed he'd judiciously conveyed the information on to the Council of Princes and the Elders of the Ouranatha and other officials of the Service.

Cliopher had no cause to be disappointed that it was not, in fact, personal.

He put everything back into his writing kit, and turned his thoughts to what he would do if Aioru did not wish to stay on in the Service.

His glance went to the books of Protocols on one of the bookshelves. Protocols for disaster after disaster, everything Cliopher or his department had been able to think of, so that if something terrible happened there would be a ke'ea to follow.

He shook his head, smiling at himself. He'd noticed Islander words were coming more and more into his mind, even his vocabulary, as his thoughts were turning more and more towards home, towards what he would do when he was no longer Cliopher Lord Mdang, Viceroy of Zunidh and Hands of the Emperor, head of the Imperial Bureaucratic Service, acting head of state—but only everyone's Cousin Kip, the rising tanà. The one who'd left.

He would be the one who came home, eventually. He had promised them—promised himself—that.

If Aioru wanted to resign or move laterally, Cliopher would manage. His government would manage.

The government would manage. Soon enough it would not be *his*.

~

Cliopher had come back from a whirlwind visit home via a long series of legal cases requiring him to act as supreme judge, and he was tired.

The day—not even a day, a *night*—at home had been splendid. He had wanted to take the occasion of his cousin Enya's restaurant opening for a real visit, but the requirements of being Viceroy had gradually absorbed all of his planned holiday, and it had only been an accident that he'd been able to steal enough time to get to Gorjo City for a single, dreamlike night.

He was still not sure if it had been the mad exhilaration of playing truant from his responsibilities that had led him to feeling, for the first time, as if he truly belonged, as if he had been accepted, as if his rank in the wider world had *finally* translated to some form of status at home. He had even been invited to sit with the uncles.

It had been wonderful, and it was not anywhere near enough.

And he knew, for it had always been the case before, that if he'd stayed longer— even three days—the bright perfection of that one evening would have faded, would have diminished, into something full of ordinary goods and ordinary complaints, and the business of ordinary life, and ... well.

The truth was, he was almost ready for those, too. He *wanted* his mother to complain about his hair being too short and his clothes too fine; he wanted his aunts to gossip over his romantic relationships and lack thereof; he wanted to go to the pubs and cafés with his old friends; and he wanted his friends from Solaara to be there, too.

And ... and he wanted some things that were still treasonous, even now.

At any rate, there was still work to be done here.

Cliopher was tired.

And ... a day (a night) at home, an hour or two sitting with the uncles, still deferential because for all he was Viceroy of Zunidh, wearing court costume of ahalo cloth and pearls, he was, still, *always*, the one who left ...

It had not been enough.

It had been enough for him to taste what *home* could be, once he retired. Once he *stayed*.

It had been painfully difficult to return to those heartrending, terrible trials, judging the worst of crimes and wondering if the people who committed them were truly the worst of people, wishing he had the energy to come up with a better justice system and knowing he did not.

That was a bitter mouthful to swallow. Being tired had never been reason to stop before.

But he was tired. He wanted to go home.

He wanted home. And he wanted people there who were not there, who *could* not be there, and he did not know what to do.

He had been entrusted with the world, with this fire at the heart of the Palace, and so he put on the robes of judgment and listened with all the intelligence and compassion he could to the plaintiffs and defendants, and he tried, he tried. His heart was sore, and he missed his Radiancy, and he felt guilty for missing him, for his Radiancy was free from the weight he had carried for more than half his lifetime, and surely Cliopher could bear it another handful of months.

And so he did what he always did: he set himself to the task before him, and performed it to the best of his abilities.

And if part of that task were to slowly and carefully unwind his multitude of positions and responsibilities and delegate them to others—

He felt guilty for his relief. He was not doing this to make his life easier, but because it was proper, better, *right*. His goal had never been to be king of the world. He was, in the customs of his people, the tanà, who was not the chief or the paramount chief, but to whom, when he spoke, the chiefs listened. He Held the Fire: he did not run from its burn.

Part of holding the fire was teaching others to light and tend their own, and whenever he felt guilty about handing over yet another aspect of his job to someone else, he reminded himself of that. It was not about him.

It was about all those who came after him and his Radiancy, who would not hold the entire weight of the world upon their shoulders.

He still felt guilty, whenever he realized he had another quarter-hour in his day that was no longer devoted to five different tasks.

~

Aioru came in at the third bell precisely. He had dressed up, in the finest version of the Upper Secretariat uniform; the only departure was the addition of a bracelet made of woven silk and wooden beads. He looked better in the deep ochre-brown robes that Cliopher ever had.

"Good morning, sir," he said when he entered the office.

Cliopher regarded him for a long moment, noting the slight nervousness in his bearing, the cautious excitement in his dark eyes, the thick sheaf of papers in his hand. His own heart started to beat a little with anticipation. This did not seem as if Aioru were about to resign and go home.

"Good morning, Aioru," he replied, and stood up from his desk. "Come with me."

He led the younger man through the austere, elegant rooms he did not use until he landed in his private study. He had already told Franzel, his majordomo, to serve them with tea there, and the pot and cups were laid out on a table between two comfortable chairs. Aioru followed him with watchful, curious eyes.

"Sit down, please," Cliopher invited him, gesturing at the second chair as he took his own. "Have you ever had tea before?"

"No, sir."

"This type is usually taken with lemon. Some people like it with honey," he told him, gesturing at the condiments. He poured the fragrant copper-hued beverage into the cups, dropping a thin slice of lemon into his own and half a teaspoon of clear honey. Aioru watched him carefully and then—Cliopher was very pleased to see—tasted his drink before adding the lemon.

In some ways, that indication that Aioru would think things through for himself was all he needed to know. But—

He still needed to be *sure* that Aioru wanted what Cliopher thought he did.

He smiled politely at the younger man. "To what do I owe the pleasure of this meeting?"

Aioru hesitated. Cliopher made sure his posture was relaxed, affable, approachable, respectful, and waited.

He waited, at ease with himself, listening to his heart beating with steady curiosity, rising hope. Cliopher had spent a long, long time learning how to sit like this, open to whatever came to him.

Look first, listen first, his Buru Tovo had taught him. *Questions later.*

He had discovered, over his years in the Service, how powerful that simple mantra was. *Look first, listen first*. Think for yourself, see what there is to be seen, hear what people say and do not say, look at what they do and what they do not do. And then ask whatever questions are necessary.

And thus, having asked his open-ended question, Cliopher asked no further leading ones. He waited to hear what Aioru would say.

And he watched what Aioru did.

Aioru sat there, sipping his tea, betraying his nerves by his slightly-too-wide eyes and his painfully upright posture. Aioru was no aristocrat, and had grown up in a squatting culture: he was comfortable with Solaaran furniture, of course, by this point, but he had been the champion of alternative desks from his earliest days in Cliopher's offices.

That had been one of the first indications, to Cliopher, that this young man had a spark of something worth cherishing very carefully. For one thing, Aioru had been very young—if he did not mistake the matter, Aioru still held the record for the youngest successful application to the Imperial Service—and for him to have been confident enough in himself and his ideas to suggest desks that could be used standing or squatting?

Oh, Cliopher could remember the ache in own legs, the small of his back, when he had first gone to Astandalas and been confronted with sitting at a desk for all his working hours. When Cliopher was growing up, the schools at home in the Vangavaye-ve—even in Gorjo City—even at the University of the Wide Seas—had been strongly inclined towards squatting and sitting cross-legged on the floor.

He crossed his feet the other way, and Aioru took a deep breath, set down his tea cup, and said: "Lord Mdang, sir, I'd like to be considered for additional responsibilities."

Brief, polite, and to the point. Cliopher approved.

He took another sip of his own tea. Aioru was clearly tense, but also solid, settled in this decision. Now that he had made his move in this conversational game, he waited, his hands folded in his lap so they would not tremble very obviously.

Cliopher had spent a long time observing those around him, and he had watched Aioru grow into himself as he grew into an adult, and he knew the younger man's habits and tells.

Cliopher had been working to this point for more than half of his life. So had Aioru—he had been hardly sixteen when he joined the Service, and was now in his early thirties, with a lifetime ahead of him.

He savoured the moment, which hung there, as full of possibilities as that moment when you turned the sail to the wind but had not yet released the painter—and then he smiled with his full heart on Aioru, and said, "What part of my job did you want, exactly?"

Aioru blinked rapidly. His hands were tightly clenched upon each other, his knuckles nearly white. He had deep brown skin, and curly black hair he had been slowly growing out over the past year: it now stood in a three-inch cloud all around his head. "Sir," he whispered.

Cliopher could not help himself, and laughed. "Come now, Aioru! We both know you've been working towards the chancellorship for as long as it's existed as a position. If you're ready—"

"Do you think I am, sir?"

"Do *you* think you are, Aioru?"

The question hung there. Cliopher held onto the rope, waiting—

Aioru lifted his chin and met his eyes. "Yes."

—And let go.

His heart caught the wind and leapt forth, over the waves, into the open ocean. All his being seemed to say *yes*.

But he was not only the Islander who could jump into his canoe and sail across the lagoon when the mood took him. Cliopher had worked far too long and too hard to not be *sure*.

He was sure of Aioru's skill and knowledge and ability and competence. But was he *ready*?

Cliopher had spent more than three-quarters of his life studying to be tanà, and it was only in the past few months, since his Radiancy had left on his quest for an heir and Cliopher had been left holding the world on his shoulders, this fire in his hand, that he had been absolutely certain that he was ready to go home and leave all this power and glory for the quieter, less visible responsibilities awaiting him there.

Aioru was watching him attentively.

He had been impatient, when he first came to the Service. Cliopher remembered sitting down with him, talking about *looking first, listening first, questions later*.

Aioru had not learned any of Cliopher's dances, nor more than the handful of sayings from the *Lays* that Cliopher had chosen to share with his people here, but he knew almost everything else about being a tanà. Certainly more than Cliopher himself had, at thirty-two.

He'd been thirty-two when Astandalas fell. He'd thought he'd known so much, and he hadn't.

Oh, it was a long time since then, and the world had changed.

Cliopher said, "Tell me a story about why you want this position."

Aioru glanced at the sheaf of papers and then back up at him. "Sir ..." But then he frowned slightly, and his face cleared. "You already know all my ... official skills, of course."

Cliopher waited, sipping his tea, while Aioru gathered his thoughts together. He'd evidently been prepared to go through the logical arguments first—and why would he not have expected to?—and was now sorting through what story he might tell.

At last Aioru said, "There is a proverb in my tribe: *Galaroo goygillarrah foh.* Literally I'd translate it as, *The man who came looking for the sea.* Usually people would say it means something like, *Dreaming makes you foolish.*

"My tribe's territory is the very centre of the Hutabarrah, the Great Desert Basin of Jilkano. We are as far away from the sea as you can get, and traditionally there would never be any reason to go there. The closest someone might get is a medicine man on a vision quest going to the mountains that encircle the Hutabarrah. If you climbed up maybe you could see the sea, I'm not sure."

Cliopher nodded, putting this together with what he knew of Aioru. Inland, yes —and tribal, yes. Aioru had come into the Service late enough that although he'd certainly faced suspicion and condescension for his origin, he hadn't had to *hide* it.

"The phrase is used to mean someone who's an idiot, naive, a fool, doing something difficult and impossible. *Don't be a fool, don't go looking for the sea, don't be like the man who came looking for the sea.*"

Aioru paused to sip his tea. He looked seriously at Cliopher. "We had stories that long ago we'd been part of an empire—connected to the outside world—but it was really only in my father's day that we started to be part of things again. The coastal princes started to send surveyors out, looking for ores and gems and the like. At first there were not many, and they were welcomed, shown how to live in the desert.

"Then someone realized there was gold in our territory, and the Prince of Jilkano-Lozoi sent people to build a mine. They brought soldiers with them, and the things they needed for a small town, as well as caravans to travel safely across the desert. We were less happy with that, because we were not consulted, and they had built their mine close to a sacred site of ours.

"That was when I was young. There was some violence back and forth, and other forms of conflict, not too much but enough for people to get worried. Eventually it was decided that some of the tribe's children should go to the little school the miners had set up for their families, and learn Shaian so that communication would be easier. I was one of them."

Cliopher nodded in encouragement, and poured them each another cup of tea.

"I learned quickly, and soon was among the most fluent. Often I had to act as a translator, for the miners wanted to expand and the elders of my tribe did not wish them to. There came a kind of stalemate, and the miners, we learned later, sent off for assistance."

Aioru smiled at him with a sudden brightness. "You came."

"I remember," Cliopher said: the heat, the stark beauty, the wrangling between self-assured miners and the local tribe, the surprise everyone had shown when he had supported the tribe, the eventual agreement that had created a flourishing mixed community there in the desert.

"You may not remember me," Aioru said modestly, "except perhaps that there was a boy who interpreted for you. But I was that boy, and I remember you: how carefully you listened, how polite your questions were, how interested you were in what *we* had to say. I thought it was amazing.

"You were interested in *me*, too, this tribal boy learning Shaian and maths and so on in the mine school. When I asked you how you came to your position, you told me all about how you were from as far away as me, and how you'd written to the governor for the examination books, and that even though you'd failed at first you persisted until you won a place."

Cliopher had undoubtedly told that story to many young people in hinterland villages and tribes around the world. He remembered that trip, even vaguely remembered the boy, but he had never imagined it was Aioru.

"My elders knew I wasn't translating everything when I started asking you about that," Aioru said. "They made me tell them, and then they told me, Galaroo goygillarrah foh! Don't be a fool, boy! The sea is not for you."

"We call it *chasing a viau*," Cliopher murmured. "They all said that to me, too."

Aioru smiled at him, a tight, shy, conspiratorial expression. "Before you left, sir, we took you on a small tour of one of our special places, which we hadn't shown anyone for a long time—there was an old legend about them—that's not relevant.

The Kirralah, we call them: great water-sculpted stones that stand out from the desert, from long ago before people lived there, when our desert was the floor of a sea. We say they are the very centre of the Hutabarrah, the navel of the world."

Those Cliopher remembered very well. Half a dozen or so red and orange sandstone monoliths, tall as mountains, curved and carved by wind and rain into immense, sinuous shapes without obvious meaning but enormous, incontestable significance. They were sacred, beautiful, nearly unearthly.

"I am so honoured to have seen them," he said. "And seen them twice, actually. Once that trip, and once after the Fall, when I was crossing Jilkano trying to find my way home ..."

Aioru nodded solemnly. "You told us that story then, too. How you had walked across the Hutabarrah along the songlines, tribe to tribe, following the stars home. How our ancestors had laughed when you asked them for directions to the sea."

Cliopher startled. "You mean ..."

Aioru's expression was glimmering with amusement, though it was serious enough as well. "Yes—*you* were the man from the proverb! We all realized it—surely you saw how surprised we were?"

"I thought it was just because of the strange difference in time—that I could remember crossing the desert in a time generations upon generations back in your tribe's history."

"Well, that was surprising too, of course. But really it was that you were the man from the proverb."

Cliopher sat back, digesting this. "There have been many over the years who think me the consummate fool, it's true."

(So many people, over the years. Still—always—he was chasing that viau, looking for that sea, dreaming dreams no one else did.)

Aioru smiled slowly. "Sir, that's not what I mean."

"You must be prepared for it."

"Oh, I've been called a fool many times over," he said airily. "No, sir: you don't understand. You were the man from the proverb—the person I'd always been told not to imitate—*the man who came looking for the sea*—and then I learned that *you found it.*"

Cliopher considered that. And then he said, "Tell me what the sea is that you went looking for, Aioru."

And oh—what an *ocean* of possibility it was!

CHAPTER THREE
A NEW OCEAN

I t was one of the best conversations Cliopher had had in a very long while—perhaps one of the best he had ever had. Aioru had never been shy about telling him ideas, which Cliopher in any case had often solicited from him as well as others in his various departments, but there was a difference between the diffident suggestion for a tweak, and ... this.

This was the vision Aioru unfolded for him of what the world could be.

Cliopher listened, rapt, at points, and at others found himself leaning forward, asking question after question, following up hints and suggestions and trains of thought. Aioru answered hesitantly at first, a little bashfully, until at one point he said, "Sir, are you sure this isn't—too much?"

"Too much?" Cliopher laughed: of course he laughed, loud and heartily, such as he very rarely laughed in the Palace. "Oh, Aioru, this is *splendid*!"

Aioru had spent most of the past half hour, if time had any meaning—Cliopher had certainly not been paying very much attention—explaining all the problems with the justice system as it currently stood, and how reparative justice was far better than retributive. He was from a very harsh environment: it was rare for the community to decide to send someone out alone into the desert, and much more common and critically important to work out how to restore the broken lines snapped by the crime.

Cliopher wished ... not that he'd thought of it, because he would not have come up with this, but that he'd been *able* to begin thinking about it.

There had been other things to do, first. So many things.

"I'm going against what you've done," Aioru said doubtfully. "You're not ... angry? Or no, angry isn't the right word ... upset?"

He felt a twinge of regret. Chagrin, even. But only a twinge, because he *had* done his best. He had. And it was because of what he had done that Aioru could do this, and that was a legacy he could be proud of. He smiled at Aioru.

"I have recently come back from a tour of all the principalities as supreme judge. I am absolutely *not* upset that you have some better ideas."

"I don't want you to think I don't appreciate what you've done, sir."

Cliopher forced himself to sit back, take a breath, listen to what Aioru was saying and not saying. He sought out a metaphor to explain his views.

As they always did, the *Lays* provided him with a guide.

"We have patterns in our histories," Cliopher said. "It is the Islander tradition to look to those who came before to show the way to those who came after. One of the patterns in the *Lays* concerns what happens when a chief or a lore-holder hands over the primary duties to those who come after."

"And what do your patterns say?" Aioru asked, peering down into his tea cup as if it held answers. Cliopher waited, for it seemed as if the young man had something else to say; finally, Aioru added, "In our stories that does not always go well."

Nor did it in the historical record of Astandalas, and it had been known to be a bit precarious, this handing-over of power, in Solaara since the Fall.

Over and over again, the *Lays* told a story—of the gods, perhaps, and those other beings who peopled Sky Ocean—and then told it again, this time as exemplified by the great mythic heroes of the legendary past—and then again, as one or another historical human being looked to the *Lays* to guide their actions and dance the same pattern once more, in a new way.

"It's a very important pattern, in the *Lays*—the *Lays of the Wide Seas*. Two stories speak to me. One." He lifted his hand, and brought the efetana out from where it had lain hidden by the collar of his robes. "This is the efetana, fire coral, to represent that I am the tanà."

"You Hold the Fire."

"Yes." When he had started giving Aioru more responsibilities, he had spoken about that position and how it related to his understanding of his work in the Service. He could see, looking at Aioru now, that he was also remembering that conversation.

Indeed, Aioru did not wait for him to go on. He said, "You said that your duty— no, not duty—your *calling* was to light and tend fires, and also ..." His shoulders relaxed, and he smiled shyly. "And also to teach others to light them and tend them."

"Ember to ember, I pass down the fire that was given to me. Each fire new, each fire old."

Aioru blinked hard for a moment. "And the other pattern?"

"This comes from ... every story, practically. My people, the Wide Seas Islanders, were great voyagers—we sailed across the Wide Seas, finding new islands, naming them, settling them. That pattern is a fundamental one: the idea that there might come a time when you go looking for a new island."

Cliopher was a little surprised to realize his own hands were trembling. He would have thought the fire analogy ...

But it was this story that made his hands tremble and his heart thud in his throat.

"The other pattern is to acknowledge that there comes a time when it is time for someone to leave the island you have settled and find a new one."

Aioru set his tea cup down sharply. It clacked on its saucer. "Sir."

Cliopher met his eyes squarely. He was not able to smile, but he hoped it was as obvious in his eyes as it was in his heart that he meant every word of this. "Aioru, I have brought us to this island. Now it is time for you to look out at the horizon and seek a new one. I built the ship that brought us here, but it is not necessarily the ship that will take you to the next. No. I am not upset to hear your thoughts. I am proud."

"Sir ..."

Aioru's voice trailed off. They looked at each other for a long, intent moment, and then Aioru flushed and he murmured a long passage in his own language. Cliopher waited, listening to the unfamiliar rhythm of sounds and tones, and it came to him with a sudden, confusing shock, that even as he had waited for Aioru to be ready to claim this fullness of his vocation, so too those at home must have been waiting for Cliopher.

For a moment he felt as if the wind had thrown him back against the mast.

It was a sailing term, *being taken aback*. Not something that happened on Islander boats, with their triangular or claw-shaped sails, but something he had experienced once, on a square-rigged Astandalan ship.

When he was a young man, full of dreams and ideals, certain of his course, he had worked his passage from the Vangavaye-ve to Kavanor. He had sailed on one of Astandalas's huge lumbering trading ships, with acres of sails and an isolation from the sea against the hull, the wind in the rigging. Cliopher had not liked the ship, nor most of the crew, but he had done his best.

Cliopher had been young, and fearless—reckless, even. He'd had the voices of his Varga cousins in his ears, laughing at him for being too safety-conscious, too timid.

He was the only one who had decided to go to Astandalas, to leave the expansiveness of the Wide Seas, familiar from their *Lays* if not from their own experiences. Looking back on it now, he could see how his Varga cousins had been jealous of his daring, shamed by their own refusal to go so far, take such a risk. But at the time ...

Oh, at the time he had heard only the jeers and the laughter, and so when he climbed high up in the rigging of those Astandalan ships, he had eschewed any sop to prudence.

He had, understandably, been given the worst jobs, the most dangerous and vertiginous.

He had not had a rope around his waist when the ship was *taken aback*.

He was on the bare mast leading up above even the crow's-nest look-out, reaching up to the magic lantern on its peak, when the contrary wind caught the front of the sails and pushed them back against the masts.

The whole ship had shaken and juddered and groaned as it came to a ferociously unpleasant and unnatural halt in the water.

Half the crew had fallen over; at least one had fallen overboard.

Cliopher had not fallen. He had been watching that shadow, that ruffle across the face of the sea, and he had held onto the loops that held the magic lantern in place, and he had been shaken to the roots of his soul, but he had not been thrown off.

Someone always leaves, Buru Tovo had told Cliopher when he'd asked him for stories about Elonoa'a.

But why did they go? The young Kip had asked him, listening to the full cycle of the *Lays* over and over again, worrying at the stories of Elonoa'a and his crew on the *He'eanka* and that strange story of Elonoa'a's dear friend, the Emperor Aurelius

Magnus, who had been stolen by the Sun. Whom Elonoa'a had gone seeking after, in that ship that became the comet, the wandering star, the *He'eanka*.

You tell me, Buru Tovo had said, settling in to whatever task they were undertaking.

I will go one day, Kip had declared, though no one had gone very far, not in his family. *I will find out.*

And who will you be?

Another question that had echoed in his heart, down all the years since then.

I will be as the third son of Vonou'a, he had declared proudly to Buru Tovo and to anyone who would listen. *I will sit at the feet of the Sun.*

What will you bring home?

He'd been unable to answer anything beyond *A new fire, of course!*—for the third son of Vonou'a had gone to the House of the Sun and brought home fire, the first flame of that same fire Cliopher had learned to light, and the lore and the *Lays* that were the fire of culture he had tended his whole life long.

When he had met that old man, that odd seller of shells, that god, in the market on Lesuia, the efelauni—for there were enough stories of such odd, god-touched shell-merchants around the Ring, that they had their own name—the efelauni had challenged him with the questions from the *Lays*, and asked him also that same question that had been ringing in Cliopher's ears since the first time he had heard Buru Tovo ask it.

What will you bring home from the House of the Sun?

A new life for the hearth of the world, Cliopher had said that time, and thereby won an efela of forty-nine sundrop cowries, the efela nai, and the weight of legend.

Well. He had brought the fire home. He would be a poor tanà if he did not *share* it.

Aioru stopped his recitation, and lifted his head. He had tears standing in his eyes, and he very carefully and cautiously set the tea cup and saucer on the side table before he set his hands flat on his knees.

They sat there, looking at each other, not saying anything, until Aioru leaned forward and said, "In that case, then, sir, I should like to suggest we *entirely* separate the auditing department from the government. You should not have been doing that, sir, and I certainly ought not! The Lord Emperor should not have let you do it—it is a *clear* conflict of interest."

For a moment Cliopher could only sit there, stunned.

And then he sat up, all the way up, let go of anything resembling professional distance and decorum, rallied himself for a real discussion, grinned in what was probably a somewhat feral manner, and said, "Go on. Tell me more."

And so Aioru did: all the way until the noon bell rang and Tully knocked on the door and said, "Sir—sorry to interrupt—the Ouranatha."

Aioru stopped, a little embarrassed at his enthusiasm now that he'd been interrupted. Cliopher laughed and clapped his hand on the other man's shoulder as he stood and gathered himself together for this meeting. "You don't need to come to this one," he said. "We'll hardly be finishing the budget today. I'll see you at the Council of Princes meeting this afternoon."

"Yes, sir." Aioru hesitated; Cliopher turned back from the door, enquiringly. "Sir —how—that is, when does this become official?"

One of the things Aioru had pointed out was the obscenely vast amount of power Cliopher currently wielded, given that he was both Viceroy and also still Lord Chancellor and thus head of the Imperial Service.

He considered the general protocol for such things. "Do you have a preference? I believe we should give unofficial notice to the various pillars of government today, then make an official pronouncement to the Private Offices—if you'd like to tell them *unofficially* now, please do so. We'll have to meet with the person you want to succeed you as Minister of the Common Weal, as well. Perhaps you can arrange that while I'm with the Ouranatha."

"Whom you should not leave waiting," Aioru said, grinning at him suddenly. "The princes won't be over-pleased that you tell the Ouranatha first. Good politics, sir."

"Thank you," said Cliopher, smiling back, quite as if they'd planned it.

Inside the council chamber the nine Elders of the Ouranatha were gathered around an oval table. They had left the seat at one end for him; his secretaries and their various attendants were settled at tables to the side.

Cliopher swept in and gave them a courteous partial bow. The Ouranatha was the collective name for the upper college of the priest-wizards, who as a body were one of the five pillars of the government. The Elders were theoretically equivalent to the Council of Princes and the High Command of the Imperial Guard, and thus while a step down from Cliopher's current position, only that step down.

"My apologies for my tardiness," he said as the Elders returned his greeting. "I was meeting with my successor to the chancellorship. Please, sit down."

They all did so except for the Elder opposite Cliopher, who remained standing. Cliopher inclined his head in their direction. "Would you like to speak first, Elder?"

"Thank you."

The Elder's voice was a mellow contralto. The Ouranatha wore a uniform of loose, floor-length robes in a deep, somber grey, with hooded mantles in silvery grey overtop. The Elders added carved metal masks. Cliopher found the intricate silver masks eerie; he was secretly grateful he had very little to do with the Ouranatha, generally speaking. Even this year without his Radiancy, who was the highest priest and chief wizard of the world, he had managed to keep to only the ordinary meetings and status reports. The Mother of the Abbey of the Mountains, a wizard from Old Damara, was seeing to any magical problems, none of which had been serious enough to involve Cliopher at any level beyond reading reports.

Even better—for to become the Viceroy had required an excessive number of ceremonies of purification, which had been onerous—he didn't even have anything to do with the two chief priest-wizards. They were busy with the rituals and ceremonials of their calling, which did not, thankfully, involve him. Thankfully, the preparations for his Radiancy's abdication and the coronation of his successor (whenever he returned with one—but Cliopher could not begrudge his lord this adventure) had not yet required Cliopher's involvement.

"I hope there is nothing amiss with the magic of the world?" he enquired politely, when it appeared nothing more would be forthcoming.

The Elder opposite shook their head. "No. All is well. All waits, but patiently."

"I am glad to hear that."

He waited again (if less patiently than the world according to the Ouranatha). His papers were in a neat stack before him, outlines of arguments regarding the Ouranatha's annual budget. They would not get through it today—they never did—but he did need to ensure he had more or less aligned their priorities with his when it came to finances. Even workers of magic had to obey certain fundamental laws of economics.

The Elders regarded him through their masks, a circle of near-identical figures. Cliopher was reminded of shamans back home, and refused to shudder at the thought. He had had little to do with the shamans, either, except for a few encounters as a youth when he had studied the old ways with his great-uncle. The Mdangs Held the Fire, but his great-uncle had felt he should know the basic studies of each of the great lore-keeping lineages.

The Ela, Those Who Went Furthest, adopted anyone interested in shamanism into their lineage. It was a little surprising that none of Cliopher's fifty-nine cousins had been so inclined, actually.

And still the Elders of the Ouranatha said nothing. Cliopher kept his eyes up and his posture and expression patient and attentive, and ran through his arguments about their budget in his mind.

"Did you go to see the comet last night?" the Elder said at last, sitting down.

This was so far from the question of the amount needed to maintain their buildings in the city that for a moment Cliopher could only blink in surprise. After a moment he collected himself. "Yes, I did," he replied, and then, when the silence seemed expectant, added, "Thank you for letting me know about it. I'm afraid I have been far from attentive to Sky Ocean of late."

The silence took on a strange crystalline quality.

Cliopher caught his breath, unsure, but he refused to be embarrassed for using the names he had grown up with, for calling the stars according to his people's traditions.

The Elders almost certainly thought him an overweening barbarian (other members of the court had never shied away from saying so), but Cliopher was the duly appointed and ceremoniously anointed Viceroy of Zunidh, and out of respect for their own traditions and for his Radiancy if not for himself they would keep their opinions to themselves.

The Elder opposite leaned forward slightly. Their mask gleamed in the lights illuminating the room. "And where was the comet, when you saw it?"

This was a long way from the budget, and Cliopher was well aware that the Ouranatha had insisted that the meeting fall between noon and the first hour, and *only* noon and the first hour, that day. Still, they were priest-wizards, and that meant their priorities were different than his.

Perhaps if he gave them this they would be more inclined to give him some leeway there.

He repressed a sigh and instead nodded politely, but his irritation came out in the defiant use of Islander names. "I do not know your name for the constellation. My people call it the Fisherman, and the comet, whose name we say is He'eanka, was near his heart, with its nose pointing into the Lulai'aviyë, what you call the River of Stars, over the Palace and towards my home island."

A very soft murmur ran around the table, with the Elders nodding to themselves as if in confirmation of something. Cliopher held himself in his court poise despite his unease.

"Can you name many stars in Shaian?" the same Elder asked him.

"I have never studied them," Cliopher replied.

"And in your own language?"

It was rare, even for a hinterland tribesman—which Cliopher, for all that his family were solidly middle-class urban professionals, nevertheless was—to admit they had kept use of their own language instead of the Empire's Shaian.

Even without the strange effects of the Fall of Astandalas on the flow of time, it had been nearly two thousand years since the Vangavaye-ve joined the Empire, and admittedly it was only those out along the Outer Ring who grew up with it as their primary language. Cliopher himself had only gained fluency as a teenager, sitting at his great-uncle's feet.

Well. If they wanted him to answer according to his traditions, by the gods he *would* answer in terms of his people's traditions.

"I am not Nga," he said, smiling but serious. "I do not Name the Stars; I am a Mdang, and I Hold the Fire. My knowledge is, you might say, practical. I know the Sixteen Bright Guides and the forty constellations of the year, and the rising and the setting of the stars whose paths mark the islands it was necessary for me to know."

Loaloa, his ancestral island, was one of the boundary islands of the Western Ring. He had been able to stand at the Leaping-Place, where the spirits went to join the ancestors in the ancient homeland after their sojourn on the island of the dead, and name each star-path leading to every major island of the Ring and also the major islands and archipelagos across the Wide Seas.

He could draw up the images in his mind's eye even now; even if he wondered how accurate he would be. The traditional knowledge lay quietly in the back of his mind, parallel and distinct from the trained memory and habits of thought of a career bureaucrat. One focused on writing and numbers and organized paperwork, the other on the oral recitation of ancient songs and the physical embodiments of knowledge in dance and design.

Yet when he danced each morning, the songs came to his lips, and the steps to his feet, and the words were in language, not in Shaian.

The Elder said, "And where is your island, your excellency?"

Cliopher gave them a long look, then raised his hand and pointed behind him and to the right in the direction of *home*, which he kept in a corner of his mind.

It was a matter of pride to any Islander raised in the old ways that they *always* knew where their island was.

He had lost his way, a few times. Typhoons had blown him off course, when he had sailed home across the Wide Seas in the strange years after the Fall. He had never felt so entirely bewildered as the first time he had washed up on an island after capsizing and realized that in the tumult and terror of the storm he had lost himself. His island was *gone*, and it was not until he had finally cracked the riddle of the fire dance and been able to place himself in the Wide Seas again that he had been able to reorient himself.

And then in the next storm he had once again lost it, and again and again.

But he had found his way in the end, and since then—however tenuous the intimation, however much he had consciously ignored it—he had never quite lost his sense of home.

His silent, confident gesture caused another susurrus of murmuring, the Elders turning to each other in pairs. Only the Elder at the far end, opposite him, sat unmoving. Cliopher felt distinctly perturbed by this. Just what had the wizard-priests been up to?

"Lord Mdang," the Elder said, "you have always been respectful to us. Your traditions are not our traditions; your gods are not our gods; your stars are not our stars. A comet comes and goes and crosses above the paths of many men and women, many lands and many peoples. It can be read in many ways."

They paused there, glancing around, if the movement of the mask was anything to judge by, at the other Elders. One after another nodded meaningfully. At length the Elder who had spoken turned to face Cliopher squarely.

"Lord Mdang, you mentioned your successor?"

"Yes," he said, as if this was not new. (It was not: he had been nurturing Aioru towards this eventual point for years.) "Aioru of the Kallarrahroo will be taking on the position of chancellor."

Another pause; another silent regard; another circle of masked faces nodding one after the other. Cliopher felt the hair on the back of his neck rise.

"Lord Mdang," the Elder said a third time. "This comet means many things to many people. It heralds change to us all. No surprise there when it is the year that the old order changes to a new one, when the Lord Emperor returns with his heir, when *you* hand over your authority. May we ask what it means in your tradition?"

He said, "It is said to be the ship of Elonoa'a, last of the Paramount Chiefs before the coming of the Empire, ally and comrade and great friend of the Emperor Aurelius Magnus. It is said that when Aurelius Magnus went to the House of the Sun, his friend Elonoa'a took ship with a crew from the Vangavaye-ve and went to find him. Since then they have sailed across Sky Ocean on their quest. When the comet becomes visible it is said that Elonoa'a is searching in our quarter of the sky. Whether he found Aurelius Magnus or not our stories do not say."

The Elders nodded again. The one at the end said, "According to all our readings, in the bones and the smoke and the ink on water, in the hands of the casters and the dreams of the dream-walkers and the visions of the seers, the comet has come for you."

Cliopher stared at them, nonplussed.

They, being priest-wizards and therefore delighting in ambiguity and rendering their audience disquieted, waited silently for him to absorb this.

Finally he came up with, "I thank you for the message, although I do not know how I can be of such interest to the gods."

All the stories said it was a very dangerous thing, to be of such interest to the gods.

He hoped he didn't blanch too obviously at the thought. They didn't say anything, so he went on. "With regards to the budget—"

"We accept it," said the Elder at the end of the table, with an airy wave of their hand. "There is a total eclipse of the Sun that will fall on the tenth day of the tenth month of next year, the thousandth of Artorin Damara's reign according to the ledgers we have kept. This is the date set by the heavens for the abdication of his Radiancy, the Sun-on-Earth. We will present the tables of ceremonies to your offices soon, your excellency."

"Ah, thank you," he managed. "And ... are you willing to sign off on the proposed budget?"

"Yes, yes," the Elder said, gesturing at one of their own attendants, who hastened over to Cliopher with a stack of papers, all already properly signed and sealed. "You understood that we would need more funds for the increased ceremonies this year, and we have no other points that need to be raised at this time."

Cliopher flipped through the stack to see that the Ouranatha had, in fact, done what not a single other government body in his entire career had ever done, and accepted the first iteration of a budget.

"Lord Mdang," said the Elder, as they all shifted as if wanting him to give them permission to depart.

He could barely form words out of his shock. "Yes, Elder?"

"The comet has come for you, but not only for you," they said. "Remember that."

CHAPTER FOUR
THE PILLARS OF THE GOVERNMENT

O ne of his household attendants had laid out a tray of food for him on the desk in his study. He placed his writing kit down and picked up the tray to take into his sitting room, kicking off his sandals as he went.

It was a small luxury, this quarter-hour to eat a meal in his sitting room. That was what came of delegating even so small a task as unofficially informing the Private Offices—the upper echelon of the Secretariat, Cliopher's department—about Aioru's promotion.

Cliopher would make the official pronouncement tomorrow. The protocol was quite strict: the Ouranatha, the Council of Princes, the Command Staff of the Imperial Guard, the Imperial Bureaucratic Service, and his Radiancy.

His Radiancy properly came first, but in this case ...

Cliopher had been writing reports for him, of course, though he was unable to guess where his Radiancy might next end up on his quest and could therefore not *send* them. He kept the folder containing the reports in one of the magically expanded pockets of his writing kit. At some point—

He sighed. At some point his Radiancy would return, and Cliopher would be able to make his reports in person.

He did not have long enough to read anything for pleasure, and so he sat moodily eating his lentil salad and stared at the portrait of his great-uncle on the wall.

The portrait was the original used for the *Atlas of Imperial Peoples*, that more than slightly biased but still invaluable record of the many peoples who had lived under the banner of Astandalas. As a young man, Cliopher's Buru Tovo had gone sailing across the Wide Seas, exploring the islands sailed and settled by his ancestors, sung in the *Lays*.

Somewhere along the coast of Kavanor he had encountered a cortege of ships and barges containing both the then-heir (later the Emperor Eritanyr, his Radiancy's uncle) and also the painter recording the progress and depicting the various locals it encountered.

Cliopher's great-uncle, his teacher in the lore, was quite literally the exemplar for the Wide Seas Islanders. Whenever someone who did not know them thought of Cliopher's people, it was the young Tovo inDaino of Loaloa he pictured.

He'd tried, Cliopher had, to live up to his model.

Cliopher looked at his great-uncle in the traditional finery, the efela necklaces, the body-paint, the grass skirt, the arm-bands of fresh leaves, all those meaningful and significant ornaments and choices that the court called *barbaric*.

There was a challenge in the young Tovo's eyes and humour in his face, because he'd posed for this painting for his own reasons.

Cliopher finished his salad, and then he got up and changed into half court costume. He wished his Radiancy were there.

Of all his many committees and councils, the Council of Princes was Cliopher's least favourite.

They met in an elegant room in the central block of the Palace, not far from the council chamber where he'd met the Ouranatha. Cliopher entered with his two honour guards at his back and a recording secretary at his side. Today's scribe was Eldo, Prince Rufus's third son (a careful choice for this occasion—Cliopher rotated between Zaoul of the Tkinele, his own nephew Gaudy, and Lord Eldo, who were all superb secretaries in their own rights and brought disparate skills and social perspectives to the table), and his guards were Zerafin and Oginu.

As Viceroy he took his Radiancy's place as Chair of the council. He continued to sit where he had long been accustomed to sitting, first as his Radiancy's secretary and the recording secretary for the meetings, at a small table set in the opening of the squared-off U-shape of the princes' arrangement. In the past his Radiancy had sat directly opposite him; in his Radiancy's absence, the near-throne was left empty.

There had been suggestions Cliopher sit in it, but he had not, at the time, wished to lose the advantage gained by facing the princes.

Over the months of his Radiancy's absence, they had modified a few of the ancient arrangements. His desk was somewhat larger now, and contained a chair to his left for the new recording secretary, and another to his right for one or other of Cliopher's 'apprentices'. Aioru was thus a familiar face to the princes.

Prince Rufus was the self-chosen leader of the council, being by far the most outspoken and stubborn of the lot—though Jiano, the most recent addition, had spent the not-quite-year since his induction learning the ways of the council, and had recently started to speak up more and more frequently.

After the replacement of the ineffective Princess Oriana, who had Jilkanese connections and hated Cliopher, with the Islander Paramount Chief (*not* Prince) Jiano, the balance had shifted. Some of the quieter members of the council were finding their voice now that there was a second figure to rally around.

Cliopher guessed that his Radiancy's absence had contributed to that new dynamic, together with the fact that Jiano, while he certainly respected Cliopher, was also quite willing to push back and argue with him. It was a headier combination than he'd realized.

~

An hour passed; two; servants brought in refreshments, and they took a short, welcome break. Cliopher had deferred several times to Aioru, which the princes did not find strange, for he had been doing so more and more over the past months, and as Minister of the Common Weal, the mundial budget was very much within Aioru's remit.

Cliopher's head was prickling with the headache dealing with the princes always gave him. Even Jiano's stalwart support (as far as Islanders ever gave such; Jiano was certainly not backing down over proposed budget cuts any more than Prince Rufus, but unlike Prince Rufus, Jiano at least shared most of the same cultural priorities as Cliopher) was not enough to make this *easy*.

He glanced at Aioru, who had taken the opportunity of the break to get up and talk to the Princess of Kavanduru, who was the next-youngest after Jiano; they appeared to be having an intensely stimulating conversation, from the bright interest on both their faces. The Prince of Jilkano-Lozoi joined them, saying something in what seemed an almost teasing tone to Aioru.

Cliopher felt some small concern dissipate and blow away. If Aioru could smile and laugh like that to the Prince of Jilkano-Lozoi—the prince of his own province—then there was no need to worry about his ability to hold his own in this council's more vitriolic debates.

As they returned to their seats for the final items on the agenda, Cliopher revolved ways of making this announcement. It was hardly a surprise, except insofar as they were not expecting anything materially to change in their interactions with him until his formal retirement.

Maybe it would be a surprise, at that. None of the princes had ever *retired*.

Before Cliopher could begin, Prince Rufus harrumphed and stood up. "Lord Mdang," he said, as usual mangling Cliopher's name almost to *Madon*, "before we continue, I should like to say something about this line in the budget you have devoted to the justice system—"

He continued on, as he always continued on, at vast oratorical length. Cliopher listened, or tried to. His blood seemed to be roaring in his ears. Aioru had talked about this same budget line, had had such brilliant ideas—

Prince Rufus took a breath, and Cliopher said, "Sayo Aioru has some very interesting ideas on the potential reformation of the judicial system. I should like to suggest that he form a committee—"

"I am amazed," Prince Rufus interrupted before he could go on. "Lord Mdang, without an idea of his own? Handing off such an *important* subject to someone else? Surely we have fallen into a dream-world! Are you quite well, Lord Mdang? Or are you over-worked? Is it, conceivably, time for you to step back?"

Cliopher stared at him.

The room was dead silent, for that was a line Prince Rufus had not crossed in some time.

They were all looking at him, these princes and princesses, the one Grand Duchess and the one Paramount Chief, and Aioru and Lord Eldo and no doubt the guards behind him as well: all watching, their faces intent, even anticipatory.

Waiting for him to seize the opening Prince Rufus had given him, to lift up the weapons of his tongue and his wit, to charge forward as he had always charged forward. He could see that Prince Rufus was ready, intent, *expectant*, his eyes eager. He and Cliopher had clashed over and over again, debated for hours and days and years, until they had wrested a government both of them could be proud of.

Cliopher stared at the prince, and for a moment his mind was completely blank.

The wind was changing.

That was all he could think: that the sail was for this one moment uncertain, the ropes slack in his hand, as he looked at Prince Rufus: his bushy red eyebrows jutting forward, his pale eyes hot and intense, his pale skin ruddy under the freckles. The wind was changing and it was up to Cliopher to decide what to do.

Did he keep the course he had set so long ago, relentless in the face of any cross wind or uncertain weather? Did he take his arms up, as he always had, and do battle with Prince Rufus?

Or—

His Radiancy was not there, with a smile and a challenge hidden in his eyes, a solid place to stand, a star to follow.

No. Even absent—

Even absent, he was a solid place to stand, and Cliopher wanted nothing more than to follow the star-path his Radiancy had set off upon.

He was not here because he was looking for his own successor. Cliopher's stood beside him.

Cliopher took a breath, a diver's breath, as if he were about to dive deep for a pearl, and the future opened out in front of him.

There was a horizon he had never crossed, a sea he had never sailed, an island he had never found. A star that burned steadily before him, whose ke'ea he might follow.

He smiled, genuinely smiled, at Prince Rufus, and said words that had almost never crossed his lips before, in this council or out of it: "You're right."

Prince Rufus reared back. "I am?—that is, of course I am, Lord Mdang—"

"It's *Mdang*," Cliopher said, without heat but with full emphasis. He looked around the room, deliberately meeting the eyes of each of the seventeen princes seated around the table. Their expressions had changed: they were no longer idly amused and anticipatory, but confused. Even a little perturbed.

Not Jiano. The Paramount Chief of the Vangavaye-ve met his eyes, his face grave, his eyes sparkling, and spoke forth one of the great challenges: "What island have you seen? What wind fills your sails? What star is calling you?"

Cliopher nearly flinched, because Jiano knew the words that echoed in Cliopher's heart and mind and all this government he had created out of the ruins of Astandalas.

Those questions were the ones Anyë, the first woman, asked her brother, the third son of Vonou'a, in the *Lays*.

Cliopher replied with the third son's words: "Sama e'lolōna. Lulai'aviyë dinai'o. Ke'ea moa'alani anonōna."

The sound of Islander rolled through the silent room like thunder, like the breakers on a reef.

He turned to Prince Rufus, chin up, voice level, as court-formal as he had ever been. "The Wind That Rises At Dawn fills my sails. The Wake of the Ancestors' Ships have I seen. The star-paths of Sky Ocean are singing to me."

He took another breath. The room was *so* quiet. He relished it, for just this one moment, as he gathered himself and then let the little ship of his soul follow this new wind where it blew him.

"I am the longest serving member of the civil service. Commander Omo joined the Imperial Guard a little after I entered the Service. Princess Anastasiya and the Grand Duchess—" He bowed his head to indicate the two women, his Radiancy's great-aunt and sister respectively— "have served longer than I, and of course so has the Lord Emperor himself."

The formal title sat ill in his mouth. Most often Cliopher called him *his Radiancy*, but that was too intimate a term, a *name*, for this assemblage. His Radiancy's household called him that.

(Cliopher had been granted permission to call him *Tor*. But that was not a name he could use here.)

He turned back to Prince Rufus. "You are right, Prince Rufus. It is time for me to step back. Aioru of the Kallarrahroo will be taking up the position of Chancellor." He took a deep breath. "I shall continue as Viceroy of Zunidh, as my lord has entrusted me with the ceremonial and legal position, but I shall take this opportunity to announce my resignation as Lord Chancellor and Secretary in Chief of the Offices of the Lords of State, effective immediately."

Prince Rufus said, "But—Lord Mdang—"

Cliopher relished the confusion and bewilderment and total shock in his long-time political opponent's face and voice and bearing. Prince Rufus had never fully grasped just how many times Cliopher had won his destination by yielding his way. The prince was no sailor: he did not understand that sometimes the ke'ea of an island was not in the straight line at all.

Oh, it was sweet, to win this last bout by the simplest possible means, to win by conceding his ground.

Cliopher nodded amiably to Aioru and sat down.

The princes were murmuring and whispering to each other, broken out of their stupor by his movement.

"As Viceroy, I believe you continue as Chair of this council, do you not?" Aioru said, and his voice was at once so professional and so steady that Cliopher could only admire it, even as he hoped the trembling in his own hands was hidden by the solid front of his desk. "I'm sure we would all be grateful if you were continue to moderate today's session, Lord Mdang."

"Indeed," Jiano said. His eyes were wide, but he had governed his face to something plausibly neutral. He turned to Aioru. "I would be interested in sitting on a committee to consider the judicial system, Chancellor Aioru, if you do indeed intend to form one on the topic."

"I do, yes," Aioru replied, and proceeded to take charge just as if he had done so a thousand times before.

~

The rest of the Council of Princes meeting went smoothly. Cliopher had little to do besides ensure they did not stray overly far from the agenda. He positioned himself in his best courtly mode, back straight, chin up, face polite, smile affable, and watched as the dynamics of the room slowly began to flux.

Kurakura was the Islander word for the sort of rough water caused by intersecting waves; where deepwater swells or two currents met, or a tide turned through the pass in a reef. Cliopher felt as if he had entered into such a patch, as if his small canoe were crossing over a submerged reef, as if he were slipping to a new current, as if he were negotiating the Gate of the Sea at the mouth of the Ring of the Vangavaye-ve.

He had only sailed that pass once, in his little *Tui-tanata*, the small boat he had made with his own hands (over and over again he had built it, mending it after shipwreck after shipwreck, all the way across the Wide Seas in that incomprehensible time after the Fall). He had waited outside the Ring the night before, listening to the seabirds crying on the barrier islands.

In the dawn he had seen a shell floating on the waves towards him: Ani's Tear, the coiled shell green-blue and white as the sea. He had always wondered if it were truly for him, that shell: recognition, perhaps, of his long journey across the Wide Seas ...

But yet, was it not also a warning? The gifts of Ani were all the bounty of the sea, and also all its many dangers.

Ani had wept for her son Vonou'a sailing away across the horizon in the first boat, as he went off to seek a wife for himself, and had sung the first song, the lament for his going.

Vou'a, the god of mysteries, the Son of Laughter, had heard the weeping of Ani and raised up the first island for her.

In those days Ani had been able to walk on the land. Later, she had lost—

Prince Rufus exclaimed, "No!" And banged his hand on the table, and Aioru laughed out loud.

Cliopher focused on the room before him. Prince Rufus was laughing too. He'd never laughed for Cliopher.

He should probably care. But he didn't; he didn't.

Cliopher had often wondered if his Radiancy grew bored with being a living symbol of power and authority. Cliopher had spent all of half an hour as one and he was already calculating how soon this meeting could possibly be over. They'd already sorted out the budget—

He suppressed a sigh, took a sip of water, and listened to the four Jilkanese princes argue about Nijan for only, oh, the thousandth time. This year.

~

The second hour after sunset was the usual time for dining in Palace culture, unless there was a formal court supper. When Cliopher finally arrived, almost half an hour late, he was not surprised to find his friends already gathered in the dining room, drinking wine and picking over small and delectable tidbits. Cliopher's stomach rumbled: it had been a long time since that hurriedly snatched lentil salad.

"Ah! There he is!" Rhodin cried. "Cliopher, stop dallying in the doorway and come sit with us. We were just debating whether we should call for another round of appetizers."

"The theme appears to be Southern Dairese today," Conju observed. "Have one of these stuffed grape leaves, we haven't eaten them all."

"They're good," Ludvic rumbled when Cliopher hesitated over the only plate that didn't seem to be entirely picked over. "Came out last."

"Good to know," Cliopher said mildly, and felt a great weight lift off his shoulders at the ease of their company. It was good to be amongst such dear friends.

(Even if one were missing—

But his Radiancy had only ever joined them like this on that holiday to Lesuia. Before then they had never dared to presume so far against court etiquette and the ancient, unalterable taboos; afterwards they had still felt the constraints of court culture.)

"The moping has started again, has it," Conju said in a bored tone. "Come sit down, Cliopher. You've weathered the Council of Princes. *And* the Ouranatha, Tully told us."

"You're looking most distracted," Rhodin said. "Was the Council of Princes that bad?"

Cliopher looked around at the faces of his dear friends. "I resigned," he said, and sat down harder than he intended.

Rhodin said, "From the Service, I take it?"

"I'm still Viceroy, yes. Aioru's Chancellor." Cliopher's voice was strange in his ears. "I told the Ouranatha and the Council of Princes and—and—"

"And Ludvic and I represent the Command Staff of the Guard," Rhodin concluded. "Well. *Well*."

There was a pause, and then Conju passed him a full goblet of Amboloyan red wine. "About time, I say."

Cliopher laughed, almost hysterically relieved at their response. It was so friendly —so—so *familiar*.

"I knew I should have put myself on guard duty this afternoon," Rhodin said irritably. "How did you say it? Tell us everything."

"You will have to get Zerafin and Oginu's report." He shook his head, and laughed again, more normally. "His Radiancy would have enjoyed it. I agreed with Prince Rufus."

Conju raised his eyebrow elegantly—quite as his Radiancy did, in fact. "Prince Rufus said you should resign, and you *did*?"

"I'd already talked it over with Aioru," he protested. They laughed and it was...it was *good*.

How he wanted his Radiancy to be there, sitting with them, sharing such a meal, such a conversation, such a *life* with him. One day, he told himself. One day.

His Radiancy's quest was a fine and necessary thing. Surely he was loving all the new experiences, the vast differences between life in the Palace of Stars as His Holy and Serene Radiancy, the Last Emperor of Astandalas, the Lord of Zunidh, the Sun-on-Earth.

He turned to Conju. "Are you ready for your trip? And—" He fought for the name of Conju's current boyfriend. Rovert? Linnel? Augustinius?— "Antonio?"

Conju rolled his eyes. "Don't strain yourself, Cliopher," he said astringently, and described his meticulously planned itinerary at humorous length.

～

The reverberations from Cliopher's resignation were quiet, but they rippled through the palace and out into the wider world like the aftershocks of an undersea volcano not yet become an island.

First there was the froth of rumours; the editorial in the *Csiven Flyer* querying the state of his health. After the formal announcements, the investiture of Aioru as Chancellor, the various shuffling of senior members of the Secretariat into new positions, more junior ones promoted, the following headlines lauded Cliopher's commitment to the proper distribution of authority.

The editor of the *Csiven Flyer* liked Cliopher, admittedly. The newspaper's caricaturist enjoyed very much the opportunity to sketch the imagined reactions of everyone they could think of.

There were meetings with everyone.

Kiri, his longtime deputy in the Private Offices, told him she'd scooped the Service-wide bet on whether he would resign before he retired or died.

"Of course, I know you, sir," she said, grinning; Cliopher smiled back. The primary reason *she* wasn't his successor to the Chancellorship was that she didn't want to be, being not far off retirement age herself.

"Meaning?"

"Oh, you started to look for a way out as soon as Himself left." She laughed at his instinctively denial. "I doubt I'll stay long without you, sir. Just till Aioru's settled. Bosses matter."

Which of course was true.

(It had been a long time since Cliopher thought of his Radiancy as *his boss*.)

～

He met with every one of the princes. Princess Anastasiya of Xiputl, his Radiancy's great-aunt, gave him a beady stare and informed him that *she* planned on seeing the Jubilee out.

She'd once told his Radiancy in Cliopher's hearing that she intended to outlast him, so this was not the surprise to Cliopher she evidently thought it would be.

"I *had* thought your devotion to your vocation admirable," she said, magisterially disapproving, as she swept out.

～

The Grand Duchess Melissa, his Radiancy's sister, congratulated him on following his heart after so long tethered to his duty. Unlike her great-aunt, she looked wistful at the thought. Cliopher tentatively said, "You can do the same, your Grace."

She smiled sadly. "My heart was lost long ago, Lord Mdang. It is a liability for one such as I."

"What was lost can be found, your Grace."

"It's been far too long for me, I'm afraid."

"Then perhaps another," he suggested delicately, but she shook her head and took her leave, leaving him wishing he knew how to help her. He barely knew her, save that she loved her brother, and that due to their respective positions they had never been able to be *close*.

There was a story in the *Lays* about an irreparable loss: a pattern for resignation, dignified acceptance, strength despite adversity. Cliopher had always hated it.

He wished his Radiancy were there: to laugh with him about Prince Rufus and Princess Anastasiya, to come up with something for Melissa, to—

To talk to.

As if they were real people, with whole hearts and private lives and privacy.

Jiano came last, shortly before the Paramount Chief was to leave the Palace for the Vangavaye-ve. "For the festival," he explained, and then blinked. "Of course you know that."

"I do," Cliopher replied quietly, guilt washing through him. "Please give my regards to Aya, and to everyone, when you go home. I'm sorry I shall miss the festivities."

Again, he did not say.

He had missed every one since he had left to go to Astandalas. He had been home since then—for months, that first visit home after the Fall—but never for the most important festival of his culture. It fell right at what had always been the busiest part of the court year. If he had chosen to go home *then*—

It would have been the choice to *go home* for good.

Every year, all the long years of his time in the service, in Solaara—every year, when the time came for the festival, Cliopher would sit in his room and sing over the *Lays*. Sometimes he would practice Aōteketētana, the greater fire dance.

Every time his heart would ache and he would doubt his choices. He would yearn to be home, to be the person they had all wanted him to be, to take up his position as tanà and achieve status and respect at home, in the ways his family understood, in the ways his family valued. Every time.

But every year he had calculated the cost of going, the price of staying, and every time he had stayed.

He had stayed: for his Radiancy, as his secretary, doing that long, slow, stubborn work of trying to rebuild the world from the devastation wrought by the Fall of

Astandalas, that magical cataclysm that had broken time as well as society. For years, decades (centuries, the Ouranatha said, though Cliopher had never been able to understand how the years of his remembrance turned into the centuries they counted), he had worked invisibly, laying foundations for what would come.

Each year he would think about going home, to sit at the feet of Uncle Lazo and Buru Tovo, the tanà and the tana-tai, to become what they had all wanted him to be, and each year he ... didn't.

And so, back home, because they had no tanà who could dance Aōteketētana— for Uncle Lazo had an injured knee, and Buru Tovo no longer had the stamina—the festival was never quite complete, never quite right.

Jiano regarded him gravely. "You are thinking about the festival?"

Cliopher realized he was fingering his efetana. He tucked it away, more reluctantly than usual. He wanted—

There was no one around, and Jiano had asked him that in language. "I regret it," Cliopher replied lowly. "I know people have wanted—that because I am not there— that it means that—the Greater Festival—"

Jiano interrupted him. "It is not all on your account, you know. That the Greater Festival has not been held since before the Fall."

Cliopher looked at him. "Isn't it? You need the tanà—"

"We need everyone. Every lore-keeper."

Cliopher had known that, once. Buru Tovo had been able to dance when he was teaching Cliopher—but still they had not had the greater festival, because the rukà had been sick with a terrible cough, and—

"It is there in the stories of the beginning," Jiano said seriously. "When Ani could no longer come to land, the Great Dance was ... halted. Iki could go down to the caves in the heart of the sea to visit her, but he could not do their dance without her."

Ani had been tricked and lost her mirimiri (that was an ancient word: no one knew what it was, but for its obvious importance; the word now was used to mean any mysterious quintessence whose presence made something alive and whole, but which could not be defined), and Vou'a had tried to enlist the help of some other god to barter it back. But as he travelled to the House of the Sun, he had lost the feather he had been granted by the other god, the item that was needed for the exchange, and ... that was that.

Ani could not come out of her waters, and had retreated to deep caves under the floor of the sea to sleep through the long ages. And Vou'a, Jiano's Iki, the god of mysteries, moved through the worlds of gods and men, making mischief, offering riddles, doing this and that, and always, always, looking for the feather he had lost.

The lesson was that there were some things that *could not* be changed or fixed or remedied.

Cliopher did not like the story any more than he had when he thought of it in context of Melissa Damara's ancient heartbreak, for all it had given him a cold comfort after far too many impossible, irreparable problems in the history of the world.

(He still held the grief of Woodlark in his heart, for all it had not been his decision, in the end. Cliopher had only been the witness, standing beside Commander

Omo when he gave a terrible order to enforce the quarantine with death, standing beside his Radiancy when he had raised up that terrible magical fire.

Nothing had been able to be fixed: the curse had been too strong, the only possible remedy to burn the island to its bedrock. The island was still scorched bare, all these years later.

He had been comforted to think of the grief of Vou'a when Ani could no longer come onto the land, then.)

"Tanà Tovo could have danced the fire for years when you were gone," Jiano said gently. "But the Ela had lost their zamà during the Fall—they were stuck in the Isolates by the wall of storms across the Wide Seas—and even after the zamà found their way back to the Ring, then there was a year when the rukà had a terrible bronchitis, and her apprentices were not yet ready. And ... there were other times. It is only in the last few years, Kip, that it's been you ..."

Jiano paused there, as Cliopher stared at him, feeling a strange shifting in his heart as this ancient guilt was touched.

So few people called him Kip in the Palace. It was ... disconcerting.

"Tanà Tovo has counselled us to be patient," Jiano said finally. "He is respected, you know."

Cliopher did know. He bit his lip, and then he offered a quiet, binding promise: "Soon."

"Soon," Jiano agreed, and then winked at him. "It's good that we'll *all* have time to practice."

CHAPTER FIVE
A CERTAIN SECRET

C liopher finished the last page of the report in front of him, considered it briefly, and then signed off on it with a flourish. He stacked the pages together neatly, bound them with the archival ribbon, sealed that, with a momentary appreciation for the scent of the hot wax as his seal made its impression, and finally set the bundle in the outgoing dispatch case.

There was something so satisfying about finishing a report. He was quite grateful, all told, that he had never lost that sense. It would have made for a miserable life had he not taken such satisfaction in completing them.

He reached automatically to the box containing the day's reports, ready for the next, and stopped short.

There weren't any.

It was a week since Aioru had become Chancellor, and the reports had been dwindling in number as Cliopher's various duties were handed over.

Not that all of them were handed over to Aioru. ("Sir, it's against both the spirit and the letter of the law on appropriate working hours.")

Cliopher pulled out his agenda and contemplated his schedule. He had, as usual, blocked off the morning for the reports and related decisions, and the afternoon was a meeting with the Command Staff of the Imperial Guard—much more formally than just Ludvic and Rhodin in his rooms for a meal—to go over their protocols for the transition of government to his Radiancy's successor.

He hesitated—drank another mouthful of lukewarm coffee—and then went to see if his friend Suzen wanted a live modelling session for the state portraits she was painting of him.

~

It happened again the next day. Cliopher finished his reports before the second bell of the morning, leaving him three and a half hours before he had an afternoon meeting with Aioru. This left Cliopher with the next three items on his List of Projects, of which, unfortunately, two had already been completed in the course of enacting other ideas and the third quickly turned out to be untenable.

He sat back in his chair and looked up at the ceiling, which had a pattern in the plasterwork he'd never noticed before, and found himself literally twiddling his thumbs before he gave up and started answering letters from his family. He'd been putting off a fifteen-page screed from his eccentric cousin Louya. Even that sounded like a good use of his time today.

He unfolded the first page, and rubbed his temples.

Dear Kip, I know you respect the sea, but you Need to know that SEA TURTLES are the Gardeners of Ani and should be Respected as the LORE-HOLDERS they ARE.

Then he imagined his Radiancy's joy in this letter, and, suddenly in much better temper, read on.

∿

The third day he gave up entirely on make-work and decided to figure out what the recent rumours of the return of Fitzroy Angursell were about.

There had been a lot of them of late, ever since his Radiancy's departure on his quest.

Usually an eruption of stories about the Red Company was localized and indicated that something was awry. Far before anyone would be sufficiently moved to action—or at least, usually well before action—people started muttering about the heroes who championed freedom and culture and a joyous sort of justice very hard to accomplish when one also had to think about legal precedents and balancing the budget the next year.

In this case it was probably the current succession causing all the excitement.

Most likely.

Almost certainly.

Cliopher spent a pleasantly unhurried half-hour gathering together the reports and summaries he needed. His usual practice, in a case such as this, was to lay out all the possibly related incidents in both chronological and geographical order to see what might have prompted the resurgence.

(This had already been assessed and dismissed as a threat by his own offices and Rhodin's people alike. He distinctly recalled Aioru laughing through half the report of "and Fitzroy Angursell is supposed to have been *in* the First Emperor's tomb this whole time, can you imagine?")

Cliopher had, from time to time, had occasion to read through the dossiers on the Red Company. His Radiancy had always been particularly sensitive to the rumours of their activity, and Rhodin reported to him directly. While Cliopher did receive the summaries of Rhodin's findings, he had also learned where in the Archives to find the necessary documents of some of the Red Company's more obscure deeds.

Although every rumour of their actual return so far had turned out to be a matter of impostors, impersonators, and occasional lunatics, it was good for him to be thoroughly aware of all the details.

It had long been a plausible excuse.

In truth, Cliopher had simply always been fascinated by the Red Company.

This particular cluster of incidents had started, he determined quite quickly, around the time his Radiancy had departed on his quest. Mutterings from Aigurxe in the Dagger Islands were the earliest, from a month or two before his Radiancy had left. Cliopher tentatively ascribed them as the source. Their complaints were legitimate and were one of Aioru's first tests of governance. Cliopher, thus, did not need to worry about them.

Or at least he didn't need to *do* anything about them.

Then there was a cluster of rumours and story-telling in the immediate vicinity of Solaara itself. But not, he was interested to note, *in* the city, where these sorts of things usually took hold first. No, the stories were being told and the songs sung by the Voribu, who lived in the long wedge of marginal lands bounded by the northern limits of the city, the Escarpment, and the Solamen Fens.

Along with being farmers, the Voribu historically managed the Imperial Necropolis. Pikabe was Voribu, and had once told him he'd joined the Imperial Guard so he didn't have to become a stonemason-custodian like his brothers.

Almost simultaneous with the situation outside Solaara was a cluster of strange incidents around the Abbey of the Mountains in central Damara. There were also a few more scattered reports from Boloyo City and Tsilo far in the north of Amboloyo that were just barely possibly part of the same phenomenon.

Nothing connected them, as far as Cliopher could tell, except for the kind of incidents being reported. Amongst the Voribu, in Boloyo City, in Tsilo,—oh, and there was a note of someone being fined for selling copies of Fitzroy Angursell's banned poems on the island of Dobu, which was in an entirely different hemisphere—people were chattering about the return of Fitzroy Angursell and telling over all the funniest stories about him.

They were not calling for the return of Fitzroy Angursell, Cliopher noted. They were celebrating it as something that had already happened.

Around the Abbey of the Mountains it was much the same, except that the name being celebrated was Masseo Umrit the Smith, not Fitzroy Angursell the Poet.

He looked up at the huge wall map of Zunidh that occupied most of the space opposite his desk. It showed the major cities and political divisions. Asterisks represented the location of the Lights, and faint silverpoint lines showed the main sky ship routes and sea train tracks.

The Dagger Islands were on the sea train route between Port Izhathi, which served Solaara, and Boloyo City. But if he excluded the Aigurxe from his considerations, what then? There was no clear route connecting the Voribu, Boloyo City, Tsilo, and the Abbey of the Mountains. Let alone Dobu, which was off the coast of Western Dair.

The sky ship route from Solaara to Tsilo passed over the Fens. As did most of the other eastbound ones. There was nothing he knew of to connect any of the ships with the herders who lived between Escarpment and Fens.

Cliopher was curious, and a thorough man—and bored. He returned to the files and sought out the original reports of the incidents to see what he might find. He seemed to recall something peculiar from the sky ship reports the week after his Radiancy had set off on his quest. Hadn't the postal run to Tsilo been delayed for nearly a week because the ship had had to leave its course? ...

Tsilo again, he thought, tapping his pen on his lip.

He read the report with a frown at his own carelessness.

The captain of the *Northern Joy* had reported that she had rescued a man from the Fens, which were on fire. She had thought the man a wandering lunatic of good family, and intended to hand him over to the authorities in Tsilo when she arrived so he could be returned to wherever he'd escaped from. Their route had been disrupted by encountering the sky forest over Amboloyo during the night, and in the confusion of avoiding collision in the dark the stranger had jumped overboard.

He had, the captain noted, been dressed almost exactly like the stories described of Fitzroy Angursell, whom he had all but explicitly stated he was. He was in his sixties or thereabouts, she guessed, of extremely excellent address and character but for the apparent lunacy.

Cliopher's immediate suspicion was utterly ludicrous.

Completely, impossibly, absolutely *risible*.

He set the captain's report aside and turned to the events in the Solamen Fens.

The Fens had burned down the night of his Radiancy's departure—Cliopher had observed the glow from the Palace windows. Three Voribu men had been apprehended on suspicion of arson, but released without charges when it became clear that they had not set the fire themselves.

They had reported that as they made their way into the centre of the Fens, where their people's histories held a deity resided, they had encountered a strange man bicycling along the boardwalk. He had claimed to be looking for the River-Horse Inn but was actually headed directly towards the most forbidden, sacred, and extremely dangerous part of the marshes. This man had been the one to actually light the Fens on fire, using magic, all the while playing a harp.

The men had alluded to ancient spirits awakening and greeting the stranger as an equal. They thought he might be one of the ancient Emperors, perhaps Yr himself, come on the sacred day.

A second, slightly contradictory point was that the actual arsonist (was it technically arson, Cliopher wondered, if the lord magus did it for magical purposes? But regardless—it still should have been *announced*, so that any potential disasters that might result from *burning down a magically-bound swamp next to the capital city at the end of the dry season* could be mitigated)—the arsonist, at any rate, had claimed he'd been given the bicycle by one of the custodians at the Imperial Necropolis.

It took Cliopher some time to find the report from the Necropolis, but after a further half-hour of searching the Archives he learned that a man who looked just like the emperor carved on the sarcophagus had been found by the custodian *inside* the tomb of Yr the Conqueror.

This man, the custodian said, claimed to have opened the tomb by means of a magic wand; he had not stolen anything; and he had denied being Fitzroy Angursell. (Which was a strange comment to make, either in the report or in real life, surely. Unless the custodian had asked him first ...) The tomb magic had not done anything until the custodian had stepped past the tunnel threshold, at which point the stranger had shoved the custodian out by magic and then shut the tomb behind them.

Cliopher contemplated this array of reports.

How lonely he'd been, that first fortnight after his Radiancy's departure. He'd thrown himself so deeply into his tasks as Viceroy—delegated all this sort of thing—all he'd received was the bare report stating that the burning of the Fens had been investigated and there was a warrant out for the arrest of the suspected arsonist.

He turned to the reports from the Abbey of the Mountains, and the remarkable account there of the sudden, inexplicable arrival of Aurelius Magnus to answer the prayers of a local postulant nun before spiriting away the local smith, unnamed but widely presumed to be Masseo Umrit, on a journey into the Qavaliun Basin.

All these events had all occurred within a few days of each other; some of them within hours. He got up and stood before the world map.

He touched the emblem marking Solaara. The Imperial Necropolis was named—it was the original reason why Solaara had been anything more than a tiny village in the years before it became the capital—as were the Solamen Fens. He walked his fingers down the tiny space representing ten or twelve miles of land, stopping at the silvery line demarcating the sky ship route to Tsilo.

He traced out the arc across the Eastern Ocean, over Copper Eyot and the Lissurian Sea and coastal Amboloyo before landing on the empty savannah where the *Northern Joy* had left its course and turned north to avoid the sky forest, which floated on the wind between the Lissurian coast and the mountains to the east.

The ship had sailed first to Boloyo City and thence to Tsilo, taking with it stories of a noble lunatic who carefully declined to state outright he was Fitzroy Angursell, but definitely knew all the stories and dressed the part.

Said 'lunatic' had jumped off the ship as it swerved to avoid a forest of flying trees.

Assuming he had not fallen to his death—he was a great mage, after all—he had likely landed in the sky forest, and been thus borne—Cliopher slid his hand east—straight to that part of the mountain chain that was home to the Abbey of the Mountains at the headwaters of the Qavaliun River.

He looked at the map, a little in awe of how his Radiancy had managed to illicitly, if not exactly secretly, cross half the world in three days.

Why had his Radiancy decided to pretend to be Fitzroy Angursell?

His eyes were drawn to the circle of the Vangavaye-ve, on the opposite side of the map from the Qavaliun Basin.

On that one memorable holiday to the Outer Ring of the Vangavaye-ve with his Radiancy, the Moon had come down during the course of a lunar eclipse and called his Radiancy *her beloved*. She had offered him her embrace, a share in her immortality, pleasure and life beyond human ken.

He had refused, saying that that was not his heart's desire, and she had given him a quest, and a promise of half a hundred poems instead.

On another occasion, Pali Avramapul had come on a scholar's mission, and had offered his Radiancy something that *was* his heart's desire, which he had not been able to take because neither his government, nor Cliopher, nor even he himself were ready.

And Cliopher had missed it.

All of it.

He'd never *seen* it.

A hundred moments came into Cliopher's mind, a hundred comments or strange snippets of knowledge or lightning-flash expressions, here then gone.

Of course his Radiancy was actually the notorious outlaw and trickster poet Fitzroy Angursell.

Of course he was.

Cliopher stared at the map, his throat tight, his hands cold, sick to his stomach. Of course his Radiancy was Fitzroy Angursell. Of *course* he was.

He'd never, ever seen it.

He rubbed his cold fingers across his face, biting his lip, unable to get past that brute fact. That rock—that *reef* he'd just crashed upon.

≈

He returned to his desk and cleaned up his papers. Set the reports into a box to go back to the Archives. Resolutely did not look at any of his illicit copies of Fitzroy Angursell's poetry.

Resolutely did not let himself think—

≈

It was no good.

Ten minutes of staring at his desk later, he went out, searching for someone to talk to. It would have to be one of his friends in his Radiancy's household—and that meant Ludvic. Conju was away, and Rhodin would be busy—so would Ludvic—but Conju and Rhodin were both aristocrats. They did not understand the role Fitzroy Angursell and the Red Company played in the hearts of the people.

They would not understand what this meant to Cliopher.

And Ludvic was—was—Ludvic was *steady*. That was the thing. Cliopher was so jumbled up inside himself he couldn't tell what he was feeling.

Perhaps it was indigestion.

(It was not indigestion.)

He did not miss things like this. He *didn't*.

(—He had.)

He found the Commander of the Imperial Guard sitting at his desk with his own reports. He was wearing his reading glasses and appeared the very picture of sober industry, but even in his discomposure Cliopher noted that his friend's pen nib was dry.

Ludvic took off his glasses with a vaguely expectant look and an inquisitive grunt.

Cliopher's heart was fluttery—perhaps it *was* indigestion?—but he had forced himself into his court face, and his voice did not shake. He was proud of that. It was something he could hold on to. He sounded fine. Normal. Collected. Courtly

He said, precisely, "Can we talk about Fitzroy Angursell for a bit?"

Ludvic let out a great breath. "About time."

~

Ludvic led him out by the same door they'd used for when his Radiancy left on his quest.

His Radiancy, who was Fitzroy Angursell.

His Radiancy, who had chosen to wear a scarlet silk mantle over his plain linen tunic when he set out.

At some point he had stopped and put on the sky-blue robes that the custodian at the Necropolis had mentioned. It was the costume of Fitzroy Angursell in half his songs.

Cliopher strode faster, eager to get wherever Ludvic was taking him.

He could not *believe* he'd not seen it. His Radiancy had done everything bar *saying* it—

—And why *hadn't* he said it?

Cliopher stopped short. He'd gotten ahead of Ludvic, who strode at a steady, unhurried pace.

"It's too hot to walk that fast," Ludvic observed, catching up.

"It is hot," Cliopher agreed, glad after all he'd taken Ludvic's suggestion for changing his clothing while Ludvic put on his 'civvies', which were nothing like court clothing in the least, but rather an Azilinti-style cotton drape in a dull, dusty blue over his white linen kilt.

("We're skiving off," Ludvic had said with a sudden, surprising grin. "We should dress appropriately.")

Cliopher did not care about wearing appropriate clothing. What sort of clothes were *appropriate* for discovering the Last Emperor of Astandalas, the man he had served and loved and, he'd thought, come to be friends with—*good* friends with—was actually the infamous rebel poet Fitzroy Angursell?

His Radiancy had trusted Cliopher to run the world in his absence, but he hadn't trusted him with *that*.

Cliopher did not know what to think. Or feel. Perhaps his Radiancy did not actually care if he ran the world into the ground, after all. Perhaps that trust had been as tenuous as—

He'd put on a simple Vangavayen-style tunic and trews. His shoulders felt naked without the usual court mantle over them. He shivered.

The worn linen was very soft and light on his skin, though he could feel sweat already starting to bead at his temples and down his spine. The gardens were green and lush but slightly dusty, this end of the dry season. It would be another few weeks yet before the rains came; there was a system of purifying cisterns and pumps from the river to water the Palace and its gardens.

Ludvic took him down a gravel path that led through a quiet, private copse of banana trees, their huge leaves shading the ground below. Cliopher took a breath. The scent was earthy and rich, not quite familiar—these were some sort of red lady-finger, not what they had at home—*nothing* felt right. Why hadn't his Radiancy *told* him?

(Why hadn't Cliopher *guessed*?)

They passed out of the bananas into a copse of high palms shading coffee bushes, and then through a stone wall with a pointed-arch opening. "Left here," Ludvic said, and Cliopher took the next path.

These gardens were wilder, ornamental gingers with red and yellow and orange flowers and vivid green leaves arching overhead. Within a dozen steps the path had twisted and all outside light was shut out.

His thoughts felt as claustrophobic and twisting, and he kept stumbling on roots.

There had been so much circumstantial evidence. A pattern he had never seen, he who was so good at patterns. A secret he'd never been told, he who—

He had *asked* for his Radiancy's secret name.

His Radiancy had promised him he'd tell him. One day.

Cliopher's eyes burned.

The path twisted into rough steps down the face of a fairly steep embankment. Small animals darted away from their passing, creatures and birds he never quite caught glimpses of. The ornamental gingers gave way to thicker and wilder vegetation, palms and broadleaved trees, shrubs and festoons of vines. Cliopher could not see where they were going, or more than a few bare yards into the growth. He recognized ipomoea of various sorts, their trumpet-flowers crumpled and faded this late in the day.

In the morning they would be sky-blue and scarlet; his Radiancy's—*Fitzroy Angursell's*—favourite colours.

"I've never been into this part of the gardens before," he forced himself to say. He could keep his voice even, though his jaw and neck were tensed.

"It was full of wild magic for a long time," Ludvic replied. "But not the twisted magic of the broken bits of the gardens. This was wild magic. Bright magic. *He* was very pleased to see it, when he came to the fixing of it. I remember him coming out several times just to sit near the heart of it. Once he said, 'This is what magic should be'."

Magic wild and bright. What magic *should* be.

Cliopher dug his fingers into his palms to stop a sudden, odd flood of emotion prickling his eyes and nose.

Ludvic continued quietly, down through the dim green forest on what seemed an endless series of flights of stairs and landings, all made of rough-cut wood anchored with metal pegs and backfilled with pounded rubble. There were boulders and outcroppings of the rocks on either side of the stair as well, damp with humidity.

Cliopher was damp with sweat. He was accustomed to the stairs of the Palace, and could take the five long flights from ground floor to his own apartments with relative ease, but he was not used to the proportions—or rather mis-proportions, for the steps were not at all even—and concentration required to keep his footing.

Not that he could concentrate, really.

"Are we going all the way down to the river bottom?" he asked, finally conceding defeat and having to pause to catch his breath and straighten his knees and shoulders.

Ludvic gave him one of his imperturbable expressions; his eyes were laughing. "Something like that."

Cliopher waved his hand at him. It was easier to keep to the surface the immediate: his footing, Ludvic's pace, his own careful breathing. "Yes, yes, you win."

"You're doing well," Ludvic replied encouragingly, and seemed to mean it, for he continued down without moderating his pace.

Eventually they reached the bottom. The stair stopped unceremoniously, hidden behind an enormous multi-stemmed curtain fig. Ludvic wove his way with certainty through the tangled curtains of roots and branches, and suddenly they were out of the dim, cool, chimney of wilderness and at the edge of a road.

Cliopher blinked at the bright sunlight, too white and yellow after the green. The air was hot and sultry, and smelled of food: frying things, sizzling meat, something honeyed wafting through the air.

They had descended the entirety of the longest vertical face of the volcanic plug upon which the Palace perched. Black stone draped in dusty green rose up out of the bight of the river around the plug.

This side was the Levels, one of the poorer quarters of the city. It had once been nearly a slum, but over the years in which Cliopher and his Radiancy had slowly reformed the government—and especially those more recent years of the annual stipend—it had shifted to a colourful, noisy, and pleasant place to live.

Cliopher and his Radiancy. Who was Fitzroy Angursell.

He rubbed his face again.

"This way," said Ludvic.

The buildings were still vaguely ramshackle in appearance, entirely unstandardized in design, built out of all sorts of materials. But now they were painted, decorated, illuminated with magic and stamped tinwork lanterns, and gardens exploded out of every corner and most roofs.

Ludvic led him along alleys and through courtyards, past chicken coops and communal piggeries and a few enterprising raisers of guinea pigs, goats, and other small food and fibre animals; there were also little factories for pungent sauces or regional specialties. They passed tiny businesses, tailors and embroiderers, tinsmiths, plumbers, gardeners, people who made shovels or cartwheels or protective amulets.

Cliopher held on to his sense of *home*.

In that direction, like an anchor-rock holding his tether, was his own island, Loaloa of the Western Ring of the Vangavaye-ve. He did not need anything else if he had that.

(That was a lie. He had spent his life looking for something he'd never been able to find there.)

There were not really any roads in the Levels. People, animals, bicycles, donkeys appeared and disappeared through doorways and crooked pathways. Nothing seemed particularly private.

Cliopher took a deep breath and followed Ludvic through a crowded yard full of the sizzle and smoke of a barbecue, people laughing, something tangy in the air. It was all red and yellow, piles of hot peppers being strung on lines to dry.

And then they were out of that yard and into the next, which was full instead of beans and lentils and dried seeds he could not recognize out of the corners of his eyes, and old women dipping their hands into the pulses, the sifting, shurring noise like the sound of waves lapping on a beach.

He felt anxious, surrounded by so many people and so much noise: it was like home and yet unlike, for the sounds, sights, smells were most of them unfamiliar, and all the faces were. At home there would always have been some hint of the sea—a sea turtle shell mounted on a wall, a row of fish hanging to smoke over a fire—and it would have been more spacious in general.

And he would have known *someone* in the masses of strangers.

Would not have been so—so—so discombobulated.

(That was another lie. He didn't fit in there, either. He never had.)

Ludvic seemed well at home. He nodded to people as they passed, many of whom nodded back or called things in sharp or lilting accents. They were in an Azilinti region now: people wore clothes in the same style Ludvic had chosen for his civvies, and carved staves of every wood were propped up against walls, close to hand, leaned on.

Eventually they stopped at a bead-curtained doorway occupied by a tall, muscular woman with burn scars down her bare arms. She wore dark pink and orange and yellow, sunrise colours: her hair was wrapped in striped orange and white cloth, gold rings in her ears, brass bracelets down her wrists. Her face shared Ludvic's broad features, and her colouring was the same rich dark brown. She was smoking a narrow cigar, absently watching the ash form at the tip.

"Good afternoon, Giya," Ludvic said, stopping before her.

Giya took another draw of her cigar, holding the smoke in her mouth for a moment, before slowly, deliberately tapping the ash off her cigar. It drifted down around her bare feet, pale specks against her skin. Her feet had burn scars as well, Cliopher saw uneasily; her toenails were painted pink.

"Go on, then," she said at last, jerking her head. "Rós or beer for your friend?"

Ludvic glanced at him. Cliopher rarely drank beer, but he had heard of rós, the ferocious distilled liqueur of the Azilint, and it didn't take more than half a moment before Ludvic said, "Beer for us both. Giya." With another nod he led the way through the hanging, clacking beads of the curtain and into the dim space beyond.

Cliopher stumbled on a step and was caught by his friend. "This way," Ludvic said, keeping hold of his arm as they threaded their way through a space crowded with chairs and small tables but otherwise empty. The air smelled of cigars and old beer, with an overlay of frying food. By the time Ludvic had led him to the back Cliopher had finally realized it was a bar.

There were several booths along the back wall, wooden-framed with more beads hanging down in front of them for privacy. Ludvic led him to the one to one side, not apparently any different from the others except that when Cliopher ducked through the beads he felt a wash and tingle of powerful magic.

He bit back an exclamation and sat down hard on the bench behind him.

Ludvic busied himself lighting the oil lamp in the middle of the table with a firestarter he pulled out of his pocket. Cliopher was grateful for the light, as the room still seemed extremely dim.

The booth was carved wood—elaborately carved wood. He knew enough, from his times spent haunting the Imperial Museum, to know that these were Azilinti motifs: pigs, snakes, wingfingers, hammerhead sharks, bats. The wingfingers, flying lizards with long beaks and long crests, had nested on Woodlark until the destruction of the island.

The table was dark wood, scuffed and scratched and marked with water rings. He could see out through the beaded curtain. Giya was moving around on the far side of the room. The air felt fizzy on his tongue.

"Protective magics," Ludvic said, gesturing at the carvings, the beads (themselves carved, Cliopher now saw, with runes and other sigils). "Privacy, silence, discretion ... No one can hear anything we say here but ourselves. Or recognize us through the curtain."

Cliopher regarded him in astonishment. "Why is that not something we have in the Palace?"

"It was to be kept in the community," Ludvic replied, shrugging, which was an unusual motion from him. Cliopher realized his friend had relaxed considerably, no longer on anything resembling parade rest, and tried to imitate him. The wooden bench was padded, and was surprisingly comfortable. Or perhaps unsurprisingly, if this were Ludvic's retreat from the demands of his position.

Cliopher could wish he'd had such a retreat outside the Palace.

His Radiancy—*Fitzroy Angursell*—he had only had his private study, and that barely had a window.

He folded his hands together, surprised they were trembling. He wanted his Radiancy there—

No. He wanted...someone he'd thought he knew.

A dark, heavy fire seemed to smoulder into sullen life. Cliopher hastily suppressed any hint of anger. He should not be *angry*. Undoubted his Radiancy—*Fitzroy Angursell*—had had his reasons.

His thoughts were sour in the back of his throat.

He'd always thought he'd be *excited* to discover what had happened to Fitzroy Angursell after his mysterious disappearance. Daydreamed he'd be the one to find him; even to rescue him.

Ludvic sighed. "I miss him," he said simply. "It's not the same with him gone."

"Fitzroy Angursell," Cliopher said flatly. It didn't sound like a name of anyone they could know personally.

"Yes," said Ludvic, and they sat there with that radical truth a large silence between them.

Giya knocked on the edge of the booth, a rat-tat-tat that was at once brusque and familiar. Ludvic reached out and parted the bead curtain with his hand. Giya ducked in through the opening. Her hands were full of green glass bottles cloudy with condensation, fingers stuck inside upside-down glasses.

"Thank you," Ludvic said politely.

She grunted. Cliopher hid a smile at this reversal of Ludvic's usual practice and accepted his own glass and bottle with murmured thanks. Giya gave him a short, absent nod, her attention barely acknowledging his existence.

"How is she?" Ludvic asked.

"The same," Giya replied, and went out again, the beads falling together with a wild clatter.

Ludvic untwisted the metal hood holding the cork on his bottle. Cliopher watched him before following suit. The beer came out in a thin golden stream as he poured it into his glass, effervescent and yeasty with an almost bitter-lemon overtone to the aroma.

Rat-tat-tat. Ludvic opened the still-swinging curtain. Giya thrust a large clay jug at him, followed by a plate of something fried, still steaming, and incontestably appetizing.

"Corn fritters," Ludvic said as he set the items down. There was a little bowl of some red chutney with the fritters, and a thin green sauce. Cliopher regarded them both with great interest. It seemed a long time since he had last eaten.

Ludvic ate two corn fritters. Cliopher picked one up and set it down immediately when the heat stung his fingers. The guard then poured himself water into his glass—Cliopher realized he was probably supposed to drink the beer from the bottle—took a long, thoughtful swig, and then said: "I really thought you were going to hold out till the very last minute, Cliopher, resolutely refusing to admit it."

Cliopher choked on a corn kernel; washed it down with beer; sneezed as the bubbles went up his nose, spluttered a little more, and finally demanded, "What do you mean?—When did *you* find out?"

Ludvic gave him one of the familiar blank-faced, laughing-eyed *looks*. "Oh, I've known since the beginning."

Chapter Six
Bar Talk

Cliopher had known Ludvic for the better half of his life. He was familiar with the guard's laconic habit, his insightful nature, and his occasional tendency to come out with staggering pronouncements.

This had not been one he'd expected.

"What do you mean, since the beginning?" he asked weakly. "Since you joined the guard?"

Ludvic smiled at his beer, fingers tracing the beading condensation. "Since himself awoke after the Fall."

"You were standing guard that day." Cliopher had not been there—at the time he had been nothing more than a lowly undersecretary, working for Princess Indrogan to try to restore order—but he'd been there when Ludvic had told his Radiancy what he remembered, back when his Radiancy had discovered a way to—

A way to leave the Palace and all that went with it behind, and set off on a *quest*.

A way to become Fitzroy Angursell again.

Cliopher wrenched his attention back to the conversation. Ludvic was still smiling. The gold smudges on his hands and forearms were dimly reflective in the light of the oil lamp.

"Did he tell you?" Cliopher asked abruptly.

Did he sound jealous? He didn't mean to. Ludvic could have—did have—his own close relationship with the lord he had served so long as well. With the man whose *friend* he was. They could both be friends.

"We have a different relationship than you do, Cliopher," Ludvic said. "It is more ... paternal."

"Paternal?"

Cliopher stared frankly at his friend. He and Ludvic were within a couple of years of each other in age. That was hardly a decade younger than his Radiancy.

"Perhaps ... avuncular is the better word," Ludvic allowed. "As if he were my father's younger brother."

That made more sense—Cliopher certainly had any number of cousins and uncle or aunts or close family friends in that sort of—

"You're counting out cousins of yours who have families like that, aren't you?"

Cliopher met Ludvic's eyes. The guard was still smiling, deeply amused. Cliopher flushed and took a sip of his beer. It was light, hoppy, a bit lemony.

Ludvic actually laughed. He really was much more relaxed here, in his carved booth behind the privacy curtain, far from the Palace.

For a moment Cliopher wished this moment would extend, suspended out of their real lives, a moment of friendship between them, more solid than almost any other.

"He did not tell me outright, no," Ludvic eventually went on. His eyes dropped to his bottle, the cloudy green glass, his brown-and-gold hands. "After he woke, the other guards were ... discomposed. I sent one for water, one fainted, the other for something else. To find out where Lady Jivane was, I think. Himself was on a platform on the lower daïs. He sat there for a bit and then came down the steps, stretching his legs. I stayed at the bottom of the steps while he walked around."

Cliopher pictured it. The high wall at the western end of the throne room, with the huge banner of Astandalas hanging down (black and white and the gold sun-in-glory), the names of the hundred emperors of Astandalas inscribed on the white limestone to either side. The golden throne on the upper daïs, reached (as he knew now) by a special door hidden behind it, used only by the Emperor himself and his closest bodyguards.

Five steps down to the lower daïs, where he himself stood often in the course of his duties. The lower daïs was quite large, extending out in a sweep, some ten feet above the main floor of the hall. The facing wall of the daïs was carved with scenes depicting the conquered lands and peoples of Astandalas, all bearing tribute to the Emperor at the centre.

Directly beneath the throne were inscribed the names of the official Terrors of Astandalas, vanquished by its might. The topmost were the names of the Red Company, a coup of propaganda Cliopher had long admired and despised in almost equal measure: for they had disappeared, not been destroyed.

"He stopped at the petitioners' spot, where the lower daïs swings out to the little bay where they stand, before the list."

Cliopher nodded in agreement. He could see it in his mind's eye; had stood there himself, with the weight of Astandalas pressing down upon him. Even in the empty hall—especially in the empty hall—the power was silently, oppressively magnificent.

"He stood there, looking up at his throne. All the ... display of it."

The throne room was very clearly designed to focus all awareness on the Emperor who sat on that high golden throne.

"He would have no reason to know about the acoustics in that spot, that it is designed so a petitioner's mumbles can be heard by the heralds at the bottom of the stair," Ludvic said.

Cliopher looked at him. Ludvic wasn't laughing now: his face was pensive, even a little sad. His eyes were solemn.

"He said, 'So, Fitzroy, do you think you've served your full sentence yet?' as he stood there looking up at the throne. I ... I did not take in his meaning at first, but I think I coughed or moved—so he remembered I was there—he didn't know I'd heard him, I'm sure of that. He came over and asked me questions about the Fall, what had happened, what I thought of it all."

He stopped there, thinking. Remembering.

"The other guards came back. We went to find Lady Jivane. She handed him the crown of Zunidh immediately. I was standing behind him, watching. I saw ... just for a moment, when she was sobbing at his feet and thrusting all the responsibility onto him—he'd clasped his hands behind his back, where I stood—and he—for a moment I thought he'd break his own fingers."

Ludvic gestured with his own hands, bending the fingers of one backwards with the other. Even in demonstration it looked painfully unnatural.

Cliopher forced himself not to say anything.

After a moment, Ludvic went on. "That was when I knew. And I swore then I would always stand behind him, because I have never admired anyone so much as that moment. He had no choice to become emperor, you know. But he could have said no then, and he didn't. He didn't."

Ludvic sat back in his chair, his expression pensive. Cliopher let these new details settle into his knowledge of his Radiancy. (*Fitzroy Angursell.*)

He would not have thought, if someone had asked him, that *Fitzroy Angursell* would have quite that splendid sense of duty. And yet—

And yet.

His Radiancy was the same man. The person Cliopher had known all these years. He had to be. Cliopher had a hundred arguments for why Fitzroy Angursell's banned comic epic *Aurora* was the greatest work of poetry to come out of the latter centuries of the Empire of Astandalas. He had drawn any number of useful and beautiful concepts out of it to apply to the question of good government.

Perhaps it was not a surprise, after all, that the man who was both Fitzroy Angursell, the renegade poet and revolutionary and folk hero, and Artorin Damara, hundredth and last Emperor of Astandalas, had nearly broken his hands out of grief and dismay, but yet taken the crown handed him.

Cliopher swallowed against tears and shrank into himself. He knew how painful and unwelcome that duty had been to his Radiancy. He had done his level best to reduce the load—to take it upon his own shoulders—

He should not be this angry. Not at *him*.

"I should have known," he whispered, gripping his sweaty glass of beer. "I should have known."

Giya came back with another tray, another *rat-tat-tat* on the edge of the booth. Ludvic parted the beads for her, letting in a wave of noise from the now-crowded bar outside. She set another pair of bottles on the table, a plate containing some other type of fried item, this time with a yellowish-orange sauce in the accompanying bowl.

"Thank you," Ludvic said.

Giya nodded shortly and swept off again, the beads clattering behind her. They swayed and clacked and slowly stopped, slowly fell silent. Ludvic opened the second bottle of beer and pushed the first to the side. Cliopher had barely drunk half his. His stomach was rumbling, and he took one of the fried things. It was a prawn, very hot, and he dropped it onto the table in front of him.

Ludvic actually laughed, his face creasing, as Cliopher sat there sucking on his fingers and inwardly cursing.

It broke the solemnity of the moment, at any rate. When Cliopher had finished recovering from the sting, he found Ludvic smiling at him the way the guard sometimes did, his eyes alight but the planes of his face heavy and still.

"So, when *did* you find out?" Ludvic asked.

"Earlier today," Cliopher admitted.

Ludvic's laughter came in great rolling eruptions, like the deepwater swells rocking a boat, his shoulders shaking and his hands fisted.

Cliopher sat there, face burning.

Eventually Ludvic started to gasp out his inner thoughts, much-interrupted by his laughter: "You mean ... you didn't realize when he ... told you Fitzroy Angursell was in an oubliette? Or ... when he told you he had a *red book* he wanted published ... you blithely agreed to publish it ... even when he said *it would be much harder than you know*?"

"Ludvic ..."

But Ludvic was laughing far too hard to stop. His eyes were watering. "You mean ... not when he ... not when he ... never said *anything* when you ... were humming *Aurora* ..."

"When was I humming *Aurora*?" Cliopher asked, stung.

Ludvic laughed so hard he actually started to cough in order to catch his breath. "When are you *not* humming *Aurora*?"

"I don't—"

"You don't know ... that you hum ... banned songs ... when you're making a good copy ... of your notes?"

"I *don't*!"

Ludvic devolved into hiccoughs, and swallowed half his beer in a great gulp. Cliopher decided that midday or not, it was clearly the sort of conversation that needed some lubrication.

"You do," Ludvic assured him. "Have I not stood guard all these years? You always hum! And almost all the time it's Fitzroy Angursell's music! Are you telling me you *didn't know*? You were humming them in front of the *Last Emperor of Astandalas*!"

Cliopher slumped down into his seat in mortification. He'd thought of a hundred oblique comments, a thousand speaking glances, moments where he had said to himself, *oh yes, his Radiancy must be named in one of Fitzroy Angursell's songs*.

"*Pali Avramapul* came to see him."

"I know," he said, his voice cracking with his embarrassment.

"You recognized her."

"Who else was going to have visited him in his tower of exile?"

"Indeed," said Ludvic, his face shining.

Cliopher gave up on sipping his beer and swigged it back. The deep-fried prawns were cool enough to handle now, at least. He dipped it experimentally into the sauce, forgetting that Azilinti food tended to be much spicier than anything he routinely ate.

"Have some more beer," Ludvic advised as he spluttered into the water.

"Thanks," Cliopher replied dourly.

Ludvic watched him, calmer now but no less amused. He waited until Cliopher had settled down, his face still hot but no longer quite flaming. Then he said, "Not *even* when you and he both played *Aurora* together? I was *sure* you knew at that point. Absolutely, completely certain."

Cliopher bit his lip, recognizing the out for what it was, but he could hardly *lie*, could he?

"I didn't," he snapped. "Give it a rest, would you? I feel foolish enough."

More than foolish. *Furious.*

With himself, with his Radiancy, with—

Fitzroy Angursell was *known* for his sense of his mischief, his convincing air, his *verisimilitude.*

Surely he hadn't been acting the whole time? Surely that—that friendship, if he dared call it that—surely it had not been *fake?*

Surely that hesitation, that doubt, that ... anxiety he had seen in his Radiancy's face, before he left, had not been feigned?

Ludvic sobered. "I'm sorry, Cliopher. I don't mean to diminish your feelings. Or make you feel bad."

"I can do that on my own," Cliopher muttered in reply. His jumbled emotions were settling into a heavy sludge of dismay. Disappointment.

He did not want to look too closely at that disappointment.

"Why didn't you ever say anything?" he asked.

Ludvic shrugged, his face calm, unruffled. "So long as he showed no desire to be seen as anything other than his Radiancy, I followed suit."

There was a simplicity, an assurance, to his words that Cliopher could never have achieved.

If *he* had known—

He would not have been able to stay silent.

He recalled that holiday on Lesuia, when his Radiancy—Fitzroy Angursell—had broken out of his customary behaviour, and Ludvic had immediately supported him, suggested he retire, showed him the door to freedom.

"Oh," Cliopher said slowly, chagrinned all over again. He hadn't *realized*. He had seen the bleakness in his Radiancy's eyes, the gradual ... sorrowing ... and he had responded as best he could, but until Ludvic had pointed the way he had never tried to break him free. It had never *occurred* to him to try.

"Also," Ludvic said pragmatically, "I ensured his primary guards were ... let's say, of a romantic disposition. In case he decided to throw it all over and go."

Cliopher closed his eyes. "I would have helped him, if he'd told me."

"You did help him," Ludvic replied gently.

Too gently, after all that beer.

In defiance of every hard-learned lesson of court etiquette, Cliopher pillowed his head down on his arms and let himself weep.

Ludvic made him climb all the way back up that steep, narrow, hidden stair.

"We practice on it," he told him, the second time Cliopher had to stop for breath. "The guards. Make them run up and down."

Cliopher shuddered at the thought. His lungs were burning and his thighs trembling already, and they were hardly more than two-thirds of the way up. The air was much more humid than it had been, here in the chimney of jungle running up the cleft in the stone. Water trickling down, and the rains coming inexorably closer.

Ludvic clearly ran up and down the stairs multiple times a week, because he walked up them as lightly as if it were one familiar flight.

Mountain folk. Ludvic's lung capacity was probably twice Cliopher's.

Cliopher had his pride, foolish as it was. He pushed himself, refusing to stop a third time until he reached the top. Reach the top he did, his lungs and throat and face and thighs burning, and had to stand there, bent over, hands on his knees, gasping for breath.

He was glad for the privacy granted by the vegetation, that was for certain.

He was still red-faced and breathing hard when a troupe of young guards came jogging around the corner and staggered to an incredulous halt on seeing him.

Rhodin was at the back, and pushed forward with a few brief, pungent comments demanding why they'd stopped. He raised one eyebrow at seeing Cliopher and Ludvic in their civilian clothes at the top of the stair.

Ludvic was leaning against the wooden railing at the top of the cliff, and Cliopher was woefully certain it was obvious how much he was still catching his breath.

"Lord Mdang. Commander Omo," Rhodin said eventually, saluting. All the young guards followed suit. Cliopher recognized his old friend Bertie's son Parno in the mix, gazing at him in astonished amusement, and mustered a smile for the young men. Oh, and women. There were four young women in the group, which was unusual—

Of course, he thought a moment later. The new lord magus was very likely to be a lady, given the way that historically the lords magi of Zunidh had alternated with each succession. Rhodin would be training a coterie of female guards for the most intimate duties in case she preferred them.

He wondered briefly why his Radiancy had always preferred male attendants.

His Radiancy. Who was Fitzroy Angursell. Who had never—

"Ser Rhodin," Ludvic said easily.

Cliopher weighed the embarrassment of gasping over the embarrassment of not saying anything at all, and forced himself to say, "Ser Rhodin. Guards." He was still breathless, and he coughed at the end, and Parno really didn't need to be grinning at him like that, did he? Had his accent come out that strongly?

"We were about to take a run up and down the Needle," Rhodin went on with an evil grin. The lithe young guards shifted in unpleasant anticipation. "They've been grumbling that it's impossible."

Cliopher could not deny that he felt substantially better as several of the young guards muttered and nodded and grimaced or grinned sheepishly. He knew his expression was probably quite sheepish himself.

"How many breaks did you need to take, s-sir?" Parno said daringly.

"Two," Ludvic answered for him, with a blandness Cliopher could not have managed at the moment. "Ready, Lord Mdang?"

"Yes," Cliopher said, because no matter that he would need another break at the top of the next stretch through the woods, he did have his little vanities.

How he wanted to tell his Radiancy—

Fitzroy Angursell. Would *he* still want ...

That was unfair. Cliopher *knew* him. Now that he knew this truth, he could see all the ways in which the inner man beneath the façade of the Last Emperor could have been the Fitzroy Angursell of all the stories.

Could have been. Had been. Was.

He was still the man Cliopher had loved and served for so long.

Up the steep slope, through the wild garden, to the cool, eerie, ornamental gingers.

His Radiancy was still that man. He just ... he just had even more secrets than Cliopher had suspected. That was allowed. Cliopher had never assumed his friends told him *everything*.

Cliopher didn't feel betrayed that Ludvic had never told him *he* knew, that he thought of his Radiancy in an avuncular fashion. He was *disappointed* Ludvic had never shown him that bar before, had never taken him to that private space, but that was because he would have liked to be better friends, not because he felt betrayed.

He ducked his head under a hanging branch, a terrible thought. *Betrayed* was the wrong word. It was.

It was.

He was disappointed, that was all. He'd thought—he'd wanted—something that could not be. In the end, there was an unbridgeable gap between his Radiancy and his servants; this only underscored that reality.

They were coming back to the more popular parts of the gardens. Cliopher put on his court face, lifted his chin, straightened his shoulders, lengthened his stride. He was Viceroy of Zunidh, and he was the rising tanà. He would wait fruitlessly like the tui trees no longer. So his lord was not what he'd thought—and so? He did not need to chase that viau, seek that sea, any longer.

There were other seas to seek, to find, to sail. He could be content with them.

(All of this was a lie.)

CHAPTER SEVEN
PORTRAITS OF A VICEROY

Cliopher's friend, the great artist Suzen—Saya Vho Suzen, as her customary address was—had first come to the Palace as the winner of a world-wide competition to find a new artist to paint a portrait of his Radiancy. Cliopher had organized the competition, though his Radiancy had been the actual judge of the finalists, and he had been immediately impressed by the woman who had won.

Suzen was about his age, perhaps a few years younger, and belonged to the ethnic majority of coastal Jilkano. They were entirely unrelated to the interior tribes such as Aioru's, instead being the result of successive waves of Astandalan-era settlement and colonial activities. Most of those who lived in and around the City of Emeralds were a mix of Western Voonran and Loroshians, who had long ago left their somewhat malarial and strife-torn homelands for the better climate and potential of coastal Jilkano.

Suzen was thus fairly pale-skinned, though not nearly so much as the Amboloyans—she had tan skin, a round face, very straight and shiny black hair, and dark eyes that were, Conju had once told Cliopher, a perfect example of the classical Voonran shape called Peach Leaf.

Cliopher had once said something unthinking about Rhodin's eyes being 'almond-shaped' to Conju and subsequently been treated to an impromptu history of Voonran maquillage and the names for various shapes of eyes amongst different cultures. Rhodin himself had laughed and agreed that he had inherited his mother's Jade Phoenix eyes and been glad for it, too.

When he arrived back in his rooms, he found Suzen chatting with Tully, his appointments secretary, in the reception room. Tully was enquiring about her wheeled chair, which was made of bamboo and wicker, with wheels rather like a bicycle's.

Cliopher took a breath, unregarded for a moment, and ruthlessly shoved down all his lingering distress. He had a lot of practice in packing away awkward emotions; he might as well use the skill.

She turned and saw him standing there; her face lit up. "Cliopher! What an outfit!"

Tully giggled. Cliopher winked at the young woman and smiled easily at his friend. "I like your chair. Did you get it here in Solaara?"

She'd been in the Palace for three weeks, painting his state portraits, and her previous chair, while lovely, had been all sinuous copper snakes.

"No, it's just arrived," Suzen said, wheeling around in a pirouette so he could admire the exquisite fan-shaped back. "No doubt the enchanter wanted to make sure it would be seen at the Palace ..."

"No doubt," he replied dryly. "Will you join me for a drink?"

"Tea would be lovely, if you've the time."

"You've nothing till court tomorrow," Tully put in helpfully.

"Spiffing!" said Suzen, and followed him in.

He bathed quickly and dressed court-casual, a knee-length linen tunic with an over-mantle of silk: deep midnight blue for the one, and bronze-brown shot silk for the other, which was a little on-the-nose for the heraldry of Zunidh but fortunately were also two of his favourite colours.

Suzen was waiting for him in his sitting room when he came out, a tray of tea already sitting on the low side table. She laughed as he sat down in his chair, which creaked.

"I cannot believe you still have those chairs, Cliopher! Surely you could have gotten new ones?"

Cliopher had had to expend a great deal of energy and persuasion to *keep* his beloved and battered old furniture, and he frowned at her. "I happen to like them, Suzen."

"And will you take them home to Gorjo City with you?"

He looked down, awash suddenly in doubt. He had not let himself imagine living at home so far as to imagine what furnishings he would have in his new house. "Oh, I don't know," he murmured, swirling the teapot so the fragrant steam rose up.

"I think I'll stick with my chair," she declared, grinning. She parked herself at an angle to his seat, where she could look at him and the portrait of his great-uncle with ease. "What a painting that is," she said, not for the first time. "A challenge to me, to make your portrait speak to that one and also be very clear about your status ..." She trailed off, gazing at him with that slightly disconcerting stare that meant she was looking at his features and not himself.

Cliopher was used to it, and he did not mind it from Suzen.

Especially not when she had so immediately understood that his portrait was to be the culmination of his entire life, his Islander culture and his court achievements alike.

He might not be able to be the Last Emperor of Astandalas' greatest friend—Fitzroy Angursell had his own great friends of the Red Company, friendships honoured and lauded in song and story—but Cliopher had done his best in his Radiancy's service. Done *well* in that service.

"Yes, there's the spark," Suzen murmured. "No—don't move." She reached into one of the side pockets of her chair for a leather-bound sketchbook. She pulled out a charcoal stick, flipped to a blank page, and started swiftly sketching. "Yes—stand like that—please—I've just had an idea ..."

There had been far too many times when Cliopher had been caught by the germ of new ideas and had to reach for his writing kit for him to do anything more than endeavour to keep his roiling emotions from showing on his face.

He found himself silently reciting a passage from *Aurora* to keep himself settled, and stopped short with an internal dislocation.

And then, carefully, consciously, with the greatest deliberation, he started silently reciting the *Lays* instead.

Both of them started when the sunset bell rang.

"I'll stop," Suzen said reluctantly, letting her charcoal come to rest.

Cliopher moved creakily, feeling his age. He always forgot, when he was deep into the *Lays*; somehow he always expected himself to be twelve again, learning the Islander version for the first time.

He rang the bell pull. Shoänie appeared in due course with a tray of wine and light appetizers, smiling shyly when Suzen asked her how she was getting on with some project of her own. Over the past few weeks Shoänie had begun to ask questions of the artist, as painting turned out to be one of her hobbies.

People always had more depths to them than you ever knew—look at Ludvic clearly friends with Giya at that bar down in the Levels (not to mention all the deep secrets he'd shared with Cliopher), or Shoänie with a strong artistic bent. Cliopher had thought her main hobby was cooking, as she often talked about being half-apprentice to his cook.

And then there was ... his Radiancy. Secretly being Fitzroy Angursell this whole time.

Perhaps Cliopher was the only one who did not have such hidden depths. He had his Islander culture, his knowledge of the old ways, which he had not had much cause to make much of in the Palace ...

He crossed the room to the old Voonran chest he'd bought in Astandalas, where the branch from the tui tree rested in a vase Rhodin had once given him. It was an extraordinary piece of pottery, a heavy, ancient piece—Rhodin said it was thousands of years old, found on his grandmother's land when she was excavating for a new building—made of reddish clay with incised geometric slashes.

It would always have been beautiful, carefully constructed and beautifully proportioned as it was, with the patina of age and much use on its exterior. It was made extraordinary because someone had smoothed and lacquered the interior and then coated it in a thin, brilliantly burnished slip of gold.

He went to adjust the placement of the branch in the vase, and his hand stilled.

The beautiful exterior ... the superlative interior, unexpected, even hidden at first, only revealed if you looked for it, at the right angle...

He closed his eyes for a moment, swallowing hard. He loved this vase *for* its outward beauty, its unexpected interior.

"Cliopher, what is it?" Suzen asked, her voice soft with concern.

He blinked back the moisture in his eyes. Shoänie had gone: they were alone. "I ... learned something today," he said thickly. "A secret. About someone I thought ... I thought might have ..."

"You wished they had told you?" she said shrewdly.

He nodded reluctantly. "It's foolish of me ... I'm torn between being angry at myself for not seeing it before, and—"

"And them for not telling you? Of course."

After a while, Cliopher said, "I'm conflicted, Suzen. My friend ... why wouldn't he tell me, if he were truly ..."

"Why wouldn't he?" she asked quietly.

Too many times had he turned the question back, in a negotiation. Repeated the end of a sentence, and the person would probably expand, unable to let the silence stand.

He knew what she was doing, but he was not immune to the tricks of his trade, either. He stared down at the smooth golden interior of the rough old vase, the branch with its blossom. "I don't know," he said, but Suzen was quiet for so long, in such an empathetic silence, that the words came unbidden. "I don't understand why he wouldn't have trusted me with that."

Suzen tilted her head at him. "Are you sure it was a matter of *trust*?" He stared at her, unable to parse what she meant. She was unsmiling. "I brought my earlier sketches of you with me, you know. I'd thought they would help—provide a baseline for my portraits. They don't, though."

He did not understand; did not want to understand. "Not at all?"

She allowed that, judiciously. "Of course, no good practice is ever *wasted*. And they add a depth to what I see now, have seen these past week. But I can't use them for the basis of these portraits. Your carriage, the look in your eyes ... something fundamental has changed. You're much more yourself than you used to be."

How he wanted to be, at least.

Now she smiled at him, gently, her eyes full of sympathy. "You've never lied to me, have you? On purpose?"

"Of course not."

"And yet," she said, "when I look at you now, I see not only how you have changed since your elevation to Viceroy, but also how you have always had those qualities of character. You are very different than you used to be, and yet far more yourself than you ever were before."

His breath hitched, as if his boat had suddenly spun from an area of kurakura into the shelter of a lagoon.

Ludvic had said—Ludvic had said that until his Radiancy had shown movement to reclaiming himself as Fitzroy Angursell, he had held himself to their formal role.

Cliopher had never, quite, been able to hold himself back. He had reached out first—and when he had reached out to the inner man, his Radiancy had reached back.

Fitzroy Angursell had reached back. (He remembered the joy with which his Radiancy had greeted that harp, hidden away in a closet in Navikiani, and the recovered copy of *Aurora* that had been hidden with it. That sudden eruption of music; the glee in surprising his household with that skill. Cliopher had only grieved that he had not had the space, the leisure, for something that gave him such joy; he had not felt betrayed, then, that his Radiancy had never told him he could play.)

Cliopher had seen the inner man, even if he had not been able to name him. His Radiancy *knew* that, and had appreciated that; had told him so, and Cliopher did not believe he'd lied, then. He could not believe that.

No. It was not his Radiancy who had lied. Omitted a few things, perhaps, but ... Cliopher could not say with any honesty that he had not done the same.

"Thank you," he said out loud to Suzen, and went to sit down.

"It's a big secret, I take it?"

He breathed, "Oh, yes." He smiled; he could not help it, at the thought once more crashing through his mind. His Radiancy was Fitzroy Angursell. He *was*. He was.

And Cliopher had helped him: had assisted him in dismantling the very Empire of Astandalas; had opened the door for freedom wide; and he held the fire for his return so he *could* leave.

He blinked back his tears.

After a while Suzen started to tell him new details about her new home, which was perched on a rock at the edge of the sea in the City of Emeralds.

Over supper they talked about Suzen's recent commissions and the set of 'People of the City of Emeralds' she'd been undertaking for a new gallery show. "It's just as well I had nearly finished the series," she said at one point. "Once word gets out I'm painting you, I'll be popular."

"I hope that's a good thing."

"I don't object to selling a few pieces. At some point one's walls fill up." She looked around the sitting room, whither they'd returned after dining. "This room, for instance, is probably full ... but you *do* have a lot of bare walls elsewhere ..."

He laughed. "My house at home will be smaller."

"So the rumours are true? Will you actually be retiring? Handing over your power and everything?"

Cliopher was struck by the light teasing tone, and the serious question in her eyes. "I've already begun," he replied, as lightly and as seriously. "Aioru's taken over as Chancellor, and various other people my other positions. I'm down to just Viceroy, and that's only in my lord's absence. When he comes back ..."

Suzen cast a glance at Rhodin's vase and the fragrant tui blossoms. "And will *he* truly want to abdicate? It seems inconceivable."

He hesitated a moment, for he could not say the truth, which was that his Radiancy had never wanted to be Lord of Zunidh in the first place.

Had never wanted to be *Emperor of Astandalas* in the first place.

Was, in fact, the great rebel Fitzroy Angursell.

Cliopher was suddenly ... glad, yes, *glad* was the word, that he'd never actually invited his Radiancy to live with him. It had always been a ... pipe dream, as Rhodin called it; a viau, in the Islander parlance. Something beautiful but impossible, in short. His Radiancy, the Last Emperor of Astandalas, *might* have been willing to settle in a fairly ordinary middle-class residence in Gorjo City with the chief members of his household.

Fitzroy Angursell, newly released from his gilded prison (his oubliette, as his Radiancy had once called it: *Fitzroy Angursell is in an oubliette*, he had told Cliopher, when he lay in his canopied bed recovering from a heart attack), was never going to want to ... confine himself like that.

Perhaps, Cliopher thought wistfully, he might visit once in a while. Come in with as much unexpected, splendid merriment as all those reports had said, and go again, free as the wind.

He drank a sip of his wine, remembered what Suzen had just asked, and then he said, "Suzen, I have spent my entire career picking apart the power structures and systems of the empire of Astandalas with my lord's full awareness and approval. He will not stay past the solar eclipse next year—neither of us will. We will not be *able* to."

She caught her breath. "Why am I surprised, Cliopher? I know you."

"I never wanted to be king of the world," he said, and Suzen laughed.

"Tell me," she said once she had subsided, "how exactly do you think of this retirement of yours?"

"What do you mean?"

She regarded him with an unexpected and expectant intensity. "Just what I ask, Cliopher. Are you leaving a job? Or an art?"

"Neither," he said, as forthrightly and candidly as he could. "It was a great work of art, this government I have built, but it belongs to others now." It was getting easier, each time he thought that, each time he said it. "There will be other works for me."

He could not imagine them right this moment, but perhaps he didn't to, not yet. He still had all the time before the Jubilee to think of what he would do thereafter.

Suzen continued to regard him, her eyes almost unblinking, and then she said, "You always know just what to say, Cliopher Mdang, to get the creative juices flowing. Shall we?"

For a moment he didn't know what she meant, and his thoughts wandered once more to his Radiancy—to *Fitzroy Angursell*—and his poetry. Then he looked at the painter again, her warm smile, her intense eyes, the deliberate placement of her hand on his thigh, and he felt an answering stir.

"If it'll make a better painting," he said, smiling back.

"I always appreciate your willingness to do whatever it takes," she replied gravely, and they retired to her room.

∾

Cliopher had always preferred a somewhat leisurely, even languid approach to love-making. This had surprised his few lovers, who seemed to have expected him to be as brisk and efficient in bed as he was out of it.

In his younger days this had amused him, for he had relished the distinction between the orderly, efficient, effective bureaucrat and the rather more casual and (he might even say) passionate private man.

Passionate was perhaps pushing it a trifle; at least as far as most thought of it. Sex had never been a great preoccupation of his, and if he and Suzen hadn't already had that sort of relationship he doubted the activity would have occurred to him.

They made love slowly, using their hands a great deal, and in the rosy aftermath Suzen drifted quickly off to sleep. Cliopher lay awake a while longer, stroking her short, spiky hair.

Was this what it would be like to be married? To be able to eat together any evening; to fall asleep every night beside someone; to wake and know they would still be part of your life that next day.

To fight, no doubt: quarrel and argument, compromise and reconciliation.

Cliopher had never had a partner in life of that sort. When he and Ghilly had been together as young people he had been too dominant, and they had quarrelled often, for Ghilly was no door-mat to be walked on. He had, he had come to realize over time, never treated her as his equal. It was one of those galling, shameful realizations, for he had always thought he did. But when it came down to it he would have expected her to follow him, and not he her.

Suzen and he had a deep friendship, not as long-standing as those with Bertie and Ghilly and Toucan, but the closest he had with anyone outside the Palace. She was his only recurring lover; he knew she had had others, intermittently between episodes of intense creative activity.

Suzen and he were equals in their own fashion. For both of them, the work *always* came first. She had never married nor had any long-term relationships precisely because of that, because when her muse was calling her she followed wherever the call led. She and Cliopher met as their lives intersected, and for a few hours or days enjoyed the other's company, before those mysterious calls grew too loud to ignore. She'd not be interested once she returned to her paintings, he knew that—and to be honest, was relieved to know that.

Cliopher was not exactly an artist, not the way that Suzen was, but he came from a family of musicians, and he knew what that look in her eyes meant. He could hardly describe it, except to say that he knew what an inspiration looked like—like a fire catching from a struck spark—and he was a Mdang, and trying to be tanà, and it was *his* calling to tend the fire.

And he turned to follow that call whenever it came, though to everyone else it seemed as if he was simply that overly dedicated and efficient bureaucrat without a spark of creativity in his mind.

He drifted off, thinking that perhaps the fundamental problem between him and Ghilly was that he had never been able to understand how she could have no vocation, nor she that he was following his.

Chapter Eight
Secret Passages

Cliopher awoke, the soft bulk of Suzen beside him, and felt entirely disoriented.

There was no slip of light through the louvred shutters of his windows, which he often left slightly open. Of course; they were not his windows. The room was almost completely dark, bar a distant glow from one of Suzen's enchanted lights showing the way to the privy.

He unwound himself from the sheets, drew the soft linen up around his friend's shoulders, and gathered his clothing together as best he could in the dark. They were all tangled together on the seat of Suzen's wheelchair, which he nearly crashed right over as he made his way around the bed.

He set it back as near its original placement as he could determine, slipped into the trews, and draped the mantle over his shoulders. He felt much more awake than he should, given the likely hour. He hadn't heard any of the quarter-bells in the period of his wakening, which suggested it was well before dawn.

He was grateful there was another light, an enchanted stone about the size of his fist that glowed with a cool, starlike light, in the room Suzen had decided would work as her studio. This room had a window, and he opened the shutter to look out at the paleness of the eastern sky. It was nearly dawn, the comet a bright smudge like a thumbprint on the sky.

Perhaps he'd dance, he decided, opening a door on the window-side of the room in the hopes it might lead into his study, but discovered instead a small room he'd never entered before. It had two large windows on the outer wall, extremely deep-set in order to afford cozy-looking window seats, upholstered in faded tapestry-work cushions. The windows let in just enough light for him to see that the room was a kind of cabinet of curiosities: there were cases all around the room, many of them containing things such as dead white coral of exquisite form.

He shut the door to Suzen's rooms and then clapped four times in the pattern to trigger the magic lights. He ambled around looking at the cases, yawning, increasingly alert.

It was not a large room, hardly more than a closet; when he opened the next door, he discovered he was in the back of what he'd always taken for a shallow cabinet in his study. He pushed back the stand that usually held his Islander finery—currently in Suzen's custody for detail work—and stepped down to the parquet floor.

He did not usually look at the room from this angle: from here his glance went straight to the leather-bound set of the Law-Code of Astandalas.

He walked across the room and pulled out the slender last volume, which actually contained a copy of Fitzroy Angursell's masterpiece, *Aurora*.

His Radiancy's masterpiece, *Aurora*.

Cliopher had long considered it the greatest poem to be written in Shaian, and also the most piercing critique of the Astandalan legal code he'd ever read. It had not been merely an eye to clever hiding-spaces that had caused him to bind it with the rest of the set.

(He'd not had it printed with the rest. He'd asked for three blank volumes for his own notes—and two were, indeed, filled with them. The third contained *Aurora*, copied out in Cliopher's best script. His formal hand had been used as the model for two type-fonts, as well as the Secretariat's short-hand and archival scripts; the poem looked, he thought, good.)

No. His Radiancy had not lied to him. He'd promised Cliopher, twice, that he would tell him the name he had named himself as soon as he could. And when Cliopher had come close—so close, once or twice, but then his thoughts had gone off in different lines—his Radiancy had been ... disappointed.

Cliopher's heart twisted. Right before his Radiancy had left, Cliopher had told him of a dream he'd had, how in the dream he'd known his Radiancy's secret name, and his Radiancy had listened so carefully, so intently, so—*hopefully*—

But Cliopher had not, in his waking mind, known the name. He'd not been able to offer it to his lord. His friend—they had been friends, then, or close to it. As close as Cliopher had ever dared come.

His Radiancy could have told him then, right before he left on his quest.

Cliopher tried to imagine it: either up there on the high tower below the bells, or a bit later, in his Radiancy's private study, talking about his Radiancy's private fears and anxieties. Could anyone, confessing he was afraid to go out into the world, turn immediately and say he was Fitzroy Angursell?

Fitzroy Angursell had been *famous* for his merriment, his wit, his courtesy, his gallantry ... and for being afraid of absolutely nothing.

Perhaps Cliopher had offered him a service, making space for that confession of all too human fears.

(But he wished he'd been able to make that space for that confession and *also* reassure him that it did not mean he had lost all of what he'd once known, all of what he'd once been, as Fitzroy Angursell. Cliopher could see how the two personae were the same person, were two expressions of the same man he had loved and served for so long. He hoped his Radiancy knew that.)

He flipped through the pages, murmuring favourite lines to himself, trying to imagine them written in his Radiancy's strong, slanting hand.

He should have known; he really should have. They had *talked* over these points. Half of Cliopher's reforms had been shaped by *Aurora*. Why, he'd once joked in a letter (unanswered, like all the rest) to his cousin Basil that Fitzroy Angursell really ought to be poet laureate of Zunidh—

Cliopher stopped where he stood, all his emotions rising up again. He was no longer so angry—Suzen's words had helped settle that sense of betrayal—but he felt a strange debt.

A debt. Something owing. A challenge unmet.

He closed *Aurora*, weighing the book in his hand, and then he sat down at his desk and set up his pens.

It was very quiet, the hour before dawn. No sound from the windows or elsewhere in his rooms. Cliopher might have been alone in the Palace.

As alone as he'd been in the horrible aftermath of the Fall of Astandalas, when his entire floor had been emptied, leaving him alone in his room. *Aurora* had comforted him then, *Aurora* and the *Lays*.

He dipped his pen, and then, in his fine, practiced hand, he wrote all the reasons he'd ever imagined for why Fitzroy Angursell the great rebel *should* be Poet Laureate of Zunidh.

No one would ever see it, of course, unless he worked up the nerve to show it one day to his Radiancy—to *Fitzroy Angursell* himself—but at least—

But at least he could respond to the challenge implicit in the unspoken secret identity. A secret answer to a secret challenge. It seemed fitting.

～

The dawn bell rang; the morning chorus of birds sang; Cliopher wrote.

Shoänie came in with hot chocolate and a pastry. He ate, and stretched, and wrote.

At length he set down his pen, set the papers deep into the most private drawer of his desk, and went to bathe and dress for the day.

Out of curiosity he returned to the little closet behind the cabinet in his study, which was not, after all, a figment of his half-sleeping imagination.

When he turned around and discovered Rhodin behind him, he jumped a good foot.

"Cliopher," Rhodin said, nodding as if this were entirely to be expected.

"Rh-Rhodin," Cliopher returned, staring at his friend as his heart raced madly. "What are you *doing*?"

"Oh, just keeping an eye on things," his friend said airily, waving a hand in the air. He regarded Cliopher with sudden speculation. "Are you yourself?"

Despite the early hour, Rhodin was dressed in a beautifully fitted black silk tunic with gold buttons. For one wild moment Cliopher wondered if it really *was* Rhodin. At one point Rhodin had expressed a concern that in his Radiancy's absence, villains (Rhodin's word) might try to infiltrate the Palace in disguise. What were the Protocols in case of impersonations? They had discussed some—Ludvic had, straight-faced, agreed it was a potential concern. "Are you?"

Rhodin frowned. "Yes. What is your name?"

"Cliopher Mdang," Cliopher replied promptly. "My island is Loaloa."

"In which province?"

"The Vangavaye-ve."

Rhodin grunted. Cliopher grinned at him, knowing that thanks to his (somewhat relentless) exhortations *most* of the court was able to pronounce that word correctly. "And," he went on, letting his accent thicken. "My dances are Aōteketētana."

No one ever got *that* word right. Rhodin relaxed.

Cliopher felt he should show willing. "And so? What was your favourite restaurant in Astandalas, Rhodin?"

"The White Tree," Rhodin said absently, which Cliopher was fairly certain was the correct answer. "I've never seen you here before! Nor did I hear you—were you about to go in?"

Cliopher stared. "Go in where?"

"Oh, *you* know—the passage connecting your rooms to his Radiancy's."

"What passage? Where?"

Rhodin snickered. "Oh, don't be coy! How else would you attend your secret assignations?"

～

There was, in fact, a secret passage.

Cliopher stared at the door Rhodin had opened by twisting one of the wall sconces, so that the apparently solid stone wall between the windows opened on a pivot.

The inside was a small landing and a narrow stair, the stone treads clear but for a thin film of dust.

"I swept it regularly while his Radiancy was in residence, naturally," Rhodin said.

"For ... spies?"

"Of course not—no one else knows about it. But it would hardly have stayed *secret* if he got his hems dusty. Only he and I know how far the passages extend. Ludvic knows the ones relevant to his Radiancy's needs—he doesn't like enclosed spaces so left me to the rest. His Radiancy never showed you?"

Cliopher could only shake his head.

His Radiancy showed up sometimes, unannounced—

But always attended, even if the guards had been left at the door. If only Ludvic and Rhodin knew of the passages, surely he didn't come visiting Cliopher through this secret door?

Cliopher had been *in* his study when his Radiancy had come calling. He certainly hadn't exited through the shallow cabinet ...

(A thousand glances and meaningful pauses and *puns* came to mind. He'd been so *oblivious*.)

"Not that *he* had much occasion to use them, of course," Rhodin said, snapping his finger so a small ball of light appeared to hover in front of them. Cliopher regarded this facility with some amazement, glad to be distracted.

"Could you always do that?"

Rhodin looked pleased. "No. It has taken me a great deal of meditation and refinement to achieve it. My friend—the Impostor, you know, my correspondent?"

"Ah ... yes?" Cliopher was vaguely aware that Rhodin had struck up a correspondence with one of the lunatics or copycats who (not infrequently) decided to pretend to be one or other member of the Red Company. There was always at least one every year—one year there'd been *five* separate instances of people claiming to be Fitzroy Angursell.

His Radiancy's scrupulous attention to all those otherwise very minor criminals made much more sense, in retrospect.

Cliopher could not remember which of the Red Company Rhodin's correspondent was supposed to be, if Rhodin had ever in fact told him. He was surprised to hear Rhodin describe them as his *friend*—though he had, once, once or twice, mentioned that some peculiarly apt advice or even more peculiarly bizarre (and also, very often, irritatingly apt) aphorism had come from 'his correspondent'.

But then he did have a very wide range of acquaintance, and there were so very many eccentrics in his spy network—someone who wanted to use an infamous criminal's name as their alias was hardly the most bizarre anecdote Rhodin had ever shared.

Cliopher waved at the light. "It's impressive."

"My magic is more earth-wise," Rhodin went on, entering the passage and evidently expecting Cliopher to follow him, for after he did so he gave the door a slight shove so it rotated back into place. It was eerily silent on the pivot; Cliopher was immensely aware of the stone walls pressing close. He had no sense at all that there was clear air on the other side of the blocks. Just the tight landing and then a narrow stair leading up at a slant into the darkness.

Rhodin's light cast a circle of warm gold perhaps ten feet above them, save where their warped shadows loomed black and thick. Cliopher pulled his mantle close around his shoulders.

"I found these passages ... oh, before he had even awakened after the Fall." Rhodin started climbing, his voice and pace both conversational. Cliopher kept close behind him, his fingers brushing at the edge of Rhodin's tunic, reassuring himself that he was not too far.

He had not spent much time in caves. He had never realized he might dislike them so.

"The air is fresh," he managed, tasting it above the dust.

"Yes, there are plenty of airways. Watch your head—yes, there we are." They manoeuvred around an awkward corner and found themselves in a flat corridor stretching into an impenetrable blackness. Rhodin led him for fifty or a hundred yards before fussing with something and opening another stair, this one a tight spiral.

"I believe these were originally the emperor's escape ways. They run through all the oldest parts of the Palace, from the Imperial Apartments down past the throne room, all the way to the foundation-stone beside the Treasury. I don't think anyone had been in them for years and years before me."

"How enterprising of you."

"I try. I was very enterprising in those days—building up my network, conveying news from the village, then town, up to the Palace, back down again ... Say, I was thinking it over not long ago, and realized I'd met you then, before *he* awoke."

"Really?"

The stair was not so narrow as all that, Cliopher told himself. Rhodin had a light, it was clearly well-maintained, Rhodin knew where he was. He had only to trust his friend.

"Yes, you gave me letters to send on."

Cliopher had given so many people so many letters. They blurred in his mind: he had been so tired, working so hard, trying to block out the inner voice that wanted to do nothing more than scream.

He wrenched his thoughts back from that remembered—from that. "Yes. I'm sure I did."

"I have been thinking over our friendship," Rhodin said, as if in explanation. "Oh —watch your step here, we've come to the stairs—we'll go up first, shall we?"

"As you wish."

The spiral stair had a worn stone railing spiralling up alongside the wall. There were occasional landings, more than seemed right for the number of floors in the central block of the Palace. His rooms were only two flights down from the Imperial Apartments ...

"Ah, here we are," Rhodin said, apropos of nothing Cliopher could see, until the guard stepped to one side and brought his little magic light to hover above their heads.

There was a sketch of a radiant sun carved onto the stone, one section rubbed smooth and oily with the touch of many hands. Rhodin set his hand to it. "Be quiet here," he whispered. "Conju's away and I don't think anyone else should be in here, but they might be cleaning ... it's good practice, anyway."

Cliopher forbore stating that he rarely sneaked around, in secret passages or otherwise, but the spirit of the adventure was starting to come upon him now that they had come upon another door *out*.

Rhodin pressed the worn spot, and the stone door opened as silently as had the one in Cliopher's rooms.

On the other side was a small square vestibule, faintly illuminated by light coming through a band of carved alabaster tracery. Cliopher walked forward, drawn by the light, and peered in on a place he had only visited rarely, his Radiancy's small private library. They were high up, looking down over the top of one set of bookcases towards the desk where his Radiancy had been used to study.

He edged back to Rhodin. "How does one get into the rooms?"

"Along to the side there's a door into the old privy closet off the bedchamber. I was disappointed to discover no one knew about it. What a potential security breach! I made sure the guard positions were in good sightlines for it, even though his Radiancy didn't want me to tell anyone bar Ludvic as the commander about the secret passage."

He nodded, then gestured at Cliopher to return to the stairs. "Would you like to see any of the other entrances?"

"Does his Radiancy know them all?"

"Indeed, yes. We went through them all one day, he and I."

Cliopher looked down at the dark spiralling stair as Rhodin shut the door again behind them. "Where do they run?"

"All the way down, as I said, and then there are side passages branching to all the lord magi's suites, and two different exits—one directly from a passage behind the throne, another that goes from the Imperial Apartments through a different route."

A secret entrance into the Palace, known only to his Radiancy and his two chief guards, and now also Cliopher. His Radiancy, who was also—

This was a secret entrance known to *Fitzroy Angursell*. And what a delightful secret for him to hold close in his heart. Perhaps ... perhaps it had been that, a small, secret joy ... a treasure, just for him? Cliopher could not stop himself from grinning at the thought.

Rhodin looked back over his shoulder, apparently to see if he were following, and startled considerably at his expression. "Cliopher!"

Cliopher could only laugh. "Rhodin! What is it?"

Rhodin hesitated, then shook his head. "You looked so happy, for a moment."

"Do I not usually?"

Rhodin turned forward, starting down the stair quite slowly, his light bobbing along just in front of him. "Not quite like that, no."

"I don't think of myself as unhappy."

Which was a lie, a voice whispered in his mind. He wanted—oh, he wanted.

He concentrated on his footing. Rhodin was silent for a few turns. A cool, damp air came up the stairwell, earthy. It was hard to believe they were still inside the Palace.

Rhodin said, "You miss him."

There was, always, only one *him* any of them ever spoke without other antecedent. "I do."

"I admire how you're handing over your work to Aioru. I am not *surprised*," Rhodin added hastily, as if Cliopher had voiced some objection or criticism. "I never doubted that *you* would hand over your power when the time came."

That statement seemed to hover around them. Cliopher stopped walking; struck.

Rhodin stopped, looked up at him, for once shorter than Cliopher. It was so dark and close around them, outside the circle of light Rhodin had summoned, the stair rising above them, falling away below them, the heavy blocks of stone solid and eternal.

Not eternal. No work of hands was.

"I am trying," Cliopher said, his voice coming soft. "I am trying so hard, Rhodin."

He sank down to the stone, cold and hard through the thin cloth of his trews. The dust rose and fell in fine, feathery masses, glinting as did the white sand of home.

It had been a *week* and he was already at such a loss. So *lost*.

Rhodin regarded him steadily. "You are not trying, Cliopher. You *are* handing over the reins. You *are* giving others the power. You *are* showing everyone else what it means to follow your convictions to the very end. You have told everyone who ever asked you that you would accept the power so you could hand it back ... and you are. That is not a small thing."

He pressed his hands against his knees. "I must stay here until his Radiancy returns."

Rhodin lifted puzzled eyebrows at his abrupt change of subject.

"That is your concern? You are not, let us say, unhappy at seeing Aioru at your old desk?"

Cliopher smiled involuntarily. "He's doing so well. He has so many splendid ideas, Rhodin, all these things I never thought of—I never had the *time* to think of."

"And now that you have time to think, you are ... unhappy."

"No. Yes. I don't know."

"That does cover most of the options."

Cliopher chuckled wryly. "It does, doesn't it."

Rhodin waited for a long moment, then asked, "What do you *want*, Cliopher?"

He had an answer for that; of course he did. "I want to see the world safe and sound for—"

"No. Not that sort of answer."

Cliopher took a deep breath, but he could not say it. "I can't, Rhodin," he whispered, after Rhodin let the silence spool out, velvet and heavy and cold, pressing in from above, welling up from below. "I can't ... not yet."

"What are you not saying?"

He stared down at his friend, golden in his own magic light. Rhodin didn't have half so many grey hairs as Cliopher did, he thought irrelevantly. He had two distinguished silver bars, one at each temple, and a few wrinkles at the corners of his Jade Phoenix eyes, and otherwise looked much the same as he must have looked when the young and angry Kip had asked him to take a letter—somewhere.

"My friend, my correspondent, the Impostor—"

Cliopher wondered distantly why Rhodin always prefaced his references to them in this manner. He did understand the concept of friends, and that Rhodin could have a friend outside of the Household—perhaps it was a reminder to Rhodin himself, that his friend, his correspondent, the Impostor, was all those things. A secret he could hold to himself, a chain of words like an efela or a line in a song, just for him.

"... She says you must articulate your wants, your true wants, that it is not selfish to have dreams that are just for yourself."

"Is that not the definition of selfish?"

"No, Cliopher. You can talk circles around me—we both know that. I wish you would write to her yourself ... I'm sure she'd have excellent advice. But no matter. I'm here. Cliopher, you must have dreams that are for yourself."

The man from Aioru's proverb, who asked a landlocked tribe in the middle of a desert the way to the sea.

He was still looking for the sea, wasn't he? Still chasing that viau.

East first, then west and home.

His hands were cold. He bunched them in the hem of his tunic. "What is your dream, then? For ... after."

"I have it all planned out," Rhodin said. "I am going to Voonra to visit my friend, my correspondent, the Impostor, that is, and then she has said she will show me the way to the Merrions. She met them, you know."

Who on earth were the Merrions? He cleared his throat to cover his momentary confusion, and made a mental note to look them up in the *Atlas of Imperial Peoples*. "Did she?"

"Indeed she did! And then, if the Merrions permit, I shall return bearing what wisdom and enlightenment and messages of peace they see fit to give me, and come live with you in your wonderful house in the Vangavaye-ve."

"Spreading ... enlightenment."

Not in the *Atlas of Imperial Peoples*, then.

"If I am so honoured, yes."

Probably not in the atlas, at least. They might be a religious rather than an ethnic group; that was not one of Cliopher's particular interests. He hadn't thought it was one of Rhodin's, but then again—because it wasn't one of Cliopher's—he'd never really talked about religion with any of his friends.

He'd wondered, of course he had, what it was like for his Radiancy to be worshipped as a god. But any discussion of religion would come crashing down on the very real reef of official emperor-worship, which was *not* a topic Cliopher had ever much wanted to discuss with any of his friends in the Household.

Rhodin was humming; Cliopher didn't recognize the tune, but then ... well, Rhodin had many gifts, but musicality was not one of them.

"Will you invite your friend?"

Rhodin blushed. "She has a life where she is, she may well prefer to stay a correspondent. But I should like to spend some time with her, in person."

Cliopher understood that, oh, all too well. "Yes."

"And yours?" Rhodin prompted after a small silence. He smiled at Cliopher. "It doesn't need to be a big dream, Cliopher. I know you have had such grand dreams for the world ... yours can be whatever size it is. That is what my friend, my correspondent, the Impostor, says. You can have dreams of all sizes, and all of them can be beautiful and true. She is a very wise woman."

Cliopher was trying not to flinch at those words. "She must be," he said thickly, and coughed to clear his throat. "I can see why you look forward so to seeing her."

"It is a good dream," Rhodin acknowledged modestly. "And if it turns out she *is* Sardeet Avramapul, I should like to fence with Pali Avramapul. Just once."

Cliopher thought of the short, fierce, beautiful woman, who had stalked through the Imperial Apartments with her chin held high and her eyes unflinching, unintimidated.

Even if Rhodin's correspondent was nothing more than an impostor, his Radiancy was *truly* Fitzroy Angursell, and he could very likely arrange for such a match as a favour for Rhodin.

For whatever else, whoever else he was, his Radiancy would not forget those who had served him so long and with the whole of themselves.

"Why Pali Avramapul? Not—" Who was the other superlative fencer in the Red Company?—"Not Damian Raskae?"

Rhodin smiled. "Oh, I should like to fence him, too, of course! The difference is... he is renowned for his consistency, you know. Undefeated, except for that one duel with Pali Avramapul—what a reputation! I've spoken to those who fenced him— some of the soldiers from the company he defeated, I'm sure you know the song—"

"'The Company of Armed Gentlemen'."

"Just so. Testing myself against his blade appeals, indeed it does. But Pali Avramapul ... she is unpredictable. Her utmost is higher—she is, after all, the only one who ever *has* defeated Damian Raskae—but she is not, perhaps, so consistent. And that suggests to me that she is more ... curious, more inventive, more of a challenge. Because I might win. You understand. You much prefer Prince Rufus as an opponent to the Ouranatha."

This was an attitude Cliopher had not much thought about, when it came to his political ... *opponents* was not entirely inapt a word. And it was true he preferred Prince Rufus's bluster and erratic temperament to the Ouranatha's collected and (he sometimes felt) inhumanly consistent approach.

It wasn't—they weren't—actually inhuman. They just worked hard to seem so.

"That's true, yes," he agreed. And then, since they were on the topic—or at least as close to it as they'd ever come—Cliopher hesitated, but there in the dark, close quarters of the hidden stair, the secret passage, it did not seem such a folly, such an impossibility, and he asked outright, "Have you ever thought *he* might be ... Fitzroy Angursell?"

Rhodin laughed. "Oh, Cliopher, where did you drag that out from? That's *ancient* gossip! Indeed, those were the very first rumours I ever investigated." He laughed again, long and heartily. "Oh, how his Radiancy laughed when I apologized to him for daring to suspect, even for a moment, that the true Artorin Damara had been replaced after the Fall by Fitzroy Angursell! I was suspicious of his sudden gift at magic, you see."

Cliopher felt jolted, as if he had missed a step going down the stairs. He twisted his hands in his mantle. He was still sitting on the cold stone. Nothing had moved. "Ah."

"I spent ages looking into it. That's how I ended up his spymaster, you know. His Radiancy said anyone who went to such trouble to investigate a matter of such sublime importance should be encouraged, not suppressed, and made the position official. I was already bribing half a dozen people to provide me with all the details."

"How his Radiancy laughed," Rhodin repeated, shaking his head with a fond smile. "It was the first time I'd ever seen him so purely delighted. I confessed my crimes to him and instead of pushing me away he embraced me. Metaphorically, that is, of course."

Cliopher imagined being Fitzroy Angursell, resolutely devoting himself to the unwanted and deeply disliked task of being Lord Magus of Zunidh, and being granted the—the—the *gift* of that conversation.

Oh, indeed he could see why he would draw Rhodin close and keep him there. Both prudence and his deep, deep sense of the absurd would require it; not to mention that Rhodin *was* an excellent spymaster.

"I know you were looking into those rumours about the return of Fitzroy Angursell," Rhodin went on, suavely reassuring. (How? Someone in the Archives must have mentioned his researches there.) "Nothing to them, alas."

"You didn't find anything ... odd?"

"Oh, everything about them was *odd*, but it wasn't anything nefarious. Nor aught to do with the Merrions, alas. I think his Radiancy was giving us a little going-away present. He knows how much I enjoy these little puzzles—and he adores you, of course. He wouldn't want you to think he'd forgotten about you as soon as he went out the door."

Cliopher felt a lump come into his throat, and he worked to regather his composure.

"You are looking sad again. You miss him. You feel obliged to stay here—"

"I *am* obliged to stay here. I promised."

"Mm." Rhodin made a gesture, as if to say, ignore that; his light cast the shadow of his hand across the stairwell, swift as a bird against the sun. "You have mentioned this several times now. May I presume to think you therefore want something involving leaving? Where do you want to go?"

The question hung there, as it had always hung there, every time Cliopher had ever expressed his desire to—go.

Where do you want to go? Is this where you stop?

He still—still!—wanted to enter legend. Despite everything, he still wanted to sail to the House of the Sun and bring home a new fire, a literal new fire, a flame of the sun.

Despite *everything.* He knew—*he knew*—he could not have any of these things— after a lifetime of seeking, of trying his utmost, he had reached this point and stopped, poised as on the crest of a wave—and there was no beach, no island, ahead of him; only the open ocean to the horizon.

All those things he had wanted, had dreamed of—all those viaus he had chased, that sea he had sought. Did the heart never rest? Could *his* heart never find ease? Could there never be a point where he could let his vaha go and know the currents and the winds would carry him sweetly and straight on the ke'ea that led home?

He had wanted to go adventuring with the Red Company, even if he could never be more than a footnote to a poem, a minor character in a song, a nameless bit part.

He had wanted to sail the Wide Seas with his Radiancy beside him, as Elonoa'a had sailed with Aurelius Magnus; he had wanted to find a new island, a new star, the currents that would open up the gates between worlds.

He bit his lip, hard, and forced himself to find other dreams, ones he could achieve. They existed ... they did.

(They seemed small, in comparison with the dreams he had been cherishing since he was a boy. But Rhodin was right: dreams did not need to be grand and epic to be good, to be worthwhile, to be ... beloved.)

He wanted to be the tanà in truth, and dance the fire before all his family and his people.

He wanted to look at Fitzroy Angursell, and see him happy and free.

He wanted to have Fitzroy Angursell look on him, on Cliopher Mdang who had devoted his life to his—to *his Radiancy's*—service—

No. That was not one of the dreams he could fulfil. He took a long, controlled breath, as if he were about to dive for a pearl.

He wanted to go home, and be finally, finally, finally *at home.*

"I want to go to Alinor and learn what happened to my cousin Basil," he said roughly, swallowing hard against all those other *wants* jostling against his teeth.

Rhodin waited, but Cliopher shook his head, his lips pressed tight, his hands gripping each other, unable to express any more. There were truths he held close in his heart, shut tight from the outer world as the secrets at the heart of a clam.

"My friend would say it's a good start," Rhodin said. "You might want to think about what happens *after* you get there. Perhaps I could travel with you and we could continue on to Voonra together."

Cliopher forced down all the words, all the thoughts, all the *wants*, and stood up, brushing off his garments. Féonie would no doubt chide him for the dust, since Conju was still on his holiday.

He missed Conju. But it would be hard for him—

It was going to be *terrible* for Conju to adjust to his Radiancy being Fitzroy Angursell.

"Tell me more about her, your friend," he asked politely, and as Rhodin started telling him about how she had given over impersonating Sardeet Avramapul to follow her true vocation as a baker of fine pastries (and there, Cliopher thought, amused, might well be the true point of connection), they continued back to his apartments and the responsibilities awaiting them there.

At the door to his rooms—what Cliopher hoped was the door to his rooms—Rhodin stopped, and looked once more at him. Cliopher regarded him politely, attentively, feeling like a cork stuck in the bottle of the hidden stair.

Rhodin said nothing, but his expression was oddly vulnerable, his face working as he tried to find words for whatever his thought was.

Cliopher waited, trying to be patient, but he could sense Rhodin gathering himself back into the courtly imperviousness, the suave assurance, with which he was much more familiar, and to stop that—to stop, perhaps, his own heart from beating so loud—Cliopher said, "Rhodin. I—I'm sorry. I don't know who the Merrions are. You've mentioned them as if I ought to ..."

Rhodin tilted his head, frowning slightly. "Do you not know because his Radiancy has never told you, seeing as he knows how important the subject is to me?" Cliopher opened his mouth to agree, relieved at this, but then Rhodin continued: "Or is it because your memories were blotted out when the Merrions granted you enlightenment?"

Cliopher could only blink for a long, long moment. Then he cleared his throat. "I ... I'm not sure how I would know if my memories had been ... blotted out."

"A good point," Rhodin allowed.

"Nor do I think I've been granted enlightenment."

Which Cliopher thought was self-evident, but—well—apparently Rhodin thought it a possibility?

"Must be his Radiancy's discretion, then," Rhodin said cheerfully. "I'll come by your place later this afternoon to explain—if we're going to speak of the Merrions, I need to ensure the Palace is wholly secure."

That sounded ... serious. "Thank you for your diligence," he said out loud.

Rhodin beamed. "May I ask you something in return?"

That also sounded serious. Cliopher tried to be discreet about bracing himself. "If you'd like."

"When we went on holiday that time," Rhodin said, "you recall the lunar eclipse party?"

"It was a quite memorable occasion, yes."

Seeing as the Moon Lady herself had appeared in person to address his Radiancy.

Fitzroy Angursell. Who had once written a poem about how he had seduced the Moon.

("Beloved," she had called him.)

"Aya and Jiano told us to ... make wishes, to the bonfire."

"Yes."

"Did you ask for yourself?"

Cliopher felt his hands curling again, as if he needed to stretch them after a long day of writing. He didn't have to answer. He didn't.

Rhodin was his friend, who had offered him his own dreams, his own *wants*, who had trusted him with his own secret yearnings.

"No," he said plainly, if quietly.

Rhodin nodded, entirely unsurprised, and set his hand on the door. Before he opened it, he said: "You're allowed to."

CHAPTER NINE
OPEN COURT

Open court was something he'd instituted as Lord Chancellor in a reduced form—once a month he'd held open days when anyone could come talk with him. Once his Radiancy left and Cliopher was Viceroy in act as well as name, he'd increased it to once a fortnight, and took more care to dress up.

Thus he sat on the ebony throne in his bronze and blue ahalo cloth, in the jewels and fancy hat. He gave each person who came before him the same quarter-hour block he gave anyone. This was not enough time to solve any but the rarest, nearly-mythical simple problem (he had, perhaps, had three such, in the years he had been doing this), but it was long enough for someone to articulate their problem or petition.

It amused him that most of the petitioners who came to the open courts were significantly more succinct and forthright in their statements than any of the bureaucrats and courtiers and politicians with whom he spent most of his time.

With whom he *had* spent most of his time.

Cliopher asked questions to clarify the situations, assuring the petitioners that they were heard, that though their problems might not be resolved in their favour, they could rest secure in the knowledge that they would not be *ignored*. Cliopher had worked hard for many years to be that resolute, reassuring person, to be known not only as the solver of problems great and small, but as the one who listened, no matter how humble or shy the speaker.

Aioru would do this, and whoever his Radiancy found for his heir.

(Fitzroy Angursell. But he *was* looking—he'd sent Cliopher that one letter—he hadn't *forgotten* his quest in the excitement of being free.)

The morning spooled on, one person at a time. He heard the bells toll out the hours, with only a vague awareness of the time passing. He was aware of a growing hunger, and wished he'd had more than the one pastry that morning.

Perhaps, he thought hopefully even as the current petitioner moved off and he gave a few comments to the recording secretary of points to follow up, this would be a morning where he finished a few minutes early and would be able to grab something to eat before the Helma Council meeting.

The announcing secretary said, "Of the Vangavaye-ve—"

But Cliopher had already turned with his polite smile to the next petitioners, only to discover they were his oldest friends.

Bertie Kindraa of the great bushy eyebrows and ferocious scowls, the milder and nearly dapper Toucan, the always-lovely Ghilly—

He faltered for a moment with the utter surreality of them being there, in that room, standing forward with bashful smiles and—

—And his mind stopped on the fact that they were *here*, they had come at last to see him, and without thinking about anything he leaped out of his chair and engulfed Ghilly in a great embrace.

"Oh, Ghilly!" he cried, and knew he was beaming. "You came!" He let her go and turned to Bertie and embraced him too, and then Toucan, and Ghilly again, and then it finally occurred to him that they had not mentioned this visit in any letter, and had come to the court, and if they had a petition—

"Well," he said, stepping back and casting a glance around at all the secretaries and pages and the remaining petitioner, who all had expressions demonstrating varying degrees of 'gobsmacked'. "Now that I have completely destroyed any possible pretence of impartiality, did you come with a petition? Or just to see me?"

He hoped his heart wasn't nearly as audible in his voice as he suspected it was.

Ghilly's eyes were bright, and Bertie's bushy eyebrows were drawn together in one of his great furrowed scowls. Toucan was the one to clear his throat and say, with a careless air, "No, we came to pay our respects to our countryman. We have all recently retired, you know, and had the time, so it seemed the thing to do."

Out of the corner of his vision Cliopher could see one of the pages gaping with flat astonishment. His own surprise bubbled forth in joyous laughter. "Oh, I *am* so glad to see you! What a wonderful surprise!"

"I can't believe none of your relations let it slip," Ghilly proclaimed, patting him on the arm and then stroking the ahalo cloth as if despite herself.

"Would you mind waiting over there?" he said, rallying his thoughts back to his job. "I'll finish with court, and then we can talk."

As they smirked slightly and obeyed the request, and he turned back towards the chair that suddenly seemed ridiculously ornate, he thought of the comet He'eanka, the ship of Elonoa'a, with its nose pointing to the Palace and to the Vangavaye-ve far, far beyond it.

And he had thought no one would ever come.

⁓

The final petitioner attended to, he gave his summary statements to the recording secretary, dismissed everyone to their luncheons and follow-up work, and turned to see that his friends were clustered awkwardly in the corner away from the secretaries. He went over to them and clasped Bertie on the shoulder, feeling a trifle shy.

"Hullo," he said, and then, catching a tilt of Toucan's eye that probably meant his court accent was stronger than they'd heard before, added, "Tē ke'e'vina-tē zēnava parahë'ala!"

Both Toucan's eyebrows went up at that, but he replied, "Tō mo'ea-tō avivayë o rai'ivayë," in the ancient Islander greeting.

"Come this way—er, please," Cliopher said, realizing as he was speaking that he was perhaps still in an official and therefore somewhat officious mode of speech. He caught Ghilly's sudden smile and had to suppress a laugh as he led them out the back door and along the narrow hall on that side of the audience chamber. It was not one of the service passageways but was certainly not a public route either, being attractive but not greatly ornamented.

"I have another meeting before lunch," he told them regretfully. "I'll take you up to my rooms so you can wait there, if you don't mind? Then you can tell me all your news!"

"That seems fine," Ghilly assured him, even as he opened a door and held it for her to pass through. He smiled unapologetically to Zerafin and Varro, this morning's guards, who were frowning at his poor decorum.

"Excellent." He led them at a brisk pace down the hall and up the staircase at its end, which led to the top floor of this wing. It went up five long flights, which Cliopher—who climbed the matching stair on his wing multiple times most days—took in stride, but Varro touched his shoulder at the top and indicated that his friends were lagging.

Cliopher was embarrassed. "Gorjo City hardly runs to so many stairs," he said apologetically to Ghilly, the first up behind him.

Toucan, who had just reached the top step in time to hear this, gave him a sly glance even through his panting. "I hadn't thought to practice going up and down the Spire."

"Or the Reserve," Ghilly put in, rubbing her throat. "No wonder you're so fit! I always thought your job so sedentary."

"There's a lot of sitting, too." Cliopher smiled at Bertie. "All right there?"

At his friend's curt nod he looked around for something to talk about, and hit on the general structure of the Palace. By the time he'd explained about the starfish shape, the importance of one's relative proximity to the Emperor's Tower, and that they were going along the Ystharian Wing towards the Zuni one, even Bertie seemed to have properly caught his breath.

Leading them further along, Cliopher tried to moderate his pace, but he knew from visits home that even what he considered an amble was a fast walk back home in Gorjo City. Still—he cast a sidelong glance at them—they were keeping up, more or less, so he started describing random features of the art and architecture as they passed them.

The top of the stair opened onto the grand central hall of the uppermost public floor of the Ystharian wing. There were service rooms on the floor above, cunningly disguised so that from the outside there did not appear to be another full storey, merely ornamental carvings and clerestory windows. Yet up there were bedchambers and storage rooms and even small workshops, primarily for the use of those who took care of all the practical details ignored (except in their absence) by the great lords of state who inhabited the floor below.

Not to mention Rhodin's very secret passages.

They moved towards the centre, through a series of doors that increased in their magnificence with each passage. "Officially the doors are in case of fire, in which case they close automatically by magic to seal off the wing," Cliopher said, as they passed through doors of some wood that glowed golden with its polish and was carved into shallow relief of the rose emblem of Ysthar.

"Entirely incidentally, of course, they are used to demarcate different ranks. We are moving now through to the innermost and most prestigious hall, where the Lord of Ysthar, should he ever come on a state visit, would be housed. Down a level is where his ambassador has rooms."

He gestured at a pair of sumptuously decorated doors set into an elaborate carved-stone frame. "That is the Lord of Ysthar's suite. As the host lord magus, when the Palace was in Astandalas on Ysthar, he naturally had the most resplendent rooms after the Emperor himself."

"Oh," said Ghilly.

Cliopher led them along the curving hall the linked the upper storeys of the wings to the Emperor's Tower. "There are audience chambers in the centre," he said, "used by his Radiancy and other great lords for various functions. Meetings of the Ouranatha, the Council of Princes, that sort of thing. The Offices of the Lords of State are their official name."

"That's one of your titles, isn't it?" Toucan asked. "Secretary in Chief of the Offices of the Lords of State."

"Previously, yes. Official head of the Imperial Bureaucratic Service, unofficial head of the government. Yes," said Cliopher, passing the butterflies-snakes-and-peonies insignia on the doors to the Voonran wing, grateful that the Zuni wing, his own, was next along. "I resigned last week. You probably didn't get the letter."

"Resigned?" Ghilly cried, before faltering as they came to the Zuni wing.

It was unavoidably obvious that his rooms were those intended for the Lord of Zunidh.

Cliopher coughed. "It seemed time."

"Better to hand it over while you're still around to mentor your replacement," Toucan agreed, and Cliopher was grateful for his ready understanding.

The doors to Cliopher's apartments were set into a similar stone frame to those of the Ystharian suite. His were black ebony, inset with bronze and gold wires and lapis lazuli and tiger eyes and various other gems. The circular central design was the tiger insignia of Zunidh, the great cat's eye a huge yellow diamond, with peacock feathers in the frame surrounding it.

His were manned by a pair of footmen in blue and orange livery who saluted, right fists over their hearts, as he approached. He smiled at them as the one on the left opened the door. "Thank you, Hurin," he said, and nodded at the one on the right. "I'm glad to see you're feeling better, Baion."

Zerafin and Varro stayed at the outer door as was their custom, by their presence indicating he was within the chambers, and Cliopher led his friends inside. The first room was a large antechamber, where Tully had her desk and a couple of pages sat waiting on a bench. Tully looked up in surprise as he came in.

"Yes, yes, I know, I'm nearly late," he said, grinning at her, but not stopping. He went through one of the doors behind her, not the one leading to his public office and meeting rooms, but the one that led to the private quarters in the back. He glanced at Ghilly; Bertie wouldn't meet his eye. "That's Tully—you met her in Gorjo City briefly, I think. She's my appointments secretary ... through here."

Through another two rooms, which he did not really use. "I don't understand the logic behind the design," he went on. "I feel a hallway would make the whole thing much more efficient. We use hardly half the rooms! Well, I'm not an architect. I'll give you a proper tour later, if you'd like. We're nearly at the private rooms—here we are."

As he went briskly through his study, a stack of unfinished letters caught his eye. He detoured to pick them up, sorting through for the ones for these particular friends. "I can't believe you never let slip you were on your way," he said, marvelling. "My family has been making arch comments, but I had no idea."

"It does amaze me that they didn't say anything," Toucan agreed. "This is your study?"

"Yes—and through here is my sitting room—ah! Franzel!"

Cliopher's majordomo was in the sitting room, replenishing the small cupboard of refreshments Cliopher kept there for when he didn't fancy calling any of his staff. "Sir," he said, inclining his head.

"These are my friends," Cliopher said. "They'll be staying with me for a while." How long? Dared he even ask—no. Not yet. However long it was would be marvellous. "Could you arrange rooms for them, please? And refreshments—I have to get to a meeting. I'll be back for lunch in about an hour," he said, pausing automatically for the noon bell to sound its deep, resonant note. "I'm sorry to rush, but I must go." He smiled again at them. "It *is* wonderful to see you. Franzel—"

"You can rely on me, Sir."

"Of course," said Cliopher, who had long since learned to do so. He recalled the letters he held, and handed them over. "These aren't finished, but you may as well have them to read. I'll see you soon."

"Don't worry about us," Ghilly said. "Go to your meeting."

Cliopher went.

The Helma Council meeting was quick—a matter of finalizing the budgets—and Aioru kept it expeditious. Cliopher approved, made certain to congratulate him on his efficiency, and returned to his apartments with all due haste. He changed out of his court costume, and found his friends in his sitting room.

Toucan looked disappointed. "I was hoping for more grandeur, after this morning's outfit. That looks almost ordinary. I like the colour, at least."

It was a medium bluish-green with a block print pattern of yellow chevrons on it, which Cliopher also liked. He grinned at his friend. "I'm sure you'll see me in all manner of garb over the course of your visit. Though not court costume every day! Speaking of which—where are your belongings?"

"They're down in Bertie's boat at the docks," Ghilly said, putting down the book she'd been holding and standing up.

Sailing around the world had been Bertie's lifelong ambition. Cliopher was inordinately pleased to hear that he'd achieved at least the first half of that circumnavigation. "You *did* sail here, then? I was wondering."

"Why don't you wonder over lunch," Ghilly said. "I'm hungry, and I didn't spend all morning holding court."

"Yes, it has been a while since breakfast," he murmured, leading them in to the dining room. It was already laid with a generous collection of dishes in the Southern Dairese style, half a dozen or more plates accompanied by a basket of flatbreads. Cold water and several different juices rounded out the selection. "Please, sit down and serve yourselves," he said, sitting down in his accustomed chair and gesturing at his friends, feeling awash with pleasure at the fact of them being there, dining with him.

And to think, when he retired, he would be able to do this ... all the time. Any time he wanted.

(He refused to be sad that his Radiancy would not be there. He never had been... and Cliopher could not begrudge him his freedom. Cliopher and Rhodin and Ludvic and Conju were the senior members of his household; they could not be anything other than constant reminders of...everything. Cliopher did not like that thought, and refused to entertain it. His Radiancy, *Fitzroy Angursell*, could come and go as he pleased, and if it did not please him to come, well, Cliopher had no claim on him beyond the service he had already offered, and the honours he had already received in return.)

Ghilly sat to his right, with Toucan next to her and Bertie on his left. She said, "I'm afraid I only recognize the bread and the tomatoes ..."

Cliopher probably ate some variant on this meal twice a week, and was surprised to recall that it was so different from anything one might get in Gorjo City.

(Grateful, too, for the interruption to his thoughts.)

"You didn't come round Southern Dair, I take it?" He pointed at different dishes. "Olives, a kind of marinated sheep's milk cheese, roasted sweet peppers in oil, that's a dip with roasted aubergines and garlic, those are stuffed vine leaves—probably lamb and rice, though sometimes it's rice and pine nuts—calamari, I'm sure you recognize that—oh, and that's called diab, it's a kind of parsley salad. It usually is a lot spicier than this one, but I don't like it too hot, so they don't put in as much in the way of hot peppers. And that is a lentil salad."

"I recognized that," Toucan offered. "Bertie, I vote we go back around that way. This food looks amazing."

"We came across up the Line Islands to Amboloyo, through the Northern Passage, then south along the Xiputl coastline," Bertie said, watching Cliopher carefully as he spooned some of everything onto his plate and took the bread in his hands, then following suit with exactly the same quantities.

Cliopher grinned at him. "And you kept writing as if from home!"

Ghilly swallowed a hesitant mouthful of the stuffed vine leaves. "Mm, this is good. Cora and Vinyë arranged for your letters to be forwarded on to us, so we could pick them up in various towns along the way. It was a lot of fun to go into the post offices and ask for our mail in all these places we'd never even heard of before."

"I'm still amazed no one let slip. No offence, Kip, but I would never have believed *your* family could keep a secret like this quiet for so long!"

"It does seem unlike them," he agreed. "You must have left right after Enya's restaurant opening?"

"About the next week," Bertie agreed.

Toucan spooned a second helping of the lentils onto his plate. "If you'd stayed for more than just the one night I'm sure you would have found us out, and all our cunning planning would have been for naught. We were disappointed not to spend more time with you, of course, but we *did* want to surprise you. Cora was a great help in planning, her and Vinyë."

They gave him the abbreviated version, full of random anecdotes. Cliopher listened attentively, drinking in their conversation, their presence, the familiar laughs and the new stories.

Bertie said proudly, "We came across the northern trades after we left Madurat, set the sails and lashed the tiller, and the wind was so regular we didn't have to touch it again for seventeen days, not until we came in sight of Chizarephu, even though Toucan didn't believe me for all he is a Nevan, and insisted we check our direction with the compass every hour."

"You were using a compass?" Cliopher asked, surprised.

"During the day," Bertie replied. "The stars are fine at night, but during the daytime, in unfamiliar waters—I was glad for the charts and the compass, let me tell you! Your cousin Quintus was a great help in setting a route. He's sailed all across the Wide Seas, you know, all the way to Lorosh in the west and the City of Emeralds in Jilkano in the east."

Cliopher had never actually asked whether Quintus or Bertie sailed according to the old ways or more modern methods. He found himself a little disgruntled at the thought that they didn't make use of their great history, and then embarrassed at the thought of saying so. Who was *he* to tell anyone they should do such-and-such as an Islander?

"Have we broken you?" Toucan asked, snickering. "You do understand that the world is round, right? And therefore—"

"Get away with you!" He turned to Bertie with a show of dignity. "Tell me, Bertie, is this as much a surprise to Parno as to me, or has he known for all the last three or four months what you've been up to?"

Bertie blinked at him. "He knew we were coming, so as to keep him from crossing paths with us by taking a holiday home at the same time, but not when exactly we'd get here. We weren't exactly *rushing*."

"We spent a whole week in the Dagger Islands, looking at the floating castles," Ghilly put in.

"And another week in what's-it-called, Rwassalago, looking at gardens," Toucan added. Ghilly, a Poyë, retired Provincial Inspector of Agriculture, and likely impetus for this, smiled blithely and sipped at her juice.

"And anyway," Toucan added, "it was closer to six months. We weren't really counting ..."

"I was keeping a log," Bertie said, nettled. "It took us six months and three weeks to get here. Depending on how long we stay—"

"As long as you'd like," Cliopher assured him. "You can see I have the room."

Bertie harrumphed. "At any rate, we reckon we'll be home for the next Singing of the Waters."

Cliopher raised his eyebrows at him. "What, this week?"

They all paused. Ghilly said, "What do you mean? We left—oh, six weeks before the festival, wasn't it?"

"It's a small one this year, anyway," Toucan agreed.

"So you see, if we left six weeks before, and took six and a half months, nearly seven, on our voyage, we can't possibly make ..." Ghilly trailed off, no doubt at the amusement on Cliopher's face. "You don't mean it's only been a *month* at home?"

Cliopher had spent most of his life bewildered by and trying to ignore the strange temporal effects still lingering since the Fall. "Don't think about it too much," he advised.

"It doesn't make any sense," she complained.

"Don't look at me like that! No one knows why it's this way, not even my lord. Since he finished the Lights, in general things have been much more stable and uniform, but not always."

Ghilly stared at him in perturbation. "Has it been six months for you, then? Or six weeks? Or ...?"

"*Or*," he agreed. "The Ouranatha are the ones who work it out. I just go by what they tell me and try not to worry about it too much."

"Seriously, how long has it been since you came home for that visit?"

Cliopher gave Ghilly an amused if somewhat chiding glance. "On the one hand, officially I have one year until his Radiancy retires, and it was two years when I was appointed Viceroy. On the other hand ... maybe two months? Or not. I really do mean not to think about it too hard. The Ouranatha told me off for worrying about it once; apparently it makes things worse."

"No wonder you were our best correspondent," Toucan murmured.

"Am I not always your best correspondent?" Cliopher returned, and turned to Bertie. "Regardless, Bertie, if you'd like to startle your son at work *almost* as much as you did me, you can find him on duty at the Menagerie this afternoon into the evening. Rhodin said he would look into Parno's leave for next week, because apparently he's been chosen to go to Kavanduru for the training camp—which is a great honour, it means he's been promoted to the next stage of the Guards."

Bertie looked pleased. "I suppose he hasn't made it up to guarding *you* yet, then?"

Cliopher laughed; he currently had his Radiancy's usual household guards guarding him in his Radiancy's absence. "No, not yet."

"I imagine you have more meetings this afternoon?" Toucan asked.

"I have one with Rhodin, but I expect it to be short." Cliopher reached for the pocket in his linen tunic and pulled out the paper Tully had given him, though he didn't need the blank page as proof for anyone but himself. "Yes, that's it."

Inconceivable though it was; it was true.

"I'm astonished," Ghilly said.

There was no sense in prevaricating; they had known him far too long for that. "Well," he said, and coughed. "It seemed time to put all my fine words about succession planning into practice."

They regarded him, as seriously as he was looking at them, and then Ghilly said, very gravely, "How long has it been?"

"A week."

That made them all crack up. "It's good we arrived when we did, then!" Ghilly cried. "Oh, Kip, are you terribly bored?"

The comment was a little too true to be funny. "I was planning to invite Gaudy and Parno and my friends—Ludvic and Rhodin—for a kind of special meal in honour of the Singing of the Waters."

"What about Conju?" Toucan asked.

"He's on holiday in Amboloyo. Anyway, I thought we could have an Islander meal and maybe sing over a few of the passages from the *Lays* ..."

"That's a lovely idea," Ghilly said approvingly. "Do you think you'd be up for making it a little larger? Because—"

Toucan shook his head. "Ghilly, he might not want to have to deal with perfect strangers."

"It's the Singing of the Waters," Ghilly retorted, and smiled winsomely at Cliopher. "We met wontok down in the city, when we were trying to get the—what's the phrase? The *lay of the land*. We arrived yesterday, you see, but we got a little lost trying to find the Palace, and, well, then we met Alun and Nala at this market with music and things, and they invited us for dinner tomorrow, you too—we didn't say you were *you*, of course, we just told them we'd come to visit our friend in the Service—"

"Take a breath, Ghilly," Cliopher advised. "I'd love to come."

As if it were *easy*. But—perhaps it was.

"And if you like them, and they seem interested," Bertie said practically, "you could think about inviting them for your party."

"Making it into a party, yes," Cliopher murmured, but he was not entirely unhappy at the idea.

CHAPTER TEN
THE MERRIONS

Rhodin arrived precisely on time, his black silk tunic as fresh and unwrinkled as it had been that morning in the secret passages.

He bowed formally as he came in—through the usual door. Cliopher, startled, rose from his desk to return the courtesy. He'd decided to meet in his study, which was less formal than his official reception rooms but not so informal as his private living space. Given Rhodin's behaviour, this seemed to have been the correct choice.

"Good afternoon, Rh—Ser Rhodin," he said. "Thank you for coming to explain this … grave matter."

"It is my pleasure, your excellency," Rhodin replied, and made a slow perimeter of the room, examining the windows and opening the various doors, including the hidden panel concealing the door to the secret cabinet.

And he had apparently spent the entire morning ensuring the Palace was *secure*.

Finally he deemed the room safe—or so Cliopher assumed—for he came to stand before the desk at attention.

Cliopher considered this, considered inviting him to have a cup of coffee or tea, decided that Rhodin was not in a mood for friendly conversation, and set his shoulders and chin in his court posture. Some tiny tension went out of Rhodin's shoulders, and Cliopher was glad.

"His Radiancy," Rhodin said, "has always preferred me to report in person on the results of my special investigations."

Cliopher kept his face very still. He'd once asked his Radiancy about those special investigations, reckoning that if he were to be the Lord Chancellor he should probably know about them. They kept it very quiet but Rhodin *was* the head of the Intelligence Service, after all. His *special investigations* were surely of paramount importance.

His Radiancy had regarded Cliopher with an intent, intense expression. "Rhodin is always most *precise* in his written reports," he had said; "his verbal reports are somewhat more fanciful. Trust me that anything of relevance is passed on to you."

That had done nothing at all to assuage Cliopher's curiosity, of course, but he had put it aside in the face of such a concrete instruction, and, reading the reports coming from Intelligence, wondered mightily what the *special investigations* could possibly involve.

The Merrions, who spread enlightenment. But what did that *mean*?

And now he knew that his Radiancy was actually *Fitzroy Angursell*, a man rumoured to be the literal child of Mischief.

Not that he was a son of Vou'a—the Vangavayen trickster god of mysteries—but perhaps there was a Shaian equivalent. Cliopher had never really understood Astandalan religion beyond the complexities of its ceremonial magic and emperor-worship. Rhodin's expression was earnest. Very earnest.

Cliopher's heart started to beat a little faster with anticipation. "I see," he said, as slowly and levelly as he could. Should he take notes? Perhaps not. He made a show of cleaning his pen before setting it aside.

Rhodin relaxed another infinitesimal fraction, but instead of speaking he made another circuit of the room.

"It is unfortunate," he said on his return to the point in front of Cliopher's desk, "that you cannot raise the Wall of Silence."

"I'm sorry," Cliopher replied.

Rhodin shook his head, and went to lean on the windowsill, staring moodily out at the city visible through the louvred shutters. "After the Fall, before I started working for his Radiancy, I explored the Palace. I found the secret passages, and deep down—deep in the oldest part of the Palace—I found ancient carvings. I sought out further knowledge—anywhere I could—in the libraries—in the mysteries—and gradually I pieced together the truth. The carvings are the relics of the ancient and brilliant civilization whose architects the Emperor Yr employed to build the Palace. The Merrions."

Cliopher had never looked into the architectural history of the Palace. He nodded, deeply intrigued.

"They objected to Yr's continued war," Rhodin went on, "and retreated from the world. They took shelter underground."

Cliopher blinked. "Underground?"

"Yes. In beautiful caves of crystal, where they could commune with the Mysteries and become transcendent gods themselves."

That was ... not what he'd expected. But gods, well, gods and mysteries ... that meant this *was* a matter of religion for Rhodin, and no one had ever said religions had to be *logical*. There were at least four different accounts of how the Vangavayeve had come to be settled, and logically it could not be true that the Ring had been settled by the Wayfinders from across the sea *and* inhabited by people who had climbed up out of caves deep in the rock, *and* that Mama Ituri, the volcano overlooking Gorjo City, had given birth to the first people in a great outpouring of lava.

The rest of Cliopher's mind was caught up on the logistics of living underground. "What do they eat?" he asked curiously.

Rhodin waved that aside. "They have mushrooms and places where the sunlight comes down through the crystal so they can garden."

"And it's just them?"

"Just them," Rhodin said reverently. "And their dinosaur soulmates, of course." He looked intently at Cliopher. "Dinosaurs are another word for thunder lizards, you know. We—those of us who are seekers after the wisdom of the Merrions—use *dinosaur*, or sometimes you will hear *saurian*, when we are speaking of the hyperintelligent telepathic cousins of the brute thunder lizards."

All of this *had* been making sense. "Telepathic?" Cliopher asked hesitantly.

"It means 'mind-to-mind'. Silent speech, as it were." Rhodin nodded sharply. "It is a gift from the Merrions. That is why I had thought you were enlightened—well, that and your great practical wisdom."

He stared out the window mistily, apparently reflecting on this.

Cliopher considered, and discarded, any number of responses. "What sort of ..."

"Evidence?" Rhodin sighed heavily and turned so he could regard Cliopher pensively. "So much circumstantial evidence, and nothing concrete. But I believe I will one day be judged worthy to know the truth, Cliopher. You and his Radiancy vibrate on such an exquisite frequency ... it is beautiful to observe. Each time I see you communicate silently, telepathically, I myself come a little closer to the secrets. I regret that you must keep your soulmate secret. But I understand," he added sincerely.

Cliopher considered and discarded another set of responses to that. If Rhodin were spinning a new religion—or had stumbled into a very old one (for all Cliopher knew it was quite possible that an ancient civilization had assisted Yr in building the Palace and then retreated—perhaps not to live literally underground, but there they might have found a passage to another world in a cave or something)—it behoved him to be polite about it.

Even if he and his Radiancy did not actually communicate *telepathically*. Or have a hyperintelligent dinosaur soulmate.

Finally he offered, "When ... when you retire you can spend more time on it."

Rhodin nodded gravely. "Thank you, Cliopher. Each time I am discouraged there comes someone to hearten me, remind me that the best and most important things do not come easily. I take great comfort in reflecting on how long it has taken you to achieve your ends. I had envied how far ahead of me you were, but then when we were in Gorjo City, you told that lovely story about seeing his Radiancy's portrait and beginning your long journey, and that put your hard work and patience into perspective for me."

"I'm glad you found it ... helpful."

Rhodin gave him a small smile. "That's what friends are for, isn't it? To help each other along the way."

Cliopher could respond to that without any hesitation. "And to enjoy each other's company, too."

Rhodin sat down in the chair he had previously eschewed, relaxed and apparently chatty. Cliopher wondered if he had somehow passed a test; he had not been aware there was one underway. "You must find the days very empty without his Radiancy here. I'm glad your friends are visiting."

"So am I." Cliopher hesitated, but he always had been far too curious for his own good. "And so, you seek contact with the Merrions?"

Rhodin's expression lit with pure joy. "I *do*! May I tell you about them?"

Cliopher got drunk that night, which never happened.

His conversation with Rhodin had gone on long enough for his friends to have decided that they would take advantage of Cliopher's rank while he still had it. They were thus happily exploring his rooms while the footmen went down with careful descriptions to Bertie's boat; in fact, it was only when they stumbled into his study and interrupted Rhodin's explanation of how his correspondent, his friend, the Impostor Claiming to Be Sardeet Avramapul had *met* the Merrions that Cliopher recalled the time and returned to their company.

Rhodin stopped talking, refused any invitations to join them—"I am not done my day—I shall return later, thank you—oh yes, Ghilly, of course I can show you the way back out to the reception room—"

Why Ghilly wanted to go back to the reception room she did not say. Cliopher was still reeling from an hour and a half deep-dive into the world of hyperintelligent dinosaur soulmates and the wisdom of the ancients and did not think to ask her until the two of them had left.

"We met your friend Suzen," Toucan told him as they went into his sitting room. "What a glorious artist she is! Her sketches are brilliant. I can't wait to see the final portraits."

"Nor I," he admitted, "though it seems a bit conceited to say so."

"Don't be absurd," Toucan replied. "She's got the vision, you can see it. Watching her for even a few moments is a lesson in itself. She did say she'd be interested in seeing some of my landscapes—I painted along our journey, you know."

"Took up half the storage space," Bertie grumbled good-naturedly before continuing on to the room Franzel had given him.

"Tui flowers?" Toucan said curiously, coming up to look at Rhodin's splendidly incongruous vase of them. Cliopher stepped back—the scent was making his eyes prickle, foolishly—and looked into the cupboard where Franzel kept refreshments. "Where did those come from?—I suppose *you* could have had them brought by sky ship."

"I suppose I could, but it's never occurred to me. I brought a cutting, years ago, for the Imperial Botanical Gardens."

"You'll have to show Ghilly where it is."

"No gardens for you?"

Toucan laughed. "*Many* gardens for me. She just likes plants better. I prefer questions of the overall aesthetic."

"The difference between the botanist and the painter."

"Indeed! Is that wine I see?"

"It is." Cliopher found the decanter of wine and pulled out four glasses. There was a bowl of pistachios as well, which he set on the table between his seat and the one Toucan had taken next to him.

"This is lovely wine—I suppose I should stop being surprised at the quality of things in here. ... You know, Kip, we've spent the past six months sailing here and it was like you were this ghost in the room. Always there but not there at the same time. Bertie's been planning for weeks what he was going to say to you when we saw you, and then he didn't say anything!"

Cliopher didn't particularly appreciate the idea of being a ghost in anyone's life, metaphorical or not. "I see," he said slowly.

Toucan laughed. "Don't be absurd, Kip. We missed you, and kept talking about you, that's all. And then we kept coming across people talking about you as Viceroy and it was so strange to think that *that* is you, too."

"I suppose so," he said, and then Suzen and Ghilly appeared from a door that they had not expected, by the looks on their faces, to lead to the sitting room.

"Huh," said Ghilly. "I was sure this door was going to be that library again."

"I don't have a library," Cliopher said, but they all heard the doubt in his voice.

Ghilly started to laugh. "Give us a tour, then," she challenged, "and you can tell us what it *is* in that case."

He showed them around the rooms he used most often: sitting room, dining room, study, his own bedroom and the dressing and bathing rooms next to it, and the dancing room.

"You can use this," he said hesitantly, "if you'd like to practice. There are other mats on the wall, there, that don't have the patterns on them."

Toucan looked down at the swirling lines inscribed in chalk and charcoal on the bamboo mats that were laid down across half the floor, with a portion covered with plain mats from where Cliopher had been practicing that morning, and said nothing.

They found the library, which must have belonged to a previous inhabitant of the rooms for the books were not Cliopher's. He wondered how long the room had rested unused; magic kept it mostly free of dust, but the books and scrolls in elegant glass-fronted cases seemed untouched.

"So this isn't yours, then?" Ghilly asked.

Cliopher opened one of the cases, which was full of wooden-ended scrolls, and took one out, unrolling it partway. It was written in Old Shaian ideographs. Without a syllabary and some thought he could only make out it was something to do with *flowers* and *war*.

He probably could probably have guessed that from what little he knew of Old Shaian literature, which tended to be very interested in the contrasts between bucolic countryside and strife-torn cities.

He rolled up the scroll again and set it back on its rack. Whatever magic was in the room had kept the parchment supple, the ink dark and clear. "No," he said. "I've never been in here before. I'll have to ask Franzel if he knows anything about it."

As they went out, he looked back at the tiles surrounding the door frame. The central one showed what appeared to be an octopus drawn by someone who'd never seen one in reality.

"What are you looking at?" Toucan asked.

"Each of the doors have tiles along the top," he said, pointing them out. "The central one tells you what room is next—back to the, er, Octopus Room, and out—" he ducked back in the doorway to show the ones on the inside—"to the Lion Room.

The Sun and the Moon sigils show whether that next room goes to the private areas, the Moon side, or the public ones, following the Sun."

"Following the Sun right out to civilization," Toucan said, grinning at this echo of the Islander tradition, which held that a great adventurer, the third son of Vonou'a, had gone to the House of the Sun and brought back the fire of civilization to the people. "I don't think I would have figured that out any time soon."

"I was only told about them after a week of getting thoroughly lost," Cliopher admitted. "Here, take note as we go so we can find the library again. Octopus, Lion, Wavy Leaf—"

"You don't know what kind?"

"No more than the artist knew what an octopus actually looked like. It's probably some temperate-climate tree from Ysthar. Wavy Leaf, and there's the Deer, which takes us back to my sitting room."

He opened the door with a flourish, and there it was, homely and cluttered after the spare elegance of the empty rooms they'd just gone through.

"Come sit down and have a glass of wine," he said, ushering them in.

"I want to hear all about your trip, please," Suzen added, positioning herself next to Ghilly. "It sounds fantastic."

∼

They talked and laughed all through supper. Cliopher made sure to question all of them, including the often-reticent Bertie, about how they were finding their lives now that even Ghilly was retired. Apart from a soured relationship with his wife Irela, it appeared that all was well. Parno had been happily surprised by their arrival that afternoon, and Bertie's older son Faldo was doing well; he'd finished his apprenticeship to a glass artist and was now building up his own business.

"That annual stipend of yours has helped," Bertie admitted as he poured out another round of wine from the bottle Shoänie had brought in. This was a problem with having staff: he was not entirely aware of how many bottles they'd had, since Franzel kept taking them away whenever he brought a new one.

"I'm sure it has," Suzen said warmly. "I can see the difference in the City of Emeralds already. There was a period where we had some problems with supplies—people deciding they didn't actually want to work in the mines or refineries, mostly—and prices of some goods have gone up quite a bit, but others have dropped now that no one's as worried about making a living. There are a lot of farmers who just like growing things."

"I think it's meant that more people can live like artists do," Ghilly said, smiling at Suzen. "And many people are perfectly willing to work half days at boring jobs to earn some extra cash for their hobbies."

Cliopher had planned for this—he had *so many* Protocols in Case of Worldwide Trade Disruption due to the stipend (or any other cause—*he* had not forgotten the Fall)—but he had gambled on the certainty that trade and entrepreneurship were as fundamental human activities as gardening or art.

"I hadn't realized how much of an artist Faldo wanted to be," Bertie went on, sinking back into his chair with an appreciative rumble. "I thought he just liked working with dangerous things like molten glass and hot furnaces."

Cliopher laughed. "Not Cora's son!" He turned to Suzen. "Cora's an archaeologist but her hobbies are mountain climbing and surfing."

That love of danger had been one of the crisis points in Bertie and Cora's marriage, if Cliopher remembered correctly. Bertie had felt she was irresponsible, and she had not liked him constraining her. His second wife. Irela, by contrast, was almost theatrically timid.

"Has she come to the City—our city, that is—for the big-wave competition?" Suzen asked. "There's a standing wave just down the coast all through the trades, and it's becoming increasingly popular. Not my hobby, of course—I get sea sick," she added, with a straight face.

Ghilly laughed. "I bet you'd be able to develop a fantastic surfboard with your enchanter friend, if you tried ..."

Suzen looked immediately intrigued, and Ghilly said, "You should come to Gorjo City and see Kip's boat—Cora's been restoring it for him. It's a vaha—that's a traditional outrigger canoe—he sailed home all the way from Nijan, after the Fall."

Cliopher shifted uncomfortably. He had made the vaha and sailed it across the Wide Seas, and then abandoned it behind a warehouse for half a lifetime. Cora had rescued it before it had entirely sunk, then repaired it with the aid of her students, and he had no idea how to repay her for that.

"Having now sailed across the northwestern part of the Wide Seas," Toucan said, "in a rather bigger boat, and with someone who has been sailing regularly his whole life, *I* can't believe you actually made it across safely."

Safely?

He had capsized and rebuilt that boat on island after island after typhoons had overturned him.

He had cut his leg badly once, on a piece of broken coral, and feared he would die alone from sepsis.

He had lain there on his back at midnight, looking at strange zenith stars, trying to identify the desolated islands he had found, unable to bear wondering what had happened to the people who had once lived there, terrified to imagine what might have happened at home.

He had lost his island, which no Islander ever ought to do.

"It was a long journey," he said, and glanced at Bertie. "How is Irela?"

"Bertie's second wife," Ghilly whispered to Suzen. "Cora's my best friend and was his first wife."

Suzen looked politely intrigued—or indeed rather more than politely—at this gossip.

"I keep forgetting you weren't with us on our journey," Toucan said, as Bertie ducked his head with a fierce scowl. "We were all thinking about you so much ... Anyhow. Irela was not exactly pleased with the idea of Bertie sailing around the world for an indefinite length of time."

"We're divorcing," Bertie said bluntly. "Papers served and all."

"If it's only been six weeks at home, no wonder it seems like she's taking forever with her end of the paperwork," Ghilly muttered.

Shoänie came in with a coffee service and a bowl of tropical fruits, as well as a small plate of exceedingly decorative chocolates. She grinned at him and said nothing as she set it down. As she exited, he could see that she was deliberately swinging her hips to make her skirts sway, with a sultry look directed towards Bertie.

Cliopher did not understand the general fascination Bertie seemed to hold for women. He could understand why Rhodin (fantastically muscled from all the exercise, second-in-command of the Imperial Guard, decidedly handsome with those Jade Phoenix eyes, etc.) was the object of desire. Shambling and scowling Bertie, on the other hand ... Perhaps it was the eyebrows.

Bertie shrugged. "Anyway, instead of keeping on with making fancy goblets and things for Noro's store along the Asu Canal, Faldo saved up all his money so he could rent a poky little workshop over in Haloloa, and has since been producing these fantastic glass sculptures. I don't think he's sold more than a handful but he doesn't care."

"How *wonderful*," Suzen said in delight. "The stipend covers what he needs?"

"He says that he's sold enough to pay for the materials, and the stipend pays for what else he needs. Instead he's beautifying that portion of the canal, and he gives some away to people who happen by and admire them."

"Perfect," said Suzen. "Absolutely perfect. You must be so proud, Cliopher."

Cliopher's cheeks heated with embarrassment. The annual stipend—and all the infrastructure that supported it—was his life's work. But it was hard to say that, even to his friends. Perhaps especially to his friends.

(He missed his Radiancy—Fitzroy Angursell—who knew just how hard that work had been. He missed Basil, who didn't know about it. He wanted...oh, why *couldn't* he have that house with all his friends nearby, his cousin alive and well and home from Alinor? Might as well dream of that voyage to the House of the Sun!)

Ghilly laughed. "It's true. You see them walking along the canals sometimes, holding a blown-glass sculpture, looking astonished. I stopped and asked one man whether it was one of Faldo's, and he said that he didn't know the artist's name, but wasn't it magnificent, and did I think he'd really meant for him just to *take* it without payment or anything?"

"And?"

"Artists," Bertie rumbled, in a tone that did not in the least disguise his pride. Suzen beamed at him.

"People keep coming back and leaving him return gifts," Ghilly said. "It's very old-fashioned, really. Cora told me that Faldo has so far been the recipient of several efela, a selection of highland feathers, numerous yams, and a rather lovely Nijani jade pendant. He'll be a wealthy man without ever selling a thing, if you ask me."

"Oh, I like that idea," Suzen said, her eyes calculating. "We don't have that tradition ..."

"Come to Gorjo City and I'm sure you could find something worth trading," Ghilly said.

"Faldo's pieces are beautiful," Toucan said. He glanced at Bertie, who rumbled something, and at Ghilly, who nodded. "We brought you one, actually. If you'd like it."

"Why wouldn't I?"

They looked at him. Finally Ghilly said, "You do know these are the fanciest rooms we've ever been in, right?"

Cliopher raised his eyebrows at them. "And so?"

Bertie harrumphed, but he got up and went out of the room, returning shortly with a stoutly woven basket about a foot square. Cliopher opened it curiously, prepared to admire whatever it was, and found himself speechless at the object inside.

A *glass sculpture* could have meant anything. For Faldo, for the gift his father brought to Cliopher, it meant a clamshell of milky-white glass with a golden-yellow interior.

Suzen gasped as Cliopher drew it out of the basket and its enveloping wrapping. He set it on the table, where the glass caught the light, revealing the subtle variations representing the growth rings of the shell, the cunningly shaped folds of the mantle, tiny white-touched beads of golden glass representing flame pearls, others of brilliant blue the mollusk's eyes.

"A nefalao," Cliopher said, touching the glass with trembling fingers. "How utterly perfect."

~

When he prepared for bed that night, Cliopher reflected that he had learned a deeply unexpected secret held close to Ludvic's heart, and another now from Rhodin—who certainly gave every evidence of being utterly and completely sincere—

And Bertie divorcing Irela, and Faldo's surprising, stupendous gift at glass-making—

And of course, there was that astonishing, incredible, and yet so indisputably *true* secret that his Radiancy was Fitzroy Angursell ...

He glanced at himself in the mirror as he washed his face. That respectable bureaucrat, grey-haired and sober, eyes crinkling with humour as he could not help but laugh at himself for the immediate thought that he surely was not *that* sober and respectable—

What secrets did *he* yet hold in his heart that he himself had yet to uncover?

(He was not at all sober, just that moment.)

CHAPTER ELEVEN
THE MUSEUM

The next morning, Cliopher woke up late. He did not feel his usual alert self; he was a trifle hungover.

He decided not to practice his dances but instead settled himself in his sitting room with his lap desk and a few sheets of paper, and wrote a letter to his cousin Basil about his friends.

He was just in the midst of explaining how wonderfully they had surprised him when Toucan appeared in the doorway.

"Oh—good morning, Kip."

"Good morning, Toucan." He surveyed his friend, who was yawning and, though dressed, still sleepy. "Coffee?"

"Please ..."

Cliopher rang the magical bell that informed whoever was on morning duty to come in. Shoänie appeared in due course with another cup of chocolate. She grinned at him and took Toucan's preference with a pretence at solemnity. Toucan sat down in the chair next to Cliopher.

"Sorry—do go on. I didn't mean to interrupt."

"It's not work," Cliopher replied. "I was writing a letter."

"Oh, to your sister?"

He hesitated, for he had never told anyone about his extended, one-sided correspondence with his lost cousin. "No. My cousin Basil."

For a moment he thought Toucan wouldn't catch that; he had forgotten that Toucan and Basil had once been as close friends as Cliopher and Bertie. Toucan paled. "Basil ... You mean you've heard from—you've never said—"

"No, no, I've not kept any news from you," Cliopher said hastily, and then of course he had to explain, because Toucan was looking at him in confusion. "I send the letters to Alinor with the embassies, to send on once they arrive, but I've never had any replies."

Toucan regarded him. "How often do you write?"

Cliopher found he was fiddling with his pen. He set it down carefully in the groove carved into the lap desk for the purpose. "Every few months, I suppose."

"And never a reply."

"No."

"You don't think ..."

"Of course I think that's *possible*," he replied sharply. "Even probable." Toucan simply kept watching him, and in the early-morning silence, the fragrance of the hot chocolate, mingled with the nearly-similar scent of the tui blossoms in their vase, Cliopher found the urge, the need, to explain.

"But I don't *know*, you see. There are other explanations. My letters might not get there at all; there were a number of ambassadors to Alinor who did not like me, and it is possible they did not send them along. They might be sent, but not arrive at the proper place; I understand that the post in Northwest Oriole is not as secure as it was before the Fall. They might arrive, but Basil's responses go astray; every Alinorel ambassador or scholar or what-have-you I've asked says that there's been very little news out of that part of the world since the Fall, and even the famed Noirell honey is increasingly hard to acquire. Then again, he might be dead, or incapacitated, but in that case, if someone is receiving the letters you'd think they'd reply at some point to give his rather dedicated correspondent the news."

"And so you write," Toucan said. "Because you do not *know*."

Cliopher traced his fingers across the page he had been writing. "And if it is the case that he has received them, but for one reason or another has been unable to reply ... I do not want him to think we have forgotten him."

Toucan shifted in his seat, and looked down at his hands. "If I wrote a letter, will you include it with yours?"

"Of course," Cliopher said. Shoänie came in then with Toucan's coffee, and the bells rang the next quarter-hour, and Cliopher put away the lap desk and the unfinished letter and wondered what his friend really thought of his entirely unsubstantiated hope that Basil might still be alive.

It was an ember he held for so long ...

~

When Ghilly came out, she was bright-eyed and much more alert than either of them. "Hungover?" she said slyly, stealing Toucan's coffee for a drink. "You know what would be a good plan for today? The museum! It'll be quiet and cool, right? And they might have a bookstore nearby ... I've been getting back into reading properly, Kip. All that time on the boat, and suddenly I can only think about philosophers from uni."

"To our regret," whispered Toucan.

Ghilly rolled her eyes. "To your eternal admiration, husband of mine. And then we can go to Alun and Nala's later in the afternoon."

"I'll have to have a guard of some form," Cliopher said, though he was getting a little excited at the prospect of a whole day *off*, just like that, like a regular person. (*He* hadn't read much philosophy, and perishingly few books at all, for years, either.)

"Rhodin and Ludvic get a little stroppy if I go off by myself. Something about being the acting head of state and the dignity of my station and nonsense like that."

"Utter nonsense, absolutely," Ghilly said, grinning, and surprised him by giving him a sudden embrace and a peck on the cheek. "Oh, Kip, it's so good to be here with you!"

≈

Rhodin, notified by a duly-sent page, arrived before they had finished breakfast and informed Cliopher he had assigned himself and Pikabe as the day's guards. Neither were in their uniform; they arrived in civvies, their undoubted weapons hidden.

"I haven't been to the museum in some time," Rhodin stated when Cliopher regarded his presence curiously.

"I've not been to the museum at all," Pikabe added cheerfully. "I go to the plays on my days off. I like the comedies best. Ato goes with Féonie, sometimes."

Cliopher himself dressed in his good common wear, or what amounted to common wear according to Féonie. (She had blushed when he asked about her visits to the museum with Ato, and mumbled something about inspiration; he'd laughed at this excuse for a courtship the entire Imperial Guard and viceregal household were enjoying watching progress.)

He wore the usual white cotton culottes and tunic, sleeveless in deference to the heat outdoors, plus an overgarment like an open robe of finely woven linen, light and airy and a pleasant striped green and yellow. Cliopher felt a little as if he were playing dress-up, for the style was neither Vangavayen nor fully Solaaran, but Féonie assured him the colour suited him well.

They went out, down one of the side stairs to the gardens on the north side of the Palace, not far from the menagerie. It was hot and humid even this early, with white clouds building up over the western mountains.

"The rains will start in ten days or so," Cliopher told his friends, gesturing at the mountains.

"I confess this might be the strangest thing to me," Toucan said, coming up beside him as they started down the gravelled path that cut through a grove of giant birds-of-paradise plants. The huge paddle-shaped leaves arched high overhead, a good twenty feet above them. Weaverbirds were moving around the flower heads, pecking at insects, their yellow and black feathers nearly velvety in the sunlight.

"That there's a rainy season?"

"That it's so precise. The whole thing with time is incomprehensible, I leave that as a mystery in Vou'a's bag. But this seems as if it should be simply untrue."

"It's magic," Cliopher said. "The Astandalan wizards could do it for huge stretches of Ysthar. The Ouranatha only do it here because of his Radiancy."

Not that his Radiancy cared about such orderliness of season.

Because he was Fitzroy Angursell.

Cliopher caught his breath, coughed, pretended he had swallowed a fly, and then flushed when Toucan eyed him with a strangely knowing expression.

"You miss him, don't you?"

A whole cascade of emotions rushed through Cliopher, as unexpected and inexpressible as ... as anything he could imagine. He glanced out, rearranging the fall of the mantle. He should have put on a hat; the sun was heavy on his unprotected head, unaccustomed as he was to going out in the middle of the day.

"It's only natural," he said stiffly. "I was hitherto accustomed to spending much of the day in his presence."

Toucan gave him an incredulous glance. "Hitherto?"

Cliopher did not know where to look or what to do with his hands. He accidentally caught Rhodin's glance. The guard was maintaining his respectable sober face, but there was a wild, amused glint in his eye. Cliopher coughed again. He could wish he knew more botany, for this part of the garden was full of beautiful plants he could not name.

"It *is* only natural," Toucan said, gently teasing. "We miss our friends when they are gone."

Was it only that morning they had spoken of Basil, of Cliopher's long, one-sided correspondence? He did not need to be embarrassed for ... loving people, surely.

And it was no secret that he was devoted to his Radiancy.

"Yes," he said, far too long after Toucan had last spoken.

Toucan laughed. "Tell me about this museum, then. This is the one you've been after them to rename, correct?"

Now that was a topic Cliopher could expound upon without any difficulty at all. "Yes," he said, and at Toucan's encouraging expression—he carefully did not look again at Rhodin—he told them all about the splendid holdings and the ridiculous imperialistic settings they were about to experience.

～

One of the things about being the Viceroy of Zunidh was that people had begun to recognize him by sight.

They never had even as Lord Chancellor. They might or might not know his name— the court pronunciation of *Lord Madon* had been as good as an alibi. People were thus split between knowing him primarily from verbal introductions, which meant most of those in the Palace, or from seeing his name written down, which meant they knew it was *Mdang* but generally had no idea of its pronunciation. Cliopher could forgive the latter.

The Curator in Chief at the Primitive Cultures Gallery was one of those who had been surprised to discover what name went with what face. Cliopher had invited him to the Palace when he had danced the fire before the throne, and finally, finally, set in motion the slow process of renaming an important building.

The museums were in a cluster next to the university. Most had been built after the Fall, though several of the university buildings were repurposed minor palaces from before, their architecture incongruous and only made habitable by magic. The Museum of Comparative Anthropology was a fine stone building, limestone carved with many different kinds of animals and plants.

Cliopher had assumed that only the curator was at all likely to recognize him, and so was rather startled when the young man on the desk took one look at their party and went a shocked, pasty grey.

The museums were free to visitors—an innovation Cliopher had caused to be instituted ages and ages ago—but because the wing was undergoing renovations, he'd heard it was necessary to request admission, as they were only letting small parties in at a time.

"Your—your excellency," the young man said, in a voice that echoed in the vaulted entrance hall. He bowed jerkily, catching the attention of anybody who had not heard him. "We were not expecting you today?"

Cliopher sighed inwardly and set himself into his courtliest expression. "Good morning," he said, ignoring the implication he ought to have sent one of the pages or secretaries down to make the appointment. He would have if he'd wanted a private tour of the holdings.

Perhaps he ought to have, so that Bertie could have a private tour.

Well, it was done now. He smiled mildly at the young man. "Might we visit the Western Galleries? No need for a guide; I am well acquainted with the route."

He would not call it the Primitive Cultures Gallery. Not now they had finally decided on a new name, describing both the location in the building and the hemisphere of the world thus covered.

Assuming a central point in Solaara, of course. But Cliopher had never quite dared suggest they pick a centre for directions and distance measurements that was not the Palace of Stars.

It was not as if his centre in the Vangavaye-ve was any more absolute a centre for the world. His island was his ground and anchor, no one else's.

Or no one else's but those whose island it also was.

Toucan was from the Epalos, and Ghilly from Tisiamo, and Bertie from Gorjo City itself, and all of those had different zenith stars and were slightly different centres.

The young receptionist had stammered something and was waiting expectantly for Cliopher to reply.

Rhodin stepped up beside him and said, "That will do admirably."

"Yes, thank you," Cliopher replied belatedly, and followed Rhodin where he led. Which was not the usual route at all.

"Where are we going?" he whispered once they were far enough from the receptionist.

Rhodin grinned out of the side of his mouth. "Side door. The main door's closed while they work on the entrance exhibit."

"They're renovating the galleries before they have the grand reopening with the new name," Cliopher told his friends, his steps once more assured now that he knew where they were going. He'd once—oh years and years ago, long before he was a Somebody in the eyes of the court, or anyone's, come to think of it—at any rate, once he'd been escorted out of the gallery through the side door for being too loudly opinionated about an exhibit on boat design in the Sociable Isles.

They had included examples of vahas from the Isolates. The Isolates were on the far side of the Wide Seas from the Vangavaye-ve, and most of an ocean away from the Sociable Isles, which were archipelagos extending out through the trade latitudes from Nijan.

It wasn't as if they weren't *related*, admittedly. The Isolate Islanders were part of the same widespread culture. But the boat designs were very different.

"When do they expect to do that?" Bertie asked curiously.

"I believe it's to coincide with the Jubilee ceremonies around his Radiancy's retirement," Cliopher replied. "They were supposed to open a year or two ago but then discovered a structural problem with the building. You know how it goes."

"Oh yes. Renovations always take so much longer and are so much more expensive than you think," Ghilly said. She was looking around the hall curiously, interested in the artefacts displayed in niches along the route. These were all from the Grey Mountains of Southern Dair: blowguns three yards long, and the brightly-coloured darts, the length of a hand, that went with them. A stuffed jaguar perched on sculpted tree limb forty feet away, showing the range and accuracy of the weapon.

"Goodness," Ghilly said, pausing to look again at the darts. "These can take down a great cat like that?"

"They poison them using toxins from the frogs," Cliopher said, pointing to the ceramic figurines of the bright-skinned poison dart frogs next to the quiver of darts. These were red and green, not the tiny golden ones he'd once seen in person.

"How efficient," Ghilly replied, shivering.

"Someone tried to assassinate Cliopher with one of those last month," Rhodin said conversationally, peering down at it. "One of the ex-Princess Oriana's weaker efforts, I thought. Everyone knows the Hagen Pass folk don't hunt people with them, so it was easy enough to find the rogue." He tutted disapprovingly.

Cliopher, to be honest, had no idea what to say. There'd been a report or two about 'ex-Princess Oriana's various incompetencies with conspiracies to murder and discredit'—she was just competent enough to keep the indisputable train of evidence from directly implicating her. Rhodin had had some sort of convoluted explanation for why it was better to let her fail consistently rather than arrest her and perhaps not be able to convict her.

Cliopher had not had much interest in sitting in judgment on a case of high treason, and Rhodin and Ludvic were, after all, in charge of security in the Palace and the world, and he had listened to them.

"I didn't realize it had come anywhere close to succeeding," he ventured hesitantly.

Rhodin scoffed. "Don't be absurd. The assassin didn't get past the outermost door to the suite you were in. I *do* know my job, you know."

～

They left the ceramic frogs and the gaily coloured darts and entered the side door of the western gallery.

The lights were dim, brightening as they entered and Rhodin clapped the four sharp doublets that usually served in public buildings. Ghilly jumped at the sound, which echoed, and then gasped as she caught sight of the doubled prow of a parahë angled before them.

The great voyaging canoe was set so that those entering by the main doors would see it first. They walked up to it, drawn as any Islanders were by the ships of their ancestors.

"Is it a replica?" Toucan asked hoarsely.

A year or two (or three, or four...) ago, Cliopher had spent several long and pleasant afternoons with the curator, discussing various aspects of the Islander display.

"It's the remains of the *Au'o'eakanë*," he replied quietly, walking forward to place a hand on the hull of the ship that Elonoa'a had first sailed when Aurelius Magnus had requested his aid. Bertie frowned at him, and he guiltily removed his hand. "It was sunk off the coast of Kavanor, Sayo Giron—the curator, that is—told me. The Kavanduru fishermen dive down to the sunken cities, searching for treasure. They found the prow and raised it when they found out what it was."

"And how," Ghilly asked, "did they know what it was?"

Cliopher blushed. Out of the corner of his eye he saw Rhodin leaning forward, eyes gleaming with interest. "I saw the reports," he murmured. "His Radiancy was interested in what they found, so the lists were sent up to him. I went to see it ... I told Cora ..."

"I remember," Ghilly said. "She told me you'd written about an Islander ship they'd found, wondering if it was the *Au'o'eakanë*."

"It could have been another ship, I suppose," Cliopher said, "but the designs are the ones mentioned in the *Lays*, and its location matched the accounts." He walked down the length of the hull facing them, his hand hovering over the flowers inlaid with mother-of-pearl, the curving lines of the Kindraa carvings, the cross-hatched manta rays that had been the signature of one of the ship-building families.

The parahë was incomplete, ravaged by woodworm and the broken stern from hitting a submerged rock (so said the *Lays*), but—broken as it was—it was incomparable.

"I don't recall those sorts of details," Toucan said, frowning.

Here in this room, with the light shining on the ship—so out of place, rising high above them, its hulls lifted above the floor so they could nearly duck beneath, its mast rising up, sailless but yet seeming ready for any new seas—

Oh, it was easy to bring up the old words.

Cliopher sang the lines softly, the Islander words coming forth from that deep part of his memory that ran parallel to his Palace life and preoccupations. A dozen lines, describing a ship; this ship. He had known it as soon as he saw the cross-hatched manta rays.

Pikabe and Rhodin stood a little apart from his friends, one on each side of their group. Rhodin was looking down the gallery, but his head was cocked towards Cliopher. Pikabe was not even pretending not to listen, was staring at him in amazement.

Cliopher finished the passage and fumbled a moment, not able to say any of the formal ways of concluding such a singing—he had not *begun* it with any of the formalities he ought to have done—he had not lit a fire or passed around a bowl of kava or water or palm wine—he had not offered food or hospitality. He had not even started with the proper words.

"It's from the sixth of the *Lays*," he said, half-explaining to Ghilly and Bertie, half to Rhodin and Pikabe. "It treats the coming of the Emperor Aurelius Magnus across the Wide Seas to meet the Islanders."

"Ilona, right?" Pikabe said. "The one with the comet."

"Elonoa'a, yes," Cliopher corrected gently, pleased that Pikabe had remembered that midnight conversation so well as that. Soft steps made him look up, to see that the curator was coming along the hall towards them. He nodded at the man and continued. "The *He'eanka* was the ship he took to sail Sky Ocean. The *Au'o'eakanë*, this ship, was the one he took when Aurelius Magnus asked him to navigate for him, to find the ke'ea—the way—to Colhélhé. It sank off Kavanor on his return, and they parted ways, Aurelius Magnus to continue north to meet his army, Elonoa'a to return home in a borrowed Shaian ship."

"You have a splendid voice, Lord Mdang," Sayo Giron complimented him as he reached them. "Was that the passage you paraphrased for me when the wreck was found?"

Cliopher nodded shortly, wishing the man had waited a moment longer before coming. He did not sing in public; whatever courtly blandishments the curator might offer, he knew he was not actually skilled in the art.

"It describes the carvings," Ghilly said, moving around Toucan. "Tell us about them, Kip? Or Bertie?"

Sayo Giron's attention suddenly sharpened on Bertie. "Bertie—you're not Falbert Kindraa, are you?"

"Indeed," Bertie replied, his voice warm even as his eyebrows drew together. "And you're Chisra Giron, I take it?"

"It is a great pleasure to meet you at last, not simply through your letters," the curator said, clasping Bertie's hands in the Solaaran greeting and then immediately drawing him over to the side to launch into a discussion that waxed technical beyond Cliopher's knowledge in a matter of seconds.

He shrugged apologetically at Ghilly and Toucan. "I suppose that's that. The *Lays* describe this as *the kurakura lines of the manta rays*—kurakura is, ah, the way the ripples are when two sets of waves cross each other."

It was, as ever, difficult to switch from Islander to Shaian and back again. Cliopher's accent had strengthened with even so small an impetus as a handful of lines from the *Lays*.

"It was Uruyë Ena'a who carved them so," he said. "Ena'a is what they called the Gēnangs before they took the name of the island for their lineage. It's still used in the Epalos, isn't it, Toucan?"

"Ena'a? Yes—one of my cousins has that name."

Toucan was regarding him oddly. Cliopher gave him as enquiring a glance as he could, but Toucan merely shook his head and drew Ghilly's arm through his. "You do have a good voice, Kip," he said.

Cliopher stole a glance across at the curator, who was pointing at something in the direction of the main entrance door. "Not good enough," he muttered, and turned the other way.

He would have left it at that, but Ghilly caught at his elbow with her free hand. "Kip."

He stopped perforce and looked at her. "Yes?"

"What do you mean, *not good enough*?"

He looked at Sayo Giron, who seemed thoroughly engrossed with Bertie, judging from how close they were standing and how enthusiastically Bertie was nodding. Cliopher stepped back from them automatically, unthinking of anything except that Sayo Giron always stood slightly too close for comfort. Toucan and Ghilly followed him, Ghilly's expression challenging.

"My singing voice is adequate," Cliopher said, looking at the great ship. "That's all."

Even broken, riddled with wormholes, still encrusted with barnacles towards the broken stern, it was a magnificent, heart-lifting sight. He ached with pride in his people. The Ke'e Lulai, Those Who Lived Under the Wake. What an ancestral ship to imagine sailing Sky Ocean above him!

"I don't think I've ever heard you just ... sing," Toucan said.

Cliopher smiled slightly, forcing his shoulders to loosen. There was no reason to be bothered by this. No use in still being disappointed, all these years on. "No reason to, most of the time."

Ghilly did not have a good singing voice. Toucan's was better, but both of them had been surprised—he recalled any number of proud, mystified letters—when their daughter turned out to have a splendid voice, one of the great gifts of her generation.

Cliopher had written back to his friends with compliments and congratulations, and written to Lara directly as well, with thoughts on what it took to follow a vocation. He had not tried to offer her any advice on singing or music, merely on how much practice and dedication meant over and above raw talent.

"Didn't your mother want you to develop your talent?" Toucan asked.

Cliopher laughed. "What talent? I didn't have what Vinyë did with music, you know enough to know that, Toucan. I was never going to be ..."

"Good enough," Ghilly finished.

"Exactly." He looked at Rhodin and Pikabe, standing foursquare and sober a few feet away, suddenly invisible guards rather than companionable friends. Back at Ghilly and Toucan, whose expressions were still odd. He took in their postures, the way Toucan had Ghilly's arm drawn through his, the way that Ghilly had furrowed her brow, Toucan quirked his mouth.

"You don't believe me," he said, a little blankly.

Ghilly sighed. "We just heard you sing."

"Yes."

"You could have had a *great* voice," she said. "I can't sing but I can hear that—I spent enough time taking Lara to teachers to work on her voice."

"Lara does have a great voice."

"Why are you so *stubborn*?" she hissed, glancing down at where Bertie and the curator had drifted farther from them and were peering at something in a glass case down the hall. "You must know your voice is ..."

"My mother is one of the greatest sopranos of the Ring," he said flatly. "My aunt Malania and uncle Haido are the lead singers of the opera. My sister is the director of the symphony orchestra. Dozens of other family members are musicians. I think I know my quality, thank you. They always made it perfectly plain."

Ghilly stepped back, her hand slipping to grip Toucan's forearm. "Kip."

Cliopher took a deep, raggedy breath. There was no need to take out his temper on his friends. "I went to my uncle Haido once, after my voice changed and I was relearning how to sing. Before I knew you. I had hoped I could ... I was never going to be a pearl hunter," he said, trying to keep his voice calm, polite.

How *embarrassing* that his youthful disappointment still rankled so obviously.

"I sang for him, a passage from the *Lays* I had learned from my Buru Tovo. Thinking I might apprentice ..." He shook his head sharply. "That didn't happen, obviously."

"What did he say?" Toucan asked.

"It was him and the director of the opera choir. They looked at each other—" Cliopher could picture it so clearly, no doubt because he had gone over and over this moment in his imagination until he had eventually been able to put it aside. "And then the director said, 'Maybe in fifty years you'll be able to sing,' and Uncle Haido ... laughed."

There. He had said it. He didn't think he'd *ever* said it out loud.

He worked his jaw and turned away, staring fiercely at the ship. It was mounted on steel posts, set discreetly far back under the ship. There had been magic involved in the raising of the vessel and strengthening the ancient wood, but Cliopher had been adamant that it not be *restored* by magic.

How dared he speak for the Islanders? But there had been no one else to do so, no one else who cared and was in a position to be able to do something about it. Jiano had not yet become Paramount Chief—Sayo Giron had been working on this ship, this exhibit, for years.

There were so many things buried in the minutiae of Cliopher's days, weeks, months, years, decades. Centuries. So many things that when they were before him were crucially important, and then, once dealt with, what could he do but put his mind to the next task, and the next, and the next? There was always something else to do.

"You know, Kip," Ghilly said, and he turned his head to look at her, hoping the tears stinging at his eyes were not evident. It was the ship, his friends, the words from the *Lays* still round and rich in his mouth, that made his emotions so close to the surface.

"What do I know, Ghilly," he said, suddenly exhausted.

"Lara went to sit at your aunt Malania's feet for a time," Ghilly said. "She said— Lara did—that you'd given her advice on how to follow a ... dream, if she'd decided on one."

He shifted position, uncomfortable. "I write to many people."

Toucan met his glance and Cliopher guessed he was also thinking once more of Cliopher's unanswered letters to Basil.

"Your aunt Malania told Lara, at the end of something she'd been doing, that if she kept working she might one day be said to *have a voice*. Lara came home positively glowing at the compliment."

"Yes."

"But you, told the same thing—"

"It wasn't the same," he snapped. "I wasn't cut out to be a pearl hunter, and I wasn't cut out to be a musician, and I wasn't ever going to be—" He stopped, realizing his voice had raised, and he took three deep, rattling breaths, clenched his fists, and walked down the hall, away from Sayo Giron and his friends.

Past the stern of the ship was a collection of masks from the high islands of the Eastern Ring. Cliopher forced himself to identify the patterns he knew: island, family, legend.

Toucan came up to him a few moments later, standing at his shoulder, a warm, comforting presence. They stared at the masks.

"Your family," Toucan said eventually, "are known for cutting down the tall poppies to size."

Cliopher nodded jerkily. He had always been too clever by half, too opinionated, too obnoxious. His family had resolutely tried to direct his energies into suitable, acceptable paths.

None of which he had been able to stand.

He was not good enough for the ones he wanted, and the ones they wanted were not for him.

It had been such a relief to have that sense of a vocation when he saw the portrait of the newly crowned Artorin Damara and realized that *there* was a path he could take, something he could cleave to, something he could work at.

"You're not a tall poppy, Kip," Toucan said.

Cliopher stared at the masks. That one was surely a Koromahi design, red ochre and white clay marking out the grooves, tiny shells traded from the Western Ring embedded into the wood.

Toucan put his hand on Cliopher's shoulder, turning him to face him. Cliopher looked at his friend's expression, serious, intense, almost sad.

Cliopher wanted nothing so much as to laugh, to scoff, but he couldn't move. The dimly lit hall, the beautiful displays of familiar artifacts, the cool air, the distance from Ghilly, who was talking with Rhodin and Pikabe, and Bertie, still with the curator ...

"I was never good enough at any of those things," Cliopher said lowly. "I wanted ..."

"Basil told me," Toucan said. "He was my best friend, you know that. He told me how when he came from the islands and was lost in the city, you plucked him out of all your cousins to be your brother. He didn't know Shaian, so you spoke Islander with him. He didn't know the city, so you explored it with him. He would get overwhelmed with all the people, so you took him to the quiet, private, solitary places you knew."

Cliopher could not stand Toucan's intense gaze. He looked down. "Basil and I were ..."

"Two of the three sons of Vonou'a, everyone said. People said that when you left, you know. They said, 'Oh, Kip has gone to sit at the feet of the Sun. Basil, are you going to go look for your heart's desire?' And eventually he did. He and Dimiter left to visit you."

Toucan's voice dropped into silence, then lifted again, a hint of chagrin in it. "I always wish I'd gone with them. Basil invited me, but it was so far—I was afraid. I told myself it was that I didn't want to lose my job, but it wasn't that. It was so far, and so strange, and I was afraid."

"You've come now," Cliopher said, not sure if that was reassuring.

"I have. Cliopher ... please."

It was extremely rare for any of his Islander friends to call him *Cliopher*. He looked sharply at Toucan.

"Cliopher. We love you as you are. Let yourself be yourself."

As if it were that easy.

Chapter Twelve
Ke'ea and Ke'e

Nala and Alun were Ghilly's new friends. Nala was a pleasant-featured woman with intelligent eyes and waist-length hair that crackled like smoke around her as she moved. Cliopher was a little in awe of her hair, which seemed almost to be its own entity. She also had a lovely voice, cool and smooth like an abalone shell, accented with the Nijani inflections.

Alun was taller even than Bertie, and rounder, with a comfortable belly and much more ordinary curly hair flecked with white. His accent was stronger than his wife's; Cliopher could place it to a specific neighbourhood in Zangoraville, an old warehouse district now home to many artisans' workshops.

After the initial wave of greetings and proclamations of hospitality and welcome and so forth were performed, Cliopher and his friends were ushered into a comfortable sitting room. There was no hesitation about welcoming them, perhaps because they'd left Rhodin and Pikabe outside.

(When they'd arrived at the house, Rhodin had informed Cliopher that he and Pikabe would keep watch on the two entrances.

"You'll not be bored?" Ghilly asked tentatively.

Rhodin smiled at her, and gave Cliopher a significant look. What it was supposed to signify was less clear. "I shall sit in the shade," he said, gesturing at a tree with a bench placed below it that stood at the corner of the street. "I have some things to think about."

Which suggested ... Cliopher thought of that mad conversation about the Merrions and their telepathic dinosaur soulmates, and suddenly *did not want to know* just what Rhodin was planning on thinking about.

"I'm sure they wouldn't mind you coming in. We told them it might not just be Kip—we weren't sure ..."

But Rhodin refused to be moved. He sent Pikabe around to the back, gave Cliopher a look that he took to mean he was to be good and not cause a ruckus—though since this was Rhodin and not Ludvic, there was also an amused, amusing gleam almost daring him to do so—and retreated to the tree.)

Cliopher looked around curiously. It had been a while since he was last in a stranger's home. The room was furnished largely in the Nijani style, with airy white wickerwork furniture cushioned in brightly patterned fabric, mostly red and yellow. The floors were a pale gold wood, the walls painted a rich bright blue, and the deep-set windows framed in white. Books and many plants with intriguing leaves were the primary decorations, along with several good pieces of art on the walls.

One was a dramatic wooden storyboard in an Islander style Cliopher didn't quite recognize. The storyboard was teardrop-shaped, wider than it was tall: perhaps seven feet across, and five high. It took up the majority of one wall, and was the clear focal point of the room. A few abstract woven textiles hung on the side walls, and between two of the window embrasures was a small square painting of a meticulously detailed cowrie shell, in a style he knew.

He turned to Nala, who had come back in with a tray of refreshments. "This is by Vho Suzen from the City of Emeralds, isn't it?"

Nala seemed astonished. "It is! We got it on our honeymoon. We couldn't afford to get a portrait done, but this ... I just loved it. You're a connoisseur, then, Kip?"

Cliopher laughed. "Hardly. I know Suzen, that's all, and recognized her work." He gestured at the storyboard. "Where is that from? I'd say Eastern Sociables, probably east of Korivo, but I don't know the tradition."

Ghilly uttered an inelegant snort from her seat on the sofa, next to Toucan and under the abstract weavings.

"Yes?" said Cliopher, raising his eyebrows at her.

Toucan grinned. "'You are unbelievable', I believe is the phrase."

"I shall ignore that," Cliopher proclaimed loftily. (He was, surely, able to ignore the way it sparked thoughts of Toucan's comments in the museum.)

"It comes from Alun's family. But we don't know where exactly," Nala explained, gesturing him to a chair and handing him a glass of fruit juice. "They moved to Nijan after the Fall, but as I'm sure you know, many of the records are confused from then."

"Yes, I am aware," he murmured, sipping the juice (guava, and obviously freshly squeezed; it was delicious). He studied the storyboard. Its central image was a yam house with a richly decorated façade, surrounded with clusters of people, pandanus, coconut palms, parrots, and several repetitions of a long eel-like fish. The bas-relief carvings were picked out in white and red pigments, but no blue or yellow or green.

"It must be a high island, to have the wood for a carving this large," he said, thinking it through. A coral atoll would not grow a tree that could be carved to these dimensions, and it was a single piece, not several fixed together. He'd already thought the style Eastern Wide Seas—farther west, towards the Vangavaye-ve, there would be blue and green pigments from crushed uzu shells.

What were the high islands between Nijan and Korivo? The Otoroye-ve were atolls. The Rarikiki were volcanic, but they were far south, and still populated. He tried to visualize the maps of the Wide Seas, but could only think of the snaking route of the sea train. Which had broken down *again*—

But that was not today's work. Not *his* work, at all, any longer.

He turned back to the storyboard.

The only terrestrial animals depicted were ones the Islanders would have brought with them: pigs, dogs, the Jilkanese marsupial known as a *toutou*, which some Eastern Wide Seas communities kept as pets. The canoes were of a design that did not show precise origin to Cliopher, at least. The sails were the half-claws common to the entire eastern Wide Seas, and the double outriggers only narrowed it down to the Sociable Isles.

He'd missed that entire group of archipelagos, the most extensive in the Wide Seas, on his journey home. One or other of the typhoons had cast him far south of the Tiatuoan Line, which marked the eastern edge of the Sociable Isles, and he had limped along through the lonely southern archipelagos, most of them long-since uninhabited.

He looked again at the storyboard, then to his friends, who continued to be amused. "Do you know, Toucan?"

"No, and Bertie doesn't either," Toucan replied.

"Bertie doesn't what?" said Bertie, who had disappeared with Alun earlier and now returned with him.

"The origin of the storyboard. Kip was asking."

Alun regarded Cliopher curiously. "People here are always intrigued by it, but I'm surprised you find it so exotic?"

"He's trying, in a round-about way, to find out your island," Toucan explained. "This is the Islander question: where do you come from and how might you be related to me? But Kip has spent too long away, and so he no longer asks directly."

"Thank you, Toucan," Cliopher replied dryly. "I do appreciate your willingness to interpret."

"Any time, Kip."

Alun laughed, shoulders relaxing from a defensiveness Cliopher knew all too well. "I see. I'm afraid I don't know what island my family came from originally. My grandparents left when my father was young, to move to Zangoraville, and they died before he could really ask them about it."

Cliopher could guess, from his knowledge of Nijani culture and the experience of émigrés everywhere, that the grandparents had felt a certain reluctance to speak of the past (even as they inevitably lived it and what elements of their culture that they could), while the father in his turn had probably tried to assimilate to his present and dominant culture, and not desired to ask about family history until it was too late.

Zangoraville had been founded by Wide Sea Islanders, but was much more a part of Imperial culture than the Vangavaye-ve or the other islands had ever been, and had created their own culture with only a tenuous historic relation to the more remote traditional communities. They regarded Cliopher as one of their own, but no one he had ever spoken to had ever given a hint of knowing even a word in the old Islander language. The Sociable Isles were, to them, exotic: the Vangavaye-ve on the other side of the ocean was almost mythical.

Alun appeared wistful at this gap in his knowledge. Cliopher hesitated, then asked: "What is your surname? Many are quite local to certain islands or archipelagos."

"It's Ke'e Ofuluente," Alun replied, "but your friends have already said that's a direction, not a historic name. Like being called 'west'."

"Doesn't help very much to know what star to follow if you don't know where to start from," Toucan said.

Cliopher set down his guava juice on the glass-topped table beside him and leaned forward. "I thought you said *Ke'e* Ofuluente? Or is it *Ke'ea*?"

"Ke'e," Alun said. "Is there a difference?"

Cliopher looked at his friends, but Toucan was grinning and the others appeared vaguely mystified and more obviously amused. Alun and Nala, for their parts, were intrigued.

He took a breath. He had always loved to explain things others didn't know. This was no different than proclaiming a new—a new postal system.

(It was of course, entirely different.)

This went deep into that parallel sea of knowledge, learned at the feet of his Buru Tovo, kept secret for so long from the court.

He smiled at Alun and Nala, easy, courtly, as if this were nothing at all significant. They could not see his sweaty palms. "Ke'ea is the direction word. It's usually translated as 'star path' or 'star road'."

Nala tilted her head. "What does that mean? Like a constellation?"

"Not a fixed one, no." Cliopher thought about how to explain it. "It's easiest to give an example. Let's say you wanted to go from Loaloa, which is my ancestral island, in the Western Ring of the Vangavaye-ve, to Gorjo City, which is in the north of the Eastern Ring. The ke'ea for that route is called *Ke'ea Kaibola*, because you start with Kaibola, one of the Sixteen Bright Guides."

"So if you follow Kaibola from—no, that doesn't work," Nala objected. "Stars don't stay in the same place all night."

Cliopher had sometimes wondered if he would have had a satisfying life as a teacher. He smiled at her. "Exactly. So the star path you learn is named after the first star, but the actual teaching consists of the stars you follow through the course of the journey. You can follow any given star for about an hour or a bit more after it rises or before it sets, by the way, for a true consistent direction. There are ways to navigate by upper stars or constellation patterns, but that's more complicated."

"So for your example, you start with following Kaibola as it rises over the horizon. Then comes another star?"

Cliopher found himself gesturing in the direction the stars would be, if he stood on the beach at Loaloa preparing his canoe to sail back across the Bay of the Waters. "Yes."

His voice settled easily into the half-chant he'd had to recite so many times as a youth. "First night: Kaibola, Hinai, Osu, Re'eaka, Tina'a, Lona Kaibola, Lona Tukoa, Lona Jiano. First day: East past Blade Reef, Poliaye Reef, White Rock. Second night: Kaibola, Hinai, Itavo Nua-nui, Lona Furai'no, Tina'a, Lona Kaibola, Lona Tukoa, Lona Jiano. Sunrise over Doyano Reef, and Mama Ituri shows the way home."

They all regarded him in some surprise. Toucan—of course it was Toucan—said, "Lona means 'setting', doesn't it? What does itavo mean in this context?"

Cliopher had to think of the Shaian translation. Like the names for the stars, the constellations, Sky Ocean itself, he'd never really thought about them except in the context of Islander life, and he had learned them in language, not in Shaian. "It's a way of navigating when the star or constellation is high," he finally settled on. "I could show you but I'm not sure I can explain it very well."

He smiled apologetically at Alun and Nala. "This isn't my area of specialization. I knew a Nga woman once who Named the Stars, had trained in the lore of her family, and she could name every visible star and knew stories about at least half of them. My knowledge is very limited in comparison."

Ghilly asked, "Why do you change those two stars the second night?"

"That's to counter the drift from the currents in the middle of the bay. There are other ways of doing it, but the star-path is the easiest. My great-uncle always despaired of me ever properly learning how to read currents."

He'd gotten there in the end, but it had taken him a long time to distinguish competing patterns of currents, and those in the middle of the Bay of the Waters were renowned for their complexity.

Alun was a large man, broad-shouldered and tall in the way of many Nijani Islanders. He had Nijani tattoos as well, black lines curling down his right arm. His garments were Solaaran, and his loose outer robes hid the majority of the tattoos, unlike the traditional boga worn by men in Zangoraville. He stroked the spiral running down his forearm thoughtfully, eyes on the storyboard. "Is that something many people learn? I mean, that sounded rote, like you had to memorize it."

Cliopher nodded in agreement. "I sailed alone back and forth along that route three or four times a year from when I was twelve until I went to university. My family made me recite the directions every time. I don't think they ever believed I had learned the way. Which is also ke'ea, metaphorically speaking."

Toucan and Ghilly exchanged a quick glance, which had Toucan smiling into his cup and Ghilly muffling her snorts. Cliopher gave them an interrogative glance of his own, but Ghilly merely shook her head and, in a voice that barely trembled with poorly concealed laughter, said, "That, then, is ke'ea. What about ke'e?"

Cliopher was inclined to wonder at their mirth, but resolved to ask them about it later, when they were not in public. He vaguely wished Rhodin had agreed to come inside.

"Ke'e refers to ... the zenith star, I think is the best translation. Any given location can have a certain star that passes directly overhead—touches the zenith, you could say—and so ke'e means 'Under the star'."

His thoughts flashed to explaining this to Pikabe and Ato, to the Ouranatha. How strange that three times in three weeks he'd had the occasion.

"The ke'e of Loaloa is Furai'fa, for instance. If you are *Ke'e Ofuluente,* your island is Under Ofuluente: that is, Ofuluente is its zenith star. You can imagine it like a pillar or a rope extending up from an island to the star."

Nala appeared to be trying to wrap her head around this concept, judging by how intently she was frowning at the floor. Finally she looked up at him. "Wouldn't that just tell you the latitude? Surely many places could be under the same star."

"As many are under the Wake, yes. We, the Wide Seas Islanders—" and when had he last been in a room with *only* those of his people?— "We used to be called the Ke'e Lulai'aviyë: those who live Under the Wake of the Ancestors' Ships, that is the River of Stars for Shaian astronomers. Navigationally speaking, the zenith star gives you your latitude. Theoretically you could sail north or south from any given point until the correct star was overhead, then sail east or west until you came to it. Practically it's rather easier to have the ke'ea to work with."

"But that depends on where you're starting from, and whether you know the whole route."

"Just so. Although there are ways you can judge your direction from just the first star if you know what you're doing; star navigation can be much more complex and sophisticated than this."

Toucan nodded. "Historically, most of the islands would have fanoa—trading— relations with other islands and the navigators would know the ke'ea for them. Each island would have its own star compass, you could say."

Alun sighed. "Would someone know what island my family came from? My father said his parents told him that everyone had left—there wouldn't be anyone to keep the knowledge."

"A Nga lore-keeper—the vanà, ideally—would know."

He thought of Saya Ng, who had lived in a village outside of Zangoraville, whom all her neighbours considered mad. She had told him how to make a traditional boat and how to sail it, and started the journey across the Wide Seas with him. She had died in a storm, but he had held her memory dear all the years since; she had given him his way home.

He thought back yet farther from Saya Ng, back to what he had learned from his great-uncle that year when he was twelve and in the visits running through his teens.

All those years he had tried so hard to find a traditional path, for being the tanà was something one grew into, after learning, mastering, another role. There was always something to learn, his Uncle Lazo had said, no matter the seeming banality of the job.

Uncle Lazo was a barber. Buru Tovo had been a great pearl hunter. And Cliopher ... was here. "I used to know all the major ke'e for the Islands," he murmured. "Let me think..."

He closed his eyes and this time consciously tried to shift his thinking into traditional modes, into Islander.

Buru Tovo singing him the *Lays*, over and over again until he could recite them back word-perfect, and yet again and again until he could answer any question with the appropriate passage.

The second day of the *Lays*, as they would be sung at the Gathering of the Waters, was the one in which the Nga Named the Stars. They sang the history of exploration, the settlement of the Islands, not according to strict historicity or even geography but according to their relation to the Star Compass held by the vanà.

Cliopher had learned these verses but never thought about them in Shaian. He found himself murmuring them, running down the lists.

Adouray-ve ela a ke'e Nōsa
Erunai'a ela a ke'e Kaibola
Erunai-nui ela a ke'e Fikuluente ...

Ofuluente was a star in the constellation Ofulu, the Dolphin. Cliopher shifted in his seat, eyes still closed, imagining his Buru Tovo at the stone canoe, pointing at each section of the sky. The Dolphin was in the southern half of the sky, above Nua-nui but below the Fisherman. He hit the edge of the chair and broke himself out of his train of thought.

Their hosts were looking at him with puzzled and slightly uncomfortable expressions. Cliopher smiled apologetically at them, but he didn't want to switch into Shaian and lose the passage he had nearly found. He stood up and walked over to an open space, orienting himself until he stood with his back to the vague feeling of *there* that was the tug of Loaloa from the other side of the world.

If he closed his eyes he could imagine he stood by the stone canoe (ignoring that he was inside a building, which smelled fresh and lightly floral from the vine that was blooming in its pot in the corner), that he was pointing to each constellation in turn and reciting the corresponding passage.

He sang the *Lays* in the Islander tongue, the vowels rolling off his tongue, the glottal stops making his voice rise and fall in the ancient rhythms.

How he loved the *Lays*. The words were so sweet in his mouth.

The Dolphin was made of seven bright stars, one of which, Osu, had its own name, but only four of them were named in the *Lays* as being zenith stars:

Enaye-ve ela a ke'e Ofuluomë
Zua-nui ela a ke'e Osu
Dinaiyo-ye ela a ke'e Ofuluanto
Zirua-tō ela a ke'e Ofuluente

Cliopher slowed down as he sang those words, and repeated them twice to be sure he had it correct. Then he opened his eyes and smiled triumphantly at Alun. "Ofuluente is the zenith star of Zirua-tō, which is a high island in the Yevaya Group, if I'm not mistaken."

Alun regarded him with a strange expression halfway to shock. "What—what was that?"

"That," said Toucan, "was part of the *Lays of the Wide Seas*, which are the oral histories of our people."

"Goodness," said Alun, but was prevented from saying anything else by the arrival of a young woman, who came unceremoniously in and said, "Dad, is the barbecue supposed to be smoking?"

～

Alun and Nala had prepared a Nijani meal for them. Barbecued chicken and pork, sweet potatoes, vegetable skewers, and a large fresh salad, along with bread rolls. It was all delicious and not at all the food he got in the Palace.

The young woman's name was Mirella, and she was, it turned out, the younger of Alun and Nala's two daughters. The older, Falima, was out with friends, and would be back later, or so Mirella said airily. She turned to her parents. "Is Aioru coming today?"

"You know Aioru?" Cliopher said, surprised.

Nala beamed at him. "*You* know Aioru? Oh—he's just been promoted, so you must have heard that! We're very proud of him."

"He used to board with us, when he first came to the city," Alun explained. "He lives around the corner now, but he comes here for supper quite often." He turned to his daughter. "I believe his friend Tanaea's visiting, and of course, his new position makes him *quite* busy."

"He's the new Chancellor, can you imagine!" Mirella said, marvelling.

Cliopher did not dare look at his friends; nor could he think what to say. He was simply struck by Aioru's ease with his family, for surely Alun and Nala and Mirella were his family, here in the city. They were discussing whether or not he was walking out with this Tanaea with quite as much relish and partisanship as *his* family had ever argued about his relationships, at least.

Cliopher listened, interested. Of course he was; he had never spoken of such personal things with Aioru as his potential girlfriends. And ... *Tanaea* meant hearth, and hearth-fire, and one of the two stones with which once could strike a spark.

It didn't mean she was Islander—he might have been mishearing her name—but oh, what symbolism!

"You're in the Service too, I think Ghilly said, Kip?" Nala asked.

He could learn from Aioru, couldn't he? He should. He took a deep breath. "Actually my full name is Cliopher—Cliopher Mdang—I'm the one who just resigned so Aioru could take my job." They stared at him, and his heart sank, but he refused to back down from the absent Aioru's challenge, and he smiled as disarmingly as he could. "Which is the only reason I have an afternoon free today!"

"He'll be sorry to have missed you," Nala said after a long moment, and Mirella asked him a question about the special scripts used by the Secretariat, and—and it *was* fine, after all.

~

After lunch, they returned to the sitting room. Cliopher had just decided to ask about the woven hangings when Alun, who was regarding the storyboard with a pensive expression, suddenly turned to him.

"Is that common knowledge? The passage from the *Lays* you sang for us earlier. Is that something many people know?"

Cliopher considered how to answer. "The central twelve *Lays* are widely known. They are often sung in Shaian and I would say most people are at least familiar with them, even if they don't know them by heart. They're the ones that are printed; sometimes they're called the public *Lays*."

He glanced at his friends for confirmation. Ghilly nodded. "Yes, that's right. Everyone knows the opening of the *Lays*, and we all learn the main stories from them. How the Islands were settled, that sort of thing."

"There's talk of splitting the twelfth one to make a thirteenth," Toucan put in. "With the new stanzas covering the history since the Fall, and, and so on. I wouldn't be surprised if it's presented at the next Great Singing of the Waters."

Nala came back in with the coffee in time to hear this. "The Singing of the Waters?"

"That's an annual festival to celebrate our culture," Ghilly said.

Toucan nodded. "Each of the lineages is responsible for a certain portion of the history, so over the twelve days of the festival, the lore-keepers sing the *Lays* relating to their family line. On the Great Festivals, which happen irregularly when there's enough to warrant them, the full dances are performed and major announcements are made. New lore-keepers, for instance, an addition to the *Lays*, that sort of thing. The regular one happens around now, and the Great Festival will happen ... soon."

They all carefully did not look at Cliopher.

Alun hummed. "So the passage you sang is from one of those? One of the ones your family is responsible for?"

"You could say so," Cliopher replied awkwardly. "I studied under my great-uncle, the tanà, when I was younger."

"He's the rising tanà," Ghilly said. "The one coming into his own."

"There should always be at least three, and more usually four," Cliopher said, wishing—oh, he didn't know. He did not *regret* the choices that had led here. The world was a better place for him having chosen this ... ke'ea. He cleared his throat. "In my family, the tana-tai—the eldest keeper of the tradition—is my great-uncle, and then my uncle Lazo is the tanà proper, and I come up behind them. I should have already started teaching someone what I know. It's our responsibility to ensure the knowledge is passed on to the next generation and not lost."

Toucan nodded. "Bertie's family, the Kindraa, *Know the Wind*. Ghilly's are the Poyë, who *Hold the Seeds*. Mine, the Nevans, *Tie the Sails*. Each of the twelve lineages has people who hold the knowledge—Ghilly's family are the literal keepers of the seeds, and healers too, whatever is necessary. Some families have more than one lore-keeper. What Kip is not saying is that only two or three people ever reach the point of being named the tanà."

Nala and Alun were looking at him with admiration now, which made Cliopher flush and feel deeply uncomfortable, almost fraudulent.

It was not that he hadn't studied the old ways, or that he felt he was ignorant of them...but he could never forget that he had left, that he had not been home for the Singing of the Waters since he had left to go to Astandalas, that he had never danced Aōteketētana for his people, only here in the Palace for those who did not know what it meant.

(Jiano had said it was not only him they, the people, had been waiting upon. He had also said that they were waiting for him. But to be what? 'Himself' had never been the right answer.)

He cleared his throat. "Theoretically, each island group should have people who know each of the traditions."

"In practice it's the Outer Ring folks who keep them most rigorously," Ghilly said. "I studied agriculture because I wanted to honour my ancestors, but I didn't want to be responsible for the seeds and seed-stock myself." She chuckled. "In the end I did end up responsible for much of that, through my work, but I don't know all the songs and dances to go with them."

"I wasn't interested," Bertie said, shrugging. "It's not for everyone, and it wasn't for me."

Toucan made a face. "It wasn't for me, either, though I wanted it to be. I started studying when I was at university—I felt I was missing something, and Kip here was an example—but I didn't get very far before deciding it was too much work and too much ... There's a lot of pressure, being responsible for a twelfth of your culture's knowledge."

"How did you know it was something you wanted to do?" Mirella asked curiously.

It was easier to answer the innocent question of a young woman barely out of her teens than it was to look at Toucan and Bertie and Ghilly and wonder what they meant with their words. Cliopher set down his cup and answered Mirella seriously.

"My great-uncle, my Buru Tovo—Buru means *Honoured Elder*—was a famous pearl hunter. If you've ever seen the *Atlas of Imperial Peoples*, he's the person who was painted as the Wide Sea Islander. I went to stay with him when I was twelve. He started teaching me the old ways. I grew more and more interested, and finally asked to learn officially."

Mirella looked a little skeptical. "And that was that?"

"There are many things in life that are easy to begin, and very hard to finish," he said gently. "If ever you do finish them, before death. Some things were easy to learn, others very difficult ... If you start the study of the old ways, the lore, as Toucan put it, you begin by making what's called an efela ko."

He reached under the neck of his tunic for the pearl and obsidian necklace, fingers distinguishing it from the newer efetana with ease. Mirella leaned forward to look at it curiously.

"Efela are traditional necklaces, usually made of shells and coral, though they can be pearl and stone, as this one is, or other materials—there are various meanings to the different beads. They are your wealth, in the old tradition: you earn or buy or make them with your knowledge, your skill, the money you earned from your knowledge and skill ... And there are some that you *cannot* buy, can only be given."

He paused there. The last efela he had received from Mardo Walea, who Held the Efela (if *held* was the right translation ... *nevio* had so many nuances ... *held, kept, weighed, counted, strung* ...), was the efela nai, which was because Cliopher had been given a strand of sundrop cowries by the god of mysteries. Mardo had said that any future efela he received would not be bought, but given.

The only one Cliopher had received since then had been the efetana, just before the Viceroyship ceremonies had concluded, when he had finally claimed that part of himself before his people.

He shook his head. "And there are others that you must make yourself. The efela ko is one of those. It means the 'anchoring' or 'foundational' efela, the one that shows you have begun to study the lore. My great-uncle took me out to the edge of the outer reef of Loaloa, which is the westernmost edge of the Outer Ring of the Vangavaye-ve itself, and showed me how to dive for pearls."

He looked soberly at Mirella. "I knew after the first dive that I would never be a pearl hunter. I hated it, and knew I would never learn to love it. Some things you just know immediately."

His hand was grasping the pearls, the twelve of them he had wrested from the edge of the reef with such difficulty and over so many months.

"Where did you get yours, then?"

"Every time I came up, swearing I would never dive down again, my great-uncle asked me, *Is this where you stop?*" Cliopher dropped his hand and folded them in his lap, straightening his shoulders as if he sat in council. "And my answer was always, *No, I'll keep going*. Eighty or a hundred dives it took me to gather these pearls, and the ones I needed after I started learning to drill holes through them and shattered them instead. And again, after the cord broke and I lost them to the sea. *Is this where you stop?*"

He stopped there, not wanting to get too far into it. That had been that whole first year, while he learned the *Lays*, while he began to learn the dances, while his Buru Tovo taught him to sail a canoe and name the major constellations and start to feel the pattern of the waves and all the many things, small and large, that he thought Cliopher should know.

"I got six months in," Toucan said, "before I decided it was where I stopped. My mother's cousin was the one teaching me. He was a weaver, but he made me start my efela ko with making the beads. I managed to collect the first four types of coral, and the first three nuts for the beads, and begin shaping them, but the central pendant was supposed to be carved from the claw of a cassowary I had killed myself with a weapon I had made myself, and I stopped there. I was terrified of cassowaries." He paused. "I still am, come to that. They're horrible birds. My aunt was disembowelled by one."

"And he wanted you to hunt one?" Nala exclaimed in horror.

Toucan nodded seriously. "It is a very serious commitment, holding the knowledge. If you cannot face down your fears—or rather, overcome, conquer, *surpass* them—how can you be considered the exemplar of an Islander?"

They all looked at Cliopher, who said, reluctantly, "My father died by drowning. I still have nightmares about it, about drowning."

They looked at his hand, still on the efela ko, and with a grimace he tucked it away again.

"Is this where you stop?" Nala said, her expression sombre.

Toucan gestured at Cliopher, a little apologetically. "It's worst for the tanà. The rest of us say that the tanà holds the heart of the Islands in his hands: that so long as there is a tanà to light the fire, our culture will never fail. The rest of the lore-keepers keep the old ways for us all, but the tanà shows us what it means to be an Islander."

∽

Cliopher was still thinking about Toucan's words long after they had left Alun and Nala's house and were returning to the Palace.

The endless acrimony about his leaving (and *staying* gone) made a lot more sense, he supposed, if everyone thought *he* was supposed to show them what it meant to be an Islander.

But he knew what would happen if he tried. It was all too easy to imagine them laughing at him for being too old-fashioned and too deep in the *Lays*—they had when he was a boy, a young man, trying so hard to be what they wanted. When he had played on the beach with Basil and boasted that one day he would sail to the House of the Sun like the third son of Vonou'a, one day would stand beside an emperor as Elonoa'a had stood beside Aurelius Magnus, one day would—

Oh, they had laughed then, and they had probably been right to laugh.

And would they really listen to him, embrace him as the tanà he kept trying to be? If he sailed the Ring in the boat Cora had restored for him, would they do anything but laugh when he came to an island and said the old words Buru Tovo had always said?

(Tanaea-te imalo! Moa'a-ki imalo! Kifa'ana imai? *I bring a fire for your hearth! I bring news of the Wide Seas! Have you any problems for me?—Would* they do anything but laugh in his face?)

They climbed up the hill under the long serpentine pergola that led towards the Palace. Ghilly took his arm. He slowed his steps to match her pace, glad she didn't say anything while they climbed.

He had spent his life fighting to make the court, the Council of Princes, the *world* listen to him, to look at his beautiful, fragile dreams and make them sturdy realities, and ... and he was tired.

He did not know if he had another lifetime of fighting left in him to make his family listen.

At the end of the pergola, under an arch fragrant with night-blooming flowers, Ghilly tugged him gently to a halt.

She was looking up at the brilliant lit Palace crowning the hill in front of them.

"Is this where you stop?" she asked him softly.

Cliopher looked at the building in which he had spent the majority of his life trying to figure out what it meant to be an Islander in the wide world.

And the challenge...he could only laugh at himself, wryly, silently, on the verge of tears: for the challenge-song always pricked him. Always. He'd never been able to answer it otherwise; it was not in him to take the easy way.

Is this where you stop?

"No," he said. Her hand tightened on his elbow. "No. I'll keep going."

CHAPTER THIRTEEN
PLANNING A PARTY

The tui tree was full of blossoms, hundreds of them scenting the humid air of the botanical gardens.

Cliopher walked out one dawn. Pikabe and Ato were once more his guards, and they walked silently behind him, respectful of his quietude.

It was hard to imagine being Fitzroy Angursell, free and—and—and *free*—

Free; and then confined abruptly with the heavy chains of power and authority and magic.

What a prison the Palace must have seemed to him.

Cliopher sat on the bench and stared out at the grey expanse of the Eastern Ocean. There was a paleness ahead of him where the sun was nearly about to rise, and a wind rising softly, curling through the chocolate-weight of the tui blossoms with a scent of salt and far-off things.

Sama, the Wind That Rises At Dawn. Her daughter—Samayë, the Woman of the Dawn Wind— was the mother of the Islanders, the wife of Vonou'a whom he sailed across the sea to find.

The sky caught a few tints, peach and pink and a fine lavender. A few birds were singing behind him—the pair of lyrebirds seemed to have escaped from the menagerie again, for the male was singing lustily not far from him.

For a moment Cliopher was shaken by the sound and the scent of home, the light blazing in his eyes as the sun rose over the horizon.

If he took ship and sailed to meet its rising, what would he find?

East first, and then westward and home: that was the pattern repeated over and over again in the *Lays*. So had his ancestors sailed. Was it because he had gone west first, to Kavanor as it was in those days, that had turned everything topsy-turvy? He had always come home westward even so, across the Wide Seas and not by way of the Eastern Ocean.

He had never sailed east into that sunrise.

He blinked away the water in his eyes, the tears started by the sun, and sneezed. Once, twice. The dawn bell sounded out from behind him, setting all the birds to singing in response. A bevy of gongbirds made their tattletale knells, and somewhere a flock of macaws screeched.

The third son of Vonou'a (the third son of Samayë) had sailed east, east until he sailed out of the known and into Sky Ocean; east until he reached the island where the Sun had his house, moored his own boat.

There he had traded his name for the fire he brought home again, the law and the *Lays*.

The lyrebird scuffled in the underbrush beside him, its heavy train of tail-feathers dragging in the grass. Cliopher looked at the bird's courtly plumage, thinking of the headdress he had worn for the Viceroy ceremony, with lyrebird feathers all around its crown.

East to the sun, westward home.

He turned his back to the sunrise, facing his own distant island as his sense of *home* came into sharp, splendid focus. The Palace loomed above him, white and gold in the dawn light. High, high above where he stood he could see the smudge of red that was the canopy over his Radiancy's terrace, unfolded so one of Conju's underlings could sweep up the dust that would have settled.

Up there in his Radiancy's private study was a red book, containing some thrilling secrets that would be *hard to publish*.

Unless, of course, he had taken the book with him, in that bag he had modelled after the one Fitzroy Angursell—the one *he* had made famous—

The one he had no doubt used as a model when enchanting the writing case he had given Cliopher. How had he not *seen*?

It was truly embarrassing that he had never before realized his Radiancy was Fitzroy Angursell. He had been given nearly every hint short of outright statement.

Embarrassing, and ...

He could not articulate, even in his own mind, the curl of fire that licked around the edges of that thought. His Radiancy had trusted him with the world ... but never with that secret.

It was hard to hold onto Suzen's assurance that it might not be a lack of trust. Part of Cliopher's mind knew that, understood that; but his heart ... ached.

Above the red smudge the uppermost roof of the Emperor's Tower rose into the final gilded dome of the Palace. There was one sacred room, deeper into the Imperial Apartments than Cliopher had ever penetrated, where the light from the clerestory windows in that dome, the central aperture, focused on a stone that ran straight down through the entire height of the Palace to its foundation, passing through the throne room behind the great seat.

His Radiancy had once told him that all the magic of Astandalas had been spun about that stone, that still point of all the complex net of magic; that he the Emperor was its visible outcropping, as he the Marwn had been its invisible foundation.

Cliopher regarded the building in which he had spent the greater part of his life, and was conscious that it was no longer the mooring-post for his soul.

He dropped his gaze again, taking in the layers of carved stone, the windows and the columns, the balustrades and balconies, the outstretched arms of the wings of the building, the doors and the gardens rioting in bright colour against the white stone.

For the first time he wanted to go and not come back.

But of course he could not do that; not yet. His Radiancy had given him these reins of government to hold, and Cliopher knew his duty.

~

He went in, and posed for Suzen in his court costume, and planned a feast.

~

"How many people do you expect to feed?" the Palace quartermaster asked, frowning over her notebook. "Do you really think ... *three* pigs, your excellency?"

"Yes," he said recklessly, aware of how extravagant that would sound to anyone back home. Jiano, as Paramount Chief, might supply three pigs for a festival. No one else would even think to suggest they supply more than one, not unless they were making a bid to be seen as obscenely wealthy and high-status.

Cliopher was not obscenely wealthy, but according to Palace culture he was the highest-status Islander in the world—certainly this hemisphere of it—and he was the tanà, and according to Toucan the exemplar of what it meant to be an Islander, and he would not shame himself before his ancestors by making a poor show.

"Three pigs," the quartermaster muttered. "Really."

~

He wrote another letter to Basil, though a kind of ferocious anger underlay his words, and his pen scratched deeply into the paper.

He could not put a source to his emotion. It was not at Toucan and Ghilly and Bertie, who had come at last to visit him. Perhaps it was at Basil, who had never, ever replied.

Who was almost certainly dead, Cliopher thought glumly, staring at the messy scrawl that did not look anything like his usual hand. He began doodling, drawing stipples and little traditional designs around the swooping line of a swash he had forgotten he used to make with certain letters. The stipples turned into waves, and then he added a boat—a vaha, of course, an outrigger canoe, the lobster-claw sail not the one from the Ring but that of his own little *Tui-tanata*.

A figure took his place on the boat; and then a second, taller than the first by a head. Cliopher went to add hair to the second and hesitated, pen hovering over the paper, ink beading on its tip before splashing down to form a splotch like a black sunburst in the middle of the sail.

It wasn't *wrong* to miss him, surely. He could still be glad his Radiancy—*Fitzroy Angursell*—was free, having adventures, reconnecting with his old friends. If he had found Masseo already, surely the others would be there for him to find, too, however long the silence. He knew where to go to find Pali Avramapul, at least.

What silent, steady grief his Radiancy must have felt. Had he had a spark of hope any time Cliopher's reports or Rhodin's brought up stories of the Red Company? Had he hoped that this time—*this time*—surely the rumour would be true?

He had never let on by more than the deepest glimmer of a smile that he had any thoughts that were not those of the Last Emperor of Astandalas.

How *starved* he must have been.

Oh, Cliopher thought, his pen catching, scrawling out a jagged line he turned into a school of fish, long-nosed barracuda, sleek and predatory.

Oh, he was *glad* his Radiancy was able to drink freedom deep, able to go gallivanting, guided by nothing bar that need to find another wild mage of power to take up the reins of government.

Reins Cliopher was holding for him.

Not reins. What sort of metaphor was that for an Islander?

Cliopher held the coals, tended the fire-pot, nestled the embers into the ashes and damp ferns, feeding them as they needed, ready for the many fires to come when the new lord magus brought tinder and fuel to the hearth.

That was *who he was*. He was not only a Mdang: he was the tanà, and it was his *calling* to Hold the Fire. He had spent his whole life building and tending this one. He could not now ... just walk away from it.

He drew a diamond-shaped manta ray, cross-hatching its underside as if he were Uruyë Ena'a, carving a ship that would sail out of Islander *Lays* and into Shaian histories.

Underneath he wrote, once more in his usual clear, exemplary script, *East first, then west.*

Basil would take it—*if* he received it, if if if—

Cliopher set down his pen with suddenly trembling hands, his eyes burning.

He held the fire. He could not go. He *could not.*

～

His friends explored the city and visited with him in the evenings. Sometimes he went with them, but he felt an obscure pressure to have all the meetings, hand over the power, show everyone he was doing what he had always said he would do.

He sorted through the papers in his study, giving Aioru the important ones.

"Here are the Protocols—you know many of them, of course," he said one morning, dropping the stack of large volumes on what had once been his desk in the Offices of the Lords of State.

Aioru grinned at him. "Yes, sir. Even unto the rain of sharks."

The development of the Protocols for various disasters had been so depressing Cliopher had started salting in absurd possibilities just to relieve the relentless focus on disaster and destruction. For every devastating plague such as the one that had beset Woodlark there was a waterspout carrying rains of sharks sixty miles inland.

"That shark one happened," Cliopher said.

One of the younger secretaries made an incredulous noise, halfway between a guffaw and a choke. Cliopher gave her an amused smile.

"It's true," he said. "It was not long after the Fall ... I had become his Radiancy's secretary not long before. Everything was so grim and ... broken...and then there was this report of the Shark Queen of Dinezi."

"I'm from Dinezi," one of the pages waiting by the door blurted out loud. They all looked at her; she blushed fiercely. "We have a legend of the Shark Queen."

"I met her," Cliopher said, casting his mind back oh—so long ago. "She was one of the emissaries to the Littleridge meeting. Very fierce and very smart. She tanned the shark-skin and wore its head over her own, like a helmet, the tail hanging down as a cape. She had an alliance with the Tiourangi League out of the Azilint, and they ferried her column of elephant cavalry up to the coast of Xiputl."

"No way," the page said. "You can't—that can't possibly be true."

"There is still a breed of domestic elephants in that part of Xiputl that are the descendants of the ones she brought—she only took her core army back down with her. She was one of the great proponents of the treaty, and her elephants were the ones that broke the trail for most of the parties to come to the Palace for the formal negotiations."

They all stared at him, and Cliopher realized with a shock that this was ancient history even to those who lived in places where they might conceivably have been alive for the negotiations. Even in the Vangavaye-ve that had been at least twenty years ago.

Gods, he was getting old.

❧

Organizing a festival was like setting the budget, and took up all the time Cliopher allocated to it. Toucan expressed astonishment when he discovered that he was done.

"What do you mean?" Cliopher asked, a little distracted; he was sorting through his efela, deciding which to wear.

Well. Deciding if he really were going to wear both the efela nai and the efevoa, as he knew very well was appropriate.

They were in the sitting room; Cliopher still kept his efela in the basket in the old Voonran chest there. He was standing near the chest, Rhodin's gold-lined vase full of fresh blossoms exhaling their chocolate perfume. Toucan perched on the arm of one of the guest chairs.

"What do I mean? I am simply astonished you are not running around doing last-minute preparations."

It was the day before the festival. Cliopher rubbed his thumb along one of the shells, the soft clicking as they stirred against each other familiar, homely. He frowned at his friend. "Why would I need to?"

"You are terrifyingly efficient," Toucan said plainly. "My sister is a professional organizer, you know."

Cliopher could probably have fished that piece of information out of his memory if he'd thought about it. His knowledge of Toucan's older sister was largely confined to her love of huge earrings and an impression of boundless enthusiasm for all things floral, as well as a longstanding hobby making knotwork hangings and bags and things.

"Surely if she is a professional, she's not running around at the last-minute *all* the time."

Toucan snorted into his wine. "She loves the chaos. It's organized chaos, I am informed, but she is a whirlwind up to the last minute, when everything falls into place."

Cliopher tried not to wince in profound horror at the mere thought of that methodology. "I prefer to be somewhat more prepared."

"And do you have plans in case of, oh, I don't know, a sudden rainstorm?"

"The Ouranatha haven't been off by more than three days in their prediction for the onset of the rains in the past six or seven hundred years, but of course. And if there's a sudden eruption of a pestilence or a plague of insects or an embassy of potentially hostile hyperintelligent thunder lizards, too."

Rhodin had been very impressed at the latter, although he had gently chided Cliopher for thinking that the Merrions (or their soulmates) would be anything other than heralds of peace and enlightenment.

Toucan laughed outright. "Oh, Kip, don't ever change!"

Cliopher chuckled and raised his glass to honour the toast, but the words struck at that part of him that wanted to—go.

His gaze lifted to the portrait of Buru Tovo as a young man, sly and confident, laughing-eyed as he let the Shaian artist paint him in his festival finery.

Cliopher took a deep breath. He Held the Fire. He had claimed that before his family, before his people, before his gods. He wore efetana in earnest. He had promised his Radiancy to safeguard the world. He was not confined here; this was no prison to him, no cell whose limits he paced over and over again.

He held the fire. He could hold this one a little while longer. This was not where he stopped, not after everything. Not yet.

~

In the privacy of his own room, he fretted over the last, newest bit of the *Lays*. He tried not to let the fact that Toucan had had to teach it to him bother him. He would have had to learn it from someone, at some point.

There was a line in it referring to him.

One who holds the fire went as Elonoa'a went
To sit at the councils of the emperors and speak for the people.

He could wish for his name to be named—for his efela to be described—for him to be one of the heroes, the shining stars—

But this was the Littleridge Treaty all over again, wasn't it? What mattered was what he had done, not that he was known to have done it.

And he *was* in the *Lays*, after all.

One who holds the fire went as Elonoa'a went

He could be proud of that, proud to sing that, proud to hold his head up before the Ancestors and say he had followed the path laid before him—followed the ke'ea handed down over the generations to him—followed in the wake of the Ancestors, in the wake of Elonoa'a and of the third son of Vonou'a, who went to the House of the Sun.

He was proud. No matter that he wanted ... more.

(He had always wanted more. That did not mean he could have it. Look at—but he wasn't thinking about going home after everything, to that house he had bought in Gorjo City, making a life there with all his friends bar one.)

He put on his Islander regalia, from the grass skirt to the extraordinary headdress, all the fine, elaborate stitching and subtle dyes demonstrating to anyone who knew what they were looking at that this was a very splendid garment indeed. He was already wearing his efela ko and the efetana Buru Tovo had given him—or rather given Féonie and his Radiancy to give to him—before the viceroy ceremony. He drew out the efela nai and looked at it for a long moment, the five ranks of flame pearls heavy and warm in his hands.

He had never been able to find a flame pearl, diving off the reefs of the Western Ring for nefalao. That had been a place he stopped. He could go so far, and no farther, that way.

Had Buru Tovo actually looked disappointed, or was that only Cliopher's remembered shame shading his memory?

He had been so very disappointed in himself. *Bitterly* disappointed. He had tried; and he had failed.

You could not dive for the flame pearls if you did not, at some level, love the nefalao, and Cliopher did not. Could not.

Buru Tovo had only watched him, that last attempted dive, sobbing and coughing up water until he lay flat on his great-uncle's outrigger canoe, shaking with physical reaction to nearly drowning, shivering with his shame.

"Each of us has a line we cannot cross," Buru Tovo had said, and: "There is more than one way to find a flame pearl."

And he had sailed Cliopher, the young Kip, away from that particular part of the reef and into safer waters.

Not long after Cliopher had been sent back home, so he did not lose the city ways.

He had not wanted the city ways. He had wanted the old ways, wanted to sit at Buru Tovo's feet, wanted to be worthy of being tanà after him. He had felt, being sent home, that he was being sent away, having failed.

He touched the efetana, fire coral in a simple band around his neck, deceptively plain.

It had taken him a long, long time to find a flame pearl, and yet in the end he had been given this efela of a hundred and seventy six of them, wealth and beauty almost beyond any array even his Radiancy possessed.

There was a knock on his door, and he turned to find Féonie there. "Shall I do that up for you?" she asked, nodding at the efela nai in his hands.

Cliopher took a deep breath, and nodded. She pulled over the stool so she could reach. Her hands were warm and deft as she did up the efela nai and the efevoa, and then secured the headdress with long pins.

He looked at himself in the long mirror.

"You look magnificent," Féonie proclaimed, patting him on the shoulder before hopping back down off the stool.

She had made the skirt and the headdress. She was allowed to be a touch proprietary.

He smiled at her, genuinely touched by her innocent pride in her handiwork, and was struck at how much his face lightened as a result.

Smiling unselfconsciously, not as he usually saw in the mirror—even now his face was settling into its familiar serious lines, only his eyes bright with amusement at himself—he looked ... not *young,* but not decades older than his friends, either.

As if that didn't make him feel even *more* self-conscious, he thought, grinning outright now, and ducked away from the mirror to find his friends waiting in his sitting room in their own Islander garb, along with Rhodin, who was in his best court costume.

"Ludvic will join us there," Rhodin told him, eyeing his finery appreciatively. "He wished to see to something first."

Cliopher nodded, awash with nerves now that the event was imminent, and reprimanded himself for being so. He wished his Radiancy were there—Well. Of course he did. They were friends.

(*One who holds the fire went as Elonoa'a went, to sit at the counsels of the emperors and speak for the people.* If that were all the fame he was granted, it was enough; it was enough. He knew what all of that meant. He *had* gone desiring to dance the pattern Elonoa'a had shaped, to find an emperor worth following. And he had.)

"Let us go, then," he said, nodding sharply and being surprised by the weight of the headdress on his head, the feathers bobbing as he moved.

Ghilly laughed, her own efela simple and beautiful, her dress Nijani flax dyed in the intricate Poyë designs.

"You look so grand, Kip," she said, as she and Bertie rose and gathered their things together. Toucan did the same, but paused closer to him.

"Remember," he whispered, "let yourself be who you are. You don't have to cut yourself down to size."

~

"I've had an idea," Rhodin announced as they descended the stairs towards the planned location. "Not just an idea—"

"A suggestion?" Cliopher asked, amused.

"I've already planned it," Rhodin continued, undismayed. "It's a kind of a present. A trip to the Liaau, leaving tomorrow afternoon, staying the night, then doing that hike up through the gorge to the waterfalls you like. Another night in the lower lodge, and then back again the day after."

Cliopher regarded him in surprise. That *was* one of his favourite hikes—one of his favourite places to go. He'd often wanted to take his friends there, especially Ghilly, who loved plants.

Ghilly nudged him. "Say 'thank you', Kip. We're already all packed."

As planned, Cliopher arrived amongst the earliest. His nephew Gaudy, Bertie's son Parno, and Zerafin, who was one of the Guard and whose mother was an Isolate Islander, were there, tending the fire, along with several of their friends from amongst pages and guards. Cliopher greeted them all by name, relaxing as they returned the greetings, expressions amazed and pleased as they took in his finery.

Of course, most of them were from the hinterlands and the tribes, not the cities and the aristocracy. And the ones who weren't, like Eldo, Prince Rufus's son, had already seen this, learned what it meant, in Gorjo City.

The fires were grand. The pigs had been roasting for hours already and smelled immensely appetizing. Cliopher did a tour of the tables laden with foods and drinks and cutlery, thanking the Palace staff who had worked to make them not only be there but also look magnificent. Someone had hung lanterns and bunting all around the courtyard, and placed piles of cushions in discreet corners for those who were unaccustomed to squatting.

"It looks great," Ghilly said when he returned to their group, satisfied as if she'd done the work herself. Cliopher smiled at her, trying to hide his nerves but unable to muster his court expression. "You can't be worried that no one will show up?"

He hitched his shoulders in lieu of a shrug. It felt so *odd* to be wearing his finery here, with the Palace looming above. There were branches of the tui tree in pots here and there, blossoms in water, cuttings in soil. Those who were so inclined could take cuttings of the tree home to plant, mark themselves Islanders as the Islanders always had done.

That *had* been Ghilly's idea. Cliopher was glad she'd thought of it.

"Even if they weren't interested in the festival for its own sake, everyone is *so excited* to get to see part of the Palace—not to mention—you!"

Which part of him knew was very true; but that was not the part of him that was worried.

Fortunately Ludvic chose that moment to arrive. He was dressed not in his usual uniform but in what must have been his own Azilinti finery: simple linen kilt in pale fawn, and over his bare shoulder an immense, splendid cape woven out of different threads in a hundred shades of brown and gold. The gold smudges on his hands and arms from where his Radiancy had burned him matched exactly. And he held his staff, which Cliopher had never seen him display in public before.

Cliopher caught his breath, knowing what a rare gift this was. He walked forward to greet Ludvic formally in the Islander way, bowing over his hands as Ludvic responded with the Azilinti greeting, placing the staff directly vertical in front of him, his hands spaced well apart so the wingfinger carved on the head of the staff was facing Cliopher.

Giya from the Levels bar stood behind him, also in Azilinti garb, her strong face proud and challenging, but her eyes softer than they had seemed when Cliopher met her. She held an enormous clay jug in one hand, her other holding her own staff in the same vertical pose. Cliopher did not recognize the creature at the top of its carving, some sort of large-eyed monkey.

"We thank you for the invitation to this festival," Ludvic said.

"It is our custom to bring a gift," Giya added, offering the jug.

Cliopher accepted the jug with the gestures he remembered seeing Buru Tovo use when people insisted on giving him things.

("Don't reject an offering honestly made," Buru Tovo had told him. "People want to give gifts. You enjoy giving them, don't you? Be gracious receiving them, too.")

Giya nodded sharply at first him and then at Ludvic, then departed with her staff thumping sharply down on every other step. Ludvic turned to Cliopher, his face softening from its previous stolid impassivity. "It looks good. I am looking forward to hearing you sing."

Cliopher could only nod, clasp Ludvic on the shoulder with his free hand, and beckon Gaudy over to take possession of the jug.

"It's rós," Ludvic said. Gaudy suddenly looked very intrigued by the jug. "Giya insisted. I wanted to bring beer but rós is the better guesting-gift."

"I appreciate the thought," Cliopher replied dryly, with a stern glance at his grinning nephew. "Don't drink it here, Gaudy."

"I would never, Uncle Kip," Gaudy proclaimed with vast innocence. "Look!"

Cliopher turned at the swell of noise to see Alun and Nala and their daughters, along with Aioru and most of the upper secretariat, and dozens of other people in all variation of Solaaran, Nijani, and Islander costume hesitantly coming in. He took a deep breath, which filled his nose and mouth with the scent of roasting pork and tui flowers, and suddenly all his vacillations fell away.

He did not need to be the tanà of the Ring or the Viceroy of Zunidh: he could merely be Cliopher Mdang, once more getting to tell everyone something he thought they should know.

∾

He greeted all his guests, exerting every trick of memorization he'd ever acquired in order to remember the names and islands—or their mainland equivalents—of those new to him. Most of the strangers were confused and pleased at being there, very much excited to be able to say they'd met him, admiring of his finery and the three enormous pigs on the bonfires.

Aioru had brought with him his friend Tanaea, a young woman of about Cliopher's own height with striking vitiligo and one blue eye, bright and brilliant, and one dark brown.

"This is Tanaea of ... where *do* you say you're from?" Aioru asked her, his voice teasing. He turned to Cliopher. "Tanaea's father is a writer, and she grew up travelling *everywhere*, which she's continued as an adult. We've had some fun working out our respective timelines, haven't we? Where have you just come back from, Tanaea?"

"Voonra," she said promptly, her smile bright. She regarded Cliopher intently. He met her eyes steadily, though the hair on the back of his neck started to stand up as he felt the power rising in her. A wizard—

Or not a *wizard*, exactly. This was not the magic of the Ouranatha or the School-trained. This was wild magic. He wondered what sort. Was she a fire mage, with a name like that?

"I am Tanaea Au'auēna of Ziukurui," she said finally. So she *was* an Islander! "I never learned any of the dances; my mother didn't know them. I met a man once on the sea train, when I was quite young and he was already very old. He told me the way to name myself. I wonder if you know him? You have the same expression in your eyes he did. He taught me how to light a fire, six different ways."

Cliopher smiled back, glad when she blinked and released him. Mages. He'd have to see if Ludvic or Rhodin had any of the eyedrops that helped the sort of headache a wild mage could instill without intending—or indeed *by* intending.

"My Buru Tovo travelled by the sea train a few years ago," he agreed. "He is the tana-tai, and Holds the Fire."

"You have the same necklace he wore. Efela, I'm sorry. I don't know many Islander words. Only what I learned from him that trip. And my name, of course."

"Tanaea is the hearth-fire."

"Yes. And the stone that sparks it."

A tovo, a rock common to the Islands, was one half of a set, the tanaea from some mysterious island far away the other. It had been a long, long time since there were any tanaea found in the Ring bar the ancient ones passed down through generations. Buru Tovo had a set; Uncle Lazo did not. Cliopher had never asked whether *he* would inherit Buru Tovo's one day. It had always felt far too presumptuous a thing to ask.

Cliopher felt his goosebumps rise up with some deep sweep of mystery. "You'll learn a few more words today," Cliopher promised her, and hesitated a moment—he wished very much to talk with her, ask Aioru more about her—but the Palace bells tolled, and suddenly Nala was at his elbow, wishing to introduce her friend Trisia to him.

Trisia was blind and held a cane, but she cocked her head when Cliopher greeted her and proclaimed him a very orator, and had he ever thought of going on stage?

Cliopher was suddenly awash in strong, brilliant women; nothing could have felt more like home. He led Trisia over to where Lady Ylette and her wife, the great actress Karinna Lo, were sitting on cushions in great estate, surrounded by an enormous brood of exquisitely dressed children—surely all eleven weren't *theirs*?—and guided them easily into a conversation about elocution and oratory.

Later, when everyone had arrived, he stood up on the low platform constructed for the purpose, in the corner of the courtyard where the acoustics meant his voice would sound forth clearly to everyone. He welcomed everyone formally and laid out the plan for the rest of the afternoon: first the feast, and secondly, when everyone had their meals and was feeling replete, he would teach them some of the *Lays* and sing other portions for them.

Everyone was looking at him, interest warring with the powerful scent of the roasting pork, and he laughed and said that he would not expound further before they'd had a chance to eat. That improved everyone's mood, and he caught Ghilly's grin as he turned to step back down.

In the commotion of people moving towards the food, he almost missed a fuss by the gate, where a few of the guards stood watch. After a moment a page came running up to him.

The page looked deeply excited, wide-eyed as he took in Cliopher's outfit. Cliopher beckoned to Ludvic and Aioru and Rhodin to join him. He'd been very clear this was an important event, and he was not to be interrupted bar true emergencies.

"What is it?" he asked, running down his list of protocols.

"It's an embassy!" The page stopped and coughed. He was red-faced and breathless; his eyes bright and astonished. "From—from—"

Surely not from Rhodin's telepathic dinosaur civilization (Cliopher had become muddled in the course of Rhodin's explanation as to whether the Merrions were humans who lived with the telepathic dinosaurs, or whether they were themselves sentient thunder lizards, and had not dared ask for clarification). *Surely* not. Even this level of excitement did not betoken that. *Surely*.

Beside him Rhodin was nearly vibrating with excitement. Cliopher did not dare meet his eyes. "From whom?" he asked carefully.

They were not expecting anyone...most of the main embassies had been withdrawn in his Radiancy's absence so that the many necessary arrangements could be undergone for the Great Jubilee and the new lady to come on his return.

"From the Last Free City of Zunidh!" the page finally managed. "They only speak Antique Shaian! They were lost to a curse in the jungles of southern Damara before the Lord Emperor freed them! The Mae Irionese!"

Beside him, Rhodin whispered reverently, "The Merrions!"

CHAPTER FOURTEEN
THE MEN OF MAE IRIÓN

Cliopher glanced at Aioru, who appeared entirely flabbergasted, but stepped aside with him when Cliopher gestured him over.

"Well, Chancellor Aioru," Cliopher said quietly. "What do we do?"

Aioru sucked in a shocked breath, his eyes kindling with excitement as he realized that Cliopher was deferring to him.

"We shouldn't wait, should we?" Aioru whispered. "Do we need to go somewhere else? Change our clothes?"

Cliopher raised his eyebrows at him, and Aioru held still for a long, long moment.

"We don't, do we?" the younger man said, his voice threaded with awe. "We *don't*."

"No." It was hard to ignore the thrill running through him at the thought.

Aioru frowned and closed his eyes. "In the Protocol for—Iguwarra, this is almost the embassy for the thunder lizard society, isn't it?"

Cliopher did not trust his voice at that moment, and nodded gravely.

"I ... I ... I guess we start with—you're the host, sir, and the acting head of state, so when they arrive here you would greet them—and then—then after the main parties are introduced, they can stay here for the celebration, if you don't object, of course, sir, and meanwhile I can go to ... get their rooms ready, and arrange for translators, and, and follow the Protocols, right?"

"That is why we wrote them, yes." Cliopher waited a moment longer, glad that the main body of the audience were clustering by the food and drinks and not paying very much attention to them. "Are you ready, Aioru? This is your first great test."

Aioru met his eyes and smiled, shakily at first but then with more confidence as he took in Cliopher's carefully expectant and undismayed expression. "Yes, sir," he said, nodding. "I can do this."

And because Aioru could, Cliopher could, too. He could step back, be merely the Viceroy, hand over the rest of the duties that had for so long been his to fulfil.

He turned back to the page, who was looking around the courtyard curiously, with a wistful envy at the bonfires, and said, "By all means, invite them to join us."

The page nodded, bowed, and ran out almost as quickly as he'd entered. Ludvic and Rhodin gave Cliopher two sharp glances.

"I forgot to ask if they had a translator with them," Aioru muttered.

Cliopher was about to point out that the page had known who they were and therefore there had to be some method of communication, but Aioru seemed to make that connection a moment after he had, for his expression cleared. "The page gave their names, so they must. Well. Next is ... preparations for when they arrive." Aioru hesitated, glance cutting to Cliopher before he squared his shoulders and turned to Rhodin and Ludvic. "What do you recommend for security, Commander Omo? Ser Rhodin?"

Ludvic smiled slightly and deferred to Rhodin, who was utterly in his element and immediately led Aioru off to the gate to talk with the guards there. Ludvic stayed with Cliopher, his posture as perfectly formal as it was in his usual uniform. He looked every inch what he was.

"And so you step back," Ludvic said, so quietly Cliopher could barely hear him.

"I'm trying," he replied, straightening his own shoulders and putting himself into his best court expression. He would not change from his Islander garb—he had worked too hard to get to this point for that—but he would not, for all that, act a whit less professional.

~

His guests had all seated themselves and were busy chatting and eating and drinking, the atmosphere merry and festive as he had hoped it would be, and had started to look curiously at him standing to one side.

Another page came running up. "Lord Mdang," she said, "Sayo Aioru sent me to say that the embassy is still coming up through the city. He has gone to meet them; there was some sort of fuss with their boat at the docks, and Ser Rhodin sent some of the guard to assist. He expects they will be here within two hours."

That was clear enough. Cliopher thanked the page, offered her the opportunity to take some of the food—even after the main wave of guests there was still plenty to be found—and took himself to the raised platform, Ludvic pacing companionably beside him before moving to sit with Giya, whom he had established between Ghilly and Lady Ylette's family.

Cliopher was not sure he would ever get over the discovery that Lady Ylette was not only married to a famous actress but had eleven children. No wonder she did not live in the Palace!

Perhaps not all eleven were hers: at least a couple seemed to be friends or cousins, by their marginally less perfectly tailored clothes. They were the most exquisitely dressed children he'd ever seen, but laughing happily and romping around the fire and pig roasts for all that.

He took a breath, shifting his thoughts to the *Lays* and all that went with him.

The crowd fell mostly silent, their faces turning to him.

"Now that you have eaten and drunk, it is time for us to celebrate. You have been invited here because you bear some connection, by blood or family or friendship, with the Wide Seas Islanders. Our people were once called the Ke'e Lulai'Aviyë: we who lived Under the Wake of the Ancestors' Ships, the name of our ancestors for the great ribbon of starlight that Shaian astronomers call the River of Stars."

There was a murmur of amusement and astonishment, as people murmured over those words and ideas to themselves. Cliopher waited, fitting himself into the rhythm of this crowd, their words and their attentiveness, their interests and uncertainties.

He was not the greatest orator ever to have trod the stones of the Palace of Stars, but he had heard all of those who had so spoken in the years he had spent there, and he was a diligent student.

"We are gathered today for a version of the festival of the Singing of the Waters, which commemorates the coming of the Emperor Aurelius Magnus across the seas to seek assistance from the great Wayfinders of the Wide Seas, the Ke'e Lulai. The last of the paramount chiefs was Elonoa'a of Izurayë ..."

He told the familiar story, raising laughter and pride in his people, who were listening to him, learning from him. He was the tanà, and this was a fire he held, too. His heart swelled as he taught them the opening lines of the *Lays* in Shaian and in Islander.

I sing the Wide Seas!

They sang together, the first few stanzas, the chorus swelling as more and more became comfortable enough to join Gaudy and Ghilly and Toucan and Bertie and Parno. Nala and Alun and their daughters sang too, and Cliopher realized Toucan must have taught them some of the songs over the course of their growing friendship.

He had chosen representative passages from the *Lays*, no more than an hour's worth: the opening, the settlement of the Islands, the coming of Aurelius Magnus, the last great journey of Elonoa'a, and a great leap in time to the twelfth and last. Perhaps it was vanity to wish to sing his own contribution (oh, it was, it was) but ... he did. And they would want to know how the histories they themselves might know fit into the whole.

He sang, and had just come to the end and was, quite untraditionally, reiterating the chorus of the beginning, when there was another commotion near the courtyard gate, and the embassy arrived.

Cliopher did not stop singing, not with the music of his people thundering around him. He stood on the low platform, no more than a head above his usual height, the fires behind him and the sun casting the courtyard into cool shadow so the lanterns glowed like alabaster.

Aioru and Rhodin walked in on either side of a small party—no more than six men—two old men, far older than Cliopher, and four young men who must have been around twenty or twenty-five, and who looked around the courtyard with wide eyes. One of the old men was almost certainly the translator, as he was dressed in what Cliopher recognized as Old Damaran style; the others all wore very simple belted tunics of pale linen, caught up at the shoulders with brooches.

The velioi old man, who had a proud carriage and an expression almost as brightly interested as his young companions, strode forward towards Cliopher after one swift glance around the courtyard.

Cliopher stepped down off the platform so he could greet the ambassador properly. The translator hurried forward, but the velioi man—the ambassador, he chided himself, amused at his unthinking use of an Islander term—ignored him in favour of smiling warmly at Cliopher.

He stopped a few feet away, a polite distance. Ludvic was holding his staff, very upright and stern, at Cliopher's right shoulder. Cliopher knew that according to strict court protocol he should make some gesture to indicate the stranger should speak first.

He spread his hands in what he knew a moment after was the Islander gesture, not a court one, but before he could change to the courtly version the velioi gave him a sharp, decisive nod and cried in a clear, carrying voice, "Tē ke'e'vina-tē zēnava parahë'ala!"

Cliopher could only stare at him, utterly astonished, before his wits caught up with him and the old, old words—the old words he had just taught the people sitting in this courtyard, witnessing this historic moment—the very words the first Wayfinders had said when they met their kin upon any meeting after a long parting—before they came to his lips and spilled forth: "Tō mo'ea-tō avivayë o rai'ivayë."

The man beamed at him, and continued on in slow, accented, archaic Islander: "You are he of whom I have heard! We have seen the ships of your people. We traded, were friends, long ago." He beckoned to one of the younger men, who had followed behind and was fumbling with an object in his hands. The old man said, "Long ago, before the storms came. Before the foreigners came. When I heard of you, I knew it was good for us to sail again the world."

Cliopher listened incredulously. The old man spoke slowly enough, enunciating the words carefully enough, that he could understand them despite clear evidence of sound changes. He said *ú* where Cliopher would say *a*, and *gh* where Cliopher would say *h*, but for all that it was comprehensible.

He cleared his throat and responded as slowly, as formally, as he could: "I bid you greetings and good welcome to this fire, to our food and drink and company. We welcome those who have sailed so far and are eager to hear your stories."

The old man listened intently, nodding along. Cliopher had exaggerated his gutturals, mimicking his throatier sounds. His vowels had already shifted from the Solaaran accent.

"We bring news of the chief-of-chiefs," the old man said. "First, his message. Then, our gifts."

Cliopher could do nothing more than bow over his hands in the appropriate gesture of respect. His headdress feathers bobbed and the efela nai shifted and bumped against his collarbones, and he recalled once more what he was wearing, and was...could not be other than *proud*.

This was a meeting out of the *Lays*: it would go into the *Lays*, when he had reported it to the assembly of lore-holders.

The young man produced a rolled-up letter tied with a red ribbon. There was a dollop of sealing wax across the joint, impressed with what Cliopher's fingers knew without looking was the Imperial Seal.

The *chief-of-chiefs*. Of course. Ancient Islander had had no need of a word for *Emperor*.

He showed the seal to Ludvic, who nodded solemnly, and opened the missive.

My dear Viceroy—

He had to stop there and clench his jaw against the sudden upwelling of emotion at his Radiancy's familiar hand, this casual address. How this was ... almost what he had wanted. (Almost. He must stop yearning for more than anyone would ever give him.) After a moment he looked down again, braced against what revelations might come his way.

My dear Viceroy—

    I write you from Mae Irión, the Golden City—the 'Queen of Cities' in the Saga of the Sons of Morning. You will be given this by the hand of one of those who met the very Sons of Morning. They fought against the young empire, when Yr and Damar pressed eastward across ancient Kavanor and Kavanduru, and were steadfast to the last. They were cursed by Yr himself, for ninety generations and nine: I, hundredth in my line, lifted the curse.

Cliopher read that paragraph again, parsing its meaning. He recalled his Radiancy's trajectory. This must have been ... barely a week into his adventure. After meeting Masseo the Smith the reports from Old Damara said he'd gone into the uninhabited jungle to the east.

Not quite uninhabited, evidently.

And ... not *his* Radiancy. If he hadn't already realized—

He forced down a smile and returned to his reading. If he hadn't already realized his Radiancy was Fitzroy Angursell, he would surely have merely thought of how happy this letter showed him to be free at last.

They were doubtful at coming within the sway of my government until I stood in their treasure-room. What glories of the ancient world, Cliopher! One of them had travelled to Kithor and Zard and knew Aurdar before it was destroyed ... he is a linguist, and most likely will be their ambassador: his name is Tion.

Cliopher looked up: "Tion?" he asked, guessing at the pronunciation.

The old man inclined his head, smiling. His younger companion was looking at the letter with awe in his eyes.

"Cliopher Mdang," he replied, indicating himself equally formally, before returning to the message. These were the *actual* ancients?

. . .

Amongst their treasures was an efela of your people. I recognized it as such, and in doing so first distressed the Mae Irionéz—for they were grieved that such a proud and great people had, they thought, been conquered—and when I told them what I know of your histories, and of you yourself, they were reassured. Tion said, 'If your vizier can hold his culture such that you recognize it here for what it is, we can trust you not to destroy us in your peace as we were never destroyed by your ancestors' wars'.

(We should have given you the title of Vizier. I regret not having thought of it.)

I promised them that the Queen of Cities, Mae Irión of the sagas, would not be destroyed; that you would give them the assistance they needed to join in the world.

They need everything, Cliopher. The curse kept them within their bounds, and first sickened and then killed all the women in their community. They kept their faith but they have so little: no women, no salt, no metal, no trade-goods. They had never heard of writing before they saw me write this. And yet their citadel is clad in gold leaf from when they were great: they were the first to learn how to cross between worlds.

I trust you will be able to keep them free. They are emphatically NOT to be subsumed under the rule of Old Damara or Amboloyo or Kavanduru. Create an eighteenth principality, or whatever you wish.

As I do not know when you will receive this note, I shall leave it here. I have given them letters to show to others so they can find a scholar who knows Antique Shaian to act as a translator, when they have decided to enter the world.

They are a proud people, Cliopher. You will like them. They buckled but did not break under the weight of the curse laid upon them. They were still planting gardens twenty years after they had last had a child born to them.

—A

A for Artorin, and ... perhaps, just perhaps, for Angursell.

There was another sheet enclosed with the letter, a much more formal restatement of the first.

He folded up the more private, nearly personal letter for later re-reading and comparison with the single other letter so far to have come from his Radiancy, and handed the formal component to Aioru, who scanned it quickly even as Cliopher turned to the men of Mae Irión.

"You are twice welcome, having come from so far away and long ago," he said, first in Islander and then in Shaian, waiting while the interpreter—a scholar by his appearance—repeated his words in what must have been Antique Shaian. It was much farther from modern Shaian than the ancient Islander was to his ears.

Tion, the ambassador, smiled. "It is we who rejoice to meet you." He nodded at his assistant, adding something in what must have been their own language, which was quick and burbling, full of diphthongs and consonant clusters Cliopher was not entirely certain he would be able to pronounce clearly.

"We have brought a gift to you, a token of our esteem, a memory of those of your people who in the long-ago met ours. Two gifts, indeed," Tion said, still in his careful, slow Islander. "I remember the Keluléz well!"

The Keluléz. The Ke'e Lulai ... Cliopher's heart seemed to swell, fill his breast, almost enough he might have floated away like one of the sky ships. He waited, face as court-formal as he could manage, while the younger man brought two items, one large and one small, both wrapped in the same sort of plain linen they were wearing.

Tion said, "One was a trade-gift from your people, when they came following a certain bird, to see where it went. The other ... we knew that your people came to an island off our land, at the mouth of our river, for a certain stone. That place was lost to us under the curse. It may be you have come, many have come." He shook his head. "Not many. Only one came, not often. One man, one canoe."

The word he used for canoe, *vaha*, struck straight to the heart. Cliopher did not know what he meant. *One man, one canoe.* That had a resonance of some secret lore, some secret knowledge, held by one lineage or one lore-keeper. He did not know it, anyway.

He was given the larger parcel first. He opened it to find coiled on the linen a splendid efela.

Iridescent blue abalone beads; golden pearls; white cowries; red coral.

That kind of abalone was extinct now. There was a whole passage in the part of the *Lays* sung by the Walea on the topic of how the early Islanders had not been cautious with the resources of new islands, how they had hunted to extinction certain birds, certain fish, certain shells. There had been a great conclave, a Gathering of the Ships, to discuss how to better steward their resources.

Cliopher had spent ages thinking about that passage. How to manage an abundant resource so it was not lost? How to steward something that had never been abundant, so it could be shared? How to mediate between the greedy and the cautious and the meek but deserving?

"I know the name of this efela," he said, the words springing to his lips as he stared at it. "Its name is Mau'alanio'ina. Mau'a was the one who made it, sang its name into the *Lays*. He traded with the Pisiringali, those who...swim with dolphins."

Tion smiled sadly. "They were our friends, once, the dolphins. They left us when the curse came down."

Mau'a was one of the earliest names in the *Lays*. Cliopher could not suppress the shiver that ran through him at the realization that Tion must be 'the tall bright-eyed man, the gifted at tongues, who travelled far in the ways of his people', who had *met* Mau'a.

He had met Yr and Damar. He had met Mau'a. He had seen Aurdar before it was razed by the armies of Yr.

No wonder the Antique Shaian scholar was standing so importantly beside them, almost panting with impatience as Cliopher and Tion spoke in the slow, careful, not-quite-the-same languages of the Islanders ancient and modern.

"And here is the stone," Tion added, as Cliopher turned to find Gaudy and his other secretaries had hastened up to stand beside him and Aioru. He was glad to see Tully had a notebook out to record this historic encounter. Cliopher handed the efela to Gaudy and received the smaller linen parcel.

What stone did anyone cross the Wide Seas to find?

He unfolded the linen, and nearly dropped the contents. It was a striking rock.

He held it, trembling with a kind of awe: an ordinary enough stone, roughly oval, a good size to fit in his hand.

There were half a dozen such rocks in the Vangavaye-ve, all of them very old, so old their origins had been lost. Buru Tovo had one; he said it belonged to him as tana-tai. The others were all in the possession of descendants of ancient tanà, long since folded into other families.

Buru Tovo said that Cliopher would learn, or not, where they came from. It was not necessary, not for a Mdang; not even for the tanà.

(Was it necessary, then, for the tana-tai? What did it mean, that it had come thus to him?)

"Mau'a did not come for this," Cliopher said. Mau'a had been of the...Ela, that was it. The wide-wanderers, the shamans, *those who went farthest*.

"No, it was one who had a red necklace, like that one you wear," Tion replied. "He laughed when we said it was how we lit fires. It is a gift for you."

"Thank you," said Cliopher, trembling with awe and doubt and one of those wishes he could never articulate. "Thank you."

CHAPTER FIFTEEN
IN THE LIAAU

I f you had asked Cliopher even three weeks before—before the coming of his friends, before the comet, before the flowering of the tui tree—he would have laughed at the idea that an embassy from an ancient lost city could come, and he would still leave on a holiday.

But yet—he did.

The embassy had travelled a long, long way, and were weary with the endless novelties of the wide world. They wanted a few days to rest and continue to work on their languages.

And they did not *need* Cliopher for this stage. Not until the actual discussions were being held would he be present, and those would not begin for another week at the least.

And so—he went.

Cliopher was of a position that the Liaau park wardens would, and did, do everything necessary and many things that were not to make his visit greatly enjoyable. He and his friends (including Rhodin and Pikabe as the second guard) arrived by sky ship in the late morning and settled down to a splendid repast before being escorted on the most spectacular trail to the lodge they would be staying at that night.

This trail was not usually open to the public because of the extreme fragility of the ecosystems through which it traversed. Cliopher was a little embarrassed that his rank permitted the exception; but he could not be but delighted in the opportunity.

He walked behind Ghilly, who had cornered their guide and was asking intelligent questions about the region's botanical diversity, which was apparently legendary. Cliopher listened, recalling Aioru talking about his vision of an ecological paradise, and acknowledged that while he appreciated plants and animals and natural beauty as much as the next man, it had never been his great focus in life.

Still, he was the first one to see the mountain condor slide down a thermal to see if they were of any interest, and that was pleasing.

~

They spent the night in luxury. The food was exquisite and the beds comfortable, and to be woken by birdsong rather than bell-rings was a treat. They all rose early, Bertie and Rhodin grumbling good-naturedly about how much of a taskmaster he was being, and prepared to descend into the gorges.

The lodges were built on the eastern face of the mountains, on a high ridge with spectacular views oriented into the mountains or back across the plains towards Solaara and the distant sea. Theirs faced south, which gave it the best light for the waterfalls coming off the higher peaks. Even in the dry season the water glittered in the steely dawn light.

"How much larger are the falls in the wet season?" Ghilly asked him as they gathered on the deck before departure. Cliopher eyed Rhodin's excessively enormous rucksack with suspicion, wondering what on earth his friend had decided was necessary for an 'expedition' that would compass six or seven hours at most, but decided not to express any criticism. This whole trip was a gift from him, after all.

He pointed at the wide grooves in the rocks, stretching perhaps ten times the width of the dry-season cataract. "That whole face is water, to that outcropping that looks like a knob—it looks like a head from the other side, we'll see it later in the afternoon once we get to that side. We go down the stair, here—"

He pointed at the metal and wooden stair that started not far from their lodge and zigzagged down into the still-shadowy canyon below them.

"That takes us to the river-valley. This is one of the three sources of the Dwahaii, the river that runs through Solaara. This one is called Duvayna. We will follow the river upstream to the base of the falls, then we curve to the north, through a natural tunnel that leads to the other side of that ridge there, and then we'll be in the catchment basin of the Uyna, the second of the rivers. There's a longer trail that keeps going into the back country, but we'll cut it short, follow the cairns along a hanging valley to the Uyna gorge, which will bring us out at the lower lodge of the park before sunset. And that's where we'll spend tonight."

Ghilly regarded their proposed route with a relieved smile. "I was worried this was going to be like the staircases, but that's not too bad."

"Once we're down in the valley it's easy," Cliopher promised her. "And the rock formations and plants are amazing."

Ghilly tilted her head back to look at the clouds piling up behind the mountains, with their billowing tops just catching pink from the sunrise. "We don't need to worry about the rain?"

"One benefit of being here, rather than any other part of the world, is that the weatherworkers are both skilled and practiced. The Ouranatha say the rains will begin in three days."

"And so the rains will begin in three days."

"Hence why we are doing this walk *now*, and keeping the ones up here for later."

"You truly do think of everything, don't you?" she said, laughing.

"Rhodin does, yes." She gave him a disbelieving look, and he laughed. "Oh all right, so do I."

~

He did not think of everything.

All went well up to lunchtime. They clambered down the staircase without difficulty into the shaded and cool canyon, then turned and followed the stream-bed as it wound back into the mountains.

It was not perfectly level—in fact was noticeably sloping upwards—but the water scoured the stone clean each year and so the footing was mostly straightforward. They walked easily, or at least it was a very easy pace for Cliopher; his friends said that as they had spent the past month exploring Solaara on foot and climbing up and down the five flights of stairs to his apartments all the time they were much fitter than they had been on arrival.

There were plenty of intriguing things to observe. Strange hollows where the water had scoured out pot-holes, hanging gardens of ferns and mosses and some sort of delicate purple-and-red wild fuchsia, and many more plants than Cliopher could even begin to name. Ghilly could name some, having acquired a plant guidebook in Solaara for the purpose, and they had to keep stopping to wait for her to catch up, face alight with an impish joy in discovering this or that incredible rarity.

There were jewel-bright lizards, green and iridescent gold, somnolent as they waited for the sun to climb high and rouse them from their torpor. There were dozens of hummingbirds on the fuchsias, of at least half a dozen species—ruby-throated, gold-backed, blue-tailed, and Cliopher's favourite, black ones barely bigger than a large bee.

There were beetles and butterflies and flying insects by the multitudes, and swallows and swifts darting after them, and even bats at first, though those returned to their roosts as the day wore on. The walls were a kind of sandstone, fantastically swirled in cream and beige with thin lines of rust or charcoal. The water had carved out strange shapes, smooth and somehow organic-looking: formations like standing waves, or tall pillars, or high court costume hats.

About halfway up the canyon, Cliopher found himself walking with Bertie at a small remove from the others. He matched his step to his friend's, enjoying the cool wind coming down the mountain towards them.

"I have an apology to make, Kip," said Bertie.

Cliopher turned to him, smiling in surprise. "Do you?"

Bertie scowled at the ground. "You don't make it easy," he declared, puffing slightly. Cliopher slowed his steps again; his pace tended to increase when he didn't pay attention. "I've been trying...but it's hard to get you alone, and you're so damned impervious that when I have, I've not ..." He expelled his breath sharply. "I'm making a hash of this, aren't I?"

"I admit," Cliopher said, trying not to laugh, "that I'm not entirely clear on what you're apologizing for."

Bertie made a barking sort of a laugh. "You'd let me leave it there, wouldn't you?"

Since Cliopher had no idea what Bertie was getting at, he shrugged. "If you'd like."

Bertie muttered a few words under his breath. They came around a twist in the canyon, and saw Rhodin standing at the top of the next rise, looking back. Cliopher waved at him to go on, and Rhodin nodded once, then turned to follow the already out-of-sight Toucan and Ghilly.

Pikabe was trailing along behind Cliopher and Bertie, his expression thoughtful. He was not quite out of earshot, given that the wind was blowing towards him, but no matter what Bertie was trying to say, Cliopher was sure he could trust the guard to keep it to himself.

They got to the top of the steep bit, no doubt a foaming cascade in the wet season, and paused there to take in the view—the shadowed stone canyon, the sunlit plains beyond—while they both caught their breath. Pikabe caught up and offered them water from his pack (which was well-stocked, if not quite as full as Rhodin's ready-for-anything bag). Cliopher thanked him and then nodded at him to stay back; Pikabe smilingly acceded, and Bertie—well, Bertie looked a trifle constipated, but he said nothing until they had once more drawn ahead of the guard.

"I've been—what I think—damn it, Kip, you shouldn't have forgiven me so easily. I keep expecting you to throw it back in my face. What I *said*—I was so awful—they've been weighing on me," he finished, kicking at a rock so it bounced hard off the canyon wall. Cliopher eyed the resonating stone warily, but the echoes faded with no more than a trickle of pebbles shaken loose from directly above the rock's impact.

"Maybe don't do that," he suggested mildly to Bertie.

"I've been such a bad friend," Bertie responded, his scowl truly ferocious now, his heavy eyebrows drawing sharply together. "I said—I'm sorry—I said that *bilge* about not wanting Parno to be like you...I didn't mean it even then and I shouldn't have said it at all and I'm sorry."

Cliopher could not say he had *forgotten* Bertie's words, nor that they had not hurt him. But ... "You already apologized for that, Bertie," he said.

"Not really. Not enough."

They had to go single file for a moment, as the trail took them through a natural arch. Cliopher tried to think what to say. Perhaps if nothing had changed, he would have held those words closer to his heart.

But things *had* changed. Cliopher had tried to be more forthcoming in his letters, and Bertie had reciprocated, and he'd *come*, come at last, to visit.

"As we sailed here," Bertie said thickly once they were walking side-by-side again, "we heard so much about you. How you've made the world a better place. At home it's not—not so obvious, what the stipend means. Not for most people. It made Faldo able to follow his dream. And other people ... Lara can concentrate on singing—she's training for the kotua—and Cora—and—and *we* got it, you know, in ... Boloyo, right, because we'd hit a storm and the sail was damaged and they're expensive, especially since it wasn't the usual shape there, and...and then someone in a bar said 'You can get the stipend,' and it was this—relief."

Cliopher smiled, a little stiffly. "I'm glad."

"This gift from *you*," Bertie said roughly. "For us. For everyone. And it felt so... so personal ... and I could see how that wasn't just us feeling that. It was like we'd gone to the tanà for help, and ..."

Bertie shook his head vigorously, and Cliopher swallowed, not sure how he could respond to that. He blinked hard at a tiny black hummingbird sipping from a brilliant orange trumpet flower hanging off a rock.

"Kip. I had this moment where I realized that the reason it seemed so logical, so obvious, so *normal*, was because ... it is. It all comes out of the *Lays*, doesn't it? And I thought—I was in line to get the stipend, and I thought, if my sons were *half* the man you are—"

He stopped and blew his nose, and the honk echoed off the stone. They walked on up the cool, shadowy riverbed.

"Thank you, Bertie," Cliopher said quietly, something easing in his chest.

If Bertie—if Bertie could *see* that what he had done with his life was in service to the *Lays*—was an *interpretation* of the *Lays*—perhaps it would not, after all, be impossible to go home and be the tanà there?

Perhaps he could keep sailing another year or two across that great and endless ocean, seeking the island he knew was there.

Perhaps ... oh, he could not fool himself. Of course it would still be *hard*.

But he had faced harder impossibilities.

"Irela has a lot to answer for," Bertie rumbled unexpectedly.

Cliopher did not know quite what to say, as he didn't particularly like Bertie's second wife, and he was sure the sentiment was reciprocated.

Bertie snuffled, and then said, his voice filled with disgust: "She filled my ears with poison. Drip, drip, drip. She hates you, you know—maybe you do. I didn't realize how bad it was till we were sailing and talking about you and all these criticisms came out of my mouth, and Toucan and Ghilly said I sounded just like her."

"I didn't know I'd offended her so badly."

"It wasn't about you at all. It was all about Cora—Irela was so jealous of her. She didn't like me being such close friends with Toucan and Ghilly—Ghilly especially— but I wouldn't budge with them, so it was you she ... Every time I was confused or— or upset about something you'd written, or after your visits, she'd make it out to be your fault. Not obviously, you know." He grunted, and gave Cliopher a sidelong, pleading glance. "I can see it now."

"I'm sorry."

"It's hardly your fault I married her. You told me not to—you wrote me about how maybe I was rushing it, maybe I shouldn't let her be a rebound when I wasn't over Cora. Irela saw that letter, apparently—I'd been going through my letters from you, setting up boxes—and that was when she took against you. Picking away at our friendship. All this time I should have ..." He sighed.

Cliopher reached out and squeezed his hand gently, companionably. "It's on me, too, Bertie. I should have said something earlier."

"Don't go apologizing for that again. You've been better."

"I'm trying."

"Yeah."

They stopped for another rest. The canyon walls closed them in, bar a narrow river of bright blue. A crow flashed across the space between, striking black in the sunlight. Pikabe stopped to look up at the bird, his hands on his hips.

"I'm glad you came," Cliopher said, trying to offer something back. It was a small vulnerability—very small—and hardly *news* to Bertie, who'd seen him throw off all decorum in open court in his delight that they'd come.

"Should've come before." Bertie sighed. "I was a bit ... Irela didn't help, but it wasn't just her. I was a bit afraid that it wouldn't be ... that you had better friends, here, fancy ones, and I'd have to acknowledge that," he finished in a rush.

Cliopher stared at him as that fear hit far too close to home. "Oh," he said blankly, and swallowed hard. "I'm sorry you ever thought that, Bertie. That's—I know exactly what you mean. It's a hard thing to face."

Except that in his case his fear was not for some ... fancy noble friends, but for literal legends.

Bertie nudged his shoulder. "Yeah. I know. And I kept telling myself that, whenever I started to think that we weren't going to be grand enough for you. At least *we* don't have to measure up to the Red Company."

Cliopher caught his breath and coughed. "I beg your pardon?"

Bertie laughed, a slow rumble at first that rose up into great echoing guffaws. Pikabe glanced up at them from where he stood, then turned again to look at the riverbed winding down. Another crow, or perhaps the same one, was perched on an outcropping, high above them, and Pikabe seemed very interested in it. Cliopher ignored the bird. "Bertie."

"Kip," Bertie said, wiping his eyes. "Aya told me about your ... lord. I have to say, everything made *much* more sense after that."

Cliopher tried, and failed, to come up with anything coherent. "Aya?"

"Jiano's wife, your cousin, yeah? I went to see her before we left ... I wasn't going to go talk about you with tanà Lazo, you know, it would have been awkward. She's got half the training, and she's been to Solaara. It was Cora's idea to ask her for places it might be nice to see, wontok she'd found ..." He glanced at Cliopher, who was trying to grasp this. "She told us about your ... lord." He chuckled again. "What a thing, Kip. You never *could* do anything by halves, could you?"

"I have no idea what you're talking about," Cliopher said with great dignity.

"Does that work with your council of princes?" Bertie asked. "Because—"

"Did I say I was glad you'd come?" Cliopher interrupted. "Can't think why, now. Between you and Rhodin—"

Bertie laughed loudly enough the crow cawed back. "I'll hold my head up with your fancy friends," he promised, "if you do the same with *his*."

"Bertie."

"Kip!" His voice took on the familiar teasing tone, and Cliopher could—could not handle it.

"Bertie," he interrupted softly, "please. I ... I can't joke about him. Not ..."

Bertie glanced at him, once, something on the tip of his tongue, in his suddenly-merry face, and then he nodded once, and nudged Cliopher with his shoulder. "Not yet, eh? There'll be time for that, then, when you retire."

Cliopher released a long breath, not quite a sigh, and resolved to have a word or two with Aya about the concept of discretion. Not to mention high treason.

They reached the bottom of the great cataracts just before noon. Cliopher suggested they continue on and get through the tunnel before having lunch, for that was the hardest component of the hike and would mean that the afternoon would be easier. The others all agreed, and after a short break to eat fruit and drink water—not to mention appreciate being able to stand at the bottom of a three-hundred-foot waterfall and feel only the lightest mist reach them—they continued on.

The going here was harder, as they had to pick their way through rubble that had fallen off the cliffs. Although Rhodin had joined Cliopher on several of his previous visits to the Liaau, the guard had never accompanied him on this particular hike before, and so it was Cliopher who had to pay attention to the landmarks and ensure that everyone stayed well away from the cliff face itself.

There was no set path, for the river shifted it every rainfall. The park wardens had told him what had changed since his last visit. A portion of the cliff before the tunnel had given way the year before, which meant that they now had to swing out quite far from the rising cliff to get around the unstable ground. This took them much closer to the downslope edge of the cliff face than Cliopher quite liked.

"We're on a kind of ledge, then?" Rhodin asked when they stopped so Cliopher could find the best route. "This seems to be a different sort of rock."

It was: a much darker and greyer stone, harder and resistant to the water's erosive force. The path took them along its edge to the flank of the mountain that channelled all the water on this side into the Duvayna's course.

"Yes," Cliopher said. "Keep close to me, and single file along here. You see that cave mouth, there? That's where we're going, but because of the landslide earlier this season we have to go round a bit. The wardens told me it was safe as long as we don't stand on the loose rocks."

"Not that we'd want to," Ghilly said.

They picked their way carefully. Cliopher was glad they could stay a good fifteen feet away from the edge, which was irregular and fell a considerable way before the rubble and scree were halted by another outcropping of the grey rock. They did not make any conversation until they were past the dangerous part; he was relieved when they reached the short metal ladder that led up to the mouth of the tunnel.

"Almost there," he said, eager now to show them the view on the other side, which was the true point of this route.

"There's a good place for lunch?" Rhodin asked.

"There's a fantastic place for lunch," he promised.

Through the tunnel—they had to crawl for a short distance, which made Bertie very unhappy, but there was light visible the whole way along and the floor was surfaced in fine sand, easy enough on the knees. On the other side they paused, blinking to readjust their eyesight, and Cliopher—who had gone through first, somewhat to Pikabe's displeasure, but thus had his sight back so he could see their expressions—watched as they took in the landscape before them.

The Grey Mountains rose up here in steep heights, until their more distant peaks were snowcapped. They plunged down in stark magnificence into the heart of the

Liaau; the chain of lakes fed by those high glaciers, set in jungles of an intense, luscious green.

And this time of year, the week before the rains, the flame-of-the-forest and the gold-rain and the cloud-of-butterfly trees were in full blossom and more than living up to their names. Sunbirds rose and fell, their feathers nearly glowing in the light as they performed courting dances in advance of the great eruption of plant and insect life that would occur once the rains began.

This side of the mountain did not feel the effect of the waters cascading down the other, and so the park wardens had cleared a small area and set two benches there, angled so that everyone could see the view. There they sat to enjoy their packed lunches.

Cliopher finished first. He was content to watch his friends and regard the view for a while, but soon felt the desire to relieve himself. There was no good spot in their immediate vicinity, which was extremely open, but a hundred yards or so down the path turned to cross a secondary spur and descend not into the upper valley they were looking at but into the smaller valley of the tributary of the Uyna which they were going to follow back down to the lower lodge.

He pointed out their route to the others, then said he was going to find a clump of bushes he recalled from another hike. Rhodin laughed at his barbaric indelicacy and insisted that Pikabe accompany him.

"I hardly think anyone else is up here without the wardens knowing," Cliopher objected.

"You never know. The locals still hunt through here, don't they?"

"They're permitted to, but I shouldn't imagine they are this close to the rains— it'd be hard to get anything back out of the gorge system. Once the waters rise the canyons are impassible."

Toucan nodded sagely. "Note to self: do not climb mountains in the rainy season."

"That depends on the mountains," Rhodin objected—he had taken the Guard trainees to Kavanduru for many mountain exercises—and Cliopher laughed and left them to their discussions.

He and Pikabe climbed down silently, then made their way around the corner of the knoll. There was deeper soil here, and more plants, but it was still quite exposed so he pushed in further before he felt it private enough.

As he was finishing he heard a strange noise. He looked up to see a crow knocking a snail-shell on a rock.

Pikabe said, "Sir?"

"Yes?"

"There's something—" Pikabe appeared at the edge of the bushes Cliopher had chosen, an odd look on his face. "Did you see something?"

"A crow, that's all."

Pikabe frowned. "A crow? Sir—" He stopped, visibly troubled. The crow regarded them with a bright eye—they were, Cliopher knew, very intelligent birds— and flew up to the top of a small knoll that rose to the east. "We should ..."

"Follow?" Cliopher asked, smiling, and climbed up to the knoll. Pikabe did not seem to know whether this was the correct response or not, but came behind him. The crow flew off, leaving a solitary black feather fluttering down after it.

Cliopher moved to the side to pick up the feather, admiring its iridescence in the sunlight. It was very light in his hands, with a satisfying pattern in the way the vanes interlocked to form the pinion. He ran it through his fingers. There was a story in the *Lays* about a single black feather ... One that Vou'a had been given, and which he had carelessly lost.

The mountain spur came down in a fine sweep, hesitated where they had stopped for lunch—looking up he saw his friends looking down at them, and waved—stepped over and down to the knoll where he and Pikabe were standing—and swept down again on this front in a steep tumble of stone and very small plants that gave Cliopher minor vertigo.

Right at the top of the knoll was a perfectly round hole in the stone that was full of water. Cliopher stopped there to look into it. His head was silhouetted against the sky: it seemed very deep, though he guessed it could not be in truth. It must be some sort of spring, as the water welled up very gently and trickled over the side with a faint, musical tinkle.

Cliopher bowed over his hands and addressed a brief, silent prayer to the deity that surely dwelled here. He had nothing very suitable for a gift-offering, bar the crow's feather, but then again ... some gifts were meant to be received and immediately given on. He laid it on the lip of the stone before bowing again in the Islander fashion and stepping back.

Pikabe had gone a few yards farther to take in the view, which just here led back through a gap in the mountains towards the white gleam that was Solaara. He turned to see Cliopher watching him from the edge of the path.

"I'm coming, coming," Pikabe said genially, walking back towards him with long strides. He checked as he went past the spring. "Oh, sir, the feather."

"It's a gift," Cliopher said.

"Sir, if Crow—"

But whatever Pikabe was about to say was lost: for without any more warning than a single shout from above, barely heard than gone, the whole face of the mountain was falling and Cliopher with it.

Something struck him on the back of the head, and he was—gone.

Interlude
Falling (1)

Cliopher was drowning in an ocean of light.

He was far below the surface, in water that was not water, in light that was not light, in a sea that was not anything he had ever known.

There were voices singing.

He floated on his back, limbs outstretched like a sea star, looking up dizzying heights to where the clear water and clearer light dissolved into each other and became the sky.

The song was the song of the *Lays*.

The voices were ethereal, high, sweet, inhumanly beautiful.

They were singing the Naming, the sacred passages that named the universe: stars, winds, islands, currents, birds, trees, fish, ships, shells, gods, mysteries, people.

Cliopher floated there, drowning in light, in the *Lays*, in this water that was not water but which he still could not breathe. All he could do was listen those high, sweet, inhuman voices Name the world, the universe of the Wide Seas, all that lay Under the Wake of the Ancestors' Ships.

He found he was instinctively trying to add his voice, sing his own tiny part of the great chorus.

He had no air to breathe, let alone to sing, but he mouthed the words, anchoring himself to them, in them, with them. They were the ropes with which he might hold himself fast to the universe, these passages from the *Lays* which he knew deep in his bones, in his heart where the embers waited, smouldering, to become fire.

The great Naming went on and on, far longer than the *Lays* Cliopher knew. The familiar names in his own language expanded outward to stars he had never seen, oceans never travelled, skies never breathed. The Names came faster and faster, the chorus unimaginably vast, each voice Naming a star, an island, a current, a wind, a bird, a plant, a fish, a people, a person.

Over and over again the voices rose and fell in complexities beyond any traditional melody, beyond the intricate music of court, beyond even the patterns of populations and economies that Cliopher had tended so carefully in his life.

Cliopher forgot he was drowning, forgot he had no air to breathe, forgot that he was deep in the ocean of light, forgot that he was dying, for he had realized what this was, that he was being sung home by the Ancestors, that he was being called home across the Sky Ocean, and he was dying and if he did not now sing his name he would be lost, fall to the darkness below the luminous waters, fall into the oblivion where the Old Woman Who Lives in the Deeps would ingather him to her silent company.

He forced his mouth to shape the sounds, forced out the words, the name of himself, in the language of his ancestors that the very universe was singing in the great Naming.

O Cliopher ezū Mdang, he cried silently.
  Loaloa vayë-ba
  Aōteketētana aōtetē-ba
  O Ke'e Lulai'aviyë surū
  Nē nia ti'i'ina!

~

He woke.

ii. Chasing a Viau

CHAPTER SIXTEEN
ERANUI AND THE FIVE SHELLS

He was, strangely, in a bedroom.

He stretched experimentally, and was (he could admit it to himself) disappointed to find he was still stiff and sore.

Well. Not exactly *disappointed*, on second thought.

He slid out of the low bed, noting that the sheets were old Nijani-flax linen, and that the straw pallet seemed to be resting on twisted sisal ropes.

The room was very plain. There was the bed. There was a window, which was shuttered closed, but enough light came through the slats to suggest it was daylight. There was no art on the whitewashed walls, and only a single woven mat on the floor. Its simple stripes and natural materials could have come from anywhere.

There was a wooden door, closed. In the corner opposite was a wooden stand, which contained an ewer of water and a small cup on a saucer. All three items were made of fired red clay, again very simple in material and design. Cliopher did not know enough about pottery to be able to determine where it might have come from, though he supposed Bertie might have been able to.

The thought of his friends caused a swift pang to run through him, as he remembered the last few minutes before waking from his ... dream. That horrendous rumble, the ground suddenly disappearing from under his feet, the cries of alarm, the strike to his head, and then spinning into that ocean of light in which he was sure he had drowned.

Perhaps he *had* drowned.

He had always thought drowning would hurt more.

There were stories of people who had come back from Sky Ocean, but never from the dead.

The ewer was filled with water, which smelled good. He tasted it cautiously before drinking. He felt better afterwards, though still rather weak and shaky.

He was probably not actually dead.

He returned to sit on the bed.

The room looked, he decided slowly, like an unused guest room hastily swept out for an injured stranger. The bed was not much like anything he'd ever seen from the Grey Mountains people—the Liaau park wardens used thick mattresses on wooden frames.

This room was certainly not in the Palace. Anyway, surely he would have been taken to his own rooms in that case. It could still be one of the local villages.

He found that he was gripping the edge of the mattress tightly, and made his hands relax. The route he had chosen for their hike was about as far from any local village as it was possible to be in the Liaau, up the gorges towards the wildest and most remote part of the park, where the most magnificent scenery was. The locals did hunt through there, as they always had, but they had also always been mostly nomadic hunter-gatherers, and they did not build permanent houses with permanent beds in them. Not up there.

He folded his hands on his lap. Were these his clothes? He was wearing a tunic with short sleeves and knee-length ... culottes, that was what Féonie called the short wide-legged trousers.

If he did not recall that he had been wearing them when he went rambling, well, thinking about the hike was painful, and he was not sure he was actually remembering where he had been, or if it was part of the dream.

The cloth was very white linen, and had discreet embroidery in palest blue and bronze at the cuffs. He examined the design on the hem, feeling comforted by the discovery that it was the one Féonie had made out of the traditional Mdang patterns.

He reached up in sudden worry to grasp his efela, but they were there, his efela ko and the efetana of fire coral. His hand brushed a third necklace, and he startled, for he had not worn any others except during high ceremonies.

It was tied with the traditional knot, which never released accidentally but was easy enough to undo on purpose.

He loosed the strange efela, capturing the falling strand before it quite disappeared down his tunic.

A pair of flame pearls nestled on either side of a single perfect sundrop cowrie, which the *Lays* named efevoa, the shells of Vou'a, god of mystery.

Cliopher took a deep, unsteady breath, and with trembling fingers replaced the efela around his neck.

So. He was in his own clothes, but perhaps not what he'd actually been wearing. He wore his two customary efela, and a third that he had never worn but knew he was entitled to, more or less.

The room was architecturally and culturally unlikely for the Liaau, and if he had been removed from the park he would surely have been taken to the Palace.

This was not the Palace.

It would be very strange for people to leave the Viceroy of Zunidh alone if they knew who he was. This suggested they did not know that, either.

According to all the evidence he had, he was not dead.

Had he fallen into another world? Was this Voonra or Colhélhé?

~

His feet were bare, and looked the same as always, planted on the mat.

He looked around him, wondering. This room could easily be one in his mother's house.

There was a story in the *Lays* about a gift, or a challenge, one of the gods had once given someone ... Vou'a, or perhaps it was Ani, had once given someone, one of the great matriarchs when she was young, the gift or challenge or ... task, of going ... somewhere else ...

He could not remember the story. All he remembered was taking the lesson of *doing your best regardless of whether it seems to matter*. The rest of the story had seemed fantastical and absurd.

Whoever it was had fallen into another *place*—another version of their world, the past, the future, or—or—

~

The shuttered window was merely latched, not locked, but it was stuck. When he finally managed to jimmy it open all he could see were the vast leaves of an enormous and very healthy banana tree.

~

There was something about five shells, in the story he could not remember.

Five shells, five days ... and ... five tasks ...

And something about the past, or the future, and the choices one made.

~

There was a noise of footsteps, and soft voices, and he tensed, trying to remind himself that this could be *anything* but he was still Cliopher Mdang, Viceroy of Zunidh and tanà—

The door opened. Cliopher stood up politely, courteously, summoning his best court-impervious expression.

Kip Mdang walked in.

~

For a moment he thought it was his younger self, but then he met the other man's eyes, his own eyes, and saw—

~

Cliopher took a deep, unsteady breath, and tried hard to focus.

The man who walked in stared at him as frankly as Cliopher stared back. It was eerie, seeing his own features alive before him, bearing the marks of a life, an identity, a personhood who was *not him*.

This Kip—he was clearly *Kip*—had self-evidently chosen the Islander way and entered into it with as much devotion as Cliopher had given his own work. He stood straight and proud, his shoulders broader than Cliopher's, his frame everywhere heavier with hard muscles under a comfortable layer of fat.

He looked the very picture of a prosperous and respectable Islander.

Cliopher was very conscious of his fine linen with its discreet, superlative embroidery and its Solaaran-court cut.

Kip wore a grass skirt, intricate but not festival-fine. His efela marked his high status: he wore the efetana, and there too was the efela ko, almost identical to the one Cliopher wore. (*Almost*—had this Kip never had cause to chip away at the obsidian pendant?) He, too, wore a third efela, a beautiful double strand of matched green pearls from Kuariso, which were nearly as rare as the flame pearls of the Western Ring.

It was the sort of efela a chief would wear, but the tanà was not, ever, a chief.

Cliopher reminded himself that he had very recently handed over official control of the government of the world.

And this was, somehow, his mirror self.

Kip's hair was longer than Cliopher's bureaucratic cut, long enough to reveal the wave that Cliopher had honestly forgotten it had. This Kip had only just started to go grey, and his face was sun-weathered and healthy.

He looked in his early fifties; which Cliopher should have, had he spent the years since the Fall at home and not in the strange timeline of the Palace, and if his vocation had not weighed him down with stress and care.

The other Kip had not ventured in to see his double alone: he was accompanied by a Ghilly who was also not the Ghilly Cliopher knew. This Ghilly was holding her arms as she stared at Cliopher. Behind her was a Cora who seemed to have embraced an eccentric artist's identity far more than *his* Cora, and a man whom Cliopher vaguely recognized as some distant connection on his father's side.

"Who *are* you? Where did you come from? Why are you here?"

The vehement, hardly traditional questions came from the other Kip.

The other Ghilly frowned. She wore a kind of dress made of Nijani flax fibre, beautifully dyed and woven. The style was at once traditional and new to Cliopher's eyes. She wore two efela, one of them close to the Poyë lore-keepers' efuruma, with a rainbow of beads made from various seeds and plant material. This Ghilly had clearly studied much more of her family lore than his had, though she did not claim the greater dances.

Cora wore a grass skirt, unselfconscious as *his* Cora never had been about going about topless, with an efela of twisted strands of many beads and pearls, showing that whoever she was in this world, this universe, she had achieved much to be admired. That was an efela of note, if not quite one of name.

The other man—the distant cousin (what was his name? In Cliopher's world the man had been a sailor on one of the inter-island trading ships, had fallen afoul of drinking too much and had ended up murdered by the husband of a woman with whom he'd had an affair—Jordo, that was it, Jordo Varga)—was wearing a much more ordinary skirt, and he only wore one efela, though it was beautiful.

"So," Cora began uncertainly. "What ... I mean who ... I mean ... *how* ..."

She trailed off. None of the others were any help. Other Kip was watching him with sharp eyes. Cliopher could not help but wonder if *he* ever looked quite so fierce. Probably not.

This Kip had a fire to him that Cliopher had long since banked.

"It's like the story of Eranui and the Five Shells," Ghilly said, very thoughtfully.

Cliopher felt a surge of relief that the story was known here, and that it did not matter that *he* had not been able to dredge it up from his own memory.

He had sung over the *Lays*, preparing for his little festival. But the parts that he had only ever learned in Islander were harder to recall.

If he had time, when he got home, he would practice them until he knew them as well. What kind of tanà would he be if he did not know *all* the *Lays* equally well?

He looked at the other Kip, who was nodding slowly.

What kind of tanà was this man, who had chosen another way?

What kind of tanà might Cliopher have been, if he had chosen never to leave?

(Had this man chosen not to leave? What had happened to the wider world, if he had not?)

"Remind us of the story," the other Kip said. His voice was decisive, though his expression continued to be wary and slightly unfriendly.

Cliopher wondered if his voice sounded like that. It was lighter than he'd realized, with a pleasant richness to it, a timbre on the edge between baritone and tenor.

He did not have that sharp Vangavayen accent, not any more.

Ghilly tipped her head. "Eranui was Poyë, a great urumà, many generations ago. It was she who thought the Poyë knowledge should be split, one to focus on gardening, the other on healing. It was a lesson she'd learned on her ... adventure. She was a healer. When she was quite young, she went sailing across the Bay from Tisiliamo to visit her father's family on Iruzayë. A bad storm blew up as she returned home, but when she got there it was not the same place she had left. All the people and buildings were different, the whole island was different."

Cliopher recalled the story now, at least in vague outline: Eranui had found herself wearing a new efela of five shells. She had decided this meant there were five tasks facing her: once she fulfilled the fifth, she had sailed off, and when she reached Iruzayë she had found her father's family there, just as she expected.

The five tasks changed in different versions of the story, which was both very old and not something that had ever been fully integrated into the *Lays*, because no one knew if it were truly travel in time or some slip sideways into another ... place.

"She'd gone back in time, hadn't she?" Cora asked.

"That's one version," Ghilly agreed, and they all looked hard at Cliopher.

He took a deep breath, and locked eyes with the other Kip.

"No," the other Kip said slowly, solidly. "I cannot see how I would get to where *you* are from here."

Cliopher smiled wryly. "Yes. I can see that, Kip—you do go by Kip?"

Kip inclined his head. "And what shall we call you?"

Cliopher met his eyes squarely. "We have clearly made different decisions. If you do not think anyone will greatly object, I am well enough used to answering to Cliopher."

~

It was his mother's house, though his mother was not there. Dead, they told him, along with most of the oldest generations, in a pestilence that had swept through some decade previously.

Cliopher absorbed that blow, trying to hold on to the knowledge that *his* mother, his aunts and his uncles, his great-uncle, all the elder generation of lore-keepers—all of the people he expected to be alive—were alive, back home.

Back home. In his ... what was the word the scholars used? Not *world*, because one could step through certain gates—certain doorways, certain cave-mouths, certain waterfalls—and find oneself stepping from Zunidh to Alinor or Ysthar or Voonra or what-have-you.

This was Zunidh, but not *his* Zunidh.

He had a new efela with three elements to it, a sundrop cowrie and two flame pearls. If the tale of Eranui was the pattern from the *Lays* he had fallen into, then he needed to find what three tasks were specifically for him, not this other Kip, and complete them, and then he could go home. Then he *would* go home. He had to hold to that.

He made a mental note to add a Protocol for suddenly and mysteriously appearing strangers from ... other places ... when he got back.

Rhodin would no doubt be pleased.

~

They went downstairs, into the front parlour his mother had rarely used, and Cora and Jordo went for refreshments. Cliopher was glad of the water and sliced papaya, even if what he wanted was coffee.

Well, no. What he *wanted* was tea, but that was an extravagant habit embarrassing to admit.

Once settled downstairs, he told the story of his life to this strange audience.

All the beginnings were the same, though there was a deep, old, still-sharp grief in the other Kip's eyes when Cliopher mentioned Buru Tovo.

"He is gone, then, too?" Cliopher asked, his heart twisting.

"He sailed off one day. The old custom, you know. Later the shamans said he was sailing Sky Ocean with the Ancestors."

Cliopher inclined his head in compassion. He remembered the desolation he'd felt when he'd thought *his* Buru Tovo had died, when he had disappeared according (so they had all thought) to that same ancient custom. His Buru Tovo had showed up at the Palace of Stars, of all places, come to see what Cliopher was up to.

He had already hoped to seek out this place's Buru Tovo for his counsel and advice. It would be hard not to have it.

It must be terrible for the other Kip not to have had it. At least, if he had stayed here, he had had many more years directly under Buru Tovo's instruction and guidance than Cliopher himself had had, on the far side of the world.

Cliopher could not say that sometimes people had come back from sailing Sky Ocean, in the ancient legends. This Kip would know that, and be unable to state that faint and perhaps embarrassing hope; no more than Cliopher could state any of *his* faint and embarrassing hopes.

"Artorin Damara became Emperor of Astandalas," he said instead, continuing his story, ensuring his tone revealed nothing. "I conceived the ambition to join the Service."

Should he go into details? No; he could see from Kip's face that that was a private vocation. And if he *had* felt the vocation, but chosen not to go ... No.

(And oh gods—Vou'a, whose gift this mystery must be—what had happened to his Radiancy *here* ...?)

"It took me five tries to pass the examinations," he said instead, "but in the end I did, and went to Astandalas."

He paused, but Kip, meeting his eyes, nodded slowly. So he too had gone?

Cliopher began to suspect he knew what the true point of difference was, and did not like to have to admit it.

"I was in the Palace of Stars when the Fall occurred. Afterwards ... I did what I could. Wrote letters home that disappeared. Scoured all possible sources for news of the Vangavaye-ve. One day there came a ship, whose captain was an admiral in the navy, whose family had been in the Vangavaye-ve on holiday just before the Fall. She determined to sail east from Solaara, across the Eastern Ocean to Amboloyo and thence across the Wide Seas to the Vangavaye-ve."

He hesitated, and in his hesitation could see that both of them knew this was where their worlds diverged, with that decision that had seemed so impossibly hard at the time, and yet was so simple in retrospect. Kip's lips twisted with realization.

Cliopher said, very precisely, "It is the greatest regret of my life that I did not go with her."

Kip looked at him with a faint scorn in his eyes. "I did."

∼

The differences that choice had made to the world were staggering.

∼

This Kip had been hailed a hero for crossing the storm-wracked Wide Seas. He had been received with joy, that lost son who had come home through disaster, and when he had arrived home safe at last, he had vowed never again to leave.

The trade ships from the rest of the empire had stopped coming, and with them disappeared also the need to pay tithes or heed to imperial bureaucracy. Over the first years after the Fall the Vangavaye-ve had already lost several layers of Astandalan culture, and that was only exacerbated by Kip's reports of the disasters and anarchy besetting the rest of the world.

Cliopher thought back to his own return home. No one had blinked to see him wearing a grass skirt—was that because they were already running short of cloth, and so it was hardly unusual, as it had been when he was younger?

He had been so preoccupied by the travails of his own journey, the stripping of his soul, that he had barely seen ... anything. He had bitterly castigated his family and friends for seeing only the surface of himself, and seeing what they expected at that—but had he not done the same thing? Had he not assumed that because nothing *seemed* different, that it was not?

"Ghillian and I married," Kip said, with a fond smile for his wife, "and we went out to Loaloa for a couple of years. I returned to my studies under Buru Tovo, undertaking the next stages of the ceremonies and learning from Uncle Lazo as well."

Ghillian. That was easier, Cliopher thought gratefully. This was Ghillian, not his Ghilly. (Not ever his Ghilly.) She nodded. "I taught at the village school, Shaian language and history, but after a while we started to wonder why we were still trying so hard to be Astandalan."

"It's not as if Astandalas was doing anything for *us*," Kip said. "They never did." He looked at Cliopher in challenge. "You can't argue that anyone ever wanted to listen to you—me—us?"

"I think," Cliopher said, "that it's best if we think about it as if we were identical twins whose lives diverged." He would not wince for Basil and Dimiter, who were lost in this place as in his. "But yes, you're quite correct. No one ever did want to listen to a nobody from the Islands."

Not that *he* had ever let that stop him.

"Kip has been the leader in a resurgence of Islander culture," Jordo announced proudly, giving Kip a look of nearly fawning admiration. Cliopher regarded him dubiously, especially when Kip appeared to take this look at face value, for he murmured something self-deprecating.

"We'll show you," Kip said, complacent now that he was fully in command and control.

"I'd like that," Cliopher replied, knowing himself far too well to laugh.

Kip led him—them, for Ghillian, Cora, and Jordo accompanied them—on a meandering route towards Saya Dorn's old house.

The most immediately striking difference was the sheer quantity of *greenery*.

The giant banana tree blocking the guest room window was only an outpost of a near-jungle out of which buildings peeked. Flights of birds and butterflies filled the air, and the sound of birds was everywhere, accompanied by a distant, tuneful chiming of surprisingly harmonic wind chimes.

Cliopher looked around in astonished delight. The majority of the plants were edible as well as ornamental: fruit trees in multitudes, and huge perennial vegetables. The venerable mango tree in a pot outside the Mdang family house was joined by decorative-leaved sweet potato plants, their roots in their own sizeable baskets.

Somehow the floating docks on which Gorjo City was built had been extended to include entire living jungle ecosystems—was that a full-grown *breadfruit* on the roof of the Luvos' house across the way? Gradually, as he grew accustomed to the plants, he was able to take in the fact that while he knew most of the buildings he could see, they too had their differences.

In his Gorjo City the buildings of Tahivoa were usually painted in solid, definite colours: red and peach, aquamarine and lemon yellow, dusky purple and mauve. Their doors and windows were white or contrasting colours; it was inside that customary designs and carvings started to be visible.

In this city, the Islander designs had migrated outside, and to what glory! Cliopher took in the great carved facade of the Mdang family house. No longer simply painted red, now it had an elaborate frontage of wood or plaster or something of the sort carved and painted and gilded with the same design that was woven so subtly into Cliopher's clothes.

He turned, his smile no doubt incredulous, to see the smug satisfaction on the other Kip's face. Well, if this was *his* doing ... !

Something told him this Kip did not really do *subtle*.

Cliopher refused to acknowledge that it had taken him decades at court to learn any real appreciation of it himself.

(How delighted had he been to make that grand statement when he'd worn Islander finery to their version of the Singing of the Waters!)

The other Kip was fairly exuding pleasure at Cliopher's open amazement. Cliopher, a little wryly, acknowledged his own love of telling people about other things, and obligingly asked what this was all about.

Kip was, naturally, utterly delighted to tell him.

CHAPTER SEVENTEEN
ESA'A

Eranui had travelled in time and perhaps also from one ... place to another. No one had known her, on her own island, though the names of the people who were there were ones she thought she knew from the *Lays*.

(In the earliest part of the *Lays* there was a line, always ambiguous, about 'the stranger gifted in healing who came in our time of need'. It *might* have been Eranui visiting from the future, or ... it might not.)

Five shells, Eranui had been given. Five tasks to complete. Five gifts *she* had been given.

Even as he marvelled at the changes in the city, Cliopher was thinking hard.

∼

Like the Mdang house, Saya Dorn's was graced by the addition of a carved facade. This one owed much to Eastern Wide Seas storyboards—it immediately put Cliopher in mind of the one Alun and Nala had in their house—and even as Kip stopped to speak to some men sitting outside, Cliopher stopped to regard it and read the story there depicted.

The central image was the double ring that traditionally designated the Vangavaye-ve. Spaced around it were any number of scenes, each anchored by the emblems of the great families. A rising—or perhaps *setting*?—sun at the top probably indicated simultaneously the departure from Astandalas, the ancient story about the third son of Vonou'a, who brought home fire and the other arts of civilization from the House of the Sun, and the equally ancient tradition that the ancestors had come from the west and sailed east towards the rising sun before turning and following the sun's path to their home in the Islands to the west.

It was magnificent: as a work of art, as a piece of propaganda, as a celebration of Islander culture, as a demonstration of Mdang influence. For though all the great lineages and many smaller ones were represented with their emblems, seeds or sails or spears or drums, the familiar pattern of parallel wavy lines and dots that represented the fire was the most prominent.

"What do you think?" Ghillian asked.

"It's splendid. What is the house being used for?"

"We repurposed it for our longhouse," Kip said, bustling back over to them and giving Cliopher a look of triumph that was brutally direct. "Would you like to see inside?"

"Yes, please," Cliopher replied mildly, stifling laughter.

It *was* much more appealing than his offices in the Palace, he could say that.

Unlike Cliopher, whose own laws about the preservation of historic buildings affected what he could do with the architecturally significant house he had bought for himself, this Kip had not felt any compunction about modifying the space for his needs.

Cliopher looked at everything carefully, storing up notes of a few felicitous decorations or colour choices (he would not have thought of that bright teal for the entrance hall, but it set off a collection of Western Ring yam masks to perfection). He did not know when he might be suddenly returned home: Vou'a alone might know why he was here, and he would be the one to decide when Cliopher had fulfilled whatever mission it might be.

The ground floor was still a maze of haphazard divisions, disguising the original clean lines. It was dim as they walked through the building, and although people were certainly aware of his foreign clothes none of them remarked on his resemblance to Kip. He saw a cousin or two in the clusters—for there were many people there, talking and presumably doing some form of work—and caught murmurs in Islander of the velioi, and something about trade negotiations, before they were outside in the back courtyard.

Velioi. Trade negotiations. The faintest possible whiff of disgruntlement.

Cliopher had traded a great promise to the Son of Laughter for the efevoa. To have the sundrop cowrie on the new efela here suggested a connection.

He had not seen anything else. Gorjo City had always been a jewel, but this ... Esa'a, as it was now, was ... splendid.

Undoubtedly there were downsides to Kip's revolution. There always were. Aioru's vision for what he could do, for what the world could be, showed that well enough. But were those *Cliopher's* tasks to remedy?

He did not want one of his tasks here to be the construction of a world government. He wanted to go *home*.

He blinked back any prickling in his eyes and tried to memorize the good things he was seeing.

The courtyard was shared with the house opposite, forming a sort of private area with access on one side to a small inlet leading onto the nearest canal. In Cliopher's universe the courtyard was paved and boring; the people across the way had a jumble of useful things by their door, potted plants and a patio table and a washing line, and Cliopher's side had a bathing-house.

The bathing-house was still there, and some of the paving. The rest was utterly transformed.

Cliopher turned slowly about, taking it all in. He didn't bother hiding his interest and astonishment: it was a glorious place.

The space was oriented around a stone hearth in the centre, which held what looked like a more or less permanent fire burning merrily on it. Low woven platforms surrounded the fire, with a few wind and shade awnings strategically placed. Beautifully stacked wood encircled the seats and provided fuel as well as a visual delineation of the space. That was the centre: the fire of civilization.

The rest of the courtyard was crammed full of a riot of food plants and flowers.

"This is the heart of the new Esa'a," Kip told him, just a trifle smugly. "Esa'a is the Islander name for Gorjo City."

He made a small grimace as he said *Gorjo*. Cliopher smiled politely in acknowledgement, not saying that he knew what Esa'a referred to, or that actually 'Gorjo' referred to a short-lived brilliant star—a supernova, his Ghilly's brother, an astronomer, had told him when he'd asked what the references in a few Astandalan texts could possibly mean—which had been visible even during daylight for the full three-week period of that Singing of the Waters when it was decided to make a permanent settlement on the shores of Mama Ituri's Son.

It was true that people usually took 'Gorjo' to be a corruption of the first Astandalan's governor's name, which was Gorgen, and thus not an Islander word at all. Cliopher only knew the truth from a single line in the *Lays* and an extensive study of Astandalan tax records. This Kip would not appreciate being corrected, he was quite sure.

"It's magnificent," he said honestly. "How do you get all the plants to grow so well, given that this is all built on floating docks and there isn't soil or fresh water?"

Ghillian answered him, with vast technical details about soil and raised beds and compost and grey water re-use and desalination systems. Cliopher could follow her descriptions, but just barely, and was reduced to nodding and making mental notes.

A workable, *scalable* desalination program that leveraged geothermal and solar energy and didn't require burning vast amounts of coal or extremely complicated magical systems? That needed to be investigated at home—both in his Gorjo City and elsewhere in the world—Csiven was forever nearly running out of water and irritating the mountain tribes by wanting to build dams for aqueducts—not to mention water was a key concern of the Aigurxe on the Dagger Islands—

Not his concern. Not any longer. He must remember that. He had to let Aioru and the rest of the government make their own choices.

"We now produce over three-quarters of the city's food within the city itself. More, if you include fishing," Ghillian concluded proudly.

"Most impressive," he replied, looking at the courtyard again. Perhaps his Ghilly would be able to help him turn his courtyard into something like this. Except he wouldn't block the view.

Maybe his tasks were things *he* needed to learn?

That was an uncomfortably self-centred thought.

"Kip!"

Cliopher turned when he heard his sister call his name. The look on her face when she saw him was a blow to his gut.

"Good—good heavens," she stammered, hand coming up to her mouth in shock. "Jordo *said*, but I didn't imagine—"

She took a hesitant step forward, staring intently at him. Cliopher bore her scrutiny patiently, tabulating the differences between his sister and this Vinyë.

Most obviously she wore Islander clothes, which his Vinyë hardly ever did outside of important festivals. Her hair was longer—*much* longer, past her waist—and held up in great carved-shell combs. To his shock she had a tattoo around her wrist, though he couldn't identify the image. She was thinner, her face a little more intent.

"That's uncanny," she said at last, her eyes flicking from Kip to Cliopher. "You're the same, yet not the same at all. And of course your clothes ... Why are you here, do you think?"

The others all tensed, as if they felt he might have been holding out on them.

The five shells of Eranui. The three items on his new efela.

"I hope that will become clear. Of course, I expect my greatest skills are less necessary here." He gestured politely at Kip; then smiled at a thought of those whispers inside. "Unless you have any particularly fraught diplomatic negotiations going on? I am rather good at those."

⁓

After a tour of more of the city (keeping well away, he noted, from the slopes of Mama Ituri's Son, where the palace and the university were located) they ate a traditional meal—grilled fish, breadfruit, taro, sliced papaya—at the longhouse. Cliopher sat next to Cora, who whispered explanations in his ear of the people who came up to speak to Kip.

This Kip was a much more active community leader than Cliopher had ever thought was encompassed in the role of the tanà; but perhaps he was wrong.

Kip's behaviour reminded him, irresistibly and a little uncomfortably, of his own open court days. Kip here sat on a low bench beside a bonfire, not on a near-throne in court costume, but the petitions and the responses were much the same.

Cliopher watched him, and wondered.

It was true that people came to his uncle Lazo for advice, usually but not always under the guise of also getting a haircut, for Uncle Lazo was a barber as well as tanà.

But Cliopher had never been Uncle Lazo, and Uncle Lazo's approach was very different than Buru Tovo's. It was—apt—that Kip's manner should be his own.

(It was hard to imagine anyone at home treating *Cliopher* the way the people here were treating Kip. And yet ... looking at the way the other Kip was behaving, the confidence and conviction in his bearing, his gestures, his voice ... was that not at least partly Cliopher's fault? He had never *invited* anyone to treat him this way.)

He turned to Cora. "Thank you for sitting with me," he began. "I hope I am not keeping you from your usual activities?"

Cora gave him a considerably startled look, then laughed robustly. "You are *so* different!"

Why? Was it the expression of gratitude? That he had thought she might have something to do besides sit by him? That he should expect himself to be so interesting she would gladly drop all else?

He did not much like any of those inferences.

He watched as a small party arrived and engaged Kip's attention. Vinyë and Ghillian had left the fire-side earlier, taking their used dishes away, and now returned bearing trays of lime pots, betel nuts, and coffee. They set these around the grouping and then sat down, one on either side of Kip.

Cliopher was relieved to see they were obviously active participants in the conversation, even if Kip was dominating it.

Cora was still chuckling. "Oh—Cliopher! What do you think I do?"

She appeared quite earnest in her question.

"I don't know what the Cora of my world does all day, of course—I live in Solaara and do not see her all the time. She's a professor in the department of anthropology and history at the university. A specialist in ancient parahë and traditional boat construction techniques. She's been working to restore a traditionally made canoe that was ... abandoned ... after being sailed across the Wide Seas, as a sort of practical project with her students."

He stopped there. He did not want to say it was *his* boat. This Cora's face had flashed through a number of expressions: wistfulness, regret, pride, satisfaction, wonder.

"We still have the university, I suppose, but I left it when I divorced Bertie—too awkward! Besides, by then Kip had begun the cultural revolution. Ghillian was in the thick of it, of course, at his side, and it was so exciting to be part of something so big, so grand, so wonderful. And I'm good at organizing people!"

"I haven't seen Bertie," he asked tentatively, wondering greatly about this 'cultural revolution'. A renaissance was one thing, but a *revolution* suggested a certain amount of violence.

"Bertie? Are you still friends, then? I haven't talked with him for ages. Our Kip had a huge row with him, oh, years ago. It was about the university, actually. Kip got it into his head that it was too much an Astandalan thing, and thought it should be shut down entirely. Bertie disagreed."

Cliopher felt a strong rush of pride in his friend. Who was not *his* Bertie, of course.

His Bertie was still fully willing to tell Cliopher when he was wrong.

He shifted in his seat, watching Kip gesture grandly; the men talking to him laughed, and one accepted the bowl of betel Ghillian handed to him. That was an Islander custom Cliopher personally disliked. The narcotic drug, while admittedly fairly mild, stained the teeth black and made saliva red as blood, which he found disturbing.

Cora was shaking her head again, but when he quirked his eyebrows at her inquisitively she ignored the unspoken question and continued on the subject of Bertie.

"Yes—it was a frightful argument. Horribly divisive in the community. All the people who wanted to go back to the old ways on the one side, and those who wanted to keep the Imperial culture on the other. For a while there we feared it would become violent, but in the end Kip compromised, and let them do their own thing."

"But he never forgave Bertie?" Cliopher asked quietly. Was *this* one of his tasks?

She stilled, and turned to look at him: her face was very serious. "I admire Kip very much," she told him. "He is a truly great man: a visionary. Smart enough and strong enough to bring his visions to reality. I share those visions, those dreams. I think life is better—bolder, brighter—more beautiful, more glorious, more splendid —than it was before Kip came home and said we should stop trying to be imitation Shaians and start being *Islanders*. I am proud to have been part of that."

Cliopher could not deny the thrill that went down his spine at her words, at the idea that his other self had been such an artist as that.

His own orderly bureaucracy was efficient and effective and reasonably good government; but it was not *splendid*.

Cora was not done. He waited silently until she decided to speak forth the obvious criticism.

"You are so amiable," she said. "I wonder ..."

Cliopher said nothing. At length she continued.

"Kip has never forgiven Bertie, and I don't think he's ever compromised to that extent again, either. Not that he experiences much opposition nowadays. We've all seen how great his ideas are ... and of course, no one can forget that temper! Not very many people are as brave as poor old Bertie, standing up to Kip's tongue."

There were many things Cliopher might have said to that, but he dared not voice them here where he was the greatest of all possible strangers.

He wondered uneasily what *his* people might say about him. He could be that intransigent, that relentless, that resistant to compromise. He might have worked hard to govern his temper and his tongue, harness that inner fire to the work before him. But had he not also had a vision of what the world might be, and refused to stop until he had brought it into reality?

Cora's eyes were on her Kip. "Of course, it is different for *you*."

He looked at Kip, too, holding court beside the fire. The scene in front of him could have occurred at any point in the five or six thousand years of Islander history. (Except that the ground on which that fire was built was no island soil, but a cunningly wrought floating dock anchored to the side of Mama Ituri's Son.)

"Because I come from another ... place?"

Cora shrugged. "Maybe. You are a Mdang. You Hold the Fire: you do not run from its burn, as the rest of us prudent folk do."

~

He was still thinking over Cora's words when they returned to the Mdang house. Vinyë accompanied them back, walking beside Cliopher. She asked him what her counterpart was like.

He smiled; and how was he supposed to respond to that? He had not spent much time with this woman. "Very like you, I expect," was what he said. "She's the principal cellist and director of the Gorjo City Symphony Orchestra."

This Vinyë gave him a severe look. "We do not continue the art forms of our imperial conquerors."

Well—that was a difference.

"The Islanders were never conquered," he returned automatically, if in his habitual mild tone.

She nodded approvingly. "True. But culturally speaking the conquest was *savage*."

Cliopher had seen the places of Zunidh which the Astandalan armies had *conquered*, and most of them had no hope whatsoever of any true cultural renaissance that was not wholesale reconstruction from imperial accounts of said conquest. The people who had once dwelled on the Csiven coast were extinct, mere names in the histories. Nor had he ever met anyone from coastal Jilkano who could even name the languages their ancestors had spoken before the coming of the Empire and its colonists.

The Vangavaye-ve had experienced a certain degree of cultural imperialism, certainly, and strong influence. But its very remoteness had protected it. Not to mention that the Islanders had joined voluntarily with Astandalas as allies. They had always looked on the emperors with a certain ... interest, perhaps, he could say. There was always the hope that *this* emperor would be like Aurelius Magnus, whom Elonoa'a had loved.

(Oh, what had happened to that emperor whom Cliopher loved? What had his Radiancy become, without Cliopher at his side? He could see something of what *he* might have become, without his Radiancy to stand beside.)

"I burned my cello in the great bonfire of the artefacts we had," this Vinyë said proudly. "That was a fine and splendid day! We burned all the things that had come from the empire on the old palace grounds."

Cliopher was more than a little troubled by the fanatical gleam in this Vinyë's eyes. He had never really thought of the characteristics he shared with his sister, except insofar as she had channelled her stubbornness into music, and thus excelled in her sphere. But this—

She went on, describing the heady days of the early revolution, the persuading and convincing of the reluctant, the mobs that had captured the remaining government officials and seized their paperwork and money.

"And what did you do with the officials?" he asked.

"Those that would, joined us. Those that wouldn't ..." She shrugged unconcernedly.

"Some went to the Apologists who stayed at the university," Cora said, with a glance at Kip.

His face darkened, but he said nothing, merely greeting Jordo as the other man came up.

Cora went on. "Others went to live along the Ring—the Epalos are Apologist too, and some went with the merchants back across the ocean."

"And good riddance," Jordo put in, apparently needing no further context. He smirked slightly. "All those whinging and cringing bureaucrats ..."

Cliopher ignored the insult, but he could not ignore the questions tumbling through his mind.

Kip and Jordo were whispering together like schoolboys, Jordo full of mischief and Kip radiating privilege and self-satisfaction in a way that Cliopher found almost unbearable to observe.

Did *he* look like that when he walked down the halls of the Palace?

"You're serious about being good at negotiating?" Kip said abruptly.

Cliopher regarded him calmly, all his mind alert. "As you are at the things you have set your mind to."

Kip scowled, but apparently had nothing to say to that. "Will you come?" he said to Ghillian and Vinyë. "We'll talk it over with the others."

Jordo went with them, leaving Cora to take Cliopher back inside the house. Cora took him back to the parlour and winked at him as she opened a cabinet at the side of the room (not an imperial artefact?) and pulled out a bottle of rum, which apparently was not an imperial artefact either.

"I think you might need this," she said slyly.

Cliopher did not disagree. It was good black rum.

Cliopher sat down in a chair opposite the one Cora chose (no squatting? That would be the traditional posture) and sipped at his drink. He congratulated himself on managing to get through nearly the entire day without losing his temper, breaking into laughter, or having an hysterical fit on account of being thrown into another *place* where his other self was—

"Oh, there you are!" Cora cried happily as the door behind him opened. Cliopher's train of thought was interrupted, and he moved to set his glass down so he could greet whoever this was.

"Come and meet the other Kip—Cliopher, that is—"

The person came in: a man tall and with touches of grey at his temples, unselfconscious in his grass skirt, daubs of paint on his hands that did not seem to be deliberate.

Vinyë's decades-dead husband Erwin stood there before him.

The glass fell from his suddenly nerveless fingers and his breath stopped dead in his throat.

Cora said, "So you're not *totally* impervious, then."

And at that Cliopher's equanimity *did* break.

～

Like Jordo, Cliopher had no recent interactions with Erwin to go on. Unlike Jordo, Cliopher had liked and cared for his sister's husband a great deal. His death in a fishing accident had been a grave blow, the worse because Cliopher had learned about it by letter and had been unable to come home until the sagali feast a year later.

Once he was sure Cliopher had recovered, Erwin heaved an ostentatiously disappointed sigh. "Here I was, all excited to find out what I was like in your world, and then I turn out to be dead in it. Just my luck! Well, it's deeply strange to meet you, Kip—oh, Cliopher?—Cliopher, then."

Cliopher laughed rather more normally. Had he forgotten Erwin's sense of humour? How many evenings had they spent drinking and laughing together?

Or was it just that everyone else here had been so earnest?

He had been other places where there had been relatively recent revolutions, cultural and otherwise. The people there had all been extremely *earnest*, too.

Erwin settled himself down. He was not especially tall but was otherwise a big man, like this Kip both muscled and with a comfortable belly.

"Are you still a fisherman?" Cliopher asked.

"I do fish," Erwin replied, grinning. "Who doesn't? But not as a commercial enterprise, no. Turns out I have a bit of a talent for designing holulenui—er—"

"The house facades? I've been admiring them! Did you do the one for this house? Or the Esa'a longhouse? They're magnificent!"

Erwin nodded proudly. "I like these big projects. Fishing was always one day at a time, you know? Maybe a few days' planning, if I wanted to go across the Bay or something. But these! It takes months to work through all the elements and how to place them ... Such a great puzzle. And Vinyë's happier that I'm here. She had a hard time with our third, and the storms were so bad that year ..."

In Cliopher's world, there had been no living third child for his sister, and her husband had died in one such bad storm. There had been no discovery that Erwin had a talent for carving anything more than fishing lures or canoe prows, nor that he liked big projects.

Cliopher liked big projects. He would have loved being able to talk over that with his brother-in-law.

"And then, of course," Cora murmured, with a sly glance at Erwin, "Kip was very pleased you were taking on an old tradition and making something new and grand out of it."

"One must minister to genius, of course."

Surely he was not ... earnest?

Cliopher had never subscribed to that philosophy; he did not believe in genius as a singular phenomenon. There were individuals of talent and vision, who should be supported, of course. But so should those who were happily a part of the usual and did not have grand plans be supported, too. And those who were not *happy* needed more support, didn't they? Especially if it were physical or mental or emotional illness. And ...

Well, everyone, in short. That was why he'd instituted a *universal* annual stipend. You never knew what was hiding in someone's heart.

Look at Rhodin with his dinosaur soulmates.

Look at his Radiancy being actually *Fitzroy Angursell*.

He sipped his rum and was able, after a moment, to smile at Erwin with unfeigned pleasure. "Taking something old and making it new and magnificent is an admirable calling."

It was no longer up to him to write *policies* for such. But as tanà—

"So, Cliopher," Erwin said, leaning forward curiously. "How did I die?"

CHAPTER EIGHTEEN
TWO PEARLS AND A SHELL

I t had been mid-afternoon when Cliopher woke up in the other Esa'a. It was now the next morning, and he was antsy.

What could it mean, he wondered over and over, in his world, if his people sought to be not ersatz Shaians but true Islanders?

(If the tanà showed the community what it meant to be an Islander, what did, what *could*, Cliopher himself show? What kind of tanà would *he* be?)

It was some time before dawn. With the banana obscuring the view he could not tell quite when, but it was definitely still dark. He picked his way silently to the bathhouse, his silk robe over his arm. He'd wandered around Gorjo City—Esa'a—all day yesterday in his under-layer, aware that even in his Gorjo City it would look merely foreign.

He was, nevertheless, glad to have been given the robe by Ghillian when she came back from whatever meeting the other Kip had held. It had gotten wet, she'd told him, and they'd hung it to dry in the shade and forgotten about it in the excitement.

He bathed, knowing now why it was soap-nuts rather than any other sort of toiletries in the bathhouse. It was good, he reflected as he dried himself with a twist of banana leaf, just as if he were visiting his relatives on Loaloa. It was good to be clean. It was good to be sufficient without depending on necessities from outside. It was good that the people here were so *proud* of being Islanders.

The Mdang bathhouse was attached to the back of the house. Cliopher walked out its side door to take in the air of the courtyard on the back. The banana took up much of one side, but there was a clear space with a bench to look out on what he'd always thought of as the perfect view. Half a dozen houses all aligned to frame a long vista to Tahivoa lagoon and the distant rim of the southeastern barrier islands.

The sky was a deep, luminous blue. Cliopher stood looking down the view, barefoot, the silk robe whispering in a gentle breeze that rustled the banana leaves. The comet was perfectly visible, pointing straight down the Wake towards him.

Towards *them*.

He turned at a faint noise, barely audible, to see that the other Kip was sitting on the bench.

Cliopher stepped aside, hesitated, and approached him. "I apologize for interrupting your view."

Kip was silent for a moment. There was not really enough light to see his expression, though Cliopher's eyes had adjusted well enough not to trip over large objects.

Then: "It was hardly your doing that your life was interrupted to interrupt mine."

Cliopher smiled involuntarily. "No."

"Will you sit?"

It was the most conciliatory the other Kip had been. Cliopher sat down, and they looked at the comet in silence.

"I suppose it is the same year for us," Cliopher said, and at Kip's inquisitive noise indicated the comet. "He'eanka was visible for me, too."

Kip took a sharp breath. "You have a stressful ... job?"

"It was, yes. It has its ... compensations."

Compensations. Consolations. *Joys.*

Cliopher had not spent his lifetime away from home for no good reason.

The other Kip chuckled softly. "Louya told me the comet would bring something strange and wonderful for me. I'd thought it was just the velioi come for the trade negotiations."

"Cousin Louya?"

"Yes—she's a seer, you know."

Cliopher held his tongue for a moment. "I didn't," he said softly.

"Yes. She receives dreams from Ani ... Doesn't she in your ... place?"

"I haven't heard anyone say so."

"You should ask her," Kip suggested, his tone very much that of the tanà. "She only worked it out here after the revolution, when everyone was talking over the old traditions and what those who hadn't studied them already wanted to do. The shamans taught her."

All those letters, strange theories and stranger convictions ... but there was always that hint, that unshakable intuition, that there was a kernel of truth in them, like the sand-grain at the heart of a pearl.

"I'll ask her, when I go home," he said, something of a promise, and they fell silent.

It was a long time later—long enough that there was the sky was growing paler and the comet had nearly faded—when Kip said, "Why did you not take that ship?"

Cliopher breathed in, out. There were so many birds in this version of Esa'a. He'd always thought there were plenty in his Gorjo City, but it was not like this.

How he missed *nature* in the Palace.

He spread his hands on his knees, smoothing out the silk. It felt good under his hands. Familiar.

Was it so bad, how much he wanted to *win* against this other version of himself?

And yet, what could he say? The truth was ... hard to say.

He glanced up at the faint smudge of the comet. Hard, but not impossible, and ...

and he had come to wonder, during his time in this *other place*, just how often Kip actually spoke hard and uncomfortable truths about himself.

His Bertie had apologized to him, roughly and awkwardly, months after he had spoken the words he regretted. Cliopher could follow his example, and speak a hard truth to his other self.

Cliopher took a breath, and said, as if it were easy, "I was afraid."

"I don't believe you."

The words were simple, almost without heat: puzzled.

This was himself, if he'd made another decision. Himself, if he'd chosen a different path, a different ke'ea.

Himself, if he'd not had his Radiancy, Rhodin, Conju, Ludvic, in his life.

Himself, if he'd ... given his all to the Ring.

Cliopher looked up at the faint smudge that was all that remained of He'eanka. He could have had this. This Gorjo City, this Esa'a, where the Islanders were proud and merry and *splendid*, where they had taken what was old and tired and traditional and made it new and living and thriving. He could have had that marriage to Ghilly, that closeness with Vinyë and Erwin, that devoted friend in Jordo, the respect and admiration of all those who came to ask the tanà for advice.

And—he knew himself—he could have had the broken friendships with Bertie and Toucan, the distance from his cousins, the sharpness of tongue to go with his sharp wit. For this other Kip did not speak to the entirety of the Ring, did he? He had landed his boat here on Mama Ituri's Son, and refused to sail on.

Cliopher had very nearly decided not to sail on.

He breathed in through his nose, measured and even, just as if he sat in the Council of Princes; as he should have, whenever he faced the tribunal of his gathered family, their teasing and their love and their concern that he had broken himself in his long time away. Grown ... sun-sick, as it were.

He thought back to those hard years in the Palace after the Fall, when his Radiancy had been a sleeping mystery at the heart of it all, and all things had seemed suspended, unable to move forward or to change or be resolved while he lay there insensate and silent.

"I was doing good things there," Cliopher said honestly, his voice quiet. "I was afraid at what destruction the Fall might have wreaked here. I'd lit that fire and it seemed important, I suppose, to tend it ..."

He trailed off. He'd been afraid. He didn't have any excuses, not really. He'd been afraid.

"What fire?" the other Kip asked, almost inaudibly. Then, much more intently: "*What fire?*"

Cliopher turned to stare at him, though it was not light enough to see more than a reflected gleam on the other man's (his other self's) eyes.

"The first fire after the Fall," he said, surprised. "You know—the one in the kitchen. After I woke up—we woke up—I went to the cafeteria and there were so few people, and the cook came in crying because all the stoves were magic and had gone out ..."

Kip was silent. Too silent. Cliopher's heart started to beat faster. Had *this* been the difference? Not the ship, but the choice to light a fire, or not?

Even as he thought that, he knew it must be true.

He had come so close to giving up. So close to saying *this is where I stop*, and turning his back on the world. So close to closing his eyes, choosing the easier way. The lesser way.

So close to looking at an impossible dream and turning away from even attempting to realize it.

His hand came up in that ancient unconscious motion he'd tried so hard to train himself out of, and grasped for the obsidian pendant of his efela ko.

He touched the smooth lump of the sundrop cowrie instead, and he swallowed as his hand curved around it.

He wrenched his mind back to the horrible time after the Fall. The other Kip had left behind that ke'ea so long ago he probably did not even remember it.

"I went to the kitchens," he said, his mouth very dry. "They were carrying on in their fear and uncertainty."

"Someone said that they should barricade the doors and hoard the food," the other Kip said, his voice flat.

"Yes," Cliopher breathed as the memories stirred. "I'd forgotten ... you're right, that thin boy. He was so afraid ... He was from Voonra, did you know? Somewhere in the north ... he'd heard the story of Dimiter crossing the Northern Wastes ..." He breathed more easily. "He calmed down after the fire was lit. The cook set him to chopping something and he settled down with a job to do. He ended up the second chef for the Palace kitchens, in the end, I think, and when we managed to re-establish diplomatic relations with Voonra he came with us—I was one of the embassy—to be our cook, then learned his family had survived and went to join them."

It was good to remember something good from those days, when everything had been so terrible.

(It was good to remember that once one started on the ke'ea, star led to star, and one could learn the ways of even an unfamiliar sea, as Elonoa'a had been said to ...)

He turned at a choked noise. It was just light enough that he could see that the other Kip was grim-faced and staring.

Cliopher's half-smile faded. He held himself still for a moment, forcing himself to look at this as a stranger who needed comfort or assistance, not his other self.

His other self did not seem likely to be any better at receiving comfort than Cliopher was himself.

"You didn't listen to their fear and hate," the other Kip whispered.

"There was a cold hearth and a fire to be lit," Cliopher said, not quite gently.

"I turned away."

Cliopher could not find it in his heart to feel any of the scorn the other Kip had shown him when they'd both thought it was the ship going home that was the point of difference. He knew precisely how evenly balanced that decision had been: his own fear and desperation echoing louder and louder as the kitchen staff argued the fundamental questions of when self-care became selfishness.

(And he knew how *close* he'd been, this past fortnight, to making the same mistake.)

He could not say, *it is the office of the tanà to light the fire that needs to be lit*. The other Kip knew that perfectly well.

(What fire did *he* need to light? Cliopher hardly dared let himself speculate. Not here, not now, here in this *other place*, this Esa'a that was not his Gorjo City, sitting beside this Kip who was not himself.)

Somewhere on the other side of the world the terminator line of sunset was passing over the Palace even as the leading edge of dawn rose over the Vangavaye-ve.

Sama, the Wind That Rises At Dawn, blew over them, bringing with her the scent of salt and the distant cries of the seabirds from the Outer Ring cliffs.

"It is a beautiful thing you have built here," Cliopher offered sincerely.

The other Kip did not look at him. His face was set, his eyes brilliant with unshed tears as he stared unseeing into the bright line of the horizon.

And then he swallowed, and he set his shoulders, and he said in a tolerably composed voice, "I will take you to meet the velioi negotiators and we will see what *you* can do, Tanà Cliopher."

They wove their way through the jungle-green and exuberantly decorated city, past people dressed in feathers and shells and paint and elaborately dyed and plaited grass skirts, past any number of Islander canoes. When they came out of the houses to the wider expanse of the Paloa lagoon, which was where the ocean-going ships had always moored, Cliopher was expecting to see some sort of modern revival of the ancient parahë.

Along with a ship of a design so familiar at first he didn't realize it was strange for it to be there, there were three, but they were not as big as he had always thought—certainly not as long as the one that had been buried in state as if it were a chief, which his Cora had carefully excavated, nor the remnants of the *Au'o'eakanë* he had last seen in the museum in Solaara.

This Cora was, alas, not with them this morning. And Kip had been resolutely polite and resolutely saying very little. Cliopher said to the air, "Can you tell me about the parahë?"

"They're filuhë," Jordo stated importantly. "It's the improved modern design. They're used all around the Ring nowadays."

Bringing rum and sugar and Nijani flax fibre, if not cotton and linen and food, Cliopher surmised.

"Where else do you sail them?" he asked curiously.

"Where would we need to go?" Jordo asked, apparently seriously.

Cliopher looked at Kip, who lifted his chin just the way Cliopher did when he was refusing to be embarrassed. "There hasn't been any need to trade outside the Ring," he said, and Cliopher was sure he did not imagine the faint thread of shame that they did not go farther, as their ancestors so splendidly had. "Some of the more liberal have expressed a desire for metal tools and a few other things from outside, and so when the velioi came in sight we agreed to entertain them and enter into discussions."

"That's their ship, I take it?"

Kip frowned at it. "One of them. The other's anchored around past the old opera house."

Cliopher nodded as they proceeded not towards the opera house but cut across through the old business and hotel district towards the palace grounds. The ship's flag was limp, and the ship quite far into the lagoon (had they not dredged it recently? His cousin Quintus' ship could moor right at the wharves), but not so far that Cliopher did not catch the familiar white-and-black flag.

Thus when they reached what had been a gently sloping lawn and was now yet another food garden and met the velioi party, Cliopher was not *wholly* surprised to find his lord among them.

~

Not surprised, no.

Shocked, on the other hand—

~

This other place's Artorin Damara was in the centre, flanked by people Cliopher knew (and did not know): Ser Rhodin—not in a guard's uniform but a courtier's—Ludvic and another senior guard (Hiscaron? In Cliopher's world he had injured his leg at some point and now trained the new recruits under Rhodin's aegis); three courtiers who were obviously far more important here than they'd ever become in Cliopher's world, but by their postures and clothing, not so important he needed to pay them special attention.

Cliopher and Kip were in the centre of their group. They stopped before the Last Emperor's party, and Cliopher—under the habit of decades of practice, and more recent hours with the Master of Etiquette—went down into the formal genuflection appropriate to his station.

He felt the surprise of the Vangavayens beside him; and saw it in the hesitation before this Artorin Damara made the gesture releasing him from his bow.

Cliopher rose, deciding on his address, and met this lord who was not his lord's eyes as calmly and patiently as ever he did at home.

(And this stern man before him, cold and remote, was *also* Fitzroy Angursell?)

Artorin Damara's eyes widened when Cliopher met them without hesitation or flinch, but his expression was otherwise entirely of grave interest. His eyes slid to Kip; Cliopher automatically angled himself in response so he could see both of them and was slighting neither.

"Tanà Mdang we have met," Artorin Damara said, his voice in his most court-formal accent. "But you, sir, are a stranger to us despite the obvious practice of your courtesy. And though we note that the magic is very strange about you, nonetheless we do not see that you have any of the power indicated by your style."

Cliopher bowed in a high courtier's acknowledgement. "My name also is Cliopher Mdang," he said upon rising upright. "I am, however, the Cliopher Mdang of another ... place, where a certain decision was differently made. No doubt it is the magic of my home that you see, Glorious and Illustrious One."

Artorin Damara's interest sharpened, the weight of it the familiar strength of his Radiancy's magic, but not as friendly, not at all. Not precisely *unfriendly*, either,

Cliopher took care to note, but certainly wary and—in the most basic sense —judgmental.

(Oh, what had *happened* to this man, without Cliopher to joke with him?)

"And so," the Last Emperor said, "that one decision had great repercussions? Knowing Tanà Mdang's influence here, we are not astonished to hear it."

The truth was going to hit the other Kip harder than Cliopher liked after their conversation this morning, but he had no intention of refusing to answer this version of his lord.

"Indeed, Glorious One," he replied therefore, choosing his words carefully. "After the Fall the Cliopher Mdang of this world chose to return home and devote his attention to the Vangavaye-ve, and as a result this city, this people, this archipelago, are at a height of culture and influence unknown since the days of our Paramount Chief Elonoa'a and your Radiancy's illustrious ancestor, the emperor Aurelius Magnus."

"And you?"

"I chose to return to Solaara and devote myself to the question of a peaceful, effective, and stable world government."

Ser Rhodin and the other courtiers' attention sharpened intensely. Artorin Damara's face went that slightly more pronounced blankness that suggested he was surprised.

"And what titles do you hold in your world, sir?"

Cliopher bowed again. "I have the honour of being the Hands of the Emperor. I recently handed over my titles of Secretary in Chief of the Offices of the Lords of State, Head of the Imperial Bureaucratic Service, and Lord Chancellor of Zunidh. In my lord's current absence, I am Viceroy of Zunidh in his stead."

There was a lengthier pause. Cliopher did not look around or away, simply held himself with as unshakable a confidence as he could muster.

"We take it," Artorin Damara said at last, "that our own counterpart values you highly."

Cliopher did not, of late, bow to his lord anywhere near this often, but this was a formal occasion, however unusual, and he knew the rules. And this was not *his* lord. He bowed to acknowledge the compliment. "I am honoured by my lord's regard."

Artorin Damara smiled very slightly and inclined his head. "We have been greatly impressed by Tanà Mdang's intelligence and character. We expect that if you possess the same characteristics and have directed them to diplomacy, we should find your advice invaluable."

"The political situation on my world is naturally somewhat different, Glorious One; and yet I serve the people of Zunidh as best I can."

"We are sure of it. Have you any sense of your purpose in being here?"

Cliopher met the lion eyes, as was his long habit, and saw the surprise breaking over this Artorin Damara. He smiled, court-polite. "I have often been sent places for my skill at negotiation, Glorious One."

∾

It had not precisely been an *argument*, with the Other Kip, that morning.

Somehow that pre-dawn conversation had felt like a challenge-song. And Cliopher had to admit he had always, always, risen to those.

(When he went home, he—he—he *would* not let the fact that he was not one of the Red Company and a legend on five worlds stop him.)

❧

He was, it was true, very good at negotiations. And though none of these people knew him, he knew them; or at least he knew much *of* them.

It turned out that the negotiations were not simply between the government represented by this Artorin Damara (who was not, *not*, Cliopher's Radiancy, not at all), because—

Because, as there had been no Cliopher Mdang refusing ever to give up, no Cliopher Mdang given some indefinite length of time that might or might not have been hundreds of years, no Cliopher Mdang given also the unwavering support of his lord —because of those things, there was no world government.

The Palace party represented the magical governance of the world, which was almost but not quite entirely separate from the political governance, and then there were the two expanding kingdoms of Kavanduru and Jilkano who had met here to discuss their borders with the people who had always held the Wide Seas as their own.

Jilkano was represented by a shrewd old woman, the matriarch of the princely family of Haion City in both versions of Zunidh and the dowager queen of the Jilkanese imperium in this one.

She was perhaps a touch more respectful than Cliopher had ever found her, in his experience: she told him that he was not anywhere near so handsome as his counterpart, then cackled wildly and tried to get fifteen clauses past him.

Prince Rufus was not that different, for all that here he called himself a king.

It was all Cliopher could do not to laugh outright when he heard that the capital of Rufus's new kingdom was called Rufopolis.

❧

He had been given a challenge, and he had not forgotten that when Eranui had finished the tasks she had been sent to do, she was able to return home.

He had borne looking at the off-set mirror of himself that was the other Kip. He had been curious to learn about the cultural revolution, all the splendid things that had been achieved, all the magnificent ideas brought into reality, the ones still being spun into existence. He had been pleased to see other sides of Ghillian and Cora and Vinyë—and, he could admit, even Jordo had begun to grow on him; the man was very easy company—and he was delighted to spend the time with Erwin.

But oh, it hurt to have Rhodin and Ludvic look at him as a stranger. It had been distressing to be extensively interrogated by Rhodin as to his ontological status and purpose. It had been painful for them to look at each other in confusion when he'd asked about Conju; Rhodin had eventually said that there was a great perfume and fashion house called An Vilius in Solaara.

It was impossible to look at Artorin Damara and see a stranger looking back.

~

It took him a day and a half to finish the negotiations.

~

After the signing of the new treaty the air felt different; Cliopher's skin felt different. Tingly, almost, and tight. He wondered if it was the magic calling him home, and hoped so dreadfully. He had taken to fiddling with at the new efela, rubbing the sundrop cowrie, holding the flame pearls until they warmed in his hand.

Three shells (one of the words for *bead* was the same as for *shell*), three tasks, three gifts.

Three shells: the sundrop cowrie and the two pearls.

Three gifts: Erwin—this glimpse of what it could mean to be Islanders in truth—and oh, this example of what it might mean to be a certain sort of tanà. It was not the way Cliopher wanted to be, when he went home, but Kip was as solid and brilliant an example in his way as Uncle Lazo or Buru Tovo.

He could only count two tasks. One had to have been that conversation with the other Kip, the comet shining down on them with that ancient story hovering in the air. The second was surely the treaty negotiations.

And the third—

He frowned down at the efela in his hands, and put it back around his neck. It was late afternoon, nearly sunset, and he knew the velioi party liked to walk in the jungle-grown palace gardens as the night flowers began to bloom.

He could not leave Artorin Damara like that, without at least *trying*. He was not, after all, the Kip Mdang who had turned his back on the Palace and all within it and learned to be content within the circle of the Ring.

Cliopher had been sitting outside Saya Dorn's old house, watching Kip be the kind of tanà who was the centre of the community. It no longer seemed quite so ... impossible.

After a while, he inserted himself between conversations and told the other Kip where he was going.

His counterpart regarded him steadily. "Your last task?"

"I hope so."

"I imagine you want to go home."

Cliopher ducked his head, as if that would hide all the complicated meaning of *home* from this man who was, and was not, himself. "I do."

Kip was quiet for a long moment. "May the winds be favourable and the seas kind."

"And may your ke'ea be bright and clear," Cliopher replied, and they looked at each other for a long, silent moment, before the other Kip reached out and for the first time they touched, hand to hand and forehead to forehead in the ancient custom.

They did not go up in flames and ash, but Cliopher's heart was hammering hard in his throat when he turned and left his other self standing beside the great fire-pit at the heart of his Esa'a.

~

He could feel the tug of home, like his island in his mind.

This world's Loaloa was to the west. In his mind his island was far, far to the east.

He made his way through the familiar-unfamiliar city, boardwalk and bridge, until he reached the solid land of Mama Ituri's Son. Instead of going immediately up to the grand house that had been given to Artorin Damara's party, he turned and walked along the small stony beach facing Mama Ituri.

He took off his sandals and stood at the edge of the waves, the cool water tugging at his feet. In his ears was the sigh and sough of the pebbles tumbling and pushing against each other.

It was nearly sunset: the sky was gold in the west.

He turned, and as he stepped back onto the beach he hesitated at the way the light caught the stones and small white shells scattered along the beach, as if they were the finery one would choose for a great efela to warrant a place in the *Lays*.

He bent down and picked up one of the shells, one half of a clam no bigger than his thumbnail. In his hand it was something very simple, perfect, self-contained.

He stood there for another moment, listening to the pebbles as the waves tumbled them, breathing in the scent of home, and then he put on his sandals and continued on up the hill to where the lord that was not his lord waited.

~

The Lord Emperor met him in the gardens, his four guards standing at a wary distance. Cliopher knew them—Ato, Pikabe, Kulo, Aizurvenne. It was still hard that they did not know him.

"Thank you for the audience," he said politely.

Artorin Damara inclined his head. "We did not wish to miss any last words you might think to give us, when you have shown in such an exemplary fashion precisely why our counterpart holds you in such high esteem."

Cliopher bowed.

"And so?"

He looked at the four guards, standing very much in earshot. "Would you be willing to invoke the Wall of Silence, Glorious One? I think you would prefer what I have to say to be for your ears only."

The so-familiar and yet so-different eyebrow rose up, but without comment Artorin Damara raised his hand and made the gesture that invoked the spell to give them aural privacy. "Well?"

Cliopher took a deep breath, but he had been wondering how to say this from the moment he had seen the shadow in Artorin Damara's golden eyes. This was not *his* lord.

Not his friend. His ... great and good friend. This is what Artorin Damara, Fitzroy Angursell, might have become without Cliopher, as the other Kip was what Cliopher might have become without him.

They were both of them whole people, in their own ways, standing tall and proud and confident in themselves, and yet ... and yet there was such a depth of sorrow in this Artorin Damara, such a depth of loneliness in the other Kip.

Cliopher knew that longing, that sorrow, that empty hearth. It was the office of the tanà to light the fire that had to be lit: that was what he was doing here.

(And he knew that he could not now return to his own Gorjo City and let that hearth stand empty, that loneliness remain always unfulfilled. Perhaps he could not enter into legend as he had always desired, but he would not let the legend go ignorant of the hearth and home that awaited him if he ever desired it.)

"You have not asked me why I am Viceroy of Zunidh," he said.

"It seemed a matter you would explain, or not, as seemed best to you."

Oh, this man had indeed spent time with the other Kip.

Cliopher cleared his throat. This was not *his* lord, but he was ... he was still a man, and still Fitzroy Angursell, and still someone Cliopher could love.

"I am Viceroy," he said plainly, "because my lord decided to retire, and he learned that there is a traditional spell that was used by previous lords magi of Zunidh to find their successors."

He stopped there, and waited while Artorin Damara regained his composure. He was even less demonstrative than Cliopher's Radiancy: this was truly the Serenity.

But Cliopher knew him, and knew what that utter stillness meant.

And he remembered how *his* Radiancy had responded, when Ludvic first made that staggering suggestion that he might want to retire.

When Artorin Damara ceased breathing in rhythm, Cliopher continued on.

"The spell is a variant on Harbut Zalarin's Seeking Spell combined with the Eilmanii vision quests. It can be determined by careful study of *The Saga of the Sons of Morning*, and to perform it the Palace bells—which are made of the bronze hammers taken out of the city of Aurdar, I think it was, when it was conquered by Yr —must be rung at noon, and dried yarrow stalks cast. That is all I know of the spell— I am no wizard—but I am sure you could reconstruct it if you so wished."

At that Artorin Damara's lips twisted. "If we so wished."

Cliopher held onto his own composure with all the hard-won discipline of a lifetime at court.

"Secondly," he said, for this too was in three parts, "I cannot see that this would be made different by my counterpart's different decisions here, and so I tell you, Glorious One: Pali Avramapul is a scholar of Late Astandalan History at the University of Stoneybridge on Alinor by the name of Domina Black."

Artorin Damara once again went very still, but that was the only reaction he showed.

"And so? This is hardly something our guards could not have heard."

Dared he? For his lord, certainly. For this one ... oh, his heart might break.

But it was the third truth, and this man, this Artorin Damara, needed to hear it.

He met the lion eyes with as much certainty, as much compassion, as much *faith*, as he could muster.

And then he said, "The man known as Fitzroy Angursell is in an oubliette in the Palace: what I have learned, what I *know*, is that he can still be freed."

Artorin Damara's face was blank, hard rather than serene, still as a stone sculpture.

Cliopher paused a moment, and then, very delicately, he added: "When my lord set out on his quest, he wore a scarlet silk mantle."

"I think," Artorin Damara said plainly and firmly, the personal singular like a sharp knife after his usual rolling plurals, "that you have said quite enough, Cliopher Mdang."

Cliopher bowed, and at the gestured dismissal went, and hoped very much he had said the right thing to this man who was not his friend at all.

CHAPTER NINETEEN
PART OF THE WAY HOME

Cliopher woke up in his own bed.

He started sobbing with relief, and was glad no one else was immediately present to see him lose control so spectacularly.

This was *his* art on the walls, *his* Mgunaivë rug on the floor, *his* letters on the table beside him. That was the door to *his* bathroom.

He did not remember much after leaving the *other place*'s Artorin Damara. Perhaps he had returned to the Mdang house, perhaps he had thrown himself down for a rest on the guest bed he had been using, perhaps he had fallen asleep—

It did not matter. He did not care. He had fulfilled his three tasks. He was *home*.

Once the sobs subsided into hiccoughs, he rose and went into the bathroom. He did have a moment's fear that this was yet another world—

But it seemed wholly unlikely that if he were in another world where his other self had also become Viceroy of Zunidh that he would, in that case, be put in his other self's very bed.

That would *not* be in the Protocol.

No: these were his preferred toiletries, even if they were a little out of order.

Well, he could imagine his household had been a little out-of-order with his disappearance.

When he bent over to wash his face, his skull felt as if he'd stabbed it. Confused, he touched his head. There was a sore spot.

He'd hit his head.

He frowned at his fingers, as if they would tell him what had happened. Had it all been a dream? Some strange hallucination brought on by a concussion?

He looked at himself in the mirror, at first shocked to see his own face and not that of the other Kip, and then he caught sight of his efela. His *three* efela.

He touched the sundrop cowrie, the two pearls, with shaking hands.

What had happened?

He thought he'd remembered what had happened, when he woke in the other place. He put on a towelled robe and wandered towards his dressing room. They had been ... hiking, hadn't they? In the Liaau. He'd been talking with Bertie. They had gone through the tunnel, and on the other side ...

On the other side was a blank, filled only with the strangely distant memory of the other Esa'a, like a book he'd finished reading.

His mind felt as if it were swimming in murky water.

He stared at the wardrobe, frowning. His court costumes were in Féonie's care, but surely his fancy clothes had been on the *right* side, and his more ordinary wear on the *left*? And he was quite certain there had been rather *more* clothes than this, too.

A very simple garment in the Vangavayen style was laid out on the clothes rack. The current Vangavayen style. Not the new variations on the traditional he'd seen in the other Esa'a.

His head was starting to throb. What a day it was going to be, the return of the Viceroy after ...

He frowned. After what? *Had* he disappeared in body as well as spirit and mind, or had his friends here been left with an injured, comatose body?

He did not *feel* as if he'd been laying motionless for three days. But—he was the Viceroy of Zunidh. He would have been given the best possible care.

What had his Radiancy dreamed of, experienced, *felt*, when he spent that hundred years deep in a magical coma?

What dizzying hope he must have felt, waking to realize the weight of the Empire had lifted from his shoulders. Ludvic had heard him say so: the prisoner spying the cell door hanging off its hinges, light and free air just out of reach.

So, Fitzroy, do you think you've served your full sentence yet?

The face not of his lord but of that other Artorin Damara came into his mind. Sober, serene, fully in command of himself. So very, very shocked when Cliopher met his eyes.

That other place was no longer his concern. But oh, he hoped he had done the right thing, telling that Artorin Damara those three truths.

He turned back to the closet, and dithered until the bells rang the third hour of the morning. He jumped at the sound and plucked out the first items that came to hand: Solaaran-style undergarments, soft with age and care, and simple silk robes in a deep blue that was easy on his eyes.

It was, in fact, nearly identical to what he had been wearing in the other place.

Perhaps they'd meant to change him into the Vangavayen tunic and loose trews if he'd died of the head injury.

He looked at himself in the tall mirror set to one side, and felt a queer jolt as he saw once again the new efela. He adjusted the collar of the silk robes, but it was cut to show his efela, not hide them.

He did not look like the fierce and fine Kip of the other Esa'a. Cliopher looked old, and tired, and a little gaunt.

And grand, and respectable, and ...

He dropped his hand from his efela, and smiled wryly at his reflection.

It was amazing what good tailoring could do to lend—what was it Lady Ylette had said to him once, so long ago?—countenance and dignity. That was it.

He had that, at least.

And the smile made him look rather less *worn*. He'd have to remember that.

Cliopher put his shoulders back. Time to find out what had been happening in *his* world.

~

There were voices in the dining room, so he went there first. There were small changes in his rooms, things missing, perhaps, but he could not seem to focus on his surroundings.

Things didn't matter, anyway.

The door was ajar, and he stood with his hand on the frame as he drank in the sight before him.

His mother was there, alive and well, and sitting beside her was Uncle Lazo. Cliopher could only stare at them, relieved beyond words.

And there were *his* Ghilly, Bertie, Toucan—they all looked well—and Rhodin, looking just as he had in the other place, suave and sophisticated—and *his* Vinyë, smiling so much more easily than that other Vinyë had—and sitting next to Bertie, Cora.

It was Rhodin who noticed him first, of course: the guard, the spy, ever alert to doorways. He broke off whatever he was saying to Toucan and met Cliopher's eyes with a steady, curious challenge.

Cliopher could only smile and shrug helplessly: but Rhodin, remarkably, relaxed and smiled openly at him. "Cliopher!"

"Good morning!" Cliopher returned, moving immediately to embrace his mother. "Oh, I am so glad to see you! Mama—" He faltered there, for his stoic mother was weeping.

He rested one hand on her shoulder and looked at Vinyë for explanation.

"Oh, Kip, it *is* you, isn't it?" his sister asked. "Do you feel yourself?"

"Was I unconscious here?" he asked curiously. "For me it was ... Do you remember the story of Eranui and the Five Shells?"

Uncle Lazo lifted his head sharply. "I'd been wondering," he said.

"It was very peculiar," Cliopher said.

"It was very strange on our end," Toucan said fervently. "What do you—" He stopped when Rhodin put his hand on his arm. Toucan looked at him; Rhodin said, "Wait."

It occurred to Cliopher that something had clearly happened. Before he could ask, Shoänie hurried into the room, her face lighting when she saw him. "Chocolate, sir?" she asked hopefully.

"Yes, please," he replied. She burst into tears and hurried off again.

"Well," he said, nonplussed, and sat down in the chair Bertie had hastily inserted between Vinyë and his mother. "It appears strange things have been happening here, too. Are they as odd as what I've just experienced?"

Everyone looked at each other. Then Bertie spoke, his rumble so familiar that Cliopher felt a lump come into his throat. The other Kip did not have Bertie.

(Cliopher had almost lost that friendship, over the long years, but despite the attenuation and occasional argument and—and everything, they had managed to maintain it, and in the past year it had gotten stronger.)

"What do you remember of the past three weeks, Kip?"

"Three *weeks*?" Cliopher's heart seemed to congeal and stutter. What had happened if—if— He struggled to speak evenly. "It was only three days for me." His hand went to the new efela. "Three shells, three days, three tasks ..."

"The Son of Laughter has his own reasons," Uncle Lazo said quietly, looking with narrowed eyes at the efevoa.

Cliopher took several long breaths, realizing as he did so that he was imitating his Radiancy, that other Artorin Damara: breathing in a rhythm, a count of five heart-beats for each inhale, each exhale. But it did work.

Rhodin looked at him. "You don't recall anything of the past three weeks from here?"

That brought Cliopher up short. "No ... Do you mean I was here physically? How strange; I was definitely in my own body *there*." He shifted awkwardly in his seat. "Surely I wasn't unconscious the whole time? It doesn't feel as if I've spent the past three weeks on bed-rest."

"Does your head hurt?"

His hand went up to the soft, bruised, painful spot. "A little."

They looked at each other again. Cliopher watched the various expressions on the faces of his friends, his family, which were complicated.

He wished his head wasn't throbbing.

Rhodin leaned forward. "In the interests of—well, I'm curious!—will you humour me a moment?"

Cliopher was so relieved to be home he felt ready for the Merrions and their tele-pathic dinosaur soulmates. He smiled. "Gladly!"

Rhodin blinked, then carried on. "Yes, very well. Cliopher, I know it is an unhappy subject, but will you cast your mind back to the night of the Fall of Astandalas?"

Cliopher stared at him. "Yes ...?"

"Will you tell us about it?"

Rhodin had much worse memories of that night, Cliopher reminded himself: his entire family and the vast majority of his friends and acquaintances had perished in the Fall. Cliopher only ...

"As you wish," he said, after a moment. He settled himself, made sure his voice was even, calm, collected.

"I was in my room—down on the lowest floor of the Voonran wing. It was very quiet, being Silverheart, and I was feeling very sorry for myself because I hadn't been invited to any of the parties. I was sitting there reading, and then ... there was a kind of earthquake."

"And then?" Rhodin said gently, but his eyes were intent.

Shoänie brought him his chocolate, and he folded his hands around the warm cup. He closed his eyes, for the first time letting the memory rise up in full.

"It felt like I'd fallen into a dark and turbulent sea," he said, trying to be precise and unemotional. "I've often had dreams of drowning ..."

So far had he told people before. His family were around him, his dearest friends

—*most* of his dearest friends—where was Ludvic?—Conju?—Conju was probably still on holiday. And his Radiancy ...

Oh, what stories his Radiancy would have, once they could stand beside each other as friends, as equals, and Cliopher could ask the questions he had always wanted to ask, and never dared. And his Radiancy could, in return, ask for the stories he'd always carefully refrained from requiring.

He met Rhodin's eyes gravely, Uncle Lazo's more briefly. The cup was warm, comforting, in his hands.

He had always let people assume his fear of drowning came from his father's death in the sea. But it was not that, or not only that.

He took a breath, his back straight, his voice even. The room was very quiet; attentive.

"Once, when I was diving for pearls with Buru Tovo, I dove off the canoe and got caught by the breakers, pulled by a rip tide through the reef and down ... Down and down ..." He swallowed, his jaw working, feeling as if he had forgotten how to swallow. Uncle Lazo looked very serious. Perhaps Buru Tovo had told him about this.

"It was the outside of the Ring," he said, making a gesture as if to point it out. The Ring was so far away ... but oh, his island was there in his mind, a distant tether no matter how far he went. He could feel it, behind the small headache.

"The seafloor just kept going down and down, into the darkness and the cold and the pressure of the abyssal deep. I can still see it. How *cold* the water was. How strong the rip. I could not free myself ..."

He gripped the chocolate, reminding himself that he was not there, neither struggling to get out of the rip nor submerged in cataclysmic magic.

No one spoke. Rhodin's face was deeply interested, empathetic without being overt. Cliopher took another breath. He was not there. He was not.

"I was pulled down below the reef. I couldn't *see* the current, there was nothing to *see*, just the darkness and the reef and the fish darting out of the way. I remember trying to reach out, catch hold of something, scraping my hands bloody on the coral, breaking all these delicate, ghostly corals—all these silver fish flashing around me as I was pulled down—"

He'd forgotten those fish, until this moment, dull grey but catching the light in those streaks and splashes, like fireworks around him, silent and beautiful and so, so terrifying.

"It was so fast. I was caught, and down, and the coral breaking under my hands, the fish scattering, the ocean so dark a blue ... and then I slammed against something."

Someone gasped, and he dragged a breath, for he'd been holding it unconsciously, as if he were deep under the water, deep under that pressure. Someone else did the same, the air whistling through their teeth.

"A rock." Cliopher said it, then stopped, as he had stopped then. "A rock," he repeated, feeling the rough surface, slimy with algae, but firm, *solid*, stable, under his hands. He had landed on it, and his lungs had been compressed by the sudden blow, driving what air was in them out, and he had gripped that rock—

"The pressure was terrific," he said, his eyes closed, his voice falling softly into the silence. "I was so far down. The surface was so far above me—and I could not get there, there was this *force* holding me down, away, trying to cast me into the dark—"

He stopped, and laboured to take a deep breath, to remind himself again that he was not caught in that current, that magic, that awesome force.

Oh, sometimes it felt as if he had spent his entire life there, submerged under that pressure, looking up at the distant line of safety, clinging to one solid rock.

—But there had been that rock.

"When I was on the reef," he said carefully, eyes still shut—"I held onto that rock, and I remembered the passage from the *Lays*."

Someone—he thought perhaps Uncle Lazo—grunted. Someone else murmured a soft exclamation. He did not look. If he broke his story he did not think he would be able to tell it again, not in such a bright and illuminated room as this, not with—

Oh, not with his rock gone.

He dragged in another breath. "Buru Tovo had been singing them to me, the *Lays*. Teaching me the words. Teaching me the beginnings of what they meant. What they mean." He grimaced, gripping hard to this truth, won so hard. "I have spent my whole life learning what they mean."

Another little stir, a soft grunt. They must know this, surely? Surely he had *shown* them this? They had finally acknowledged that he had accomplished much in his life —had they not finally seen that when he had stood there for the viceregal ceremony it was *as* an Islander, it was *because* he was an Islander?

The other Kip had turned his back on the dead hearth in the Palace and had not lit the fire.

The other Kip had never found the rock; he had only found the sea.

The other Kip had built a ship out of the *Lays* and sailed the Vangavaye-ve to a glory it had never attained.

Cliopher had chased the viau, yes, had always run after the falling star. Always. But that was because he had found *this*.

"There was a rock, and it was solid under me, despite the ferocious pressure of the current. What is stronger than the ocean?"

That was a proverb every one of his family knew. It was Vinyë who murmured the answer: "The rock that holds fast."

A strange idea for the Islanders, so much of whose knowledge, whose lives, were shaped by the caprices and strengths and gifts and terrors of the sea. But the islands they sought were fixed stones, the rocks that held fast in their minds. Gift of Vou'a to his beloved Ani: the mystery of the shoreline and the sea.

He had never spoken of these things. Why they came out now ... well, he could guess. He turned his cup a precise quarter-turn, a thing his Radiancy did, and missed him fiercely.

His brain felt as if it were sloshing inside his skull, like bilge-water in the bottom of a canoe.

"On the reef that time, I held onto the rock, and I thought of the Rock that Holds Fast, about which the world turns. And I—I turned with that rock, I held onto it with all my strength, trusting that the *Lays* were true, that Buru Tovo had not drummed them into my head until I was dreaming them for no reason—"

Another conscious breath. Another quarter-turn of the cup. "I turned, my knee on the stone, my hands scraped raw, the current pushing my back down until I bent under its force ... until I reached the far side, the sheltered side, where the current did not run down, but *up*, through a kind of vent or chimney in the reef."

He breathed. What a lesson this had been; all of it. All of it.

He could do this. He had started the story. He could finish it.

"I pushed against the rock and the other current lifted me, up through the darkness to the surface where Buru Tovo could haul me onto the boat and I could breathe again ..."

How he had wept, safe on the canoe in the bright air, above the innocent glitter of the surface, for his inability to find a flame pearl, for he would never dive down again so deep, and the great secret of the pearl divers of the Western Ring was that the flame pearls were only to be found on the outside of the encircling reef.

Buru Tovo had told him there was more than one way to find a flame pearl, and brought him back into the sheltered lagoon, and never again suggested diving that side of the reef. For each person had limits, Buru Tovo had said, that they could surpass, and others that they could not.

There were limits, lines, even now, that Cliopher had never crossed in his own mind.

He thought of that other Artorin Damara, who had not had the other Kip in his life, and the other Kip, who had not had a Radiancy of his own.

Perhaps it was time to cross one or two of those lines, those limits, those horizons hiding half the world.

His heart was hammering in his throat, with memory and desire and that hope for something he had never been able to say.

He could not help but look up at a sound, as if someone had begun to reach out and decided against it. The room was too bright for him to see who it had been.

There was some purpose for Rhodin's questioning, Cliopher reminded himself, and after a silent pause he went on. "When Astandalas Fell, there was no rock, and no current up. I dreamed I was pulled down so far my bones broke and turned to water, and I was remade. I dreamed that I drowned in the darkness, and then again in an ocean of light ..."

His voice trailed off despite himself, as that odd dream he'd had before waking returned to mind. Was this what Rhodin wanted to know?

"I dreamed that again, after I fell," he murmured. "When I woke I wasn't sure I hadn't died at first ..."

"Did you have any other dreams, during the Fall?" Toucan asked. His voice was subdued.

Cliopher took a shaky sip of his chocolate as the memories welled up around him again. "I know I did. I don't remember them well." He managed a smile. "Not all of them were awful, though some were very strange. ... Everything was so ... off-kilter..."

"I'm not sure if it's a dream from then or not, but I always had this strange memory of one where I was in the Palace, but not in the Palace, and my family was there—Mama, Vinyë—but they didn't look like who they were, but yet they were ... and everyone was trying to persuade me that I'd done something important— you know the sort of dream, when you are searching and searching for something, but in this one everyone was expecting *me* to do something, or be something, and I was this imposter ... And I dreamed that they were holding a funeral for me, the whole city was in mourning, except it was not Astandalas, but yet it was the capital ..."

He stopped, his own words catching in his mouth.

They were looking at each other now in shock, in speculation, in wonder. He reached for more memories, but they were faded and dim, nothing he'd chosen to revisit. He had revisited the dreams of drowning, of being pulled under, so often.

He looked at Rhodin. "What happened here?"

Rhodin sat back, a secret smile in his eyes before he was once more professional and correct. "The mountain fell. You were caught in the landslide, you and Pikabe, but not entirely swept away. Once the rocks settled the rest of us made our way down to you. You were unconscious, and Pikabe ..."

Cliopher felt a sudden drop in his throat. "Pikabe—please say—did he—"

"He lost an arm, but we were able to keep him from bleeding out, and he is in good condition. He'll recover," Rhodin said confidently. "We were able to do field care, Bertie and I, and carry you two up to a small cave."

"It was a good thing you had your full kit, then," Cliopher murmured, remembering how over-prepared Rhodin had seemed with his enormous rucksack.

Rhodin smiled with a touch of justifiable smugness. "Indeed. Unfortunately the landslide blocked the tunnel and the rest of the path forward, as well as damming the river. I have learned that the sky ship at the ranger station was affected by the magical disturbance created by the landslide, and they could not fly over until the next morning. By then we'd had to cross over to find shelter, as the rains started a few days early —no doubt also affected by the disturbance."

Cliopher nodded, unsurprised. "Were we rescued the next day, then?"

Ghilly snorted a rueful laugh. "No. Our first shelter was too exposed to the rains, so we had to move."

"We went over the ridge into the next valley, where we found a better cave, and Ghilly foraged for food," Rhodin continued.

"I had that book on the flora of the park—it talked about edible plants." Ghilly looked around, and then continued with an air of bravery. "And then, when you woke up, you were *sure* it was the night of the Fall. You didn't remember ... *anything* past that until today."

Cliopher considered that. He cast his thoughts back a step before that dream of drowning, those strange and muddled dreams of what might have been this future. He thought of that cold, bleak winter in Astandalas, his fifth and the most difficult. Basil and Dimiter had come and gone, Basil to a happy domesticity with his new wife, his newborn son, Dimiter to that fatal traverse of the Northern Waste of Voonra.

None of the rest of his family or friends had come to see him. They had written him, letter after letter telling him he sounded miserable, telling him to come home, come home, come home.

That bitter realization that his dreams had fallen to ash in his hands, and he, who dared imagine himself a tanà in training, could find no embers to light anew.

Oh, what gall there had been in his heart, that night Astandalas fell.

He looked around at his family, his friends. None of them had seen him, known him, at that moment in time. Basil might have guessed the most, for Cliopher had always been able to tell him things he'd been unable to articulate to anyone else, but Basil was not here.

He had tried to keep the true depths of his misery and disenchantment from them, unable to bear the thought of their dark triumph in being right, that his decision to go to Astandalas had been wrong, that he had made a mistake. He had maintained all the way till that moment that he was doing something worthwhile in Astandalas, even as that very pronouncement felt more and more like a lie with every letter.

They were all watching him, as attentive as they'd been to his story, their expressions ... kind. He flushed under their regard, under the squirming embarrassment of knowing they had seen *that* part of him.

He reflected on his thirty-five-year-old self, bitter, cynical, and sharp-tongued, and quailed at the thought of what he might have said.

(And yet: he *had* lit the fire in the Palace, and built it up until the world blazed.)

He said, tentative, uncertain: "I feel I must begin by apologizing. That was not my best period."

"I," Rhodin said proudly, "was informed by your younger self that I was the only aristocrat he'd ever encountered who was of any use whatsoever."

Chapter Twenty
A Letter from his Younger Self

They told him stories of what had happened: how they had spent a week in the mountains while the rain came down in deluges, trying their best to tend to Pikabe and Cliopher, awaiting rescue. Rescue had come in the form of a local boy with a home-made canoe and the information that the search had been called off.

A dramatic journey down the river, down the rushing cataracts and all the way to the city, where they discovered that they'd all been reported dead.

Even with his head throbbing, his thoughts like water in his hand, Cliopher knew what that meant.

"The Protocols," he said blankly.

"The Protocols," Rhodin agreed gravely.

"That's why you're here, and Ludvic isn't."

Rhodin inclined his head, and smiled somewhat sardonically. "Yes. Both of us are out of a job, I'm afraid."

Cliopher could only stare at him as that sank in, his hands trembling, feeling every year of his age and every unremembered blow of the mountain. They had declared him *dead*. That meant—

There were no Protocols for doppelgängers arriving from other universes, but there assuredly were ones for how to transition power and authority when the head of state died unexpectedly.

"I'm sure, uh, Chancellor Aioru will be here to speak to you soon," Ghilly said, comfortingly.

Cliopher was staring at Rhodin, who was staring back intensely, as if trying to communicate something silently. Cliopher had no idea what his friend thought he was doing, but he could feel the wind changing around him.

෴

Cliopher had never been so glad to see his Radiancy's personal physician, Domina Audry, who arrived with due haste to examine him 'now that your memory has returned to you, Lord Mdang.' He followed her back into the comparative quiet of his bedroom, where the physician directed him to sit on his bed.

It really was a much nicer bed than the rope-slung mattress he'd had in the other universe. This mattress was stuffed with down and sat on a raised wooden frame in the old Astandalan style. Someone had made it up since he'd left that morning, and he sat on the pristine coverlet filled with amazement that this was not only more comfortable but also, somehow, more *homely*.

Domina Audry went to the windows and drew the shutters closed, though she left the louvres open so some of the bright daylight could filter through.

Cliopher sighed, astonished at how relieved the sudden dimness made him feel.

"Now then, Lord Mdang," Domina Audry said, "if I asked you to tell me how your head feels, on a scale of 'no pain at all' to 'cannot think clearly', what would you tell me?"

He glanced down at his bare feet. He hadn't put his sandals on, not even to go into the breakfast room. Usually he followed the court custom of wearing footwear in all public areas, even in the outer rooms of his own apartment, but he had never been quite comfortable about sandals in his sitting room and study, and he always removed them before entering his bedroom.

"Lord Mdang?" The physician prompted gently. "Your headache?"

Cliopher frowned at how his mind was wandering. "I apologize, domina."

"It's nothing to be concerned over," she assured him, though of course then he did worry about what other physical side effects the landslide had had on him.

"I—oh, yes," he said, when she smiled meaningfully at him. "My headache ... you want to know how ... strong it is?"

"That's right, yes."

He considered. He was used—he *had* been used—to a perpetual mild headache, which he had always assumed was a corollary of his job, and perhaps also the chronic lack of sufficient rest. This was ... "It's more than the waterline," he said, trying to find a good analogy. "Not as bad as after a Council of Princes meeting. Maybe as much as after having open court."

Domina Audry nodded and scribbled something down. "You have a constant headache? Is that what you mean by waterline?"

"Doesn't everyone with a stressful position?"

She scribbled something else down. "First of all, you are going to feel overwhelmed more easily and more frequently than usual, and when you begin to notice the headache getting worse, I'd advise you to find a quiet, dark room and *rest*."

"That'll be easier now that I don't have a job," he replied, trying to make light of it.

"Then I expect you to *follow* my instructions," she returned. "If you're feeling up to it, I should like to do some tests—it doesn't appear that you're missing any of your functions or memories now, but I should like to be certain."

Cliopher felt his headache spike at the mere thought he might be *missing a function*. "I—"

"Not today," Domina Audry went on, scribbling away. "I'll give you a potion to help with the headache, and I suggest you close your eyes and rest for a time. If you find yourself straining at anything, whether that be reading or conversation, return to a quiet, dim space. You are still healing. Your brain was bruised, so do not be surprised when you feel it."

"I don't remember ... everything about the period ... just past," he said, hoping his voice didn't sound too small.

"Naturally," she said briskly. "There are different names for that sort of amnesia, but it's known to happen—the mind, having suffered such a shock, sometimes returns to a previous, comparable moment, as if it has been returned to its beginning. I've seen it last for a day or for two months. Sometimes the patient regains his memories of the period, but sometimes not."

That was all very well and good, but Cliopher had woken up with an efela his family disclaimed any previous knowledge of.

Domina Audry went to her work-bag and pulled out a phial of an opalescent pink substance. Cliopher was generally healthy enough to avoid needing to go to the physicians, and he was only tangentially aware of the complex developments in medicines over the past decades. There had been a number of experiments done on folk and traditional medicines in order to combine them with the surgeries and Schooled magic of the Astandalan-style physicians. He knew the results had been excellent and continued to be promising as the college of healers expanded out from their initial trials, but he had not hitherto experienced the effect.

Whatever was in the pink potion was potent. He drank it down and felt the pounding in his head immediately start to lighten. He also felt immensely exhausted.

"Will it make me sleep?" he asked the physician, his voice already slurring.

"Only as much as your body needs it," she replied, almost kindly.

Cliopher had been told often enough by his friends and colleagues that he did not sleep long enough. He lay down on the bed even as Domina Audry bade him good day and quietly exited the room.

His Radiancy was also chronically exhausted; he must be. His position had required *seven* new ones to meet the law.

Cliopher's was five and two departments and then that new ministry—or no, it was not part of the government, it was precisely a non-governmental organization that had been needed, because *he* had been scrupulous and honest as he was trusted to be, but Aioru was right, that did not mean he should have been left to be ...

He woke some time later.

Someone had been in, for he was covered with a light blanket, and the louvres had been closed almost all the way. He stretched and sat up slowly. There was a slight stab of pain up the back of his skull, and a sense that the headache might return at any moment, like storm clouds off on the edge of the horizon, but for the moment the sky was clear.

Whoever had come in had also left a pitcher of water on the bedside table. He poured himself a glass and sipped it slowly, appreciating the cool, fresh liquid. He felt parched, and there was an odd taste in his mouth, no doubt from the pink potion.

His eyes had adjusted to the light, and when he set the glass down he saw the papers set on the table beside the pitcher.

This was hardly unusual; he commonly had papers on his table, most often letters to which he was in the midst of replying. He could not remember what this one might be, and so he unfolded it with a mild curiosity.

For a moment the writing was only familiar, a trained but still slightly uncertain secretarial hand—had Gaudy written him a note?

No. Not Gaudy.

To Cliopher Lord Mdang, my older self:
When I first awoke in what turned out to be your life, I was angry.

Cliopher stopped there. His head felt as if something was pinching it.

He did not want to know what his younger self thought of his life.

(This was a lie. He was desperately curious.)

You had given up everything you—I—we—ever wanted. You had all this power, this prestige, this rank—a palace, a city, a world *mourning for you. Your clothes so fine, your apartments so grand, portraits of yourself on display.*

Those most be Suzen's state portraits.

If—well, if he'd been considered dead, with no body to touch as part of the mourning and funereal rites, then yes, he could see why the paintings had been on display instead.

He rubbed his eyes. He did not know what to think about anything. He missed the clarity of the other universe, the knowledge that he had three tasks to find and complete.

He had innumerable Protocols in case of any possible disaster.

(That was also a lie. Obviously they were enumerated. Indexed. They would not be useful otherwise. Number 100 was the Embassy from the Thunder Lizards, Rhodin's Merrions. Number Two was Sudden Unexpected Death of the Head of State. Number 143 was Unexpected Return of Important Personage Considered Dead.)

Cliopher stared up at the ceiling. He did not want to put Protocol 143 into motion.

~

He fell asleep. When he woke, it was to a quiet, apologetic Shoänie. "Chancellor Aioru is here, sir," she whispered.

Cliopher sat up, winced, and grabbed at his throbbing head. Shoänie picked up the scattered pages of his letter and handed them to him before bobbing a curtsey. "Shall I bring him here, sir?"

He nodded distractedly, trying to arrange the pages back in order.

Aioru came in short order, smiling at him in relief. He looked good, a touch stressed but nowhere as much as he might have been.

"It's good to see you yourself, sir," he said earnestly, and then grinned at him. "I liked your younger self, sir. I was—glad—to get the chance to know what you were like when you were my age."

Cliopher caught his breath. If he'd had a friend like Aioru—if Aioru had been his age, and with him— "We would have changed the world together."

Aioru tilted his head, and then he smiled slowly. "We already have."

They looked at each other for a long moment, and then Cliopher blurted, "Don't follow Protocol 143."

Aioru did not pretend not to know what he was talking about, nor what he meant. "You were going to retire within the year, anyway," he agreed.

"You don't need me," Cliopher said.

Perhaps this was the gift, all the gift, the whole *purpose* of that strange episode.

"No," said Aioru, utterly confidently. "We don't. Not any more."

≈

Perhaps when his head no longer hurt he would be upset he no longer had anything to do.

All he could think of was the look in his Radiancy's eyes when he had set off on his quest.

(And the look in the other Artorin Damara's when Cliopher had told him Fitzroy Angursell could still be freed.)

He had never stopped chasing viaus, had he?

≈

I was angry. Disappointed.—More than disappointed. I spent the evening before I came here thinking that the Palace was not for me, the Service was not for me, the Empire was not for me, and that I should stop chasing viaus and go home. Beg Uncle Lazo and Buru Tovo to let me sit once more at their feet and learn to be tanà in truth.

I woke up twenty-five years in the future to discover you had not done so, had instead become—

Oh, the young Kip would have *hated* what Cliopher had learned to seem to be.

You cannot reach the sort of position you have without losing your ideals. I have spent long enough at court to know that.

I hated the idea that you had stayed, and let all that I, that we, thought most important go.

No wife, no children, only the smallest tokens of Islander identity in your private rooms—a few carvings, a few shells, one printed copy of the Lays. *Such a poor showing, I thought, of all that matters.*

All that matters.

Cliopher sat there with those harsh words ringing in his mind. *All that matters.*

This Kip—for he had been Kip then, of a certainty—was the Kip who had gone home and become the other Kip of that other universe. Brilliant, certainly; and though briefly humiliated by his doubt and his perceived failure in Astandalas, not *humbled.*

Cliopher had been humbled.

He had thought he had known so much, setting sail on his little boat, his little *Tui-tanata,* into the wall of storms across the Wide Seas.

Years—years, decades, centuries, time out of time—of shipwrecks and storms, of trying to get home, of trying so desperately to stretch what paltry understanding he had, to save himself by the knowledge he had been given by Buru Tovo and Uncle Lazo and always, always, the *Lays.*

He had learned humility on that journey across the Wide Seas. In the face of the implacability of Ani, the silence of Vou'a, he had *had* to.

Oh, he felt for that other Kip in that other universe.

And then I started to learn what you've done.

And I learned it was not you *who forgot why I, you, we, came to Astandalas in the first place. I had forgotten.*

I had made myself forget.

Cliopher discovered he was not, perhaps, quite humble enough to face this letter.

He set it down upon his chest as he lay back on the covers of his bed, eyes on the curlicued plasterwork of the ceiling. He felt the subtle variations in texture of his embroidered coverlet. His bed-furnishings were exceptionally simple and terrifyingly expensive, as he had found after requesting an itemized spending list from Franzel.

But he had to admit they were beautiful, the pure white cotton sheets, the layers of thin blankets of cloud-like wool and silk embroidery.

He read over the paragraph again.

I had made myself forget.

There was a word, which Cliopher still refused to let himself think, though it had never left him, all those years as his Radiancy's secretary, as close as he could be but still so far from the inner man, the whole self.

Cliopher had not been able to offer his whole self back, had he? He had thought he had to keep his Islander culture ... not *hidden,* but ... discreet.

How wrong he had been. How much his Radiancy had relished those raw and real elements of Cliopher's personality.

He stared up at the ceiling for a few moments, feeling the tears pooling at the back of his nose.

His Radiancy was Fitzroy Angursell. He was everything Cliopher had always loved most from the wider empire, the great emperor-mage, the even greater revolutionary poet.

His friend.

(That was another lie. There was another word.)

He took several deep, even breaths, and returned to the letter.

You will know, I guess, why I was wrong.

I can only see the hints of what is there, the wake of the ship that passed without my noticing, the things washed up on the beach after the night's storm.

Where had that poetry gone? Cliopher did not write like this any longer, did he? He did not search for such splendid metaphors. He had lifted the form of the bureaucratic report to an art; but at what cost?

One portrait, the Viceroy of Zunidh, to show power.

One portrait, the tanà of the world, to show wisdom.

Cliopher had to set the letter down again for a moment and let his eyes close, his mind rest.

The room was dim and smelled good, of beeswax polish and the faintly orange-blossom fragrance of whatever they used to wash the bed-clothes. It was quiet, bar a comfortingly distant, comfortingly familiar murmur of voices, where his family was gathered in one of his private rooms. He had not shut the doors as he came through, and the sounds filtered through the intervening rooms as the daylight through the louvred shutters.

He had seen enough of Suzen's portrait of him in his viceregal court costume to know that that portrait very certainly showed power. But how had she known what it meant to be tanà? He had spoken of his culture to her from time to time, but how could she know that even as the position of Viceroy was to power, so that of the tanà was—theoretically, traditionally, as one *hoped* to be—to wisdom?

I doubted at first—how could I not? How could I believe that I could possibly reach where you have gone?

But I asked, and learned—learned of the world in mourning for your gifts to them. Learned of the work you have done, the ideas you have realized, the imagination of a better world that you have brought into existence.

. . .

Cliopher closed his eyes and cupped one hand over his ear, listening to the sound of his blood circulating, the invisible sea in his body, the sound of the distant sea in his mind. He had been humbled before Ani and Vou'a, *by* Ani and Vou'a. He had faced the sea in her glory and terror, and by learning humility had learned how to find his way home.

He had faced Vou'a in the market in Lesuia, and traded a promise, a vow, for forty-nine sundrop cowries and the laughter of the Son of Laughter.

There were mysteries he would never plumb.

Learned, too, in a letter that came today, that you remembered what I had forgotten.

Remembered what? He had forgotten so much, by that last night in Astandalas before its Fall. He had forgotten his vocation, his calling, his ...

I think that letter is sending me home, calling you back. My head hurts with a pressure like a coming storm. I write because—because you are so close. So close, and yet, I think, perhaps still not quite there. What is the line in the Lays? You have seen the signs of the distant island, but you have not yet come into the shelter of the lagoon, not yet drawn your canoe up on the beach, not yet made your way home.

That was a sharp blow. Cliopher's breath hissed out of him, and he had to hold himself still for a moment.

He had been brilliant, thirty-five or whatever he had been, that night Astandalas Fell. He had been able to see patterns, intuit connections, ascertain truths. And even then, after five years in the Palace, he had not yet learned to hold his tongue in the speaking of that truth to power.

It hurt to know it was so obvious he had not found his way home. That he had never found his way home.

(And yet: *The dawn wind fills my sails. The Wake of the Ancestors' Ships have I seen. The star-paths are singing to me.* And—and he had promised himself, hadn't he, in that other place, that this was not where he stopped.)

The one who wrote that letter was the one I left home to find, sure our fates touched, are entwined—

Oh. *Oh.* He did not mean—

But that meant—

There must be a letter from his Radiancy that had come, that had sent home his younger self, called Cliopher back from that other place, dream or vision or whatever it was. He turned his head to look at his bedside table, but the motion sent a stabbing pain through his skull and a bloom of light across his field of vision. He forced himself to relax once more, head cradled by the soft pillow, blinking back the tears until the lights faded and the pain subsided.

After a few moments he could return to the letter.

Entwined, yes, but not yet—
   Well that is the question, isn't it?

Cliopher had been asking himself that question for ... more than half his life.

In the letter he mentions a visit to Navikiani. It took me a moment to remember that Iki is a name for Vou'a, and that therefore ... that therefore you took him, that one with whom your (our) fates are entwined, to the Meeting-Place of Iki and Ani.

Oh, he had, he had.

   Cliopher had come so close—he had even told him half the story—
   Cliopher had come that close, and no further.

He remembered his Radiancy once saying that to him, that day Cliopher had made another step towards him; the day Cliopher had held him in his study, a fine woollen throw between them to keep the taboos.

   So close, and no further.

   Cliopher was always *so close*, but never there.

He bit his lip and turned back to the final page of the letter.

You took him there and yet he is not certain of you?
   He must ask you to take his words as the words of a friend?
   He must ask you to grant him that—
   I am angry again, not at what you gave up but what you have not yet claimed.

Cliopher's breath caught, for his younger self was brilliant and insightful but not thoughtful, not *kind*, for he had not learned humility in the face of the majesty of Ani and the mystery of Vou'a.

   There were many things he had *not yet claimed*. Some days they weighed upon him, those desires for home and family and status and a place in his community he had earned but never yet dared claim.

   And yet, looking at that other Kip, the one who *had* claimed all those things—

   The other Kip had still not been *happy*, had he? Not content. Respected, admired, heeded—all those things, yes, but Cliopher was, too, in his own way, and it was not enough.

He will still chasing viaus, still that lost traveller looking for the sea in the midst of a landlocked desert.

Elonoa'a was dancing an earlier pattern, you must know that. You must remember that. You brought him to the Meeting-Place of Iki and Ani. Did you not tell him the story?

He had told his Radiancy half of it.

Even now Cliopher did not think he would dare tell him all of it—his heart would be bare as a shell broken open on a beach, under the full glare of the sun.

He had come nearly to the point where he might tell his Radiancy, that inner man behind the glorious mask ... but that was before he had realized his Radiancy was Fitzroy Angursell, and ... not for him, after all.

So close, and no further.

I am being sent home. You are being called back. I will endeavour to hold this future in my mind, this possible life I might live, this realization of so many dreams, so many hopes, so many ...

From your younger self, given a glimpse of a foreign sea, an unfamiliar sky, through a chink in the sail of his current life—

Remember that you know the steps of your ancestors' dances, and that you, too, are Under the Wake of their ships.

Kip (Cliopher)

Cliopher closed his eyes tight against that reminder, the third (or was it fourth? fifth?) in as many weeks, that he was Ke'e Lulai, that he was one of the great wayfinders, the navigators, the seafarers, who always knew their way home.

(He saw, distant and clear in his mind's eye, the other Kip standing beside that great fire in the heart of his Esa'a, the tanà of the Vangavaye-ve in its great flowering.)

He shuffled the pages of the letter together, and his eye caught on one line on the back of the last page.

One final scrawl, a postscript—

How could you let him sail off alone on his adventure? Why is he travelling without you? If he was stolen away by the Sun and the Moon, you know what to do.

Moving carefully, slowly, his head faintly but insistently painful, he set the letter from his younger self down on the bedside table. He made himself drink another glass of water, sipping it, and then rested the cool glass against his forehead until his eyes felt more or less as they ought.

And then, moving even more slowly, more delicately, he took up the other letter, which was indeed from his Radiancy, and could not make his eyes focus on the slanting letters with their extravagant flourishes.

He lay back down on the bed, holding it on his chest, over his heart, his eyes stinging.

He was the tanà. He Held the Fire. He did not run from its burn.

He felt singed.

CHAPTER TWENTY-ONE
PORTRAITS OF A TANÀ

He slept fitfully, confused by his inability to hear the Palace bells.

Franzel came in with a tray of fresh water and informed him, in response to his question, that it was the first hour after noon, and that Domina Audry had been insistent that the bells be silenced on his bedroom.

"I didn't know that was possible."

Franzel indicated, in his own inimitable way, that it had required the efforts of the Mother of the Mountains, the wizard-abbess his Radiancy had left in charge of the world's magic in his absence.

"I should thank her," Cliopher said, and struggled upright.

"Sir," Franzel said hesitantly.

"Tea in my study, please, Franzel," Cliopher said firmly.

"Sir."

~

Someone had rifled through his desk and bookcases. Aioru or one of his secretaries, he assumed, looking for—he couldn't think what they might have looked for, but if they had thought he was dead ...

He did not sit at his desk, nor write a note to the Mother of the Mountains. Someone had placed the portrait of himself in his Islander finery on his seat.

He sank into one of the chairs where he'd met with Aioru for that interview that had started this course.

(That was another lie. This course had started a thousand years ago, when Cliopher had picked up another portrait, half a world away, and felt a second star join the ke'e of his island.)

Franzel brought in the tea tray, which had a pile of freshly baked pastries on it.

"Your uncle, Tanà Lazo, is looking for you," his majordomo said.

Cliopher made a vaguely affirmative noise and gesture, and Franzel poured out his tea and departed through the door that led out towards the other parts of the apartment.

Cliopher stared at the portrait.

The tanà of the world, his younger self had said.

Suzen had perfectly rendered every different material and texture, from the feathers and shells and pandanus leaves to the small scar on his elbow where he had caught it once on a piece of coral when he'd not so much entered as flailed over a reef, some time he'd been shipwrecked crossing the Wide Seas, on some island whose name he could not recall.

His hand came up to touch first the scar, through the thin material of his sleeve, and then his efela ko. He held the obsidian pendant, looking at the one in the painting.

He had spent a long, long time trying to break himself of the habit of holding the efela ko for comfort and reassurance, that constant reminder of his home, his studies, that this was not where he stopped.

He felt the air stir as the door opened, heard the soft tapping of his uncle's cane, the shush-shush of his feet on the wooden floor.

He should have been less obviously staring at this idealized image of himself, should have moved, but he did not.

Uncle Lazo came quietly over and stood beside him, not quite touching but close enough that Cliopher could feel his bodily warmth. They looked at the painting together in silence for several minutes.

The plaque at the bottom of the painting read:

Cliopher Lord Mdang, Viceroy of Zunidh, Tanà of the Wide Seas Islanders

Cliopher could not meet his painted gaze for long. He felt small, humbled, next to the wisdom and strength Suzen had depicted. That proud lift to the chin, that good humour in his mouth, the lines of his face; that headdress.

It was an Islander headdress such as no one had worn for generations: seed pearls sewn in bands, and above them cassowary down, and above that the arcing gold-and-near-black of lyrebird feathers, and above that the red froth of a superb bird-of-paradise's wing plumes, and surmounting *that* the brilliant gold-eyed blue tailfeathers of the emperor bird-of-paradise.

It was a dizzying display. He still did not know how Féonie had come to make it.

His eyes dropped away from the headdress, his painted self's challenging gaze, to the simplicity of the splendid efela, which even to untutored eyes would surely be remarkable.

The five ranks of flame pearls had been painted with such loving attention that Cliopher did not have to count them to know that they were all there. His own efela ko. And the forty-nine efevoa, the sundrop cowries the colour of his Radiancy's eyes, in a double loop joined at the singular spiral of Ani's tear, the efani, the most perfect distillation of the colour of the sea.

They made one efela, not two as he had previously worn them, and he guessed this was due to some arcane knowledge held by the efà, Those Who Counted the Shells. Cliopher had written to him about the efela brought by the Mae Irionéz (and what had happened with *them*?) ...

One pearl is a token, and two are a promise, but five make an efela.

An efela of note, that was: the kind that began to be recognized, noted, *named*.

In the portrait, with the efani and efevoa joined together into one efela, he had four ...

He had more than that, of course. Efela *not* of note or name. The ones he had acquired over the years, hard-earned and secretly bought, most of them. Only Mardo Walea, the rising efà, knew all of them, for he owned the shop in Gorjo City where Cliopher had habitually acquired his.

Mardo Walea had told him, when he gave Cliopher the efela nai, that any future efela would be gifts of the gods: he was no longer in the society of those who bartered or bought the necklaces to show his wealth or standing.

Uncle Lazo continued to say nothing, but he sat down in the other chair.

Cliopher could have waited him out: he had learned patience, as a necessary tool for his work. But his head hurt, and he was tired, and he yearned, just for a moment, to sit at his uncle's feet and pretend he was not ignoring the weight of the world that should have been on his shoulders.

"His Radiancy has a portrait of himself, the first state portrait of when he became Emperor, in his study," Cliopher said. He did not look away from the portrait, though he felt his fingers clench on his imperfect obsidian teardrop, with the chip clearly visible in the painting. "I have always wondered why."

Uncle Lazo waited several beats before he said, "How did you come to chip the obsidian?"

Now Cliopher could look away, from the idealized tanà to the one who stood beside him, ahead of him. He smiled painfully at his uncle, and released the efela ko so he might rub at his forehead, as if he could scrub away his doubt and uncertainty and headache alike.

"The first time I was shipwrecked, crossing the Wide Seas," he said. "I found myself on a low island ... it was far to the south. I could not find anything I could use for an auger. I used the chip to make a tip for a bow drill so I could repair my boat."

Uncle Lazo nodded, and returned his attention to the painting. After a moment, so did Cliopher.

He wondered how much artistic license Suzen had taken in painting his body. He was fairly certain his musculature was nowhere near so *defined*.

Not that even this most generous representation was anything on, say, Ludvic or Rhodin or any of the other guards. But Cliopher had been looking at that other Kip in the other universe, who had somehow managed to become an exemplar of the classic Islander shape for men, all solid muscle with a layer of healthy fat.

It had looked ... good. Proper. *Right*.

The other Kip had seemed so much younger, too: he had sneered once, the first day, saying that Cliopher obviously was far too used to velio foods and luxuries to appreciate the fresh, simple, wholesome fruits and vegetables and seafood of *proper* Islander food.

Cliopher had wondered if any of those ardent revolutionaries had missed coffee, and why they had been so insistent it was a velio custom. He had always thought their voyaging ancestors had traded taro and breadfruit and bottle gourds for the coffee and sweet potato and sugarcane of Southern Dair.

(That had not been an argument he wanted to have, so it would have to remain one mystery amongst many tucked into the bag of the Son of Laughter.)

Looking at this image of himself, he thought he looked a trifle too ... intense.

More than a trifle. Cliopher Mdang had never done anything halfway in his life.

That had been so obvious in the other Kip, with the sheen of fanaticism in his eyes, the set of his jaw, the way he stood in the company of his people. And oh, in the things he—both of them—had achieved.

A man in his late middle age should have some fat about him, some indication that he enjoyed the fruit of his labours.

Cliopher Lord Mdang, Viceroy of Zunidh and Tanà of the Wide Seas Islanders, bore all the symbols of hard-earned status and knowledge ... but Cliopher could not see much sign that he had ever *enjoyed* them. He swallowed. Surely the mortifying sense of starting tears was because of the injury.

"And why, do you think," Uncle Lazo said presently, "your lord kept that portrait of himself in his study?"

Cliopher kept his hands down, folded across his stomach in the neutral resting position of the court. A proper courtier would probably have held a fan with which to indicate all the emotions he chose not to reveal in face and posture.

A proper Islander wouldn't have bothered. There was no shame in showing emotions, back at home.

Cliopher had never been either fully of the court or fully *at home*. Too much one, too much the other, never enough of either to satisfy anyone.

No, that was unfair. It had satisfied his Radiancy. And his friends. They *liked* Cliopher.

"For a long time I thought it was a kind of ... reminder that he had been young once, and was no longer. A reminder that death comes for us all, even emperors who are worshipped as gods."

That was blasphemy or even treason, or could have been argued to be, once upon a time. There had been whole years when Cliopher had walked the narrow edge of it, blasphemy and treason and anarchy.

Another emperor would undoubtedly have listened to Cliopher's enemies and detractors. Another emperor's own doubts and fears would have forced the dismissal —or no, for those crimes it would not have been a *dismissal*; it would have been death.

Another emperor would not have been Fitzroy Angursell.

Uncle Lazo had always known the virtue of the patient waiting, the pertinent question and the long, silent, space held open for the answer.

Cliopher looked at his own painted face, at the wisdom and the strength in those brown eyes, that face lined with experience, the good humour and confidence in the set of his mouth, those shoulders squared and head held straight and confident. Anyone looking at that portrait would undoubtedly think the person so shown was patient and measured and steady as a boat with the wind in the heart of its sail.

Perhaps Uncle Lazo had not always been patient, either.

"I have come to think," Cliopher went on, "that he kept it as a reminder of who he was."

The portrait seemed to mock him: the superlative headdress he had only ever worn twice, once for the final viceroyship ceremonies and once for the abbreviated Singing of the Waters; the efetana and efela nai, the efevoa and efani and efela ko, all that wealth and status in heavy links about his neck.

His voice dropped down. "Or rather, a reminder of who he seemed to be. Who he was *expected* to be."

Uncle Lazo waited, but Cliopher had nothing else to say: only the memory of his Radiancy, *Fitzroy Angursell*, pacing up and down the length of that beautiful, elegant, austere room, reminding himself at every turn that he was the hundredth and last Emperor of Astandalas.

"Have I ever told you the story of my efela ko?" Uncle Lazo asked, after a decent silence had unspooled.

Cliopher turned his head to look at him, at the efela his uncle was fishing out from the neck of his tunic. He had seen it often, of course: he knew the black obsidian pendant in the centre (which showed no sign of ever having been chipped in extreme need and failure), the doubled pairs of golden pearls, the single flame pearl on one side balanced on the other by a piece of bone or ivory Cliopher had never identified, carved about as finely as anything he had ever seen in his Radiancy's possession.

His uncle knew well that he had never told the story to him. Cliopher had asked, once, one of those years when he had been a horrible, intemperate youth, trying so hard to follow the ke'ea laid before him and failing over and over to learn any of the lessons anyone was trying to teach him.

That time he had been told it was not knowledge that was lightly shared.

He had not understood at the time. Now he had a better grasp of why. Cliopher himself had only ever told the tale of his efela ko once, in Mardo Walea's shop when Rhodin asked him in honest curiosity, and Cliopher had to explain how he had failed over and over again.

"As you studied primarily under Uncle Tovo and then secondarily, under me, so I began my studies sitting at the feet of my father's mother, who was a Nevan and Twisted the Ropes."

Cliopher must have made a soft noise of surprise, for Uncle Lazo chuckled briefly. "I had so many siblings. I wasn't sure I wanted to Hold the Fire."

There was nothing he could say to that, not yet. He was experienced enough to know it was *his* turn to wait, to be patient, to hold open the silence for as long as it took for the story to be told.

Uncle Lazo touched the cord, an intricate five-strand braid of different threads. Cliopher recognized the shimmer of ahalo thread, and one was Nijani flax, but he could not name the others by sight alone. "I believe you met her, when you were learning to make the cord for your efela ko."

Cliopher remembered the great matriarch of the Nevans, surrounded by her apprentices—he remembered being somewhat scandalized at how many there were, all of them laughing and talking and spinning as they sat in the shade at the edge of the beach and watched the fishers out on the reef.

The matriarch, the fena-tai, had not taught him directly. She had told him to sit with the youngest children, the ones who were busy playing at what they saw their elders doing in earnest, while she talked with Buru Tovo.

Cliopher, all of twelve or thirteen, had been resentful and reluctant, but he had learned enough by then to shut his mouth and do what he was told.

Over the weeks that followed, he had learned the basics of making cords that would not snap, as his first poor attempt had snapped.

"I remember her, yes," he said. "I don't think I knew she was my great-grandmother."

That was an embarrassing admission, but Uncle Lazo only laughed. "While she did not have quite so many children as my mother—only nine!—and though she was a loving woman, she was always fenà first."

Cliopher glanced sidelong at him. Uncle Lazo's eyes were far away.

"As you learned to make the fire first, so I learned how to prepare and spin thread first. The fundamental lessons." Uncle Lazo sighed. "I enjoyed it, very much. I was good at it. But there was always something missing. I could not quite ... settle."

Cliopher drew in a sharp, soundless breath, as a wave of something rushed through him. He rode it out, an anchored boat rocking across the wake of another's passing.

There had been reasons, surely, why Uncle Lazo had never told him this before.

"The beads on the efela ko are intended to be challenges, as you know. Once you know the first steps, if you are serious about wishing to study to be fenà, the first task is to make a whorl. Do you know what that is?"

"The weight on a spindle," he said. His hand found the cord of his own efela ko. "I made them later ..."

"When did you have to make a spindle, Kip?"

"I was wrecked many times on lonely islands, that journey home," he said. "I had to remember ... learn ... so many things."

All those islands across the Wide Seas, when he'd had to make the thread to sew the broken planks of his boat together; when he'd had to twist the ropes to rig the sail; when he'd had to make a fishing line, a net, a sail.

Uncle Lazo laughed, almost wheezed, but when Cliopher looked at him his eyes were full of many emotions, and humour was hardly the most prominent. "Oh, Kip," he said, his voice hoarse with the gurgle of laughter still in it.

Cliopher did not let himself grow upset or offended. Uncle Lazo's humour might well have a dozen causes, none of them amusement at Cliopher's expense.

"I wanted to make the most beautiful spindle whorl," Uncle Lazo said, "I wanted it to be a symbol of my dedication. I spent weeks scouring the beaches for something worthy of all my dreams."

"I always used tobby seeds, as they already have a hole in the middle," Cliopher admitted, for that pause begged to have a response. There had always been so many things to do, trying to repair his boat and survive on any of those innumerable desert islands, that any small convenience had felt an enormous benison.

Uncle Lazo laughed again, hard enough he started coughing. "I should have been so humble, but I was a proud and vain youth."

Cliopher smiled at that. Had Buru Tovo sent him on such a task he would undoubtedly have made much the same decision.

"My patience was rewarded, or so I saw it," Uncle Lazo went on. "One day I went to the outer reef barrier islands south of the Tirigilis, after a great storm had come up out of the south. It was one of the greatest storms anyone had seen for years—we had a big job cleaning up after it, I can tell you that. So many trees down. But I sneaked away before dawn, before we started the clean-up, to see what I could find on the beach. I found something like a ngali staff made of ivory, but natural, not carved. I thought it was from a fallen viau—you know the story, I'm sure?"

Sometimes it felt as if everything in Cliopher's life came back to that proverb about *chasing a viau*.

"That if you find a viau after it lands on the sea, it becomes something magical and mysterious, something different each time, which you can use to make something equally magical and mysterious."

You were a fool for chasing a viau.

And yet the desire lingered, for there were always stories of people who had caught one. There were ngali staffs in the Ring—not many; Cliopher had only ever seen one—symbols of the paramount chiefs in the old days, and the old legends had it that the ngali staffs were made from the caught viau.

"I learned later that it was probably the tusk of a kind of whale that lives in the frozen part of the oceans of Colhélhé. Maybe it had come through some sort of passage between worlds ... sometimes that happens, with whales. They're Ani's children, of course."

Cliopher nodded. There was such a tusk down in the museum.

"The ivory was good to work, pleasing to touch, beautiful. It was everything I wanted."

Uncle Lazo sighed, smiling at his younger self, shaking his head.

"The prince at the time fancied himself a scholarly sort, and brought all sorts of artists and scholars from other parts of the empire to live at his court. Most of them had nothing to do with us, of course, but there was one old man from Colhélhé or Voonra who traded a few of his pieces for flame pearls. He made hollow nesting spheres, carving the inner spheres through the holes in the outer layers ... I thought it was the most fantastic thing and decided to do that for my spindle whorl."

His Radiancy's bed had finials made of ivory carved in that tradition. A master of that art would absolutely be able to trade one of his pieces for a flame pearl.

"I hadn't realized," he said cautiously, "that you had such skill at carving."

"I didn't."

Uncle Lazo said it simply, honestly. Cliopher waited.

He waited, as he had learned, finally, to wait. He held open the silence, the space, the room, as he had always wanted the space to be held open for him, kept safe and ready for when he was at last able to enter into it.

His uncle's hand was touching his efela ko, just the gesture Cliopher had worked so hard to unlearn.

"The ivory horn was ... oh, five feet long. A good size for a staff. I should, I thought, be able to carve the whorl and still have the rest for trade or whatever else I could think of." He snorted. "I broke half of it, two inches at a time, trying to make something I was in no wise skilled or patient enough to make."

Another silence. Cliopher waited. The questions jostled at the back of his teeth, but he kept them there, held open this space by sheer force of will. So often a silence was all that was needed: half of his best negotiations had come because he had held open that silence long enough for the other person to haggle themselves down to the position Cliopher wanted them to take.

"This took place over the course of a year or so. I was still learning to make the threads, all the other parts of being fenà. My grandmother told me not to be so foolish, that I was using the wrong material for the purpose. I didn't listen, not then."

Cliopher let that sit there, in his heart. Strangely that had never been a hard lesson for him: he had always loved finding the right tool or material for the purpose he intended.

"One day Uncle Tovo came to visit. I think my grandmother might have invited him because of me, but I never asked. He did come to talk with me, asked me about my studies, what I was learning. I knew the tanà was the person you go to when you have a knot in your heart you cannot untie, so I showed him my efforts with the ivory and the whorl and asked him what to do."

Another long silence. Cliopher was no longer looking at the painting, but at his uncle, and he had shifted position so he could lean against his desk, for his head was throbbing painfully with the intensity with which he was listening to this story.

He did not understand why Uncle Lazo had refused to tell him this story, for the young Kip he had been had needed, badly, to hear that someone else had struggled and yet succeeded.

"Uncle Tovo listened, and he looked at all the mess I had made, and finally he asked me why I wanted to be fenà."

Uncle Lazo shook his head, meeting Cliopher's eyes for a moment before smiling ruefully. Cliopher felt a sudden shock at the camaraderie of the expression, the vulnerability it revealed, the ... *equality* it suggested.

Uncle Lazo was not telling this story as a *lesson*.

He had to grip the edge of his desk as dizziness washed through him.

"I couldn't answer him," Uncle Lazo said, watching him intently. "I finally said that I had thought there were many Mdangs, and fewer Nevans. And Uncle Tovo nodded at me, you know the way he does, and he patted me on the shoulder and he said, 'There are not so many Nevans as there are Mdangs, this is true, but there are two dozen fenà and there is only me to hold the fire."

Cliopher frowned, trying to work out the ages. Buru Tovo could hardly have been out of his thirties—extremely young to take on an apprentice of his own. "What of his own teacher?"

"Uncle Tovo had been travelling, sailing the Wide Seas, visiting all the islands. His teacher was still alive, but he was very ill—he'd had a stroke while Uncle Tovo was away, and while his memory hadn't been entirely affected, his balance and some of his speech had been. I spent a long time sitting at his feet, listening to his stories, helping him with all the things that needed doing." Uncle Lazo grinned suddenly at him. "I was about as pleased to do that as you were to help me in my shop."

Cliopher coughed and looked down sheepishly. "I learned much from you, Uncle Lazo. Some lessons took longer than others to sink in."

Uncle Lazo nodded, serious once more; his eyes strayed from Cliopher's face to the portrait. "So I went to sit at Uncle Tovo's feet, learning to hold the fire, the *Lays*, the lore. I loved it: the dancing, the singing, the quiet study, the stories. I was much more suited to it." He lifted his hand to his efela, touching the ivory bead. "The bead and the threads from my first studies. And then the pearls ..."

Cliopher suppressed the small shudder that thinking of pearl hunting always brought out in him. He watched Uncle Lazo carefully, curiously, listening to how he was speaking as well as what he was saying, what he did not say and what he laid careful emphasis upon.

And all the time his head throbbed with the knowledge that this story was equal to equal, tanà to tanà.

"You have said," Uncle Lazo said, "that you knew from the first dive that you would never be a pearl hunter. How many did it take you, to get the pearls for your efela ko?"

"Dozens. Perhaps a hundred." Not all nefalao contained pearls; and Cliopher had broken many of the pearls he had found, trying to drill holes for the thread.

"I dove once," Uncle Lazo said, "twice; three times, and found a pearl. This one." He touched the one to the left of his obsidian pendant. "And when Uncle Tovo suggested we go diving again, I burst into tears and refused."

Cliopher tried not to react. His hands were gripping the edge of his desk. He waited.

"Uncle Tovo said, *Is this where you stop?* And I said yes."

Cliopher took in another breath, sharp and deep, and held it until he could hold back his words. He held open the space. There were reasons Uncle Lazo had never told him this before. There had to be. His uncle was a great man, a great tanà, wise and humble. He would have good reasons.

"I had already quit once, of course. It made it easier to decide it wasn't for me, that challenge. I felt sorry for Uncle Tovo, but you have to be the *right* person to be tanà. You have to love the fire."

Oh, there had been times in Cliopher's life when this would have been a very good story for him to know.

"For a few weeks, a month or two, I felt all ... self-righteous. Went back to the city, got a job at a barber shop, pretended all was well. Told people the old ways were on their way out, no one needed to be as serious about them nowadays. That sort of folly."

Uncle Lazo dropped his hand from his efela ko and folded it over the other on top of his walking stick.

"And yet I found myself answering the questions people asked me with things I had learned from Uncle Tovo and his teacher, Tanà Dinyo, and one day it occurred to me that there were, as Uncle Tovo had told me once, *other ways to find a pearl.*"

"Yes," Cliopher murmured despite himself, remembering the time *he* had stopped, unable to face what it would take to find a flame pearl.

Uncle Lazo knew what it meant, that Cliopher had been unable to dive off the edge of the reef.

He glanced at the portrait, at the efela nai and its five ranks of flame pearls. He returned his attention to Uncle Lazo, who was smiling at him.

"Yes. I collected some of my whale-ivory and traded it for another pearl." He touched the one to the right of the obsidian pendant. "And then I went back to

Uncle Tovo and begged him to let me keep learning from him. He told me that if my ears were listening he would keep talking."

Cliopher had seen Buru Tovo practice that; had spent much of his life trying to hold himself to the principle of listening first, looking first, but also never refusing to reach back when someone reached out to him.

That was the lesson the other Kip had forgotten, that day after the Fall in the Palace kitchens, when Cliopher had seen the desperation and fear on the kitchen staffs' faces, and suppressed his own fear and desperation so that he could do what he knew how to do, what he had been *taught* to do, and light the fire in the bare hearth he found before him.

"So I studied, and one by one I was able to exchange what I knew for pearls. One in exchange for a perfect length of ahalo silk. Another for the complete recital of the public *Lays* for a bedridden old woman who had been unable to attend the Singing of the Waters for years and wanted to hear the old words before she left on her own last journey."

One he had dived for himself; three in fair exchange. The ivory bead. And that left the flame pearl.

"This one," Uncle Lazo said, touching it, "was last. I had finished the rest, the obsidian pendant as well—you recall that that is one of the final steps—but Uncle Tovo said the last one would come when it was time for it to come. You know how irritatingly gnomic he can be."

Cliopher was surprised into a laugh, and he covered his mouth, startled.

Uncle Lazo grinned at him, eyes bright. "So I studied the *Lays*, and danced the fire, and opened my own barbershop in the city, and married Onaya, and ... one day I was in the warehouse district to pick something up for her from the tool library, and there was a fire."

Cliopher held very still. His aunt was a toymaker: she'd made half the toys of his childhood.

"The whole building went," Uncle Lazo went on, and his hands gripped tightly on the head of his staff. "There was oil stored there, for maintaining the tools, and someone had done something stupid—you know how much easier it is to make a spark than people think. Most sparks fizzle ... some catch. That one caught."

He looked down at his hands, rubbing the thumb of one hand over the other. "We all got out—there weren't many of us there. Then we realized ... the man who kept the tools had his young daughter with him. As we were rushing out, the daughter ran back upstairs for one of her toys, the way very young children do, and was trapped."

He looked at Cliopher. "I was young, and proud, and I had studied the fire. And I wasn't thinking. I dipped a cloth in water over my mouth and nose, took another for the little girl, and ran back in to save her."

He paused a moment, and then his hands relaxed. "I did. At a cost." He thumped the staff. "The whole front of the building had gone, and the stairs. I broke a back window and was about to jump into the canal with her in my arms when the floor started to give way. I caught my leg badly, ripped the tendon in my knee, they said later, tore an artery. The only reason they could save the leg afterwards was because I'd cut it on metal hot enough to cauterize the wound."

Cliopher swallowed. He had known, in a roundabout way, that Uncle Lazo had injured his leg in a fire. That was all.

"The leg took a long time to heal," Uncle Lazo said. "And then a long, long time for me to come to terms with the fact I would never be able to dance again. For a long time I couldn't bear to go near fire. Some tanà," he added, chuckling mirthlessly.

And yet ... he *was* tanà, Uncle Lazo was, and a good one. The heart of Gorjo City, Cliopher had said once, or something along those lines, when the former princess Oriana had been particularly obnoxious. He kept the hearth-fire of the city, and tended it well.

"The girl's family gave me the flame pearl in their gratitude, but I hated it. I was not long back at work, grumpy and cranky and terrified of fire, when Uncle Tovo sent you home."

Where nearly the first question of Cliopher's mouth, after he had been sent to work for his uncle and sit at his feet, was to ask for the story of his efela ko. Cliopher took another careful breath and did not say anything.

"There you were: so sullen, so angry, so ... *aggrieved*." Uncle Lazo smiled fondly at him. "So brilliant. Spouting off the *Lays* in two languages, connecting any problem laid before you to something in the *Lays* or what you'd learned back home on Loaloa."

His uncle hesitated a moment, and his eyes went once more to the portrait. Cliopher kept watching him: the way he sat, straight-backed, his hands loose and relaxed now on his walking stick, his breathing easy, his face clear.

This, Cliopher realized, with a cold thrill, was the point. He hardly dared breathe.

Uncle Lazo returned his gaze firmly to him. "I felt such a fraud. You were a better tanà at thirteen than I was at thirty. I could see you would be the tana-tai after Uncle Tovo. All I could do was teach you how to be a good barber, I thought."

Cliopher weighed that silence and then said, honestly, "You have taught me half of what it means to hold the hearth-fire of a community, Uncle Lazo."

Uncle Lazo shook his head, and he was smiling, his eyes candid. "Half of what I know I learned from you, Kip. There was a day my leg hurt abominably and the customers had been terrible and I was certain I had made a knot of everything I touched—some days are like that—and one of the customers said something sharp to me and I couldn't think what to say, I was so hurt and angry. And you gave him one of your most aggravating scoffs—you had a great gift for scoffing when you were a teenager, you know—and rolled your eyes and said, 'And did Vou'a say that to Ani when she could no longer come up onto the islands he raised for her? Honestly, it's like you think that Uncle Lazo thinks with his knee!' He was so embarrassed he didn't come back for a month, until he was ready to apologize and listen to what I had to say. He waited till you were away, though. Doubt he ever looked you in the eye again."

Cliopher did not recall any such—

Well, no, that was a lie. There were far too many such incidents for him to recall a *specific* one. He coughed.

Uncle Lazo laughed. "And you were so rude and angry and aggrieved about him, but after he left you told me to go home and put my feet up—as if I were so decrepit, at thirty!—and you would close up the shop, and I did, for my mind was full of your words. That story." He shook his head.

Cliopher could not dredge up the story. His head was throbbing with a solid wall of pain. He was not certain he could shake his head or nod it without something coming loose. It felt as if his brain were dry inside his skull, scratching on the bone. He tried to be unobtrusive about leaning back in his chair.

Uncle Lazo's attention snapped to his faint motion, and he grimaced apologetically. "You need to rest, and here I am telling over old, old stories I should probably have told you long ago." He stood up and looked at him expectantly.

Cliopher wanted to deny it, keep talking, but his head hurt. He cleared his throat awkwardly and stood up, gripping the back of his chair to keep his balance as his head swam.

"Thank you for telling me," he said, trying to be as equal in speech as Uncle Lazo had been.

His uncle glanced once more at the portrait, and then walked forward the few steps it took to come right up to Cliopher. He leaned his walking stick against the desk and put his hands on Cliopher's shoulders so that he could look him directly in the eye before leaning to rest their foreheads together.

And then he murmured, softly, gently, "There is nothing in that painting that is not really there, Kip. You've earned all of it and more."

CHAPTER TWENTY-TWO
THE LETTER FROM HIS RADIANCY

Aioru swept in while Cliopher was writing a note to the Mother of the Mountains, his last act after leaving Lazo, before bed. It was far too laborious, even those few lines, but it would be rude to wait any longer.

"I'm sorry, sir," the new Chancellor said, grinning apologetically at him. "I feel as if our conversation yesterday suggested that I didn't *welcome* your counsel—"

Cliopher regarded him with immense fondness. "You're looking well, Aioru."

"I'm glad you're not dead, sir."

But it was more than that. Aioru was clearly thriving. He said as much, and the other man laughed. "My friend Tanaea—you remember her?—said I must have been a juggler in another life. It *is* fun."

Cliopher asked after the Mae Irionéz, but they were all doing brilliantly without him.

∾

Cliopher remembered when it had been *fun*.

Challenging, at any rate.

He did not miss those days.

He missed his Radiancy.

∾

He did not even try to look at his Radiancy's letter before he went to sleep. If he had not been able to read it after the letter from his younger self, he surely wouldn't with his head the way it was. He had barely been able to focus on what he was writing to the Mother of the Mountains.

The day felt like one of the ones after the Fall, which had felt a hundred years long.

They might have been, in some places.

There was another phial of the opalescent pink potion on his bedside table, beside the refilled carafe of water. After he wearily washed his face—he would have dearly liked a bath but could not face the thought of the exertions required—he dressed in his softest sleeping shirt and drank down the potion without hesitation.

He did not remember falling asleep, but he must have done, for he knew he was dreaming.

◇

Cliopher stood on the beach at Navikiani, near the rocky point that formed one horn of the crescent. He should have been able to see the summer house where he had brought his Radiancy on holiday, but there was no building there, nor sign of any human presence at all. The jungle was heavy and full of the sounds of coral-crested cockatoos shrieking at each other.

He was sitting on a wide, flat stone, looking out at the lagoon. The water was intensely clear; he could see the ripples on the sand. From the shadows of fish it was much deeper than he recalled from swimming with his Radiancy.

He shaded his eyes and looked out into the Bay of the Waters. On that holiday he had been able to see a smudge on the horizon that was Gorjo City, filling the space between Mama Ituri and her Son like a thumbprint.

There was no sign of the city. No boats on the water. No footprints on the beach.

Was this before the coming of the Islanders?

He waited, the sun warm on his head, letting the soft hushing murmur of the waves fill his ears, his heart, his mind. The air was fresh on his skin.

After a while he felt so immensely peaceful he wanted to swim. He picked his way down to the edge of the point and cast himself into a long low dive.

He could see underwater as clearly as if he wore a snorkel mask, and in his dream he did not need to surface to breathe any more frequently than a dolphin. He swam out, eyes wide to see all the fish around him, an abundance of fish such as he had not seen even on the reefs of the Outer Ring.

He swam out to the same low sandbar he had gone to with his Radiancy, where the reef rose above the surface. Some part of his mind knew that it could not be the same one, not if this was the ancient prehistory of the Ring, but his heart was tranquil and full, and he did not let that quibble trouble him.

He pulled himself out of the water, and lay flat on his back, feeling the waves still moving through his body.

He closed his eyes against the sun, the diamond-drops of seawater caught on his eyelashes, and he heard the sea singing her endless love-song for the lands she had once walked, hand in hand with Vou'a, before she had been tricked into giving up her ability to leave her waters by one of the clever monsters of the dark.

When he woke he was weeping, but he felt obscurely refreshed.

◇

He bathed, scrubbing himself clean of the previous day's dust and confusion. The spot on his skull was still tender when he massaged his hair. He felt much better; once again thirsty, but not so weak and shivery.

He dried himself slowly, appreciating the soft plushness of his towel before shrugging into the silk dressing gown Shoänie had laid out on the clothing rack.

One of his secret indulgences—not-so-secret, in a household with servants, but exceedingly rare—was to put on a dressing gown and get back into bed to read without getting properly ready for the day.

A daydream he had was to do this on a balcony or terrace, some space private but in the open air, with birdsong and the sound of the wind in palms around him, and if there could be the soft plash and murmur of the waves, that would be the best thing.

A balcony, a cup of tea, his book, the fresh air ... a friend.

It seemed inconceivable that this daydream was so close to realization. He had only—

He climbed back into bed, arranged his pillows as he liked them, picked up the wooden lap-desk he kept nearby, and arranged the letter and the cup of chocolate Shoänie had brought out while he was in the bath.

And then, at last, he opened the letter from his Radiancy.

He had the stray thought that it might *still* be some official correspondence—

No. His younger self had seen something much more than official correspondence when he read it.

Cliopher looked at his name in his Radiancy's hand, neatly and yet extravagantly written across the Alinorel-style envelope. He was relieved that he could read the letters easily. It was good this was his first effort of the day, he thought vaguely; he was sure it would become harder as time went on.

The letters were familiar, but looser, at once more confident and more relaxed. Cliopher had spent decades honing his writing to a perfect copybook standard. Not only the scribal shorthand was modelled after his; there were entire fonts of movable type that had been developed to match his hand.

He was sometimes slightly ... envious ... of those whose writing reflected their moods.

He did not try to decipher character from ascenders and descenders or anything of the sort, but he knew his Radiancy, and he knew that this was not what passed for his official hand.

They had never written *informal* letters to each other before. Cliopher had not dared write anything more than the odd postscript or annotation to his reports, before that holiday to Navikiani on Lesuia, and he had not gone anywhere since. The most casual letter his Radiancy had written to him was the one he'd received earlier about his Radiancy's quest.

He unfolded the letter. Unfamiliar scents rose up: something a little acrid, probably the caustic ink; a ghost of smoke from a campfire that burned wood he did not know; a lingering floral perfume.

There was no date. There were little sketches in the upper margins: stars, clouds, stylized birds, barely more than two strokes of the pen.

Not an official missive, no.

. . .

My dear Cliopher,

And there was his name, as no one ever wrote his full name, in a personal letter. Cliopher could immediately hear his Radiancy's voice in his mind as he read those firm slanting letters, angled across the page as if he wrote on an uneven surface rather than a desk.

I have been missing your counsel and humour very much these past few days. I fear you are overworking yourself as much as I am retreating into my lesser self ... for who else but you have ever dared say that the Emperor of Astandalas is a lesser man than—his inner self.

So close.

He had *come so close* to saying 'Fitzroy Angursell'.

Cliopher read over the paragraph again, though it was not that his eyes or brain could not read them.

His Radiancy feared he was retreating into his lesser self, that brilliant and serene persona he had inhabited for so long.

If that was what he meant? It was hardly true that Cliopher was the only person who would say such a thing. There were any number of people who would argue gleefully that Fitzroy Angursell was a far greater man than the Emperor of Astandalas. Fitzroy Angursell himself, for one thing, in his youth.

Cliopher frowned, and kept reading.

I write this perhaps a fortnight into my journey. You will, I expect, receive this much later. Only a few days ago did I encounter that Alinorel Scholar whom you may recall, Domina Black of Stoneybridge. In her experience it had been perhaps a month since she had departed the Palace, whereas to us, of course, it had been far longer.

He had Pali Avramapul, then, as well as Masseo. Oh, how good it was for him to have his friends.

Except—

A month for Pali Avramapul was not a long time for a woman of that intensity of emotion to even begin to sort through her feelings. She had felt betrayed upon seeing his Radiancy, and though Cliopher had been certain enough of her by the end of their following interview to be sure she loved him, deeply and dearly loved him, he knew far too well that love was not enough to ensure understanding.

Oh gods, how he knew that. His family were full of love and praise *now*, a fortnight after they had sincerely thought him dead, a week after his return without his memory and with his tongue as sharp and brutal as an obsidian knife.

Soon enough they would turn to that loving criticism and unsubtle hinting that had formed the constant swell of all his interactions with them, less obvious than the turning stars but equally as clear a direction.

What would Pali Avramapul be like?

His Radiancy knew himself well enough to see that he was retreating back, as he had learned so imperatively to retreat back, behind the serene façade.

His Radiancy knew Cliopher well enough to worry he was overworking himself.

The image of himself in the mirror came to mind: the near-gauntness of his figure, that lack of enjoyment or—or *ease*—

Faced with the other Kip of that *other place*, Cliopher had been pleased, even proud, of all *he* had attained and achieved and become.

Why did he feel now as if his life had collapsed?

He closed his eyes. They felt dry and hot and he rubbed his forehead. He breathed in. He was upset because hitting his head had disturbed all his internal equilibriums. He was unsettled because he no longer had the job he had devoted his entire life to, and because he did not want it back.

He was unhappy because every word of this letter was written with pain. He could see it in the uneven pressure of the pen-nib on the paper, the blots of ink, the choice of words.

He took a deep breath, and then another and another. He tasted the chocolate on the air, the scent of his bed-linens, the remaining fragrances of his soap and the letter's ghostly imprints. He felt the soft breeze diffusing through the half-open louvres, the dampness of his hair and the collar of his dressing gown.

He opened his eyes, blinked as they adjusted once more to the light of the room, and sipped at his chocolate until the lowering storm seemed likely to hold off, just a little longer.

Outside the window came the soft hissing noise of rain.

It never rained in the daytime in Solaara, because the Ouranatha prided themselves on keeping some of their old standards alive.

He felt perversely relieved to realize it was not only him whose equilibrium had been so disturbed by that landslide.

I hope, I think, I dare to imagine you will not think less of me for saying it is harder than I thought to be once more in the world.

Cliopher let that sentence sit there, the heartbreak of it echoing in his mind.

To walk free, to choose my own path—

He could not immediately read more. He had to stop, and read the two lines over again. He felt no disparaging impulse, no shock or disdain. He was too busy being struck to his own heart.

He was destined for these impossible letters.

Not destined. He did not believe in *destiny*.

(That was not a lie. He had felt called, summoned, that his fate was entwined with the new emperor's, when he saw that portrait, but that had been as much wishful thinking as anything. He had *chosen* to step into that pattern from the *Lays*. He could have chosen another.)

He slid down in his bed, his dressing gown rucking up around his waist but he could not seem to move his hands to smooth it out. He let his head fall into the cradle of the pillows, the pages of the letters moving on his chest with the movement of his lungs, his breath.

How had he feared his Radiancy would forget him? That he would not be enough? (That he would be too much, but in the wrong direction?) That his Radiancy did not *trust* him?

Could he imagine he felt that soft, steady movement of the waves on the beach from his dream?

The peace was harder to grasp.

He lifted his hand up to his efela ko and held the obsidian pendant, so carefully faceted that a stone whose edges were sharper than steel would not cut.

Of course he would not think less of his Radiancy, of *Fitzroy Angursell*, for finding freedom harder than he had expected. For finding it harder to be *once more in the world*.

Cliopher had had only a few weeks between handing over the majority of his responsibilities and the landslide that had removed the rest, but he had already felt that he had begun to cross some yawning gulf over a narrow and swaying rope bridge.

What it would be like, when he did not have even that fine tether to ground him?

To walk free, to choose my own path—(however guided it may be by that spell of seeking, that ritual of undertaking, that ceremony with which I began this journey), to speak to whomever I wish, even to touch, if the mood compels me ... these are simple things, Cliopher, so simple I never imagined I should find them difficult.

His Radiancy had wanted touch so badly. Cliopher knew that.

Before he had left on his quest, after he had finished his spell or ritual or ceremony—for a moment Cliopher was struck not by the wandering shapes of the letters but the words, the brief excursus into poetic diction, this flash of that inner man who was sometimes his Radiancy, hundredth and last Emperor of Astandalas and present Lord of Zunidh, and sometimes Fitzroy Angursell—

He looked up at a soft tap followed by the service door opening, as Shoänie crept in on quiet feet. She was never quite silent: Cliopher had not liked the perfectly, eerily silent service of his first days with a household staff.

Conju had told him that good servants never knocked, but Cliopher was not actually an aristocrat, and in his own house—as the Lord of Zunidh's apartments theoretically were—he did not feel he had to obey such velio tenets.

"More chocolate, sir?" she asked, smiling with carefully composed winsomeness at him. Cliopher laughed, as she intended him to, and suffered her to spend several minutes fussing over him, in the course of which he not only agreed to breakfast in bed but also learned that Conju was in the Palace.

She went off to fetch his meal. He braced himself and turned back to the letter.

But the sky is beautiful, Cliopher. I am writing this in the Borderlands, that misty and tangled region between worlds. I departed Zunidh with a step, and entered upon Alinor when my foot touched down ...

His Radiancy (Fitzroy Angursell) went on, describing where he was, the people he was travelling with—it seemed that he had found at least one more member of the Red Company than just Pali Avramapul and Masseo Umrit—and Cliopher loved it, he truly did, and he was sure he would savour these descriptions on a later re-read, but ...

But his head hurt, and he did not want a travelogue. He wanted—

Shoänie came in with his breakfast, the plate containing not only the promised pineapple buns, their crackled crust still warm when he picked one up, but also an assortment of custard tarts and sliced fruit in a rainbow of colours.

It was a very sweet breakfast. Perhaps he was not the only person who thought he was a trifle too thin.

He ate two of the buns and three slices of starfruit, carambola as they called them here, sprinkled with fine white sugar to cut the acidity. Cliopher had always loved starfruit: there were trees outside his Buru Tovo's house on Loaloa, and they always made him think of those early months learning to swim in the *Lays* as he learned to dive in the lagoon.

When he had *first* arrived on Loaloa, he'd been bitterly certain the only reason he was there was so Buru Tovo had someone else to pick up all the fallen starfruit before it rotted.

Cliopher ...

I dare to write to you as a friend. Please ... please accept it as if we sat together on the sandbar at Navikiani, far out in the lagoon, far from any ears, any guards, any need to guard ourselves. But better, for we were still so tentative and unsure then, you uncertain how far you dared reach, me uncertain if I even dared reach back. For so long it was not only my literal touch that burned.

That was the line that had so disturbed his younger self. Cliopher's heart ached. His Radiancy should not be uncertain, tentative, afraid.

His Radiancy wanted to be Cliopher's equal, and Cliopher his.

There was an old Islander word for that.

Cliopher frowned away his distraction.

. . .

I wish for your counsel, for your patience and good humour, for your capacity for love. If I did not have your example to set before my eyes I should lose my temper so often, say words I do not mean but could not take back. I can hold my tongue because I have seen through your eyes how love can be so unintentionally painful.

The pain was raw. The courteous effort to reach past it was almost worse. Oh, Cliopher could understand why his Radiancy could feel himself slipping back into his Serene and Radiant persona, the Glorious and Illustrious one who gleamed, even glowed: luminous, safe from any outward shadow.

Safe from outward shadows; safe from outward touch. Entirely vulnerable to whatever shadows and blows his heart and mind might inflict upon themselves.

Painful, yes, but perhaps it is the pain of a sleeping limb reawakening, an atrophied muscle stretching—

I hope so. I remember that there were times when this was not so hard.

When I was younger I never imagined that it could be hard.

He had to sit for a few moments over that plaintive, painful statement.

I am smiling now, imagining your voice saying 'Ah, it is no matter, my lord, worthwhile things are often hard,' the way you did when I was nearly doubtful of our ability (who am I fooling? your ability) to accomplish ... so many things. From that first proper request of mine, when I asked you for peace and you brought it back to me in the form of that quiet, subtle, revolution of a treaty—oh, all the way to the great peace you have wrought.

Worthwhile things are often hard, and that is no reason to stop, is it? 'Partway done is easily undone', you've said that too.

(I do listen, you know. I have so often wished we could just—talk.)

So had Cliopher, so very often.

They had come close to it, a handful of times. Closest that one time when his Radiancy had asked him to show him how to greet people, when he went out in the world without the structures and strictures of his role as Last Emperor of Astandalas to guide him.

Cliopher had told a halting account of a dream, ruing how his Radiancy's true name had melted out of his waking mind.

(For at some level he *had* known it. He *must* have. All those years upon years—years, decades, centuries, time out of time—working together, never reaching too far for fear of what might break if they did.

He had not been *ready* to name him.

At some level Cliopher had known he would not be able to let Fitzroy Angursell go as he could reluctantly let his Radiancy go.)

They had descended from the bell-room at the highest point of the Palace, above even his Radiancy's apartments in the Emperor's Tower, and gone into his Radiancy's private study.

It had looked ransacked: his Radiancy had packed his own choices in there, as ever refusing to let anyone else in.

"What do I do, Kip?" his Radiancy had said, after they had both sat in silence long enough for the square of sunlight to visibly shift position.

Cliopher had looked at him in the dim light of that small, cluttered room. His Radiancy's eyes had seemed huge in his dark face, the colour of sunlight in amber.

That was what he remembered most clearly: the way his Radiancy's eyes seemed the brightest thing in the room, and the way his Radiancy's hands twisted his signet ring on his finger.

They had already talked over half the ways one might greet another. Cliopher had shown him as many as he had dared, though he had felt his Radiancy's heart fluttering like a trapped bird when he went to embrace him, and had retreated to a more formal posture.

That was not what his Radiancy was asking, but Cliopher could only offer metaphors.

"If you do not wish to touch anyone," he had begun, his voice husky with the awareness that he was walking one of those swaying rope bridges, that his Radiancy was himself teetering on the edge of some deep and terrible emotion, that Cliopher's words mattered. He had cleared his throat. "If you do not wish to, for—for whatever reason—no one would be offended by a bow."

And that made his Radiancy finally blink and smile and relax his hands. "And yet I have seen many people offended by a bow in my time at court."

So. I have begun, and it is hard, but it is worthwhile, isn't it? This quest of mine not so much for an heir (though I have not forgotten that end!) but to return to myself as a human being, a person, a man. I was one once.

You are one now! some part of Cliopher cried, fury boiling up in him, overwhelming all those quiet, intense memories. *You have always been one!*

Even that first day—that first *hour*—Cliopher had seen it. *Known* it, as solidly as he had ever known anything. That man pacing the splendid study, offering him refreshments, telling a joke that could have destroyed them both—

Oh, he had been a man then, and a man through all those long years of working together, wrenching peace and prosperity out of the devastation of the Fall. A man when he burned Woodlark to the bare rock, and a man when he had sat in that study with Cliopher and confessed he was afraid to leave.

A man when he had not been able to tell Cliopher his name.

. . .

Do not let my private difficulties lead you to think ill of my friends, Cliopher. They remind me in every moment who I used to be, and that is a help. It reminds me it was not all the memory of a dream. I was once as I remember myself ... it was not always a mask, a pretense, a performance. Once I was real. I shall be so again.

I am sorry—You have always looked at me as if I were real.

I do not think I have ever told you how solid an anchor that was. Thank you.

—I can imagine your expression, that courtly mildness, that underlying intransigence, solid as a stone you do not realize is part of the bedrock.

When I asked you how I might learn once again to meet others as a man, you did not laugh or misconstrue me. Instead you opened your arms and touched my hands, my arms, my skin, my face, in those customs that are common to many but goods beyond price to me. And there was no fear on your face.

My old friends do not understand that there once was something to fear.

It is getting dark. Domina Black has just ... Never mind. It is only that I wish ... oh, that they were as happy for me to be here, as I am now, as I am happy to be here with them, as they are now.

I think ... I think I should like to play a bit, my harp, pull out some of those old songs. You gave me that gift back, too, didn't you? That holiday on Lesuia where I was able to remember myself.

We never sat beside a fire together there, did we? Not just the two of us. We should have.

There was a large spatter of ink, as if his Radiancy had stopped there, pen aloft, for a long time.

I cannot say anything else tonight. The stars are too brilliant. I wish you were here. I remain—

Several things were scratched out, thickly enough Cliopher could not decipher them.
    And then:

—Your servant, in a manner of speaking.

Cliopher did not think he was quite in the right place, physically (he refused to admit, emotionally), to consider that valediction properly, and so instead he let himself be immediately, irrationally furious with Pali Avramapul for making his Radiancy feel in the least diminished and *small*.

CHAPTER TWENTY-THREE
CONJU

He did not know how to be in the presence of his family with nothing to do. Stories of the *other place* only went so far.

He tried. It would have been easier if he'd been clearer in his mind what they wanted from him.

Another lie. He'd always known what they wanted, and after three days looking at that other Ghilly, that other Vinyë, that other Kip, he could see it.

They wanted him to be happy.

They had always, always, wanted that. Nothing more: and nothing less.

He wanted that, too.

∼

Eventually he remembered that Conju was in the Palace, and that midmorning was a perfectly reasonable time to go calling on him.

He met Rhodin at the door to his rooms.

"Were you heading out?" Rhodin asked, turning around immediately to accompany him. The two guards on duty—Zerafin and Oginu—saluted but did not follow.

Cliopher supposed he was no longer important.

Rhodin said, "Your younger self found the guards intolerable, I'm afraid."

"I'm sorry," Cliopher said, twisting around uncertainly, but Rhodin took his arm and smiled at him.

"Don't worry about it. They understand. And I may be retired now, but obviously I still have all my skills."

"Obviously."

"What a great deal we shall have to tell his Radiancy when we see him next," Rhodin said thoughtfully as they turned into the wide curving hall that encircled the central tower of the Palace. "Are you going to see Conju?"

"I'd thought so. And Ludvic—"

Rhodin shook his head. "He's deep in meetings today. Poor bugger." He laughed. "Though I have some as well, so I'll leave you once we get to Conju's. I have a lead."

Cliopher glanced at him sidelong. He was more grateful than he wanted to say for his friend's strong arm, and he did not object when Rhodin guided him to the discreet alcove that hid the lift instead of the stairs.

This was the lift Suzen had used—trying to make conversation over breakfast that morning, Cliopher had managed to determine she'd returned home to the City of Emeralds after finishing the paintings—and it was slow and sumptuous, if not as slow and sumptuous as he assumed the one reserved for the use of the emperor was.

Rhodin suddenly laughed. Cliopher looked at him enquiringly. "Oh, I *am* sorry, Cliopher! I've forgotten I can't report telepathically to you."

The lift stopped with a gentle thump. "I beg your pardon?"

"I give the special reports to his Radiancy in person," Rhodin explained glibly, "but the *very* special reports I give telepathically."

Cliopher counted to three before he answered. "Really."

"Yes. It's practice for when I find the Merrions and find my soulmate—" Rhodin blushed. "That is, if I am adjudged worthy."

It was truly fascinating, watching Rhodin spin a new religion out of—well, not nothing.

Not exactly *nothing*.

Very seriously, Cliopher said, "I cannot imagine that you would be considered unworthy if you managed to find the Merrions."

≈

Conju's rooms were two levels down from Cliopher's and on the opposite side of the Palace, off the Collian wing. Back when Cliopher had lived at the far end of the Alinorel wing he had thought Conju's apartments unimaginably grand. Conju had retained some of his family furniture and artwork, and everything was displayed with a meticulous attention to detail Cliopher had never been able to grant his living space.

Never *chosen* to grant his living space. Cliopher gave quite as much diligence to the things he did care about, after all.

Conju's majordomo greeted him with subdued enthusiasm and congratulations for his continued survival, then indicated that Conju was in his workroom. Cliopher thanked Zala for her kind words and made his way through the rooms towards the back.

There was so *much* in Conju's rooms: figurines and tchotchkes from his travels and friends occupied every surface, and there were layers of carpets on the floor and galleries of paintings and wall-hangings on the walls.

The first time Cliopher had come into his rooms, Conju had explained the Astandalan custom of displaying gifts as markers of status and alliance and friendship: for someone who knew how to read the heraldic emblems and symbolism, this room would be a legible display of Conju's rank and status within the court.

The focal point of the drawing room was the old fireplace, which had a surround of intricately carved white marble, stone garlands of curving leaves and unfamiliar fruits. There were items on its mantlepiece, candlesticks and portraits of Conju's family, and above them a large mirror in an ornate frame.

In the fireplace itself was a tree made of glowing, living magic.

It had a thick trunk of a dark brown bark, and wide-spreading branches with green leaves that whispered and shivered in mysterious winds. Sometimes the leaves turned red and golden-buff, and fell in little drifts about the fireplace. Conju always left them there until the new leaves emerged from the tree, according to some seasonality Cliopher only vaguely remembered from his time in Astandalas. It had been a gift from his Radiancy on some important anniversary, and even more than the location of Conju's rooms—which were due to his familial rank—the tree showed his status.

There was usually a table or two next to the fireplace, on which Conju displayed carefully composed vignettes that Cliopher invariably misconstrued. It was something of a game for them: Cliopher would examine the display, and Conju would ask what he thought it meant. Cliopher would inevitably miss a key component, and Conju would take great pleasure in explaining whatever it was, and then they would both laugh.

Cliopher had ceased to be dismissive of court culture when he realized that it *was* a culture, and not only that, the culture of his good friends Rhodin and Conju. He'd tried to learn its mores, but had never quite grasped the nuances.

His glance was drawn to the resplendent tree, and he frowned at a new thought. Was it also his Radiancy's culture? Did *he* think of it as such?

Something was missing from the tree. Usually there was a white crystal snake coiled about the branches, representing some aspect of the Vilius family crest.

He hesitated, but Conju would probably ask him about the displays.

He looked at the two tables, one on each side of the tree, and felt himself shiver as he recognized the objects on them.

He would not lose this challenge, not today.

The one on the left held things Cliopher had given Conju or which were otherwise associated with him: There was the carved bowl Conju had acquired in the market on Lesuia on their holiday, which he had been somewhat embarrassed to show Cliopher when he noticed it.

("It's beautiful," Conju had declared, running his hand around the flared rim.

It was a very simple bowl, with only one band of carvings around the rim, but the wood was a fine ebony and the whole shape of it satisfying to the eye.

"You do not expect me to argue that people from my homeland can create art, do you?" Cliopher had asked.

Conju grimaced at him, and then lowered his voice although no one else was in the room with them at the time. "It was made by that village carver, the one who was so rude to his Radiancy. I saw the bowl before I realized it was his work ..."

"It's a beautiful bowl," Cliopher had reassured him, and then, with laughter bubbling up, "and you know, even Prince Rufus can have a good idea from time to time.")

He smiled now as he walked past the bowl, letting his fingers run along the incised edge. Next to it was the efela Cliopher had bought Conju when they became close friends, a strand of glossy black cowries with a singular pearl he had not really been able to afford at the time.

It had been an absurd extravagance, really, but Conju had been his first real friend in the Palace, and that had seemed worth the significant gift. The single pearl was a token of friendship, as he had explained when Conju asked what it meant.

Conju had placed the efela in a bone-white porcelain bowl, and Cliopher had always looked, when he had a moment, to reassure himself it was still there in the room.

He had never quite known whether it was merely the need to dust, or some other motive, that meant that every time he looked at the bowl, the golden pearl was in a slightly different position.

For Conju to have placed this table where he had, with the efela in its bowl and the various books and meaningful trinkets he and Conju exchanged ...

This was part of his own mourning customs.

The other table, then and obviously, was for Rhodin.

Cliopher touched the salt-cellar made out of a hollowed-out emerald and then shook himself and continued on.

～

Conju was seated at his worktable, a vast desk with pigeonholes and drawers and all sorts of cunning compartments. Cliopher admired and somewhat envied that desk. He did not need any such thing—unlike Conju, he did not have an ever-increasing collection of small items to store in the multitudes of drawers—but it was a beautiful item of furniture and he not infrequently caught himself wondering what he *could* put in it, had he owned such a thing.

Conju was not doing anything, as far as Cliopher could see. He was sitting on the swivelling stool, feet tucked almost casually onto its lower bar. There was a wooden box—not a particularly well-made one, Cliopher noted—on the table before him, open to show a handful of items that he guessed were the raw materials for a perfume. Beside the box was a lump of a waxy substance, mostly white with flecks of grey and brown. It was bigger than his closed fist, and seemed to be the source of a strange, pleasant, scent: a little like sacred tobacco, a little like vanilla, a little like the sea.

Cliopher took a deep, appreciative breath. The air in the room was full of faint scents, for Conju's hobby was the creation of perfumes, and the worktable's drawers were full of the many components of the art. He had once or twice shown Cliopher the alchemy and artistry involved; Cliopher had been reminded of watching Mardo Walea at work turning shells and seeds and stones into the beads of an efela.

Conju was looking at the two items and stroking the crystalline snake that usually resided in his oak tree.

Cliopher knocked lightly on the door and when Conju absently said, "Come," entered.

He found a safe place to lean, where he would not disturb any of the experiments in progress. Conju looked up at him. He looked peaky, his bronze skin pallid, shadows under his bloodshot eyes.

"I'm sorry," Cliopher began, shocked at the sight of his friend so dishevelled.

Conju raised his eyebrows. "Whatever for?"

"I fear my younger self might have been a touch rude."

Conju regarded him for a long moment, and then his lips twisted and he said, "Not everything is about you, Cliopher."

Cliopher had prepared himself for an emotional conversation, and he was almost relieved—or to be honest, there was no *almost* about it—to discover that Conju was not about to fall weeping on his shoulder.

He should have known better. Conju did not like emotional conversations.

He settled himself a little more comfortably on the edge of the desk. "I apologize for being overly self-centred, in that case. Is it—" He racked his memory for the name of Conju's most recent boyfriend. "Did things not go well with Antonio?"

"I'm surprised you remembered his name," Conju retorted acidly. He set the crystalline snake down on the table, where it slithered itself around an amber paperweight, into a coil like the glitter of sunlight on water, and picked up an elegant blown-glass goblet to drink from.

"It seemed serious enough to remember his name, as you'd planned a three-month holiday trip with him."

Cliopher had certainly not bothered to keep track of *all* of Conju's boyfriends, as they came and went with incomprehensible frequency. Conju was not exactly like Rhodin, who rarely saw the same woman more than three or four times. Conju had deep and dramatic affairs, which usually lasted a few months before something broke.

He presumed, insofar as he understood either of them, that their respective devotion to his Radiancy got in the way of any other relationship.

Conju set his glass back down and sighed. "The first two weeks were lovely, just as I had hoped. And then we got news of the landslide, and he had the gall to say that he didn't understand why I intended to come back to the Palace immediately, as you and I were surely nothing more than *colleagues*. I did him the *honour* of explaining our friendship and he ..." Conju shook his head sharply, then winced, and rubbed his temple with one knuckle. "He said that it didn't matter how close we were, you and I, that is, we were never going to be *family*."

Cliopher was not feeling himself. He made a soft noise of distress and denial.

Conju pursed his lips. "And then the *nerve* of Prince Rufus—I came back to Solaara with him—he was determined to show everyone how close he was to you, and—"

"You are my family," Cliopher said. "And you *are* welcome."

"Of course I am." Conju sniffed. "Your mother likes me better than you."

This was almost certainly true. Cliopher laughed, then stopped himself when that set his head to throbbing. "I'm sorry about Antonio. I know you liked him."

Conju's eyes fell to the box and the waxy lump on the table. He touched them both with gentle hands. Cliopher smelled the odd fragrance once again, that hint of the sea and vanilla and something heavier and darker. "What is that?" he asked.

"This? Ambergris. My sister, Nerisse, once found a lump the size of her head, and she sent it to me. For my perfumes."

Cliopher had not recognized the ambergris on sight, but he had heard of it, and he knew without having to search his memory that it was worth more than its weight in gold. Nerisse had been Conju's next-oldest sibling, and the one to whom he was closest. She had died with the rest of his family in the Fall. "A princely gift."

"It was unimaginably generous of her." Conju touched the lump on the table, and he smiled nearly fondly. "I still have so much of it left, as you can see. Every time I use it I think of her ..." He took a deep breath. The little snake uncoiled itself and slithered across the table to drape around his wrist, like a brilliant bangle. Cliopher winced away as the magical construction caught the worktable light and sent rainbows into his eyes.

"It is a bit bright, isn't it?" Conju said, wincing almost equally. "I am also feeling somewhat delicate."

Cliopher opened his eyes and took in his friend's demeanour and general attitude. "You're hungover."

"Unbelievably."

"What happened?"

Conju smirked at him. "It wasn't about you—or not entirely. We were struggling with your younger self, Rhodin and Ludvic and I, and then you came *back*, so obviously that was something we were going to celebrate when Rhodin told us, and then ... well, and then there was ... there were letters that came from his Radiancy."

"Yes. You received one?"

"I received *three*." Conju set down the snake and reached into one of the pigeonholes of his desk. He drew out three letters, each tied with ribbon of a different colour. "One from his Radiancy, one from my sister Nerisse, and one from Terec."

Cliopher coughed in surprise. "Terec and your sister? *Both* of them?"

There had been no doubt about Nerisse, he'd thought—she'd been home on leave for the Fall, and perished there.

Terec, on the other hand—Conju's dear friend and beloved—had been a wild mage who had been unable to stand the magic of Astandalas pressing down upon him. He had disappeared well before the Fall, and thus there had always been that faint thread of possibility that he was not dead, and could return, unexpectedly, into Conju's life.

The endless parade of unsatisfactory boyfriends probably had something to do with that, in retrospect.

"He came across them—his Radiancy did." Conju's mouth quirked again, in something equally pained and reluctantly amused. "Or rather, if Nerisse is to be believed, *Fitzroy Angursell* did."

Cliopher regarded him. His head hurt too much to know how to parse this conversation. "I am beginning to see why you might be somewhat hungover today."

At least Conju had been safe, with Rhodin and Ludvic beside him. And Solaara was hardly *dangerous*, except to reputations—and theirs were nearly unassailable.

"What did they say? Are they—are they going to come here? Or will you go meet them?"

Conju tapped his fingers rapidly on the wooden box, and then he said, firmly, "I still have half of my holiday booked and paid for, and there are things I have to do before the Jubilee."

He quirked his lips, and then smiled slightly, sardonically, all emotions clearly tucked away and not coming out at the moment. "We missed you last night. Even though you would have been too prudish to play strip poker with us. Ludvic said we shouldn't take you, not with a concussion."

Cliopher took a deep breath, but this was Conju, who had, after all, lost and found two members of his family—*four* members of his family—in the past fortnight.

He grinned. "You never know, I might have been persuaded. Especially if Ludvic's rós was involved."

"How could you guess?" Conju touched the wooden box again. Cliopher guessed it must have something to do with Terec, if the ambergris were from Nerisse. "Rhodin was trying very hard to persuade me that his Radiancy had been replaced by Fitzroy Angursell, or was an imposter claiming to be Fitzroy Angursell, or—something about Aurelius Magnus being Fitzroy Angursell." He frowned delicately. "It's perhaps a touch unclear. That was later on in the evening, when we'd gone to some quaint Azilinti bar Ludvic knew, after Rhodin's dance club ... Rós is wicked stuff. Wicked."

Cliopher had tried precisely one mouthful of the jug of rós Giya and Ludvic had given him at the Singing of the Waters and then, when even that mouthful had started his head swimming and his face flushing, gave the rest of it to Gaudy with a warning that he had better water it well and share it with *all* his friends. He'd heard a few days later that Lord Eldo, generally the most reserved of the younger secretaries, had been seen in the group of people running through the waterlily gardens, nude but for some strategically placed flowers, and had barely been able to keep his countenance long enough to compliment Gaudy on his choice of friends.

"I went to another ... place, some gift of the god of mysteries, where my counterpart went home after the Fall and stayed there," Cliopher said. "You hadn't stayed in his Radiancy's service ..."

Conju regarded him with jaundiced eyes. "It really isn't *all* about you."

That would have been easier to believe if Cliopher hadn't seen that beautiful, carefully composed table display.

"The other Rhodin told me there was a great fashion and perfume house in Solaara called 'An Vilius'."

Conju considered that. "Now there's a thought."

Cliopher stared at him. He was not recovered enough for elliptical conversations.

"For retirement," Conju said astringently. "You're going to be busy being tanà and telling everyone what they should be doing, not that that's a change, and *he* is going to be all ... bardly."

"Bardly?"

"Goodness, Cliopher, are *you* drunk? It's not even noon."

"I have a head injury." And Conju was carefully skirting the topic of his sister and long-lost beloved friend. Cliopher had no idea if he should press or not, but was quite certain he *could* not.

"I suppose that's an adequate excuse." Conju sniffed. "I cannot believe you made him poet laureate. He's going to be insufferably smug."

"What? Who?"

"*Why* is the question I've been asking myself for the past fortnight," Conju said, with an elaborate gesture of ennui. "His poetry isn't even that good."

Cliopher frowned painfully. "Do you mean Fitzroy Angursell's?"

"Yes. The poet about whom you wrote a *most* impassioned essay your dear successor decided to take as your last request. I understand the general response was tears."

"Tears," Cliopher repeated blankly.

Conju reached into one of the desk's pigeonholes and pulled out a copy of the *Csiven Flyer*. Cliopher stared at the stark, simple words that took up the entire front page of the newspaper:

ZUNIDH MOURNS

"Inside," Conju said in a bored voice.

Cliopher opened the paper. Every article was about him.

"The booklet," Conju directed. "I'd ignore Prince Rufus's eulogy."

There was an insert, which the *Flyer* did every once in a while when it had something it particularly wanted to convey to its readership. Cliopher decided that no, he wasn't in a position to handle whatever backhanded compliments Prince Rufus had found to say about him, and opened it to see that the first full spread was entirely taken up by the essay he'd written after realizing his Radiancy was Fitzroy Angursell.

Lord Mdang's Last Act to Name Fitzroy Angursell Poet Laureate of Zunidh

"I didn't *ratify* this," Cliopher said.

As if that was the important point.

(He was—*had been*—the head of the government. It *was* an important point. It was.)

"Really, Cliopher," Conju said, cupping his hand around the lump of priceless ambergris. "Are you suggesting Aioru, your chosen successor, *forged* a government document? I understand his Radiancy secretly pardoned them all before he left. The Red Company, that is." His voice was precise, disapproving. "Don't *you* start crying now. You're not actually dead."

"I have a head injury," Cliopher said thickly, taking the handkerchief Conju handed him.

"So you said." Conju snorted. "So you've said. Tell me about this other world or whatever it was."

CHAPTER TWENTY-FOUR
THE MOTHER OF THE MOUNTAINS

For the rest of that day, and the next few following, Cliopher drifted. Part of that was the strange, potent medicines that Domina Audry prescribed after she did her lengthy array of tests and examinations. In other circumstances Cliopher would have been quite interested in what she did to test his brain function, but given that his head continued to ache, sometimes to the point of incapacity, he could not muster up his usual curiosity.

She did not seem concerned, but she gave him different potions to drink in the morning and the evening. The ones in the evening merely made him sleep more heavily and for longer than he was accustomed to, and he did not mind them. He did not like the ones in the morning, which made him feel both detached from his emotions and peculiarly clarified in focus.

If he'd had his work to do, he would probably have been grateful for it.

But he did not have his work to do—he did not have *any* work to do—nothing beyond a desultory handful of meetings with Aioru and various other people, all of whom assured him they were fine, all was well, he need not concern himself with anything other than healing and spending time with his family, had he not created whole systems for just this eventuality?

The worst thing was he *had*. Of course he had. He had allowed (more than allowed: deliberately shaped) the power structures of the world to consolidate and condense around himself under his Radiancy, and equally deliberately released them, one by one untwisting and distributing authority and leadership and, slowly, real power, until there was no single centre with all its strengths and weaknesses.

It was not as if he did not have his weaknesses as head of the government.

Had not had his weaknesses as head of the government.

Aioru was making small changes already, changes that would gather and grow force as their momentum grew, changes that were sometimes fixes to problems Cliopher had not even seen he had created.

He was glad of it, for the sake of the world and all its people.

Secretly, he was unutterably relieved at not having to make those changes *himself*.

Under the strange detachment and clarity of focus of Domina Audry's potions, Cliopher could look at himself and admit he wanted to be done.

It was, nonetheless, impossibly hard to *be* done.

～

He drifted.

The Mother of the Mountains arrived one evening while he was lingering over a slow meal with his family. His head was aching but not so severely he had wished to retire, though he could feel that he would shortly need to find a quieter, dimmer room. He was grateful enough to make his apologies to his mother and uncle and head to the small reception room.

The abbess was about Cliopher's own age. She was a few inches taller than him, with skin like gently bronzed porcelain, short steel-grey hair, and angular, very pale grey eyes that shone silver in certain lights. Her most notable feature, however, were her tattoos.

Cliopher had gathered, over the years they had spent together on shared committees or other projects, that the tattoos were indicators of her mastery of different elements of her school of magic.

They formed patterns of lines and dots on her face, outlining her eyes, curving across her cheeks and temples, spiralling down her arms and around each finger of her hands.

"Mother Superior," he said, greeting her as he entered the room to find her already seated on one of the two comfortable chairs. She had a cup of tea and a plate of some sort of biscuit, and made as if to rise. "No—please remain seated."

"Then you must not bow, Lord Mdang," she replied with a small smile. "Your head will not thank you, and I am well aware of your consideration for me."

"I should like to apologize for all the work you have had of late on my account," he said, taking the seat beside her. Franzel came in with a tray containing another cup and saucer, and a fresh teapot. Cliopher thanked his majordomo, who smiled austerely at them, ascertained that the abbess did not wish for anything else, and departed once more on silent feet.

"You did not set the mountain to tumbling down," she replied easily, smiling at him. "It has been a satisfying challenge. I have a new ... hmm, apprentice is not quite the word, as she is well into her journeywoman stage. She'd be a master, if she chose to focus and settle down. She has been of great assistance, full of an abundance of new ideas and cogent implications."

Cliopher was not in the right state for the lengthy of exchange of courtly compliments and questions. He nodded, sipped at his tea, and tried to gather his scattered thoughts. He had met a powerful young mage, not very long ago, hadn't he? Aioru's friend—

"Is this, ah, Tanaea Au'auēna of ..." He trailed off, trying to remember her island. It was one of the Sociable Isles, he was sure of that, and her father was a velio writer. He'd remembered Au'auēna. The name meant 'whale-song', after the constellation of the Great Whale. "She's friends with Aioru—Chancellor Aioru, that is."

The abbess regarded him, still smiling. "I am glad to see that your memory is unshaken. Tanaea of Ziukurui is indeed she of whom I speak. She is partly an Islander by descent, I understand."

"We are a matrilineal society, Mother Superior; as her mother is an Islander, she would be reckoned amongst our kin."

Her eyes were amused, not at his expense but aware of what that meant to him. "She has an unusual gift. The Glorious One would have been greatly interested in speaking with her, I expect."

"Indeed," Cliopher replied, as dryly and ironically and equally as certain.

"She and your successor do indeed work very well together. Her manners are excellent, as she has travelled so far and amongst so many different lands and peoples, and her father's name is highly respected amongst the old Astandalan aristocracy."

If Tanaea turned out to be the object of his Radiancy's quest, Cliopher thought, it would serve all of them right.

The abbess set her cup down and regarded him more intently. "I wished to speak to you immediately, not so much regarding your presumed death and the consequent shifts in the political landscape—though we may, certainly, if you wish to discuss the matter?"

Cliopher was fairly certain he *should* say yes, and also equally certain that he did not want to. He hesitated more obviously than he liked—even if she were a long-standing ally and colleague, this was still, at court, a *weakness*—and then he remembered that newspaper. He'd read the articles, eventually. All his weaknesses, all his emotions and his passions and his most vulnerable dreams, laid out as strengths.

He smiled self-deprecatingly. "Is there anything you would like to tell me?"

"Other than the valuable assistance of my student?" She smiled at him, a true smile such as he had hardly ever seen from her before. "I should like to congratulate you, Lord Mdang, on jumping before you needed to be pushed."

He blinked at her. "I'm sorry? Please forgive me, Abbess, I am still recovering from the concussion."

"Of course. That is—well, we shall come to that soon enough. Lord Mdang, you had already prepared *all* that needed to be done to hand over everything bar the most formal and ceremonial elements of your role as Viceroy to your successor. You had already begun the transition. When we necessarily called off the search, Sayu Aioru had merely to search your files for the Protocol for the Unexpected Death of the Head of State, and there were all the remaining steps laid out with the thoroughness and clarity for which your policies are justly renowned."

Cliopher hoped she would get to the point soon. Also, she'd clearly called Aioru *sayu* rather than *sayo*. He would have to talk to Aioru about that, make certain he was using the correct form of the honorific.

"I can see you are not altogether yourself," the Mother Superior said. "When I heard the glad news that you had recovered your proper memories, I wished to make my own assessment. I originally trained as a healer, as I believe you know."

"You have mentioned it in the past, yes."

Her eyes were glinting more silvery than ever. Magic stirring, he guessed, though he could not *feel* it. He never could, unless it were powerful indeed. Sometimes he noticed it when his Radiancy was working magic, but that was because Cliopher was so attuned to his lord's behaviour and demeanour that he could see, almost sense, his magic rising.

"One of the matters Tanaea and I have been discussing is the nature of wild magic and what it means, or can mean, to be a *great* mage."

Cliopher was fairly sure that was intended to be a hint. He smiled weakly. There was no way he was going to be able to tug his Radiancy away from his quest with the promise of a successor *in the Palace*—his Radiancy, having tasted freedom, having had the opportunity to reclaim his full self (his *Fitzroy Angursell* self), would not be at all ready to return.

No matter that Cliopher thought it might be easier on his successor if she had more than a month or so to work beside him.

("That is not how succession works amongst those in my position," his Radiancy had said when he broached the topic of the timing of his return. "Traditionally death is the boundary." No matter how delicately Cliopher had suggested that it might be worth *training* his successor, his Radiancy had refused to be budged. Now that Cliopher knew the truth, he understood better why, even if he still thought his Radiancy was wrong.)

"One of the little-known aspects about being a great mage of truly *wild* power," the Mother of the Mountains said presently, "is that one affects the magic around them at all times and without conscious intent. One may naturally endeavour to *increase* that effect, which may rise to the point of being called spells or enchantments or curses or the like, but it is impossible to fully remove it."

Cliopher focused back on the abbess, and tried to run those words through his mind again. "Yes?" he said tentatively.

"Even I have a small field of ... influence, let us say, though it is nothing to one such as his Radiancy."

"Oh?" Cliopher said, since she seemed to expect a response.

She smiled at him, her eyes crinkling so her tattoos seemed to shift position and emphasis. "You are not recovered, are you?" she murmured. "Let me be more explicit: The effect is most pronounced on those places and persons with whom I spend the most time and am most emotionally entangled."

For a moment Cliopher continued to wonder what on earth she was getting at, and then realized that he himself had spent a considerable amount of time in the presence of and, one might argue, emotionally entangled with, a very great *wild* mage.

"Ah," he said, sitting back in his seat.

"In your case," the abbess continued, "such an effect is compounded by the fact that you stand in the position of a great mage without actually being one. The magic of Zunidh was taught to know you because of your proximity and relationship with Lord Artorin, and when you were formally, ritually, and magically inducted as Viceroy, the world ... responded."

She must have seen Cliopher's not-quite-skeptical response to this (for apart from the strange experience following the landslide, there had been no odd magical happenings around him at all since he became Viceroy), for she smiled more openly.

"Forgive me what must sound very odd and unbelievable. This is very little studied. The Lord of Ysthar has written several essays on the topic, but I believe there is nothing else but what Tanaea and I have been discussing in response to them."

"What does it mean for me?" Cliopher managed.

The Mother of the Mountains sipped her tea, set her cup down once again, and then regarded him from under hooded eyes. Her tattoos seemed to move, the colours darkening or fading, the designs subtly shifting.

"I am not the Lord of Ysthar," she murmured, "who is said to be gifted in sight as almost none other. Yet I have studied long, performed many rituals, entered deeply into the mysteries. I see ... much."

"His Radiancy spoke of your insight and clarity of vision, when we spoke of his quest and your position in his absence."

"He is kind. His gift dwarfs mine, as the mountain the foothill." She shrugged elegantly. "Our inclinations and our studies have been different. I have sought balance between the elements, as is the way of my religion; he has worked directly with them, though his inclination is to fire and to air and his studies have been deep in the naming of names."

Oh, Cliopher knew what she meant, not from his long years as his Radiancy's secretary but from long reading of *Aurora* and Fitzroy Angursell's other poetry.

The *naming of names* had always thrilled through him, the idea that magic and poetry were inextricably linked, as in the Islander way history and philosophy and poetry were all to be found in the *Lays*.

The high, ethereal singing from the dream of drowning came back to him. He tried not to shiver.

"And so," the Mother of the Mountains said, "we come to your odd experiences. I spoke with your younger self, if so he truly was. I have heard *you* fell into another version of the world in your ... absence."

"So it seemed to me."

She nodded, neither encouraging nor disbelieving. "Thus. You are imbrangled with magic despite not being yourself a mage. Our world of Zunidh knows you as she knows few individuals. Your strange experience was, I believe, the result of the world's magic having taken a liking to you combined with a certain motivation on the part of the powers that be—so we may call them, for their names are their own—to give you ... a gift, a test, an opportunity. They are often the same, when it comes to the gods and the powers greater than any human imagination."

The Ciriths believed that the world was full of deities—almost *crammed* full. Cliopher had talked to people in Old Damara, the heartland of the religion, and been amazed at how they imagined the world. Every tree and spring and river and mountain, almost every stone, had its own protective deity; the heavens and hells (for they believed in places of torment as well as grace) were a bureaucracy more creaking and congested than even the end of the Astandalan service.

Even Cliopher had quailed at the description of the proliferation of portfolios amongst the gods.

If it turned out to be a universally true religion, and he did not sail Sky Ocean with his ancestors, then he would surely do something about it.

He did not *want* to. He wanted to sail with his ancestors, chasing viaus to his heart's content, the starry sky his ocean and the wake of his ship a blessing and a guidance to those who lived beneath it.

"We have spoken in the past of how the Cirith tradition is to consider the fourfold, under the symbolism of the four elements."

"Yes, I remember," he said. "Fire, Air, Water, and Earth." He had found the fundamental idea of a four-elemental system comprehensible, if still somewhat alien to his conception of things.

"This is not, I think, your tradition?"

In Islander culture the world was home to divinities, as it was home to human beings and plants and animals. But Vou'a and Ani were at once more distant and more engaged than the Cirithian gods.

Cliopher had never really *prayed* to Vou'a. But he had met him in that marketplace on Lesuia.

"We do not frame it so ... abstractly, no."

She nodded. "Even so, Lord Mdang, I look at you, and see how the elements know you and are known by you. If you will permit the impertinence, I think you may find it helpful to hear what I have seen."

"I understand," said Cliopher, wondering at this—diagnosis? "Please, go on."

"First, we say, there is water. All the magic around you sings of the sea. No surprise there, you have spoken often of what it means to you to be a Wide Seas Islander."

He had, yes. Undoubtedly.

She tipped her head. The tattoos around her eyes seemed to grow in prominence, though he could not quite decide why he thought that. Her eyes were glittering silver. He refused to look away. His spine was tingling with atavistic response.

Her voice went softer, more distant, as if she were sight-reading from a page someone else had written. "You have been marked by the sea. Tempest-tossed and becalmed, of the surface and yet aware of the currents of the great deeps. The sea has tested you, tried you, *known* you, given you her warnings and her gifts. The sea embraces you and says: through great fear you have passed to wisdom."

Perhaps that humbleness he had learned in the face of Ani was wisdom. Or at least the first star of wisdom's ke'ea: he had spent his lifetime trying to understand what that journey meant.

The Mother of the Mountains opened her hands to him, and the markings on her palms seemed to swirl and shimmer, as a heat mirage upon the water.

"Then there is fire." She smiled at him. "No one who witnessed it could forget your dance across the coals. No one has ever forgotten your more passionate speeches. Your inspired reforms have shaped the world. It is no surprise. You know fire by the soles of your feet and the palms of your hands and the tongue in your mouth, by your mind and your heart and your soul."

She paused there. Cliopher was shattered by that simple accounting of a lifetime's efforts to be tanà. He swallowed, and waited, seeking a patience he did not feel.

As he had so often been rewarded, when he had managed to keep his tongue still, his ears receptive, so was he rewarded, for she went on.

"You are by nature inclined to fire: quick-witted, quick-tempered, quick-tongued. Warm, sometimes hot, sometimes blazing: always brilliant, always seeking to illuminate."

Cliopher had seen that so clearly in the other Kip, what he had lost over the years.

"And yet," the abbess went on, her eyes gentle, even kind. "You have learned well the lessons of the sea. Sought to become as water: gentle, persistent, irresistible. The softest of all things, and yet when struck as hard as the strike."

Cliopher was trembling, his soul cut open and laid out to see with three deft sentences.

"There is a story I have heard," she said, her voice kind. "A sage with his disciples went to observe a river at the base of a waterfall, full of whirlpools and treacherous currents over hidden rocks. On the other side they saw a man approach the bank and dive in."

She tilted her head, a small smile on her face, luminous in her eyes. Cliopher could not tell which of her tattoos were prominent now; all he could do was wait, mouth dry, to hear her words.

"The sage and his disciples ran to the riverbank, searching for the suicide's body, for who else would dive so into that river? But the man who had dived came up on the bank, unharmed and unafraid, surprised at their fear. And when asked how he had survived, he said that he went where the water went, and so ended up where he wished."

Cliopher stared at her. He drew a deep breath, uncertain.

The Mother of the Mountains did not draw any more explicit conclusions than that. She spread her hands. "As for earth ... fire and water sing so loudly and so clearly around you that it seems inconceivable that earth could speak forth above them, but so it is. You are rooted deep in place, anchored below the very sea. Fire burns in the heart of your land. Your heart is anchored by earth, the specific local earth of your home, and yet your care expands out and across all the lands of the world."

She was the Mother of the Mountains. Earth was her element, Cliopher guessed, earth and air. She would be interested in his connection to those.

His island burned in his mind, a distant star. Furai'fa, that was the name of the ke'e of Loaloa. An unimportant star, unless you knew it as your home's zenith.

"No doubt it was the will of your gods that your strange experience took the form it did. Your uncle told me stories your people hold of such things. I believe, having performed divinations and studied the situation in the Liaau, that Earth was giving you a gift, a test, an opportunity, a warning, as is the way of these powers. They are not human and do not have human concerns. They know you because of your devotion and your dedication and because, as I said, you stand in the position of the one human they are accustomed to being able to notice. The rest is mystery."

Mystery. Vou'a was the god of mysteries, of caves and mountains, of the shoreline and all its in-betweenness. He had raised the islands for Ani.

"As for the element of air ... I think, Lord Mdang, you have not yet received that ... gift."

Cliopher held her gaze as long as he could before he broke and looked down at the tea remaining in his cup. It was an amber-brown, missing the gold of his Radiancy's eyes. He wished his Radiancy were here, to help him parse this strange, unexpected conversation.

"Do not be afraid," the Mother of the Mountains said. "You are surrounded by magic, by the love and esteem Lord Artorin bears for you, by all the protections his love and esteem have woven around you, consciously and not, over the years. There are few who would ever seek to work against such protections. No one would want to attract the ire of the one who laid them so carefully and so well."

Cliopher had very rarely had to do with any situation where that protection would be necessary.

Or—as far as he knew, he hadn't.

He had been the focus of targeted attacks before, for his reforms and for his position and for personal or political enmities. Rhodin's people had always managed to protect him from any physical harm, but magical curses could be insidious. Cliopher knew they had been in use in the Astandalan court, and every once in a while there would be some attempt made in his Radiancy's present court.

Not often. His Radiancy *was* a great mage, and when he discovered such a curse had been laid—and from Rhodin's account, he had discovered each attempt almost immediately—his wrath had been terrifying.

If Cliopher had such protections around him, and that was *known*, to those who knew such magic, that might explain quite a few things about his apparently invulnerability to certain court intrigues. He had always thought it was just that those particular factions did not think him worth the effort.

The Mother of the Mountains looked down at her hands. Each finger was tattooed with a different pattern, corresponding from right to left. Only her thumbs were different: her left thumb was a complex design of interlocking spirals, and her right seemed constellations of asterisks.

"You know of the four elements," she said slowly, and Cliopher found all his attention focused on her, for that was the voice of someone about to tell a secret. He held himself still, attentive, unthreatening, receptive but unforced.

"It is far less known," she said, "that in the deeper magics of the Cirithian religion, as one follows the fourfold path into the mysteries, that one begins to study the remaining two cardinal directions."

He looked at her, his heart thudding steadily in his chest. He could feel his physical pain as a distant cloud; all of him seemed attuned to her words.

She spread out her hands, the fingers wide, and then turned them so that her left thumb pointed down, her right up. "Together with the four elements, the four directions, there is also down, into the underworld, and up, into the heavens."

The Cirithians believed in those hierarchies of heavens and hells, those divine bureaucracies, those proliferations of portfolios and ministries and powers.

"I do not know what your beliefs are, Lord Mdang. We have never spoken of them, and I have not studied your religion. I hope I do not offend you if I ask if you have such a tradition?"

He took a deep breath, but she was sharing mysteries, and he had long respected her. And this was ... private, rather than secret.

"We say that those who die pass on to sail Sky Ocean. And we have a god of mysteries—the Son of Laughter, we call him."

He hesitated over whether he should say Vou'a's name.

"That is a very interesting title."

Cliopher hesitated again. "He has many names. He ..." He thought of Buru Tovo, who had often joked that he was married to the Son of Laughter, an old phrase meaning that he was inclined to men. "We do not have priests or a religion, not the way you do," he went on. "There are temples but they are more ... Astandalan in origin."

The abbess looked at him. "How do you—approach your gods? If you do."

"They approach you," Cliopher said automatically, the words straight out of the *Lays*. "It can happen ... anywhere."

You could meet a mysterious seller of shells in a village marketplace, for instance, who could upend your world with one grin and one question.

She hummed thoughtfully. "You stand at a crossroads, Lord Mdang."

A crossroads meant very little, on the ocean. A place where two currents or two swells crossed was a kurakura: a place, often, of much abundance, for the complicated waters would stir up sediments and attract all the creatures, great and small, that fed on them.

"A crossroads, Mother Superior?"

She gestured with her left hand, the interlocked swirls on her thumb darkening, moving whenever he wasn't looking, so he had at every moment the sensation of something flicking out of sight in the corners of his vision.

"There is darkness ahead of you," she said, and her eyes shone a pale silver, like moonlit fog upon the sea. "Darkness and danger ... deep shadows. Deeper crevasses. They go down forever ... There are monsters below." Her voice was abstract; Cliopher's spine shivered with horror. "And it is so silent."

"I see," he said. That was Vou'a's way, surely. He was the god of caves, amongst other things.

"I do not," she whispered, closing her eyes. She folded her left thumb into her fingers, made a fist of her left hand. Her right was still outstretched, the asterisks lightening until they seemed white scar-lines instead of black ink. "The other direction also holds darkness and danger for you. Deep shadows. Deeper crevasses. They go up forever ... And there are monsters above. They are not so silent."

He sat there. Sky Ocean was a place of many wonders and many terrors; so said those parts of the *Lays* that spoke of them. His father's mother, his Varga grandmother, had told him many tales of the beings that inhabited those places just past the edge of the seas the Islanders sailed.

The Mother of the Mountains folded that thumb into her fingers, made a fist of her right hand, and then, with a peculiarly ritual motion, placed her fists together in her lap. Only then did she open her eyes again to look at him; her face was troubled.

"Lord Mdang, I see and I do not understand. The gifts of the four elements stand around you, but these, the farther two ... the spiritual realm is pressing close upon you. You have gained their attention."

They being ... the gods, he presumed. Once again he recalled that efelauni in the market-place on Lesuia, laughing like a kookaburra after Cliopher dared bargain with him, his heart's desire for a strand of forty-nine sundrop cowries.

And he recalled, as if from a dream, that dreamlike dawn when he had woken at the Gates of the Sea, having reached sight of his home harbour at last after so long alone crossing the Wide Seas in his little *Tui-tanata*, and discovering there, floating upon the waves, that gift of the sea, the shell called Ani's Tear, which he had never been quite certain was for him.

His head was hurting. He did not know how to respond, to the eerie certainty of the Mother of the Mountains, to this strange account of magic and gods and things with which he had never before concerned himself.

(Except, a voice whispered, he *had* answered that challenge in the market-place, and he *had* taken up that shell.)

"Lord Mdang," the abbess said after a long silence, in which she had considered her fisted hands.

He looked up from his own lap. She had relaxed her hands, and let them spread open, palms down, on her thighs. Her eyes had returned to their more usual pale grey, no longer shining with magic. Her expression was very serious; her voice fully present.

"Mother Superior," he replied politely, attentively, not certain how curious he should permit himself to be.

(Oh but he was, he was. He had always been too curious for his own good. Too clever by half and too curious and far far *far* too stubborn.)

"You stand at a crossroads," she repeated. "The paths unfold before you. Darkness and the monsters below; darkness and the monsters above. But it is a crossroads, and one of our teachings—for I follow the fourfold way, Lord Mdang—is that one does not always need to continue *forward*. Sometimes the best way is to turn and take another road entirely."

Cliopher stared at her, trying to make sense of that. He *knew* that; surely *she* knew he knew that? He was a sailor, of a seafaring people. You had to *constantly* change course in order to keep your way.

She smiled suddenly: a small but a genuine smile. "I have known you too long," she murmured. "That is not your way, is it? Lord Mdang—" Her face went serious again, intent. "Lord Mdang, you do not need to ... perpetually *keep going*. You are allowed to be done with this task. You are allowed to stop."

Is this where you stop?

Buru Tovo's perpetual challenge—the *world's* perpetual challenge—rang in his ears, her words. And as he had then, as he always had, Cliopher responded immediately, almost unconsciously.

Almost unconsciously. For this was a true challenge, and one's response had to be conscious and deliberate, *chosen*, in return.

His chin came up, his shoulders went back, his spine straightened, and the Mother of the Mountains, who had worked with him, beside him, across from him, on so many committees and projects over the years, sighed and smiled and even chuckled ruefully.

"No, that is not in your nature, is it?"

"I have sailed across unknown seas before," he replied evenly. "One does not reach one's destination by turning back."

She closed her eyes; looking politely away from her face, he saw that she was pressing her thumbs into her thighs.

"I do not doubt your vision," he added.

"Take heed," she said urgently. "I can see nothing but darkness."

That did make him take pause. He might, after all, be setting the wrong course for his destination— He spoke in a somewhat subdued voice. "Nothing?"

She cupped her hands, fingers interlaced, and stared intently into the hollow made by her palms. He waited, while the tattoos once more seemed to move and shift, darken and lighten, slowly migrate across her skin, while yet always being what they were when he looked directly upon them.

Finally she said, her brow furrowed, "I can see nothing but darkness ... except that there is one tiny white thing ... a shell, I think ... very far in the distance."

"A tiny white shell," Cliopher repeated carefully.

"Very tiny," she agreed. "It is dwarfed by the darkness."

It would be, he thought, the image brilliant in his mind. The tiny white shell, perfect in his hand, which he had picked up in the *other place*, that last evening, flared in his memory.

Fanoa was the word for them, those tiny white shells one found on every beach, clams or cowries or anything else of the sort.

They were ... they were something he understood.

"Thank you," he said sincerely.

The Mother of the Mountains looked up at him, her eyes full of magic, of wonder, of mystery. "And for the possibility of a tiny white shell," she said, "you would face the certainty of darkness?"

"It is a common and ordinary thing," he said, and then, when her eyes sharpened, full of humour as well as wisdom, he smiled and—for he did not need to even pretend he did not know where that phrase had come from, now that Aioru had published Cliopher's carefully crafted, impassioned essay about why this was the fundamental message—the fundamental *decency*—of Fitzroy Angursell's poetry (for while Fitzroy Angursell could be scathing, he had never been *mean*)—and so he added: "It is a common and ordinary *good*."

"And for those," the Mother of the Mountains said, "you have shown over and over again you would face any darkness and doubt."

"I would," he said, for he always had.

Chapter Twenty-Five
Three Offers

Cliopher began, slowly, to feel better.

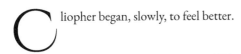

He talked to Aioru about the poet laureate business.

Aioru was unembarrassed. "It was a very good essay," he said. "Convincing."

"I hadn't exactly ratified it."

"Zaoul assisted his Radiancy with the pardons for the Red Company, so I was certain the Lord Emperor would hardly *disagree* with your last wishes."

"The ... pardons?"

"Oh yes, you missed that. His Radiancy issued official pardons for the entire Red Company, individually and as a group, though as you know he didn't announce that he'd done so. I assume he wanted to wait for the Jubilee, but he left no *instructions*, and I was sure he'd want to honour your last wishes when clearly they aligned so well with his intentions."

Cliopher could not say that Aioru had done anything *wrong*, for he hadn't. He was the one who had written the essay and left it in his desk, and he was the one who had been caught by a landslide and presumed dead according to the Protocols he himself had written. And his Radiancy was ... Fitzroy Angursell.

It was not as if Cliopher were *unhappy* about this turn of events.

Even if Vinyë and his friends teased him mightily for his long-standing love of Fitzroy Angursell's poetry.

"I've heard a few people refer to you as *sayu*," Cliopher said, letting it go. "I wanted to be sure I wasn't using the wrong honorific. Or indeed pronouns."

Aioru relaxed, his grin softening to something a bit more personally amused. "I've started going by both. Aioru sounds like it's a neutral name to most of the

Palace folk, you know. It's not in my tribe, but I don't mind—it's made me think about it more. Question some of my assumptions. And it's not," he concluded, "as if I am a very *manly* man. At home."

Cliopher blinked at him. "Both?"

"Either, sayo or sayu is fine," Aioru clarified. "I think it's neat. My family already thought something of the sort," he added, and laughed. "My siblings are going to come for the installment. They've never gone farther than the City of Emeralds before. We're trying to persuade our parents, but my father's never left the desert at all."

There was no strain there. Aioru started talking about the party his siblings had thrown when he'd left home, and then shifted towards the Mae Irionéz embassy and how he felt for them, leaving their isolated existence for the outside world, and his ideas for how to integrate them into the world without losing their fundamental culture.

Cliopher felt something ease—some uncertainty, some wistfulness, some fear —something.

∽

At some point soon his family and friends would head home. Bertie had spent a great deal of time with Cora and their sons, and Cliopher had the impression that Cora was considering sailing home on Bertie's boat with them. He was glad. Very glad.

But when his friends tentatively asked if he might like to join them, he responded with an immediate, instinctive *no*.

"Sorry," he said weakly, looking away from their surprise, that evening when he was sitting with them and Vinyë. "Thank you for the invitation."

"I'm sure you have things you will need to finish up here," his sister said comfortingly, patting his knee.

"Packing, at least," Ghilly suggested, with a sly look around the cozy sitting room.

"Yes," he said, and then, because that was not, after all, quite true, he ducked his head and mumbled, "I'm not ready to go home yet."

"We understand," Vinyë said, with an odd look on her face.

Cliopher looked at his sister, trying to parse her expression. Was it—relief? He rubbed his temple in lieu of shaking his head. Sometimes he felt as if he continuously needed to shake it, as if there were water in his ears or something loose that needed to be constantly poked back into place.

But shaking his head only made it hurt.

"Do you?" It was getting late in the day: his emotional equilibrium was faltering. So was his ability to focus. He knew he should go to bed, but it was so nice to sit with them, there in his own place, as if he were home.

He could go home. But he didn't *want* to.

He wanted that shell on the other side of the darkness.

"You'll get there," Vinyë said softly, reaching out and taking his hand away from where he was pressing his knuckle into the side of his head. "Kip, we'll be there when you're ready. You need time to ... transition."

"You need to sort out your relationship with your lord," Toucan added, and the rest of them laughed, and Cliopher, to his private embarrassment, blushed.

~

He visited Pikabe, who appeared to be relishing his convalescence.

Cliopher had no idea how he did it, and didn't want to ask how losing an arm could leave him so apparently cheerful. He felt significantly more mulish and grumbly about his concussion and summary loss of his job, and he had been planning to retire within the year. Pikabe could have had decades longer in his position, if he'd wanted.

His Radiancy's core guards had their own rooms inside the barracks: small ones, admittedly, but they had windows and privacy. Pikabe greeted him with great gusto, making a small apology for the messiness in his room and explaining that he'd been writing instead of cleaning. He had a lapdesk, and carefully turned over the pages before Cliopher could catch a peek of the writing.

Cliopher thanked him for his service and the likelihood that Pikabe had saved his life. "I'm sorry for your arm."

"It's not my writing hand," Pikabe said, as if this were the important thing. "I wasn't sure I was going to stay on, after his Radiancy retired, you know. There's a girl ..." He grinned up at Cliopher. "With the stipend, and my pension from the Guard, I'll be fine ... and I've been thinking I might take up writing. Professionally, I mean."

Cliopher honestly had no idea what to say. "I'm glad you have so many things to look forward to," he said sincerely. "I'd like to read your books, once they're published."

Pikabe laughed. "Thank you, sir. Perhaps ... perhaps I can dedicate the first to you and his Radiancy? If you're willing, of course. I'll send you the manuscript when it's done, so you can decide. It's ... inspired by ... some of the stories you told me, sir, about the emperor and his great Islander friend—the navigator."

"Elonoa'a," said Cliopher, his heart warming at this evidence that Pikabe had listened to him.

"Yes, sir."

"I'm sure his Radiancy and I will both be glad to read it."

Pikabe blushed. "Yes, sir. Thank you, sir. Appreciate the visit, sir."

~

Cliopher went out, one afternoon, to walk in the gardens.

It had rained again that morning, but he had seen a gap in the clouds and gone out forthwith. It was extraordinary that he *could*. He had never looked out the window in the middle of the day and thought the weather looked fine and he'd like to go for a walk, and simply *gone*.

The guards trailed behind him, Varro and Zerafin today. He would rather be altogether alone, but it was good to know that if he needed something he could turn to one of them. He knew it made his family feel better, when he had told them he was going out by himself, that he was not *entirely* by himself.

Most of them had never understood Cliopher's desire to go off and be alone with himself. He'd found private places even as a teenager in Gorjo City, taking his small outrigger canoe—even smaller than his *Tui-tanata*—out to the nearest of the Ring islands, pretending he had gone fishing when all he had done, quite often, was sit in the shade of a handful of palm trees and read his book.

His footsteps turned, as always, to the bench under the tui tree, the view eastwards. The sea was a deep blue with a fine rim of white. A sky ship was passing over the Fens, orange-striped sails belly-full of wind.

Perhaps it was that ship that his Radiancy had taken, when he was picked up from the Fens like a stranded mariner from a desert island.

Cliopher watched the ship until it disappeared in the distance. His head was throbbing slowly, with a different sort of headache than he was accustomed to. It felt like rolling waves coming into shore, steady as an ocean. Deepwater swells.

He leaned against the bench, grateful for the dappled shade cast by the tui's leaves. It still had a few blossoms strewn about its branches, waxy petals upon the ground. He breathed in the scents, the chocolate of the blossoms and the faintly sweet rot of the old flowers.

The river was a glittering greyish-brown line, wide and muddy from the rains. The fields and pastures on either side, cradled in the opening valley between the Escarpment and the hills to the south, were a rich, verdant green.

The eastern horizon looked so far away.

∼

He was still sitting there when Ludvic came to find him.

He heard the guards rustle and come to attention, and Zerafin cleared his throat and say, "Commander Omo, Lord Mdang."

Cliopher opened his eyes and turned his head to see that Ludvic was standing at a polite distance away, speaking softly with Varro. He smiled at Zerafin and beckoned Ludvic to join him, shifting over so there was room on the bench beside him.

Ludvic, unsurprisingly, preferred to stand, hands hooked into his belt, balanced easily on his feet. He was wearing his usual day-to-day uniform, not the panoply he wore on guard but the midnight-blue tunic and trousers and the bronze-and-gold half-cloak of his rank. He had a sword at his side, which was also a part of the official uniform.

Cliopher had put on teal-green silk this morning. He felt unmoored.

Ludvic regarded him solemnly. "Would you like to go down to the city with me?"

"If you have the time," Cliopher replied. He'd barely been able to meet with Ludvic since he'd come back from the *other place*, his friend had been so busy. He stood, and felt a wash of dizziness. He put a hand on the backrest of the bench. "I'm not sure I can walk that far."

"I know. There's a rickshaw waiting." Ludvic gave a sharp nod to Varro and Zerafin, who looked enquiringly at Cliopher. When he simply looked back at them, Ludvic rumbled a laugh. "You can stay up here. If anyone needs us—*needs*, mind you —we'll be at Giya's, down in the Levels."

Cliopher nodded belated agreement. The two guards saluted and departed, straight-backed and free-striding even as Varro had to duck his head beneath a branch of the curtain fig.

"Come along, then," Ludvic said gently.

It was nice not to be making the decisions. Cliopher told himself that. It was.

The rickshaw dropped them off at the edge of the Levels. Ludvic paid the cyclist to wait for their return, and led Cliopher into the maze of buildings.

This time they did not look as if they belonged, and they moved through a moving bubble of silence as the crowds fell silent and pulled back to give them passage.

Cliopher's headache was growing ever more noticeable, a distant storm gathering strength. He followed Ludvic's unhurried pace, keeping his eyes on his friend's dark tunic rather than the shining, shimmering cloak. Had he remembered to put one of Domina Audry's phials in his pocket? Did this outfit even *have* a pocket?

This time the courtyards were full of vegetables, leafy greens and sugarcane and piles of citrus fruits. He caught the scent of fires, wood burning in great metal braziers or clay-brick ovens. Bread baking, beans cooking, the sweet char of fresh corn grilled in its husks.

He was grateful no one called to him; that they were accorded that silent bubble of empty passage. A few people still called to Ludvic, hailing him politely—very politely, with him in his guard commander's uniform, tall and broad and official.

And a few people murmured Cliopher's name, low voices where he hardly caught a word beyond 'died'; and slightly louder comments of how he'd made Fitzroy Angursell the poet laureate.

He was glad when they reached Giya's bar.

To his surprise, it was also a café: there were tables outside with umbrellas over them for shade and to protect evening patrons against the rain, where clusters of people with Azilinti clothes and features ate pastries and drank the thick syrupy coffee of the region.

They nodded at Ludvic with a kind of wary respect. Ludvic nodded back, more stiffly than usual, and said nothing as he led Cliopher into the dark, empty room and the same bead-hung booth they had used before.

Ludvic waited till he had settled himself, then exited the booth and went unhesitatingly to the bar at the back of the room, where he filled a jug of water and collected glasses. Cliopher watched him in bemusement. Ludvic clearly had a close relationship with Giya, and the fact that he had his own booth, with his family carvings on it, suggested it was longstanding.

Cliopher was nonetheless shocked when Ludvic spent a few minutes behind the bar, then disappeared through the swinging back door of the room and returned bearing coffee and a plate of fried dough twists sprinkled with cinnamon sugar.

He grabbed cloth napkins from the bar, and plates, and set all of this on the table before taking his seat opposite Cliopher. Cliopher stared at the coffee, which was steaming and still managed to look approximately the viscosity of honey, and wrestled with his tongue.

He lost when Ludvic got up and came back with a bowl of nuts from the bar. "Should you be doing that?"

"What's that?" Ludvic asked, stolidly as ever but Cliopher flicked up his glance and saw a twinkle in his eyes.

"I'm missing something," he said, resigned. "Do you have an arrangement with Giya?"

"Naturally," Ludvic agreed, and he let his amusement show. "Look at you, so confused and uncourtly! It's unnatural. It's my bar."

Cliopher stared at him. "Yes ..."

Now Ludvic was nearly laughing, his eyes bright and his shoulders relaxed. "Literally mine. As in, I *own* it."

"Oh. Oh!"

"Yes. Yes!" Ludvic was obviously happy to have surprised him. "You didn't realize last time? Mind, you were in a somewhat *preoccupied* mood."

"Somewhat, indeed," he replied, a touch more sourly than he quite intended, for he was still embarrassed for not having figured out that particular truth sooner. His Radiancy truly had done everything bar outright telling him, and yet he *still* hadn't figured it out. "This is your place? When did you buy it? After ..." He trailed off. He wasn't going to say the name, not unless Ludvic did. One didn't mention Woodlark.

Ludvic sobered slightly. "I'd watched you, of course. Listened to you, also. When I was on duty. Heard you talking, over and over, about building communities, maintaining communities. What makes them healthy, what makes them sick. How they need ... centres. After what happened at Woodlark ... I was already almost-outcast. People knew why I'd done it, made those orders. They could ... respect that someone had to. But they could not *like* me for it."

He sipped his coffee, apparently immured to the heat; Cliopher had already burned his tongue on his and set it back down.

"I was used to not being ... *liked*. It did not stop me wishing to help. It was hard—you know that. There were refugees, not many from the highlands, but some of the coastal people escaped. They came here, when it was still so poor, and it was bad. Hard. I knew you were working on the poverty, and that I did not have enough money, myself, to help everyone that way. And they would not have accepted it, from me. A blood-price, they would have said, for something that couldn't be paid for. So I thought about what you said, and this is what I came up with."

There was so much in that ... Cliopher looked carefully at Ludvic, who did not, he suspected, wish to talk about those old wounds. Still—he could be wrong. His emotional equilibrium was unbalanced, and his thoughts kept scattering like a school of fish, and Ludvic had kept secrets from him before. He hoped his willingness to listen, to hold a space open as he had for Uncle Lazo (as Ludvic had for him, in this booth, this bar, on the other side of the landslide), would be enough. "A café-bar?"

"A gathering-place," Ludvic corrected, as Cliopher had so often corrected others. "A peaceful, pleasant place to meet, to eat together, to drink together, to be a community in." He waved towards the door. "I own two of the other buildings, too. One's a—what did you call it? A tool library. The other one's a book library."

Three things Cliopher had said a community needed; over and over again, all through the creation of the Indrogan Estates to deal with the worst of the world's slums. A place to meet, and the knowledge and tools you needed to build something.

For a moment, he was almost incandescently proud.

"Yes, yes," Ludvic said, smiling, and pushed the fried dough at him. "Your coffee should be cool enough to drink now."

It was. Each of the Azilint islands had its own way of preparing coffee—they were one of the homelands of the shrub—and the Woodlarkian form was thick and syrupy, spiced with something unfamiliar, not quite cardamom. It felt as if it would make the hair grow on his head from two sips.

"I hear," Ludvic said presently, "that Conju invited you to go with him to finish off his vacation, and you said no."

Cliopher looked down at the scarred wood of the table-top. Conju had invited him, casually but also sincerely. Now that he was caught up on Cliopher's mother's gossip—or so he put it—Conju was ready to return to his extravagant and meticulously planned holiday, Antonio or no Antonio, and make the most of it.

Cliopher had had as immediate a *no* on his lips as he had when Bertie and Toucan had made their offer.

"I hear, too, that you're not ready to go home yet, either."

He shook his head, mute. His head was hurting again, though the water helped. Perhaps it was the coffee? It was very strong.

His teal silk robes did have pockets, but they were empty.

Ludvic watched him as he resigned himself to the water as the best option. "Food will help," the guard observed, and then slid out of the booth and back behind the bar again. He came back with more nuts and a small bottle with an even smaller green-glass spoon attached to the bottle by a string. Cliopher stared at the spoon. It was probably the smallest spoon he'd ever seen, even smaller than the absurdly tiny caviar spoons sometimes brought out a court dinners, with their recurved handles and bowls intended to hold no more than twelve grains of roe.

Ludvic wiggled the cork out of the bottle and poured two drops of a heavy liquid onto the tiny spoon. It was an oily, iridescent silver; it did not look in the least appetizing.

"Two drops only, no more than twice a day, *with* food," Ludvic said. "Tell Domina Audry before you take anything other than the nirgalin."

Cliopher was mesmerized by the way the light reflected on the spoon and its silver liquid. "Nirgalin?"

"Didn't you ask what medicines you were given? That's the pain potion she gave you. This is the concentrated form. Eat the churro."

He picked up the fried dough, still lukewarm to his touch, the cinnamon sugar falling all over his hands and the table in front of him, and ate it obediently. Ludvic passed him the spoon, and he stared, unsure if he were supposed to lick it. "How do you know?"

"Just let it drop onto your tongue. Your household and guards know, so no one gives you anything that might react poorly with it. Nirgalin is safe with most things, but don't mix it with hard liquor. Beer or wine's fine."

The nirgalin tasted fruity on his tongue, not metallic at all. It might have been his imagination, but it felt as if the vise clamped on his skull was loosening already. Cliopher smiled weakly. "No rós today, then, I take it?"

Ludvic snorted, peered intently at his eyes, and then nodded in satisfaction. "Good. Finish that, Giya'll bring dinner soon."

With his headache receding—when had it gotten *that* strong? Surely he should have noticed at some point earlier—Cliopher was rather more able to focus. "Is it dinnertime already?"

"What we call dinner," Ludvic said, shrugging.

"Her food's good. A bit spicier than I'm used to, but good."

"Maybe she'll remember that." He drank down the rest of his coffee and wiped his mouth with the back of his hand in a gesture Cliopher felt shockingly and intimately casual. Ludvic looked at him, his wide face settling into its more familiar, placid lines. His eyes were intent; serious. "I'm sorry I never brought you here earlier."

"I can understand wanting something of your own culture." He smiled painfully. "I didn't invite you when I went down to the museum to look at the Wide Seas Islander artefacts, either."

"I'm sorry I didn't," Ludvic repeated, and this time Cliopher was able to be silent. He drank his thick, viscous coffee, trying to work out what spice flavoured it. He ate the rest of the churro.

Giya came, *rat-a-tat* on the edge of the booth. She brought them beer and a platter containing a bowl of something goopy and green surrounded by fried plantain chips.

Cliopher tried the gloop warily. There was a faint burn at the back of his throat, but the forward taste was creamy avocado and some bright combination of herbs and spices. Onion, cilantro, garlic—and was that firgal lime? Mellower than regular limes, just a hint of a pleasant mustiness.

He felt embarrassed to have offered Ludvic a home in Gorjo City, assuming he had none here.

Not embarrassed for the offer. For the assumption.

Ludvic said nothing, and said nothing. They finished the dish of avocado goop and all the plantain chips, and Giya came by with another ewer of cold water and more beer and more unidentifiable fried items with a deceptively innocent-looking sauce.

The fried things seemed to be sweet potatoes. The sauce was peppery and aromatic and made Cliopher sneeze.

Ludvic traced out arabesques in the water puddled on the table where the condensation had dripped off their bottles. Cliopher felt his headache slowly dwindle.

"Rhodin said you wanted to go find your cousin," Ludvic said finally.

"Yes. Basil. I ... want to find out if he's still alive."

Ludvic nodded, and was once more silent. Cliopher waited. All those years sending letters to Basil, hoping there would one day be one back. One would have been enough,

And there had never been one. Not once had any reply come. Not even from someone else from his village, or from the post-office, saying Basil was dead. *Nothing.*

Ludvic rubbed his hands down the golden smudges on his forearms, not looking quite at him

"My mother was fifteen when I was born. She loved my father—he was a year older—they got carried away. You know how it is."

"Yes." The air tasted like any cheap bar at home, this safe place of Ludvic's.

"Azilinti society places a great value on purity. Not magical purity like they have here, for *himself*, but ... sexual purity. No marriage except between a man and a woman. No sex outside of marriage."

"Oh," Cliopher said, sympathy crashing over him.

"My mother was fifteen," Ludvic repeated, touching the beads so they clacked and sparkled. "She was legally considered a child. My father was sixteen. He was an adult. Rape, they said. He would be killed for the transgression. She was ... sent to the witch, to deal with the result, but she wouldn't. My mother. She loved my father and she wanted me."

There was a different note to his voice then: a subdued wonder; a long, deep, painful love. Cliopher's heart swelled in wonder and pity. He dug his nails into his palm to keep from saying anything. It had taken half a lifetime of acquaintance, decades of friendship, for Ludvic to be able to say this. Cliopher would listen until his friend had finished what he had to say.

"My mother did not go back to the village, not really. She stayed with the witch, and she swore a blood oath to ... avenge herself. I was raised there, on the outskirts. She called me by a Shaian name, an outsider's name, because she wanted me to remember the injustice. Omo for the witch's son. Luvo was what she called me ... short for Lusseo, that would be the traditional name. Short for Ludvic. *Luvo* means 'the root of the mountain'. It is a good name. I don't know what Ludvic means."

"'Strong warrior'," Cliopher said softly, for that did seem to need a response, and he had always loved how apt a name it was for Ludvic.

Ludvic grimaced. "When I came of age, sixteen, I was an adult according to the law, and I ... wanted to leave. They gave me what they thought I should need: a knife, a cloak, a staff. By then they feared my mother, and did not stop her when she gave a proper staff to me. She would not come with me—she stayed for her work there."

The local witch—healer, herbalist, midwife—no, the village would not want to cross her or drive her away, even when she gave so important a cultural marker as an Azilinti staff to her son. Cliopher felt an odd pride in the girl who had lost so much but refused to let her village's opprobrium diminish her.

(She had raised Ludvic, who was splendid. She must have been a remarkable woman.)

"Before I left," Ludvic said, and then hesitated. Cliopher waited.

Ludvic picked up one of the crumbs from the churros and rolled it between his fingers, the sugar-dough bright against his brown skin. The gold smudges gleamed in the lantern-light.

"I went down to the sea," Ludvic went on, and Cliopher was conscious of a piercing disappointment that Ludvic would not say it. Not just for himself and his own curiosity and care, but because he thought that Ludvic might *need* to say whatever that was, to open his heart fully and let the light shine in.

But—if he was not ready, he wasn't. There were truths Cliopher held in his heart that he had never been ready to tell.

"There is always work for those who are strong, even if they are considered rather stupid." He glanced quickly at Cliopher, then down again, his cheeks flushed. "I could not read or write. It was not something that was learned in my village. I came down to the coast and everything was different. They all thought me so stupid."

Ludvic had never mocked Cliopher for not knowing how to hold a weapon. When Cliopher had asked him diffidently for exercises to increase his strength Ludvic had shown him patiently and without any whiff of condescension.

He had asked him once or twice for exercises to practice writing, which Cliopher had given him, thinking nothing more than that the guard had wanted to improve the smoothness and speed of his hand. Calligraphy was a skill like any other, and Cliopher was one of the masters of the art. He hoped he had not seemed condescending to Ludvic then.

"I was strong, because I was always given the heavy jobs to do, the ones that required no skill. I was taught to hunt, to cut and carry firewood, to carry water, to dig gardens, to move the full logs the carvers used. I was strong."

The word came out ... charged. Cliopher thought how he always thought of Ludvic as being strong—everyone thought of Ludvic as being *strong*. He was dependable, and strong in spirit and will as well as body.

And yet ... he composed romantic epics in his mind. He was kind, and thoughtful, and he watched and learned: and when a word needed to be said, he said it.

"There was a ship, going somewhere I had never heard of. But I had nowhere to go. They gave me food and a little money. It was hard work. Loading, unloading, up in the sails. All the heaviest tasks came to me." He flexed his broad shoulders. "I listened to all the others talking. They thought me stupid, illiterate and with a heavy accent, ignorant of the outside world. I listened, I watched, I learned."

Cliopher's regard for his friend, always high, surged again.

"The ship took me ... somewhere. I was paid my trifle and put ashore, and ... there I was. I worked at the dockyards of that port. I had nothing else to do, nowhere to go, no one ... no one to find."

He trailed off there, and Cliopher guessed it was something to do with that last thing he'd been told by his mother before he left his village. There was the same expression on Ludvic's face.

"There was a physician who lived there, disgraced—a drunkard—healing the dockworkers, drinking when he had the money. I used to carry people to him, because I was ... the biggest and the strongest, and ... I wanted people to live. Not die. If I could help them."

Cliopher nodded encouragingly. He took a drink to force himself to keep his mouth shut. The beer bubbled in his mouth, tickling the back of his nose. Ludvic was still not looking at him, was focused on his hands.

"I started to stay around. I wanted to learn. Healing people. Something *good*. He didn't want to teach me, he thought I was stupid and good-for-nothing, but I kept coming. Did things for him. Fixed his roof ... He started to teach me. He showed me how to read, a little."

Ludvic fell silent for a long time. Cliopher waited. The curtain of beads swayed and clacked as Giya stalked by, a tray in her hand. There were people out there in the main room now, Cliopher realized vaguely: shadowy shapes alone or in small groups, sitting at the tables with beer or rós. He couldn't hear more than a low buzz of conversation.

"I stayed there for two years, three. Artorin Damara came to the throne. Soldiers started being discharged from the armies because he wasn't expanding the Empire the same way as Eritanyr. The port city was a main disembarkation point, and grew crowded. Rougher. More fights, more crime. I was helping the physician, working the docks. I was tired all the time."

He stopped, hesitated again. Cliopher was fairly certain Ludvic had never spoken any of this out loud to anyone.

"I was asleep when some soldiers came and burned down the physician's house. He was still alive when I came, but ... I did not know enough to save him."

How *much* did Ludvic have to bear on those strong shoulders of his?

"The fire spread and took out half the city," Ludvic went on. "I helped to put it out, but in the end ... there it was. All ashes and death."

Cliopher thought he knew what city that was: the Zangoraville that was not on Nijan but had been the port at the mouth of the river Ast on Ysthar, a few hundred miles from Astandalas the Golden itself. He himself had been travelling to Astandalas, seeking his own fortune, when Zangoraville had burned down and the provincial governors had sent in the armies to restore order.

"The armies came," Ludvic said. "They rounded up many, took them to work on the roads, the mines. Others they pressed into service. I still wanted to be a healer but I could barely read, I could not write. I was so ignorant, so stupid. But strong. Always strong. So they wanted me to join, and I did. The bottom rank, always. But I learned what they had to teach me."

Cliopher could not prevent himself from smiling at that terse phrase.

Ludvic looked up, caught his expression, and for a moment appeared almost offended: and then he seemed to realize why Cliopher was smiling, and shyly smiled back.

For a moment the two of them sat there, two hinterland tribesmen who had *learned what they had to teach* until the two of them could play *their* games better than any of them, and now sat there opposite each other, the Viceroy and the Commander in Chief of Zunidh.

"Eventually my unit came to be posted in Astandalas. I was sick of fighting, killing, but I did not know how to do anything else. I did not want to go back to moving heavy things for people. I was sure I could do more. I ..."

Again, that hesitation. Longer this time, as if Cliopher's silent encouragement *was* encouraging him. It was still not enough for the deeper secret; but he kept going.

"I requested to be released and applied for the Guard. I was accepted, a few months before the Fall. I was very junior: still in training, still confined to barracks, still ... in the Palace for the Fall."

They were silent, as anyone who had lived through it always fell silent when thinking about the Fall, that crashing collapse of the Empire of Astandalas and all its magics.

"Afterwards, I was part of the Guard. I moved heavy things, stood where they told me, obeyed orders. Was given, eventually, the position of the night watch over the Last Emperor. I was there when he woke. And then ..." The pause again, even longer, before he said: "It was as I told you."

It was a long, long time before Ludvic went on. "We do not name the dead."

Cliopher sat back, knowing this was the prelude to something important. He tried to be receptive and patient with every fibre of his being, follow this current wherever it led, even while he reeled inwardly. Not name the dead!

The majority of his relations were named for other people, living and dead, names carried down with their histories into the future. Half the *Lays* listed the names of the Ancestors, telling the Islanders who they were by who had come before them. Traditionally one sought to have one's name made immortal by inclusion in the *Lays*. That was the legacy of an Islander, to be remembered far into the future, as Elonoa'a was remembered.

That the third son of Vonou'a had traded his name for the fire of the Sun, the fire of civilization, the laws and the *Lays*, was the greatest gift anyone had ever given their people. He was remembered, honoured, described, caught in a net of circumlocutions, so he was not lost, not forgotten, despite having no name to be sung in the *Lays*.

"When I thought you were dead ... you and Rhodin ... there were many things I wished I'd done. Wished I'd said. I wished I'd brought you here, because you would have liked it before, wouldn't you've? A place not ... not fancy."

Cliopher could only nod, because it was true. That had been his first thought: that this was like a bar at home. He felt at home, sitting here with Ludvic.

He would have come here with Ludvic as often as they could pry themselves out of the Palace. He would have *wanted* to pry himself out of the Palace to come here with him.

"You should go," Ludvic said suddenly, abruptly. "No—" He held up his hand, when Cliopher, surprised, made to get up and leave. "Not now. I mean—" He slapped his hands hard on the table, making the bottles and glasses and plates all ring. "You should go find your cousin. Go find *him*. Go find *yourself*."

Cliopher stared at him. "Ludvic—"

"There are other people to hold your fire here," Ludvic said, very seriously. "It will not go out because you have left it. It will stay lit *because* you have taught other people to tend it. Let them."

Cliopher's breath caught. "Can I?" he whispered.

"You *should*. You'll undermine Aioru's authority if you stay. He needs you to be away for a while."

Needs. *Needs.*

Cliopher was shivering, shuddering, as if he caught just at the edge of a rip. He gripped at the table. "The Mother of the Mountains said all she could see was darkness ahead of me. Darkness and monsters."

Ludvic raised his eyebrows at him, almost just as his Radiancy did. "*All*?"

Cliopher closed his eyes for a moment. "Darkness, and monsters, and a small, ordinary, common white shell."

"That sounds like it is in one of your stories."

Cliopher recalled then that his friend was not only patient and strong, but observant—and a poet. And poets *saw* things. Knew things. *Understood.*

"It is," he said. Ludvic waited: and Cliopher was not strong enough, not patient enough, not *willing* enough, to outlast him. "Fanoa, they're called. The tiny white shells you might find on any beach. Common shells. Ordinary shells."

"Common and ordinary goods."

"Yes."

Ludvic regarded him, straight and proud, his bronze-and-gold cloak shimmering in the faint light of the bar like the last light of sunset, the first light of dawn, on the lip of a faraway horizon. "What do your people say, when the time has come to leave a place they have rested in, after they have rebuilt their ships and feasted with their friends and allies?"

"Ke'ea anonōna," Cliopher whispered, the words like coals in his mouth. "*The star-paths are singing for me.*"

Ludvic smiled at him, once, his face brilliant: and then he took a sip of his beer and looked as he ever did.

It was the same, Cliopher thought numbly, as shocked, as comprehensively capsized, as his Radiancy had been when Ludvic had asked him whether it had occurred to him to retire, that holiday on Lesuia, and thereby upended the world.

It had taken his Radiancy all of three sentences to seize that offer, that rope thrown to a drowning man, and save himself.

His Radiancy. Fitzroy Angursell. A man who had resigned himself to being considered only a god, and never again known properly and fully for himself.

With Cliopher's ... demotion, the Commander of the Imperial Guard was the senior-most government official. He was. He knew better than Cliopher did the state of things, these days. If he said—

If he said it was fine, it was good, it was *necessary* to go, it was.

The star-paths are singing for me.

Cliopher shuddered. He did not need three sentences to know his decision.

And then Ludvic said, "We do not name the dead. But when I left my village, my mother took me aside and told me my father's name. She said he had been cast out, not thrown over the cliff for the sharks but just ... considered dead to us. It was not so strict back then, the customs. The laws were what they were, but people were less ... ready to take the hardest interpretation. But after this—the headman's daughter, the chief carver's son—there were ... years of disaster. A drought; a blight that affected the sacred woods; a monstrous snake that took the pigs ... monsters in the shadows. It was stricter as I grew up."

Cliopher understood how such things worked: how a culture might shift back and forth, sometimes more traditional, sometimes full of innovation. Sometimes they were slow tides, ebbing and flowing over years or decades; other times the switch seemed to happen in a harbour wave, a tsunami crashing down and rearranging all in its wake. A revolution.

"You must remember," Ludvic said solemnly, "that my village was very isolated. Some of the elders left—the headman to meet with other headmen, the carvers sometimes to meet with other carvers, or to fulfill commissions. My mother never left her mountain. We did not cross into other villages' territories."

"I understand."

"My mother whispered his name to me, when she gave me a bag of food for my journey." Ludvic stopped. His hands were flat on the table; while Cliopher watched they curved together, fingertips meeting. His face was not imperturbable, after all: his eyes were full of tears.

"She gave me the beads. My father carved them, when he was still an apprentice to his father, before ... My mother was the one to magic them. A gift for me, from—from both of them. And then she told me his name."

Cliopher sat there, hoping his face and bearing said how honoured he was to receive this confidence, an ember Ludvic had kept safe in his heart, guarded as carefully as ever he'd guarded his Radiancy.

"His name," said Ludvic, "was Masseo."

Cliopher was sure he'd misheard. But—

"His name was Masseo. *Umrit* means 'no-name'. I came down from the mountain, onto the coast, and thought, I will ask to see if anyone might remember another young man come down from our mountain—"

By the time Cliopher was sixteen, the Red Company were already famous. He'd been half in love with Jullanar of the Sea just from the stories. The Red Company not yet gone to That Party, not yet travelled to the Moon's country, but they had already —Masseo Umrit had already—Fitzroy Angursell had already—made their names known.

"No one else knows," Ludvic said. His hands were still pressed against each other.

Did he think Cliopher was going to—what did he fear Cliopher might do? He would hardly laugh; he did not know that he might not cry.

And then he realized. Ludvic had just told him, ordered him, given him permission to go. Go find Basil; go find *himself*, who was always, always, his Radiancy.

Go find his Radiancy, who was Fitzroy Angursell and who was undoubtedly actively looking for his old friends. Who had already found Masseo Umrit.

"I have looked at the records, always," Ludvic said quietly, "but he has never been found. I do not know ... no one knows, do they? If I may indeed still say his name."

"When I was looking into the rumours, before ... my accident," Cliopher said, in a voice that came out as his bureaucrat-of-bureaucrats voice, but ... well, sometimes that was easier, wasn't it? "I learned that someone who was taken to be maybe Aurelius Magnus or quite possibly Fitzroy Angursell had shown up in a village outside the Abbey of the Mountains and immediately invited a certain 'Master Smith' popularly rumoured to be maybe Masseo Umrit or quite possibly the god of blacksmiths to continue travelling with him."

Ludvic was silent a moment, his face very still, imperturbable once more. "He is alive."

"Yes," Cliopher replied simply.

This time he felt no urge to break the silence. He ate the last few cold fried sweet potatoes, and drank the now rather lukewarm end of his beer. He could feel the alcohol as a pleasant, buzzing lassitude; his headache seemed to have finally disappeared.

What an amazing thing, that Ludvic of all people was the son of Masseo Umrit the Smith. Masseo Ironhand, who shod the horses of the wind; who had built a bridge out of swords; who had made locks that could hold a shadow hostage; who had forged swords out of starlight.

Maybe Masseo Umrit was worthy of having Ludvic for a son. Maybe. Cliopher would have to find out.

The star-paths are singing.

It was not a rip that had caught him, but a ke'ea.

At last he knew his direction, the direction it always was, the pattern in the *Lays*: East first, and then west and home.

It was time to go.

CHAPTER TWENTY-SIX
EAST FIRST

After leaving Ludvic's bar, they sat back in the rickshaw as the bicyclist put aside his book and began to pedal with a sturdy, steady strength all the way up the long sloping hill from the Levels to the Palace. It was much slower than the way down, and Cliopher was mellow from the beer and the pain relief and the giddy decision.

"Rhodin should go with you," Ludvic said at one point, nodding sharply.

"Rhodin?"

"He wants to," Ludvic explained. "He's on leave, after that landslide. And he also should let his successors do their jobs."

Cliopher noted the plural: he wasn't the only one doing too many jobs.

"I thought he might go with Conju," he said, a little meekly. The rickshaw was shaded with lightweight cloth in pale orange and yellow stripes, which cast a warm light on their faces and kept them from being too-easily recognized. The cloth was in fluttering ribbons, so they could still see out easily enough if they wanted.

"I think they would both enjoy that for perhaps two weeks," Ludvic answered judiciously, which had been so much Cliopher's own thought that he laughed.

"What do I tell everyone?" he asked once the laughter had subsided again. "They want me to go home with them ..."

"They want you to be happy," Ludvic replied gently. "They know you haven't finished your voyage yet."

Ke'ea anonōna. *The star-paths are singing.*

The only person he said those words to was Uncle Lazo, whom he told first. The rest he told only that he wanted to follow up on Basil, answer that lingering doubt, that unresolved hope.

Uncle Lazo simply said, "I shall look forward to your tales when you return, then."

His mother voiced the thought that Conju's plan sounded so lovely and why didn't Kip take him up on that offer, and while Cliopher was trying to express his reservations without insulting or annoying anyone, Conju suddenly turned to Eidora and invited her instead.

To Cliopher's surprise, his mother hesitated, looked at Uncle Lazo, looked at Kip, looked at Vinyë, and then coloured beautifully and said 'yes'.

~

They travelled together as far as Boloyo City on one of the sky ships, and Cliopher rather thought he'd gotten along better with his mother over that day and a half than he had in perhaps his entire life.

("You see," Conju said, with one of his sniffs, "your mother *does* like me better than you.")

Conju and Eidora went off one way, to continue Conju's itinerary of wineries and olive oil producers and luxury spas, and Cliopher and Rhodin took their travel bags and went another.

~

Rhodin was a great logistical expert, and since none of this journey involved traditional Wide Seas Islander sailing techniques, Cliopher did not much object to his friend doing the planning.

Accordingly, they spent a pleasant three days in Boloyo City sampling the local specialties—Rhodin had prepared a list of restaurants he wanted to try—before boarding the sky ship that served the isolated garrison where the gate to Alinor was located.

Cliopher did not object to spending part of the journey going through their packs again.

He did object to being offered weapons.

"What if we meet up with danger?" Rhodin asked. "Robbers, for instance."

Cliopher eyed the wicked steel implements laid out on the table with distaste. "Then I will talk us out of it, and if I cannot, then you will fight," he said.

Rhodin considered this for a moment, and then nodded. "Acceptable. To each his strengths. Why are you laughing, Cliopher?"

"I'm not," Cliopher said, turning his head to hide his smile. "What do you think the weather will be like, on the other side?"

~

Two days after their arrival at the outpost they were woken at midnight to enter the gate.

They dressed in layers appropriate to the north-Amboloyan autumn, as no one ever knew the season it would be on the other side of the gate, but the gate-guards did know the Alinorel side was of a colder and harsher climate than theirs, for people stumbled through sometimes in furs and heavy cloaks, snow still glittering on their hair and shoulders.

Cliopher could not say he had truly missed snow. Rhodin, on the other hand, looked a touch wistful at the thought. More than wistful; excited.

Sometimes Cliopher did not understand his friend at all.

At any rate, he put on layers: his linen trews and tunic, his new boots with good socks, in which his feet felt immensely constricted, but he remembered wearing boots in Astandalas and knew he would need them if it were at all cold on that side. Overtop his linens two layers of robes in two shades of blue. He had a hooded cloak near the top of his pack in case it was winter on the Alinorel side.

Rhodin wore much the same, but for the sword belted at his hip and the closer cut of his garments around his torso, the slits along the hems to allow freedom of movement. He was wearing his favourite off-duty colour as well, a rich dark green that brought out the golden undertones in his skin. In the lamplight of the garrison dining room, where they were given a midnight meal, his eyes were gleaming with excitement and anticipation.

Cliopher was excited and expectant as well, of course, he told himself, but he was perhaps a little tired. Trepidatious, part of his mind whispered. He ignored that voice. He was going to find out what had happened to Basil; that was it.

The commander of the garrison ceremoniously unlocked the three iron locks of the gate in the fence surrounding the passageway.

The yard behind the fence was a bare earthen space, cleared of debris. The gate was glowing a faint, luminous purple. The space between the uprights was a swirl of violet mist. It all looked deeply uninviting.

"There you are," the commander said encouragingly.

Cliopher said a few appropriate words, and glanced at Rhodin, who accepted the commander's parting salute with a nod and then strode forward, a step ahead of Cliopher.

Cliopher followed: and with as little ado as stepping through any other open doorway, they had left Zunidh and were on Alinor.

~

It was day on the other side; Cliopher winced and shaded his eyes when the sunlight hit them. He bumped into Rhodin, who had stopped not far from the gate, and gathered himself.

They stood at the edge of a waterway; the marshy bank suggested it was the inland part of an estuary. Gulls were crying, familiar here as at home. The marsh-grasses were green, the trees above them had long flickering leaves, green one side and silver the reverse. Cliopher found them rather appealing.

He twisted around. The gate on this side was a rough opening in a cave-mouth, no hint of purple mist or anything at all. Curiously, he stepped back through it, but all there was to be found was a sandy floor and a few bits of driftwood washed there by a high tide. "Cliopher," Rhodin said.

"Rhodin," Cliopher replied, smiling at him as he stepped out of the small cave.

The strange thing about the gate from Zunidh to Alinor was that while on the Zuni side it always opened at a regular, specific location, if at irregular times, on the

Alinorel side the passage exits were scattered within a wide circle loosely centred on an ancient standing stone.

To cross the other way, from Alinor to Zunidh, there was only one gate that had a definite, consistent location, and that opened only twice a year. That was the one ambassadors, traders, and other travellers from the Alinorel side used.

But people *could* come through on other occasions, and not infrequently did so by accident, stepping through a doorway that usually led to their barn or pantry or, on one occasion, a local assembly hall, when the little garrison in north Amboloyo had had to host fifteen distraught minor gentry for a month until the gate reopened for them.

Rhodin had brought maps, of course, and immediately pulled the relevant Alinorel one out of his pocket. Cliopher set down his pack and then took off his outermost robe, rolling it carefully (as Féonie, Franzel, *and* Conju had all made certain to instruct him) and stowing it away. He fluffed up his hair, glad to feel the air on his head. The sun was too bright to stay hatless, given the physician's concern over his still-healing head, but for a few minutes surely it wouldn't be too bad.

"I believe we're here," Rhodin said, pointing at a spot on the map. "There should be a road up top of that cliff."

Cliopher put on the wide-brimmed straw hat Conju had acquired for him as a going-away gift. "I don't think I can scramble up there," Cliopher admitted after a due consideration of the cliff in question. It was perhaps twenty feet high; not enormous or unscalable, by any means, but far too high and steep for him to think himself up for the task.

"No, we can't risk you falling again. Upriver, then. We want to head south in general."

Cliopher shouldered his pack, belted it snugly as Ludvic had instructed him, and set off after Rhodin along the bank of the river, humming happily to himself.

Despite having known Rhodin for nearly half his life, and considering him one of his closest friends, Cliopher had never actually spent more than a day or so *alone* with him when neither of them had anything else to do.

While they were on familiar territory, still caught in the expectations of their ranks and (newly divested) roles, it had not been so obvious. Here, though, where everything was new and uncertain, Cliopher was struck anew both by Rhodin's great competence and his *deep* strangeness.

He was astonished to discover that Rhodin, far from being the silent guard of his official life, was downright voluble.

"I've never travelled in this exact part of Alinor," Rhodin said, "but my father had an estate somewhere near Orio City, the capital of the province, and we went once or twice before I went to court."

And he was off, telling anecdotes about his childhood, which seemed to have involved all sorts of scrapes and escapades where he'd sneaked away from his governess or tutor to practice spying.

"You wanted to be a spy from that young?" Cliopher asked, surprised.

Rhodin shrugged. "I didn't call it that—it was hardly a reputable occupation—but there was a wonderful series of novels my mother owned, all about these aristocratic intrigues, and I was much taken by them. Why, there was one winter my mother invited the author, who went by Lady N— but everyone knew was really the Countess of the Western March, for a house party, and—"

Cliopher listened with interest and amusement and a sense of baffled distance. He knew that the court was a game to many of its courtiers, that there were those who enjoyed all the intrigues and assignations and gossip and elaborate customs—Conju did, and Rhodin obviously—but he'd never thought about it in terms of such nostalgia.

It kept Rhodin happily occupied, and Cliopher's mind off his slowly gathering pains.

They had had to walk from the sky ship dock to the garrison, spending most of the day on a gentle hike through the mountains. They had been accompanied by several of the soldiers on duty, who had carried their packs with them. Cliopher had felt fine. Tired, of course, at the end of the day, but *fine.*

A couple of hours with the rucksack on his back over the rolling hills of wherever they were in Northwest Oriole was quite different.

Rhodin frowned at him when they rested at a roadside fountain. "It must be the magic," he said. "I imagine Zunidh was supporting you. It's a known phenomenon."

"Is it," Cliopher said, glad of the stone bench and the shade cast by a large tree. Birds were singing, twittering really. He leaned back, listening to them, and closed his eyes.

"We need horses," Rhodin decided. "Wait here."

～

Cliopher did not know how Rhodin did it, but within an hour of his disappearance he had returned with a place to stay for the night with some local gentry, the promise of horses for the morning, and the statement that they were surely on the path to enlightenment. On balance, Cliopher decided not to ask for details.

He regretted that choice a few hours later, when he discovered, halfway through supper, that their hosts were Rhodin's half-brother and his wife.

Cliopher's headache was fierce and he didn't have the energy to do anything but pretend Rhodin's reticence about his long-thought-dead brother made perfect sense.

Cliopher knew that Astandalan aristocrats were very odd about families—it had been one of the most jarring discoveries when he came to court. There was enough of it still remaining at his Radiancy's court for him to not forget it.

Geordin—Lord Ker, as was his title—and his wife Lady Ker ("But of course you must call me Annadel!") were kind, hospitable, and pleasant company. Annadel, Lady Ker, was particularly delightful, and fussed pleasantly over both of them, while Geordin was quieter, and kept staring at Rhodin when the other man wasn't looking. Rhodin himself seemed entirely nonchalant about the whole thing.

Cliopher eventually pleaded exhaustion and retired early to his room.

Rhodin came to find him not much later.

"We'll leave in the morning," Rhodin said happily. "It's about a hundred miles south of here, Ragnor Bella, so even granted that you've never ridden before, we should make good time."

"Rhodin ..." Cliopher said, and when his friend looked blankly at him, added weakly, "We can stay longer, if you'd like."

"No, no," Rhodin said, waving this off. "An evening's quite enough for me."

And with that he whisked himself off, leaving Cliopher deeply perturbed.

He lay down on the bed, sinking deep into what seemed to be a feather mattress. No doubt it was cozy in the winter.

~

The horses were ... horses. Cliopher knew nothing about them, save that the snorting black one was Rhodin's and the more placid brown one was his. The grooms had already saddled them and placed their rucksacks into appropriate positions, and led them out into the courtyard in front of the manor.

Rhodin had come to Cliopher's room before they'd gone down to breakfast. "About the riding."

"Yes, Rhodin?" Cliopher hoped he was going to say that had been a joke, that Geordin was not actually giving them two of his horses in a show of fraternal solidarity and love, but Rhodin clapped him on the shoulder.

"You're a dancer," he said enigmatically. "Follow the rhythm of the horse. We'll walk so long as we're in sight of the house."

"Yes ..."

"Hold the reins like this—" He pulled the cord that dangled from the cloth curtains into his hands and demonstrated how to pass the reins between fingers and thumbs. Cliopher practiced reluctantly until Rhodin nodded. "As for mounting, if you don't think you can manage the leap, there'll be a mounting block in the courtyard you can use. It's not as if you'll see Geordin or Annadel again any time soon."

Cliopher's competitiveness and pride would see him wrong one day. When they got down to the courtyard he let Rhodin mount first, watching as he took the reins in his left hand, placed it on the front of the saddle, his right hand on the back, his left foot into the—the stirrup, that was the word—and with a combination of pushing off with his right leg and his arms was able to propel himself into the saddle in one elegant motion.

Cliopher did not quite understand how Rhodin had done it, and he was shorter than his friend. But Geordin and Lady Ker were watching him, and however odd the situation—and it *was* odd—oh, he was proud, and he never had liked losing to the aristocracy, had he?

And he *was* a dancer. Cliopher took the reins as instructed, placed his left hand on the front of the saddle, and after a moment to prepare himself was able to take three small rushing dance-steps and a leap, quite as if he did one of the Varga dances at a festival.

He landed the seat with a jar he felt to his teeth, but his feet found the stirrups. One discreet glance at Rhodin and his family told him he'd managed the first test. The surge of pride was enough to keep him from falling off when his horse suddenly started walking after Rhodin's.

~

Once out of sight of the manor, Rhodin stopped him to show him how to adjust the length of his stirrups. "You're doing very well," he said encouragingly. "That was a beautiful leap. Don't try it on a nervy horse."

"I'll bear that in mind."

"We'll keep on at a walk," Rhodin said, and showed him the small leg and heel motions that apparently did most of the directing for the horse.

It was something new. Cliopher told himself he had always liked learning something new.

They had ridden for perhaps half an hour before he couldn't handle it any longer. "Rhodin," he said.

"Yes, Cliopher?"

Rhodin was smiling in a smug, secretive way, clearly very pleased with himself. Cliopher regarded him in amazement.

"We could have stayed longer, you know."

"I do."

They did not, generally, have this kind of conversation. Cliopher wasn't sure how to bring it up; it was not the sort of thing one *did*. "Did you not want to spend more time with your brother?" he finally asked directly, a little desperately.

Rhodin blinked at him as if this had never crossed his mind. "No ..." And then he started to laugh. "Oh, Cliopher!" he cried happily. "That wasn't *actually* my brother, you know. It was my bastard-born cousin *pretending* to be my brother. And doing a much better job of it than Geordin ever did, I must say. I almost felt bad blackmailing him for the horses, but then we did need them."

All Cliopher could think, after the first, shocked, disbelief, was: velioi.

"It's not illegal here," Rhodin added, as if in reassurance.

"I'm sure that's not true."

"It'll be better if you think it is. I know it's a new concept, but you could try, couldn't you? For me?" Rhodin blinked at him with a beautifully constructed pout.

Cliopher began to laugh, because his Radiancy (who was actually *Fitzroy Angursell*) was going to find this hilarious—and so would Basil (if Basil were alive—)
—

"I suppose I am on leave," he admitted, with as officious a graciousness as he could manage, which after the long months as Viceroy of Zunidh was considerable, and Rhodin faced forward with an even smugger smile on his face.

Which meant Rhodin had won, alas. It was all very irritating.

~

By the time they reached South Fiellan Cliopher could say that he no longer hated riding.

Now that the various portions of his anatomy had stopped protesting quite so loudly, it was actually, he might admit, quite pleasant.

One was at a pleasing height above the ground, high enough to see over most of the hedges and stone walls that enclosed fields in this country. It was late summer, and there was much harvesting going on around them. Cliopher enjoyed looking away from his horse's relaxed ears at the farmers about their work.

It was good distraction from his emotions, which were being pesky. *He* had nothing like the equanimity Rhodin felt about his long-lost relatives. They were travelling slowly, in deference to Cliopher's inexperience and his head, and there was too much time to think.

It was much easier to ask Rhodin about the Merrions. Cliopher found himself increasingly fascinated by the whole proto-mythology.

After the first, gentle day to get used to the horse, Rhodin insisted they spend a portion of each day practising trotting, cantering, galloping, jumping, and 'looking fantastic'.

Rather to both of their surprise, Cliopher had managed to achieve a certain basic comfort with all of these.

"It's all that time I spent watching his Radiancy," Cliopher murmured after Rhodin complimented him on his seat and poise after a short period of combining cantering and looking fantastic.

Rhodin gave him a mildly baffled look. "You reckon you learned by proximity?"

Cliopher laughed. "There was some deliberate imitation. Some of it is mere contagion of habit."

"Your seat is not in imitation with his Radiancy."

Once Cliopher had gotten over his initial fear and distrust of the horse itself, he had found the motion easy enough to match. "I am used to dancing and sailing," he said, frowning over explaining. "This is a matter of rhythm and balance. When I thought of it in terms of learning a new dance or how to read a current, it fell into place."

"I see." Rhodin rode silently, watching their surroundings pensively. They had spent much of the morning passing through an area of fields and pastures in the bight of a large loop of the river. Ahead of them was the dark mass of a forest, and a line of trees that seemed to show where the river was looping back.

The road, the old imperial highway, passed nearly due south. Ahead of them was a curve, as the road turned not to follow the river but to go into the forest. Cliopher wondered why it had been designed that way, given how much extra work it would have entailed for the wizard-engineers. A major highway played a significant role in the magical bindings on the empire: usually it was considered easier to move a river or an inconvenient hill than to bend the course of the road.

"I was wondering," Rhodin said after a considerable pause, "whether you had recalled *all* your past memories when you came back to yourself."

"I'm not certain I would know if I were missing any!" Cliopher chuckled, but Rhodin appeared very serious, and he sobered attentively. "Nothing seems to be awry."

Rhodin nodded. He glanced thoughtfully at Cliopher, then down again, at his hands holding the reins with elegant ease. He looked very much an Astandalan aristocrat.

Cliopher might be starting to, after a week under his patient but strict tutelage.

"You are changed since your experience," Rhodin went on.

On the one hand, Rhodin was obviously leading in a specific direction. On the other—

On the other, Rhodin honestly believed in a secret civilization of enlightened telepathic dinosaur people.

"It was quite the experience, yes," Cliopher allowed, and then let curiosity ask the next question. "Was there something you thought I might have remembered—or not remembered—in particular?"

Rhodin flushed lightly. Cliopher regarded him in amusement. After so long in the sun, Rhodin had developed a splash of freckles across his nose and cheekbones, which seemed to provide an even more alluring visage than usual, judging by the speculative looks and giggles that followed Rhodin wherever he went.

For his part, Cliopher had been enjoying the opportunity to chat with locals in the taprooms of whatever inn Rhodin had chosen—he did not fight over the guard's choices, since there were usually only the options of 'clean and fancy' and 'very rustic', and after a day on a horse Cliopher definitely wanted bathing facilities.

"I was wondering if it meant you had recovered all the details of your past life."

Cliopher blinked at him. "I beg your pardon?"

Rhodin glanced around, an ostentatious display given that they were riding down the middle of a forty-foot-wide road that ran through open meadows, not a covert in sight.

"I hope that you know I would never betray your secrets."

"I trust you, Rhodin," Cliopher replied with sincere alacrity.

They rode along a few more yards. Cliopher looked around. The green meadows, grazed by some exceptionally fluffy black-faced sheep. The darker woods ahead of them, heavy and somnolent in what did not feel particularly hot sun to him, after Solaara, but which seemed to have driven all the local people and wildlife to the shade.

"His Radiancy remembered, I am quite certain, after the Fall."

"Remembered ... *his* past life?"

"Yes. As Aurelius Magnus." Rhodin sighed. "I had wondered so about you, you know. There was such an immediate connection between you, but I could not imagine for so long what it could possibly mean. Not until we went to the Vangavaye-ve and I saw how well the two of you fit together *there*. Truly a romance of epic proportions."

There was ... that was a lot. There was a lot to unpack there. "You think his Radiancy is the reincarnation of Aurelius Magnus? And I am ... Elonoa'a?"

"Yes," Rhodin breathed, his face shining with something almost like pride.

Cliopher felt he should head this off quickly. "I'm not the reincarnation of Elonoa'a, Rhodin," he said plainly.

He did not believe in reincarnation, for one thing. For another—

There did not need to be *another*. There was no evidence for reincarnation, let alone for *him* to be the reincarnation of Elonoa'a.

Rhodin, admittedly, had *quite* a lot of evidence for his Radiancy being Aurelius Magnus.

CHAPTER TWENTY-SEVEN
THE BEE AT THE BORDER

The other side of the forest opened into a pleasant, rolling landscape. The highway ran at a tangent to the outside curve of the great river now, crossing a bridge over a smaller tributary. This side of the forest the crossroads were marked with tall standing stones.

"There's a lot of magic around those," Rhodin observed as they passed a tall white stone, much inscribed with mysterious runes. "Deep, old magic. Bindings."

Cliopher himself was shivering with the power bound and tied into the stone, so he could only nod, dry-mouthed, and unnecessarily urge his horse faster.

They cantered down the highway, which was better-used along this stretch though hardly busy. They passed a few farmers with wagons, a few people walking. Ahead of them was another rider, on a fine black horse, but he was going away from them.

The locals regarded them with curious eyes, but no one hailed them. Cliopher nodded at those they passed, pleased to see their general prosperity. The fields were well-tended and thriving, and apart from the eerie standing stones the place felt peaceful, even bucolic.

A little before noon they passed a public house with the sign of the Green Dragon out the front. Rhodin regarded it with a slight wistfulness, but the place didn't seem to be open. Shortly after that there was a well-travelled road heading off to the west, downhill to the main river valley, signposted to Ragnor Bella.

That was the nearest town to Basil's village. Cliopher had visited it two or three times, curious about a rural town in the Alinorel style. It had seemed very small and sleepy after several years in Astandalas.

"Do you want to head there?" Rhodin asked, and then shook his head and answered himself before Cliopher could speak. "No, of course not. We've food for lunch, and it's not far now, is it? Unless you want to ask after him here?"

Cliopher had thought of that, of course he had, but he felt a superstitious need to see for himself. "Please," he said, and had to clear his throat and start over. "I'd rather keep on."

"Of course, Cliopher," Rhodin replied easily, and kept on the highway.

Most of the traffic clearly turned off to the town, entirely the opposite of what it had been in the days of the empire proper.

Cliopher vaguely remembered there being many farms along here, and a handsome building with a tower—some religious building for this region—but as he looked around, he saw abandoned buildings and overgrown hedges and the rank growth of fields no longer fallow but feral.

They rode up a rise, and paused there of one silent accord.

Ahead of them the road ran straight down to the great circular arch of the lead-up to a border between worlds as stitched together by the Astandalan wizards. Behind the arch was a ditch, probably a stream, and behind that the woods began.

Behind the woods were the high mountains with snow on their peaks that Cliopher remembered marvelling at. Basil had led him on a few walks into their foothills, though even in the days of Astandalas it had been a difficult and dangerous country, much infolded and interwoven with the borders with other worlds.

"It will be better when you know for certain," Rhodin said quietly.

Cliopher swallowed. Sometimes he forgot how excellent a friend Rhodin was, really. "Yes," he said.

They cantered swiftly down the hill. They paused at the old gate, though the horses showed no balking. Rhodin examined it, saying he could feel the old magic, and something perhaps newer, but that there didn't seem to be any reason not to ride through it.

Cliopher did not feel anything so eerie as with the standing stones. When he rode beneath the arch there was perhaps a shiver up his spine, but that might have been in his imagination.

"We shouldn't leave the road," Rhodin said immediately after they entered the trees.

Cliopher looked to the left and the right. It was not quite the season for the trees to be blooming—that was later in the year, he remembered now; it had been the Alinorel autumn when he and Basil had first crossed over. There were a few early blossoms, and a few bees, but nothing like the astounding chorus of bee-song, so loud they'd been able to hear it on the wind on the other side of the border.

The trees had straight, dark-grey boles. There was moss underneath, green and cushiony. Patches of grass and flowers where more light broke through.

He was used to the tropical jungle. It seemed incredibly, eerily *empty*.

There were no vines climbing up, very little undergrowth, very few birds.

"Let's go," he said, nudging his horse with his heels. Rhodin smiled encouragingly at him.

It was cool under the trees, shaded and more humid than it had been out in the sun. Cliopher rode for a few yards, then paused and pulled out his upper robes.

"Excellent choice," Rhodin said approvingly. "That's such a good colour on you."

It was a rich, deep indigo, with bands of embroidery in bronze and gold in the Mdang family patterns. His lower layer, tunic and trews, were a deep caramel-brown.

Somehow Féonie and Conju had conspired with his travelling wardrobe; Cliopher was sure he'd packed far more practical and plain garments than he had actually been able to find in his bags.

"Let us practice for a few minutes," Rhodin announced. "It will take your mind off things. First: the dress trot."

Cliopher reluctantly agreed, and nudged the horse into the high-stepping trot that Rhodin had been teaching him the past two days, after he'd shown he could sit the other gaits. He posted—rose up and down in harmony with the horse—and then smoothly transitioned to a canter, which was his favourite of the faster gaits.

The road began to bend and turn, not apparently for any reason; there was some magical purpose to the wide loops it made.

"Walk but *most fantastically*," Rhodin called suddenly.

Cliopher drew the horse down back to the walk, easing down into the poise that felt as if he were about to take on the entire Council of Princes on some splendid debate.

"Excellent!" Rhodin cried, applauding, as he cantered up to join him.

Cliopher was still laughing when they came around a steep, grassy hillock and entered the village.

It looked immediately, incontestably familiar.

He must have looked around, at the castle on the heights, at the houses, the flowers, the gardens, the people, for he had a blur of colour and shapes in his mind, but all he could focus on was the rambling building off the green lawn in the middle of the village.

The door was open.

Most of the windows were boarded up; a few glass panes were broken, and there was a certain sense of dishevelment and disrepair the further from the centre he looked.

The centre was—was lived in.

Cliopher would not have been able to walk, but Rhodin rode forward and his horse followed.

There were boxes at the windows of the central building, and those boxes were filled with flowers, bright-coloured and spilling healthily down in great festoons.

Those windows were clean, the wood trim freshly painted, the roof shingles in good repair.

And the door was open. Not just open: *propped* open, with a stone in front of it, in invitation.

His horse stopped when Rhodin's did. Rhodin dismounted and looped his reins over his arm, then tugged Cliopher's gently out of his hands. "We're here," he said softly, patting Cliopher's knee where no one was likely to see. "We're here."

They were, and someone was there.

Cliopher slid down. He shook out his clothes automatically, but he couldn't quite bear to step forward. He thought Rhodin might have glanced at him, but he wasn't certain. He was staring, transfixed, at the darkness through the door.

It would probably not seem dark once he was inside and his eyes adjusted.

From the sunlit green it seemed secret, crevice-like.

Were there people around him? Behind him? There might have been—might have been villagers looking over their walls, out their doors and windows, at these two travellers in their fine clothes arriving at the inn.

Before the Fall that would have been so common as to be uninteresting. Now...

He glanced again at the boarded windows, the crumbling mortar, on the building's extended wings. There could not be many travellers who came now.

A boy, maybe twelve or thirteen, came sauntering out the door. He stopped in astonishment when he saw their horses, and stared openly at the glamorous Rhodin before his gaze travelled to Cliopher.

Cliopher caught his breath as the boy turned his head and his profile leapt out in sudden, shocking familiarity.

The boy's eyes widened. He stepped forward, one hand coming up as he examined Cliopher's face hungrily.

And then he said, his voice wavering with something like wonder, "What is your name?"

"Cliopher Mdang," Cliopher replied, his proper accent striking through his tongue like a thunderbolt.

"What is your island?" the boy breathed, taking another step forward.

Oh, this was it, this was. "My island is Loaloa."

The boy hesitated, swallowing, his eyes bright and brilliant, as any Islander's ever were when the opportunity came to say these words, enter themselves and their interlocutor into the *Lays*, announce by their questions that they too were of the great wayfinders, the Ke'e Lulai, Those Who Sailed Beneath the Wake of the Ancestors' Ships.

"And what are your dances?"

"My dances," Cliopher replied gravely, "are Aōteketētana."

The boy—his nephew, in all but the strictest definition—oh this *was* Basil's son, it was!—opened his mouth and breathed the traditional words of greeting. "Tē ke'e'v-ina-tē zēnava parahë'ala!"

"Tō mo'ea-tō avivayë o rai'ivayë," Cliopher replied, his heart singing.

"Did I say that right, Uncle Kip? May I call you Uncle Kip? That's how Dad always talks about you!"

"You did, and yes, of course—and your dad, is he—"

His nephew's eyes grew wide and round. He had blue eyes, no doubt inherited from his mother: they were very striking with his golden skin and Islander features. "Oh, *Dad*! I'll go tell him you're here!"

Without further explanation he wheeled and dashed back into the doorway, his cries of "Dad! Dad! He's here!" echoing behind him.

Cliopher sucked in a breath, as if he hadn't breathed at all since he'd dismounted. He met Rhodin's glance; Rhodin's face was about as impassive as it was when he was guarding his Radiancy, but his eyes were warm. "He's here," Cliopher said. "Basil's here."

"Yes," said Rhodin.

Cliopher felt suddenly as if he could move—indeed, as if he *must* move, or else burst. He turned away from the horses, from the dark doorway, and looked more attentively around the village.

It was organized around a green meadow, close-grazed or mown. An elaborate sort of wellhead stood before the inn. There was an arched opening to the left, along one of the boarded-up wings: if he remembered correctly that led into the stables and some private gardens attached to the inn.

There were pleasant houses around him. They were adorned with flowers in their window boxes and in large barrels beside the doors, but here, too, could be seen the effects of much-reduced trade and wealth. Cliopher's eye was too practiced to be able to ignore the signs of repair and retrenchment, reduction of space used, reuse of materials: patches on the clothes hanging out to dry, the materials clearly less dear and more local than the originals.

Part of his mind tallied what he saw. The rest of him listened to the bees humming around the flowers, the scent of something sweet and clear from pea-like blossoms in pink and white and lavender growing up a trellis near him, the people emerging curiously to investigate him.

One old woman hobbled forward, gnarled hands strong on a curiously twisted wooden staff. She was fair-skinned, her hair white, her skin wrinkled and spotted; her blue eyes were sharp and alert.

She surveyed him with something that Cliopher hoped was a favourable expression. "You're Basil's cousin Kip?" she asked, which made Rhodin catch on a laugh and start coughing. Cliopher glanced briefly at him and grinned sheepishly at the elder, who pursed her lips in amusement. "The one who wrote all those letters?"

Cliopher stared at her. "He got them, then?"

"Aye," another person said, a man in his forties, with a long rippling beard the colour of the ripe grain they'd passed coming south. "Only a couple of months ago, mind."

"In t'winter," the elder corrected.

"March, maybe, mother," the man returned. "Not even six months, for certain."

Cliopher had spent far more time than nearly anyone thought seemly thinking about postal systems. He resolutely told himself that it was none of his business why the Alinorel system had collapsed so thoroughly since the Fall—

But he was allowed to ask a personal question, wasn't he?

"Do you know why?" he asked. "If they did reach here in the end ..."

"They all went to another town," the man replied disgustedly. "It was such a mess after the Fall here we didn't expect anything, and then ... well, and then we were under the curse, and when we came out of it Basil was the one to wonder about letters. Young Master Jemis wrote to anywhere he could think of, and finally this box showed up. We were all excited but then three hundred of them were for Basil."

"From his Cousin Kip," the elder said.

"His incomprehensibly great correspondent," a voice from behind came, and it was so familiar—so entirely, easily, perfectly familiar that even as he turned Cliopher's voice was shaping his own accent.

"Not incomprehensibly, I trust, or at least not illegibly."

"They must use your hand as a model."

"They do, yes," Cliopher said, before he stopped because Basil was there.

He was *there*.

Cliopher could barely retain his manners enough to nod at the elder before he focused all his attention on his cousin.

Basil, who was standing in the doorway of the inn, leaning against the frame as if he couldn't quite support himself without its aid. Cliopher walked forward, a step, another step, gazing at his cousin as if—

As if one of them had come back from the dead.

Basil looked so *young*. Younger than Cliopher, but then Cliopher was grey-haired, his face lined, from all his years in the Palace. Younger also than Ghilly and Bertie and Toucan, who reckoned themselves in their early fifties.

Basil had been thirty-four when Astandalas Fell, a year younger than Cliopher, and now looked maybe mid-forties.

But oh, it was him. He had the Mdang family look, and as his mother was a Varga, same as Cliopher's father, they were first and second cousins, and looked close enough to be the brothers they had so often claimed to be.

Basil's hair was dark, curly, shoulder-length; he wore it pulled back in a loose braid. He wore something blue, with a white apron over it.

He was smiling, his eyes brilliant with tears.

Cliopher was smiling so hard his cheeks hurt.

He stepped forward, past Rhodin and the horses, until he stood at the bottom of the wide flagstone that formed the step into the inn. Basil and he were much of a height, so his cousin looked down on him from a few inches' superiority.

"Basil," Cliopher said, no longer easily, all the years of silence standing enormous in his throat. "Basil."

"Kip," said Basil, equally hoarsely. "Kip."

Cliopher felt as if he were pulled by an invisible rope, as strong and clear as that invisible tether to his island, which even now he could feel in his mind, as if Loaloa stood directly behind Basil, as if it were through Basil that Cliopher could find his way thence.

He stepped up, and his hands reached forward to Basil's shoulders. Basil's hands came up to his own, and they leaned to touch their foreheads together in the ancient Islander greeting.

"Oh Kip," Basil whispered, his breath scented like honey.

They held each other there for perhaps a minute—Cliopher had never felt himself so unmoored from the Palace bells as here, in this moment—and then Basil laughed, his movement rumbling in his forehead.

"Three hundred and twenty-seven letters, *really*."

～

The boy who had greeted him was his namesake Clio, by the mysterious ways of magic and some even more mysterious curse only twelve or thirteen when even to the village's reckoning he ought to have been fifteen or sixteen. Basil sent him around the back with the horses, Rhodin amiably accompanying him, while Basil drew Cliopher into the inn proper.

It was too dim after the bright sun outside for Cliopher to make sense of anything for a few moments, by which time Basil had led him through to a small back room where Basil's wife Sara sat in a rocking chair.

Sara looked faded and frail, worn. She'd long been ill with a mysterious ailment, but Cliopher remembered her vivaciousness, her tawny hair, laughing blue eyes, and his heart twisted at seeing her so unwell. Her smile was as sweet as it had ever been, and her voice gentler, kinder.

"Kip!" she cried when he entered. "Oh, Kip! Is it you?"

Cliopher could only look at her, all his words catching in his throat, and she smiled and patted the hand he had reached out towards her. "I know, I look ill," she said matter-of-factly.

"I look old," he replied without hesitation, and Basil choked on a laugh and then it was as if that was all they needed. Basil went out, muttering something he didn't hear, and Cliopher was able to move forward and embrace Sara carefully.

He knelt beside her chair, grasping her hands. He'd forgotten—let himself forget —(*made* himself forget)—how much he'd liked her, too, Basil's heart's desire, for whom he had left his island far, far behind.

"I missed you," he whispered.

"We missed you," she whispered back, and he bent over their joined hands, hot tears welling up and splashing down upon them. He had not wanted this—

(That was a lie. He had wanted to share his life with *someone*. It had just not been Ghilly.)

Sara tugged one of her hands free and set it on the back of his head, combing her fingers into his hair. "Basil has missed you so, Kip. Go to him. We'll have all the time we need to talk, later. He needs you now."

～

Basil was down the hall, standing in a messy office where there was a large wooden crate and pile after pile of familiar oilskin packets.

Cliopher did not know what to say, at first. He stared at his cousin, not quite able to believe it really was Basil.

But of course it was. His smile, the way one eye drooped a little, the little gestures he made—

It was shockingly easy. Every movement seemed to unfold a thousand memories in Cliopher's mind. Images of their shared youth and young adulthood crowded into his mind; Basil's and Dimiter's visit to Cliopher in Astandalas, Dimiter's brave request to the emperor for permission to go exploring—

"Three hundred and twenty-seven letters, all in one go," Basil said, waving at the crate.

Cliopher stared at him. Rhodin had pressed a handkerchief into his hand when they were finishing their midday meal, before they quite reached the Woods Noirell. ("You'll need it," Rhodin said, matter-of-fact.) It was still in his pocket. He pulled out it and blew his nose.

He should be mortified. He wasn't. His heart was overflowing.

"I haven't even finished reading them all. And I'm sure there were more that didn't make it. Even with the ones I've not read I'm clearly missing some."

Cliopher had no idea how many letters he'd written to Basil. The years had been uncountable; and he had written him often.

He cleared his throat. "Someone outside said you'd only got them a few months ago."

"Yes—" Basil stopped and looked intently at him. "I did write, as soon as I realized you *were* alive—P—someone last winter was going to Zunidh but I couldn't, I didn't have your *faith*—I didn't know what to write home, after so long, when you were—" Basil stopped, his chest heaving, and he bit his knuckle for a moment before he could continue.

"One of the later letters said to write to the ambassador. I did, but I'm not sure if it got through—there were troubles in Orio City this spring and with the post—and —I sent another, but they must not have reached you yet."

"The ambassador sends dispatches twice a year from the Alinorel side, so I think it's probably that she hasn't yet," Cliopher acknowledged, because this was the sort of thing he could always focus on. "The post on our side works very well."

Basil's lips twitched. "So I read."

Cliopher lifted a handful of his packets from a stool and sat down. He felt shivery and uncertain, surrounded by the letters describing the passions and preoccupations of years that he could no longer quite remember. He stroked the oilskin, the faint scent of whale-oil rising up from the thin cloth, his own writing on the outside mocking him with its even regularity.

Basil el Mdang Sayo White

Letter after letter, sent into the silence and uncertainty.

"I probably seem a great fool, for never stopping," he said, for want of anything better to say. He smiled, not quite sourly, for he could laugh at the truth of his intransigent stubbornness, his relentless refusal to be anything but optimistic, his extravagance in assuming Basil would still want all the minutest secrets of his cousin's heart.

"Kip," Basil said, and then, gently, "Cliopher."

When they'd been younger, teenagers, Basil had been the only one ever to call him Cliopher, and even then it was only ever intermittent, a kind of reverse nickname, spoken privately, in intimate moments.

Cliopher did not want to be that other Kip in that other universe, brilliant and ruthless and almost unlovable. He wanted ... he wanted to be ...

"It was probably easier when you were writing, and I never wrote back," Basil said, and Cliopher nearly dropped the oilskin packets in shock at being seen so clearly. Basil was still standing, leaning against his desk, and he reached forward to take the packages from his numb hands. "Oh, Kip, I thought you were dead until this spring."

Cliopher felt Basil's callused hands, warm around his fingers. "I'm sorry."

Basil snorted. His grip was strong, comforting. "Sorry that the post here doesn't work as well as yours? Sorry that you were the recipient of an unbelievable stroke of fortune or fate and survived the Fall? Sorry that you sent hundreds of letters refusing to believe my silence meant I was dead? Kip—I—I hoped that people at home were alive, I hoped that they'd survived the Fall, I thought they must have ... but I didn't ... I couldn't see how I could go home if you weren't there."

That was the sort of thought Cliopher was very well accustomed to ignoring.

It was a practiced deflection in his mind, so practiced he might not have noticed he was doing it at all but for the fact that Basil snorted and flicked him on the temple with his finger. Cliopher jerked back, dumbfounded.

Basil laughed, in a way Cliopher at first took as complacent but then realized hid a thread of nervousness, of concern he had overstepped.

Cliopher paused, collected himself as deliberately as in any Council of Princes meeting, and then equally deliberately tried to step away from his court expression. Which left him having to consider Basil's words and expression at their ... face value.

Would he have to spend the rest of his life choosing to work away from that other Kip's example? Surely not—there had been things he, Cliopher, had admired, in that other universe. He missed Erwin terribly. He kept thinking of the glories of that Gorjo City, that Esa'a. And he—it felt odd to say it, but he *did* admire that other Kip's solidity and confidence in his place, in his role, in being the tanà. He hoped one day he would be able to stand so firmly in his whole self.

But he would not give up half his life for it, and he would not lie to himself again. And he would not lie to Basil. He *would* not.

"I tried to go home after the Fall," he said, his hands twisting in Basil's loose grip. "And they did not want me, not the Kip who came back."

He stopped there, unable to speak any further.

Basil had always wept easily. His eyes were bright, the tears wavering at the lip of his lower eyelid, but he was smiling too, and he shifted position so he could lean against Cliopher, shoulder to shoulder, the brother Cliopher had always wanted beside him. "We can go home together, then," Basil said, "and terrorize everyone just as we always used to."

Cliopher snuffled, mortified to find his nose was full and his eyes overwelling, but Basil only laughed, and after a moment so did he, rubbing his face to feel his wet cheeks, the strange smell of horse strong around him after the day in the saddle.

"Just as we used to?" Cliopher managed.

Basil pondered a moment. "Perhaps not *exactly* the same. I've read enough of your letters to know there's someone else you'd rather be playing the role of Aurelius Magnus now!"

Cliopher's tears stopped instantly as all his blood rushed to his face instead. "Basil!"

His cousin laughed heartily, leaning in a much more relaxed fashion back against his table. "Oho, did I hit a soft spot? And here I was wondering because in all the letters extolling your lord to the skies—and let us be clear, there are a *lot* of letters extolling your lord to the skies—"

He was the (ex-)Viceroy of Zunidh. He was the tanà of the Mdangs. He held the fire. He was *not* blushing like a virginal teenager in the face of his first crush.

"Clio looks just like you when he's embarrassed," Basil said, grinning, and even through his embarrassment and his incredulity Cliopher could not help but notice how his heart and shoulders had both relaxed, as if some tight defensiveness in him was loosening—

As if some great grief, held secret as a pearl in the heart of a nefalao, had been winkled out and shown for the treasure of unstinting love it was.

"I could not help but notice there's a word you never use," Basil went on.

Cliopher stared at him. "This is the *first* thing you talk to me about?"

Basil guffawed. "I refuse to ask you to tell me about your astonishing career in one go. I *read* your letter explaining how you uncorrupted the government by firing the *entirety of the Upper Secretariat*—an action which, I must say, struck me as being perhaps a *trifle* high-handed—and only possible because of the unstinting love and affection you held for your lord. Your friend. Your *great* friend, even."

By this point in other conversations they might have slipped already into language, the Islander words falling easily off their tongues. Cliopher wasn't certain how well Basil had retained language, with no one but Sara and Clio to speak it with, and both of them needing to learn it first.

Perhaps Basil had forgotten that particular word. Cliopher was sure he himself had.

(This was *entirely* a lie.)

Basil did not say anything about Cliopher having become staid and boring. He did not suggest Kip had *let the fire go out*, as Bertie and Ghilly and Toucan once had. He simply leaned against his table, the dozens—scores—*hundreds*—of letters Cliopher had sent him scattered behind him, all the silent, eloquent witness of a life.

Cliopher looked down at his hands, and clenched his fingers so that the incipient blisters from the reins stood out white against the reddened skin. "My great friend, yes," he said quietly. It was easier to say in Shaian.

"There we are," Basil said, his entire face lighting with joy—and mischief.

Gaudy had been known to look like that, from time to time.

"What else," Cliopher said warily.

"Oh, nothing, nothing."

"Basil."

"Cliopher."

How he had missed the way Basil said his name. Basil's accent, like Cliopher's own, was thickening, becoming more familiar, more pleasing to the ear, with every sentence, almost every word, they spoke to each other.

Basil used to be able to outwait Cliopher, but that was before Cliopher had learned patience. Cliopher sat easily on the stool, hands now folded loosely, relaxed, face as calm and attentive as it ever was when he waited out someone else.

He could outwait *anyone* in Solaara.

(That was not quite true. His Radiancy could be more patient. And Ludvic, very likely. But everyone else, yes.)

Basil held out long enough that the old Kip would certainly have conceded defeat first. Cliopher simply smiled, calm and attentive, and recited the opening of the *Lays* in his mind.

He had reached halfway down the list of the ships and the lineages who had come from them when Basil heaved a great sigh and then chuckled.

"Oh, you *are* good, aren't you!" His voice was admiring and amused. "I can't wait to see what else you've learned. I'm afraid I have very little of such great note to set beside your accomplishments. I have learned to make very good mead."

Cliopher regarded him with patient interest, and let that silence fill the space between them, too. Basil had already learned the ways of a bartender before they'd ever left Gorjo City—he'd not had any one career or vocation, always restless, always saying he wanted to be the second son of Vonou'a and go seek his heart's desire—and along with having a deft hand at the pouring and the mixing, had a great gift for knowing when to speak and when to be silent.

Uncle Lazo had hoped he might sit at his feet, Cliopher rather thought, but Basil had never wanted the responsibilities that came with formal study of the lore.

"I have made one very excellent friend of my own," Basil said eventually, his face so mirthful Cliopher almost regretted his so-hard-learned mildness.

(But he was no longer Viceroy of Zunidh, except as an honorific lingering until his Radiancy—until *Fitzroy Angursell*—released him, and he could start to learn ... to let go. Basil would help him. Cliopher remembered that initial sense of *home*, of Loaloa, of his—their—island standing behind Basil, as if Basil would be his guide and navigator, one of the stars of his way. Even in this room Cliopher's distant sense of Loaloa seemed to be behind his cousin.)

"Indeed?" Cliopher asked, one piece set onto the board.

"Yes," Basil said, and his eyes crinkled up with a great and beloved joke. "I must apologize to you," he went on, sounding entirely unapologetic. "I thought you were dead, you see. So I didn't think there was any harm in describing certain ... youthful passions you had."

The most obvious one had been Cliopher's vast and embarrassingly passionate love for Fitzroy Angursell's poetry. But he knew precisely where *that* poet had been, and it was not in southern Fiellan.

"I *am* sorry, Kip, but when I became close friends with Jullanar of the Sea I simply *had* to tell her how you taught me Shaian using Fitzroy Angursell's songs about her because you were *entirely* convinced you would one day marry her." Basil gave him a sly, laughing grin. "She's recently divorced, you know. If your beloved lord isn't *quite* enough—"

"He's Fitzroy Angursell," Cliopher blurted, just as if he'd never been to court a day in his life.

Basil stared at him, for just a moment, shocked. And then he said, "Of course he is," and laughed until the tears streamed down his face and he had to sit down before his knees gave way. "Of course he is."

CHAPTER TWENTY-EIGHT
GINGER WINE

The thing about reconnecting with Basil was that it was *easy*.

Cliopher had not tried to imagine their reunion, not the way he had dreamed of returning home. Basil had been a stalwart, living presence in his mind. Cliopher could not count the number of times the off-hand thought that he should remember to tell Basil this or that in his next letter had occurred to him; nor the number of times he had duly done so.

No. Not *duly*. Even when he had wept over the pages, because sometimes when he wrote he could not help but remember the yawning silence into which he sent them, he had never quite believed Basil would turn his back on the new Kip, the Cliopher Lord Mdang who had become Viceroy of Zunidh.

The miracle was that Basil didn't.

Once Cliopher had adjusted to the strangeness that was Basil's comparative youth, there seemed almost nothing more that *had* to be adjusted. And even that first adjustment was perilously easy: indeed, by the next morning, when Cliopher woke up rather hungover in a room he remembered expatiating upon in some fulsome manner for a reason he could not now recall, and he looked in the mirror over the washbasin, he was for a moment severely disconcerted to see his own reflection so old.

He would always have been stiff after riding for a day, and it was easy, for a moment, to forget there was any other reason for his bones to ache, his joints to crack.

He looked at himself, the grey hair and the wrinkles, the muted laughter at himself in his eyes, his mouth, and wondered when the thousand years had ceased to feel at all consequential.

～

The days unfolded quietly, pleasantly, soothingly. Cliopher and Rhodin slipped into the rhythm of life in the village as if they had always belonged to it, as if a space had been left waiting for them.

Cliopher did not know how to account for it. When he went home—every time he had gone home—he had had to *fight* for the space Basil and Sara and all their neighbours gave them. Here he was Clio's Uncle Kip, Basil's cousin, *the one who wrote all those letters*, and they all looked at him with ... pride. Wonder. Almost ... possessiveness.

Basil had told them so many stories about him.

Whenever Cliopher went out, for a walk through the village, along one of the lanes that looped out into the Woods, the ones that were safe for a stranger to walk down, he was greeted by name, with smiles and questions that were ... familiar.

Basil tells us you are the ... what was the word? The tannah?

Tanà, he enunciated carefully.

Ah yes, with an easy smile, an unhurt accedence. *The tanà. You hold the fire, he says. You build communities. You do not give up.*

Cliopher did not know how to account for any of this. He wished he could speak to his Radiancy. Tell him the baffling wonderment of it all, this welcome he had longed for his whole life long from his own family, his own community, his own island.

To find it here, so far from the sea ...

Oh, he could not stay here, not even for Basil, not if his Radiancy were not here.

(He had always understood why Basil had stayed for Sara.)

And Rhodin, for his part, seemed equally delighted. He was at his best, charming and witty and debonair, telling perfectly timed anecdotes about life in the Palace, asking questions of their life there ... Cliopher's heart ached to see Rhodin trying so hard for his sake.

Rhodin spent much of his time tending their horses, which was something he must have missed, given how much attention and pleasure he seemed to take from grooming and riding them. He too explored the village, talking particularly with the elders and a few of the more middle-aged sorts who spent their evenings drinking Basil's mead and ale in the parlour of the inn.

Cliopher did not ask him what secrets he was discovering. Undoubtedly there would be some; undoubtedly Cliopher would be scandalized to hear them.

It felt a balm, those late summer days in the Woods Noirell.

It *was* a balm. He could feel himself healing, the lingering unwellness from the concussion diminishing, the even longer, older, aches of loss and grief not quite disappearing, for the bruises they had left were imprinted on his heart, but easing.

He spent long hours sitting with Sara, talking about the inn and its business. Many hours walking with Clio, fishing with him in the streams and rivers of the Woods, hearing all about his nephew's love of his mother's home and his shy dreams of seeing his father's. Clio wanted to practice the Islander his father had taught him, and Cliopher was careful never to laugh at him when he stumbled, unless it was over a word Cliopher himself had never quite managed.

Clio was very, very interested in hearing him sing the *Lays*. He had already learned some of them by heart, the most important passages and those that had always been

Basil's favourites, and he listened intently as they walked or fished or tried to teach each other various small handicrafts. By the time Cliopher had been there a fortnight he had sung the entire cycle in Shaian and many passages in language.

And that, too, was a balm.

He helped Basil in small ways, weeding in their garden, which was full of vegetables Cliopher did not know the names of, though some of the tastes he remembered, with sudden clarity, from Astandalas. His head did not like it when he lifted and carried, so he did not help with that, but then again Basil seemed to enjoy him simply being there, talking, while he himself worked.

Basil had never studied formally to be tanà, no matter how many times Uncle Lazo had offered a piece of the lore to him, but he knew the *Lays* well enough to teach his son the important parts.

Cliopher sang for Clio, remembering Buru Tovo singing for him. He remembered feeling jealous of how Uncle Lazo looked to Basil, how he simply *offered* the lore to him when Cliopher had to spend so much time *earning* it.

Basil had learned what he was given, and lived it, too. But he had never sought what Cliopher had wanted so badly.

He thought of the story Uncle Lazo had told him about his efela ko, and how he had felt when the young Cliopher had come to work with him. What had Basil been, to their uncle?

He asked Basil what he thought.

"You think Uncle Lazo wanted me to learn the lore?" Basil considered, pausing in his weeding. Cliopher was sitting on a bench next to him, shelling some sort of bean. "I always thought he was showing me how to be a mafa." He laughed. "It was good practice for running an inn!"

The mafa was the person who guided the singing of the *Lays* or otherwise made certain festivals and other events went smoothly. Cliopher ran his thumbnail down the pod and popped out the beans. "I thought ..."

"Were you jealous?" Basil grinned up at him. "He just wanted someone your own age who could keep up with you!"

～

One afternoon Clio took him to see his boat, a little coracle he had built with his own hands, as he told Cliopher proudly.

Cliopher praised his skill and his relish for the old traditions, and watched his nephew paddle about the village millpond in the tiny round boat made out of cowhide and willow and hazel withies.

He thought of that other Kip, who had proudly rejected all of this. Had he realized he would be rejecting his own namesake nephew? Had he cared?

(He was sure that other Kip had *cared*. The distant Basil and the nephew he had not seen since infancy, both of them long since lost on the other side of the Fall, would have been acceptable sacrifices to that bonfire of the artefacts.)

Uncle Lazo had told him he'd been tanà at fifteen, telling people what they should know. It had taken him till the Viceroyship ceremony to be offered the efetana—

It had taken him till then to offer the challenge that was rewarded with the efetana.

He was tanà, one way or another. Exemplar of what it meant to be an Islander.

He watched Clio splashing with his oars, scuttling across the calm, still water, the foreign trees around him, the very earth a different colour, and could only think that being a Wide Seas Islander also had to include this.

~

He was warned not to go wandering outside the village limits in the lingering twilight, but Cliopher had no interest in adventures on the edges of Fairyland. He wanted to sit with his family, eating and talking, sometimes reading, sometimes even shyly playing his oboe.

None of the villagers were truly professional musicians, and their instruments were miscellaneous: a hand-drum, round as the full moon, beaten with a short smooth stick; a silver flute, precious relic of earlier, wealthier days; two ancient curling hunting horns, mellow in their tone, rich almost as Vinyë's cello. There were two violinists, or fiddlers as they were called here, their bows dancing merrily across their strings or drawn in long, slow, melancholy songs.

They knew songs from home, too, because Basil had taught them: the work songs Basil had learned on his various jobs, for hauling nets or mending them, for the slow, tedious work of mending sails, which made it into the *Lays*, it was so important, so crucial a step in the return home: every time a voyage was concluded, after the welcome feast the sailors would go off to mend their sails, prepare their boat for the next voyage.

Cliopher had not simply *played* for a long time. That was another balm. How was it that Basil's presence filled and soothed—healed—so many bruised and ragged parts of Cliopher?

Late one morning, perhaps three weeks after he'd arrived—the days were long and sleepy, those twilit evenings long and merry, and there was no reason for him to rush anywhere else, no vius to chase, here in these woods—Cliopher stood beside his cousin in the cool cellar where Basil kept his meads and ales and all the other beverages of his trade. Basil was decanting a barrel into another barrel, and Cliopher was a companionable distance away, perched on a stool and watching with a pleasant idleness.

"Is it the same for you?"

Basil's steady hands did not falter or fumble. The golden stream of honey-wine fell in a muted thunder, the fragrance heady and warm in the cool, damp room. "Is what the same for me?"

The court felt more than a world away. Cliopher watched the wine pouring, glittering in the light of the candle-lantern Basil had brought down. It was just the colour of his Radiancy's eyes; his heart twisted a little.

But his Radiancy, *Fitzroy Angursell*, had missed his friends. No matter what Cliopher had meant to him, or might still mean to him, that ache had never healed, because there had always been that endless, impossible uncertainty. His Radiancy, also, would have to heal.

"Is it hard for you, for me to be ... here?"

Basil watched the final drops of mead fall into the second barrel, and then tipped up the first with a practiced hand so no drips spilled. He set the barrel onto the bench beside the great stone sink to one side, and wiped his hands. "Is it difficult for you? I'm sorry; I should have been more attentive. I was thinking how simply wonderful it was to have you here, as if you'd always belonged here, as if you'd just been on a trip and came ... home."

"No," he said, trying to ignore how his voice was wavering, his lips trembling as he fought for his composure.

"No?"

"It's like that for me, too," he said, and choked on his own breath as Basil smiled at him, unshadowed and happy—choked, caught his breath, hiccoughed, and then, to his shame, started to cry uncontrollably.

Basil came over and put his arm around his shoulders, so that Cliopher could turn his head and hide his face in his chest. The last time he had cried like this was when his sister Navalia had died and Basil had borrowed Quintus's canoe and sailed the two of them out to one of the quiet islets on the far side of the great lagoon surrounding the city, where Cliopher had fumbled and fought to build a fire, he who had been training to Hold the Fire for over a decade, and then when the fire had at last caught and steadied, Basil had silently handed him a bottle of rum and waited while Cliopher simply held it and then cried.

He cried now in that dark, damp, cool cellar, with the smell of earth and yeast and honey and the sharpness of alcohol in his nose, the back of his throat. He cried for all the years since he had last seen Basil, the foolishness and embarrassment he had felt about holding that one dwindling ember, that single spark, that hope that Basil had not died.

And yet Basil had not died.

Not only that, Basil had welcomed him home, as Cliopher had always wanted to be welcomed home.

And not only *that*, incalculable gift though it was: it was easy, it was simple, it was *not difficult*.

It had always been difficult.

He had had to fight to be worthy of sitting at Buru Tovo's feet, of listening to him, of learning what he had to say. Buru Tovo offered fire to any who asked for it, but that deeper knowledge had had to be *earned*. Cliopher had had to fight, over and over again, to face his fear of drowning and dive down again, seeking another pearl for the efela ko that was only the anchor, the first step, of a lifelong challenge.

He had had to fight to find his place in the city again, and he had never succeeded, had he? He had wanted to stay on Loaloa with Buru Tovo, but Buru Tovo had said no, had sent him back to the city, had told him he had to learn those ways, too, had to learn to be *modern* if he wanted to be a true tanà for the people. And—oh gods, that had been so hard, had been so nearly impossible. Cliopher had managed more or less to fit in before his father had drowned, but when he came back from Loaloa he had been ... different.

(He had not known, then, that it *was not all about him*, and that perhaps he had been sent as much for Uncle Lazo's sake as his own.)

He had tried to follow the paths his family wanted him to follow, tried to take those safe, known, conventional ke'ea. Tried, and failed, to become a pearl diver; tried, and failed, to become a singer under Uncle Haido; tried, and failed, to be traditional; tried, and failed, to be modern.

When Basil and Dimiter had come from their strange and isolated childhood, knowing only their family and the not-quite-normal dialect of Islander they had learned from their parents, Cliopher had immediately felt a kinship, for he, too, was *odd*.

And that had been a revelation, for Basil had loved him, *liked* him, as easily, as effortlessly, as immediately, as Cliopher liked him.

With Basil at his side Cliopher had become able to articulate the dreams he had always held. Everyone else laughed, but Basil had not. Basil had listened to his dreams of doing something worthy of the *Lays*, and swore that when Cliopher went to the house of the Sun, he would go seeking his heart's desire.

Cliopher sobbed into his cousin's, his brother's shoulder, Basil's arms warm and strong around him, for the first time ... *able* to do so.

He had wept in the final throes of the purification rituals leading up to the viceroyship, when magic and responsibility and far, far too much work had all conspired to overwhelm him, but that was not the same as this ... letting go.

He thought of his Radiancy, sitting in his private study where no one else had ever gone, that afternoon after Pali Avramapul had come and thrown who he seemed to be in his face, and Cliopher had been unable to do anything but throw that purple blanket around his lord's shoulders and hold him, as Basil was holding him now, while he cried.

And oh, how his heart had ached for his Radiancy, even before he had known why exactly that encounter had hurt so much.

His Radiancy. Fitzroy Angursell.

He stopped sobbing but did not immediately move away. His forehead rested against Basil's now-damp shoulder, listening to his cousin's heartbeat, his breath moving in his lungs. Basil's hand on his back was such a comfort.

It had been a long, long time since Cliopher had had someone to comfort him like this.

"Better?" Basil asked, after a long silence filled only with their breathing and the distant noises sifting down from above of Clio talking with Rhodin, the pitch and cadence of their voices distinctive even without intelligible words.

"Yes," Cliopher replied, sitting up and smiling ruefully. "I'm ..."

"Don't say you're sorry."

He ducked his head, regarding the flagstones of the cellar floor with earnest attention. They were a pale grey stone, well-swept in the area around the sink and barrels, though there was dust and cobwebs in the less frequented corners.

Sometimes Cliopher could not stand the sterile perfection of the Palace.

That was not a thought he had let himself think.

(Oh gods, how had his Radiancy, *Fitzroy Angursell*, stood it? How had he been able to inhabit that serenity, *be* the Glorious and Radiant One, distant, unapproachable, divine? How had he been able to leave that tiny, cluttered, messy study for the impersonal magnificence of that beautiful room, that unvarying schedule, which Cliopher, who was always free to leave, had therefore been able to stand?)

"Thank you," he said, fiddling at the hem of his tunic. Féonie had insisted her art was sufficient to the task of travelling clothes, but he'd had to borrow a tunic from Basil that none of them minded him getting mucky. The village laundress, who had once cleaned the garments of every traveller, high and low, who had stayed at the inn, had risen to the challenge of Cliopher and Rhodin's silks, but with pungent commentary about how Cliopher *ought* to be treating his clothes.

The thought made him snuffle a laugh, and he looked up to see that Basil did not look worried or afraid, merely gently concerned.

"There you are," Basil said, his eyes and his voice warm. He had never had to learn courtly reticence; he had laughed at Cliopher's poor attempts, back in Astandalan days. "There you are."

Cliopher caught his breath again, and bit his lip against the resurgence of the tears. "Basil," he said thickly. "Please ..."

Basil nodded sharply, and turned not to the barrel he had just decanted, but to another one that lay on a rack to the side, fitted with a spigot. There was an upturned jug drying by the sink, and squat tumblers of an unglazed red clay, satisfyingly heavy in the hand. He turned the spigot and poured them each a measure of a mead that was sharp-scented with ginger and other warm spices.

"Spiced metheglin, technically," Basil said, offering him one of the tumblers. "I think of it as ginger wine."

Cliopher sipped at his, which was as fine as anything he'd ever drunk, even unto what was served upon the Last Emperor's table—and wouldn't his Radiancy (*Fitzroy Angursell*) like this!—and regarded his cousin smiling at him with a sly amusement. "It's very good," he said, not pretending otherwise.

"And would your lord like it? I'm informed he has a sweet tooth."

Cliopher muttered one of Rhodin's ruder swearwords, but Basil grinned at him, unabashed. "I take that as a yes."

"Didn't Sara say earlier you had some ledgers I could help her with?"

Basil laughed. "Oh, Kip, how I love you."

He turned to the barrel with the jug, filling it with his spiced metheglin even while Cliopher was once more struck by the simple statement of an unfathomably simple truth, which he had found so hard to speak.

He had been able to say some such unfathomably, staggeringly simple truths to his Radiancy, in moments in-between the usual parts of their lives, when they had a moment of privacy, or what passed close enough for privacy in his Radiancy's life.

"I missed you," he said.

"I'm not entirely unaware," Basil replied, grinning at him. "I started to have my suspicions after the second or third dozen letter."

Cliopher replied with a swearword Basil had once made up, and they looked at each for a long, serious moment before breaking up into laughter.

Basil closed off the spigot and drained his tumbler before rinsing it out in the basin of water in his sink and setting it to drain. Cliopher stared at his cup, which was more than half-full, and Basil said, "Oh, bring it up with you. I'm sure you can review our ledgers with a bit of lubrication; it can hardly be as much of an impairment as being chronically exhausted. Will you bring the lantern?"

Cliopher picked up the lantern in his free hand, once more silenced by Basil's perspicacity.

The stairs were over to the side, wooden treads worn dark and smooth with age. Cliopher liked how it felt as if the inn extended as wildly and mysteriously underground as it did above, as if it were full of a secret life of its own. He wondered if people ever found themselves opening doors onto other worlds, and what they found if they did.

Basil was waiting for him at the edge of the circle of light the candle-lantern cast. Cliopher muttered an apology as he rejoined him and shone the light on the stairs so that neither of them would trip despite the ancient, irregular treads and the shadows.

"I think what it is," Basil said, "the reason why it's easy, is because I always believed you."

Cliopher stopped, one foot on the lowest stair, the lantern in one hand, Basil's ginger wine in his other. Basil stood beside him, waiting for him to go ahead. "What do you mean?"

Basil smiled at him, neither sly nor mocking. Just—a smile, of someone who loved him.

Oh, why was he jealous that Basil had had Sara all this time? Had he, Cliopher, not had his Radiancy? They were not, had never been, *could* never be, true equals, no matter how much Cliopher's principles said they were, but they were almost as much in harmony.

"Ah, you know what I mean," Basil said. "I believed you when you sang me the *Lays* and said you would go to the House of the Sun and bring back a new fire. I believed you when you said you would go meet the new emperor, whenever he came to the throne, and see if he was worthy of being Aurelius Magnus to your Elonoa'a. I even believed you when you said you would marry Jullanar of the Sea—"

"I was *fourteen*," Cliopher replied heatedly, hating that he was blushing, refusing to acknowledge anything else.

"Given the difference in aging, you're now, hmm, a little *older* than her." Basil grinned unapologetically at him, "She's heard an awful lot about you from *me*, and I can't imagine anything but that your dear and beloved friend, your—"

"My *lord*."

"Is that the best translation?"

"Basil."

Basil put up his hands. "Peace, peace. But I *know* he's why you went."

Cliopher looked down. Basil had been the first person he'd told about his sudden decision to go to Astandalas—the only person he'd told the truth of why.

There was a small silence, and then Basil said, "And because I believed you, because I believed *in* you, when you went, *because* you went, I followed." His voice softened. "And I knew that if you went to the House of the Sun and back, you wouldn't forget me."

Cliopher opened his mouth, but he could not say the snarky response he might have made when he was younger, and after a lifetime at court he could not say the sincere one, and he refused to use any of the courtly forms.

"Never," he managed, for this was Basil.

Basil patted him on the shoulder, careful not to slosh the jug of ginger wine. "I'd ask if he was worthy, except that I have three hundred and twenty-seven letters up there saying precisely why you stayed. Come on, Kip, let's get you examining ledgers. That will restore your equilibrium."

CHAPTER TWENTY-NINE
UNBALANCING THE LEDGERS

There was nothing quite so restorative, in Cliopher's opinion, as taking a muddled mess and slowly, methodically, turning it to order.

He sat down with the ledgers Basil had desultorily attempted to keep during the first, savage attacks of Sara's illness, when his own distraction and the wild magic thrashing around the inn during the Fall had worked against each other to create a vast and complicated tangle, compounded by Basil having entirely ignored the books in the years since.

Or vast and complicated for Basil's experience and knowledge. Cliopher looked at the piles of untidy notes and the half-dozen account-books and could not bite back the question of where the rest of them were.

Basil laughed, no doubt at Cliopher's resolutely blank expression. "Oh, this is nothing to you, is it? I keep forgetting you've been running the literal world government. How long do you reckon it'll take you?"

Cliopher regarded the box, and what he remembered of Basil's accountancy skills, which, he abruptly remembered, could most charitably be called *basic*. "You must have learned more business, running the inn?"

"Sara used to do this part. That was the problem."

"It's been ... years?"

"I've been busy," Basil said, shrugging.

And Sara had been sick, and the curse, and the lack of business had probably made this seem unimportant.

"At least a couple of hours, then," Cliopher decided, and smiled at Basil's incredulity. "I can't make mead."

Basil laughed again and pushed off from the doorway. "You won't need to make mead, you'll have mine. Cheese, now ... you need to be finicky and precise with that."

That *assumption*—that simple *assurance*, that Basil and his mead would be wherever Cliopher was—

He would not start crying again.

Cliopher waved him off, taking his writing kit from the crook of his arm—oh, how good it had felt to pull it out of his bags—and spent a few minutes clearing off the table and setting up his pens and inkstand and papers the way he liked them. The chair faced the open door, but that opened onto a back hallway of the inn. He could hear the murmur of voices from the taproom, where some of the locals were probably coming for a midday gossip before returning home with Basil's ale for their lunches.

The situation and surroundings were completely different from any of his previous offices, but this was another easy thing, wasn't it? For him to sit there, useful work to be done, with friendly people, *family*, just out of distraction, his own pen in his hand, a knot to untangle with his own knowledge and skill.

It felt good, he acknowledged, for this to be useful and helpful work but not have some unbearable portion of the world's wealth and health and happiness riding on it. It was a heady lack of pressure.

But he was Cliopher Mdang, and he never gave his less no matter how small the task. He opened the box and began by sorting all the receipts and notes by kind, as there was certainly no hope of doing so by date.

And if he were humming *Aurora* as he worked—

Well. At least he had started to recognize when he did so.

And it wasn't as if it weren't the greatest work to so far come from the pen of the poet laureate of Zunidh, his dear friend.

～

He finished sorting all the bits and pieces of paper, and was about to move on to analyzing them when it occurred to him he didn't need to.

It was an alien thought, and took a moment to sink in.

He stood up and stretched his neck and back. He had a small headache, the sort he had always assumed was one of the minor but unavoidable drawbacks of his job.

But—this wasn't his job, not really.

And there was no *rush*.

He looked at the desk, with its now-neat stacks of papers and ledgers. It had been obvious what had happened: six months before the Fall, Sara had been taken with a sharp attack of her mystery ailment. By that point her parents had died and left the running of the Inn entirely to her and Basil, and it was still in the days when the Bee at the Border was one of the busiest coaching inns in the Empire.

Basil had let some of the necessary records lapse—had perhaps not even realized what *were* necessary records—and certainly had not understood the nuances of book-keeping—and then he had never bothered to sort any of it.

In some ways, he was fortunate that the Fall had stopped him from mismanaging the Inn's finances into ruin.

Of course, there were other forms of ruination. Cliopher had come close ...

Someone was singing, in a sweet soprano—

Someone was singing the *Lays* in a sweet soprano.

Clio was singing the *Lays*.

Cliopher hesitated, and then he left the room, resolutely shutting the door on the unfinished work. It would still be there tomorrow.

He went for a walk with his nephew, out across the green and along a path bordered by huge pink granite boulders to where a stream went over a small waterfall.

Small compared the great falls of the Liaau, that is. The main cascade was perhaps twenty feet, falling into a deep pool where Clio liked to fish.

"What's it like to swim in the sea, Uncle Kip?" Clio asked as they sat dangling their feet in the cold water.

Cliopher looked at him, and then down at their feet, golden against the dark water. "The sea has waves that tumble on shore."

"Waves like the wind in the grass?"

Cliopher felt a sudden cognitive shock, as astonishing and impossible as when Rhodin had started talking about the Merrions.

"What does that feel like?" Clio asked. "Like the current from the waterfall?" He kicked at the water.

"Yes, something like that. The waves rock you, if you float in the water. You can feel them in your blood afterwards, when you lie on the beach. And the water is salt ... salt as tears or sweat."

"You're making that up."

Cliopher laughed. "No, I'm not."

"Where does the salt come from, then?" Clio challenged.

"Vou'a's tears," he replied promptly, and told his nephew the tale of how Vou'a's dear friend Ani, the sea, had lost her mirimiri and was no longer able to come onto the shore.

The next day he went for a short ride with Rhodin, who was concerned he would lose all of his heard-learned expertise.

"I'm hardly *expert*," Cliopher objected mildly, though he also looked at the horse with less dismay than he might have, the previous week.

"You could be."

They went for a slow, gentle ride back along the road to the gate at the edge of the Woods and back around again, following a route Sara had told them was safe. Rhodin told him about his researches into the lore of the Woods, and Cliopher, endeavouring to look fantastic and listen with due attention, found his heart lifting with another kind of pleasure.

He returned to the ledgers an hour and a half before Basil liked to serve supper. The village musicians would be by later on, and Cliopher was looking forward to playing.

No one had touched his piles of notes. Cliopher opened his writing kit upside-down by mistake, and smiled as he touched the book of poetry that was tucked into the hidden pocket.

He bent his attention to the task. It was easier today than it had been the day before, and he was glad he'd decided to rest before the small headache had become a big one. He didn't have one at all today, even after the ride through the heavy summer sunlight.

Not that it was as heavy as Solaaran sun, but Cliopher had very rarely gone out in that.

He was vaguely aware of a surge of voices, footsteps passing his door, going up and down the stairs, Clio shouting something incomprehensible but excited. No one came to get him, so he assumed it was some favoured visitors—perhaps the young viscount, of whom Basil had many good things to say, had shown up—and continued with what he was doing.

It was good to focus, and focus *deep*. Like plunging in a smooth dive into warm, welcoming water.

None of this cold freshwater for him!

It was the best kind of work: requiring focus, but not exactly *thought*. He was able to let himself remember that holiday on Lesuia, when he and his Radiancy had gone swimming together off Navikiani.

He could almost hear his Radiancy's voice, laughter barely suppressed: "Hard at work, Lord Mdang?"

"Always, my lord," he replied out loud, and then chuckled quietly at himself for his fancies. He dipped his pen and finished adding up a column of figures, double-checked it against his previous notes, and only then registered there was someone at the door.

He looked up, pen forgotten mid-air.

Leaning against the doorway was a man his eyes insisted was a stranger.

Tall—taller by a head than Basil, who stood grinning behind him—lanky in dark green leggings and a knee-length sleeveless surcoat in rich teal-blue over a soft white shirt, leather boots crossed casually, an expression of studied amusement on his face. One ring on his left hand, a simple gold signet ring, gleaming brilliantly against his dark skin.

Cliopher set his pen down onto Basil's inkstand, with careful, exaggerated precision.

This was not his Radiancy. This was Fitzroy Angursell.

He took a breath, trying to marshal suitable words. How was he expected to greet—

He looked up, as he had always looked up, to meet the other man's eyes.

Limpid gold as the glimmering amber paperweight Conju kept on his worktable, as the smudges all up Ludvic's arms, as the efevoa Cliopher had won from the Son of Laughter.

His heart was thundering. They had talked about names, hadn't they? They had talked about that name his Radiancy had named himself, the name he had never told Cliopher but which Cliopher had finally learned for himself. Cliopher had wept secret tears for not being able to offer it to him, when his Radiancy had been heart-broken and wanted only to be recognized for himself.

Cliopher was not less himself when he was called Kip by his family than when he was called Cliopher by his friends, was he? Or even when he was called Lord Mdang or Sir by his underlings and household?

"Cat got your tongue, Lord Mdang?" his Radiancy said, his voice as serene as it had ever been, but Cliopher was looking into his eyes and he could see the hesitation there, the all-too-human doubt, the hope—

"My lord," he said, and then, his words tumbling over themselves even as he stood up and thrust the chair back. It fell over, shaking all his pens and the inkstand and the ledgers and his notes. "My lord. My—Tor." And then, as he came around the desk, and he did not know what to do besides that he could not, he must not, fall into that habitual formal prostration, his tongue ran away from him and he said, "Fitzroy Angursell."

He was still looking into his Radiancy's eyes, and he saw the doubt waver and vanish, like a fog dissipating at the rising of the sun.

Saw the solid satisfaction of hearing that name, spoken by Cliopher.

Could not think, in that moment, how he had ever been nervous for this meeting. This was not a stranger. Cliopher had always seen this man, from the earliest moment when they had first shared a joke until that last farewell when he left on his quest.

His Radiancy straightened, his eyes lightening with one of those smiles Cliopher treasured. Cliopher dropped his eyes, unable to stand the magic, the joy, the reciprocal love in them, but even as he hesitated a step away, still not certain of what he should do, for all that he had broken half a dozen sacred laws simply by standing and stepping forth as he had—

Even with all that, he was conscious of Basil rolling his eyes and then ambling off, muttering something about drinks, a smug grin radiating from his entire being—

And then Cliopher's hands came up, and without any further hesitation he stepped forward and grasped his Radiancy by his upper arms, and felt his Radiancy's startlement, even as his hands came up to return the gesture, and they leaned together and touched their foreheads in the ancient Islander custom.

That word he had refused ever to utter, to write down, to *think*, seemed to echo in his head. He closed his eyes more tightly, his hands gripping, but his Radiancy murmured, "It's good to see you."

"I missed you," Cliopher replied without thinking, and let go instantly. He stepped back, his face hot and fiery with an emotion that was not shame but which he did not know how to parse.

His Radiancy took a deep, shuddering breath, and then he smiled, truly smiled, gave Cliopher a *Fitzroy Angursell* smile, and Cliopher wondered for a short, incredulous, furious moment if he were going to be like his cousin Zemius and faint from sheer astonishment.

His Radiancy stepped forward and took his elbow in a firm grip. Cliopher collected himself, cleared his throat, and did his best to present something approaching a normal expression. "Good, er, good afternoon, my lord. Tor ..."

He trailed off.

"You know my name," his Radiancy said in a low voice, naked longing on his face. "You said it, a moment ago."

Cliopher had to look away, for he knew that longing for one's heart's desire.

In that moment, he understood why his Radiancy had never told it to him: his Radiancy had wanted him to *see* him despite all the masks and the layers and the taboos between them. Had wanted—had desperately wanted—that assurance that he was not wholly lost.

(And it had taken Cliopher so long—but he *had*. He could give him this gift, after all.)

"Fitzroy Angursell," he said, the name like Basil's ginger wine in his mouth. He let his right hand come up and rest upon his Radiancy's hand, still holding onto his elbow, just as if he were an ordinary man, his friend.

His fanoa, Basil's laughing voice said in his ear. Cliopher shivered violently.

"I'm sorry," his Radiancy said, instantly contrite. "Basil gave me a few moments to compose myself after he told me you were here, whereas I ... surprised you."

Cliopher could only laugh. "Indeed you did, my lord."

They separated, his Radiancy's hand dropping a moment after Cliopher stepped back. They looked at each other. Cliopher dropped his eyes a moment later, no longer inured to his Radiancy's brilliant regard. There was mud on his Radiancy's boots, red as the clay tumbler still on the desk.

"You're looking well," his Radiancy said. "More ... relaxed."

He was supposed to be on Zunidh holding the world safe in his Radiancy's absence, not *relaxed*. Cliopher felt as if he had been dipped into boiling water.

"I—things are well at home, my lord," he stammered, stepping back to the proper distance, his posture automatically shifting to the appropriate demeanour, his court accent flattening his vowels. "I didn't abandon my—"

"Cliopher."

Cliopher stopped his inarticulate apologies and met his lord's gaze again.

His Radiancy tipped his head with a faintly puzzled air, then smiled. "Cliopher. I have no doubt all is well, and more than well, if you were able to take a holiday to come find Basil. I am *glad* you found him. I have been regretting ... leaving all that on your shoulders."

All that. The weight of the world.

Cliopher shifted uncomfortably. He *wanted* to fall into easy conversation, *wanted* to respond to his Radiancy with as much assurance and equality as he did to Rhodin or Basil, *wanted* to be ... Sincere was not the right word. Nor was *genuine*.

Informal. Casual. *Ordinary*.

"When I considered your position and sought to modify it to follow the laws on appropriate hours of work, my lord," he said finally, which was too formal—he could see his Radiancy was not happy with it—but he *could* not simply be—he did not know *how*—

He knew what he wanted, as he had always known his aim, his destination, his island. He wanted his Radiancy to be his fanoa (now that he had permitted the word into his mind it chanted there, his heart singing and straining for it to be said, aloud, *claimed*). He wanted his Radiancy to live with him in that beautiful tower solarium in the house Cliopher had bought at home. He wanted them to be at ease with each other.

And he did not know how to get there from here. If it were even still possible.

"Yes, my Lord Mdang?" his Radiancy said, retreating a half-step to the familiar, comfortable degree of intimacy to which they were accustomed.

Cliopher tried not to exhale with relief. "To bring your job into alignment with that law, my lord, required me to create *seven* positions to fulfil its duties."

His Radiancy closed his eyes, just for a moment, his face very serene. "Seven. And for yours?"

"Five." His Radiancy raised an eyebrow, and Cliopher managed a small smile. "Also two new departments. And an extra-governmental organization."

His Radiancy laughed. Cliopher listened to the sound with something nearly approaching awe.

He had heard his Radiancy laugh, of course—had always quietly celebrated every time he managed to elicit laughter—but very rarely had he heard him laugh like *this*.

This was Fitzroy Angursell laughing, whom everyone who had ever met him—Cliopher had read account after account—had described as having *a splendid laugh. A merry laugh. The sort of laugh you can't help but join. Joyous.*

It rang in the air, merry and splendid and joyous, delighted. Free.

Cliopher remembered the half-hysterical laughter in his Radiancy's private study, that time when they'd both been far more than half-drunk in the wake of Pali Avramapul's visit, and how the magic had sifted down like falling fireworks around them.

His heart was full, luminous, effervescent as that light had been, that laughter had been, but he did not himself feel inclined to laughter. He gazed at his Radiancy, his friend, Fitzroy Angursell, his fanoa (oh, if *only*) and did not know what to say.

His Radiancy lifted his hand to his mouth to hide his lingering smile, which was surely not what he did when he was free to fully be himself. Cliopher's heart twisted, remembering that letter and knowing how hard it was for his Radiancy to be released from the strictures and structures of his position.

For all the virtuoso magic, for all the reputed divinity, for all the epic atmosphere that surrounded his very name—*all his names*—he was a man.

Cliopher looked at him and had to remind himself once again of that fundamental truth. It was almost harder with Fitzroy Angursell standing there in muddy boots, tears of laughter standing in his eyes, his hand at his mouth, than it had ever been in the Palace with all the glory and splendour of power standing about the Lord of Rising Stars.

Back then there had been a kind of subversiveness in upholding that truth, hadn't there? In the Palace so few had ever looked at his Radiancy as a human being, as a person, as a man, that Cliopher had been able to set his back to the weight of their expectations, just as if he set his sail against their bloviating wind.

People did not look on Fitzroy Angursell as if he were quite human, either, but for the opposite reason. Not because he was a god, elevated and serene, but because he was *too much*, too human, too brilliant to be quite real.

But he was real. He was. And he was Cliopher's dearest friend.

(His fanoa, and oh by the gods, now that he had thought it he could not unthink it, and yet he could not say it, either. He had dared to imagine that an emperor with no empire might step off the upper daïs to join the man he had raised to the lower one. He could not imagine that Fitzroy Angursell of the Red Company would reach out his hand to Cliopher Mdang of Tahivoa, still only daydreaming of legendary deeds.)

They stood there, as they had stood any number of times, except his Radiancy had not stood like that, hand over his mouth, eyes dancing, laughter in his face, his shoulders, his stance, as he had never allowed it to be—not once—in the Palace.

Cliopher's heart twisted again.

"Come now," his Radiancy began, his voice coming out with the softened accent that must have been his preferred one, his *Fitzroy Angursell* accent, not the pure court elocution but something much rounder and more resonant, and Cliopher tried to look attentive, because he did not think he knew how to smile.

He had never been so grateful to be interrupted as he was at that moment, when there came a sharp rap on the door-frame and then Rhodin came in, two glasses held in one hand and a jug in the other, and said, "Cliopher, you can't still be working! You know the physician said—Oh! I do beg your pardon. I didn't realize you had company. I assumed the two glasses were for me and you."

Cliopher and his Radiancy both looked at him.

Rhodin regarded his Radiancy with an alert, intrigued expression, smiling and friendly as he'd been for all of Cliopher's family here in the Woods.

"You're Fitzroy Angursell, I take it?" he asked after a moment, his voice appreciative.

"Indeed," his Radiancy said in his most imperial voice, though he had not otherwise changed posture or expression.

Rhodin had begun to turn to Cliopher to offer him the drinks, but his head whipped back as he took in that one, singular word. His eyes went wide. "Glorious and Illustrious One!" he cried, dropping the glasses and jug into Cliopher's hands so he could execute a perfect salute.

Cliopher struggled to catch the glasses, not drop the jug, not shatter into a hundred thousand pieces.

"Ser Rhodin," his Radiancy said, nodding, a small smile playing about his mouth.

"My lord!" Rhodin paused; his Radiancy said nothing, and Cliopher was trying to straighten the jug so it would not drip over his fingers without turning away from the tableau. Then the guard said, with just the smallest hint of reproachfulness, "I had been given to understand that certain of my theories were incorrect, my lord."

"They were," his Radiancy said equably, and gave a mirthful look at Cliopher, who found himself able to turn away and set the glasses and jug down. It was the nutty brown ale Rhodin had decided he'd favoured. Cliopher had determined that between Ludvic and Rhodin and Basil he was due for a thorough overview of beers and ales whether he quite wanted one or not.

Ser Rhodin's face brightened alarmingly. "Do you mean this is a *disguise*?"

"Only incidentally, I'm afraid."

Rhodin cast Cliopher a deeply meaningful look, which Cliopher resolutely refused to consider indicative of his Radiancy *actually* being the reincarnation of Aurelius Magnus. "I think," he said therefore, "that his Radiancy means it is not a mere alias."

No more than it was an alias, or a costume, when Cliopher was called *Kip* by his family and dressed in Islander finery.

No more than it was an alias, or a costume, when Kip was called *Cliopher* by his friend and wore court garb.

Rhodin subsided only slightly. "But then, my lord, was I therefore incorrect in thinking you—or I apologize, the true Artorin Damara, the *original* Artorin Damara —had been replaced by you—by Fitzroy Angursell, that is—in the dark years after the Fall?"

His Radiancy said, "As I believe I told you then, Rhodin, I have always been myself." He cut a sideways glance to Cliopher, and a wry smile turned the corner of his mouth. "To the best of my ability and under the given circumstances, of course."

He watched his Radiancy smiling at Rhodin, who appeared so resolutely focused on disentangling which of his many (*many*) theories about Fitzroy Angursell were actually correct that he felt no difficulty whatsoever in accepting that his Radiancy was the man in question.

No. That was not quite correct. Rhodin clearly had many qualms on the topic. They were simply not the same ones Cliopher possessed.

Finally his Radiancy said, his voice warm, "Rhodin: I am Artorin Damara, son of Lamissa of the House of Yr and Mantorin Damara. I was dedicated as the Marwn shortly after birth. When I was sixteen I was exiled; when I was eighteen I left that exile, taking the name of Fitzroy Angursell. When I was thirty-two I was summoned back from my exile and crowned Artorin Damara, hundredth emperor of Astandalas. After the Fall I remained myself—both parts of myself."

His voice was firm, but his eyes held a wavering uncertainty, hints of an inner kurakura, as two lives met and crossed and left behind them a turbulent sea.

Those were rich fishing grounds, where currents met, Cliopher thought vaguely.

Rhodin did not ask about Aurelius Magnus, for which small mercy Cliopher was grateful. He did give his Radiancy a very intense and meaningful stare, which … which might well have been a telepathic communication on the subject. Or at least an attempt thereat. His Radiancy gave no outward response.

"It is good to see you, my lord," Rhodin finally said, giving him another salute and then standing at his professional ease. His Radiancy had, over the course of the conversation, once more resumed what had passed for his informal manner, back home.

"And I am pleased to see you, Rhodin. You have been taking good care of Cliopher for me, I can see. But what did you mean, when you said that he must remember what the physician said? Nothing of great moment, I hope?"

Cliopher exchanged a glance with the guard, uncertain where to begin. "I am, as you can see, quite recovered," he essayed. "It was not all that serious, really."

"Certainly not," Rhodin agreed, "if you consider causing the entire government to go into the protocol for the unexpected death of its acting head of state *not all that serious.*"

"I *beg* your pardon?" his Radiancy snapped, wheeling around to stare at Cliopher even as a wind out of nowhere whipped through the room and scattered all his careful piles.

CHAPTER THIRTY
KURAKURA

Cliopher let Rhodin explain, which he did with precision and panache. *He cleaned up the desk.*

Rhodin summarized the eight months since his Radiancy had left as, "Business mostly as usual, my lord, although there were some developments in some of my special investigations—"

"I shall be *delighted* to hear those reports in good time, Ser Rhodin."

"Of course, Glorious One."

Cliopher fiddled with the ledgers and straightened out the disarrayed receipts, and tried not to think of anything else.

Ser Rhodin explained how Cliopher had fulfilled all the hopes ever vested in him, and simultaneously spited all the doubters, by actively and openly handing over power to Aioru and those other people and departments and that extra-governmental bodies who should have been doing the work long since.

"Thus, when his friends from the Vangavaye-ve came," Rhodin explained, "we—Ludvic and I, and Aioru—all thought he ought take a proper holiday."

"And so you came here?" his Radiancy said, turning his smile on Cliopher, who had to look away, uncertain, the currents rocking the surface under his feet. This was his Radiancy, his lord, his friend, his ... Fitzroy Angursell, whom he knew as well as anyone could know another man, and not at all.

That was a lie. He could see how the tales and poetry of Fitzroy Angursell fit with what he knew of his Radiancy, two halves of a shell fitting seamlessly together.

He recalled that letter. Perhaps not *seamlessly*. And perhaps that was the wrong metaphor. It was more ... the tovo and the tanaea, the striking rock and the struck, together making a fire.

"We went to the Liaau, Cliopher, his friends, Pikabe, and I, and halfway through a day-hike beyond the waterfalls—"

"Cliopher has spoken of the path, yes."

"No doubt, my lord."

Rhodin went on to describe the landslide and the resulting disaster, and Cliopher turned to replacing his things into his writing kit. His head was throbbing.

His Radiancy kept looking across at him, his face more openly concerned than Cliopher had ever seen it.

"And so," Rhodin concluded, "since the transition had already been effected, there seemed no reason we could not come here and see if Cliopher's cousin Basil was alive."

Cliopher looked up when his Radiancy turned towards him. He swallowed. "I'm fine," he said. "Truly."

There was nothing serene in his Radiancy's eyes, face, voice. "Cliopher. Kip. You were caught in a landslide."

"Pikabe lost his arm."

"Pikabe isn't here," his Radiancy said, his eyes nearly liquid gold. "Nor is he you."

Cliopher could not stand to be the recipient of that gaze, that care, that phrase—not when his boat rocked on such cross-currents and swells as surrounded him, not when he did not know how to get from where he was to where he wanted to be.

His Radiancy: the sun of his life, he had told Buru Tovo. He was burning more brightly before him than he ever had in all the pomp and majesty of his role as Sun-on-Earth.

Cliopher looked down and caught a glimpse of the special insert from the *Csiven Flyer* he had placed into his writing kit, and because he had no words to offer—*he!*—he tugged out the paper and shoved it across the table to his Radiancy.

His Radiancy took the paper, his concern fading into curiosity, and Cliopher released a silent sigh of relief from a tension he could feel but not name.

When you were caught in cross-currents—

He couldn't think what to do. His mind was full of a white noise not far off the roar of the mountain falling down.

He had spent the past *month* thinking about how his Radiancy was Fitzroy Angursell. This should not be so *hard*.

He was lying to himself. This was not hard, not at all. It was frighteningly easy.

Easy as being caught in a rip.

He had gone to Astandalas because of this man, and he had stayed in Solaara for him, and he had lifted up the world so that he could step down from his throne without falling—

His Radiancy read the front page, that absurd eulogy by Prince Rufus, with a set mouth and the nearly-inaudible comment that *his* eulogy would have been far better —and now flipped through to the inner leaf.

Cliopher held his breath.

He had stared at the inner page until the image of it was burned in his mind's eye. *Lord Mdang's Last Wishes to Declare Fitzroy Angursell Poet Laureate!*

And then Aioru had given the *Csiven Flyer* the entire text of his little essay on why.

"Kip," his Radiancy said, his voice uncertain.

"Read it," Cliopher replied hoarsely, barely above a whisper.

His Radiancy gave him a searching glance. Cliopher did not know what he had expected—surprise, certainly. (There was none.) Laughter? (None of that, either.) A sense of a shared joke, a jest against the world?

Certainly not betrayal, for all that this had been treason until Aioru had excavated that well-hidden formal pardon for the Red Company from where it had been filed deep in the Archives—

His Radiancy's face was full of ... awe.

His Radiancy read over the little essay, once, twice, a third time. He was a swift reader, though careful and retentive; Cliopher could time his progress.

"Aurora *is the greatest commentary on the laws of Astandalas ever written*," his Radiancy read, barely audibly. "*No revision to the law code could be considered either complete or just that did not take its criticisms into account.*"

"My lord," Cliopher said, for although he had tried (oh, how he had tried), he had never quite learned when to speak and when to be silent. Not when it mattered most.

"Kip," said his Radiancy, and made a vague beckoning gesture.

Cliopher obeyed out of impossibly long habit, impossibly deep regard. Rhodin had faded into the background after giving his report—more than faded, had in fact left the room, shut the door—he was vaguely aware of the latch clicking.

He came around the table, and once again hesitated in that strange in-between distance, neither what was appropriate for his formal role nor quite where he would stand with his dearest friends.

His Radiancy, Fitzroy, stepped forward, arms outstretched, and seized him in a fierce embrace.

"Thank you, Kip," he whispered into his ear. "Thank you."

Cliopher remembered the uncertainty with which his Radiancy had said he did not know how to greet people, just before he had left on his quest, and his heart twisted again.

"When did you find out?" his Radiancy asked, with nearly his usual equanimity.

Cliopher flushed, embarrassed, stepped back out of the embrace. "Not very long ago."

His Radiancy lifted one eyebrow in the familiar gesture. "As in ..."

"About six weeks ago," he mumbled.

His Radiancy laughed. "I had wondered *so* much!" His voice was warm, delighted, even teasing, his eyes bright. "All that humming of *Aurora* ..."

"Ludvic's already teased me about that," he said grumpily. "I'm sorry I didn't ..."

"You did *everything*," his Radiancy replied immediately, and then there was a pause while they both failed to meet the other's eye.

At length Cliopher felt he could change the subject. "You weren't surprised. About the poet laureate business."

"My friend Sardeet has a penpal—"

Cliopher jerked his head up. "No."

His Radiancy's eyes were brilliant with unshed tears, but his grin was blinding. "She's upstairs."

"*No.* It can't be true."

"I myself was *greatly* surprised." His Radiancy suddenly frowned at him. "Don't tell me *she's* one of your vast correspondents. I knew it had to be someone in the Palace—"

Cliopher buried his face in his hands for a moment, trying to compose himself. "It's Rhodin."

His Radiancy made a valiant effort at keeping a straight face, he really did. "Rhodin. My spymaster. Second-in-command of the Imperial Guard. Has for a penpal Sardeet Avramapul of the Red Company."

"No, no," Cliopher corrected, feeling near-hysterical laughter bubbling up. "Has for his dear friend, his correspondent, his penpal, the Impostor Claiming to be Sardeet Avramapul."

His Radiancy met his eyes for a long moment. The hilarity was beautiful to see. "We can't tell him."

"Certainly not."

"I've never seen Rhodin *actually* surprised, you know, before just now. He's so hard to ruffle."

"Indeed," Cliopher said, and told him about the strange, strange encounter with Rhodin's not-brother.

They were both snickering like schoolboys when someone knocked on the door and made them hastily attempt to be decorous.

"Enter," his Radiancy said, his voice even and courtly, and Basil came in with a grin that made Cliopher wish he *could* faint on command. "Sayo Mdang—White, that is, my apologies."

"Basil, please," said Basil, shutting the door behind him and then leaning against it. His hands were tucked into the sides of his apron, where the tied strings made a kind of pouch, and he simply grinned at them. "We're basically in-laws at this point, aren't we?"

His Radiancy held terrifically still.

Cliopher caught his breath, but Basil had three hundred and twenty-seven letters in which Cliopher had poured his heart out, and his heart was full of what everyone had always seen so much more clearly than him.

To think he had thought, he had *genuinely* thought, that he had stayed merely because he wanted to change the world.

He *had* wanted to change the world. It had also taken a bare fortnight after his Radiancy left for him to begin planning how to hand everything over to Aioru.

"I'm not certain Kip's ready to say that," his Radiancy said, but his hand was still on Cliopher's shoulder, and Cliopher could feel how his fingers were trembling.

"Oh, is there something you want to tell me, Kip? I was thinking of how Fitzroy's beloved friend Jullanar is like a sister to me, you know." He winked. "Speaking of whom, she asked me to make certain you hadn't gone wandering off picking elf-candles in the gloaming."

"I can't say that was something I was *planning* on doing," his Radiancy said equably, and Cliopher was once more able to grasp a certain equilibrium, for his Radiancy had landed on that polite, courteous, friendly manner he had displayed to Cliopher's friends and family back home—which was, now that Cliopher had the comparison so closely to hand, not entirely unlike Rhodin's own efforts—and Cliopher knew how to respond to that.

"We'll be serving supper fairly soon," Basil went on, opening the door and politely gesturing his Radiancy through first. "We're all eating together, these days. Kip hasn't given me a complete plan for rebuilding custom, unfortunately."

Cliopher latched onto that topic with alacrity. "Did you want me to? I've been making notes towards it, of course," he went on, refusing to falter as Basil and his Radiancy exchanged glances and then simultaneously started to laugh. He waited them out, chin lifted, and when they'd subsided, Basil wheezing a touch, added: "I didn't wish to presume overmuch."

His Radiancy swept out, as effectively as he ever did in his robes of office. "Really, my lord Mdang? You never cease to astonish me."

~

Cliopher's step hesitated, just for a moment, as they crossed into the parlour and he saw half the Red Company waiting for them. But it was a long, long time since he had last quailed in front of strangers, and he knew how to deal with people.

He straightened his back and his shoulders, set his face into its habitual mild smile, and refused to be intimidated to stand in the presence of even such legends as these.

They were gathered already, at the large rectangular table Sara had told him had been made by her great-great-grandfather. It was of a warm honey-brown wood, polished by generations of beeswax and companionable use, and Cliopher loved it.

Cliopher knew how to swiftly and carefully assess a room without giving offence or seeming to take much time about it. He stood a step behind and beside his Radiancy, who had stopped to put his hand on Rhodin's shoulder and murmur something in the guard's ear.

They were ten to dine, by the number of seats drawn up to the table. Sara sat at the head, nearest the fireplace, with Jullanar of the Sea—it had to be Jullanar of the Sea—beside her.

Sara was in her shawls, her eyes and smile bright as she inclined her head to her friend's comments.

Jullanar of the Sea was a pleasant-featured woman, neither pretty nor plain. She was pale-skinned, freckled, her nose a touch sunburnt red. Her hair was twisted up on her head in a style Cliopher had seen amongst a few of the local women in the village, held in place by long pins. It caught a stray shaft of sunlight coming in the window, which crowned her with a splendid combination of colours, strange to Cliopher's eyes: brown and blond and silver and auburn. It reminded him of nothing so much as the dappled light as the sun shone through a woven pandanus-mat sail.

Cliopher was too professional to gaze too long on her, or too curiously. Not when Basil was coming in and out with trays containing piled loaves of fresh bread, pats of butter, full wheels of cheese, honey, fruit, fresh salad leaves, cold cooked sausages, the tangy mustards they made in the Woods. Basil was trying to catch his eye, his cheeks dimpling as he smirked at him, so Cliopher made himself keep looking.

Beside Jullanar were two empty spaces, and then the fierce Domina Black, Pali

Avramapul, looking even fiercer and more beautiful than she had when she'd come to the Palace.

Cliopher nodded at her when she lifted her chin and met his eyes. Her expression was challenging, and he felt his heart thud a little in readiness. He had not forgotten how sad and sorrowful his Radiancy had been in the letter he had written, nor how badly Pali Avramapul had hurt him when she came.

"Ah!" his Radiancy said, stepping forward and effortlessly commanding all their attention. "Cliopher, let me introduce my friends of the Red Company! This is the resplendent Jullanar of the Sea. The redoubtable Pali Avramapul you have met—"

Cliopher bowed over his hands in the Islander courtesy. Jullanar's eyebrows quirked; Pali's face seemed to grow still and statue-like.

His Radiancy said, "Sardeet will be joining us soon, I hope?"

"She was sorting out her pets," Jullanar explained.

"Next along is Masseo Umrit," Fitzroy continued. "Everyone, this is my wonderful Viceroy! My magnificent former secretary! My friend! Basil's Cousin Kip! The incomparable Cliopher Mdang, whom I've mentioned."

"Once or twice," Pali Avramapul muttered, just loud enough for Cliopher to hear. His heart warmed slightly even as he tried desperately not to stare at Masseo Umrit, who looked so astonishingly like Ludvic he could not imagine how neither Rhodin nor his Radiancy saw it.

He glanced at Rhodin, who had apparently already been introduced, for he was smiling happily and accepting Sara's suggestion he sit on her other side.

Masseo Umrit was tall and broad, if not quite so tall and broad as Ludvic. He had the same wide features and flattish nose, the same sense of solid dependability, the same visible strength of muscles and frame. His tight-curled wiry hair was longer, and his eyes were less widely set, but there was no mistaking their relation.

The smith caught Cliopher's eye and said, "I should like to thank you, Lord Mdang, for all—"

Cliopher, scandalized to the foundation of his being, said, "Cliopher, *please.*"

Masseo stopped, and the expression on his face—puzzled, amused, quickly glancing past him to look at his Radiancy, looking back with a frank, relaxed confidence—was not one Cliopher had ever seen on Ludvic's.

And his voice was different: his accent unrecognizable; his timbre and pacing unfamiliar.

Cliopher recalled, as if from a great distance, how Rhodin quite likely would not have recognized his Radiancy had he not spoken in his customary tone and accent. Perhaps it was not so strange that someone who did not know the truth would not guess it, without the two men standing side-by-side for the comparison.

And though he was excellent with faces, his Radiancy did recognize people faster by voice than by face. Cliopher knew that from any number of committee meetings and courts.

"Cliopher, then," Masseo said, with a smile of great good humour. "Please let me thank you, as a citizen of Zunidh, for all the work you've done on our behalf. Fitzroy has made it clear it was mostly your doing."

Cliopher forced himself to not say *His Radiancy* or *My lord*, and instead managed, "He is being somewhat modest, then."

"Not on your behalf," his Radiancy said, his voice warm. He drew Cliopher forward with a glance to one of the two seats left on the nearer side of the table.

This put Cliopher at his Radiancy's right hand, which was the sort of position that—well, it did not mean what it would mean at court, did it? Or in any of the poems and tales of court. For all he was officially the Hands of the Emperor, he had never sat *beside* him in any official court function.

It meant that his Radiancy was pleased to see him, and pleased to have him beside him. Nothing more.

Nothing less, either. Cliopher was a little embarrassed at how pleased he was to sit next to him. He was glad Basil was directing Clio in placing cups on the table, and not looking at Cliopher. Clio whispered something to his father before disappearing through the door into the main part of the inn. He didn't come back, and Cliopher vaguely remembered him saying something about going fishing with one of his friends that evening.

He wouldn't have missed the chance to sit with the Red Company, but perhaps that said more about him than his nephew.

Pali Avramapul was directly opposite Cliopher, and she gave him another stiff, formal nod as he sat down.

She didn't say anything before there was a small commotion, as if a warm and friendly wind had suddenly flung itself around the room, and they all shifted around to see that Sardeet Avramapul had arrived.

In a dozen songs Fitzroy Angursell had called her *the most beautiful woman in the Nine Worlds*, and after seeing her sister, Cliopher had formed the vague impression that she would be like Pali Avramapul but ... more so.

In many ways that was quite correct. He had not expected the *more so* to include being about three times as large as her sister, and he regarded her with a sense of stunning *rightness*.

She looked just as he had always imagined Ani would look, if the sea-goddess took human form. Copper-skinned, full-figured, even fat—*generous as the whole width and depth of the Wide Seas*, whispered a line from an old, old song—her obsidian-black hair fell about her shoulders in shining waves, held back from her face by a wide head-kerchief in a fine and unapologetic scarlet. She wore a layered dress in green and purple with a wide white sash, but Cliopher was caught, as so many people in so many stories had been caught—as the gods themselves, so said one of Fitzroy Angursell's songs, had been caught—by the smile she turned on him.

The only word he could think of was *ravishing*.

Pali Avramapul had smiled at him and shook him like a small boat tossed on a large wave, when she walked past him to an interview with his Radiancy and he had not yet known who she was.

Sardeet Avramapul smiled at him and he felt his heart shift and refocus, as if he had been lost at sea and was now granted a sunrise to show him precisely where he was.

He was unexpectedly breathless.

The only other person he had ever met with that immediate *presence* was his Radiancy himself. He could see immediately why the gods had taken notice of Sardeet Avramapul of the Red Company.

"We would usually say a prayer or two before we eat, traditionally to the Emperor," Sara said, grinning down from her seat at the end at his Radiancy, who smiled back and actually nudged Cliopher's knee with his own.

Cliopher's thoughts had gone to that first public meal with the villagers on Lesuia island on their holiday, when it had fallen to him to make the prayer to the Lord Emperor because said Lord Emperor refused to with mirth in his face and anarchy in his words, but he was so flabbergasted by the friendly, companionable nudge he could do nothing besides hope his hard-learned court poise had not entirely deserted him.

"I'll say a blessing, if you like," his Radiancy said, and when Sara agreed, smiled at her and Jullanar beside her, and said: "We call upon the Lady of the Green and White to bless this house and this meal." He turned to the sisters Avramapul. "May we find in this fellowship the brimming joy that is the gift of your Arvoliin." Sardeet blushed happily; Pali was quite stern, her brows knitted. His Radiancy turned to Masseo. "May the four elements provide us their nourishment." He smiled at Basil and Cliopher. "May the god of mysteries and the great sea grant us their blessings." And finally, to Rhodin, with great solemnity, "And may we be granted enlightenment and peace."

His Radiancy hesitated a bare moment, and concluded with the rolling formal words of the blessing he used at court, which never sounded insincere no matter his private thoughts.

Cliopher's thoughts felt like the islands scattered across the Wide Seas.

(*Once I was a man*, his Radiancy had written. *Once I was real.*)

Cliopher decided it was best to focus on getting a true measure of Pali Avramapul, who had hurt his Radiancy so, but whom he loved and who loved him. The Red Company was part of his Radiancy's family. Cliopher had to remember that. This was a family, as full of love and argument and mutual support and contention as his own. His Radiancy would not like him to be at permanent odds with Pali Avramapul any more than Cliopher would like it if his Radiancy were with Vinyë.

After the benediction they all started passing the food around, as casually as if this *were* all Cliopher's family, joined together. Jullanar was part of Basil's, he had said as much, as Rhodin was a part of Cliopher's. And—

He was a bit dizzied. And Sardeet Avramapul was Rhodin's secret penpal, and Masseo Umrit was Ludvic's *father*.

"Here's the bread," his Radiancy said, taking a round bun and examining it with delight even as he somewhat desultorily handed the basket to Cliopher.

Cliopher regarded his lord's plate with curiosity. His Radiancy had taken small quantities of everything, but focused on lavishing the bread with vast quantities of butter.

Into a lull in the small conversations that had started up, his Radiancy said cheerfully, "I have found out the explanation for how I was named Poet Laureate of Zunidh. It's Cliopher's doing, of course."

He cast a laughing, sidelong glance at Cliopher, who hoped he was not blushing.

Rhodin looked up. "I am astonished to learn you've already heard the news, my lord."

His Radiancy quirked his eyebrows and Cliopher shrugged very slightly, apologetically. Beneath the table his Radiancy nudged their knees together again.

"I have a penpal on Zunidh," Sardeet Avramapul said happily. "He told me all about it."

Rhodin dropped his knife.

CHAPTER THIRTY-ONE
RHODIN'S CORRESPONDENT, HIS DEAR FRIEND, THE IMPOSTOR CLAIMING TO BE SARDEET AVRAMAPUL

Court manners delighted in the absurdities of etiquette, and any long-term courtier in the Palace of Stars would probably have rather broken a finger than one of the established rules.

Even Cliopher did not drop cutlery, no matter the provocation.

They all looked at Rhodin, who was heedless of his dropped knife and was gazing searchingly at Sardeet Avramapul.

Cliopher very carefully did not let anything show on his face.

"It is I," Rhodin said, his voice almost wavering. He reached into his pocket and pulled out some sort of stone carving on a string. "I have here that mystical amulet you kindly bestowed upon me—"

"Oh my dear friend!" Sardeet Avramapul cried, bouncing out of her seat and granting Rhodin a smile beyond metaphor. "Can it be? My *dear* friend! My correspondent! My penpal! My heart!"

His Radiancy, beside Cliopher, actually murmured, "Astonishing."

It was uttered so quietly—and his face was almost as serene as ever—that probably no one would have heard, had he been seated as was his wont upon that isolated golden throne. Not even his guards, probably, could have heard it.

But Cliopher heard it, and he turned his head to meet his Radiancy's mirthful gaze, and let himself smile in shared amusement.

Rhodin had risen, and he and Sardeet were now holding each other's hands and gazing raptly at each other. "My dear friend!" Rhodin said. "Can you forgive me for never believing it to be true?"

"It wasn't a particularly believable claim," Sardeet replied, her voice warm with forgiveness. "Not when those investigators had decided it was untrue ..."

"I believed the rest," Rhodin assured her. "How are Kissie and Pea? Have you closed your café while you go adventuring, or is Lily able to manage? Did Sayo Kivim like this year's cake?"

Sardeet laughed. Cliopher was slightly surprised that flowers did not start blooming at the sound.

"He didn't get it!" She turned, beaming, at his Radiancy. "It was Fitzroy's birthday cake, you know! And he came just in time. I knew he would, one day."

Her voice was full of such emotion, as if her whole heart was overflowing, that Cliopher was not very surprised to see that his Radiancy had retreated into his most inviolably serene posture and expression.

Sardeet sat down beside Rhodin, even as they promised each other a proper conversation once the meal was finished. Cliopher noted that everyone else, Red Company included, were exchanging amused and incredulous glances. It was the most human expression he'd seen on Pali Avramapul's face.

He looked at his Radiancy, whose expression was no longer either amused or incredulous, but that impenetrable calmness that hid any ruffle of emotion. It would have been painful to see, had Cliopher not been equally unwilling to reveal all of his own sentiments and thoughts.

Into the quiet that followed as they all tried to pick up their food and conversations where they'd left them, his Radiancy said, "I was surprised to learn of your correspondence with Sardeet, Rhodin."

Rhodin shifted just enough to demonstrate his cognizance of this rebuke. "I had mentioned the circumstances, my lord, when I ... decided to embark upon a ... frequent correspondence ... but it was around the time of Woodlark, my lord. And later ..."

Later Rhodin had probably made, or at least attempted to make, telepathic reports.

His Radiancy's face was very, very still. Cliopher wondered if he dared, and found he did: he nudged his Radiancy with his own knee, offering that small comfort, which he had never been able to do before.

Some of the bleakness of memory passed from out of his Radiancy's eyes. Cliopher was relieved, but as he turned to survey the reactions from everyone else at the table, he saw the frown on Masseo Umrit's face, and recalled with a coldness down his spine that if Masseo Umrit was Ludvic Omo's father, then he too was from Woodlark.

He'd been living on Zunidh ... but no one talked about Woodlark, if they could avoid it. Even the mention of it was largely seen as a cursed subject.

"What happened with Woodlark? Is it a ... place?" Pali Avramapul asked, frowning as she looked at his Radiancy.

"An island," his Radiancy said, his voice utterly, terribly neutral.

"Oh?" she asked, leaning forward intently, ignoring any of his Radiancy's indications that he did not want to talk about this. Cliopher caught his breath at her rudeness.

Even distracted by his dear friend and correspondent, Rhodin also saw it. He said, briefly, seriously, "It was the worst disaster on Zunidh since the Fall."

Pali Avramapul refused to be quelled. "What happened?"

Cliopher could not hold both Masseo Umrit and his Radiancy in his vision at once. He looked away from Pali Avramapul, whose expression was almost *eager*, caught Basil's eye—his cousin was regarding him with confusion—and shrugged slightly even as he saw the smith trying not to show his concern.

Masseo Umrit did not have a courtier's mask. His emotions were writ naked on his face, for anyone who was accustomed to looking for them.

His Radiancy was not looking at his friend, but at Pali. Cliopher found his simmering grudge against her rising up, for why was she looking like that, as if this was something to dig into, to investigate, to *study*.

She did not know what it was, he reminded himself. She did not know what it meant to his Radiancy ... except that surely she *should*? Could she not see his distress, his bleakness, the shadow that had fallen across his eyes?

"Woodlark was an island in the Azilint," his Radiancy said, his voice precise and coolly unemotional. "Through a strange and unfortunate set of circumstances, its inhabitants became subject to a terrible plague." He paused. Cliopher knew his distress, and so with his knee pressed against his, offering that small consolation and comfort, he turned his head just enough that he could keep Masseo Umrit in his field of vision. The smith was leaning forward, intent, serious.

"If you recall the ghouls we encountered in the Trigoon Wastes, you will have a sense of the ... problem." His Radiancy cut his glance to the visibly confused Basil. "They were ... monsters, haunting the battlefields around the Golden Fortress, ravening the dead. They could pass their ... condition on, if they ate one who was not entirely dead ..." He hesitated, and then added, even more flatly, "The contagion on Woodlark was passed by touch."

His Radiancy was almost never that hesitant. But then they never talked about Woodlark.

"What happened?" Masseo asked in a subdued voice.

Cliopher could not be angry at *him* for asking that question, for all he wished his Radiancy did not have to think about the decisions he had had to make about Woodlark. The only small mercy was that Ludvic was not here.

He was glad Clio had not stayed to eat with them.

His Radiancy's face and voice were imperturbable. "We quarantined the island, and when it became clear there was no magic nor science that could prevent the spread, we ... I ... burned the island to the bare rock. It is a cursed place."

Everyone shrank back. His Radiancy held himself very still, very serene; but his knee against Cliopher's was trembling. Cliopher's hands were above the table in the court custom, where everyone could see them. All he could do was press his knee against his lord's, offering that small comfort.

(How often must his Radiancy have hidden his emotions upon that golden throne, behind that serene mask, those robes of state, pretended to be unmoved and unshaken by *anything*?)

Cliopher did not like to leave Masseo Umrit with that horrifying knowledge.

He recalled Ludvic telling him about the concern with *purity* in his village, how his father, this man, had been exiled, declared dead, for transgressing one of their laws. Would Masseo be remembering that? Would he be thinking of how when he was sixteen he had been cast out for bringing that upon his family, his village, his island? Would he be wondering, despite himself—for he was not mired in bitterness —whether this tragedy was something to do with that?

Cliopher could not let anyone sit there with that suspicion, however faint, in his mind.

"The investigation was necessarily inconclusive," he said, in what was probably far too formal and dry a phrasing, but he had stood beside Ludvic when he had given that order, beside his Radiancy when he had called up the fire. He had been the *witness*. "But from what I was told by those of Woodlark who had left the island before the contagion spread, there was a coterie of sorcerers who were seeking to strengthen their authority by necromantic arts."

"Rarely a good idea," his Radiancy said, with a twist to his mouth.

Cliopher nodded grimly. "They claimed it was in service of the community."

"They paid the price for it."

So had everyone and everything else on Woodlark, and many far from that island who bore the weight of it on their hearts, but Cliopher was not going to say that. "Some of the people had fled in time," he said, hoping to provide some comfort to Masseo. "There is a sizeable community now in Solaara."

It had been easier to imagine interrogating Masseo Umrit to assure himself that he would not hurt Ludvic, who had lost so much else, before this subject had arisen.

It was one thing to be far from one's island by choice, as Cliopher and Basil were. It was another to be exiled, declared dead and anathema. Masseo Umrit had probably never expected, or perhaps even wanted, to return to the family and community who had expelled him, but it could nevertheless not come as anything but a grievous shock to hear that one's island was dead.

More than dead. *Killed.*

No one was speaking; they were all looking at his Radiancy with variations on shock and horror. Cliopher wanted to take them to task for such a discourteous response, but that would hardly help. He said, "It was a deeply unpleasant and unfortunate situation, indeed." He turned in his seat slightly, catching Rhodin's eye. "I can entirely see why your new correspondent's potential identity went unheeded! How wonderful that you have been able to maintain it so long, even across worlds." He looked at Basil, smiling ruefully. "My letters reached Alinor but did not quite make it all the way here, alas, until very recently."

"I'm not nearly so great of a correspondent as you," Rhodin said, picking up the conversational thread as the experienced courtier he was.

"You write magnificent letters," Sardeet Avramapul protested. Cliopher was grateful she was gracious enough to heed the change of subject.

"Nothing like Cliopher—of course, he has a simply *enormous* family, and he writes to all of them."

"They have come to enjoy the thrill of having a correspondent in the Palace of Stars," Cliopher replied, and slowly, but with increasing engagement, he and Rhodin managed to pull the rest of the table back into a lighter and more pleasant conversation as they finished their meal.

His Radiancy pushed his remaining food around on his plate and drank the wine Basil had offered him with careful, controlled sips. He kept his hands around the clay tumbler when he was not lifting it, turning the vessel in those precise quarter-turns from time to time.

He also kept his knee pressed against Cliopher's, who wished fruitlessly and furiously that he had been able to offer any such comfort in the past.

By the time the food was mostly eaten, the wine had flowed liberally and the conversation had become once more genuinely merry. Only Masseo Umrit and his Radiancy continued quiet, and Cliopher could see that no one was particularly surprised at the smith's reticence. Cliopher kept having to fend off interjections directed at his Radiancy from Pali Avramapul, which was irritating.

At least his Radiancy had eaten a few more bites—perhaps half the plate he'd taken at the beginning, which Cliopher considered a small victory. Sara eventually suggested they move into the taproom for more drinks for those who wanted them and conversation.

"Perhaps," Cliopher added, "some music?"

His Radiancy smiled at him, and though the shadow still lay on his eyes the smile was genuine. "Will you be playing, Cliopher?"

Cliopher smiled back. "Would you grant me the honour of playing as well?"

"I should be delighted."

His Radiancy went off to whatever room Basil had given him, and Cliopher, left alone for a moment near the door, took a moment to close his eyes. He jumped when Rhodin touched him on the elbow.

"My apologies," Rhodin said, and drew him away from the door. He nodded as Jullanar of the Sea passed by them, Sara leaning companionably on her arm. When they were a discreet distance apart from the others, Rhodin spoke in a low voice. "He doesn't like to be reminded of Woodlark."

"I know."

"We may have managed to head it off ... especially if you're to play with him, he'll like that."

Cliopher shrugged. "I can hope so."

"You play very well, you know that." Rhodin looked up as Sardeet Avramapul waved cheerfully at them from across the room. He made a gesture as if to say "one moment" and looked doubtfully at Cliopher before speaking in an even lower voice. "You mightn't know this, perhaps, but he gets nightmares, often, after thinking about Woodlark."

Cliopher closed his eyes against all the layers in that. Just for a moment, he wished ... well. It was all done and over now, wasn't it? Palace life would not be the same, no matter that they would have to go back, eventually, for at least a short while. But his Radiancy was never going to go back to that isolation and loneliness, surrounded by guards he could not touch. Cliopher would not permit it. Neither would Ludvic. Or Rhodin.

"What does he do, on such nights?"

"Sometimes he paces in his rooms. Other times he goes into his study, or the gardens—on bad occasions he walks all night."

Wishing he could be anywhere else, no doubt.

"Thank you for telling me," he said, opening his eyes so he could smile reassuringly. "I'll see what I can do. You should go visit with your friend. She's waiting for you."

Rhodin glowed at the mention of his correspondent. "If you're certain—"

"Entirely."

"We'll listen, later."

"Can't miss the opportunity to hear Fitzroy Angursell himself perform?"

Rhodin laughed, clapped him on the shoulder, and hastened off to meet his friend, who gave him another one of those extraordinary smiles. Cliopher admired her beauty, but he could not stop himself from thinking of the light in his Radiancy's eyes when Cliopher had finally called him by his name.

He went to his room to wash in the basin and fetch his oboe. It helped to compose himself, even to comport himself in something close to his courtly poise. Otherwise he might become entirely discomfited by his Radiancy being there ... by the *Red Company* being there ...

Yes, better to be on his guard, as it were. The Red Company were not his enemies, but they were not yet his friends; barely even his allies at this point. Jullanar of the Sea was in her own category, and his Radiancy of course, and Sardeet Avramapul was preoccupied with Rhodin ...

Pali Avramapul was the one he had to watch out for. And Masseo Umrit, for Ludvic's sake and his own, after that devastating news of what had happened with Woodlark.

As he returned towards the central taproom he encountered his cousin in the hall.

"Kip! I was looking for you."

Cliopher stopped politely. "What can I do for you, Basil?"

Basil hesitated, then opened a door beside him and gestured Cliopher into what turned out to be a somewhat dusty private parlour. Cliopher glanced around it curiously, noting the beautiful details of the carved wooden panelling on the walls, the painted glass lights in the windows. "This is a lovely room."

"The Silver Room—used to be popular with the aristocrats—look, Kip, I wanted to ask you how you were."

"I beg your pardon?"

Basil twiddled the loose end of his apron string. "That was a hard topic, wasn't it?"

"Yes. His Radiancy does not like to be reminded of it. It was a terrible situation for him."

His cousin tilted his head to regard him with sober intensity. "And you?"

"What of me?" Basil simply continued to look at him, so Cliopher essayed a small, polite, courtly smile. "I don't particularly enjoy the reminder either, no." He swung his oboe delicately.

Basil huffed a short, not-quite-a-laugh. "And that's me told, is it? In two sentences and a smile. I had wondered what exactly your 'court face' looked like, and here it is. Impervious, impermeable, impersonal, and very polite. I admired the way you managed the conversation over dinner, Kip. You and Rhodin work very well together."

It was easiest to sail straight above, a sky ship above the restless sea. "We do, yes."

(Easiest, but perhaps not best. Cliopher did not yearn to fly; he loved the sea.)

"Perhaps it is because I only read the letter you wrote after Woodlark quite recently that I am concerned about you."

(Not best. But easiest.) He nodded as amiably as he could manage. "It was quite some time ago, for me."

Basil sighed. "I had to put down a rabid dog once, oh, it must be fifteen years ago now at least. I still think about it sometimes. It had to be done, but ..."

"There are many such decisions when one is the ruler," Cliopher said evenly. "I do my best to support—"

"You make those decisions too."

"Of late, though I am grateful there have not been any such tremendous crises since his Radiancy left on his quest."

"Kip."

Cliopher waited, fully in command of himself.

(This was a lie. The concussion still lingered, and he could not hold to any internal calm. But he could pretend to it, and that helped with the inner perturbation.)

Basil twiddled with his apron strings again. "Kip. I know with Woodlark you were the one synthesizing all the reports and presenting the few, very terrible options. Perhaps you didn't make the final decision, but you were still very much involved."

"That is—was—my job, Basil."

"I know—*Kip*. You're deflecting."

Cliopher would usually have continued to deflect until the conversation was fully reoriented, but ... but this was his favourite cousin, and he did not want to *manage* Basil, as if he were ... someone else.

"Probably," he said, and let himself smile ruefully. "I'm not certain what you want to hear."

Basil made a strange sort of noise, almost blowing a raspberry but not quite so loud and rude. "Pfft. I want ... Kip, I want *you* to say what you need to."

Cliopher could only stare at him blankly. He felt no need to say anything further at the moment. He wanted to go and play his oboe, and make certain his Radiancy was not dwelling on memories of Woodlark or any other disaster that might have come to mind, and let his own memories return to their quiet rest.

"You don't say it, do you?" Basil went on, and his face was sad, almost pitying. "What do you usually do, Kip? After a bad situation, or the reminder of one. Do you talk with your friends?"

This was not court, where vulnerabilities were weakness. This was Basil's inn, and Cliopher had always been able to tell Basil the secrets of his heart.

Or he had,

"If they were also affected, yes," Cliopher said. "Rhodin wasn't involved, so he's fine. His Radiancy ... I am worried about him, yes, but we do not usually speak of such things directly, not unless he wishes to."

Basil twisted his mouth, but then nodded as if he had understood something. "And then?"

"And then I would do something else. There's always more work to be done."

"And if you were ... particularly bothered? *Yourself*?"

Cliopher had learned not to shift or fidget and thus display his tells to those who would be watching for such signs of weakness or doubt. He kept his hands still, shoulders down and relaxed, expression—oh, undoubtedly as Basil had described it. *Impervious, impermeable, impersonal.* But polite, always.

Almost always.

He had to do Basil the courtesy of considering the question seriously. They could not return to the depths of friendship, of love, they had once shared if he did not.

The truth was, he didn't talk about such things. There was no one to talk about them *with*. Conju and Rhodin were courtiers, and culturally as well as personally very much did not like to talk about such things.

Perhaps Cliopher could have had that with Ludvic, if they'd reached out earlier. (If Ludvic had shown him his bar earlier. If Cliopher had invited *him* to come home on holiday with him, as he had Conju. If.)

The only other person who ever might come and ask him how he was feeling about something, who would want to hear him fumble to articulate his emotions, was his Radiancy. And they would never talk about Woodlark.

Or at least, they *had* never talked about Woodlark.

"On other matters," Cliopher said hesitantly. Honestly. (He was trying to be honest. He had never thought of himself as a deceitful man, but in speaking to Basil he was reminded over and over again how much he concealed.) "On other matters his Radiancy might ask me about it." He bit his lip, shook his head. "I shouldn't call him that ... it is hard to get out of the habit."

Basil waited, and this time Cliopher was not sufficiently grounded in himself to be able to wait him out first.

"Otherwise I suppose, if it were something that would not leave me alone, I suppose I would write to you about them ..." The reality of Basil receiving those letters struck him, and he winced. "I'm sorry ... I shouldn't have burdened you with them. I didn't think—" He stopped, and it took a moment before he could get the words out. "I didn't think you would mind. If you got them. I didn't think ..."

Basil stepped forward and grabbed his shoulders, almost roughly. Cliopher focused on him, blinking against the traitorous tears.

"Kip. I *don't mind*. I am so glad you had those letters, those memories of me, that *comfort*. I am trying—Lady take it!—I am trying to tell you to come *talk to me*, that I am here, that I am listening. You don't have to keep it inside. You can *tell me* what you're feeling."

Cliopher stood there, his hands still caught in their opposite's sleeves, pinned by Basil's strong, comforting hands. He caught his breath. "Basil ..."

Basil gazed searchingly into his face. Cliopher closed his eyes against the concern and pity and love he saw, directed full on him. It was an impossible gift, and he did not know how to accept it.

That other Kip flicked into his mind, when they sat looking at the comet in the dawning, speaking deep and uncomfortable truths, able to offer nothing to each other bar the truth and a willingness to hear it.

"Thank you," Cliopher whispered.

Basil's hands tightened, and then he relaxed them, and they stood together with his hands resting solidly and comfortingly. "I had not realized how honest you were being when you said all your introspection happened in your letters to me. Perhaps the first step is to admit your own emotions."

"What a thought!" Cliopher said lightly, ironically, the courtly response; but then he leaned forward and rested his forehead against Basil's, and more quietly he said, "That's another hard habit to unlearn."

"It'll be worth it," Basil whispered back. "I promise you."

Cliopher held very still for a moment, because Basil had never broken any of his promises to him.

"I'll try," he promised, with all the weight of a sacred oath, for he had never broken any of his to Basil, either.

CHAPTER THIRTY-TWO
AN EVENING AT THE INN

Cliopher was not a *great* courtier—he was neither Conju nor Rhodin—and he usually relied on *himself* not losing control of his emotions when others did.

It was Basil, therefore, who changed the subject. His cousin stepped back and leaned on the back of one of the elegant chairs furnishing the room. "How were you making out with the ledgers, anyway? I meant to ask earlier but you were a trifle distracted."

Cliopher raised his eyebrows at him, which unexpectedly made Basil guffaw. "What?"

"That was so much—I've only *just* met him but that's one of his gestures, isn't it? The way you held your head ..."

"We've worked together for many years," Cliopher said, resolutely calm.

"Ah, yes, that was *definitely* the look I'd expect to see on the face of a loyal colleague, when you looked up to see your lord standing there in all his Fitzroy Angursellian glory. Don't splutter, you know it's true."

"Basil!"

"He dressed up for you, you know. He came in with Jullanar and the others, and he came right up to me and said: 'You're Kip's Cousin Basil! He's told me so much about you!' So I looked at him, and I said, right back, 'You're Kip's dear friend! He's told *me* so much about *you*!' And then, while he was still spluttering a bit, I said: 'He's here.'"

Cliopher sat down on one of the other chairs. He hadn't had enough time to think through the wherefores of that earlier encounter. "Oh?" he said, which was weak, but this was Basil.

Basil laughed. "He looked *immensely* pleased and said, 'Oh? Is he organizing all your accounts for you?' And I could only laugh, because he *does* know you, and ask if he wanted to surprise you. And then he insisted on having a bath and changing clothes first."

Cliopher had just promised to acknowledge his emotions. He said, quite carefully, "Did he."

"In*deed*," Basil said happily. And then he peered hard at Cliopher. "Now. I wasn't *sure*, given your past ... inclinations, or rather the scarcity thereof, but I *do* take pride in my vocation as an innkeeper—"

Cliopher was somewhat concerned he knew exactly where his cousin was going with this. "Basil."

"Now, now, Kip, this is serious. I gave him the room next to yours, but do I need to tell him that there was a problem and you need to share?"

That was—that was—"That's not *true*."

His cousin rolled his eyes. "It could be. A leak or some sort of magical problem—"

"He's the *lord magus of Zunidh*."

"We have our own weird magic in the Woods, you know." Basil leaned forward, hands on his knees, grinning at him. "I can tell him you need to share. Only one room left, et cetera."

"That would be a lie."

"By the Lady, Kip, I thought you'd spent your life in government? Surely you're well aware of the usefulness of certain untruths?" Basil laughed when Cliopher just stared at him. "Oh, very well, it's not like that, I take it?"

"No. It's *not*."

"And yet you won't say what it *is*."

The challenge hung there. Cliopher bit his lip, and then he lifted his chin, and he said, "It has to be equal to be true. You know that, Basil."

Basil had stopped grinning, but now he smiled, slowly, an appreciative light in his eyes. "And you don't think you stand equal to Fitzroy Angursell, last Emperor of Astandalas? Perhaps you should ask *him* what he thinks. I'd say he'd be *quite* happy to be Aurelius Magnus to your Elonoa'a."

"You don't know him."

"Don't I? I've only had twenty years of hearing about Fitzroy Angursell and three hundred and twenty-seven letters about 'my lord'." Cliopher made an involuntary noise, and Basil grinned, unrepentant. "Sorry. Three hundred and twenty-six. I'm pretty sure there was one that was *only* about the postal system."

Cliopher opened his mouth to reply, and then sagged in defeat. "I think I want a drink."

"Fortunately, I happen to have an excellent supply."

He nodded, and stood up, trying to smile at his cousin, for that had not been a *bad* conversation, not at all. But nonetheless he felt shaky and uncertain.

His cousin clearly saw something in his face, for he caught at Cliopher's arm and gave him a quick embrace. "I'm sorry to keep pushing you when you're already off-balance."

Cliopher looked dourly at him. "I have not managed to reach where I have, nor put through the changes I have implemented, without knowing precisely how effective it is to keep pushing when someone is off-balance."

Basil sucked in his breath, and then laughed in surprise. "The Lady! I expect not." He shrugged, and changed the subject. "I like Sara's Lady of the Green and White. She's a friendly god, most of the time, at least as the Woodlanders think of her."

They went out into the hall, and Cliopher said lightly, "Did I tell you I met Vou'a?"

"Do you mean Buru Tovo's husband?" Basil laughed uproariously. "Good in bed, he said."

Cliopher was appalled to realize he was blushing. "No!"

"I'm sure he did."

"He said he was *chosen* by him. All it means is he likes men! He's got that hermit—"

Basil gave him a pitying glance. "Who did you *think* that efelauni of his was?"

Efelauni. The strange shell-merchant Cliopher had met in the market-place on Lesuia, who had very likely been Vou'a.

Cliopher thought of how his family had for so long thought his statements that he was the Lord Emperor's secretary were all part of a long and complicated joke.

He groaned as several—be honest—*many* comments his Buru Tovo had said over the years fell into place. How had he done exactly what he had castigated his family for doing?

Basil snickered. "No wonder you took it with such equanimity back then! The rest of us were all very scandalized. I always used to wonder if I dared ask for details, but you were so adamant there was nothing going on—"

Buru Tovo's sex life was not a topic Cliopher had ever spent very much time thinking about. He was about to respond when his Radiancy came down the stairs at the end of the hall and came up to them with one of his blazing Fitzroy Angursell smiles. Cliopher caught his breath and did not know where to look.

"I caught only the tail end of your statement and am *very* curious, Basil! Is Cliopher scandalizing you?"

"No, our Buru Tovo—our great-uncle, who taught Kip—"

"How to be tanà, of course. I have the utmost respect for your Buru Tovo. He came to see Kip, you know." His Radiancy gave Cliopher a sly smile. "He *did* seem to enjoy being scandalous. Told me all about how he'd attempted to show *my* uncle the 'give and the take' but didn't find him receptive. So to speak."

Cliopher felt intensely, piercingly embarrassed on behalf of his great-uncle, who had undoubtedly felt no shame or embarrassment at all.

Neither did Basil, who hooted with laughter. "Oh he did, did he? Your uncle—now that would be—"

"Emperor Eritanyr. Before he was emperor, of course, and the taboos came into effect."

Cliopher had undoubtedly written of the taboos, for Basil nodded with a hint of sober sympathy at their mention before returning to the happier subject. "Ah, he would have gone looking to see if he was worth it. I'm *sure* Cliopher's told you of Elonoa'a and his emperor."

"Once or twice, yes."

His Radiancy should not have looked at him like that, with his Fitzroy Angursell smile and the depth of meaning that their long acquaintanceship had given them.

Cliopher's face was tight and hot and he gripped his oboe, unable to muster the proper reserve and decorum.

"Let's play," he said, even as his Radiancy gave him a look that seemed barely a step off from a question, or an answer, or—or something.

Cliopher could not let himself name, let alone articulate, what he was feeling, for he would go up in flames as the driest tinder under a spark from two striking rocks.

Basil seemed to recognize he'd pushed Cliopher as far as he could go for the moment, for he only grinned and said, "Of course, of course, I have wanted to hear you play ever since Cliopher taught me Shaian using *Aurora* and your songs about Jullanar of the Sea."

≈

His Radiancy let Basil lead him to the taproom. He cast one amused look over his shoulder at Cliopher as he went, as if to check that he was ... all right. Cliopher nodded reassuringly, and his Radiancy turned at a polite question from Basil and said, "Oh, this harp? It's one I found when I was on holiday with Cliopher at a place called Navikiani. ... Yes, on Lesuia ..."

And they were gone, though Basil gave one brilliant, incredulous look at him as they turned the corner.

Cliopher was *all right*. He just needed a moment.

He leaned against the wall, gripping his oboe case, concentrating on his breathing. Basil must not have read the letter in which Cliopher had talked about that holiday. Letters. It had changed his life as much as his Radiancy's.

You took him there and he is not certain?

His younger self had written that to him about that very holiday. His Radiancy had thought about Cliopher, about swimming out to that sandbar, about that first deliberate reaching towards true friendship, when he was off with his friends of the Red Company learning again how to be a free man.

Cliopher took a deep breath. He would show his Radiancy. He would show *Fitzroy Angursell*. That he was a man—that they both were men—that they both were *people*. People who might choose to be friends.

His Radiancy was Fitzroy Angursell. He knew what it meant to have friends whom one would follow wherever they needed to go.

He could choose Cliopher, if Cliopher let him.

Cliopher opened his eyes, prepared to go into the taproom, when he saw that Pali Avramapul was coming down the hall towards him.

His emotions sloshed up rancourously. "Domina," he said politely, refusing to be anything less than perfectly courteous to her. His Radiancy had said *do not think ill of my friends*.

"Lord Mdang," she replied with a brusque nod.

He should have said *Cliopher, please*, as he had when Masseo Umrit had said the same, but he could not. He could only nod back at her. "Are you going into the taproom?"

"Yes." She glanced down at the case in his hand as they started walking beside each other. "What instrument do you play?"

"The oboe. It's a woodwind."

She nodded, though whether or not that meant anything to her he couldn't tell. The twenty or so steps to the hexagonal main taproom of the inn seemed a thousand paces long. She was frowning pensively; Cliopher decided he didn't need to say anything else.

"Fitzroy has talked about you," she said as they came in the door. He governed his face, hoping to hide the rush of warmth he felt at the thought, just as she glanced at him. "The oboe seems apt—I've heard it's a finicky instrument."

Cliopher gave her a very polite smile, even as his Radiancy turned towards them from where he'd been talking with Rhodin and Basil.

Pali Avramapul smiled tightly at Cliopher. "You really are the perfect bureaucrat, aren't you?"

"I have tried," Cliopher replied evenly.

His Radiancy, *Fitzroy Angursell*, merely smiled with almost his most benevolently serene smile.

Basil handed Cliopher a drink, which he took with a muttered thanks, and went over to sit with the village musicians.

He still had his court face wrapped about him: he could see the confusion in the village musicians' eyes, with whom he had played without any such need to hold himself aloof and alert, but then their eyes slid to his Radiancy and the cold countenance of Pali Avramapul, the bright interest of Jullanar of the Sea, the gloomily distracted Masseo Umrit, and Alfred with the hand-drum leaned to Harry, one of the fiddlers, and whispered something behind his hand, and Harry winked at Cliopher, and it was all right.

They had told him of great players who had sat in that taproom and performed. The Bee at the Border, where everyone stayed, had been known for it: the greatest performers in the Empire had polished their sets there before the run-up to the capital and all its competition and potential glory.

Fitzroy Angursell had played here, in the old days. Sara had told him how she had snuck out of her room one night when the Red Company had stayed at the inn, ostensibly incognito but recognizable for all that. She had always remembered his smile, the firelight shining in his eyes, the way the crowded inn had fallen silent and heedful before he had ever set hand to harp or opened his mouth.

Cliopher would have been nervous, had he let himself be.

He opened his case and fitted the pieces of his oboe together, and then hesitated a moment as he chose his reed.

(The oboe *was* a finicky instrument, in some ways. That didn't mean he had to ignore the challenge in Pali Avramapul's proud face.)

Cliopher had spent several hours each day over the past weeks with Clio at the edge of the millpond, Clio playing with his coracle and asking questions about the Vangavaye-ve, Cliopher with a pen-knife and a handful of canes for his oboe reeds.

It was a slow, meditative process, *finicky* and requiring both care and practice, but Cliopher had been making his own reeds for long enough that he could talk at the same time, at least for some of the less complex elements.

He'd learned how as a teenager, skipping out from school or work at Uncle Lazo's barber shop for music lessons. He was full of the *Lays*, and the importance of the old traditions he'd been learning from Buru Tovo, and he had insisted on being taught how to make the reeds himself. He could have bought them pre-made, only bothered with the final adjustments; but that had not been the sort of person he was even back then.

He chose one of his new reeds, the one that had felt the best in his hand as he was shaping it. He put it in his mouth to wet, glad as so often that this meant he was obviously preoccupied and unable to talk.

His Radiancy—*Fitzroy Angursell*—was chatting with Pali Avramapul, laughing and apparently fully recovered from the earlier conversation. He was holding his harp in one hand. The harp from Navikiani, which his Radiancy had found in a hidden closet alongside an illicit copy of *Aurora*.

Cliopher was quite certain, watching them as he looked over his oboe and positioned his stool so it was at a comfortable distance from the other musicians, that this was quite as much a performance, a persona, as Cliopher's court face or his Radiancy's usual serenity. Pali Avramapul herself was smiling up at him, her face as cold and beautiful and brilliant as the moon.

Cliopher set his other reeds back into the case, the linen wrap of his specialized tools—an awl, gouges, a pen-knife, the wire he used to bind the reeds together—nestled into its pouch in the lid, and sucked at the reed while his Radiancy finally got around to tuning his harp.

Pali Avramapul was wearing some sort of golden hair-clip; from where Cliopher sat, it looked like a frog.

Perhaps it was because he had spent so much time over the past week shaping reeds out of cane that the hair-clip made him think of a poison-dart frog.

On his return home after the Fall, when he had not taken the ship that the Other Kip had so easily taken, he had travelled south, across the plains and the hills and then the wide uplands slanting up towards the jungled heights of the Southern Grey Mountains. Somewhere near the headwaters of the Orcholon he'd been caught by a raiding party out of the mountains.

The raiding party had been to capture a jaguar for a ceremony before they commenced a period of making their weapons. They hunted with poisoned darts and blowpipes two or even three yards long. They had caught him easily: he'd had no weapons, and no wood-craft. He'd been following the old road, overgrown down to a narrow trail, when a dart had thudded out of nowhere to land one inch before his sandal, and a second one inch behind, and then, as he'd stood there befuddled and feeling the first trickles of fear, the raiders had melted out of the jungle in a circle around him.

Once in their camp, Cliopher had watched the hunters making the darts and pipes, laughing and joking as they carved. It had been interesting, watching them: how they split a long palm-tree stem, used a soot-blackened line to mark the course of the hole, then some sort of teeth—crocodile, from the river, he guessed, or maybe jaguar or ocelot—to carve the long groove.

(He did not remember now if he had thought of shaping oboe reeds then. Such a peace-time frivolity had been far from his mind; he had not taken his oboe with him when he left the Palace. He had found it, along with his furniture and books, exactly where he'd left it, when he returned and discovered no one had bothered with even opening the unlocked door to his room.)

It took months, he learned, to make a blow-pipe: to hollow the core, ensuring both halves matched exactly, and then to shape the cylinder, wrap it with bast, coat it with the tree latex that acted as waterproofing.

He'd had plenty of time to observe the hunters at their work. They were young men, teenagers; it was part of their initiation into manhood to create their own weapons. It was forbidden to kill once they began, and so they kept him a prisoner instead.

One day they had brought a basket of tiny yellow frogs to show him, laughing as they held it up to his face. He remembered how pretty they were, gold against the green moss lining the basket, their skins glistening in the sunlight.

(Pali Avramapul's hair-piece was pretty, incongruously so for such a stern woman; and she was wearing green, just the colour of new leaves, in an Alinorel-style dress. And of course her deadliness was legend.)

They'd told him how some of the other tribes, who lived where the frogs were less poisonous, drew out the exudate to coat their darts and spears. They had relished the description: how those hunters took a sharp stick and skewered the living frog through the mouth and out the leg, so that the panicked and tormented creatures would start to release their poison.

"We do not do that," he was told, as the basket of golden frogs was held under his nose. He could still smell the strange scent of the frogs, feel the terror washing down his back as the amphibians crawled and hopped about their cage, three inches from his face. He could have stepped back, but he was helplessly lonely.

They'd fenced him like an animal, tethered to a post, with a decrepit lean-to his only shelter from rain or sun, a single hollowed gourd for his water. They tossed him food when they remembered, which was not every day. He might have been a half-starved bear, kept for desultory entertainment.

His enclosure was a semi-circle of stout stakes with sharpened points. The other side was a sheer drop down at least five hundred feet before the uppermost levels of the tree canopy. Occasionally flights of parrots or other birds came up out of the foliage, but never so high.

There was one rock in the enclosure, which had one rough edge. He could have used it to saw through the rope of the tether. He could have jumped.

As weak as he was by this point he did not have the strength to get out of the stakes, nor the knowledge necessary to survive outside of them.

But still, he didn't jump. He thought of it, too often at times. But he didn't jump.

He looked down at the tiny golden frogs, and up again at his captors, and said, with as much polite curiosity as he could manage, "Oh?"

The young men grinned and jeered. The oldest, their leader, took two large leaves and used them to pick up one of the golden frogs. It squirmed a little in his grip, but it was terrified, and barely moved.

With his other hand he drew one of the darts he'd spent the previous afternoon fashioning from the bamboo quiver at his waist. He smiled at Cliopher, satisfied with his horror, and with a delicate, even gentle motion, stroked the spiral-grooved tip of the dart along the back of the frog. Once, twice, three times.

"Three times is enough to kill anything," he'd said, and tossed the stunned but still-living frog at Cliopher, laughing when he scrambled away from the deadly animal as far as his tether would let him.

"Are you ready, Kip?" his Radiancy asked him.

Cliopher looked up with his most perfectly polite and impersonal courtier's face, scanning the room to gauge the audience's mood. For a moment he met Pali Avrama-pul's eyes, and she condescended to smile at him, *the perfect bureaucrat*, and with the fire rising in his heart he took the reed out of his mouth, fixed it into the neck of his oboe, and said, "Indeed."

His Radiancy raised one eyebrow and then, when Cliopher didn't look away, but set his hands and his breath ready to play, smiled slowly and began, without an ounce of hesitation, to play the introduction to *Aurora*.

Well, everybody knew it, of course.

CHAPTER THIRTY-THREE
THE SECRET COLLECTION

I t was not the full poem set to music, of course—that would not have been as long as the *Lays*, but certainly longer than was comfortable to sing in one go, of an evening, unrehearsed. Fitzroy Angursell (his Radiancy, sitting not five feet away, playing his harp as he had played it before the villagers of Ikialo on Lesuia for the lunar eclipse party) had written two different shorter versions. One, it was generally assumed, had been his first foray into telling the story; the other a kind of synopsis or advertisement for the full poem once published.

Most of the time one played the second. It was a better song by any metric.

They played the second version, and then in the easy pause after *Aurora* had finished, Harry the fiddler took up the refrain of *In the Company of Armed Gentlemen*, which had always been a favourite on Alinor. Cliopher remembered Basil writing to tell him so, back when letters from the inn to Astandalas had taken a day and a half to reach him.

They went around the little cluster of musicians, each of them starting the next song without consultation or hesitation. *Aurora* into *In the Company of Armed Gentlemen* into *White Stone and Ivy* into *The Seven Winds* into *The Red Roses of Katharmoon* into the far less popular *Donkey Ears*, which was about an ancient emperor who had made several disastrous mistakes when it came to interacting with a fairy, and made his Radiancy's eyes brighten in appreciation and delight.

And then it was Cliopher's turn. Without hesitation, he chose one of the Islander songs he knew the rest knew: Basil's favourite of all the tales of Aurelius Magnus and Elonoa'a.

His Radiancy took half a verse to catch up, but he knew the words to more than the chorus, and a variation on the melody that Cliopher knew had come from Vinyë's hand.

His Radiancy quirked his eyebrows at Cliopher, and chose *The Lay of Fo Wakailunte*, which was an Islander song.

An Islander song about Lesuia, where they'd gone on that holiday.

Cliopher glanced at Pali Avramapul, whose face was sharply intent as she watched his Radiancy play, and when it was next his turn he chose another of Fitzroy Angursell's songs. Still one of the legal ones; for now.

And each time it was his Radiancy's turn, he chose an Islander song. His voice really was as beautiful as Sara had said it was, as every story had said it was, as Cliopher had known full well it was.

After four or five rounds the horn-players called for a break, and Basil brought over great foaming mugs of ale, cool and refreshing after their exertions. The summer night was bright out the door, what Cliopher had learned were frogs and crickets singing loudly, and some bird Sara called nightingales, which he had thought were purely mythical.

There was a jewelled nightingale, a mechanical bird, set in a golden cage in his Radiancy's private study. It had been a gift to a previous emperor, one of his ancestors, and sang, once a year, on what had been the longest night in Astandalas.

Cliopher had been in the room, taking dictation for some long series of depressing decisions, when it had suddenly burst out singing. He remembered the way his Radiancy had held himself, still as a stone thrown up on the beach when the tide receded. How they had both listened, for a moment drawn away from the litany of disasters and hard choices, and then, refreshed, returned to the grinding work.

There was no Fitzroy Angursell song about that mechanical nightingale; or not yet.

Probably his Radiancy was not yet ready to address the long years he'd spent in his golden cage. He'd called it an oubliette ... Cliopher did not know whether to hope he had been able to forget, for a time, what he'd lost.

He had sometimes thought it would be easier if he just gave up on his cultural identity, stopped caring when people mispronounced *Mdang*, stopped forcing them to pronounce *Vangavaye-ve* correctly, let his accent become entirely court.

But Cliopher had never been able to take the easy way, had he?

Neither the stories of Fitzroy Angursell nor Cliopher's knowledge of his Radiancy suggested that the man drinking his ale, wiping his mouth with the back of his hand as easily as Ludvic had, knew how to take the easy way either.

His Radiancy set down his mug and stretched his hands, his golden signet ring flashing in the candlelight. His eyes were as bright as the firelit gold.

He did not say anything, and neither did anyone else. Cliopher knew they had an audience, of half the Red Company and Basil and Sara and Rhodin, and all the villagers he had come to know and generally like over the weeks of his sojourn there, but he did not look at them. He did not look at the other musicians, either.

He was not entirely surprised that when his Radiancy picked up his harp once more, and Cliopher his oboe, they were the only two playing.

They looked at each other. There was a gleam in his Radiancy's eye that Cliopher could not quite read. There was challenge, to be sure, and amusement, but also something else ...

He wondered if it were the same incomprehensible anger he felt, rising up like his gorge. All those years in the Palace, respectively doing their best, never crossing this line. All those endless days of work, hard work, pretending that neither of them knew these songs, these stories, these dreams. All those unspoken thoughts.

All these years when Basil had been alive, and none of his letters had gone through.

All these years Rhodin, of all people, had been penpals with Sardeet Avramapul, of all people.

All these years his Radiancy had been trapped in his tower, that oubliette into which he'd thrust half of himself, hidden in plain sight, and Cliopher had pretended that he was only inconsequentially an Islander, that half of himself was a mere decorative flourish, unimportant.

He felt sick to himself with his own anger. Always before he had tried to focus his fury and despair onto the things he could change, tackled the impossible interlocking systems of society and government one at a time, with dogged intensity, refusing ever to give up, to back down, to *stop*.

You're allowed to stop, the Mother of the Mountains had told him. But Cliopher had never been allowed to stop, never allowed himself to stop, never *dared* to stop.

He had seen what that looked like from the outside, in that other universe where the other Kip had sparked a revolution.

How glorious it had been. When he'd been there he'd thought he would be one of the Apologists, but now—

He understood the desire to burn it all down.

Cliopher and his Radiancy were still looking at each other. It had probably not been as long as it felt, that exchange of a glance, as quick as one of their glances in a Council of Princes meeting to ascertain the other was ready, before they manoeuvred the conversation where they wished it to go.

As he did—*had always done*—on those occasions, Cliopher cast one look around their audience. In the flickering candlelight it was hard to focus on expressions, but he could see how Pali Avramapul was sitting, a glass of wine in her hand and a just slightly amused and more than slightly patronizing smile on her face.

He took in a deep breath and set the oboe in his mouth, and his Radiancy tilted his head, smiled one of his Fitzroy Angursell smiles, and began the introduction to one of his rather more seditious songs.

～

To the Islanders, challenge-songs were important. The *Lays* were full of them.

When faced with a challenge, you had to meet it, surpass what was asked of you. That was how you won: and Cliopher had always liked winning.

His Radiancy, Fitzroy Angursell, had a wicked look in his eyes. A challenging look; a *dare*.

It was like that, was it?

(His heart was singing, like the stars calling him home.)

Cliopher played *That Party,* which had been banned for mocking the emperor and his immediate kin.

His Radiancy returned with *Kissing the Moon,* which like *Aurora* was one of his longer poems and also a cycle of three or five shorter ballads—three that were considered generally acceptable, and two that decidedly were not.

It was, perhaps fortunately, difficult to smile while playing the oboe. Cliopher swept smoothly into the second of the permissible songs, and into the third when his Radiancy began it, and then, without missing a beat, began the fourth himself. He heard someone gasp; he did not look around, but Alfred began to drum, just a soft, insistent beat, matching the underlying rhythms of the songs.

For everyone knew Fitzroy Angursell's songs, after all.

And so they went on: spiralling down further into less and less common songs, more and more seditious ones, Cliopher meeting and surpassing each step of the challenge, until at length they were playing pure treason in the form of the alternate version of *Donkey Ears*.

Cliopher had never heard it performed: by his time in the capital the more seditious songs had mostly been suppressed. But he had been on polite terms with the Imperial Censors in the office next to him. One day they asked him to help box all the submitted materials to be burned in the incinerators used by the priest-wizards for ritual purification. When he'd helped (reluctantly, but he was grateful to them for even acknowledging he existed), he'd found the stacks upon stacks of works by that notorious poet and outlaw ...

The book of censored poetry was the only thing he'd ever stolen from the Palace.

Well. Except for the government, of course.

Song by song they matched each other. Cliopher did not know what to think about the fact that his Radiancy remembered all the words, except that his Radiancy had a prodigious memory.

Perhaps, like Cliopher, he had sometimes gone over these songs when the unending efforts to effect meaningful change were crushing his spirit, and, as everyone always had, taken heart from the verve and joy and humour with which Fitzroy Angursell had written them.

Except that for Cliopher there had only been the thrill of something forbidden, dangerous, *illegal*. For his Radiancy there would also have been the constant knowledge that *that* was who he had been, that these poems and songs had come from a part of himself that he could not reveal openly.

Well, he could now, Cliopher thought truculently, playing a little variation because he could not quite recall the proper flourishes for an early and musically overly complex song.

He lost track entirely of time or his physical state or his audience. There was the gleam in his Radiancy's eyes—still a touch wicked, but more appreciative, almost hilarious—and there were the strange harmonies of oboe and harp, and there was song after song after song.

Cliopher started one, and his Radiancy broke off playing in a flurry of laughter and broken notes. "I was hoping you wouldn't play that one," he said, his eyes a brilliant, liquid gold with delight. "I can't remember how the second verse goes."

There was a little pause. Cliopher lowered his oboe, and then he cleared his throat and sang it.

His voice did not sound so ill as that, in that taproom of such history and good acoustics.

When he finished, his Radiancy didn't say anything for a moment. Cliopher felt suspended in the moment, in this place beyond all physical awareness but the music thrumming through his bones and his blood, the metal keys of his oboe warm under his fingers.

His Radiancy, eyes luminous, face intent, started a song he did not know at all.

This time, his concentration wavered and broke.

His hands were tight, his fingers cold, and he felt thirsty like a solid brick in his head.

He should not have done that.

But oh, the light in his Radiancy's eyes—

Cliopher turned his head, grateful to see that Basil was hurrying up beside him with a great tankard. He drank half of it down in one go, not even grimacing at the slight bitterness of the cool brown ale.

Basil set his hand on his shoulder, warm and solid. Cliopher leaned back against his cousin, and sipped the ale more circumspectly.

His Radiancy sang a verse, a chorus, another verse, the chorus again, and then he faltered and looked over at Jullanar. Cliopher hoped suddenly that it was a *new* song, though he had not quite registered the words well enough to tell—something about a unicorn, was it? The villagers had told him about how one of the local gentry had somehow acquired a unicorn foal—

Jullanar laughed. "I don't think you ever finished that one, Fitzroy."

"Pity," his Radiancy said, playing the melody of the chorus again. "It had potential." He looked intently at Cliopher, who was nearly quivering with exhaustion.

"I'm not sure," Basil said, squeezing his shoulder, "whether I should be proud or mortified at your comprehensive knowledge of Fitzroy Angursell's body of works, Kip."

"Proud, surely," his Radiancy said with a grin, setting down his harp and reaching for a clay tumbler that Harry the fiddler offered him. "Thank you."

"How do you even know all t'at?" Harry asked. "Not you, sir, I remember you coming through here in t' old days. En't *you* head of the Zuni government or summat?"

"Or summat," Cliopher agreed wearily. Basil's hand clenched on his shoulder, digging right into a knot, and Cliopher could barely prevent himself from hissing. He looked up instead, to see that Pali Avramapul was regarding him with a speculative, surmising sort of expression—his own response of smug victoriousness he buried deep beneath his court face but nevertheless felt keenly—and Jullanar of the Sea had jumped up to draw chairs over beside her and Sara.

"Come sit with us," she said, beckoning to both of them.

"Aye, we'll play a bit," Alfred said, winking.

Cliopher was not too loath to put away his oboe—his lips were rubbery with the strain of playing for however long that had been (hours? Fitzroy Angursell had written a lot of songs, and Cliopher felt as if he had played all of them)—and he was glad Basil stayed beside him, for he might have stumbled, standing, otherwise.

He ended up seated between Sara and his Radiancy, Jullanar of the Sea facing him. She spoke laughingly to his Radiancy, referring to their shared past adventures.

Not adventures. She was teasing him about an ordinary sort of thing, when his Radiancy had been genuinely young.

"Did you play your fingers bloody again?" she asked, laughing at him. Cliopher liked the way she laughed, how warm and friendly and pleasant the sound was, and the way that his Radiancy smiled back without any strain or unease showing in his jaw or eyes.

"They're not raw," his Radiancy objected, displaying his fingertips to her. "A bit sore."

"You should know better," she scolded him, but gently. "Do you need me to kiss them better?"

Her tone was so maternal that his Radiancy instantly gave her an innocent, pleading expression—something Cliopher had certainly *never* seen on his face before —and let her grab them. Jullanar was laughing so hard that her kiss was more of a splutter.

When he smiled back, she bounced a little in her seat before turning her bright smile on Cliopher. Her eyes was gleaming with intrigue. "You've seen *The Secret Collection*."

It was not the same sort of ravishing smile as Sardeet Avramapul had bestowed, but Cliopher felt a certain, unexpected delight and could not help but smile back. He'd heard stories from Basil and Sara about what she was like as a person, not a legend, and he hoped he might be able to become friends with her. It did not seem as if it would be hard—not like Pali.

"What's that?" his Radiancy asked, regarding the small bowls of nuts and fruit and baked goods laid on the table before them and choosing a bunch of something with small and translucent golden-green berries.

Jullanar stole one of the berries, tasted it experimentally, then shrugged and got her own bunch. "After the Silver Forest, I ended up east of Galderon. I told you I went back to the university and examined for a degree, I think?"

"And assisted with the embassy that was sent to Astandalas," his Radiancy added.

"How dull a way to put it," Jullanar murmured thoughtfully. "And here we were, thinking we were so grand and revolutionary, sneaking an envoy through enemy lines to the highest power in all the land! Pity I didn't go," she added, with a rueful glint in her eyes as she looked at his Radiancy. "We might have been able to do something ... *greatly* unexpected."

His Radiancy was obviously not ready to talk about such things, for he kept his face and voice light. "Indeed! Instead I was left with this nagging sense of familiarity in some of the phrasing."

"One does one's best," Jullanar replied, with a mock bow. She grinned at Cliopher. "While under siege I put together a collected edition of Fitzroy's works. *All* his works."

"All of them?"

"Well—not *Aurora* or the other long ones that were already published. All the *important* ones."

There was something to be said, Cliopher thought, for a person who came back from heartbreak—for it was clear the dissolution of the Red Company had been hard on her as on his Radiancy—by taking up the editor's pen under the standard of truth no matter how incendiary.

"There weren't any printers able to do what I wanted in Galderon—or rather, with the distribution network, and Galderon was nowhere near anywhere useful for disseminating a collection of Fitzroy's more scandalous works—so I came back to Northwest Oriole where I knew where to find a printer I knew to be sympathetic. Hence the *Secret Collection*."

"I've never heard of it," Pali Avramapul said suddenly from his Radiancy's other side. Cliopher suppressed a jump; he hadn't realized the two sisters Avramapul and Rhodin had drawn up chairs to their table. Only Masseo Umrit was still sitting aloof, within hearing distance but closer to the small fire that was all Basil kept burning on this warm summer's night.

"One of the printer's employees was *not* so sympathetic, alas, and called for the authorities. There were only half a dozen copies printed before they seized the works and destroyed the plates and all the unfinished books—I didn't think anything survived. But you couldn't have known those songs in those variations unless you'd seen it. I just can't think *how*."

Cliopher mustered his most impregnably dignified expression, just as if he were explaining to Prince Rufus some small detail of Islander culture, and said, "I stole my copy from the Censors."

His Radiancy went instantly and perfectly serene, but when Cliopher very solemnly met his lord's gaze, he could see the subterranean mirth bubbling up like Basil's ginger wine.

"There's got to be a story in that," Jullanar said, laughing. She had a cheerful cast to her face, as if she smiled a great deal, and a delightful splash of freckles over her nose and cheekbones. "Basil told me you'd joined the Service before the Fall, so—did this happen in Astandalas?"

Now his Radiancy had turned inwards and secretive, just as he did when he was waiting for Cliopher to make one of his speeches to the Council of Princes, and change the world.

Cliopher forced himself to keep his posture relaxed, friendly, not adversarial. He chuckled wryly. "For a while I worked in this closet of an office next to the Censors. One day they asked me to help them take some of the materials to be incinerated, and I ... kept one back."

Rhodin paused, considering. "Where did you keep it? You have a lot of enemies who would have *loved* to find that."

His Radiancy knew Cliopher, knew the way his mind worked. "Cliopher, did you put it back in the Censors' office?"

Cliopher bit his lip and nodded, grinning bashfully, at this ancient trick.

Jullanar of the Sea laughed, the sound ringing out. "How clever of you!"

For a moment he could only stare at her, remembering youthful daydreams of making the legendary Jullanar of the Sea laugh in admiration and delight.

It felt—strange, to have it happen.

He was unaccountably flustered, and hastily explained. (So dryly; so *boringly*. But this was who he was ...) "I've never met anyone who did less work than those Censors. They would open everything that was sent to them and then just pile it up in their offices. At the end of every week they were supposed to produce the List of Banned Texts. Whatever twelve items were on top of a random stack were the ones that got banned."

"That's terrible," Pali Avramapul said flatly.

"It was, yes," he replied, trying not to let his hackles rise. "They don't do that any longer."

"They don't exist any longer," Rhodin said; that had been an early reform, when Cliopher had first started to make real changes.

"The only time I saw them clean out the room was the time I helped them, and that was only because they couldn't physically close the doors any longer. After I realized what the book was, I'd borrow it from time to time."

"They never saw you? Surely even they would have reported that. I put *everything* I knew by heart in there." Jullanar grinned at his Radiancy, whose expression was nearly serene, as if his emotions were too strong. She turned to Cliopher. "What happened after the Fall? Was it lost?"

"The offices were in the lowest level of the Collian wing, which was badly damaged in the Fall. All blocked off. I was the Hands of the Emperor—the head of the Imperial Bureaucratic Service—by the time the restorations and renovations reached those cellars. They brought all the documents and books for me to decide on."

Basil hooted with laughter. "Don't tell me *you* ended up being the last Censor?"

"I was nothing of the sort, dear cousin," Cliopher retorted with great dignity. "I went through the entire collection and had it all put into the Imperial Library and Archives."

"That book wasn't in there," Rhodin said, suddenly intent. "I've read through all the material on the Red Company."

"So have I," his Radiancy murmured, his eyes hooded as he met Cliopher's gaze.

There were so many emotions. Cliopher had no idea if his Radiancy were delighted or upset or merely neutral—no. He could not possibly be *neutral*. Cliopher sought the right words. "Perhaps I kept that one book."

His Radiancy lifted his hand to cover his smile, his eyes full of a sudden delight, and Cliopher was so glad he'd found the right words.

"Where did you keep it?" Rhodin asked, frowning. "I know where you keep your copy of *Aurora*—"

"Do you?" his Radiancy asked, almost normally.

"It's bound as the last volume of the Law-Code of Astandalas," Rhodin informed him, which made Jullanar and Basil both catch their breath on laughter. "But of course you were well aware of Cliopher's appreciation of *that* poem."

His Radiancy's eyes glittered. "Indeed."

Cliopher was glad he was still mostly wrapped in his court persona, for he did not want to sink into his seat in mortification at the reminder of the constant humming Ludvic had told him he did.

"It's not as if *I* felt the need to go through your belongings," Rhodin assured him, "but it was always a good exercise for my most promising agents. The only thing to find was *Aurora*, and that was well-enough hidden that I knew if they didn't find *that* then they weren't going to be any good at all."

"That's a bit of a backwards compliment, Rhodin," Cliopher managed dryly.

"You're the person who is both infamously loyal and wrote an essay explaining why Fitzroy Angursell should be the poet laureate."

Which was really the same thing, of course.

His Radiancy had turned to a kind of serenity, his eyes a touch hooded, his posture uninformative. He was definitely feeling emotionally off-kilter. Cliopher sympathized.

"So where is it?" Jullanar of the Sea asked. Her cheeks were flushed, and her eyes flashing, and her wonderfully multi-shaded hair coming out of its twisted braids. "I cannot imagine, even on so short an acquaintance as we have, that you *destroyed* it."

"Of course not," Cliopher said, and felt, for just a moment, as if she were not a *stranger*, for all that this was the first time they'd met.

It must be all the stories he'd heard of her, and she'd heard of *him*. He nodded. "If you'll give me a moment ..." Before anyone could say anything, he got up and went to Basil's office, where he retrieved his writing kit.

The few moments away from the group helped him regain his composure.

Mostly.

It didn't help his composure any that his Radiancy broke decorum to grin when he saw it. "Of *course*."

"Your writing kit?" Rhodin asked, apparently equally delighted. "It was a gift from his Radiancy," he explained to Jullanar, who was leaning forward to look at it. "Nearly always on his person."

"Yes," Cliopher said, with a sidelong glance at him, as he set the wooden box on the table. He opened the lid and showed the neat compartments for his inks and inkstone, brushes and pens and pen-knife and the metal nibs he sometimes used, and the deeper-by-magic sections for papers and parchments and so on.

He had found out its more obviously hidden qualities—that nothing inside would break even if he dropped it; the extra depth of the containers—but it had taken him years and a trip home to explore further.

That journey—on a trading ship, but one where he was solely a passenger, not part of the crew—had been long and lonely and boring, and at one point Cliopher had resorted to taking everything out of the writing kit and cleaning it thoroughly. Examining the wood for any signs of rot or damage, he had discovered that if he turned it upside down and pressed one of the hinges in a certain way that the back would open as a new lid to an entirely new set of compartments.

There had been a single note in there, the first time Cliopher had received anything like a personal note from his Radiancy.

Ah, you found it! Well done. Always going above and beyond.

He would not be embarrassed that he kept all his private notes from his Radiancy in the secret back compartment. No one but his Radiancy, and perhaps Rhodin, had any chance of recognizing them, and that was only if he brought them out.

He slid his hand in and pulled out the slim volume.

"I feel as if I wrote far more poems than that," his Radiancy murmured, taking it out of Cliopher's grasp.

"I didn't include *Aurora* or *Kissing the Moon* or any of the long ones," Jullanar of the Sea said, craning her neck to see the book. "The paper was very thin—it was a new invention, the font and the paper ... we had this idea that it should be very easy to smuggle. It would have been, if that rat hadn't told on us," she added bitterly.

"It's lovely," his Radiancy assured her, flipping through the book. "You even had most of the music down."

"All those times you made me take notes for you," she said with good-natured pragmatism.

Cliopher shut the back lid of the case with a quiet click.

"What a clever thing!" Sardeet Avramapul said, leaning over her sister's shoulder to peer down at the writing kit curiously. "Such a pretty piece of magic. Very subtle, and useful too."

Pali Avramapul shifted, annoyance on her face as she looked down at the writing kit. Cliopher made sure his face was court-polite. He'd won the challenge she'd offered him this evening—he the perfect bureaucrat! pah!—and he did not think she was particularly pleased about it.

Well, he was not particularly pleased about how she'd treated his Radiancy, either.

"Yes, it is," Cliopher said in response to Sardeet Avramapul's statement.

"And a superb move in the game of courts," Rhodin added, nodding towards his Radiancy, who was still absorbed in the book of his songs. "Not that Cliopher ever thought about it like that, of course."

Sardeet tipped her head, smiling, and Cliopher smiled back, and then her face suddenly grew intensely focused.

"*You* ..." she breathed. "Oh, it's *you*."

Cliopher's heart caught, because no one could have had Sardeet Avramapul look at them like that, *say* that, and not have their heart skip a beat in anticipation and holy awe.

She reached into her pocket and pulled out a small leather pouch. "I was given this in trust," she began, before offering it to him. "I was told that I would know the person I should hand it on to."

"What is it, Sardeet?" Rhodin asked, and then his face changed with wonder. "It's not—not that item you were given by the Merrions—?"

No.

Surely not.

Surely not.

Sardeet Avramapul smiled radiantly at Rhodin. "It *is*, yes!" She turned back to Cliopher. "It is not for you, I'm afraid—but I can trust you to pass it on to the right person, can't I?"

"Of course," said his Radiancy, with the kind of certainty that had been the stone upon which Cliopher could turn the world.

"Who is the right person?" Cliopher asked, though his hand was already reaching out for whatever-it-was that had come from the Merrions—and it was not merely curiosity that drove his motion. This was Rhodin's dear friend, his correspondent; his Radiancy's friend.

"You'll know," Sardeet Avramapul said complacently. "Just as I did, just now, with you. You'll *know*."

"How wise the Merrions are," Rhodin murmured.

Cliopher refused to look at his Radiancy. He said, "May I open it?"

"Of course, I put it in there so it wouldn't get damaged," she replied, nodding encouragingly at him.

He opened the little leather pouch. It was closed with a kind of drawstring, the knot easy to untie. Whatever was inside was very light—

Feather-light, in fact.

CHAPTER THIRTY-FOUR
FIREFLIES

The scent of roses and fire and tea billowed up, filling the air around them. Cliopher breathed it in deeply even as his mind tried to take in what he was seeing.

It was clearly a feather. He could see the fine downy filaments on the lower part of the shaft, the smooth vanes curving to a rounded point.

Except ... it was also made of fire.

The feather was not the ivory-gold he had seen in the living phoenix that was the Lord of Ysthar's familiar companion, and which Cliopher had had the honour of meeting on his embassy to Ysthar. Nor was it the ruddy gold, just the colour of banked embers as the breath stirred their surfaces, of the fantastically, impossibly legendary Veil of Shahargan, which the Lord of Ysthar had shown him as proof of his victory in the Great Game Aurieleteer he had played with the enchantress Circe.

This was the orange-and-lilac of a young fire. It was beautiful, and Cliopher knew that it was quite possibly the only remaining feather in the Nine Worlds from whatever phoenix it had come from.

"I shall keep this in trust, and hand it to the one who seems intended to receive it." He spoke the oath solemnly, not breaking eye-contact with Sardeet Avramapul, letting the words pool around him as his fingers felt the strange warmth of a fire that burned without consuming itself, without burning his hand.

"Thank you," she replied equally gravely, and then they nodded at each other and Cliopher tucked the feather back into the pouch, and all the noise started up and his head felt as if it were about to explode.

He drank the end of his ale grimly, wanting water and a quiet room, knowing it would be impolite to leave so soon, while his Radiancy's friends were talking over the music and the feather and the book of poetry.

Then Sara leaned towards him and said, "Kip, will you give me your arm, please? It is getting late—I don't usually stay up so long," she added with a disarming smile to the group, who had fallen quiet to let her speak. "But I could not have missed that performance!"

"Of course, Sara," Cliopher replied, putting the leather pouch into his writing kit before standing. He gave the assembly a polite bow, though the motion made his head slosh and seethe, and was glad to move slowly and gently, Sara's hand on his elbow, through the room and to the back door.

"To the kitchen first, Kip," Sara directed, and he obeyed. They both sighed with relief when the door swung shut behind them, blocking off the noise from the taproom. "It's been a long time since we were so busy," she added, as they moved into the kitchen. One hearth contained a bed of coals perfect for grilling; Cliopher felt a small pang of regret that he had to stir them up for the kettle to boil.

Sara sat down on her padded chair, and directed him to bring down two teapots from the cupboard and set them on a tray. "That jar, there—put two large spoonfuls in each pot." She smiled at him. "It will help your headache. I know you've not been taking anything."

"The physician said I was healing well," he protested.

"There's no shame in seeking comfort when you're hurting," she replied quietly.

She had a chronic illness none of the local healers had ever understood. Basil had wanted to bring her to Astandalas when Cliopher was there, to see a specialist, but people of the Woods rarely did well going far from their homes, and Sara could not face the idea of crossing the border between worlds for such an expensive uncertainty.

The healers of Astandalas had been the best, if you could afford them. If.

"Thank you," Cliopher said, humbled. "I forget, sometimes. Headaches are not ... unfamiliar."

"I forget I have a different baseline than most people ... what does Basil call it? The usual level for something."

"The waterline ... it's the mark on a ship or a canoe for how deep its draft is. How high or low it floats. It can change depending on the weight of the cargo."

"Just so."

He glanced at her as the already-warm kettle began to splutter, and watched for the steam to come out its spout in a steady stream. "The extra cargo feels heavy tonight," he admitted.

"Yes. You might want honey in your tea. That blend is quite bitter." She smiled crookedly. "So many useful things are."

He nodded, and when the kettle fully boiled he made the tea, so that the fruity-bitter scent of herbs rose up, and he took little pots of the famous honey of the Woods and set it on the tray beside more of the heavy clay mugs, and then he carried the tray first to Sara and Basil's room on the ground floor, where he left her to retire, and then, gratefully, he went upstairs to his own room.

～

Not that he could sleep.

He drank the tea, and puttered around slowly picking up his room, arranging the clothes that had come back, clean and folded, from the village launderer, sorting through his books.

He lay down on the bed, still in his day clothes, the candle casting warm ruddy light on the ceiling, odd shadows in the corners.

Sardeet Avramapul had given him a phoenix feather to hand on to ... someone.

He lay there, but even with his headache slowly diminishing, the kurakura of his emotions was so impossibly rough he knew he was never going to be able to sleep.

Well. Not *never*. He did, after all, have things he did on such occasions. There was work, and ... walking outside in the gardens, and ... writing to Basil.

Cliopher got up and went to the small wooden desk under the window, where he could look down on the village green during the day, and pulled together his notes on how the business of the inn—always the heart of this village—could be increased. It would probably never be able to return to its heyday as an important stop on the route to the capital, but it could become something new and equally good for the community. Perhaps, depending on what said community wanted, even better.

He had already made most of the notes. It did not take him long to organize them into a concise report, analysis and evidence and suggestions all in their categories.

The sounds from below had grown quiet by the time he was done. He'd noticed when many of the villagers departed the inn and dispersed like so many shadows across the green to their own homes, and then the sounds of feet on the stairs as the guests made their way to their rooms.

And then, silence, but not full silence, for the inn was an old, old building and it had its own quiet noises in the night.

Cliopher finished his report for Basil, and cleaned his pen before putting it away in his writing kit. There was the leather pouch.

He could not resist looking at the feather again. It was extraordinary that he'd seen feathers from three different phoenixes—almost unbelievable. There was only ever one phoenix at a time, the Lord of Ysthar had told him, while his ivory-gold phoenix preened and sang softly in the background.

This feather, lilac-gold, felt good in his hands. It made his heart lift simply to look at it. He knew he shouldn't, knew it was not for him, but he could not help stroking the feather down the creased line of his forehead, the bridge of his nose. All the tense and pained muscles of his face seemed suddenly to quiver and relax, and Cliopher felt the tears prickle his eyes.

He set the feather down, intending to return it to its pouch and that to his writing kit, when a thought struck him.

A phoenix feather was, quite literally, a legendary item. And there were stories in the *Lays* for what you did if you were handed a legendary item and asked to pass it on.

A legendary *feather*, even.

You kept it on your person.

The stories were very clear about that. It made sense, from an historical point of view—in the old days, the days of the voyages, you were never going to be sure of anything that was not physically on your person. And in those days no Islander, no one who was Ke'e Lulai, would have anything like a pocket. Bilums and other kinds of bags or pouches were for shore, not long months at sea.

Cliopher hesitated, old songs running through his mind, verses of the *Lays* he had not thought of for ... years. There were a few verses in the public *Lays* mentioning this story, and more in those additional lays Buru Tovo had taught him in Islander.

Regardless of the truth behind that old joke (if it *were* a joke?), Buru Tovo *had* always had a special connection to Vou'a.

He had been very careful to ensure that Cliopher knew all the songs and stories and lays to do with Vou'a, and Cliopher had been very careful to learn them.

Cliopher put his hand to his neck and released the knots of the three efela he was wearing.

He spread them out on the table, shivering and rubbing his neck at the odd lightness and discomfort he felt at removing the efela ko. He had not gone without any efela—without *that* efela—since he had made it when he was twelve.

He had taken it off only once before, that first terrible shipwreck on his journey home across the Wide Seas. He had lost Saya Ng to the storm, and then all the tools and supplies and a goodly portion of the boat itself.

He'd hauled the battered wreck onto that low islet, which was barely high enough above the waterline to support a small copse of coconut palms, but there were coconut palms, and on a slightly larger islet farther along the ring of the atoll he had found three breadfruit trees and a pandanus and a tobby shrub, and a swampy area with wild-gone taro growing in it, and in the lagoon there had been the old stone foundations of fishing weirs, and so he had had enough, after all, to rebuild.

He'd had to take off his efela ko and carefully chip a flake of the obsidian to use as ... well, as everything. A drill-bit, an auger, a knife to split open the hard rind of the tobby nuts so he could eat the nutritious meat and have the seed to use as the whorl of a spindle, so he could use banana leaves and the pandanus to make fishing line and to repair his sail.

That was the last time he had removed it.

He did not like seeing his efela ko laid out before him, the burnished pearls, the imperfect obsidian teardrop. But this was the pattern of the *Lays*.

So had Vou'a spread out his efela when he was given a feather by Akuava'a (the 'dark god', who was only mentioned in this story), and asked to carry it ... somewhere.

Cliopher could not quite bring himself to think of the full story, now. It was long and involved many secret stories of the gods and why Ani no longer came out of her waters. His head hurt too much to think of the challenge-songs, and the negotiations between all the gods under the sky for their territories and peoples, and all the rest of the rich detail Buru Tovo had delighted in telling him. But he remembered this part.

In the story Vou'a had spread out his efela, and he considered which one was most appropriate for the task, which was able to hold the feather he had been entrusted with, and that was the one he had used.

So. Cliopher had his efela ko, a dozen golden pearls evenly arrayed on either side of the obsidian pendant. He had his efetana, an unbroken ring of fire coral cut into tubular beads of different lengths, representing all the many types of fires. And he had that efela from the dream-world, a flame pearl on either side of a sundrop cowrie.

One pearl for a token, and two for a promise, and five to make an efela.

These two flame pearls represented that promise Cliopher had made to Vou'a, whose shell was the sundrop cowrie, the efevoa: that he would bring home a new hearth-fire for the world.

And he had, hadn't he? He had tried.

He looked at the feather, phoenix fire glimmering with its uncanny light, and thought about symbolism and the *Lays* and the story of Vou'a and Akuava'a, and the feather Vou'a had been tasked to carry and had, to his great shame and eternal regret, lost.

Cliopher studied the phoenix feather. Vou'a had not pierced his feather, but had simply tied it on to his efela, and it had worked its way loose and fallen.

It seemed a crying shame, but—

But the lesson was clear.

Cliopher wondered for a moment if he should ask Sardeet Avramapul her opinion, but then he decided against it. This task had been passed to him, and it was up to him to stand by his decision, for good or for ill.

He got out the reed-making tools from his oboe case and carefully used the awl to pierce a hole through the shaft of the feather. He had a length of fine wire for tying his reeds together, and he threaded it through.

He twisted the wire around the shaft, and considered his three efela again.

And then Cliopher tied the feather with which he'd been entrusted to the new efela, for he had always believed in second chances.

The little feather curled neatly into the hollow of the sundrop cowrie, as if it had been meant to be there.

He replaced the three efela around his neck. When the efela ko settled into the familiar hollow of his throat he sighed with relief. It was not a superstition, really—or at least Cliopher did not think of himself as a superstitious man—but it was said that the efela ko was anchor for more than simply your studies, if you sought to become one of the lore keepers.

It was said that the gods noticed the lore keepers more than other people. The efela ko *protected* the one who set out on that path. Somehow.

Cliopher bit his lip in lieu of shaking his head, which felt as if it were going to rattle again. Nothing terrible had happened after he took the efela ko off last time—

Well. Nothing so terrible he couldn't survive it. He'd made it home, in the end.

He replaced the other two efela, tucking them safely below the neck of his tunic.

He left his writing kit where it was, but took the neat sheaf of papers. He would set them on the newly tidied desk in Basil's office, and then sit on the bench by the front door of the inn and look out across the calm, quiet green. The trees made a splendid noise, whispering in the wind, and there were those frogs and night insects and the nightingales that sang almost as melodiously as the poets suggested.

The hall was quiet, the doors shut. One or two had light shining beneath them, and he wondered whose they were. Which one Basil had given his Radiancy, in the end. The one immediately beside Cliopher's room had a line of light that looked brighter and clearer than a candle's. He almost knocked on it—but it might not have been his Radiancy's. And if it were, what would Cliopher say, anyway, that would not be better said in the light of day?

He moved slowly down the stairs, candle in one hand to light his way. The inn was eerie in the night: strange half-lights coming in the windows, which were never quite where he thought he'd seen them in the daytime; strange shadows in corners that contained doors he was almost certain were not there except when he turned his head away.

For all its eeriness it was a friendly building, and Cliopher felt no danger in walking down the main stair to the hexagonal taproom and the door whose latch Basil had shown him for just this reason.

He would not, however, have gone into the cellars by himself.

He set the sheaf of papers on the desk in Basil's office, and then continued down the hall to the taproom, where he discovered he was not alone in his wakefulness.

His Radiancy—Fitzroy Angursell—sat before the dying embers of the fire, his harp gleaming on the floor beside him. Its strings set up a shimmering resonance, more light than sound, in time to Cliopher's soft footsteps as he hesitated and then crossed the room to join his lord. His friend.

His fanoa, Basil's voice sounded once more in his ear.

Fanoa meant the tiny white shells you found on every beach, every tideline: clams and cowries and slipper shells, sea snails and bleached starfish the size of your thumb-nail. But that was a later meaning. Or perhaps an earlier one. Cliopher had never been able to decide.

He had spent a long time very deliberately not thinking about that word.

And yet he had told the Mother of the Mountains he would face any darkness for the chance to find such a shell on the other side.

"Kip," his Radiancy said, his voice a very low, quiet rumble. He didn't look up, but Cliopher moved around the chair, stepping carefully over his outstretched legs, and leaned against the faintly warm breast of the stone chimney.

"Fitzroy," Cliopher said, hoping it did not sound as if he wanted to say *my lord* instead.

His Radiancy lifted his eyes briefly to him, and smiled slightly.

He was sitting with his elbow propped on the arm of the chair, his chin in his hand. It was an intensely un-emperor-like pose. Cliopher was not sure how to respond to it.

He studied, for want of anything else, the candle in his hand. Candles were not common at home, and were something of a small luxury in the Palace, where magic was much more common. Cliopher sometimes lit them, in lieu of a proper fire.

None of them smelled as good as this candle, with its strong honey-scent, its thick yellow wax, the light that seemed to contain half-a-dozen phoenixes in its small flame.

The silence puddled in the room, warm and comforting, full of tiny noises as if the inn were breathing and gently snoring around them. In the candlelight Cliopher could see that his Radiancy's head was not perfectly shaven smooth, but instead showed the faint shadows of new hair.

He was perturbed at how off-kilter that discovery made him. He frowned at the candle, the soft wax below the wick, the liquid puddle right below the flame, the scent that was at once heavy and fresh. Like full sunlight on a windy day.

The harp his Radiancy had taken from Navikiani was on the floor beside him, the golden wood gleaming in the candlelight.

Back then Cliopher had buried so much of himself he had not let himself even *think* of the significance of taking this man, this emperor of Astandalas, to that particular spot of that particular island. He had told his Radiancy half the story of its significance, and pretended there was nothing more.

One day, he promised himself, one day he would tell his Radiancy the rest of that story. One day it would be the right time for it.

"I thought I might go outside for a bit," Cliopher said at length, when the candle had burned down nearly to his fingers and his Radiancy had not moved nor spoken again. "Take in the air."

That should have been an obvious enough invitation, but then again—

But then again, this was his Radiancy, for whom every relationship was hedged around with taboos and protocols; for whom the language of friendship and family and love had been co-opted to express something formal and official and impersonal. Cliopher knew better than most how hard it was for his Radiancy to judge that anyone truly *consented* to anything that could be taken as an order, howsoever much an invitation it might be expressed.

"I'd be happy for the company, my lord, if you wished to join me."

Now his Radiancy moved: he lifted his head, so that the candlelight reflected in his eyes.

It would have been eerie, even fey, but Cliopher had looked into those eyes when they were full of magic, and he did not flinch or blink or look away.

His Radiancy nodded once, and stayed where he was.

He should probably not have said *my lord*.

Cliopher held out his hand, and after a long moment his Radiancy took it and let him pull him upright.

His Radiancy felt distant, as if his thoughts were far away. Cliopher tucked his hand into the crook of his elbow, just the way he had with Sara earlier, and was relieved to feel his Radiancy's fingers grasp the sleeve of his tunic. His Radiancy made a soft noise, and Cliopher waited while he hesitated and then picked up the harp and slung its strap over his shoulder.

The outside door was not even latched tonight. Cliopher opened it, and they went outside to find that the green was full of fireflies.

"Goodness," his Radiancy breathed, hesitating at the top of the stairs before going down them in what was almost a controlled fall, given how he clutched at the strangely elaborate wellhead at the edge of the green to stop himself. Cliopher followed his tug, wondering if his Radiancy were drunk, remembering, despite himself, the stories upon stories of how Fitzroy Angursell could drink anyone under the table, and the knowledge of how little his Radiancy drank as a rule, and the memory of the light sifting down in his Radiancy's private study that time he had first let Cliopher in.

The fireflies were thick in the trees surrounding the green. Cliopher stood beside his Radiancy, who had let go of him to hold onto the wellhead.

"Aren't they beautiful," his Radiancy said.

They were. They filled the trees as thick as the stars over the Wide Seas, and drifted in ones and twos and swirls across the green. The grass was a flat grey space, more like water than land.

"I saw jellyfish like these once," Cliopher said, the memories rising up out of the deep waters of his mind. "I was in the doldrums ... during the day the water was the colour of amethyst. One night the moon jellyfish came to the surface, not in a great horde but like this, ones and twos and small clusters, as far as the eye could see."

"When I was young," his Radiancy said, "I was exiled to a tower at the edge of the world—the Long Edge of Colhélhé—and the stars went all the way down."

His voice was rough, full of an ancient grief. Cliopher set his hand on his Radiancy's shoulder, as he would for Basil or Rhodin. His Radiancy's breath hitched.

Then the fireflies moved, swirled away from a dark shape darting across the green. Cliopher focused on it, wondering who it was—his Radiancy tensed, then chuckled. "It's your nephew."

Cliopher's heart warmed, though he should not have been surprised that his Radiancy knew what Clio would mean to him. He smiled easily at Clio when he came into the circle of light cast by the candle Cliopher still held.

"Uncle Kip," Clio said, a little warily, and nodded at his Radiancy. "Sir."

"What are you doing out here?" his Radiancy said—demanded, really. "Isn't it past your bedtime?"

For a moment Cliopher did not know what he meant, for in Islander culture children were hardly managed so intensely as that, and at twelve or thirteen Clio was not, to his mind, a *child*.

Sara seemed to have the stronger influence there, for Clio looked down and scuffed at the ground with his foot. "Dad doesn't mind if I'm out late."

"And your mother?"

"Don't tell her! She worries."

Cliopher raised his eyebrows at that. His Radiancy said, "What drew you out that was so much more interesting than hearing us play?"

"I've been listening to Uncle Kip play the past few weeks," Clio returned immediately, "and I'll be hearing you a lot, won't I? Since you're Uncle Kip's—" Cliopher coughed, and Clio gave him a strange look, then continued, "fanoa."

He just *said* it.

Cliopher was simply speechless. Clio had just *said* it, as if it were easy, as if it were normal, as if it were a common and ordinary thing.

For a brief, dazzling moment, Cliopher wondered if he'd been wrong, and it *was* that simple.

"It's the first night the fireflies are out, that's always a special night. You know that waterfall I took you to, Uncle Kip? It's amazing. You should go see it."

Perhaps it was the head injury, or the lingering effects of Basil's brown ale, or ... or something, for Cliopher *knew* he should say no, and instead he said, "Should we?"

His Radiancy shut his mouth sharply—Cliopher heard his teeth click together— and Clio said, "You know how to get there, right, Uncle Kip? You can't miss it. It's perfectly safe so long as you stay on the path. Straight to the oak and then you follow the big stones."

"I remember," Cliopher said.

"Give me the candle, though," Clio went on. "It's not a good ... it's better not to take a light. You get a better view without one, anyway. Don't leave the path."

"We won't," his Radiancy said, and there was amusement in his voice as he plucked the candle out of Cliopher's hand and gave it to Clio, who pointed vaguely into the darkness and then disappeared behind them.

"We don't have to go," Cliopher said as soon as they were alone. "I don't know what I was thinking. Everyone's said not to go wandering alone at night in the Woods."

His Radiancy turned his head. His eyes caught odd reflections of the fireflies' green-gold flashes, little trails of illumination searing across the dark. He grinned; his teeth gleamed briefly. "But you are not alone, my dear Kip."

And he reached out—*he* reached out—and took not Cliopher's arm but his hand, and he drew him out into the open space of the green. "Come now," his Radiancy murmured, as Cliopher found his feet and started to walk, to direct them, first towards the huge oak that towered over the far side of the green and then the short walk on the lane towards Clio's favourite fishing-hole. "You are in the company of Fitzroy Angursell. What's the worst that could happen?"

Which was always something of a disconcerting question to be asked, even irrespective of an entirely rash meander through a haunted wood at the very edge of Faerie on a night when the fireflies were out.

"I have not fully prepared the Protocols in question," Cliopher replied almost at random, and made his Radiancy laugh. The harp strings jangled in quiet, eerie, harmonies.

"That was a splendid set-down you gave Pali," his Radiancy said as they crossed the green. "I had wondered, when she made that comment about you being the perfect bureaucrat, what you would do ... playing every single one of my most seditious songs and then telling us with your most beautifully polite court face that you'd stolen them from the censors ... ah! *What* a delight you are. I hope you realize that Pali is about as competitive as you. I told her you would debate with her."

"I'll look forward to it," he said, honestly, and that made his Radiancy laugh again, until he trailed off with a happy sigh.

Cliopher decided it was not a good moment to explain his general disenchantment with Pali Avramapul's attitude towards his Radiancy—for it was possible, he managed to remind himself, that she *had* amended her behaviour since that letter—and said nothing more.

They walked on together, under the wide branches of the oak and past the big boulders, a glittery pink stone in the daytime, pale mounds in the dark. Cliopher worried his hand was sweaty, but his Radiancy's was dry and warm and strong, and if Cliopher's was damp he didn't seem to mind.

"What does fanoa mean?"

Cliopher felt his hand tensing, and he forced himself to relax, not to grip his Radiancy's too tightly. The fireflies were more numerous now that they were out of the village, not enough to cast shadows but enough to outline trees and shrubs and stones. His Radiancy was a dark silhouette. Their strides matched well.

"It has many meanings," he said after a moment. "The most common means ... the small white shells you find on the beach."

His Radiancy laughed. "Any particular kind of small white shell?"

Cliopher licked his lips and nudged them a little to the right, so they kept to the middle of the wide path, a lane really, that curved past the next boulder to arrive at the edge of the stream a little up from the waterfall. He could hear its muted rumble

—the night was very still, windless, and the fireflies made an an almost inaudible sort of buzz.

A bird started a liquid cascade of notes, and his Radiancy gripped Cliopher's hand in turn. "A thrush," he said rapturously. "Oh, it's been a long time since I last heard one so fine!"

"A clam, in particular," Cliopher blurted, just as they came to the river and stopped.

His Radiancy did not answer immediately. He was looking around; and Cliopher did too, though he could feel his pulse increasing, and his palm *was* getting sweaty, he was sure it was.

It was surely not only that afternoon that Basil had said the word aloud.

Fanoa, fanoa, fanoa. The very stream seemed to be whispering it as it rushed over the rocks to the cascade.

"It is beautiful," his Radiancy said. "The air, the fireflies, the trees, the way the water is glowing."

"Is it?" Cliopher said, stupidly.

"Not to you?"

He blinked. The water was black as a freshly struck piece of obsidian, shot with green-gold sparks, the reflection of the innumerable fireflies in the air around them.

"This reminds me of when we rowed down the River of Stars," his Radiancy said, stepping forward to the very brink of the stream. The harp strings shimmered, their sound just on the very edge of hearing. "It was very like this. Do you know what happens if you touch the water here? Does it cast you into an enchanted sleep?"

"We ate the fish yesterday," Cliopher said, even more stupidly. The thrush's voice was mingling with the stream, with the ringing in his ears, with the muted buzz and crackle of the fireflies, which sounded so much like tinder catching.

One more push and he would fall all to pieces.

"It seems as if Clio meant something other than a small clam-shell, such as one might find on a beach," his Radiancy observed, peering down at the stream and then stepping carefully onto a flat stone above the water. "Since he does not, as far as I can tell, have any experience of beaches bar the anecdotal."

Cliopher hesitated before stepping out, but he did not want to let go of his Radiancy's hand—and he did not want to be left behind again. "The other meaning is ... archaic."

His Radiancy stepped to another stone, and another, and Cliopher forced himself to find his balance (he was a dancer, he should not feel unbalanced on these stones, for all they were damp and unstable and slick) and step with him.

"I like archaic words," his Radiancy murmured, stopping in the very middle of the stream.

Cliopher followed him onto the stone. There was just enough room for them both to stand there. The fireflies were all around them, making the dark night a flickering curtain, like the light catching the jewels in the throne room and making it blaze.

"So do I," Cliopher admitted.

And then he stood there, unable to see his Radiancy's expression, with the river rushing and singing around them, the bird trilling a harmony, the fireflies humming just that sound of a fire starting to burn.

"And so, this tiny, white clam, such as you might find on any beach?"

Cliopher closed his eyes. The afterimages of the fireflies reminded him of that vision of the great song of creation, the great Naming, he'd had when the landslide had struck him.

He was probably gripping his Radiancy's hand too tightly.

His Radiancy made no move to let go.

"It's an old word for *friend*," he said, for he would not start lying to his Radiancy now. "A ... pair. Two halves of a shell."

"I see," his Radiancy, Fitzroy Angursell, said, barely louder than the strings of his harp chiming with the motion of his breathing.

They stood there, still, the water rushing below them and the fireflies crackling and the wind in the trees sounding like the sound of the sea when Cliopher held his hand to his ear in lieu of a shell.

"Is it fated, such a friendship?"

"I don't believe in destiny," Cliopher replied, wondering if *he* were drunk, somehow. He could smell salt water, the scent of the ocean, as if this water, this wind, were somewhere else entirely. "There are systems ... patterns ... paths." Currents. Crosscurrents. Ke'ea. "It's a matter of choosing ... of continuing to choose. It is not ... determined."

"Tell me more," his Radiancy, Fitzroy Angursell, said, his hand gripping tight.

Cliopher said, "It is a common and ordinary good."

His Radiancy stepped closer to him, his other hand coming up to grip Cliopher's shoulder. The harp sounded like the song the stars had sung in his dream. "Is it?"

The wind gusted from behind him, and if Cliopher had been a square-sailed ship like that Astandalan trading vessel he would have been taken aback, halted by the obverse wind—

He turned his head to that wind, to the scent of the salt on the air. They were right at the top of the cascade, and the water rushing past him *was* glowing silver, and he caught his breath and took an instinctive step backwards, and there was the scent of the sea suddenly in his nose, and he wavered with a thousand legends crowding into his mind, wanting to sing them, and he took another step backwards, and his Radiancy cried, "Kip!"

The stone tilted and tipped.

He fell—

His Radiancy's hand was tight in his.

They fell.

INTERLUDE
FALLING (II)

They fell.

Not hard. Not fast. Not a dozen feet into Clio's favourite fishing spot.

They fell slowly into the silver and black water, so black and so silver it was blue.

All Cliopher could hold onto was his Radiancy's hand tight in his and the songs of the *Lays* in his mind.

They fell.

Not like a stone or a shipwreck or a heart—

They fell like a bird coming to roost, like a shell set adrift, like a viau caught in the waves.

They floated gently through the water that was not water, this light that was not light, the black and the silver and the blue the colour of Ani's Tear, their hands joined, the harp singing in their ears, all the way down to the floor of the sea, where all lost things might be eventually come to be found.

III. THE STAR PATHS

CHAPTER THIRTY-FIVE
THE ISLAND

They landed with a great splash and a jangle of harp notes.

Cliopher made for the surface with an instinctive kick, his Radiancy flailing beside him—he was holding his harp in one hand and Cliopher's hand in the other—and they both gasped and coughed and spluttered as the waves caught at them.

"There's an island there," his Radiancy said unexpectedly, and tugged him with the waves.

Cliopher was still trying to blink water out of his eyes, which were dazzled by the fireflies and the lights around him, the stars swarming close. He swam as directed.

Everything was black and silver in his eyes, his mouth full of water salt and warm.

The water dragged at his clothes, his sandals. He should kick off his sandals ... He made to let go of his Radiancy's hand, but his Radiancy was having none of it.

His Radiancy, *Fitzroy Angursell*, was a great mage and had been on many strange adventures. If he wanted to keep holding hands ...

Cliopher held hands.

~

The island was not so very different from any other island Cliopher had ever seen.

It had a fine white sand beach, soft underfoot. There were palm trees, dark against the sky, the wind in their leaves familiar, comforting.

They staggered up the beach and cast themselves down on the sand.

Water was running down his face. It had an odd, almost effervescent taste to it.

Cliopher felt odd. Effervescent, perhaps, or buoyant. Untethered. He gripped his Radiancy's hand, anchoring himself. *He* was real, his skin warm, his fingers gripping Cliopher's back.

What had Cliopher been saying, on the other side of that fall?

What had he said *that* they fell like this? He had slipped off the rock, tumbled backwards over the cascade, and—

And here they were, with salt water on their tongues and a warm wind that smelled like home on their faces and a sky that was dizzying in its beauty.

Cliopher stared upwards. The stars looked ... wrong.

Wrong was not the right word.

They were ... they were ...

His heart was singing, looking at these stars. They were ... they were ... they were *too much*. They looked like stars in a dream or a picture. They were too *close*.

He felt a strange tug in his heart.

The star-paths are singing.

His ears were singing as if he held cupped shells to them. He was so light in this strange, honey-sweet air, his thoughts swimming in all directions like a coral reef's worth of fish.

His Radiancy touched the strings of his harp. It sounded forth and scattered all the fish.

Cliopher wondered if he'd hit his head again. The air was thick, delicious. The harp music was too beautiful. So were the stars.

"Where *are* we?" he said. Tried to say. His voice did not sound like his own; it too was too beautiful.

The water was luminous, not with the luminescence of plankton stirred by keel or fin but with its own glimmering depth of darkness.

"I think we've fallen into the Divine Lands," his Radiancy said, his voice brimming with delight.

More notes from the harp, the melody from part of *Kissing the Moon*.

Not *his Radiancy*. Fitzroy Angursell. He'd let his accent soften again, and his tone was warm, friendly, personal. *Fitzroy*, Cliopher tried in his mind. This was Fitzroy. Not his Radiancy. Fitzroy Angursell, who had been here before.

Cliopher stared at the sea.

It didn't look right. (It looked far *too* right, too much itself, too perfect.) The huge and gleaming stars did not look far distant, as if they were painted on a curving sphere the way the Ouranatha said. They looked as if they—as if Cliopher and his Radiancy—he and *Fitzroy*—sat *among* them. As if they sat on a star, and the sky and the sea were all part of the same ... firmament.

"Sky Ocean, you say," his Radiancy—Fitzroy—said. His voice was so ... pleased.

He'd said the Islander word. Moa'alani.

Cliopher felt dizzy.

"I'll keep watch, if you want to sleep," his Radiancy—*Fitzroy*—said, his voice reassuring.

Cliopher did not precisely want to *sleep*, but he needed to do ... something. His head didn't exactly *hurt*, but it was ... confusing.

He was uncomfortably wet. He fought with the sopping cloth of his robes and tunic until he could get the garments off, ruing the complicated buttons on the trews.

He lay down on the warm sand.

The sound of the waves lapping on the shore was familiar.

He'd dreamed of it so often ...

His Radiancy played something that sounded like the Song of the Breaking Waves from the *Lays*, though how he knew it Cliopher had no idea.

∾

He woke just at dawn. The birds cried and sang around him, seabirds and a tangle of impossibly beautiful voices from high above.

Cliopher sat up. His Radiancy lay curled on the sand beside him, asleep, one hand touching the harp as if for comfort. His face was relaxed, almost happy. Cliopher, looking at him, thought uncomfortably that it was the most vulnerable and exposed he'd ever seen his Radiancy.

Fitzroy Angursell.

Fitzroy, Fitzroy, Fitzroy. He *must* start calling him that.

In the Palace, his Radiancy had curtains around his bed, the only concession to privacy granted him. No one usually looked at him when he was sleeping. To see him undressed—he'd also taken off most of his clothing—seemed ... wrong.

Cliopher looked away. The sand stretched at a gentle slope along the beach, and the waves splashed lightly, gently. There did not seem to be much of a tide here, judging by the distribution of ... fanoa.

He picked at the scattering of tiny white shells around them, searching for matching clam-shells, because there was no one to see him, either. Perhaps ... Perhaps one day he might be able ...

One day. He blinked as he tried to recall what exactly he'd said, the night before.

His memory of the conversation was a dazzle of lights and darkness and his Radiancy's hand in his and the warm wind blowing from ... somewhere.

Here, presumably. Wherever *here* was.

The sea was a clear, lucid grey, exactly the colour of the sky before dawn. Looking out past the too-white line of the breakers, Cliopher could not tell at all where sea finished and sky began.

Sea. Sky. Sky Ocean.

The air was so *rich*.

He felt ... drunk. And thirsty. The sun was rising somewhere behind him, and the birds were singing madly. The sea and the sky were almost light.

The wind in the palms had had a familiar sound last night, and now, when he turned where he sat to look over his shoulder, he could see coconuts.

There was a circle marked in the sand around them. He stared at it, bewildered. There were no footprints on its outside, so he decided his Radiancy must have drawn it.

I'll keep watch, he'd said, and then fallen asleep, but not before drawing that line.

His Radiancy was a great mage. Fitzroy Angursell had travelled ... far.

Cliopher was *very* thirsty.

The birds were loud, and the sky was lightening, and his Radiancy slept on.

He decided that the circle was surely intended for *protection*, and so it would be very unlikely to harm him if he stepped over it. Probably it would just wake his Radiancy up.

He rose, steeled himself, and stepped over. He felt nothing at all.

It had been a long time since Cliopher had last climbed a coconut tree. He made his way over to the edge of the vegetation and considered the available options.

Inhabited islands, or ones within the jurisdiction of an inhabited island, were usually divided up into areas managed and used by certain villages or families. Many of the lesser family dances and songs had to do with such rights, whether to fish a certain reef or grow and harvest taro in a certain portion of the swamp.

Usually one negotiated with the owners before one made use of their places.

It was not ideal to use first and then negotiate, but of course there *were* provisions for people who drifted or were wrecked upon an island. It was considered a grave crime to take more than your share, but it was a worse one to refuse sustenance or hospitality or take advantage of their need.

They would explore the island for other inhabitants later. Right now they needed something to drink.

Cliopher found a tree at the edge of the beach that was not too tall and seemed to have a good crop of coconuts at its peak. He stared at it.

It had been a *long* time since he'd last climbed a coconut tree.

At least he had no witnesses. He was already stripped down to his drawers, which were unpleasantly crisp with salt but would presumably provide some protection against scratches until he could ... He laughed softly. Until he could do as his Buru Tovo had taught him, and make the things he needed—from knives to grass skirt—from the gifts of Ani and Vou'a.

He'd lost his sandals in the lagoon. His feet were soft after so long in the Palace, never walking barefoot outside his handful of private rooms.

He stared up at the tall palm. Was he thirsty enough to climb it?

After a long, reluctant moment he decided that even if *he* wasn't, his Radiancy would be.

He picked every coconut he could safely reach, throwing them down onto the beach with a certain satisfaction in the process, and then carefully made his way back down the tree.

He sat down on the sandy ground at the bottom, back against the trunk, and stared at the unearthly water while the spots swirled in his vision and both heart and lungs returned to their usual steadiness.

It had been a *long* time since he had last climbed a coconut tree. He hoped, with the cynical knowledge that it could not be so, that it would be a long, long time before he had to do so again.

Nonetheless: no matter how many years it had been since he'd last had the need, he'd spent a long, long time crossing the Wide Seas alone, and he could do everything he needed to do in any emotional and nearly any physical state.

It was reluctantly and somewhat mechanically done, but he sighed, levered himself up once more from the sand, and searched the beach until he found a handful of casoa shells, a sizeable lump of coral, and a harder stone that fit well in his hand.

He set up the lump of coral, balanced the first shell on it, and knelt on the sand as he had so often before. His hands knew what to do: one deft blow with the other stone at the right angle and with the right force snapped off the upper layers of the shell. That gave him a knife, not particularly strong but very sharp on its cutting edge.

Three more strikes on a second shell gave him a narrow blade like a chisel or a gouge, and that gave him the tools he needed to open one of the coconuts.

He cut a stout stick, used the shell knife to sharpen one end, and sank it securely in the sand. Then he thrust a coconut down onto the spike, shucked the outer shell, and finally, finally, he could give the green inner nut a solid blow with the stone to crack it in half.

It had been a long, long time but his hands knew exactly how to turn the two halves to keep the liquid from spilling out.

It would always have been the best coconut he'd ever tasted, he knew. Each time he'd been shipwrecked he'd discovered that.

～

After drinking his fill, he remembered that his Radiancy—Fitzroy—would be thirsty as well. He opened a second coconut and walked back towards where he'd left him.

His footsteps were clear enough, but they went up to nothing.

Cliopher stood at the edge of his steps, amazed. There wasn't anything there to *feel*—he couldn't kick or touch the magical shield his Radiancy had made—he could walk straight over the ground where he was sure his friend still lay sleeping.

It was very odd.

He called Fitzroy's name a few times. There was no response, but Cliopher refused to be worried, not when he'd seen how he lay sleeping—not when he might well be exhausted.

There was no response, and so Cliopher retreated the short distance back to where he'd left his coconuts scattered upon the ground. He drank the one he'd opened for his Radiancy, scooping out some of the gelatinous interior meat while he was about it, and then considered the situation.

Not that he really needed to *consider* it. He found himself moving almost without volition, piling the coconuts together in a neat cluster, exploring the vegetation for what useful things he could find. It was not a *cultivated* island, that was obvious, but as he went along he was able to find a wild banana with ripe fruit.

Bananas were useful plants, almost as useful as breadfruit and coconuts, which between them provided the majority of the necessities of life. He broke off a number of leaves, returned to his initial site, and set to work.

～

By the time his Radiancy—Fitzroy—wandered up, harp over his shoulder and a bundle of clothes under his arm, the sun was high and Cliopher had made a fire, a windbreak, several baskets, gathered pandanus leaves and a number of other useful plant materials, waded out to the reef to catch an octopus, and begun making fishhooks.

His Radiancy regarded him with sleepy interest as he set down his burdens. "You've been busy!"

"Your protective circle was very effective," Cliopher replied, setting down the shells he'd been working with and opening one of the green coconuts for his friend. "I couldn't find it at all, even following my footsteps back."

His Radiancy—Fitzroy—sat down with a quiet grunt. "It didn't occur to me you'd leave it without my waking. I haven't set that kind of ward in a long time." Cliopher handed him one half of the coconut. "Thank you ..."

"You drink it," Cliopher said, demonstrating with the other half. "I've food as well. Fruit, and there's an octopus."

His Radiancy drank the coconut water and then leaned back against the palm Cliopher had used in the construction of his shelter. "What an excellent person you are to find myself on an adventure with!" He gave Cliopher a sideways kind of smile. "You're a man of many surprises, Kip Mdang. I suppose I should have known, from that long tale of the sea you told us when your Buru Tovo came to the Palace, that you could do all of these things and well, but I hadn't ever ... pictured it."

He looked around Cliopher's small campsite with an appreciative air.

Cliopher wondered if he were being a trifle condescending. His Radiancy rarely was, to him at least, but ... but his Radiancy was Fitzroy Angursell, who had travelled farther than practically anyone. He had seen more, done more, *been* more, than Cliopher.

He was confident in his Radiancy's, in *Fitzroy Angursell's*, respect for him as a bureaucrat and a secretary and a reformer of governments. In the moonlight, surrounded by fireflies, the wind blowing from the lands of fable, drunk on music and daring, it had been easier to imagine that he, Cliopher Mdang, could be the equal, the fanoa even, of his dear friend.

In the clear, honeyed light of a morning in the heart of Sky Ocean, Cliopher felt much more uncertain.

His Radiancy, Fitzroy, looked as if he belonged. He had been wearing a tunic and leggings and sleeveless over-robe yesterday, but somehow had turned some element of his garments into a kind of knee-length sarong knotted casually at his waist. The cloth was a rich, purplish-red, gorgeous against his ebony skin.

It was more obvious in the daylight that his hair had started to grow out. It was still mostly fuzz, shadowing the gleam of his skull, a few silver hairs like stars seen through hazy clouds.

Cliopher regarded him, his stomach twisting with uncertainty. His Radiancy looked so much *better* than he had when he'd left the Palace. Healthier, for one—his skin was a richer colour, and he was no longer on the edge of drawn and gaunt.

Healthier, and happier, too. At rest, his head turned up to the sky, his eyes closed, his expression was not the unshakable serenity of the Lord of Rising Stars, the Sun-on-Earth, the Last Emperor—it was instead a peace brimming with happiness.

And he had found it by leaving the Palace and all who lived there, all that life that he had lived there, and returning to his old friends and companions of the Red Company, whose very names were legends.

Cliopher could not begrudge him that happiness, that healthfulness ... those friends. Nor that he had managed to work through the griefs that had been expressed in that letter. He *had* written that letter to Cliopher, had not forgotten him once off on those adventures with his old friends.

"So tell me," his Radiancy said, opening his eyes and grinning at Cliopher with a brilliance and an openness that struck him like a blow to the solar plexus, "we're cast ashore on a desert island in the middle of Sky Ocean. We've secured our boat. Metaphorically, in this case. What do we do next?"

It took Cliopher a moment to catch his breath. His tone came out calm, mild, the *bureaucrat of bureaucrats*. "We find water and food ..."

"Which you've already done." His Radiancy nodded happily at the beginnings of a camp which Cliopher had made. "I've been at work too, this morning," he announced, reaching for the bundle of clothes and handing it to Cliopher. "I did ... *laundry*."

He said it as if it were a great and wondrous thing. It probably was, for the Last Emperor of Astandalas.

Cliopher shook out the garments, discovering that they all felt fresh and clean, even the silk robe apparently unmarred by its dousing in the sea. "How ...?"

"Magic," his Radiancy said happily. He gestured at his knotted sarong. "Admittedly my first efforts took apart all the stitching, but we hardly need to hold to court standards."

Cliopher tried to parse that statement, but he hardly knew what to do. He put on the tunic and trews, leaving off the silk robe as somewhat impractical for his day's likely tasks.

His Radiancy ate a skewer of grilled octopus with every evidence of enjoyment. "So: fire, water, food, shelter, clothing ... I see you are making tools ... Do we make a boat next?"

He sounded excited at the thought. Cliopher smiled, for his Radiancy (*Fitzroy Angursell*) knew what it meant to an Islander, to make a boat with his own hands, but he shook his head.

"First we see if it is truly a desert island."

～

It wasn't.

～

The island was a coral atoll with a fairly small and shallow lagoon. They had landed between the outer reef and the beach, in a band of dark blue water bordered by paler aquamarine sections where the coral came close to the surface.

The island was irregularly shaped, with spits like the arms of a sea star. After discussing the matter for a few moments he and his Radiancy—*Fitzroy*—decided to head to the left, as the trees seemed thicker and the land higher in that direction.

"This sort of island, I would expect there to be trees near the beach, and then a lower, swampier area in the middle," Cliopher explained as they walked along the beach. The sun was high but it was not very hot, and he found it very pleasant to walk on the firm sand at the edge of the water, the waves splashing and foaming about his feet. The water seemed to glitter more than it ought to, but his Ra —Fitzroy did not seem to be in the least concerned, and Cliopher felt that Fitzroy Angursell, of all people, ought to know if there was something magical to worry about.

Fitzroy Angursell had his harp over his shoulder. He'd not explained why, but Cliopher assumed it was in case there *were* other people on this island—or indeed, in case they fell out of this universe and into another. He'd put his silk robes back on, just in case.

(He should not have removed his efela ko again. He touched his efela; the sundrop cowrie felt warm, as if the tiny phoenix feather curled inside its hollow was an ember being kept safe in a firepot.)

There were no other islands in sight, and only one other islet in the middle distance, hardly big enough to host more than a couple of coconut trees. Cliopher had waded out through the shallows most of the way to the islet when he sought the octopus they'd eaten for breakfast, and there had not been anything there.

"Swampy, really? With salt water?" Fitzroy asked curiously.

"There's a kind of freshwater lens that forms under coral islands. That's what supports the plant life."

"How remarkable. I suppose I'd always assumed it was all rainwater."

"It is, but freshwater is lighter—less dense—than salt water, and it floats."

Fitzroy regarded the blue water, the white sand, the green trees. "That explains times out at sea when there would be freshwater in the midst of the ocean ... we were never in the *midst*, then, it always turned out a great river was somewhere just out of sight ..."

He told a few stories, small anecdotes really, nothing ... nothing out of the ordinary.

Or nothing out of the ordinary save that they were tales of Fitzroy Angursell and the Red Company having incomparable adventures out of epics and ballads.

What had Cliopher done? No one—not even Fitzroy Angursell—had ever wanted to write a *song* about his postal system reforms.

They crossed the neck of the spit bounding their stretch of beach, climbing up and over a short rise, and came to a sheltered cove of quite implausible beauty.

This was the ocean side: the water and the sky alike were a deep, luminous blue, alive in a way that water and air were not, in the ordinary world. The breakers shone like clouds catching the sun.

"Well, well, well," his Radiancy—Fitzroy said, his voice full of admiring wonder.

Cliopher wrenched his gaze away from the horizon to stare at Fitzroy, whose face was brilliant with the very moment of inspiration kindling.

He could not have looked away, not from such a fire as that.

"Not me," Fitzroy said. He smiled at Cliopher, just a glimmer in his eyes, a tug at the corner of his lip. His harp slid off his shoulder, and he caught it with one hand, the other coming up to pluck a handful of notes. The imperial seal, which he wore as a signet ring on his finger, glittered in the light.

"Over there," Fitzroy said, gesturing down the beach. "Isn't this *perfect*."

He played a few notes, very softly, matching the rippling water lapping at their feet.

Cliopher made himself look.

A hundred yards away, or perhaps two hundred—the strange light and thick air made distances hard to judge—two figures were making love at the edge of the water.

Cliopher stared.

The diamond water foamed gold and white against the sparkling sand, flung out into the air in impossible arabesques and fountaining droplets like streamers of foam-work and flame pearls and glittering diamonds. The gentle waves rolling on shore were smooth and shimmering silver-blue, iridescent as ahalo cloth in the sunlight.

"The magic is ... ardent," Fitzroy said, the harp music rippling around them as if the air itself was fathomlessly clear and yet liquid as the water beside them. "*What a feeling!*"

The lower person—from this distance Cliopher could not tell if it was male or female or, indeed, a human being at all—was dark as a shadow, as the undersides of the waves, as the night sky when the wind rose invisible but for its sound. The upper figure was golden, burnished by the sun and the foaming waves into radiance.

His—Fitzroy was playing, the same notes over and over again, a questioning, querying, delighted arpeggio.

The wind was whirling around the two lovers, the sea breaking over them, the sand white as shells.

"We should not be watching this," Cliopher said unsteadily.

"Why? They're not trying to be very *private*."

That broke Cliopher's reverie. He turned to his—to Fitzroy, feeling as if he were stepping out of the cobwebs of an enchantment and into the familiar, comforting *solidity* of their long acquaintanceship.

"This is Sky Ocean."

Fitzroy played another handful of notes; this time Cliopher recognized it as part of the sequence of *Stealing the Sheep of the Sun*. He had to cover his mouth to hide his scandalized smile at that choice. Fitzroy laughed, far too loudly for the situation, but let Cliopher lead him back over the neck of the spit and once more towards their own campsite.

"Well?" Fitzroy demanded once they were well away. "You seem in a tizzy. It is not a look I am accustomed to on you. Usually you do not notice even such magic as that."

He did not sound either dismayed or distressed by this; rather more intrigued. Cliopher shook away that thought. "This is *Sky Ocean*."

"So you've said. Several times now."

"That could be *anyone*."

His Radiancy regarded him with polite attention, just as if Cliopher had come in with some new plan, innocuous on its surface, revolutionary in its effect. "Indeed."

There were too many stories in Cliopher's head to speak forth. Stories his Varga grandmother had told him about the gods and the days before people were made.

Stories from the *Lays*. Plays and songs out of Astandalas, and fables of their childhoods that sometimes Conju and Rhodin could be persuaded to share. Tales Fitzroy Angursell had himself written.

"*Anyone*," Cliopher repeated, dazed at the very thought. "That could have been— could have been—Night and Day. The Earth and the Sky. The—"

"The Sea and the Land?" Fitzroy suggested, smiling. "They *were* right at the edge of both."

"They're not *lovers*," Cliopher replied instantly, out of some deep, disregarded certainty. "Ani and Vou'a are *friends*."

Fanoa, in fact. The first fanoa; the model for all who came after. The shoreline and the sea, matching at every step, every wave, every grain of sand and drop of water.

Those lovers at the edge of the sea were a vision of the most fundamental act of creation.

He did not think he would ever forget them, that sight, the blue water and the white foam and the glittering diamond-drops on the whirling wind, the black and the gold bodies obscured and revealed by the waves and the wind.

But that was not Vou'a and Ani—that *could not be* Vou'a and Ani. They were friends, not lovers—and Ani was unable to come up out of the water, that was in all the stories. Ever since she had lost her mirimiri, she could not lift her head into the air.

Fitzroy played a passage, seemingly unbothered by walking at the same time. His voice was musing, curious. "Vou'a is the god of the land?"

"He raised the islands for Ani. He is the god of mysteries, the Son of Laughter ..."

Buru Tovo's *husband*.

Cliopher did not want to imagine that he had just seen some mystic vision of his great-uncle and the Son of Laughter making love at the edge of the sea. There were things he did not need to have in his mind's eye.

Fitzroy laughed. "There was certainly *something* going on. The magic was *glorious*. I shall have to write a song about it. Will you tell me the story of Night and Day? I don't know that one."

～

Cliopher told the story—one of the stories—of creation. His hands carved fishhooks as he spoke, and he felt a strange, impossible disconnect.

Here he was, just as if he were on Loaloa learning the old ways, or cast ashore on any of those multitudes of desert islands across the Wide Seas, telling stories of home, of creation, of secret legends ...

And he spoke in Shaian, his court accent in his mouth, wearing the clothes of a great lord on holiday, to a man he both knew and did not know.

His Radiancy. *Fitzroy Angursell*. Fitzroy.

"Do you know," Fitzroy began, after Cliopher had finished his story, "that I had never imagined—"

He stopped, all his attention suddenly focused outwards.

Cliopher caught his breath when he saw what he was looking at.

The lovers from the edge of the sea were walking towards them.

Two men, at least in form.

Their heads were tilted towards each other, clasped hands swinging as they walked in synchrony.

(The shoreline and the sea. But ... they had been making love. And Ani was female, in all the stories she was female, and even in Sky Ocean—so the *Lays* said— she could not come up out of her waters, not since she lost her mirimiri and Vou'a lost what he needed to bargain it back for her.)

The one on the left, inland, was tall and broad-shouldered, golden-skinned in the sunlight. He wore what seemed to Cliopher an old-fashioned grass skirt, red and buff in colour, and efela around his neck. The one on the right, the seaward side, wore a thigh-length open vest of some sort of reddish cloth over a pale kilt-like affair. He was very dark; black, even.

Cliopher sucked in a deep, rattling breath.

"I don't think those are the Night and the Day," Fitzroy said softly.

Cliopher's attention skittered back to the one on the right just as the man saw them. His step faltered, catching his lover's attention, and both turned immediately towards them.

At close range, Cliopher could see they were both remarkably beautiful in face and figure. He could not tell their ages—mid-thirties, perhaps? It did not seem to be something he could answer, and the question itself seemed to fall out of his mind even as he formulated it to himself.

They moved elegantly, at ease in their bodies, their positions, themselves. There was something—a light, perhaps? something in their eyes, their expressions, the way they held their hands?—that limned them with something like grace or glory.

(The waves had broken over them, like ahalo cloth and foamwork, flame pearls and diamonds, the glory of the Vangavaye-ve and the most beautiful gems of the Empire.)

Cliopher had seen that light gilding his Radiancy, a sense that divinity had touched him. He had always thought it was because his Radiancy was the Last Emperor of Astandalas, a great mage in the lineage of the Sun.

(He had seen it in Fitzroy this morning, and known they were not and perhaps could never be equals.)

His Radiancy—Fitzroy—stood up. Cliopher couldn't move.

He knew the names of the efela the man on the right wore, and why he might have that touch of grace on him.

Izurunayë: fire coral and falao shell beads interspersed with flame pearls and green pearls from Kuari, and in the centre (*seven and three and five and one* went the pattern in the *Lays*), the disk of a seed that was said to come from the tui trees of the ancient legendary homeland of the Ke'e Lulai.

Uvavina'a: an efela out of legend, the white-and-blue spiral of Ani's Tear strung on lines of the black pearls from the Isolates and dozens of white and gold and black diamonds from Astandalas.

Efâla to show that he was a'alà, lore-keeper for the Kindraa.

There was only one person who this could be, Elonoa'a of Izurayë, last of the Paramount Chiefs before the coming of the Empire, greatest navigator of all the great wayfinders, most renowned of all the Ke'e Lulai; and that meant the man still holding hands with him, dark-skinned and golden-eyed as his Radiancy, was Aurelius Magnus, forty-ninth Emperor of Astandalas, who had been stolen away by the Sun.

The fanoa who had been Cliopher's image and dream and ideal of friendship his entire life long.

They had been making love in the surf.

They were not—

That was not what fanoa *meant*. It couldn't be. It *couldn't* be.

"*Kip*," his Radiancy hissed, and Cliopher realized to his utter mortification that he was staring in abject shock at the man he had admired above all others, who did not look in the least pleased.

CHAPTER THIRTY-SIX
AURI AND EL

S omehow he stood. The two legendary heroes regarded him with frowning countenances.

They looked *exactly* as he had pictured them.

Except—

Except he had never imagined that they had *that* relationship, and in none of his daydreams of meeting Elonoa'a had he ever imagined he would be *frowning*.

Elonoa'a had thick eyebrows, eerily like Bertie's.

Cliopher wished he could have a few minutes to himself to think over this complete shattering of his conception of—of everything.

He took a breath, and then he bowed deeply, hand over hand in the Islander gesture of sincere apology. "I am so sorry," he said. "I was not expecting to see the Ancestors!"

He forced himself to stand upright, shoulders back, spine straight, chin up, ready for anything, as if he were facing Prince Rufus in the Council of Princes and saying (for once in their lives) that he was right.

Cliopher had not been right, after all, about what fanoa meant.

Not right *at all*.

He felt sick with loss, as if his heart had been pierced and all his wistful dreams had gushed out of it, disappearing into the sand below their feet.

"I am no one's ancestor," Elonoa'a replied flatly. His voice was deeper than Cliopher had imagined, his accent not the sharp nasally twang of modern-day Islanders, but more lilting and rounded. His expression was stern and rather forbidding as he regarded Cliopher with a disapproving air. Cliopher's heart sank.

He hoped his decades at court were worth *something*, at least, and that he did not look anywhere near as embarrassed as he was.

Aurelius Magnus glanced once at Elonoa'a, who did not remove his piercing gaze from Cliopher, and then smiled politely at his Radiancy. "You, on the other hand, look as if you could indeed be a relative of mine. Who are you?"

His Radiancy made a graceful half-bow, equal to equal. "My given name is Artorin Damara, though I prefer Fitzroy. If I am not mistaken, you would be Aurelius Magnus, forty-ninth Emperor of Astandalas?"

Cliopher had a bare moment of astonishment at realizing that his Radiancy —*Fitzroy*—was speaking *Islander*.

A little haltingly, with hesitation, but ... Islander. Islander!

Cliopher had not taught him more than a handful of words. He'd never dared offer, and his Radiancy had never asked. Only words that had come up when they were in the Vangavaye-ve, and a few that Cliopher had used when he could find no Shaian equivalent.

"Aurelius, yes, and such was my title in the world," the ancient emperor replied, with a glimmer of amusement. He paused a moment, head tilted, and then he continued on in a dialect of Shaian that sounded extremely rural to Cliopher's ears. "I can't say I call *myself* 'the Great' in the usual run of conversation. Is that what they came to call me?"

Not rural. *Remote*.

Two thousand years remote, they reckoned at home, ignoring the strange impossibilities of time since the Fall.

The two emperors *did* look extraordinarily similar, as if they could be father and son, rather than fifty-odd generations apart. (Except that his Radiancy was the elder to his own ancestor, a dizzying inversion. Cliopher swallowed unsteadily.)

"Indeed," his Radiancy said, switching to his usual court-formal Shaian, "you are reckoned one of the pre-eminent mages and emperors in Astandalan history."

"And how many generations are there between us? Not many, I should think, given the resemblance."

"I was the hundredth and last Emperor of Astandalas," his Radiancy said imperturbably. "I am in your direct line, forty-nine generations removed."

Aurelius Magnus seemed to have no difficulty about appearing genuinely surprised at this. "Goodness!" he said, with feeling.

Two thousand years of legends accumulating around the stories told in the *Lays*, like sand around a log or a stone breakwater. And yet Elonoa'a *was* as beautiful as the stories said, and his efela were described accurately.

(They had not described his eyebrows. They were *so* much like Bertie's.)

And he and Aurelius Magnus *were* ... close.

It did not matter, Cliopher told himself fiercely, that they were lovers as well as friends. They could still *be* the greatest of friends. They could still be fanoa, reaching across cultures and across oceans and even across the divide between the human worlds and Sky Ocean, the realms of the gods.

It did not matter what he, Cliopher, had thought they were, or what he wanted. It did not.

Two thousand years was a long time. Much could be lost in that time, even with written records—even with such careful effort, full of contingencies and countermeasures, as the transmission of the *Lays* over time.

And yet—

He would not have thought that the knowledge that they were lovers (more than lovers: they stood beside each other as spouses did; as Cliopher had always thought fanoa *should*) would be lost.

People understood the idea that a lover might follow his beloved anywhere. It had always been a strange and difficult idea that one might love a friend that deeply.

The kind of friendship meant by the word fanoa had always been a strange and difficult concept. Archaic, he had told his Radiancy. Little-used.

Much changed in meaning, apparently.

Cliopher made certain his face was as polite and impervious as it could be. Elonoa'a was frowning even more sternly.

Oh, this was not at all how Cliopher had dreamed of this encounter going.

He had thought he would sing forth his accomplishments and his deeds, that he would place himself in the current of culture that had swept down from this man to him, that he would be able to be *proud* of who he was.

He had wanted, he had *dreamed*, that he would have his fanoa at his side, his own emperor he had followed across the sea, his own beloved friend. And his Radiancy *was* there, but it was not that—and Elonoa'a and Aurelius Magnus were not that, either.

Cliopher felt awash in confusion and dismay.

Elonoa'a made a gesture indicating himself and Aurelius Magnus. "And in so many hundreds of years, this is still unacceptable?"

Cliopher stared. "I beg your pardon?"

The words came out in Shaian. Elonoa'a seemed to understand, for his countenance darkened. Aurelius Magnus put his hand on his elbow, steadying him.

Or holding him back. Elonoa'a did *not* look pleased.

"That we are together," Aurelius Magnus said, and he was no longer smiling, either. Cliopher was suddenly reminded that Aurelius was not only supposed to be one of the greatest mages of Astandalan history but also one of its greatest generals.

He wished he could sink into the sand. He was being *unconscionably* rude. He could not say that they were fanoa whose love had been sung across the intervening centuries, could he? That would come across as obsequious. And—and Cliopher was not ready to talk about what fanoa had come to mean for him. They would not like that their love had been ... diminished.

That was how people always talked about romantic, sexual love. As if that sort of love was necessarily better, greater, *more*, than friendship. As if being the greatest of friends was a step down.

It had always been so *important* to Cliopher that Elonoa'a and Aurelius Magnus were celebrated *for* their great friendship, and that no one had ever hinted at that sort of romance. Even for the Islanders there were many stories of lovers loving that profoundly ... and there was this one story of the greatest of friends, the human iteration of Ani and Vou'a's friendship.

Cliopher had never thought it was a *step down*.

He had wanted—

He had wanted what no one else did, apparently. There were reasons why that meaning of fanoa was archaic, obsolete, unused.

And no one would like it if their *true* relationship was ignored.

Cliopher cleared his throat and then smiled. He had faced his counterpart in *another universe*. He could do this. "Cross-cultural relationships are not that common, no, but I think that is mostly because the Vangavaye-ve remains remote."

There was a pause. His Radiancy—Fitzroy—was amused, his eyes glimmering. (Of course, *he* did not know what Cliopher was experiencing. Cliopher was suddenly impossibly grateful he hadn't told him what fanoa *really* meant. He did not think he could have borne Fitzroy Angursell looking at him with ... pity.)

Aurelius Magnus looked surprised, thoughtful, and then pleased. Elonoa'a's expression softened marginally. "You do not mind," Aurelius said carefully, "that we are both men?"

Cliopher blinked at him. "No? I mean—no, of course not! I was simply exceedingly surprised that the two of you, specifically, are, er, together. It is not mentioned in the histories or the stories, you see."

"And after forty-nine generations," Elonoa'a said skeptically, "you can consider yourself such an expert?"

Cliopher had gone over every stanza of the sixth of the *Lays* until he knew it better than most of the Kindraa lore-keepers. He had sought out every song, every snippet of a story, every variation on the legend. When he walked the Ring with his great-uncle he had asked in every village, on every island.

He had read through every document in the Archives he could find about the meetings of Aurelius Magnus and the Islanders. He had transcribed papyrus and parchment scrolls that no one had unrolled for two thousand years, read official reports that had never been unsealed, sifted through thousands of letters and tax records for any hint of a reference.

He was far too mortified to say any such thing.

"Come, El," Aurelius Magnus said softly, "there would have been *some* mentions."

"Of an Emperor of Astandalas, yes," Elonoa'a replied. "But his fanoa from the Ke'e Lulai?'

Cliopher felt dizzy at hearing the word, *that* word, from Elonoa'a himself. And the tone he'd used! As if it were—a common, ordinary, usual sort of thing.

Perhaps it had been, in his day. There was a great deal about ancient Islander culture that Cliopher did not know. There had only been so much that Tion of Mae Irión had been able to tell him of Mau'a and the tanà who had sailed to find striking rocks on the island at the edge of his country.

And Mau'a had been another two thousand years *before* Elonoa'a and Aurelius Magnus, ancient history even to them.

"Indeed," his Radiancy said, smiling at Cliopher, who realized with yet another surge of mortification that he had not given any of the appropriate traditional greetings.

Could someone die of embarrassment? He felt as if he might.

He bowed over his hands again. His efela flapped against his collarbones as he rose, and he could not stop himself from lifting his hand to grip his efela ko for reassurance. He made himself lower his hand again as he saw both Elonoa'a and Aurelius Magnus follow his gesture.

He was inordinately and guiltily grateful that his efela were hidden beneath the collar of his robes. He felt too vulnerable to vaunt.

He took a deep breath. He was an esteemed courtier. He had stopped making mortal enemies at the court *years* ago. He could do this. "I must apologize. My manners have all deserted me in my surprise at meeting you. Tē ke'e'vina-tē zēnava parahë'ala!"

Both of the ancient men startled. And then Elonoa'a slowly said the traditional reply, "Tō mo'ea-tō avivayë o rai'ivayë."

The words fit in his voice as they never did, quite, for Cliopher. His consonants were more pronounced, the vowels beautifully enunciated, but yet they were *words* for him, not rote sounds.

Cliopher wondered—oh, how could he not?—whether he might be able to converse with this man in Islander, learn the nuances that had been lost over time.

If he had not destroyed any hope of a courteous and friendly relationship by his shock and rudeness.

Oh, this was not *at all* how he had imagined this meeting.

With a tinge of solemn curiosity, Elonoa'a said, "I had never expected a stranger to say those words to me. And you speak my language, if with a strange accent. Are you then an Islander? Do you—do you then know my name?"

Cliopher pushed aside his confusion and dismay, the cracking in his heart, the fact that he would have to remake his understanding of the *Lays*—

He would have to tell Basil about this. He would have to tell Basil how he was *wrong*, how he had entirely misunderstood Elonoa'a's relationship with Aurelius Magnus, how fanoa did not mean what he had always thought it meant—

But he *could* tell Basil. Basil was alive and well and on the other side of the sky, and Cliopher was with Fitzroy Angursell, and they would be able to return with this strange and wonderful news.

And despite everything, Cliopher got to tell Elonoa'a *this*.

"I am of the Ke'e Lulai," he said, smiling, his heart swelling, wonder rising. "I know by your efela that you are Elonoa'a of Izurayë, the last of the Paramount Chiefs before the coming of the Empire."

Elonoa'a had a very stern expression on his face, but Cliopher, now that necessary step more distant from his own emotions, guessed it was due to the surprise of being *remembered*.

Cliopher could barely imagine that someone, fifty generations on from him, would say that they knew him by his efela. And how *he* might react if they did so?

Aurelius Magnus glanced at his lover (his *fanoa*) and seemed to see something of the sort, for he turned with an easy smile to his Radiancy—to *Fitzroy*.

"We have seen few people of any sort since we began our journeys in these places," the ancient emperor said. "Even if you were strangers from far-distant peoples we should offer you hospitality and ask to hear your stories. Since you are kinsmen, however remote, and bear news of our own peoples, you are thrice welcome! Will it please you to come with us?"

"We should be honoured," his Radiancy—Fitzroy—said formally.

Aurelius Magnus took his—Fitzroy's—arm and started off back down the beach the way they had come. "To tell you a truth, descendant, I am all agog. Walk with me and bolster my self-image by telling me what tall tales people say about Aurelius *Magnus*."

~

Cliopher walked silently beside Elonoa'a, his hands in his sleeves. The paramount chief said nothing, and Cliopher did not know how to begin asking any of the multitudes of questions in his mind.

He regretted how little he knew of the ancient Islander customs. The *Lays* all said that it was the chief's responsibility and dignity to speak first. The tanà stood *beside*, not below, the chief ... but Cliopher had not claimed that status, not truly, not *here*, and Elonoa'a was a Paramount Chief out of legend.

Ahead of them his Radiancy and Aurelius Magnus were talking enthusiastically, both of them making wide sweeping gestures and laughing often.

Cliopher watched the swinging hem of Aurelius Magnus's garment and allowed himself to feel the astonishment and awe that was creeping over him. He was rather grateful Elonoa'a was preoccupied with his own thoughts. Much as he wished to start declaiming his family name and history, place himself into the current of culture that flowed from this man beside him down to him, there was too much of that history entwined in Cliopher's imaginings of Elonoa'a to know how to begin.

They walked along the beach in the opposite direction from that which Fitzroy and Cliopher had taken earlier. From where Aurelius Magnus and Elonoa'a had been making love in the waves.

Which was ... fine. It was not as if he had never seen such things before, nor heard of far more salacious things, at court and at home. He should not be disappointed that they had such physical expression of their love. He knew very well that most people wanted that far more than he.

They were aiming for a distant promontory thickly set with coconut palms. Cliopher wondered whether the star-farers had a permanent camp here, or if it was coincidence that they had arrived at the same time; and then whether it was possible for there to *be* coincidence, here on an island in the middle of the Sky Ocean. Perhaps all was fated, or guided by the gods.

He did not believe in fate, but it was hard not to imagine that this was somehow connected with his decision to remove his efela ko when he considered what he should do with the phoenix feather.

He lifted his hand and touched the sundrop cowrie with a trembling hand. It was warm under his touch, comforting.

Elonoa'a looked at him, and Cliopher responded with polite attention. For a moment they walked in a different silence, until the paramount chief shook his head, lips firming, and turned his head forward.

Cliopher had received that look from any number of aristocrats who had decided that he was not, quite, worthy of their confidence.

Stung, he forced himself into his court expression, hoping the momentary prickle in his eyes was not visible.

Elonoa'a did not know him. All he saw was a later-middle-aged man in untraditional clothing, obviously no form of a physical paragon, no efela or other cultural markings visible, who had just brutally embarrassed himself.

The rational part of him knew the Paramount Chief's reaction was perfectly understandable, but that was not the part of him that had taken Elonoa'a as his life-long model of what it meant to be an Islander.

On the whole, it was perhaps just as well he continued silent.

In a slight—not *panic*, Cliopher would not say he was *panicking*—in a slight *anxiety*, because Cliopher was here and *he* was going to have be the one to stand before the Ancestors and show them what their descendants had done and made of their lives—whatever the emotion that was making him have to concentrate on breathing evenly and regularly, Cliopher began running through the passages of the *Lays* that told the story of Elonoa'a and Aurelius Magnus and their final voyage.

Or not so final, to be found here on this side of the Sky Ocean.

On the other side of the promontory was a fair-sized cove. Cliopher scanned the scene, desultorily noting the large fire partway along the beach, wind-shelters arranged around it: his attention was caught by his first sight of the legendary *He'eanka*.

In his mind's eye the comet blazed against the night sky; the uplifted remnants of the *Au'o'eakanë* hovered mid-air, illuminated by magic, inside the new western wing of the museum; this parahë rested with its two great keels drawn halfway up on the sand.

Aurelius Magnus had turned to look at Cliopher's face as they came into sight of the ship.

Cliopher did not know what was on his face, but the ancient emperor smiled proudly. "She's a beauty, isn't she?"

"The *He'eanka*, which Elonoa'a sailed out of the world," Cliopher murmured, the line from the *Lays* coming unbidden to his lips.

Elonoa'a stood beside him; when Cliopher glanced sidelong in his direction, he saw that the man had a fierce pride in his eyes as he looked on his ship. Something in Cliopher roused in admiration, awe crashing over him as it suddenly became real that this was Elonoa'a himself, that that was the *He'eanka* herself, that those people gathered amongst the shelters and fires were the legendary star-sailors who had dared sail out of the world to go in search of Aurelius Magnus.

"You will be able to see it more easily when we're closer," Aurelius Magnus pointed out. Cliopher realized he was still standing, staring, and blushed for his inattention. Before he could muster up an apology for delaying them, his Radiancy asked a question about the size of the island.

Cliopher was grateful for the deft change of subject. Elonoa'a was watching him with a kind of suspicion, as if he were waiting for Cliopher to embarrass himself yet again.

He felt a gauche fifteen, hovering between youth and manhood, sharp-tongued and hot-tempered and so proud, and yet with nothing particular to be proud of, except that he had begun to study the lore, and thought he knew so much.

To be fifty (or sixty, or whatever it was) and still stumble over his tongue, his gestures, his words, after a lifetime at court was, to be truthful, hideously embarrassing. Cliopher redoubled his efforts to maintain an even expression even as the description of the *He'eanka* from the *Lays* passed through his mind. The spiral pattern on the carved fore-mounts really was unmistakable, as was the design of the asterisks on the sails, which shaped out the constellation of Nua-nui, the Great Bird. From this angle the wings looked enormous, like an albatross's.

They reached the encampment soon after it came in sight. Aurelius Magnus explained to his Radiancy that they had been on the island for a week or so, getting ready to restock and perform some necessary repairs to the ship before they continued on their journey. He did not say what that journey was in search of, and his Radiancy—Fitzroy—didn't ask him, though Cliopher could guess he felt much the same burning curiosity as he.

The sailors were gathering amongst the fire, obviously having seen that their two leaders had come back with strangers. Cliopher didn't know where to look first—at the woven-palm shelters, which could have been made by his family on Loaloa, or the fires, which his Buru Tovo could have made, or the fact that the men and women facing him all shared the same general colouring and features as he did.

His first clear thought, as they stared and murmured in astonishment to see him and his Radiancy, was that they all seemed so *young*.

In appearance they ranged from their mid-twenties to their thirties. There was one older man, but he was still clearly younger than Cliopher himself. Perhaps in his later forties or early fifties, hale and hearty, his grey hair his only clear marker of age.

Cliopher had grown up with these people as names in the *Lays*: the greatest heroes, the ones to be respected, admired, emulated.

The great wayfinders, of whom Elonoa'a was the greatest, who had sailed for Aurelius Magnus across all the oceans of Zunidh and out across the strange sea-current passages to then-unexplored (and certainly unconquered) Colhélhé, up to the ice walls of Ysthar, through the volcanic mazes of the edge of Fairyland, straight out of history and into myth.

How many times had he held up the model of Elonoa'a, the one who had gone before him to stand beside an emperor?

(The one who had found his fanoa in the emperor from across the sea, and stood beside him, as Ani stood beside Vou'a.)

How many times he had held true to his course in emulation of the courage and daring of the Star-Farers, who sailed the comet across the Sky Ocean.

For them to be the age of Aioru was utterly incredible.

Cliopher usually had no problem admiring and respecting those younger than he. Why their age, rather than their very existence, was the point to trip him, he didn't know, but there it was.

Perhaps it was that the Red Company, who seemed to exist in the cultural imagination as always young (always in their twenties or early thirties, in fact), had been older adults when he met them. Instinctively he must have decided that his youthful heroes would age with him, if they were real.

"Who did you find, Auri?" one of the sailors asked, stepping forward to regard his Radiancy—*Fitzroy*—with amazement. "Is this a relative of yours?"

"Yes," Aurelius Magnus said with enormous pride. "This is my descendant after forty-nine generations, Fitzroy who was the hundredth Emperor of Astandalas."

Someone whistled. There was another burst of whispered comments. Cliopher tried to assess the groupings before him as if he were meeting any other group for the first time. There were twenty-six—were the *Lays* wrong? They listed thirty-two—people here, plus Aurelius Magnus and Elonoa'a. They were gathered in little clusters of two or three, as well as a few of five or six. Friends, allies—lovers, potentially—all curious, all focused, of course, mostly on Fitzroy.

"It has been so long?" the first speaker said. "Back there, I mean."

"So it seems," Aurelius replied. "I'm sure my descendant will be able to tell us some of the history since we left."

"Gladly, though I must say I am more knowledgeable about Astandalan history than about that of your Islands. Fortunately my friend here will be able to speak to your own histories."

That made everyone turn to focus on Cliopher, who felt himself flushing again. He bowed in the Islander greeting, palm over fist.

Aurelius Magnus looked expectantly at Elonoa'a, who stared back. After a long, silent moment Aurelius Magnus let loose an incredulous laugh. "Didn't you ask him his name? Whatever have you been talking about?"

Elonoa'a looked down, his expression darkening.

Personal reactions apart, there was no way Cliopher wanted to begin a relationship with a new group of people by embarrassing their leader, however unintentionally. He smiled mildly and said, "I'm sure there have been many cultural changes over the years, which will have led to different expectations."

Aurelius Magnus did not look convinced, but his disapproval was focused on Elonoa'a. Elonoa'a, for his part, frowned even more sternly, his eyes sharp under thick eyebrows.

"Do you mean to say that elders are no longer accorded respect?" he demanded.

Cliopher glanced involuntarily at his Radiancy, who had lifted his hand to his mouth in a gesture much more like one of Rhodin's than anything Cliopher had seen of him before. The mirth and sympathy in his eyes were hard to bear.

"Ah, no," he said at last. "I would not say that."

He stopped there, unable to say that he'd never been *treated* as an elder by anyone, and didn't actually know what should have been his response, let alone that he still thought Elonoa'a was far above him in status.

As out of a dream, Cliopher recalled when Jiano had called his Radiancy *ivani*, honoured elder, and his Radiancy had said something along the lines of it being hard to reconcile oneself to the discovery one had joined the ranks of the elders.

"Oh El," Aurelius Magnus said, laughing and coming over to give his lover a brief one-armed embrace. "Have you put your foot in it!" He glanced at Cliopher, with something like a warning in his eyes though his face was smiling. "It's been a long time since we last met strangers."

There was a general laugh from the crew, who were smiling at the stern (or embarrassed?) Paramount Chief with about the same sort of fond respect and amusement as Cliopher would have expected from those immediately under him in his office. Aioru had laughed at him like that, when Cliopher had first been appointed Lord Chancellor and was short-tempered and bewildered with all the changes in his status as a result.

"I apologize," Elonoa'a said stiffly, offering a short bow over his hands in just the way Cliopher had earlier. "You remind me very much of my uncle, who was a great stickler for the formalities. He would never have respected a younger man who spoke out of turn."

There was another murmur in the watching crew, and a brief grimace from Aurelius Magnus, which told Cliopher that there was a deeper history and significance to reminding Elonoa'a of his uncle. Had the uncle been his teacher of the lore?

But that meant he had perhaps not embarrassed himself as direly as he had thought. He smiled at Elonoa'a, relief making him nearly dizzy. "I hope I would never lack respect for one whose name is sung through history, nor be unwilling to offer precedence to one so admired and accomplished, regardless of his age."

That silenced the crew, who looked at each other with astonishment. The oldest among them was standing forward, but had not yet spoken. Elonoa'a glanced at him, and he came up. Cliopher immediately noticed the fire-coral efetana, and he bowed again in respect. "Tupaia of Manaroa, I believe?" he said, his heart thumping in his throat. "I am honoured to meet you."

Tupaia drew in his breath sharply. "You know *my* name? How can you recognize me?"

He was the tanà of all tanà. Others might not remember his name, only that he had danced the fire before the Astandalan envoys and thus passed into velio legend, but Buru Tovo and Uncle Lazo had not forgotten him.

"Your name is not forgotten in the *Lays*." Cliopher looked around at the visibly flabbergasted crew. "None of you are: the *Lays* name those who sailed the *He'eanka* out of the world, when, so the stories say, Aurelius Magnus was stolen away by the Sun."

"Not exactly *stolen*," Aurelius Magnus muttered. This time Elonoa'a was the one to put his hand on his lover's arm.

"When we left," Tupaia said slowly, "we were told that we left our people behind, and brought shame to our islands."

Cliopher was shocked: the way you were shocked when someone broke a taboo. It took a moment to speak. "That is not how history has come to remember you."

Into the ensuing silence, Aurelius Magnus clapped his hands lightly, which made more than one person jump. "Now that we have determined that you and El are each of such exquisite courtesy that you refused to say anything so that the other might have the honour of being first, I hope you will not mind if I ask you the proper questions: What is your name? What is your island? What are your dances?"

The last time he had been asked that had been by an old man, a seller of shells, an efelauni—Vou'a, the Son of Laughter, the god of mysteries. Cliopher smiled slowly at Aurelius Magnus, for this meeting that was surely as unexpected and incomprehensible as that, and spoke clearly and with a stunning sense of *rightness*.

"My name is Cliopher Mdang of Tahivoa. My island is Loaloa. And my dances are Aōteketētana."

One of the crew members said, "A Mdang from Loaloa? We must be cousins!"

CHAPTER THIRTY-SEVEN
THE CREW OF THE HE'EANKA

After that, it was much easier.

The person who had claimed relation was a muscular, handsome woman, her long hair piled high on her head with shell combs. She didn't look very like any of Cliopher's relatives—certainly nothing like the clear resemblance between Aurelius Magnus and his Radiancy (or Elonoa'a and Bertie's eyebrows)—but she did look as if she might have come from Loaloa or Manaroa or any of the other neighbouring islands in their group.

An *Ancestor*, he thought with dizzying delight. *His* ancestor, even?

(She looked so young. But ... they were in Sky Ocean, what his Radiancy had called the Divine Lands. Who knew how time and aging worked here?)

"This is Pinyë, my daughter," Tupaia introduced, voice warming with pride.

"My sister's name is Vinyë," Cliopher replied, smiling even as he went through the order of names again from the *Lays*. There was certainly no Pinyë in the version he knew; the only incontestably feminine name was Hiru, though there were a few of ambivalent gender that people occasionally argued about.

"Now that is a traditional name," Pinyë said, sounding so much like his niece Leona that Cliopher was taken aback. "What was your name again? Kiofa?"

"Cliopher," he repeated, enunciating carefully. "It is a Shaian name ... I was named for my uncle, and he for his great-grandfather. There was a time a few centuries ago when it was popular to use Shaian names, and then of course later generations were named for their elder relatives."

"I have always wondered about that," his Radiancy murmured beside him.

"I'm also called Kip, if you find that easier to say."

"I can learn," Pinyë assured him, a touch pugnaciously. "Now, where is Tahivoa? That's not the name of any village I remember—"

Tupaia said, "Pinyë."

She looked at her father, who made an unmistakable 'calm down' gesture, and bit her lip. "I apologize," she said, not sounding particularly sorry. "We haven't seen anyone new for so long, and then for you to be a *relative ...*"

This *was* a pattern in the *Lays*, how you were to meet seafarers who arrived bearing news to an isolated island, how those seafarers were to respond to the hospitality offered them.

"I bear you news of the Vangavaye-ve and our people," Cliopher said, the traditional words falling off his tongue without effort. He smiled, his curiosity overtaking the solemnity. "I am glad to meet you particularly, Pinyë. I had thought there was only Hiru of Tisiamo—"

A slim, athletic woman stepped forward, her face considerably shocked. "That's me. What—I apologize, ivani, what were you going to say?"

Did he really look that old?

"That respectable, Kip," his Radiancy said quietly, in Shaian.

Cliopher took a breath. "I was going to say, yours is the only name certainly female mentioned in the *Lays*. Pinyë—I'm sorry, it is said that Tupaia's son Kuaso was the one to sail."

Pinyë's face went blank, and the atmosphere was abruptly replete with tension. She glanced at her father, whose face was supportive, if concerned, then faced Cliopher with visible bravery. "That was once my name."

"Ah," he said, nodding in understanding as her meaning sank in. "I have cousins who will be overjoyed to hear it."

Pinyë furrowed her brow at him. "You do?"

Cliopher remembered with a sharp chill that it was clear in the *Lays*, in Shaian records, that it had not always been the case that those who were born with a man's heart or a woman's in a body apparently otherwise were able to fully pursue their inner truths. There had always been those who dressed as men or women and lived that way, but the magics and surgeries and other medical procedures had not always existed.

He had forgotten, too, that the social mores must also have changed. Even now there were places on Zunidh—the Azilint, for instance—where such things were considered deeply aberrant.

Perhaps in the distant past, it had not been *acceptable*. There was a distinct sense of challenge in the air, as the crew of the *He'eanka* closed in protectively.

Cliopher met Pinyë's gaze steadily, solidly, certain now of his footing. "My cousin Clia was named Cliopher when she was born. My cousin Tiza'a holds Aōnēnizana. My cousin Lazizo and second cousin Koro were once called women's names; Koro holds the men's dances. They will," he added with a quiet emphasis, "be *overjoyed* to hear that they follow in the steps of one who sailed on the *He'eanka*." He paused, and then smiled slowly. "One who *sails* on the *He'eanka*."

"And my name is known in the *Lays* as a woman's name," Hiru said slowly.

Cliopher could not tell if she were bemused by that, or by being known in the *Lays* at all.

"It is," he said gravely. "I will see to it that Pinyë's name is corrected, when I return."

He turned then to Elonoa'a, who was regarding him still with that stern, forbidding expression—was it his version of Cliopher's court face, to protect himself from his emotions becoming weaknesses?

Social mores had changed. And that question Aurelius Magnus had asked—their response to Cliopher's answer—

They were not called *lovers* in the *Lays*, not married spouses, but fanoa—

Cliopher was not Rhodin or Conju, not a great courtier, but he had successfully navigated the shoals and reefs of the Palace of Stars for the majority of his life, and he *was* a great negotiator. He ensured his whole body—his expression, his posture, his face, his voice—was pleasant, pleasing, *confident*.

No matter his private grief. He had seen them walk together hand-in-hand along the shoreline at the edge of the sea, and he had seen them make love like the first stories of creation, and he had seen the expression on their faces when they asked him if, in so many years, their relationship was not acceptable.

He would not let his own wishing stand in the way of righting a wrong.

Cliopher said, very precisely, "You are known as the greatest of friends." Fanoa, fanoa, fanoa. The word lingered in his mouth, the taste of it so beautiful on his tongue. He took a breath. "I shall be glad to take home the truth of your relationship."

Elonoa'a's surprise broke through his sternness, and he bit his lip, but he turned not to Aurelius Magnus, whose arm he was still gripping tightly, but to Tupaia.

The ancient tanà said, "You say that very confidently. You do not think it will be hard to change something that has stood for so many centuries?"

Cliopher could not resist a glance at his Radiancy. They simultaneously burst out laughing.

~

Aurelius Magnus gave them a tour around the encampment, as he called it, while Elonoa'a and Tupaia went off together and the rest of the crew scattered about their tasks. Cliopher enjoyed seeing the ease and comfort with which the crew worked together and the affection and respect with which they treated Aurelius Magnus.

And, to be honest, he also enjoyed seeing so much of *home* in what they were doing. Oh, styles had changed in innumerable ways, and there were many items and activities he could not immediately recognize, but so much of what the crew were doing were things anyone might do, at home.

He relaxed as they walked around. His Radiancy, *Fitzroy*, spoke pleasantly with the ancient emperor, engaged and interested in what they were looking at. Cliopher walked beside them, mostly silently, looking and listening very carefully.

Look first. Listen first. Questions later.

They came around to the edge of the encampment, where Elonoa'a and Tupaia were standing beside a small shelter set slightly away from the next nearest.

Elonoa'a gave Cliopher a reserved nod before smiling more easily at his Radiancy. "This shelter is yours, so long as you stay with us," he said. "We have set it to the edge so that you may have some privacy for your sail-mending."

"Thank you," *Fitzroy* replied. Cliopher murmured something polite and probably inaudible, even as his mind raced. He'd clearly offended Elonoa'a. Was it his silence as they walked to the encampment? Or—

No. It was that first dismayed reaction on seeing him and Aurelius walk hand-in-hand towards them. Cliopher did not know what his face had been doing while—while he had been trying to re-evaluate what fanoa meant. Evidently it had been more obvious than he'd like.

(He had spent a *lifetime* at court. His face should be under better control than that, even at such a revelation. He was healed from the concussion, surely?)

He could not leave things like this. It was poor politics for one thing, and terrible behaviour from a guest, and ... and he wanted—oh, he wanted Elonoa'a to *like* him.

His Radiancy glanced at him and then returned his attention to Aurelius Magnus, asking something that took them a few steps away.

Cliopher was, by this strange and astonishing chance, the example facing Elonoa'a and Tupaia of what their descendants had *become*.

Islander was a forthright language: it was hard to perform courtly euphemisms in it. That was good, he told himself fiercely. He was a worthy descendant of these ancestors, a tanà in the line of Tupaia, and he would not shame his family and friends by suggesting by his example that they were rude and hurtful and did not know how to apologize when they were wrong.

He lifted his chin, put his shoulders back, ensured his feet were firmly planted on the sand, and looked straight at Elonoa'a. "I'm sorry," he said therefore, quietly and clearly. "I believe I offended you when we first met. It was entirely unintentional. I would like to offer amends."

Tupaia regarded him with interest, but said nothing. Elonoa'a clenched his jaw, his eyebrows furrowed (*so* much like Bertie—). "You seemed shocked and appalled when Auri and I walked up," he said tightly. "Yet your words to Pinyë were not as I would expect one such as you to hold."

"One such as I?" Cliopher asked, carefully neutral.

He could not pretend it didn't matter what Elonoa'a thought of him, but—but he had been wrong before, and for all that they shared a culture, so much time had passed that there *must* have been shifts in values. And—Cliopher had spent so long at court he was sometimes shocked by his own family's values and expectations, and they with his.

Elonoa'a made a vague gesture. "You are an elder ... you hold Aōteketētana ..." He paused. "You remind me of my uncle." Another pause; Cliopher waited patiently. Elonoa'a folded his arms across his chest, a gesture at once guarded and sharply dismissive. "He was my teacher of the lore. He ... was greatly disapproving of my relationship with Auri." Another pause, and again Cliopher waited, sure the Paramount Chief was not finished. Eventually Elonoa'a continued on in a lower voice, still tense but a trifle less aggressive. "I took your dismay to be his. Even when you said it was only surprise at it being *us* I thought that was ... courtesy."

Cliopher met his eyes gravely. But this was a dance he knew, and he knew from a thousand previous times establishing a diplomatic relationship that his personal sentiments were of no importance.

"I went to Astandalas to see if the emperor was worthy of standing beside, as you stood beside Aurelius Magnus," he said. Elonoa'a rocked back a little on his feet. At one level Cliopher was aware of his reactions, cataloguing the other man's tells and responses, mirroring his pose in a softer, more open key.

"He was," Cliopher went on, glancing once at his Radiancy, who still stood a plausible distance away—certainly in earshot but politely pretending not to be. He returned his attention to Elonoa'a, smiling with a self-deprecating shrug, keenly aware of how Elonoa'a was slowly relaxing, his offense and hurt turning to wary interest. "I have spent considerable time thinking about all that is said of your relationship to your emperor and how my actions might be seen when held up to that model."

Elonoa'a frowned, but Tupaia touched his elbow gently, and after one sharp look across at his tanà, he held his peace.

Elonoa'a had been a canny politician by all accounts (more so, Cliopher had suspected after reading those reports and letters, sifting over and over through the *Lays*, than Aurelius Magnus), chosen as Paramount Chief to negotiate with the velioi for good reason.

But it had been a long time since the *He'eanka* sailed mortal seas, and this *was* Cliopher's core expertise. He was the Viceroy of Zunidh, tanà of the world. He would hold his head up before the Ancestors not for himself but for his people's sakes.

"Nowhere has it come down that you were lovers, spouses," he said, and decided not to get into the meanings of fanoa. He had spent a long, long time not thinking that word, not *using* that word; he did not need it now. "It truly surprised me. And I was deeply dismayed, for one does not like to think that the *Lays*, which hold so much truth—even unto the very shells of your efela—could be silent or even lie on such a matter."

Tupaia nodded once, slowly. Elonoa'a had loosened his posture, his arms falling to his sides, and somewhere deep inside Cliopher knew he would win this negotiation.

"You were quick to see that," Elonoa'a said, and though his expression was still stern there was a glimmer of amusement starting to show. "I had not thought we were *quite* so obvious."

Cliopher felt himself flush as the image of the two lovers at the edge of the surf flashed brilliantly into his mind again. It was not hard to imagine this young man in the prime of his life as that golden divinity. "We—my lord and I—had begun to circle the island, to see if there were anyone else here, and we saw you. On the beach, that is. Before we knew who you were."

Elonoa'a actually blushed. "We didn't notice you."

"You did seem quite thoroughly preoccupied," Cliopher said immediately, immediately hoping the small joke would be well received.

He was nonetheless surprised when Tupaia laughed and nudged Elonoa'a with his shoulder.

Tupaia said genially, "They never notice. We've all had to get *very* good at not noticing ourselves, if we want any peace when we're at sea."

Cliopher laughed, and was glad that Elonoa'a and Tupaia both were now reflecting his loose and easy posture, the wariness and hurt nearly gone. *Nearly* was not *fully* however, and though some of that could only come with time and with

Cliopher's continued, emphatic, shows of respect, he should say something to clinch it.

"I am very interested in hearing your tales of what has happened since you sailed the *He'eanka* out of the world," he said therefore, gesturing at the legendary ship with a sudden stab of longing to stand on it, to feel for himself what it was like to be aboard a parahë under sail. "The sixth day of the *Lays* ends with your leaving."

He chuckled, once more self-deprecating, once more confident, pleasant, the bureaucrat of bureaucrats who had wrought a world's disparate factions into a solid peace. He could see their interest sharpening: in their time the *Lays* would have ended with what was now the fifth day. "I dare say I know it as well as the Kindraa lore keepers, if you'd like me to sing it."

Elonoa'a regarded him with a kind of troubled awe. Cliopher smiled at him, thinking of Aioru taking up the ship of the government so he could sail the world to the next island, the one Cliopher himself had never imagined finding; thinking of himself, reading the *Csiven Flyer*'s memorial issue; thinking of himself, looking at that other Kip in that other universe and struggling to tally his deeds and his character with what else he might have become.

(And if, by some bizarre chance, he met some distant descendant, some Islander from another fifty generations hence, who said, *I know by your efela that you are Cliopher of Loaloa, who was Viceroy of Zunidh after the fall of the empire* ... in such a case, so too would Cliopher no doubt look, knowing he had worked hard to perform deeds worthy of the *Lays*, unable to ask just what the judgment of his posterity had been ...)

And thus: one more knot in the rope of this negotiation, to anchor this truth (and it was true, all of it; it was): "Your name is not forgotten, Elonoa'a, and your deeds are still sung. I am honoured to be the one who sings them for you."

～

They returned through the encampment to where the crew had gathered the makings of a feast around a pit-oven. The conversation had turned to his Radiancy's —Fitzroy's—harp, and his skill as a musician. The prospect of new music was exciting for everyone, even Aurelius Magnus, who confessed to Cliopher that he was entirely unmusical but did enjoy listening.

"Which is just as well," Aurelius Magnus went on, "given that I am informed that the Vangavaye-ve is the homeland of music." He laughed.

Elonoa'a rolled his eyes at what was clearly an old joke, and turned to Cliopher. "We'll have a feast, and if you would be willing to sing for us the passage from the *Lays* you have mentioned, Buru Cliopher, we should all be most grateful."

For a moment Cliopher was *certain* his ears had stopped working. Certainly his feet had. His Radiancy put his hand on his elbow to steady him.

Aurelius Magnus looked at him and then at Elonoa'a and then back at him. "Has that word changed in meaning?" Aurelius asked carefully. "It was my understanding that one used it for an elder deeply versed in the *Lays*, even more so than the common knowledge of the lore-keepers, one greatly to be respected."

The politician in Cliopher was deeply appreciative that he'd managed to achieve this degree of respect from Elonoa'a.

The rest of him had crashed on the reef of *Buru*. He opened his mouth, and then shut again, unable to think of a single thing to say.

"My understanding," his Radiancy said, "is that it's still used, but only for *very* elder elders. Cliopher's teacher of the lore, his great-uncle, is still alive, and he is the one called Buru Tovo."

Only by Cliopher, really, but that didn't matter.

"I see," Aurelius said, his lips twitching.

Elonoa'a also appeared to be unable to think of anything to say, but he was flushing.

"This is *not* how I used to imagine meeting you when I was fifteen," Cliopher managed.

"This is almost exactly how *I* used to imagine meeting you," his Radiancy said cheerfully to his distant ancestor. "Although I never thought I'd be *older* than you, either! I always thought I'd be able to do some grand work of magic and heroism to assist you in whatever strange quest you were on." He plucked a few notes from his harp: the opening cadence of *Kissing the Moon*, Cliopher noted distractedly.

"That's still possible," Aurelius said, and they all laughed and made their way to the fire. *That* at least was as comforting as it ever was.

~

Cliopher had not had any clear sense of the day's passing, but the sun was now going down behind them in a great splendour of red and gold. He was quite grateful to be able to sit down on the sand and eat familiar foods, and that no one pressed him for more complicated answers than whether he'd like another piece of fish.

Cliopher sat next to his Radiancy, grateful for the familiar presence, the known humour, their deep synchrony and knowledge of each other's humours and megrims.

He found himself staring over the fire at the strange luminous water behind the ship. The sky was darkening and so too was the water, not quite in the way of reflections.

The *He'eanka* glimmered a faint silvery-green, as if it were reflecting earthshine like the dark side of the moon, or the lingering radiance of the comet.

The star-farers had been on the island long enough to have made arrak. Cliopher had had an overwhelming enough day that he accepted a cup of the palm liquor with gratitude. It was rough and burned the back of his throat.

The water dimmed to a deeper royal blue, rich as Cliopher's best court costume, and from then down to a colour that hovered between black velvet and the blue iridescence of a superb bird-of-paradise. The luminescence in the heart of each wave was the colour of starlight.

He drank down his coconut-shell cup, glanced at Elonoa'a and Aurelius Magnus and at Tupaia, met his Radiancy's solemn, familiar, encouraging nod, and stood.

The crew turned towards him, their conversations falling silent. The fire hummed before him, crackling from time to time as a log split and cast up sparks. The familiarity of it steadied him.

He had sung the *Lays* before the Palace of Stars. He could sing it here, with Sky Ocean spread out before him, before the Ancestors.

He was a Mdang, and the rising tanà. He Held the Fire. He did not run from its burn.

He took a deep breath, and then he smiled at them.

"I sing the Wide Seas," he sang clearly, casting out his voice like a net across the face of the waters. "Hear now of Elonoa'a and the coming of the emperor from across the sea."

CHAPTER THIRTY-EIGHT
MENDING SAILS

In the morning, Cliopher woke to find his Radiancy leaning right over him. He recoiled instinctively; his Radiancy flinched back, and both of them sat up, flustered and half-laughing.

"There was something crawling over your head," his Radiancy explained. "A crab, I think."

Cliopher put his hand to his hair where something was prickling his scalp, and drew off a small pale-green crab. It was barely larger than his thumbnail, and sat in his palm waving its front claws at him in curiosity or warning.

His Radiancy leaned in to peer at it. Cliopher looked at him, wished devoutly for coffee or at the very least chocolate, and tipped the crab into his hand. "I'm going to find somewhere to wash my face," he stated, yawning.

His Radiancy gave him a desultory wave, his attention focused on the crab. "There's a spring of some sort just inland. One of the sailors showed me it earlier. The path's next to a pink hibiscus."

Cliopher simply nodded before crawling out of the shelter and standing up to stretch. He wished he had fresh clothes to wear, and eyed the grass skirts worn by the people closest to him thoughtfully as he brushed down his tunic. He probably shouldn't feel as self-conscious about his appearance as he did.

He hadn't worried about it so much since he was a university student, trying to balance his traditional studies with his intense desire to learn the ways of the Empire.

He scoffed to himself as he peered around, finding a path cut into the vegetation not far from their tent. A large hibiscus with enormous flowers in a shocking magenta-pink stood next to it, so he headed off in that direction.

He had not been able to *balance* those competing desires at all, not when he was in university. Either he'd been out on the Outer Ring and comporting himself entirely traditionally, or he'd been in town and wholly modern. He'd never been able to blend the two.

Probably he still hadn't. That other Kip had chosen to follow the traditional and violently abandoned all the rest. But Cliopher couldn't do that—didn't *want* to do that. He wanted to keep books, and tea, and magical lights, and foods and trade goods from across the former Empire, and his friendships and his clothes ...

And yet he *also* wanted more of the ancient traditions to be alive and thriving. The other Kip's Esa'a had been so *splendid*.

He found the spring, which was fresh and bubbling, and knelt to wash his face and hands and drink deeply.

He felt much better afterwards. The tangle of growth around the spring was lush, almost luxuriant—more so than one usually found on coral atolls. He did not recognize many of the plants, though there was a tobby shrub with its gnarled nuts, and what seemed like some variant of a breadfruit growing tall and spreading a fine shade.

All the colours seemed so *vivid*.

He picked a couple of tobby nuts, which he hadn't had for years and years. They were available, probably, in Gorjo City, but it had never occurred to him to look for them. There were other foods he liked better, and anyway, he hadn't ever cooked at home. Either he was at his mother's house, or out with friends or family ...

When he went home for good, he would have to learn to do all those things.

At least he did know how to cook. Simple foods, admittedly—the kinds of things one could find on an atoll—but it wasn't as if there weren't plenty of restaurants in Gorjo City, and ... and there would be his friends there, too. Conju had spent years running his Radiancy's household. Would that make him more or less inclined to running such a smaller and simpler one?

Did Cliopher *want* to let Conju run it?

He had to admit he ate much better because of having Franzel and Shoänie bringing him food or reminding him of meals. Left alone, he had a tendency to get absorbed in his work and eat whatever was easiest and quickest to hand, or try to replace solid nutrition with coffee.

There he was going chasing after viaus again, assuming that Ludvic and Rhodin and Conju would all still want to come to Gorjo City with him. Well, Conju was most likely, seeing as he was (presumably happily) gallivanting around Amboloyo with Cliopher's mother—

Except that now Conju's long-lost beloved friend Terec and his sister Nerisse were found.

And Ludvic had Giya and his bar down in the Levels, not to mention now he knew that his father was alive, and even with only an evening in Masseo Umrit's presence, Cliopher felt confident saying that Ludvic would not be hurt in reaching out to him.

His Radiancy loved both of them, and that was ... that was recommendation enough.

Cliopher frowned a scuffling noise in the undergrowth. When he turned his head he saw a large coconut crab edging backwards out of sight. He relaxed, though he also noted the crustacean's presence. He *did* miss crab in the Palace. Sometimes they had mud crabs from the coast, but they were not nearly as delicious as coconut crabs.

He could not hold Conju and Ludvic back from reuniting with their families. He could not.

And Rhodin had his dear friend, his correspondent, the not-actually-an-Impostor Sardeet Avramapul.

And his Radiancy *was* Fitzroy Angursell.

Cliopher looked at the tobby nuts in his hand. They clicked against each other, the hard shells hiding the succulent flesh and spindle-whorl seeds in their centres. His father had used them as weights when he worked on his nets, Cliopher remembered from a long distance. There had been many evenings when his father mended his nets in the courtyard behind their house. His mother would sing as she did one of her own handicrafts—usually mending clothes or sometimes spinning twine for his father—and Cliopher would play games with his sisters.

Even then he'd always wanted to play at being the three sons of Vonou'a, sailing off on their grand adventures, or as Elonoa'a and Aurelius Magnus and the Tanà (he did not remember when he learned Tupaia's name, but it had been later) having *their* adventures.

Navalia and Vinyë had been willing to play along, some of the time. Vinyë used to argue she got to be Elonoa'a, being the eldest, leaving Navalia and Cliopher to bicker over who got to be Aurelius or the Tanà—getting to pretend to do great works of magic had always been a great draw.

And here he was, coming out of the edge of the trees and seeing before him the very *He'eanka*.

He could not stop himself from smiling.

It was hard to feel worried that his Radiancy would choose his old friends of the Red Company over him when they were here, together, at an island at the edge of Sky Ocean.

Why, Cliopher was at last on a proper *adventure* of his own. He—he!—had sung the sixth Lay to Elonoa'a and Tupaia and Aurelius Magnus themselves.

He resolved not to worry about that distant future when he and his Radiancy had returned to Zunidh. Cliopher had sworn once to do whatever it took to ensure his Radiancy was free. That had not changed with the discovery he was Fitzroy Angursell —quite the contrary.

Cliopher would not, could not, bind *him* with guilt or recriminations or his secret fears.

He wandered back to the encampment. His Radiancy was standing with Pinyë outside their shelter. There was no sign of Aurelius Magnus or Elonoa'a; when Cliopher looked around, all the sailors seemed to be busy about their own tasks.

"I'm on cooking duty today," Pinyë said cheerfully, and indicated several covered baskets. "Here's food for you ... Auri and El said to say that you should feel welcome to spend as long about the sail-mending as you need. My father thought we might have overwhelmed you yesterday."

Dead silence had greeted Cliopher's conclusion of the sixth day of the *Lays*—the *full* sixth day, the version that he had never sung aloud to anyone, that was never sung aloud except for the greater festival.

Dead silence, and many tears.

Cliopher himself had had tears streaming down his face. He had been unable to feel embarrassed for showing such emotion, not when he was also singing the favourable judgment of posterity to people who had thought themselves disregarded and lost.

"Thank you," he said.

"You're very welcome." Pinyë hesitated, glancing around to see if anyone was paying them attention. She leaned closer. "I should leave you be, but I must ask —*where* is Tahivoa? It sounds so familiar but I can't place it!"

"It's a neighbourhood around a lagoon of the same name in Gorjo City," Cliopher replied. She was so much like his niece!

"Gorjo *city*? Like the Astandalans have? All those people crowded together in stone buildings? Did you take up the whole of Loaloa to build it?"

Cliopher came up short. "Er, no, it's not on Loaloa, though it's named for the point off Daino village there. Gorjo City is built at the edge of Mama Ituri's Son— where the Gathering of the Ships used to be held. The old Esa'a."

He might not have so easily remembered that name for it, if not for the other Kip.

Pinyë's eyes went wide with scandal. "*Used* to be?" She bit her lip. "I'm sorry. I shouldn't have asked out of turn. Please—enjoy the food." The young woman turned and hastened off, leaving Cliopher to feel deeply nonplussed. He looked at his Radiancy, who smiled sympathetically at him.

"Come, Kip, sit and eat. It will seem less strange when you are not hungry."

"Will it?" Cliopher replied dryly, but he sat down beside his Radiancy and opened the baskets.

The simple food was familiar: breadfruit, plantain, broiled fish. Cliopher sighed as he opened a green coconut.

His Radiancy leaned over to him. "I am regretting not having my bag. It has tea in it."

"And coffee?"

"All the necessities."

Cliopher sighed again with extravagant disappointment. "I'm sure your friends will keep it safe for when you meet them again."

"Yes, Jullanar had kept my original bag all these years, can you imagine? It is still just as full and mysterious as it ever was. It was distressing to me that my new bag is so organized. Your influence, no doubt."

Cliopher smiled, even as the realization that his Radiancy was really and truly Fitzroy Angursell thrilled through him again. That bag was famous in its own right. (There were always attempts by various wizards to recreate it, almost always to spectacular failure. Cliopher had once narrowly missed being hit by a fast-flying boot as one such bag exploded in his vicinity.) He cleared his throat. "Not Conju's?"

"Conju likes things to be in a precise and perfect order, preferably according to the chromatic spectrum, the alphabet, or the numerical sequence. None of those are exactly my style. You, on the other hand, are the most eminently practical person I have ever met, and organize according to need." He shook his head. "You are, in fact, that most terrible of creatures: a patient revolutionary."

Cliopher laughed, mostly at the non sequitur. "I'm not always that patient, nor that revolutionary."

"Oh, you underestimate yourself."

Perhaps—

No. Cliopher had resolved not to worry about the future. He finished his piece of fish and rubbed his fingers in the sand to clean them. The grains felt strangely alive against his skin.

He felt strangely alive.

Their shelter faced the lagoon. They had seated themselves a little to the side, where they could see the crew busy about their tasks. The *He'eanka* was nearly in front of them, anchored a little way out from the shore. It was an extraordinary sight, so much *bigger* than Cliopher had realized it would be.

"What does *faravia* mean?" his Radiancy asked after a while.

Cliopher turned his gaze to him. "I don't know," he admitted. "Literally it means something like 'mending sails', but they must mean something else, as obviously we don't have them."

His Radiancy murmured the word over to himself. "Is there another word for sails? I thought it was *tina*?"

"It depends on the kind of sails ..." Cliopher pondered. "*Fia* means a large sail, and *fara'a* is the mending word."

"Perhaps it's an idiom for refreshing ourselves. Polite of them, to assure us we needn't bestir ourselves to work before we are ready." He smirked when Cliopher glanced at him. "Of course, your ability to simply *be* while other people work is no doubt entirely atrophied."

Cliopher consciously made himself relax.

"How do you know Islander?" he asked abruptly. "I never ..." He stopped himself.

"You never taught me any?" His Radiancy grinned at him. *Fitzroy* grinned at him. Cliopher must call him that.

(It had taken him longer than he liked with some of his cousins, as well. Clia had been easy—she'd refused to answer to Clio from about the age of seven—but Lazizo had tried out several names before settling and Cliopher still sometimes found himself almost calling one of the others when he caught sight of his cousin in the distance. One mortifying occasion on a visit home after a long gap—thankfully years ago now—Cliopher had called him *all* of them before finally landing on Lazizo.)

"It started when we went to Lesuia," *Fitzroy* said thoughtfully. "At the market. There was a word-book there, of Islander words and Shaian, and I picked it up out of curiosity." He glanced sidelong at Cliopher, and laughed softly. "That sounds so idle and desultory, doesn't it? When really I wanted to know what you'd said to that shell-merchant."

Cliopher blinked at him in confusion. "What do you mean? I didn't think anyone had heard."

No had been near him, and no one had mentioned it, either. And—he frowned —he was sure he'd been speaking in Shaian ...

His—Fitzroy laughed merrily. "No one hear? When a god asked you a question, and your voice lifted up in an answer that cracked through the air like thunder? I have walked into stories before, Cliopher Mdang, and I know a legend when I see one spun around me."

Cliopher stared at him, unable to formulate a reply. "I ..."

Fitzroy was still laughing to himself, mirth bubbling in his eyes, his voice, in the relaxed posture of his shoulders, the entirely un-emperor-like mobility of his face. "My dear Kip! No one in that marketplace could have missed that encounter."

"You didn't say anything," he said weakly.

"Neither did you," Fitzroy replied easily. "And I repeat: I have walked into stories before. That one wasn't mine. It was something of your people, and I ... I had not realized, until that holiday, quite what that meant to you."

I will bring a new fire to the hearth of the world, Cliopher had promised the Son of Laughter, the god of mysteries.

He lifted his hand to his throat, to the sundrop cowrie on the new efela.

"Indeed," his—Fitzroy said. "I noticed the new efela." He flickered his eyebrows at Cliopher. "Shall I ask you about it now, or would you prefer me to wait till this evening before the fire, so that you have the opportunity to tell your deeds before your ancestors?"

For a moment, Cliopher could only stare at him, caught on conflicting desires.

I know a legend when I see one spun around me.

Fitzroy Angursell watched him, smiling, his eyes intent, the challenge resonating in the air.

Cliopher wanted to be his equal. He wanted to walk in legends. He wanted *his* name sung in the *Lays*.

"Tonight, please," he said, chin coming up.

"There you are," Fitzroy said, satisfaction welling in his voice. "Go get something to do with your hands, Kip, I can't bear watching you shred the plates all day."

Cliopher looked down at the banana leaves left from their breakfast, which he had unthinkingly been tearing into small pieces. He took another breath. How did Fitzroy *know* him so well?

(His Radiancy had spent exactly as much time with Cliopher as Cliopher had spent with him. Albeit Cliopher had always assumed his Radiancy did not spend as much of the rest of his day *thinking* about Cliopher as Cliopher necessarily thought about him—that being a very large part of his job—and of course they had become friends—)

"Yes," he said foolishly, and got up, grateful for a few moments to compose himself.

~

He came back with the components of a grass skirt, which despite the name was generally made with banana-leaf fibres. Fitzroy regarded the neat bundles with interest. "What are you making?"

"A grass skirt." Cliopher regarded the materials disconsolately, then shook off his regret for the dyes available at home and began arranging the fibres into smaller bundles. "Aroha of Lo'o'ena—that's the old name of Looenna—he's Poyë and knowledgeable about plants—was very excited about seeing 'the designs of the future', but I'm afraid I'm going to disappoint him."

"I have faith in your ability to dredge up long-unused knowledge and make great use of it," Fitzroy replied lightly. "It's been a great consolation and encouragement to me, on my recent travels. The knowledge that you could spend so long and so much of your life at court, in the Service, and yet when the challenges came you can step up to them with the whole of yourself."

Cliopher looked sharply at him. Fitzroy's expression was closer to the imperturbable serenity than he liked to see. Already it had become foreign, alien, *unwelcome*.

"I'm glad to be of service," he said, equally lightly, equally seriously, and brushed his hand across the rustling fibres. "It's not so much the making of a skirt, but I'm hardly Féonie—any decorative elements I can do always came from choosing coloured materials." He regarded his bundles, all minutely varying tones of buff and beige. "Even Féonie might be challenged by this."

"Oh, she'd decide to do something of such understated magnificence anyone who knew what they were looking at would be overwhelmed with admiration, and everyone else would just think it looked very fine indeed." Fitzroy leaned over the bundles. "I might be able to colour those for you." He glanced under his eyelashes at Cliopher. "Assuming you don't mind the risk of me setting them on fire instead."

"Aroha did mention that if I were so out of practice that I ruined my first effort, there was a sufficiency to replace it."

"It's useful that you can get so much by walking off into the jungle. What colours do you want? No—let me guess."

Cliopher sat back, rejoicing in the glinting, glimmering mischief and delight in his Radiancy's—in *Fitzroy's*—eyes. This was what he wanted, he told himself. He wanted to sit with his friend and talk and do small, friendly things together.

The magic gathered in Fitzroy's eyes like liquid gold, the air sparkling around his hands as he passed them over the bundles. Cliopher watched the expression on his face: his heart seemed to open to the magic, like a plant turning to the sun, the tides to the moon.

Not that he could feel the magic. But he could see it in his friend's eyes, in the pleasure and joy he took in his art, just the way his face had kindled with inspiration as he looked upon Aurelius and Elonoa'a making love in the surf.

"There," Fitzroy said, and Cliopher looked down, blushing for his staring, to see the banana fibres were now all the rich shades of red-orange and bronze and blue of his regalia as Viceroy of Zunidh.

"Fitzroy," he said, picking up a midnight-blue bundle and tilting it this way and that in the light to see how it subtly glimmered.

Fitzroy smiled innocently. "To continue answering your question: after we left Lesuia, I picked up a grammar in Gorjo City while you were visiting with your family, and after that ..."

"But you never told me," Cliopher said.

He shrugged. "At first, it was something for me. I'd forgotten how much ... how much *fun* it is, to learn something new, just because I wanted to learn it."

That was *such* a hard thing to hear.

He could hardly bear to remember his Radiancy pacing in his study.

When was the last time *Cliopher* had learned something new, just because he wanted to learn it?

Fitzroy shifted position until he was lying relaxed on the sand, long legs extended out, weight supported on an elbow. He looked, to Cliopher, like a hundred historical illustrations of aristocrats debauching themselves at the court.

That was unfair. There had been a long period where the court custom was to recline to eat. His Radiancy—*Fitzroy*—had been the one to change that, in fact. There were a few of the older courtiers who still held the old custom, in their own rooms—Cliopher had had to attend a few salons and dinners that way, and hated everything about the position.

Fitzroy appeared perfectly content and relaxed, thoughtful and at ease. So it wasn't physical dislike that had made him change that custom.

"Also ... perhaps you've forgotten how little you ever talked about your culture, Kip. I didn't want to *make* you tell me things."

So much of his life had been constrained by such considerations. Cliopher's heart twisted, and he covered his reflexive pity and grief by deciding on the midnight blue as a base layer and began to knot the bundles together. So long as he didn't think too hard about it, his hands knew their work.

"Later on I practiced with Gaudy," Fitzroy continued on blithely.

"Gaudy? I didn't think he was fluent."

"He wasn't," Fitzroy said, his lips twitching. "He was much better after several years of weekly lessons with me. I think he's well on his way to an expert under-standing of comparative linguistics, after all the unanswerable questions I inflicted on him. I believe he made great use of the resources offered by your family."

"You practiced with Gaudy," Cliopher said, biting his lip and making himself stop talking, before a foolish jealousy could colour his voice too much.

His Radiancy—*Fitzroy*—ignored his tone, though his eyes were kind. Cliopher focused on the bundles before him, the knots in his twine, the length he wanted, the patterns he could make with these hues.

"As you started to claim your culture more publicly, as *we* became closer friends, I conceived the idea that I wanted to ... surprise you. Make it a gift."

Cliopher stopped and regarded him, speechless.

"I did surprise you," Fitzroy said smugly.

"You don't have a Gorjo City accent," Cliopher said, which was not what he wanted to say at all, at all.

"Well, I also asked Jiano for a few lessons ... and Aya was quite insistent I learn a *Western* accent ... and then there's been the past few weeks, after I discovered that Jullanar *is* fluent in Islander from being friends with Basil, so we've been practicing."

There was so much. Cliopher reached the end of his first length and decided bronze would be the next layer. He spent a few moments fussing with the bundles, arranging them more easily to hand.

It was not fair of his—*Fitzroy*—to say things like that. What could Cliopher offer in return?

All these people he'd known for so long, thought he'd known so well, who had *such* secrets in their hearts.

What did he have?

An unspoken desire for something that had never been true.

He swallowed down a rising tide of tears. "What sort of adventures have you had, since you set out on your quest?"

Fitzroy had been tense, as if he might reach out, and now he relaxed, flopping down so he was laying flat on the sand, his face shaded by their windbreak, the edges of his sarong fluttering in the gentle breeze.

"Oh, there have been no adventures at all, nothing to speak of."

Cliopher raised his eyebrows at him, though Fitzroy was not looking. "I *did* meet the Mae Irionéz, my lord."

A slip, but perhaps a necessary one, to return them to an even keel. Fitzroy's voice was full of laughter. "Well, I did learn to turn into a crow."

That was surely not true. Cliopher risked a glance, and saw to his shock that there was a hint of tension limning his Radiancy's face, his jaw and eyes. The challenge to *prove it, then!* reached his lips and died there. After a moment he said, "I'll be delighted to witness it, when you're in the mood."

That had been the right choice: Fitzroy's face relaxed, and he smiled, his eyes closed. "Perhaps when we're no longer in the Divine Lands, where such transformations can be rather more permanent than one might desire."

Cliopher hummed in lieu of saying anything, and they fell silent.

After a while his Radiancy said, "My friends of the Red Company find me greatly changed. They keep asking if I am well; they cannot understand why I do not speak or show all my emotions as I used to. They tease me for my posture, my manners at table, the serenity of my expression, that they never catch me being, as they say, *natural*."

Cliopher added a thin layer of fire-red to his skirt. "My friend Toucan told me that everyone looks to the tanà to be the one who shows them what it means to be an Islander."

He could not be Buru Tovo—he certainly could *not* be *Buru Cliopher*—nor could he be Uncle Lazo, or Tupaia, or even the other Kip. He was ... himself. The one who left.

Cliopher thought of that portrait of the newly crowned Artorin Damara, the one that had shocked him to his core, that sudden sense of *this, this man, him!*—and his conscious decision to step into a certain pattern in the *Lays*, and go to Astandalas after him.

It was so easy to talk to his—Fitzroy.

His voice dropped. "I don't know how to be what they want of me. I am always the one who left. No matter how many times I have come home. It never changes, no matter what I do."

The confidence with which the other Kip had claimed his place niggled at him. Shamed him. *Worried* him.

(Challenged him.)

He did not yet know how to respond.

His Radiancy turned to smile wryly at him. "And somehow most people manage to come to themselves and stay there the rest of their lives."

Cliopher raised his eyebrows at him. "Or at least they pretend to."

"Cynic," his Radiancy said without heat. "Come, will you sing with me if I play? I've wanted—"

He stopped, and smiled crookedly without finishing the thought.

There had been so many years when they could have been such better friends.

They had time now, Cliopher told himself. He would not think about the future, what would come when they were no longer in this dream of an adventure, but for the here and now they *were*, and he could enjoy this.

"So have I," he said, and left everything else unsaid.

CHAPTER THIRTY-NINE
THE APOTHEOSIS OF AURELIUS MAGNUS

T hey were deep in hashing out possible harmonies for one of the songs out of the *Aurora* cycle when Fitzroy's hands stilled on his harp.

Cliopher broke into laughter as he continued singing a line too far, and looked up from his half-completed skirt to see that Elonoa'a and Aurelius Magnus had approached them.

"Good afternoon," Cliopher said, guessing the time. He made to stand, but Elonoa'a forestalled him by squatting down instead. Aurelius Magnus followed suit, though he sank to a cross-legged pose much like Cliopher's own.

"I've never gotten into the habit of squatting," he said with a smile.

"Neither have I," Fitzroy replied, sitting up and brushing the sand off his torso. Cliopher focused on tying off his knot. He'd learned to sit; it was a more natural pose, now.

"What are you making?" Aurelius Magnus asked politely. "It's very colourful!"

"A grass skirt," Cliopher replied, refusing to be discomfited by doing something, once again, that was not what anyone considered quite appropriate.

He never managed to have the right clothing. What he liked was never *right*. It was too fancy or too foreign or too ... primitive. The word sat ill in his mind. He looked instead at Elonoa'a, who was the most physically beautiful man Cliopher had ever seen, and tried to enjoy the effect rather than quail at the inevitable comparison.

It was hard to remember, after the weeks with Basil, that to Elonoa'a's eyes Cliopher looked of an age to be called ivani and ... *buru*.

Buru *hurt*.

One day Cliopher would like to be Buru, to someone—Gaudy's children, perhaps, if his nephew had them, or Leona's. Toucan and Ghilly's grandchildren. The grandchildren of his cousins.

Another full generation down, in short.

"We apologize for interrupting your faravia," Elonoa'a said abruptly. "We wished to be sure you had all you needed."

"It's been a long time since we had guests," Aurelius Magnus replied with a twinkling smile. "We keep turning to each other to ask what else we should be doing."

Fitzroy laughed. "I understand—I only left my position in the Palace two months ago, and it has been quite hard enough to recall all the ways of being in the world." Before either of the other men could query that (surely strange) comment, he went on: "We did want to ask about faravia. I had thought my lack of understanding was due to my imperfect knowledge of language, but Cliopher says that he knows only the literal meaning. As we fell through a crack in the world, we have no boat, so consequently no sails to mend."

Elonoa'a frowned. (His eyebrows *were* like Bertie's. Every time he moved them Cliopher recalled that point anew and was once more flabbergasted. He otherwise looked nothing like Bertie—but those eyebrows!) "What do you call it, then, the time after a journey when the one who left grows accustomed to being back, once more part of the community?"

"I don't think anyone does that, not intentionally," Cliopher said slowly.

"How do you mark the homecoming, then?"

He thought of his own homecomings after voyages, whether the short ones on the sky ships or the longer ones in the past on the sea train and trading ships or the longest one across the Wide Seas in his little boat.

The dried bundles crinkled as his hands clenched. He glanced down, smoothing out the fibres. The reds were all shades from scarlet to a rusty orange. Fire colours.

This was interesting, this exchange of knowledge, of customs. If it had been another culture entirely Cliopher would have found it *fascinating*.

He smiled. "There is a feast, sometimes, depending on the situation. Other than that, one is expected to take up one's place."

The Paramount Chief's face and voice were very stern, as if Cliopher had transgressed some sacred duty. "There should be a feast, yes, but then we always have the faravia. After a voyage? Always."

Cliopher wanted to defend the generations between them, who had let this custom lapse along with the great voyages. Perhaps they had not needed it, those people coming home from short trading voyages around the Ring, or after a stint on an Astandalan ship.

But he had been unable to find his way back to being *part of the community*.

Elonoa'a said, "If it is a short journey, one might spend only a day or two there, at the edge of the community but not part of it, until one is ready to join fully in its life. If it was a long journey, many months or many years, it might take a month or more for the voyager to be ready. Until then the village or his family brings food to the door, but leaves him be until he is ready to speak."

Aurelius put his hand on his lover's knee. Elonoa'a looked at him, the frown lightening with a softness Cliopher had not expected to see from him.

His heart was beating in his throat.

All those dismal homecomings. No time set aside deliberately for that necessary adjustment back to the society of his family and people after so long away.

How much better it would have been if, when he had come home after that long voyage in his *Tui-tanata*, he had been feasted and welcomed and then left to recover his equilibrium and his own sense of self-in-community.

He might not have left, if they had given him that.

He looked down at the crumpled fibres in his hands, and consciously smoothed them out. He would not cry with longing for what might have been, had this tradition come down through the years.

"That sounds like a very good idea," he said quietly.

Fitzroy put his hand on Cliopher's shoulder, and when Cliopher looked at him, half-consciously noting the mirroring of Aurelius's gesture to Elonoa'a, his friend said, "It does, indeed. We've only just started our journey together—well," he added, laughing, "let me rephrase that. We have only started *this* part of our journey together yesterday."

"You've been together long?" Aurelius asked.

Fitzroy's hand gripped Cliopher's shoulder tightly for a moment. "Yes," Fitzroy said, his voice warm, clear, strong as the brilliant waters of Sky Ocean. "Half our lives." He turned his head and smiled at Cliopher, who could only regard him silently, his heart open as the proverbial clam on the beach.

If he had had that faravia, that time to mend the metaphorical sails of his ship, he might have stayed, and then he would not have had *this*.

(The stray thought came streaking through his mind that he hoped that the other Lord Artorin of that other universe had found his way back to being Fitzroy Angursell, and that the other Kip—could Cliopher hope for this, for his counterpart, the self he might have been?—that the other Kip found his way to friendship with him. It was ... possible. Cliopher had left them with a peace treaty and a trading agreement. They *could* meet again.)

"Astonishing," Aurelius murmured in Shaian, looking at them. Cliopher realized he was still gazing at his—Fitzroy, and looked hastily away. Fitzroy himself was grinning at him as he turned unhurriedly towards his ancestor, who went on in Islander. "In ... in that case, you are most welcome to join us about the bonfire this evening. If you'd be willing to play, we'd love to hear you."

"We enjoyed hearing your music as we came up," Elonoa'a said, less abruptly. He too was looking at Cliopher with a pensive, puzzled expression.

No doubt it was because he'd automatically put on his court face. But he *could* not simply show ... everything.

"I'd be glad to, if you don't want Cliopher to sing the rest of the *Lays* tonight."

That was a conversational gambit Cliopher could gladly pick up. He relaxed, easy, courtly, pleasant. "I could hardly sing them *all* tonight! I don't think my voice would stand for it, for one thing."

"We can take turns," Fitzroy promised him, and then turned with a bright interest to his ancestor. "Actually, I'd love to hear *your* story—what really happened to you?"

Aurelius Magnus and Elonoa'a looked at each other. Then Aurelius settled himself more comfortably while simultaneously waving at his lover. "Go on, then, El, you don't have to listen to it again." He winked at Fitzroy as Elonoa'a stood up smoothly. "I think it's a good story, but everyone else disagrees."

"We've just heard it a thousand times," Elonoa'a said, with a sharp scoffing noise. He then flushed and bowed over his hands to Cliopher. "Until later, ivani."

Cliopher nodded, taken once more aback, and then privately resolved he was going to find an equally awkward title for Elonoa'a. Perhaps ezaru—the word for a former chief—would do.

◈

"The tale told in the *Lays* is true," Aurelius began. He sat easily, his hands quiet in his lap, much as Fitzroy was now sitting. Cliopher quietly continued with the next layers of his skirt, bronze and the lighter but still rich blues Fitzroy had made for him. They shimmered slightly, like the water in the shade of the *He'eanka*. "But like all histories, it does not include everything, and it stops where its writers—or singers, in this case—thought best."

"I have also noticed this," Fitzroy said, with a small quirk of his mouth.

Given that he and Cliopher had certainly made use of this particular aspect of histories in their efforts at reform—never *lying* or deliberately misleading, of course, but if there had to be a bias—and there was, of necessity, always a bias—then it might as well be in their favour instead of against them.

So had Cliopher shaped the government of the world. If it had to tilt in some-one's favour, let it be in favour of the many instead of the few. If the histories had to be written for the victors, let it tell the great deeds of those who ruled wisely and well and celebrate those who worked for the betterment of their peoples.

It had worked: Prince Rufus was a better leader than he might otherwise have been, because of the models Cliopher had had placed before him.

(He *could* have been King Rufus of Rufopolis, petty emperor of half of Zunidh. Cliopher had seen the pride and insatiable hunger in that version of the man, and though he could allow that the highest peak of culture in Rufopolis was perhaps higher than it was in Boloyo City, he had spent enough time talking of trade and exports with the king to know precisely how much lower the lowest trough of poverty was.)

"I was raised to war," Aurelius Magnus said, his eyes and voice tranquil, the sorrow blunted. "My father took me to battle when I was twelve; by fourteen I was leading men; by sixteen I was emperor of Astandalas, and leading armies. It took me longer to learn the value of peace."

Aurelius Magnus had been renowned for his magic and his beauty and for his genius as a general: he had personally conquered half of the imperial possessions of Alinor and opened the sea-routes to the conquest of Colhélhé.

It had been easier to condemn his drive to expansion when Cliopher had not known he'd been sixteen.

"I came into magic later," he went on. "It was not much like the powers of the magicians and soothsayers I knew. My mother's people knew something of wild magic, enough to point me to the beginning stages. I searched through the scrolls and books in the Palace, but there was very little. A handful of rumours that the early emperors had golden eyes and a wild magic more powerful than any seen since."

Aurelius and Fitzroy looked at each other, the two golden-eyed magi.

"It *is* a strange colour," Aurelius said, as if he were judging a new wine. The air hummed and made the hair on Cliopher's arms stand up.

He was not a mage. That testing, questioning magic was not for him. He continued, if more slowly, knotting the bundles to the twine.

"It's different than looking in a mirror," Fitzroy agreed after a moment. "I'd always wondered ... People have such odd reactions. Amber, do you think?"

"El says mine are the colour of molten gold, but I'm not sure he's ever actually seen gold smelting."

"I have," Fitzroy said, his eyes crinkling as he grinned. "And that's a good description. Don't you think, Kip? What colour would you say?"

There were no words for the colour of magic moving in their eyes. Cliopher was dizzy with it: two of the greatest magi in history, casually swirling the air around them, bringing up scents that could not possibly come from anything growing even on this island on the edge of Sky Ocean.

Cliopher was too ordinary for this company.

—No. He was here, for whatever reason, and he refused to back down from this challenge.

"I have thought your eyes much the colour of the sundrop cowries," he said, just barely biting off 'my lord'.

"Ah ..." Fitzroy turned back to his ancestor and regarded him intently. "Yes, I can see that."

"I've never seen that shell," Aurelius said curiously. "But no matter—you can tell me of it later. Else I shall never finish." He sighed. "I sought knowledge, and since I knew no other way, I took my armies with me as I searched. My reputation grew: I was already accounted a great general by my one-and-twentieth winter, and over the years following, kingdoms fell when they heard my approach."

Fitzroy murmured a list of names; some of them Cliopher knew, as place-names on Alinor or the old Ysthar or parts of Zunidh.

Aurelius Magnus winced, but his voice was steady. "Yes. I found out many secrets, in the libraries of the ancient universities of Alinor and the monasteries of Kavanduru in the north. I learned much, but always I hungered, for none of it answered the questions I had of my magic. And always there were the battles. I did not find peace. She does not travel with armies." He glanced searchingly at Fitzroy. "Did you find peace, descendant of mine?"

"After the Fall of Astandalas," Fitzroy replied gently. He glanced at Cliopher, who remembered suddenly all those splendid titles he had loved so deeply. The Sun-on-Earth, the Lion-Eyed, the Lord of Rising Stars. "All was broken—the magic of four thousand years shattered, the governments ruined. And yet Cliopher brought me peace."

"Not with armies?" Aurelius asked, and reached out to take Cliopher's hands in his. Cliopher did not resist as Aurelius turned them over, running his thumbs over the pads of Cliopher's fingers. "No. Your hands bear none of the calluses of sword or spear or bow. You are a man of peace."

Cliopher swallowed dryly as he was caught by those so-similar lion eyes, the magic in them almost singing even to his ears, but the emotions, the thoughts, nothing that he knew.

He had lifted up his voice to the Son of Laughter in answer to the challenges given him. He could hold his head before the ancestors.

"I am the tanà," he said softly. "When the hearth of the world was cold and dark, I lit a new fire and held it until it blazed well enough to give to another to tend."

Aurelius's hands closed around his for a moment, his face full of a respect Cliopher told himself he had earned. He could not doubt that; he had built something good that Aioru could now make into something better.

His hands were still held; he could not lift one to grasp his efela ko for comfort.

"He danced the fire in the throne room of the Palace of Stars," Fitzroy said, too proudly for Cliopher to parse. "It was one of the three most magnificent things I have ever seen, and I saw the greatest swordsman in the Nine Worlds—at least in my day—defeat a hundred and forty-nine soldiers in single combat."

"What was the third thing?" Aurelius asked with immediate curiosity.

Cliopher told himself he was ... curious, that was it, he too was *curious*. He took his hands back so he could continue with his skirt. Aurelius didn't seem to notice, given the intensity of his focus on Fitzroy.

"When Pali Avramapul defeated Damian in single combat. Fourth ... Ah, there's too many to count. I was involved in stealing sheep from the pastures of the Sun, and we had *quite* the adventure trying to escape with the boats of the constellations ... but that's a story for another day. You were telling us how *you* came to be stolen by the Sun."

Aurelius laughed. "True. I am going far off-course, aren't I? I am not the navigator El is."

"No one is," Cliopher said with the solid assurance of two thousand years of the *Lays* in his voice.

"I am glad," Aurelius said gravely, "that his reputation has endured. Mine ... well! Let me try to be a little shorter, or else we will miss supper. I sought knowledge, thinking to find peace, and instead brought war wherever I went. I met El, and left him again ... met the woman who would bear my children ...."

"Tassakar the Magnificent, Fhiar Tanteyr," Fitzroy said immediately, the name rolling off his tongue.

Aurelius startled. "I'm *very* surprised you know that title!"

"My friend Damian—the superlative swordsman I mentioned just now, in fact— is a descendant on the Tanteyr side. He's as pale as we are dark, and it amused us greatly we had even one shared ancestor."

"We shall have to speak more of the Tanteyr," Aurelius said. "Suffice it to say that I came eventually to hear that there was a tower—far, far away, on the other side of an ocean no one knew how to sail—where my—our—ancestor Harbut Zalarin had lived and studied and worked great magics, and that there was, so it was said, the key to peace."

"I know that tower," Fitzroy said quietly, and Cliopher was struck by the memory of the two of them standing before the great woven map of the empire of Astandalas. His Radiancy—he had been far, far from Fitzroy Angursell then, before that holiday, in that conversation that had made Cliopher want to do *something* to relieve the bleak desolation in his eyes—the conversation that had led to ... *this*—his Radiancy had pointed at five isolated outposts where the Empire had anchored its magic. One of them had been where he'd been exiled.

"Do you?" Aurelius said, and they looked at each other again. Something seemed to pass between them, for Fitzroy grimaced, and Aurelius said, "It was a lonely place."

"Yes. But I found ..." Fitzroy smiled suddenly. "I found the key to freedom there."

"The peace I found was one of binding," Aurelius said. He looked at Cliopher. "You know how I came there—I had a handful of directions, barely more than the outlines of a myth, but they all said this was a tower on an island on the far side of a great sea. And I knew one great navigator who found islands."

"Elonoa'a."

"Yes. I learned much, in that tower. Perhaps too much—perhaps more than was wise, or more than I was wise enough to know. All I knew was war, save for those travels with Elonoa'a, and I wanted my people to know peace." He grimaced. "I came up with a way that seemed good to me, at the time. A great work of magic, one which would bind the pieces of my empire together, which would let the many kinds of magic work together in harmony."

"The Pax Astandalatis," Fitzroy said.

That was a term, and a concept, Cliopher knew. By his Radiancy's day it had been a heavy weight and a burden, the empire a glory built out on a hidden foundation of grief.

All empires were, Cliopher had studied enough history to know that. But there had been an element to the magical bindings on Astandalas that he had always found horrendous.

"It seemed good to me at the time," Aurelius said. "I have had time to think about it, to wonder what else I wrought ..."

Fitzroy did not say how he had been bound by that magic, that so-called peace. "It was a great thing. We can only do our best with the tools and knowledge we have. We cannot know what results our actions will have."

"Unless some distant descendant comes to tell you," Aurelius replied wryly. "I know I left many wars, many enemies, many threats behind me. Magic—wild magic —works in strange and mysterious ways, and I was trying to marry mine with the magic of the wizards and sorcerers of the empire."

"I learned much from your writings," Fitzroy assured him. "We can speak of the other results later, if you'd like."

"The judgment of posterity ..." Aurelius laughed shortly. "I suppose I deserve it. There is much blood on my hands."

Because he'd been taken to war at twelve.

At twelve Cliopher had been sitting at Buru Tovo's feet, learning how to dive for pearls and all the lessons that radiated out from the circle of stones on the beach with a handful of embers burning in its heart.

He was nearly finished with the skirt. One more layer to form the waistband would do it. Usually he'd woven that ... this would have to be something simpler, the way he'd done when he'd been shipwrecked.

"El was not happy with my plan ... We fought, but I did not think we could be together, not if I didn't do this ... there were other things going on, of course, I was still emperor and I had been gone a long time from the heartlands." He waved away what must have been a complicated and difficult period, politically and personally, with a deceptively airy wave. "El went home to tell the stories of his travels—you sang those last night—I went to a magically significant location, a great mountain that was said to be a place where all the directions and elements came together."

Fitzroy sat up with a gleam of excitement in his eyes. "Ousanadh? The three-headed mountain in central Damara, where the Abbey of the Mountains is?"

"It was a hermitage then," Aurelius said, sounding entirely bemused. "You know it?"

"They say that's where you ... disappeared." Fitzroy grinned. "There's a shrine to you there. I was mistaken for you on my last visit, which was somewhat ... informal."

"Just somewhat," Cliopher murmured, recalling those reports. He wondered if Rhodin would take actually *meeting* Aurelius Magnus and Elonoa'a as sufficient proof Fitzroy and Cliopher were not their reincarnations.

Probably not. That sojourn in a dream-world had sparked some alarming ideas in Rhodin's mind.

"I prepared for my spell ..." Aurelius hesitated. "It was a great work of magic."

"It bound the Empire."

"Yes ... I was focused for many weeks ... it's hard to remember now. It all centred around the date of a great eclipse of the sun, when the final binding would happen. I was ..." Aurelius hesitated, and gazed beseechingly at Fitzroy. "One is vulnerable, working magic such as that."

"Yes."

That was all Fitzroy said, but it was a solid reassurance. Aurelius firmed his lips. "Yes."

There were very few magi at their level. Cliopher knew that—that was the whole reason for his—for Fitzroy's quest, so he could *find* another one—but he had never thought of how *lonely* it must be, to have that kind of power and no one to share the burden of it.

It was bad enough bearing the weight of the world's government on one's shoulders—and Cliopher knew that weight—but to have that power beyond the lot of mortals?

"While I was deep in my magic, weaving the net of peace I hoped for my people, I ... I felt a sting." His hand came up to his shoulder. "My brother—my half-brother, Haultan—had come to ... I imagine he said to see I was well, to tend to me—and he'd struck me with a dart or a needle."

"Poison?"

"It was the moment of the eclipse," Aurelius went on as if he hadn't heard Cliopher's quiet question. His voice was calm, abstracted, his eyes cloudy with memory. "I was deep in my magic. I felt it ... felt the sting, felt the poison, felt death coming for me ..." He took a breath. "And then the Sun came down."

"Yes ..." Fitzroy murmured.

On the beach on Lesuia, there had been an eclipse of the Moon, when the Moon lady came down for Fitzroy. (Her beloved, she had called him, and Cliopher, fool that he was, had thought only that his Radiancy was a great mage and of the descent of the Sun and ... oh, there had been *so many* clues that his Radiancy was Fitzroy Angursell, and Cliopher had not let himself look at any of them.)

"He offered—the Sun did—to save my life, if I would join his court." Aurelius looked down for a moment, his hands digging into the sand. "How long was your reign?" he asked abruptly.

"Fourteen years as emperor," Fitzroy said, "and ... well, time was one of the things broken with the Fall of Astandalas. Twenty-five years, by some reckonings. A thousand years, by others."

"A thousand years," Aurelius whispered, his voice breaking. "You must think less of me, to know how ... self-serving it was. I was so tired of war."

Cliopher did not know what to say. He'd finished his skirt and tidied the mess, and he had nothing left to do with his hands.

Fitzroy leaned forward and carefully, cautiously, took Aurelius's hands. "I would not have survived so long, sitting on my throne after all, after the Fall, had I not had Cliopher."

"El and I had quarrelled, on the way home from the tower. He wouldn't come to the mountain with me. He thought ... he thought the magics I had already done were enough, would be enough. I'd practiced a new way of bringing his islands within the magic of the Empire, but I couldn't do the same, other places ... their magics didn't respond ... it was so much *harder*, without ..."

He gave a small, sad smile to Fitzroy. "You know, don't you? It's much easier when you love."

Aurelius's love for Elonoa'a had been renowned for two thousand years in the histories of two cultures.

"Yes," said Fitzroy. "It is."

"I was so tired of war ..." Aurelius took a deep breath. "And I knew, in that moment, with the poison in my veins and the Sun standing before me in the shadow of the eclipse, that if I could offer a great sacrifice, it would do more than anything else possibly could. I could use my ... my wish to be done, my desire for peace, my *love* ..."

"You sacrificed your future to anchor the Pax."

Aurelius closed his eyes, and he twisted his hands to grip Fitzroy's. "You have no idea what it is to hear someone who *understands* ..."

Fitzroy did—he must—but he did not speak.

Cliopher had tried so hard to be a rock for him, somewhere he could stand, someone who looked at him as a person, someone who loved him for who he was. He had lifted as much of the burden of the world off his shoulders as he could, taking it upon his own.

He had not been able to help shoulder this burden, this magic and this loneliness.

"I had a moment to whisper a message to El," Aurelius said. "My magic always liked the air ... the winds listened to me ... and I knew El heard them ..."

Half a world away—the whole of the western Wide Seas away—

Elonoa'a of Izurayë, who Hears the Wind, who sails the night sky, whose fanoa came over the sea ...

No, Cliopher could not begrudge them that meaning of the word.

"*I'm sorry*, I said, to the north wind," Aurelius whispered. "*I'm sorry*, I said, to the east wind. *I'm sorry*, I said, to the south wind. *I am going to the House of the Sun*, I said to the winds that circle round the sky, the deep winds of the earth, the sea. And to the west wind, blowing towards him: *I love you. I love you. I love you.* Three times, as in a tale. Three times to the west wind, hoping El would hear my words, hoping he would forgive me for that quarrel, hoping he would ... not forget me. ... And then ... and then I took the hand of the Sun and went with him."

Cliopher only realized he was weeping when a tear dripped off his nose and landed on his hand. He wiped at his face, pressing his knuckles across his mouth, trying to hold back his grief and pity for this young man—and he *was* young—who had brought so much grief and so much glory upon his people, who was worshipped as a god, whose love was sung but not the love he had had.

No, Cliopher could not begrudge them this, not at all.

Aurelius had disappeared in a flash of light, taken to the Divine Lands by the Sun himself, after a promise no one had heard him speak.

The murderous prince, his half-brother, had taken up the crown of Astandalas.

The Pax Astandalatis spun out across Zunidh and Ysthar and Alinor—eventually also Colhélhé and Voonra—and over the brutal years of Haultan's reign and those of his successors, peace had been wrought out of the magic and steel that had been Aurelius's tools.

And on the far side of the world, Elonoa'a had heard that message sent to him by the dying breath of his beloved, and—

"Elonoa'a followed you," Cliopher said, his voice falling into the air like stones into the sea.

Aurelius caught his breath, and he smiled gratefully at Cliopher, the sun breaking forth in his eyes like the waves breaking over a reef. "He did. He came—they all came—they came to the House of the Sun and they won my freedom."

"I would like to hear that tale," Fitzroy said softly.

"It is not mine to tell. They ..." Aurelius made a face. "El challenged the Sun for my freedom, and won it, so I could go with him ..."

He rubbed the spot on his shoulder again.

"The poison is still in my veins. It is dormant so long as I remain in the Divine Lands ... We search for a remedy, but ..." He trailed off, and then he visibly rallied himself, forced his voice and his expression to lighten. "It gives us something to do. Enough! It is nearly time for the evening meal."

He jumped to his feet, Cliopher and Fitzroy following hastily, if somewhat stiffly—though less stiffly than Cliopher might have expected, after hours seated before his work—and the ancient emperor gave them a straightforward, solemn look, before he nodded once and strode off.

Cliopher let out a long breath.

"Yes," Fitzroy murmured. "That was a *very* interesting story. I can see why El doesn't like hearing it. I have much to think on."

He gestured down at the brilliantly coloured skirt Cliopher had made. "Let's get ready. As good guests I think it behoves us to entertain our hosts, don't you think?"

"Sing for our supper, you mean?" Cliopher replied dryly, but he bent over and picked up the skirt.

"I've always had good luck with that," Fitzroy proclaimed, not turning around even when Cliopher took off his tunic. Cliopher felt somewhat battered by Aurelius's story and decided he did not have the emotional wherewithal to be self-conscious.

So many things were easier with that resolution.

"In fact, I had *such* good luck with singing for my supper, back in the old days—when I was with the Red Company—that I don't think I ever *paid* for a meal."

"I'm sure that's not true."

Fitzroy laughed. "It sounds good, though, doesn't it? Which is the most important thing, after all."

Cliopher fastened his skirt and gave him a dour glance. "I *know* that's not true."

Fitzroy laughed. "Oh, and I suppose you've never *tried* to live up to the story you hope people will tell about you? Come now, my lord Mdang, I've known you far too long for that. You didn't get that new efela by being *prosaic*."

CHAPTER FORTY
THE PHOENIX DREAM

"Splendid," Fitzroy declared when Cliopher had finished settling his new grass skirt around his hips.

"Thank you," Cliopher replied dryly, reaching up to ensure his efela had not twisted around. His hand lingered on the three strands, the efela ko, the efetana, the third one with the sundrop cowrie and the two flame pearls.

"No one else has one quite that bright."

"*Thank* you."

"You're very welcome!" Fitzroy laughed, his eyes glittering. "Your hair is growing out."

Cliopher hadn't cut it since his accident with the landslide. He ran his fingers across his scalp, wincing as he caught a few tangles. It had been years since the last time it'd been long enough to *knot*. "I'll have to carve a comb," he said.

"I won't need one of those for a while," Fitzroy said mournfully. "Mine seems to be growing slowly. Very slowly."

Conju had once given Cliopher an extensive discourse on the depilatory creams he concocted for his Radiancy, which apparently inhibited hair growth for months. "It's Conju's work," he said therefore as they left their shelter and made their way along the beach to the great bonfire lit against the westering sun.

"I should have known. I was worried I was going to be bald *naturally*."

Cliopher laughed. "I look forward to seeing what it looks like once it grows out further."

Fitzroy spent the remaining yards of their short walk describing the more memorable hairdos he had once sported, which Cliopher listened to with a feeling of utter incredulity. He'd read reports that described those hairstyles, the braids and the beads and the elaborately curled locks of Fitzroy Angursell.

It seemed such a stupidly small grief, that his Radiancy had not been able to wear his hair as he liked. A small matter, nearly frivolous.

Hair had never been very important to Cliopher—nothing like the pronunciation of his name—nothing like the fact he'd had to hide his efela ko—but it *was* important to many people, so important he'd enshrined hairstyles and head coverings as something that could not be regulated by employers. The Imperial Service had suggestions, guidelines, which when he'd joined had in fact been *requirements*, but they were not now.

Cliopher had not let his hair grow to the more usual Islander length when he became Viceroy, but he hadn't shaved it as the high aristocracy did, either. The latter had been an immediate, easy decision; the former had not actually occurred to him.

He ran his fingers through his hair again, remembering the wave in the other Kip's hair, the way it had framed his face and come down to his shoulders. Cliopher's would be greyer, but he could—

He could experiment, he supposed. He could always cut it off again if he didn't like it.

They reached the fire before the sun had fully set. They were greeted by the crew of the *He'eanka* with a welcome that felt at once equally as genuine and less artificial than the previous day.

Artificial was not really quite the right word. There had been an impersonality to their greetings, to these two strangers met after however long it had been for these young people (certainly not two—or three—thousand years, any more than the thousand years since the Fall were shown on Cliopher's face, held in his mind).

Today, after he had sung the sixth Lay, after Aurelius and Elonoa'a had said whatever they'd said ... today they looked at him with friendly, half-familiar interest.

Their interest sharpened as they looked at his grass skirt and efela.

Tupaia came up as they hesitated at the fringes of the circle around the fire, deciding where best to sit. He greeted them pleasantly before looking intently at Cliopher. "We had thought the traditions had changed and people did not wear grass skirts," he said, gesturing at Cliopher's change of dress.

Cliopher smiled. "It's brighter than the usual style at home—"

"My fault," Fitzroy chimed in. "I picked the colours."

"It's very striking," Tupaia said, a trifle uncertainly. Cliopher lifted his chin reflexively, and the ancient tanà dropped his gaze to look at his efela. "What," he said sharply, "you hold efevoa?"

"I do," Cliopher said, and then could think of no way to further answer that question.

"He does," Fitzroy said, "and he promised he would tell me the story of this *new* efela tonight, as I know that he holds the efela nai and therefore this efela was a gift."

From the gods. That's what Mardo Walea had told Cliopher.

(His younger self had not been given this efela during Cliopher's time in the other universe. None of his family could explain its appearance; not even Uncle Lazo. They'd already sent his efela, including the efela nai and the full length of efevoa, home to Gorjo City so that Mardo Walea could make the funerary efela that would pass to his heirs.)

(His Radiancy would have hated to come back and discover what Cliopher had left him in his will.)

Tupaia whistled softly.

"He is a man of *many* surprises," Fitzroy said.

"So I have already begun to learn," Tupaia said, gaze lingering on the efevoa as they found a place to sit down. "So I have."

Eranui and the Five Shells was a story from the eighth of the *Lays*, so Cliopher had to explain everything about his adventure in the other place.

He wasn't certain if it were his explanation of *his* role in the government of Zunidh or the other Kip's desire to cast off all that came from Astandalas that astonished his audience more.

It was even harder to parse Fitzroy's reaction: he sat very quietly, almost serenely, as Cliopher described meeting the Lord Artorin of the other place, the one who had not ...

He did feel particularly gratified when he described his homecoming and Fitzroy leaned over and said, "Rhodin must have been *delighted* by this development."

He did not sing any of the *Lays* that night—he and Fitzroy agreed without having to speak to each other that tonight was not the night to tell the stories of what exactly had happened after Aurelius Magnus's disappearance—and instead Fitzroy played.

As he tuned his harp, and Cliopher moved to drink thirstily of what he'd thought was a drinking gourd full of water but which turned out to be slightly watered arrak, Fitzroy gave him a glimmering smile. "What should I play first, Kip?"

"*Aurora*," Cliopher said without needing to think about it, and then spent quite a bit of time coughing as the potent alcohol burned all the way down.

"Ah yes, your favourite."

"If I had to pick one, my lord," Cliopher retorted, voice husky with his cough, and met the interested gaze of Tupaia. "He—he's a very prolific songwriter."

"In my youth," Fitzroy replied mildly, his expression ... distant.

Cliopher listened to him play and wondered, not for the first time, if he had written anything new.

On that holiday on Lesuia, the first night his Radiancy had played for them, they had asked if he wrote his own songs, and he'd said, flatly as an imperial pronouncement, *Not for a long time.*

Inspiration was not a gift Cliopher had in his possession. He could not strike that spark for him, nor nurse it into a flame, a fire, a blaze.

He could sing, though, if only the chorus.

As they returned home along the beach some time quite late in the evening, replete with the meal and the music and the company, they stopped to look at the elegant lines of the *He'eanka*, a dark silhouette against the brilliant stars, the glowing ocean.

"They could go home," Fitzroy said, very softly, plucking a few low notes from his harp. "Any time they pleased. They could ... go."

Cliopher listened to the soft brush of the wind in his hair, the sea lapping cool and pleasant against his toes, some fish briefly surfacing in a tiny noise that sent circles of brilliant phosphorescence ever wider.

Long ago, they had sat beside each other next to the lighthouse on the breakwater edging the Palao lagoon, looking back on the city Cliopher loved and left, over and over again.

Beside each other, and always apart, with a gulf as great as the ocean between them.

Cliopher reached out and took Fitzroy's hand. "Elonoa'a would never leave Aurelius."

"Do you think they *do* want to go home?" Fitzroy said. Out in the water the silver ripples faded back into the gleaming, shining waters. "Do you think they get ... homesick?"

Cliopher picked his words with care. "They spent most of their lives sailing to find new lands. I'm sure sailing waters no other human beings have sailed has its own consolations and joys."

Fitzroy's hand tightened on his, then relaxed, settled more comfortably in his grip. "They have done so much already for Auri ... They must be tired ..."

Resentful hovered in the air between them, unspoken.

"They came for their own reasons," Cliopher said. "They stay for love."

Fitzroy was silent, his hand in Cliopher's, his pulse fluttering under Cliopher's thumb though his body was still, a shadow as dark as the ship. And then he shook his head, once, sharply, and started once more to walk.

Cliopher followed, as he had always followed, concentrating on his footing in the surge and wash of the sea at the very edge of the land.

They were nearly back at their shelter when Fitzroy cleared his throat and said, "It's a pity you don't have that feather Sardeet gave you."

Cliopher had perhaps had a mouthful or two more arrak than he ought to have had. "What do you mean?"

"If you lay a phoenix feather under your pillow before you go to sleep, you'll dream an answer to your question." Fitzroy sighed. "It might have given them the next star in their ke'ea ..."

Cliopher's hand went up to the sundrop cowrie as his heart seemed to beat once, hard. They'd heard bits and pieces of the star-sailors' adventures in Sky Ocean, seeking wisdom from the gods and monsters and legends who dwelled there.

"But I do have it," he said, and stopped where he stood.

Fitzroy looked at him, his eyes brilliant in the starlight. "It wasn't in your pockets. I checked."

Cliopher could only stare. "What? Why?"

"Jullanar said it was important before you do laundry. Don't you check your pockets first?"

"I've never done my own laundry."

"What? Jullanar said—never mind! What do you mean, you have it?" His gaze dropped to Cliopher's hand. "On your efela? How ..."

"It's a very small feather," Cliopher said. "It fit in the cowrie ..."

They looked at each other for a long moment. Cliopher was very aware of the warmth of the feather in its shell, the huge stars like fireworks behind his Radiancy's head, the soft plash and murmur of the waves against his feet.

"Imagine that," Fitzroy said, very softly. As one they retraced their steps to Elonoa'a and Aurelius's shelter.

∿

The next morning, Aurelius was shaken, his eyes haunted not by grief but by a profound joy. Elonoa'a was, as ever, more serious.

Their descriptions of their dream were full of a strange, unsettling certainty. Cliopher was oddly reminded of some of his cousin Louya's pronouncements about sea turtles.

Fitzroy appeared entirely certain of the veracity of their shared dream, and asked questions about it.

"We were sailing," Elonoa'a began, "through the night sky, a great star upon the prow of the ship." He pointed at where the two keels of the *He'eanka* curved up out of the water, carved with the stars and patterns that were named in the *Lays*. "On the right-hand keel, to show our own direction."

One of the words for *right* was kēo, an old word for star.

"We sailed, and then we saw a great light coming towards us, guided by our star," Aurelius said. "A goddess took form out of the night: her hair black as the sky and netted with starlight, her face gleaming, her eyes as dark and brilliant as if they were holes to the heart of the night."

Elonoa'a nodded, his voice softer than Cliopher had yet heard it. "She held a viau in her arms."

"How did she come?" Fitzroy asked. "Was she flying?"

"She stood upon a manta ray the colour of the sunset," Elonoa'a said.

"I thought it was a sea serpent," Aurelius objected mildly.

Elonoa'a gave him a small smile. "It could be. Coloured like the sunset, yes?"

"Yes." Aurelius sighed. "Her robes were the colour of night, like the sheen of the waves under the stars. She came to us, as we sailed with the star on our prow."

"I made note of the constellations around us, our ke'e and the currents of Sky Ocean beneath our hulls, the voices of the winds in our sails—"

Aurelius shivered, with awe and longing and a deep, deep hope. "I guided her with the star, drew her close to us, and she held up the viau to us, its radiance spreading out all around me. I took the viau in my hands, and it was warm and living in my touch, against my skin, and I held it to myself—"

His hand went to the place on his shoulder where he'd been struck by the poisoned dart.

Elonoa'a placed his own hand upon Aurelius's, and they were silent.

They looked at each other, somber, intent. Then Elonoa'a said, quietly, "It is an impossible task. The star that brought her to us, that let her *find* us, was a flame of the Sun, we both knew it."

"It is an impossible task," Aurelius said, not hopelessly but with a certain resignation, for when had such things ever been *easy*? "We have been to the House of the Sun," he went on, gesturing at himself and his beloved, and then again, taking in the whole of the crew at work on the *He'eanka* and their other tasks.

"No mortal can visit the House of the Sun more than once," Fitzroy said quietly, a shattering regret in his voice. "I have been there also."

Cliopher thought of Buru Tovo asking him—over and over asking him—*Is this where you stop?*

Uncle Lazo saying, *yes*, and then finding a pearl another way, and thus returning to the challenge set by the tana-tai.

Is this where you stop?

He lifted his glance to the strange brilliance of Sky Ocean, the cerulean sky and the cerulean water, the horizon that was not far enough away, the sense that this air was richer than ordinary air, that that water was not water, that this very land they stood upon was not land, but the stuff of which stars were made.

Is this where you stop?

Darkness everywhere he went, the Mother of the Mountains had told him, if he did not stop, did not turn back, did not decide he had done enough.

Darkness, and monsters, and the possibility of a small, ordinary, common white shell.

He cleared his throat.

Fitzroy met his glance with a solemn curiosity, which was quickly leavened by an alarming delight. "Kip ..."

Is this where you stop?

For one brief, astonishing moment Cliopher could not believe he was about to say this.

He had played at this game, as a boy with his sisters and cousins playing the court-yard under the nets his father mended. As an adolescent he had talked the legends over and over with Basil, wondering how they could be true. He had lived his whole life according to the metaphorical meaning—

He took one deep breath, before straightening his shoulders, lifting his chin, fully in his battle mode.

Is this where you stop?

He was not Aurelius Magnus, had never lifted a sword or a spear or a bow, had never conquered worlds.

He was not Elonoa'a, the greatest navigator, the greatest of all the Ke'e Lulai, who could dream of a goddess and imagine he could find his ke'ea to that fateful meeting.

He was not Tupaia, the model and exemplar of all the tanà who came after.

He was not Fitzroy Angursell, his beloved Radiancy, the Sun-on-Earth, the greatest poet of an age.

He was Cliopher Mdang of Tahivoa, who had gone to serve his own emperor in the deliberate imitation of Elonoa'a, who had himself gone after his fanoa as Vou'a had gone for Ani when she lost her mirimiri, and he knew the steps of this dance from all the *Lays*.

This was a task he could face, an injustice he could remedy, a fire he could hold.

He looked straight at Aurelius Magnus, as if the ancient emperor were any of the hundreds of thousands of people whom Cliopher had promised a better life.

He had given hope to those hundreds of thousands, those *millions*, all his people. Hope, and better than hope, results.

Is this where you stop?

He lifted his chin. That answer had always been the same.

"I have never been to the House of the Sun. I am Cliopher Mdang of Tahivoa, tanà of Zunidh and Hands of the Emperor, and I will go there and bring you the flame you need."

The words sang in his mouth. The ancient star-farers stared at him in perturbation, Elonoa'a and Aurelius and Tupaia.

"It is a long and difficult journey, full of many perils," Elonoa'a said slowly.

"The Sun is not accustomed to giving up anything he has claimed," Aurelius added.

Tupaia merely tilted his head and regarded Cliopher with an unnerving intensity.

"Don't worry," his Radiancy said, his voice ringing in the air. "Cliopher has often accomplished the impossible when I have sent him to negotiate with people who didn't think he had any possible right to be there."

Cliopher assumed, insofar as he assumed anything after his declaration, that he would have to build his own boat.

He went for a solitary walk out along one of the spits, thinking over his decision and accumulating casao shells as he went to use as tools. By the time he returned, the crew of the *He'eanka* had already cut down a breadfruit tree and hollowed out its trunk.

Even with the addition of Aurelius's magic, this was quite inconceivable.

He set his shells down by his shelter and walked up to the area where the crew had begun their work. Fitzroy stood next to Elonoa'a, watching. He turned to smile at Cliopher when he came up. "Aren't they impressive!" he said gleefully.

"I don't understand," Cliopher replied, which was a silly thing to say, but he could not quite grasp what he was seeing. Elonoa'a furrowed his brows at him (*so* like Bertie), and Cliopher offered up a smile. It felt wan. He probably looked utterly asinine.

"It took me so much longer, when I built my vaha ... even the last time, with all that practice ..." He trailed off in the face of Elonoa'a's visible astonishment. "I sailed across the Wide Seas, after the Fall. It was full of storms—typhoons—I was wrecked so many times ..."

He flushed, biting his lip. So much for sounding confident and capable of sailing Sky Ocean!

(*Why* must he keep oscillating between a comfortable avuncularity and a gauche fifteen?)

"You built a vaha and sailed it across the Wide Seas?" Elonoa'a asked. "I had not thought you were trained as a navigator?"

Cliopher opened his mouth and then shut it again with a click of his teeth that seemed to jolt him to the soles of his feet. "I'm not," he said after a moment. "I did my best with the knowledge I had."

Elonoa'a regarded him for a long, disturbing moment. "*Many* surprises," he murmured; he must have spoken to Tupaia about their conversation. "Will you tell me?"

How humbled he had been before the might and majesty of Ani.

He could bear the recounting of that tale of how he had lost himself and his island and his way to the greatest of all navigators.

He had, after all, found his way home in the end.

"It is a long tale of the sea," Cliopher said, the ritual words, and found the entire crew listening intently as they built him a craft with which to sail the sky.

Oh, this was not how he had ever thought meeting the ancestors would go.

(A quiet voice said that it was ... better.)

Over the next few days, the crew of the *He'eanka* built Cliopher a vaha.

He assisted in places—"It's good for the person a boat is for to put his hand to the work," Hiru told him as she handed him a stone adze—but for the most part he spent his time with Elonoa'a, being examined on his scanty knowledge of navigation.

It was a strange situation all round. Cliopher could not help but be astonished, every once in a while, at the sudden realization that he was being given *direct* instruction by Elonoa'a himself, that the Ancestors were *literally* building him a boat, and awe would wash over him with a cold thrill that made him shudder to the roots of his being.

The rest of the time he was scrambling to pull long-disregarded knowledge to the forefront of his mind.

His knowledge of specific stars and constellations and wind and current patterns was useless, here at the edge of Sky Ocean. He had instead to fumble to formulate principles, which he'd never learned.

Elonoa'a questioned him sternly, resolutely, uncompromisingly.

(Cliopher knew why. The sea was uncompromising, unforgiving, resolute. If he did not know this perfectly, if he could not respond, he would die.)

But the questions were *hard*. He'd tried—he'd tried so hard, that long journey of the sea—but he had only had a handful of skills, and cobbled together the rest. If he hadn't been crossing the Wide Seas, he would never have found his way.

Elonoa'a could find his way *anywhere*. He had discovered new islands, found the currents that led to other worlds, used the vague descriptions of stars and winds and waves to form a ke'ea that led him straight to that tower at the edge of Colhélhé where Aurelius had found what he sought.

Cliopher was left, at the end of each day, with the dispiriting awareness of just how little he knew, and how much had been lost. He did not think any of his contemporary navigators were this capable.

"But that's why Elonoa'a is the greatest navigator," Fitzroy reminded him, one evening when Cliopher had pled exhaustion and left the communal fire early. "And you know just as much, in your own fields."

"Not that reforming governments is a *particularly* useful skill, out here," Cliopher retorted.

"Auri says that El thinks you're doing very well."

"It's kind of him to say so." Cliopher lay back on the warm sand with a quiet grunt. He'd spent the day laying on a raft while Auri changed the rhythm of the waves to match swell patterns El whispered to him, and he felt sore and exhausted from simply paying such *physical* attention. "What did you do today?"

"I laid spells of protection and good fortune on your vaha."

Cliopher rolled over onto his side to look at his friend. Fitzroy was laying beside him, their small fire between them, casting a warm light on his skin. Fitzroy had changed, over the days they'd spent on the island: he looked healthier, happier, more relaxed. Almost younger ... or not *younger*, but ... less aged and worn. His hair was starting to show a tight curling pattern.

Cliopher could not count the number of days they'd been there. Not *many*, he thought, but they would not stay in his mind when he tried to tally them. "How long do you think we've been here?" he asked.

"A week," Fitzroy said, smiling. "A year. A lifetime. It doesn't matter. It's not Fairyland; we'll not return home to find centuries have passed while we dallied here. This is the time of the soul."

"I suppose it's just as well I have practice not thinking too hard about the vagaries of time."

"You are remarkably good at not thinking about things you don't want to think about."

Fitzroy's voice and face were both more neutral than anything. Cliopher regarded him pensively, taking the words at face value. "I suppose so," he agreed after a few moments. The wind was scudding softly across them, making the sand grains dance against his skin but not getting into his eyes.

"Do you ever get tired of it?"

"Keeping secrets?"

"Keeping secrets secret from even yourself."

Cliopher did not think Fitzroy was talking about ... things he still wasn't thinking about. "Sometimes," he admitted. "Most of the time it's easier. Some things are best left where they rest."

Fitzroy rolled over on his back, staring up at the sky. Cliopher followed suit, relaxing into the sand, the scudding airs, the sky that was too close and too three-dimensional and so unutterably beautiful he was still being brought to the point of tears on contemplating it.

After Elonoa'a's instruction the night sky was no longer quite so alien as it had been at first. None of these huge, splendid stars had names that they knew, but for all their unknowable constellations and nebulae they still moved in patterns that could be discerned.

Cliopher stared into the sky, which felt like looking out across the horizon rather than looking *up*; as if he could sail as easily that way as along the thin line of the horizon between sea and sky.

This was Sky Ocean. Perhaps the horizon meant something different, here.

"You had a nightmare last night," Fitzroy said softly.

There were things he was not thinking about. Some of them had been crowding into his dreams.

Cliopher sifted the effervescent sand between his fingers. "It's been a long time since I sailed alone."

"You were ... I'm sorry," Fitzroy said, his voice low. "I could not help but hear. I tried to wake you, and you cried 'No! No! Don't leave me!'"

"My father died by drowning," Cliopher said. "I saw his face."

In his dreams, his father was often alive. That was better than in his memories.

Fitzroy breathed hard for a moment. "I shouldn't have asked Tupaia about the missing crew. I didn't think ..."

"I need to know the dangers," Cliopher said, as firmly as he could.

He had been singing the *Lays*, not every night—he was tired, and the star-sailors wanted to talk over what he told them, the histories of their peoples after their departure from the mortal worlds. Cliopher did not think they had fully grasped what *fifty generations* meant, not until he started to unfold two thousand years of names they did not know, stories they had never heard, discoveries and inventions and developments they had never imagined.

Other nights Fitzroy sang for them, or they sang their own songs: songs of the ancient Islanders, of Aurelius's court and the places these sailors had visited on their journeys, and songs they had composed over the course of their journeys in the sky.

Some of those songs were the tales of their friends who had been lost.

There were monsters, out there in the dark.

"I have put what protections I can on your boat," Fitzroy said, his voice uncertain. "Auri has as well."

Cliopher thrust his fingers into the sand, feeling the cooler, damper texture below the surface warmth. "I talked to the Mother of the Mountains," he said, almost dreamily, as the fire chuckled and crackled between them. "She told me that a great mage's attention tangles magic around one. That *your* attention and ... regard ... had drawn magic around me."

"My love," Fitzroy said, very quietly.

Cliopher had told Fitzroy he loved him: years ago, when that secret had grown too full to be hidden in his heart. He'd had to say it, because he could not touch his lord, not then; could only offer his best work for him, the minutes and hours of his waking life, the choices of his heart and mind.

He had told his Radiancy, Fitzroy Angursell, that he was the sun of his life, who had given him his direction.

Fitzroy had never said anything in return. He couldn't, not then. Cliopher had known that: had spent a long time building the steps so he could climb down from that high pedestal the world had put him on.

"I don't want to leave you," Cliopher said helplessly, a truth he could not keep silent.

Fitzroy was quiet for a moment, but his breath was coming hard, and his muscles were tense and quivering. Cliopher waited, wondering, listening.

Look first. Listen first. Questions later.

(One day it would be time for the questions they had never asked each other.)

Fitzroy's voice came out in a thin, hard tone, very unlike him. "I don't want you to go."

It was good that Fitzroy could *say* that. It was.

Cliopher wanted ... things he *still* could not name.

He had wanted to sail into legend—into *this* legend—from his earliest memory.

"I hate seeing people go," Fitzroy said, and his voice was flat, dispirited, defeated. "Always ... always. I had to give the orders, and they go, and so often they do not come back ..."

"I will come back."

"You cannot promise me that."

"I always have."

The waves splashed on the shore, the endless dance Ani had given to Vou'a, her gift to him in return for the islands he had raised from the underworld for her, her gift continuing long after she had lost her mirimiri and could no longer come to meet him where the shoreline met the sea.

"The first time I saw you," Fitzroy said, "I had a vision—a glimpse—two people on a boat, a vaha, in the dark, with the stars around them ..."

"That hasn't happened yet," Cliopher said, shaken.

"It might not have been *us*."

"Who else would it have been?"

It could have been Elonoa'a and Aurelius, whose stories of their adventures had included a few such starlit sails together. It could have been any number of Cliopher's ancestors or current relatives or even descendants, in the broader sense.

"I will come back," Cliopher said, as the wind washed over them and the fire murmured to itself in the hollow between them. "I have always come back. That hasn't happened yet, and it will."

"I wish I could have your faith," Fitzroy said, his voice wavering. "I seem to have lost mine."

Cliopher stared up at the sky. The wind had caught the palms now, and they whispered like spirits. He did not want to mouth empty platitudes.

He said, "The Mother of the Mountains told me there was darkness before me, in the depths, in the heights, if I did not turn back."

Fitzroy was silent for a long time. The winds gusted in the palms, and the waves danced on the shore, more loudly now. If he sat up to look he would probably see them full of brilliance, radiant like the viau in the arms of the goddess Aurelius and Elonoa'a had seen in their vision.

He was still chasing a viau.

He was the man from the proverb, who had gone looking for the sea.

(And he had found it. He had. He had.)

"Why didn't you turn back, Kip?"

Cliopher stared up at the radiant night above him, the stars in their glory, the living darkness like the whelm and murmur of the sea. He could feel tears gathering at the corners of his eyes. He breathed long, slowly, echoing the rhythm of the waves against the shore, the constant song of the island.

There were things he could not say, even to himself. But—

Oh, he still wanted them.

The sky was suddenly full of shooting stars streaking white-and-gold, as if the sky were a halo cloth shaken in the wind.

"She said she saw a shell on the other side," he whispered.

Fitzroy said nothing, but after a moment he reached out and took Cliopher's hand in his own.

They lay there, the fire between them, the night sky full of unknowable, unnameable stars, the viau flashing like flying fish across the waves, the crew of a comet singing distantly behind them, until at last they slept.

Or Fitzroy did. Cliopher stared at the sky for a long, long time.

CHAPTER FORTY-ONE
THE FIRE-POT

Eventually, the vaha was made.

Eventually, Elonoa'a sighed and said he had taught Cliopher everything he could, for now, for this ocean.

Eventually it was time to go.

Cliopher could not believe it.

~

He loaded the vaha with supplies, though he was warned that he would likely not feel much need to eat or drink as he travelled further into the Divine Lands.

Fitzroy gave him a piece of coral he'd shaped by magic into an elegant, smooth-sided lidded dish.

Cliopher took the object in his hands. They were sitting in their shelter, the afternoon of the day Cliopher would leave. Elonoa'a had told him he should leave at sunset, so he could set his ke'ea in practice for a full night before the rising sun showed him the accuracy of his navigation.

The dish, the bowl, was heavy and cool, the weight of it satisfying in his hands. The coral was a dully lustrous white, like the porcelain bowl in which Conju kept the black cowrie efela Cliopher had given him.

"It's a firepot," Fitzroy explained, when Cliopher had sat there in silence, running his fingers around the lip, the curving hollow, white dust on his hands, his heart overflowing as if he held his cupped hands in a spring of fresh water. "Tupaia said you wouldn't need one, for the flame of the Sun ..."

He hesitated a moment, and then he smiled at Cliopher, his face crinkling, his eyes full of that familiar glimmer of mirth. He looked—he looked like *himself*, all of himself, come finally into focus.

Then he said, his voice serene, threaded through with laughter, with concern, with *love*, "I thought you might like to take a fire with you."

Cliopher's breath hitched, but he was able to say, "Thank you, my l—Thank you, Fitzroy," in a tolerably composed manner.

"What a song I shall write of this," Fitzroy added, in a low voice, when Cliopher looked down once more at the pot in his hands. "Of you."

～

No one had ever had such assistance, pushing their canoe off the beach into the waters of a lagoon. Cliopher set his shoulder to the boat, with Fitzroy Angursell on one side and Elonoa'a and Aurelius Magnus on the other.

It was a few minutes before sunset. The shadows of the palm-trees and people on the beach were long and dark, the western sky brilliant red and blue as Cliopher's grass skirt, the eastern sky a deep royal blue like the bird-of-paradise's tail plumes.

Cliopher looked at the stars coming out, like lanterns lit in windows, held by wayfarers going before him.

The star-paths are singing.

The words stuck in his throat. Under his hand the vaha was quivering with the soft lap and pulse of the waves, the wind from the west. The wind stirred his hair, the line of feathers tied to the mast, the woven pandanus-leaf sail.

"May your ke'ea be clear and bright before you," Elonoa'a said, his stance and tone confident, secure, solid.

Cliopher had had to put on his court face, odd as it felt in this location, this company, to gird himself for the journey ahead of him.

But he had not lost that. His voice could still be calm, mild, ready.

"Thank you for your teachings, Elonoa'a," he said.

"Safe travels and fair winds," Aurelius said. His eyes were full of the same muffled grief Fitzroy had expressed, that sorrow of a leader asking someone to go on a long and arduous journey in their stead.

"I am glad to go where you cannot, Aurelius," he said.

Fitzroy looked at him intently, his eyes full of magic, brilliant as the sun touching the sea behind him. Cliopher stood with the warm water lapping against his thighs, half-turned from the island, half-turned to the open ocean, caught there by his—

By his fanoa's eyes, hands, smile.

He was allowed to use that word, in his mind, here where he stood, the star-paths singing for him, about to climb on board his vaha and set sail into a legend of his own.

He had never been able to go for himself. But for those he loved—

His Radiancy, Fitzroy, reached forward. He placed his hands on Cliopher's shoulders, and drew them together for a moment in the Islander way, forehead to forehead.

"East first," he murmured, his breath warm and sweet on Cliopher's face. "Then west and home. Come home to me, Kip. Come home."

Cliopher stood there for a moment, feeling Fitzroy's hands trembling on his shoulders, the words echoing deep into the vaults of his heart. Then Fitzroy took a step back, and his expression lit with a pure and splendid merriment, and he spoke the words Cliopher had spoken to him when Fitzroy left him behind in the Palace, uncertain when they would next see one another, save that all things would have changed when they did.

(And they had. They had.)

"Have fun."

~

He sailed east towards the sunrise.

Once past the fringing reef he was on the open ocean. There were no other islands visible before him, and when he turned to look back the island he had just left was gone.

He would not fear the return voyage. Elonoa'a had taught him the ke'e he should seek out, when he had reached the uttermost east and fulfilled his commission and turned once more westward and home.

The wind was steady from the west. He could lash the tiller after he set the sails, and trust that the vaha would continue on its course.

The first hour or so was filled with things like ensuring nothing had shifted going over the breakers by the reef, checking the lines and sails yet again, getting the feel for the vaha on this ocean.

Elonoa'a had given him his ke'ea, and the great stars in their unfamiliar patterns rose as the navigator had taught him.

~

He dipped his hand into the water. It was salt as tears.

~

He sailed east.

East first, then west and home.

That was the pattern of the *Lays*.

East first.

The vaha was easy under his hands, this vessel crafted by the Ancestors, the voice of Elonoa'a in his ears, the unknowable stars of Sky Ocean granted meaning and order by the great navigator's hard-won experience and observation.

Cliopher would have been lost within an hour of the first star's rising, if he had not had that.

But he did.

He did.

~

He dozed, waking at every minute variation in wind and current, eyes on the stars he could not name.

Once, so silently he did not know if he were awake or dreaming, a pure white fin whale surfaced beside him. She was enormous: it seemed to take forever as the long forehead crested the water until an eye, dark and wise and curious, looked at him.

Cliopher looked back, solemn and unafraid and dazed with sleep, with the sky, with the sea, with the solitude after such a long time in company, with the white whale on the black-and-silver water.

The whale blew once, and a fine spray of water fell onto Cliopher like a benediction. When he had blinked the water out of his eyes the whale was gone.

~

The sun rose, for a moment balancing like a star on the prow of his vaha.

Cliopher took a deep, relieved breath, for though he'd believed in Elonoa'a's skill with all the fibres of his being, with all the resolution of his soul, with all the logic of his rational mind, it was still ...

It was still *good* to have that faith confirmed.

But the sun rose precisely where it was supposed to, for the ke'ea was true.

~

It had been a long, long time since Cliopher had simply ... *been*.

He sang the *Lays*, and Fitzroy's songs, and the new-old tales and songs he had been learning from the crew of the *He'eanka*, and the ke'ea-chant Elonoa'a had taught him.

He had so much time to *think*.

He did not force his thoughts into disciplined assessment, consideration, doubt. He let himself remember all the long years of his service to his Radiancy, all the time they had spent together, all the stories he knew of Fitzroy Angursell, all the imaginations he had ever had of Elonoa'a and Aurelius Magnus, the reality of the two men.

~

The second night a flock of small dark birds, shadows against the stars in the sky and in the water, came circling around him.

They cried to one another, deep guttural sounds, somehow merry and wild.

They might be some form of storm petrel: small, swift, stout. They whirled around him once, twice, three times, and then they were gone and the world was once more the steady compass of the silver horizon and the steady wind and the sky and sky ocean mirroring each other so exactly.

~

He tended the embers in the firepot Fitzroy had made him, the coral dish warm in his hands, the embers lit from a fire Tupaia had made.

~

The third day he fell asleep heavily in the afternoon. He was not used to staying awake for so long; did not have the facility for attentive dozing that the great navigators of the past showed. It was said that Elonoa'a had sailed to the Isolates without faltering, discovering the islands when all the rest of his crew were asleep.

Cliopher had asked him, and Elonoa'a had promised the story on his return.

Cliopher slept, and dreamed.

His Radiancy—Fitzroy, Fitzroy, Fitzroy—stood on the star-island's beach not with Tupaia and Elonoa'a and Aurelius Magnus, but with Rhodin and Ludvic and for some reason, Cousin Louya. Cousin Louya was explaining her theories about sea turtles, and Fitzroy was nodding solemnly.

Rhodin and Ludvic were not wearing their guard uniforms, rather garments made out of ahalo cloth the colour of water. Their spears were tipped with points made of shells.

"It is because the sea was swallowed by the sky," Cousin Louya said earnestly. "Oh look! There's the Other Kip. What is *he* doing here?"

Cliopher turned, but it was not the Other Kip he had met in the other universe, but rather himself as a young man. He was dressed in the costume of a secretary before the Fall, and even in his dream he thought how he had never realized how silly the hat looked before.

The Other Kip came up to Fitzroy and started to say that *he* was not taken in by their disguises, thank you very much.

Fitzroy smiled sadly at him and began to list names.

"Those are the stars to cross the Wide Seas?" Rhodin asked Ludvic.

"If you don't have a boat," Ludvic affirmed.

Cliopher wanted to ask what possible use a ke'ea with no canoe was, but the wind changed then and he was buffeted by a rocky, choppy current. It felt like he was stumbling over his feet on a low stair, a lurch and then a catch and then another lurch.

He thrust himself out of the dream with a gasp, sitting upright. The wind was still in the sail, steady as the trades, but the outrigger and the hull of the canoe was juddering with the motion of his dream.

It was much less pronounced when he sat up, but he could feel it, the lurch and the catch and the other lurch.

Elonoa'a's voice came to mind, solemnly describing the currents the *He'eanka* had met with in the course of their journeys across Sky Ocean.

There is a current, he had said, *which seems to follow its own path, which is not to our good. You will know it by its rhythm: a lurch and a catch and another lurch, as if you are stumbling and about to fall. If you come across it, the thing to do is to turn* immediately *against it. It doesn't matter what other direction you are sailing,* you must *turn yourself counter to that current as soon as you encounter it.*

What happens if you don't? Cliopher had asked, for he was always curious.

But Elonoa'a had only shaken his head, tight-lipped, and reiterated his directions. Aurelius Magnus had come to him later, and said quietly that the *He'eanka* had met with that current before they had found him, and it had taken them a long, long way out of their way.

That current is no holy way, said Aurelius Magnus. *It leads to dark and troubled waters.*

That was enough, Cliopher told himself sharply. He had always been taught —*always*—to follow the guidance of the Ancestors.

("Who are we if we do not learn from those who have gone before us?" Buru Tovo had asked him more than once. And Uncle Lazo had smiled at him and ruffled his hair and said, in his quiet, thoughtful way: "Do you not hope that those who come after you will remember your name and what you have done? You honour our ancestors by remembering what they did and following their teachings.")

Cliopher unlashed the sail and swung the tiller so the boat swung out below him, skipping across the surface of the water. The wind was quartering the sail or barely that, and the vaha bucked and strained against facing head-on into that current.

He held the lines and the tiller grimly.

The sail pulled in his hands and the tiller strained away from him, but Cliopher gripped both, his mind on Elonoa'a, on Tupaia, on all his friends of the *He'eanka*, and of Aurelius Magnus waiting for him to return with a flame of the fire of the Sun, on Fitzroy waiting for him to come home.

"My way lies elsewhere," he snarled at the current. "I go towards the Sun."

The current seemed to redouble in strength, the boat ploughing down into waves that had not been there a moment ago, surging up crests that were not the steady cerulean blue of the past days but a livid grey.

And then he saw, caught in a whirling tangle of magic and water and what seemed to be netting of shadows, a sea turtle thrashing and lost.

He was growing dizzy with the motion, half sea-sick (he who had not been sick more than once or twice through all those typhoons across the Wide Seas), gripping onto the tiller even as the sail slackened and swung back towards him.

He ducked out of its way, but that was no good. He didn't want it uncontrolled, catching the wind when he wasn't ready for it.

Cousin Louya's earnest voice was in his ear: *The sea turtles are lore-keepers! Honour them!*

Cliopher would not have left anyone to that violent despair, that agony and possibility of drowning.

He followed the Ancestors, yes, but—

But he would not be himself if he did not help the needy before him, if he could do anything about it. It did not matter if it made the voyage longer, harder, more perilous—

He had never believed the ends justified the means.

The turtle thrashed and struggled, the wind and the current strained against his control of the sail, his arms pulled from their sockets with its strength and fierceness.

One hearth, one problem, one task at a time, and this was the task that had come before him. He could not know where it led, save being lost; but he held his island in his mind, one a star and one like a star, and in this little clear space of half a moment's thought, he made the decision he had always made.

It was terrible, that the turtle made no noise, no scream, no grunt. Just the heavy helpless motions of its flippers, its eye dull with panic and exhaustion.

Cliopher took a breath, one breath, and then he focused down, as he always focused down on the work in front of him.

He had been in storms before, cross-currents, kurakura. He had his ke'ea and his destination was the uttermost East, the easiest of all destinations.

He wrestled with the lines, the tiller, the vaha screaming against the water as the wind howled at the current. He heeled around hard, right against the current, the wind, until the sails slacked and boomed and the vaha slipped out of the choppy current and into the wheeling eddy that had caught the turtle.

He lashed the sail, the tiller, holding them firm against the wind, holding a course in a tight circle—how it worked he did not know, but he did not need to know, he had sailed through storm after storm in the Wide Seas, had lived a lifetime negotiating the conflicting and confused kurakura at court—he could do this.

He *would* do this.

He lashed a rope around his waist, grabbed one of his shell knives and as the boat came around, leaned out as far as he dared and slashed at the shadows binding the turtle.

They are lore-keepers, Kip! Honour them!

It was the dream Louya who spoke, but Cliopher could not do less for his cousin than he did for Rhodin.

The other Kip had said the other Louya was a seer, gifted by the sea, taught by the shamans.

All of *his* Louya's most comprehensible comments had been to do with the ocean.

"Ani, help me!" he cried, knowing she was not this water, this sea, this ocean made of star-stuff and shadows.

The shadows were tough and heavy, living as the tentacles of a great octopus.

The wind strained, and the rigging screamed.

Cliopher set his teeth and slashed hard, his shell knife bouncing off the turtle's shell with an unholy screech and a spray of sparks.

He lost the shell in his hand as he stared, shocked, at the sparks, his hands ringing with the blow.

But the shadows parted, and the turtle was suddenly gone, without a word or a whisper or a splash, and he spun around and around the eddy, lost.

It took him a long time to navigate out of the whirlpool, the wicked current, the doldrums that followed after.

A mist rose up, and hid the stars.

The wind was gone, silent; his sail hung limply, the streamer of feathers lank and lifeless.

The sun rose, refracted endlessly through the mist until he could see nothing but white clouds.

Cliopher let the vaha drift. He lay flat on the deck, listening to his heart race and his breath gasp and pant, his muscles spasming and cramped, his mind empty of thought and desire and hope.

Without a star, without the sun, without a wind, without a current, what was there?

~

His firepot needed tending.

Nothing else, perhaps, would have made him sit up, groaning with all the years of his life, and clumsily manoeuvre himself around the boat. He fed tiny bits of tinder to the embers until they glowed gently in their cocoons of ash, their bed of damp sand.

He sat there with the pot cradled in his lap, the warmth radiating into his cold and clammy skin.

And then, because he was Cliopher Mdang, and this was not where he stopped, he closed his eyes and listened with the fullness of his being until he felt the deepwater swells of Sky Ocean and knew his direction.

East meant nothing, in the silver haze of starlit fog, but Loaloa burned still in his mind, the hearth and harbour of his soul, and the star-island where he had left Fitzroy was there, angled across the currents, the anchorage of his heart and his journey.

He took one of the coals from his fire-pot and set it upon one of the unused casoa shells, cradled in a little nest of twisted fibres, and he blew on it gently until the fire caught.

So had the third son of Vonou'a done, when he lost his way in Sky Ocean.

Cliopher was no mage. He could not hear the wind calling him; he could not call a wind to his hand.

But he could whisper a secret to the fire, and offer it to the gods, and see what wind would come in response.

Nothing happened.

~

Nothing happened.

Cliopher sang the *Lays*.

He tended his fire, holding the shell in his hands, sheltering it against the damp fog.

He sang *Aurora*.

He held the fire-pot cradled in his lap, the steady warmth the stone upon which the world might turn, the strength that had held him as he re-rigged the world's sail and sent it along a new ke'ea.

He studied the deepwater swell until his breathing matched his rhythm, holding it against the wide wash of the sunrise, the sunset, until he could orient himself.

He waited for a wind.

~

Nothing happened.

He sang the *Lays*.

He sang Fitzroy's music, all the songs he knew.

He tended his fire.

~

A wind rose, and the fog parted, and he saw an island on the eastern horizon.

It was a low island, and a small one.

The irregular loop of the encircling reef enclosed an area no larger than the expanse of water in Tahivoa Lagoon, which Cliopher could not quite throw a rock across. Scattered along the reef were a string of islets, each of which was occupied by throngs of dark, booby-like birds. The birds all turned to stare at him as he passed.

They did not have scarlet feet, these boobies, nor the electric blue he'd seen in the Western Dairese species, but an intense, indisputable white, shocking against their black feathers. They were larger than the birds he knew, almost as tall standing as he was seated. Like all boobies it seemed as if they wore masks, their beaks and the area between their eyes the same leathery white featherless skin.

Their eyes were a paler gold than his Radiancy's, but just as bright and just as knowing, if as sombre as his darkest moods. The birds muttered like old men as he sailed slowly past their islets, heading for the only island in the group large enough to host trees.

The island was barely more than two yards above sea level. Cliopher used his rudder to shift direction between two outcroppings of bleached-white coral. Were there storms here, on this sea that was not water, this ocean that was also the sky?

He looked up, at the dizzying depths of reflected water-and-light, and had to swallow down vertigo. After so long in the blank fog he did not know how to take this brilliance; he felt as if he should be crouching down, hiding his face from the stars, the pitiless sun.

He did not need to land. Theoretically he could keep sailing, past this island, into the silent reaches of Sky Ocean.

He looked at his vaha, the sail taut in the wind, the water skimming below his feet where he stood on the platform between keel and outrigger. The white coral fire-pot sat snugly in its place.

Sailing past was not how the story went.

It did not, in fact, make a good story.

What a song I shall write of this. Of you, Fitzroy had said, and for all the things Cliopher had achieved in his life, for all the many honours his Radiancy had poured upon him, for all the reputation he had so slowly built for himself, he still had that longing, that yearning ...

He wanted his name to be sung in the *Lays*, with all that he had done an example to those who came after.

He wanted Fitzroy Angursell to write a song about him.

He wanted it to be a *good* song.

Cliopher turned the tiller and beached his vaha on the island with a quiet crunch and a sigh of water falling back.

He had forgotten how those first few moments off the sea were incomprehensibly unbalanced.

The discomfort passed eventually. He disembarked and tugged the vaha farther out of the water, ensuring a stray wave wouldn't capture his vessel and steal her for the sea's use. That was always the first rule of arriving at an island: *secure your boat*.

Second was *look around. Assess*, he might say: look, listen, taste, think.

There were no boobies on this island. The sand was unmarked by any footprints of bird or animal, not even the scuttling lines of a crab or the scoops of a turtle. Why the birds had not landed here he did not know. Two feet farther up from where he stood, the sand was garlanded with tiny white clamshells and even tinier garnet-red pebbles.

He stood beside his boat, breathing the air, assessing.

There was the faintest possible hint of smoke in the air.

His mind woke.

He did not move. He looked. Listened.

Look first. Listen first. Questions later.

The island was three dozen paces across and perhaps twice that again in length, with the cluster of vegetation at the centre blocking his view. The clear water rippled on the shore with the gentlest of motions, as still as if the wind had never blown here.

He picked up the tiny fire he had whispered his secrets to, cupping the shell in the palm of his hand.

The sand below the line of shells and garnet-red stones was smooth and damp, firm underfoot. Above the line it was dry, brilliant white; as he stood considering it, wondering where the smoke could possibly be coming from, he realized that there were no stones or shells above that line, either.

He had sung the *Lays* a thousand times, in that fog-bound doldrums.

There was a line in the third day about the sea-witch's efela, which she strung about the necks of those islands she had claimed as her own.

White shells and red stones edge the island that swallowed the sea, went the line. *Beware your step if you choose to cross; the sea-witch will trade what you want for what you have.*

It was, Cliopher thought, an ambiguous warning.

The *Lays*, which dealt mostly in history, said little else about the sea-witch, but there were tales he'd heard from his grandmothers when he was a little boy. His father's mother, far less of a fearsome matriarch than his mother's mother, had been full of warmth and sweets and fantastic stories.

He wished she were still alive so he could tell her that he had come to the country of stories, after all.

He'd been so snotty as a boy, so dismissive of the possible veracity of the tales, eager to hear them but absolutely certain they were nothing more than fiction.

"One day you'll see," his grandmother had said, tapping him on the nose while he crinkled it up in protest. "All these old stories have more truth in them than you think."

And she had told him how the sea-witch protected her home, which looked like a bush-material hovel on the outside but was as beautiful as a chief's house on the inside.

When he was older Cliopher had taken that as a lesson to remember that external appearances really didn't mean much.

It had been a good lesson, all in all.

"She has long, long nails," said his grandmother, tugging at his fingers to show how long they were.

"If her nails are so long," he had protested, "how can she do anything?"

"Foolish boys like you go knocking on her door asking her for the sun and the moon and all the stars on the sea, and she tells them to do her work for her."

"*I* wouldn't!"

"You would," said his grandmother, grinning at him. "Because if you didn't, you'd be turned into a big black booby, for a big booby you would be, asking the sea-witch for something and not doing what she told you in return!"

"*I* wouldn't!"

"You wouldn't?"

"I would do whatever she told me, and I would get the sun and the moon and all the stars on the sea, and bring them back home to you."

"No, no, that wouldn't do," his grandmother said, shaking her head soberly. "You'd have to do much more than that, to win the sun and the moon and all the stars on the sea—and where would I put them, anyway? And what would everyone else do, with no light?"

"We wouldn't *keep* them," he assured her. "We'd just *borrow* them for a while."

He hadn't understood then why she'd laughed as much as she had, before giving him a starfruit as 'all the star you can handle right now, my love', and sending him off to play.

The tiny fire crawled over the embers in the shell, a tingling warmth in his fingers.

He glanced at the multitudes of boobies crowded on the islets of the atoll, watching him with their bright eyes, muttering like old men, and for a moment the fantastic idea hit him that they looked just like the elders in the villages when Buru Tovo had taken the young Kip walking the Ring.

They had greeted every island, set each into the *Lays*, named them.

Buru Tovo had talked with the elders, the village leaders, the chiefs, tending communities, lighting fires, teaching those who wished to know how they could do so themselves.

Cliopher had asked for tales of Elonoa'a and Aurelius Magnus, and the three sons of Vonou'a.

He nodded respectfully to the boobies, and then he centred himself, checked once more that his vaha was safely out of the water, and stepped resolutely over the line of tiny white shells and tinier garnets.

Just out of sight of the waterline was a hut made out of bush materials that stood on white webbed feet. Cliopher strode forward. The feet quivered but did not move. The door was a dark curtain of bones, clicking and clacking as they swayed for a breeze he could not feel.

He had never said the words himself, but he knew what Buru Tovo had said, each time he had come to an island.

He looked down at the fire cupped in his hands, the white shell warm against his brown skin, and he took heart.

He was Cliopher Mdang of Tahivoa, tanà of the world, and he had a commission from his emperor to fulfill.

His voice rang out into the air, silencing the boobies in a great ripple of astonishment.

"Tanaea-te imalo! Moa'alani-ki imalo! Kifa'ana imai?"

CHAPTER FORTY-TWO
THE SEA-WITCH

An old crone with very long fingernails answered the door. She had eyes like beetles, black and glittering-green, and wore layers and layers of rags that might have been made of kelp, brown and green and a strange olive-grey, all glistening in the strange luminescence. The scent of smoke was stronger here, and something pungent, peppery, wild. Her mouth twisted in a scar of a smile.

"It is a long, long time since I heard those words spoken," she said.

Her voice was low and breathy, like the wind in the palms before the hurricane hit.

Cliopher bowed to her, hand over fist, as he had when he came unexpectedly before the Ancestors.

If she had a name his grandmother's stories had never given it, but there was a word in the old Islander tongue for addressing elder women to whom one was not related, and no one, perhaps, was as much of an elder as the sea-witch.

"Urumë," he said therefore, "I bring fire for your hearth." He lifted the shell towards her, the tiny fire burning like a winking eye. "I bring news of Sky Ocean, if you would hear it. Have you problems to bring before me?"

"Why do I need your fire, sailor-man? What news could you tell me that I have not heard? What problems could you possibly solve for me?"

The challenge rang in the air. Cliopher did not lower his hands, remembering many occasions when he had stood, some great symbolic object in his hands, as magic poured through him from the Sun-on-Earth on his high throne, separate from the world.

"I share the fire that was entrusted to me, as is my calling," he said. "I know the news of my own heart, if you have heard all the news of the sea. And perhaps you might trade me a problem to solve for an answer to a question of mine."

How do I go home shivered in his mind, the question he had been asking his whole life long.

She tilted her head, her eyes glittering. "You should ask for safe passage as well, sailor-man. Very well. I will trade the answer to your question if you do one thing for me."

"Yes," he said, prepared for this by all his grandmother's stories, all the tales he had heard from Fitzroy's pen, all the surety of the *Lays*.

"Come," she said, and let him into her hut. It had one room, small and dark and crowded with strange bundles and glass bottles full of murky liquids and all manner of pots and cauldrons and bones and shells and things Cliopher felt he probably ought not look too closely at. The sea witch closed the door behind him, thrusting him into a blind dimness but for the fire in his hands.

Silently, ceremoniously, he offered her the shell.

She laughed, low and breathy, the wind at the edge of the storm, the waves at the edge of the breakers, the deep rumble of an earthquake. "Ah, you're a canny one, sailor-man."

He did not move, did not speak, did not smile.

She took the shell, casually, easily, setting it on top of a great pile of skulls, whose gaping eye-sockets all seemed to watch him, catching the fire in their hidden hollows.

The sea-witch took his wrist with her hand, the long, horny nails digging into the soft flesh above his pulse-point. "I lost a golden bead in a pile of grains," she told him. "Find it for me."

"I do not see the grains, Urumë," he replied softly.

"Through here," she said, and thrust him through a doorway—the same one by which he'd entered? He stumbled, caught himself, and coughed on dust even as the door closed behind him with a decided sort of click.

Cliopher settled his breathing, shook out his hands, and as he had done so often before, surveyed the job before him.

The room was made of a dark brown wood and was very large. Perhaps half the size of the throne room in the Palace of Stars, he estimated absently, taking in the double row of tall, tall posts shaped like coconut palms, the carved fronds arches holding up the woven-thatch ceiling. Skylights shaped into the spaces between the arches provided the obvious source of illumination, but did not seem anywhere near bright enough to account for all the light available.

There was the door by which he had entered, and another at the other end of the long hall. Undoubtedly that would be locked as well, or if it wasn't he would fail at his task by escaping that way. Cliopher knew enough folk stories and fables to know that he would not like what he found if he shirked his task by that manner.

Not that he had ever been someone given to shirking his task.

He made one slow circuit of the enormous pile of corn in the middle of the room. He guessed it was perhaps twenty feet tall and twice that in diameter at the base, for a volume of ... over eight thousand feet cubed.

That was not a helpful thought. Sometimes he wished he wasn't any good with maths. His—Fitzroy would not have had that thought.

The pile was not solely of loose kernels, but was rather a mixture of stalks, leaves, husks, whole and broken ears, and multitudes of individual kernels. These seemed to be of a thousand different colours, but as he examined the pile more carefully, working out his plan, he saw that there were really only a dozen or so.

He picked up a handful of the loose kernels from where they'd spilled onto the floor, relishing the smooth, firm texture, the brilliant colours. He had known corn could be yellow or cream or dark red, but he hadn't known it could also be deep purple and bright lavender, turquoise-blue and navy, gold, caramel, ivory, maroon, blood-red, black, even a fine leaf-green. Not to mention spotted, striped, speckled. Some of the ears had all the colours mixed together. Some of the kernels were dented, some opaque, others shiny and translucent like glass beads.

So his task was to find the gold bead in the midst of the pile, was it?

No doubt if he were a proper hero on a quest, he would have somehow or other made friends with a finch or a mouse or a whole family of uncannily wise birds who would be delighted to do the sorting for him.

Fitzroy would have made such a friend.

Cliopher was not a proper hero, and the only creature he had assisted was a sea turtle, quite possibly the least useful animal for this task he could imagine.

The image of the sea turtle swimming its way into the heart of the pile flashed into his mind, and he laughed with pure, absurd, delight in the idea.

The turtle was nowhere in sight, whether to assist or be offended at his laughter.

And anyway, this was *Cliopher's* task, and there were some things that could not be delegated.

The only difference between sorting through this pile for the golden kernel it held and diving deep into the Archives looking for some specific detail to solve one of the world's problems was that he *knew* the golden kernel was actually here.

And so he set to work.

Cliopher was no Oyinaa, but anyone who spent any time along the Ring learned at least the basic method of making a basket. It was too vital a skill to leave to the experts; too often one would need a basket for fish or yams or taro, or for shells or coconuts or water, or for any of the other million things one might wish to carry from one place to another.

He did not know the thousands of weaves or patterns or their significance, nor more than a handful of the most common of the hundreds of materials with which an expert could weave any shape imaginable. But then, he did not need to know all those things. He had his own lore, his own traditions, and enough of that vital skill to be going on with.

He walked around the pile again, looking at all the different kinds of corn. He seemed to recall, from some visit to a corn-growing region of Dair, that the different colours had different flavours and uses.

The least he could do was what the sea-witch had tasked him with.

He wanted a *good* answer to his question: she would match what he offered her, the way of every challenge-song in his tradition.

Cliopher had done enough impossible deeds in his day, in his own quiet and bureaucratic fashion, to know that the exact parameters of the job as laid out were never enough for the desired final result.

Thus he pulled out all the stalks and husks and leaves he could easily reach. The stalks were tougher than he'd expected, but he bent and worked the stems until the fibres were flexible enough to interweave without simply snapping.

He did not have any tools, which annoyed him; a knife or a shell would have made this easier. After a bit of searching he managed to find an ear that had dried out a little more than the others, leaving an almost sharp point. With this he was able to burrow a hole in the middle of three of his stalks. The stalks were about twelve feet long, which would give him an approximately three by four foot cylinder.

He carefully did not deliberately figure out the volume of such a cylinder, but some inner voice pointed out gleefully that it would be somewhere around a hundred and ten or a hundred and twenty cubic feet, which meant the pile would need something like sixty-five baskets.

It wouldn't be that many, he told himself, because he was using the stalks and husks to make the baskets, and that would reduce the volume somewhat.

He started with a simple four-way cross, pushing two of the stalks into the holes he had made in the centre of the other two. The slath thus formed, he spent another interminable period twisting the husks until he had something like the beginnings of a rope. This rope he used to spiral around the centre, locking the slath into place. After three turns he splayed the six stalks to form an evenly radiating star, recalled that if he didn't have an odd number of rods he would have problems alternating his weavers, and eventually remembered that he could add a second rope to twist the alternate direction.

Then it was a simple matter of weaving each rope over and under, under and over, holding the stalks to keep them evenly spaced, adding in leaves as necessary to extend his rope, until he had the three-foot base.

Six upright strakes would hardly form a tight weave. He collected some more stalks, stripping the leaves and the corn for later, before he worked the ends until they would bend to form the uprights. He then inserted two on each side of the stalks he'd used for the base, bending them carefully upright and gathering them there with another twist of leaves.

And *then* he could go back to the stalks, utilize some of his impatience to stamp on them until the fibres started to split and he could use his pointy ear of corn to split them into something like lathes.

And then he wove the uprights, and after some length of time he did not want to contemplate he had a single basket made.

He reminded himself that he had nothing else to do, just at present, and returned to his task.

◇

Seventeen baskets later, the pile was looking somewhat lopsided from his ransacking it for stalks and his hands were aching from the unaccustomed work. (Cliopher had always rather admired the basket-weavers, but now he was impressed at their physical fortitude. Bending all that material was no joke.)

He was desperately thirsty. He made a full circuit of the hall, swinging his arms to loosen his shoulders, but there was nothing in it but the pile of corn.

He sighed, wishing vaguely for the helpful mice, the uncanny birds, even the sea turtle—surely its flippers could be of *some* use? They were able to dig holes for their eggs, after all—and made one more basket, this one more of a scoop. And then he started sorting the kernels by colour.

~

This was, he might have admitted to Fitzroy, something he actually enjoyed.

There was something unutterably soothing about taking a muddled pile and turning it into *order*. He had done it metaphorically so many times—his whole career —to do it now, so physically, with such immediately apparent result, was deeply gratifying.

He had half-consciously made an almost-correct rainbow with his initial pass, only the pink and the black kernels out of order. After enough passes that the bottoms of each basket were fully covered this discrepancy irritated him enough to lug the pink kernels all the way around the pile to the other side, where they belonged. Rather than sliding everything over to even out the circle—he had spaced them more or less evenly around the pile—he decided the open space was where he would put the stems and husks as he found them.

It was meditative, this process. He dipped his scoop into the pile and walked around his circle, picking out all the yellow kernels, all the orange, all the red; the crimson, the black, the deepest purple, the lavender, the rosy-pink; the speckled and spotted and striped all went into their own basket; and then it was navy, and turquoise, and green, and a pale straw-yellow, and rich caramel-gold, and ivory-cream, and finally a glassy pure white.

~

He was perhaps a third of the way through the pile when he found the golden bead.

He eyed it curiously, then tucked it away in a fold of husk in the waist-band of his grass skirt and kept going.

~

Some time later—was he halfway through? The pile had collapsed and even Cliopher's inner mathematician had no desire to work out the volume left before him —the door to the hall opened. Cliopher was singing the *Lays* to himself, and was on the fourth day of them, so it had been ... a while.

A while, yes, he would go with that.

He paused politely when the door opened, smiling a greeting at the sea-witch who shuffled in. She was clutching something to her chest. She peered at the pile and then at him, and said in a croaking voice, "There's water."

He was so grateful for this consideration that he stumbled over his words thanking her for the water. She cackled and retreated out the door, locking it behind her, as he drank deeply. He was not certain if he'd ever had water that tasted so refreshing before, not even when he'd been shipwrecked on islands after a storm at sea.

It wasn't until he found the second kernel, deep in the heart of the mound, that he realized he had forgotten to tell the sea-witch he had found the first one.

～

He needed forty-three baskets in the end, once all the excess stalks and husks and so on were stacked neatly in bundles to one side.

The husks reminded him of the women's wealth people made along the Eastern Ring. Those were bundles of specially prepared dried banana leaves, which were used for mortuary ceremonies and to make some forms of grass skirts.

Even though he believed corn husks were not valued in the same way, he wasn't sure, and so he gathered them together in case they were needed. Who knew what customs were practiced here in this island in the midst of Sky Ocean? The sea-witch might be in the stories his grandmother had told him, but that did not mean she was of, or only of, his culture.

There were whispered stories about what the sea-witch did with those adventurers who failed at her tasks and became the great black birds huddled in their throngs. Some tales said that she sent them to dive after those who died at sea, bringing their spirits home to the Ancestors.

You did not wish to die a traitor and have them sent after you. But a clean death to the sea? That was considered a sweet death, cradled in the bosom of Ani, sung home by the waves.

His last job was to build a rough broom and sweep all the chaff and loose kernels into a pile. Cliopher took his time over that job, glad to move his arms in a different motion, poking his corn-husk besom into the corners behind the pillars. In one he found three blue kernels and a third golden one.

He put the golden kernel in the husk envelope with the other two, placed the blue kernels in their basket, and considered his pile of sweepings. His shoulders and back ached, and his hands felt as if he'd wrung them in a laundry mangle. He massaged them slowly, staring at the pile.

But another thing he was proud of was that he did not leave jobs unfinished, and cleaning up at the end was always the last important (and always, always, the most tedious) part of the task. And so he fashioned yet one more basket to use as his dustbin, filled it with some difficulty—he could have done with a board to use as a pan, he grumbled to himself as he scooped up the chaff with his hands and two outspread corn husks—and finally set his broom aside.

The jug of water was not only miraculously refreshing but also miraculously refilling, for each time he had drained it he returned to find it once again full. In the strange way of this place he was not hungry, nor did he need to relieve himself of all that water; but he was thirsty, and was glad to drink.

He took a long draught and surveyed the results of his labours with a certain pride. The stout baskets with their beautifully pigmented kernels stood in their rainbow array. The stalks were bundled to one side, easy to transport, and the husks in their own parcels, ready for their next use. Even the broom and dustbin were satisfying in their own ways.

"Very good," he said, massaging his hands again, and clapped smartly at the door to let the sea-witch know he was done.

The crone surveyed the baskets, the bundles, and most especially the broom.

Finally she turned to him. "And did you find the kernel, in the end?"

Cliopher reached for the little corn-husk packet and presented it to her with the bow and gesture he would give when passing a tithe-offering to his Radiancy. She took the packet in her knobbly, long-nailed hands, and unfolded it so the corn husk balanced on the palm of her left hand. The three golden kernels glittered; so did her eyes.

She poked at the kernels with her right index finger, whose nail was a yellow horn, three inches long, with a twist in the grain. It was a very distinctive physical characteristic, but it still surprised him that his grandmother had known to speak of it, but not the sea-witch's glittering-green eyes, or the white bird's feet of the hut, or the garments seemingly made of kelp.

The sea-witch regarded him. Cliopher had the uncomfortable sensation that she knew exactly what was going through his mind. He smiled at her, his mild, inoffensive bureaucrat's smile, and she cackled aloud.

"Why didn't you stop when you found the first one, I wonder, hmm?"

Cliopher had never backed down before Prince Rufus of Amboloyo on a matter of principle, and he would not back down before the sea-witch, either. "My grandmother always told me that 'half-done is easily undone'."

"Oh, very easily," the sea-witch replied, scuttling closer and closer to him. He did not back down, nor let his expression shift to discomfort, not even when her neck seemed to elongate so that she could thrust her face directly at his. Her breath was cool and smelled like fresh seaweed thrown up on the sand, all briny and slightly rotten and more than slightly fishy.

She waited there, breath on his face, eyes meeting his from too-close a distance. Her hands came up and grasped his elbows, those long horny nails digging into the soft flesh on the back of his arms. For a wild moment Cliopher was suddenly reminded of his Buru Tovo, how he always smelled of dried fish, and then he chastised himself for his discourtesy, and bent his forehead to meet the sea-witch's in the ancient Islander greeting.

Her skin was velvety-smooth, though a few stray hairs tickled the bridge of his nose. She held him there for a moment. Cliopher was not sure if anyone would ever believe him that he had touched foreheads with the sea-witch.

Of course, that was assuming he would get home and be able to tell them anything.

The sea-witch released him and stepped back, her neck retracting as she did, like a turtle recoiling into its shell. Cliopher felt oddly discombobulated. Most of that was the mortification of missing the social cue for the gesture; but some of it was ... something else.

"They should send grown men on quests more often," the sea-witch said, giving him a deeply unsettling smile. "I had forgotten I had lost these other two beads, you see. Now, what shall I give you in return ...?"

Cliopher hoped the instinctive shiver that washed over him at her words was not visible. Her eyes glittered.

The sea-witch unfolded her left hand again. In her palm were the three golden beads. She poked one with her long index nail. "One for the answer to your question. One for ... good advice. And the third ..." She met his eyes again, and he *knew* she was seeing straight into his mind, his heart, what the poets called his soul.

For one utterly helpless moment he was entirely in her power. She had only to speak the word, and he would be one of those white-masked black boobies, muttering over their follies on the islets that followed after the sea-witch's home. One word, and he would be undone, lost forever.

"Not even one," the sea-witch crooned.

Her voice was not in his ears but in his mind, which was crashing away into word-lessness, into an uneasy ease, the human dissolved away with the colour of his eyes.

Would he still go to the Ancestors? Would they accept him, after this?

"So proud," the sea-witch's voice whispered, slinking around inside him. "And yet you do not think your lord would come seeking after you?"

His Radiancy, the Lord of Rising Stars, the Sun-on-Earth, who always supported him, the strong pillar to which Cliopher could set his back, the stone that does not move, on which he could set his foot, and thereby change the world ... Fitzroy Angursell, who was not on this quest because he had already been to the House of the Sun, and drunk honey-mead there.

His fanoa, who had bid him come home.

Cliopher sank to the floor in an ungainly heap. But he was still human, those were his feet and his hands and if he were weak as a babe at least he was not one of those black boobies, lost to himself and to all the mortal worlds. He stared at the sea-witch, who gave him yet another unsettling smile.

"I think I like you, my patient fire-starter. Would you not care to stay with me?"

He nearly started sobbing when she spoke out loud and not in his mind. He lifted his hand to bite his fist. All his muscles were trembling with exhaustion.

He worked to speak for several moments before his voice would utter forth. He had never been so glad to hear the sound of his own voice, no matter how it was quavering and weak. "I thank you, Urumë, but I seek something I may find at the House of the Sun, and my way home thence."

"Oh, the things you might ask for, for finding that third golden bead I had lost. It is precious to me."

Cliopher looked steadily at her, for all he was sitting akimbo on the floor. He had made his offers: it was up to her to return the trade.

The sea-witch tilted her head, very like a bird. "One for sorrow, two for joy ..." she said obscurely. "But the third, oh, the third is for a mystery. Come, fire-starter, come away and rest the night in safety, and in the morrow I shall give you your mete rewards."

Cliopher could not walk, and his pride was humbled enough by her insights that he was willing to crawl. He did not get far before he fainted.

CHAPTER FORTY-THREE
NUA-NUI

He woke from his swoon to find himself on a sleeping platform in a room that could have been from any traditional Islander house. Everything was eerily reminiscent of being home on Loaloa, sleeping in his great-uncle's house as he learned the lore.

When he crawled out the doorway he was almost certain he would find himself in the village.

But he did not. He was still on the improbably tiny islet, outside the bird-footed hut. There was no sign of the sea-witch.

Cliopher walked down to the shore, reassured beyond measure that his vaha was still drawn up on the sand. He did not try to cross the protective line of white shells and blood-red garnets, instead turning to follow the shore around.

The motu was no bigger than he'd seen it on arriving. It stood to one end of an irregular loop of reefs and islets, all of which were filled with the crowds of muttering black boobies. They watched him as he walked past them, their pale eyes keen and sorrowful. They reminded him too much of his Radiancy's eyes, in the long years of work, when his Radiancy had asked for peace and Cliopher had, at first, been able only to bring him hope.

He was glad when he came to the outer side of the motu, even though that meant he was looking out onto the impossible vistas of the Sky Ocean.

He breathed deeply. There was still that faint wisp of smoke in the air, and something richer, more savoury. Grilling fish, he identified after a moment, the scent so familiar he almost couldn't name it. His stomach rumbled loudly. Embarrassed, he pressed his hand flat on his belly, though no one was around to see him but the distant boobies.

The sea-witch cackled from directly behind him. He jumped, sure she had not been there a moment before, and she gave him one of her unsettling grins.

"So proud and so fine," she said, advancing towards him. He stood his ground, ready this time to give her the Islander greeting, but she instead reached out with her hand and brushed her long, long nails down the muscles of his torso. His skin twitched and shivered involuntarily.

"Such a handsome man," she murmured, her hand rather lower than Cliopher liked, from a sea-witch so early in the morning. She cackled at his response, patting his hip before finally letting go. "Not so old as all that, eh?"

He blushed fiercely, and she gave him a smile that any of his elder female relations might have produced.

"Come," she said, clicking her nails. "Break your fast, and then away. It is a long sail yet to the House of the Sun."

~

She gave him grilled fish, which relieved him, for he was not sure he could have borne accepting pork from the sea-witch. Not when the only cannibal of his acquaintance had informed him that human flesh was called 'long pig'; not when he knew only some of the stories of what the sea-witch had done.

Most of them had to do with turning foolish men into black boobies when they failed in her tasks, but there were other stories.

"Oh yes, many stories," she said, answering the thought rather than any words Cliopher had spoken aloud. "Some of them are so. Some of them might be so. Some of them will be so. And some ..." She cackled, high and wild. Out on the islets the boobies shifted and muttered more loudly, their heads weaving back and forth. "Some of them are not so at all."

"Thank you for the fish, Urumë," Cliopher said.

"All done?" She clapped her hands, and the banana leaves they had been using as plates shrivelled up and blew away, the fish skin and bones tumbling with them. Only the heads and tails remained, still silvery in the light.

Cliopher did not ask what she'd kept them for, and very much hoped it was soup stock.

She led him to his vaha, which was just as he'd left it, except that the house had walked down the beach to squat beside them.

The sea-witch squatted down between her house and the boat, just on the inside of the line of shells and stones. Cliopher followed suit, resting back on his heels. He arranged the fibres of his skirt to fall more decorously, glad to see the reds and blues and bronzes as bright as when Fitzroy had first coloured them. He lifted his hand to touch his efela. He was reassured by the familiarity of his efela ko, the warmth of the phoenix feather curled into the sundrop cowrie.

"And so, the trade," the sea-witch said, soft as the sands rubbing against his feet. He turned his full attention on her, dropping his hands to rest on his knees. He wished he had his writing kit in his hands.

"No need to write," she said contemptuously. "Are you not an Islander? Do you not sing the ways of your people?"

"This is not our sea, Urumë," he replied.

"So polite!"

He waited respectfully. The sea-witch, for all that it was his Varga grandmother who had told him the stories, reminded him much more of his mother's mother, the great matriarch of the Mdangs. She had been a short woman, short and plump, able to command attention as easily as his Radiancy.

Cliopher had loved her, deeply. No one wanted to get on her bad side; she could not turn you literally into a booby, but metaphorically ...

The fleeting thought came that it had been the difference in how Astandalan culture treated elder women that had been his downfall, those first few attempts at the exams to enter the bureaucratic service.

"Aye, you're a sight more courteous to an old crone than many of those young men who stumble on me," the sea-witch said. A certain biting amusement was in her voice. Cliopher could not stop himself from glancing at the black boobies at the next islet over. The sea-witch laughed; all the boobies fell silent.

"I like you," she declared. "Your mother raised you well, and your grandmothers too. Not a lot of men can say the same. And what of your fathers and forefathers?"

Islander culture was matrilineal: names and lineages passed down the female line.

From his father Cliopher had learned to love and fear the sea in equal measure. He remembered going out to fish with his father, being shown how to knot a net, how to sail a small boat, being told stories of the sea.

He had seen his father drowned, brought home in silence, the flags lowered and the sails booming too cheerfully.

His grandfather on that side had been Kindraa, making him some distant cousin many-times-removed of Bertie's. (Distant enough not to count, when the Mdangs reckoned their relations and worked out degrees of consanguinity for acceptable marriages.) He had died when Cliopher was in his teens. What he remembered of that old man (was he so old? He could hardly have been much older than Cliopher was now, could he?) was him singing Kindraa voyaging chants, the names of the winds.

It was he who had taught Cliopher his first words in Islander, enough that when he was sent to Loaloa after his father's death he had been able to greet his kin there and understand when he was offered food and water.

His most vivid memory of his grandfather involved his father, come to think of it. Cliopher had been eight or nine at most, precocious and as yet unfocused. One day his father and grandfather had taken him out in his grandfather's boat—his grandfather was also a fisherman—to Pau'lo'en'lai, the Island of the Dead, to make offerings to their ancestors.

It was the first time he had been considered mature enough to go there. He did not understand what death was, not really: none of his close relations had yet died, and though he understood the words, he did not know what they meant.

They had run up onto the shore of the island. Pau'lo'en'lai was of the same volcanic stone as Mama Ituri, the mother volcano of the Vangavaye-ve, and quite a large island. It did not have much in the way of accessible beaches: on the outer side it formed one of the walls of the Ring, steep cliffs thronged with seabirds. On the bay side was the one beach between stony outcroppings, which led back to a kind of low plateau. This was kept cleared by those who tended the stone houses; behind and beyond it was a jungle that no one entered.

There was a monolith at the end of the beach to mark the boundary between the living and the dead. Only those who served or sought death went past it. Everyone else left their offerings at the stele, in baskets designed according to their family patterns. The shamans would come and take them and place them in the open mouths of the stone houses, where the bones of the dead were laid.

Cliopher had found it eerie and uncomfortable. His father and grandfather had bracketed him as they walked up the beach to the stele. There were few such massive stone works in the Vangavaye-ve, and none that Cliopher had seen before; he did not know then what lay under the floating docks and houses of Gorjo City. He would later hear of the stone monuments of the other islands, even see some of them himself. But that was the first time he had ever seen stone carved in Islander patterns.

The stele was a column of basalt, perhaps twenty feet high. It was carved like a ngali staff, twelve spiralling bands to represent the twelve ships that had first reached the Vangavaye-ve and settled there. His grandfather said it marked the spot where the first man to land had died, and that it was the model for the ngali staffs thereafter. A ngali staff was the emblem of leadership, used by the paramount chiefs in the past, who were reminded each time they looked on it of the twelve original ships of the voyagers, and that death could come at any moment.

They had stopped at the stele, and his grandfather said, "Look. Do you see the stone houses?"

They were like longhouses out in the villages, but Cliopher did not yet know that. What he saw were huge warehouse-like constructions made out of blocks of basalt he could not imagine anyone moving. He counted twelve, arranged in a fan whose centre was the mountain.

"They have their backs to us," he said.

"We follow behind them," his grandfather had replied. "They go ahead. Never forget that!"

"Good enough," said the sea-witch.

Cliopher startled badly, nearly losing his balance. He put his hand out, touching the shoulder of the sea-witch. "My apologies, Urumë," he said when he realized what he had done. He could not help but notice that what looked like seaweed also felt like seaweed: cool, slimy, rubbery.

"I am known as the *sea*-witch," the crone said, that sharp amusement threading through her voice again.

"Yes, Urumë," Cliopher replied, knowing he was once again blushing.

"So your father and your grandfather were fishermen, fire-maker. Hunter and wind-speaker, eh?"

Neither had studied the lore intensely, so far as he knew. But he had not known to ask them before they died, and did not know much of who they had been to themselves.

"Few of you know much of that," the sea-witch said. "You hold fire in your hands and hardly know the sound of your own voice in your ears. No matter that! You will learn, or not, in time." She leered at him. "Best be on your way, my lad, if you don't want me to change my mind!"

He did not move. There was an unfinished challenge between them, and it was her turn to answer.

"Ah! So polite! Three golden beads did you collect for me, didn't you? One for sorrow, two for joy, and three for a mystery." She clicked her fingers, the long nails clacking, but nothing seemed to happen.

Cliopher waited patiently, as if through some courtier's delicate innuendoes before the negotiations proper could begin.

She cackled. "I like you, yes I do! Are you sure you won't stay here with me a trifle longer?"

"I am sure it would be an experience to make a story," he replied politely, "but I am sent to the House of the Sun."

"Very well, then, my fine man. Sail out the channel, yonder, and keep your back to my island until you meet an albatross. Follow him—only him, do you hear?—where he leads you."

The sea-witch picked up one of the red stones from the beach. Cliopher accepted it graciously, wondering silently (but apparently *clearly*) what it signified. It was seemingly the same as all the other red stones on the beach.

Seemingly.

"So many questions, and so polite!"

"My great-uncle told me to look and listen first."

"You are allowed to ask questions at some point," the sea-witch replied tartly.

Every story Cliopher had ever heard made it clear one should not question the gods, among whose company he certainly was inclined to class the sea-witch. Her powers were perhaps not so widespread as those of Ani, goddess of the sea, but they were not trivial.

"No," the sea-witch murmured. She reached forward and traced her hand in a spiral over Cliopher's heart, her long nails tickling his skin. "One for sorrow, two for joy, and three for a mystery."

Cliopher felt something cool and wet twist itself around his torso. He hoped his face did not show his anxiety over what exactly the sea-witch had just done.

"No telling what you might meet, sailing across this ocean," she said, "and I do not like keeping debts unpaid."

He glanced despite himself at the boobies, and she laughed again, her cackle high and loud.

She squatted down and dug with her hands in the sand. Cliopher watched as she cleared away the dry surface sand and dug down—not until she hit damp sand, nor coral rock, but until she came to a thin layer of some silvery liquid that he did not think was water, though he knew that there was a layer of fresh water underneath an atoll.

"Mm, in some waters," the sea-witch replied. She reached behind her and drew a dry gourd from some invisible location, which she used to scoop up the silvery liquid. She then proceeded to sprinkle this all over Cliopher's vaha, as if she were a priestess sparging it in the course of the ceremony.

"Not so far off," she agreed, coming back to scoop up more water and continuing to anoint the boat until it glittered wherever the water had landed. "Good enough," she declared eventually, once she'd thrown water in a silvery spray all up the sail, even to the still-bright feather pennant at the peak of the mast. "That should see you to your destination, by the albatross's route, but do be careful not to get the sail wet with salt water!"

He regarded her silently, trying to keep his mind clear of any questions bar the one standing huge before him, which was how these were trade goods.

"One," the sea-witch said, touching him on the nose with her horny yellow nail. "The stone of memory, for I do not forget, and neither shall you." She tapped him again on the nose. "Two. Safe passage across the sea no one may cross alone, until the salt water touches your sail."

"I'll endeavour not to capsize it," he replied solemnly.

"Human endeavours will only take you so far, fire-tender-me-lad," she said, her mouth twisting in her sardonic smile, her eyes glittering like the sheen on a beetle's wing. "And three. A gift, for that third golden bead I had thought I lost, which will be a surprise to you and to many others."

He could not prevent the shiver that rose along his spine.

She cackled. "Ah, I look forward to what you do with it! It's been long and long since someone won a boon from me, sailor-man! No one has brought a fire to my hearth in many a day, or news of such a love burning in the heart and mind of a mortal man, or completed a task I set him."

He glanced unwillingly at the white-masked birds watching him.

"Aye," she said, "that is not your fate."

He did not believe in fate. Only patterns, and choices, and consequences.

The sea-witch cackled. She beckoned him to lean forward for the traditional greeting, forehead to forehead, then surprised him by adding a sudden messy buss of a kiss to his cheek.

"Couldn't resist such a handsome man!" she cried, patting his cheek. "Now, be off with you before the day turns!"

～

He threaded his way through the channels of the barrier reef, focusing on negotiating the surges of the ocean-side breakers. Once in the open ocean he settled himself with a deep breath and turned to align himself on the sea-witch's house. From here you could not see anything of the white feet, and it looked like a derelict mound of palm fronds, someone's abandoned hut.

When he turned to look again out to sea, there was a great albatross in front of him. It gave him an entirely dismissive once-over, as cynical and judgmental as the starchiest aristocrat at the Palace, then uttered a low screeching cry that echoed all over the sea and set all the boobies yammering madly behind them.

"Good to meet you, too," Cliopher muttered, setting his sail to follow the bird as best he could with the wind from the north and the great bird heading east.

～

The ocean, the sky, the sky ocean ...

On this side of the sea-witch's atoll it was a deeper colour. Every time he glanced at the water (the sky) sidelong it was a bright sapphire, brilliant as the stones at the edges of the ceiling of the throne room of the Palace of Stars.

When he looked at it directly it was a sombre flat dark blue, so that he kept looking for storm clouds that were never there.

The wind filled the sail.

∿

The white albatross had a wingspan longer than his vaha, and a beak that surely could have stabbed his heart out if it had so chosen.

∿

Albatrosses, Cliopher knew vaguely, flew thousands of leagues each year. He had even heard someone claim that they could spend years aloft, sleeping on the wing, dipping down to fish the surface before rising again on one smooth arc.

He had always wondered how anyone had determined this. Had someone followed one, patiently noting its behaviour?—The thought made him laugh. He could be persistent and stubborn and a fool in his passions, but that was not one of them.

Would it have been better, he wondered, if he had followed an albatross for the sheer desire to know and understand the bird, rather than on a perilous journey to the House of the Sun?

The albatross soared in a mesmerizing pattern. It made arcs as if it were a sailboat tacking across the sea, except that its tacks were not horizontal but angled: first up into the wind, then a smooth slanting turn to leeward, down again nearly to the water's surface, sometimes even disappearing between the troughs as it made another curve, this one to windward, and up again to curve again leeward, and so on endlessly.

Amazingly, it had only flapped its wings once before setting off. Cliopher was having to work much harder to tack back and forth across the wind in pursuit, and he was much slower. So much slower that he feared he would lose the bird entirely if the waves grew much higher. Or the sky darker; it was getting alarmingly close to sunset.

(The sun was going down behind him; the wake of its light rippled as he tacked back and forth across it.)

The albatross seemed to be aware of its task, for just as he feared he had lost it entirely it circled back. If possible it looked even more disdainful.

"I'm sorry," Cliopher said, wiping his brow and wishing he could leave the tiller and sail for just one moment, but the wind was too strong and the bird's flight pattern just uncertain enough he had to strain to keep aware at all times. "I can't sail up and down the wind like you!"

The albatross gave him a jaundiced stare. Its beak was bright pink, and it had strange tubular nostrils; Cliopher wondered what they were for.

"Really, I'd love to try," he said, thinking of its beauty and the mesmerizing glory of its flight, the way it soared so dynamically with the wind, windward to leeward, up and around and down and around and up and—

The albatross cried out again, in a voice that made his hair stand all on end. Cliopher stared at it: it was suddenly far too close to him, making it obvious that its wingspan was indeed wider than the vaha was long, at least fourteen feet. It swirled around him, looking most aggrieved that it had to flap its wings again, and positioned itself directly in front of the canoe. In the strange gloaming light of the sunset it was nearly the colour of the pearlescent stone lights in the Palace.

The wind gusted madly in all directions, and he was sure he heard the sea-witch cackle. He was too busy with holding the sail, which was quartering the wind and bucking his control, and with the tiller that suddenly lost its gripping power, but then there was a sudden tingling rumble vibrating through the wood of outrigger and keel, and the tiller came alive in his hands and the sail thrummed happily, perfectly, taut.

He was nearly thrown backwards overboard, for with no more ado than that the ship had lifted out of the water and was indeed following the albatross's path.

Up twenty feet windward, curve to the leeward—adjust the sail so it catches the wind—swoop down to the surface, curve again with the speed of the descent, gather strength as the wind once again fills the sail—

After a dozen scrambling curves he realized it was the rhythm of the Kindraa songs he just remembered his grandfather singing, and the words came from somewhere deep in his memory, buried beneath all the conscious learning of the *Lays* and all that came after, and he sang them out and matched his motion to the chants, and suddenly he was no longer breathless and tense but everything was smooth and steady. The albatross looked indisputably smug.

From this angle, as he followed it up and down the wind, it looked just like the constellation of Nua-Nui, the Great Bird, who pointed the way to the southern celestial pole and was one of the most significant guides in the night sky.

~

Beneath him, the waves foamed across a thousand reefs, a maze of coral, impassible.

~

The sun—the Sun? Was that great flaming orb truly a person? Could Cliopher *truly* sail to his house in the uttermost east and bargain for a flame of his fire?

He touched his efevoa, bound now with strands of fibre from his skirt. The garnet the sea-witch had given him was not something he wanted to lose, but he had neither the time nor the tools to form a bow-drill to pierce it.

He could have taken the time, could have chipped a flake off his efela ko's obsidian pendant, could have dallied there on the Island that Swallowed the Sea, and been, perhaps, himself swallowed.

Fitzroy had told him that such choices could be unexpectedly permanent, here in Sky Ocean, and Fitzroy Angursell would know.

Thus Cliopher had worked the garnet pebble into the hollow of the sundrop cowrie, where it nestled against the downy phoenix feather, catching a glow of warm firelight when he tilted the shell.

It was really only the furled coil at the base of the cowrie that was large enough for the pebble to fall out. He'd wrapped the fibres from his skirt around the shell, red and blue and bronze, the colours of Zunidh, of the sunset, the sunrise, home.

The stone felt heavy around his neck, against his throat, for all its minuscule size.

∼

If half his nightmares were of drowning, a goodly portion of them began with being in a small boat at sea.

They usually went like this: he would be sailing along happily, absorbed in the small actions involved in sailing open ocean. He would usually be singing, and he was, in the dreams, nearly always oblivious to the way the weather was changing.

He would look up when the light changed to discover it was far too late.

∼

He was sailing along in the albatross's wake: upward, down, windward, lee, tacking at an angle to the waves. The albatross was a luminous white both by day and night, and never rested.

Cliopher had more work to do to manage the vaha than it seemed the albatross had to manage its own flight, for it never flapped its wings, merely shifted side to side as it twisted against the air, whereas Cliopher had to manage tiller and sail to do the same.

He grew tired but couldn't rest. He had to follow the albatross; he was only grateful to the sea-witch that she had done whatever enchantment it was that let the boat sail the same winds the albatross flew.

Down below him, the coral maze extended endlessly, as far as he could see. By day or night the sea was white with the foam; the reefs themselves were lines of rusty-brown in the day, glowing gold in the night.

His attention narrowed, and narrowed again.

His eyes on the albatross, always half a turn ahead of him (when Cliopher was rounding the bottom, the albatross would be reaching the peak of the upper curve; he would chase it up the wind to find it already down in the trough of the waves and curving effortlessly upwards again), his hands on the tiller and the sail, performing the minute necessary adjustments.

He sang the wind-songs of his grandfather, wishing he knew more of the words; half the time he had to hum, or sing nonsense syllables to make up the metre.

The stone was heavy in the cowrie, and his arms were tired, his eyes tired, his body achey and strained.

And still the albatross flew, as constant as the constellation of the Great Bird, though he flew with his beak pointing east, not south.

Loaloa and the star-island where he'd left Fitzroy and the others burned in his mind, the evening star, brilliant as a teardrop, as the memory of a smile, as the embers he cherished in his fire-pot.

∼

The light changed suddenly, and he looked up, attention broken, to find a rogue wave high as a mountain between him and the sun.

The albatross was climbing, and continued to climb: it disappeared over the wave's shoulder.

Cliopher was still at the bottom of the curve.

For a moment carved out of terror he dared to think he could follow the great bird, skim the surface of the mountain-wave as it had done, continue to fly.

But he was mortal, and no mage, and the wave broke.

The water tumbled down over his head, salty and cold and so very wet.

It soaked him instantly, and the vaha too, the force of the water plunging him down and down, out of the air and then deep below the surface.

Cliopher had wrapped the anchor rope around his waist when he had realized the canoe was flying in the wake of the albatross, in case he should lose control and fall. He was still gripping the tiller, still holding the sail-rope.

The water pushed him down and down, the bubbles rising furiously around him, the impact tearing all his breath out of his lungs and his mind out of his head.

Down, and down, like the riptide between reefs, like the Fall of Astandalas, like half his dreams.

Down, and down—and then the wave was past, and his vaha was buoyant, and resurfaced with a pop.

Upside down, and resolutely water-bound, and him at the end of the rope tugged every-which-way by the canoe and the slowly settling cross-waves.

Around him, in every direction, were the reefs.

CHAPTER FORTY-FOUR
THE REEFS

Cliopher did not try to do anything past survival.

The vaha had flipped, but that had been an early lesson from his father, his grandfather, his kin on Loaloa, underscored by all those storms across the Wide Seas. He swam to the boat, and wearily used the outrigger and mast to leverage it upright.

Water sheeted off everything. Cliopher held on to the outrigger, draped across it, his shoulders aching.

He thought he could hear singing around him, high voices, sweet and clear. He shook his head, shaking water out of his hair, his eyes, his ears, and focused on the problems immediately before him. Sweet voices were unlikely to be anything *helpful*, and if they were—well, they could come help him.

He scrambled even more wearily onto the deck platform, and assessed what he had lost in this fall.

Somehow, miraculously, gift of the sea-witch or the spells of protection and good fortune laid on it by his Radiancy and Aurelius Magnus—Cliopher's hands had known to ensure all his supplies were properly contained, closed under the hatches of the hollow keel.

He checked his fire-pot, the stoppered gourds containing his tools, his supplies. All were well.

His fingers trembled as he fed his embers. But the craft of the Ancestors was sound, and though the decking had been washed clean by the great wave, and every-thing had tumbled every-which-way in the hatches, those things that had needed to be dry remained so.

He furled the sail, lashed the tiller, heaved anchors made of netted coral boulders overboard, and then lay flat on the deck and let himself recover from that terrific plunge.

Every dream, every memory, every imagination of a storm ran through his mind.

He could still hear singing all around him, as if the reefs were full of music.

Finally he crawled once more to the fire-pot, so he could curl around its warmth and let the fire and the art of the one who had made it comfort him.

He was not alone, though he sailed alone in the midst of Sky Ocean. He was not drowned, though his vaha had been doused. He was not lost, for the stars Elonoa'a had taught him still shone as night came blooming across the sky like ink dropped into water, though he could not now follow the ke'ea directly through the reefs.

And there were three birds, flying low and straight, just before the light faded, even if he could not quite recall their names.

Navigating a strange coral reef was the sort of skill that people who lived in the archipelagos of the eastern Wide Seas went in for, and were highly respected for their knowledge. The Giloruogi were the most famous: they made stick and shell charts of refraction patterns, and were said to be able to tell from a curl of foam the shape of the reef below.

Cliopher knew that there was usually a channel opposite a freshwater runoff, and knew to circle an island looking for the gullies that marked such. Atolls were always harder, and he had foundered on several in his halting, limping journey across the Wide Seas after the Fall.

He took a line on the three birds, holding the wind against his back, the sunset against his cheek, watching for the first star to rise in that ke'ea: barely a pinprick of light, but there was a cluster of four brighter stars in the shape of a diamond just a ziva'a, a handsbreadth, to its east, and that gave him a line.

As the sky darkened so too did the water, and the eastern wind fell quiet. Half an hour or so after sunset a southerly wind started, not too strong but enough to propel the boat. Cliopher bit his lip, for that seemed far too helpful, but ...

He had done a good deed for the sea turtle, and in stories such things would be recompensed. If three sooty terns (that was their name!) flew by in a straight line at dusk, and a southern wind blew so he could sail after ... well. Well.

He readied the sail and hauled up the anchor. The darker water, ruffling in a different direction under this new breeze, showed different currents. They were mixed and confused with all the reefs, but there did seem to be a way through if he angled the vaha just a little to the west of where he wanted to go.

An hour after sunset he remembered to watch the horizon for the next star in his embryonic ke'ea. At first he could find nothing, but then behind him was something like the cross of Nua-Nui, and he smiled at the thought of the cynical albatross who had guided him so well, and carried on.

The waves foamed about the reefs. Under the surface they glowed.

The water was deeper than he had thought at first: the coral came up in great ridges. It was very clear down many fathoms before fading imperceptibly into a velvety midnight blue. There were luminous specks down there, jellyfish perhaps, glowing like stars.

Or stars, floating like jellyfish.

Would they sting him as a jellyfish might?

Picking his way through the reefs was exhausting, dispiriting work. There was always another channel, but they required all his concentration to find, and he kept forgetting to look up to mark the next star. First a little straight passage, and his heart would lift (every time, his heart would lift), then the safe channel would curve the other way, and he would come to a kind of cul-de-sac of teeming aquatic life but—no safe passage for his boat.

As the night wore on he fumbled the tiller and the sail and sometimes the boat slipped drunkenly from one side to another. At one point he found what nearly amounted to a lead and he took it gratefully even though it went far too far to the west and he had to pick his way back for a while until he found the next portion.

Before dawn the friendly south wind faded. Cliopher let the vaha glide for a few yards before he realized what had happened. To the east the sky was paling. He glanced around, marking the last star of the ke'ea as best he could. In the north one particularly bright one, nearly red in its light, hung low over the horizon. He decided that might be the ke'e of the island he was seeking, and wondered how far he might have yet to go to reach it.

The sooty terns flew past him, back out to wherever their daily fishing grounds were, and he lowered the anchor rock with a relieved sigh, grateful beyond words that he could rest.

The next three nights passed in the same manner. He refined his ke'ea, and began to gain a better sense of what ripples and lines of foam meant in terms of the underlying reefs; which lay far enough under the surface that he could safely pass over, and which even his vaha's slight draft could not take.

He sang the *Lays* and wished he had Elonoa'a or a Giloruogi navigator at his right hand to teach him the ways of a coral reef; and he lay in the shade of the sail during the day and wished he had someone to talk to.

On the fifth night the albatross came back, but he did not stay.

On the sixth night, if Cliopher had not lost his count—he was finding it increasingly difficult to hold ordinary time in his head, the longer he sailed on this ocean that was the *origin* of time to his people, who had never needed any timepieces other than the sun and the moon and the stars (and where was the moon? He had not seen it—her?—since—he could not recall when)—on the sixth night, at any rate, he came to the edge of the coral reefs.

He looked up to see the sooty terns coming straight at him, and on the edge of the horizon the smokey haze of an island.

~

He reached the island—a large moakili, a raised reef, half coral and half stone folded into strange and wild contortions—as the seventh night fell.

There was a fire on the beach, and after hesitating a moment—what if it were like a Shaian lighthouse, not a beacon of safety but a warning of danger?—he turned his vaha and sailed straight towards it.

It was not a beacon of danger, though he could hear the waves booming against rocks to his right and left. The water ahead of him was clear, the backs of the waves smooth and shining, and he was able to run his vaha upon a shingly beach.

He sat there, breathing hard.

Ahead of him was a fire, and food cooking, and an old man singing.

Cliopher sat there, adjusting to the land. The sun had gone down in its orange and red glory behind him, and the land was fading quickly into shadows and darkness.

But a fire, and a song Cliopher was sure he knew, and the smell of food cooking. His stomach rumbled, hungry for the first time in what seemed a long, long while.

He checked his fire-pot, to make certain it would be safe while he investigated this fire, greeted the old man singing, and then he hesitated, remembering his Buru Tovo once more.

Every village they had met around the Ring had had its own fires, of course; they had not *needed* him to bring a new coal, but he still had.

"It's polite," he'd told the young Kip. "Shows graciousness. Connects us. My fire, their fire, mixing together, becoming one, forming a new thing out of the old. Builds community and trust, eh."

Cliopher was too exhausted to think, so he picked up the coral pot and carried it with him to the fire.

The old man he had last met in the market-place in Lesuia squatted beside his fire, tending something in a pot. He broke off singing as Cliopher came to the edge of his light, and looked up at him, his eyes gleaming.

Cliopher took a deep breath. He should have known—should have guessed—

This was the efelauni who had given him the great strand of forty-nine sundrop cowries, and the one who had secretly tied the single efevoa and two flame pearls around his neck as he lay dreaming of another version of himself.

This was, Basil maintained, his great-uncle's husband.

(Buru Tovo had *delighted* in scandalizing the young Kip with tales of his lover. Cliopher knew *far* more about Vou'a's prowess in bed than he had ever wanted to know about anyone, let alone the god of mysteries.)

The god looked up at him, grinning.

"Buru Vou'a," said Cliopher, and set the fire-pot on the ground so he could kneel beside the old man—the figure of an old man—and offer him the same greeting he would give his great-uncle.

"Kip Mdang," said the Son of Laughter, and let him touch foreheads together. "Fancy seeing you here."

~

Cliopher sat down beside the god, grateful for the fire and the cool air and the feeling of being, at last, for the time being—for a certain value of the word—safe.

Vou'a smirked at him and began dishing out the soup into deep wooden bowls. He passed one to Cliopher along with a spoon carved out of a shell, and sat down cross-legged on the other side of the fire with his own bowl.

The soup seemed to have a coconut-milk base, red with chiles and some sort of oil, redolent of lemongrass and ginger and lime and prawns. Cliopher stirred the liquid with his spoon, breathing deeply of the steam. There was some sort of small round vegetable in there as well. Possibly a form of eggplant. It smelled wonderful.

It tasted wonderful, too, if just on the edge of too spicy for his tastes. The old man grinned at him when he slurped. Cliopher flushed but continued to eat, if a little slower and more carefully. All those endless court banquets seemed to be whole lifetimes away.

It was much better than anything Buru Tovo had ever made.

"Thank you," he said hoarsely. "It's very good. Better than—" He flushed.

"Yes?" Vou'a asked with bright amusement. "Better than ...?"

"You're not reading my thoughts, as the sea-witch did?" Cliopher asked, hesitant.

"Not very polite," Vou'a replied, just a hint of scorn in his voice. "Not to mention cheating!"

He was the god of mysteries, of edges, of the land against the sea, of laughter. A trickster, always.

Cliopher decided it was best to treat his words at face value while paying very close attention to all the underlying meanings, as he did at court.

"Better than anything my Buru Tovo makes," he said therefore, eating another few spoonfuls of the soup.

"Aye," Vou'a said, grinning. "Tovo's never been as interested in what you can do *with* the fire as you. Too distracted, I expect." He made a slightly rude gesture.

Cliopher tried not to blush, to little avail. (A *lifetime* at court, really.)

"Not like you," Vou'a went on. "You didn't even *notice* the sirens."

Cliopher blinked at him. "There were sirens? I heard singing ..."

The god cackled like a kookaburra. "Not a glance at them! They came crying to me, all those lusty beauties. A mortal man sailing by, caught on the reefs, lonely—so lonely! And then! Not even a glance! Too busy thinking about your fanoa, eh?" He nudged him with his elbow. Cliopher startled and bit down on a chile.

He registered a brief burst of citrus before the heat became fire, almost as bad as when he had swallowed the coal after lighting a new fire in the ceremony making him viceroy.

His eyes immediately began to water even as he cast around for water or something to ease the pain. The old man snickered and pressed something warm and rough into his hand. Cliopher brought it to his nose, not at all sure what it was, and was surprised to realize it was a small loaf of bread.

"Better than water, trust me," the old man said.

Cliopher had eaten enough with Rhodin to know that bread was better for counteracting spiciness than water. He tried not to stuff the whole loaf in his mouth at once, and instead eat it somewhat decorously, but he was far and away from anything like court manners—even ordinary manners—and he was embarrassed by more than his tears by the time he'd recovered.

"Er, my apologies, Buru," he said eventually.

The old man was laughing outright, like a whole tree full of kookaburras.

Cliopher wiped his watering eyes with the back of his hand, brushed his hair from his face—and how was his hair long enough to fall into his eyes?—and nibbled at the remnants of the bread in his hand. It had been a round loaf, white crumb and golden crust, delicious and entirely foreign to anything Cliopher had ever eaten at home.

If he had ever thought about what the gods might eat, he would not have thought of a soup that might have come from the Azilint and bread that might have come from northern Amboloyo.

"Oh, I've been known to travel. Not all of us do," Vou'a said companionably. "We have our boundaries and borders, so we do."

The Cirithian idea of heavenly bureaucracies came into his mind, all those hierarchies and portfolios and ministries and departments, like the Imperial Service at its very worst—

"Your departments?" Cliopher managed.

Vou'a chuckled and rapped him on the hand with his spoon. "None of that, not for me! You know what I mean: Ani in her waters and my friend Akuava'a in his skies, and me at the edges, the shadows, the deeps and the hidden places, finding out what there is to know, talking to those I want to."

Vou'a, who had raised up the islands for Ani, danced with her at the edge of the sea, where the waves washed upon the land.

"You and Ani," Cliopher said, not very certain what he wanted to ask, what he *dared* to ask.

"Aye," Vou'a said, a little sadly. "It's been a long time since I could dance with my fanoa properly. She's retreated down, deep down, where she's not so tempted by the sky. Sleeps most of the time, nowadays. Wakes once in a while, enough to send a dream, a message—perhaps a shell—when one of your folk sails in the old ways, singing the songs she taught you."

"She sent me the efani," Cliopher said, a little blankly.

Vou'a grinned at him, the shadow lifted from his face. "Always liked you, Kip Mdang. A man of the edges, the limits, the boundaries, aren't you? Never quite of one place, nor of the other, but doing your best for each, and for those who fall between the cracks."

Cliopher found his hand going up to his neck, not the efevoa but the chipped obsidian pendant.

"How do I go home, Buru Vou'a?" he asked, helplessly. "I've tried so hard to follow the ke'ea given me, to dance the patterns handed down, to be the tanà."

Vou'a rapped him with the spoon again. "You've brought fire to my fire."

"Buru Tovo said—"

"And are you the same tanà as him?"

The challenge made him lift his chin, as challenges always did. He met the god's eyes. "No."

"Well then," Vou'a said, sitting back on his heels, grinning at him. "What are you doing here, Kip Mdang?"

"I am going to the house of the Sun on behalf of Aurelius Magnus and Elonoa'a, who need a flame to be a star at their prow," he replied promptly.

Vou'a rolled his eyes. "You never stop, do you?" There was fondness in his voice, affection, a certain ... respect.

Cliopher shook his head silently.

(*Is this where you stop?*)

"And why not?"

It was not as if Vou'a was not using the word. Had not already used the word. "My fanoa," he mumbled.

"Was that so hard to say? All for a shell on the other side of the darkness, eh?"

Cliopher looked down, at the fire before him. It was a fire, no different than any he'd ever made; nothing strange about its colours or its fuel, its scent or its sound. "Yes," he said quietly.

"Always liked you, Kip Mdang," Vou'a repeated. "A fool, mind you, but what's life without a little folly? You'll catch your viau one day, if you keep chasing."

Cliopher looked at him, taking in the god's teasing tone, the glint in his dark, fathomless eyes, the sense that his words meant more than human words. By calling him *buru* Cliopher had entered into a certain relation with Vou'a ...

He took a breath, but he *was* Cliopher Mdang, and no, this was not where he stopped. He grinned back, at his ease, in his element, a challenge to make and some great future to negotiate. "Tanaea-te imalo! Moa'alani-ki imalo! Kifa'ana imai?"

Vou'a laughed. "A fire for my hearth! News of Sky Ocean! What gifts you offer me, that I already have, that I already gave you!"

Cliopher waited, settled in himself, not sure of anything but that this was the next star of his ke'ea, and he must pass under it to find his way.

"As for problems ..." Vou'a sucked at his teeth thoughtfully. "Not really a problem, not for me—unless of course, you want to try your hand at negotiating for Ani's mirimiri when you're in the house of the Sun!"

"I'd be glad to do what I can," Cliopher replied in his most courtly manner.

Vou'a cackled. "Perhaps you can push the negotiations forward a step or two. Tovo tells me you've got a gift for it. I've been banned from the Sun's house—a bit of a fuss with his old doorkeeper—perhaps you might be able to persuade them I can come again, eh? I miss that honey-mead."

Fitzroy had described that honey-mead, and Cliopher could barely keep from smiling as he nodded solemnly. There were many stories about why Vou'a was banned from the house of the Sun.

"Not an easy task," he said, managing expectations. "But that was not what you were going to say first, I think, Buru Vou'a?" Cliopher replied politely.

The god shrugged and spat in the fire, which hissed. Strange shapes curved up in the steam, and Vou'a regarded them intensely, as if they provided omens. "Perhaps they do, Kip Mdang, perhaps they do. You're not much of one for those sorts of visions, are you? Leave those to others."

"I have had more of late," he said, thinking of that other place. His hand went to the new efela. "Thank you ..."

"And you think that was all for *you*? I have many cares, you know, and perhaps I cared about those poor lost fools on the other side, one hiding deep down as my dear Ani, one as proud as proud can be and never asking for help, let alone the path home to his fanoa."

The word echoed. Cliopher hoped, savagely, that the other Lord Artorin found his way to freedom, and the other Kip to happiness.

"I'm glad," he said. "That it wasn't for me."

"Oh, it was for you as well, don't get me wrong," Vou'a assured him. "I like things that do more than one thing at once." He waggled his eyebrows suddenly. "Like my Tovo! Goodness me, he can do things with his hands *you* never thought of."

"I'm sure that's very true," Cliopher replied, and wondered despite himself what Vou'a was trying to deflect from telling him.

Vou'a laughed until his eyes streamed tears. "Very true! Very true! Well, Kip Mdang, Cliopher of the courts, you want to know what you could do to help me, eh?"

The question hung there, resonant as that challenge in the market-place in Lesuia, which apparently everyone had heard.

"*What will you bring home?*" Cliopher said, the words Vou'a had spoken fluttering in his own mouth.

"Oh yes," Vou'a murmured, very soft and very clearly, "some words the world turns on. You know this."

He did. He did.

Cliopher lifted his eyes and met the god's, straightforward, unafraid, hundreds of stories and songs and passages from the *Lays* in his mind, his own desire to step into them in his heart. "Yes," he said. "I bring you a fire to your fire, and news from Sky Ocean. One thing you asked me—to advance a token in the negotiations for your fanoa's lost mirimiri. A second thing—to win passage for you with the doorkeeper at the house of the Sun, that you might return to the halls from which you have been barred. And third?"

Vou'a shook his head. "You never do anything by halves, do you, Kip Mdang? One for a token, two for a promise, and three—" He grinned. "Three for a mystery."

CHAPTER FORTY-FIVE
THE SECRET WAYS

Cliopher looked into the mouth of the cave. He had never before considered himself afraid of the dark.

"You're the god of caves," he said after a bit. "What can I find in there that you cannot?"

It was early morning, and even after however long it had been, he still wished for coffee. Or chocolate. He would *love* a cup of chocolate. And a book. And—

"Told you," Vou'a replied, quite unruffled and sounding very much like Buru Tovo. "It's not polite to go into other people's minds. Or their hearts."

Cliopher turned from the dark crevasse to the Son of Laughter. "You said there was a treasure deep inside the mountain ..."

"There will be," Vou'a said. "Always is, with you lot. Humans," he clarified at Cliopher's continuing puzzlement. "You've always got surprises, deep down." He tilted his head and grinned. "*Deep* down."

Ludvic and Rhodin and Conju and Fitzroy all had their secrets, and Elonoa'a and Tupaia too, and Buru Tovo—

And himself?

Cliopher looked back at the cave, rocking a little on his feet, half-doubting, half-curious.

"You don't have to go in, of course," Vou'a said. "I can get something else for Ani, next time I visit her. It's just that you asked, and she always liked seeing what surprises I could come up with."

"And this would be a good surprise."

"A treasure from the depth of *your* heart? I would think so. Could be wrong, of course. You'd know best."

As if Cliopher was going to back down from that challenge.

He squatted down beside his fire-pot, intending to make a torch or some other form of illumination, but had not gotten far when he looked up to see Vou'a regarding him with a wry, somewhat pitying amusement.

"What? Should I not take a light, into a cave?"

"And *have* you taken a light, into that cave? You get what you have, Kip Mdang."

Cliopher stayed where he was, his hands around the shoulders of the fire-pot, the coral like alabaster warm, comforting, familiar.

"I see," he said, staring down into the coals, the wrinkles of ash and the gleams of fire.

"Yes," Vou'a murmured, "I think you do."

Cliopher took a deep breath and stood up. He looked around at the plants growing around the face of the cliff, at the bright daylight, the way that the god cast no shadow, his own vaha drawn up on the beach, visible through a gap in the trees.

There was a stand of bamboo near him, one long cane tilted over, broken off at its base. He picked it up, remembering, as from a long distance, Nala's blind friend Trisia, who had come to his Solaaran version of the Singing of the Waters. Cliopher had fumbled clumsily into the upper regions of his heart, from time to time, never going very deep.

"How far is it?" he asked, clutching the cane too vertically, too tightly, to be of any use.

"No one can answer that question," Vou'a said. "Only you know the depths of your own heart."

Did he?

Dared he?

For Vou'a's fanoa Ani, and for his own—yes.

The first part of the passage was level: narrow, illuminated by the cave mouth, extending high above him in a ravine. He might have been in a narrow gorge, like the one he hiked in the Liaau, winding its way along an ancient riverbed into the heart of the mountains.

The stones were plain at first, a thousand shades of grey, occasionally catching gleams and glitters of brilliance, narrow openings leading to chambers he knew well. He passed a gallery of tovo and tanaea and obsidian and cowries, the stones and shells glittering in a stray shaft of light from an invisible hole far, far above. He hesitated there, head tilting, hearing the distant echo of singing.

(The Vangavaye-ve, it must be.)

He went on. He traced his free hand along a twisting seam of copper, dripping peacock-blue and teal tears, a bare trace on the main wall of the passage, but which formed a brilliant gallery in one of the chambers, another shaft of light dancing upon the living metal.

(The Palace, clearly.)

Past the two illuminated chambers the passage twisted.

He looked back before he turned the corner. The mouth of the cave was a strange pale glow behind him; alluring.

He had rarely gone farther than this. There was little need to, when those bright galleries contained more than enough to occupy him.

These were not worthy gifts, a striking rock or a frond of copper, the fruits of his life.

Cliopher could not offer these to Vou'a to give Ani, for Cliopher to say, *here is a surprise I drew from the deep heart of me.*

Fitzroy would look at him with disappointment. He would say, *that is not like you, my lord Mdang,* and *is that* really *what you wanted me to put in the song?*

No.

He had always wanted more than that, hadn't he?

He turned away from the light, gripped the cane, and stepped into the darkness. There were spots before his eyes, green and orange. He blinked, but as they faded there was nothing else to see.

Eventually he closed his eyes.

It was extremely quiet.

The passage was not straight, but although it turned and twisted, it stayed roughly the same width, with a level, sandy floor. He formed a rhythm, sweeping the tip of the cane from one wall to the next, determining it would catch anything larger than a pebble. After the first few steps he was confident enough to walk almost normally.

This was a mistake. When the passage floor dropped down abruptly, he was going too fast to catch himself easily. His leading foot was already coming forward when the cane drooped in his hand, and although he twisted and tried to halt, his forward momentum was strong, and all he did was tangle himself down in a heap. The cane fell from his startled grip and clattered away.

He sat there, listening as it clattered down some sort of deep well, judging by the way the echoes gathered before finally petering away.

Oh, he had tumbled down this hole before.

He was used to the darkness of the Palace, where there was always a glimmer of light: from the hall, when he had lived in simpler rooms; from the next rooms out, where his attendants usually left a lamp burning low in case he rose in the night. And at home, there was the lights from the stars and the moon or the phosphorescence on the reefs; in Gorjo City there was always someone up, no matter the time of the day or the night.

In Basil's inn, or on the star-island, there were stars and candles and the sounds of others nearby.

He had not known this sort of darkness, this sort of silence, since that horrible night when Astandalas Fell.

But this hole was not that; it was too close to the entrance. This was ... the way he could unpleasantly surprise himself, with his temper or his tongue or his haste.

Cliopher sat there, rubbing at a scrape on his shin. Panic was hovering around him, a cloudy weight to the darkness.

He grasped the obsidian pendant of his efela ko, fingers curving automatically around the first of the pearls on either side. The side of his palm rested on the knobbly coral of the efetana, half-enclosing the sundrop cowrie with its secret contents, the sea-witch's garnet and the phoenix feather Sardeet Avramapul had entrusted to him.

He took in several long, slow breaths. The near-panic retreated; he lifted his chin and straightened his shoulders, as if he sat in one of the council rooms of the Palace, facing a hostile audience.

Look first. Listen first. Questions after.

Look first.

The blackness was absolute. The air was still cool, moist—clammy, even. The scent of stone was mingled with his own sweat, though that dissipated quickly. Cliopher took one deep breath after another, letting his exhale go out with great solemn slowness, tasting the air.

Listen first.

At first the sounds of his own body were too loud. He could hear his breath, the air rasping in his nose and mouth. He could hear the fibres of his skirt rustling as he shifted position, the scrape of his skin against stone and sand. He fancied he could hear his blood circulating in his veins, it was so very quiet; like being on the inside of a shell held up to the ear.

He cupped his hands over his ears and listened to his blood, the sound of his fore-mother the sea, Ani who had sung the first song, Ani who was the fanoa of Vou'a, Ani for whom he was doing this, until the panic receded once more.

It was so very quiet. Somewhere very far away was the plink ... plink ... plink of a steady, thin drip of water. Closer to there was no sound, just the sense of the air moving gently over his skin.

Cliopher sat there, eyes closing once more, attention focusing on the faint motions of the air, remembering Aurelius changing the wave patterns so that Elonoa'a could teach them to him. Look first. Listen first.

A draught was good. A draught meant there was an opening somewhere ahead of him, that this tunnel did not simply stop.

He had always thought there was more down there, in his heart, where he had never gone.

The tunnel mouth was curved smooth as if water-worn, as if polished, narrow enough to grasp. He grasped it and took a breath, another, another. He pressed forward again, his skirt bunching up under him, his feet tilting down now—another inch, another, another, and his right foot bounced off a ledge and his left foot caught.

He had not, truthfully, been expecting a ledge.

He had learned from his earlier heedlessness, and went down, step by step, on his rear.

There were four hundred and seventy-one steps, and at the bottom was the cane.

$$\sim$$

He was more cautious going along the next part of the tunnel.

The air was moving more briskly now, and sometimes it brought hints of something sweet and fresh. It reminded him somewhat of frangipani, when one caught a waft of fragrance through an open window.

After what seemed almost no time at all the echoes of his movement changed. He slowed his steps, moving forward cautiously. It did not seem open and echoey as had the abrupt stair: this time the echoes were more confused, muffled, as if he were coming to the end of the cave.

(As if he came to a place where the air was full of crosscurrents, a kurakura of emotions, dreams, desires, fears.)

Cliopher walked forward, free arm extended, and touched the stone. This was as smooth as the upper passage, but this time also wet. When he lifted his fingers to his mouth, the water tasted like ash.

He ran his hand down the damp stone. There, too low for his skill with the cane to find it, was an overhang.

He would have to crawl to pass through it, assuming it led somewhere.

He had always been too curious for his own good.

Too curious, and too stubborn, and too clever by half.

He scuttled forward on his belly. The stone here was smooth and wet, cold on his skin. It tingled like the sand on the island in the Sky Ocean, sand made out of the coral that was somehow what he knew in his world as stars.

What was this water, if that sand had been the stuff of which stars were made?

What was this darkness? This stone?

How far is it? he had asked Vou'a, the Son of Laughter, the god of mysteries.

No one can answer that question, he had replied. *Only you know the depths of your own heart.*

When he was young and foolish and proud, he had thought himself special, and had looked down on others, more ordinary in their surface lives, as being somehow boring, somehow lesser. He had rejoiced in learning the old ways and the knowledge of the tanà. He had been so proud of being fluent in the Islander language, in knowing the entire cycle of the *Lays* by heart.

(And was that entirely contained in that one small chamber already high above him, where the tovo and tanaea and obsidian and cowries lay in glittering piles?)

That other Kip in that other universe had never grown out of that. He had not had that endless journey across the Wide Seas, capsized again and again, lost time after time, humbled by the very pittance of his knowledge.

If Cliopher had not had any of the knowledge—if he had not thought he *knew* so much of the old ways—he would never have dared set off across the Wide Seas in that small boat. He would have stayed in Nijan and made a life for himself there with all the other exiles, all those others who had left their islands in the wake of the Fall and never been able to return home.

But he had had that knowledge, and thought he understood it. He had set off on that boat, Saya Ng beside him, into the wall of storms he should have known was entirely unnatural and would make mockery of his scant knowledge of the sea-ways.

How deep was his heart?

He pushed forward, and suddenly he was in a great open cave full of water.

The sound here was totally different, the water's noise multiplying in demonic choruses. It sounded like the time he'd gone through the edge of a hurricane in a sky ship, all cataracts of water and wind.

This was his heart. He knew that cataract, this cavern. This cavity.

He had built that stair, painful block by painful block, climbing out of the darkness of the Fall and the long loneliness of that journey across the Wide Seas, that even longer and harder loneliness of his work in the Palace, following the ke'ea of a sun he wanted to be a man, and his friend.

He rubbed his knees, the cane laid across his thighs, his hands hot, his legs feeling almost as if they belonged to someone else. He pressed his palms flat, as if by pressure he could assure himself he was real.

The floor was trembling under him, vibrating with the thunder of the waters, the broken waves he had tried so hard to leave behind.

(And thus he stayed up there in the shallows, in those caves safely within the reach of the light, very rarely descending down here.)

Did he have to let go, let himself fall? Did he have to let himself fall into the current, slide helplessly into the pit, fall into the darkness?

He did not believe that. How could he return bearing a gift out of that churning cataract?

No.

He edged backwards. The cane caught in something, a crack or a stone, and in the momentary loosening of his grip the water stole it away. He nearly reached after it, nearly lost his balance, nearly fell after all; but his other hand was still wedged into a crevice at the base of the wall, and he could not loose himself in time to fall.

There was something to be said, perhaps, for stubbornness and a tendency towards failsafes.

(And what was the Protocol for blindly plumbing the depths of a cave that was somehow also his heart, on an island far into Sky Ocean?)

He put his right side against the wall and followed the curve of the cave in that direction. Widdershins in the north, sun-wise in the south. Almost immediately it felt better: a little drier, a little warmer, a little less horrifically tilted. And there was that fragrance again.

As near as he could tell he was opposite the great cataract when he found the next passage.

He explored the size of the entrance as best he could with his hands. It was perhaps a foot high, and just over two feet wide. It was dry, and seemed to be floored with a fine shingly gravel, smooth like pearls or wave-worn stones.

The scent pouring out along the wind was almost enough to cause him to swoon. *How deep is your heart?*

If he did not want to descend into the chaos of the pit behind him, this was the clear opposite. One a gaping maw, too easy to fall into; the other a tiny opening, difficult of access and probably even more difficult of egress. That was always the way of such things.

There were monsters in the dark, the Mother of the Mountains had told him. Above him, below him, in the realms of the gods and the spirits.

And on the other side of the dark, a small white shell.

Cliopher bent his head and pushed off with his feet into the dark.

≈

He crept down the slanting tunnel, a wriggling worm of a human being, rubbing his belly and his thighs and his chest and all the rest of him on the pebbles, the sand, the smooth bare rock that felt soft as skin by comparison. His head was downward, with a feeling like his stomach was climbing into his throat, acid an aftertaste when he swallowed. His hands were throbbing with his pulse as the blood circulated sluggishly.

He flexed his hands, his shoulders, his stomach, his calves, his feet. He felt dizzy and lightheaded with the endless downward push. Nevertheless, he persisted.

He persisted.

He crawled, wriggled, abased himself in the darkness.

Once the ceiling lowered even more, so he had to move with his head turned to the side, eyes closed against the dust, cheek scraping, pelvis scraping against the stone floor. His abused grass skirt did not offer much protection, but it was better, he told himself, than nothing. Still the rock scraped across his back, bumping across every vertebra in his spine.

There was, he told himself through gritted teeth, ashamed of his weakness, a shell on the other side. A common, ordinary good: his.

He continued.

Down, and down, and down again even more steeply, until he had to brace himself not to slide, not to fall—and then suddenly he tumbled out of the tunnel and was in a cavern of blinding brilliance.

~

At last the tears washed away the pain, and he could remove his hands from his eyes.

The chamber was not large, but felt enormous after the constraints of the tunnel. It was not bright, save in comparison: the illumination came from a circle of embers burning on a ledge around the perimeter of the space.

He unfolded himself, standing upright for the first time in what felt like centuries, stretching out stiff muscles, stiffer joints.

There was treasure here, tucked into shelves cut out of the stone.

Cliopher walked around, looking at this secret cavern, the depths of his heart, the treasures he had stored up here, deep below his conscious mind.

Stones and feathers, gems and wrought gold, books and shells; all his efela, hung proudly on the walls.

One clam shell, missing its pair.

Cliopher knelt before the shell, which sat on a patch of sand that formed a kind of beach before a triangular seep of black obsidian, opposite the dark tunnel mouth halfway up the wall opposite. The seep was large, four or five feet back, a dozen across, utterly flat, utterly still, utterly black. When he leaned over his face reflected, a faded gold in the ember-light. The white shell blazed in comparison.

Half a bivalve.

He looked around, conscious of disappointment. Was this really all he was, in the depths of his heart? Was this really the store of secrets he had never shared?

He knew what each of those things represented, and they were not ...

They were not worthy of the gift he wanted Vou'a to give to Ani. They were not worthy of an epic song by Fitzroy Angursell. They were not worthy of who he, Cliopher Mdang, wanted to *be*.

Who he *was*.

The flowers were not here. He could smell them—the air was tantalizing with their fragrance—frangipani, tui, tiarë—but here there were just the *things* of his life. Nothing alive. Nothing growing. Nothing ... grand.

He shifted position, sitting down, half-unbalancing and putting his hand down on the obsidian.

It was so cold for a moment he thought he'd cut himself, but when he lifted his hand to his lips—in the dull ember-light all looked red—it was not blood, but water, he tasted.

He stared at the triangular seep.

Water, not obsidian.

How far down had he come?

How deep is your heart?

("A treasure from the depth of *your* heart? I would think so. Could be wrong, of course. You'd know best.")

This cave, this cavern, which held all the treasures of his life—all the things he had *accomplished* with his life—all the things he would boast of, if he boasted of them. A cave illuminated by the coals of his fires, containing all the pieces of his life, all the things he thought about.

He did not think anyone's life was bounded by what they had *done*.

Fitzroy was his beloved not *because* he was the Sun-on-Earth or the great poet, but because he was funny, and intelligent, and sorrowful, and because he loved.

Cliopher looked around again.

Where was *his* love?

He did not—would not—believe that this was the depths of his heart. He had never gone farther than this: he knew that. He had never gone past the fear, the seal with which he had bound the deepest secrets of his heart, his fear of *never being good enough* ... his fear of his own love.

He would not be good enough, if he took one of these trinkets and returned up that long, terrible, tunnel. That was the life he had lived: it had brought him here, to the edge of the Sun's country, most of the way across Sky Ocean.

Most of the way. Not all of the way.

It came down to this: did he trust Vou'a, trickster-god, Son of Laughter, to have spoken the truth? That there was, deep in his heart, a worthy gift?

Cliopher breathed deeply, his ribcage expanding as he saturated his body with life-giving air.

Hints of fragrance, wisps of scent, frangipani from Solaara and jasmine and roses from far-away Astandalas and tui and tiarë from *home*, and mingled with them flowers he could not name, but which did not grow *here*.

It seemed back in the prehistory of the world that he had learned to dive for pearls, and known from the first dive he would never love it.

He picked up the shell, and knew that that was *his* half, and the other half was on the other side of the darkness.

He gripped it in his hand, and then he dove down into the black seep, uncertain of anything but that he wanted to know what was on the other side.

The slope of the rock went down at an angle.

He kicked strongly, following the slant downwards. He held the shell tight in his left hand, something real in the darkness, his right hand on the wall.

Down, and down, and down. Still the ceiling plunged. There was a sense of depth below him, and he felt turned upside-down, the floor above him, the openness below him.

The pearl-divers of the Azilint went down farther than this, free-diving on one long breath like a whale, down and down and down a hundred feet, two hundred feet, until they could touch bottom and claim the small oyster shells that formed the brilliant white pearls for which their islands were famous.

The pearl-bearing nefalao of the Western Ring of the Vangavaye-ve were not so far down, but still deep enough that Cliopher knew what it meant when he passed the point of buoyancy and his rib cage suddenly compressed.

The desire to breathe, the panicked fear that he would run out of air, was nearly overpowering.

His mind groped for some distraction. He had to keep himself from panicking: that way lay death indeed. If he blacked out now he would die.

He gripped the shell in his left hand.

Over and over a single line looped in his thoughts.

How deep is your heart?

Once he passed the point of buoyancy it was easier and easier to drop, gravity claiming him. Cliopher kept his hand on the wall, his back on the roof, the scrape of stone against skin numbed by the cold water. He kicked his feet gently, just enough to keep his momentum. His heartbeat was slowing; he imagined he could feel his body shifting under the pressure of the water, the air held in his lungs transferring to his blood with each steady pulse.

The water was black.

This was no friendly lagoon in the embrace of the Ring, not even the terrifying majesty of the open ocean on the outer edge of the reefs. This was water cold as death, cold as doubt, cold as fear.

How deep is your heart?

The ceiling lifted from his back. Cliopher drifted down in the black water, his downward momentum slow, steady, the water still around him. He was perfectly balanced: no current, no air, no light. Just him drifting downwards in the dark.

He was beyond panic. If he died here, here in the dark, drowning in the dark water, it would be the fulfillment of a lifetime of nightmares. He had always feared he would die by drowning.

How deep is your heart?

Deeper than this. He could feel the drop below him, the plunge to the roots of the mountain, to the bed of the sea, to whatever floor there was to the sky.

(The only floor to the sky was the earth.)

His fingertips on the stone beside him, the shell in his palm, were the only anchor he had. His chest was compressed, his ears roaring with the sound of the sea, as if he held a shell pressed to his ear.

He remembered, as if in a dream, Buru Tovo showing him how to even the pressure in his ears, his nose. He had instinctively been performing the moves, pressing the back of his tongue against his epiglottis, *pushing* air into his sinus cavities, ears, the inner parts of his body.

Not instinctively, but with that persistent teaching, that education that had woven itself into his very being.

In his left hand, half of a fanoa.

Is this where you stop?

Every time that question had come to him, Cliopher had answered: no.

He would not stop despite his hatred of diving. He would not stop despite his fear of drowning. He would not stop when the storms capsized him again and again. He would not stop when all the world stood against him. He would not stop when he was the proverbial fool. He would not stop when the winds blew athwart him, or failed to blow at all.

He would not stop here, in this black depth. He wanted to know what was on the other side.

He had not drowned in the plunge over the reef when he was a boy, nor in the Fall of Astandalas, nor in any of those storms across the Wide Seas. He had gathered those treasures in that room on the other side, and never dared pass through that fear of drowning, of never being good enough, of being unworthy.

Is this where you stop?

He turned around himself and kicked down: against no rock but that of his own stubbornness, but it was enough, just barely enough to get him moving upwards, to follow the trajectory of the rock as it led up out of its depths. He moved slowly, languidly, his mind burning with the need for air, for light, for warmth.

He was so slow, kicking against the downward pull. Was he truly going upwards? Or had he drifted into that dangerous madness that sometimes took those who dove deep? Would he drown because he had not realized it would be so deep?

Something changed in the pressure, his lungs starting to inflate. He kicked once, twice, then stopped. He was still moving upwards, his hand still on the stone. The *Lays* in his mind, his great-uncle's voice in his ear, the shell in his hand.

Is this where you stop?

No. He made that promise to himself, as he had made it so many times. No, and no, and no. This was not where he stopped.

His fanoa was waiting for him, the other side of the dark.

He felt a sudden ringing in his ears and he opened his eyes involuntarily.

There, above him, wavering in the water, was a light.

CHAPTER FORTY-SIX
TREASURE

Cliopher reached a stone ledge and draped himself across it, suddenly unable to move at all. He breathed out gently, in again quickly, the sweet air tasting of flowers and fresh water and sunlight. His eyes were dazzled and he had to close them again to concentrate on his breathing.

He breathed slowly, pausing at each inhale, each exhale. Buru Tovo had worked with him on the breathing for weeks before he was ever allowed to dive beyond what all the children did in their games. Cliopher had thought himself a good swimmer, before that time on the Outer Ring. All of his cousins there could swim circles around him.

The breathing came automatically, drilled into him as deeply as the *Lays*. Before and after a dive one breathed slowly, gently, calming the heart, relaxing the muscles, bringing the mind to that spiritual serenity that his Buru Tovo thought appropriate for pearl-hunting.

Long, slow, even breaths, the diver's breathing, deliberate pauses after each inhalation, each exhalation.

Eventually he was able to drag himself the rest of the way out of the water, over the sharp lip of the ledge, and onto deep, soft moss. He rolled over onto his back, listening to the water still rippling.

The air was heady with scent.

He breathed it in, those long slow even breaths, the diver's breaths. He had not found a pearl, down there in the dark, but he had found ... something.

Something good, by the moss and the soft air and the gentle lap of the water and that fragrance.

He lay there, body cushioned by the deep moss, the scent of green growing things and fresh water in his nose, his mouth, his throat ... his heart.

This was his heart, on the other side of that icy, black, terrifying plunge.

This was the home of his deepest secrets, the part of himself that he had never dared explore.

He had reached that ember-lit chamber before, where he kept the things he had achieved by doing, by thinking, by striving always forward against the dark and narrow and the intense weight of expectations crushing him close.

This ...

This was the other side.

He was still holding the shell tight against his palm. He brought his hand to chest, feeling his ribs move with his breathing, afraid of what he would find.

He was not the tanà on this side of that cold water; not the bureaucrat of bureaucrats; not the man with those proud efela and those books. This was who he was without all of that.

This was the self he wanted to believe was equal to Fitzroy Angursell.

He had never thought that self was ... soft, but this moss was, deep and welcoming, comforting.

He gripped the shell. He would not get where he wanted by refusing to claim it, would he?

He opened his eyes.

~

Once, on a visit to Nijan, he had been taken by his hosts into a cave system. They had a small boat, almost a ferry, tied to a rope at either end. The rope was threaded through the caves, so they did not need to row: they could pull themselves along, neither losing their way nor distracting their guests with fear that they might become lost in the dark caverns.

They had set up lights in the earlier parts of the caves to show off the incredible formations there: stalactites and stalagmites, waterfalls of stone, shapes carved out of stone and water and time. There had been a cave where the limestone was white and creamy and sculpted into marvels.

Then they had gone through the mouth of a tunnel, and the lights had faded. Their guides had told them it was to let their eyes adjust, so that they could appreciate what was to come.

On the other side was a huge cave with a ceiling covered in glow-worms, like the sky writ somehow larger for its constraints.

Cliopher lay on his back in the depths of the mountain, in deep moss, and stared upwards in wonder at what might have been the night sky from the other side of the sun.

And then, so very faintly at first, he heard the singing.

He had heard it before, in that dream between falling down a mountain and waking up in the other place. He was not spinning, was instead anchored, and he was not drowning in a sea of light, nor in the black water he had so recently left. But he still heard the singing, the song of the *Lays*, the Naming of Names.

Was it the glow-worms? Or were those the stars? Unfamiliar in their positions, on this side of the sky?

Cliopher didn't care. He lay there, murmuring the star-names to himself, a baritone counterpoint to the high, clear, inhuman voices above him.

The song went on and on. First the names he knew, and then those other ones he did not, in melodies increasingly complex, counterpoints and harmonies and fugues working together as elaborately as the whole of creation.

His heart was so much vaster than he had ever realized.

He wanted to go home.

The stars above him were singing.

He wanted Fitzroy to be his fanoa.

He wanted ... this.

At last he sang his own name, placed himself into the song of the *Lays*.

O Cliopher in Mdang ezū, he sang softly, so much less beautifully than the stars above. But—this was the voice he had, these were the words he had, this was who he was.

◆

He sat up.

◆

The cave was large but not enormous. Roomy. He got the sense there were side chambers, galleries, leading off into the dimmer recesses.

The ceiling was crowded with the stars (or the glow-worms, or the glowing jewels, or whatever they were). The lights came down in a great arc over his head, not the hemisphere of the sky but something distinctly closer.

The moss covered the floor, which sloped up from the water to a kind of ridge and then descended again into a wide and shallow trough. At the bottom of this trough was a river whose current was gentle enough that the waters were a quiet rush, hardly louder than the sound of the blood in his ears, once more sounding like a shell held to the ear.

Dotted across the moss and floating in the river were flowers. They were all luminescent.

In the centre of the cave there was a hearth made of what looked like pearls, and burning merrily in the hearth was a fire.

Cliopher started down to the fire immediately, and equally immediately turned his foot on something buried in the moss.

He knelt down on his unhurt side, letting his ankle rest for a moment. He dug gently into the moss, peeling away the layers from a small wooden boat.

He held the item in his hand. He had not thought about it for years, but he knew it—his father had carved this toy for him—and it was also the *Tui-tanata* he had built with his own two hands and sailed across the Wide Seas.

It was battered, nicked with play, with disregard, with neglect.

He had left the *Tui-tanata* tied up at the back of an abandoned warehouse. He had walked across the city in his grass skirt, hiding from anyone he knew, who might know him, ashamed in a way he had never understood for all the failures that had led to him arriving there in that boat.

(Elonoa'a had not thought it a failure, that he, an untrained navigator, had made his way across the Wide Seas alone. Cliopher had claimed that journey in the course of the viceroyship ceremonies, the first time.)

He turned the toy over in his hand, the scrap of a sail tattered, the outrigger hanging by only one strut. How he had had loved this boat, when he was a boy. Carried it everywhere with him, mumbling adventures—even then it had been the adventures of Elonoa'a, of the third son of Vonou'a, his own fancied voyages—while he sat at his mother's feet, his father's, his grand-parents, all the aunts and uncles who had been in his life.

He had thrown the toy boat into the lagoon the week after his father died, enraged at the stupidity of it all, the unnecessariness. Cliopher had been so furious at the sea for taking his father, who had loved Ani best of all the gods.

It had taken him a long time to forget that anger. What was the sea, after all, he had eventually convinced himself. Impersonal, implacable, terrible and great.

The fanoa of Vou'a, his Buru Tovo's husband.

Cliopher set down the boat on the moss, just for a moment, while he covered his face with his hands and breathed deeply, trying to compose himself.

But he was deep inside his heart, and there was no composure here: only what he had brought in, all the secrets he had never told anyone.

Now that he was looking, he could see lumps and bumps everywhere, their shapes blurred by the deep, dark moss growing over everything.

He picked up the boat, cradling it in the hand that still held the shell, and went on his knees to the next lump.

He moved the moss carefully, cautiously, braced for what he would find.

～

The efela he had given Ghilly before he left to go to Astandalas, and which she had unclasped from her neck and handed back to him when they sat on the top of Mama Ituri's Son, and she told him she would wait no longer; that though he had come back, at last, he was not the man she would marry.

～

The notebook, a fancy hard-bound one, which Uncle Lazo had given him for a birthday in his teens, because he thought Kip liked words and writing.

Cliopher had never used it, unable to think of anything worth writing down, except for one page, right in the middle of the book, where in tiny letters he had written his great dream.

He knelt there now, remembering that he had burned the notebook before he went to Astandalas, hoping no one would ever need to know he had never been joking.

∽

A tobby seed his sister Navalia had given him, which she'd carved with the Mdang family patterns, when he'd written to tell her he had to learn how to spin in order to make his efela ko.

It was probably still in a box in his room in his mother's house, the one with his letters to her when she'd been out on the Ring and he'd been at university, the one he'd never opened after she died.

∽

A furled leaflet enclosed in a glass bottle. The brown glass bottle still smelled of Basil's mead. The leaflet was advertising the Yrchester Cheese Festival, for the year Astandalas Fell. "We'll go next year!" Basil had scribbled across it. "Sara's already making plans!"

∽

A stuffed toy in the shape of a whale his toymaker Aunt Onaya, Uncle Lazo's wife, had made for him. Au'aua, he'd named the whale—the name of the Great Whale, the constellation, whose eye was the brightest star in the sky—and she had been his constant companion.

Aunt Onaya had made her eyes out of a scrap of golden ahalo cloth, and he had thought it the most wonderful thing he'd ever seen.

It was still wonderful. Aunt Onaya was a great toymaker, and although most of the velvet was rubbed bare, and there was a tear in the tail where the stuffing was coming out, and one eye was gone, the other eye twinkled up at him as beautifully as ever.

He still remembered his mother telling him he was too old for such toys, and when he refused—for he had always been far too stubborn, and he had loved that whale—she had taken Au'aua from him and placed her high in a cupboard he could not reach.

(His father had given him the boat a few days later, but Cliopher, the young Kip, had mourned Au'aua with a depth of grief he had not understood for years; when his father died that had been the only point of reference he had had, that devastating loss.)

∽

His arms were full when he reached the fire.

He sat down quietly on the bare stone that extended in a wide radius outside the hearth. It was cool to the touch, but sooty—singed, he might say.

This was the fire at the heart of him.

This was the fire *of* the heart of him.

It was a proper bonfire, like the ones he and Tupaia had built on the sand for the nightly gatherings of the crew of the *He'eanka*, or the fire he had built in the courtyard of the Palace of Stars for his festival, or the fire the other Kip had built in the courtyard of his house in Esa'a.

Or like the fires he had built some of those lonely beaches across the Wide Seas. He had built some of them up high—far higher than he needed, even to rake the coals out afterwards for the fire dance—hoping, with a fury and a fear he had never told anyone, that someone would see the fire and come find him.

No one had ever found him, though he'd screamed with rage and impotence and grief and confusion. He'd piled branch on branch, sheaves of coconut fronds, driftwood that made the flames green or purple, towering up towards the crown of stars, and no one had ever seen it but him.

He sat there on the scorched stone where the soft, gentle moss had been burned back by his flares of temper and grief, righteousness and fear, and his relentlessness, and he cradled lost loves to his chest, and he looked at the fire burning there.

The pearls were the size of his closed fists (his heart? his brain?), golden as the ones on his efela ko, some of them marked with the white flames as the ones on the efela nai. Some were burnished to an amber the colour of the efevoa, his Fitzroy's eyes.

The fire was fire, the colour of every fire he had ever lit.

It *was* every fire he had ever lit. The fine and brilliant ones, the tiny hopeless ones, the furious blazing ones: the fire he had lit in the cold hearth of the Palace, and the metaphorical firebrand he had handed to his Radiancy, to Fitzroy, when all his researches said that Woodlark must burn. The fires he had lit on each of those lonely beaches, and the ones he had lit when he and Conju went camping together, laughing their way into friendship.

The fires he had lit in Basil's inn, and the one he had lit when he and Fitzroy had landed on that island that was a star, and the one that had once started a war.

The fires he had lit under Buru Tovo's instruction, and the ones he had taught Clio to make, small hands under his on the bow-drill, a stone instead of a shell over the butt of the stick.

The fires he had lit in the hearths of the world, by working so hard, so relentlessly, towards a peace that was made of a home and a hearth, food and friendship and family, and the possibilities of art.

The fires he had seen kindled in his Radiancy's eyes, back when Cliopher had not known the truth, when all he had seen was a man drowning under the weight of all that was placed upon him, and since Cliopher could not reach out his hand he had, instead, offered—

He could not say *his heart*.

Cliopher had never been this far into himself. He had felt the flames here, nourished them, been nourished by them: that warming glow of something well done, that flame of indignation and righteousness (again and again he came back to that word; but he had seen it in the other Kip, and known it in himself), that terrifying volcanic fury that choked him.

He had never been this far into himself, and so he had not been able to offer this to anyone, not even his Radiancy.

He had offered his Radiancy the coals of that other chamber on the other side of the water-blocked tunnel, all the treasures in that cavern, all those things that had seemed so secret and so grand.

He had not offered him these things, these broken parts of himself, the sharp edges of the mirror he had shattered when Navalia died, the gift he had intended to give the friend who had not invited him to the party (the gift that had been a weight on him all these years since, when he had looked at it with guilt and relief; for if Dwian had invited him to that party as he had hoped, as he had expected, then Cliopher would have died in the Fall; and yet Cliopher had been so hurt by the rejection).

The fires of resentment, grumbling in the coals. All the snubs and misunderstandings with his family, which he tried so hard to suppress but which bided their time, banked embers, until a breath of air stirred them once more to hot and rancorous life.

The fires of his love, all his loves—his friends, his handful of lovers, his ideals, his family, his people in the Secretariat, his dreams—

All the fires he had ever lit.

He set the broken, battered relics of his life in his lap, Au'aua and the boat set carefully on top of the book, the shell guarded between them, and reached out to the nearest of the pearls. It was warm in his hand, warm as that black water had been cold, warm the sun on his face, warm as a hand in his.

He turned his left hand over. The shell had left its curved lines imprinted on the folds and creases of his palm, cutting across the lines and scars already there. A white shell, tinted gold in the firelight, perfect, missing its other half.

And what, then, was the gift he would offer the god of mysteries to bring to his fanoa?

Ani had taken his father from him, and given him the shell called her tear.

(It was not Ani's tears that made the sea salt, so the old story went, but Vou'a's.)

Cliopher bent his head over his treasures, his own face wet, his tears falling like rain.

And if he had ever been willing to dare that dive before, would this have always been here?

He closed his eyes for a moment, the flames dancing in afterimages on his eyelids. That was not an answer he could give, even to himself.

He was not imaginative that way. He had what he had found, what he was.

Here in the heart of himself was unexpected moss, and stars like the other side of the night sky, and all the fires he had ever lit, encircled by the pearls he had worked so hard to collect. And there were also all the broken parts of himself, the parts he had loved and been unable to let go, unable to keep. A well of dark water leading down, and down, with another treasure-store on its other side, and a long, difficult, endless journey back up.

And there were flowers, and stones, and ... a river ...

He set his things carefully beside the fire, where they would be safe, and he walked to the river.

It was very clear, diamond-bright, with a bed like the gemstones that made up the floor of the throne room in the Palace. The fire hummed behind him, a mature blaze, steady. The river sang softly, rushing, fast, still going somewhere.

He knelt and drank from his cupped hands. It tasted of starlight and grief.

He looked to his right, where the river poured out of one of the darker recesses of the cave, and to his left, where it went to an opening, from which came that wind that smelled of green and growing things, flowers, like coming across the scent of an island at night.

He turned to his left and followed the river to the mouth of the cave. There was some sort of open space before him, verdant and rich; the stars of Sky Ocean hung low over him, the glow-worms writ large and resplendent. Mountains encircled him, with the silvery line of the river disappearing like the tail of a snake.

To the right was darkness; to the left, darkness, and a narrow gap through which he could see a red light like an eye, and behind it the glimmering line of the sea.

Vou'a had asked for a treasure from the heart of him, with which he could surprise Ani.

He turned and went back to his fire, and he looked again at the things he had brought out of the moss.

He sat down before Au'aua and the little boat and the shell, and imagined giving any of those to—

Vou'a would not come into his mind, and Cliopher had never seen anything but the impersonal might of Ani.

He could imagine sitting on the beach of the star-island, on the balcony of the house he'd bought in Gorjo City, in his Radiancy's private room, with Fitzroy, and telling him the stories behind the stuffed whale and the boat, the tobby seed and the bottle with its ghostly scent of mead, and even that notebook in which he'd written the truth in tiny, untidy letters.

He stared at the fire, the flames licking over embers and logs. The longer he looked at them the more it seemed as if each stick, each coal, held a story, a moment, a love; for even his grief and his anger burned with that flame.

In the centre of the fire, the very centre of the fire, there was a coal that burned like the heart of the sun.

Cliopher stared at that coal, Au'aua and the boat and the shell from the other side of his heart in his hands, the pearls in the corners of his vision, the moss stretching behind him, the fire and the river in his ears, the scent of the flowers in his nose and mouth.

This was a gift from one god to another, whose love for each other was the pattern Cliopher wanted to follow.

His fanoa—the man he wanted to be his pair, his match, his equal—was a great mage and a great poet, who could bear the weight of the world upon his shoulders and laugh when he saw something new, and who always chose the action that was best for the story.

Cliopher had been wanting to be part of a story his whole life long.

He breathed those diver's breaths, long and slow and even, counting them out as his Radiancy counted out his breaths when he worked magic or sought inner peace, and then he leaned forward into the fire at the heart of himself and brought out that one brilliant coal.

For a moment it burned, the concentrated fire of all of Cliopher's love for his Radiancy, for Fitzroy, for the idea and dream of what fanoa could be—all the disappointments he had faced in the reality of reaching up to that emperor on his high golden throne, that legendary long-lost poet—all the devastation he had known when he saw what fanoa meant to Elonoa'a and Aurelius, and the understanding he had gained in knowing them as people—

For a moment it burned, and then his tears fell upon it, and in a great upwelling of steam the coal went out and left, in the palm of his hand, the second half of a common, ordinary, simple white shell.

CHAPTER FORTY-SEVEN
THE UTTERMOST EAST

Cliopher held the shell in his hand, and then he could not resist, and tried to fit the two half-shells together.

The new shell was bigger.

He turned them around in his hand, but though they were the same shape, the size difference was unmistakable.

Eventually he nestled them together, the one from the other side of the water sitting neatly within the other. In his hand they sat there, mute and immutable, two halves of his own heart.

He should have known. This was *his* heart—not Fitzroy's. Fitzroy's treasure-house of forgotten loves lay deep within himself, perhaps in that private study full of cloth and pens and books and the dusty detritus rescued from a life that was supposed to be without flaw.

—Fitzroy had let Cliopher in. Cliopher had knocked, and Fitzroy had *let him in*—

He bent his head, the tears falling again, watching as they were caught by the creamy white shells, barely gold from the firelight, and puddled there like liquid fire, scarlet and gold.

The image blurred as the tears fell faster, and he lifted his hands to his mouth, the shells pressing against his lips, and tried to compose himself.

But this was, still, his innermost heart, and it was where he sent things to be buried in that thick moss, forgotten, ignored. He could not, sitting in the midst of ancient memories, compose himself.

He did not even know why he was weeping.

Eventually he stopped, and set the shells down so he could take in several deep, shuddering breaths, and then he wiped his face with the heels of his hands.

He sat there for a moment, hands over his eyes, breathing, listening to the fire crackle, wondering what he was possibly going to be able to give up to Vou'a.

The flowers were sweet and the air was fresh, and the fire was warm in his heart, on his skin, and he could hear the stars singing the *Lays*.

He knew what he had to give, what he had to offer. He laughed softly to himself, surprised by the sound of his laugh in his mouth.

No one *worshipped* Vou'a, really (except his Buru Tovo, with a salacious wink and a comment about what making love to his god *meant*—), and while Ani was worshipped in Shaian dress in the Astandalan temples built in the city, Cliopher had never felt drawn to her there.

No. Ani had known his tears, and his fires, and his stubbornness and his persistence and his pride.

He opened his eyes, and arranged the relics of his lost loves more carefully at the edge of the burnt and scorched circle, where they would be safe from the encroaching moss and the occasional flares of fire. His hand lingered on the small wooden boat his father had carved, and the battered and piebald form of Au'aua, her single ahalo-cloth button eye still gleaming in the firelight.

No one was here. He caught her up and kissed her on the curve of her head, just as he had when he was a little boy, before he'd been told he was too old for such toys, and then he set her on top of a stone that emerged like a daïs out of the moss.

He took the wooden boat with him. Unlike the stuffed toy, which might well still sit mouldering in the cupboard where his mother had placed her, the boat was long since sunk into the sea.

And then he bent to pick up the shells, only to find they had transformed under the effects of his tears again.

A coal sat burning, gleaming like a fire seen from far across a bay, in the heart of a cowrie made of glass shading from clear as tears to the opaque white of any common cowrie.

He balanced the shell on his palm. It was warm to the point just below pain, and seemed to pulse in time with his heart.

He laughed again, closing his fingers around its warmth and light, and then he lifted it up to his mouth and whispered a secret.

He went first to look at the pool of water that led to that other chamber on the other side of the water-logged tunnel. The water was black, glistening, significant even: it reminded him of the finest ink, the ink he'd use for a great proclamation, the ones that he wrote and his Radiancy sealed and then stored in the Archives as witness of some moment that had changed the world.

He knelt down on the stone ledge and dipped in his hand. The water ran out of his palm, clear as tears and cold as grief.

In his other hand he held the fire-lit shell, and the little wooden boat. His tears were warm on his cheeks, and grief no longer seemed a necessary corollary of the choices he made.

For most of his life he had been the person who took the hard way, when he knew it was the right way. He had never let difficulty, or pain, or fear, or even unending tedium turn him aside from his ke'ea. He had set his course by that brilliant daystar, the sun of his life, and followed him ... here.

Cliopher could dive down into that dark water, down and down until he passed the point of buoyancy. He could find his way back up to that small, dimly illuminated chamber. He could force himself back into that long, narrow, low tunnel and wriggle his way inch by inch up through all the density and weight of the mountain to that cavern of the cataract.

He could find that other entrance, and the dark stair he had built out of past despair and stubbornness, and come to the mouth of the cave once more, and down the slope to the edge of the sea where his vaha was beached and Vou'a had lit his fire.

He could do all those things.

He might still need to, if the other way was impassible after all.

He did not want to—oh, he desperately did not *want* to—but he could. And if he needed, he *would*.

He knew that: for he was still stubborn, and persistent, and he had been fitting himself into shapes and spaces he had never been made to fit for his entire life, and he could do so again if he had to.

He rubbed his hand dry on his chest, and then he shifted the cowrie to that hand, where its warmth could warm his cold fingers.

And then he turned and walked down the river to the mouth of the cave.

He stepped out onto the flowery meadow that unfurled beside the diamond river like a snake endlessly burrowing into the hills.

He walked the undulating path in the open air, the flowers unfurling around him, perfuming the soft and mild airs.

He was no longer the Cliopher Mdang who knew only the hard way home.

He was Cliopher Mdang of Loaloa, whose island still burned in his mind, whose fanoa was waiting for him, who had sailed to the edge of the uttermost east, and who was on his way to the House of the Sun to win a flame of the Sun's fire.

He, too, walked in legends.

And—

And it *was* easy, for once.

(And if the thought of how Fitzroy always chose the onward route—if he thought that this was a choice that his beloved friend could gladly write into a song—well. He was allowed to.)

❧

Vou'a sat beside his fire, Cliopher's fire-pot beside him, spinning the last shadows of the night into a line.

Cliopher sat down beside him. The sky was lightening to his left, and he watched a great palace take shape in the delicately tinted clouds of dawn. There were pillars, and domes, and balconies, and windows like the huge stars that were now almost familiar, and great sweeping canopies of cloth-of-gold.

White birds suddenly came pouring out of nests on the gables and galleries, hundreds and thousands of them. They sang as they came, a high, sweet song without words.

Cliopher watched them go overhead, the white froth at the breaking wave that was the dawn.

"And what did you find, in that mountain?" Vou'a asked quietly, one hand drawing out the darkness that drained out of the hidden corners of the island into the spindle, the other twirling the shaft against his thigh.

The motion was mesmerizing. Cliopher had used the old-fashioned long spindles —made them, too, sometimes—but he had never been able to make so even and fine a thread as Vou'a was spinning out of shadows.

Cliopher was reminded suddenly that in one of the stories, Vou'a was said to have flung his fishing line to pull up the islands.

"Did you lose your tongue down there?" Vou'a continued after a moment, as the last shadows slithered out of the mouth of the cave. He touched his hand to the spindle, and held the line there, humming with the stored motion, even as he met Cliopher's eyes with his own.

Cliopher smiled. "No, Buru Vou'a."

The god grunted. "Good. Tovo wouldn't like it if I sent you home speechless."

That made him laugh outright. "I'm sure there's been a time or two he wished I would stop talking."

"Not so many as you might have thought, Kip Mdang. That wasn't the treasure you found, I take it."

"No, Buru Vou'a," he said, and held out his hand.

The Son of Laughter pursed his lips, laughter glittering in his dark eyes. "You've brought me a shell to give to the sea?"

"She doesn't have this one," Cliopher replied, his heart thundering in his throat.

Vou'a regarded him steadily for a long, long moment, and then he set down the spindle, wedging it beneath his thigh, and delicately lifted the cowrie. The back was white, opaque, plain as any cowrie—any fanoa—on any beach.

Turned over, revealing the corrugated ridges of the curved opening, the shell showed its crystalline clarity, and the coal that burned with a white-gold heat in its heart.

That secret, the fire at the heart of him, that love for his own fanoa (that was not the secret; it had never been a secret to anyone but himself), this shell made out of all the conscious work of his mind and all the fires of his soul, his heart, his spirit—

"No," Vou'a agreed after a moment. "She doesn't have this one. This is the best of you, Cliopher Mdang. Are you truly willing to give it up?"

Cliopher took a deep breath, and met the god's eyes as steadily as he had ever done anything in his life. "It is the best of what I have been, not who I will be, Buru Vou'a," he replied, "and I do not lose the fire by giving it to another."

Vou'a did not move for another long, long moment. And then he closed his fingers around the shell, cackled like a kookaburra, and said, "Oh, you Mdangs! Always ready with yet another metaphor about fire!"

"Buru Tovo taught me well," Cliopher agreed demurely, keeping the small wooden boat close in his other hand.

∾

Vou'a gave him a breakfast made out of leftover soup—"No sense wasting it!" the god said gleefully—and pointed at the half-transparent palace in the eastern clouds. "That's your destination, right enough, young Kip."

"Yes," said Cliopher. He hesitated a moment. "Why were you banned from visiting?"

Vou'a tapped the side of his nose. "Ah, that's the business of the gods. You've got enough to be working with, don't you? Tovo tells me you're quite the brilliant negotiator."

"Usually I try to gather all the information I can first."

"I might have said something about the Moon that was not particularly tactful." Vou'a snorted magnificently, rolling his eyes. "How was I to know she was *actually* pregnant?"

"The Moon?" Cliopher asked, astounded. "You've been exiled that long?"

"What?"

"The Moon's the mother of the sons of Harbut Zalarin," Cliopher said; the old imperial fiction felt at once more and less plausible than usual. "One of them was the first emperor of Astandalas."

Vou'a waved his hand dismissively. "Could be, could be. Doesn't seem like that long, but I don't always pay that much attention to which way I'm going. Time's one of mine, you know? A mystery."

That explained far too much, really.

"The Moon, though. She's a bit flighty, if you take my meaning. Falls for any mortal with a bit of magic and a singing voice." He peered hard at Cliopher. "You sing, don't you?"

Cliopher remembered the cold beauty of the Moon when she had come down in that moment of the lunar eclipse. She had not looked twice at *him*! "No magic," he said, gratefully.

"Nor much interest, eh?" Vou'a cackled. "Those poor sirens! They've been off collecting reinforcements, by the way. Don't be too cruel to the poor tirului, they're not used to being entirely ignored. Now, that's enough gossip, young Kip! Best be on your way. You've a long journey yet before you have that flame you've promised to get."

～

There were sirens—

Frolicking like dolphins under and over the waves and the foam, as he sailed eastward through the silvery light of a perpetual dawn, though the sun moved westward as he ever did.

There were dolphins, too, a whole pod of them, and mixed in with the dolphins were the sirens, male and female in face and torsos, dolphin-like in their tails as they swam.

Their hair streamed out behind them, copper and gold, silver and black, red and greeny-brown like kelp, and the blue water shivered and shook with the white bubbles of their powerful tails.

They called to one another and sang, leaping in and out of the water with the dolphins, their voices rising up in sweet harmonies, echoing down into the lower registers, as fine as he'd ever heard under his aunt's and uncle's direction at the Gorjo City opera house.

Cliopher smiled at them, admiring their lithe motions, their beautiful faces, their flashing eyes and their superb voices, but he felt no urge to do anything but keep his sail well-trimmed and the rudder pointing the vaha due east.

He'd been at court far too long to have his head turned by that look in someone's eye.

To be fair he'd *never* had his head turned by that look in someone's eye.

A brilliant conversation, now—

Not to mention tirului meant 'dear little ones', and once Vou'a had put *that* image into his head, Cliopher could not but look at all those beautiful young things the way he looked at Gaudy's friends.

He might have hired one or two of the sirens, if they'd been willing to apply themselves to something other than seduction and swimming.

(Back home—at the Palace, that was—Rhodin usually siphoned off the ones who were *particularly* interested in seduction, as he felt a roving eye a potential asset in court espionage.)

~

He sailed east, in the silvery light of dawn, towards the fragile palace in the clouds, with the sirens singing around him. They peeled off eventually, the sirens and their pod of dolphins, and Cliopher was left with the blue ocean and the silver sky and the distant cloud-castle slowly tinting with sunset-colours, sunrise-light, the lanterns of the stars hung around its halls in the impossible brilliance of the night, this close to the palace of day.

He could see reefs below the surface, but they seemed much deeper than the ones in that shallow maze on the other side of Vou'a's island.

The wind was constant from the west, and Cliopher was able to set his sail, lash it into position, lash the tiller, and simply sit, cross-legged and calm, on the decking, watching for anything that might come into sight.

Seven silver swordfish breached the surface and danced past, poised on their tails as if for a court dance or a fencing-lesson.

The white birds passed overhead, their wordless song like the break of dawn.

At night the stars were huger and more brilliant than ever, like the pearls that had formed the hearth of his fire in his heart.

Cliopher held the little model boat in his lap and imagined himself walking back along that grassy meadow, back along the shining river, back into that cave where the moss both covered and cradled all his past loves.

In his mind's eye, his heart's eye, he could spend all the time he needed uncovering each item, brushing off the moss, remembering the joys and heartbreaks and fears and hopes of his life, some of them as great as his love for Fitzroy, some of them as small as the lingering grudge he still felt for the Alinorel ambassador who had, he was almost certain, burned his letters to Basil.

Some he burned in the fire.

Most he set in a circle around the fire of his heart, where they could be watched over by the wise, one-eyed Au'aua.

Some he brought out into the light outside the cave, where the clean air and sunlight might help them ... heal.

～

The cloud-castle was growing large: it seemed to occupy half the horizon, like approaching Solaara from the river and seeing the Palace of Stars rising high above the city.

He did not know if it was his own imagination being shaped by his long experience that made the House of the Sun look so very much like the familiar palace of his working life, or if the ancient emperors who had designed it had seen this palace in Sky Ocean and tried to recreate it in mortal stone.

He considered the lost treasures of his heart, and he pondered the challenges Vou'a had given him, and he thought, when he could discipline his mind to the task, of all the stories he had heard about the House of the Sun.

Mostly he listened to the white birds singing—he could hear them even in the day and night, from their roosts all across the face of the Sun's palace—and looked at the great stars in the night, the white clouds and blue sky and silvery light of the eastern day—and let himself be who he was.

～

He had begun to hear the booming of the breakers on the fringing reefs of the House of the Sun, the farther shore of Sky Ocean, when the sea turtle came for him.

～

It might not, of course, have been the *same* turtle. He had not been able to notice any idiosyncrasies of shell markings or colouring when he rescued the one (so long ago, it seemed!) caught in that cross-current.

He wondered, looking into its dark and alien eye, what he might have met along this journey, had he not stopped for the turtle.

That was not a question anyone could answer, not even Vou'a; all the stories were clear that the journey was different for each person who hazarded the voyage, and each person could only do so once.

("It's not a matter of desire," Fitzroy had explained to him before he left. "It's a matter of ... *ability*. One *cannot* find one's way to the House of the Sun twice. If I tried, or El, or Auri, we would grow increasingly lost the further we tried to go.")

Cliopher inclined his head with great politeness to the sea turtle. "Greetings to you, donà," he said, the word for 'lore-keeper' falling from his lips with barely a conscious effort.

The turtle kept pace with him a few dozen yards, watching him with its strangely solemn eyes. From the two oblong scales between its eyes he would have identified it as a green sea turtle, but it was much larger than any he'd seen at home—easily as long as his vaha.

He'd had any number of long letters from his cousin Louya about sea turtles in the last year or so, he thought idly, smiling at the thought of her. Her letters were sometimes a trifle incoherent, often exasperating, occasionally useful, and always deeply entertaining.

The other Kip had said Louya was a seer; the other Louya, whom Cliopher had not encountered, had been trained in her visions by the shamans.

His Louya had always been considered odd, a bit risible, but ... if she *did* have visions, and had never been granted or sought out what she needed to know to determine which were fancies and which were true—

If that were the case, would she not develop that wild jumble of strange theories and impossibilities and relentless truths?

(The shamans were treated with respect, but no Mdang had gone to their number in a long, long time—for all Cliopher's multitudes of cousins, not one of them had joined that branch of the Ela lore keepers, Those Who Went Furthest.)

The sea turtle slowed. Cliopher hesitated just a moment, and then he unlashed the tiller and the sail and followed suit.

He sat there, bobbing gently in the easterly swell that swept to those waves thundering against the edge of the sky.

The turtle watched him, and then rolled sideways in the water before stabilizing and looking at him, he could not quite but think, *expectantly*.

He stared, uncomprehending.

The turtle rolled again.

TRUST THE SEA TURTLES, Louya had written in one her screeds. *THEY ARE LORE-KEEPERS AND KNOW MUCH.*

He touched the mast, the rope he would need to untie and pull if he wanted to—

The turtle rolled a third time, and then dove down into the water.

Cliopher swallowed, but this was a realm where—oh, where his cousin's mad starts might hold a truth he had never before seen.

Every story of Sky Ocean, of the realms of the gods, said that if you did a good turn, you would be rewarded.

Cliopher took a deep breath, as if he were diving for nefalao—as if he were diving into the dark water at what he hoped was not the bottom of his heart—and then he took the rope in one hand, stepped over to the outrigger, and deliberately capsized his boat.

The boat hesitated, tipped, splashed down into the water—

And was once again in the air.

Cliopher had closed his eyes instinctively, and now opened them in astonishment. He was wet with the dousing, but he was not submerged.

He blinked at his hands, the water dripping off them, and pushed back his suddenly-sodden hair.

And he breathed.

He breathed, controlled, steady, careful, for he would not panic.

The air was heavy, rich, cool, delicious. *Air.*

For a moment his eyes simply would not take in what he was seeing; his mind could not comprehend it.

There had been times when he stood at the edge of a puddle on the kind of day it had been on the other side, when there were clouds piled high in a limpid blue air. Sometimes (it was a sort of game he had played on occasion, if no one was around to see) he would adjust his positioning so that he stood just *so*, so that there was no glimpse *into* the puddle, and all it showed was sky.

The whole ocean around him was ... sky.

He didn't even look up for a few minutes, so astonished was he with the glowing clouds of the House of the Sun rising up—falling *down*—below him.

It was not the same as flying above the clouds in a sky ship, for he and his vaha were still clearly beneath them: he could see the flat bellies of the cloud-sheep where they were pressed against the floor of the winds, with the clouds mounding up above them.

But that *above* was *below*, and the whole sky opened up *under* him.

He looked up, and cringed.

The sky ... the ocean ... rose up, pellucid at first and darker as it extended away, until the lines of white sand and purple seagrass and umber and green kelp traced out their mysteries.

Cliopher slid down until he was laying flat, dizzy. He was beside the hatch beneath which was his fire-pot, and he reached in.

The coral-alabaster gleamed, warm and friendly and comforting, Fitzroy's friendship and regard (his *love*, Fitzroy himself had said, before Cliopher left on this quest), holding Cliopher's fire safe.

He closed the hatch and held the fire-pot in one arm, the little wooden boat safe in his other hand.

The turtle took the red feathers of the pennant on the mast in its mouth, and swam down. The vaha followed as if this were the most natural thing in the world.

~

The sea turtle spiralled in all dimensions, silent, graceful, stately. Cliopher kept flinching away from the coral formations until he realized that he was not steering, did not need to worry, was able to sit back and let his tense jaw and shoulders relax, his hands loosen their grip, and actually *look* at the sea around him.

The corals: smooth ones wrinkled like brains, ones branched like trees, others like deer horns, still others like tubes piled all on top of each other. And the colours! Green and blue, slate-grey and orange, red and pink and purple. Here were clusters of sea anemones with their attendant clownfish (not just orange and white, but also an intense violet and white); there were sea pens and tall, delicate sponges. Spotted sea slugs and perfectly transparent jellies, angelfish in black-and-white and blue-and-yellow and green-and-pink, and so many other fish and plants and sponges and shells Cliopher was dizzy with the surfeit of colour and form.

The sea turtle led his vaha through an arch in the reef, into a blue cave, right into the middle of a great cloud of silver fish. All the fish scattered away as one to form a ring, their movements each matched to each to form a mesmerizing whole.

The sea turtle spun through the fish again and again, forcing them together and apart. Cliopher watched, dazzled by the light glinting on the silver scales, the turtle's massy presence, the blue water. The sea turtle turned again and again, the vaha obediently following, until Cliopher was no longer able to distinguish up from down and he had to press himself, dizzy and dazed, against the smooth planking of his canoe, his little boat in one hand, his fire-pot in the other.

The sea turtle dove down, the vaha following in its wake, and Cliopher caught his breath despite himself, for they were plunging deep into the ultramarine depths below him.

Down and down, past a cloud of great translucent-gold jellyfish, their stingers streaming down like rays of sunlight. Down, past streams of tiny bubbles rising up; down, past huge shadowy fish, long and sleek and dangerous; down, into the topmost reaches of a kelp forest.

Down, and down, and suddenly Cliopher realized he was no longer thinking of this as *up*, for at some point during the play with the fish the sea turtle had turned the world around and gravity no longer was reversed for him.

And still they went down: to the very roots of the kelp, where purple sea urchins with gold-tipped spines crawled over a shingly floor, and crabs with magnificently jewelled and resplendent carapaces paced like courtiers across the sand.

There were eels down here, green and grey, cloudy purple and stippled with white and blue and silver. The kelp had stems as wide around as his wrist, seemingly delicate for such long fronds waving above them.

The sea turtle wove through the stems, the vaha pressing close behind, and then they came to the root of a mountain, in the face of which was a door.

CHAPTER FORTY-EIGHT
THE LONG STAIR

The sea turtle glanced over its shoulder at Cliopher, with an expression in its eyes that suddenly shocked him with its uncanniness. The invitation was clear: the vaha had come to a halt just beside the door, settling to a level just above the sea floor. He leaned forward, careful not to tumble off the canoe—who knew what would happen then?—and knocked three times.

When he glanced at the sea turtle it was to see it swimming off between the kelp. Shafts of light reached down from high above, illuminating a swath of its shell, one leg, one glinting eye.

"Thank you," he called.

"I haven't done anything yet," a voice said.

He swung around hastily. The door had opened, and an old, old woman stood there, peering at him. Her hair was a pure white, her eyes a sharp, brilliant brown. She was stooped with age, her hands knobbly with arthritis, her bronze skin loose and wrinkled, and she wore a Nijani flax dress with subtle patterns in the weave. Cliopher, looking on her, was struck with an intense pang of longing for his distant family.

He bowed over his hands. "I bid you greetings, Grandmother," he said, for she felt so much akin to him that he could not call her by any less familiar term.

"Few come to this door," the Grandmother said, "and I have never seen *you* before. What business brings you across the Sea of Stars?"

Cliopher swallowed, but he had the fire-pot between his knees, and he was who he was—and who he wanted to be. He smiled at her. "Tanaea-te imalo," he said. "Moa'alani-ki imalo! Kifa'ana imai?"

The words were solid, ritual, *true*.

The Grandmother tilted her head at him, her eyes so sharp and striking. "A hearth-fire to the house of the Sun? News of Sky Ocean? And you ask *me* if I have problems to set before *you*? Who are you?"

He stayed where he was, kneeling on the decking of his vaha, the fire-pot before him. "I am Cliopher Mdang of Tahivoa. My island is Loaloa. My dances are Aōteketētana."

"You are very free with your name for one who sails this ocean."

"It is my own, and I do not lose it by sharing it with you," he replied, as serene as Fitzroy ever was at his imperial best. "I am the tanà of my people, and it is my place to light fires and share them."

The Grandmother weighed his words; more than his words, himself.

But Cliopher had weighed the merits of those who came before him, and he had done his best, both sides of that secret water in the heart of the mountain. He had tried to be just, when he sat unwillingly in judgment, and when Aioru had come with ideas of a better form of justice—a *juster* form—Cliopher had given him the opportunity and support to see it done.

"You are mortal," the Grandmother said, surprise in her voice. "How came you to the Lower Door?"

"The sea turtle brought me, Grandmother."

Her eyebrows raised. "And why was that, I wonder?" That did not seem to be a question she expected him to answer, for she suddenly laughed, light and clear like a young girl's. Cliopher stared at her in wonder, wondering who this was: this old woman, this goddess, who kept the secret door at the bottom of the sea that led into the House of the Sun.

"Come in and be welcome, Cliopher Mdang of Loaloa, by the door that no one enters. Yes, your vaha will fit through—there you are."

Cliopher did not need to do anything, for once given permission the vaha floated in of its own accord. The Grandmother stepped aside—had she been standing on water? Or had there been no water until she invited him? He had been unable to see past her, until she let him in.

Whatever had been, what he saw now was this: a circular stone room with exceedingly tall walls, like the very bottom of a well. The vaha slid in through the door into a small pool that took up perhaps half the space. The other half was a shore of dark basalt rocks, much encrusted with barnacles and green-lipped mussels, with a few soft, glistening mounds of dormant anemones in a rainbow of colours. Between the rocks was a thick mud, of a strange greenish-brown.

Cliopher took up his fire-pot and the little wooden boat. His hair fell into his eyes, and he brushed it back with the back of his hand, even as he stepped off the boat onto the land. His legs felt weak and wobbly after so long at sea, and the mud squelched oddly between his toes.

He had made his challenge: now was the time to see what came of it.

The Grandmother stood with the end of a very long rope in her hand. It rose up and out of sight, lost in the brightness at the top of the well.

"Here," the Grandmother said. "You may tie your vaha to this, I suppose."

"Thank you," he said, setting his fire-pot down on a rock beside him so that he could fasten his painter to the rope. The air here was cool, but he could not smell anything, which was disconcerting. He finished his knot and picked up his fire-pot again. He could hold it with one arm, though it was an awkward size, roughly the size of his head.

He had made landfall, and he had secured his boat, the first, fundamental step.

Next was what it always was, to assess the situation.

Look first. Listen first. Questions later.

"Come, come," the Grandmother said, hobbling over to an arched opening in the wall. She had a stick in her hand, which he hadn't noticed before. It too was curved and bent and seemed very old, driftwood shaped to her need over years of use.

He hastened after, to find that there was a stair cut into the rock. A basket of mud sat there, as if the Grandmother had been collecting it when he knocked. It was large, with straps to go over the shoulders.

"If you'd truly like to do something for me," the Grandmother said, "you could carry that up for me."

"Of course," he said easily.

"It's a long stair," she warned him, her eyes twinkling.

"Of course," he said, even more easily.

"You're a strange one, aren't you?"

He smiled even as he once more set down his pot and knelt down so he could put his arms into the straps of the basket. "Some have told me so," he agreed as he felt the weight of the mud settle onto his shoulders. Before he stood he took up the fire-pot once more, tucking it under his left arm so he could hold the little model boat in that hand and have one free for balance.

The Grandmother nodded once, and then grinned at him. "See you at the top, if you can make it!"

～

As soon as he stepped foot on the stair Cliopher was finally aware of *smells* again. He took several deep, nearly gulping breaths: tasting brine, and cold stone, and salty air, and the scent of tui blossoms that must have been from the Grandmother's clothes or hair. He climbed after her, the stone cold and rough under his bare feet.

There were barnacles on the walls, from tiny white ones to huge goose barnacles the size of his hand. They were interspersed with patches of mussels, green-lipped and then, as they climbed higher, ones with silver rims and others with shining blue shells and others the colour of jet.

The stair twisted in a tight spiral, with really only just enough room to set one foot at a time. The Grandmother's staff plunked down beside her, unerringly hitting the narrowest possible part of the wedge. Cliopher kept to the outside, though that meant his shoulder occasionally scraped on the barnacles and mussels.

Up, and up, and up. The basket was very heavy, digging into his shoulder.

He could not recall the last time he had carried something so heavy.

He could not recall if he'd ever carried anything like this. Surely he must have? When he was young he'd helped with the yam harvest on Loaloa, as everyone did: if one didn't help with the harvest, one didn't get to eat the yams except as a guest, and no one who lived there wanted to be seen as a *guest*. He had helped with gusto, digging the great tubers and helping bear them to the village yam-house for storage. Thus was Loaloa *his* island. He could feel a dim sense of it in the far distance, a soft, gentle reminder that he had not lost his way.

Up, and up, and up. His knees were creaking audibly.

He'd carried baskets of coral rubble for Buru Tovo, helping to build a platform for some reason he couldn't quite recall. He'd felt rather unjustly used that time, if he remembered correctly—that was it, he had never been told what the platform *was* for. It was taboo for those uninitiated, apparently, and he had never been initiated into that secret.

He still didn't know how many things he had not been initiated into because he had chosen to go to Astandalas and then to stay in Solaara.

The other Kip had said he'd gone back to Loaloa and been initiated.

Cliopher did not want to be the kind of tanà the other Kip was.

Up, and up, and up. The sweat was pouring down him, hot and steaming in the coolness of the well. He shifted the basket to the other shoulder, then hastily back again when he nearly unbalanced and fell.

"It's a long way back down!" the Grandmother said.

He didn't dare lift his head from his cautious regard of the stairs directly before him. Her feet and staff danced up lightly, tirelessly.

He was not tireless or light. He plodded. There were still barnacles and mussels, and bits of seaweed attached to the corners of the stairs, the central pillar. The widest part of the steps were kept clear, but the edges of his feet kept squishing on plants. He didn't mind the texture, but he was worried about slipping.

Up, and up, and up. The Grandmother was far ahead of him now, her pattering feet out of sight, and then only a faint echo.

He had carried the world on his shoulders, too.

Cliopher kept climbing.

～

He came to a landing, and stopped, the basket pressed against the wall for support, trying not to retch with the exertion.

He did not dare set the basket down, but he gripped the fire-pot and breathed in the fragments of familiar smoke that escaped under its coral lid, almost as delicious and dear to him now as incense.

(Conju had somehow created a perfume for him that gave the impression of a burning fire without smelling in the least like smoke or ash. Cliopher disliked wearing perfumes, a courtly custom he had never been able to appreciate, but he let Shoänie scent his clothes delicately with the one Conju had made for him, because it was both a gift from a dear friend and somehow, mysteriously, a comforting sense of home.)

His breath came in great heaves. His ribs were sore from the gasping, his eyes streaming.

Eventually he caught his breath, and could lift his head stiffly, wary of the high back of the basket, to look around him.

The spiral stair led into a corridor, illuminated by windows that cast a speckled golden light across the dark stone. In the distance was another dark opening, and a pale-coloured stair going once more up.

Cliopher did not in the least want to continue climbing, but this was the Grandmother's response to his challenge, and how he did with this task would shape his negotiations to come.

He pushed off the wall with a great groan that rumbled embarrassingly through the hollow stone, and staggered forward a few steps before he got the trick of walking with the heavy basket on his shoulders.

He passed into the hall. The windows opened not on lights or fires or lamps, or stars in their daytime slumbers, or anything of the sort.

There were apertures high, high above him, that cast down great shafts of sunlight like the beams piercing through clouds.

The sunbeams bounced off the treasure-hoard of the Sun.

Cliopher staggered past the arched and open doors, admiring the glint of gold and jewels, uninterested in looking closer.

He had spent decades assessing the tithes sent in to the last Emperor of Astandalas, the Lord of Rising Stars, the Sun-on-Earth. He was sure there were items in the Sun's possession that were finer than anything he'd ever seen before, but he had no lust for them.

He came to the second stair, which climbed up in a single flight out of his sight, like one of those sunbeams falling down from the high vaulted roof of that enormous treasure-chamber, and dared not hesitate even a moment before setting his shoulders against the backward drag of the basket and continuing up.

∾

They did not have climbing songs at home, but they had any number of other repetitive tasks about as boring and monotonous and potentially dangerous. Cliopher picked a coral-crushing song almost at random, as the stresses matched well with his steps.

And still the stair went up.

∾

There was a library, the scent of leather and parchment and paper and ink unmistakable.

There were windows that opened onto gardens, full of water and greenery and wind chimes.

There were rooms that opened into store-rooms full of all the foods and drinks the gods could desire or human beings could imagine.

There were baths, and bedchambers, and places full of all the tools and materials for any craft or art or activity Cliopher could think of.

∾

He was tempted—of course he was tempted—but he had been offered bribes many times before, and he wanted something none of those tempters had ever understood, nor that the way to it lay far from the things they offered.

∾

At last he came to the top of the long, straight stair.

He staggered forward a few steps, enough to realize that he had come upon a wide, airy place—enough to stop, and slide the heavy basket off his back, and set it down as gently as he could upon the stone flags.

He set down his fire-pot and the little wooden boat, and then he bent over, hands on his thighs, every part of his body burning.

When he could look around, he did so, curiosity warring with a deep, deep exhaustion. But he was curious—too curious for his own good—too clever by half— too *stubborn* by half—and he had been tired before.

Half his life, it felt like.

He stood on a pavement of a pale stone, which extended in a wide semi-circle out from a cliff of living stone. The stair had come out at one end of the cliff. In the distance on the opposite side of the half-moon he could see a dark circle, which he guessed was the top of the well.

The cliff formed a wall halfway around the circle; the other half of the arc was formed of a colonnade of white pillars joined by stone arches the same semicircular curve as the door. The whole area was open to the sky above: when he looked up, it *was* sky, though there was something odd about it, a crystalline clarity and a purple depth to the blue and a certain sense that it did not extend as far as it usually did.

There was no sign of the Grandmother.

He waited, patient because he had begun the negotiations, and he could be patient—terribly patient, terrifyingly patient to others—when it came to achieving what he had set out to do.

Peace, prosperity, the complete dismantling of the power structures of Astandalas … oh those had been long, long endeavours, requiring him to bank the fire of his heart again and again, until the embers burned like the coals of the fire dance, and he could go dancing across the gaps he had cut in them, his political opponents and counterparts left puzzled by how he did it.

They thought there were tricks, but there were no tricks.

Only patience, and hard work, and careful preparations, and long, long practice, and the readiness to move as soon as the cue came.

～

He waited.

～

No one came, though the light coming through the colonnade changed in quality and degree. The sun was setting, he thought idly, squatting beside the basket of mud, his fire-pot, his little wooden boat.

Sunset.

Above him, the sky was darkening, deepening in colour: a deeper blue, a richer violet. The star-lanterns burned, their people coming in and out of sight, ever more seemingly figures instead of points or pearls of light.

Cliopher could be patient, terrifyingly patient, but—

But he stood here on some sort of landing-place or ledge, halfway or more up the cloud-mountain on which was built the cloud-palace of the Sun, and it was sunset, and there was no sign of the Grandmother.

He started to grow perhaps the triflingest bit irritated.

～

The sun was definitely setting on the other side of the Wide Seas, which meant, theoretically, that the Sun would be coming home to this house of his soon.

Cliopher was muddy, and tired, and a little irritated, and more than a little hungry.

This was not what he'd thought his arrival would be. He'd thought—

He glanced at the basket of mud, and rubbed at the streaks of greening-brown ooze drying on his arms and torso. His grass skirt was tattered, worn, its bright sunset-colours not exactly *faded*, but dimmed by wear and dirt.

He'd thought he'd arrive in glory, like a hero of old, like the third son of Vonou'a or Aurelius Magnus or Fitzroy Angursell and the Red Company. He'd thought ...

He'd thought he was *important*, somehow. He'd forgotten he wasn't here for himself, but with a task—several tasks—entrusted to him.

He laughed, until the air rang with it, until he started to hiccough and cry, until the star-people seemed almost to notice him.

And then he shouldered that basket of mud one more time, picked up his fire-pot and his little wooden boat as the talismans they were, and he felt a little spark of indignation.

Oh, he didn't need to be noticed by the gods to be named in the *Lays*—or in Fitzroy's song of this journey—but that didn't mean he deserved to be *ignored*.

He had sailed across Sky Ocean! He had fulfilled the tasks given him—*even* this terrible basket of mud up that horrendous stair—and for what? for the person who met him to disappear without further instruction (or even *thanks*), for the stars to look blankly down, for the House of the Sun to be silent and unwelcoming and, frankly, *cold*?

No.

He was Cliopher Mdang of Tahivoa. His island was Loaloa. His dances were Aōteketētana. He was the tanà of the world and the Hands of the Emperor, and he was on a *quest*.

His arrival into Astandalas—his return home—his subsequent return to Solaara —had been equally ignominious, and look what had happened *there*.

He'd said he could run the government better than the rest, and he *had*.

He shouldered that heavy, heavy basket, though his legs quivered under its weight, and he walked along the cliff-wall until he found the stair that led up.

The stair was carved out of the outer wall, without handrail or retaining wall. It was vertiginous, the zigzags across the face difficult to manoeuvre with that basket on his shoulders, his hands full of his two treasures, and the winds—half-seen figures all hair and feathery wings and long narrow fingers—seemed to pluck at his hair and the fibres of his skirt and even the mud in the basket.

The sky darkened to its lustrous black, but the stair was the white of moonlit clouds, each edge rimmed in black shadow, and he knew his way.

He set himself against the wind, resolutely ignored the way the cliff seemed to fall all the way down into the mortal worlds below, the way the high back of the basket had caught his wind-blown hair, the way his legs quivered and his lungs burned and his heart thundered, and instead nurtured a fine and splendid flame of righteous fury in his heart as he climbed all the way up to the open front door of the House of the Sun.

He didn't bother knocking. His hands were full.

CHAPTER FORTY-NINE
THE GOLDEN HALL

The double doors were open, to the brilliant night sky behind him that, Cliopher was quite sure, looked like an extension of the room before him.

His first thought was that it was not as grand as the throne room of the Palace of Stars.

His second was that it was far lovelier.

The Palace of Stars was designed to impress upon all onlookers the fundamental claim of the Emperors of Astandalas to divinity. In its throne room, every line and every ornament was in service to that singular idea, converging on the resplendent inhabitant of the throne at its focal point.

In the House of the Sun, the double doors opened onto a great and welcoming hall. White marble pillars marched down each side, with come-and-go walls between them: sometimes Cliopher could see stone walls and wooden doors, other times they were half-transparent, or fully invisible, and he could see the rolling midnight meadows and silver-edged cloud-sheep drifting beyond.

The floor was a smoothly polished limestone, cool and pleasant under Cliopher's bare feet. He bounced on the balls of his feet, the heavy weight of the basket of mud nearly familiar, nearly easy.

Not easy. The weight of the government had never been *easy*, even after he had grown accustomed to it. He had still felt it, in his bones and the hollows of his mind, his grey hairs and the long, lonesome hours at his desk. But he had learned to bear it, and he bore this weight now, with his shoulders braced under the burden but his back straight and his head up for all that.

He looked up, to find the hall open to the heavens. The luminous faces of the stars—and they *were* faces—were looking down with mild interest, but none of those gazes were directed at him.

There was a throne in the centre, a carved wooden seat set beside a great semicircular basin that looked as if it were made of gold but probably wasn't. It held a fire, which possessed all the qualities of the sun without being blinding in the same degree.

The throne was made of ebony bound, he thought, with gold, and had a blue cushion upon it. The Sun lounged upon it, a giant with skin the colour of the shadows he cast, the children he had sired, all the way down that long line of emperors to the one Cliopher knew and loved.

The ones he knew; on whose behalf he had come.

The hall, like its walls, was both empty and full. Empty at one angle of his head, full of figures at another. They were each supernaturally beautiful, displaying all the human colours of skin and hair Cliopher had ever seen or imagined, all the shapes and heights a person might be. Some were as slender as the sylphs in the stories, others even fuller in figure than Sardeet Avramapul.

All seemed young, as young as his niece Leona, and it made him smile to imagine Leona and all her friends chattering and laughing like this.

He could not help but wonder what, in the allegorical scheme of things, they represented. Who might be the attendants of the Sun?

He seemed to recall a line of poetry saying that *the Hours are the handmaidens of the Sun*, but it did not come from the *Lays* and he did not know if it were just some poet's fancy speaking.

Did it come from one of Fitzroy's poems? *He* knew such things.

Fitzroy would not have stood here in the doorway of the hall, a basket of mud oozing slime down his torso, his hair caught in the wickerwork, clutching a child's toy and a priceless gift in his hands.

Fitzroy would have somehow contrived to have a bath and a change of clothes, and no doubt swept in with his harp and his laughter and his golden voice. He would have spun all these fine Hours into an eager audience, warmed the Sun on his throne with his rhetoric and his kinship, made of this encounter a story worthy of his pen.

Cliopher had not contrived a bath and a change of clothes, and he did not have his writing kit with him, and not a single person in that hall was giving him so much as a curious glance.

Well. They would learn better soon enough that he had his tongue and his right hand, his mind and his heart, the *Lays* on the one hand and all the stories Fitzroy and Aurelius and Elonoa'a had told him on the other, and—far better than kinship with the Sun—the strength and expectation of his fanoa behind him.

With that rock under his foot, that direction given, Cliopher had reformed the world.

Look first. Listen first.

Cliopher assessed the space, thinking about what it implied about the Sun at its centre.

That basin of fire was the flame he sought, surely.

The Sun was proud, and vain, and generous; but he was not so vain as the Emperors of Astandalas had been, for he had no need to be. He could be far more generous, for he was the Sun whose flame would not go out so long as the worlds endured, and his glory was paramount.

(*Or*, said a voice in the back of Cliopher's mind, the part of him that had always taken a step back to look at the wider picture: *or the Sun's glory was the* image *of the paramount, as the Emperors had sought to be image of the Sun to their subjects.*)

A white bird landed beside Cliopher with a rustle of wings. It had intelligent eyes and a beak sharp as the sunlight when you had a hangover, and spoke to him in a voice that prickled like sunburn.

"Deliveries," it whispered, "to the *back*."

Cliopher had received any number of such remarks, and without quipping anything about what *possible* deliveries there could need to be, to the House of the Sun, he smiled affably at the bird and ignored it in favour of taking a breath, firming his diaphragm, and projecting his voice across the entire length of the hall.

"And is this," he said, his voice ringing through the hall, "the vaunted hospitality of the House of the Sun?"

The whispering hours fell silent, and the stars were suddenly sharper, more brilliant, like the ones above a high mountain. The white bird screeched with indignation, and made as if to peck the boat from his hands.

Cliopher did not move, did not look aside, did not do anything but lift his chin and look straight into the Sun.

"Tanaea-te imalo," he cried, even as he imagined the song Fitzroy would write of this. "Moa'alani-ki imalo!" And then, with a finely judged sliver of sarcasm, for he had spent his lifetime at court and he knew this dance, "Kifa'ana imai?"

How he loved these moments before the negotiation started. Every step a step in the dance, though the other party did not yet know Cliopher was shaping the very possibilities and probabilities of the answers that would be given, the offers made, the trades accepted.

The Sun looked back at him, as his challenge echoed in the distant corners of the hall.

Cliopher let the silence unfold, unfurl, unroll. At precisely the moment before another would break it—he imagined he heard the Sun draw in his breath—Cliopher said, "I had not heard that one who sailed across Sky Ocean would be greeted with such *disdain*."

The white bird squawked and protested, but the Sun lifted his hand, and it fell silent.

The Sun was frowning, the faintest shadow across his radiance, just the hint that he was taken aback. Cliopher did not look down, no matter that his eyes were watering with the power and light facing him.

Then the Sun spoke, his voice like a great golden bell, shivering into the corners of his hall. "Come in, then, and be a guest at my hearth, you who have brought your own fire, and tell me the news of an ocean that is not my sky, for I did not see you sail it, and perhaps I can do something for you, since you presume to be able to do something for *me*."

Cliopher did not smile in exultation, for that would be unprofessional, but he could not deny the lightness of his heart and step as he set foot across the threshold not as a supplicant, but as one with guest-right and answers to give and the promise of an unspecified boon.

Honestly, it was as if the Sun wasn't even *trying*.

He walked down the half-empty, half-thronged hall, his feet slapping on the white limestone, the stars looking down.

No one said anything, nor came too close.

Cliopher was aware that the mud smelled oozy and organic, and he himself was encrusted with salt and grime, the bright sunset colours of his grass skirt discoloured by rough use and the vile liquor trailing down his skin.

At what would have been the requisite distance for the Sun-on-Earth—at least for the Viceroy of Zunidh, the Hands of the Emperor, his dear friend—Cliopher stopped and stood solidly before the throne.

This close, he could see that the Sun was massive and yet perfectly proportionate, an exquisitely formed giant, black of skin and gold of impression. He might have been wearing cloth-of-gold or he might simply have been garbed in his own splendid light for all Cliopher could tell of his garments.

The Sun stared down at Cliopher with burning eyes, taking in every detail of his appearance and demeanour.

It felt absurdly like being examined by Prince Rufus of Amboloyo, who had never ceased to consider Cliopher as some extraordinary fluke of nature that had to be constantly watched *in case.*

(In case of what? Prince Rufus had never successfully prevented Cliopher from doing anything he wanted, though admittedly he thought he had; his entire eulogy had insisted on it.)

"And so," said the Sun in a rumble that sounded at once very close and very far away, "you stand before me in your ... grime. Is this what is expected of a guest come to a house?"

Cliopher said nothing. He slid one arm out of the basket, balancing the great weight just for a moment on one shoulder, so that he could transfer his fire-pot and toy boat to the other hand. When he made to release the other strap, he remembered painfully how his hair was caught in the basket's weave. He gritted his teeth to keep from over-balancing, and bent over as he set the basket down.

He tried to be gentle, but it nevertheless landed with a thud that reverberated like an earthquake.

Cliopher did not notice what reaction, if any, either the Sun or his half-invisible courtiers made to this. He was too busy trying to tug his hair out of the wickerwork in anything resembling a graceful fashion, and with only one hand free this was not happening at all.

He finally tore a handful of hairs out and straightened with them fluttering in his hand, eyes swimming with tears, light-headed and dizzy with exertion. He breathed, re-centering himself.

How much Fitzroy would laugh! *He* would not have had this happen to him!— but then again, Fitzroy would hardly have carried the basket up that whole long stair in the first place. His stubbornness took other forms.

Cliopher rolled back his shoulders and lifted his chin to look again at the Sun.

The Sun was staring at his hand, shock on his face and in every line of his bearing.

Cliopher dropped his own gaze. Along with a cluster of wavy black and silver strands of hair, he held a single black feather the length of his forearm.

He felt a cold thrill shiver along his back. Surely that wasn't—that wasn't *the* black feather, the one that had been lost?

(It had not been in the basket, not when he had set it down on any of the landings between the bottom of the sea and the feet of the Sun. Not until he had climbed all the way up that long, long stair.)

He set himself, staring proudly at the Sun, ready to negotiate on behalf of those who had sent him.

"Who *are* you?" the Sun demanded. "How did you come here? What do you want?"

What questions to be asked! *These* could go in the *Lays*!

Cliopher smiled at the Sun with his best bureaucrat's expression, the one that had driven Pali Avramapul to such distraction.

"I am Cliopher Mdang of Tahivoa," he said, his voice clear, ringing through the hall. "My island is Loaloa, and my dances are Aōteketētana. I came here in a boat my ancestors made for me, following the ke'ea I was told to take to the best of my abilities. As for what I want, O Sun—" He smiled, moving his hands to indicate their miscellaneous contents. "I am the tanà of my people, and when the tanà travels to a new island, he brings a fire to add to the lore-keepers, and news of the seas he has crossed, the peoples he has met, and he asks the ones he meets if there is anything he can do for them."

The Sun seemed for a moment just as stunned as Cliopher could have wished for.

"What could I want with your puny pot of fire, when I have my own?" the Sun growled. "What news can *you* have that I have not seen with my own eyes? And what problems do you think I have? What sort of person are you, to trespass in my house and traipse *dirt* all over my floor?"

Cliopher lifted his chin, for he was not Aurelius Magnus, that wizard and warrior, nor Elonoa'a the great navigator with his stalwart crew, nor Fitzroy Angursell with his music and his brilliance and all his friends at his side.

He was himself, and he would not be made lesser, not though he stood at the feet of the Sun.

"I am Cliopher Mdang of Tahivoa," he said again. "My island is Loaloa, and my dances are Aōteketētana. And I had never heard, O Sun, that you were so *churlish*. Your generosity is legend in the worlds below: your light and your warmth and your wisdom given freely to all. So I was told when I said I was travelling hither—'Ah! I remember the sweetness of the mead made in the House of the Sun!' 'I remember the music! Listen well when you go, for the songs they sing now!' 'Sit at the feet of the Sun and learn wisdom from the fount of it, as the third son of Vonou'a learned wisdom, the lore and the *Lays*!'"

His voice dropped, scathing. Without that basket on his back the fire-pot seemed light in his hands, the boat and the feather insubstantial. "And instead, what do I find? I knocked on the door, and was invited in. I told the old woman who met me, the Grandmother as I called her, that I brought fire for the hearth of this house and news of the seas, and when I asked her if she had any task I might do for her, she asked me to carry this basket up from the bottom of the sea."

He indicated the oozy, stinking mud. The Sun looked upon it, his expression clouding.

The thronging courtiers had left the circle containing throne and fire-bowl and Cliopher truly empty; the flames roared, at once very soft and enormously loud (like the rolling thunder of the breakers on the edge of the sky, which he had heard before he followed the sea turtle down into the depths of the sea), and the courtiers whispered and rustled to each other like distant air, the memories of distant hours.

"I have carried the basket up the spiral stair, and up the straight stair, and up the stair that zig-zags its way up and across the face of the cliff," he said, "and I did not cross that upper threshold until you invited me in, O Sun. I am no trespasser."

"Your hands and feet are muddied and bloodied and bruised," the Sun said, "but you bear no stains of silver or gold or the glitter of my treasure."

"What need have I to steal from you?" Cliopher retorted. "The Grandmother gave me her task. If you do not wish her gift, then tell me where to take it, and I shall continue on my way."

He moved as if to pick the basket back up, his motions slow but smooth, showing neither his exhaustion nor his cunning, and before he had done more than once more switch around what he was holding so he had a hand free, the Sun said, "Wait."

Cliopher straightened and waited, patient as a fisherman. The Sun frowned down upon him.

The Sun was proud, and vain, and generous—and *curious*.

That, truly, was the best possible characteristic to encounter in a Power.

"Who are you, who came to the Lower Door?" the Sun cried into his silence. "Why did the Old Woman Who Dwells in the Deeps give you a basket full of the firmament to carry up? *How* did you carry it so far as you did? What must I give in return for these gifts you have brought me?"

He stopped there, his voice echoing off the columns like the sunspots Cliopher had once seen in Astandalas.

Cliopher waited politely, and then he met those burning eyes again. They were not gold as were those of his descendants: they seemed to burn with a white fire, like the magic rising up in Aurelius's eyes, in Fitzroy's.

"I am Cliopher Mdang of Tahivoa," Cliopher said, steady as the rock upon which the world turns. "My island is Loaloa. My dances are Aōteketētana. I asked the Grandmother what I might do for her, and that was what she asked of me. I climbed the stair one step at a time, as I must, O Sun, for I am a mortal man, though I have carried the world upon my shoulders before. I offer you the fire for your hearth and the news of the seas I have crossed freely to you, for I am the tanà of my people, and we Hold the Fire that was entrusted to us from the first fire my far-distant ancestor brought us from you."

The Sun stared at him.

The courtiers murmured to each other, their voices like any sunny morning, any afternoon, limpid, clear, lively. Cliopher could imagine sweet hours speaking with his friends, sitting with his family, feasting with his community; afternoons spent engrossed in his work, winkling out improvements one by one, pearls out of the massy shells of a government like the great barrier reef around the island of the Sun.

Each step of this dance was one he had practiced until it came without thought or strain, and he waited for the fish to swim into his net.

One pearl for a token, and two for a promise, and five for an efela. If the Sun had stopped with three questions—

But he hadn't.

The Sun flung up his hands in a sudden exasperation. "What do you *want*? I will give you a boon, if only you tell me how you came here without my knowledge!"

Cliopher smiled.

CHAPTER FIFTY
THE SUN

In the golden hall, standing before the Sun, with the mud drying as it dripped off him, Cliopher used his words and his actions to position one specific sequence of responses as the one his opponent would naturally and happily take.

No matter it was the very Sun from out of the sky: Cliopher knew his nature from observation and all the stories he had heard.

He was proud, and vain, and generous, and curious.

"Well?" the Sun demanded, moving restlessly in his throne. "You have a strange notion of what it means to be a guest, that you come with such challenges and offer nothing in return."

And *impatient*.

Cliopher blessed all those long years facing off against Prince Rufus.

"I have offered you fire, and knowledge, and my ear to your problems," Cliopher replied evenly. "So far you have offered me nothing bar empty promises. Not a sip of water, not a morsel of food, not a cloth with which to clean my face, not a place to sit and rest, not even a song of welcome."

The Sun stiffened on his throne.

Oh, Cliopher knew the steps of this dance. He smiled up. "And yet, what am I, before you? I am not one of the heroes out of legend, your descendants with eyes the colour of your light! I have no magic of my own. All that I am is shaped and guided by those who have gone before me. I bring you the fire that has been lit, flame to flame, from that first fire you gave to my distant ancestor, the third son of Vonou'a, who sailed hither to sit at your feet and know wisdom."

"I note that *you* do not sit."

"How should I dare to, for myself? I am nothing in your eyes, O Sun. I sailed here in a boat of my ancestors' making. I carry the fire that I lit, in a pot that was made for me by the magic of one of your descendants."

He held out his hands, coral fire-pot balanced in one palm, the toy boat on the other.

"And that black feather?" the Sun asked, with an intensity that belied his effort at studied neutrality.

Cliopher held the feather pinched between finger and thumb in his left hand, where it rose up above the toy boat like a great standard.

"This?" He regarded it with a careful appearance of nonchalance. It was a black feather, nearly the length of his forearm, gleaming with the shining, almost purple-blue iridescence of obsidian or midnight or a crow's wing.

Akuava'a, the Black God, had given just such a feather to Vou'a.

"Yes, that," the Sun said, and now he was leaning forward. "What will you—what do you want for it?"

Cliopher blinked at him, face court-neutral, hastily rearranging his plan for the next few steps. A child in a marketplace knew not to begin a prospective barter with *that*!

"What, then? A flame of my fire? Knowledge that you have lost? The solution to *your* problems?"

The Sun was not very good at sarcasm, either.

Cliopher had irritated *any* number of people by taking what they said to him at face value.

"Your generosity is indeed the stuff of legend! I agree to your offer: A flame of your fire, in return for my own. The name of the third son of Vonou'a, in return for my tale of how I crossed Sky Ocean, since I was too small and unimportant for you to notice. And for the feather: the mirimiri of Ani."

The Sun stared, and then laughed, so that the whole hall shivered and shuddered and shimmered with light. "What cleverness is this? How dare you ask for such things? A flame of *my* fire? A name torn from the Great Naming? Something that I won by my own hard work and effort?"

Cliopher smiled at him, serene as the Sun-on-Earth. "As the fire may be shared without losing any of its nature, so ask I for your flame, and so shall I share mine. And as you share a name to my ears without losing it yourself, so shall I share my story with you, and keep it for my own memories as well."

"That is not the nature of *my* fire," the Sun grumbled.

"You share your light and warmth in the worlds below without stint or ceasing. I had never thought to hear you so chary here, in your own hall. But no matter my thoughts! It is your reputation, O Sun, that will be shaped by the songs I sing on my return home."

The Sun shifted and grumbled on his throne, the floor vibrating with his displeasure. The Hours whispered and murmured: the anxious hours, the worried ones, the dismal and shadowed ones, the ones that seemed to drag on indefinitely.

Cliopher was a professional. He did not roll his eyes or smirk or do anything but raise his eyebrows, and then, when the Sun still gave no reply, he shrugged, and rearranged his grip of fire-pot and boat and feather once again so he could shoulder the basket of mud.

It was even heavier than he'd remembered, but he managed to get it up on his back without throwing all his muscles into a spasm.

He had gotten as far as the door when the Sun said, "Wait."

Cliopher turned, hoping his face showed none of the strain of that basket on his back, none of his satisfaction with the progress of this negotiation.

"Come back," the Sun said, a distinct whine entering his voice. "I am not finished."

Cliopher walked back at a moderate pace, his face court-polite and curious. "I do apologize, O Sun," he said easily. "I had taken the discussion as complete."

The Sun grimaced and squirmed on his seat, and finally burst out: "I will have that boat made by your ancestors as well!"

"This one?" Cliopher said, indicating the toy in his hand. "In return, then, I expect hospitality for myself and any of my kith and kin who find their way to your hall, especially including my great-uncle's husband, who desires greatly to drink your honey-mead."

"Done," said the Sun, with a relief Cliopher was quite sure he would rue when the Son of Laughter once more showed up at his door.

That was four things, and in Cliopher's culture, things came in threes or fives; four was not a number for a fairy tale.

Nor was it the joy of poetry; or at least not Fitzroy's, either.

On one of the evenings before Cliopher set off, Fitzroy had said something about the artistic preferability of odd numbers, but he had been a little drunk on arrak and Cliopher had not followed the entirety of his argument. Odd numbers were more satisfying to the soul, as even numbers to the reason, Fitzroy had said, and gone off on a long digression about Cliopher's excessive enjoyment of censuses combined with something about the ballad form being an exception to the rule.

Cliopher did not want a ballad made out of this quest; he wanted an epic.

He wanted the *Lays* to sing of him.

And so—four trades was not enough.

Cliopher pondered what he would be taking back with him. Something for Elonoa'a and Aurelius—something for Ani—something for his people (the very name of the third son of Vonou'a! Tales of Elonoa'a! Songs and knowledge from the Ancestors!)—something for Vou'a and Cliopher's own family—

He was missing something for Fitzroy.

Fitzroy would undoubtedly say something about how the tale of this adventure was more than enough, but ... But that did not seem enough to Cliopher. He should bring a gift for his fanoa, too.

The Sun had sent one of the attendants to fetch something—the mirimiri? a witness?—and Cliopher stood there with his shins pressing against the cool, wet exterior of the basket of mud, trying to physically prevent himself from trembling with exhaustion. He still held the fire-pot in one hand, the model boat and mysterious feather in the other, and now that the mud had mostly dried he felt itchy and full of grit.

But he watched the Sun steadily. Until he was on his way, all the trade-goods safely in his possession, he would not consider the negotiation *finished*.

The Sun slumped on the throne, elbow on the armrest, chin on his fist, glowering heavily at him. Cliopher was sure his increasing headache was due at least in part to incipient sunstroke, which was vastly irritating.

But he waited, glad of the cool stone under his feet, the wetness on the basket against his skin, the cool breezes swirling around his shoulders, in his hair.

And he waited.

Outside, the midnight meadows rolled endlessly on, the unceasing swell of Sky Ocean, the starry fields of the sky. The silver-edged cloud-sheep had drifted off, and the night sky spread out with a vastness Cliopher had never before seen.

Looking at the Sun, here in the uttermost East, Cliopher *knew* with a solid certainty that his island stood behind him, as far to the west as he was now in the east.

(*East first, then west and home.*)

He waited. He had been waiting a long time to go home, and he could wait as long as this negotiation took.

He had to come up with a fifth thing. He had planned for three—the feather had been *greatly* unexpected—and now he had to come up with a fifth thing that was his to give up.

He looked up at the Sun on his throne, from that distance he had held standing before his Radiancy on the throne of the Emperors of Astandalas. His Radiancy, the Sun-on-Earth, the Lord of Rising Stars.

There was something else that Cliopher might be able to offer.

He centred himself, feet solid on the floor, though his head swam with fatigue and the headache grew in force. It was all too familiar, and he gritted his teeth and set his shoulders back. How quickly he'd grown accustomed to being without that constant, persistent headache, that tight jaw, those weary muscles.

He waited: and then, suddenly, so unexpectedly he caught his breath, nearly swayed, nearly fell, everything was in motion around him.

He closed his eyes against the swirling hours and the people who came into the Sun's golden hall. They were strange people, figures of sylph-like wispiness, half invisible as they drifted through the place. Some had wings: feathered or butterfly-bright or dragonfly-faceted, and some wore gauze and some wore white linen and others seemed to be wearing nothing but a drapery of light.

And with them, it seemed, all the winds of the sky.

A strong hand touched his shoulder, and he opened his eyes, shocked and embarrassed at himself, to see the brilliant brown ones of the Grandmother, the Old Woman Who Lives in the Deeps of the Sea.

Cliopher had not let himself think too much about that title, for it was one of the euphemisms given to death.

"Ah, you're one of Vou'a's, aren't you?" she whispered in his ear. "Clever as they come, I see. And patient, too. People forget that he's patient, that Son of Laughter! They remember the jokes and the tricks and forget the long, long practice that goes into pulling something like that off. Well done, Cliopher Mdang of Tahivoa!"

She laughed, that girlish, beautiful laugh, the one that had struck him so in that strange encounter at the very bottom of the sea, and then the Grandmother let go of his shoulder and turned to the Sun, who was glaring now at her. She said, "What is this? What folly are you about, child of Day?"

The Sun harrumphed. "What are you talking about, Old One?"

"So rude!" the Grandmother tutted. "Here you have a guest in your house—oh yes, I heard you promise him hearth-right!—and you have given him neither food nor water, neither offered him a chance to be clean nor to rest, and not only that, not a gesture of respect!"

"What respect do I owe him?" the Sun said sulkily. "He is a mortal come by some trickster's path to con me out of all my treasures."

Cliopher kept his mouth shut.

The Grandmother tutted again and rapped her gnarled stick loudly on the floor. "You have let your own light blind you! Did you not look at his hands and his feet? Not a step off the path did he take, not a treasure did he touch!"

"He cannot have found that feather himself. It was lost—we all sought it."

Cliopher listened carefully. (*Look first! Listen first!*) His Varga grandmother had said—it was a bit of a refrain— "And all the gods sought what Vou'a had lost, but it was nowhere to be found ..."

"You all sought, but *I* was the one to find," the Grandmother replied tartly. "All things come to me in the end! Yes—even so shall you, child of Day! And then you will be glad to know I do not forget where I have put any of what has come to me, nor what might be best done with it!"

"And instead of giving that feather to me, who had looked for it and wanted it, you gave it to *him*?"

The Sun gave Cliopher a gesture he would have found very rude, if he had not been accustomed to Prince Rufus.

The Grandmother laughed merrily. "He earned it! *You* have never offered me fire and news and an ear for my problems!" She grinned at Cliopher, whose expression was probably not quite as neutral as he would like, and pinched his cheek. "He came to the Lower Door."

"That was lost," the Sun muttered.

"To *your* sight," the Grandmother replied. "Tell me, Cliopher Mdang of Tahivoa, why have you tied reeds about that golden cowrie of yours?"

Cliopher could not touch his efela, as his hands were still full (and felt both leaden and full of prickles; he wondered how much his forearms would ache, once he finally was permitted to set down his offerings), so he lifted his chin. "The sea-witch of the Island That Swallowed the Sea gave me a garnet, and I did not wish it to fall out of the shell where I stowed it."

The Sun lifted his eyes suddenly to meet Cliopher's full-on. He bit his lip at the pain, and he hoped that he would not be blinded.

"Enough," the Grandmother said sharply. "He earned that gift too, I am sure—and I heard you traded a name for his story, so we shall hear how! That answers a question: his mind is his own, for that stone from that isle, and no doubt you will learn why he was able to sail in such secrecy across that long sea. What else were your trades, Cliopher Mdang of Tahivoa? No—*you* can be quiet, child of Day! You have spoken quite enough for one night."

Cliopher smiled, eyes still watering, afterimages dancing, and let his voice roll through the hall. "For my fire: a flame of the Sun's. For my tale: the name of the third son of Vonou'a, shared without loss on either part. For the feather: the mirimiri of

Ani. And for my father's boat, hospitality for me and any of my kin who should come to this hall, and especially my great-uncle's husband, who desires greatly to drink the mead of the Sun."

He blinked, his eyes finally clearing, and he added: "The Sun offered me also a boon, in return for crossing the threshold, but I do not wish for there to be any ill-will or resentment, and so I offer this as my gift in return: that when I return safely home to the mortal worlds, I shall see to it that the title of the Sun-on-Earth be repudiated. It was taken by the descendants of the Sun, those Emperors of Astandalas who sought to be as the Sun for their peoples, though their glory and majesty could not rival yours."

The Grandmother gave him a sly, sidelong glance, and another whisper came to his ear, though she did not move her head closer to him: *Truly you are one of Vou'a's!* She tapped her stick again. "Five treasures offered in return for four treasures and a boon that should have been a free gift! Speak your assent to these terms, child of Day, unless you have any further counter-offers to make?"

The Sun squirmed on his throne, as any chief chided by the matriarch of his family, and he grumbled and he hesitated, but at last he said, "In return for that promise, I shall give you a message for the last to hold that title, and you shall keep that boon as a gift to you. To the rest of the terms: I agree!"

The Grandmother rapped her stick on the floor, with a crack Cliopher felt up his spine. Thunder rolled out across the great expanses of the sky, and all the hours and winds of the Sun's court stopped moving for one endless moment.

"And done," whispered the Grandmother, when the thunder fell silent. "Come, Cliopher Mdang of Tahivoa, and I shall show you the glories of this house while the trading feast is prepared. You can leave your offerings here: no one will take them till the trade is complete! No—leave the basket. I'll want that later."

She grinned at the Sun, who glowered severely, and took Cliopher's arm in her own before he could even think of bowing.

∼

The Grandmother led him to the back of the hall, and through a warren of corridors that did not hold in his mind: sometimes he thought he walked outdoors, on bridges of silver or shining gold or crystal, and sometimes he was in the cool halls of pale stone and paler wood.

Cliopher followed her wearily, no dance left in his step and barely a word left in his mind. The headache throbbed where the mountain had hit it, and he had to concentrate to stay upright, glad of the old woman's hand on his elbow.

The Old Woman Who Lives in the Deeps of the Sea. Grandmother Death. Leading him, Cliopher Mdang, through the House of the Sun.

He decided it was best not to think too hard about anything other than keeping his footing, and was pleased when they entered a splendid hall, the stonework mirror of the one where he'd sorted grains for the sea-witch. It was dim, comforting on his eyes, cool against his skin.

Hurrying towards them was a woman, or woman in figure and face: tall and slender, her hair all shades of silver and grey, her skin a rosy gold, with wings arched around her, their feathers peach and lavender and the tenderest of greys. Her eyes were a deep, burnished silver, and flashing with curiosity even as she covered a yawn with one curved wing.

She halted as she saw the Grandmother, and her face fell. "Did I miss everything? I was so hoping to hear—"

"He is here," the Grandmother said, indicating Cliopher. "This is Cliopher Mdang of Tahivoa. He's one of Vou'a's."

"One of Vou'a's! Is he also one of ..." the wind trailed off, her wings curling up, so that a soft, fragrant air blew in his face and stirred his hair.

He was sure he knew that wind, the scent and the feel of it, from ten thousand mornings.

"Are you the Wind That Rises At Dawn?" he asked her.

"I am," the wind replied. "Do you know my name?"

"Sama is what my people call you." He hesitated, for she was looking at him almost beseechingly, and that was such a *strange* expression—

Except that he had seen it not long ago, had he not? On the faces of Tupaia and Pinyë and the crew of the *He'eanka*, when he stepped forward and said he knew their names; when Basil's son Clio had come out of the inn and seen him and asked him those questions out of the *Lays* ...

He bowed over his hands, fist over palm. "I am Cliopher Mdang of Tahivoa, of the Ke'e Lulai, as we call ourselves. We trace our descent from a man named Vonou'a, who was the son of Ani, and his wife Samayë, the Woman of the Dawn Wind, who is said to be your daughter ..."

"Ah!" cried the wind, and she laughed, her wings fluttering with a kind of astonished joy. "You remember my name! Not my daughter's—my own! Three sons had I, and my daughter was Anyë."

"And the name of the third son, which was lost in trade," the Grandmother said, "has been won back by this son after many generations."

The Wind That Rises At Dawn stepped forward and took his hands, and Cliopher, looking at her eyes, was certain, absolutely certain, with a surety like knowing where his island was—back there, down the whole length of Sky Ocean, in the farthest West as he stood here in the uttermost East—he knew, just like that, that she was the one to whom he should give the phoenix feather.

He said, "I have something for you, foremother."

She let go of her his hands when he tugged them loose, and watched curiously as he undid the third efela. The Grandmother folded her hands about her stick and watched him with a grin that did remind him very much of the Son of Laughter.

She peered down at the shells in his hand. "Is it the necklace that is for me?"

"No," he replied, and flipped the cowrie in his hand, the pearls nestled beside it, so he could unwind the coils of wire and tug the downy phoenix feather from its shelter. The sea-witch's garnet clattered like the bead in a rattle as the feather moved.

He held the feather up to the wind.

Her eyes were very large, and very silver. "That is for me?"

"Yes." His voice was solid, certain, as the stone beneath his feet, the weight of that mud in the basket, the embers that burned in his fire-pot. "I was given it to give on, when I met the person for whom it was ... intended. You are that person."

She smiled, a slow, secret smile. "For *me*. Do you know why this is mine, Cliopher Mdang of Tahivoa?"

"No," he replied honestly. "It may be yours; it may be that you meet someone to whom you will pass it on."

She held the feather pinched between forefinger and thumb. It glowed in her hand, like a thin cloud catching the sunrise, the lavender-violet of a flame coiling above the hottest coals, like the stars before the dawn overpasses them.

"You are full of surprises, aren't you?" the Grandmother observed. "I like you." And when both Cliopher and the Wind That Rises At Dawn gave her equally astonished glances—though Cliopher hoped his was not quite so obviously perturbed—she laughed her silvery laugh. "Oh yes, I do indeed. Come along now."

CHAPTER FIFTY-ONE
THE WIND THAT RISES AT DAWN

He was led to a bath-chamber, where the airy sylphs bathed him.
He felt no embarrassment at their assistance, except insofar as he had always bathed alone and it seemed odd to have light fingers carding through his hair and rubbing soaps into lather on his back.

Scents rose up around him, clean floral scents, satisfying and soothing. The steam billowed up, so he saw even less of the sylphs: a flash of hand or wing, a bright eye, a flare of something that might have been steam or might have been hair or might have been a flowing garment.

The water in the pool grew clouded and murky with the filth drawn off his skin. They tutted and twittered and the water gushed out, but before he could grow the least chilled fresh water poured in from somewhere overhead.

Three times they changed the water. Great clots of foam and hair and dirt washed off him, more than he could fathom producing. They scrubbed at his skin with pleasantly scratchy sponges, rinsed with cool, fresh water, and then he was led out of the pool to be dried in towels that surely were made with the cloud-sheep's fleeces, anointed with oils and lotions that his thirsty skin absorbed joyfully.

Finally he was given clean garments to wear, a white tunic as soft on his skin as the towels. It was belted with a sash of bronze and gold, pleasantly tight against his waist.

The Wind That Rises At Dawn surveyed him with a pleased eye. "Much better," she said, and reached out with one slender hand to brush his hair back from his face. Her eyes were very sad. "You remind me of the one I loved, very long ago," she said, and then she smiled at him. She bade him sit, and then brushed out his hair with her fingers and a delicate comb that seemed made of a fine, iridescent shell, and then braided his hair in complicated fashion. "This is how I braided my dear love's hair," she told him, "and my sons' and daughter's too, the way that my brethren of winds and stars do. It is a gift to see that our line has not died! There was one, long ago by your reckoning, who came from our people, searching after his beloved here. He was quite as clever as you ..."

And while she braided his hair the way the winds and stars did, she told him her version of the tale he had heard from Elonoa'a about the rescue of Aurelius from the House of the Sun.

~

The Wind That Rises At Dawn gave him three feathers from one wing, for her three sons, and two from her other wing, for herself and her daughter. She braided them into his hair, all those pale dawn colours—lavender, silver, dove-grey, pale rose, and one like a soft line of charcoal.

She'd braided the phoenix feather into her own hair, so although he had no mirror with which to see himself, he could imagine a hint of the effect.

(Some of those who lived on the high islands of the Eastern Ring wore feathers in their hair, but usually as headdresses, not as hair ornaments. He had seen only a few people who wore feathers like this, his Buru Tovo among them.)

He was, somehow, no longer tired and sore. He followed the wind back through the house of the Sun, along the quiet corridors and across the bridges of silver and shining gold and crystal.

"These are rainbows," the Wind That Rises At Dawn said of the crystal arches. "It is very beautiful here in the day, though no one sees it who does not stay."

Aurelius would have seen those rainbows, these halls fully illuminated. They were not precisely dark—even the nightscape he could see beyond the come-and-go walls was not *dark*, without illumination. But the halls were lit with a gentle, soft radiance, the light before dawn.

"We still have a feast, the Grandmother said," Cliopher murmured, though he was so relaxed and at ease after that deep cleansing that he could not find it in his heart to be worried.

"The night will be the length it needs to be," the wind said, "and then, when the Sun takes his leave for the day, I shall carry your boat forth, back towards your destination."

"Thank you," Cliopher said sincerely, touching her hand lightly as it swung in the space between them.

She smiled at him, his foremother after all the generations his people had ever reckoned. "Might I sail with you a time? I shall ask one of my sisters to carry the boat through the night. It has been a long time since I stood on such human craft ..."

"Of course," Cliopher said, through a lump in his throat. "I should be honoured."

~

The feast was impossible: foods he could not name in unstinting abundance.

The mead was like drinking liquid gold, and he could stand no more than three sips before he was forced to set it aside in favour of the pure water.

After they ate and drank, the Grandmother set forth their trade.

It was the same pattern Cliopher knew from many other occasions: as the one who had begun the negotiations, he presented his trades first.

The fire-pot with its coals; the black feather; the little wooden boat; his promise; and his story.

All the while Cliopher told the story of his journey across the Wide Seas, the Sun dipped his fingers into the fire-pot and ate the coals, one at a time.

At one point he noticed Cliopher staring, mesmerized, and in a pause in his description of the Albatross, offered him the pot. "Would you like one?"

His tone was far more courteous than it had been: perhaps because Cliopher's account of the sea-witch had suggested to him that it was her gift of the watery benediction that had kept Cliopher from the Sun's notice.

"Ah, no thank you," Cliopher said, politely gesturing a refusal of the fire-pot. "One was enough for me."

The Sun had started to chuckle, but stopped. "I beg your pardon? I did not think mortals could bear such tastes!"

"Only once," said Cliopher, and shrugged self-deprecatingly. "It is perhaps a long story, and this one is already the length of Sky Ocean!"

The Sun nodded and crunched another coal, then licked the sand from his fingers as if it were sugar.

～

In time, he finished his story; the food was long since reduced to fragments. The Sun regarded him pensively, but the Wind That Rises At Dawn and the Grandmother sat beside him, one to each side.

Cliopher did not know why the Grandmother set such store by the sea turtle guiding him to the Lower Door, but he was glad—very glad—he had for once listened to Cousin Louya.

"It is not quite dawn," the Sun said abruptly. "There is time for a dance before you go."

He clapped his hands and a wild and free music erupted from the corners of the room.

The Hours and the winds danced, their hair and wings and clothes flying as their feet and hands met floor and partner and they whirled and stamped and their voices cried out for joy.

Cliopher watched the dance, longing to join but knowing that no matter how skilled he might be in his familiar dances he did not—could not—dance this one— when suddenly the Sun gave a huge cry, a ringing call that shot through the music like a thunderbolt through the sky.

He reached out his hand to one of the Hours, and his other to Cliopher, and he laughed at Cliopher's expression. "Come, come!" he cried. "Come and dance with me, Cliopher Mdang of Tahivoa, who travelled so far and bargained so cunningly, and who will go forth from hence to sing of the glory of my hall! Come and dance!"

Who was he to say *no* to that invitation?

He danced.

~

While most Islander dances were done in pairs or groups, the one Cliopher knew best and had practised most was solitary.

In the fire dance it was just him and the coals, the drum and the song and the touch of feet and hand in the air. When he had danced it island to island across the Wide Seas there had not been any drum but his heart, and he had had to sing the words himself.

In the hall of the Sun he was the only mortal dancing there, and it was him and the coals, the drum and the song and the touch of feet and hand on air. The hours and the winds had the form of goddesses, and the Sun was blazing-warm to the touch. He danced around the flame at the centre, now circling it in a waving, bowing dance, now dipping under the arch made of two others' arms, now forming the arch himself: and the winds bore him up, and the hours whirled him around, and he grew drunk and merry with the honey-wine and the light in the eyes of the Sun.

There was honey on his lips when the stars grew faint above them. The Wind That Rises At Dawn whirled him around and around until they came to a still point at the centre of the gyre, the golden flame at his back.

She gestured at the golden basin of the Sun's fire. "Will you take what you are owed?"

"I will receive what I am given," Cliopher replied firmly. He was not so drunk as that!

"Well spoken," said the Grandmother from right beside him. Cliopher jumped. She laughed, still incongruously merrily with her stooped and elderly frame. "Show me your efela."

He did so, slowly and shyly: the efela ko, the efetana, and the nameless one with efevoa and flame pearls and a red garnet hidden away.

"Kiofa'a is the name of this efela," she told him: "He who Barters with the Sun."

Cliopher felt something run through him, a bolt of magic or power, as if this Islander rendition of his Shaian name had always been a part of him, as if the name his mother had given him had always led ... here.

"You understand that necessity is always still a choice, don't you?" The Grandmother murmured, cupping his cheeks with her hands and staring deep into his eyes. Cliopher stared back, his mind whirling with images from his life, as if his soul were cradled in her hands and she stirred his memories. He landed on the moment of the first time he had gone swimming with his Radiancy, with Fitzroy, and set all this in motion.

He was named for his uncle, and there were at least a dozen other *Cliophers* scattered amongst the Mdang family; but he was the one who stood here.

"I am the one to whom all thing come in the end," the Grandmother murmured. "And every choice you have ever made has been free."

Had he not seen that with that brief glimpse of the other place, the other Kip?

Her hands were warm and dry, comforting, secure.

"I hold the world in my hands," she said. "And so have you." She let go of his face. He stared at her, wondering mightily, with no questions on his tongue.

The Sun came leaping through the throngs of winds and hours, broad shoulders and strong legs ready to embark on the next day's journey.

"It's been a long time since you last took a favourite," the Sun said to the Grandmother.

"It's been a long time since someone came to the Lower Door," she replied imperturbably. "What of the things you promised?"

The Sun sighed. "I am here, am I not?" He turned to Cliopher, who was still standing, but felt very small beside his giant frame. "In return for the story which he told of your journey, I give you the name of the one who took it from me: Samayo Atēatamai."

The Wind That Rises At Dawn made a soft cry, even as Cliopher felt a lump come into his throat, the tears hot in his eyes.

It was a splendid name: the Son of Dawn, the Seeker After Wisdom.

"And the flame?" the Grandmother said.

The Sun picked up the coral fire-pot, and showed it to first the Grandmother and then Cliopher himself that it was empty, clean even of the sand. "I have rinsed it in the last dew of the night, the first dew of the morning," he said, and then turned to the brazier and thrust the pot into the heart of the flames, where they burned so white-hot Cliopher could not follow his movements.

He drew his hand out, and now the fire burned within the pot: a piece of the Sun, not reflected nor radiated, but radiant and warm in itself.

For a moment the Sun breathed heavily, obviously reluctant, and then he set the lid snugly on the pot and handed it to Cliopher.

Cliopher cradled it close. It radiated a fine, splendid warmth through the coral, and glowed very faintly. It was not heavy—far lighter than it had been when filled with sand and embers—but somehow also far more massive and weighty.

"The feather," the Sun said, and paused.

Cliopher was holding the black feather, and offered it to him.

The Sun hesitated.

Cliopher said, "The greatest poet of the Nine Worlds will write the song of this, I promise you."

It was half the threat he'd used it as, and the Sun knew it, for he grimaced and produced a shimmering, supple length of cloth, the very colour of the froth of a wave caught in the air.

"The mirimiri of Ani, and much good may it do to you!"

"The feather that was lost," Cliopher replied, and took the strange, glistening cloth in his hands. It did not feel like ahalo cloth on his skin; more like the faintest breath of air. And yet something told him it was the memory of this that had inspired his ancestors to turn the byssal threads of certain molluscs into that glimmering iridescent cloth.

"It's nearly time to go," the Wind That Rises At Dawn said, glancing at the Sun and then up at the faintly glowing sky. "The horses are ready."

Horses?

"We do not all follow your love of boats," the Sun said, his expression brightening as if this condescending comment was all that was required to put them once more in their proper relation.

Reminded once again of Prince Rufus, of that other Kip, Cliopher resolutely did not smile, but instead handed over the boat his father had made him.

The Sun took it with every pleasure, and reiterated formally the promise that any of Cliopher's kith and kin, and especially his great-uncle's husband, would be welcome to the hearth of the Sun to drink mead there.

"And the last is my promise to you. There is, on my world of Zunidh, a solar eclipse coming: it shall be done upon that day, this repudiation of the title of the Sun-on-Earth by the last to hold it."

"Good," said the Sun, and beckoned him closer to whisper a secret in his ear. "Tell him that."

Cliopher bowed over his hands, as several things upended themselves entirely.

And then it was the moment before dawn, and the House of the Sun roused in readiness.

The Wind That Rises At Dawn smiled at him. "You must make haste, but once you are upon your boat I will carry you home." And she was off, her wings more like the dawn clouds than ever as she dashed after the Sun.

Cliopher turned then to the Grandmother, but she had once again disappeared.

All the winds and the hours swirled out, leaving an empty hall full of dust motes, Cliopher standing there with a coral fire-pot full of sunlight in one hand and the mirimiri of Ani in the other.

He went out the front door, and found the stair. It was even more vertiginous going down, the zigzags tight and the drop ever more alarming, but after climbing up it with that basket—and even more, after the bath and the mead and food—Cliopher found himself able to run swiftly and sure-footed down the stairs until he came to the great pillared hall.

The water was even higher than it had been when he left the boat there, pouring out of the well and over the lip of the colonnade.

Hurry—hurry—hurry! came the faint cry of the Sun, echoing off the mountain-tops and startling the white birds into flying, out across the rolling meadows, the brilliant sky.

Cliopher undid the painter and leaped aboard the vaha before the current could sweep it off. He tucked the fire-pot into the hatch, but before he could put the cloth anywhere a high voice called out: "The day has come! We must away!"

It was taken up by a chorus of voices, words and birdsong weaving in and out of each other, as the huge white birds he had seen on the other side of the morning came plummeting down from the heights behind him.

Cliopher twisted the mirimiri about his waist, loose ends tucked into itself, and made haste to raise the sail.

The vaha hesitated at the edge of the colonnade, attentive to his own hesitation, but the water was pouring down onto the Sky Ocean and Cliopher had to trust that the wind would catch it, the sky hold it, the waters bear him down to the rolling waves of Sky Ocean.

The vaha hesitated, tilted—he leaned his weight carefully, cautiously—and then he passed the fulcrum and there was no returning, not now, and so he threw caution to the winds and cried out, "Away! Away! The day has come!"

And the Wind That Rises At Dawn rose from underneath him, and the vaha *flew.*

~

He trusted the wind; he had always trusted the wind.

He took note of the direction she was taking him, feeling the faint, attenuated awareness of his distant home flicker, an ember suddenly catching as his attention and his face were both turned in that direction.

She was singing, or the white birds were singing. They flew beside him, above him, below him, their great wings beating, their necks stretched out and tail feathers streaming. They were something like swans and something like birds-of-paradise: white, strong, splendid. Their beaks and their eyes were both of gold, and in their beaks each held what seemed to be a single flaring ember. Or perhaps it was a rose, for Cliopher could smell the fire of roses, heady and rich and heartening.

He had danced with the hours: he could not help but lift his voice to sing with the birds of the dawning. He did not know their song. It was wordless and endless, longing and love, fulfillment and desire—

But he could sing the *Lays* to rise up through and with their melodies.

Far below him he suddenly caught sight of a marvellous thing: the shadow of the night running ahead of them, the Sun's illumination running before, the white birds of the dawn at the very cusp between day and night.

Above him thundered the hooves of the white horses carrying the chariot of the sun, but Cliopher could no longer look directly on him, for all that he carried a flame of his fire with him.

~

Eventually the Sun outpaced the Wind that Rises at Dawn, and the shadow of twilight came rising up behind them. The white birds had long since flown on, and Cliopher had come to the end of his voice for the day, and was sitting cross-legged with his back to the mast, the sail thrumming above him.

He noticed the movement slowly; the sail boomed as the wind flickered.

The Wind That Rises At Dawn took form out of the invisible airs, her face and her wings all Cliopher could see. She smiled down at him. "I cannot carry you any farther."

"Then join me, and rest awhile here," he offered.

She smiled, his foremother, and with a flurry of feathers was suddenly human in form and landing softly beside him, one hand on the mast to steady herself.

"Thank you, descendant of mine," she murmured. "My sister is here, the Wind of the Evening Star, and she will take you the rest of the way. I shall rest for a while, and remember my love of long ago."

Cliopher looked politely away from her, to see that there was another face taking shape out of the shadows: this wind's eyes were a deep purple-blue, her hair smokey black, her wings all shades of purple and indigo and grey.

"Hina'ui," he greeted her. "I thank you for your kindness."

"I hope your great ships will follow me once more," she said. "It has been a long time since the pennants flew across the seas and the songs in our honour were sung!"

"They will be sung again, or new ones if the old ones have been forgotten," Cliopher promised her. Some of the songs he had learned from the crew of the *He'eanka* were wind-songs, and surely Elonoa'a would know some specifically for these two winds.

Behind her dark hair the sky was filling with stars. The wind beat her wings once, twice, three times, and the sail filled, the vaha skimming once more through, rather than across, the luminous sky.

The Wind of the Evening Star faded into invisibility. The Wind That Rises At Dawn sat by the mast, her wings folded around her. She was facing forward, westward, as the night sky bloomed around them.

She sang, in a language Cliopher did not know. A star-song, a wind-song, a song of the four quarters and the constellations and the winds that rose and fell under them. He listened, as the evening wind bore them through the night and the stars grew ever grander above and around them.

The wind shifted a little, and Cliopher moved to change the angle of the tiller, but the Wind That Rises At Dawn broke off her song and said, "Wait."

He waited. The wind bore them at an angle, cutting across to where there were the faint hints of luminescence, of some sort of sky-plankton glowing in the currents of Sky Ocean.

"Lift up your star," the Wind That Rises At Dawn said.

"It is not for me," Cliopher said. "I was sent for it."

"This is a gift for you and for me, a boon from the Grandmother," the wind said. "Lift up your star."

He looked at her: her face and eyes were intent, pale as the earliest dawn, drawn with a tiredness that came, he assumed, from being so far from her usual place.

"Lift up your star," she said a third time, and Cliopher, moved by the pleading in her voice, her eyes, her face, turned to the hatch where he had stowed the fire-pot.

He held it in his hands for a moment, and then at her nod he lifted the lid.

And—

"There!" she cried, and he looked, for the faint swirls and outlines of luminescence had become full of the flashing lights of viau, each of them like a fish, like a diving bird, like a star—and the flame of the sun blazed in his hands and illuminated all the ships of his ancestors, for he sailed on a steady current down the very centre of their wake.

"And there," said the Wind That Rises At Dawn, her voice soft, "there they are."

A man stood on a ship of an ancient style—far more ancient than any Cliopher had ever seen—but yet, hardly impossible, its sail and his outrigger clear cousins to his own—a man, and with him three younger men, and a daughter.

And they were looking back.

~

Cliopher could not name many by sight, not with only a glimpse of an efela or a nose or eyebrows just like Bertie's (like Elonoa'a's). He could cry out across the water, in a voice that he did not know if they heard, the name of the third son of Vonou'a, the name that had been so long lost.

He tried; his voice seemed to fall into a great silence, and by then they were past that ship, as his vaha was propelled by a faster current, a stronger wind.

"Ahh," cried the Wind That Rises At Dawn, "thank you, thank you!"

She embraced him, forehead to forehead, and then, with one backward smile, unfurled her wings and launched herself across the great gulf between his living vaha and the vessels of the dead.

Cliopher saw, and wondered—but he saw, and wondered, at an older man, perhaps a bit older than him, who saw his boat sailing by and leaned intently, peering across the distance, his face for a moment—hopeful?

Was that the uncle of Elonoa'a? The father of one of the crew of the *He'eanka?*— Cliopher could do nothing but nod his head in acknowledgement and let the wind carry him on, the star in his hand.

It was growing hot and heavy, but he could not close the lid and hide this vision, not until he had seen the last, the latest ships—

~

There was no time but for the day and the night on that ocean, but it was some time closer to dawn when the Wind of the Evening Star withdrew from his sail and silently departed.

Cliopher had closed the lid of the fire-pot and laid himself down on the deck of his vaha, for he could hear an echo of the songs the ancestors were singing that way, though when he sat up he could hear only himself. He lay facing up, the sky dizzying in its glory above him, the ghostly ships keeping him company even after he had let the close vision fade.

But he would hold that last ship in his heart, his mind's eye, his hope of what came after he too joined that great flotilla voyaging he knew not where.

When the wind faded he sat up. The main current bent away from him, the starry luminescence shaping its curves and curlicues, the great ocean-going parahë and vaha and all the other craft of his ancestors following its line.

All of them, all the way down to his father's boat, with his father and grandfather and Navalia and Erwin looking across at him, pride on their faces, for they *saw* him, they knew *him* for who he was.

Cliopher's vaha was moving slowly but surely across deep-black water towards a glimmering white sand beach.

There was a bonfire on the beach, and the black bulk of a ship against the starlit water. Cliopher put his hand on the tiller, but he did not need to steer: the last breath of wind had set him true to his destination.

The ship glided closer and closer. There had been a reef, he remembered, but it seemed so far beneath the surface he did not worry about his vaha grounding on it.

The waves were gentle, hardly breaking at all except right at the beach. The swell carried him over the coral.

Once he was within the line of the breakers he could hear the sound of voices carrying across the water. Not the ethereal voices of the stars or the winds or the hours or the birds of dawn, but human voices; and not just human voices, but ones he recognized. He would know his Fitzroy's resonant laugh anywhere.

They had not seen him yet, of course.

The canoe was aiming at the bonfire, which was the red of a long, cheerful burning. Cliopher looked back once, to see the Wake of the Ancestors' Ships fading as his own wake rippled away into imperceptibility.

He took a deep breath, as if he was about to dive into the unknown dark, but instead of the water closing over him he lifted up the fire-pot and once more removed the lid.

The sunlight kindled, a star in his hand, eclipsing the bonfire in its sudden brilliance.

Out of the blinding light came the voices of Elonoa'a and Tupaia singing out the passage from the *Lays* in which the third son of Vonou'a came home.

(And now he knew his name, Samayo Atēatamai!)

Cliopher was crying when the vaha touched the shore, and he struggled to disembark. Many hands dragged the canoe to a safe anchorage. At last he stood there with the light of the sun in his hands and the stars at his back, the ancestors behind him, before him.

Cliopher looked past them all to his friend who stood at the edge of the light, his harp hanging loose in his hands.

Cliopher could not resist, and passed through the crew of the *He'eanka* to his lord, his friend, his fanoa.

This time he did not hesitate; this time he reached out and embraced him first, as tightly as he had ever held onto anything.

"Kip," Fitzroy breathed, his breath stirring Cliopher's hair, and then was silent, before he shifted position, just enough for Fitzroy to rest his forehead upon Cliopher's. Cliopher's hands fell from the embrace, fire-pot in one hand, lid in the other, and then he stepped back and regarded him directly.

They looked at each other for a long, intense moment. Fitzroy's hair had grown out, too: it was four or five inches long, finger-thick coils of black threaded with strands of silver, just the colour of the night sky.

That reminded him of the fragment of day he still held in his hand. Cliopher turned to the others, who were staring at the fire-pot, the light illuminating them clearly; none of them had yet noticed the mirimiri still wrapped like as a sash about his waist.

Elonoa'a and Aurelius Magnus stood closest to him, their expressions full of a relief so strong it was nearly awe.

The weight of what he had just done was suddenly very heavy on his shoulders.

Cliopher swallowed dryly, then straightened his back and composed himself into his best matter-of-fact bureaucratic manner, which he knew always amused his —Fitzroy when he reported something magnificent, impossible, entirely absurd.

"As I was bid, I have sailed to the House of the Sun and bring back a flame of his fire," he said as nonchalantly as possible. "While I was there, I was able to attain a few other items, which, small as they may be to some, will be of interest to you, my lord."

This had been the preface to any number of reports.

Fitzroy lifted one eyebrow and spoke in his most imperial manner. "You astonish me, my lord Mdang."

There was a beat of silence, and then they both burst out laughing, unable to maintain that pretence for any longer at all. Elonoa'a and Aurelius regarded them in fascination, which just made Cliopher laugh harder.

"Enough," Fitzroy said eventually, "we all long to hear your story."

"It is a long tale of the sea," Cliopher replied, smiling at Elonoa'a and Aurelius and all the others.

"We shall sit by the fire to hear it," Fitzroy returned, which was almost the correct phrasing, and took him by the hand to lead him there.

CHAPTER FIFTY-TWO
THE STAR

He did not tell them the story immediately, of course—not the *whole* story. It was late, and they were all tired.

"We could see the star coming towards us," Elonoa'a told him when they had sat down before the fire. "Each night larger, so we knew you were returning to us."

Aurelius had not yet spoken. He held the fire-pot Fitzroy had made, which Cliopher had given him, cradled on his lap where he sat cross-legged beside them. Elonoa'a sat close beside him, his arm around his beloved's shoulders. Aurelius stared down at the coral pot, the glimmer of daylight coming from under its lid, the promise of a cure for the poison in his veins.

"We knew you had embarked across the last sea," Fitzroy said. "Vou'a came to visit us, after you left his island. An old man in an old canoe—at first I thought it was your Buru Tovo. It wouldn't have surprised me to find him here."

Cliopher laughed till the tears started, for it was too much—the sudden stabbing hope that his great-uncle *was* here—the knowledge that if he had left the world behind it was to join that great flotilla of those who had gone before them—the promises he had extracted from the Sun—the *everything* of his journey.

He wept until he began to hiccough, and then he sat there, face burning, and wished for ...

Wished for someone else to take up the burden of decisions and directions, just for a moment.

Tupaia, seated on Fitzroy's other side, said firmly, "We can hear this story later. It is nearly dawn, and you are tired. You may want a longer faravia this time, my friend."

"I have news to tell you of Sky Ocean," Cliopher managed through the hiccoughs, even as the tears began to flow again.

"You have brought a fire to our hearth and scouted for us the next ke'ea of our quest," Tupaia said gently. "The news will wait."

The encampment was more elaborate, though in the dark Cliopher could not quite see how. Fitzroy walked him along the beach, the familiar waves running gently over Cliopher's toes as he paced on the wet sand at the edge of the sea. His mind felt adrift in a sea fog.

"I can leave you to rest," Fitzroy said when they turned to the shelter.

Cliopher's eyes had adjusted to the starlight, but he could not see his friend's expression, nor more than that the shelter was a little bigger and seemed to have more in the way of things within it.

Fitzroy's words penetrated the fog. Cliopher instinctively grabbed on his arm, though he had not actually moved away.

"Please stay," he mumbled, embarrassed. "If you don't mind ..."

"Of course not," Fitzroy said, the relief audible, and he flung himself down on what was apparently his side of the shelter. "That mat's for you."

The serene assurance that Cliopher would return undid him.

Cliopher sat down, the tears streaming down, unable to speak or do anything but bury his face in his hands.

This time Fitzroy sat down beside him and reached his arm around him, just the way Elonoa'a had comforted Aurelius.

"Shh," said Fitzroy, rubbing his hand gently down Cliopher's hair. "Shh. You are home safe."

Cliopher wept until he surely had no more tears left, and then he sat there, echoingly empty, aware only of Fitzroy's warmth enclosing him.

Fitzroy moved his arm, and Cliopher made a small protest.

"Shhh," Fitzroy murmured, tugging him gently until he relaxed and let himself fall backwards to lie next to him. Fitzroy caught his hand and entwined their fingers together. "There, that's better, isn't it?"

"I've been so long alone," Cliopher said, gripping hard.

"I know. I know. I'm here."

Cliopher turned his head. Fitzroy was facing him, his eyes just catching the faintest glimmer of starlight or magic. "You are."

"Yes."

He stared, glad of the dark for hiding the intensity of his expression, glad of the starlight for showing him that Fitzroy was looking back at him.

"I have so much to tell you."

"I have not been entirely idle myself," Fitzroy said, his voice just a little amused, curling like the scent of something good into the hollowness in Cliopher's heart. "Auri and I have spoken much of magic and history and ... how to leave off being an emperor. El and the crew and I have exchanged many songs."

"Not Auri—Aurelius?"

"I'm sure he'd like you to call him Auri," Fitzroy replied, the amusement breaking the surface of his voice, so his tone was breathy with suppressed laughter. "And no—for all his many excellences, music is not one of his gifts. He's better at math than I am, however."

"Not difficult," Cliopher murmured, starting to relax.

"Vou'a showed me how to spin shadows, as one does."

"He was doing that when I met him."

"So he said, and I was most curious ... it's a perfectly useless hobby, exactly what I was missing in my life. When I find my heir ..." He trailed off, and then, a moment later, said, "You are squeezing my hand very hard."

"Sorry—I—" Cliopher took a deep breath. Fitzroy's eyes were wide, brighter, gleaming with amusement and curiosity. "I have something to tell you. A secret the Sun traded for the promise you would repudiate the title of Sun-on-Earth at your abdication."

Fitzroy laughed. "I always appreciate it when you manage to trade something we were fully planning to do anyway. What secret is this?"

Cliopher took several deep breaths, bracing himself. He was glad he was already holding Fitzroy's hand.

"You begin to worry me, my dear Kip."

Fitzroy always knew what to say to provoke Cliopher over whatever hurdle faced him. "You have a daughter by the Moon," he blurted, and then waited, heart pounding, for the response.

"I? A daughter? By the Moon?" Fitzroy said, his voice blank and astonished, and then, his tone changing to something like wonder, like grief, like the expression Aurelius had had when he looked down on that fire-pot holding the promise of a new life ahead of him: "I have a *daughter*? Me?"

"Yes," said Cliopher, gripping his hand tightly. "You do."

Fitzroy was quiet for a long moment. Then he said hoarsely, "We must go find her, Kip. I dreamed of someone, in that tower at the edge of the Abyss—"

Cliopher's heart might melt, if it were ice instead of fire. "She might not be your heir."

"She might be my daughter," Fitzroy replied instantly, and then was silent, struck by his own vehemence. After another long while, so long Cliopher had almost fallen asleep, he murmured, softly, "My family. My very own."

The island was not large; Cliopher could walk around it in an afternoon.

It was coral, rimmed with a barrier reef that formed a small lagoon. It had several spits, as if it were a sea star, splayed out against the cerulean water of Sky Ocean.

This island was a star, seen on the other side of the sky.

Cliopher walked the perimeter often, after he returned from his journey to the House of the Sun. He needed the space, the quiet, the expansiveness beyond the reef, as he gazed on the breakers that foamed like sparks, the horizon where the water became sky.

The air was soft, limpid, neither hot nor cool. The winds brushed gently across his cheek, his back, ruffled his hair. Sometimes he could see them: faces taking shape out of the sky, wings and long hair, stars in their eyes, music in their voices.

He walked the island's beaches, the smooth sand cool underfoot, where the water had washed it firm, the waves breaking over his feet. There were hundreds of tiny white clams that lived where the waves splashed and ran back, and he loved to watch them wriggling frantically into the sand after the waves tossed them up.

There were birds here, gulls and terns, great predatory skuas patrolling the barrier reef. There were tropicbirds, their long white tails banners in the sky. He wondered— oh, how he wondered—what those white birds were.

He did not always walk alone. Often Fitzroy joined him, walking silently beside him or humming softly, sometimes singing under his breath. He had spent much of the time of Cliopher's journey learning old songs from the sailors of the *He'eanka*, and practiced them still to ensure they were firmly in his mind and his throat.

Other times Cliopher was joined by Elonoa'a or Tupaia or Pinyë or Hiru or one of the other sailors. When it was Tupaia they spoke long of what it had meant in Tupaia's day to be tanà, what Cliopher understood it to mean in his.

"The tanà holds the fire," Tupaia said, as they walked on the far side of the island. Coconut palms waved in a stiff breeze, and Cliopher turned his head when he caught a glimpse of green and gold: a flash of wings like a great parrot's, hair whipping through the air until it became invisible wind, an echo of laughter ringing down from that other way of being.

"You still see them?" Tupaia asked softly.

"Sometimes," Cliopher said, blushing for his distraction. "Most often as a glimpse in the corner of my eye."

"You have changed," Tupaia told him solemnly.

Cliopher could only nod agreement. He did not know how to account for all the changes in him, the internal shifts arising from experience and thought, of the challenges he had made and met, and especially that deep descent into the secret chambers of his heart.

He hoped that he would not lose all the ease and limberness he had also been granted from his journey. He walked more easily than he used to, his breathing easier and the steps of the dances coming more lightly, more readily, to his feet. He often found himself drawn into the dances around the fire. Some of the steps he knew, and he was forever humbled when he thought of that proud claim, *I know the steps of my ancestors' dances.*

He did. He *did*. He had always meant it metaphorically—but oh, it was not. The steps were there, woven into the truth of the *Lays*, the common dances for weddings and festivals, the dances done for the Singing of the Waters.

He walked, and danced, and he sang, too.

He sang more than he had since he was a youth. Learning as many of the lost old songs as he could, and teaching some of the newer ones as well. The singers amongst the sailors had learned from Fitzroy while he learned from them, and had a wealth of new songs to sing on their long voyages. They teased Cliopher for wanting their tired old songs, but he never grew tired of the voyaging chants or all the songs that went with them.

It was a timeless place, that island that was also a star. The night fell, and other stars came out, unfamiliar constellations that here could be sailed to, could be reached, could prove themselves to be places out of myth.

The sun rose, heralded by the white birds with fiery eyes, who flew overhead singing that high, ethereal song, the Naming of Names in a language Cliopher did not know. He had seen their nests, those white birds, on the eaves of the House of the Sun.

The sun sailed his boat (drove his chariot) (ran his race) through the sky, a blaze against the blue.

Day succeeded night, and night day, and the stars turned, but there was no way to understand how many days there had been, how many nights. Cliopher tried, once, to keep a tally, but the numbers would not hold in his mind. He made a dozen scores in a piece of wood before he forgot to tally a day, and when he returned to his wood he could not account for any specific number of days he might have missed.

He asked Fitzroy how long he had been away on his journey.

Fitzroy leaned back on the sand outside their shelter. They were taking a respite from the bright sun overhead—it was not overly hot but nevertheless it was pleasant to sit in the shade and watch the terns fishing the barrier reef, listen to the wind in the tangle of trees behind them, smell the rich scent of a nameless shrub blooming with tiny yellow flowers of incomparable fragrance, speak over unimportant things.

"A long time," Fitzroy said eventually. "A month." He smiled without strain. "A lifetime."

Cliopher dug his hand into the sand, which felt effervescent against his fingers. "How long do you think its been back home?"

"Hardly long enough for them to believe we've had an adventure."

Cliopher looked at his friend—yes, friend. He did not look very much like his Radiancy now, with his hair grown out in those black-and-silver corkscrew curls, his muscles lean and taut as a panther's, his face mobile and emotive, full of laughter and wonder. He perhaps looked younger, though ages did not seem to mean much, here on this star, and Cliopher did not know how to describe the changes he saw. Fitzroy did not look as if he'd dived into the Fountain of Youth he had once mocked in one of his own youthful songs.

He looked as if the weight of the world had been lifted from him. No more, and no less.

He was a wild mage, a poet, a great man in his prime. Far more godly than he had ever seemed even in the height of his worship, and yet no more so than Elonoa'a or Aurelius Magnus or Tupaia.

"In my experience," Fitzroy said placidly, his eyes gleaming with mirth, "the Divine Lands are less like Fairyland than people suppose. There things take the time the fair folk desire; here they take the time necessary to the soul."

"It does not seem the same timelessness as it used to be on Zunidh," Cliopher said. "I cannot count the days, but it is not that they fall through my fingers like the sand, more that days do not mean anything at all."

"We will not return home to find all our loved ones centuries dead."

Fitzroy's certainty was palpable and reassuring. It matched Cliopher's desires, certainly, but also some faint intuition of things.

They were silent a while, watching the terns fish, black caps jaunty against their white bodies, their coral-red beaks.

Cliopher tried to pay attention to how long it was they sat there, how many minutes or hours, but all that would stay in his mind were the laughing faces of the sunlit Hours.

He laughed, and when Fitzroy asked him why, told him again of his time in the House of the Sun.

He had told the stories over and over again, teasing out all the layers of meanings any of them could hope to know. They had all wondered at the mirimiri of Ani, the news brought to Fitzroy of his daughter by the Moon, laughed at how Cliopher had outwitted the Sun for the hearth-right of Vou'a.

The sun was descending infinitesimally towards the west; towards that faint tug in the corner of Cliopher's mind that said *home.*

"You have started to talk more about home," Fitzroy observed at length.

"So have you."

Fitzroy nodded. He had been telling more stories of the Red Company, of his flamboyant youth; and had spoken from time to time of Zunidh as they had left it, of his household, of Conju and Ludvic and Rhodin and Lady Ylette.

There were no stories from his time as Emperor. Each time his reign was mentioned he would answer the question politely, economically, soberly as if he read from some academic or bureaucratic report. There was a hurt there, the memory of a terrible imprisonment, not yet healed.

"It is nearly time to go," Cliopher said.

They had come to Sky Ocean, to that star-island where they had met the *He'eanka* and her legendary crew, by the sort of accident that might have been fate, if Cliopher had believed in fate.

He believed in choices. He had chosen to step back, and thus slipped; Fitzroy had chosen to not let go of his hand, and thus fallen with him.

That night full of fireflies and magic, with Fairyland pressing close.

Cliopher had fallen hand-in hand with a wild mage, a great poet, a legendary hero: together they had fallen out of the Nine Worlds and into the heart of the sky.

And yet it was Cliopher's sky they had found. Aurelius Magnus was Fitzroy's ancestor after forty-nine generations, but the island and the ship and the rest of the crew were all from his *Lays.* And though he had found in the House of the Sun a Sun who acknowledged his fire still flowing in the veins of his descendants, nevertheless the rest of his journey had been through his own stories, his own constellations, his own heart.

To return home, then, would be his journey.

The crew gave Cliopher the vaha with which he had sailed to the House of the Sun.

"Your hand is on it, now," Pinyë said, stroking the carvings along the top edge of the outrigger.

They were variants of patterns he had seen all his life. Pinyë was Mdang, back when they had not yet taken the practice of surnames in regular speech, but the lineages were true. She had written her lineage, his lineage, the fire and the history of Loaloa, there in the spirals and curved lines and the speckles of red ochre.

"I will never forget that it was your hands that made it," Cliopher told her. "I have often enough said I sailed the ships my ancestors made for me, meaning that I have taken the lore and the *Lays* and brought them into my own life. To sail an *actual* ship made by my ancestors home! The heart leaps with joy."

Pinyë laughed. "You know I am not actually one of your ancestors. Not like Auri for your Fitzroy."

Cliopher smiled at her, remembering the tension and fear with which she had told him of her changed name, her changed appearance. "You are my kin. When I look at the Wake of the Ancestors' ships, I have more names by which to call them. If ever I see the comet again, I will know not only the names as they came down to me, but also your faces."

Pinyë swallowed. "And you will see to it that my name is ... my own?"

"I will," Cliopher promised, solid and certain as he had ever promised anything to his lord. He had told the god of mysteries in his guise as an efelauni that he would bring a new fire to the hearth of the world; and he had a coal lit from the flame of the fire of the Sun to take back to his people, along with the names so long lost or unknown.

"I will be singing the *Lays* over and over again," he murmured, as Pinyë fussed with ropes that did not need to be adjusted. "Telling the name of the third son of Vonou'a. Telling the names of the sailors of the *He'eanka*. Telling the love of Elonoa'a and Aurelius Magnus. Telling my long journey across Sky Ocean."

"They will give you a new song in the *Lays*," Pinyë said.

Cliopher grinned at her. Here, on this island, with the gifts of the Divine Lands still on him, he could believe that without difficulty. "We'll see," he said.

❦

A while later the faint, niggling desire grew a little stronger, and he took the opportunity of a walk with Tupaia to broach the subject.

Tupaia listened to him, nodding. "It is coming to our time to continue as well."

Certainly the *He'eanka* was fully refurbished, and the crew had turned towards stocking food and water and other supplies for the next stage of their voyage. Cliopher had been assisting where he could, helping the rope-makers and sail-weavers, building drying racks for fish and fruit, helping Hiru examine every inch of the parahë. She had taught him the songs of ship-building, anchoring the words to the physical shape of the ship, until, she thought, Cliopher would be able to take the song to the shipwrights of his day and build parahë of their own.

Cliopher and Tupaia walked the now-familiar scalloped edge of the island, the blue water fizzing white and clear about their feet. It was nearing evening, and the Wind of the Evening Star was blowing all the tints of the evening against the western sky.

Somewhere that way was *home*.

"I should like," Tupaia said studiously, "to dance the fire with you before we part ways."

~

They built up the bonfire hugely, the last day before he and Fitzroy intended to leave. They had a feast of all the good things of the island, fish and fruit and crabs and eggs.

And then, as the sun lowered towards the west (toward *home*, burning ever more brightly in Cliopher's mind), Cliopher and Tupaia used the rakes they had fashioned earlier out of palm-branches and drew the coals out into the patterns of the fire dance.

Cliopher had not told anyone their plan. Neither had Tupaia, it seemed, for the laughter and chatter died down as he and Tupaia pulled apart the fire.

There were a few places where Tupaia said, "That curve isn't quite—"

Cliopher double-checked the curves, feeling the rightness of the line in the scars on his feet. "Perhaps the currents have shifted a trifle," he offered.

They were on the ocean side, far from the earshot of the others. Fitzroy had struck up a song, and there were billows of music wafting over the smoke.

Tupaia smiled at him, his eyes intent in the last light of the sun. "Remember that."

Cliopher thought through what the other man meant. "That the dances shift according to later knowledge?"

"For a thing to be alive," Tupaia said, "it must change and grow."

Cliopher had a dizzying memory of that other Kip in that other place, holding on with all his considerable might to the ancient past. He had been trying to remake it into something new, but he had cast out half of what it might mean to be an Islander in his eagerness to be genuinely one.

Cliopher had stacked those two shells, the two halves of his heart, together.

It was not simply a matter of *correcting* the *Lays* to what had always been true but had never been known or had been forgotten or had been deliberately suppressed. He knew that—did he not have six nights after the last *Lay* Elonoa'a and Tupaia knew to sing for them?

"Your field is wider than mine," Tupaia said a little while later.

Cliopher looked up from where he was inscribing the curves of the islands to the west of the Vangavaye-ve, the Isolates to the south, the Line Islands to the north.

"The Wide Seas are wider for you," Tupaia went on, his face kindling with a kind of wonder. "I look forward to your dance."

~

Cliopher had *dreamed* of Tupaia's dance.

He sat next to Fitzroy, beside Elonoa'a and Aurelius. There was a drum—many drums. He had never loved the drum, never sought to become a master of it. He could, nevertheless, play the beat of the dance.

They were not doing the formal, festival dance. If the Fisherman were in this sky, his stars were all different, in an order Cliopher did not, could not recognize. Tupaia might start at sunset, but Cliopher's dance would not.

They had found the kind of sea cucumber whose slimy exudates protected against burning. That was a secret of the Mdangs, the various unguents one could use to protect the legs against an hour of dancing over coals.

"An hour!" Tupaia had cried, laughing, when they discussed the order of the dance. "Mine is not so long as that."

Until they raked out the coals Cliopher had not been able to fathom why that would be so. But Tupaia's dance showed the middle reaches of the Wide Seas, the Sociable Isles and the scattered atolls and archipelagos along the equator: the map of the journey from the mysterious beginnings in the west to the east, into the sunrise, until the first voyagers had found a continent and turned back, uninterested in conquest, and explored instead the unknown, uninhabited islands to the south.

Elonoa'a himself had been the one to find the Isolates, hearing their voices singing down the wind to him.

Cliopher had asked him about that discovery; how had he known there was a land far to the south and west, where there was otherwise nothing for thousands of miles in any direction?

"The wind blew the scent of flowers I did not know," Elonoa'a said eventually, pondering. "I followed, and soon enough found other evidence: birds migrating to their nesting grounds, flotsam along the currants, certain kinds of phosphorescence, certain kinds of fish ..."

Cliopher listened carefully, awed at the skill Elonoa'a dismissed so casually. He remembered too many islands he had sought nearly in vain to dismiss the discovery of a new archipelago.

Elonoa'a looked at him, his expression a little perplexed. "This is new to you, isn't it?"

And somehow there was enough time for all those conversations; and yet somehow also it came to be the time for their last evening, the great feast and the coals raked out across the sand.

Cliopher glanced up at Tupaia, who stood at the eastern end of the coals, and at the other man's nod began the same insistent beat his own Buru Tovo and nephew Gaudy had played for the last time *he'd* danced the fire.

The sailors fell silent and attentive, all eyes on the figure across the coals, the air wavering with rising heat.

Cliopher beat the drum, and at the right moment began to sing.

The familiar words tasted rich and right in his mouth. His hand was stinging with the unaccustomed vibration of the sticks on the drum. It was a slit-log drum, a kona'a such as he had seen a thousand times before. The design had not changed in two thousand years, not for this.

He sang the song of the fire dance, his eyes on Tupaia.

He had not seen anyone else dance it, not since his Buru Tovo had shown him. Never seen anyone else dance it before an audience.

Tupaia's motions were precise, settled, calm. His feet fell into the white sand channels between the coals, his hands curved in the motions Cliopher knew, pointed to stars he could name. The tears pricked his own eyes, but he blinked them furiously until he could see, for he would not miss a moment of this dance, of the tanà of all tanà dancing the fire before him.

He could see—oh, how could he not!—exactly why this man's dance had come down into the legends the Shaians told of the Seafarers.

And yet ... and yet ... there were differences. Tupaia's hands and feet shaped currents and winds, pointed to stars and star-roads, stepped from island to island across the Wide Seas ... and it was all elegant and beautiful and so full of meaning Cliopher's voice was thick with emotion, the song coming forth without his conscious mind attending, his hands beating the beat as if it were his heart, unable to be forgotten while he yet drew breath.

Tupaia finished his dance at the end of what Cliopher knew as the second of the five parts of the song. He nearly started the third, the rhythm so ingrained in him he could hardly refrain, but Tupaia had stopped, stepped out of the coals, was meeting their eyes and bowing, hand over fist, just the way Cliopher had done for the court.

He stopped the drum and let the song linger in his throat for a moment longer before the humming vibrations stilled.

Tupaia walked over to him, his face lit with exertion and joy, and he reached down his hand.

Cliopher took it, let himself be drawn up, let the kona'a fall to the sand. Pinyë took up the strikers and pulled the slit log over to herself.

Tupaia smiled at him and then looked at his friends, his family, this crew for whom he was the tanà on all their journeys no matter how far or dangerous, and he said, "Now it is time for our Cliopher, our One Who Barters with the Sun, to dance the fire."

And so he did.

CHAPTER FIFTY-THREE
THE EYE OF AU'AUA

They left in the cool, silvery light before dawn.

It was more traditional to leave at dusk, when sunset and the stars would provide the ke'ea, but Cliopher had his island in his mind and he felt an odd certainty that he should begin this next stage of his voyage as he had the last, with the Sun behind him.

Aurelius and Elonoa'a and Tupaia—along with the rest of the crew—gathered close as he and Fitzroy prepared to embark. They had already said most of their farewells, readied their supplies, prepared themselves.

Cliopher did not know how to leave the star-farers to their long journey. He hesitated at the edge of the sea, the waves lapping against his feet, unable to take the steps to push the vaha out into the water.

They did not seem to know what to say, either, Auri and El and Tupaia. They looked at each other, grief in their eyes at this parting.

Cliopher did not know how his ancestors had done it; not though he had left, time and again had he left, and seen that grief in his mother's eyes.

Fitzroy put his hand on Cliopher's elbow, though whether it was to steady himself or him Cliopher could not tell.

"We have gifts for you to take," El said abruptly, his fierce eyebrows coming together in that familiar scowl. He looked at Cliopher, who was suddenly glad for Fitzroy's hand on his elbow, at the intensity of emotion in El's eyes, at the fact that El put his hands to his neck and unfastened Izurunayë.

"This was the efela of the Paramount Chiefs," El said, holding it up so Cliopher could see the beads. The green pearls of Kuari, the flame pearls of the Western Ring, the powdery white beads carved out of falao shells ... the iridescent blue ones made from the same shells Cliopher had seen on the efela Tion of Mae Irión had given him ... and in the centre, a single bead polished until it glistened like fresh blood.

El looked at the efela. Cliopher wondered if his neck felt bare after so long wearing it. "This centre bead," he said, "was passed down, Paramount Chief to Paramount Chief, as the seed of a tui tree. They do not set fruit, the tui trees," El went on. "This came from our ancestors when they crossed into our histories." He looked gravely at Cliopher, and then smiled, the way Cliopher had come to realize meant his deep humour was surfacing. "It is not for you, but to give to the one who is now Paramount Chief."

Cliopher could accept that efela for that, and he bowed over his hands in acknowledgement.

"Here," said Elonoa'a, stepping forward, and when Cliopher looked up at him, he fastened the efela about his neck. "Wear it lightly until you may hand it over as you are bid."

Cliopher put his hand up to feel where the efela had settled between his efela ko and the efela the Grandmother had named Kiofa'a. The tui seed felt as warm as the efevoa had when it had held the phoenix feather close in its folds.

"We have a gift that is for you," Tupaia said, stepping forward as El stepped back. He held in his hands a small pot of alabaster-like coral, very like the one Fitzroy had made for his fire-pot. "It is from all of us, in thanks for the gift you have brought us."

He reached out, and Cliopher opened his hands for the fire-pot. As soon as the coral touched his hands and he felt the familiar warmth he knew it was a flame of the Sun.

"The fire was for you," he said, stammered almost.

Tupaia smiled at him. "And have we not spoken long about what it means to be tanà, Cliopher of Loaloa? It is right that you should take a share of this fire from the hands of your ancestors and bear it to those who come after you. You know that the fire is not lessened for lighting another."

Cliopher curled his hands around the pot, unable to say anything more. He looked instead at Aurelius, who was smiling at him almost shyly, before his expression changed into something fierce and blazing.

Cliopher took a step back, nearly knocking into Fitzroy, at this sudden emergence of the fabled warrior.

But Aurelius met his eyes with the magic in his own. "We shall meet again," the ancient emperor said, certainty ringing in his voice.

Cliopher's mouth was full of words he could not say, but they died on his tongue.

"Then we shall say fair winds and fair seas, and an island full of all you need when you are ready to land," Elonoa'a said.

"And to you," Fitzroy replied for them both, his voice thick. "And to you."

Tupaia stepped forward and they embraced, then pulled apart so they could touch foreheads together. "Thank you," Cliopher murmured.

"Thank you," Tupaia replied. He stepped back, his expression full of respect, full of amusement. "Who knows when we shall meet? Or where? Or why? You met the Old Woman Who Lives in the Deeps of the Sea, and she gave you the feather that Vou'a lost, so that you might reclaim the mirimiri that Ani lost."

Cliopher's hand dropped to the mirimiri, which he wore like a court mantle so that it would not be lost by his carelessness. He had learned the importance of keeping such things upon his person! He swallowed, and then he said, "May the winds be swift and the seas favourable, and your ke'ea clear before you!"

Fitzroy embraced his ancestor fiercely. He laughed when Aurelius whispered something into his ear, and refused utterly to tell Cliopher what Auri had said even after they had launched their boat.

∾

They sailed west.

Cliopher felt an incontestable sense of rightness as he lifted his sail and felt the Wind That Rises At Dawn catch it. The wind smiled at him, for a moment visible, her face pink and gold, until the white birds came singing out from behind her. Their wings covered her face, their voices overlaid the soft rush of the wind, and the vaha leapt forward, through the dark channel in the reef, out into Sky Ocean.

Fitzroy sat neatly on the outrigger, working the sails while Cliopher navigated with the tiller. He had spent many hours learning how to sail while Cliopher was gone, though his magic was not entirely happy with the waters even of Sky Ocean.

"I am learning to learn to love it," Fitzroy said once they had set the sail to the steadiness of the wind. Samayë guided them steadily west, along the line of Cliopher's heart's desire.

Half his heart's desire looked at him from where Fitzroy had seated himself near the prow with his golden harp in his hands, dipping his feet down so they skimmed over the water, the odd wave breaking white and gold across his black skin.

"I am so glad you are here with me," Cliopher said, his heart overflowing like one of those waves, crashing upon himself with a sudden effervescence of white and gold and joy, joy, joy. He was going home with a flame of the Sun and news of Sky Ocean and Fitzroy, his friend, his *fanoa* sailed with him.

Fitzroy plucked a few notes from his harp, which segued into something liquid and beautiful, which Cliopher thought perhaps he'd played that night of the lunar eclipse, when Cliopher had thrown a small white shell into the bonfire and asked for his Radiancy to learn to be happy, for he had not, then, been willing to articulate his own deepest desire.

Cliopher sat near the tiller, letting his own legs dangle down to skim the waves, watching a flock of bronze and jewelled flying fish suddenly come skipping around the vaha, as if they too desired to hear Fitzroy Angursell's music.

He did not think he had ever been so happy before.

∾

The sun climbed high overhead, a fiery disc, a bright canoe, a chariot pulled by white horses, a giant black as Fitzroy running a race, a golden orb in his hands.

"We sail due west?" Fitzroy asked, as Cliopher made a minute adjustment to the tiller, the sail, to make up for the afternoon shift of the wind. Samayë—or rather Sama, the wind in herself, not her human form—returning to her rest, and one of her sisters taking her place.

"For now, yes."

The silence was as companionable as it had been on any of those walks around the star island, any of those quiet afternoons or merry evenings on the beach. Cliopher felt the thrum of the water against the hull, the taut quiver of the boat in the belly of the wind, the slow rollicking motion of the deepwater swells coming from north of west.

"We shall follow the sun's path during the day," Cliopher said presently, "and the westerly ke'ea through the night, until we come to the ... Aya'e'alu'ova, it is called in the old, old stories, the ones about the third son of Vonou'a—about Samayo Atēatamai."

Fitzroy murmured over the word, parsing out the Islander meaning. "The Song of the ... Breaking of the Waves?"

"That's what it's named."

"What do you think it means?"

Cliopher felt a certain thrill of mischief. "Not even Elonoa'a knows. We shall be the ones to tell them. Tell everyone."

Fitzroy grinned at him, his face illuminating with that glow that was not majesty or glory or youth but joy.

No wonder half the Nine Worlds had fallen in love with him.

"What a gift you are to me," Fitzroy said. "And here I nearly took you for merely an incomparable secretary!"

Cliopher had been unlearning courtly reticence. He laughed. "And here I nearly took you for merely one of the five aristocrats in the Palace who actually did something useful."

Fitzroy lifted his hand to his heart. "You wound me, Lord Mdang!" Then his nose twitched. "Who are the other three?"

"I am not counting myself in that number."

"I was presuming either Rhodin or Conju made the cut."

Cliopher pretended to consider. "Perhaps. Rhodin did waver a little in my estimation when he started telling me about how his heart's desire was to find his dinosaur soulmate amongst the Merrions."

"Rhodin's special reports on his investigations into the Merrions give me *enormous* joy."

"I know." Cliopher nodded judiciously. "After much thought, I decided that Rhodin's telepathic communication with you probably counted for something."

This was one of the very few times Cliopher had ever seen Fitzroy genuinely gobsmacked, and he relished it.

"Unless, of course—"

"I swear I *don't*—"

They stopped simultaneously, and regarded each other with just a hint of challenge. Fitzroy—well, Cliopher did not know quite why he had flicked up his eyebrow like that.

Unless it was because Cliopher had never spoken over him like that before. But then again, Cliopher had not sailed to the House of the Sun and won legendary treasures for his people before. He smirked, just a little, and Fitzroy laughed. "Oh, you *are* sly!" His voice was warm with delight. "What did you say the Grandmother called you? *One of Vou'a's?* Runs in the family, I see."

Cliopher took that as a point for himself. "But not telepathic communication with Rhodin?"

"Outside of very few, very particular moments of great magic and great emotion, I have never had a telepathic communication with anyone."

They looked at each other. Cliopher felt a little breathless, the unspoken challenge not dissipated, but strengthening. Challenge, and something else—a gleam of—hope?—a wavering of doubt—

Doubt. Hope. Challenge. Works of great magic, great emotion ...

There had been that moment, when Cliopher first touched Fitzroy, at the conclusion of the viceroyship ceremony, when he had *felt* Fitzroy's emotions, and known Fitzroy had felt his.

Beloved had been the word spoken silently between them, heart to heart as they held that curving okana shell with its single ember between their cupped and entwined hands.

It was not the single shell, symbol of the Vangavaye-ve, that Cliopher wanted to hold the flame he had nurtured from that tiny spark of their first encounter.

Challenge was to be met with challenge: that was the way of his people. He did not look away from Fitzroy, who was smiling crookedly with some subterranean amusement.

"You've never asked me to finish explaining what fanoa means," he said, his heart thundering. He had said enough, surely he had said enough, for Fitzroy to begin to understand why he said that—

Fitzroy played a few bars of a song ... it was Astandalan, not one of his, nor one of the Islander songs that had been so much in Cliopher's ears. He knew it, he knew he did—Fitzroy played the bridge, a sudden complicated flurry of notes, and then the so-familiar chorus ...

And suddenly Cliopher recognized it: one of the many ballads that went under the title of *Aurelius Magnus and the Seafarer King*.

Oh, how he loved the man before him.

Fitzroy spoke desultorily, his attention apparently more on the notes he was playing. Apparently. Cliopher knew him too well not to know that this nonchalance was half-feigned. Only half ... but still half. "After Vou'a left to go wherever he was going, I asked El and Tupaia all the stories they knew about Vou'a and Ani."

Fitzroy looked across at him, his black and silver curls elegantly windswept, his eyes golden in the sunlight, his bright grin illuminating his face.

Cliopher flushed, some deep part of him fluttering madly. "I was perhaps not entirely clear."

"Those fireflies were very distracting, admittedly."

"Yes," he said, remembering that night, the scent of the flowers, the magic on the wind, the fireflies and the shadows, the soft summer airs of that dark and enchanted wood. He opened his mouth, not sure what he was going to say, for he had only articulated this once, in that secret cave of his heart, offering it to the coal he tucked into that shell for Ani—

Before he could speak, Fitzroy abruptly looked down and away, letting his hair flop over his face, and began playing the long version of *Aurora*.

Cliopher tucked the mirimiri of Ani more securely around his shoulders, not sure of anything except that Fitzroy had cared enough to ask Tupaia and El about what fanoa meant.

~

The day unspooled with light, pleasant conversation. Both of them laughed a great deal, and they talked over much of what they had already talked over, Cliopher's journey and Fitzroy's time with the star-sailors.

"Has magic not developed greatly from Auri's time?" Cliopher asked, some time when the sun was nearly full in their eyes and he had to turn sideways so he would not be blinded by its radiance. Fitzroy had investigated their stores of food and opened a green coconut for each of them, using his shell knife with much more facility than he had when they'd first come to Sky Ocean.

"Wild magic is like poetry. There are some principles, some rules, that can be learned—that can be taught. But if one wishes to move beyond the rote, beyond the trite ... it is all down to the imagination, the heart and the soul of the poet, the mage. Auri sees magic in the air, in the wind ... He truly does match El."

Cliopher glanced away from Fitzroy's brilliant gaze, which was fixed on him. He drank his coconut, savouring the taste. The sea was golden on the sunward side, deep blue and silver on the shadowed. The sky was a deeper blue, lavender; black-and-white terns winged back past them, returning to their island to roost.

His island burned in his mind, on the other side of the sunset.

He cleared his throat. "And you?—How do you perceive magic, that is?"

Fitzroy smiled slyly at him. "We already know how well we work together, don't we?" He set down his coconut so he could lean back against the mast. "I do not hear or see magic, not unless I am deep inside it, in a trance, but I feel it ... I know the taste and texture of it, the temperature and the weight of it."

Cliopher clutched his coconut, the weight of it an anchor in his hands. "What does it feel like here?"

"What does the sea look like to you?"

He could not look away from Fitzroy's face, the wrinkles around his eyes, the relaxed set of his smiling mouth, the way the heavy coils of his hair tumbled in the wind.

"It looks like the sea, but more," Cliopher said softly. "More itself. More real. More ... than it seemed to be, at home, but not other than what it is."

Fitzroy raised his hand: light gathered around it, as like the foaming breakers of the reef around the island as Cliopher could imagine. "It is much the same with the magic. I cannot go into the deeper trance ... or rather I *can*, but there is no point. When I turn away from my own heart, I see nothing different. Everything is so much itself there is no magic beyond that."

Cliopher watched him, dipping his hand down so the sparks fell down, foam upon the wave.

Fitzroy looked up at him, his eyes golden as the water. Neither said anything. Cliopher was thinking of that moment he had first seen the portrait of the new emperor and known with that sudden shock, as if someone had called his name, that their fates were entwined.

"What are you thinking?" Fitzroy asked softly.

Challenge and counter; the pull of the current and the push of the wind; the movements of the fire dance, each step precisely into the safe channel between the reefs of burning coals.

He could have stepped back, could have said a true dissimilation, could have paraphrased with some plausible denial. Cliopher had lived his lifetime at court; that dance was easy.

He would not do that to Fitzroy, nor to himself. He had sailed across Sky Ocean to the uttermost East, and he had stood at the feet of the Sun and bargained well with him.

"When you became emperor," Cliopher said, "a copy of your first state portrait was sent to a friend of mine in Gorjo City. She'd gone to Astandalas in your grandmother's day, to study magic ..."

"To see if Anyoë was worth staying for."

What could he say to that? Fitzroy knew he had stayed: stayed his whole life an arm's length away, unable to breach that barrier, unwilling to leave.

Cliopher nodded, his mouth dry. "When I saw the portrait, when I saw *you*, it was as if someone called my name. As if our fates were entwined, I told Basil."

Fitzroy looked at him, frowning slightly, all his formidable attention focused onto Cliopher. "You don't believe in fate. You've told me that."

"The patterns are there," Cliopher said, gesturing at the sea, the sky—the Sky Ocean—all around them. "We choose which ones we follow." He was silent for a moment; Fitzroy said nothing, merely regarded him carefully, as if waiting for the moment it was his turn to dance.

"I never imagined," Cliopher said, his voice soft as the pitter-patter of the flying fish on the surface of the waves, "no matter how proudly I pretended so to others, that when I went to Astandalas I would one day truly cross Sky Ocean to stand at the feet of the sun, and come home with you."

Fitzroy's eyes were very bright. "For so long I thought I would never be able to have friends such as I had known in my youth ... and yet it was you, not they, who saw I was bound, and freed me."

Cliopher's heart was singing, each step, each turn, this dance he knew and did not know, had never danced before for all the times he had imagined what it might be. "It took me so long ..."

"You did not shatter the chains and burn down the Empire, which is what my friends of the Red Company would have done if they had come for me."

They looked at each other, and Cliopher saw something, some deep emotion, moving just below the surface of Fitzroy's expression. His friend's (his fanoa's) expression lightened, into something like awe, like amusement, like love. "No. You picked apart the knots and made the locks no longer necessary—for me, or for anyone. Neither my heir nor my—my—my daughter will be chained into that throne as I was, unable to touch or to look or to love or to *leave*."

This time it was Cliopher who looked away, his hands plucking at the cloud-soft fabric of his tunic, and him who cleared his throat and began to sing a song.

His was about Vou'a lifting the islands out of the sea for Ani.

≈

The sun set, and the stars came out.

The sea was glassy, glossy black. It looked as if it were made of obsidian, as if touching the edge of a wave would cut his hand.

The wind was steady out of the east, the current bearing them due west. He had not had to shift tiller or sail since they they had set it.

Fitzroy was lying flat on his back upon the deck, looking up past the sail to the stars.

Cliopher lay down opposite him, face-down at first, the swells rocking into his ribcage, and gently reached down past the edge of the deck to touch his fingers to the smooth back of the wave. Five furrows raised, white-edged with bubbles, but the water itself was warm, welcoming.

He rolled over, hand still trailing, and looked up at the sky. It was a vast luminous black, spangled with the stars that were so much larger, so much *more*. The sail glimmered with a light like phosphorescence or earthshine on the dark side of the moon.

The stars were closer, too, even than they had been on his journey to the uttermost east. They looked close enough to touch, half dancers and half burning lanterns.

They were drifting around him, like the glowworms in the cave at the heart of the mountain, not falling but stepping, dancing down invisible staircases, their light in their hands, their hair, their eyes.

Cliopher turned his head to see that Fitzroy had rolled to meet him, their heads close enough that their hair mingled. His eyes were luminous in the starlight.

"Look," he said softly, his voice low and rich.

Cliopher looked away from the bright eyes to the bright stars, the night air on his face fragrant with the sea, with the faint hint of some distant island's impossible flowers. He slid over another few inches closer. Fitzroy caught his hand and held it, his fingers warm, his grip snug.

How long had he spent unable to touch? How hungry must he have become for that simple, simple connection. Cliopher had yearned sometimes for another's touch, and he had had no taboos or customs preventing it, merely loneliness. Even after he had come to be proper friends with Conju and Rhodin and Ludvic they rarely touched each other, as if that were an intimacy too far.

Not the Islander way, not at all. Cliopher touched his family, his friends, his acquaintances, often even strangers: hands on the forearms in the Astandalan greeting, foreheads touching in the ancient Islander way, hands clasping hands or shoulders or elbows or knees, shoulders or hips bumping as they walked, embraces, the odd kiss on forehead or cheek.

He left his hand in Fitzroy's, glad for the touch, and looked again at the water passing so smoothly underneath them, the faint hissing of the hulls through the water the music of his childhood. His father used to take him out, he remembered suddenly; they would spend afternoons with him playing in the bottom of the boat as his father tended his nets and told him stories.

The River of Stars was above them, and also below.

Cliopher looked down, his cheek against the wood, the swells thrumming, forming the underlying beat of ... something.

He wondered what Ghilly's brother and the Ouranatha had seen, when that star flared bright in his hand as he held it high, a beacon across the night sky. Their little fragment of day was tucked safe in the hollow of the hull, nestled within the mirimiri of Ani inside a water-tight basket Pinyë had made for them.

He sailed the night sky, now. The ocean was still water below him, still salt when he lifted his hand to taste it, but yet when he looked to one side or the other he could not quite tell where Sky Ocean left off and sky began.

The stars were still stepping down the winds, taking up their place for some dance he could almost see was about to begin.

What dance did they do here, in this place where time was meaningless because all the markers of time had their own beings?

Cliopher looked down, at the water below him. At the sky below him, for the stars were there, too, in clusters like the nebulae he had seen through the telescope, clouds of stars, bright faces walking there, waking there, looking up at him and Fitzroy on the infinitesimally small vaha running down the River of Stars away from the gods and towards home.

Was one of those stars Furai'fa, burning high above Loaloa?

He sought some familiarity, some constellation, one of the Bright Guides, Nua-Nui back before him, wanting to know what raiment those stars wore, this side of the sky, but none of them showed any sign he recognized.

He was looking down when something rose from the deeps.

A shadow, black in the black water, starlit like the nebulae, vast as any vaunting Cliopher had ever done.

He gripped Fitzroy's hand tight, fear and excitement warring.

The lights were moving: a nebula rising: and then it curved away from the vaha, and curved back again, so he could see a fin, an eye, the arc of a tail—

"It's a *whale*," Fitzroy said, the delight in his voice audible, ringing with the magic of it.

Cliopher looked into the whale's eye. It was deep and wise, huge as an island, brilliant as a star.

There was a northern constellation of the Whale, one of the ones that dipped over and under the equator, visible half the year in the latter half of the night. The ke'e of the midmost of the Line Islands was the star in the fork of the tail; the ke'e for the Mae Irionéz, when he had found their names in the *Lays* as Those Who Swim with Dolphins, was the Eye of Au'aua, the Great Whale, the brightest star in the north of Zunidh.

He met the eye of this celestial whale and knew, as he had known when he flew with the Albatross, that this was the constellation, this *was* the Great Whale herself, as that albatross who had guided him across Sky Ocean had been Nua-Nui the Great Bird.

He gripped Fitzroy's hand tight, his breath catching. Au'aua kept pace with them, looking deep into Cliopher's eyes.

He thought first of that tiny toy, the stuffed whale his aunt had made for him, the one he had loved so deeply, so dearly.

Au'aua had a question in her eye, the star of the north.

Unlike the Sun and the Grandmother, Cliopher was sure she could see into him.

He did not mind: he had loved the constellation with all the love he had ever given that small toy, and he would open his heart to her.

The night darkened around him, the sky as black and glossy as the waves, as the wavering blade of an obsidian knife, the volcanic glass that was sharper than any forged steel and yet brittle if struck wrong.

Au'aua blinked once, the star winking out like the opposite of a viau, a streak of black against the nebulae, and Cliopher put his hand to his efela ko and the obsidian pendant at its centre.

He had not thought of this for ... so long. So much of his memory was contingent, requiring something to spark a thought. How could he have worn his efela ko all these years, held onto that obsidian pendant, looked upon Mama Ituri on every visit home, and not think of this?

Yet he did not. He remembered the shaping of the obsidian until he could fasten the twine around it securely, so it did not scratch or cut his throat; he had not thought about where the obsidian came from.

The Great Whale stared at him, thoughtful, intelligent, kind. She reminded him a little of Ludvic, who watched, mostly silent, holding his thoughts and emotions deep, deep within.

Ludvic with those smudges of gold down his arms, Ludvic who had stood beside the man he thought of as his uncle, Ludvic who had never known his father but for the songs Fitzroy had written of him. Ludvic who had been illiterate until adulthood and yet composed romantic epics; Ludvic who was the great soldier and guard and yet yearned for the arts of healing, of peace; Ludvic who was so strong and yet had shown Cliopher how he was brave enough to be weak.

The Great Whale seemed almost amused as his thoughts skittered away. Cliopher was aware that the stars were clustering closer, as if they were listening, as if he was the hearth at the centre of the dance, he and his Radiancy lying hand-in-hand on a vaha in the midst of Sky Ocean.

"What is the whale asking you?" Fitzroy asked, his voice soft, part of the air and the soft shurring hiss of the vaha across the shining water.

"She is asking how I came to have the obsidian on my efela ko ... I climbed Mama Ituri for it ..." He hesitated, picking his words as he had picked his way up that difficult path. "There is a path ... a secret way ... up through the broken rock, up to the caldera ... I climbed up, the way I had been told to follow, all the way up to the very peak of the mountain ... At the top the crest curled over, like a wave of liquid fire turned into stone ..."

Fitzroy's breath hitched, and his hand squeezed Cliopher's, though he did not say anything.

Fitzroy knew poetry: knew symbolism the way Cliopher knew the *Lays*. He knew why that was the central metaphor of the Mdang family's efela ko.

"Coming down was hard," Cliopher said vaguely, remembering the bruises and scrapes on his feet, the haste with which he had carried that fist-sized globule of obsidian ... "I dropped the stone on my foot at the bottom, and it split in half ..."

Buru Tovo had set the two pieces together, matching perfectly, as if the crack had meant something significant to him. He'd said *well done*; the first time Cliopher remembered him using any words of praise, though he'd shown his pleasure and approbation many other ways.

Au'aua regarded him calmly, with a vast sorrow that was yet vastly comforting.

The question rose in Cliopher's mind: *why?* But the whale merely regarded him, and returned the question, silent and yet opening up in Cliopher's mind like a flower.

Why did he find the whale's sorrow comforting?

—No. That was not the question; not quite the question. And he was not certain it was sorrow, after all. It was a solemn joy, deep as the lowest note of his sister's cello, humming deep as the whale song he had sometimes heard when he lay like this on his *Tui-tanata*, listening.

Why?

The whale blinked at him—*winked* at him—amused as vastly, as deeply, as slowly as her sorrow, her joy, and then Au'Aua exhaled a great vast plume of starlight and even as Cliopher and Fitzroy both sat up, spluttering, laughing at the way the starlight glittered and fell and clung to them, illuminated them, hung smudged and glorious in their hair, on their eyelashes, the sails and spars of the vaha, the Great Whale dove down and disappeared once more into the night.

Cliopher relinquished Fitzroy's hand so he could brush the spume from his face. Fitzroy was laughing, as glittering and radiant as he had ever been as emperor, in his most formal raiment, but laughing, eyes as bright as his smile, as he never had.

"This is such a different River of Stars to the one I sailed down with the Red Company," Fitzroy said. Cliopher did not tell him he still had starlight dusting his cheeks, his nose, smudged across one ear. No doubt he did as well. The thought was warming.

"These are my people's stories."

"Yes ... last time it was mine, I think. Mine and Jullanar's ... we share much of the same imaginative universe, I suppose you could say. We read all the same books, you see."

The stars were dancing around them, more lanterns than people, now, save that their shadowy, nebulous robes swept like shadows, like wings, like waves, through sky and Sky Ocean.

Their vaha was moving quickly, quickly as if caught in a river-current.

The ke'ea in the story of the third son of Vonou'a—of Samayo Atēatamai—was to follow the sun to the uttermost west, where they would find Aya'e'alu'ova, the *Song of the Breaking of the Waves.*

It was a somewhat ominous term. One might use it, poetically, for the breakers over a reef, or the cataract of a great waterfall from a high island.

They would find out in due time. Cliopher smiled at Fitzroy. "Would you sing me the songs you wrote of that journey?"

Fitzroy smiled at him, swift as a sunrise, and lifted his voice in the second half of those poems he had called *Kissing the Moon.*

～

They were still in what Fitzroy called the Divine Lands, and did not feel any regular need to eat or drink or sleep or fulfil any other bodily function. They opened green coconuts from time to time, sipping the sweet water held inside the nuts, playing games with the shells. Fitzroy spent some hours breaking the shells into a set of pieces, and then inscribed a cross-hatched board on the main platform of the vaha.

He set the coconut shells in front of Cliopher, and a pile of pebbles in front of himself.

"Draughts?" Cliopher asked, considering.

"If you play."

Cliopher raised his eyebrows at him. "We were accustomed to the occasional game, if you recall. When you were disinclined to trouncing me at chess."

Fitzroy gave him a slightly sheepish grin, ducking his head so he could look up at Cliopher through his lashes. "You are the only person I ever regularly beat who didn't simply let me win."

"I've never been particularly good at truckling to authority," he acknowledged.

"Even at your most obsequious—" Fitzroy started to laugh. "Your most obsequious lasted all of an hour, that second day you were my secretary."

"After I looked you in the eyes."

"After you corrected my pronunciation, capped my joke, and ... saved me."

Cliopher had known that without ever saying it aloud. It sounded weightier, said aloud. He spread out his game pieces.

Fitzroy followed suit, his hand setting the pale pebbles down with quiet, assured clicks. The vaha rolled with a calm, steady motion, caught in the current, riding the slow, gentle swells that were now coming from dead astern.

"Perhaps," Cliopher said softly, "it would be good for you to talk about your time as emperor."

Fitzroy hesitated over one of his pebbles, then moved it forward, starting the game. Cliopher followed suit, playing out move after move in silence. Finally his friend said, "Perhaps it would. One day."

Cliopher nodded, and let the game focus him. He had played draughts with Buru Tovo many times. His cousins had laughed at him playing with the elders—draughts and dominoes were their games—but Cliopher had felt proud to sit with the elders, proud to lose (very occasionally to win) against them. He had usually been sent off to fetch coffee or juice or refreshments at some point, while the conversation ran on, half in Islander, half in Shaian, lines from the *Lays* woven into everyday concerns.

"I only have metaphors," Fitzroy said after the game was finished—Cliopher won handily—and the board set again.

Cliopher waited patiently, curious—how could he not be curious?—but aware this was not the time to ask questions.

"The fire at the heart of me, down to a handful of embers, buried in ash. The garden of my poetry, blighted, frosted, burned, sere as a northern winter. No clear wind, only stagnant, heavy air ... doldrums. My whole ... myself, thrust down so far below the surface I thought I should never return. They were trying to make me a god, you know."

He nodded. He did know. The Ouranatha had done so deliberately, building on the old imperial fiction until those desperate for a god who was not so distant and unreachable as the ones who had let the Fall happen looked upon the god at the centre of the palace, the god on the golden throne, whose magic brought rain or sunshine—

"I almost let go, let ... myself ... float away ... until you caught me. For so long all I had was that morning ritual, of you looking at me and saying 'good morning' when I looked at you and said 'good morning'—that was *it*, Cliopher, that was all I had to remind myself that I was a person, a human being, a man. You, never quite able to look at me as you were supposed to. Never quite able," and here Fitzroy smiled, tilting his head up so he could look through his lashes again, the smile tugging at the corner of his mouth, crinkling the corners of his eyes. "Never quite able to, as you say, truckle to authority."

It was Cliopher's turn to grin sheepishly.

Fitzroy leaned forward and caught his hand, turning it over so he could rub his own thumb over Cliopher's palm. "Thank you."

He was caught, Cliopher was, in the golden eyes, magic-brilliant, still with starlight smudged across his nose, streaked in his magnificently curly hair.

Cliopher had met his lord's, his emperor's, his friend's, eyes—each morning, greeting him, rising up after his bows, sitting down to the table. Golden eyes shadowed brown, sorrowful and sombre as the Great Whale's eye.

The shadows now were softer, hovering on the edge of joy.

Cliopher had no magic, still. He could not see it, taste it, feel it, touch it, hear it. He could not hold fire in his hands or call light or hear the secret calls of far-away islands.

He knew where his island was, and he had been to the uttermost east, to the house of the Sun, and looked full into his eyes.

He smiled and looked down, as if there were nothing holding him in Fitzroy's but the emotion rising up into a crooked smile.

Cliopher felt a shift, a change, something coming to a point of balance.

The sail was still taut, curved with the wind. Somewhere distant was a dark shadow of wings, of long streaming hair, of starlit eyes, prettily curved mouth. The tiller was lashed into position, holding the vaha true to its course, cleaving down the centre of the current.

All around them were the stars, stately and luminous, impossibly large, impossibly bright, the sky between them, the water, the shimmering, shining curve of freshly exposed obsidian.

And something, something, steady and poised, the vaha balanced on its two keels, sailing under a fair wind, the ke'ea home clear and straightforward.

This was what he had always wanted.

This is what he *had*.

He had lifted up the world so that the emperor on his golden throne could step down without falling. He had lifted himself up to be worthy of being the equal, the fanoa, the match of Fitzroy Angursell, fulfilling a quest out of myth that he might walk beside legends.

Cliopher lay down, holding Fitzroy's hand.

"What is it?" Fitzroy asked, laughing, breath hitching as he made a surprised mewling sound when Cliopher tugged him down.

"Lay on your back," Cliopher said, turning his head so his cheek was on the deck of the vaha, his face towards Fitzroy's. The little current of air that ran just above the boards of the vaha tickled as it moved across his skin.

Fitzroy let go of his hand to brush back some of the hair that had fallen into Cliopher's face, his fingers lingering a little on the feathers the Wind That Rises At Dawn had tied into the braids. "I like this style," he said, playing with the braids. "I like your hair grown out. It softens your face."

"I like how your hair looks, too," Cliopher said, a little shyly. He knew Fitzroy had been experimenting with various unctuous substances—oil from the coconuts, from the tobby nuts, from some seed of a plant that had never been named—and the coils gleamed black and silver in the sun. It seemed odd to give him such a personal compliment, when for so long Fitzroy had been at all times perfect, the very model of what was correct; but that had been Conju's artistry, not his own.

Fitzroy tucked the feathers behind Cliopher's ear before arranging himself so he was cushioning his head on his outstretched arm, that hand curving around Cliopher's head. Cliopher smiled at his refusal to take instruction—on his side was not his back—and took Fitzroy's free hand and pressed it to the deck. "Do you feel the rhythm?" Cliopher asked softly. "The waves, first."

The great rocking swell, smooth and stately, comforting, easy. Fitzroy hummed a note, so exactly right Cliopher chuckled against the wood. They were very close to each other; Fitzroy's hum was in his chest, touching his heartbeat.

"And the current," he murmured, humming a beat, not urgent but deliberate, certain, steady. Fitzroy added another note, harmonizing with his, picking up the higher, faster rhythm of the counter-current Cliopher had just noticed.

"Very good," he said, very quietly, nearly whispering. "That's the one that will take us home."

Fitzroy smiled at him. His eyes really were an extraordinary colour. Cliopher smiled back, listening to the waves thrumming, the keels hissing, the wind bringing with it those hints of flowers from islands he would never see.

He was purely content, resting his eyes on the sky, which was such a soft black, iridescent like ahalo cloth dyed for his Radiancy's black garments, catching soft purples and blues, bronzes and golds.

Fitzroy was there, his hand a little sweaty in his, his pulse beating steadily, a little fast.

Cliopher wanted, dreamily, to offer a further intimacy. "On the island where I met Vou'a, I went down into the cave of my heart ..."

In his recounting of his voyage, Cliopher had told the outline of this story; none of the private details. He'd told them of finding the one chamber, and the dark, cold dive into the darkness, and the one on the other side.

"I knew the first chamber could not be all there was to me," he said, still looking at the sky. A great school of silver viau swam there, or flew there, catching brilliance as they came in and out of the stars. He squeezed Fitzroy's hand. "I knew because my love for you was not there. All the things I had *done* ... but not the fire at the heart of me. That was on the other side, in a hearth made of pearls ..."

His free hand came up to his efela ko, the obsidian and the pearls.

"When I look at my magic," Fitzroy said, his voice very quiet, "the fire at the heart of me is protected by a ring of golden pearls, flame pearls, all the gifts you have given me ..."

How many times had Cliopher laid on his back on a canoe with his cousins as a youth, talking over all the concerns of youth! Wondering what it meant to be human, to see the colour of the sky, to love or to yearn. He felt a great warm surge of love, and squeezed Fitzroy's hand.

"Do you ever dream about kissing?" Fitzroy asked him.

"No," he said easily, dreamily, as easily as he had when he and Basil had whispered over their questions. Cliopher had never dreamed of love as Basil had; never woken with those thoughts in his mind, his body.

"I see," Fitzroy said, his voice trembling. He turned his head, to see that Fitzroy had closed his eyes and appeared to be trying not to laugh out loud.

Basil had laughed at him, too, sometimes. Teased him, in a way that had never hurt. He had not intended to make Fitzroy laugh ... but he was glad he could bring that joy to him.

The wind shifted, just a trifle, just enough that Cliopher reluctantly let go of Fitzroy's hand in order to sit up so he could adjust the tiller.

"It's never been one of my great concerns," he added, for Fitzroy's silence seemed expectant of further revelation. "Sex, that is. It doesn't really ... come to my mind."

That did make Fitzroy laugh, his shoulders shaking, his whole body given over to merriment.

It was a delight to see him so relaxed, so happy. Cliopher fixed the tiller into its new orientation and then lay down again. Fitzroy quivered for a few moments with the little after-shocks of hilarity, his hands folded over his stomach. His signet ring, the Imperial Seal, glinted.

Cliopher had almost forgotten he wore it. He was reminded of how much touch meant to Fitzroy, and how perhaps that had been enough. He let his hands rest gently at his sides.

The vaha was humming, Cliopher's chest vibrating with song, some ancient wordless song he could not remember hearing before. Deep, echoing so much lower down the high ethereal song of the distant stars, the glowworms in the flowery cave, the lights when he thought he had drowned.

And yet ... he had not drowned. And he was here with Fitzroy, his fanoa, crossing Sky Ocean together on their way home, waiting for the white birds of the dawn to come surging across the sky towards them.

CHAPTER FIFTY-FOUR
THE SONG OF THE BREAKING WAVES

Cliopher must have fallen asleep at some point, for he woke to the singing of the white birds.

Fitzroy lay beside him; he'd turned in his sleep, so Cliopher could see the structure of the muscles on his back, the way the reflected ripples of starlight and dawnlight played upon his skin, the stark contrast of the pale sarong draped over his hips.

Sunrise came like a tsunami of light, shining through air and water with an equal luminosity, an equal radiance.

The stars softened, faded, for a moment shone like candles in glass, then the sky, the sea, the Sky Ocean flooded with colour, and the stars became sparkles on the crest of innumerable waves, on tiny pure white clouds keeping pace with them.

Cliopher sat up, and from their stores chose a mango, as perfectly ripe as any fruit had ever been. He offered half to Fitzroy, who took it with a yawn and a faint, ironic smile.

He ate the fruit with a curious concentration. Cliopher wondered whether Fitzroy still felt a sense of broken taboo when he ate fresh fruit. Cliopher still felt that thrill when he looked directly at him, after so many years; even more when they touched, as friends did, easily, companionably, lovingly.

Fitzroy was much less tactile this morning than he had been last night. They moved without comment to sit on opposite sides of the boat, Fitzroy perched near the mast, Cliopher on the outrigger. The new current was stronger this morning; he could feel it without needing to lay flat and calm against the deck.

It was a perfectly beautiful day. The sun seemed to take a long time crossing the sky towards them. Cliopher hummed passages from the *Lays*, songs of the third son of Vonou'a, of Samayo Atēatamai, trying to find any hint of what might lie before them when they sought to cross from Sky Ocean back to the waters of his own Wide Seas.

The water was a pure cerulean, clear impossible fathoms deep. It was so nearly the same colour as the sky that Cliopher could not look at it for long before he started to doubt which way was up and which down.

He looked across at Fitzroy, who was regarding the distant northern horizon pensively.

It was strange that Fitzroy had offered so little speech this morning. He had been so full of smiles and laughing looks last night ...

Cliopher considered, staring pensively off at the horizon himself. He was facing to the west, admiring the clouds piling up there, great curving domes all white and tints of gold and lavender-grey, just what they had tried to imitate when building the Palace of Stars.

Home was that way, dead ahead, true as a wind or a star whose name he knew. Cliopher could almost hear the distant rumble of breakers, but perhaps that was his imagination.

Had Fitzroy had a nightmare? Had all that touching been too much, too soon?

Fitzroy had not had nightmares all the time they had spent sharing the shelter on the star-island. But perhaps he had felt safer there ...

Cliopher sat with that creeping uncertainty. He looked at his friend, who had finished his mango and had knelt down to dip his hands in the water, one at a time, and wash them in the running seas. He did not look ... harrowed, or haunted. Fitzroy looked up at him as he stood, nodded with a small, wry smile at the corner of his mouth, and sat down with his harp in his lap.

In some confusion, Cliopher checked the sails and tiller, the fire-pot (not though the flame of the Sun needed *his* attention). He unwound the mirimiri of Ani and coiled it around the fire-pot, cradling both inside the close-woven basket. This morning it did not seem right to wear it. And if there *were* breakers ahead, a reef to navigate, it would be better for the fire-pot to be held snug and fast.

Fitzroy was playing the complicated instrumental passage from the middle of *Aurora*, when the eponymous princess rebuffed her suitor and disappeared triumphantly into the night.

The thought presented itself to him, and then would not leave again.

Cliopher watched the clouds, turning that thought in his mind. There were birds fishing, the pelagic birds of the open ocean. No albatrosses he could see, but flocks of storm petrels and shearwaters. They dipped in and out of the swells, lines of them breaking the surface into liquid gold.

Cliopher had long since realized Fitzroy liked to play songs that matched his mood. Sometimes this was clearly on purpose; other times, it seemed—or he wanted it to seem—less deliberate.

If deliberate, that suggested that—

Cliopher watched the birds fishing. What could possibly have made Fitzroy want to imply *Cliopher* was rejecting *him*?

No, that was not the way to think about it.

Take away the specific people involved: take away what Cliopher knew of Fitzroy, what he knew of himself.

He imagined looking on two men having the conversation he and Fitzroy had had last night; two people having the *sort* of conversation they had had. Imagined the one smiling, laughing, touching, humming, in harmony; the other smiling, laughing, touching, humming, in harmony; until the moment where the one asked about kissing, and the other ...

He glanced over at his friend, who was regarding him with studiously polite attention, and the blush rose hot and fierce to his cheeks.

Cliopher had never, not *once*, imagined that Fitzroy found him attractive.

It had never even arisen as a question in his mind: it had never *occurred* to him to wonder. Cliopher had never dreamed of kissing him (that question!); but that was because he had never dreamed of kissing anyone, really.

He had felt a few flickers of physical interest, sparks he had never bothered to fan into flame, but all of them had been for women, and it had just ... never occurred to him. The discovery that Auri and El were lovers had not made him think of Fitzroy that way.

Had it made Fitzroy think of *him* that way?

Cliopher had wanted ... what they had last night. That closeness, that intimacy, that shared joy, the conversation ranging from the depths of his heart to poetry to common, ordinary things.

The two keels of a vaha singing under the wind, over the water, their ke'ea home clear before them.

And Fitzroy, asking that question, had responded to Cliopher's unthinking answer by ... laughing.

Laughing nearly to the point of tears.

Cliopher felt a shiver, a frisson, of doubt, as reason gave him a sequence of likely responses.

Most people did not—did not think fanoa meant what Cliopher had always wanted it to mean.

He had wanted to be *chosen*, to be equal, to be the other half of the shell that was half-formed by Fitzroy. He had not wanted ... sex.

Fitzroy Angursell had written a hundred songs about his lovers and those he wanted to love. It had been quite clear in the songs that the physical act of making love was important to him. Cliopher knew that—knew that this was a man who loved as much as anyone ever had, as much as El loved Auri—

El and Auri had made love in the foam at the edge of the sea, the air full of magic, as if they were the night and the day giving form to the lights of the sky.

Fitzroy Angursell had engendered a child on the Moon herself.

Cliopher had ... literally never entertained this idea before.

He glanced at Fitzroy, who was studiously plucking notes from his harp, his beautiful long hands moving slowly over the shimmering strings. He let each note sound in the air until the vibrations disappeared into the wind.

This was not merely the Fitzroy Angursell of song and story, of legend and rumour.

This was *his* Radiancy, whom Cliopher had served and loved for more than half his life.

And Fitzroy had been under touch taboos for so long. If whatever there had once been between him and Pali Avramapul had not survived the long distance and the changes in them both (for she had not been able to *see* the man he was now, that great-souled man who had survived all that time and the gods threw at him)—whom else might Fitzroy be inclined to reach towards? Who else was *safe*?

There was Jullanar of the Sea ... Cliopher frowned, remembering how they had looked at each other. He had not thought the way they were with each other suggested that Fitzroy and she had that sort of relationship, that sort of desire lingering between them.

Then again, Cliopher had not thought that *he* and Fitzroy had that sort of relationship, that sort of desire.

But perhaps Fitzroy had not meant it like *that*. Perhaps he wanted a kiss, a close embrace, nothing more. After so long constrained by the taboos and restrictions on his person, perhaps he wanted what Cliopher did ... To be *chosen*. To be someone's. To be close, to have permission to love with his whole heart ...

Cliopher did not want to be the person who was offered a heart and dropped it, unthinking.

And yet he had, last night, when Fitzroy had looked at him that way and Cliopher had not dared to ask the question on the tip of his tongue, the hope that burned in the centre of the very fire at the heart of him.

He had to make this right, for his Fitzroy, his friend, his ...

His fanoa, if ...

If only Cliopher dared *ask* him to be. It was not real until he spoke it out loud, and Fitzroy answered. Until they stacked their own half-shells together, and saw how they matched.

He cleared his throat, and then again. There was a scattering of the coconut husk game-pieces around him. He picked them up, worrying at the fibres with his fingers.

"Fitzroy," he said, hoarsely.

"Yes, my lord Mdang," Fitzroy said, his voice so much his Radiancy's that Cliopher dropped all the husks from suddenly nerveless fingers.

No. He would not let this happen. They had travelled too far together to return to that.

A rebuff, was it? Say a challenge, rather.

Cliopher scuttled over and took Fitzroy's hand in his.

Fitzroy let him, but did not grip back the way he had last night, either. The harp sat on his lap, his other hand holding it steady, like a shield between them.

Perhaps his music had always been a shield; Cliopher had not yet learned enough to ask, or answer, that.

If there seemed no way to lead up to something, Buru Tovo had told him, sometimes the only thing to do was leap right in. "I'm sorry," he said.

Fitzroy's voice was too even. "I cannot think there is anything for which you need to apologize."

"Fitzroy ..." He hesitated, but there really wasn't a subtle way in to this conversation. The courtier in him would never have broached it; such a rebuff would have been the end of it, polite enough not to make an enemy, firm enough never to be discussed.

Cliopher had taken the most precious thing he had ever held and *dropped* it.

"Fitzroy," he said, holding to his friend's hand, his name, trying to find his way to the truth. "You seem distant this morning, and I think it is my fault."

He knew, from comments Rhodin or Conju had made, that this was not the first time he had politely and firmly rebuffed someone by not realizing in the least that such an invitation had been made at all.

Fitzroy looked at him, one swift, sharp glance, before looking away again, his face not quite serene.

Oh, it was his fault. Cliopher swallowed, but he had crawled down into the depths of his heart, dived through the black, icy tunnel of water, found his lost loves and that great fire.

That time he had taken the forward way, the new way, the easy way.

This was not easy, but he needed to step forward into the *new*, if he wanted to reach that place on the other side, that island or that star where he might find the other half of that shell.

"I did not realize what you were proposing, last night," Cliopher said in a rush. "I rarely do. Conju and Rhodin have told me all the people they claimed were flirting with me, but I ... I never see it."

There was a pause. Fitzroy forgot himself sufficiently to stare at him in astonishment. "You didn't *realize*? I did everything bar—" He stopped, biting his lip. He was definitely blushing.

Cliopher rubbed his face with his free hand. His hair tumbled down, and he brushed it back. Fitzroy had brushed it back the night before, played with the feathers, brushed his fingers so lightly, so tenderly, over Cliopher's skin. How had he missed *that*?

It did not feel good to be the one who was missing all the steps of the dance the other person had led him into.

He breathed deeply, the diver's breath, hoping—oh, he was *sick* with the hope he had nurtured for his whole life. Last night he thought he had reached it—he had been so *happy*, so content—and ... and Fitzroy had wanted something else.

"I love you," he said, his voice thick with the emotions he was trying to bite back. Perhaps Fitzroy had only meant kissing—

"But not that way."

Cliopher listened to the rawness in that statement, the loneliness and grief, and was devastated at the depth of it.

Not only kissing, no.

The great poet, whom Cliopher loved so very much, but not ... apparently not in the right way. He had always loved things too much or not enough or in the wrong way.

He was sick to himself. He was never going to be enough, was he? Not unless he could—

Cliopher had never been interested in men—had never been interested in any specific man—had hardly ever been interested in *anyone*—

But this was *Fitzroy*.

He had never loved anyone as he loved Fitzroy. He had loved him enough to stay for him, always an arm's-length away, through all those grinding years of work. He had loved him enough, he had always told himself, that if his Radiancy had been taken away by the Sun and the Moon, Cliopher would have built another boat with his own two hands and sailed after him.

He could reach out, now, to offer what Fitzroy wanted.

He swivelled around so they were facing each other. Fitzroy was looking at him, his eyes burning-brilliant. His hand still lay quietly in Cliopher's hand, but his pulse was swift and strong.

Cliopher thought of the slowly awakening flame of desire he had felt for Suzen, for Ghilly in their youth, for his other two or three lovers, when the brilliant conversations had turned to touches and finally to questions of beds and pillow-talk.

He knew Fitzroy far more deeply than any of them. He *loved* Fitzroy far more deeply. He had always admired his long fingers, his beautiful hands, the timbre of his voice and the way he looked at Cliopher when they greeted each other in the mornings or caught glances in some fraught moment of a Council of Princes meeting.

He had admired Fitzroy Angursell since his own youth, when the songs and stories started to circulate.

He had always been drawn more to Jullanar of the Sea—how could he not be, him an Islander and her with an epithet like that?—

But this was Fitzroy. His Radiancy.

Cliopher licked his dry lips, trying to be as certain, as steady, as the vaha gliding west into the brilliant gold air, just the colour of Fitzroy's eyes. Fitzroy was staring at his face; his glance flicked down to his lips, and his own parted slightly.

"What are you thinking?" Fitzroy asked, soft as the air

Moving slowly, Cliopher lifted the harp from Fitzroy's light grasp and set it safely beside the mast. He knelt in front of Fitzroy, so their faces were level. "I liked being close to you," he said. "If you'd still like to ..."

Fitzroy hitched his breath, his eyes widening and then narrowing with speculation. He smiled, a crooked, imperfectly, beautifully human smile as he lifted his hand and traced Cliopher's face with light touches, light and comforting as when Cliopher touched a nefalao, seeking out a pearl.

He brushed Cliopher's hair back, and ran the back of his hand down his cheek, along the line of his jaw, then along his hairline to cup the back of his neck.

Cliopher leaned forward, obedient to the touch, his hand gripping Fitzroy's other hand, steadying himself. Fitzroy did have beautiful eyes, and long eyelashes, gently curved. His skin was so dark, his eyebrows were usually nearly invisible. It was hard to know what to feel. He hoped Fitzroy remembered what they should be doing.

Fitzroy leaned forward and touched their foreheads together, his hand still cupped around Cliopher's neck.

"You said last night this wasn't something you cared much for."

"I don't mind," Cliopher replied earnestly, then blushed, and wondered if Fitzroy could feel his skin heating. Neither words nor tone were at all appropriate to the mood. To what the mood *should* have been.

"I confess I have never been interested unless *both* parties were enthusiastic," Fitzroy said, releasing him and sitting back.

His voice was light but his face was disappointed.

More than disappointed. Devastated. He let Cliopher look for a moment, then shifted position so he was looking away, out at the horizon, the westering glory of the sun.

Cliopher did not know what to do.

He had tried—He breathed out through his nose, tried to govern his breathing, his expression, his thoughts. What was he supposed to *do*?

Fitzroy's expression was far more than someone disappointed because a frolic was not going to occur. He was not wrestling with undue arousal. This was deeper than that.

If he wanted more than enthusiasm, that suggested a desire for ... intimacy.

What greater intimacy could sex *possibly* give? He had not magically become more intimate with Suzen—or even with Ghilly—because they'd had sex. It didn't work like that.

It didn't work like that for Cliopher.

Cliopher's hands were cold. He sat back on his heels, his hands on his thighs. This was Fitzroy. He did not have to be afraid. He breathed through his nose, ensuring his voice was warm, and reached forward again for Fitzroy's hands. "You wanted to be ... more intimate?"

"It doesn't matter what I wanted." His voice was too calm, too steady, too ... formal. Cliopher's breath hitched, and he moved his hand convulsively. Fitzroy nodded once, his eyes distant, opaque, and tugged his hands free from Cliopher's. "Forget last night. We can continue on as we have been. It's served us well enough, hasn't it? Better all round, I think."

Cliopher did not know what to say. He had been so happy last night. He had wanted that for so long ... and it had been just what he'd imagined.

What *he'd* imagined. Not what Fitzroy had. Not what Fitzroy had wanted.

Fitzroy stared at the horizon, the clouds piling up there in golden glory, hiding his face. He'd folded his hands on his lap, his back as straight as if he sat on his throne in full public view.

Cliopher had offered him all that he was, had told him the secrets he had found in the depths of his heart—what more could he give?

But even as he thought that, he knew it wasn't true.

He had not told him that secret that burned in the shell. He had not asked him to be his fanoa. He had not even asked him—

Cliopher closed his eyes for a moment, but Fitzroy deserved better than this, and Cliopher—Cliopher could do better than this. He could. He had to. He had to try, once more. Had he not successfully bartered with the Sun?

He breathed in, out, trying to find the calm mind and calm heart before a dive. He could hear the distant rumble of the breakers, a soft vibration echoing back through the current, the swells, the limpid, liquid air.

And then, the slip into the deep waters, his voice soft: "When I was in Gorjo City for the viceroy ceremonies, I bought a house."

There was a great silence. Fitzroy looked down, his hands gripping each other tightly. "Rhodin told me."

Cliopher refused to be put off by the cool, unemotional (... the hurting, grieving ...) tone. "There's space for you. Private rooms you could have. If you wanted them. If you wanted to live there ... "

Fitzroy's expression twisted, curdled, broke.

"Fitzroy," Cliopher said, forgetting what he was saying, scrambling forward, but his friend thrust him back with a gesture that was more a blow of magic than of physical force.

Cliopher sat back hard, stunned.

Fitzroy snapped out, "You don't need to *pity* me. Why would I want to—why would I choose—why—"

He stopped, his breath coming hard, his face hard and ferocious, his eyes bright. He didn't say anything else, but what else was there to say?

Cliopher had heard enough to know this negotiation was not going to end in his favour. He was a great negotiator: he knew when he'd failed.

Three things he had offered, and none of them the right good for this trade.

He had never done well when he tried to negotiate on his own behalf. Never. He always wanted what no one else wanted to give.

"I see," he said, and crawled back across the boat to sit at the tiller.

He was not able to keep the tears from welling up and falling hot on his cheeks.

He had told Clio the sea was salt because of Vou'a's tears. Vou'a had wept for his fanoa, after Ani lost her mirimiri and could no longer come onto dry land.

He breathed hard, the tears pouring down his face. He had wanted—he had always wanted this—he had wanted a fanoa. He had wanted it since he had first heard the story of Elonoa'a and his emperor, since he first learned what it might mean to love and be loved that deeply. He had wanted—

He had wanted someone who was *his*, and who would choose *him*, as his equal, his match, his outrigger, as so much more than *friend*.

He had wanted to love someone as the sea loved the land, or the land the sea, caught in that endless dance of shoreline and wave. He had wanted to love someone enough to go chasing them across the sky; he had wanted someone to love him enough to raise an island for him. He had wanted—

He had wanted to catch that viau he had seen shining in the distance, that brilliant star darting across the sky, that beautiful, impossible, joy.

He had tried *so hard* to do enough—be good enough—to step into legends as his equal and match.

But he had to be chosen *back*, and now that he had finally dared offer up the secret treasures of his heart, they were not what Fitzroy wanted.

"Cliopher," Fitzroy said, sharply.

Cliopher said nothing, only wept, his face buried in his hands. He could not bear any witness to his folly and his heartbreak, the death of this dream.

"Cliopher. Kip."

He shook his head at the imperative, dumb with grief, wishing he could howl his emotions in a song or a rising wind, a storm, a wave, a great tumult.

He could not. He was not Aurelius, whose magic stirred the sky. He was not Elonoa'a, who could hear the winds whisper of far islands. He was not Fitzroy fucking Angursell, who had written the best poem of an age.

He was Cliopher Mdang, and he was not good enough.

He wept, his vision blinded by the westering light in his tears, his fingers glowing pink against the diamond brilliance. Oh, he understood what the stories meant when they said that Ani had grieved so deeply for the loss of Vou'a she had torn her heart in two and set the pieces in the sky as the sun and moon.

Not that he could do that, either.

There was a noise, which he ignored, and then warm fingers grasped his and gently but firmly pulled his hands from his face.

"Kip," Fitzroy said, his voice no longer cold and hurt, but confused and concerned. "Kip. Look at me."

Cliopher shook his head, lips pressed together, and turned his head away.

Fitzroy held on too tightly. Cliopher tried to pull his hands loose, but could not without a struggle. "Let go."

"No."

His tone was unmovable.

Cliopher glared at him and tugged at his grip. "Please let go."

"Kip. You're upset."

"So are you."

That was self-evidently true, at least for Cliopher, who knew him too well not to be able to see the tension around his eyes and mouth.

Fitzroy paused, and then said. "Kip. I am upset because ... I am misunderstanding something. Talk to me—please. I'm trying but—I'm making things worse—*Please*. Set me right! You've never hesitated before. Don't let me spoil everything."

Cliopher stared at him, unable to formulate words. Everything around them was a liquid, luminous gold, the colour of Fitzroy's eyes, so full of magic he could hardly swallow from the ache in his chest.

"Don't," he whispered. "Don't say things like that."

Fitzroy gripped his hands. "Don't say things like what? That I misunderstood something? I've hurt you."

"It's my fault. I've ruined everything."

Fitzroy stared at him.

His heart was going to choke him, it was thundering so hard. The tears were leaking out of his eyes, running down his cheeks, dripping. Cliopher wanted to rub them away, wanted to hide his face, but he could not, with Fitzroy holding his hands and sitting so close their knees pressed together.

"I should tend the vaha."

"It's fine. We're on course. The wind and the waves are the same."

They were the same, but Cliopher was different. He wanted to crawl away into a hole, into that dark cave on Vou'a's island, and hide away from the light and the question in Fitzroy's eyes.

"Cliopher," Fitzroy said quietly, "what does fanoa mean *to you*?"

He could not answer. His whole life stood in his throat.

Fitzroy hesitated, as if he faced a precipice and did not dare step out.

No.

Fitzroy Angursell cared nothing for *falling*.

He hesitated as if he were going to have to put himself back in the cage.

Cliopher did not want Fitzroy to go back into the cage. Not for him. Nothing was worth that. But he had no words, not with that question enormous as the sky, the entirety of the world, silent.

Fitzroy breathed in, delicately, and said, "While you were gone, I asked Tupaia and El and the others. They said ... they said fanoa was the word they used because they didn't have any other, not for what El and Auri were to each other. And I thought ... of course it was. The old Shaian word for that kind of relationship—for Conju and Terec—is fayna, which is clearly derived from it. And I thought ... the way Clio said it ... the way *you* responded ... the way Basil joked about us being in-laws ...'"

Cliopher looked down at their clasped hands. Fitzroy's nails were bare of any lacquer or polish. He had new calluses from playing the harp.

His hands had new calluses, too, from handling the ropes on the vaha.

"I thought that was what you wanted," Fitzroy said. "And what I ... I wanted it, too. I wanted to ... Kip, I thought ... I've misunderstood *something*. What does it *mean*? You're so quiet about this ... it's so important to you. I want to know. *Please*."

This time, when Cliopher tried to draw his hands free, Fitzroy let him. Cliopher rubbed his palms together, feeling the ghost of his friend's touch. The sky was so heavy and resplendent of light he could not tell any distinction between sea and sky. The wind was scented like ambergris.

He took a deep breath. He owed Fitzroy this, at least.

(He would not let himself hope. He could not, not now. Fitzroy wanted to know what it meant; that was all. He did not want to be it.)

"Fanoa is an old word, as I told you."

"The shells on the beach. The small, white, common, *ordinary* shells. Specifically, clam shells."

Cliopher rubbed at his face, the sticky tracks of the drying tears, feeling in the hot prickle at the back of his nose that it would take barely a push to set him off again.

He would not let himself hope. He could not. And yet ... oh, he was still that fool looking for the sea, wasn't he?

"Yes," he said, his voice low, as if he told a secret. "A fanoa is a matched-but-different pair of something. Two halves of a clam shell, a pair of sandals ..." He gestured at the vaha. "The keel and outrigger on a boat."

"Go on."

"In the *Lays* ..." He had to brace himself, one hand on the taut line he'd lashed, the other flat on the decking, where he could feel the wind over the back of his hand, the vibrations of the sea on his palm. "It's also used to mean a ... trading partner. Someone you meet on equal grounds and have a special relationship with."

"Auri and El began with that meaning." Fitzroy's voice was carefully neutral.

Cliopher closed his eyes, scrunching them against the bright sun, his friend's face, his own ... disequilibrium. "That's not how the *Lays* use it for them," he said, very quietly. "It means ... what we say it means ... what *I* always thought it meant ... is ... someone you love so deeply you would leave the world to sail Sky Ocean for them."

His voice wavered and the tears started to come, hot on his cheeks, dripping off his jaw. Cliopher breathed in a hitching breath, not quite a sob, and made himself continue. "A relationship like Vou'a and Ani have. Vou'a raised up the islands for Ani. She brought forth all the living creatures for him. The greatest of friends, we say, though that's thin. A euphemism. Fanoa means the person who is worth ... everything."

Cliopher scrubbed at his face, as if hiding his mouth behind his hand would hide the vulnerability of the words he spoke. "I was so shocked when we met Auri and El because ... because it had always been so important to me that in the stories they were *not* lovers. That two people could love each other like that, but it didn't need to be about sex. That you could find someone who was your match. Your other half. Your equal."

Fitzroy was silent.

"I shall correct the *Lays*," Cliopher added stiffly. "It doesn't matter what ... fancies I have. Had. I shall make sure that people know the truth of Auri and El. It's not as if anyone *uses* the word. Fanoa, that is. In its social meaning. No one else will have ... lost anything. They've all always thought me a fool for taking that meaning. Chasing a viau." Looking for the sea. He swallowed, forced out: "It's very old-fashioned."

"Archaic, I believe you said," Fitzroy said, in a voice that was so soft and tender that Cliopher could not help but look at him.

It was not fair that Fitzroy was looking at him even more softly, more tenderly, his face full of something that almost seemed like wonder, even though that was surely the wrong word for it.

Fitzroy took his hands again. This time Cliopher did not try to pull away. He did not think he had anything left in his heart but the yawning ocean of grief, the rumbling thunder of despair, that cataract in the cauldron-cave.

Fitzroy said, still very softly, very gently: "You think of me as your equal?"

It was not really a question. Cliopher did not have to answer it. He spoke anyway. "I do."

The words hung there. The whole sky seemed to be suspended around them, their vaha moving in a great wash of golden light. Cliopher could not look away from Fitzroy's face.

"Your equal. Your match. Your ... mirror, even? To bring in a Shaian conceit. The other shoe. The outrigger." His voice warmed with something like humour, and he squeezed Cliopher's hands. "Your other hand."

"All those things," Cliopher said, his voice airless and faint.

He had been so *foolish*—

He was still such a fool, still chasing that one viau he had set his heart on so long ago.

They held there for a long moment.

Cliopher did not know what to think. His mind was flat and blank as the doldrums, though his heart seemed to be full of the same golden light as Sky Ocean, traitorous organ that it was.

Fool fool fool

And then Fitzroy released him, and leaned back, and said, "Why does it matter what Auri and El made of it?"

Cliopher stared at him. His heart *hurt*.

"We are not Aurelius Magnus and Elonoa'a. We are ourselves. Fitzroy and Cliopher."

His breath ratcheted in his throat. Was this—was this—this was the spark, wasn't it? The tanaea striking his tovo—

"Yes," Cliopher breathed, something kindling in his heart, a new fire. This one would not destroy all those lost loves, but give them warmth, new life.

Fitzroy smiled. His eyes were full of joy and hope and *relief*, because this meant they were not alone, this meant they were good enough, this meant they could *choose* each other.

His friend's eyes. His *fanoa's* eyes.

Please—

Before Cliopher could speak, Fitzroy suddenly leaned forward again, grabbed his hands in his, and drew Cliopher's up to his heart. "Cliopher, Kip, you are my right hand, my outrigger, my mirror that shows me my better side. My people do not have a word for this, but yours do."

Now he had too much air in his lungs to speak, as if all the winds of the whole sky were contained inside him. "Yes."

"Ask me," Fitzroy whispered. "Ask me so I can say yes."

They held there, hands clasped, the air thundering around them, roaring like a bonfire.

Then Cliopher spoke, his quiet words falling clear as water drops. "You are my fanoa. My beloved. My own. Will you let me be yours?"

"Not *let*," said Fitzroy. "You are. You are."

Cliopher's eyes were wet, the light reflecting diamond-rainbows in them. He blinked, tried to lift his hands to wipe them, but Fitzroy would not let go, would only lean forward for a moment so their foreheads touched. "My fanoa," Fitzroy said, whispered, and Cliopher blinked the stars from his eyes so he could lean back and smile at him.

Fitzroy's eyes were the colour of the sky, the sunset, the ocean, the clouds rising like steam around them, not covering the Sun but glowing with his light. The thunder was growing enormous, loud as Cliopher's heart, as if his heart were shaking the foundations of the sky with how full it was.

They were sailing into the very sunset. The clouds billowed up out of the sea, rising up like fountains, like flowers, like whale-spouts. There was a whole pod of sky-whales, the thunder their breath, the clouds rising up under their flukes and plumes, the whole sky shivering as they fountained fiery light into golden clouds.

There were huge shapes out of the corners of his eyes, the ruddy shadows of a hundred cloud-whales swimming beside them, the crests of the waves breaking over them in a flurry and a froth of sparks, a wave of sunset-fire in a thunderous echo of water upon water, air upon air, all the colour of fire as they hovered right at the edge of the horizon, the clouds and the whales and water orange-red like the embers ready to be raked apart for the fire dance.

Cliopher's heart was loud as the great shouting joy of the sky. He asked the question that had so nearly capsized them. "Would you like to come home with me?"

A pause, and then Fitzroy flicked one eyebrow up in his familiar, beloved gesture. "Goodness, my lord Mdang, you say that as if I did not fall half in love with you on sight." And then he smiled, lifted Cliopher's hands to his lips, and said: "Yes." His voice was raw, husky, certain. "Yes. Let's go home, Kip."

"Together," said Cliopher, dazzled. "Home."

"Yes. Home."

And with that Sky Ocean dropped out from below them and became suddenly, incontrovertibly, absolutely, sky.

INTERLUDE
FALLING (III)

They fell.

Straight down, in a fulsome plunge.

Cliopher was still holding Fitzroy, and in the first, astonished moment as he felt himself lift into the air, he grabbed for the harp.

It was if all the water had turned in a flash to air, and they were falling down straight as a rainshower.

They fell through the sunset: from gold to orange to red, blazing all around them, shooting stars of white and blazing violet, down and down with the air stolen away from him as if he danced the fire, his mind exalted by the focus and the music and the flame and the steady placement of his feet as the world moved around him and he stood still.

Down, and down, until they broke through the fire, silver air rising around them in streams of bubbles, the pressure as hard, as relentless, as that time he had been pulled down by the riptide, that time he had been pulled down by the Fall of Astandalas.

Down, and down, into a depth of colour like indigo ink, spreading like a pool of ink to the horizon, puddling indigo across gold.

Down, and down, the wind screaming in his ears, his eyes blurred with tears struck by the wind, all the breath pushing out of him.

But there was—something else there, something else in his ears, something black and solid next to him, holding onto his arm in a tight, ineluctable grip.

With extreme difficulty, Cliopher turned his head to see that Fitzroy was laughing.

Indigo ink with a sudden starburst at its centre, a sun-in-glory as golden fire suddenly erupted on every surface of the vaha, running along the lines and spars and sail, along the pennant of feathers and flowers standing vertical in their descent. Like Ani's Fire, but not the same colour—

It was Fitzroy's magic, holding, cradling the vaha, slowing their descent, softening their plummet.

Holding them, cradling them, keeping them safe as they fell.

Cliopher drew in a deep, forceful breath, pushing against the panic and fear wanting to rise in his gorge. He would trust in Fitzroy's magic. He would.

This time he was not falling alone; neither of them were.

And then they hit the sea.

IV. Faravia

CHAPTER FIFTY-FIVE
LOST AND FOUND

Water plumed up around them, sheets of it arcing against the sky, catching gold from the magic, turning silver and black as the waves plunged back under the surface.

The vaha went down, and a great spray of water washed right over them, but Cliopher was holding firm to the harp, firm to Fitzroy, and Fitzroy was holding to the mast, his magic like a great hand on Cliopher's shoulders, keeping him safe.

The vaha rose up again safely and bobbed on the surface in the centre of a huge ring of spreading circles.

It was terrifically quiet after the noise of their landing.

Cliopher sat there, his rear throbbing from the hard landing, listening to the thunder in his ears, unable to move.

The water spread out, black and silver. All the colour was washed out of the world, out of his eyes, out of his heart. The air seemed cold and lifeless; the sea unfriendly.

The horizon was so far away.

He tipped back his head and felt the tears leaking from his eyes when he saw the sky was lidded with thick grey clouds. All the exhilaration, the joy, the wonder was gone, extinguished—

No, not *extinguished*. He would not believe that. Hidden, perhaps, as the glory of Sky Ocean was hidden behind the clouds and thickness of the ordinary, human world.

Fitzroy finally said, "I think you can let go now, Kip."

Cliopher wanted to wipe his face. To do that he would have to let go of something.

He was gripping Fitzroy's knee in one hand and his harp in the other. Fitzroy had just let go of the mast; his other hand was still on Cliopher's elbow, albeit no longer in a solid grip. His magic no longer felt like a weight, but a tentative, feathery brush of warmth.

It took Cliopher conscious effort to unclench his fingers from the sarong.

Fitzroy smiled at him and gently tugged the harp from his grip. "There," he said soothingly. "We're home."

Cliopher looked around blankly, taking in the huge drab emptiness of the sea around them.

"Well," Fitzroy amended, undaunted, "we're on our way."

Cliopher woke some time in the morning, utterly lost.

It took him a while to recall falling asleep in the first place. It had been dark and grey, and the stars hidden by clouds, and Fitzroy had told him to rest. He had not intended to, but he had been so weary he had flopped down and immediately slept.

He sat up slowly. He felt old, old, old. Everything creaked. The ship was too loud, and his bones scraped across each other.

Everything was so *heavy*.

He forced himself to sit up, wincing as his joints protested. His head was hurting, as if some taloned bird had grabbed his skull in its pincer-claws. The sky was a hard, unforgiving curve of grey, the sun blazing hot behind the cloud cover. The sea was a dark, unfriendly blue, stretching undifferentiated to the horizon.

He dragged himself to lean against the mast. Fitzroy was sitting on the other side of the platform, wearing the hat he'd woven himself before they'd left ... the others.

"All right there, Kip?"

Cliopher rubbed his eyes with his knuckles. His heart was aching, desolate. "I'm fine," he muttered.

"Lying through your teeth now, are you?" Fitzroy's voice was nowhere near as sharp as his words. Cliopher looked up at him, though the motion hurt, his bones unlubricated. Fitzroy was smiling with a certain sympathy. "You feel inexplicably bereft. Your heart is aching. Your bones are heavy and your jaw feels as if it's been wound up like a spring. Your head is full and empty at the same time. All you can see is desolation and loss."

Cliopher swallowed hard, painfully, as if he'd forgotten how. "I hadn't noticed my jaw," he whispered, rubbing his fingers down the joints and wincing as the muscles quivered with tension and pain. "You don't seem ..."

"I'm used to it," Fitzroy replied, almost indifferently. He crawled over the platform to sit next to Cliopher, and offered him one of the green coconuts. "You'll feel better if you drink something."

He'd already opened the coconut, which was just as well as Cliopher did not think his muscles would stand for anything at the moment.

"I'd forgotten what it felt like to be *old*," he said mournfully, after he had taken a few sips of the sweet rich liquid.

"It'll pass."

"Old age?" He couldn't muster up the energy for a laugh, but he did manage to quirk his mouth in an approximation of a smile.

"There we are," Fitzroy murmured. "It's the return to the mortal worlds, Kip. That's what you're feeling."

"And you're *used* to it?" Cliopher regarded him doubtfully. Was this the prelude to some confession? What was he supposed to say, if Fitzroy told him he really *was* a god?

He wasn't. Cliopher knew that. And even if he were ... well, Buru Tovo loved a god, in person and *as* a person, and was loved in return. It could be done.

"Every time I come out of a deep trance of magic, it's like this. You get used to it."

"Do you?"

Fitzroy looked at him, and then he huffed a laugh. "Yes, as a matter of fact, you do. Otherwise you go mad. And I mean that quite literally—if you refuse to come out, to just *stay* there, you lose your ability to be in the world. You may have visions of the truth you can share, but you are no longer ... part of things. And the world is far too full of excellent things for me to want to stay in that glorious simplicity."

Cliopher drank some more of the coconut water. He could not imagine how he'd climbed up that stair; he could barely lift the coconut to his mouth, and his hands were stiff and clumsy. He wiped at his mouth. "It was simpler up there, wasn't it?"

"Simple as the most important things. It's like living inside a poem." Fitzroy gave him one of those sly, wry, glinting grins. "Which even I can find tedious eventually."

Because he was a real person, and real people were messy. Cliopher finished the water and poked at the gelatinous coconut meat with his finger. "I'm almost hungry." It was a strange sensation, after so long dreamily hungry only when the meal was ... *significant*.

"Oh yes, we have to get used to that again. Food, sleep, drink ... the results of eating and drinking."

Cliopher sighed with weariness at the very thought.

Fitzroy patted his shoulder, his face half sympathetic, half gently amused. He nodded and went on. "Also we need to figure out where we are and what we should do about it. I can contribute the fact that we're back on Zunidh. Observation suggests we're on the ocean."

Cliopher looked around at the circle of the horizon and rolled his eyes.

"Oh, come now, wasn't that worth a smile? Maybe even a snicker?"

"It wasn't a very good joke."

"You wound me!" But Fitzroy laughed, and Cliopher managed to smile. They were on Zunidh, and that meant—that meant they were not so far from home.

(What *ocean* were they sailing?)

Fitzroy regarded him with a familiar steadiness, a familiar intensity, so out-of-place and so comforting that Cliopher felt his throat close with tears. He brought one hand up to pinch the bridge of his nose. He should not miss his Radiancy (who was the Fitzroy before him; he was; he *was*), even if he missed the ... simplicity of that relationship.

This was better. To be not secretary and lord, but ... fanoa. Even if they had to determine what that could indicate from nearly the foundational meaning of the word.

That was how the Islander language worked. You had a root word, an anchor meaning, and suffixes and prefixes and metaphorical transferences built words and meanings out from there. *Ta* was a fire, and *fa* was a shell, and *moa* was the great undifferentiated ocean around them.

"You always feel better with something to do," Fitzroy observed. "So, then: what shall we do? Where shall we head? Would you rather sail or sleep?"

Cliopher's thoughts ground like rocks together. He had been storm-lost many, many times before. But that had all been decades ago, by any measure, and he had always started off with knowing approximately where he was, and certainly what ocean he was sailing. He'd never sat on a boat and sincerely wondered what *hemisphere* he was in.

Wearily, he considered their provisions. They had plenty of coconuts, fermented breadfruit, dried papaya and mango, and various other stores of vegetable foods. They had fishing lines and hooks. They had all the necessary tools for sailing and mending the vaha. They had a fire-pot containing a fragment of the sun.

They just needed a *direction*. Cliopher looked around at the flat grey sky and the flat grey sea and he just ... couldn't.

"I don't know," he said, rubbing his face. "I don't know, Fitzroy. I don't know where we are or where we should go or ... or ..."

Fitzroy knelt down beside him, and hesitated for a moment, as if he were about to embrace him, before instead slowly, gently, laying his hand over Cliopher's. His skin was warm, comforting, full of the sparkling *realness* that had drained out of everything else. Magic.

"It's all right, Kip," he said. "I can handle things for once."

"I don't know where we should go," Cliopher repeated. He had no magic. He had no ... no *heart* for anything. No strength in his bones or his spirit or his mind.

Is this where you stop?

If someone had asked him that old challenge, he might have had to say yes.

"We're on Zunidh, you said?" he said, trying not to break down. "We could go ..." He could not say it, not with his mind cringing away from hope.

But Fitzroy knew him, as well, perhaps, as Cliopher had ever known himself.

"Home," Fitzroy said, savouring the word. "We can go home. We can't be more than half a world away, can we?" He smiled at Cliopher, who was staring, speechless. "Don't worry. I'll get us *somewhere*."

For a long moment Cliopher was unable to find words even in his own mind. All he felt was a rising swell, like a current catching him and turning him in a new direction. He could not comprehend his own emotions, only the sense of the anchor letting go.

"Trust me," Fitzroy said, smiling like the sunrise, like all the lost magic and wonder of Sky Ocean, like the embers of sunlight burning in the fire-pot. "If my fanoa is so fantastically competent, I can't be entirely useless."

"Not at all," Cliopher replied, his voice gravelly and catching in his throat. "Not at all."

~

Cliopher could not fathom it, but he felt a terrible invalid—even worse than immediately after the landslide. Shaky, his thoughts scattering, barely able to focus enough to respond to Fitzroy's occasional comment or question. The bird dug its talons into his skull whenever he moved too quickly.

Perhaps the fall out of Sky Ocean had rattled loose his healing brain. He could do nothing about it but endure.

Despite the sun, the wind was cold out of the south. Cliopher did not realize how violently he was shivering until Fitzroy brushed against his shoulder as he tended the vaha and exclaimed aloud at the goosebumps on his skin.

Cliopher had been wearing the grass skirt he'd made on the star-island, but the garments the Grandmother had given him were in the hatch, stowed carefully in a tightly-woven basket. Fitzroy pulled them out and assisted him into the tunic. Whether it was the clothes or Fitzroy's magic Cliopher could not tell, but they seemed to be warmer than simple cloth would be.

He could not ask. He curled up, hugging his knees to his chest, his back against the mast, and tried to gather the fragments of his self together. The drop out of Sky Ocean had been more than the loss of magic; it was if the parts of himself had cracked and splayed open with the sudden blow of hitting the ocean's surface.

He could not imagine how Fitzroy was so blasé about the situation, but he was.

Fitzroy was the one to unroll one of the mats in the hatch and attach it to the poles as a sunshade when the clouds started to break up and dissipate under a stiffening wind.

Fitzroy was the one to set the sail and choose a ke'ea.

Possibly Fitzroy was the one to set the wind.

Cliopher lay in the shade Fitzroy had made for him, letting Fitzroy's music fill the desolation left by the loss of Sky Ocean. He tried to attune himself to the swells below him, tried to decipher the rhythm of current and wave and swell, but he could not hear the sea, as if he were suddenly unable to hear music.

He was grateful to have Fitzroy there, his friend, his fanoa. It felt wrong to leave him to do all the work, and he hated his helplessness ... but Fitzroy was tender, careful, caring, and Cliopher remembered over and over again how long it had been since *Fitzroy* had been allowed to take care of someone else.

Cliopher and all the rest of Fitzroy's household—of *his Radiancy's* household—had worked very hard to ensure he didn't have to worry about anything but his work. Watching Fitzroy delight in his activity, delight in his *ability*, even delight—not in Cliopher's current infirmity, but in being *able to help*—Cliopher could only feel sorrow and a kind of suffocating rage that they had misunderstood human nature so terribly.

He and Conju, back when Cliopher was his Radiancy's secretary, had done *everything* to keep their own troubles from his Radiancy. Cliopher did not think Fitzroy had ever learned that he had spent months flattened by bonebreak fever during the aftermath of the in-Palace negotiations following the initial signing of the Littleridge Treaty.

He had worked very hard to ensure his Radiancy did not know. It all seemed so ... useless.

Cliopher did not enjoy being so infirm, but every time the guilt rose up, he caught Fitzroy's obvious *care* (love, he told himself defiantly; he was allowed to use that word, though Fitzroy never had; he did not *need* the word, not when he could see it so clearly in his fanoa's face and actions). Somehow, this was a gift to Fitzroy; Cliopher had only to accept the reciprocal gifts of care with as much graciousness as his Radiancy had taken his.

Fitzroy sang as he worked, happy songs from the youth of the Red Company. Cliopher had first heard these songs on the docks of Gorjo City when he was a young teenager, learned them with delight when they were still anonymous. Ballads and folk stories from all sorts of places, the catchy tunes Fitzroy had once created with seemingly inexhaustible joy.

A joy that had been snuffed out by the heavy weight of the crown of Astandalas coming down over his head, binding his heart and his magic and his physical being within the net of taboos and customs and grinding responsibilities.

There were no new songs yet, nothing Cliopher could point to as being the fruit of the long disciplines of Fitzroy's life as emperor, but they would come, surely? Fitzroy was not like Cliopher, who had never had any songs in him to create.

Cliopher had the love, but not the gift ... but he had other gifts, did he not? He had set his hand to the shape of the world, even if no song had ever come forth newborn from his pen.

(He should not be weeping for the things Fitzroy had lost, that Cliopher had never had. Had he not reclaimed the very mirimiri of Ani when Vou'a could not? Had he not stood before the Sun with fire in his heart and upon his tongue?)

Fitzroy cast fishing lines off the boat, once he'd set the sail and lashed the tiller in place. He caught some kind of mackerel, the silver and charcoal patterns on the fish's scales looking like the court costumes of the Ouranatha.

Cliopher watched as Fitzroy slipped the curved edge of a shell knife into the side of another fish and expertly removed the fillet without snagging on the bones. That spoke of long experience: all that time when Cliopher was on his solitary voyage, reinforcing skills learned long ago, in his days with the Red Company.

Fitzroy offered him the fillets, raw, presented on a small piece of banana leaf brought from Sky Ocean.

Cliopher had eaten raw fish before, of course, when it was necessary, but never with such ... deliberate intention. "Thank you," he said, trying not to sound either puzzled or ungrateful.

"This is a delicacy, parts of Colhélhé in particular," Fitzroy replied. "Better with the sauce they use—something fermented and salty, if I remember correctly. They eat it with rice, as well, make little shapes out of it."

"The fish?"

"The fish and the rice together. It's an art form, how the flavours and the textures and the shapes and the colours all fit together."

"Ah," said Cliopher regarding the leaf in his hand.

"I was never a great cook," Fitzroy murmured, running his fingers down the mottled scales of the remaining mackerel, its flank like a sky ribbed with stripes of cloud. "Never very good at following directions, I suppose. Nor being consistent ... not one of my natural strengths." He smiled down at the fish. "I always enjoyed it when it was my turn, though. Travelling. Trying new things. Trying to make some grand meal we'd had in someone's house or an inn on a campfire or ... a boat."

Cliopher's heart twisted, remembering Fitzroy in the Palace, hedged around with taboos. There had been no raw fish for him, however fresh and exquisitely prepared.

The fish was much better than he'd expected, like a distillation of the sea on a cool morning, a sharp wind blowing out of the south. "That's good!"

Fitzroy glanced at him, and smiled, just a little, shyly.

Cliopher ate the second fillet and sat back, the banana leaf cool, comforting under his hand. As he watched Fitzroy sit down with his harp to play some rippling instrumental music, something eased in his heart, his mind, his soul.

Not yet his body, alas, but you couldn't have everything.

He watched the shadow on the mast slowly move, and then, as the sun rose higher, suddenly realized that it could tell him how far north or south they were, and in which hemisphere. He watched more intently for a few minutes, Fitzroy's music ripping gently over him, the sea running fresh and clear below the vaha.

The shadow was longer than he'd expect it to be in the Vangavaye-ve, but it was on the southern side of the mast.

"We're quite far south," Cliopher said, rolling over to look at the way the light prickled in the small gaps of the woven sunshade. "Southern hemisphere of Zunidh, south of the Vangavaye-ve by latitude."

"Oh, well done! I thought you'd need the stars to tell that?"

"I'll know our latitude more precisely when I can see a ke'e," Cliopher agreed, smiling with relief.

Even this small degree of orientation, of using his own skills and knowledge to place himself, made him feel much better. He watched Fitzroy consider the sail and adjust the lines slightly to account for a small variation in the wind. "Where are you taking us?"

"Home ... well, somewhere," Fitzroy amended. "If we're in the Southern Hemisphere I suppose it could be ... all sorts of places, couldn't it? Southern Dair, Lorosh, one of the Wide Seas islands ... Jilkano, even Kavanor ..."

"We're too far south for Kavanor or Jilkano," Cliopher said. "The shadow was too long at noon."

Fitzroy gave him a smug smile, as if Cliopher had passed a challenge. He tried not to feel too pleased about winning—wayfinding wasn't a *competition*.

(It was splendid that Fitzroy could take the lead. Cliopher had always been able to trust following where he led, hadn't he? He had followed Fitzroy Angursell long before knowing who the man was, trusting his fundamental decency and sense of humour; he had trusted his Radiancy as the sun of his life.)

"There's human magic that direction," Fitzroy said, pointing ahead so his signet ring flashed in the light. "I can't tell more than that, but it does not seem so widespread as to be a city, which suggests an island, and I assume you can get us home once we know where we are. And once you're feeling better," he added hastily. "But if you tell me where to go I can probably get us there. El and the others taught me how to sail while you were gone."

He grinned, half-proud and half-shy, and Cliopher's heart nearly broke. "Thank you," he whispered.

"It seemed about my turn," Fitzroy said lightly, then picked up his harp. "Any requests?"

Cliopher wanted to ask if he had something new, but—

But he'd recognized almost everything Fitzroy had played so far, and the ones he didn't he knew came from other musical traditions. He could not forget the way Fitzroy had looked, back when Cliopher had first learned he played at all (back so long ago, at Navikiani on Lesuia, when he had first reached out for—this—), and they'd asked if he wrote his own music. *Not for a long time*, he'd said, flat and final, and ...

And Cliopher did not want to rake that up, if Fitzroy had not yet been able to recover.

And *he* had not recovered enough to assist. He could see the tangled knots, but not what he should do about them.

"Something you've learned on your adventures, please," he said, relaxing as best he could on the hard decking of the vaha.

"This was all the rage in Mae Irión, four thousand years ago," Fitzroy said, and began playing some very weird music indeed.

~

When he woke, it was night. Fitzroy was sleeping, curled up not far from Cliopher. The tiller and the sail were set, and Cliopher could tell after a few moments that they were holding true to their course. The deepwater swells were coming at the same angle to the vaha, and the wind was steady out of the southwest.

They were going north and east. North was good; wherever they were, in whichever ocean, land was north.

Cliopher crawled to their food stores and ate several pieces of fruit, slowly. He felt better, able to open a coconut for himself and drink the sweet water thirstily.

The stars were veiled by a high haze. Cliopher picked out the brightest, glad to see Nua-Nui steady to the south. They were far south indeed, with Nua-Nui that high in the sky.

He recalled, as in a dream, the albatross canting against the wind, watching his efforts to follow with such a jaundiced, cynical eye, and wished he could write a song that would convey any part of that.

He'd never had the gift of composition. He wished he did, wished he could take the fragments of images in his mind and turn them into words, phrases, poems, musical passages. He'd managed a few fragmentary compositions, but nothing he'd ever felt able to share with anyone else.

He watched Fitzroy sleeping, a dark hummock with a faint glimmer of golden magic draped over him, as light and ethereal as the hazy clouds over the stars. It was not bright enough magic to illuminate his features, though it brightened and dimmed in synchrony with his breathing.

Cliopher dipped his hands into the cool water, and then sat back against the mast.

It was good to be back in the world, even if he had to be old and stiff and full of aches. Fitzroy was right: that splendid simplicity, that living inside a poem, was wonderful for a time, but not ... enough.

This was better.

Cliopher watched the clouds tinted with starlight and the black sea hissing beneath the hulls of the vaha as it ran beneath the fresh wind, listening to Fitzroy's soft and steady breathing.

Yes, this was better.

~

The next morning, their third, Cliopher felt alert and awake enough to hold a conversation. Fitzroy was visibly relieved when he ate a proper meal.

"I was beginning to worry a little," Fitzroy said, then immediately shrugged off his own anxiety when Cliopher regarded him in surprise, a fragment of dried papaya in his hand. "That is, I could hardly return you home to your family all skin and bones."

"Indeed not," Cliopher replied gravely. He'd seen Fitzroy's *care*: the anxiety had not been anywhere near so obvious. But Fitzroy did not like showing—

Well, Cliopher actually had no idea whether he liked or disliked showing negative emotions. Fitzroy had spent so long forced to a benevolent serenity, his stern disapproval strong enough to cause stalwart generals to quail, that he had perhaps suppressed the ability to *show* them at all.

All the insistent offers of food and drink and warmth made more sense.

"I'll be glad to reach land," Fitzroy said, nibbling at a piece of coconut meat. "Whatever land it is. Fresh water for a wash would be *greatly* appreciated."

"Would it?"

Fitzroy laughed. "It would!"

"How far away are we?" Cliopher asked.

"I don't know," Fitzroy replied readily, unperturbed.

Cliopher blinked at him. "How *are* you navigating? The winds?"

"It's hard to explain." Fitzroy pondered, and made a sort of vague gesture with his hands, golden magic sparkling briefly around his fingers. It occurred to Cliopher that he hadn't seen Fitzroy gesturing much at all of late, not since they fell out of Sky Ocean.

Perhaps that was how he demonstrated anxiety and concern. His stillness was still a sign to Cliopher to tread carefully, not out of fear of his anger but out of concern that he might bruise a vulnerable heart.

"Without going fully down into a deep trance, I can't *perceive* magic that precisely, or at such a vast distance. And I don't want to go that far down because ..."

He trailed off, but Cliopher waited patiently. At last Fitzroy said, "Because it's hard, and we're in the middle of the ocean, and my magic doesn't like water, so it's even harder than usual, and ... and what if you'd needed me? I couldn't *leave* you like that. I don't know how long it would take me to come out, with no one around me. Conju used to help ..."

He shook his head sharply, as if the mention of Conju had pricked him unexpectedly. "We don't *need* to, do we? You'll be able to get us home once we reach one island, right?"

There were a lot of things in that. Cliopher answered the central point.

"Assuming we can figure out what quarter of what ocean we're in, then yes." He paused, but it did not seem the moment to talk about Conju or any of the others they had left behind.

"There are definitely people at this place ... or if not people, very old and very strongly worked magic. There will be *something* we recognize. It's calling me. Unmissable. It's overwhelming everything else anywhere near here."

"I'll take your word for it."

"Why, thank you, my lord Mdang!" Fitzroy laughed, but he also looked carefully at Cliopher, as if to see how the title hit.

There was nothing standoffish or hurtful about his tone, so Cliopher smiled easily at him. It was rather nice, really; almost as if it were a nickname Fitzroy had devised for him, instead of a title that Cliopher would be giving up at the Jubilee.

"I was wondering," Fitzroy said after a moment, "whether there was a special efela for fanoa."

Cliopher looked sharply at him, but Fitzroy was fussing with the knot on his sarong, his hair flopped over his face. "Were you?" he said faintly, uselessly.

"I was." Fitzroy peered up at him through his hair, which the wind was tossing merrily and no doubt tangling horrendously. "When Vou'a came to the island, when I was waiting for you, I saw his efela."

"Driftwood and white cowries?" Cliopher asked, from some deep well of memory he could not provide with a source.

"Yes, exactly. Well, not all of them were cowries ..." Fitzroy smiled slowly. "But then fanoa means any and all of the little white shells you might find on the beach, doesn't it? I thought that must be it, the ... efelafanoa?"

"Efanoa," Cliopher corrected absently. He frowned, visualizing Vou'a by his fire, spinning shadows, tending the soup. "I've never seen his efela. And I didn't *notice* that I hadn't."

"Perhaps he was hiding it from you. You know the description ... there can't be that many mysterious old men who wear efela of driftwood and white shells, or strings of flame pearls twisted into a rope. He said that was the wedding efela from your Buru Tovo."

And what a thought that was. If Cliopher had ever seen such an efela he would have *known* ... perhaps that was why Vou'a had never shown him. Some things were not simply *given*; they had to be asked for.

Fitzroy was regarding him thoughtfully. Cliopher smiled, a touch weakly. "It's called efelēla. The marriage efela."

"Oh? It's not a wedding one?"

"Weddings aren't that important," Cliopher said, yawning and brushing at his hair; his fingers tangled in the knots, which was dispiriting. All that time sailing Sky Ocean he'd not had to do anything with his hair. Now it felt crunchy with salt and sweat. "Weddings are for the community, to announce the relationship. Marriages are for the people involved."

Fitzroy shifted position, lifted up a wooden comb with four widely-spaced teeth, and asked, quite neutrally, "Would you like me to comb your hair?"

Cliopher opened his mouth to say *no*, but he remembered, again, how long it had been since Fitzroy had been *permitted* to offer such a thing.

(They had spent however long it was in Sky Ocean, but that was a dream—a beautiful dream—a *true* dream, even—but a dream. This was reality, where their hair was knotted, not braided, by the wind, and the strain and stain of taboos and habits and human foibles worked upon their better intentions.)

"Yes, thank you," he said quietly, and turned around so his back was to his friend, his eyes to the wide rim of the ocean to the north.

Fitzroy gently worked his comb into the bottom of Cliopher's hair. "And so, the efelēla?"

Cliopher had to force his thoughts from the pure strangeness of *his Radiancy* combing his hair. (Why was he suddenly *his Radiancy*? He shouldn't be. He wasn't, any longer.) He swallowed, watching the distant spout of a whale. The column of spray was tall and didn't fan out till quite high: a blue whale, perhaps, one of the giants of the sea.

Not Au'aua, who was a northern constellation down here in the world, not a whale swimming this ocean.

But he was glad to see the whale. Whales belonged to Ani, and were good luck.

He cleared his throat. "Not everyone does the efelēla nowadays—not in the city. Aya and Jiano wear efelēla. Jiano's is the one with the two golden pearls and the carved pendant in the centre; Aya's has the pendant and two green pearls from Kuariso island. The other beads will be ones they've added over the years."

"They'd have dived for the pearls?"

"Probably. The green pearls are rare ... Kuariso is an isolated island, quite dangerous to reach."

"So they exchanged pearls to represent themselves?"

The symbolism clearly spoke to Fitzroy, the great poet. Cliopher wanted to feel nervous about explaining this, but his fanoa's hands were gentle on his hair, untangling the knots, reforming the braids, and all Cliopher could think of was the long years of devoted service and loving patronage.

That had been enough, for so long; enough to hold him there in the Palace, climbing that endless stair with that heavy basket of mud, hoping that the end would be worth the work.

It was no longer enough. Cliopher could never go back to that devoted service of vassal and lord, not when they could be equals, fanoa, mirror and match.

"The old tradition is that you would exchange efela koro, which are unfinished efela. You'd give the line and a bead or a shell representing yourself or your relationship together. Pearls, usually, but not necessarily. *One for a token, two for a promise, and five make an efela* is what the Walea say."

"So two for the promise of the life together? Or one as a token of intent? Or would that count as the betrothal?"

"We don't really do betrothals. Most of the time people have already been living together for a while before they get married ... it's a statement of commitment."

"In the eyes of the community and your families."

"Yes." Cliopher was silent for a moment as Fitzroy gently worked through some of the knots in his hair. Or perhaps he was undoing the braids the Wind That Rises At Dawn had made? Either way, it felt good. He felt better all around, with the wind and the swells so steady, and Fitzroy's certainty that there was an island not far away.

"And then, over time, with the efelēla, each year—or if something big happens, you might add another—you would exchange another shell or pearl or what-have-you."

Fitzroy hummed, his fingers massaging more than combing. Either way it felt great. Cliopher relaxed, knowing he should probably offer to reciprocate but unable to do anything but enjoy the gift. "Vou'a had a lot of pearls on his efelēla."

"Buru Tovo was a great pearl diver."

"They've been together for that long? Decades?"

"I never really believed him when he said he was married to the Son of Laughter," he confessed. "I always thought he just meant that he liked men ... It's an old-fashioned phrase, but then Buru Tovo is very old-fashioned. I'd met his boyfriend before ... I thought he was a hermit out on the Ring somewhere. Buru Tovo told me he'd met him when he came back from his journey across the Wide Seas when he was young, the one when he was painted for the *Atlas of Imperial Peoples*."

Fitzroy laughed. "That sounds about right. After he'd decided my uncle Eritanyr was not an emperor worth staying for."

Cliopher had shown by his life that Fitzroy had been worth staying for. He did not need to *say* it. "An efanoa is similar to the efelēla," he said instead, relaxing as Fitzroy tucked away the comb and began to re-braid his hair. He knocked his elbow against Fitzroy's harp, which was never far from him, and moved it onto his lap, out of the way.

"Do we use any little white shell from off the beach? Or may we add some fancier elements? Not that we need to—I will wear it with pride and joy, whatever it's made out of."

"Any, both, all," he said, laughing in sudden delight, "We can de—*Oh!*"

The wind slammed out of nowhere, a blow that slew the vaha around. Cliopher grabbed at the mast as the vaha tilted, crushing the harp in a jangle of strings as it caught against his ribcage. He caught his balance and crawled to the tiller, as Fitzroy had grabbed at the lines for the sail.

With the harp safely between his knees, Cliopher gripped the tiller and held it steady against the monstrous waves. The vaha slew around to a more stable angle.

There had been no sense of an incoming squall—

Nor of the island looming above them.

"Fitzroy!" Cliopher cried, moving the tiller so that they didn't crash headlong onto the jagged black rocks heaving out of the surf. It must have been a trick on his eyes after so long at sea—he could have sworn there was nothing there, and the rocks had *literally* jumped out of the sea, surging up like the gaping maws of lunging sharks. Cliopher hove the tiller the other way as another rock loomed out of nowhere. "Fitzroy!"

"I'm trying—the knot's stuck—the wind—" Fitzroy cried out three pungent swear-words and a fourth word of such crackling magic Cliopher flinched down in atavistic response.

He cringed over the tiller as the vaha surged forward and up—*up?*—over the crest of a huge wave and then, as if the wave had thrown them, catapulted them even, straight on into the air and up through a rippling thickness of air to a landing that shook him to his teeth.

"Fuck," said Fitzroy. "I wasn't expecting that."

Chapter Fifty-Six
The Tower

The land was heaving around him. Cliopher let go of the tiller and carefully let himself slide off the deck, but though he felt stable grass under his feet, his eyes insisted everything was moving.

He closed his eyes, but that didn't help, and he staggered two steps, fell to his knees, and was sick for several minutes.

Then suddenly he felt gentle hands on his temples, and a wash of something—magic?—running over his skin, sinking into him like the warmth from a fire, the welcome coolness of a shadow, and as quickly as it had come, his dizziness was gone.

He rubbed the moisture from his eyes until he could see. The land was solid and steady in his vision. The air was cool, a fresh breeze blowing off the ocean. His heart was still beating too fast, his breath coming at a speed some more calculating portion of his mind knew was dangerously close to hyperventilation.

Fitzroy was counting, slowly, steadily: up to five and back down to one, over and over again. Cliopher latched onto the sound, trying to match his breathing to the rhythm, and finally he was able to catch his breath and his composure.

Finally he was able to breathe, focus his vision, and even speak. "My goodness," he said forcefully. "I can't think what came over me."

"I can," Fitzroy said grimly, helping him up to his feet. "I apologize. There are strong magical protections on this island. I should have realized, but they didn't affect me."

"Because you're Lord of Zunidh?" Cliopher said, straightening his tunic and efela. He rubbed his hands together; they were tingling, as if with returning blood circulation. His whole body felt like that, in fact, pins-and-needles without surcease. Cliopher was glad Fitzroy was still holding onto his arm.

"Because I was Emperor of Astandalas," Fitzroy said even more grimly. "This was one of the anchors of the empire. No wonder it blazed such a beacon for me."

That came out in Fitzroy's most serene and dispassionate tone. He looked serene and dispassionate, too, as if he was going down to sit in judgment. Cliopher shivered at how distant and bleak an expression it was, but he did not know quite what to say. If Fitzroy *needed* that distance—

He looked around, and his heart quailed.

It was not a large island: they could see the entirety of it from where they stood. The stone was a rusty-black stone, basalt probably, which fell down in staggered cliffs to a boiling sea. The rocks in the water were even more obviously unnatural from up here, arranged like the serrated teeth of a lamprey in rings around the island.

The island consisted of a squat stone tower of decidedly unfriendly appearance, situated not far from them in a wide meadow covered in a short, tussocky grass, grey-green and flatted by the wind. There were hardly any flowers and no visible birds, which disturbed Cliopher on a fundamental level. There were *always* birds on an island.

Fitzroy let go of his elbow so he could take a few steps forward, and Cliopher shuddered comprehensively.

The island was silent but for the wind, which whistled over the tussocks and around the jagged cliffs rising up before them. The crags almost looked like ruins, he thought vaguely, before turning to examine the vaha for any damage done by the surprise magical landing.

"What are you doing, Kip?"

Cliopher looked up. Fitzroy had walked the half-dozen strides over to the nearest crag, one hand on the stone. "Checking on the vaha," he called back, running his hand along the tiller. The harp was safely resting on the deck, if tipped over. Cliopher set it upright solicitously.

However unexpectedly put into use, Fitzroy's magic had sufficed to cradle the vaha safely to land. Or so he hoped. There weren't any breadfruit trees to tap for their gummy sap if there were unseen cracks.

"Kip," Fitzroy said, half-exasperated, half-amused. "Surely the boat can wait? I know the first rule is to *secure your vessel*, but I hardly think it's going to wash away from up here!"

"It might blow away," Cliopher returned, and stepped onto the deck. He took his time in furling the sails and tying them down properly, then unfastened the shade cloth so it didn't act as a sail and tip the vaha. The two hulls would hardly be good sledges, but the wind was stiff enough it might be able to set the vaha moving across the grass; even into the crags Fitzroy found so fascinating.

Fitzroy watched him impatiently. When Cliopher opened the hatch to check on the fire-pot and mirimiri, he sighed audibly over the wind, but when Cliopher then moved on to checking on the rest of their stores, he uttered an incredulous exclamation and stomped back over. "What is *wrong* with you?" he demanded. "How can you not show *any* curiosity at this?"

He waved at the crags. Cliopher peered at them, and then looked back. "They're rocks," he said, and then, with a bit of an effort—he felt physically better than he had on their arrival, but he couldn't deny that his mind still felt a little slow and stupid after the brilliance of the time upon Sky Ocean—he remembered what had drawn his friend to this island in the first place. "I can't see what makes them magically interesting, Fitzroy ..."

"Can't see—" Fitzroy swore again, and grabbed Cliopher by the hand.

Cliopher jumped at the wave of magic that crashed over him and set all his hair on end. "Wh—what—"

"Look now."

He looked. The crags were not crags; the stones formed a squat tower with many dark windows. "Fitzroy ... What *is* it?"

"Magic most powerful," Fitzroy replied blackly. "Old magic ... I think I'm going to have to keep hold of you while we explore. Unless you'd prefer to wait out here?"

"I'm not sure what use I'll be in there, but I'd prefer to accompany you."

That made Fitzroy relax, just a trifle, and give him a lightning-quick smile. "What use? The man who climbed from the deeps of the sea to the top of the sky, and won from the Sun the mirimiri of Ani? I should be able to manage any magic we find within. What use could you be? ... You have been my right hand for a long time, Kip Mdang."

Cliopher swallowed. "You're too kind."

"Indubitably. Shall we?"

Cliopher jumped down off the vaha, and hand in hand they went to what he could now see was a heavy wooden door. There did not seem to be a handle, but when Fitzroy set his hand to the wood it silently opened.

Cool, heavy air washed over them. It tasted of stale spices, and both of them sneezed. The entry was very dark.

"I don't think anyone is here," Fitzroy said, and conjured several balls of golden light to illuminate their way with a single snap of his fingers. Cliopher was reminded of Rhodin doing the same thing, as they crept through the secret passages of the Palace. It heartened him to recall that moment, that question Rhodin had asked him —*did you wish for something for yourself, when you cast your wish into the bonfire? You're allowed to*—

He had cast his wish into the bonfire of his own heart, and it blazed in the shell he had given Vou'a to give to Ani. He had said it out loud to Fitzroy, and here they were, exploring a strange and terrible place together.

"Come in," Fitzroy said, tugging him across the threshold.

～

The ground floor seemed to consist of a bare stone cellar, feathery grey dust inches deep over whatever else might be there.

"No tracks of vermin," Fitzroy murmured, making his lights brighten so the whole room was clearly illuminated. "Mice or rats or whatnot. Not for a long time, at least."

There were no windows, but a stone stair zig-zagged up the squared walls. They walked across the floor, Fitzroy apparently unbothered by the dust on his bare feet. Cliopher found the sensation of the dust collapsing onto his skin disturbing, and there was invisible grit underneath. He wished Fitzroy hadn't mentioned *vermin*.

"I counted three sets of windows," Fitzroy said as they climbed towards the trapdoor set between two huge wooden beams. "Four floors. That's an important number for certain types of magic ... For Schooled magic, especially. Two pairs, balancing each other. This floor empty; the top floor full. The middle two will be paired as well."

The trapdoor had a cord hanging down, which appeared to open a lock, by the grinding of ancient and little-used gears when Fitzroy pulled it. They retreated down the stairs as the two leaves of the trapdoor unfolded and permitted them access up. Cliopher felt another shivering wash of magic as he stepped off the stairs onto the wooden floor. It was suddenly much warmer, and there was no dust.

Fitzroy said, "I'm going to try letting go of your hand, Kip. Go stand by the wall first, in case you get dizzy."

Cliopher obeyed, moving well away from the open stair, but when Fitzroy let go of his hand, nothing seemed to happen. He shrugged, smiling uncertainly, when Fitzroy peered intently at him and then sighed explosively. "I thought so," he said. "We're inside the protections now. The air is clearer, can you tell?"

"It's warmer," Cliopher agreed. "And cleaner." They were in what seemed like a small anteroom, plain stone with another wooden door facing them. He brushed at his feet; the grit seemed to be broken shells and stone fragments rather than petrified rat droppings, which was something.

Fitzroy squatted down to examine the trapdoor; when he rose, his face was set into a stern but otherwise calm countenance. "We'll leave it open," he said quietly. "There's no easy way to open it from this side."

Cliopher looked down at the trapdoor, shivering with the implications. "Is this— was this—a prison?"

"It would have felt like one, I expect. ... Mine did."

"Fitzroy—"

But Fitzroy shook his head firmly. "Never mind me. Let's see what secrets this place holds."

One of the anchor-points of the magic of Astandalas. Fitzroy had once pointed them out to Cliopher, standing in his study before that huge embroidered tapestry map of the five worlds of the empire.

One of the anchors for the Empire's magic, he'd said, pointing at the narrow crescent of the island known as the Long Edge of Colhélhé, where there was a tower. *There were five.* He'd walked down the map; Cliopher could see it in his mind's eye, how his Radiancy had touched the tapestry, setting tiny gems to glittering. *Outside the Vale of Astandalas on Ysthar. Far northern Voonra. Out past the Outer Reaches of Alinor. Somewhere past the Isolates there was one.*

He'd implied that was the one where he'd been exiled, but that could not be so. This was not *that* tower. Surely—surely he'd told Cliopher since then?

But Cliopher could not remember anything but his Radiancy standing at the map, looking down the long length of his empire at Cliopher, his eyes far away. (Thinking, no doubt, of that lonely youth, that extraordinary young adulthood with the Red Company, the unexpected burdens of the crown.) His Radiancy's words echoed in his mind:

I was exiled there. Before I became Emperor. That was where I lived.

Those words, that look in his eyes, that ... that everything ... that was what had made Cliopher rent the house at Navikiani on Lesuia for him, offer him that holiday that changed everything.

"This wasn't yours," he said, as Fitzroy set his hand on the door, which had a handle but no lock; but something clicked and the air shivered.

Fitzroy looked back at him, his face at its most serene, his eyes distant, overlaid with golden magic. "No," he said, his voice cool, unemotional. "Mine was the tower of Harbut Zalarin on Colhélhé."

Auri had talked about visiting that tower, studying the books Fitzroy must also have studied, two thousand years on. It was there that Aurelius Magnus had designed the incredible work of magic that came to be called the Pax Astandalatis, which had brought peace to his troubled empire ... and bound his descendants ever more tightly in the chains of their own power.

He didn't know what to expect as he followed Fitzroy into the main part of the tower. He found himself standing in his long-accustomed position, a few steps away and behind, well out of reach. Cliopher made himself come closer, provide a physically near presence; no matter how distant and serene Fitzroy looked, he could not possibly be that calm inwardly.

Perhaps he had never been serene inwardly.

The room was entirely empty. There were windows on all four walls, the thick glass panes letting in a wan daylight. There was no dust in here; a faint air moved about them. It tasted like cinnamon.

An ironwork staircase rose in a tight spiral in the centre of the room, though this time there was no trapdoor, but a circular opening. Cliopher looked up the stair, and saw that it continued on past the next floor, presumably all the way to the top of the tower.

"A place for exercise, I suspect," Fitzroy said, making one circuit of the room before joining Cliopher by the staircase. "One does need some movement, after all."

Cliopher looked at him in concern, but could not think what to say. "Yes," he said quietly.

"I was given all that I needed to keep me content, theoretically," Fitzroy said as they climbed up. The stair was solid, though the iron quivered under the vibrations of their movements. "Books, food, writing supplies ... musical instruments ..."

"Did you have attendants?"

Fitzroy laughed shortly. "There were sprites bound into servitude. According to the books they're sentient and have a kind of culture of their own, but the ones that *attended* me acted mindlessly. Either they had no true intelligence or they could not perceive me as a fellow being. They did their work as mechanically as I did the rituals I was bound to do. Ah, this is more like it."

They stepped off the stair onto the next floor. This one was again one square room, but it was subdivided with screens and had furniture, of a sort. Very old-fashioned Shaian furniture to Cliopher's eyes, but he did not know enough to be able to identify any of it more precisely than that.

"I don't see anything more recent than Zangora XII," Fitzroy murmured, regarding the painted birds on one of the screens. "This is Voonran from around that period ... and behind it we have ... a bath, also in the Voonran style."

It was a large, beautifully carved wooden tub, deep rather than long. Cliopher had experienced them on his embassy to Voonra, and he looked for the washing area that would be nearby; like the Islanders, Voonrans tended to consider that baths were for soaking only, and washed before-hand with dippers and sponges. One of the other corners held the expected area, with a smoothly tiled floor and the humming sense of magic in the air.

Cliopher touched the elegant metal spigot that came out of the wall, and a shower of hot water obediently poured out.

"Nothing stinted here," Fitzroy said. "Mine was the same. The second heir to the Empire should want for nothing that could be given them ..."

Nothing but friends, family, companionship, *humanity*.

"There are sacrifices that must be made, you know," Fitzroy said, his voice as steady as a rock, his eyes opaque, his entire body in his most perfect posture.

"I know," said Cliopher, who had stood beside him for so many impossible decisions.

"I couldn't make this one," Fitzroy said, tapping the spigot so the water ceased its flow. "I couldn't put anyone in this position. No matter how necessary the good for the many. I *couldn't*." He was silent for a moment, looking at the beautiful antique furnishings. "And how many people died in the Fall because I couldn't?"

"You don't know that that was the cause, Fitzroy," Cliopher said carefully, because all their years of study and analysis had never conclusively answered that question.

"Perhaps not," Fitzroy said, very distantly. "Perhaps not."

They went silently up another flight.

~

The topmost floor was, indeed, as *full* as the ground floor had been empty. It was crowded, reminding him rather of Fitzroy's private study. There were more *tools* here than Fitzroy had there—telescopes at two windows, a sextant on a table, other similar devices of bronze and iron. But the papers, the books, the small objects, the cushions, the *cloth* ...

He shivered.

The room had been divided into segments radiating out from the staircase, each terminating in a lobed alcove containing a window. One was the sleeping area, with a kind of daybed piled high with bedding and cushions in rich jewel-tones. Then a table, more sturdy than elegant, which contained more piles of things— papers and inkwells and quills, and leather-bound books and scrolls and paper-weights.

Cliopher was drawn to the papers. At a glance he could see that they were written in a fine courtly hand, feminine in inflection—there had been a period where the fashion was for male and female courtiers to develop different hands—the script suggested Fitzroy's identification of the most recent furniture being from the reign of Zangora XII was correct. He only caught a few words—most of it seemed to be mathematical notations—when Fitzroy exclaimed softly.

Fitzroy was standing beside a brass telescope, but he was looking down at the caramel-brown velvet at his feet. His face was stark, so grey that Cliopher ran across the room to his side—only to be stopped with an inexorable wall of magic. "Fitzroy!"

"I'm sorry," Fitzroy said, releasing the magic. He wasn't looking at Cliopher; he was looking down at the cloth, and though his face was still and serene, his eyes were filling with tears. "I'm so sorry."

Cliopher looked down, and saw the bones.

The tower's resident had died there, fallen away from her telescope, still wrapped in the sumptuous velvet gown that had been her clothes. Over the centuries, her flesh had fallen away into dust, but the perfectly articulated tiny bones of her hands, outstretched upon the floor, still showed how she had reached out in her last moments.

His throat closed, and he had to stand where he was for a moment. Then he looked at his friend, who was taking the slow, controlled breaths of his long training, and had forced the tears back.

"Oh Fitzroy," Cliopher said, stepping carefully around the cloth so he could gently take Fitzroy's arm and guide him away from the skeleton. He made for a comfortable chair set before an archway that held a fire—still burning by magic—but did not trust the plush fabric to hold them, and instead fetched over the hard wooden chair from the table.

Only one chair in each place. This was not a person who had expected visitors.

He pushed Fitzroy gently into the chair. Fitzroy sat down, back perfectly straight, chin up, eyes fixed on nothing Cliopher could see.

He did not know what to do. He stood beside his friend, his *fanoa*, hand on his shoulder, providing his presence for whatever comfort that might be.

"That was supposed to be my fate," Fitzroy said suddenly. His voice was no longer serene and distant, but sharp, biting. His accent had shifted to its court one; it scraped across Cliopher's nerves like freshly-snapped obsidian. "The Marwn, bound as one of the anchors of Astandalas, ensorcelled within an enchanted tower. Left there, unknown, unspoken of, unthought of ... our very names sacrificed to the empire."

Cliopher squeezed his shoulder. Fitzroy was wearing his sarong, and his hair was viciously tangled (because he had combed Cliopher's hair, and not his own; because Cliopher had been the one hurting and panicked), but he nevertheless looked every inch the emperor he had been.

"Left to die and rot alone and forgotten for *centuries*, his life—hers? I don't even know!—no one knows—I tried to find out the names of the Marwns before me, but the records were deep in the Ouranatha's archives, and they said they were unwilling to relinquish them for my *mere curiosity*."

"She," Cliopher said, his voice trembling with the effort of keeping quiet and level. "Her hand is a feminine one, in her papers. There was a fashion ..."

"And she chose that form." Fitzroy closed his eyes. "She was ... Some ancestor—not a *direct* one, obviously, no Marwn was expected to *procreate*—we were the spares, the back-ups, the fail-safes. The unwanted. But an ancestor, the way you could claim Tupaia and Pinyë as yours. She was a sister or a cousin of some ancestor of mine. If it was like me she was sent here when she was sixteen ..."

They both looked around. Just the papers bore the evidence of years, if not decades, of life.

"Left here, sustained by magic, until she died. Alone." Fitzroy's voice rose up in anguish, and he stopped, as if shocked that his emotions had broken through all those endless years of discipline. He bent his head and buried his face in his hands, breathing hard, while Cliopher stood uselessly beside him. After a long, uneasy silence, Fitzroy said, "What do I do, Kip?"

That was asked in exactly the tone Fitzroy had used when asking him for the solution to some impossibly complicated problem. Cliopher closed his eyes and tried to centre himself. The white bones of the dead woman's hand were fixed in his mind's eye.

"We can bury her," he began, trying to make his voice the calm, dispassionate bureaucrat's voice, offering a slate of solutions in the hope one or more would be palatable. "On the island, or at sea. We can take her bones to Solaara, if you want to bury her in the Imperial Necropolis." Fitzroy gave him an odd, almost baleful glance between his fingers, his eyes glinting. Cliopher swallowed. "You—we could build a memorial to the Marwns in that last space in the necropolis."

"The one everyone thinks is for my tomb?"

"Did you want to be buried there?"

Fitzroy shook his head convulsively. "No. I want to be cremated and my ashes scattered. You'll see that done, if I die before you?"

"Of course," Cliopher said, forbearing any protests or the grief that rose up in his throat at the mere thought. "Of course."

"Of course," Fitzroy repeated, not quite sarcastically, and stared, dry-eyed, at the bones of his distant relative. "I suppose you'd want to be taken to the Island of the Dead? Someone pointed it out—To lie with your ancestors? In the manner of your people?"

Cliopher was about to say *of course*, but there was a note in Fitzroy's voice—

And he recalled the stories that the Sea-Witch sent her birds down to fetch the spirits of those lost at sea, to return them home.

The Sea-Witch had given him the garnet that still rattled in the efela the Grandmother (The Old Woman Who Lives in the Deeps, the in-gatherer of all life, in the end) had named Kiofa'a. Cliopher carried the mirimiri of Ani, to give to Vou'a to take to his fanoa. Vou'a was his great-uncle's husband.

He would not be lost, though he did not follow the traditions of his people.

"If I die first," he said, "cremate me and keep the ashes until—until—until they can be scattered with yours. So you can be free but you don't have to be—alone—we can sail with the Ancestors together—"

Fitzroy said, "Kip."

His voice was not the serene one, but fighting for equanimity.

"I will not be lost, and neither will you," Cliopher replied fiercely. "The Sea-Witch likes me. The Old Woman Who Lives in the Deeps likes me. Your ancestors have not forgotten you."

Fitzroy breathed in deeply and visibly worked to compose himself. He gripped Cliopher's hand once, tightly, and then straightened his shoulders and spoke evenly. "I like the idea of taking that space up with a monument—no, you're right, a *memorial*—to all those ... forgotten ones."

Cliopher nodded, smiling painfully, following his cue. "When we reach Gorjo City you can send a letter to the Ouranatha to research their names. And to Aioru about starting construction of the memorial. You can think about what you'd like it to look like as we continue our voyage."

Fitzroy smiled twistedly. "What would I do without you?" He pushed himself up. "Let's look through her papers. Perhaps there's something we can see published, in honour of her life's work. I would have wanted someone to bring my poems or music to life, if I'd never been able to share them."

"Perhaps we can find her name," Cliopher said.

"She won't have known it," Fitzroy replied flatly. "I only learned mine when I was crowned."

Cliopher set his jaw, refusing to falter. He spoke firmly. "Then we will force the Ouranatha to find it for you in their records."

Fitzroy looked at him, and then he huffed. "They will not want to face you now."

"They never liked my temerity," Cliopher agreed, offering him his hand as he rose.

"No, they didn't. But they came to respect you, and that was before you sailed Sky Ocean to the House of the Sun. You will see."

Fitzroy looked at the table with its papers and pens, but then set his shoulders and they went first to the telescope embrasure, and he and Cliopher carefully gathered every last tiny bone together into a beautiful enamelled box, empty of whatever it had once contained, that Fitzroy found by the fireplace.

CHAPTER FIFTY-SEVEN
WAYFINDING

After a few hours, Cliopher went down for food and to ensure the incessant wind had not blown the vaha over. As soon as he stepped across the threshold he grew confused and bewildered at what he was doing and, even worse, what *Fitzroy* was doing.

He spent a good hour in increasingly frantic searching of the empty island before Fitzroy came to find him.

"I'm sorry," he said, when Fitzroy had collected him and helped him recollect where they were and what had happened. His head was spinning, and he had to grip Fitzroy's elbow to keep his balance when they turned their backs to the wind. He was bewildered and upset: with himself, with the magic, with the whole situation. "I'm so sorry."

"You have nothing to be sorry about," Fitzroy replied. They walked back together across the tussocks, the wind buffeting at them. Cliopher had been nearly ready to try climbing down the cliffs to make sure Fitzroy had not fallen off. So long as he could see Fitzroy, Cliopher did not fret, and he could remember that there was a tower, though he could not see it without touching him.

It was all very disturbing. He did not like this slippery, subtle magic.

"It's good to be in the fresh air," Fitzroy said, subdued in demeanour and voice though his hair crackled with magic in the wind. It was about as long as Cliopher's hand, perhaps six inches, at rest: the wind caught the coils and extended them out nearly twice as far. "We should eat out here."

"As you wish," Cliopher agreed, reassured that the enchantments had not tangled and ensnared Fitzroy as they had made him stumble over his own perceptions. The wind was cold, blowing straight out of the south, and made him shiver, but the sun was bright and cheerful.

They sat on the grass in the lee of the vaha. The hulls were decorated with a handful of opportunistic barnacles and streamers of seaweed, drying now after the hours out of the water. Cliopher regarded the vegetation thoughtfully. These were creatures out of Sky Ocean, presumably.

"It's hard to be in there," Fitzroy said out of nowhere. "I had thought ..." He picked at the grass, plucking blades and letting the gusts that curled over their shelter take them out of his hand. "That was supposed to be my fate, Kip. I had thought ... I thought I'd left it behind long ago." He fretted at the tiny flowering spike of the grass, pulling apart each of the dangling pollen-laden bits. "Perhaps I've never been able to leave it. In my head. I've always been stuck in a tower."

There was no sign the Marwn of this tower had paced, as his Radiancy had paced, endlessly. But neither Cliopher nor Fitzroy knew what use she'd made of that empty room 'for exercise'.

"I've never been able to finish that voyage home after the Fall," Cliopher offered, returning confession for confession, soul-shaping secret for secret. "It has haunted me, the way nearly drowning when I was twelve, unable to dive successfully for a flame pearl, has haunted me."

Fitzroy glanced at him, his golden eyes shadowed brown, his eyebrows drawn together. "Do you feel as if this voyage is helping? We are heading towards your home."

"East first, then west and home ..." Cliopher quoted from the *Lays*, and then sighed. "Yes." He smiled at his fanoa. "Yes. It is helping. I'm not the person I was when I left, but that person wanted something he could not find there."

"And now?"

Cliopher lifted a blade of grass up so it fluttered in the constant wind. "I have found what I was looking for," he murmured. He looked at his friend. "You can find your way home too, Fitzroy. You're a great poet—you can write a new story for yourself."

Fitzroy looked down. "I haven't written anything new since ... since the Fall, Kip. Not a line of poetry, not a bar of music. It comes into my heart, even into my mind, but when I lift up my pen or my harp it's ... gone."

"I've seen you writing," Cliopher said tentatively. "When we were on holiday on Lesuia."

"At Navikiani, where Vou'a first met Ani." Fitzroy smiled at him; Cliopher blushed. Fitzroy laughed, then sobered. "Prose. I can write prose ... memoirs ... essays ... It's not the same. I don't *want* to be a novelist. I am a poet.—Was. I was a poet."

"You can find your way home to that, too," Cliopher told him, in perhaps a somewhat more pugnacious tone than was warranted.

Fitzroy laughed again, more genuinely. "Will you take my inability to create as your next problem to fix, Kip?" But he did not let Cliopher answer: he jumped up instead and reached out a hand, so that he could see and enter the enchanted tower.

They spent several days there, sorting through the long-dead Marwn's belongings. Fitzroy was very quiet, much of the time; occasionally he would mention something off-handedly about his own tower of exile, but he always hurriedly changed the subject when he realized Cliopher was listening.

Cliopher did not like the picture painted by the off-hand comments, but he was careful to follow Fitzroy's cues.

He had already spent most of his life meticulously deconstructing the governance and political systems of the former Empire of Astandalas. He had worked very hard to free the last emperor from his chains. The empire had already collapsed under its own weight and excess. There was nothing more he could *do*.

Nevertheless, he seethed with anger.

He helped sort through the papers. The Marwn's writing was elegant and clear. She had clearly prided herself in her hand, and justly so, in Cliopher's opinion. Once he was used to her idiosyncrasies, it was a pleasant, easy script to read.

She'd been meticulous; it was quickly apparent that her passion was the sky. Her notes were full of carefully constructed arguments about astronomy and the nature of clouds and the wind patterns she'd observed over her decades in her tower.

She had lived in this tower—in these three floors, and the small open roof—for something like seventy years.

She did not know that *back in the world*, as she described the rest of the empire, five empresses had come and gone. One of them had been her older sister; one had been her mother.

It felt wrong to call her the Marwn, but that was who she had been, her name and all the life she might have had *back in the world* sacrificed to the empire she had never known.

No, Cliopher did not blame Fitzroy for being quiet and changing the subject too frequently.

He almost wished they had the Empire of Astandalas back, simply so they could destroy it even more thoroughly.

~

The wind was incessant and cold out of the south. Fitzroy and Cliopher dithered, neither of them speaking out loud, when it came towards evening of the first day and they had to decide where to sleep.

They did not have a tent, and there were no materials on the island save what was in the tower for making of anything like a shelter. The tower was full of things that Cliopher thought should have disintegrated over the centuries, but Fitzroy said there was magic on all the non-living things to keep them sound.

"They would have stocked it ready for her lifetime," he said, picking up a soft blanket off the reading chair.

"What about food?"

Fitzroy glanced at the table by one window, where a solitary dinner set was laid out: plates, bowls, glasses, two-pronged forks and deep-bowled spoons, whatever had been considered appropriate all those centuries ago. The lack of dust on the dishes bothered Cliopher more than the rest of the room, somehow. It made it too apparent what magic lasted here.

"It would have come from ... somewhere. I never figured out where mine came from ... it just appeared, along with the correct utensils for the rituals I was supposed to perform." Fitzroy shook himself. "That magic would have failed with Astandalas, if it persisted past her death."

"It amazes me that the rest of the enchantments have lasted so well."

"These anchorages were so far from the centre, their magic necessarily had to partake of the wild magic outside the boundary of the empire. These were great, great works of magic, Kip: I wouldn't be surprised if the persistence of this tower and the power generated and bound by the Marwn's life and death here is part of why Zunidh was less fragmented than Ysthar."

Time had fragmented, fractured, in ways that had still not entirely healed. The idea that it could have been *worse* was terrifying.

He had read accounts of Ysthar since the Fall: the devastating advances of the continent-sized sheets of ice that had been held at bay by the magic of Astandalas; the very fact that millennia had passed when mere decades had in other parts of the former empire. The Lord of Ysthar had spent his entire working life cleansing and piecing together the fragments of magic so that they would flow smoothly as a whole; the fragmentation was still visible in the strife-torn lands and unstable weather.

Admittedly, Ysthar was also known for its wild exuberance of invention, artistic and political and scientific and technological—everything, in fact, but the magic for which the world had once been renowned. Magic-workers there were limited in scope and vision, secretive, often very ineffectual.

So said the books Cliopher had read, and what he had seen and learned for himself from his one embassy to the Lord of Ysthar.

"I'd like to go to Ysthar again," he said, a little at random, and Fitzroy relaxed away from his fixed staring at the dining table and started talking instead about some essay on magic that the Lord of Ysthar had written. It was so abstruse Cliopher could understand nothing beyond "he has a whole *method* for studying magic *rationally*, or so he says, but his actual *practice* is extremely artistic, which makes for this effect like someone using a very formal structure in order to write an extremely silly song—"

The end result of the long disquisition about theoretical magic was that Fitzroy declared the tower safe to bathe and sleep in.

Safe, but not exactly *comforting*, though they were clean and warm and had soft bedding for the first time in what felt like months.

Neither of them could bear the thought of sleeping on the Marwn's bed, so they piled the blankets before the fire, where they could hear each other's breathing.

Cliopher had odd dreams he could not recall the next morning, save that he felt both unsettled and somehow accepted and welcome. Fitzroy was quiet and shaken: he'd had a vision of his long-dead ancestor, but he would or could say nothing more of her but that she'd asked to be laid to rest with her family, which meant the Imperial Necropolis outside of Solaara.

~

Fitzroy spent half a day enchanting a box to hold everything they wished to take and to keep it safe from water and salt, and then Cliopher had the truly magical experience of putting a lifetime's worth of papers into something approximately two feet square.

They did not empty the tower fully: they left many of the books, most of the cloth, and all of the furniture and tools.

"Someone else may come here one day," Fitzroy said. "Let us leave what they need."

They took the Marwn's reams of notes, and Fitzroy took one blanket and something small that Cliopher did not see before he'd wrapped it in a handkerchief and stowed it in the box with the papers. "She'd like you to take something to remember her by as well," he told Cliopher.

Cliopher shivered, unsure why it felt so different for Fitzroy to have had such a message from his ancestor, when he himself had not only sailed with the crew of the *He'eanka*—which had sailed, living, out of the mortal worlds—but had looked across that gulf to his own dead family members, and seen them looking back.

He walked around the tower room, thinking, and eventually chose a beautiful rock-crystal inkwell. He would use it, and every time he did he would remember this nameless woman who had given her all to an empire who knew nothing about her existence.

He wrapped it in another handkerchief from the store Fitzroy had found, and then they were done.

They carried the boxes down: Fitzroy the one containing his ancestor's bones, and Cliopher the one with her papers. It was a solid weight in his hands, though easy enough to carry.

Cliopher stowed the boxes away in the covered hatch and unfurled the sails while Fitzroy closed the doors to the tower and worked some magic that made his teeth tingle and his bones seem to hum.

"What do you see now?" Fitzroy asked, coming back to the vaha.

Cliopher regarded the tower, and then realized he *could* see it without strain or effort. "It's there," he said. "Did you remove the protections?"

"Only the ones for concealment. If anyone else lands on this lonely isle I'd like them to be able to take shelter. There's nothing dangerous in there now." He brushed his hands and hopped up beside Cliopher. "Are you ready?—Why are you looking at me like that?"

Cliopher was smiling, a vast fondness rising in his heart, as he watched Fitzroy check the sails with easy competence, the magic he'd been working still limning him with a sense of solidity and grace. *Solidity* was perhaps the wrong word. It was as if he were more densely himself, more concentrated, more real.

"If you lift us off the island where you set us, I can sail us home," he said.

"We do work well together, don't we?" Fitzroy said, and then, for the first time since they'd entered the tower, he laughed. He lifted his hands, palms up, and the constant southern wind eddied and swirled around them, under the vaha, cradling them for a moment before launching them like a slung rock far out across the sea.

"I hope you wanted to go north," Fitzroy said when they'd skimmed and skipped across the surface a dozen times before sinking to a normal depth. "I should have asked."

Cliopher caught his breath and loosened his hands from their death grip on the tiller, and coughed, and coughed again, and looked across to see that Fitzroy was bright-eyed and mischievous and so full of laughter the air around him seemed to be brimming with it.

He coughed again, and payed out the ropes to set their course at an angle to the southern wind. "All I know is what you told me," he said, "which is that that island is somewhere 'past the Isolates'—which means west of them. But we were definitely far too far south, so yes, north was good."

"Excellent," Fitzroy said, relaxing, and then he stretched, yawned, and relaxed all the way down to drape himself across the outrigger, boneless as a cat. "Wake me if you need me."

"It can be my turn to watch over you," Cliopher said softly, but the wind stole his words and Fitzroy had already closed his eyes, his hand cupped beneath his cheek.

They were west and south of the Isolates, which left the majority of the Wide Seas before them.

Technically the Wide Seas flowed into the so-called Eastern Ocean—so called by those who lived on its western shores—the Islanders had named the Ke'e Kiaruë, which meant 'Under the Setting Sun'. Sometimes people called the ocean Across the Horizon, a kenning Cliopher had long loved, looking at the silver line of the eastern horizon from his rooms in the Palace.

Past the Isolates, Under the Wake, there was nothing bar a handful of small islands and island chains until you reached the continent of Kavanduru in the north or, even further to the west, the island continent of Lorosh. The Islanders had visited Lorosh, but rarely; the Loroshi did not live on their eastern shore, which was full of volcanic activity, and the ancient Islanders had turned back after sailing for weeks along the boiling seas.

Home was north and east. Cliopher knew quite clearly how far north they had to go—until Furai'fa, the ke'e of Loaloa, was the zenith star—but how far west they were, and consequently how far east they had to travel, was an unknown number.

Thus he set their course mostly north—easy with a southerly wind—and a little east.

They had all the fish of the sea for food, and their stores of fermented breadfruit and dried papaya and so on were sufficient for several more weeks, but they could do with finding an island that had coconuts for more water.

He supposed Fitzroy could probably summon up a rain cloud, if it came to that, and felt a certain mischief at the thought—it was surely cheating to sail with a great mage who could lift their vaha up and send it skipping across the sea as Fitzroy just had.

Cliopher's great mage was soundly asleep and drooling slightly. Cliopher chuckled to himself and set up the sun-screen to shade Fitzroy, and then he laid himself down beside his fanoa and let the deep swell of the sea fill his bones.

They sailed for several days. Cliopher did not pay much attention to how many of them there were, as it seemed unnecessary—their northward progress was obvious each day in the gradual shortening of the sun's noontide shadow, each night as the stars slowly changed their relative positions.

Fitzroy was quiet, for the most part, and Cliopher did not press. He himself did not feel like speaking: he enjoyed their easy companionship, their occasional conversation, the music Fitzroy played on his harp or Cliopher sang. Their conversations were almost entirely to do with the business of sailing or the star-stories each of them knew. For some reason, most of Fitzroy's knowledge was of the constellations of Colhélhé, which Cliopher had never seen.

"One day, Kip, we shall go to Yedoen—to the Grand Bazaar—it is the greatest market in the Nine Worlds. You'll love it."

"One day," Cliopher agreed. "After we retire."

"We're not going back to the Palace after we visit the Vangavaye-ve," Fitzroy proclaimed, smiling and utterly serious. "I'm not done with my quest."

"Not to mention we left all our friends behind."

Fitzroy relaxed from a tension Cliopher had almost missed noticing. But then Cliopher had no desire to return to the Palace, that life of a great lord of the court, the weight of the world upon their shoulders.

"We can't just travel indefinitely," he murmured, watching a jaeger emerge from behind a swell and cut low and swift across the waves before the prow of their boat. Jaegers were pelagic birds, so its presence did not indicate land was near, but it was still good to feel there was life above the waves.

"Perhaps not," Fitzroy replied, slumping bonelessly down into the shade. "But we can still go *somewhere*."

"Anywhere you'd like."

Fitzroy smiled, his eyes closed. "Everywhere you've ever wanted to see."

The third or fourth day, just after sunset, they shared fish and fermented breadfruit, and Fitzroy sighed and said, "I feel terribly spoiled, but I would *love* some variety. Are there no islands between that one and the Isolates?"

Cliopher regarded him, smiling. "Not that I know of. There are none named in the *Lays*—not this far south. There are more to the north—the Line Islands, and the Zizura-ve, an archipelago of volcanic islands, right on the equator, almost all the way to Lorosh ... that's the furthest west the Islanders ever settled, but there's a strong Loroshi presence there and culturally they look more to Lorosh than us."

"Zizura-ve ... Zizar, you mean?" Fitzroy was laughing silently; Cliopher rolled his eyes. Fitzroy chuckled out loud, then leaned down to dip his hands into the water below them. "I do like travelling with you," he said after he'd rinsed his fingers. "Shall you want to come adventuring on land as well, do you think?"

Cliopher snapped his glance to him, but Fitzroy was looking down at his coconut, his hair bouncing in the wind, his face serenely intent. Their conversation from earlier came forcibly to mind.

"It would seem a waste of many adolescent daydreams not to," he replied, just as lightly as Fitzroy asked him. "Not to mention a great disappointment to Rhodin, who was insistent I learn to ride specifically so I could keep up with the Red Company."

Fitzroy did not say anything, but his shoulders relaxed out of formal, posed tranquility and into his more usual semi-slouch.

It was only a few moments later that Cliopher realized that the casual posture *had* become usual.

He was so perturbed he exclaimed aloud, but when Fitzroy looked at him with polite curiosity, he did not know how to express his whirling thoughts, and so he said, "This is very different than my journey home after the Fall."

Fitzroy hummed quietly and shifted position so he sat cross-legged, his sarong draped smoothly over his knees, his weight back on his hands, his face open and attentive.

(How he had changed since that first reunion in Basil's inn. How *both* of them had changed.)

"I was alone, and I knew so much less about sailing," Cliopher murmured, looking around. The steady rolling swells, the wind out of the south, the vaha running freely across the water, the soft hiss of her hulls friendly and familiar as the lapping of waves on a lagoon-side shore. "Having you here to help keep our course ... to talk to ... simply your *company* ..."

Fitzroy smiled at him, and Cliopher grinned back, his heart singing. "And of course, your earlier work with the typhoons is much appreciated, my lord."

It was Fitzroy's turn to roll his eyes and snicker, and Cliopher shrugged and turned at a flash of white, only to catch his breath when he realized what the black-capped tern *meant*.

"What is it, Kip?"

"It's a tern—a *tern*!"

"Naua, right?"

"Yes—no—naua is the general name but specifically means a brown tern—this is another kind—but the point is, terns roost on shore. On *shore*. This kind flies out for fifty miles or so—"

Fitzroy took a moment, and then his eyes lit up. "An island?"

Cliopher grinned at him. "An island."

※

Now all the things he had learned from Elonoa'a truly came into practice. He'd set his ke'ea towards the north, aiming at the latitude where Furai'fa was the zenith star. They were nowhere near that latitude, and so he was quite certain—middle of the day though it was—that they must be nearing either one of the Isolates or else one of the smaller, uninhabited islands scattered across this vast and mostly empty quarter of the seas.

They held to their same course that day, but Cliopher was alert for any signs of approaching land. His best indicators were the birds: first the terns, whose fishing grounds they sailed through for an hour before leaving behind, and then the little tuko'o, who flew in long lines home from their fishing grounds just before sunset.

They were on the wrong side for the currents to bring them any driftwood or sea wrack originating on land, and the waters here were very dark, showing no sign of rising reefs. The deep swells continued to roll on unabated from the south and west, so there were no complicated refractions to indicate an island chain.

Elonoa'a had had all those gifts showing him that an island chain was approaching, when he'd sailed with his face to that distant wind offering him rumours of land. Cliopher had none of them, but thanks to Elonoa'a and those who had gone after him, he *did* have the *Lays*.

And he knew, therefore, when the midnight stars passed overhead, that they were too far south still for the majority of the Isolates, which clustered under Jiano as their ke'e. They were nearly under Fe'eluente, one of the stars that made up the Octopus, which meant the island ahead of them was most likely one of the southeastern outliers of the Isolates.

The wind changed just after midnight, shifting to come nearly due west. Cliopher shivered at this gift, wondering whether it was coincidence or part of travelling with a great mage or the action of one of the gods. Did Ani know he bore her mirimiri back to her fanoa, that Vou'a could carry it down safely to whichever cavern deep in the heart of the oceans she had taken for her home?

(Did Sama, the Wind That Rises At Dawn, still watch over him, nudge one of her sisters to assist them as best they could, here in the world?)

He reset the sails so they continued on their previous course, quartering the wind now but with the deep swells constant in their pattern. There was a high haze, veiling all but the brightest stars, but those were enough.

Just before dawn, he woke from a deep doze at a change in the swells. There was a fine, lacy sea fog, wisping across the smooth backs of the waves. Sea fog came when the water was cooler than the air, which meant that the seafloor might be rising steeply below them, forcing the cold water of the depths to the surface.

Fitzroy was awake, playing his harp softly. "It'll be light soon," he said.

They waited, listening for birds, but the wind was behind them, while the sky lightened with the casual slowness of these latitudes.

And then silhouetted against the rising sun, was the shark's-tooth pinnacle of Nivomano, which he had never seen but which he recognized immediately from the descriptions in the *Lays* and the instructions Elonoa'a had given him.

And knowing where he was, where he had been, he knew exactly how to go home at last.

CHAPTER FIFTY-EIGHT
THE LEAPING-PLACE

It usually took over a month to sail from the Vangavaye-ve to the Isolates. That journey went against the winds: the ke'ea was to travel north, to catch the westward equatorial current, and then drop south once one had reached Gaeva, a lonely and uninhabited atoll on the way to the Line Islands. One had to wait for the annual reversal of the trade winds for it to be anything like a pleasant journey; there were often cyclones that formed in the western Wide Seas.

The return journey left from Tizia'ano, the largest of the Isolates and location of the capital, and it took around three weeks for a small ship.

Nivomano, the Shark Tooth, was at least seven days' sail southeast of Tizia'ano. Cliopher saw no benefit in trying to run against the wind to go up the archipelago, when Tizia'ano would be farther from home, for all that that was a known and well-travelled route.

They spent two nights on the island, camping on its narrow beach and relishing the opportunity to bathe in the stream that formed pools as it came down from the heights. The Isolates were high islands and very wet in climate: Nivomano and its neighbour Rikoro were unbelievably green and lush.

No one lived on Nivomano, which was mostly vertical jungle, so Cliopher built up a fire on the beach while Fitzroy went for a second bath in the deep pool upstream. He came back in the gloaming—the Isolates had more of a twilight than the Vangavaye-ve—golden magic gleaming around him like a constellation of fireflies.

Cliopher was enjoying the opportunity to roast breadfruit and the sea urchins he'd gathered along the reef that afternoon. And there was fresh fruit! Although the island was uninhabited, it was not infrequently visited, and the local Islanders had planted many useful and fruitful trees and shrubs in the narrow band of soil between beach and cliffs.

"This is the best papaya I have ever had," Fitzroy said, sitting down beside the fire after his second bath. "I'm sure of it."

"Mine is too," Cliopher agreed. "They always are. The first fruit after a long time at sea."

"You cannot *imagine* how delicious was the first orange I had after—after leaving the Palace." Fitzroy sighed. "And the strawberries—they're a northern fruit, I had them in Masseo's village—and the *cherries* in Fiellan! Cherries are Jullanar's favourite but they're one of mine, too."

Cliopher smiled at him and set another branch of driftwood on the fire. Fitzroy sighed and scratched at his shoulder, where his wet hair was dripping. He had spent much of the afternoon picking out the knots in his hair so he could wash it, and now it gleamed black and silver, the weight of the water tugging it down past his earlobes.

They finished their meal in companionable silence. It was good to have some variety, even if still variations on the theme of traditional Islander foods; Cliopher kept finding himself daydreaming of the meals he'd been accustomed to in the Palace. And the bread and cheese he'd had at Basil's inn ...

Fitzroy wiped his hands in the sand. "I miss them. Jullanar and Masseo, Pali and Sardeet ... the others I haven't found yet ... and Rhodin and Conju and Ludvic ..."

"I miss them, too."

"I'm sure Rhodin is having a good time with Sardeet and the others," Fitzroy said, a little anxiously. "And Ludvic and Conju are together ..." He frowned. "They're not as close friends as Conju and Rhodin, are they?"

"No, I'd say I'm closer to Ludvic than Conju is."

"Ludvic's a great mystery to me, you know," Fitzroy said. He touched his hair, then shook his head. "I'm trying hard not to wring it out. Auri told me that wasn't very good for it ... our hair ... I didn't remember, it's been so long since I *had* hair. He was—not amused—I think he was a little baffled that I asked him how to take care of it." Fitzroy laughed, his eyes on the fire. "When I was younger—when I first left *my* tower, my hair started to grow, and I had no idea what to do with it. Jullanar tried, but her hair is totally different."

"What sort of hairstyles did you try?" Cliopher touched his own hair, feeling the braids Fitzroy had put in, the soft, somehow gentle feathers from the Wind That Rises At Dawn barely there to his touch. "This is by far the most interesting style I've ever had. When I was younger I just let it grow out in the traditional fashion, and as an adult it was in the bureaucratic cut. I suppose I could have let it grow out when we changed the uniform to not regulate hair, but by then I was so used to it being short it never occurred to me."

"This looks better," Fitzroy said earnestly, and then grinned. "Of course, it's your hair—"

Cliopher reached out and lightly pushed on his knee. "It *is* my hair and I shall wear it precisely as I wish. Which at the moment, is how you've done it. We'll see if I change my mind once I see what it looks like in a mirror."

Fitzroy laughed. "It looks fantastic and you'll be amazed." He looked as if he were about to add something else, but instead said, "Would you help me with mine?"

His voice was matter-of-fact, but his body was still; *serene* came the unwelcome thought. The long and hard-learned serenity of his Radiancy, which showed nothing at all to the onlooker.

But Fitzroy was not only his Radiancy, and when he grew serene and still it was because his emotions were strong below the surface, like the shining smoothness of a rip in amongst the froth and flurry of the breaking waves.

"I only know how to do basic braiding," Cliopher warned him, keeping his tone light and warm, as matter-of-fact as Fitzroy's had been, asking.

Fitzroy kept his eyes down, as if to hide his emotions. "You don't need to braid it at all." He took a segment of his hair and split it in half, then twisted the two pieces together so they formed a helix, curling the very end around his finger in a neat spiral. "Like this ..."

"That looks fairly straightforward," Cliopher agreed. "Do you have your comb?"

"I'll get it." Fitzroy got up and fetched the comb, his harp, and a small basket from the compartment in the hull of the vaha. As he opened the hull the covered fire-pot suddenly cast a winking daylight radiance across them.

"Do you think anyone will believe that I really went to the House of the Sun?" Cliopher said, when Fitzroy closed away the light. "It is entirely impossible."

Fitzroy raised his eyebrows at him, his mouth quirking, before he dropped easily down to sit cross-legged before Cliopher. He was holding two combs, the ebony one Cliopher had already seen and another made of nacreous abalone. "Trust me, Kip, they will."

"I suppose I do have you for corroboration."

"Oh, no one believes me when I tell such vast truths as that! You should have seen the expressions when I told unsuspecting people I was Fitzroy Angursell, returned from his exile at last! But you, Kip: you bring home great treasures, and ... and Kip, there's an *effect* to visiting the Divine Realms."

Cliopher could feel the changes in himself, the physical effects—his stiffness and creakiness were definitely much diminished, and his stamina was far better than it had been. He was still learning the depths of his internal changes. He cleared his throat, wondering what Fitzroy saw in him, that he could say so definitely that people would be able to *tell*. "Well yes. Our hair has grown exuberantly."

Fitzroy snorted. "It's more than that. You'll see." He twisted around to offer Cliopher the basket and the comb. "There's oil in there—take a small amount, maybe the size of a pebble, and ... massage it in, if you would?"

"Of course," Cliopher said, focusing on being gentle and slow with his motions. This was the first time he had ever touched Fitzroy's hair—perhaps the first time anyone had, since those long-ago days when Jullanar had tried to help him learn what to do—and he wanted it to be a good experience for his friend (his fanoa, and oh ... *what* a treasure that was! That he could think that word, and not just wish for something that could never be, but ... for it to be true).

He opened the basket, and discovered it contained a small clay pot nestled in what looked like shadows and starlight.

He stared long enough that Fitzroy said, "Kip?"

"Just when I'd started to think I'd been imagining it," he murmured. "The clay pot must have come from the *He'eanka*?"

"Yes, apparently they'd spent time on a high island at one point and made a bunch of pottery."

"And the ... shadows?"

"Oh!" Fitzroy grinned at him. "I told you Vou'a visited, didn't I? And taught me how to spin shadows? Those are my threads. The silvery ones are when I tried spinning starlight."

Cliopher touched the shadows, which gave softly under his fingers. They felt a little like the mirimiri, as if they were too fine, too subtle, for his ability to feel. "They're beautiful," he said.

"I should try to see if I can do it here," Fitzroy murmured. "Perhaps when we set sail again." He turned back, settling down more comfortably into the sand, his back very straight but in a relaxed way, as if that *was* more comfortable for him, after so long sitting perfectly upright on thrones. "Do you mind if I play while you work?"

"Not at all," Cliopher replied. He opened the lid of the pot, which was a spiral-woven pad of fibres with a shell handle. A delicious waft of toasted coconut came up.

"Auri showed me two ways to make the oil," Fitzroy said, plucking a few soft notes. "One was fermented but I liked the heated one better. It has a nice smell, don't you think? I thought the oil was a bit more lustrous as well. Auri said we should also be using a kind of cream, after the oil—water first, then oil, then cream—but I've run out of what he gave me, and I don't know what it was made out of. Some kind of nut, maybe. It didn't grow on that island, at least."

Cliopher smiled fondly at the back of his head, and scooped a small amount of oil onto his hands. He combed gently through Fitzroy's hair with his fingers, the wet coils and curls seeming to absorb the oil as he worked. The skin of his scalp was warm, his hair cool and thicker than Cliopher's own. "Does it matter where I start?" he asked after a while. Fitzroy was playing one of the rippling instrumentals that suited the harp so well.

"I think the back is easier. There should be two combs, so you can pin some of it up."

"You'd think I'd remember this more from when I worked in Uncle Lazo's barbershop," Cliopher murmured, taking several attempts before he could gather the majority of Fitzroy's hair out of the way and pin it in place with the abalone-shell comb. "Your hair is very different from Islander hair."

"I don't think you'll need to cut it."

"Probably better to wait for scissors," he agreed, and gathered together a small section of hair. It was damp but seemed thirsty in his hand, and he added more oil as he ran his fingers through, making sure each strand was coated. The twists worked better, he soon found, if he grasped the hair closer to the scalp, and looked better if the segments were even.

He was slow, but it was meditative work, with Fitzroy humming along with his harp-music, the fire crackling merrily, the sea lapping at the beach with a soft, steady breathing. The wind was soft, and it was good to hear the quiet calls of birds and bats after so long with only the wind in their ears.

After a while, he said, "What did you mean, that Ludvic is a mystery to you?"

Fitzroy did not answer immediately, but his shoulders had not tensed, and he did not pull away from Cliopher's slow, gentle touch.

"He's so constant, so steady," Fitzroy said at length. "And yet ... such poetry in him. Has he ever shown you his writing?"

"No."

Fitzroy sighed. "I didn't think so. He's such a private man. It's ... it's not *great* poetry, technically, but it has such *heart* to it. I was humbled, when he recited it to me. You and Conju were away on holiday, that was when he did—I think it was to distract me—and it was so surprising to me, and I felt so bad I was that surprised."

"It surprised me, to learn of it, too."

There was a silence. Cliopher could feel Fitzroy's tension in the way he held his head terrifically still. He worked more oil into the next section of hair, running his fingers through the strands over and over again until he relaxed under the touch. Fitzroy's hair was thick, slightly coarse, and felt good in Cliopher's hands: springy, increasingly sleek, *alive*.

"What is he going to do, Kip?" Fitzroy whispered. "Ludvic's always been so ... *steady*. Ever since I woke up after the Fall, he's been there, no matter what. He's so *loyal*. How can I face him and tell him that the emperor he loved was a—How can I tell him?"

What had he been going to say there? That the emperor Ludvic loved was an outlaw? An accused traitor? A wanted criminal?

Cliopher made himself wait through three twists before he responded, but Fitzroy said nothing further. He picked his words carefully. "You tell him the truth. You are Fitzroy Angursell and you are also Artorin Damara."

"That name means *nothing* to me."

Although that could not possibly be true—there was far too much venom in his tone for it to be true—Cliopher left it alone. "Ludvic loves *you*, not the Emperor."

"You don't know that."

"He told me."

That silenced Fitzroy, who knew as well as Cliopher that Ludvic far preferred saying nothing to lying. Cliopher waited again—one twist, two, a third—and then he said, "When I went to talk to Ludvic about you being Fitzroy Angursell, he told me he'd known since the beginning."

"He can't have."

"He did."

One twist, two, a third—Cliopher was nearly done, only a few segments left. He put a dab more oil on his hands, running his fingers gently along the exposed portions of scalp. The sea shushed gently beside them.

It was such a good sound, the waves on the shore.

He had missed the sounds of the natural world, all that time in Solaara. Only a few bird-cries had come to the window in his rooms—when he'd lived at the far end of the Alinorel wing, he'd been closer to the ground, and there had been a tree outside his window where weaverbirds had nested. Their scraping, bubbling, one-note chatter had grown to be a companionable noise, whenever he was there during the day.

"How did Ludvic know?" Fitzroy asked in a subdued voice.

Cliopher was glad he'd obtained Ludvic's permission to tell this story, which he did, gently, softly, as he finished his hair.

"All that time," Fitzroy said blankly when he'd finished. "The whole time. He knew. He never said—not once. He never gave *any* indication." And then, when Cliopher said nothing, merely continued to work on his hair, he went on, his voice worryingly neutral: "Not until I showed that I wanted something different, when we went to Navikiani. That's when he stepped forward and suggested I retire ..."

"He loves you," Cliopher repeated gently, running his hands through Fitzroy's hair, the glossy twists he'd just made, reminding him that the taboos and restrictions no longer bound him. "You."

Fitzroy was silent for a long, long time. And then he said: "Would you mind if I ... went for a walk by myself for a bit, Kip? I ..."

That was something else Fitzroy had not been able to do, all the time in the Palace. And of course, being at sea in a small boat as they had been, there had been no opportunity for privacy or solitude.

"Of course."

"I won't be long."

"You know where to find me when you're ready," Cliopher replied, letting his hands fall, just for a moment, to Fitzroy's shoulders, before he scooted back to give him the space to rise.

Fitzroy stood, and looked down at him for a moment, his face gleaming with the red-gold firelight, his eyes like coals. Then he smiled, and he was once more Fitzroy, full of magic and power but human for all that.

"Thank you for doing my hair," he said.

He did not mean only that: it was in his eyes, his face, his voice.

"You're very welcome," Cliopher replied, and let him go.

After they had replenished their stores of fresh coconuts and other fruits of lagoon and land, they set off again at dusk along one of the lesser ke'ea of the *Lays*.

Cliopher resolved to track the days this time, though the Vangavaye-ve had a very wide 'screen', given the quantity of birds that nested on its islands, and he had no fear of sailing past it unawares. He guessed that with the helpful west-by-southwest wind and more eastern launching-point their journey would be well under three weeks, but the ke'ea was so little-used he knew only the stars of its progression, and not its length.

And yet—his island was clear in his mind at last, and they were going home.

On the ninth sunset after leaving Nivomano they met the first of the Vangavaye-ve's birds, and the morning after that they saw the clouds that gathered over the islands of the Ring.

Fitzroy stood, one arm around the mast, shading his eyes against the sunrise. "We're almost there."

His voice was a little doubtful, as if he could not quite believe it, or, believing it, could not quite decide whether to be glad or sad.

Or perhaps that was just how Cliopher was feeling. The journey from Nivomano had passed like a pleasant dream, full of easy conversations and companionship. Perhaps he should have pushed Fitzroy on how he felt—perhaps Cliopher should have pushed himself on how he felt—but it had been so lovely just to spend the time together, Fitzroy and Cliopher, the two of them in their small vaha under the great wheeling glory of Sky Ocean.

Fitzroy played his harp; Cliopher sang; they talked about books they had read, places they had been, the friends they shared and the ones they didn't. Cliopher asked many questions about the Red Company, eager to learn what they were as *people*, not legends. He was glad for every story about Masseo that showed that the smith was a good man, a good friend, someone Ludvic could safely love.

They had not talked much about what would happen once they finished this journey. A few light comments—"We'll return to Alinor and Basil's inn, of course"— "We'll have to write to Aioru and Ludvic and let them know all is well"—and the rest had been discussion of the happier parts of the past and the historic present of literature and philosophy.

"Do we have to sail all the way around to the Gates of the Sea?" Fitzroy asked, late one afternoon while Cliopher was fishing, the wind fresh on his shoulders and the sky taking on rose and orange tints behind them. "On the maps I've seen there doesn't seem to be another navigable passage into the Ring."

Cliopher laughed and returned to his lackadaisical jigging. "If we had a larger boat —a trading ship or a parahë like the *He'eanka*—we would, yes. That's the only passage wide and deep enough."

Fitzroy sat down beside him. "And since we have a small, light vaha?"

"You won't have to lift it across any reefs," Cliopher retorted. "I know the passage near Loaloa."

"The westernmost of the islands, of course," Fitzroy said, his eyes shining. "Your island. I am looking forward to seeing it, Kip."

"So am I," he replied, though now it was his turn to sound a little doubtful, a little hesitant.

"It's practice," Fitzroy said comfortingly. "Before we go to the city and have to face all your relatives."

Cliopher gave him a wry smile. "Half the people who live there *are* my relatives."

Fitzroy snickered, just for a moment. "Still, practice."

※

Loaloa was a low island, though not a coral atoll; its core was basalt, created in the ancient explosion that had created the Outer Ring, eroded in the hundreds or thousands of millennia since, and lifted again in occasional bouts of volcanism.

Cliopher's Varga grandmother had told him that Ani slept in a cave at the deepest point of the Bay of the Waters, where the ultramarine blue became nearly black with the depths falling away below. Sometimes she turned in her sleep, and the islands she had once loved and danced upon, the islands Vou'a had raised for her, shook and trembled and held still a moment, waiting to see if she would wake and come dance upon their shorelines again.

Cliopher looked at the basket containing the mirimiri of Ani, the shimmering cloth so subtle and fine his hands could barely hold it, his eyes barely see it, and he shivered with a deep fear and wonder at what he might waken.

The tenth morning they were well within sight of the Ring, mere hours away from landfall. Cliopher felt far more nervous than he had arriving at the House of the Sun.

(He had always been so much better at the challenges of strangers than he was with those of his family.)

He and Fitzroy groomed themselves as best they could, without water or tools other than their few remaining casoa shells. Fitzroy combed Cliopher's hair again, making sure the braided feathers sat properly, discreet but visible. Or so he said; having no mirror, Cliopher could only trust him that his hair looked reasonable.

Cliopher untwisted Fitzroy's hair, oiling the glossy spirals, and used the abalone shell comb to arrange them into a swept-back style that looked deliberate and (he thought) fairly attractive. Fitzroy insisted on using part of his much-modified clothing (which looked nothing like the tunic, shirt, and leggings he'd started with) as a head-scarf to protect his new style against the wind.

Both the dramatic curls and the scarlet headscarf were very much a Fitzroy Angursell effect, not something that his Radiancy would ever have chosen—or rather, not something that Conju or Lady Ylette would ever have chosen for his Radiancy—and seeing him sweep his hair up into the scarlet cloth allowed Cliopher to ask a question that had been strengthening in his mind since their conversation on Nivomano.

"What do you want me to call you?" he asked finally. "Amongst other people."

Fitzroy looked across the gradually diminishing space between them and the land that, just here, still looked more a mirage than reality. The clouds and the birds were their most reliable indicators that land was there: the higher islands of the northern part of the Ring were still hardly more than a dark blur.

"I can't lie to your family," Fitzroy said. "I don't want to."

"No," Cliopher replied, speaking to his own gratitude—no, his fanoa did not want to lie to his family—and also understanding the pain and doubt that was rearing up in Fitzroy's heart and mind, as they came inexorably closer to the world they had left behind.

The last time they had been in the Vangavaye-ve together, he had been so strictly *his Radiancy* that not even Aya had dared imply otherwise. Cliopher had certainly heard no more of her suspicion that his lord was Fitzroy Angursell after her journey to Solaara when she had realized who he was. Whether that was because she had changed her mind or because she had simply decided not to *say* it again, he didn't know, but no one had joked about it to him, and they would have, if it were common gossip.

"I want to be Fitzroy," Fitzroy said. "But they will not understand why you have such a relationship with him—with me—I mean—they know you have spent your life s-serving the Lord Emperor."

Cliopher looked up at a wheeling frigatebird, tail feathers streaming, and felt his heart lift with this indication they were coming so near land. And not just any land: Loaloa. His island.

(His island, which he had not visited for years. *That* was going to add a complication even without the rest of it. He felt nervous, uncertain, out of place. And yet it *was* his island, the anchorage of his soul. Or so he had always proudly claimed. What his family there actually thought remained to be seen.)

"They will remember that I spent my teenaged years equally obsessed with the *Lays* and the music and poetry of Fitzroy Angursell," he said, not looking at Fitzroy; he was blushing. "They are going to remember that I made a great fuss over how I wanted to be Elonoa'a to my own Aurelius Magnus; how I wanted to be as the third son of Vonou'a, and sail to the House of the Sun; and ... and how I used to go around singing your songs and declaring I would marry Jullanar of the Sea one day."

Fitzroy turned and leaned back on one elbow, his face suddenly intrigued. "I'd forgotten that—Basil told me, and Jullanar too."

Surely he hadn't heard that correctly. "Jullanar told *you* that *I* wanted to marry her?"

"Jullanar told me many stories that Basil told her about his Cousin Kip, and that was one of them. I thought it very funny." Fitzroy lifted his eyebrows suddenly, eyes gleaming in impish delight. "I could help you with that goal, if you like."

"If I still *had* it," Cliopher retorted, laughing. "To return to the point at hand: if you wish to be Tor, I will endeavour to call you that."

"No," Fitzroy said instantly. "That was for you."

Cliopher had arranged all his letters of reference for banks and minor lordlings who would not recognize the Last Emperor but would grant hospitality and aid to a gentleman wizard under the absurdly grandiose pseudonym of *The Wizard Tor*. Even then he had guessed his Radiancy was going to go back to the name he had once chosen for himself, but ... but his Radiancy (Fitzroy) had never told him that secret name.

He'd said he would, one day, but he hadn't.

—Because he had wanted Cliopher to see him for who he was, and find his name himself. The look on his face, back in Basil's inn when they had reunited, had said that.

That was for you. The only name Cliopher had had to call him that was even remotely his own, since *Artorin Damara* had never been his.

He cleared his throat. "If you wish to be his Radiancy—"

"No. I—I can't, Kip. Not yet."

Not ever was obvious in the sudden distress in his eyes.

"Very well, Fitzroy," Cliopher went on, lightly emphasizing the name. "I don't want to call you nothing, so we are left with the question of whether you are ready to let people know you are both."

"You make it sound so easy," said Fitzroy. He sighed. "Will it get out, do you think?"

"Get out where? The rumours will run the Ring, I'm sure, and reach Gorjo City eventually. Will they go further than that? Possibly. But no one pays very much attention to the Vangavaye-ve, you know."

Fitzroy gave him a small smile. "You've mentioned it, once or twice." He took a breath. "I'll think about it."

"I'll try not to refer to you directly until you've decided," Cliopher said, gently teasing. "It'll be difficult, but I shall do my best."

~

The land swept up suddenly: first the water was a deep, dark, blue, and then the air was full of gulls and the white fairy terns that fished the onshore waters; and then the water was coloured teal and aquamarine; and then they could see the land clearly; and then they were there.

It was early afternoon, the tenth full day after leaving Nivomano. The western wind, their friend for so long, had fallen away into a breeze. They were coming dead on the westernmost point of the Vangavaye-ve, the spit of stone that reached a great buttress out into the deep water. It fell down in sheer cliffs, and the two arms of the Outer Ring curved back away from them to the east.

"That's the Leaping-Place," Cliopher said, guiding the vaha to the south of the spit.

"We don't land there, I take it?"

"It's the place where the spirits of the dead are said to leap forth into Sky Ocean," he explained. "So no." The current was swift along the side of the spit, and he had to concentrate to guide the vaha. After so long on the open sea, he was utterly familiar with the canoe; and it did not seem so hard to navigate this narrow channel after the great maze of reefs in Sky Ocean. "It's sacred."

"Ah," said Fitzroy, looking curiously on the great spit before turning his attention firmly to the island.

The spit bent inwards and rose to an undercut arch. Cliopher guided the vaha away from the eddies passing through the arch, catching the swells that were suddenly sounding loudly in their ears as they came to the edge of the reefs.

He sailed a few hundred yards, remembering this sound, the crash and suck of the waves, in his bones. He had had so many nightmares featuring that sound: sometimes he simply heard it, echoing into his bones.

"Are you all right, Kip?" Fitzroy asked, when he turned the vaha away from the land in a wide curve.

"I missed the passage," he muttered, bringing the vaha to face the land again, but keeping to the deeper water.

"The white column marks it?"

"There are two columns, yes," he said. Stacks of white coral, stark against the vegetation. He had built the second one; Buru Tovo had been a better inshore sailor, and had said one was sufficient to remind him of the correct approach for the passage. Cliopher had set a second column behind the first, so that he knew to position his canoe so he could see the two columns exactly superimposed.

"Kip," said Fitzroy, and set one warm hand over Cliopher's cold one, which held the line of the sail. "What's wrong?"

Cliopher looked quickly at him, and then away, at the white froth of the breaking waves, the deceptively smooth water of the rip.

"This is where I nearly drowned," he said finally, because Fitzroy had been able to tell him some of his secrets, and Cliopher had to offer his own back, didn't he? If he wanted to be true equals, mirrors, matches—fanoa—he had to offer back equally for what he was given. He swallowed, his fingers tight on the smooth wood of the tiller. Fitzroy's hand was so comforting on his. "This is Buru Tovo's range—the place where he dives for pearls—or dove, he's retired now, of course—I don't know who holds it now. Not me." He laughed shortly. The vaha was quivering under him, the line holding the sail out of the wind taut in his other hand, wanting to swing around and let the onshore wind bear them against the rip to land.

It was a perfect situation for crossing the reef in that passage. But Cliopher looked at the dark water, the glimpses of colour from the reef under the foam and dazzle of the surface, and his muscles froze.

"I should dive again," he said, distantly. "Face that fear. See if I can find you a flame pearl for your efanoa."

Fitzroy was silent for a moment, and then he said, "Kip. Look at me."

He did, of course, for a moment, meeting the familiar golden eyes. There was magic in them, and sympathy, and a deep ... respect?

"Cliopher, if you want to dive—if you *want* to, mind—to face that fear, then I will watch for you, and I will save you with my magic if the water seizes you again. But do not do it because you think I should have a flame pearl for my efanoa. That's ..." He smiled suddenly, wryly. "Kip, we both have plenty of flame pearls. I'd rather have a thousand common, ordinary white clamshells strung together than all the jewels in my treasury, because we could find those together. I can't dive down for a pearl for you. I don't know how, and frankly, I don't want to learn. I like swimming but I have no desire to swim in this current. I can't believe your great-uncle made you try when you were twelve."

"I wanted to," Cliopher whispered. "So badly. I wanted to make him proud. But this was where I failed ..."

"What did you fail at, Kip? You didn't find a flame pearl that way; you learned a limit, and respected it."

Cliopher looked at him, unable to bring words to his tongue.

Fitzroy said, "Kip, I'm certain you could fight against this current and find a flame pearl. You've never let anything stop you from something you truly wanted to achieve. You don't have to prove anything. Not to me, not to your Buru Tovo—who is immensely proud of you—not to Elonoa'a—not to Tupaia—not to anyone. Do you *want* to dive for a pearl?"

"No," Cliopher said, the truth torn from him. "I hated it. I hated it every time."

Fitzroy leaned forward and rested his forehead on his, just for a moment, and then he whispered, "Don't drown yourself to make a point, Cliopher Mdang. You don't need to be anything but who you are."

Cliopher closed his eyes against the tears in them, letting those words sink deep into his bones, his blood, the very depths of his heart where that fire burned in the starlit cave, and then he nodded once and turned the vaha. He fed the ropes through the fingers of one hand, the tiller in his other, Fitzroy's hand resting above his, working together.

He let his breathing even out and match the deep swells that had carried them all the way across the Wide Seas to this westernmost point of home.

There were two columns of bleached coral. If he lined himself up—

Yes. There was the channel, with the waves seething through the gap, the rip that had caught him, so long ago, and plunged him down and down.

Down, and down, until he found the rock that did not move, and with his foot upon it he had been able to find his way to the sunlight and safety, and the life that had brought him back here in a great circle that encompassed not only his love and study of the lore and *Lays* but also all the time in Astandalas and Solaara and Sky Ocean.

And not only his hope for a fanoa, for an emperor he could love as Elonoa'a loved Aurelius Magnus, but his love and admiration for the great Astandalan poet Fitzroy Angursell.

He was ready for the next gust of wind that met with the ninth wave, the greater swell—

The wind caught the sail, and with a cry of exultation he rode a wave safely over the rip and into the calmer waters of the narrow band inside the fringing reef.

He tuned a triumphant look on Fitzroy, who patted his hand and then lounged theatrically on the decking. "Nicely done, my lord Mdang."

"Thank you, my lord," Cliopher replied equally sardonically, and they grinned at each other. "Welcome to Loaloa, Fitzroy."

CHAPTER FIFTY-NINE
LOALOA

Cliopher kept the vaha in the middle of the narrow lagoon between the fringing reef and shore, where the aquamarine water showed by its cerulean and lapis blues that there was a deeper channel along the course of the gentle current formed by the water channelled through arch and passage.

He gestured at the reef to their right, where the breakers sounded their familiar muted thunder. "This is Buru Tovo's stretch of the reef—that is, he holds the fishing and pearl-hunting rights, and is responsible, I suppose you could say, for maintaining it." He frowned at the tranquil lagoon, the tall coral column just moving out of sight. "I'm not sure if he's given the rights over to someone else to hold."

Fitzroy looked around curiously. "Not you, I presume?"

"I'm not really his heir," Cliopher explained. "My uncle Lazo would come first."

"Is he a diver?"

"No. He told me he hated diving, too."

Fitzroy smiled at him. "It's that awful, is it?"

"Plenty of my cousins here love it," Cliopher said, gesturing vaguely at the island. "But not me, no."

"Someone's waving back."

Cliopher looked at Fitzroy. "I beg your pardon?" His friend nodded in the direction of the land, where someone was standing on the shore with his arms loose at his sides, his whole posture almost comically shocked.

He felt almost comically shocked, if it came to it. It had been so long since they'd seen another human being that for a moment he could not resolve the man into a fellow person.

But his hands were wiser than his scattered and uncertain thoughts, and turned the vaha smartly across the current so the westerly wind could drive them up to the beach.

The man did not move.

"He looks just like you did when you saw Auri and El," Fitzroy whispered glee-fully. "Quite understandable, really."

Cliopher gave him a quelling glance, and smiled at the man. He was in his early thirties, wearing a cloth sarong and with an efela of variously red and cream seeds around his neck to show that he had studied the Poyë traditions. His hair—after their own recent efforts, Cliopher could not help but notice it—was shoulder length and wavy.

He was looking back from Fitzroy to Cliopher with his mouth open.

"I didn't look *that* gobsmacked, did I?" Cliopher murmured very softly in Shaian.

"Absolutely," Fitzroy whispered back, his face almost court-serene but his eyes bright with hilarity.

The young man snapped his teeth together, his cheeks flushing, and bowed over his hands. "Tē ke'e'vina-tē zēnava parahë'ala!"

His accent sounded strange to Cliopher's ears, after so long hearing El and the crew of the *He'eanka*, or Fitzroy with his deeply variable vowels. But he almost knew the young man's name—he'd come to the city once or twice when Cliopher was home—and he had Poyë relations close enough to learn their lore—

His Uncle Haido's unexpected son by a Poyë kinswoman of Ghilly's, born after the kotua fertility festival at the sugarcane harvest. What *was* his name?

Cliopher bowed back, buying time as he frantically thought through all his cousins. "Tō mo'ea-tō avivayë o rai'ivayë."

The young man's eyes were full of hero-worship as he took in Fitzroy's dark skin and golden eyes, and Cliopher's efela—

Which included one which was named and described as belonging to Elonoa'a in the *Lays*, and which he had entirely forgotten he was wearing.

Cliopher hastily said, "I'm not Elonoa'a—I'm Cliopher—Kip Mdang—you're my uncle Haido's son, Haunui."

Haunui's eyes went even rounder. "I am—you *can't* be. That efela—"

Cliopher refused to blush for his mistake. He nodded gravely, conscious that Fitzroy was vibrating with nearly-concealed amusement beside him. "I was given it in trust, to hand to the Paramount Chief."

"Then it—it's really—" Haunui could not fathom this, and his eyes rolled back and he collapsed onto the sand in a full faint.

Cliopher and Fitzroy hastily disembarked, but Haunui hadn't hurt himself on the soft sand. While Fitzroy ensured the vaha wouldn't float away, Cliopher brought his young cousin into the shade of the sail. Haunui had apparently been collecting coconuts, for there were several green ones in a pile near where he'd been standing.

"I don't think he'll mind sharing with us," Cliopher said pragmatically, passing three to Fitzroy to open. "He can climb another tree if he needs more."

He took off Izurunayë, because *that* was a mistake he did not want to have to deal with twice. It was so good to be on land—he was able to take one of their shell knives, walk a few steps, and cut a banana leaf to shape into a pouch to contain the legendary efela.

"Oh, come on," Fitzroy said in Shaian once they had settled down with their coconuts and were waiting for Haunui to come around. "That was hilarious. I love how your cousins occasionally faint with surprise. It's most gratifying."

"I'm glad to provide you amusement," Cliopher replied sarcastically, which of course was the moment his cousin awoke. He smiled down at him and switched back to language. "Are you feeling better, Haunui?"

The young man nodded, rather too many times—he was red with embarrassment —and scrambled to a more dignified position. Cliopher offered him the open coconut, which he accepted but did not drink from.

"You're really Cousin Kip? You look ... different."

Fitzroy was looking suspiciously innocent. Cliopher refused to lift his hand self-consciously to his head. "My hair has grown out, I know," he said, smiling self-deprecatingly to set his cousin at ease.

"You *were* wearing another efela, weren't you?" Haunui said cautiously. "I might have imagined it ..."

"You didn't," Cliopher assured him. He spread the banana leaf on his lap and laid Izurunayë upon it. In the shade the impossible shells seemed to glow with the same kind of light Cliopher had seen limning Auri and El. "This is Izurunayë," he said, as his cousin gazed at it in reverent bewilderment. "I sailed to the House of the Sun, and on my way I met the *He'eanka* and her crew. Including," and he smiled at Fitzroy over his cousin's bent head, "including Elonoa'a and Aurelius Magnus."

Haunui lifted a trembling finger to stroke the tui seed at the centre of the efela, which he might well have been particularly aware of, having studied the Poyë lore. He swallowed. "You went and sailed to the House of the Sun, c-cousin Kip?"

Cliopher tried not to look too smug. "I have."

His cousin regarded him for a long, uncertain moment. "You're coming to the village?" he said abruptly, letting his hand fall away from the efela. "You'll have to sail around ... I'll run across the middle and let them know you're—you're—you're coming."

"Thank you," said Cliopher, and had not even begun to think of standing before Haunui had leaped agilely to his feet, bowed very deeply indeed over his hands, and darted off into the jungle.

Cliopher stared after him, mildly nonplussed.

Fitzroy chuckled, but when Cliopher looked at him, he only smiled brightly and said, "I hope that means we shall get a feast."

≈

"There are three villages on Loaloa," Cliopher explained as they sailed along the southwestern shore of the island. They were moving much more slowly than they had on the open ocean, but it felt faster because of the visible change in the landscape. "Dovo and Daina are close together on the eastern side, and Dako is at the southern tip—we'll pass it as we go around the point."

"Is it a rule that they all start with *d*?" Fitzroy asked curiously.

Cliopher had never noticed, and had to think about it for a moment. "I think they're named after three siblings," he said finally. "There are several stories—one that they came out of the caves in the centre of the island, and another that they were sailors on the *Ouvaya-ve*, which is—"

"Your ancestral ship."

"Yes." Cliopher should not have been surprised that Fitzroy remembered that— had he not seen over and over again how much Fitzroy knew about people? How much he cared about those in his household?—but somehow it felt different when it was *his* culture and history. "Yes," he repeated, and cleared his throat awkwardly. "Aya's family is from Dovo … inDovo is how you say it, here, the place-name. Tovo inDaina, Aya inDovo … In the old days, you didn't use your family name, though you knew it, of course."

"Important for intermarriage, I expect."

"Oh yes, one whole branch of the Walea lore-keepers is concerned with the genealogies for each island."

"A lot of memorization."

Cliopher laughed. "Yes, yes it is. Family matriarchs usually know their own lineages well enough to ensure their children don't marry too closely. I know some cultures have tribes or clans—they do in the Isolates—with rules about which ones you can marry into, but here it's connected to your island and your lineage."

"Does your vast number of Mdang relations affect that?"

"Undoubtedly." Cliopher grinned. "I'm related by blood or marriage to a full quarter of Gorjo City. The posà have their work cut out for them. Consanguinity is traced out to four removes, usually."

"I find that unfathomable," Fitzroy declared. "My family tree looks like a cordon-pruned fruit tree, whereas yours is like one of those vines that runs underground as well as overground, and pops up in all sorts of strange places."

"There's *always* another Mdang," Cliopher agreed gravely, and they laughed.

It took a couple of hours to sail around Loaloa, which was not a large island— certainly not compared with some of the high islands of the northerly part of the Ring—but was quite long. It would have been much quicker, Cliopher explained to Fitzroy, to go around the northern tip, but apart from the lack of an accessible channel on that side, the northern side of the Leaping-Place was sacred to the spirits.

They didn't see anyone as they sailed down the ocean-side length, which was to be expected—this shore bore the brunt of the salt-laden winds, and the fruit trees and vegetable plots would be on the more sheltered lagoon side of the island. The fishers and pearl-divers would have been and gone in the morning, as well.

It was a little eerie, despite knowing that, to sail along an island Cliopher knew held a thousand or twelve hundred inhabitants, and see no one.

They manoeuvred easily around the tricky currents at the southern point of the island, where a spit of basalt jutted out into the ocean; a stream coming down on its inner side formed another open channel where the water was too fresh for the coral to grow. The water in the channel was seething with a ball of baitfish, held in place by the dark shadows of sharks cutting through the clear waters to feed on them.

Fitzroy stared down in fascination. "It amazes me how little we saw on the ocean, when there's all this life here."

Cliopher cut through the silver baitfish, which split into two balls, each with its attendant black-tipped reef sharks. "The open ocean surface is like a desert," he said, concentrating on the tiller to ensure it didn't foul. "All the life is hidden from view. Reefs are where all the resources are."

"It's amazing."

"Don't put your hand in the water," Cliopher said in exasperation when he saw his friend preparing to reach down. "Those sharks will take it for a fish if you're not careful."

"Well—"

"No."

Fitzroy laughed and obediently sat up. "Spoilsport. Is that the third village? Daka?"

Cliopher looked up to where he could see a handful of bush-material houses clustered in the sheltered cove on this side of the basalt spit. "Dako, yes."

"Also quite empty," Fitzroy observed. "Oh—I take it back! There were some children playing in the shade. They've run off into the trees now. Watching for us, do you think?"

"Everyone will have gone to Daina, I expect."

"That's your village?"

Cliopher sighed with relief once they were out of the tricky spot, and angled the sail to catch as much of the onshore wind as was blowing this side. It was rather more than he'd expected, given that they'd had a westerly wind the whole day: to go around the spit and suddenly have a southeasterly wind seemed suspiciously convenient.

Fitzroy gave no indication he was doing anything, but then again he usually didn't.

"I was born in Gorjo City, which is why I say I am Cliopher Mdang of Tahivoa— that's my 'village', as far as these things go." The lagoon was wider here, and Cliopher let the vaha move further away from the land, where the wind blew more freely. "My village here is Daina because that's where my mother was born, and because I lived here with Buru Tovo when I studied with him."

"Would you be Cliopher inTahivoa, then? Or inDaina?"

"I'd probably go with inTahivoa," he replied thoughtfully, and then, more quietly, admitted, "I've never quite felt at home on Loaloa."

Fitzroy nudged him gently with his foot, just enough to show he was present. "It's most interesting to me," he declared. "How connected you are with your family and your place of origin, that is. Both your own and your family's and, of course, your people's as a whole ... I was born on Ysthar, in my father's house there ... I found the records once, when I was looking for ... something." Fitzroy sighed, watching the white beach, the coconut palms, the tangle of vegetation that Cliopher knew included well-tended fruit and other useful trees. "I do feel more *from* Zunidh, having been raised here, and of course as Lord of Zunidh, my magic was tied permanently to this world. Even when I hand over the crown and the authority to someone else, I shall still be of Zunidh."

"Will it change your magical power?" Cliopher asked.

Fitzroy gave him a sly grin. "Could be. Probably not as much as most people would expect."

Which wasn't worrying at all. Not in the least.

~

They reached the wide cove that held Dovo and Daina villages, one on each horn. There were people in Dovo, who waved when they caught sight of Cliopher and Fitzroy on the vaha.

Cliopher was feeling nervous; there were so many people. "There's only a thousand people on the island," he muttered. "*And* I'm related to most of them."

"Are you feeling a touch of stage-fright?" Fitzroy laughed, but he too was shifting his posture and accent closer to his court serenity.

Oddly, that made Cliopher feel better. "We have been a long while at sea," he reassured himself out loud.

"This is why faravia exists as a concept," Fitzroy said. "We will have a feast and give them our news. And then we can leave again until we can handle people."

"I'm very glad we came here first," Cliopher admitted, as they came closer to the beach and he could begin to identify people. There were maybe a dozen people waiting for them on the beach. Amongst their number was a very old man leaning on a stick, his elbow held by a tall woman with long black hair. For a moment he thought, hope hot in his heart, that they were Buru Tovo and Aya, but then the vaha was running up on the last waves onto the beach, and Cliopher realized both were strangers.

"You can do this," Fitzroy murmured softly. "You've been to the House of the Sun. *Own* it."

Cliopher closed his eyes, adjusting to being on the land, and then he lifted his chin, and stood up, undoubtedly more in his court face than he should be. It had been easier to face the Sea-Witch, the Grandmother, the Sun himself, than it was to look at his cousin Afu, who was chief, and who was looking very doubtful indeed.

But Afu held two leis in his hands, strings of fragrant tiarë flowers, and for just a moment Cliopher's throat closed. It had been *so long* since he had come to Loaloa, to his family here, been greeted with a lei around his neck and a flower to tuck behind his ear.

Cliopher tried to make himself say the words he had spoken so proudly to the Sea-Witch, the Grandmother, the Sun himself—the traditional words for the tanà come to an island—but he could not utter a sound.

"Is that really you, Kip?" Afu demanded. "Is what Haunui told us true?" His glance dropped to Cliopher's efela, and his expression wavered.

The efetana was unmistakable, even in the unlikely situation that his relatives here did not recall the young Kip's efforts to make his efela ko.

He had put aside the legendary efela of Elonoa'a, but his third efela, the one the Grandmother had named Kiofa'a, was also his, and his alone, with the sundrop cowrie and the two flame pearls and the hidden garnet from the Sea-Witch's island.

Cliopher felt suddenly certain of himself. He *had* been given that garnet by the

Sea-Witch; he *had* been granted that name for his efela by the Grandmother; he *had* bartered with the Sun.

"Yes," he said, "it is true."

He stepped off the vaha and handed Fitzroy down. Cliopher bowed politely to Afu and the two women wearing the chiefly efela beside him—presumably the chiefs of Dako and Dovo villages—and to the old man with the walking stick. The old man looked vaguely familiar; Cliopher was sure he'd seen him (and his efela; he wore the Kindraa efàla) before, but he was not one of his relatives. He was at least Buru Tovo's age, though wiry and spry.

"I bring you greetings," Cliopher said. "I am sorry it has been so long since last I came home to Loaloa." He smiled, and then, into the expectant silence, he said: "Tanaea-te imalo! Moa'alani-ki imalo! Kifa'ana imai?"

There was as utter and complete a silence as Cliopher could ever have hoped for, in any of dreams of this moment. And then the old, old man with the Kindraa efàla wheezed out a laugh. "And here I'd long doubted what it meant that the rising tana-tai had left, chosen the ways of the outside world, turned his back on us and our islands."

Cliopher met his eyes gravely, refusing to look down. He *had* made those choices, and he knew that no one had looked to see his sail coming from the west, along the traditional path.

And—he did not know what to say, that the old man called him *the rising tana-tai*. It sent a thrill through his veins. Cliopher was trembling from all the strangeness of this homecoming.

The old man snorted, as if despite himself, and then he hobbled forward to offer his wrinkled forehead up to Cliopher in the traditional greeting, while Afu stood there with the leis in his hands, motionless.

"Tovo always has said that you'd come back when it was time," the old man said. "I should know better than to wager against *him*."

∾

The news was too grand, too unexpected, too impossible: it was only the fact of Cliopher on a vaha coming from the west that had brought the three chiefs to meet its arrival.

But Daina was full of Cliopher's relatives, and they had mustered up a small welcome feast for him. There had not been enough time to roast a pig, but they'd started an earth oven and even the scent of cooking chicken was enough to make Cliopher seriously worry he might faint.

He was glad, really, that only a few dozen people were there at first, sitting around the bonfire on the beach. Fitzroy was very quiet, a steady, supportive presence, answering questions, asking a few of his own, mostly letting Cliopher take the lead.

Cliopher did not know what to do.

No one was quite certain of the customs, as it had been so long since anyone had come across the Wide Seas to Loaloa as their first landing, but Cliopher was the tanà, at least, and he decided in consultation with Afu that they would eat and drink and talk over local news, and afterwards Cliopher could tell the story of his travels.

"It is a long tale of the sea," he murmured, and the old Kiịndraa chief—Kuaso, Buru Tovo's friend, the former chief of Izurayë, El's own island—coughed as he laughed at his words.

"You ever going to tell us what's in that pot you've been keeping such good care of?" Kuaso asked.

Cliopher wiped his fingers in the sand beside him. He'd tried not to be greedy with the fresh fruit and cooked food and, wonder of wonders, *honeycakes*, and was able to be sparing with the liquor offered to them.

But then they had coffee.

He knew perfectly well he would regret drinking coffee after supper after so long without it, but the scent of the dark-roasted brew was unbelievably alluring.

Fitzroy was sitting next to him, the creamy tiarë flowers on his lei dramatic against his dark skin, chatting amiably with Afu. When he saw Cliopher hesitate and then accept the sturdy clay mug offered him, he grinned and said, "You were able to say *no* to the sirens, and *no* to all the temptations across Sky Ocean, and coffee is where you falter?"

"I don't see you refusing," Cliopher replied, taking a cautious sip with great dignity.

"Oh, surely that would be impolite," Fitzroy replied airily, which made everyone in earshot laugh. "But you're quite devastating enough without coffee to wake up your tongue and your wits. You didn't have coffee when you bargained with the Sun, did you?"

"No," Cliopher replied, his heart thudding—no doubt from the coffee.

(No doubt.)

"Perhaps," Afu said, "you might tell us your story, Kip. Last we heard you hadn't died."

Cliopher took in the people who had been chatting in their clusters, enjoying the meal and curious about his arrival. He looked at Fitzroy, who smiled encouragingly, his teeth gleaming in the firelight.

It was dusk; he could see fires and lights in Dovo village across the horn, where people were busy with their ordinary lives.

After so long in Sky Ocean, alone with Fitzroy on the sea, the dislocation was unnerving.

This was his island, Cliopher reminded himself. The anchor of his heart, the place he could always find. These were his relations, his people. They were ready to listen to what he told them.

He picked up the fire-pot, and he spoke forth as clearly as he could.

"East first have I gone, to the uttermost East, and then west to the sunset, and east again home. I have sailed to the House of the Sun, and bring a new flame home to our people."

They looked at him in disbelief, in amusement, in dawning curiosity, and he lifted up the fire-pot, lifting off the lid so the fragment of daylight shone like a star in his hand.

"I sing of Sky Ocean," he said, into the silence that was changing quality, that was becoming crystalline with awe. "I sing of the ship *He'eanka* and its crew, of Elonoa'a and his emperor Aurelius Magnus. I sing of the Sea-Witch of the Island That Swallowed the Sea, of the Grandmother who gathers all things in, and of the Wind That Rises At Dawn, our distant ancestor. I sing of the House of the Sun, and what I found there."

He took a deep, juddering breath, his heart racing, and knew they were listening to him at last.

CHAPTER SIXTY
THE LORE-KEEPERS

One or other of his cousins swept out Buru Tovo's house for him and Fitzroy. Cliopher appreciated the consideration, even with the arch glances they garnered when he and Fitzroy went in together with a handful of their belongings. They took Fitzroy's harp, Cliopher's fire-pot, and El's efela, and left everything else, including the mirimiri of Ani and the boxes from the Marwn's tower, safely tucked away in the hatch of the vaha, some discreet protective magic of Fitzroy's gently encouraging everyone to stay away. They would decide what to do with those items once they decided what exactly they were doing.

Fitzroy lit one of his magic lights, softer and fainter than the flame in the fire-pot, and they sat down cross-legged facing each other.

"That went well, I think," Cliopher said, anxious.

Fitzroy smiled fondly at him. "Let's talk about that tomorrow. We should probably sleep now." He regarded the room, which was very plain. "Do you think your great-uncle and Vou'a sleep here often?"

Cliopher was not able to say anything immediately, which was just as well as Fitzroy spent a happy few minutes making broader and broader innuendoes and double entendres. Cliopher listened with half an ear as he arranged their belongings to be out of the way and set out the sleeping mats.

"That's it?" Fitzroy said, when Cliopher was done.

All there was to do in Buru Tovo's house was talk and sleep (and, Cliopher supposed, make love, if one were so inclined). His great-uncle lived very simply: all his wealth was in the relationships he had with his community, their respect and his own skill.

"When I was a boy, living here," he told Fitzroy, "I never understood why Buru Tovo had so little."

Fitzroy shifted position so he could lay out his full length on the mat. "These are all beautiful," he observed, running his fingers down the subtle weave. "The mats, the hangings."

"He was—is, I suppose—poor, in the ways of the outside world. He never had money."

"I cannot imagine he ever wanted it. He could have sold a pearl or two if he did."

"Yes." Cliopher lay down, facing his friend. His fanoa. He felt bewildered by the solidity of the floor under him. The deck of the vaha had been no softer, but there had always been that give and take of the water beneath its keels. "He always told me his wealth was in his efela, in what he knew, what he taught, the fires he lit."

Fitzroy chuckled softly. "This explains many things about you, Kip."

"I suppose so." Why did he feel so disheartened? As he told his tale other people from the villages had come to hear his news, see what was the source of that bright light, learn what he had to tell them. It was what he had always wanted.

"I think," Fitzroy said, his voice very low, and yet ... certain, too, "that you have tried very hard to be of *use*, Kip. You give and give and give so that you can feel as if you are part of things, don't you?"

Cliopher swallowed, his lips wobbling. It had been a long day, and he had spoken for what must have been hours, after so long where he and Fitzroy had been able to be quiet with each other. It was hard to meet Fitzroy's eyes, but he did. He could not say anything, but he nodded, his cheek scraping against the mat.

"I have felt the same, you know," Fitzroy went on. His eyes bored into Cliopher, dark amber in the shadows cast by his light. "Felt that since I could not be myself, all I had was what I could give to the role I was expected to play. I could not ... write my songs any longer, go on adventures, be who I wanted to be. But I could be what my people wanted me to be, what they *needed* me to be."

"You are worthy in yourself," Cliopher whispered. "You don't have to write a song or go on an adventure to have a place with me."

Fitzroy smiled at him, his eyes gleaming gold as he shifted his head. "Neither do you, Kip. Your family, your friends, your people, they respect the wealth you have given them, because how could they not? But they welcomed you home because you belong to them."

"They didn't believe Haunui, that's for certain," Cliopher muttered.

"No," Fitzroy agreed. "But your cousin Afu was waiting with the leis even so."

∿

He couldn't sleep.

Fitzroy seemed to have no difficulties, but Cliopher lay awake, anxious, alert.

He could hear too many insects in the thatch, and the sound of the palms overhead was unnerving instead of soothing when he could not feel the wind that stirred them. He could not hear the sound of the waves, not over the rustle of leaves and Fitzroy's breathing. He could not see the stars or the glimmering phosphorescent wake of the vaha in the sea.

It was too much to take. He was full of the jittery energy of the coffee—the months without any had clearly had an effect; there had certainly been a time when a single cup would have had no appreciable effect whatsoever—and the newness of being here, this home that had never quite been his, with Fitzroy.

He moved as quietly as he could, rolling off the mat and crawling to the low door. The house was built in the old Western Ring style, and consisted of a single room on a platform raised six or so feet off the ground on stilts. Buru Tovo did not keep pigs; he had stacks of firewood curing under his house, and some miscellaneous rocks and pottery shards.

Cliopher pushed aside the tapa cloth curtaining the entry and sat for a few moments on the platform, feet curled around the bars of the ladder. He wasn't wearing sandals, and it felt odd to think he would have to go back to such things.

For a moment he didn't dare look down, in case the house had turned into the sea-witch's, and instead of stilts had white seabird's feet. But of course it was Buru Tovo's old house, familiar in its position at the edge of the village, nearest the sea.

It was a beautiful night, the stars above burning brilliantly, the low embers of the bonfire a rich red-gold. A few insects buzzed around curiously, but did not bite. Cliopher sat there, breathing in the night. Now the wind in the palms was comforting instead of eerie.

A dark shadow moved in front of the bonfire. Someone else was awake. Cliopher sat there for a moment longer, then slid down the ladder to the ground. Suddenly he was overcome with the desire to be in company, to speak to someone who was not Fitzroy.

It was Afu. He'd put another log on the fire: new yellow-orange flames were licking at it when Cliopher reached him.

The bonfire had been built on the beach, where the entire population of the three villages had been able to gather to hear the story. Fitzroy had quietly done some small magic that enabled Cliopher's voice to be heard clearly by each and every one of them, so although his voice grew hoarse after so much speaking, he had not had to shout or strain.

Afu was sitting where he had been for the feast and the tale, though he'd acquired a woven robe to throw over his shoulders. The wind was cool, coming off the ocean and over the island to sweep out into the Bay.

Cliopher sat down quietly a few feet away. Close enough to have a conversation; far enough not to require one. The sand was still a little warm from the sun on the surface, cool underneath. It all felt very fresh and pleasant after the stuffy enclosed sleeping chamber.

They sat together quietly for a while, long enough for Cliopher to decide he could add another log to the fire. He did so, taking a branch from the pile off to the side. When he sat down again, Afu said, "That was quite the story, Kip."

"Thank you for listening."

Afu laughed quietly, in the back of his throat. "You've never let people ignore you."

Cliopher thought of all those years in the Palace, slowly forcing the powers to take him seriously, to listen when he spoke, to learn that he—hinterland tribesman as they thought him—that he was worthy of attention, of being heard, of being taken seriously, of being *listened to*. "Not always to my credit," he murmured.

"I remember you saying once that you would sail to the House of the Sun," Afu said. "It was before you left ... I must have been ten, eleven. You would have been—eighteen? Nineteen?"

"Something like that."

"You were so serious." Afu laughed again, softly. His eyes had a liquid sheen in the firelight. "I thought it was great. This idea that you could just *decide* to be great, to walk in legends, to enter the *Lays* ..." He was silent for a moment, drawing his robe over his shoulders. "Then you left, and you stayed away, and gradually you changed, and we came to think you had forgotten those dreams. I was so disappointed. I really looked up to you, Kip. How you sat at Buru Tovo's feet and studied with him, how you went to the city and studied there too, how you were bringing the two parts together."

Cliopher did not know what to say, but he felt the need to say something. "I'm sorry for disappointing you."

Afu snorted and then made a strange snuffling noise into his hands. "When we heard about the viceroyship—after the ceremony—I was sorry I didn't come to the city for it. You'd sent me an invitation."

Cliopher had told Gaudy to send invitations to all the chiefs and lore-keepers around the Ring, knowing few of them would come for a palace function but also refusing not to acknowledge their status. "I learned, rather too late, that Princess Oriana had not been disseminating proclamations and news from Solaara, as she was supposed to. I had misunderstood why no one here seemed to be interested."

"It's certainly been very different since Jiano became Paramount Chief," Afu agreed. "And now you've come back having achieved everything you ever set out to do ..." He grinned at Cliopher, the firelight picking out the creases at the corners of his eyes and his sly amusement. "Except for marrying Jullanar of the Sea."

"Yes, alas, he's just got me," Fitzroy said, and made both of them jump. "My apologies, Kip, Chief Afu." He sat down with a quiet grunt, but there was a sense of almost manic energy thrumming in his body.

"Did you have too much coffee, too?" Cliopher asked sympathetically. (It was a good excuse, the coffee. Their earlier conversation wavered in his memory, like a bubble caught in his hands, too delicate to be examined.) "Between that and all our time at sea ... I couldn't handle sleeping inside."

"I am becoming more and more appreciative of the concept of faravia," Fitzroy declared, stretching out his legs so his toes were nearly in the fire. Magic kept him safe, presumably.

"Sail-mending?" Afu asked, his brow furrowing.

"No, it's a metaphor for ... adjusting back into the community."

"Ah, yes, yes. That makes much more sense than the literal meaning. I had always wondered why they had such poor sails."

"Hadn't we all," Cliopher murmured.

"Do you want to stay here, on Loaloa, for your faravia? You'd be very welcome. You have the tanà's house, of course, and that part of the reef ... Leina has been tending that land, which she does happily, don't worry, but she's gone to the Tirigilis for a visit. If you stayed longer than she's away, well, you *are* the tanà."

Cliopher had never—*never*—thought it would be so simple.

Fitzroy put his hand on his knee. Cliopher looked at him; his fanoa smiled, the crooked small smile of sympathetic amusement, and then Fitzroy leaned to Afu. "We were intending to continue on to the city first. Cliopher wishes to give his news to his Buru Tovo as soon as possible."

"Of course," Afu said.

Cliopher was surprised to hear the honest disappointment in his cousin's voice, and his heart clenched. "Thank you for your welcome," he said, suddenly uncertain.

"You're always welcome here, Kip," Afu said, sounding very chiefly and also very much Cliopher's younger cousin whom he'd played with and told stories to. "We honour the tanà and the tana-tai." He cleared his throat, and went on in a less professional tone. "When do you plan to continue to the city?"

"We should probably stay," Cliopher said. "We've just got here, after all, and ... I've been away so long, I don't want to disappoint anyone."

Fitzroy looked at him, and then at their vaha drawn up just down the beach, and back at Cliopher. "I'm not exactly wise in the ways of family obligations," Fitzroy said, in one of those neutral tones that always made Cliopher furiously angry at those who had raised him with such lovelessness and lack. "Whatever you think is best."

Cliopher did not want to stay. He vacillated, busying himself with adding another stick to the fire, stirring the coals so they would not go out too soon.

Afu regarded him with a frown, visibly thinking. "Don't stay because people didn't come to listen right away. That's their problem, not yours. I'll tell them so— you told me the news, and the other chiefs. *You've* fulfilled all your responsibilities. And you'll walk the Ring soon enough, won't you, Kip? When you're ready."

Cliopher swallowed again. "Yes. After the Greater Singing of the Waters."

Afu nodded: the chief, secure in his role, his status, his place. "Exactly."

The wind was fresh, soft in his face; the bonfire flickering. Cliopher turned to Fitzroy, who was sitting with his face serene, attentive.

The tanà was not the chief or the paramount chief, but when he spoke, the chiefs listened. So said the old tradition. Cliopher felt like laughing hysterically. Why was it so hard to follow his own heart's desire?

("You can wish for what *you* want," Rhodin had told him—it felt so long ago now.)

"Perhaps we should go now," Cliopher said, with the same sense of terror and abandon as when he had dived into that black seep of water in the depths of the mountain. He sought a reason; came up with an excuse. "There will be *so* many questions tomorrow ..."

Afu laughed abruptly. "Yes, best run off now if you want to leave any time soon. I'll let everyone know why."

"Thank you," Fitzroy said, almost regally, and as they stood up, his hand grazed Cliopher's shoulder as if to say *well done.*

"Have you enough supplies?" Afu asked.

"We took Haunui's coconuts when he ran off to tell you we were coming," Cliopher said, "and we had everything else we needed."

"I'll get our things," Fitzroy said, and dashed quickly back into Buru Tovo's house for the fire-pot, the efela from Elonoa'a, and his harp.

Cliopher turned to his cousin. "Thank you again, Afu."

Afu embraced him swiftly, and then stood back, his robes slipping off his shoulders as he bowed. "Fair winds and gentle seas, Kip."

"And wisdom in your heart and your tongue, Afu," Cliopher replied, the words those he had heard Buru Tovo use when leaving a village. "I'll not wait so long before I come back, I promise you."

"And next time you invite me to something, I'll come," Afu retorted. "I'll help push you off."

Fitzroy jumped on board, and after stowing his harp and the fire-pot, positioned himself to manage the sail and tiller, and the two cousins put their shoulders to the keels to set the vaha afloat. Cliopher grabbed his fanoa's outstretched hand to jump up, and waved once to Afu, a dark figure on the grey sand, the gorgeous red coals of the bonfire blocking any hope of seeing the village.

Fitzroy managed the line expertly, and the westerly wind coming off the ocean, over Loaloa, caught the sail and sent the vaha skimming, light as a bird, across the Bay of the Waters.

For a moment Cliopher, looking up from his island, thought he saw the silver-glinting wings of the wind, and he caught his breath.

But then they were sailing swiftly, away from the dark island and the red eye of the fire, and the stars were brilliant. The moon was low in the west. Cliopher looked up, to see Furai'fa directly above them.

"The ke'e," Fitzroy murmured, and then pointed at a star at the edge of the Wake, just to their south. It had a noticeably golden hue to it. "What star is that, Kip, do you know?"

"No, I don't." It wasn't part of any of the constellations he knew, nor was it one of the Sixteen Bright Guides. He frowned at it. "I feel as if I *should*, but I don't think I've ever noticed it before."

Fitzroy smiled. "I'll see if I can find a book—there will be *books* soon, O happy thought!—Or no, I should find a Nga lore-holder, shouldn't I?"

Cliopher grinned at him. "Depends if you want the Shaian name or the Islander one."

"The Nga lore-holders are the vanà, am I right? Or no, there's also the rukà ..."

"The vanà and the rukà both Name the Stars," Cliopher explained, and minutely adjusted the tiller as Tina'a came over the horizon. That was a star he knew well. "The rukà are the trained navigators, whereas the vanà hold more of the legends and stories of the sky, and the ways of leadership."

"So I probably want a vanà, then." Fitzroy nodded, satisfied. "Is that star the ke'e for an island, I wonder?"

Cliopher glanced at the star, judging its relative altitude to stars he did know. "I think it's a bit too far south for the Ring proper. We can go explore one day, if you'd like."

"What a thought," Fitzroy murmured, holding himself very still for a moment. Cliopher settled himself down on the deck, facing where his friend (his fanoa) leaned against the mast. "The idea," he went on, "that we could do something because we *wanted* to."

"It is a strange thought."

"Heady, even. The world is *full* of invitations, ideas, possibilities—"

Cliopher laughed. "That's probably the coffee."

~

The ke'ea from Loaloa to Gorjo City was so familiar Cliopher hardly needed to think about any of it. He taught Fitzroy the chant he'd learned as a boy, showing him the stars as they rose, the reefs as they came to them. Fitzroy learned the names and pattern swiftly, and on the second night was proud to take the late watch.

He woke Cliopher as the first light was stealing across the sky.

"Look," Fitzroy said softly.

Cliopher looked. First at Fitzroy, whose face was soft and full of wonder, his eyes brilliant with gold though his hands were full of the thread of starlight and shadow he'd been spinning while Cliopher slept.

Then up, at the east, where the sun was a brilliant, blinding spot on the horizon, visible from this approach down the narrow gap of the Gates of the Sea.

"We passed the reef in the middle of the night," Fitzroy said gleefully, pointing back to the east. "It was all lit with some sort of phosphorescent bloom ... I nearly woke you, but the wind was stiff and we were gone too quickly."

Doyano was a deep reef, rising no more than ten or twelve feet below the surface, and broad rather than narrow. That made it a good marker for anyone crossing this portion of the Bay of the Waters, but one did not sail *along* it very far.

"But look! The sun in the pass! I'm right on the ke'ea, Kip!"

"You are," Cliopher said, smiling. "Well done."

"I am appreciating your casual competence at wayfinding even more."

When Cliopher had sailed the route in the past—several times a year, all through his teens and into his university years—he would leave Loaloa at sunset and arrive in Tahivoa in the late morning of the second day.

His thoughts halted on what Fitzroy had said. "What do you mean, we passed the reef in the night? We left *later* than usual—we shouldn't be coming onto it until midday."

Fitzroy lifted his hands to fiddle with the red scarf he'd wrapped around his hair again, and mumbled something incomprehensible.

"I beg your pardon?"

"I was maybe a bit excited at the idea of a real bath and called up a wind in the night," Fitzroy said in a rush.

Cliopher stared at him.

"Look," Fitzroy said, "I've had *one* hot bath since we left Basil's inn. Washing with a bucket of water in your ancestral village was fine, I guess, but it's not—it's not the same. You know what I mean, don't you? Conju is going to *despair* over my skin. It's peeling, Kip."

"Where?" Cliopher asked, somewhat helplessly. Fitzroy extended his hand dramatically, pointing at the well-defined curve of his left bicep, where there was a handful of very small spots of faintly white-edged new skin. "Ah," he said, trying to sound sympathetic. "My condolences."

Fitzroy sniffed. "I know you don't care so much for appearances as I do ..." He suddenly stopped speaking and frowned. "Speaking of, Cliopher, I wanted to ask you about our arrival in Gorjo City."

"We'll go find Uncle Lazo—Buru Tovo should be there, too."

Fitzroy gazed at him expectantly.

"What?"

"You can do better than that." Fitzroy sat down crosslegged, in an attitude of intense instruction. "Cliopher. Cliopher Mdang. *Kip.* What is my area of expertise?"

Cliopher raised his eyebrows, then settled himself in the mirror posture of attentive listening, though he couldn't stop himself from smirking slightly at the idea. "High drama."

Fitzroy nodded judiciously. "Exactly." He waited expectantly.

"I don't think my story needs any more drama than it already has, Fitzroy."

"Kip! Honestly, this is why Ylette and I had to dress you. I let you take the lead on Loaloa, and what did you do?"

Cliopher folded his arms. Fitzroy *was* dramatic, that was the problem. He said, patiently, "I told the story."

"Kip. You downplayed yourself so successfully that Haunui would have *believed* you hadn't done anything out of the ordinary if you hadn't had El's legendary efela visible on your lap the whole time! You tried to change the subject and ask about him and his family *twice*! And then when we got to Daino village, you didn't explain you'd sailed Sky Ocean *to the House of the Sun* for a full hour. An *hour.*"

"And what would you have me do?" Cliopher asked, meaning it sarcastically, but it came out plaintive. "You say I should be myself, and then when I *am* myself you say I'm doing it wrong!"

Fitzroy sighed explosively. "That's not what I mean, and you know it. You're not boring, Kip! Why do you *insist* on acting as if you are? I know you know how to claim yourself and your culture and your own deeds—I've seen you bring the entire court of the Palace of Stars to its knees."

Cliopher opened his mouth to retort, and then stopped.

"Kip," Fitzroy said in a softer voice, "listen to me. You are coming home in triumph, having stepped into legend. Am I right?"

He waited, eyebrow raised in the familiar challenge. "Yes," Cliopher replied hoarsely.

"And, forgive me: you've complained that your family, your people, your friends here, that they don't take you seriously, that they don't *appreciate* the great things you've done."

"Yes," he said, in an even smaller voice, wishing he could sink down. "I have."

"Do you not want them to appreciate that you've sailed to the House of the Sun on behalf of Elonoa'a and Aurelius Magnus? That you have come back with the actual mirimiri of Ani? That you won guest-right to the House of the Sun for your *entire extended family* including the Son of Laughter? That you bring home the name of the third son of Vonou'a, which he traded for *fire*?"

Cliopher stared at him. "Fitzroy ..."

"No, Kip," Fitzroy said firmly. "I let you take the lead on Loaloa, to see what you would do, and it was ... well, it was *acceptable*, I'll grant you that. I can't speak as to whether it was worthy of the *Lays*. But you made it sound as if it were too boring for me to write a song about, and I was *there*." Cliopher opened his mouth, to say quite what he was not sure, but his fanoa continued on, his voice intense, his eyes brilliant. "Cliopher, trust me. *You* are worthy, and you *deserve* to be seen for the brilliant man you are. Your people are waiting for you to step up and take your place. It's time."

Cliopher licked his lips, which were suddenly dry, and could not form words. Had he not had this very thought himself? Had he not, seeing Aioru step forward to claim the chancellorship, thought that his people were waiting for him to claim himself?

Fitzroy smiled at him, a little sadly, and leaned forward to take his hands. "Kip, let me help you. I'm your fanoa, am I not? Your mirror and your match, your equal? The other keel of your vaha, your other hand, the other half of the shell?"

He nodded. His fingers felt cold in Fitzroy's; the two of them were a little too far apart for comfort, and he could feel the strain in his shoulders and back as he leaned forward to keep contact.

"Well then," Fitzroy said. "You don't need to be something other than you are, Kip. You just need to be *fully* yourself." His voice went soft. "Both halves, Kip. The carefully contained embers and the blazing fire."

The two chambers of his heart, which he'd promised to himself he would not let go.

"I made that dive between them," he said. "In the dark mountain."

"And you can do it here." Fitzroy said, releasing him. "You know I'm right."

Cliopher smiled, a little reluctantly. "You are."

"Precisely." Fitzroy tossed his head, obviously relishing the way his hair bounced at the gesture. "Now, let's get down to specifics. Your diction and oratorical control are splendid, of course, but it's a matter of posture and presence, no? You don't want to be the Hands of the Emperor here. You want to be the man who stood at the feet of the Sun and took him to the cleaners. No, don't laugh, you know it's true. Do you think that people all fell silent when I first started to play? Of course not! They had seen a thousand would-be minstrels. But I wasn't a minstrel—I was a bard, like the bards of old, and I taught them to listen. And *you*, my dear Kip, have walked with the gods and the heroes of myth. I don't believe *they* pussy-footed into declaring their deeds. What do the *Lays* say?"

Cliopher closed his mouth, which was gaping foolishly—for this was Fitzroy Angursell in his full flowering, his fanoa, his Radiancy, and he was soliciting the pattern in the *Lays*—Cliopher found himself answering automatically, rising to this challenge, describing the pattern of Vonou'a returning from his quest, and his third son (Samayo Atēatamai) returning from his, and Mau'a who had gone to trade with Tion (whom Cliopher had *met*), and Elonoa'a after his voyages to Colhélhé, and Eranui coming back from her dream-vision, and—

And all these patterns that he had chosen to follow into the adventures—

He could follow them home, too.

～

They sailed into the city in the late morning. Fitzroy had offered options for the most dramatic moment to arrive—"We used to hide so we could arrive at the best moment, the Red Company, that is," he explained, laughing. "It used to drive Damian mad. Never one for drama, Damian."—but Cliopher could not bear to wait.

Fitzroy spent some time ensuring Cliopher's hair looked its best. "I've never done this much with my hair before," he said.

"Your hair has always been very boring before," Fitzroy returned. "Hold still. There—that's better." Fitzroy ran his hand over Cliopher's head, some sort of tingling, ticklish magic running behind him.

"What are you doing?"

"Making sure it doesn't get blown around in an unbecoming fashion. Now. What are you wearing?"

Cliopher laughed. "What, you're not going to choose for me?"

"I was trying to give you agency," Fitzroy said with great dignity. "This is an important moment for me, too, you know. Watching you come into your own. Not being the centre of attention for once."

His tone and face were light, but Cliopher could feel a weight behind his words. He smiled wryly, hoping Fitzroy could see that he saw his vulnerability, the truth of this gift of stepping back—oh, all the emotions Cliopher himself did not know quite how to express. "What," he said, and had to clear his throat. "What do you think I should wear?"

"Oh, the traditional option, certainly. The grass skirt you made on the island. Which you're conveniently already wearing."

"They used to mock me for being too traditional," Cliopher muttered, but he brushed out the skirt. "You can wear the clothes from the House of the Sun, then."

"You cannot possibly have been more traditional than your Buru Tovo."

"He's your Buru Tovo, too," Cliopher said, as he reached into the hatch and regarded the items there. The fire-pot of daylight set into a nest of woven shadows; the basket containing the mirimiri of Ani; the efela of Elonoa'a in its simple packet; the boxes from the Marwn's tower with her bones and her life's work.

Cliopher needed to live up to them, didn't he? He took a breath, and lifted out the shining cloud-soft garments from the hatch. He handed them to Fitzroy. "It's not really a familial title ... and even if it were you're—you'd still be allowed."

Fitzroy tugged the tunic over his head and looked down as he adjusted its hang. It seemed to fit him perfectly (as it had also fit Cliopher perfectly; but then it had come from the hands of a deity), and he looked even more like the Sun than he ever had in his full robes of office. The white was so brilliant it seemed to be shining like a cloud with the sun behind it. His hair looked magnificent: the coils formed by the twists gleamed in the sunlight, smooth and sleek, the black coal-dark, the grey threads a true shining silver. Cliopher could only hope, wistfully, that his hair looked half as healthy.

They came to the first of the pilings marking the channel that led past the barrier reef to the city proper, and Cliopher caught his breath at the sight of the cormorants clustered on its rocky top. For a moment he was cast back to his arrival on the sea-witch's island, the Island That Swallowed the Sea, and the stares and mutters of the white-masked boobies on its islets.

But he had lifted his chin and crossed the garnets and fanoa garlanding her shores, guarding her island, and armed with his knowledge of the *Lays* and the stories of his grandmother and his own long learning and practice in government and court and as tanà, he had succeeded.

"There you are," Fitzroy said, and canted the vaha swiftly into the channel that led to Tahivoa lagoon.

Past the familiar buildings—past a handful of familiar faces, along with strangers who pointed at their antique vaha, the strange legendariness of who they were to the outer eye, the black-skinned Shaian mage, the Islander with feathers in his hair—

Cliopher's heart was thudding in his chest, very loud but very steady, steady as the swells that had carried them from the uttermost East to the uttermost West, where Sky Ocean fell down into sunset sky, and eastward home again.

Fitzroy let him bring the vaha into the berth at the floating dock in front of Uncle Lazo's shop, beside another canoe.

"I've seen that vaha before," Fitzroy said quietly as Cliopher tied up theirs. "Not long ago."

Cliopher glanced across at the other canoe, and it seemed as if a shadow passed from across his eyes; now he could see the patterns carved into its prow looked like clouds or shadows or islands. Vou'a's, then, hidden until he knew what it might be.

He shivered. So had it always been with Vou'a, whom he had met time and again but never recognized until that fire on the side of the dark island.

They climbed up the stair-ladder onto the boardwalk, and discovered that Fitzroy's wild magic or Vou'a's love of the dramatic moment had been at work, for not only Jiano but also what looked like every principal lore-keeper were gathered outside of Uncle Lazo's shop, taking in small clusters as if a meeting were just breaking up.

Only Vou'a saw them. The Son of Laughter was seated where the elders often played dominoes, under the canopy outside the shop, and Cliopher, meeting his gaze, was reminded of all the times he had met Buru Tovo's friend—whom he had eventually realized was his great-uncle's boyfriend—and now knew to be his husband.

Now that he knew it was Vou'a, he could see the Son of Laughter's efela. The efanoa of driftwood and small white shells, and the efelēla of an extravagant number of pearls, and the third, the efela of shark teeth and curved silver-black claws, whose story he had never heard.

Fitzroy stood beside him, silent, all his exhortations made. Cliopher wished he had a ngali staff to strike down, to announce himself, to require response—but they were rare as a caught viau, and he had only ever seen one in his life.

Well. He had still never caught a viau, but he had achieved greater things. Cliopher took a deep breath, set himself for rhetorical battle, and looked in proud challenge at the god of mysteries.

"Well, well, well," the Son of Laughter said, his voice cutting through the chattering lore-keepers. One by one they turned to look at Cliopher and Fitzroy; one by one they fell into a thrumming, expectant silence.

The god waited until the very air seemed to shimmer and sing with intensity, and then he grinned and spoke. His voice slammed through the silence like lightning.

"Who is this that comes out of the sunrise?"

CHAPTER SIXTY-ONE
THE PATTERN

And there it was, the pattern in the *Lays*: what someone had said to Vonou'a, to Samayo Atēatamai when he came home without a name, to Mau'a, to Elonoa'a, to Eranui—to Cliopher Mdang.

He drew on every ounce of experience he had to make certain his voice rang out with all the clarity of the sunlight in his hands.

"I am Cliopher Mdang of Tahivoa," he said. "My island is Loaloa, and my dances are Aōteketētana. I come with my friend beside me, the last emperor of those who came from across the sea, who has sailed far with me."

Beside him, Fitzroy nodded once, magisterial, and was serene.

"Your great-nephew is so old-fashioned, Tovo!" one of the elders said, and many of them laughed.

In the past that would have been enough for Cliopher to step back, tone it down, pretend he was not serious. When he was young—when he had last been called *old-fashioned*—he had not been able to express what the *Lays* meant to him any other way. Even though he'd been sure that the pattern was there, that the truth was there —that even he could be great, despite growing up in the shadow of Astandalas, the backwater tribesman at the fringes of a great empire, from a people who no longer considered themselves great.

He had taken himself to Astandalas, and to Solaara, and he lived the truth of that belief. He had lived the *Lays* as best he could, wrought a better world out of their lessons, sailed all the way to the House of the Sun and back following them.

The elders were still laughing. Vou'a's eyes were glittering with amusement. And Buru Tovo was grinning, but he was looking straight at Cliopher, and his eyes were proud and certain.

Cliopher took a breath, but he had answered the first call of the challenge, and he would wait until the second question was asked.

Vou'a did not speak; Buru Tovo did not speak; but one of the lore-keepers, voice full of laughter, not quite mocking, not quite welcoming, said, "Well then, Cliopher Mdang, in what boat have you sailed?"

Was this all it took? All it would ever have taken? Had all he had to do was *not* step back, *not* tone it down, *not* pretend this wasn't serious?

(The thought came to him that of course that was it: he had known that through all his time in Solaara, where he persisted against all obstacles and obstreperousness because he had chosen his destination and his ke'ea and the only way to arrive was to follow it. And was this not what the Other Kip in that other place had done? Had he not refused to let them laugh him to scorn or smallness? That other Kip had wrested greatness out of what he'd had to work with, and so too would Cliopher.)

He spoke clearly, his voice ringing through their laughter and stirring disbelief.

"I sailed in a boat made by my hands and those of the Ancestors. The hand of Tupaia and Elonoa'a is upon my vaha, and the hand of the emperor Aurelius called Magnus and my own emperor here beside me. My own hand is upon it, and the hands of those who crewed the *He'eanka* into Sky Ocean."

They fell silent.

His heart was thundering, his ears roaring. The sun was so bright in his hand, in his eyes, in the air that shimmered and shivered with the moment like the spray and fume around the waves that broke upon the edges of the sky.

Oh, what a song this would be, when they placed this into the *Lays*, when it was sung by all the people, when Cliopher's own distant descendants learned of this.

The story that would be told in the *Lays* was how the Son of Laughter challenged Cliopher Mdang, and Cliopher Mdang *won*.

Vou'a leaned forward, the third of the great questions upon his lips. "Where have you sailed, Cliopher Mdang of Tahivoa?"

Cliopher had spent so many hours of his youth dreaming of this moment, imagining the question, the challenge, the answer that he would return forth.

Fitzroy was right, he had to be as magnificent as he had ever wanted to be, ever imagined he *could* be. He owed it to the young Kip Mdang, running around with Basil pretending to be Aurelius and Elonoa'a, the three sons of Vonou'a, any of their ancestors.

He owed it to all the children who were still doing the same.

He owed it to *himself*.

His heart swelled with pride, with joy, with the incontestable triumph of this moment. He had done this—*he* had, and shown all his people that it was not too late to enter into legend. To be great. To be the Ke'e Lulai, equals to anyone.

He set himself as for any moment of declamation in the court, before the Council of Princes, before all the great lords of the world. He was Cliopher Mdang of Tahivoa, and he was the equal to any of the elders and lore-keepers gathered here before him. Vou'a had brought them together, but they stayed to hear Cliopher.

"I have sailed in the boat my ancestors made for me across Sky Ocean, from an island that is a star where the *He'eanka* rested all the way to the House of the Sun—to the uttermost East and back again to the uttermost West, from the dawn unto the very sunset, and I have brought home a new fire to the hearth of the world."

Someone hissed, sharp with astonishment.

Doubt, too, probably. Cliopher knew that with part of his mind, the part that said he *must* present himself as he wanted to be seen, the part that Fitzroy had so thoroughly diagnosed. He knew that the elders were reserving judgment. They all knew how much he had *wanted* this, how he had claimed as a boy, as a youth, as a young man that he would go to the House of the Sun and bring back fire; how, during the Viceroy ceremonies, he had said he had achieved that metaphorically.

This was no metaphor, and he was the one who had done this.

As they always had, the *Lays* showed him the way. He was so grateful—so immensely, unbelievably grateful—that his ancestors had understood just how hard it could be to claim yourself and your deeds, and had provided this model.

"One for a token, a promise once made and now kept," said Vou'a, his face full of laughter, he the Son of Laughter. "Is there a second, Cliopher Mdang of Tahivoa, for a promise?"

And now the elders were silent, still, intent, watching sharp as a spear-fisher for the fish to come into range. They had heard, but did not yet believe. Even the fire-pot of day in his hands was not enough, was it?

But Cliopher was no longer mired in the doubt and confusion of *not being enough*. He had Fitzroy beside him, his fanoa, the other half of his heart: the sun of his life, the rock that held fast, upon which the world turned.

Cliopher had to answer in a way befitting the *Lays*, the song Fitzroy Angursell would write of this moment, the exemplar of what the Islanders were and could be, here and now in this moment of the history of the world.

It was a negotiation, wasn't it? For his own reputation and legacy, admittedly, but Cliopher knew what he wanted to achieve—thanks to Fitzroy's questions he had articulated it—and he knew how to get there.

"I bring a flame of the Sun, given to me by the Ancestors for whom I sailed to fetch it," Cliopher declared. "From the House of the Sun do I also bring knowledge that was lost, that name of the third son of Vonou'a, the third son of Samayë, who traded his name for the first fire of all, and greetings from our foremother, the Wind That Rises At Dawn."

Vou'a's eyes were glittering. But it was Buru Tovo who spoke next, who asked the question: "What tokens do you show us?"

What proof are you offering?

Cliopher knew his great-uncle, could see the pride in his eyes; and he remembered Kuaso of Izurayë's words that *Tovo always said you would come home when it was time.*

Buru Tovo had never let that ember go out, and Cliopher was ready to show him that he was ready to fan it to a flame.

He lifted the fire-pot, and with a slow, ceremonious gesture, one of the ones he had learned at the court of the Palace of Stars, he opened the lid so the daylight shone out, a star held cupped in his hands.

"I show you a flame of the fire of the Sun," he said, his voice falling with the solidity and certainty of his feet in the steps of the fire dance. "I sailed to the Uttermost East on behalf of Elonoa'a and Aurelius Magnus, for they needed a new star for the prow of the *He'eanka* and they had been once already to the House of the Sun, and could not go again. I brought them the fire, and they gave me a flame of it, for as our lore has long held, a fire shared is a fire that will not go out."

Buru Tovo closed his eyes, just for a moment, and the tears running down his creased and wrinkled face caught the sunlight like molten gold.

Now Cliopher looked around the gathered elders, the lore-keepers, the paramount chief and the god of mysteries. He touched the feathers in his hair.

"I wear feathers given me from the hand of the Wind That Rises At Dawn, Sama who was called Samayë when she took human form to wed the son of Ani, Vonou'a who first took sail."

"And what do those feathers betoken?" the Kindraa lore-keeper said, her eyes full of baffled wonder; the Kindraa Named the Winds.

Cliopher met her eyes steadily, his heart steady now, steady as the vaha in that westward wind that had carried them to the sunset, the Song of the Breaking Waves, home. "Five feathers," he said, touching them, "taken from the wings of the Wind That Rises At Dawn, one for herself and each of her children who were our ancestors." He touched them one by one: soft peach and dove-grey, lavender and silver, tenderest rose. "Sama herself; her daughter Anyë, the first weaver; Aho who sailed to find new islands; Pokuli who sought his heart's desire; and Samayo Ateatamai, who traded his name for the first fire."

Silence.

"That is a name that was long since lost," said Vou'a, the god of mysteries.

"It is not the only thing that was lost that I regained from the House of the Sun," Cliopher replied simply.

No one spoke: the elders watched with their expressions closed, intent, curious, intrigued. Listening.

They would listen, for he had been challenged and was challenging in return.

"One for a token, and two for a promise," said Vou'a, his face intent now, knowing what he had asked of Cliopher—perhaps there was the merest hint of hope there, that Cliopher had in fact been able to make progress on the ancient negotiations of Vou'a to recover the mirimiri of Ani. Just wait, thought Cliopher, far beyond doubt, beyond fear, beyond anxiety. Just you *wait*.

Buru Tovo said, "And is there a third?"

Cliopher stepped forward into this opening, this challenge, as he had done before the sea-witch, the Grandmother, the Sun himself.

"One for a token, and two for a promise, but five make an efela of name," he declared, nodding at Mardo Walea, who stood beside his grandfather, the efa-tai. "First: a flame of the Sun for my people, a new fire for the hearth of the world."

Cliopher looked around the elders, his bearing as proud, as confident, as true to himself as he could be. "Second, the name of Samayo Ateatamai, to be sung in the *Lays* as we have always sung his deeds and honoured his memory."

The Kindraa lore-keeper nodded, her eyes lingering on the feathers in Cliopher's hair. Cliopher took a breath.

"Third, a secret for my lord, which is not mine to share."

Fitzroy nodded again, imperious, mysterious, in magnificent display. Cliopher handed him the fire-pot, which garbed him in radiance like the radiance that had clothed his ancestor the Sun, and took instead the banana-leaf envelope.

"Fourth," he said, taking a deep breath. "Fourth, I bring news from the *Lays* of our ancestors: of Elonoa'a and the crew of the *He'eanka*, of the ship we call the comet;

of the fanoa of Elonoa'a, the emperor Aurelius Magnus, whom he rescued from the House of the Sun. For them did I sail across Sky Ocean, and much news do I bring home, stories and songs and changes to the *Lays*. The sea-witch of the Island That Swallowed the Sea did I meet, and Nua-Nui who guides us well. The god of mysteries did I meet upon an island of mystery," he said, smiling at Vou'a, who grinned back, unrepentant, "and much did I learn within the House of the Sun."

There was a stir then, but no one spoke: no one, he thought, thrilled with the thought, no one *dared* speak.

"And as token of that journey, of the truth of my account, I bring also a gift for the first Paramount Chief since the Fall of the Empire, from the last Paramount Chief before the coming of the Empire from across the sea."

He opened the banana-leaf envelope and displayed the legendary efela, which shone in the sunlight. He could see that several recognized it immediately; Mardo Walea was silently mouthing the pattern of the shells. He turned to Jiano, whose bearing was full of shock, the tears standing in his eyes, shining in his face, and held out the efela. Jiano's hands were shaking violently as he stepped forward, expression beseeching.

Cliopher smiled at him, knowing just that terror and awe, that sense of holiness met unexpectedly in the light of day. He took a step forward so he met Jiano coming towards him, and tucked the younger man's hands safely around the efela. "Thus do I show you Izurunayë, the efela of Elonoa'a, and hand it over to our new paramount chief, that Jiano of Lesuia might add his own deeds to its tale."

A moment of silence, of weight, as Jiano looked speechless at the efela in his hands.

Cliopher judged the moment, the oratorical rhythm, the story that would enter into the *Lays*.

"And fifth?" said Vou'a, regarding him with an intensity that might have made him quail, the other side of his journey.

"And fifth," Cliopher said, turning to the god, grateful beyond measure that Fitzroy stood there behind him, the rock that held fast, the sun and stars of the ke'ea Cliopher had always followed, his friend, his fanoa, his beloved, his own.

"Fifth," Cliopher said again, "I bring guest-right to the House of the Sun for any of my family who should ever reach it, including most explicitly my great-uncle's husband, who desires strongly to drink of the honey-mead there."

Buru Tovo uttered a short, crackling laugh, and looked up at Vou'a.

But Vou'a was looking down at Cliopher, because Cliopher was still standing forth in challenge, had not finished his answer. "What is it?" the god of mysteries asked. "You look smug, Cliopher Mdang. And your emperor has something else hidden in his hands."

Cliopher smiled at him, his heart thundering, for this was a moment beyond any he had ever dreamed of.

This was a moment that reached out of legend into myth, that would have ramifications he could not even begin to imagine. What could it mean, that the sea could come once more above upon the land? What *was* the dance that Vou'a and Ani had once performed, the shoreline and the sea, ever meeting, ever parting?

He would find out. They would all find out.

"There is one other thing," he said, taking the basket from Fitzroy. "As my great-uncle the tana-tai is a pearl-diver, and my uncle the tanà is a barber, so am I the rising tanà, the rising tana-tai, and I am a diplomat and a bureaucrat and one who knows how to gain more than he was asked to achieve in negotiation."

Beside him, Fitzroy smiled with an expression at once imperially serene and sly.

"And so," said Vou'a, no laughter in his voice, his bearing, his expression. He leaned forward, and the power stood around him like the weight of the mountain upon Cliopher's back, when he dove down into that cold, black water.

But Cliopher had dived down into that black water, and found the light on its other side.

He lifted his head. "When I stood at the feet of the Sun, in the House of the Sun, I bargained for the things I have told you," he said, "and I won also something that was lost long, long ago. And thus this I present this to you, O Son of Laughter, to give to your fanoa below the waves." And he lifted out the ethereal cloth of the mirimiri of Ani.

Vou'a said nothing: nothing at all.

Cliopher held up the mirimiri, which shone in the air like a mirage, like a sea-fog in the sun, like the faintest glint of spray from a distant whale's spout. Vou'a took it from him. And then the god held there, inhumanly still, something churning deep below the surface of Cliopher's ability to sense it.

Fitzroy took two steps forward, so he stood exactly beside Cliopher, and he said, "This is a gift beyond that which you asked Cliopher to negotiate for you, and thus the recompense will be beyond that which you have promised in the past."

Vou'a nodded, once, sharply, with a motion that seemed far more significant than any human nod, and abruptly disappeared.

∾

Cliopher stood there in the rippling pool of magic and noise left by the departure of the god, all the elders suddenly speaking. He tried to look as magnificent as Fitzroy had said he could, tried not to let the surprise and shock turn into opprobrium in his mind. The elders and lore-keepers gathered around him were *shocked*. That was all. They were not disapproving.

Perhaps they had never been. Perhaps that had always been in his head. Perhaps it had always been his own doubts that had shadowed their faces, their voices, in his understanding of them.

He had stood firm against the swirling cross-currents of the court. He could stand firm—or sail smoothly—across this kurakura of his own culture, his own people, the very council he hoped to join. He had shocked people before, and often revelled in it.

(He had shocked Vou'a, the very god of mysteries, in whose bag were all the riddles and mysteries of the world. He had given Vou'a a new riddle, and that was a story for the ages.)

Buru Tovo came over to Cliopher, who reached immediately towards him, then flushed and bowed over his hands.

His great-uncle shook his head and instead stepped forward, hands on Cliopher's upper arms, and they greeted each other in the traditional fashion. Buru Tovo's hands were trembling, and that broke through Cliopher's composure as perhaps nothing else could have. He closed his eyes, forehead resting on his beloved teacher and great-uncle, the tears leaking from the corners of his eyes. Buru Tovo's breath smelled of coffee and caramel; he'd fallen in love with the sticky sweet on his visit to Solaara.

"There you are, boy," Buru Tovo said hoarsely, his hands gripping tightly.

"Here I am, Buru Tovo," Cliopher said back, his voice almost as hoarse. "Here I am."

Buru Tovo gripped hard, and then he lifted his head, nodded sharply. "Is *this* where you stop, boy?"

Buru Tovo had always said it was no shame to weep; that there was strength in showing your heart. Cliopher knew his own eyes were tearing up; he swallowed hard, but he made no effort to wipe away the tears. "I still couldn't dive for a flame pearl," he whispered. "We sailed across the reef at the channel to Loaloa, and I looked at the waters ... and I could not, Buru Tovo."

Buru Tovo snorted, and then he laughed, and he squeezed Cliopher's arms tightly. "What are we going to do with you, boy?"

"Sing a new song in the *Lays*," Cliopher said promptly, the words jumping out of his adolescent certainty that he *would* do something worthy of them. But it was true, and he had. He *had*.

Fitzroy stepped forward to stand beside him, their shoulders touching.

His fanoa. His own.

He had wanted this. He had always wanted this. He had *earned* this.

(He had sailed to the House of the Sun in the boat the Ancestors had made. He had brought home the mirimiri of Ani and a flame of the Sun. He had everything to be proud of. He need feel no shame or embarrassment for having done *too much*.)

Jiano said, "I'm almost afraid to ask, but—what changes to the *Lays*? Beyond the name of the third son of Vonou'a and—and the recovery of the mirimiri of Ani and —and—" He stopped and laughed weakly. "And there's more, isn't there?"

Cliopher swung to look at him; Buru Tovo stepped back. The young Paramount Chief was holding up the efela Izurunayë, staring at its resplendent shells, the gleaming tui seed, the incontrovertible existence of it. Mardo Walea and his grandfather had drifted closer to look at it, murmuring to each other as they examined the shells.

"Yes," said Cliopher. "There is."

And he told the story of his journey.

Not in the fullest length—not all the details—but he described leaving Solaara to travel to Alinor to find Basil, and finding both his cousin and then Fitzroy, his fanoa, the last emperor, there. How they had walked in the woods and fallen into Sky Ocean ... How they had discovered that Auri and El were lovers, husbands even, and that the crew of the *He'eanka* had sailed thinking they had lost their people's admiration ... oh, all of it.

Towards the end, he spoke of visiting Vou'a's island, the god's request that he see if he could regain his guest-right to the House of the Sun. "And then I continued on," Cliopher said.

Uncle Lazo said, "How did you come by the—the—" He halted, as if unable to speak the vast impossibility that had happened next.

Buru Tovo exhaled in a long, quiet whistle. "The mirimiri of Ani."

"Yes," Uncle Lazo said, "but more ... the stories say the feather was lost, the feather that was the only trade for it. How did you come by that?"

Now they were all listening, for this was—was far beyond any story there had been so far, in the *Lays*. This was Cliopher not following the ke'ea of Elonoa'a, the ke'ea of Samayo Ateatamai, but finding his own.

He took a deep breath. "A sea turtle came, and I followed it down to the depths of the sea."

"How did you breathe?" Jiano asked in fascination.

"I don't know," he replied, smiling a little. "It didn't seem to be a problem."

"Why did you follow the turtle?" one of the elders asked.

He hesitated, but this was a time for truths, and for the mending of breaks, for the finding of things lost, and so he said: "My cousin Louya told me they were the lore-keepers of the sea, and I should honour them accordingly."

Everyone knew Louya; and knew, probably, the way she had written screeds of varying degrees of coherency to Cliopher. The elder grunted. "She is not known for her insight," someone else muttered.

Cliopher nodded, and then he said: "I do not know if you have heard, from my family who came when I was ... considered dead, but I had an experience earlier that was like unto Eranui and the Five Shells. And in that other place, wherever it was, my ... other self told me that their Louya had gone to the Ela shamans and learned to be a seer."

There was a stir, and the Ela lore-holder looked struck. "I shall speak with your cousin," he said. "Perhaps we missed a gift."

"She has always been wisest when it came to matters of the sea," Cliopher offered. "And by following what she said, I was able to follow the sea turtle to the depths of the sea, where I came to a door. The Lower Door, the Sun called it."

"I have never heard of such," someone said.

Cliopher nodded, unsurprised, but also—this was *his* story, his tale, his pattern he was making for those who came after. The exemplar showed what had been and what could be and what *was*, and what the Islanders were included Cliopher Mdang, Viceroy of Zunidh.

"I knocked upon the Lower Door, and was invited across the threshold by the Grandmother, whom the Sun named the Old Woman Who Lives in the Deeps of the Sea."

The elders looked at him in consternation. *Buru Tovo* looked at him in consternation. That was a name they knew from the stories.

Buru Tovo said, "The Old Woman Who Lives in the Deeps of the Sea let you in? What did you *offer* her?"

Fitzroy put his hand on Cliopher's shoulder, which was a comfort he had been lacking for ... for so long, and so Cliopher did not minimize or deflect, but instead he said, "I said, 'Tanaea-te imalo! Moa'alani-ki imalo! Kifa'ana imai?'"

Buru Tovo laughed a cackle almost like Vou'a's, hard enough that the tears started in his eyes. One of the other lore-keepers cried, "Ah, you can tell he sat at *your* feet, Tovo! And what did she say, that old woman? What problem did she give you?"

"She asked me to carry a basket of mud up the long stair," Cliopher said evenly, "and I did."

Buru Tovo stopped laughing, and watched him with narrowed eyes.

"All the way up the spiral stair," he went on, shifting unconsciously as he remembered the weight of that basket, one hand coming up to touch his shoulder where the straps had pressed. "All the way up the straight stair, past the treasure-rooms of the Sun. All the way up the zigzag stair across the face of the mountain, above the vast emptiness of the sky. All the way to the door, where I was ... eventually ... invited across the threshold as a guest by the Sun. When I set down the basket, I found my hair had tangled with the straps, and when I pulled it free, I found a certain black feather also in my hand."

Uncle Lazo took in a hissing breath. "The Old Woman Who Lives in the Deeps had it."

"She is the gatherer-in of all things."

"She does not often let things go from her grasp," Buru Tovo said, and he looked down for a moment, then smiled with a certain sly respect at Cliopher. "You never did like that story, did you?"

"No," said Cliopher, solid as the rock on which the world turns. "Perhaps a person cannot fix the mistake they made, but that does not mean the mistake can never be fixed. After all, as I have been told many times, there is more than one way to find a flame pearl."

CHAPTER SIXTY-TWO
LOW-HANGING OBSTACLES

It seemed as if they would have to spend hours answering questions. Cliopher did not know quite how to say that he was feeling dizzy and gradually deflating from his grand pronouncements, that he was tired and hungry and thirsty, and Fitzroy was being *so* quiet even though some of the elders were asking for his part in the story.

And then his Aunt Onaya came out of the living area above the barbershop to see why the elders had not dispersed. She greeted Cliopher with a fierce embrace and kisses on his cheeks and forehead, stood back and looked at him intently, and immediately stated that Cliopher and his lord must be exhausted, and surely there would be plenty of other opportunities for him to tell the story of his travels over, and what sort of hospitality and welcome home was this, anyway?

Cliopher was so overcome by gratitude at this that he could not say anything. Fitzroy smiled at her. "Thank you for your consideration," he said, his voice deep and rich, court-accented, neutral. It was as it had been for so long, and that was fine—they were back in the world, after all, with all the claims and roles that came with that—but Cliopher still found it hard to hear.

Fitzroy went on, "We learned from Aurelius and Elonoa'a that faravia was meant to be taken metaphorically—'mending sails' as a way of saying, taking the time needed to recover from the trials of the voyage."

"How clever," Aunt Onaya said. "Well, you've paid your respects to the elders and piled up your news for them to chew over, so what's next?" She tapped her lips with her fingers. "Kip's house is ready, I suppose. Eidora's still away," she added at his surprised look. "Oura's there so of course you *can* stay, but you'll want more privacy than that, won't you? Let's see ... Most everyone's looking to Malania, in her absence. Eidora's having a grand old time with your friend Conju, Kip, from her letters home. They've gone to stay with Vinyë's friend in Old Damara, so Vinyë went to join them and took Leona with her."

"Vinyë has a friend in Old Damara?" Cliopher asked in some bewilderment. "A musician? I thought her friends were from Amboloyo ..."

"Hugon is, yes, but no ... it's someone she met when she visited you." Aunt Onaya thought a moment, then brightened and turned to Fitzroy. "I do think it might be your sister. Vinyë thought she should make an effort, since we could all see ... well, Kip talks about you a lot."

Cliopher's cheeks were burning. It didn't help that Fitzroy merely laughed. "Vinyë's made friends with my sister Melissa? How wonderful! What a splendid thing, Kip—the idea of Conju and your mother and your sister and your niece ..."

"Indeed," Cliopher said weakly.

"Well, be off with you, then," Aunt Onaya said, flicking her fingers at them. "All these will talk your ears off, and you've been sailing a long time. Malania's at rehearsal today, so you go on home. I'll stop by your place after I've talked to your aunts."

"Thank you," Cliopher said. It was easier to accept this gift—and it *was* a gift— when it was his aunt Malania he was not immediately visiting, not his mother. "Aunt Onaya," he said, kissing her on the cheek. "Thank you."

"My pleasure, Kip," she replied, her eyes bright.

She'd been a constant figure of his youth, what with him hanging around Uncle Lazo's shop most of the time. "You didn't hear this part—Aunt Onaya, I found Basil. He's alive. He and Sara and their son, Clio. They're well."

She drew in her breath sharply, and Uncle Lazo wrapped his arm around her shoulders. "Well. Well. I'll—I'll ask you more about that, later, then. But really?"

"Really and truly." Cliopher looked at Fitzroy, who nodded and put his hand on Cliopher's shoulder. Cliopher had never had that before, and he did not know what to do. He did not feel right relaxing against Fitzroy as Aunt Onaya was against her husband, but ... but it *was* a comfort, to have Fitzroy touch him, his hand warm.

"We'll be returning there after our faravia," Fitzroy said. "If you would like to write a letter for us to take with you." He smiled with a hint of the familiar mischief. "Their postal system has not had Kip's hand shaping it."

"Pity," said Uncle Lazo, the teasing familiar—pleasing, even. Cliopher's heart was overflowing, and he did not know what to do with the emotions upwelling in him.

Aunt Onaya said, "We'll come by later, Kip. We're glad to see you home."

"And for your news," Uncle Lazo added, his eyes full of wonder and pride.

Cliopher smiled back, equal to equal, and he nodded respectfully to the elders before he and Fitzroy descended to their vaha and continued on.

"Will we be able to fit down the back canals?" Fitzroy asked as Cliopher guided them along the edge of Tahivoa lagoon. "Or are there bridges?"

Cliopher had not thought at all about this. "There are, yes."

They both looked up at the tall mast. "Do we take it down?" Fitzroy asked, with an academic interest. "Or would you like me to try something magical?"

"Is that even a question?"

Fitzroy laughed. "I was all set to hear you had a Protocol in place for low-hanging obstacles."

"Asking the great mage currently aboard with me for assistance is a perfectly reasonable plan," Cliopher protested, though he could not manage a straight face for the entire statement. They both laughed, and he barely made the turn into the large canal that led down past a small section of warehouses into the neighbourhood around Zaviya Square.

Fitzroy regarded him narrowly. "Are you thinking what I'm thinking, Kip?"

That was a challenge, if not as fraught as the ones Cliopher had just answered. He met his fanoa's gaze; Fitzroy looked a little manic, as if the brief moment of imperial dignity had concentrated all his mischievousness.

There were stories Fitzroy had told him of his time with the Red Company. Legends Cliopher had heard; songs and tales of fantastic deeds. He tried to let them rise up, as the vaha slowly sailed against the current towards their new home.

And then he had it. "I've heard a story," he said cautiously, "of when you first went to the Grand Bazaar of Yedoen."

Fitzroy's face lit up. "The lights! The music! The marvellous size-shifting ship! Exactly! But I would not wish to repeat myself—"

"Naturally not," he replied dryly, waving at his cousin Haro, who was walking along the side of the canal. Haro waved back absently, then did a magnificent double take that made Fitzroy laugh himself into hiccoughs.

Cliopher considered the vaha. "It's mostly the mast and sail," he murmured. "I think we'll fit into the bywater, if only just, but there's at least one bridge before we get there."

"Are we going to our house?" Fitzroy asked, a little absently. "Do you have a key for it? Or shall I try to recall what I once knew about housebreaking? I was once quite good at it, you know."

"So I've heard," Cliopher replied even more dryly. "I'm sure we'll be able to manage."

He'd not come by water for decades—not since he'd gone to Astandalas—but he knew the route. There was the big warehouse, empty for years, on the corner of the grand canal and the smaller one that led by several waters eventually to the theatre district. The big warehouse looked as if someone had bought it and was renovating it: a huge mural of a flight of coral-crested cockatoos was in the process of being painted along its façade.

Cliopher's attention was necessarily on negotiating the faint airs and slight currents and obstacles in the way of reaching the quiet bywater that would lead towards Saya Dorn's house.

His house. *Their* house. His heart warmed, and he smiled at Fitzroy, who was regarding him with a quiet amusement. "What?"

"I've always enjoyed watching you concentrate. Are we nearly there?"

"Are you ready for your working?"

"Naturally."

Cliopher trusted Fitzroy to know himself and his abilities, and so he moved around a small flotilla of dories painted in bright colours and into the dim tunnel that led to their backwater. A bridge loomed overhead; someone had planted it with some sort of vine that draped great festoons of scarlet and blue flowers almost to the water. The vines were alive with movement: insects and iridescent blue and green butterflies the size of his hand and roly-poly honeycreepers with long beaks and longer tongues to reach into the trumpet-shaped flowers.

Fitzroy broke off a spray of the blossoms as they passed underneath the bridge, their mast glittering with golden magic, passing through the stone and the blossoms as if it were insubstantial.

And yet the wind still belled the woven pandanus leaves, and the vaha continued to move without a jerk or a judder.

Cliopher swallowed. The story from the Grand Bazaar of Yedoen had been full of laughter and comedy, as the changing shape of the ship knocked all its passengers and crew akimbo.

"I shall take you to Yedoen one day," Fitzroy murmured, as lights—white, gold, blue, red, orange, green—rippled and glinted upon the mast and sail, the ropes and hulls, of their vaha, hardly visible even in the dim daylight of the back-water.

Fitzroy passed Cliopher the spray of flowers, his smile crooked, as if he were doing no magic at all. The mast and sail wavered, solid, the magic settling into their matter. "The perfect colours—scarlet for the Red Company, and blue for Zunidh. Fire, obviously, and the sea that we have sailed across together. And of course, they're my favourite colours."

"Mine too," Cliopher admitted.

"Nonsense," Fitzroy said sternly. "You like orange-red, not pure scarlet, and royal blue, not cerulean. It makes *all* the difference."

"Does it."

"It does."

They both laughed, and Cliopher bumped the nose of the vaha against the pier.

"Careful there!" a voice called from above, and Cliopher, his face burning, looked up to see that Saya Dorn's long-standing neighbour, Tiru Oyinaa, was standing at the edge of the boardwalk that extended out from the courtyard between their houses.

He hastily manoeuvred the vaha into the generous pool that served the two houses—a small gust of wind was suspiciously convenient, but he did not dare look at Fitzroy—and as he furled the sail, Fitzroy jumped onto the dock and took the painter.

"How do you do," he said politely to the elderly woman watching them, hands folded over her walking stick. "We're your new neighbours."

"Kip Mdang I know," Saya Oyinaa said, "and you must be his lord."

"In a manner of speaking," Fitzroy agreed, and bounded up the short set of stairs leading to the courtyard. He gave the woman a florid bow. "I bid you good day!"

Cliopher had by this point finished tying up the vaha, and he set their few important possessions on the edge of the courtyard before he joined them. He felt very young, knowing that Saya Oyinaa had seen him at his most gauche and most obnoxious, but after he handed Fitzroy his harp he bowed over the fire-pot in his hands. "Saya Oyinaa," he said. "It's good to see you again."

She regarded him with narrowed eyes. "There's magic upon you."

"Yes," Cliopher said, smiling at her. "I have been to the House of the Sun, Saya Oyinaa."

"You always said you would." She glanced at Fitzroy. "You also used to say that you would go see if the emperor was worth staying for. You stayed, so we thought you must have decided he was," she added, her eyes twinkling.

"I certainly have found Kip incalculably worthy," Fitzroy replied serenely.

Saya Oyinaa regarded him for a long moment, and then shook her head. "I imagine you'll be wanting to settle in." She regarded them, and peered down at the vaha. "I'll bring you some food in a bit."

Fitzroy began to disclaim any need for this, but Cliopher knew how these things worked, and he smiled and said, "Thank you very much, Saya Oyinaa," and nodded politely to her. Fitzroy followed suit, and they watched as she hobbled across the courtyard to her own door.

There were only the two houses on this courtyard: Saya Oyinaa's had a bit of an addition that formed an ell with the main building, whereas Saya Dorn's old house —*their* house—rambled across the other side of the square. The public square was reached through an alley between the Oyinaa house's extension and a shed of some form beside theirs. Then the house, and beside them a miniature of the large house down to its little cupola on the roof.

"It's lovely," Fitzroy said quietly. And then, tentatively, even more quietly, "Home."

Cliopher nodded, his heart in his mouth. "Home."

The first one Fitzroy had ever had, really.

It was very strange to look at the house rising up in all its quirks of architectural flourish—the spiral stair painted a clear bright blue, the upper balcony, more of a covered terrace, running along the courtyard side of the house; the little balconies off various other rooms, some of them at odd heights because of internal stairs; the arched windows at the top.

Cliopher had a dizzying memory of the version of this house in the other universe. He clutched his pot of daylight to him, trying to imagine how it would look to have a golden basin full of it in this courtyard. Would it be too bright, in the night? He wouldn't want to bother his—their—new neighbours.

"It really is lovely," Fitzroy said again, and walked forward, his arm slipping out of Cliopher's hand as he walked across the courtyard. "What's this little building?"

"The bathhouse," Cliopher replied, suddenly nervous now that it was far too late.

Fitzroy turned to grin at him. "A proper bathhouse! Cliopher!"

"You can go first," he said generously. "I know you've been wanting a bath."

"Dreaming of baths. Perishing for one. Not literally, of course, though I have sometimes wondered ...—By which door do we enter?"

There was a ground-floor courtyard door, but Cliopher led Fitzroy up the spiral stair first. "The kitchen's on the main floor," he said, "but let's look up here first."

"As you see fit," Fitzroy replied agreeably. "Show me the house first, and then a bath. And then we should go acquire supplies. Food. Books. Clothes. Other necessities."

"Things to furnish the house," Cliopher suggested, wondering if the bank would let him withdraw anything. Fitzroy laughed, and Cliopher decided not to worry about it. He didn't *always* have to be the practical one, did he? He was more than that. He could be spontaneous and casual and follow Fitzroy's caprice if he so chose.

"Is there only the one bath-house?" Fitzroy asked. "What about privies?"

"There are water-closets indoors," Cliopher promised. "All the facilities."

"Imagine that," Fitzroy murmured.

And then they were on the upper balcony, and looking in the windows, and coming up to the door.

Leona had done a *fine* job.

Everywhere he looked he saw not the many small signs of neglect and disrepair, but instead a renovation that showed no ... seams.

Seams was the wrong word. It was more—he could still see the history of the building, the wear and repair that came with being alive. It was not the sterile perfection of the Palace of Stars, where anything broken was immediately whisked away to be magically fixed or else entirely replaced, whole and entire and as if nothing had ever happened.

This was ... was like repairs he'd seen done on his embassy to Voonra, where they had taken the broken pieces of a beautiful pot and shown the repair by the lacquer that held the sherds together. He'd even seen ones where the lacquer had then been brushed with silver or gold.

"The cracks show its history, but what is damaged is not destroyed," his Voonran counterpart had told him, when they sat together drinking wine out of bowls made of such splendid craft. "We were damaged by the Fall, but we are not destroyed."

It was not *clumsily* done. That was what it was. There were a few places where Leona and her craftspeople had highlighted some element—the carved cornices were painted the same blue of the stair railing and white and a deep ultramarine, so they looked like curling waves carved out of wood; but the one that had broken was painted to look as if the snapped wood was the foam breaking out out of the shape of the wave.

"This door *is* unlocked," Fitzroy said, trying the handle. He stared at it with a slight perplexity.

"Everyone knows it's mine, and currently empty."

"But what about vandalism?" Fitzroy opened the door, then hesitated. "You should go in first, Kip. It's your house."

"Ours."

"Magically, you go in first."

"Well, if it's *magic* ..." Cliopher grinned at him, feeling suddenly boyish, and carefully took his fanoa's hand before he stepped across the threshold.

Fitzroy, tugged off-balance, knocked against him, rested his chin upon Cliopher's shoulder, and uttered a long, satisfied, "Ahhh."

Cliopher was speechless.

The main common room had been appealing before Leona's renovations, but it had seemed dim and a bit ... tired. Cliopher most remembered the carved plasterwork around the dumbwaiter leading up from the kitchen.

The plasterwork had been cleaned and painted—the whole room had been—and now the floor was a fine golden wood, smoothly sanded and pleasant underfoot. The walls were a pale cream, the arches around the doors and windows picking up the same blues from the outside of the house.

The room was so *beautiful*. The glass windows, newly cleaned, sparkled in the sunlight pouring in. The upper floor projected out above the courtyard, with the balcony running along part of the frontage, and the sitting room was thus full of light. And the view ... out across the canal to a vista of Tahivoa lagoon, Mama Ituri to one side, the darker Bay of the Waters extending westward along the waters they had so recently sailed.

He let out a deep sigh of ... relief? Was it relief?

"It needs decoration," Fitzroy murmured. "And art, in general.—Assuming you agree? Of course you do—you have beautiful art in your rooms in the Palace. What are you looking so intently at? Ah. Naturally."

This was because Cliopher was staring at the brazier set in the centre of the room, a copper-coated basin quite large enough to hold a sizeable flame.

He looked up, at a small circular opening high above, showing a bright disc of cerulean blue.

"That's a clever magic," Fitzroy said, waving his hand generally. "It'll carry the smoke straight up to the skylight. I can see what you meant about it being a bit ... convoluted, this magic. Mostly it just wants someone to belong to, you know? It's curling around me like ... a cat, cats do that, don't they? Or a dog? Like it wants me to pet it. The house misses your Saya Dorn."

Cliopher felt his throat close. "I miss her too," he said softly. "She was very good to me."

Fitzroy had heard a number of stories about her, all that long journey across the sea, and he nodded solemnly. "I look forward to hearing more about her."

They stood beside the empty brazier. Cliopher stared down at it. "I should light a fire here," he murmured.

"Yes, that will anchor the magic properly."

Leona had set a basket of firewood and tinder beside the brazier. Cliopher laid the fire carefully, and then hesitated over the best method for actually lighting it.

"It would best if it were with the tovo and tanaea," he murmured, "but those are in my bag at Basil's inn."

But that was the correct symbolism, wasn't it? A rock from the islands, a rock from the other side of the world, together striking a new flame.

He looked at Fitzroy, who was watching him intently. "Would you light it for me, Fitzroy?"

Fitzroy drew in a sharp breath. "Kip. You can't mean that."

Cliopher did not know if he could smile, but he nodded. His voice was hoarse. "Please."

"Are you *certain*?" Fitzroy asked, after a silent, suspended moment, his eyes soft and full of golden magic, his face intent, curious, almost ...

Cliopher could not name that emotion. It was too raw.

"I am," he said.

Fitzroy stepped forward, until they stood shoulder-to-shoulder. Cliopher did not move, even when Fitzroy picked up Cliopher's left hand with his right and wove their fingers together.

Cliopher felt the magic move, a warm tide through Fitzroy's veins, through his own fingers, and the fire spilled from between their joined palms like a handful of water or sunlight.

The wood caught, and crackled, and for a moment Cliopher touched the fire, as he had always wanted to touch it, as if it were a living thing tame to his hand.

And then they stepped back, and all he could say was *thank you*.

~

There were three suites on the upper floor, their doors a darker wood than the floors, very simple but pleasing in the clean lines.

"This is a traditional style of house, here in Gorjo City," he explained to Fitzroy. "Intended for an extended family to live as one household." Fitzroy nodded, his eyes alert though his face was calm, almost serene, and he was very quiet as Cliopher led him into the first suite. "So each family, or person, would have their own private spaces ... a sitting room, a bedchamber, some storage rooms, that sort of thing. Oh look, these have privies too—not every house would, you know. Then you share the kitchen and bath-house and main areas."

"I see," said Fitzroy, looking curiously at the rooms. Cliopher hadn't been into this suite before, and he was delighted to see a deep embrasure in the arched window facing on the courtyard; perfect for a window seat. One room had a pair of glazed doors opening onto the long balcony leading to the stairs.

"I like this," Fitzroy said quietly. "Have you already picked one for yourself?"

"The one I liked before was on the other side, facing Zaviya Square," Cliopher said, not sure what else to say. "You could certainly have this one, if you like it best ..."

Fitzroy glanced at him and quickly away, but not before Cliopher saw the slight frown, the brown shadow in his eyes.

"There are three on this floor, and two more, suites that is, on the ground floor," he said hastily, hoping that was the right thing to say. Fitzroy hummed noncommittally. Yet—he *knew* that Cliopher had asked Rhodin and Ludvic and Conju to join them.

But there were the Red Company. Fitzroy had been quite definite that he wanted to go back to Basil's inn to reunite with his friends as soon as possible.

And he had been trapped for so long ...

Cliopher led the way not to the other suites but over to the narrow stair leading upwards. He had offered a house ... a *home* ... and Fitzroy had sounded as if he wanted a home, as if he yearned for one. And he had *said* he wanted to be Cliopher's fanoa— had seemed so pleased by it—

For the first time in many days, Cliopher remembered the misunderstanding before their conversation about what fanoa meant to him; what it had meant to El and Auri; what Fitzroy had *thought* it meant, at first.

Had wanted it to mean.

Was that still an issue? Was what Cliopher had offered not enough, after all? Should he ask?

But Fitzroy was smiling again, pleased with the space, the house, and ... and he would say something, wouldn't he? If he wanted—

"Up here," Cliopher said, his voice rough, and started up.

The stair was still dark and close, though without the effect of being nearly grimy that it had had previously. Now the short, curving stair felt rather like a moment of meditative darkness.

Or so he hoped. He almost wanted to stay there, suspended between floors, in a warm, welcoming, smooth-textured dimness, the curve of the handrail a delight to the touch.

He was reminded, suddenly, of that conversation with Rhodin in the secret passages between his rooms and his Radiancy's—the Imperial Apartments. *You're allowed to ask for what you want*, Rhodin had told him. And *it doesn't matter the size of your dream.*

He had fulfilled the grandest of his dreams. Now he wanted—the smallest one.

The small white shell on the beach, matched to another.

"Is this where those upper windows are, Kip?" Fitzroy asked politely, and made him start and continue walking.

"Sorry," he muttered. "I was ... thinking."

"A delightfully dangerous propensity."

Cliopher felt a smile tug at him as stepped aside from the top of the stair to let Fitzroy come up the last few steps.

It took a moment for his eyes to adjust. And then he eased himself to sit on a bench built to run under one of the great curved windows, and watched the unnervingly silent Fitzroy turn around, his sarong flaring, his hair crackling around his head —was magic building in it?—as he took in the space.

Leona had painted the walls and refinished the floor and fixed the cracked panes in the windows, and dusted each of the scores of glass fishing floats so they gleamed as they caught the light.

It was a high-ceilinged room, round, windows curving around the entirety of the space and offering a view that looked across Gorjo City to the Gates of the Sea in the east. One huge beam, bent by steam (and perhaps magic) into a perfect circle, held the ribbed beams of the ceiling and walls in what felt like the perfect marriage of tension and repose.

It was still cool and airy and full of light, the wide eaves and some lingering magics keeping the air fresh, and the hundreds of glass fishing floats hung around the room, catching the sun and spangling the richly polished wooden floor.

Fitzroy stood in the centre of the room, where there was another circular aperture opening to the sky. It did not line up with the one in the sitting room below, and Cliopher wondered vaguely if there were more rooms on the upper levels that he had not yet noticed. Perhaps there might even be a hidden stair; Rhodin would like that, if there were.

He smiled, and Fitzroy caught his glance and stilled, as if caught in the same moment.

His eyes were full of light, of magic, of delight in this space.

For a moment Cliopher could not speak; was literally speechless, as if the Sea-Witch had stolen all his words away.

"This must have been your Saya Dorn's workroom," Fitzroy said.

"I thought it could be yours," Cliopher replied, and then folded his hands tight on his lap, shoulders back, chin up, in sudden apprehension.

It was nothing, he told himself. A cloud passing in front of the sun, casting a shadow upon the bright room. It would pass, and the light would return.

It did pass, and the air brightened, and he let out his breath in a shaky sort of exhale.

And then Fitzroy said, "Because it's a tower?"

CHAPTER SIXTY-THREE
THE HOUSE TOUR

Cliopher's blood congealed, and he forced himself to breathe evenly, slowly, calmly. "No," he said, croaked really; coughed, cleared his throat, swallowed hard, and spoke again. "No. Because it was beautiful."

Fitzroy strode across the room to the windows on the other side, and he fussed awkwardly with it until he was able to undo the latches and slide the sash up. It moved easily enough, and Cliopher recalled, for the first time in a long while, that as the emperor Fitzroy had been barred from almost all manual activity.

Certainly he would never have opened his own windows; even if the ones in the Imperial Apartments had opened. He would not have leaned out, the warm air gusting into the room behind him, sending dust motes flying up and sparkling.

He would not have had Cliopher walk softly across the floor—they were both still barefoot, of course, after their long time at sea—and gently place his hand on his shoulder.

His skin twitched, but he did not move away, though Cliopher left him the space to do so.

Cliopher breathed in, out, tasting the fragrance of tiarë; he could see the glossy-leaved shrub growing in a pot outside their neighbours' door. He breathed in deeply, letting the fragrance fill his heart. He would have to get a plant for their side, or several.

"I'm sorry," Fitzroy said after a moment, still leaning out with his arms folded on the sill. "I didn't mean that."

Cliopher hummed acknowledgement, and, being uncertain of what to say, stayed silent. He had been able to hold this space open for Ludvic, for Uncle Lazo, for Aurelius Magnus himself: he could do so for Fitzroy.

Fitzroy had spent a lifetime holding all of his emotions and thoughts back, far below the serene surface of his face, his voice, even his body. Even after that long sojourn in Sky Ocean, the long sail across the Wide Seas, it was clearly not easy for him to speak.

"It's beautiful," he said, his voice muffled by the wind swirling past. "And you thought of me."

"I did," Cliopher said quietly.

And silence.

"The house wants me to belong here," Fitzroy said, slumping down so he was resting on his forearms. "I want to belong here. I do, Kip. I do."

More silence.

Cliopher waited quietly. The silence seemed to need something more from him, and he wondered what else he should say. "There is a place for you," he said finally. "A home, here, with me, and with Ludvic and Conju and Rhodin."

"Five suites."

"Just so." Cliopher pressed lightly with the hand that still rested on his friend's (his fanoa's) shoulder, gripping gently to remind Fitzroy that he was not alone, that he was not bound by the taboos and restrictions that had held him so far removed. "And if you want to go adventuring with your friends, free as a bird, that's ... that's entirely your choice."

"I do," Fitzroy whispered. "I do, and I don't."

The wind was warm, coming through the window, the sunlight pouring across them in a splash of rainbow spangles from the fishing floats.

Cliopher nudged closer, so he was embracing Fitzroy, holding his broad shoulders, their heads knocking together. "It's a long way home, isn't it?" Cliopher murmured. "You showed me my way."

Fitzroy's eyes were closed. "As you will show me mine? Will you do that for me, Kip?"

"I will hold that ember safe," Cliopher said into his ear. "The star to guide you home."

Fitzroy hiccoughed, his face twisting. "Will you be my ke'e, Cliopher Mdang?"

"As you are mine," Cliopher said. "My fanoa."

"You didn't call me that. When you introduced me. You said I was your emperor and your friend."

Cliopher looked sharply at him. "No. I'm sure I said fanoa."

Fitzroy pulled his head back in from the window and stepped back, so they were a little apart. He was tense, controlled, his face very still. "I was listening very carefully. You said *friend*."

"I meant fanoa," Cliopher said, almost helplessly. "I ... I'm sorry ... I meant to say it. I spent so long not letting myself even *think* it ..."

"What? Why would you do that?" Fitzroy asked, his eyebrows plunging together.

"It meant too much. I wanted it too much."

Another long, fraught silence; this time they were staring at each other. Cliopher did not know what else to say, what else he *could* say. "I'm sorry."

"I was imprisoned in a tower once, with the Red Company," Fitzroy said in a toneless voice, his eyes opaque, his whole body wound tight. "I lost control of my magic and burned it down, but I couldn't escape ... Pali rescued me, in the end. She carried me out through the fires I'd lit and let go out of control."

He'd never written a song about that, but other musicians had, and Cliopher knew that it was rumoured that that forest was still burning. He swallowed, but his voice, though low, came out clearly, fiercely, firmly. "I will be the star showing you the way home, and the rock that holds fast under your foot. I would sail a second time to the House of the Sun for you, and I would spend another lifetime making a better world with you. And," he drew in a deep, trembling breath, but it had to be said: "And I will help Pali or anyone else rescue you if I cannot."

"You will show me how to love this tower, won't you?" Fitzroy said, very softly, as all the ice and iron melted out of him, and he was once more golden-eyed and smiling with an almost convincing ease. Cliopher nodded, once, and Fitzroy let his face and voice lighten. "Will you show me the rest of the house? What's on the ground floor, besides the other two suites?"

"There's the kitchen," Cliopher said, and felt his heart twist at how Fitzroy's eyes lit up.

~

"Is there no inside stair?" Fitzroy asked as they returned to the wrought-iron masterpieces leading down off the balcony.

"It would certainly be unusual for there *not* to be one at all," he said slowly, wrenching his thoughts to the present.

"Does that mean you don't know where it is?" The thought seemed to give Fitzroy great joy. "Could it possibly be a *hidden* stair? What a thought!"

Leona's skill and thoughtfulness showed even more strongly on the lower level. The kitchen nearly glowed with its careful restoration, and the rest of the main floor, which Cliopher remembered as being cluttered and congested (and in his mind's eye oddly, eerily, overlaid with the version of the house he had seen in the *other place*), was as airy and pleasing to be in as the upstairs.

They didn't find a stair, though they investigated the two suites, and then the dancing room with the reinforced floor—"Not a fencing room?" Fitzroy teased gently, moving forward suddenly with a flurry of quick, light steps, clearly according to a pattern. Equally clearly he had not realized he remembered the steps, for he reached the centre of the room and stuttered to a halt.

"Rhodin thought it might be big enough to practice in," Cliopher agreed placidly.

"I used to know how to fence," Fitzroy said. "Damian and Pali taught me."

And he was the swashbuckling hero of at least half a dozen songs, not all of them his own.

"Rhodin will probably be pleased to fence with you—Ludvic too."

"Ludvic doesn't *fence*," Fitzroy replied, sounding nearly shocked. "He *fights*."

~

The front door was not locked either, which fact made Fitzroy shake his head in mystification. He pushed open the heavy wooden door and then leaned against it as he looked across the small square in front of them. A freshwater pool filled with waterlilies rested at its centre; the periphery did not contain as many trees as Cliopher's youthful memory suggested should be there.

A later, more despondent memory came up; how many of the great trees, grown in huge containers resting on heavy stone piers, had toppled during the extreme weather after the Fall.

When he'd come home, he'd gone eventually to visit with Saya Dorn. She'd seemed very old by then, and frail; the magical disruption of the Fall had aged her even more than her years, and the fallen giants of the square had seemed too symbolic.

He'd written to her from Astandalas, describing the places she'd known and the ones he'd discovered, and they sat, for a while, and she reminisced about the two years she'd spent studying wizardry there.

She'd asked him if he were staying home, and when he said he was—for at that point he was—she'd reached forward with one trembling hand and laid it across his.

"My dear," she said in her soft voice, "it will all be well in the end. Trust in the sea and the sky and the sun."

He had thought of the shell he'd found floating on the waves, and how he'd hidden it deep in his closet, told no one at all that he'd received it.

He might have been able to tell Saya Dorn about his long journey across the Wide Seas, but her twenty-year-old grandson was living with her, and he did not like leaving Cliopher alone with his grandmother.

Later family gossip said it was because he'd been afraid Saya Dorn would leave her house and wealth to Cliopher instead of her own blood kin, but at the time Cliopher had not known that, and had been in no state to protest being edged out of her life. He'd assumed (he remembered this now, watching Fitzroy watch a pair of crested pigeons cooing and bobbing at each other on the lip of the waterlily pool) that she had liked having a young person around to carry her groceries and run other small errands, and that her grandson naturally fulfilled that role better than the Kip who'd come home from Astandalas broken and not what anyone wanted.

She'd been hurt by the magic of the Fall—though the Vangavaye-ve in general had not been badly damaged, wizards had fared the worst—and she was *old*. And Cliopher had not known to push back against the grandson, had assumed Saya Dorn preferred her own relations; had assumed she, too, did not want the Kip who had come home.

How hurt he'd been by the Fall, by that long and lonely journey, that homecoming with no faravia.

And so, after a few months, he'd gone once more eastward, always eastward, looking for the sun.

Fitzroy turned around and pattered up to the door, which he patted with a strangely intimate expression, as if it were a living animal he were greeting. He tilted his head at Cliopher. "Is everything all right, Kip?"

Cliopher did not know what to say, but he wiped his eyes with his fingers. "Remembering Saya Dorn," he said thickly, which was true.

All his family had ever wanted was for him to be happy. And they'd seen that he wasn't, that he hadn't been, that in some indefinable way he'd lost himself.

~

They went back to the kitchen, and discovered that Saya Oyinaa had to have been by while they were out in the front of the house, for there was a basket of pastries wrapped in a cloth sitting on the table, and the basket was far too complex and lovely a thing to have come from Cliopher's family.

There was a bench and a chair at the table; Cliopher slid unthinkingly onto the bench, the familiar seat of his youth. Fitzroy touched the back of the chair, shook his head, and wandered around the kitchen opening cupboard doors and peering into the many nooks of the space. He disappeared into the pantry, and Cliopher thoughtfully ate one of the pastries.

It was spiced chicken with some sort of mango salsa, and it was delicious.

He had not consciously been wearied by the monotony of food at sea until the last few days, but he was delighted indeed to be back in the city with all its resources and luxuries.

Fitzroy came back, a pleased smile on his face, and chuckled at seeing Cliopher licking the crumbs off his fingers. "That good?"

"I can't tell," Cliopher admitted. "After so long at sea any pastry would be superlative."

"That crust looks good, at any rate." Fitzroy snagged one of the pastries and ate it in three large bites. He nodded solemnly. "Excellent, at least. Superlative may need some comparators."

"I see."

The shadow upstairs seemed to have passed, which was a relief. Fitzroy opened a cupboard and discovered a set of plain glass tumblers. He turned the tap over the great stone sink experimentally, and watched with fascination as it burbled and hissed for a moment before the water came gushing out.

"I assume it's safe to drink?" he asked Cliopher without turning his head.

"It should be, if the magic is working."

Fitzroy glanced at him, the golden magic stirring in his eyes, and he stuck his hand into the stream. "Seems fine to me," he said blandly, and filled two of the glasses, handing one over before he sat down in the chair. "What a luxury!"

"The chair?"

"Don't tease. Fresh clean water at the turn of a tap! There are whole worlds that have never thought of such a thing."

It was good water, sweet and cool. It was good to have fresh water, neither rainwater nor coconut-flavoured. Cliopher ate another pastry, discovering it to be some sort of greens-and-cheese, and sighed with great contentment.

Fitzroy ate a second pastry and then, apparently restless, got up to refill his glass and look around the rest of the kitchen. He came to the small door which used to hold Saya Dorn's private shrine, and before Cliopher thought to say anything, opened it to find the old state portrait of himself inside.

"Oh," Fitzroy said, grimacing, and dropped the painted board on the table as if it had burned his fingers.

Cliopher made a noise of protest and reached for the picture to check for damage, and only after he had done so did he look up to see that Fitzroy was staring at him, face completely wiped clean of expression and posture forcibly tranquil.

"Fitzroy," he exclaimed, and then glanced down at the painting cradled in his hands, and did not know what to say. "Fitzroy ..."

Fitzroy pressed his lips firmly together and turned his head away. He did sit down, but as if the homely kitchen chair were his unwelcome throne.

Had they not already untangled this knot?—except that Cliopher knew (oh, how he knew) how many times one had to go over something to learn the new pattern, to ingrain it into one's heart and mind. This was not about him, was it? It was about Fitzroy and that prison he had spent half his life caged within. Cliopher scrambled to find words. "It's not—not—it's not what you're thinking."

"What am I thinking?" Fitzroy said, his voice low, controlled. Furious.

"It was Saya Dorn's shrine," Cliopher said intently. "Not mine. *Never* mine." That was reckless—and then he chided himself for that thought, for who was going to charge *him* with treason and blasphemy and sacrilege? The very god-emperor who sat at the table with him, all his defences raised?

This was not court, where that would have been a fatal misstep, if he'd made it in public.

He took a breath, a second one, a third. He set down the wooden board further down the table. Fitzroy had folded his hands together on his lap and so he could not hold them, but Cliopher set his own hands on the table, relaxed, friendly, unthreatening. A mirrored posture in a muted, calmer, gentler mode.

"When you came to the throne," he said, "that state portrait you kept in your official study was painted, and copies were made to disseminate, correct?"

He waited; Fitzroy nodded stiffly. Someone who did not know him might have believed the feigned serenity, the imperial façade.

"Such things rarely made it all the way out here, but Saya Dorn had a friend in Astandalas who used to send her parcels every once in a while." He smiled, inviting Fitzroy to relax; Fitzroy did not unbend in the least, but he was listening, his eyes lowered and yet intent on Cliopher's hands. "When I was thirteen or fourteen it was a copy of *Aurora*. The first printing, I think it must have been."

A memory stirred, no doubt closer to the surface because of the encounter outside Uncle Lazo's shop earlier.

"My first time reading it, I spent half the afternoon translating it for Buru Tovo and his ... friend ..." He trailed off as he realized just who that friend had been. "Vou'a. I translated it for Buru Tovo and Vou'a."

Fitzroy said nothing, but his lips twitched, just a little, and Cliopher pressed forward into the hint of softening.

"I loved it. *Aurora*. I read it over and over again, until I had it memorized, and then I bullied everyone I could into reading it, until the spine cracked and someone refused to give it back." Fitzroy grimaced reflexively. Cliopher spoke gently. "We'd only just barely heard there was a new emperor when Saya Dorn's friend sent her a package containing this portrait." He gestured at the board.

The gilded eyes of the icon stared up at the ceiling; the real man stared down at the table.

Cliopher picked his next words carefully. "I was twenty-one, twenty-two, something like that. Trying to find my way, unsure of my vocation, how to be the tanà I wanted to be. Studying at the university, thinking about becoming an accountant, because in those days most of people's problems seemed to be about money, and I was good with numbers." He smiled ruefully. "And then I came to visit with Saya Dorn one day. She showed me this portrait, and I ... felt my ke'ea shift. I knew, right then, that you were the emperor I would go seeking; that somehow you were my ke'e; that our fates were entwined."

There was a silence, which Cliopher let unroll. He had nowhere to be and nothing more important to do than work out this knot.

At last Fitzroy said, "I thought you didn't believe in fate."

"I believe in choices," he agreed. "I had spent my childhood dreaming of a fanoa like Aurelius was for Elonoa'a—like I thought Aurelius was for Elonoa'a—and I fell in love with your vision from the first lines of *Aurora*. But I did not know that the poet was the one who would be my fanoa. It was when I saw this portrait that I felt as if someone called my name, and I chose to turn and follow that call wherever it led."

Another long, long silence. Cliopher sat there, patient, remembering ... it felt as if he were remembering his entire life of service and loyalty, and yet nothing at all came to his mind but the great surging love he had for this very human man sitting across the kitchen table from him.

Fitzroy lifted his eyes; they were shining with tears that did not fall. They had spoken of ke'e upstairs, in that tower that would not be a cage; Cliopher had promised to be his zenith star, marking *home*.

"I promise you," he said softly, "that particular painting matters to me because it is the one that told me the ke'ea of my life. Not for any other reason." He smiled, gently teasing, and added: "I'm fairly certain there's an old 'Wanted' poster of you in my room at my mother's house. We could put it in a matching frame."

Fitzroy looked down, not smiling but starting to relax. He slowly unclenched his hands. "Will you keep it somewhere else?"

"Of course," Cliopher said in a great rush of relief, of fondness, of hope. "Of course."

≈

They finished the pastries, and Fitzroy proclaimed himself perishing for a bath. Cliopher saw him out the door, spent a few moments playing with the tap of water (which did seem magical, after the long privations of life on a small vaha at sea), and then he took the portrait upstairs and wondered where he should hide it. If Fitzroy wanted him to destroy it ... but he had not asked him to do so. Not yet. If he did, then Cliopher would deal with the request.

He stood in the middle of the main room, the flame of the sun filling the space with soft, kindly light, and ... simply stood there some more.

Cliopher had never had a house to himself before, and he did not know what to do with it.

He was grateful on so many levels that Fitzroy was there with him, even if it was going to be complicated and difficult negotiating their way through all the unexpected hurts and vulnerabilities of a house, a relationship, a *home*.

It was helpful that Fitzroy had decided he needed a bath, and left Cliopher alone for a bit, so they could both recover their equilibriums.

(Fitzroy had assured him that the bath was surely not so wholly incomprehensible that he—"surely one of the greatest connoisseurs of baths in the whole of the Nine Worlds"—could not figure it out.)

It was incomprehensible that it was the same day Cliopher had so proudly told the assembled elders and the Son of Laughter himself all of what he had achieved in the House of the Sun.

Oh, he was glad he knew what faravia meant. He could not imagine having to simply ... act part of things.

He did not think he could feign anything, after that journey. He had never been given to lying, but he found a deep distaste at the passing thought of pretending to be what he was not.

Just as well that he was not going to go back to the Palace as a courtier.

He would have to get paper and ink, he mused, going through the suites he had imagined being homes for Ludvic, Fitzroy, himself. He'd need to write to Ludvic—Fitzroy probably would as well—and to Aioru—

He stopped in the second room of the suite he'd half-fancied might be the one he chose. There was a beautiful desk he'd never seen before placed against the wall, between two windows looking onto the square.

It was made of striped mahogany, polished to a lustrous shine, with clean lines and a modest set of pigeonholes and drawers. It didn't have anywhere near the number of either that Conju's splendid worktable did, but it was still—it was something he had always wanted, and never quite found.

He pressed his hand against his mouth, trying to hold back the prickle of tears. It was exactly what he'd always wanted. And someone—someone had *known* that, and had put it here.

Who could it be? Conju might have noticed his admiration of his desk, but he wouldn't have commissioned one for Gorjo City.

Cliopher opened the drawers and discovered a selection of excellent papers and envelopes and inks, a selection of calligraphy brushes and pens, and one of the scribal pens.

There was, in one of the pigeonholes, an envelope.

It was addressed to *Kip*, in Vinyë's hand.

My darling Kip,

I found this desk at an estate sale over on Looenna, and thought immediately of how you'd once told me you wanted a desk like this. I didn't see that you had one in the Palace (and why not?), so here you are. I'm sure the papers and inks and so on are not quite what you'd buy for yourself, since when I asked Gaudy his explanations grew more technical by the sentence, so I went over to Lori's Stationery over near the opera house and asked for assistance. When I said who it was for Lori herself came out, and wouldn't let me pay anything at all. I went back the next day and played my cello for them all afternoon, which seemed to be a fair exchange. I must say I do like how people are much more willing to do that sort of thing now that the stipend eases things so.

(Though of course I do appreciate money as well! Sometimes it's inconvenient to barter.)

Love, Vinyë

He folded it up, and stood there for a moment, feeling foolish for the tears starting.

Then he placed the portrait inside one of the drawers, carefully out of sight, and stood there, not sure what to do.

He was still standing there when Fitzroy slammed into the common room and cried, "Cliopher! Kip! Where are you?"

Cliopher had barely managed to turn when Fitzroy came barrelling into the room, his eyes wild and sarong trailing uselessly from one hand.

"What is it?" Cliopher asked with some trepidation.

"Kip, there is an *iguana* in the bathhouse. No—let me rephrase that. There is an iguana *in the bath*. My bath. With me. An *iguana*."

Cliopher blinked at him, his thoughts feeling as if they had been bodily hauled to a different direction. "Oh," he said faintly, a very distant memory rising up. "Saya Dorn had an iguana—a familiar—" He smiled involuntarily at the memory. "It was about eight inches long. Very sweet."

"It's not eight inches any more," Fitzroy said darkly. "It must be six feet if it's an inch."

Chapter Sixty-Four
The Annual Stipend

Fitzroy insisted Cliopher return with him to the bathhouse, which was full of steam.

"Steam?" Cliopher asked.

"There's a boiler," Fitzroy said, gesturing vaguely at a huge copper pot half-visible through a door to the side. "I didn't bother with a fire, I just heated the water. I was having a *great* time. And then the *iguana* showed up. Out of nowhere. As if it appeared by magic."

"And ... could it have?"

"It's an *iguana*." And Fitzroy was one of the greatest magi in the Nine Worlds. If he had felt no magic stir, most likely there had been none.

Cliopher had last been inside the bathhouse most of his lifetime ago, after helping Saya Dorn whitewash the small shed in the courtyard. He looked around curiously. The bath-house was well-lit from skylights. The floor was newly tiled in lovely grey and blue tiles of a sort he'd never seen in the Vangavaye-ve; the walls were covered in a mosaic of waves.

"I am going to set wards," Fitzroy announced, glaring down at the bath, which was about eight feet square and currently entirely empty of a six-foot lizard. "See how the iguana likes *that*."

"You don't think that's a touch excessive?"

"Do *you* want to be surprised by an iguana in your bath?"

"Not particularly," he admitted, trying not to laugh. Fitzroy's expression did not suggest he was in any mood for a joke, and after the tumultuous emotions earlier Cliopher did not want to ruffle him further. He cast around for something innocuous to say. "Is the enchantment on the tank still there?" he asked Fitzroy, who was grumbling mostly silently at the pool. "To clean the water."

Fitzroy frowned at him. "There's magic there ..." But his face was lightening.

Cliopher grinned with relief. "Unlike the iguana."

"It was here," Fitzroy insisted. "I wouldn't make up an *iguana*."

"I didn't think you had! Perhaps it was the magical ghost of her familiar."

"Am I the great mage or not?" Fitzroy flounced over to the corner where pipes came down from the cistern for a shower. "Yes, the magic in here is still working fine. Clever of your Saya Dorn to tie it so thoroughly into the local, natural magic—but of course this was always far from the centre of the Empire, so she couldn't have been *only* a Schooled wizard in practice, no matter her training."

"Excellent," Cliopher said. Fresh water—or clean salt-water—was always a matter of concern in Gorjo City. Most drinking water was collected from rain in rooftop cisterns and then purified by a combination of physical and magical filters—that was presumably what fed the kitchen tap—while waste-water was cleansed by both and the addition of some complex biological filters involving certain plants and other microbiotic organisms before being directed into watering plants and similar. The general goal was to keep the city's freshwater circulating above sea level, so as to avoid affecting the marine flora and fauna that proliferated in the city's waterways. Or so Ghilly had once explained to him.

"Would you like to finish your bath?" Cliopher asked solicitously. "I can stand guard, if you'd like."

"No," Fitzroy replied shortly. "I've been put off. By the *iguana*." He strode out, desultorily wrapping his sarong around his waist as he did so.

Cliopher hesitated a moment, looking around one more time, but the iguana failed to materialize. He did not know quite what to do. He'd thought he could read Fitzroy's emotions so well—

It was good Fitzroy felt comfortable enough to lash out, he supposed. Not that it made being the recipient of the poor temper any better.

~

They sat on the steps and ate the rest of the pastries, which certainly improved Fitzroy's mood after Cliopher had persuaded him to eat several. "It's getting late in the day," he said after they'd mostly finished. "What do you want to do?"

Fitzroy looked longingly in the direction of the bath-house. "I didn't really *finish*," he said, half-defensively. "And you probably want a bath, too?"

"I wouldn't object," Cliopher replied cheerfully. "We should take the rest of our supplies in from the vaha and make sure it's sea-worthy."

"In case of a sudden need for further adventure?" But Fitzroy was grinning. "I do approve, L—Kip."

Too soon for the titles, even as jokes, Cliopher noted. "Indeed, I thought you might, Fitzroy."

Fitzroy yawned mightily. "I know we need supplies, Kip, but I don't think I can handle any more people tonight," he said quietly.

If Cliopher were honest with himself, neither could he. "I'll check over the boat, then, while you have your bath," he said, "and you can decide what to do about sleeping arrangements while I have mine."

"You'd let me make such an important decision?" Fitzroy asked, one eyebrow rising.

"Unless you'd prefer otherwise, of course."

Fitzroy looked actually struck. "No, no, I'll do it. Thank you, Kip."

Cliopher had no idea why that was such a momentous request to his friend, but he was glad he seemed to have landed (however inadvertently) on such a good idea. "Enjoy your bath," he said, laughing, and went over to the vaha to carry all the rest of their goods inside.

∾

Fitzroy's harp and the fire-pot went into places of honour in the sitting room. The boxes from the Marwn's tower were more difficult; after some thought, he tucked them away in one of the storage rooms on the main floor, from whence they could be easily moved as seemed good. They still had a fair amount of supplies on the vaha. He sorted through fishing lines and hooks, husks and broken casoa shells, and made sure everything was ready for an adventure of a moment's notice.

This was something he remembered his father being insistent upon, that you *always* left your boat ready. You never knew, he'd said, when what was supposed to be a simple pleasure-jaunt might not become an emergency by a turn of the wind or an unexpected encounter. It could be a matter of life or death to have a fishing line and a few green coconuts on a boat.

That done, and Fitzroy happily ensconced in the bath-house—from the fragments of singing Cliopher could hear as he went back and forth past the building, the iguana had not made a reappearance—Cliopher arranged their few supplies in the kitchen and then went upstairs to the sitting room.

It felt a remarkable luxury to be able to go to the desk Vinyë had left for him, choose paper and pen and ink, and then go sit in front of the fire he and Fitzroy had lit, and *write*.

They'd need to get a few books, he decided as he set himself up. He was hungry for something to read. He considered the room. There were places they could put up shelves, surely—he'd always wanted a library of his own.

How would they organize it? *Did* Fitzroy organize his books, left to his own devices? Had he ever had a place where he *kept* them? There were so many questions whose answers Cliopher still did not know.

But it would be ... fun, he thought, to learn them.

∾

By the time Fitzroy came in, Cliopher had written most of a letter to Basil, who was, always, the easiest to write to. It was such a lovely thing to know that his cousin might actually *receive* it. Whether the letter arrived before Cliopher and Fitzroy did was less certain. Though now that Cliopher knew more about the situation with the garrison in northern Amboloyo and the Alinorel side of the equation, he felt more secure in sending the letter straight to the garrison to pass through with the next traveller who crossed over.

Fitzroy was much more relaxed when he came up. He'd put on his sarong (changed to a deep purple in colour) and held the tunic from the Grandmother folded untidily over his hand. He stared intently at Cliopher. "Where did you get *writing materials?*"

Cliopher laughed. "Vinyë left me a desk full of them. I thought I'd write a few letters. There's plenty if you'd like to as well."

"How *perfect,*" Fitzroy expressed. "Were there any books?"

"No, we'll have to get them tomorrow."

"Good, good. I left the boiler properly hot, if you want to bathe," Fitzroy said. "Do you mind if I fossick in the desk for what I'd like?"

"Go ahead," Cliopher said, finishing off his letter when Fitzroy did so, and only when he'd set down his pen did he recall he'd put the portrait in the desk.

He followed Fitzroy to the room, apologies on his lips, but Fitzroy was so cheerfully trying out the different inks he must not have looked further down. "Did you find everything you need?" Cliopher asked.

"For now," Fitzroy agreed, and gathered up the chosen ink (the peacock-blue one, of course; Cliopher rather regretted his immediate choice of the pure black) and pens, as well as a few sheets of good paper that the stationer had probably included in the hopes Cliopher would start supplying himself from that shop.

"What a thing this is," Fitzroy said suddenly, as they entered the sitting room and looked at the merry fire in the brazier, the harp gleaming, the sky a deep royal blue through the ceiling aperture. "To be in a house, and for it to be ... ours."

"Utterly fantastic," Cliopher agreed, brushing his hand gently across Fitzroy's elbow as he passed him.

∾

Cliopher's bath remained uninterrupted by any visitors, reptilian or otherwise. Even without any toiletries, it was a great and splendid luxury to bathe in as much hot water as he desired.

He added *towels* to his list of supplies when he came out and realized he had nothing but his grass skirt, and accordingly had to drip his way back to the house.

He went into the kitchen, thinking he might as well take some of their leftover fermented breadfruit as an evening snack, and discovered they'd had a visitor. Who had brought *food.*

On the kitchen table was a basket of bread and a covered clay pot containing some sort of fragrant soup full of vegetables and dumplings. There was no note or other indication of who it might be from. His eyes pricked with tears at this consideration, and he carefully carried both objects upstairs. It wasn't as if they had any dishes anyway.

"We do have *neighbours,*" Fitzroy said, after a moment of stunned appreciation at the sight of the soup, and before Cliopher could say anything, off he went outside. He came back a bare few minutes later with two bowls, carved wooden spoons, and several blankets.

Cliopher told himself that he was probably justified in his smugness.

"Since we don't have any furniture yet," Fitzroy said, when they had put away the dishes and returned upstairs to finish their letters before the fire, "I thought we could sleep out here. The fire is cozy, you know."

"A good plan," Cliopher agreed, who did not want to sleep in an empty room by himself, either.

He finished five letters—to Basil, to Ludvic, to Conju, to Aioru, to Vinyë—while Fitzroy wrote his own and then shifted to playing his harp. The rippling music was familiar after their long journey together, but it sounded different, in the confines of the room, when Cliopher was writing, when there was no sea or stars to bound their horizon, but walls.

He slept well, even on a simple mat with a blanket for a pillow, even indoors. The fire was a comfort, and the air was fresh and warm.

It was a comfort to hear Fitzroy breathing, a few feet away from him.

They woke near dawn the next morning, and ate the rest of the bread on the balcony for their morning meal. While they did so, Cliopher thought over what they were going to need and how they were going to acquire it.

"Coffee," said Fitzroy dreamily. "And tea. You can get tea here, can't you?"

"It's expensive, of course, but yes."

"And chocolate."

"All sorts of things," Cliopher replied. "Anything we want. Within reason," he added hastily, as certain logistical concerns immediately came to mind. "I wonder if I can get any money out of my bank." A small, colourful finch was hopping around on the floor in front of them in the hopes for crumbs. He threw a piece of his crust down, which the bird accepted, and then it fluttered up to sit on Fitzroy's hand.

"Magic," Fitzroy said with a straight face, making a kissing noise at the finch.

"I suppose we can trade skills for money, yes. Bartering." Cliopher didn't object to that, of course, but it was a tedious thought when it came to every necessity. "I think there will be some clothes at my mother's house that will fit me ... probably we can find something for you, too. Gaudy's taller than I am, and he might have left things behind."

"Or," Fitzroy said, after the bird flew off and he was able to give what Cliopher thought was appropriate consideration to this problem, "*or* we can go and get the annual stipend, and have plenty of money for what we need."

Cliopher opened his mouth, and then stopped.

"It was for *everybody*," Fitzroy said smugly. "You were very insistent about that, if I recall. You never know a person's situation, you said. The rich can be trapped by their circumstances as much as the poor, you said. How do you know, you cried in the midst of your seven-hour oratorical masterpiece on the subject, that one of us—us being those in the Council of Princes—might not one day need it?"

Cliopher realized his mouth was still open, and shut it.

"Exactly," Fitzroy said. "Come on, my Lord Mdang! Let us be off!"

"Of course, my lord," he replied automatically.

Fitzroy wrinkled his nose at him, finished off his last mouthful, and brushed off his fingers with some delicacy. "Lead the way. May I request that we walk, unless it is substantially quicker by boat? I'd like to get a sense of the neighbourhood."

"A good idea," Cliopher replied, and adjusted the grass skirt. Fitzroy was wearing the tunic, which he'd belted with the scarlet cloth he'd previously used around his hair. Cliopher was glad to see this departure from the rigid sartorial rules of the emperor, who wore white, black, gold, and Imperial yellow in public.

Neither of them had sandals, but their feet were fairly well hardened after the time on the vaha; he hadn't felt it very awkward to walk on the paths on Loaloa.

"This is the edge of Zaviya Square," he said, as they entered the small, leafy square in front of the house. There were several very old and wide-spreading trees in large pots on the corners, and a central fresh-water pool filled with waterlilies. "There's a market here once a week. They used to do puppet shows over on the corner, there. My cousin Faila runs the company now, but I'm not sure if they still do them here or if they've moved to one of the bigger squares."

"How splendid! What sort of market?"

Cliopher thought. "I'm not sure. When I was a boy it was a daily market, but this has become a less desirable quarter since the Fall, mostly inhabited by the old and sometimes foreign."

"We fit both those categories," Fitzroy said, elbowing him gently. "And I expect it will become a *most* desirable neighbourhood once we're living here properly."

"Could be," Cliopher replied, smiling at the thought. They passed through a gap between houses on a lane that wound for several hundred yards alongside a curving canal, before turning a sharp corner, arching over a bridge, and landing them at the edge of the main commercial district.

Fitzroy walked with a long, swinging stride, his mood seemingly returned to bright vivacity. Cliopher's stride was shorter but faster; he kept pace easily. It was ... well, it wasn't *odd*, was it, that Fitzroy should be somewhat mercurial? His Radiancy—

He frowned at the internal usage of the term. While Cliopher had known *his Radiancy* as well as anyone could, as well as anyone had been *permitted* to, he had spent the past months travelling with Fitzroy, and he knew *him*.

Fitzroy had not been this mercurial on the vaha, but then again there hadn't been much occasion for such swings of mood. There hadn't been much to trigger any change of emotion. Before Nivomano Cliopher had been sick, or whatever you called that reaction to returning to Zunidh, and after the bleak tower where the Marwn had been exiled, Fitzroy had naturally been quiet and withdrawn.

After Nivomano they had both kept the conversations light.

Cliopher's own emotions were a bit tumultuous, walking through the familiar-unfamiliar neighbourhoods of Gorjo City, in the familiar-unfamiliar Islander garments, with the familiar-unfamiliar man beside him.

His head, for the first time in ages, was throbbing gently.

They cut through the tail end of a market, where Fitzroy promptly charmed an amulet in exchange for two pairs of sandals, and where one of Cliopher's younger cousins commented on his appearance.

"You really are following Uncle Tovo, aren't you?" Tuaso said, rolling his eyes. "Look at you in a grass skirt and feathers in your hair. Anyone would think you just came from the Ring."

"We did," Cliopher said. "We sailed Sky Ocean and came in through Loaloa."

"Really?" But Tuaso did not seem particularly interested. "Maybe that explains it." He shrugged off Cliopher's eccentricities—which really was just as well, Cliopher did not really want to get into all the details of his adventures. (Not even Fitzroy's studiously bland expression could make him!) "Louya's looking for you, something about the sea turtles? She seemed very excited to talk to you, whatever it was." His tone suggested Cliopher and Louya went together in his estimation.

Cliopher pretended his grimace was for the not-exactly-perfect fit of his new sandals and was glad to take his leave.

$\sim$

They passed five more cousins, three of their spouses, and no fewer than seven of their children—though five of these were together in a school outing—all of whom greeted Cliopher and 'his lord' with bright smiles and laughter about his grass skirt and his hair and the feathers ("Oh, Kip, *surely* you know you can still be tanà without dressing like Great-Uncle Tovo!"), and a strange undercurrent he could not name.

He almost brought up the undercurrent, wondering what Fitzroy made of it, but then they were at the newly relocated Department of the Common Weal—Tuaso had told them the new address—and the moment seemed to pass.

"Am I to expect any more relations in here?" Fitzroy said as they came to the door.

"Probably," Cliopher replied, already exhausted from those they had encountered. His head was throbbing, waves from a distant storm-front. But he was home ... and he'd eaten ... his stomach wasn't rebelling against the rich, unaccustomed food ... and he'd slept last night. "Sorry," he mumbled.

"For your scores of relatives? It's an experience, admittedly. One day I shall write a song about all your cousins and your uncles and your aunts. Shall we?" Without waiting any further he pulled open the door, and they went in to a blessedly dim room. Five or six people were waiting, one at the counter and the rest sitting in chairs set around the walls. They looked up with desultory interest when the door opened; Fitzroy beamed at them, and Cliopher smiled depreciatingly, and the curiosity sharpened almost unbearably.

"Cousin Kip!" a woman called from the front of the room.

This was the official behind the counter, a tall, handsome woman in her late thirties; Uncle Cliopher's youngest daughter. His flashcards of family members came to mind, and he was able to smile and advance a few steps into the room. "Cousin Nora!"

"Fancy seeing you here!" she cried with a great grin. "Are you here to summarily fire everyone again?"

Cliopher flushed. "No ..."

"I don't expect we need to, and if we do, Kip will write a letter to the new Chancellor Aioru and ask him to deal with it," Fitzroy declared, advancing on the counter with a smile that made Nora preen happily and twinkle up at him. Cliopher was too professional—too *polite*—to roll his eyes, but he wanted to. "No," Fitzroy went on, leaning his elbow on the counter and turning his head to address the entire room, "we've just arrived from a long sail across Sky Ocean—Kip sailed all the way to the House of the Sun and back, you know—and have no money at all."

There was a faint, incredulous murmur.

"Kip was all up for bartering but I reminded him that he was *extremely* eloquent on the topic of the necessity of it being a *universal* annual stipend, and so here we are. Do we take a seat to wait?"

Nora stared, which was probably the effect Fitzroy had been going for, if his brilliant smile was any indication.

"I don't mind waiting!" one of the people who'd been near the front of the room said, moving back three steps with alacrity. "Good on you, Kip." His glance flickered from Fitzroy to the feathers in his hair, and Cliopher stifled a sigh and the desire to say, again, *It's not like that.*

Because it wasn't—and yet it was. The declaration that they were fanoa was a tender flame but a brightly blazing one in his heart.

"Have you the book and the pen?" Fitzroy asked Nora, who moved slowly, a small smile on her face, to draw out the enchanted objects. "I've done this before," he added to Cliopher, "because the post office in—you know, I never learned the village's name—the village by the Abbey of the Mountains, at any rate—"

"Oussel," Cliopher supplied from some recess of memory housing the reports about those strange doings when Possibly Aurelius Magnus or Maybe Fitzroy Angursell fell out of the sky in answer to a postulant nun's prayers.

"Oussel, really? Doesn't sound very Damaran ... at any rate, the post officer, who also served as the local administrator for the stipend, had an assortment of Alinorel and Ystharian money he gave to me in lieu of the regular monthly stipend."

Nora, by this time, had set a huge book on the counter, and beside it a silver-chased ebony pen with an ivory tip. Cliopher regarded these with ... amusement, he could call it at this remove. The long hours of debate over the aesthetics of the annual stipend had seemed irksome and unnecessary at the time—but he did know just how much the aesthetics could matter, in the end.

There was a certain *awe* encoded in a grand old book and a beautiful, fancy pen. The magic required the silver and ivory, a certain sort of solution involved in making the paper for the book: the rest of it was all for show.

Fitzroy looked entirely in his element as he took up the pen and signed his name with an elegant flourish before moving over so that Cliopher could follow suit.

The pen was a goodly weight in his hand: it felt substantial, important, signing his name beneath *Artorin Damara of Solaara*, which was in turn below *Tia Mdang of Tahivoa.*

There was no ink. Magic was at work here, magic identifying the truth of his identity and whether he had claimed the stipend that month already, and when he wrote his legal name on the paper the magic would funnel ink to form the contract.

He was a citizen of Zunidh and he could therefore receive the stipend. That was it: nothing more, and nothing less.

The pen didn't write.

He frowned and instead of *Cliopher* tried *Kip*, but that didn't work, either.

Fitzroy said, "Is there a problem, Kip?" He looked over Cliopher's shoulder and hummed. "Please say you didn't deliberately exclude yourself from the categories covered by the stipend? That sounds like something you would do out of some misbegotten sense of ... appropriateness."

Nora snorted and then giggled, and Cliopher flushed.

"I couldn't have," he said. "It should work."

"It's not setting off the alarms," Nora murmured, taking the book back to consider it. "You tried *Kip* as well as *Cliopher*?"

"I did. Neither are working."

"How strange ..." She frowned, then absently bent down to pull out a small sack with the seal of the Treasury on it—the actual amount of the stipend, Cliopher presumed, and then, still thoughtfully, pulled out a second one and set it on the counter.

"Oh, no," Cliopher protested immediately. "It isn't working, Nora."

Nora gave him a steady look, somewhat tempered by her smirk. "Did you get the stipend this month, while you were up on Sky Ocean, Cousin Kip?"

He tried to answer and stumbled over his words, flushing. "But it's not the right *procedure*," he mumbled.

"I think it's probably because you were legally announced to be dead, and all the stuff after that," Nora said, nodding as she spoke. "I bet it got recorded and then didn't get fixed again, don't you think?"

Fitzroy was happily flipping through the pages of the book, which was almost certainly against the spirit of the law—although as the Lord Emperor theoretically he *was* allowed to look at whatever governmental records there were—Cliopher's headache was starting to be much more prominent, and he struggled with not being distracted by all the people *looking* at him.

He wanted to shrink away, hide in a doorway as he had when he had first come home after the Fall, duck his head and not be seen ...

But he was not a young man, and he had looked the very Sun in his eyes and won back the mirimiri of Ani. He let himself clench his jaw, just for a moment, and then he smiled at Nora.

In the moment before he spoke, Fitzroy said, "I'm fairly certain at some point in your lengthy peroration on the subject of the annual stipend—in one of your several perorations on the subject—you made much of the fact that while corruption is always to be deplored and guarded against, a bureaucracy with no room for personal judgment or agency on the part of its bureaucrats was ... oh, what did you say? *Soulless, inhumane,* and ... *likely to destroy the very things it purports to serve,* I believe was your phrase."

Nora snickered and pushed the second bag over to Cliopher. "There you are, Cousin Kip, your boss thinks you should let me have agency and personal judgment in order to prevent the collapse of society. Will you pass me back the book, sir—or is *sire* the right term?"

"It is my understanding that the Islanders have never had *kings*," Fitzroy replied with a straight face, flipping back to the last page of the book and regarding it with an odd expression; almost a challenge, but to whom Cliopher could not tell. "Actually, let me try something, will you?"

Fitzroy did not wait for Nora to reply. He plucked the elegant pen from Cliopher's hand and with a much more fluid movement of his hand, signed *Fitzroy Angursell of Nowhere in Particular* underneath his legal name.

The magic sparkled and settled into ink, and Nora and Cliopher and Fitzroy himself all stared at the book.

"Well," said Nora, faintly, and then more loudly: "Fitzroy Angursell. Imagine that."

Fitzroy bit his lip and then grinned up at Cliopher with an expression of winsome apology and delighted mischief at war.

"I used to think you were so subtle," Cliopher said, because there was nothing else in his head. Not a word, not an idea, not an image. Not an idea.

Fitzroy just grinned at him, and deliberately set the pen down in the gutter of the book.

Nora said, "Ah, I'll, hmm, just make a notation ..." She picked up another pen from her side of the desk and wrote *Kip Mdang of Tahivoa [erroneously presumed deceased]* in the book.

Right under *Fitzroy Angursell of Nowhere In Particular.*

"Why did that work?" Cliopher cried in exasperation.

"Did you leave a loophole, Lord Mdang?" Fitzroy said, with *inordinate* delight. It was almost obscene how much enjoyment he was taking, really.

"No, I didn't," Cliopher growled, glaring as Nora diligently—nearly defiantly—set a third stipend bag on the counter. "*Why did that work.*"

"Because I have two legal identities," Fitzroy replied, his eyes bright. "Which have never been connected in any official capacity. I gave the whole Red Company official pardons, if you recall—"

"Oh, I do. Once we unearthed them from where you'd stuck the folder."

"I thought you might appreciate my discretion."

Cliopher could not help but laugh, even if reluctantly. "And by our own laws that means all of them—all of *you*—have citizenship and all the rights and responsibilities that appertain thereto."

"Including the stipend," said Nora.

"And *responsibilities*," he repeated.

"Have I ever paid taxes?" Fitzroy said, wonderingly, with a terrifying glint in his eye.

Cliopher glanced around at the avidly attentive audience, recognized one man as a jobbing journalist for the *Ring o'News*, and grabbed the three stipend bags with one hand and Fitzroy's elbow with the other.

"Thank you, Nora, we'd best be going. Lots of supplies to acquire. Things to talk about. You know how it is."

"Definitely, Cousin Kip," said Nora, and mercifully managed to avoid laughing until the office door had shut behind them.

"That was splendid," Fitzroy said, once they were a few buildings down. He was still laughing, tossing one of the bags up and down in the air.

"Really," said Cliopher, biting off the words, and strode off almost at random.

CHAPTER SIXTY-FIVE
ISLAND TIME

T his part of the city overlapped with the sections he'd toured in the *other place*'s Esa'a, and Cliopher looked at the buildings with a strange, terrifying sense of dislocation. Fitzroy's slightly manic mood appeared entirely undimmed, and Cliopher wondered, still rather disgruntled by the scene in the Common Weal office, how much of it was a pretence.

"What shall we get first?" Fitzroy asked happily. "I need something to read, Kip. I am perishing for new words. Do you think Aya has a new book out? The last one of hers I read was *The Case of the Lost Parrot*."

"I think there's been another one since then," Cliopher replied, forcing his thoughts to stop gibbering insistently at the lack of fruit trees, vegetables, traditional clothes, great carved house frontages. Those weren't *real*—not in *his* city.

Not yet. Not ever, probably. Cliopher was not going to be the person forcing a cultural revolution on his people.

"A bookstore, then, is a certain necessity," Fitzroy murmured. "And we need food, yes? And soap."

He sang a snatch of a song—one of his own, from those bright-lit youthful days of the Red Company—Cliopher knew it, but nothing would come to his mind, his lips. Not the title of Aya's most recent mystery novel, not the words or title of the song, not a smile or a suggestion of what they needed to get for their house.

He, himself, was at least four books behind on Aya's mystery series, and he thought he'd been doing so well after reducing his hours.

They came into a more open area, bordering along the main canal leading towards the Tahivoa lagoon, and now there were people.

Many people. Looking at him and Fitzroy, some greeting them—Cliopher replied mechanically, a smile and a greeting, a name if he could bring it to mind, just a nod if he couldn't—*yes, I've just arrived—yes, we sailed Sky Ocean—yes, this is my lord—*

He wanted to say *my fanoa*, but he could not. The word was too precious, too important, too real.

Yes, it's good to be alive; yes, it's strange to be retired; yes, it's good to be home; yes, I do have feathers in my hair; yes, I did make this grass skirt—

Cousin after cousin, and spouses and children, and in the distance an uncle, an aunt, his dead sister Navalia's best friend from childhood, the son of his old teacher, neither of whom had ever liked him—

He set his shoulders, his chin, his smile.

No, I hadn't heard that news—no, I haven't seen Aunt Malania—no, I didn't know Cousin Fina was seeing anyone—no, I'm not trying *to start a new fashion—*

He had so many relatives. The Mdangs had spread across the city, of course, but they were concentrated in Tahivoa, and as they came around the lagoon towards the covered market where Cliopher's mother had always bought her household wares, he could barely focus past the next familiar-unfamiliar face that looked at him in disbelief and shock and then, with a faltering smile, cried, "Kip! And his lord! Goodness, look at your *hair*."

Fitzroy took it all in stride, as if this was not simply to be expected, but to be desired.

Cliopher wondered if drowning felt like this. His mind felt as it had deep in that dark, cold water between the two halves of his heart, the weight of his life and the fear pressing close on his lungs, the blood sluggish in his veins, wondering if he'd passed the point of no return.

He could have kept going, down. He had not touched the bottom of that dark water, that tunnel that opened only down—

"And perhaps something to—Kip!"

That voice, that tone, would always cut through his preoccupations.

He spoke automatically: "My lord?—Fitzroy."

Fitzroy's eyebrows plunged together and his lips thinned, but he seemed to deliberately refuse to comment on that. Or so Cliopher guessed, but his head was throbbing and his thoughts were scattered as the sunlight on the waves.

Had he *dreamed* the whole of that voyage through the sky?

"You're looking very peaky," Fitzroy said. "Let's—here's a bench." And without waiting he bustled Cliopher to a bench set along a wall all overhung with white star jasmine. The fragrance was nearly overpowering, and his headache seemed to gather reinforcements.

He closed his eyes. "I'm sorry," he said. "Fitzroy."

"Kip, what's wrong?"

"Nothing."

"Most convincing," Fitzroy replied dryly. "The truth, now."

"It's too much," Cliopher whispered, refusing to shrink back when someone walking by gave him a bright, excited smile and a wave. He waved, if desultorily, but Fitzroy must have done something for the man kept walking on with just a complicated sort of gesture in their direction.

"Who was that?" Fitzroy asked.

"I have no idea," Cliopher said tiredly. "We're probably related."

"Fifty-nine cousins sounded like a lot in the abstract, but it's even more in the flesh."

Cliopher closed his eyes, placing his hands over his face in the hopes that might relieve some of the strain. "It's more than that," he managed hoarsely. "We reckon relation out to the fourth degree ... Bertie and I figured it out once, I'm related by blood or marriage to fully a quarter of Gorjo City."

"Maths is not my strongest subject, as you know, but that sounds improbable."

"Lots of Mdangs moved here. Other islands have other dominant lineages ... the Epalos tend towards Nevans and a few Kindraa, the Poyë are strong on Tisiliamo—that's where Ghilly's from."

"Yes, yes, I understand. What do you want to do, Kip?"

"We need supplies. I've been trying to make a list ..."

"You and your lists." But his voice was fond. "Tell me what you have so far."

"Food. Some dishes. Clothes—though we can get some from my mother's house."

"We have money, and I have never liked wearing cast-offs unless as part of a costume—and even then there are arguments to be made for proper tailoring ..."

"We shouldn't spend *all* our money at once."

Fitzroy laughed. "The budget—oh, it's a pity I don't have my bag! I was doing so well with keeping track of my spending, Kip. You'll be astonished."

"I am," Cliopher assured him, removing his hands and blinking at the strange, over-saturated appearance of the world around him. He felt even more oddly like he'd strayed into the *other place*, the Esa'a of the other Kip's vision of what the Islanders could be.

But the other Kip's vision had not included coffee or—or Fitzroy—

Fitzroy was peering down at him. "Are we close to your uncle Lazo's? Or your mother's house? Somewhere you could lie down for a while? I can do the shopping. Food, dishes, clothes I can manage."

"We're nearly at the market where there are stores for housewares and things ..."

"I'm almost entirely certain I can find someone to guide me," Fitzroy said, and stood up, then carefully set his hand under Cliopher's elbow to lever him up. "There you are. I've got our money, and—yes, there we are."

"We need the next bridge," Cliopher said, but he felt better for having sat down out of the way, despite the star jasmine (and usually he loved flower-scents ... had the landslide taken that from him?), and he could smile with better humour at the various neighbours he'd known all his life and who looked at him with strange expressions on their faces.

"What am I supposed to *do*, Fitzroy?" he whispered, as they came around the corner, and the house was there, familiar, a faded red, the mango tree still straggling in its pot next to the door, and Cliopher felt as if he had never come home at all.

"Rest, first," Fitzroy said, "and let me take care of things."

"You make it sound easy," Cliopher replied, trying not to sob, to flinch, as someone called a greeting from a boat in the canal.

"I learned to trust you," Fitzroy said. "You trusted me with the boat, didn't you?"

Cliopher nodded, something stabbing in his head at the motion. "What a tanà I am," he muttered, gripping tightly to Fitzroy's elbow.

"Showing that you can accept care and support when you need it? That you need not be perfect to be great? That if you light a new hearth-fire for the world that there might be a cost? All that is a fine example to set for others," Fitzroy said.

For the first time in a long time Cliopher thought of the portrait Suzen had painted of him, the tanà of the world, with strength and wisdom in his eyes.

"You're right," he said, wishing for that strength, that wisdom, that certainty.

"I often am."

Despite Fitzroy's light tone he smiled gently, compassionately down at Cliopher, and then they were at his mother's house. Fitzroy opened the front door without ringing the bell. They stepped inside the cool, dim front hall. The heavy door swung shut behind them, and the bright noise and colour of the world outside cut off sharply.

"No one's here," Fitzroy said, a swirl of air presumably reacting to his magic to inform him so. "Your room's upstairs?"

"I'm not that unwell," Cliopher said, but he was glad for his friend's company as he struggled up the two flights of stairs to his childhood bedroom.

He got the sense that Fitzroy was very intrigued by the remnant decorations of many layers of his life, but Cliopher's eyes were entirely for the bed. "I think I might lie down," he declared.

"A good idea," Fitzroy said, shoving him gently in that direction. Cliopher more or less collapsed onto the mattress, which felt incredibly soft and receptive. "I believe I recall where the privy is ... I'll come back in a couple of hours, shall I?"

"Island time," Cliopher mumbled, face down into the pillow. "Sunset's a bit later than the Palace ... Don't get lost?"

"I could find you anywhere," Fitzroy said softly, or he thought he did ... Cliopher felt as if he were whirling around, as if he were falling ...

(That landslide; that waterfall; those sunset clouds at the edge of the sky)

(He was not imagining the blanket placed over his shoulders. It was there when he woke.)

He woke what must have been several hours later. It was dark, for one thing, and he felt much better.

He sat up, the blanket falling off his shoulders. He stroked the soft material, a woven blanket in soft blues and greens that had been on his bed since he'd been a child. It had a few holes, and one edge was fraying, but it was still soft and warm, and it smelled, comfortingly, of the sweet-fern distillation Aunt Oura—who had always been primarily responsible for the laundry—always used.

His door was shut, but Cliopher knew this room. He stood up, stretching gratefully, brushing his hair back from his face, and yawned extravagantly. He grinned at himself for feeling as if that were a trifle daring, a trifle *uncouth*, and ambled the few steps necessary to his old desk. There was a box on top where most of his lingering belongings were stored, and he felt through it—careful of any sharp-pointed quills or pencils left behind—for the smooth glass globe that had served as his study-light for many years.

He'd won it as a prize in a competition for debate in school, having managed to argue quite successfully—with an irony certainly not lost on him or anyone else who remembered the occasion—that a bureaucracy was a burden and a waste of money.

He tapped the globe in a short pattern, and a soft clear light slowly welled up from its heart.

He sat back on the bed, and looked at the room thus illuminated.

Familiar, yes, and unfamiliar, too. The walls were still the soft, creamy white he'd painted them when he went to university, smudged and nicked here and there with the wear and tear of time; the single bed with a mattress that felt splendid after so long sleeping on the bare boards of the vaha but which was, he knew, actually quite mediocre; the one wide window, shuttered closed. The desk, its companion chair, the closet containing the rest of his things.

He'd not bothered with art, so there was the hanging Navalia had given him when he finished school and the painting Vinyë had given him for another birthday, and his university degree. And the 'Wanted' poster of Fitzroy Angursell, which, now that he knew just who *was* Fitzroy Angursell, was clearly of someone else.

Someone else had added a frame since his last time home, and he got up to look at it, the globe in his hands throwing a soft shadow across the floor.

The frame held the official proclamation of his appointment to the Viceroyship —Cliopher was somewhat astonished to realize it was an original copy, the ink his Radiancy had used gleaming with faint flecks of gold, the wax of the seal thick and resonant with magic. His mother must have had it framed, which was a pleasing thought ... why she'd then placed it here, hidden away from visitors to the house, was a little more perplexing.

It was hard to feel anything but a little tired and mostly amused about the endless efforts to impress his mother. She did love him; he had never doubted that. She was proud of him, too; he knew that, at an intellectual level, even if he'd never quite been able to reconcile that knowledge with what he'd always seen as her endless disappointment with his choices and actions.

But what had he shown *her*? A life far-distant, far-removed from his family, his culture, seemingly himself ... a son who had banked that blazing fire of the secret, deeply personal half of his heart down to the smouldering coals of the room holding the more public-facing triumphs of which he could be proud.

She'd wanted him to be happy, and to be successful—and being *successful* meant according to the values and customs and mores of their family, their people. He was not married, had no children, had not claimed the dances of the tanà until that extraordinary viceroyship ceremony—and so until he had done so, his status had remained uncertain, unclear.

And now he had come back from Sky Ocean, full of the news of walking legends, with a fanoa.

Traditionally, to have a fanoa *was* acceptable, was to be as firmly part of the nexus of relationships as a spouse or a child; a fanoa had legal claim on inheritance, and ... and no one had used that meaning of the word in decades or more. Established, inherited trading partnerships were still called fanoa networks, but they went in the category of customary usage of distant uninhabited islands. It was not part of everyday life.

Cliopher did not want people to mock him for being old-fashioned and foolish for having a fanoa, as they had when he had merely expressed the desire for one.

Cliopher did not want anyone to laugh at Fitzroy for *being* his fanoa.

He swallowed, and forced that unlikelihood away (*surely* it was unlikely, surely it was not his reason speaking, surely it was just him feeling down-hearted and bewildered). If they laughed, well, what then? They had laughed at Cliopher before, and he had proven them all wrong. He *had* run the government better than those hitherto in power; he *had* found an emperor worthy of standing beside; he *had* sailed to the House of the Sun and brought home fire; and he *was* the rising tanà, and he would give them a new model of fanoa to go with the rest.

He had not dived down through that dark and terrible black water to find the secret half of his heart to ignore it now that he was on the other side.

He sat down on his bed, but he was no longer tired, and the thought of that cave with its hearth made of pearls made him remember the little stuffed whale, and he wondered—he had to—whether it might indeed still be in the house.

Not in his closet—he'd gone through it too many times over the years. Which meant, most likely in the attic, where the unwanted detritus of the household inevitably ended up.

He took his glass light with him, climbing slowly to the upper floor of the house. The attic latch was stiff, but he jimmied it open and held up the light.

Someone had cleaned the attic recently, and organized it. It took him only a few minutes to find the pile of boxes labelled "Kip" in his sister's writing.

He sat down beside the boxes, sneezing at the dust as he opened them.

His old notebooks from school and university. He flipped through a few pages, smiling at his unpracticed hand, the wildly varying letters depending on his mood and engagement with whatever he was writing. Loose, erratic scrawls of reminders for himself—a party for Bertie's birthday; a present for Ghilly's; mentions of one or other cousin's events for which he had to send a card—Small, cramped notes for his secret meditations on *what might be*, those first attempts at combining the *Lays* with the wider world of Astandalas.

He closed the box and decided he would bring it to his new house at some point. Fitzroy had suggested he consider writing a memoir of his time in government, and although Cliopher was not certain he really wanted to write such a thing—surely it would be terribly boring to anyone *not* already involved?—

No. That was untrue. He was afraid of telling the truth of what it had been like.

He turned quickly to the next box, which held letters addressed to him. He flipped through a few, not opening the envelopes, tears rising from simply seeing his name in all those hands. His sisters, his mother, his grandfather, his grandmothers ... letters from his time on Loaloa, these must be. He'd been at home the rest of the time.

The third box held miscellaneous items: toys, gifts, little treasures he'd found on the beach. Nestled deep into the bottom was the scruffy, faded velvet of Au'aua, with its one remaining ahalo-cloth eye still gleaming, as if she had been waiting for him all this time.

~

He was sitting there, staring at the detritus of childhood, remembering the deep, soft moss of that innermost cave, the lumps and bumps of forgotten loves, the fire with its encircling hearth of pearls, when someone knocked on the door.

"Come in," he said, not moving.

"See, I found you," Fitzroy said happily, entering the attic with a bounce in his step and a sudden flurry of—not exactly wind, or light, but the sense that there was more light, more air, in the room than there had been before he'd entered.

Of course, literally there *was*, as the door was open and there were lights in the hall, fresh air coming in the entry, but still ... Cliopher shook his head and smiled. "You're back?"

"I've been back for half an hour or more. Helping your aunt Oura with supper. She sent me up to bring you down." Fitzroy grinned at him, and flopped down beside him without further comment. "What's that?"

Cliopher clutched the whale defensively. Fitzroy tilted his head, curious, but not pressing.

Fitzroy was his fanoa. He wouldn't laugh at Cliopher's sentimentality, would he? "It's a toy from when I was small," he said at last, and shyly showed it to him. "When I was down in that dark island, I remembered her ... it's Au'aua, you see."

"The great whale. I do see," Fitzroy replied gravely, looking closely at the toy but not touching. "You loved her."

"Yes," Cliopher breathed, and had to wipe his eyes. "It's silly, I'm sure. My mother took her away from me at one point ... said I was too old for stuffed toys ..."

"How foolish. We shall give her a place of honour, if you like."

He swallowed, and brushed his thumb down the worn velvet of her back. "Yes." He cleared his throat, trying to regain his equilibrium.

But then Fitzroy scuttled over and embraced him fiercely. "There's no shame," he whispered, "in loving something, however big, however small."

Cliopher rested there, the whale in his hand, his head against his fanoa's shoulder, held in comfort, in strength, in love. After a while he stirred. "You said Aunt Oura had made us supper?"

Fitzroy looked at him carefully. "Yes, but we don't have to stay, if you would prefer to go home."

"You've been shopping, and I've been sleeping," Cliopher said, wiping his face. "How are you so full of energy?"

"Magic," Fitzroy replied easily. " Don't look so shocked, Kip! I don't mean ... whatever you're worried about. I'm a mage, and not doing very much magic," he went on. "So it's sort of ... pooling, I suppose. Building up resources for some great working ... which is what I've trained it to do. Since I'm not doing any such great working, it's providing me with extra vim. It's one reason why great magi so often have excellent health and a great memory well into old age—the magic compensates for physical infirmities."

That seemed entirely unfair, but then again, the distribution of gifts was never fair.

"Oh," said Cliopher, and looked at the toy in his hand. Au'aua's ahalo-cloth eye seemed just as full of wisdom and compassion as the Great Whale of Sky Ocean had been. He touched his efela ko, the obsidian pendant comforting in his hands. "I'd like to see my aunt," he said at last.

"Go wash your face," Fitzroy advised. "Then we can go down for supper. It's just us and your aunt and your other aunt, though I didn't catch which one. She wasn't here yet, but will be in the next half-hour or so, Oura said."

"Yes," said Cliopher. "I didn't look for any clothes ..."

"Oh, I brought you some—they're hanging over the railing in the hall."

"Thank you."

"My great pleasure!" Fitzroy stretched languorously and then jumped spryly to his feet. He had changed his garments, and was wearing cream-coloured trousers and a Vangavayen-style knee-length tunic in a pale lavender embroidered with brown and violet and cream. "Go on, Kip," he instructed. "Don't spend too long staring at yourself in the mirror."

As if that wasn't a strange thing to say at all. Cliopher hesitated a moment, and then gave Fitzroy the whale to keep safe.

～

The new clothes were nice in his hands—good linen and silk, he noted absently—but he was yawning again as he went into the room, the light winking on as he entered (Vinyë's first boyfriend had been proud of his magic, and had enchanted the lights in all the house's privies and wash-rooms to work automatically—the relationship had not lasted but his magic continued), and he was immediately distracted from the clothes Fitzroy had chosen for him by the stranger's reflection in the mirror.

Not a stranger, except in time ...

Cliopher let the door swing quietly shut behind him, and was glad for the weight of the clothes in his hands, for his hands were trembling and that was hard even for himself to see.

The man in the mirror did not look *young*; not any more than Fitzroy looked *young*. But he did not look old, either, and Cliopher *had* looked old—he had looked old in the portraits Suzen had painted; in comparison to the other Kip of the *other place*; in comparison to his friends, his family, Basil; in the mirror of his rooms in the Palace.

He did not look *old*, not as he had.

His hair was down to his shoulders, which he'd known, pushing it back from his face, letting Fitzroy brush it and braid it. Cliopher extracted one hand from the clothes so he could touch the feathers the Wind That Rises At Dawn had given him, the soft greys and lavenders and faintest, tenderest rosy-peach of the morning. His hair was lustrous, shining in rich, healthy waves, the black like the night waters of Sky Ocean, the grey not as bright a silver as that in Fitzroy's hair, but shining, gleaming, silvery-grey like the shadows and starlight Fitzroy had spun into thread.

His face was still creased with wrinkles, still showing his experiences, his preoccu-pations, his *life*—but his skin was no longer loose and worn, but visibly healthy. Visibly ... *alive*. Strong. In his prime.

And his eyes ... Cliopher did not know quite what they might look like to other people, but to him ... well, he could see a glimmer of why no one had voiced or even hinted at any doubt at his statement that he had sailed to the House of the Sun. There was a look in his eyes, even staring at himself in the bath-room of his mother's house, that said he had drunk of the honey-mead of the Sun, and heard the voices of the white birds of dawn.

He made use of the water-closet, and washed his hands and his face in the basin, and was not surprised that Fitzroy had brought him garments almost the match of his own, though the tunic was a warm orange-red raw silk that rasped pleasantly against his skin and made his colouring seem to glow.

This tunic had a vee-shaped neck, letting his efela show to the world: the efetana, the efela ko, and the one the Grandmother had called Kiofa'a, with the sea-witch's garnet pebble rattling quietly inside the sundrop cowrie.

Well.

He didn't have anything else in his mind. Just ... *well*.

He tucked a few loose strands of hair behind his ear, settled himself, and went out. There was a light shining from his room, where he discovered that Fitzroy was lounging on the bed, playing with the whale Au'aua: he was floating the stuffed toy around the room with his magic, agitating little sparkling stars to ripple around her, and humming a tripping, rippling sort of melody.

Cliopher stood in the door, listening, until the whale came zooming up to his face and bopped him on the nose, and Fitzroy laughed robustly before swinging himself upright.

"What was that you were humming?" Cliopher asked, plucking Au'aua out of the air. He cradled her protectively.

Fitzroy sat up. "Oh, was I?" He sang a few notes, none of them what he'd just been humming. "Some old song, I suspect."

Over the course of their journey from the star-island, Cliopher was fairly certain both of them had gone through their entire repertoires three times over, and that song had not been one of them. But he remembered Fitzroy's anguish about his lost muse, and he said, "No doubt," and left it at that.

Aunt Oura had set the long wooden table on the back porch. Though there were only four settings, clustered at the end nearest the door, she'd lit the glass-chimneyed candles that ran all the way down the long table.

"How many does it seat?" Fitzroy asked in awe. "Eighteen?"

"We've had as many as thirty, though that was a squish on the benches."

"Fascinating," Fitzroy declared, admiring the coloured-glass bowls filled with water to catch the candlelight, each bowl containing one floating flower—hibiscus in several shades of white and red and pink, a few tiarë to waft their rich, clear scent into the air.

Cliopher turned to see if his aunt needed help carrying, but was prevented by her emergence through the doorway with a great tray in her hands. She set it down on the table and immediately swept him up into a fierce embrace unusual in his rather reserved aunt.

"Oh, Kip!" she said. "I couldn't *believe* it when they said you were dead!"

He thought, of course, of the fiasco with the stipend, but he grinned sheepishly at her. "I'm sorry, Aunt Oura. I didn't mean to trouble everyone."

"Stopped the whole world, you did," she said, wiping her eyes with the edge of her apron. "And then! You went off and came back just as you always said you would."

"With a flame of the Sun and an efela out of legend and, somehow, *both* Fitzroy Angursell *and* the Lord Emperor at your side," his aunt Malania said, coming from behind Aunt Oura and surprising Cliopher considerably. "You look shocked to see me, Kip! I'm not such a great surprise, am I?"

"I didn't expect to see you *here*," he stammered, embracing her in turn. "Is—is anyone else here?"

"Onaya said not to overwhelm you," Aunt Malania said, "so I told everyone I would come greet you and they could all *wait* until you were ready."

There could be a first time for everything. Even that.

(It was inconceivable. He'd been bracing himself for his family's inevitable *muchness* the whole way home.)

"Thank you," he said, which was thin, but ... it was a gift. *Another* gift. "I found the city surprisingly overwhelming this afternoon, after so long at sea."

"Understandable," Aunt Oura said briskly, setting down the plates and gesturing them to their seats. "Why, after I went to the Line Islands for my research, it took me *months* to feel comfortable in the house again."

"You went and spent a month back on Loaloa, didn't you?" Aunt Malania agreed, passing Fitzroy a basket of soft, warm bread. "There you are, dear.—Sir, rather," she added in confusion.

"Please don't bother," Fitzroy said with a grin. "You'll find that I'm actually *profoundly* informal. What was your research, Oura? You're a natural philosopher, I understand?"

"I studied sea horses and their relatives—pipefish and sea dragons. The Line Islands have a fantastic assortment of sea dragons—the giant ruby was my focus, but I also discovered three new species ..."

She told several stories of the year she'd spent diving down to look at the strange creatures of the reef: the pygmy sea horses that spent their entire lives defending a tiny stretch of a fan coral; how male sea horses were the ones that gestated their young; that the sea dragons could be up to two feet long.

Cliopher ate the food: egg pie and green mango salad and a spicy legume mixture he didn't recognize, and the bread and golden-green olive oil from Southern Dair, and he listened to his aunt Oura speak more about her studies than he'd ever heard from her before, and he ... realized that it was not only himself who had perhaps not been able to speak forth the truths of their heart to their family before.

～

He and Fitzroy walked along the canals quietly, slowly, almost ambling.

Before they left, Aunt Oura had given them a basket with more food, and told them not to *worry*, and Cliopher was almost able not to.

"Were you able to get everything?" he asked Fitzroy abruptly, as they climbed up over the arched bridge across the main canal.

"I believe so," Fitzroy replied demurely, then nudged him gently with his elbow. "All the necessities."

"We've been sleeping on the vaha this whole time," Cliopher murmured.

"I may have forgotten a tent, but I did not forget cushions," Fitzroy declared. "Trust me."

Which—of course he did.

He smiled at his friend, his fanoa, and then they had passed under the great tree on the edge of Zaviya Square, and then there was the front door of their house, with magic gleaming in the windows, just as if ... someone really lived there.

As if they were home.

Oh, he still could hardly fathom it.

CHAPTER SIXTY-SIX
THE NECESSITIES

The front hall was illuminated by a soft star of golden light, as bright as a candle, which hovered at the place where the ribbed arches of the entryway came together. Cliopher looked up, bemused. "I hadn't noticed the ceiling before," he said. "If you'd asked me I would have said it was flat."

"Nothing about this house is boring," Fitzroy replied, ushering him down the hall to the kitchen. He ducked inside the pantry while Cliopher leaned against the table, smiling as Fitzroy mumbled incomprehensibly to himself before emerging with a bottle. "What I am told is adequate wine from Looenna," Fitzroy told him. "There's food as well, for later. Or tomorrow, I suppose."

"I am well replete from supper," Cliopher agreed, though after the walk and the fresh evening air he no longer felt nearly so sleepy. He followed his friend back outside —waved at Tiru Oyinaa and her wife, the Nga lore-keeper, who were sitting outside their door in a pool of torchlight—he caught a glimpse of their vaha, a dark shape against the water glittering with scattered reflections from the windows and court-yards facing onto the backwater—and up the stairs to their main living area.

"Suzen would find it hard to visit," he commented. "My friend—"

"The painter, of course. Yes—she uses a wheelchair, doesn't she?"

"Her newest one is splendidly enchanted, but I think she said it could only handle short flights of stairs."

"Perhaps we can devise a lift of some form. Your uncle Lazo probably doesn't do well with stairs either. Surely it couldn't be that hard to add a platform at the end, could it? That could be raised and lowered with—oh, I've seen it done—a counter-weight, that's it. Masseo would probably know. He's good at that sort of thing. Mechanics."

"Not my area of study."

"Nor mine," Fitzroy returned, with a bright flashing grin, and then they were inside.

The room with the brazier—the sitting room—was very dim; there was a rim of light shining out from the lid of the fire-pot, next to the brazier, and Fitzroy lit a cluster of sparkling lights to show that there was a considerable pile of boxes, baskets, crates, and blankets on top of what appeared to be a set of rattan furniture in the middle of the room.

Cliopher raised his eyebrows but edged past the accumulation to reach the brazier, which was down to embers. "You had fun, I see. I'm impressed at you managing to lug it all here."

"Oh, I had it delivered," Fitzroy replied airily, and opened the fire-pot.

The sunlight welled up slowly, gently, like sunrise in the uttermost east. It overflowed the lip of the fire-pot, pooled briefly in his cupped hands, and then spread out like an opening flower, a softly whelming wave, to fill the room.

Cliopher stared at him: his hands, even more beautiful than usual, the signet ring glittering like a distant star against the night. His face, intent, wondering, for a moment full of peace, his hair falling around him in twists of silver and shadow.

"I hope the light doesn't bother everyone else," he said, and wished immediately he'd phrased that differently, because Fitzroy's face shuttered down and he closed the lid on the fire-pot.

"I meant ... because I liked it," Cliopher said, awkwardly, and Fitzroy smiled at him as if there'd been no moment of beauty broken by his words. Cliopher did not know what to say, how to fix it, how to bring back the still, splendid communion.

"We'd be illuminated like a stage-play, without any curtains," Fitzroy said.

"Curtains weren't one of the necessities?" Cliopher meant it to be a gentle tease, but Fitzroy went still.

"I tried to think what you'd want, Kip."

"I'm sure it's fine. More than fine." Cliopher walked around the brazier so he faced his friend (his fanoa!) across the pile. He felt strangely ... shy, now that they were here, together, alone after the time in the city, in this house that Cliopher had bought in hopes of a new kind of life.

It felt different than being alone on the vaha, caught out of the possibilities and realities of ordinary life by the constraints and demands of sailing in a small boat. In clothes, in the house, with Fitzroy's choice of furnishings in front of them, Cliopher felt strangely as if he'd fallen upon that unexpected stair in the dark caves of Vou'a's island.

Cliopher's heart should not be racing, simply at the sight of Fitzroy regarding his purchases with a pensive eye.

"Shall we start unpacking?" he asked tentatively.

Fitzroy opened a handsome basket—just right for storing extra mats or perhaps throws in—and nodded as he drew out several gaily embroidered cushions before stuffing them back inside. "Do you want to stay down here? Or we could go upstairs," he said abruptly, jerking his chin at the stairway leading to the solarium. "Look at the stars."

That sounded infinitely better. "Yes," he said, his voice coming out a croak. "Yes."

It was so much harder than he'd ever imagined it would be, to set a new ke'ea. He was *home*: literally home, in his own house, with his own fanoa right in front of him. Why did he feel so adrift? So lost?

(It could not be the concussion still, could it? Even excluding the time in Sky Ocean it had been *months*.)

Fitzroy tucked the wine bottle into the basket of cushions, added a rolled-up mat Cliopher hadn't seen at first, and almost scampered up the stairs.

Cliopher didn't feel *creaky*, precisely, but he was too full from supper to scamper anywhere. He probably hadn't since he was a teenager, anyway. He'd been far too full of his own dignity in his twenties.

He climbed up, the wine-glasses in his hands, and found that Fitzroy had spread out the mats and cushions in the middle of the room, under the great windows. Though the items were all things he'd acquired in Gorjo City, the effect was subtly foreign. Perhaps it was the wine bottle, or the way he was lounging on one elbow, or the starlight pouring in through the windows. Perhaps it was just that they were inside, after so long on the vaha.

Cliopher sat down next to him and watched while Fitzroy used a small folding knife he pulled out from a pocket to pry out the cork.

"That's clever," he said, holding out the glasses to be filled.

"Pali showed me. Again, I mean. Though I suppose it was her who showed me the first time, too, come to think of it." Fitzroy's voice was fond. "She didn't think Damian's method was impressive enough. They used to compete ... slicing the tops of the bottles off with their swords, that sort of thing."

"And you didn't master the art?"

Fitzroy laughed. "I had my own tricks."

Cliopher sipped the wine, which seemed good to him, but then again he hadn't had any wine to speak of since Basil's inn.

"I should mail our letters," he murmured, setting his glass down so he could lie back on the cushions. The windows faced south, and the golden star he couldn't name shone brightly, high in the sky.

"I dropped them off at a post office this afternoon," Fitzroy replied. "Don't look so shocked, Kip! I too have my moments of effectiveness."

"You are wonderful," Cliopher said honestly, and then blushed and looked firmly at the sky. "I should know that star," he said. "That golden one."

"I asked our neighbours. You hadn't said Saya Tiru's wife is the rukà."

"I forgot," Cliopher said, slightly taken aback at Fitzroy's tone. "I ..." He didn't know what to say. (He was the great diplomat. Why was it always so *hard* with those he loved?) "What did she say?"

"She just smiled at me and said I should ask you. Have you been holding out on me?"

His voice was still light and lilting, what Cliopher had come to name his *Fitzroy Angursell* tone: not just the softened accent, but the richer timbre, and the sense of great and glorious merriment held barely back.

"No," he replied, wishing he'd not drunk any of the wine. Even half a glass was too much, after so long without. His head was swirling. What was Fitzroy trying to say? (What was he *actually* saying?) His eyes landed once more on that bright star, what he almost thought was a *new* star—

And his thoughts stuttered on the idea, for had he not, himself, gone to the

House of the Sun and brought a great gleaming flame of the Sun to be a new star at the prow of the *He'eanka?*

It was inconceivable that he and Fitzroy had sailed through that night sky; that Auri and El and Tupaia and all the others were up there now, the new star at their prow, seeking the remedy for the poison that still ran in Auri's veins.

Inconceivable, and yet true.

It was inconceivable that his aunts Malania and Oura had heard he had come home from that adventure and that he was overwhelmed by the busyness and bustle of the city, and they had listened to his request that he not have to deal with the entire Mdang clan all at once. And yet that was true, too.

He sat up so he could look directly at Fitzroy, who was still lounging on his elbow, expression indiscernible in the dim light.

Cliopher did not need to see his expression to know it would be either the impenetrable serenity of his Radiancy or the madcap grin of Fitzroy Angursell.

He waited, but if he had learned patience at the court, how much moreso had the man before him? The quicksilver poet forced to become that golden idol.

His Radiancy could outlast Cliopher Mdang any day of the week.

Cliopher waited, though mostly he was trying to calm his whirling thoughts. There was the star above them and the house below, and the glass fishing floats Saya Dorn had collected gleaming and chiming in a circle all around them, like a visual representation of the magic circle of protection Fitzroy had drawn around them on their first night to the star-island.

He waited—*look first! Listen first!*—but he was listening to his heart thudding in his ears, the faint breath of wind bringing flowers and smoke to his nose, the light of the star he had caused to be shining down upon them, the taste of dark wine velvety on his tongue, the wooden floor soft as his silk tunic under his hands, the sea-grass matting cool, almost damp, under his feet.

His own ruffled emotions settled, stilled, and he realized Fitzroy's sharpness was because *Cliopher* had hurt him. He did not know how, but he *knew* this man, and he knew that. He waited, looking, listening, to a deep and abiding—a deeply *stubborn* —patience.

And then he realized it was long past time to move past the looking and the listening to the asking of questions.

"Fitzroy," Cliopher said carefully, "what's wrong?"

Fitzroy emitted a rough sound that was probably supposed to be a laugh, but it was so strangled and strained not even he could pretend it was any true humour. "There's nothing wrong," he tried next, and swigged back his wine.

Perhaps the Red Company would have believed that tone, but Cliopher doubted it; and anyway he was not the Red Company, but the man who had been his Radiancy's secretary and second for decades.

(*How long have you known each other?* Auri had asked—it was Auri, wasn't it?— and Fitzroy had smiled and said *Half our lives.*)

Auri, who was sailing that golden star.

"Nothing's wrong," Fitzroy repeated, but he fumbled picking up the wine bottle to refill his glass.

Cliopher said nothing, but he held out his glass for a refill, and shifted position so he was sitting cross-legged. Fitzroy gathered several more cushions around him, and rubbed his hand down the velveteen surface of one with a soft whispering noise.

Perhaps it was real velvet, not velveteen. He might well have decided to splurge on such a thing.

"It's only—it's foolish," Fitzroy said, cutting himself off with a sharp gesture. Magic sparkled in the wake of his motion, illuminating the path his hand had taken like the phosphorescence in the wake of a ship.

"I don't think it can be, if it's bothering you," Cliopher replied as gently as he could manage.

"I'm not *bothered. Stop that!*—No, not you. I—Kip—It's just—just that the magic of this house is very *insistent*. It's twining around me and, and, I keep pushing it away, but it won't. It's insisting."

Cliopher blinked, but the sentence made no more sense on reflection. He ventured, "What is it insisting on?"

"It won't leave me alone." Fitzroy made another sharp gesture, another brilliant swirl of magic following the curlicues of air behind his hand. "It's just that my magic's calling to it. It's not as if it's *my* house."

"What?" he said, which was not the diplomat's answer, not at all.

"I told you," Fitzroy said, with a dangerous edge to his tone. "The house wants to belong to someone, and for some reason it's chosen *me*."

"But why can't it belong to you?" Cliopher asked, and then bit his lip as all the blood surged to his face. He'd *promised* Fitzroy he wouldn't cage him. He'd promised Fitzroy would be free as a bird, able to choose to come or to go, that he would never bind him. "I'm sorry," he added in a low, unhappy voice. "I ... I don't mean to ... if you don't want to be—if you don't want—"

Fitzroy's voice cracked out in imperial order. "*Stop it.*"

"Yes, my lord," Cliopher replied automatically, and then cringed.

They stared at each other in the darkness. Cliopher's heart was beating too obviously, and he felt a cold trickle of guilt, a thick heaviness in his mind.

How had it been so easy, all that time on the vaha? And yet here they were, just as he had barely let himself imagine, and it was ...

At one level it *was* just what he had always wanted. Had he not wanted to be *family*? That meant love, and miscommunication, and the slow effort to speak across hurt and confusion.

(He had always thought he *understood* his Radiancy so well; and he had thought that Fitzroy Angursell could not be so great a mystery. But *did* one ever know another person? Cliopher did not even know all of *himself*. Look what deep mysteries there had been in that cave.)

He shivered at the memory of the cold, cold water, the pressure, the dark, that moment where he had hung suspended, drifting downwards.

The fishing floats gleamed and chimed softly as they moved in a wind from the window Fitzroy had left open that afternoon. The air was cool, faintly scented from whatever flowers the cushion-sellers had used to store their wares, just a hint of smoke coming from someone's barbecue out in the city.

"I miss the sound of the sea," he said, as if in offering. He turned the words over in his mind, wondering why he felt vulnerable, saying that.

"I don't miss the vaha," Fitzroy replied, equally stiffly.

They sat there silently, and Cliopher did not know what to say. He took a mouthful of his wine and grimaced, unable to stand any more.

"You were calling me *my lord* all day in town," Fitzroy said finally.

Cliopher caught his breath. "You told me not to call you by any of your names. What else was I supposed to call you?"

Fitzroy shifted uncomfortably, and rearranged all the pillows so they were cradling his back, and finally he muttered, "You could have said I was your fanoa."

Cliopher gritted his teeth and let his first instinctive response wash over him, a wave crashing over his head. Then the tug back out to sea, but he could sit here, steady, on the shore. He could. (He dug his hands into a stray cushion. He couldn't.)

"You said you didn't *mean* not to say it aloud to Vou'a and the lore-keepers," Fitzroy said, in a ferocious, scathing tone. "Which I could accept. But to say *nothing* to any of the hundreds of cousins who asked you who I was? 'Oh, it's Kip and your lord, isn't it?'—why didn't you say, *My fanoa* then?"

Cliopher's breath hitched. He could not prevaricate, and he stammered silently, unable to speak the truth. Where was the guidance of the *Lays* for this?

He had never turned to the *Lays* for how to speak forth the secret, splendid, shy dreams of his soul. It had been Fitzroy Angursell's poetry that had taught him that, and he did not dare—*not a line* from any of his songs was in his head.

"It's—it's—" Oh gods, where were his *words*?

"Private?" Still mocking; still sharp; scathing.

Cliopher drew in his breath. This *was* Fitzroy, who had written those beautiful, tender lines of love and dreams and inspiration and hope; and also the Fitzroy who had excoriated the cowards and the hypocrites and the *fools*.

Cliopher was still a fool, chasing the viau, looking for the sea. This was what he had always wanted and still he *could not find the words*. He nodded, face tight. The face of the other Artorin Damara of the *other place* came to his mind, that serenity and that bleakness and that deep, deep grief, and Cliopher could do nothing but press his hands tightly to the floor, as if he could anchor himself that way.

Fitzroy spoke in a detached, brittle tone. "I didn't think it was anything to be ashamed of. I thought it was something rather fine, in fact."

Cliopher's heart seemed to stutter, crying out for him to *do something*, but he couldn't—he couldn't. He was caught in the rip, and he was going down. "Fitzroy—"

"I see I was wrong."

"You weren't wrong. *Fitzroy*."

"Perhaps we should reconsider, if it's not something you feel can be announced. I've had enough of being a *secret*."

Even here, even now, when Fitzroy's tone was calculated to hurt, he was still the rock that held fast, upon which Cliopher could set his foot.

It was as if a lock on his tongue broke with the sudden flood of boiling emotion.

"Why would you say that?" he cried, his voice cracking.

"Oh, I couldn't say! Perhaps it's related to the many other times I've seen you compulsively squirrel away anything you assume your family won't immediately understand and approve of!" A beat of silence. "Do you deny it?"

"No," Cliopher said quietly, his voice startling raw to his own ears. "No, I don't." He wished he could. He wished he could say otherwise, but ... but he couldn't.

He heard Fitzroy take a slow, unsteady breath. "Then perhaps it's up to me, *again*, to make speeches about you before a great gathering of your relations? 'I bring you greetings, O great assembly of Mdangs! I'm Kip's fanoa. I apologize for the inconvenience but I will not be taking the sixty-odd nearly identical iterations of your three questions about it at this time, as I have barely more information than you do.'"

"Fitzroy."

"No, we're not lovers, though he'll sleep beside me and hold me when I'm upset. Quite possibly this is because he feels sorry for me, but who knows what Kip Mdang is ever thinking? He called me 'my beloved, my own', once. And that we could be each other's zenith stars. And he'll say he loves me, but only on special occasions when I've been dramatically inconvenient enough to bait him into making it a setdown! Oh, and I do have a place in his house! I have my own little collection of empty rooms.'"

"*Fitzroy*, that's—"

"'I thought we were going to be like Aurelius and Elonoa'a, but then we weren't, and we agreed we were just going to be ourselves.'" Fitzroy's voice was growing sharper, brighter, louder. "'But then we didn't discuss it again—of *course* we didn't discuss it again, we only had weeks alone on a boat with nothing much else to do *but* talk.'"

"Fitzroy ..."

But Fitzroy talked right over his hesitant interruption. "'*And,* now that you mention it, *no*, I'm not sure who I am, or who I'm suppose to be, or what I'm supposed to be doing as his fanoa, or how I'm supposed to be behaving to all of *you*. The only people who were willing to have a technical conversation with me about what the word means made up their own definition and have missed the last two thousand years of linguistic evolution. But please don't ask Kip any questions about it, you know how he digs in his heels when he's pushed.' Yes, I'm sure that would all go very well."

Cliopher sucked in air, wishing he could make the air to rage and sparkle with his emotions, show forth in the word around him the great fire suddenly blazing in his heart. "I don't feel sorry for you. That wasn't—I *don't*. I cared, I was worried, I—"

"Is this the part where you say you love me as a set-down? I do so enjoy that part, truly I do, but if it's inconvenient for you, we can skip to the end when I feel very impressed and foolish and put in my place—"

"Will you let me speak!" Cliopher snapped. The wave overwhelmed him, and he surged forward, rising up on his knees, reaching out so he could hold Fitzroy, cupping his face as gently as he could manage in his hands.

"Kip," Fitzroy said, not pulling back, the starlight and his own magic showing only his eyes, wide with his own churning emotions.

"Fitzroy," Cliopher growled. "Why did you never tell me you were Fitzroy Angursell? *You* kept that secret—why?" He didn't allow Fitzroy to answer, to fall away from his justified hurt and anger. "If you were ashamed, was it because you wondered if the best of you was too much more than you had become?" Cliopher was panting, but he focused on keeping his hands gentle, though his voice surely wasn't. "I thought about it, you know. I was hurt you didn't tell me. You'd promised you would—but you wanted *me* to see it, didn't you? So you could know you hadn't lost yourself?"

"Yes," said Fitzroy, on a long breath.

"Is that the only reason?"

He could feel Fitzroy's jaw work under his palms for a moment before he spoke. "I was afraid."

"That I wouldn't love you?"

It was nearly a full minute before Fitzroy answered. "You'd been humming *Aurora* forever."

Cliopher closed his eyes, just for a moment. "It doesn't have to make sense. You were still afraid."

A slow, shuddering breath. "Yes."

"Fitzroy," he said, looking into his eyes. "I saw you. You could have told me at any point and I would have believed you, wholly and utterly."

"Nobody believes me when I tell the truth," Fitzroy said.

"You know what it is to have a truth too big, too real, too much the ground of your soul. That is what I feel for you, for calling you my fanoa."

Fitzroy was trembling, but he lifted his hands to hold Cliopher's face in turn. His hands were cold, but Cliopher did not flinch.

"No shame. No regret. There is *nothing* to reconsider," Cliopher said fiercely. He did not believe Fitzroy wanted to back out, not here, not now. There was no world (no, not even the strange mirror-world of his dream-vision!) in which he would suddenly decide Cliopher was unworthy of him.

"I sorted the corn for the sea-witch, and I plunged to the heart of that black island for Vou'a, and I followed the turtle to the Lower Door where Grandmother Death gathers all things in, all so that I could hold my head up before you as your equal," he said, low and strong.

"I climbed the entire stair from the bottom of the sky to the door of the Hall of the Sun with a world on my shoulders, as I did for you through all the years I stood at your right hand, the tanà to the chief-of-chiefs though you did not know what that meant—*all* so the song you would write would be the better for it."

Fitzroy was holding him as tightly as he held Fitzroy.

He dropped his voice, so it rumbled in his stomach, deep as the deepest tremors of an earthquake rolling through the islands. "I whispered the truth of my love for you into the coal of the fire of the heart of me, as a gift worthy of being given by Vou'a to Ani. *The best of me*, Vou'a said when I gave him the shell holding the coal, and I told him no, it was the best of who I had been, but not the best of who I would be, because I had not yet built the new life with you."

"Kip—"

"No," he said. He could not call light with his will: but he could pour fire into his voice. "It's not a set-down, and you haven't baited me, and you *aren't* being inconvenient, and I am *not* saying this to put you in your place or make you feel foolish for what you feel. You have a right to be angry; you have a right to be hurt." The fire wavered. "I'm sorry. I'm sorry. I am. I hate that we keep stumbling over each other—that you have to keep stumbling over me—that I ... that I need ..."

"Time," Fitzroy whispered. "Faravia. Adjusting to your community."

"Yes." He swallowed hard. "I keep remembering that *other place*, and the time when I came home after the Fall, and I couldn't—"

"When you had no faravia, and could not stay."

"I didn't have my fanoa with me, then," Cliopher said, his lips wobbling as he tried to keep hold of the swift fire. "I am so *tired*, Fitzroy. There is so much work left to do that if I think of it I'll cry, and I'm sorry I'm ... like this. Too much, and not enough." He managed a shaky laugh. "I always have been, you know."

Fitzroy's thumbs moved against his cheeks. "So have I," he said softly. "Fanoa, you know."

He gently tugged on Cliopher's head, and they touched their foreheads together. "The other half of your heart."

"I am the other half of yours," Cliopher said.

They held there for a long time, and then Cliopher could not sustain the awkward angle any longer, and he tumbled over to lie beside Fitzroy. Fitzroy tangled their hands together, and they stared up at the stars in the sky. The moon was setting in the west, waxing gibbous and pale gold.

After a while, Fitzroy gave a soft, sniffling sort of laugh, and said, "You know, I'm lying here thinking, 'What would Jullanar do?' But the answer is 'healthy communication' and 'ask useful questions.'"

"We're doomed," said Cliopher without missing a beat, and was gratified when Fitzroy laughed properly, out loud. He turned his head, nudging his forehead against his fanoa's shoulder. "Divide and conquer? I've been trying to practice asking useful questions."

"I'd noticed. Picked the easier one, I see, and left me the harder."

Cliopher squeezed his hand. "You said ... perhaps we should reconsider?"

"That's ... useful to be clear on, I suppose. I didn't mean it. I was hurt."

"And scared. And you thought I might be reconsidering?"

"Yes."

"I'm not. I never will. Not for another dozen lifetimes." He swallowed. "Nonetheless ... Fitzroy, if *you* wish to, if you cannot bear the thought of such a permanence —if you cannot bear to be part of my family—they can be overbearing, I know—if you cannot bear to live in this house—if it is going to be a *cage*, then I don't want you here. I refuse to trap you. I refuse to hold you here. I refuse to bind you, even with my love. It is—I want it to be—a gift. Freely offered."

Fitzroy squeezed his hand back. "Freely taken," he said, very quietly. "I'm not reconsidering, and I don't wish to." He took a breath, another, long, slow, controlled, and then he said, "My turn?"

Cliopher nodded, afloat on a welling tide of relief, lifting him over the reef they had crashed upon.

Fitzroy said, "You don't need to be the tanà with me. If I don't have to be your lord."

"You don't have to be my lord. I'm trying not to call you that ... it's force of habit, not because I mean it. I prefer you as my friend. My fanoa."

He could hear the smile in Fitzroy's voice when he spoke next. "I think we should name the iguana My Lord. Then every time you slip up I can make gentle mock back."

"Probably a good idea," Cliopher replied, smiling back into the dark and squeezing Fitzroy's hand. The silence was easing, softening, becoming comfortable. "You know," he murmured after a while. "It probably *is* your house."

"Tell that to My Lord of the very fitting name, he clearly thinks he owns the place," Fitzroy retorted, then paused. "What do you mean?"

"Legally. If my death wasn't repudiated in the records. I left it to you in my will."

Another silence. "You left it to *me*? Not—Ludvic? Or Rhodin? Or Conju?"

"It was before I discovered your name. I thought ..." This was not any more vulnerable a thing to say, was it? He was glad for the dark, and that Fitzroy was still holding his hand. "I thought you'd want it. A place of your own. A home filled with laughter and music and family, for you and your household." He hesitated, but it had to be said—after that argument, he *had* to say it. "I have long ... it wasn't proper, I know, not without talking to you about it—not without all—all that we've been through—but I have long ... secretly ... even to myself, I mean, it was a word I never even let myself *think* ..."

"You're rambling, Kip," Fitzroy said gently.

"Fanoa is a legal relationship. Here. Or it used to be. It's ... old-fashioned, this usage."

"Archaic, I think you said."

"Yes ... but to me, to *me*, it's meant ... the way you leave something to your spouse or your sibling or your child, to me I wanted you to have this house if I died because I wanted you to know you were part of my family. Even if I could never claim it outright. It was still true."

Fitzroy laughed very quietly. "You and your set-downs," he said, his hand gripping tightly, his voice faint.

"Don't feel foolish. Please. You're not a fool—and even if you are, you're in good company. I've been chasing this viau my whole life. Look at my stuffed whale with the golden eyes. I thought she was the most wonderful thing in the world. I thought her golden eyes were so beautiful."

Fitzroy was silent for a long few minutes, but this time Cliopher felt no need to fill the silence. He waited, and at last Fitzroy said, "I've always thought you hung the stars, you know. But you literally did hang that new one, didn't you?"

Cliopher turned his head, and now he wished he could see Fitzroy's face. He had to offer something—some gift—not something in trade, because they had been trading gifts between them for half their lives, but something that would be for both of them, that they could do together, that would be shared and *theirs*.

He didn't want to be fanoa in the old sense of trading partners; he didn't want to be fanoa like Auri and El—he wanted—

The old want surged up, but it was no longer bitter in his mouth, but sweet. Fitzroy gripped his hand tightly.

Cliopher looked up at the new star, hanging in the sky to the south. "I know you said you didn't miss the vaha," he said slowly, "but would you like to go see if there is an island under that star?"

"I would, but I know *you* said you were tired. We should sleep, and there are things to unpack, and—" He stopped, and he laughed softly. "And I used to be noted for my spontaneity, didn't I?"

"Yes," said Cliopher, who knew dozens of stories about Fitzroy Angursell's yen for adventure. "And I used to be the solid, staid, responsible bureaucrat of bureaucrats, who could be trusted with the world's government."

"You've never been that boring," Fitzroy returned, "and I would still trust you with the world."

"Do you want to go?" Cliopher pushed himself up onto one elbow and looked at his fanoa frankly. "Fitzroy. Do you *want* to?"

Slowly, Fitzroy nodded. "Yes. Kip. *Yes.*"

CHAPTER SIXTY-SEVEN
THE BAY OF THE WATERS

Cliopher had prepared the vaha for sailing at any moment, but he ducked into the kitchen to collect some food and fresh water for later.

The iguana was reclining on the table.

Fitzroy came crowding behind him, drawn by his short exclamation.

"You see," he said, complacently. "There *is* an iguana."

"And it is six feet long," Cliopher replied faintly. The lizard was green, with a fringe of spikes all down its back, and seemed entirely at home stretched out along the table, its tail hanging off the further end. It was chomping happily on what appeared to be fruit.

"That can't be hygienic," Fitzroy said.

"You can move it if you'd like." Cliopher nodded at the iguana, though it wasn't particularly clear to him if the creature was intelligent. If it had lived surrounded by magic it could well be smarter than the usual run of lizards.

For that matter, he had no idea whether iguanas were particularly intelligent at all.

"Rhodin is going to be so pleased with this development," Fitzroy declared, extending his hand to see if the lizard would sniff it. The iguana ignored him entirely, even when he stroked its side with a gentle finger. "Our very own household lizard."

Cliopher picked up one of the baskets left from Fitzroy's shopping and opened the door to the pantry. "I am simply pleased it's not a hyperintelligent dinosaur soul-mate with whom I am expected to have telepathic communications."

"That is a good point," Fitzroy said brightly, and when Cliopher turned around to look at him, he said: "We're getting off very lightly, when you put it like that. It's only six feet long, and it's not going to be communicating mind-to-mind with us."

"Merely eating all our fruit and being unhygienic in the kitchen."

"And bath-house." Fitzroy frowned. "On second thought, perhaps it's a trifle ... tacky. Do you think your cousin Louya might want it?"

They were still laughing as they scrambled down the stairs to the vaha. Fitzroy raised the sails while Cliopher undid the painter mooring the vaha.

He glanced upwards at the sky as he pushed off. "It's a couple of hours till midnight ... we might not be able to get across to the southern edge of the Ring before that star reaches its zenith. It used to take three or four hours to get to the nearest islands, if I recall correctly. I used to go when I needed time by myself."

"Hmm," said Fitzroy, and the fitful breeze swirled around them a little more strongly. "I might be able to assist with that."

It should have felt like cheating, but it didn't. Nor did the magic glinting and glittering on the mast as it passed *through* the bridge. Cliopher directed Fitzroy to angle them to the main canal leading to the southern edge of the city.

It was a quiet night, music and laughter spilling out of houses and courtyards as they passed; some houses were brilliantly lit, others already asleep. There were many night-scented flowers, their fragrance billowing in wafts; smoke from fire-pits and barbecues mingled with it, bringing savoury odours in their wake. The water was black and rippled gold-and-white from the reflected lights, and they passed with a soft skimming hiss between the piers and boardwalks of the city.

They passed a few others out on their own boats, fishers out for a night's catch, lovers or friends having a romantic sail, a party of teenagers daring each other to jump off the upper deck of a yacht. One came down, limbs tucked into a ball, and sent a great fountain of water up and over the vaha.

"Sorry!" one of her friends cried through her laughter.

Fitzroy waved acknowledgement of the apology, with a curious flick of his wrist, and then, smugly, called up a brisker wind.

"What did you do?" Cliopher asked, lounging in his familiar position by the tiller.

"Nothing dreadful."

Behind them, there was an exclamation and then a great upsurge of laughter from the teenagers, and a single shockwave ran counter to the tide under the vaha. Cliopher twisted back, but all he could see was water sheeting off the teenagers' boat.

He turned back to his friend, his fanoa, who was grinning. "I held the water up a couple of moments longer than it should have," he explained. "Just long enough for them to wonder what was going on before it landed on them."

It shouldn't have landed *on* them, either, but it was water and the teenagers had all been soaked anyway; and Cliopher was also damp from their splashing. "Mm," he said, and then he laughed.

They navigated a small marina and then went past an open area full of music and people dancing and a small night market, and then they were out in the open water of the south lagoon and they both relaxed at the sudden open space around them.

"You're not feeling seasick?" Cliopher asked him as they rocked over the currents coming from the channel between Mama Ituri and her Son.

"*Now* you ask me!" Fitzroy smiled at him, fondly. "Not with all the wild magic I've been doing. Makes a great difference. Which direction?"

"East of south, please." Cliopher set the sails and tiller as the wind swirled, gusted, subsided, and then swelled to a steady current. It bore the city's faint sounds of merriment with it, and the flowers and smoke; and yet there before them was the great shining expanse of the Bay of the Waters, with luminescence in their wake.

It was another moonless night, and the stars were clear once they were out of the city's lights and airs. The new star hung above them, huge and gold; below it was the deeper black of the southern rim islands, garlanded with the foamy surf in a white and gleaming ruff. The Bay was calm, the currents on this side of the city easy.

The wind, steady now, sent them flying across the water at an exhilarating speed.

Cliopher ensured everything was shipshape, as the phrase went, and then moved to sit again in his spot by the tiller. Fitzroy laid himself along the outrigger.

"What a beautiful evening," Cliopher said.

"Back there," Fitzroy said abruptly, gesturing in the direction of the city. "With the water. Was it very undignified and unworthy of me?"

"Do you think it was?"

"I feel as if I've lost my entire sense of humour," Fitzroy said. "I can't tell."

"You've been making me laugh for as long as I've known you. All the way from that first joke—you capped it and it was perfect."

"I don't remember the joke, do you?" Fitzroy asked, his voice subdued.

"No. But the exact words don't matter, do they? I'd been struggling so long in the court, and there, where I should have been most out of place, most ill at ease—that was where I found *you*."

"I wasn't much of a person, back then."

"You were yourself."

Fitzroy sighed heavily, and flopped over so he could drop his hand into the water, where his touch lit the black water with green phosphorescence.

Their wake was luminous as the Lulai'aviyë high above them, the golden star at its southern edge but still within its band. Cliopher shifted position to sit cross-legged, and imagined Tupaia and Auri and El, Hiru and Pinyë and all the others on the *He'eanka*, sailing high above them with that golden star at their prow.

"You didn't bring your harp," he said.

Fitzroy sighed. "No." He rolled onto his back so he could look up at the sail, the sky. "It's easier out here, isn't it? Simpler."

They passed through a jewelled cloud of flying fish, leaping high out of the water in great skittering skips, the starlight catching their translucent fins, the water droplets falling back into the sea, the ripples cutting across the waves.

"Yes," he said. The wind was steady, warm, friendly. "It's not so difficult to be ... just Cliopher, here. There doesn't seem to be the contradiction."

"But you never have a contradiction," Fitzroy said bitterly. "You're so *thoroughly* yourself. It's not as if you *change* at court or at home. You're just the same wherever you are."

"Doesn't seem to stop the arguments," Cliopher breathed, and Fitzroy snorted, and his posture seemed to melt against the support of the outrigger.

"No, I don't suppose it does." Fitzroy lifted one hand, and a soft gold-tinged glow jumped from his palm to run along the ropes and spars of the sail. "It's because you had a happy childhood, isn't it? Mostly, I mean. I know there were difficulties. But you're like Jullanar—or Pali—or Damian. You're all so *solid* in yourself. Sometimes I used to think it *had* to be a front, a façade, some sort of *performance*, but it was never an act. When you came to me and said 'I can fix this but I need a staff of ten,' you weren't making some bid for power and prestige and to line your own pockets—you *fixed* it. I went along with it at first because at least you were *interesting* and you seemed to like me—you seemed to *see* me—you *looked* at me—"

"I did," said Cliopher. "I tried."

"You saw me," he whispered. "I would have lost myself, Kip. I was so close to just letting myself float away. I don't know what that would have been ... the magic would have done *something*—perhaps it would have been a second self? Under torture people sometimes send part of themselves away, to protect it, and there's another part that comes to the fore and is only ... awake, I guess you could say, under those conditions, and it doesn't always grow or change, and it's not *whole* ..."

"Your parts are not that separate, Fitzroy. Even if they were, I would love them each and the whole company they formed."

"You make it sound like a playhouse," Fitzroy grumbled. "Why must it always be a performance?"

"We show different aspects of ourselves in different company. That doesn't make them false."

"Not for *you*," Fitzroy retorted, and then seemed to shrink back against the boat, as if that had been too true a statement.

"What do you mean?" Cliopher asked gently. He checked the sails and tiller against the fast-approaching islands of this portion of the Ring, and waited.

"Sometimes," Fitzroy said very quietly, "I'm afraid there's nothing beneath the performance. I can't—Kip, I'm not like you. If we're fanoa, two halves of a shell, you're the whole one and I'm the empty curve. I don't have—there's nothing *there*. It's *all* an act."

"Is that what you meant, back at the house?" Cliopher asked.

"Our house," Fitzroy corrected him, almost fiercely, and then he uttered a low cry. "Our house. O gods, Kip, I have *two legal identities*, and neither of them are truly me." He laughed harshly, like a crow's caw. "And here we are, coming *back* to this point—"

"We'll come back as many times as you need," Cliopher said sturdily. "You are not going to be able to reconcile everything in one grand action."

"Not in the real world, no. I wish—" He stopped, his breath coming fast. "I wish I could. I wish I could just say *this is who I am*, and that would be enough. But it's not, is it?"

"No," Cliopher said. "Unfortunately."

"Perhaps we should talk about something else. This is a very boring topic for our romantic night sail under a new star."

Cliopher could only speak the truth. "I love you."

Fitzroy flopped back dramatically. "The *efficiency* of your set-downs nowadays, Kip, it is entirely unbecoming." He sat up, as if to continue in the same vein, and then shook his head vehemently, almost violently, and, as if some barrier or barricade had burst, words spilled forth, his accent slipping, his chest heaving.

"I don't have anything like you do. *Who are you?* someone—anyone—asks you, and you lift your chin and put back your shoulders and you say *I am Cliopher Mdang of Tahivoa. My island is Loaloa. My dances are Aōteketētana.* It doesn't matter *who* asks you that. It could be some random child on the street or one of the princes of the court or the very sun in the sky! *I am Cliopher Mdang of Tahivoa.* Nothing shakes you. *Nothing.* You just let the wave crash over you and then you pick yourself and your boat back up and off you go wherever you wanted to be.

"I don't have that, Kip. *Who are you?*" His voice took on a mocking, singsong quality, and he sat up so he could gesture furiously. "Who *am* I? I am Fitzroy Angursell—or I *was*, once. But who was he? He was always a pretence, an act, a *sham*. He was just a collection of faces mirroring back whatever anyone wanted. I wanted to be a bard and speak forth the truth—I wanted so *badly* to be real—and what did I get? A legend spun around me."

He slapped his hand on the outrigger, making the boat jerk and jump under the impetus of his magic. Cliopher did not look away from his fanoa, nor jump in reaction. The sails held under the swift wind, and they were still far enough from the rim islands not to have to worry about reefs just yet.

"The worst is that I did it myself. I didn't know what else to do—what else to *be*. I met Jullanar and Damian and—and it was—all I knew how to do was what made them smile, what made them like me. I made them laugh—Jullanar liked to listen to my music—Damian wanted us to learn to fight—but there wasn't anything else—I didn't know how to do anything else. I was locked in my fucking tower like that Marwn who died and I was *supposed* to have died there, like she did, nothing but a vessel for the Empire."

He stopped for a moment, his breast heaving, and then he laughed, hard and sharp. "I didn't want to be that. I couldn't *bear* to be that. And yet what have I ever been, but that?"

Cliopher cast a worried eye on their distance from the fringing reefs, the strong and steady wind, and did not dare leave his position to join Fitzroy on the outrigger. "Come to the middle," he said, and, miracle of miracles, Fitzroy *did*.

He was still gesticulating, still speaking, still taut with emotion: but he came.

Cliopher inched forward so he could sit beside his friend, his fanoa, and still be within reach of the tiller.

"When they asked me where I had come from I could not answer with anything but *behind me*, and when they asked where I was going I could only ever say *ahead of me*. There was nothing else there. There has never been anything else. Either the walls of the tower, or the empty horizon. Nothing else."

Fitzroy had not brought his harp to help him articulate this—or to help him hide from this. Cliopher hummed; after a moment he realized it was one of the passages from the *Lays* about waiting through a storm for the clear weather that would come behind.

Whether he recognized it or no Cliopher could not tell, but Fitzroy slumped suddenly against him. Cliopher put his arm around his shoulder. He could witness this, and comfort him, and *listen*.

"And then I *was* the vessel for the Empire, and I was very literally nothing else. A name and a gold mask and another bloody tower."

Fitzroy flung his hands out, and sparks fluttered around him, illuminating the edge of the wind with velvety midnight feathers shining with gold-tinted iridescence.

"What could I do? Tell me that, Kip? I could have told them I was Fitzroy—and then what? No one would have believed me! I used to think—oh, maybe they'll imprison me down in the dungeons—maybe they'll execute me—maybe they'll confine me to some rooms as a lunatic—but then I realized they wouldn't. They didn't *need* to. Who could I possibly have told? The commanders of the armies would have gladly sided with the Ouranatha to bind me even more than I was, and I would have been nothing more than a puppet.

"I didn't want to be a *puppet*—drugged as well as enchanted? lost entirely to myself—I couldn't. And I couldn't—I didn't want to kill myself—Kip—I wanted—I thought for a while maybe I could *be* someone, being Fitzroy seemed such a dream I convinced myself that I'd only ever imagined it. I pretended I'd been in that tower the whole time, just imagined all the adventures and friendships and that I could create something worth living for—"

He caught his breath and coughed hard for a long time. Cliopher squeezed his shoulder, took the moment to look up at the sail, awestruck that the wind was holding steady at the same force; for all his emotional upheaval Fitzroy was keeping close control on his magic.

Another quarter-hour and they would be at the edge of the Ring. The star was nearing its zenith, but even without laying flat so he could use the mast as a plumb-line he could see that it was ke'e for none of the islands of the ring.

"I fit myself to the mask they held up to me," Fitzroy said coolly, staring unseeing at the coming reef. "My voice, my posture, my expression, my words ... soon enough also my thoughts, my opinions, my actions. Pali told me I was starting to become a decent emperor, by the end. I used to imagine what Jullanar would do, to help me keep my moral compass. She ..."

"She loves you."

"The gods know I tried hard enough to be what everyone wanted of me."

Cliopher hugged him more tightly, and then thought better of it and kissed him on the top of his bent head, in a part of the spiralling hair.

Fitzroy shuddered convulsively, and clutched at his hand. "No. That's not true. Not everyone. I had enough of Fitzroy Angursell left in me that I tried to pick the *greatest* image. The most resplendent, the most glorious, the most ... magnificent." His voice was very sour. "If I were to be the Sun-on-Earth I was determined to play the part properly.

"Then the Fall, and I knew, when I fell down into myself, that I would find nothing there. And there wasn't," Fitzroy declared, voice ringing out into the still, soft air. "It was all shadows and emptiness, after all."

Cliopher had crawled down a deep cave at the heart of himself, and he did not believe that Fitzroy would have found nothing if he had been able to continue on.

He was not certain that he believed Fitzroy when he said he had found nothing but shadows and emptiness; but he could believe that whatever dark places he wandered under the magical catastrophe of the Fall of Astandalas had shown him very little that was true.

The pain had been real. But that did not mean that that was the truth of all things.

"I would have gone afterwards, I would have gone back to being Fitzroy, but there wasn't anything there. I couldn't *find* anything. The costume didn't fit any longer." He shrugged; Cliopher could see the movement against what now seemed to be luminous water.

The reefs rising up as they came towards the edge of the Ring. Moving slowly, calmly, reluctantly, Cliopher edged away from Fitzroy to unlash the tiller and adjust the sails so the vaha slowed to a more moderate pace. Fitzroy said something, one of those words that Cliopher could never hear quite correctly, and the stiff wind dissolved into a much more natural and more fitful breeze. For a moment Cliopher thought he felt the touch of a velvet-feathered wing brush against his cheek, though he saw nothing.

"How do you *do* it?" Fitzroy said, his voice softer, though no less emotional. "How can you be so much yourself all the time? How do you even know who you are?"

I am Cliopher Mdang of Tahivoa, Cliopher thought, and bit his lower lip.

"Fitzroy, I don't know any more than you do," he said. "When I look at you— whenever I've looked at you—I've never seen *only* a mask and nothing underneath it."

"That can't be true," Fitzroy scoffed.

"It is," he said, quietly, intensely. "The man who met my eyes when I made a joke and capped it? The man who let me—*helped* me—dismantle the residue of the Empire of Astandalas? The man who never failed to look at *me* as a person? The man who asked me to be Viceroy with a terrible prank about the Duke of Ikiano? The man who vocally forbade Ylette to dress me in satin or the colour olive, in front of multiple people? The man who cared so much for his people he was willing to stay in a cage until he was sure *they* were free? The man who learned *Islander* in *secret* just to please me? The man who always, always, *always* listened to *me*?"

"Kip," Fitzroy said, and then: "What a pair we are."

The reefs were luminous below them, fish flashing silver and gold, the coral a shining silver-green. Their vaha slid silently along the darker channel between the reefs, where the water was black and speckled with tiny white motes of luminescence. The breakers were louder now, filling the air.

"It sounds like the edge of the sky," Fitzroy said, his voice for a moment full of longing.

It did; and Cliopher, remembering reaching the sunset, felt the tears rise hot and stinging to his eyes.

But the simplicity of Sky Ocean had long since been replaced with the convoluted and forever backtracking kurakura of the mortal worlds. Well—he knew what it meant, to follow a long and arduous ke'ea, his eyes fixed upon the star shining above the island at the end of the journey.

"For a moment, when I first realized you were Fitzroy Angursell," Cliopher said resolutely, "I feared that everything you had ever shown me had been an act. That you had only pretended to respect me, to trust me, to care for me. I was very upset that you could trust me with the world and not with such a truth as that."

"Kip—"

"No," he said, moving the tiller somewhat too aggressively and having to compensate with the sails. The reefs were breaking the surface now, though the swell was still calm, this side of the barrier islands. He picked another line, half-remembering sailing these waters when he was a teenager. This was where he'd often come to escape the city, the uninhabited islands—sacred, people said—of the southeastern curve of the Ring.

"No?" Fitzroy said, his voice airless and faint.

"No," Cliopher replied firmly. "I was angry, and upset, and after a short wallow in my emotions Ludvic and I went to this Azilinti bar down in the city he knew, where we could be private, and we talked about it. That's when he told me the story I told you, of how he had learned."

"From the beginning."

"Yes."

Cliopher caught sight of a tall chimney of basalt he recognized. There would be a very shallow reef to its east, and so if they went to the west—yes—there was the channel that hooked around the Oa Kiva and would take them to the more substantial island of Piripiki.

"And then?" Fitzroy muttered, his tone somewhere between reluctant and curious.

"And then I spent a while being very upset and angry *with myself* for never having seen it, because you did everything bar telling me outright, didn't you? And I thought to myself that of course you had—you must have wanted someone to see *you* for who you were."

"Yes," said Fitzroy, almost inaudibly.

"I could not name you, Fitzroy, until far too recently. But I always saw you. Who are you when you are not the Lord Emperor? When you are not the great poet Fitzroy Angursell? When you are yourself, all by yourself, sitting on a small boat in the middle of the ocean with no mirrors or masks before you?"

"Nothing," he whispered. "There's nothing there, Kip."

"The more fool me, then," said Cliopher, smiling at him, as the wind gusted fitfully and tangled the feathers and braids in his hair. "Since I took you for my equal."

"Kip ..."

"I cannot answer for you," he said, for he was not Buru Tovo, not Uncle Lazo, not Tupaia, not even the other Kip of the *other place*. He was himself, and they had promised each other they did not need to be lord and tanà, not to each other: he was this man's fanoa, whose face he could barely even see, silhouetted as it was against the brilliant night sky, the white sand of the beach, the luminous foamwork surf pounding against the edge of the Ring. "I can only ask you the questions, and listen to your answers."

"Kip, don't ... Kip, I can't ..."

Cliopher ran the vaha onto the beach with a soft crunch of sand and the soughing fall of the waves back into the sea. The breakers were loud on the other side of the island, and the star gleamed golden, just barely off its zenith.

"You can," he said relentlessly, as quietly and confidently as he had crossed Sky Ocean, as he had climbed that long stair, as he had lived in the world. "You *must*."

Fitzroy stood up then, in one smooth motion jumped off the vaha and strode up and over the crest of the island. Just before he disappeared down the slope on the other side Cliopher saw him clearly: the starlight caught a gleam on his bare arms, the whites of his eyes, the signet ring he still wore on one hand. And then he was gone, and the fitful wind died down completely.

The surf was very loud.

Cliopher quietly lowered the sails and lashed them in place, and slid over so he could disembark.

The vaha was not high on the beach, but high enough for this side of the Ring, he decided, and followed Fitzroy across the island to the other side, the ocean side, where the waves broke relentlessly upon the Ring and the rest of the world lay spread out in its glory before them.

CHAPTER SIXTY-EIGHT
THRESHOLDS

Piripiki was a typical island for this part of the Ring, barely a lip of black basalt catching a shallow crescent of sand in its lee. From the sky ship one could see clearly how the Vangavaye-ve was the remnant of an enormous supervolcano, the main islands a ring around the deep, deep caldera.

The Ring was tilted, with the northern islands much higher and more complete; the southernmost portion was much lower, rarely higher than half a dozen yards above sea level, and formed a maze as complex and dangerous as the one that Cliopher had found blocking his eastward progress in the sky.

He passed between two basalt boulders and found that the rocks stepped down to a kind of ledge where a layer of stone had been eaten out by the waves. Fitzroy's pale tunic shone like a flag against the black stone; for a moment Cliopher was frightened that he'd jumped in and left only his tunic behind, but when his eyes adjusted he saw that the shadows were playing tricks on his eyes.

He felt his way down, skinning his palm on a broken edge, stubbing his toe on an unexpected protrusion, and was alarmed by how steep the slope of the ledge proved to be. But eventually Cliopher managed to reach his friend's side in safety. He sat down cross-legged, sighing with relief that neither of them had tipped headfirst into the boiling surf surging and crashing on the rocks some dozen feet below them.

The stone was vibrating with the force of the water striking it.

"Are we in danger of falling in?" Fitzroy asked absently. He was sitting with his knees drawn up, his arms wrapped around. His signet ring caught the glint of starlight, the brilliantly luminous waves crashing upon the stones; his head turned towards Cliopher, but his eyes were closed.

Cliopher took a breath. He knew the rhythm of these waves and breakers: they were driven by the constant swell that had accompanied them all the way from the far side of the Isolates. "If we're careful not to lose our balance."

"One must always strive for equilibrium, I suppose," Fitzroy said.

"Equilibrium can be overrated," Cliopher replied seriously, and was delighted to surprise even so much as the huff of breath he heard from his friend.

"You believed me, didn't you, that there was a six-foot iguana in the bath-house."

That was an unexpected sequitur, but Cliopher went with it. "Of course."

"People don't, you know. Believe me when I tell such a strange and ridiculous truth as that."

"I did know there had once been an iguana there," he pointed out.

"I told Masseo I was the Emperor of Astandalas and he *laughed*. I tried to tell Pali —" He stopped. "Kip. Tell me why *you* see something below the masquerade, and they don't."

"First of all," Cliopher said carefully, "you don't know that."

"Pali said—"

"Pali Avramapul strikes me as a person who does not like to feel confused and guilty."

Fitzroy laughed shortly. "That's true. She did apologize ..."

"I'm glad to hear it." Cliopher paused, watching the surge and retreat of the waves, those breakers breaking after travelling a third of the way around the world. They had fallen out of the glorious simplicity and splendour of the sunset into the grey and troubled world they had both loved and served so long.

And yet these waves were full of a glinting, glittering phosphorescence, the lulai created by the thousands of millions of infinitesimal creatures of the sea.

The world was beautiful in and through its troubles. He pressed his knee against Fitzroy's side.

"I feel," he said thoughtfully, feeling his way to words that articulated something he had never consciously realized before, "that I am only now starting to have the *space* to ... think, and feel, and *see* truly. I keep thinking about all the ways I have misunderstood and been misunderstood by my family, and how so much of it could have been remedied if I'd ..."

"Talked about it with them like adults?" Fitzroy asked sardonically, as if he were quoting someone.

"That sounds like more of what-would-Jullanar-do," Cliopher said. "The useful questions and healthy communication and so on."

"She's appalling." Fitzroy's voice dropped. "I wish she were here."

"Me too," Cliopher said, nudging with his knee. "If it would make this easier for you."

Fitzroy nodded, but his posture loosened slightly.

"Basil's that for me. Always right, too. It's terribly irritating. And I miss him even more now that I've found him again, and I didn't think that could be possible."

Fitzroy chuckled wetly. "I've noticed that in your family. The terribly irritating tendency towards very often being right, especially about awkward and uncomfortable truths."

"We do have a cousin for every occasion."

After a moment, Fitzroy said, "I like the one I have for this occasion." Then he stirred without fully unfolding his position, shuffling over so their shoulders touched.

Cliopher felt the tears come to the back of his nose at the simple, small moment of physical closeness. And then he had a clear thought—why *was* he hesitating?—and he reached out with his right arm and hugged Fitzroy.

His fanoa tilted his head into Cliopher's neck, his hair tickling across his mouth and nose. Cliopher carefully lifted his chin so he could tuck the hair out of his way. "Most of the time, I have come to realize, our loved ones wish for two things: that they are happy, and that we are happy."

"Very simple."

"Indeed. The problem comes when they think they know what makes us happy —or even more, when they see us *unhappy* and assume that if only we did what they think is right, we would be content."

"Ah. I can see—that is, I understand from meeting your—"

"Do you think Pali or Sardeet or Jullanar or Masseo love you any less than my sister or my cousin Basil love me?" Cliopher interrupted gently. "They want you to be happy, Fitzroy, and they thought you were before."

The sea surged and splashed on the rocks, fine spray reaching them with a refreshing mist. Above them the new star must have been at its zenith; it was barely a finger's-width off the true ke'e of Piripiki.

Out there was the shining emptiness of the sea surrounding the Ring, where the steep slopes of the ancient volcano's rim plunged down into the abyssal deep.

"I thought I was, before," Fitzroy said thickly, his face still turned into Cliopher's body, his voice muffled. The stone vibrated with the force of the sea; Cliopher's chest was buzzing with it. "I thought I was happy. They thought I was happy. But it was always hollow ... always just a surface. I didn't know any better, then. I thought that was all there was. I thought everyone was like that. We were all so *young* ..."

"Many of us have a more fragile happiness in our twenties than we would like anyone else to know."

"I feel as if this is where you would normally bring out a story from the *Lays* or else about one of your cousins."

Cliopher smiled, chuckling softly. "I don't need a cousin for this. My happiness was fragile and built on sand back then, too."

"And the *Lays*?"

"Elonoa'a was young, too," he said quietly, and they both sat there, remembering Auri and El and the love so great even the deliberate erasure of its true nature had been unable to tarnish that legend.

"We're not young now, but are we any happier?"

"I am. Are you?"

Fitzroy pulled away from the close embrace, stretching out his legs so his feet dangled over the cliff edge. His eyes glimmered faintly in the starlight as he turned to face Cliopher. "Strangely, yes, despite my megrims."

"I don't think I know what that word means."

"I'm *sure* I've heard you use it."

"Doesn't mean I know what it means," Cliopher retorted, and Fitzroy laughed outright.

"My glumbles."

"That's not a real word."

"I could make it one," Fitzroy countered, and he was grinning; Cliopher could hear it in his voice, the familiar amusement welling up. "Oh, Kip, I'd ask how you grew so wise except I know."

Cliopher felt his eyebrows raise at that. "You're more knowledgeable than me, in that case."

"Well, yes, I *am* very well read.—Kip, I've watched you growing into yourself. All these years. And all these past months—how you have let your *Lays* burgeon—like a thieves' lantern that has always been hidden, lit only for you, openly revealed at last."

He smiled at the metaphor, and nudged Fitzroy with his elbow. "And you haven't been letting yourself come out of your shell? Is the thieves' lantern not even more apt a metaphor for you? If you feel as if there's nothing underneath—as if the lantern has gone out—you know, you can relight it."

Fitzroy laughed softly. "You and your fire metaphors."

"I thought you might be tired of the nautical imagery."

"I," said Fitzroy very gravely, "shall never tire of your nautical imagery."

"It takes time to light a fire," Cliopher said. "You need to gather tinder, kindling, wood ..."

Fitzroy held up his hand, snapped his fingers, and a fire blossomed in the palm of his hand.

Cliopher rolled his eyes. "A garden, then? They do not grow overnight ... No, no," he added hastily, laughing out loud, as Fitzroy turned to grin at him and lifted up his other hand. "I believe you could call up an island's worth of vegetation in an instant."

"Please go on," Fitzroy said, as the fire turned into some sort of small spiky animal and nuzzled his fingers. He set the creature on his knee and stroked the space between its ears. "I am enjoying your metaphors for the rebuilding of a self from nothing."

"It's not from nothing," Cliopher said. "You always start from *somewhere*, and you start from my fanoa and the Red Company's Fitzroy Angursell and the Imperial Household's beloved Radiancy. I know you don't like that title," he added, when Fitzroy's gentle stroking of the fire-creature faltered, "but it was always an endearment. No one outside your household called you that. It is a name of love and respect."

Fitzroy sighed. "So I start with three disparate selves."

"So you start with an island where you *feel* as if you have three disparate selves," Cliopher corrected gently, "and you go on from there."

They both looked at the wide, shining waters filling the whole world in front of them, from the white foam of the breakers crashing at their feet all the way out across the obsidian-black sea to the faintly silver line of the horizon, where Nua-Nui turned about the southern pole.

"The sea is too big," Fitzroy said, his voice small. He moved his hands so he could cup the fire in them. It sniffed his fingers and then settled down in a round, compact ball, feet and snout tucked safely in. "I don't know where to go, Kip. How ... Where do you start? *You* start with the *Lays*—where do *I* start?"

"With *Aurora*, if you like," said Cliopher, pointing to the eastern horizon. "Or with the poem you will one day write about the glorious abdication of the Sun-on-Earth," he went on, pointing to the west. "With Au'aua behind us, her eye the brightest star in the sky. The Star of the North ... you stole the diamond named for it, didn't you?"

"The Diamond of Gaesion," Fitzroy murmured. "I enchanted my heart in that diamond, Kip, that false star. My heart and my ability to fly ..."

"You said you'd learned to turn into a crow."

"Jullanar had the diamond, and I was able to ... reclaim myself."

Cliopher smiled at him, the tears starting in his eyes at that simple statement. "There, you see? There was one star for your ke'ea. The Star of the North—the Eye of Au'aua. What's next?"

"Not *Aurora*," Fitzroy said. "Not yet. And I haven't had any new poetry, Kip."

Cliopher did not bring up that new song Fitzroy had been humming when playing with the toy of the Great Whale. "Well, then," he said, and he made a broad, sweeping gesture to take in the sky. "We sit with Au'aua behind us, Nua-Nui before us. Where do you want to go next?"

"Where should I go, Kip? What star should I rest my head under?"

"Would you like to know the ke'e I know for you?"

Fitzroy nodded once, his eyes huge, reflecting the red flames of his creation. "Please."

Cliopher thought for a moment, turning so many half-articulated thoughts into words. "I know you are my favourite poet. I know you have a great mind for legal niceties, and an alarmingly loose grasp of what a triangle is. I know your eyes glaze over whenever I start to speak about budgets. I know you try your hardest at whatever you set your hand to, except for math and, apparently, other things involving precise directions. I know you love with your whole heart, and that your heart is as broad and deep and splendid as the Wide Seas. I know you have excellent taste in friends. I know you are immensely curious, and delighted with all things, big and small. I know you love the common and ordinary goods with an intensity greater than the sun."

"That's ... that's not one thing," Fitzroy said unsteadily.

"One thing I have learned over the years, is that people are not islands, but archipelagoes."

"Don't say it like that, Kip. Don't make it easy."

"It *is* easy, as easy as a poem, and it is hard, hard as living in the world."

Fitzroy snuffled, and the fire-creature unrolled itself from its ball to snuffle back curiously. Cliopher and Fitzroy both laughed.

"See, your creature agrees with me, you were magnificent as Fitzroy Angursell and you were glorious as Artorin Damara and you will be even more wonderful as whoever you choose to be next."

"It's a tiger," Fitzroy said, and kissed the creature on its fiery nose. It sneezed minutely.

"An alarmingly loose grasp of what triangles *and* tigers are."

"When we go back to Basil's inn, I'll introduce you to Sardeet's tigers. You'll adore them."

Cliopher reached out to hug Fitzroy again. "If I am wise, you must be as well, my fanoa."

"I thought you were foolish."

"We can be both. As long as the song of our deeds is good enough, isn't that right?"

"I'll be the best fanoa, you'll see."

Cliopher grinned. "You do have some unusually stiff competition there—"

"I cannot believe you're making dick jokes about Auri and El."

"I meant—honestly, Fitzroy, I wasn't thinking about them."

"For once," Fitzroy muttered, snickering, but he also leaned into Cliopher's embrace. "I thought they were your model and mentors?"

He hesitated for just a moment, but not because he was afraid of speaking such a deep and secret truth. No ... it was that this was a gift they could share. "I was thinking of Vou'a and Ani," he murmured. "The original pattern."

"*Were* you now," said Fitzroy, with a sudden strangely speculative tone to his voice. "Now there's a challenge ... to do something as splendid and grand for my fanoa as Vou'a ever did for his ..."

"Vou'a raised up the islands for Ani," Cliopher said, laughing.

Fitzroy turned to him, face stern. "And you don't think I, Fitzroy Angursell, cannot come up with something equally impressive? They may be gods but *I* am your favourite poet."

"You are," said Cliopher, and, much daring, reached out to pet the fire-tiger (though it was assuredly not a *tiger*, with its small quivering snout and its tiny paws and its alert ears). He could only stand it for a moment before he had to snatch his hand away.

"Did it burn you?" Fitzroy asked, and shifted the creature to one hand so he could pick up Cliopher's with his other. "Does it hurt?"

"Nothing to speak of."

"Nonsense," Fitzroy said, with a sly smile, and he lifted Cliopher's hand to his lips. "I'll kiss it better for you."

Cliopher laughed helplessly, and could not stop even when Fitzroy drew his hand down and then tipped the fire-tiger so it sat on Cliopher's palm instead.

Fitzroy tilted his head back up so he could look up at the star hanging nearly overhead. "Even the sky changes, doesn't it?"

Cliopher looked out, at the wide sweep of the horizon, Nua-Nui the Great Bird with his wings stretched across the sky, his beak pointing firmly south. The albatross had guided him across Sky Ocean with such a jaundiced eye ... but he was true, as true as the sea and the sky and the stars that slowly changed their course, so that Cliopher's pattern in the fire dance was almost but not quite the same as Tupaia's.

"For a thing to be alive it must change and grow ..."

Fitzroy caught his breath. "Who said that?"

"Tupaia said it to me, but I'm sure others have said such a thing," he replied. The sea was such a shining, gleaming black (like the obsidian high on the peak of Mama Ituri; like the depths of Au'aua's eye; like the black, black water reflecting the fires at the heart of him). The waves that came out of the sunset and the south surged against the island, and the ancient stones thrummed against their bones.

The foam was as brilliant as foamwork, as the white birds of dawn, as the stars garlanding the sky. There was a dark shape down there, a shadow cutting through the currents marked out by the infinitesimal glowing creatures of the sea. A shark?—it was far too large for any that would come near the reef.

A flick of a tail, up-and-down rather than side-to-side, and he realized it was a whale.

Whales were dear to Ani, said all the stories. They were wise, those daughters of Au'aua, those children of the sea, whose songs (it was said) echoed across oceans, all the way down to the floors of the sea where the Grandmother in-gathered all.

A shadow of a whale, where no whale should be, so close to the reefs.

The wind gusted, velvet-soft, warm, and scented with something like the perfume Conju made for Cliopher, which had no hint of smoke but somehow seemed to smell like *fire*.

Fitzroy lifted his head, and his eyes were gleaming, gold as the star above them.

Gold as the stars, for the viau were running, shooting stars splashing across the sky, arrows shot from a bow, fish darting away from a spear—

Cliopher felt a hard shiver run up and down his back, and he swallowed. The fire trembled in his hand. "Look in the water," he said.

"Look at the sky," said Fitzroy, his voice full of wonder, his hand closing over Cliopher's, over the tiger, which was an orb of fire between their palms, shining between their fingers, like the star Cliopher had set in the sky.

The whale dove down and then came up, a great shadow, a sleek darkness silvered by the water sheeting off it, as it rose up and breached the water in a sudden tumultuous crash, its spume flaring out in a great splash.

At the same moment, the viau fell down in a great cataract, and the air rang like the great bronze bells of the Palace had rung when the Last Emperor had awoken from his enchanted sleep; as they had rung when he claimed his freedom to leave and find his heir.

"This must be what it looked like when we landed," Fitzroy said, his voice exultant. "Isn't it *magnificent!*"

Cliopher knew that kindling spark, the moment of creation catching fire. It was in him, too, but he had no way to express it—he was no poet, no musician, no artist —he could sing others' songs, but had never written his own. He had only ever been able to shape policies and systems to be a little easier, a little more gracious, a little more ... beautiful.

But he knew the question he had to ask.

"Who are you?" he said, the tears streaming down his face. The viau were still falling, and the whale was dancing, breaching the surface and flinging herself down in great plumes of water, and the stone was thrumming and Fitzroy was singing under his breath, notes for a song Cliopher had never heard, half-rhymes and words that seemed in their half-unheard, half-unspoken state to open whole new vistas of meaning.

Cliopher listened to the words, the music, the song being spun out of nothing, committing it fiercely to memory in case Fitzroy could not convey it to his pen, for no, he might not be able to *create* himself but he had spent his entire life opening the space for other people to do so, and if he could do it for the meanest beggar in the once-slums of the Levels, he could do it for his fanoa.

He could do that. He was Cliopher Mdang of Tahivoa, and his island was Loaloa, and his dances were the dances of Those Who Hold the Fire, and he had held every fire ever handed to him and tended them well.

"Who are you?" he whispered again.

He held a fire in his hand, that living fire his fanoa had made for him, held between their clasped hands.

"Ask me again," Fitzroy said, as the whale slapped her tail upon the sea and the sound ricocheted off the low cliffs of the Ring. "A third time, Kip. Ask me the questions."

He was breathless; Cliopher was too. The island was vibrating, the sea churning in the wake of the whale's great fins. The viau seemed to be rising and settling upon the waves, like terns diving for fish in their multitudes. He felt dizzy with the power washing around him, and was grateful to feel Fitzroy's strong hand close firmly around his.

"The questions, Kip."

Cliopher was shaking now; the sea was boiling. Was this kurakura in Fitzroy's heart, released out into the water? Or had Vou'a dived down to his fanoa, to Ani deep in her cave hidden at the heart of the Ring, and the great goddess of the sea was wakening?

"Beloved," he said, "what is your name?"

And all the world stopped.

The whale vanished below the surface; the viau settled in the hollow troughs of the waves; the waves themselves did not crash upon the stones, but were still.

Cliopher turned his head in terror and awe. Fitzroy's face was exalted, radiant in the reflected light of the viau.

Things that are alive change and grow.

And everything around them, the sea and the stones and the air, were *listening*.

Cliopher was shaking, his teeth chattering, his hair rising with the power surging around him. But he was the tanà of the Wide Seas Islanders, the tanà of the world, and he was the fanoa of Fitzroy Angursell, and he would ask the questions that needed to be asked.

"My name," his fanoa said, solid as the earth, "is Fitzroy Angursell."

He was looking at Fitzroy; then there was an eerie sense of a sudden drop of pressure, and they both turned their heads to look at the sea.

The waters were receding.

The land opened below them, stone gleaming with the wetness, with the phosphorescence, the waters falling away, as if a great harbour wave were pulling them back—and yet they fell, farther and farther, the basalt cliffs of the ancient volcano emerging from their long slumber, as if the wave that would come would be enough to swallow the world.

Or at least the world contained within the embrace of the Ring, which contained three-quarters of Cliopher's heart.

"Are you doing this," he whispered, his hand clenching around Fitzroy's in atavistic terror.

"I am not," replied Fitzroy, with exhilaration in his voice. "We are being invited."

Now Cliopher could see that it was not the whole sweep of the Wide Seas that had retreated, but only a section directly in front of them, offering them a narrowing channel into the vastness before them.

"Do you trust me, Cliopher Mdang?"

"I do," said Cliopher, for he did; he did.

"This is a song, a story, a legend for us. For *us*."

"I trust you," Cliopher said, not moving.

"I can take us down there by magic, if you will let me?"

Now Cliopher looked at him. The fire in his hands seemed to blaze up, no tiger now but a wavering bonfire of power, of strength.

One for a token, and two for a promise. This fire promised a doorway into legend.

"I trust you," Cliopher said, his voice squeaking. "Yes."

"Come with me," Fitzroy said, his voice suddenly warm, delighted, enticing—as enticing as every story, as that picture had been (however poor a portrait, with the eyes hidden behind gold leaf, the serene mask of the emperor hiding such wealth of joy and sorrow)—and—

And then he was dissolving, his bones and flesh falling away, his hands no longer grasping anything but air—

And he was flying.

≈

He tumbled in the cool air, the great wind from the warm sky sucked along with the waters into the depths, and his human mind and the avian form were at war, but he was flying and he was able to follow the black shape in front of him, down and down—

≈

Voiceless, handless, lost; darkness before him, behind him, pressing close, and behind the faintly luminous edges of the cliffs of waters held back for them there were the great curling shapes of monsters.

They slid down the air falling from the sky down the exposed slopes of the volcano, down and down into the roots of the sea.

Thunder behind him, and a leading edge of a more urgent wind, as the walls of water crashed together in their wake.

≈

Down, and down, and now there were only gleams of a strange green light flashing far away in the cold waters hemming them in, except—except there were gleams like shot-silk, like ahalo cloth shaken in the sunlight, like the mirimiri of Ani when Vou'a had held it crumpled in his hands—

The viau, keeping them company, streaking down through the water as they had streaked down the air, faster now than the wind bore them, faster than they could fly, disappearing into the darkness—

～

Down, and down, and down, and then there was something ahead of them: a pinprick of white, a star, and he did not remember the depths of the sky above them, for he had something to look for, something against which he could see the other bird, the black feathers and the shining beak and the golden eyes, and though the water was nipping at him and he was tired, so tired, he flew harder—

～

And then they reached the floor of the sea, and there on a rocky outcropping that was steaming as if it were the chimney of some great subterranean oven was a small, white shell.

～

For a moment he tried instinctively to land; and then he was human again, fumbling to find his balance, flailing until Fitzroy caught and steadied him, and there they stood upon a stone at the bottom of the sea.

Cliopher opened his mouth and could think of literally nothing to say.

Once he was sure Cliopher would not fall, Fitzroy lifted up his hands. Light welled up from his palms, a soft golden light like the light Cliopher had brought back from the House of the Sun. It expanded slowly out in a wavering circle, catching the curved edge of what must be a bubble of air, illuminating what seemed to be a desolate wasteland of feathery dust.

Cliopher found his voice. "That was ... was ... matter for a song."

Fitzroy smiled at him, slow and secret, his delight welling as slowly as the light. "Yes. One day."

"I will help you," Cliopher promised, almost soundlessly.

"I will help you write your memoirs," Fitzroy replied. "Rhodin told me he'd thought of a title for you—what was it?"

"This is so bizarre." They were perched on the edge of some underwater vent—volcano?—with the black water pressing close, strange lights pinpricks in the invisible distance. Cliopher shuddered and focused on Fitzroy, who was grinning at him.

"*Unexpected Appearances in Unlikely Places*," he muttered.

"Perfect!" Fitzroy said exultantly. "Look where we are, Kip! Do you think anyone has ever stood on the floor of the sea before?"

"It seems unlikely."

"A very unlikely place, indeed! Look at those!" Fitzroy pointed down between his feet to a stand of feathery sponges in a searing scarlet. An attenuated crab minced past, entirely ignoring the intruders to its space. "I've discovered something, Kip."

"Have you?"

"I want to have adventures with you for the rest of my life."

"They'll be better memoirs for it," Cliopher replied, giddy, unable to stop grinning. "That's not a ke'e, Fitzroy."

"No, it's a ke'ea," Fitzroy returned complacently, though his brilliant smile showed that he meant every word. "Did you even notice the shell?"

Cliopher could only laugh helplessly. "Of course. The small white shell on the other side of the darkness. The Mother of the Mountains promised me ..."

Oh, there were monsters in the deeps, outside the bubble of safety. He was sure of it: the pinpricks of light winked on and off with the sense of huge shapes swirling past. Drawn, no doubt, to the light. It would be precious, this far down.

A flicker of an eyebrow, and all Cliopher's fear evaporated. Fitzroy would keep him safe; or they would fight the dark and the cold together. Hand in hand, as Ani and Vou'a had once walked, the shoreline and the sea.

"I do appreciate that even after all that time spent together on a small boat with, let me reiterate, nothing much to do besides talk, you *still* managed not to tell me half your stories."

"I didn't want to run out," Cliopher replied, and Fitzroy laughed.

"The first shells for our efanoa," Fitzroy said, transferring his grin to the shell. "We should pick it up together, shouldn't we?"

"Probably," said Cliopher, who felt unbelievably light-headed. Moving slowly, carefully—he was not sure of the cause but he felt as if he might float off if he moved too quickly—they both extended their hands so they could touch the shell at the same moment.

Nothing happened, though as they straightened the two halves came apart and left them each holding one.

"A matched pair," said Fitzroy, with what Cliopher could not help think was *slightly* misplaced smugness.

"You're so beautiful," Cliopher blurted, and when Fitzroy gave him an incredulous look, refused to do anything but be as earnest as his heart wished. "With the shell in your hand and the magic in your face and your ... your ... everything ..."

Fitzroy smiled at him, blazing as the Sun, far more wonderful. "You're rather splendid yourself, Cliopher Mdang."

They both nodded at each other, as if acknowledging an absolute truth.

"Now what?" Cliopher asked, clutching his half of the shell tightly in his hand. "What comes next in the song?"

"Ask me the second question," said Fitzroy, his eyes almost glowing.

"What," he said steadily, not letting his gaze waver for a moment from Fitzroy's, "is your island?"

Fitzroy did not look away. He reached his arms out, the shell in one, magic stirring the air, the water, the feathery dust of the seafloor, the rumbling fire deep within the vent. "Are you ready, Cliopher?" his fanoa asked, one soft breath as the magic gathered underneath them.

They stood at the bottom of the sea, in a bubble of air, on top of fire and stone, with the monsters of the dark all around. And Fitzroy had taken his question as a *challenge*.

Cliopher had not thought he could love him more, but he had been wrong. Every time, he had been wrong. He stared at him, breathless, as if he stood upon a rope bridge with each strand parting as he waited, but he was no longer afraid—now he knew what it meant to be able to fly—

He met his fanoa's eyes. "Are *you*?"

Fitzroy smiled slowly, like the sunrise. "Let us walk in legends, Kip Mdang."

Cliopher's heart was hammering. "Yes," he breathed. "*Yes*. What—What is your island, Fitzroy Angursell?"

"This one."

Fitzroy dropped his hands.

The fire at the heart of the world rose up.

INTERLUDE
FALLING (IV)

Cliopher had tumbled head-over-heels in love with Fitzroy Angursell from the first few lines of *Aurora*, the glimpse of the man in the icon of the Emperor, a joke and a laugh and the meeting of eyes across habit and taboos.

He had fallen over and over again, deeper and deeper, until here they were at the bottom of the sea, where the stones no longer held fast but were transfigured into flame.

Fitzroy reached out, almost casually, and grabbed Cliopher close about his waist, holding him tightly within the narrow column of air within the fire and the water and stone rising up underfoot.

They were rising, shot up through the ocean like a cork out of a bottle of sparkling wine, and it felt like falling.

He could hear nothing: the noise was a physical force as strong as silence, as heavy as the sea, as impossible.

There was lightning under the water, under the waves, in the billowing clouds of ash and steam shaped against the midnight waters.

Fitzroy's magic held him, holding the awesome forces back, so the living rock boiling up underneath them, turning from fire to stone under their very soles, did not burn them; so the great weight of all the Wide Seas crashing together upon their heads did not crush them.

Up he fell, up and up and up: through the black water now stained like coloured glass blue and red and gold and green, the land rising under his feet, the lava becoming stone, forcing him up, up up—

He gripped the shell in his hand, himself held safe by his fanoa, and he looked up at the golden eyes so full of magic, so full of brilliant intellect and indomitable will, so full of the fundamental joy of creation. Fitzroy knew what he was doing. He was smiling, and he was raising the fire around them, and he was the rock that held fast, and the sun and the stars in the sky, and Cliopher was as safe in his arms as Fitzroy had ever been in his.

Though the sea was boiling it would not scald him; though the land was shattering it would not swallow him; though the air had evaporated into silver bubbles he would not drown; though the fire he held in his heart surrounded him, he would not burn.

They fell, together, magic around him, love welling between them, up.

One star burning in his mind's eyes: his own ke'e, Furai'fa above Loaloa.

A second star, burning bright: the new star, Fitzroy's ke'e, the unnamed star above this island that had never existed before.

A third star, in front of his eyes, holding him in his arms: the glowing magic, the shadow caught in the net of light, the black figure in the gold and white of fire and air, the earth bubbling below and the water pressing close on every side.

They fell in parallel, magic around them, spiralling around each other as they had spent half their lives doing, no longer apart but safe at last to hold each other as tightly as they had ever wanted to.

Two halves of a shell, not identical but because of that fitting together.

Up through the dark (and up, and up); up through the twilight zone, where the fish had long since scattered; up through water full of silver and blue and then gold and green; and still the fire bubbled up beneath them, fire to stone underfoot, and still they fell, out of the night and into the day.

v. The Rising Horizon

CHAPTER SIXTY-NINE
NAVANOA

They broke the surface in a huge plume of steam and spray.

Cliopher drew a deep, astonished breath. Fitzroy held him close.

The island kept rising, higher and higher, and the wind blew sweet air across his flushed face, and Fitzroy conducted the fire out of the sea.

Cliopher was held in the circle of his arms. He could feel the magic thrumming through Fitzroy's bones, the stone coming alive under their feet, in the air and the plunging waters around them.

Molten stone arced out of blue water: fire-red and gold and white, hissing in great billows of white steam, plunging down and leaping up, so many dolphins, so many viau, solidifying in a bubble or an arch that caught the light like blown glass.

And still the island rose out of the sea.

His ears were ringing. His head felt as it had in the very moment of the landslide, that echoing, ringing uncertainty whether he was alive or dead—that dream he'd had of dissolving into light, into the great Naming of Names—

And *still* the magic raced around them, fire coming up out of the sea, dancing in the air, turning to stone that glittered with rainbows, a wave of fire that became a towering curve shading them like the sail of their vaha.

Fitzroy smiled, his eyes blazing, his arms holding Cliopher tightly, and he was singing wordlessly, deep in his throat, calling up the fire and the stone, quenching his creation with the sea, lightning crackling through the smoke.

Cliopher had stood beside him when he called the fire down upon Woodlark. This was entirely different.

This was not a rain of destruction, but of pure, primordial creation.

And *still* the island rose up.

They stood now on a flat place, a valley cradled by that great translucent wave, magic still gleaming in rainbow sheens across and through the obsidian. Fantastic columns rose up, twisting, curling, coiling, curved, crying out for vines to gild them with flowers. There were humps and hillocks, pillows and curving rivers of stone, and all of it was gleaming like the night sky when Au'aua had come swimming up out of the constellations to greet them.

Only when the island stood a hundred feet proud of the sea did Fitzroy cease.

He smiled at Cliopher, his eyes focusing from magic onto him, and let go. Cliopher stood there, trembling with awe and delight.

Fitzroy stepped back, only a few paces, so he had enough room to shake out his hands, careful not to drop the shell he held in his right hand. And then, as Cliopher watched—as he watched the master calligrapher about to set his pen to the page for the last letter—as he watched the musician take the final breath before the finale—as he had watched Tupaia set his feet down in the fire dance— Fitzroy lifted his arms up high and dropped them down in a decisive gesture.

The island shuddered once, and was still.

The steam and smoke and vapours rising from the ground continued to rise, and dissipated as they did so, until the great plume was caught by some high wind and borne off to the southwest.

The stone was warm as a hearth under Cliopher's feet.

He could not make his hand unfold from where it was clutching his half of the shell. He stared at Fitzroy, whose face was exhilarated, dazzling as the sun, and he thought that he had thought he could not love that man any more, and he had been wrong.

He tried to say it, but nothing came out.

Fitzroy replied—or at least mouthed words—but Cliopher could hear nothing but the tinkling tintinnabulation of the liquid stones settling into solid materiality.

Fitzroy stepped back across the small space between them, and he cupped both his hands over Cliopher's ears. He murmured something that Cliopher probably would not have been able to understand even if he'd been able to hear it properly.

With a strange *pop* the silence in his ears dissipated.

"There," said Fitzroy. "Can you hear me now?"

"Yes." His voice was rough. Had he screamed? He did not remember screaming. "Yes ... Did you heal me?"

He had not thought that was one of Fitzroy's skills, magical or otherwise. But he was so entirely amazed he could be wrong.

"No ... I put a protective bubble around you, around both of us, so the explosion wouldn't deafen or destroy us, and the spell upon your ears lasted longer than mine."

Fitzroy shook his head, a deep satisfaction in his eyes. Cliopher knew that satisfaction. He had felt it, when he let himself feel it, when he and Fitzroy had been in financially straitened circumstances and been able to collect the stipend. *He* had done that —had made the world a place where that could happen—

Fitzroy had made the world a place where *this* could happen.

"Thank you," Cliopher said, dazed, unable to do anything but smile.

"You're welcome," Fitzroy replied with a royal graciousness, and then his lips twitched. The serenity dissolved into a purely, gloriously human joy. "Kip! Look what I just did!"

"You made an island."

"I made an island."

They grinned at each other, each as astonished by the magnitude of Fitzroy's daring as a person could be.

"You made an *island*," Cliopher said again.

"I *did*."

The fire of Cliopher's heart, deep in that cave full of moss and secret lights, corralled within the hearth of the fire pearls he had never been able to dive deep enough to find—oh, the fire at the heart of him was blazing like the star in the sky they could not see.

Fitzroy was dazzled with his magic, smiling with such power in him that Cliopher felt that inner flame rise up just a little further. He said, "Fitzroy. You made *me* an island."

Fitzroy's smile grew wider, and the air fluttered around them both, stirring their hair and their garments, bringing with it the scent of flowers from the older islands of the Ring.

Cliopher reached forward and grabbed Fitzroy's shoulders tightly. Fitzroy grinned, and Cliopher could not stand it, that delight and that hope and that creativity given full flood. He could only grab onto Fitzroy and embrace him as tightly as Fitzroy had held him, rising up out of the depths of the sea, tears running freely from his eyes in pure, singing joy.

"You're digging into my back with that shell," Fitzroy said after a decent interval, pulling back. He was weeping as well, and rubbed at his face with his elbow before turning his hand so his shell balanced on his palm.

Cliopher did the same.

A white clam-shell, not as big as his palm. It looked like every clamshell you could find on the beach, and he smiled down at it, at that thought, at the idea that he and Fitzroy would have these so apparently ordinary shells for their efanoa and no one would know except for the stories they had to tell them.

Or perhaps Mardo Walea and the other efà would know. Perhaps there was something about the shape, the curve that made it not a true triangle, the pattern of the overlapping layers of the shell, the very colour of it, that would say to one who knew to look that this was no ordinary, no common shell.

Fitzroy turned his over, and they saw the glowing red interior, resplendent as a drop of blood. Cliopher tilted his, and saw how the red caught an inner brilliance, as if the red overlay a smooth polished gold interior like that ancient Voonran vase Rhodin had once given him.

"Do you know what kind of shell this is?" Fitzroy asked.

"No." Cliopher cleared his throat. "No."

"A gift from Ani. For our efanoa."

He nodded, his throat closing with ... everything.

Fitzroy closed his hand around the shell, gently, delicately, and then he moved so he was standing next to Cliopher and they could hold hands. "Look at what I made, Kip."

They looked; they *admired*.

"It's made of obsidian," Cliopher said, turning his head as he caught sight of fleeting glimpses of iridescent fire, red and gold and green and blue and even purple, as if there were an infinitesimally thin layer beneath the dark glossy surface that caught the light when he turned his head just right. "It's ... perfect."

They stood, on the second-highest point: the wave rose another fifty feet above them, caught just as it crested and broke: the wedge of the crest was luminous with the sun, and dark rainbows speckled them.

The columns and arches, high spirals and flowing drapery of stone spun around them, down the back of the wave and in a curve to enclose a perfectly circular protected harbour.

From where they stood, the waves of obsidian rippled down, forming a kind of long, shallow stair angling down towards the south-east, where a sort of raised lip seemed to sparkle as a protective barrier against the deepwater swells.

They were facing the open ocean; the long ridge of the obsidian wave blocked the main view back across the Ring, so Cliopher couldn't see Piripiki, but he could look to the east and position them in relation to the islands running out to the southernmost of the Gates of the Sea.

"We're quite far out," he said, squinting against the sun.

"I hope we're under the new star, after all that," replied Fitzroy, and then they both laughed.

"Not even Auri ever made an *island* for El," Cliopher said.

"I thank you to remember that we are not Auri and El, and we are setting our own grand example—exemplar, even—for those who come after us."

Fitzroy's tone was grand and tolerably smug. Cliopher grinned at him again. "You made me an island."

His fanoa's eyes were sparkling like the sea. "I did." And then, with a small, brilliant grin. "Not just for you."

"You made *us* an island."

"That's better, yes." Fitzroy stretched out, sighing as he opened his fingers to their greatest extent. "Oh, I can feel that flight."

"What kind of bird did you turn us into?" Cliopher asked. He felt light-headed—lack of sleep and food and then all those excitements—not to mention all that *magic*—and he sat down onto the stone, the warmth cradling his bones. "My shoulders hurt from that flying."

Fitzroy leaned over him, tucking the braid of feathers back behind his ear, and then sat down beside him with a quiet, happy grunt. "So do mine. Crows, of course. I told you I'd learned how."

It felt a long, long time ago that Fitzroy had mentioned that. "You did, yes. I'd forgotten all about it." The whole descent through the crevasse in the ocean felt like something out of a nightmare. "We really flew down to the bottom of the sea?"

"We did."

"And then you made an island."

"I did."

Fitzroy lowered himself onto his back, groaning slightly as his vertebrae cracked audibly. They both shifted until their heads were close to each other. Fitzroy hummed, just the beat of the waves below them, then spoke dreamily. "Do we get to name it? Is that the usual practice for discovering a new island?"

"Discovering, yes, but since *you* were the one to raise it from the sea—"

Fitzroy laughed, and the wind blew over them, tangling their hair together. "You were the first to *discover* it, then. We should name it together."

"It's your island."

"Oh, just as it's *your house*, hmm?"

"It's our—" Cliopher stopped, and laughed, and started again. "I take your point. What are you thinking?"

Fitzroy hummed. "It should be an Islander name."

"Then you should be able to come up with something, given all your secret lessons in language. Go on," he said, in challenge, in invitation, in shared and certain joy.

Fitzroy lifted his half-shell up against the sun and made an admiring noise as the light gleamed against the rich lustre. "Look at this colour. Scarlet and a subtle gold."

Cliopher was immensely glad they were not pure gold and white, which would have been far too close to the colours of Astandalas. But red—scarlet, even—oh, that was a good colour for both of them. "Fire and the Red Company," Cliopher said. His heart could not take much more of this, surely?

He smiled up at the sky, the far-distant clouds, a handful of curious seabirds starting to circle into the air and investigate this strange new place created for them.

Fitzroy hummed again. "It should be something about fanoa, then—or so I'm thinking."

Was his music starting to come back? New music? (It was not wrong of him, was it, to hope so dearly that it was? It was not *merely* that Cliopher would love to hear new music by Fitzroy Angursell—)

He coughed. "It's a good thought."

"I thought you might think so."

Was he smiling too much? His cheeks were hurting. But the sky was so beautiful, the gulls and long-tailed frigate birds, circling in ever increasing numbers, attracted by change and newness and the roiling kurakura still around the island as the waves crashed upon its new stones.

"Would it be—would a formation like—would it be—navifanoa?"

The meeting-place of the fanoa. A clear echo to Navikiani, the meeting-place of Iki and Ani, where Vou'a—called Iki that side of the Ring—had raised the first island for the goddess of the sea. Where Cliopher and Fitzroy had first started to see the hidden interiorities of the other ...

Where Cliopher had picked up a cowrie, and given it to the bonfire with a wish for Fitzroy's happiness, because he could not, then, name what he wanted even to himself. Because he could not, at that point, bear to pick up only the one half of a clamshell.

He lay back, the warmth below him and the shade cast from above him equally wonderful.

This was what he had wanted, all that time.

"Or would it be navivanoa?" Fitzroy asked.

"Almost," said Cliopher, for he could not say anything else.

Fitzroy hummed again, and from the number of syllables Cliopher knew he'd come up with something.

He had to say the words; the right words. The sea was thrumming against the stone, spouting up through hidden holes and crevices between the pillars and arches, rising up in parallel plumes like the pod of whales that circled them as they sailed through Sky Ocean's sunset.

Moving slowly, deliberately, Cliopher sat up and turned until he faced his fanoa.

Cliopher held his shell in his right hand and reached out his left to take Fitzroy's. Fitzroy's hand was warm, and tingled, as if the magic were still thrumming in him.

(The magic was always thrumming in him, as the *Lays* were always sounding in Cliopher's ears.)

"What is your name?" Fitzroy asked, his eyes kindling.

"My name is Cliopher Mdang of Tahivoa," he replied gravely. "What is yours?"

"Fitzroy Angursell of Nowhere in Particular." Fitzroy invested the epithet with all the glory of his entire reputation. His face grew intent, still, his eyes burning, as he held Cliopher's gaze, his hands, his heart. "What—what is your island?"

Cliopher smiled at him, just a little, just enough. "My island is Loaloa. What is yours?"

Fitzroy drew in a deep breath, and his voice was full of joy. "My island is Navanoa."

"Perfect," Cliopher breathed, as something—magic?—rippled through the air, the stone, the sea, the fires deep in the heart of this new land. "Navanoa." The word settled, perfect, solid, a new name in the Great Naming, as this was a new place, a new island, to be added to the lists held by the lore-keepers.

"Don't ask me the third question," Fitzroy said, as Cliopher was about to turn his head to do so. "I don't have a clever answer for it yet."

∾

They lay there for a while. Cliopher dozed off, listening to the pops and creaks as the stone settled into itself, the click-clack of pumice boulders floating in the new harbour and knocking against each other, the cries of the curious birds above, the surge and roar of the oceanside breakers. The great obsidian wave hung over them, smooth and gleaming-black as the nighttime swells of Sky Ocean.

Had he dreamed that Au'aua had come sporting through the living mortal waters under the golden star?

A new ke'e for a new island ...

Fitzroy had raised that island from the sea, but it was Cliopher who had set that star in the sky.

He slept.

∾

He woke long past noon, thirsty. Fitzroy was curled up, cheek pillowed by his hands, but he stirred when Cliopher sat up.

"What do you think?" Cliopher asked him, stretching and then wincing at the stiffness in his arms and shoulders. He did not think he even had the same muscles as the crow, but that did not stop his body from being quite certain he'd abused it.

"I think," Fitzroy said, pushing himself up and then falling back down as he was interrupted by an enormous yawn, "that I am going to have to leave it to your inge-nuity as to how we get off this new island of mine, Kip."

"Magic?" Cliopher suggested.

"Mm, no." Fitzroy shook his head and then wriggled as if finding a comfortable position. "No magic from me for a while. Don't play with magma without proper precautions, Kip. Didn't want to set off any *other* volcanoes. Playing with fire is dangerous."

And with that he firmly closed his eyes. He wasn't pretending, either; within a very few seconds his breath had evened out.

Cliopher watched him for a while, almost as nonplussed as he had ever been.

He imagined Vou'a hadn't fallen asleep after raising the islands for Ani.

Eventually he decided it would be better if he moved, and accordingly got up and stretched, slowly at first, and then as his muscles loosened he moved into the stretches for the practice dances.

They were on a wide and relatively flat area; the island sloped down gently in the layers of curving pillows to the sea on the south, more steeply to the north. Quite the opposite of the Ring islands, but then this was a *new* island, and it had been formed by a new eruption.

He looked at the curving stone of the obsidian wave, and admired its translu-cency, the beauty of its curve, the curl of the breaking wave caught in the very moment of spilling into foam; the impossible smoothness and sharpness and recurve of its shape.

He would not be crossing to the other side of the island over that barrier.

He walked as far as he could to the west, where the wave curled over into a tunnel and then into huge boulders where the stone, smooth as if already polished, showed a filigree of lacy shapes, like stars or ... or snowflakes, he thought, remembering that winter marvel from his time in Astandalas.

The boulders were too smooth and large for him to climb over. He turned back, walking now along the lower lip of the island, where the stone stepped down to form a ledge. One day, he imagined, regarding them with wonder, with surmise, almost with a kind of satisfaction—as if *he* had had anything to do with it!—one day that would be a beach, and his descendants would run their boats up to this island, this Navanoa, with a line or two from the *Lays* in their mouths.

A new star in the sky, and a new island in the Ring.

It was impossible, and yet it was true.

He did not even care that they had no food or fresh water or shade or shelter or means of leaving. They had a new island and a pair of shells for the first beads on their efanoa, and ... and that was enough.

∾

He returned up to where Fitzroy was still curled up asleep. The wave was shading him now, as the sun was lowering to the west.

He looked once more out to sea, wondering if the whales would come as close as the birds from the Ring were, to investigate this island.

There, not all that distant, was a boat. He lifted his hand, and saw some answering movement as the sails angled differently and the boat headed swiftly into shore, towards that sheltered harbour Fitzroy had made.

Wild mages, he thought fondly, and the gift, perhaps, of Ani—or Vou'a—or whatever deities Fitzroy believed in.

It was not just any boat, either. It was Bertie's yacht.

CHAPTER SEVENTY
THE RESCUERS

He watched the boat sail smoothly into the harbour, Toucan at the sails, Bertie at the tiller. Ghilly and Cora were at the prow, Ghilly with a rope coiled in her hands, Cora preparing to jump onto the island.

Even silhouetted against the bright water, he could tell who they were: heavy-set Bertie, short and dapper Toucan, slim Ghilly, tall and broad-shouldered Cora.

Cliopher checked on Fitzroy, who was still sleeping soundly, and scrambled down the long, sloping steps to the harbour. By the time he was within hailing distance Cora had lashed the mooring rope to one of the obsidian pillars and Toucan and Ghilly were sliding out a gangway.

"Cora!" he cried, hastening towards her, then halting a few feet away when she regarded him with utter confusion.

He brushed his hair back away from his face and shrugged, grinning sheepishly.

"Kip Mdang," she declared, her expression mellowing towards humour. She gave him a second, more thorough once-over. "You look as if you've been having adventures."

"So do you," he replied, admiring her bare shoulders and the black tattoos curving across them. "Tattoos, Cora?"

"Feathers, Kip?" She laughed, and came over to embrace him. "It's the custom for Islanders who surf in the great waves off Jilkano," she told him, and spun around slowly so he could admire the interlocking waves. "Seven waves, for the seven times I rode the Great Wave off the City of Emeralds."

Cliopher vaguely remembered Suzen mentioning the idea. He'd seen the wave, once or twice: a constant feature of the coastline a little away from the City of Emeralds, where an underwater canyon was angled precisely into the prevailing ocean swells. After a storm, the Great Wave could be a hundred feet high.

Cora tipped her head up at the high obsidian crest catching the sunlight in a wash of liquid fire. "It was like that," she told him, grinning at his discomfiture. "And it was fantastic."

"I could never do that," he said honestly.

"Kip Mdang, admitting he can't do something!" Cora cried, and turned triumphantly to the others, who had by this time crossed to land. Bertie was just standing up from drawing the plank safely to shore, but Ghilly leapt nimbly forward and threw her arms around him in a great embrace.

"Kip!" She batted him lightly on the shoulder. "Kip!"

"Ghilly!"

"I cannot believe you're here," Ghilly said, and stamped her foot. "And looking amazing. Have you had another strange otherworldly experience? Besides the experience of going to Alinor, that is, we knew you were doing that."

"I—we—Fitzroy and I—my lord, that is, but—no, he's my fanoa—we sailed Sky Ocean to the House of the Sun." Cliopher was quite proud of himself for managing to get that all out.

Bertie grunted. Toucan looked away, whistling innocently. Cora tilted her head, eyebrows raised. Ghilly appeared satisfied. "Doesn't contravene the Zboleti Paradigm, then," she murmured. "Have you read Salenge recently, Kip? I worked out a theorem to account for the time dilation we experienced going to Solaara, but the return voyage has been—"

"It has been *full* of math," Toucan said, and nodded exaggeratedly at Cliopher. "*Full* of math."

"And philosophy," Bertie rumbled.

Ghilly tutted at them fondly. "Kip understands philosophy. And math. Don't you, dear? You wrote that great paper in uni about the logical underpinnings of Hiskae's Two Theories of the Self, do you think you still have a copy?"

Cliopher felt too sozzled by surprise and magic and pure happiness to answer that. "I have no idea," he said. "Fitzroy made me an island this morning. I cannot think about philosophy right now. I have only poetry in my heart."

"Fitzroy Angursell made you an island," Toucan said, and then crowed with great delight. He turned and pointed a finger at Bertie. "You owe me a meal at Enya's, Falbert Kindraa! Didn't I tell you?" He turned back to Cliopher. "When we saw the plume go up and then felt the shockwave hit the boat, we were afraid Mama Ituri had gone at first, of course—"

"But then we saw the plume was too low, and too close to us—" Ghilly interjected.

Cora nodded. "Yes, we saw the fire coming up out of the water in the night. And the lightning!"

"So then we started telling stories to ourselves about a new island in the Ring, and what it could mean, and—and I said—" But Toucan could not keep talking; he was laughing so hard he started to splutter.

Ghilly's face was bright red, and she'd stuffed her hand into her mouth (futilely) to suppress her giggles.

"And then we started to speculate," Cora said, her eyes brimming with amusement, "how Vou'a raised the islands for Ani, and we *wondered* if it could *possibly* be the case that you and—"

She could not get out the rest of the sentence, either.

"I am so glad," Toucan said, wiping his eyes, "that you have finally claimed that relationship. I'm so proud of you."

"We're very proud of you," Ghilly got out breathlessly. "Where—where is he? I can't wait to meet him now that I know for sure. We've been *so good*," she added. "We have, haven't we?" She nodded earnestly at the others.

"Absolutely," Cora said with wide-eyed innocence. "All the way across the Wide Seas we were *very* good."

"Fitzroy Angursell," Bertie rumbled, and then smiled slowly at Cliopher. "I didn't tell them until we were past the last of the Sociable Isles."

"We were very good," Cora repeated. "We didn't throw Bertie overboard for not telling us that your beloved lord, your very dear friend, your Aurelius Magnus, was actually *Fitzroy Angursell*."

"Your *fanoa*," Ghilly said, in between little eruptions of giggles. "Which meaning are you going with? I don't seem to recall ever hearing any rumours of what you thought was its meaning. Trading partner, right? Husband? *Work* husband? Lover? Clamshell?"

"Fanoa," said Cliopher, very simply. "My dearest friend."

"You can do better than that, Kip," Ghilly said. "He raised an island for you, the least you could do is, I don't know—"

"Hang a star?" Cliopher replied, and winked at her when she stopped, flustered. "I have a great deal to tell you all."

"Indeed. Have you named your island?" Toucan asked, putting his hand over his wife's mouth. She wrinkled her nose and wriggled out from underneath, so that his arm draped instead over her shoulders.

That made Cliopher grin, his heart swelling what felt like several sizes. "Welcome to Navanoa."

Toucan said, "Of course you called it that."

Cliopher turned to look up the hill at the pale tunic of Fitzroy under the shelter of his wave. "We did, yes."

"Sickening," Ghilly said, and took his arm. "Simply sickening. Shall we go wake him?"

"He told me he'd done enough magic and it was up to me to figure out how we got *off* the island. I would be much obliged, therefore—" But he could not manage a courtly phrasing any more than his friends, and he subsided into snickering. "I have so much to tell you."

"I'm sure you do," Bertie rumbled.

"Seeing," Toucan went on, "that we left you resolutely heading east to the sunrise and Alinor so you could find Basil."

"Not that we didn't think that you wouldn't also be looking for your fanoa," Ghilly said. "Since you have *finally* stopped pretending that word doesn't exist."

He flushed. "Ah ..."

"You really do look fantastic," Ghilly said, surveying him thoroughly. "Your hair is splendid. And your face ... your eyes ..." She tilted her head, and began muttering the names of people Cliopher very distantly recalled from university debates on ethics and ontology and the philosophy of time and the gods, most of which he hadn't thought of since.

"You don't look anywhere near so drawn and tired," Bertie said bluntly.

Toucan nodded. "So! Give us the short—very short—version, and then we can help you off this island of yours. As you seem to have misplaced your boat?"

"We left it on Piripiki."

"We'll take you around Navanoa—*what* a name, Kip! But of course you wanted something that would sound excellent in the *Lays*. Stop sniggering, Cora, we all know Kip has absolutely planned his life around it."

Cliopher refused to answer that. Verbally, at least; his face felt sunburned. This had been *such* a long-held dream ...

(So had Bertie's dream of circumnavigating the world. And he had done that, too. Cliopher did not think his heart could grow any larger, and then something like this happened!)

Bertie snorted. "We should be able to get close enough to land safely, though the waters are chaotic at the moment, I expect."

"But first, the short version?" Cora gave him a winsome smile.

Cliopher considered for a moment. "I found Basil and his family well, if at the mercy of a terrible postal system. Fitzroy and half of the Red Company showed up at the inn while Rhodin and I were staying there, and Fitzroy and I went out for a walk one evening and fell through a gap in the worlds into Sky Ocean. After various adventures there we came home."

He nodded firmly. They stared at him. At last Toucan said, "Okay, I want a bit more than that."

Cliopher grinned at them. "I'm terribly thirsty, and it's a long tale of the sea to tell it."

Toucan rolled his eyes. "Bertie, come help me carry Kip's beloved ... renegade."

≈

Fitzroy did not wake up for the conveyance to Bertie's yacht. They got him on board without too much trouble—for all his long limbs and lean muscle he was surprisingly light in weight—and settled him into a nest of cushions and blankets on deck, where Cliopher could keep an eye on him.

"Did we interrupt your honeymoon?" Toucan asked in all seriousness, when Cliopher fussed with making sure Fitzroy's hair wasn't being pulled by a fold of blanket.

"Our faravia," Cliopher replied, settling back on his heels. Fitzroy was sleeping deeply, his face calm, the magic quiescent.

"Sail-mending?" Toucan raised his eyebrows. "As in the *Lays*?"

"We met Elonoa'a and Aurelius Magnus on that island in Sky Ocean," Cliopher said, and smiled at his flabbergasted friend. "We learned a great deal—old songs and stories, and—" He glanced up at Cora, who had joined them, Ghilly a step behind her. "I learned the ship-building songs for the *He'eanka* ... and we learned that *faravia* used to mean a period of adjustment after a long voyage, where you stayed on the edge of the community until you were ready to be part of things again."

Toucan considered him for a long moment. "And somehow this involved raising a new island?"

Cliopher's eyes strayed to Fitzroy. "We might have gotten a little bored."

∽

Ghilly came out with a platter of warmly spiced fruitcake, which was unexpected.

Cliopher ate a piece, hummed in pleasure, and ate a second, and only then did he think to say, "Thank you. I'm impressed at your supplies this close to the end of the voyage."

"You're ridiculous," Ghilly said fondly, and kissed Toucan on the cheek. "We met your cousin Quintus at Little Palo, and he traded news for a few fresh things. He must have left before you arrived? He didn't have any gossip about you at all."

"Must be the first time," Cora said, and they all laughed.

Fitzroy stirred, but only to curl more deeply into his blankets. Cliopher adjusted a pillow. "It was a great work of magic," he said defensively when he saw how Toucan was smirking at him. "He needs to rest, after that."

"I am merely enjoying this unexpectedly domestic side of you," Toucan replied. "I find it greatly amusing that it required a voyage to Sky Ocean to draw it out of you. Did you go to the House of the Sun, then?"

Cliopher nodded. "I did."

"You know that you were going to be in the *Lays* from your work in the world, right?"

"I didn't fall into Sky Ocean on *purpose*, Toucan."

Toucan laughed; and Ghilly said, "As if you wouldn't have if you'd known it was an option!"

He glanced at her, to find her looking down at him. She smiled, not exactly wistfully, but with memories standing clearly in her eyes.

Once, long ago, they had climbed up to the park on the peak of Mama Ituri's Son and looked out at the Ring and the distant horizon spread before them. Cliopher had asked her to marry him, and she had said no.

She had not wanted to come second, she'd said; and that he followed another star.

"We made the right choices," she murmured, as the boat heeled and Bertie set the sails to another tack. "This was what you always wanted, wasn't it?"

"I wanted you to be part of my life, too," he replied, a little helplessly, for it was.

She smiled at him, with a sudden sweetness, a sudden mischief. "And you have me, and I you, after all is said and done. Will you be able to be happy now, do you think?"

He closed his eyes for a moment, but in the shade, the soft wind cool on his face, the new island behind him, home ahead of him, laying asleep at his side, all he could answer was the truth. "I am, Ghilly. I am."

"So am I," she said, and then: "but I *will* be very glad to be home in my own bed, too!"

∽

Navanoa turned out to be perhaps a mile and a half away from the main arc of the Ring. The water was dark, deep, and Bertie was able to set a clear course across the intervening channel without any difficulty.

"How did you get to your new island, anyway?" Toucan asked once they were out of its complex currents and heading towards the familiar channel alongside the fringing reef. "You surely didn't swim from Piripiki?"

Cliopher blinked at him. The excitements of the night seemed to be hitting him, and he was not looking forward to sailing the vaha back across the bay, especially since he would not have the very convenient wind to assist him. "It was very strange," he offered.

"Yes?" Toucan said. "Would you like some coffee?"

"Please ..." They were sitting under the awning, or Cliopher was sitting cross-legged beside Fitzroy and the others were sitting on their own deck-chairs, save for Bertie who was leaning on the railing keeping an eye on the sails and tiller.

Ghilly passed him a mug with fresh coffee, which was something he'd nearly forgotten could just be had, whenever you wanted, and Cliopher sipped it with great enjoyment. "We'd gone to Piripiki for a ... an outing ..." He flushed at Toucan's amused smirk, and forced himself to continue. "A whale came up, and the viau were running, and then a great canyon opened up in the sea ..." He shook his head. "I can't tell you the tale as it should be told."

"You are looking tired now," Ghilly agreed bluntly. "We will accept that the *proper* story is full of the great questions and a challenge-song for the ages, shall we?"

Her tone was fond, and Cliopher's heart stuttered with gratitude. "Yes ..." He rallied himself, glancing down at his fanoa (and he could use that word! Just like that!) "The great canyon was a gift from Ani, or Vou'a, or them both ... I'd done them a favour ... Fitzroy turned us into birds, into crows, and we flew down the channel all the way to the bottom of the sea, and ... and then there was a shell ..." He showed them his half, which he was still holding tightly in his hand; he'd tucked Fitzroy's safely away. "And then Fitzroy raised the island."

"Right underneath you?" Bertie asked.

"Yes ..." Cliopher twisted around to look at the island behind them. From this side the great obsidian wave looked like the back of a whale, and he felt the tears prickle in his eyes. "It was all a bit ... unexpected."

"You deserve each other," Ghilly declared. "Because that sounds totally mad, I hope you know that?"

He grinned sheepishly at her. "I know."

Toucan was regarding him intently. "And what sort of favour did you do Ani *and* Vou'a, that they did *that* in return?"

Cliopher looked at the brilliant ripples, the swift shadows of tiny white clouds such as the sheep he'd seen in Sky Ocean, the glittering foam of the breakers upon the black rocks and white sand beaches of the Ring islands.

"It's a long story of the sea to tell it," he said. "But I brought home the mirimiri of Ani from the House of the Sun."

~

They came to Piripiki, but Bertie's yacht had too deep of a draft to get over the fringing reef. He had a small single-hulled canoe tucked along one side of the boat for just this purpose, and Cliopher and Toucan paddled together to the beach so Cliopher could reclaim his vaha.

They beached the canoe and clambered over the low crest of the island. There were chunks of freshly broken coral and other seawrack quite high—several yards above the usual high-tide mark, if Cliopher recalled the patterns correctly. He frowned at the detritus, and bumped into Toucan, who had stopped at the crest.

"So," said Toucan, "your boat."

"Yes."

"Which I notice is not here."

Cliopher stared at the very definite absence of the vaha that had taken him to the House of the Sun and back. "Yes."

"I'm certain—absolutely *certain*—that you are aware of the first, fundamental rule."

"*Secure your boat.* Yes. I am aware."

"And yet—"

Cliopher sighed. "And yet it is very clearly not here. I am also aware."

"I thought you might be," Toucan said, grinning so broadly Cliopher could only shrug and chuckle in response. "Didn't you tie it up to anything?"

The beach on this side was smooth enough to suggest that there had never been a boat there at all, which he knew was untrue. Cliopher looked around, but was not particularly surprised that he could not see the boat. "No, it was a clear night and the wind was off the bay ..."

"Until your fanoa lifted up an island and set off a small tsunami."

Cliopher picked up a piece of broken coral, scarlet fading quickly as the polyps died, and nodded despondently. "It seems to have washed quite over Piripiki ... the gods only know where my vaha ended up."

"Ani probably took good care of it," Toucan said soothingly. "It was enough of a wave to get over Piripiki and carry an outrigger canoe across the reefs into the open bay, but I doubt it did more than slosh up over the boardwalks in the city, if that. Don't worry."

"I had not even begun worrying about the possible damage in the city, but thank you, Toucan."

Toucan laughed and turned around to head back to Bertie's boat. "Look at you! Not securing your boat enough for any eventuality, and not thinking of a very logical eventuality at all! You *have* changed from your travels. One might almost think you were becoming spontaneous."

There was not much he could do about the surge that Fitzroy must have caused by that small, controlled volcanic eruption. He looked across the shimmering blue water to the shining black rock of Navanoa. The white gulls were circling, catching the deepening light of the sun with a golden flare.

"It was worth it," he murmured, and Toucan laughed.

≈

Fitzroy slept solidly the whole journey from the new Navanoa to the university marina where Bertie routinely moored his boat. Cliopher enjoyed being able to sit on the deck of the yacht and talk with his friends.

He had forgotten how intensely focused Ghilly could get with a philosophical puzzle, and the strangeness of time as she had now personally experienced it was a puzzle that lay right at the intersection of all her interests.

He did not, in short, get much further than Basil's inn and what he'd found there. Ghilly was far too intrigued in how this new evidence fit into what she'd learned since leaving Solaara.

Cliopher did not care. There would be time—all the time in the world, even if he did not dare say such a phrase out loud in Ghilly's presence—to tell them all his stories. To hear all theirs.

Toucan had been equally intent on his art, and upon Cora's exhortations was persuaded to bring out his sketchbooks of the Sociable Isles. They'd stopped at dozens of islands, inhabited and not. His drawings were clear-sighted depictions of people and places, wittily capturing the subtly different atmospheres of each island.

Cliopher enjoyed seeing them, and wished (not for the first time) that he had any such artistic skill of his own. "What were you doing, Bertie," he asked, "while Toucan was drawing and Cora was seeking out the local dare-devils? Did you develop a new —or old—hobby?"

"Nah, I just fished and chatted with the locals."

"Don't listen to him," Cora said, grinning up at her ex-(and future?) husband. "He's nearly done his textbook about the First Principles of Anthropological Study."

~

Fitzroy began to rouse when they entered the city, with its noises and smells and, no doubt, changed magic. He blinked blearily when Cliopher whispered, "We're nearly home; Bertie picked us up," and drew himself together so he could offer etiquette-book-perfect thanks to Bertie.

"Yes, thank you for the lift," Cliopher added, clasping Bertie's shoulder for a moment.

"Any time," Bertie rumbled, eyebrows drawing together (and they *did* resemble El's, though Cliopher had not yet told him so); and then he repeated it, with emphasis: "*Any* time."

They made their way along the edge of the canal with Ghilly and Toucan, who lived in a flat not far from Saya Dorn's old house.

"It's fun to think we'll be living so close," Ghilly said. "We'll stop by tomorrow, shall we? Or the next day?"

"Any time," Cliopher said, his heart swelling with the fact that he *could* say that, that his friends were here and so was he, and he had a place to welcome them to, and ... and they still had very little furniture and almost no dishes and hardly anything but a stack of books three feet tall, but Ghilly and Toucan had known him for literal decades.

"You're not rushing off?" Ghilly said, with a slight frown. "Is your quest done, then?"

"Not yet," Fitzroy admitted. "It's well underway ... We have plans ..." He yawned again, hand over his mouth. "We'll be here at least a few days more. Auspicious dates, that sort of thing." He waved vaguely, not making Cliopher think that there were any such *auspicious dates* to be considering. Fitzroy was not, after all, a Schooled wizard.

"Please don't come too early," Fitzroy added. "Or if you do, please make the coffee. The kitchen's quite obvious, though you might have to manoeuvre around the resident iguana."

"The resident—" Toucan burst out laughing. "You've encountered it, then!"

"We have indeed," Fitzroy said darkly.

Cliopher considered his friend. "You knew about the iguana?"

"Your cousin Melo was *quite* concerned about the fact he'd not disclosed the existence of the iguana before you bought the house."

"He *knew*?"

"Oh, yes, it's apparently incapable of being removed. He'd not told you because he hoped their last efforts—which I think involved putting it on a trading ship bound across the Wide Seas—would work. But it's got some sort of magic, and it arrived back just after you returned to Solaara after Enya's restaurant opening."

"He could have written to me about it," Cliopher muttered, and then a thought struck him. "So could've Leona. So could've *you*, for that matter."

Ghilly laughed. "This was much funnier."

Fitzroy gave her an approving nod. "Ghilly, you and I are going to get along *tremendously*."

"Like a house on fire?" She grinned impishly at them, darted forward and kissed first Cliopher and then Fitzroy on the forehead, and grabbed her day-bag before disappearing into her house. At Fitzroy's inarticulate response, Toucan snickered again and followed suit—kisses and all.

Cliopher and Fitzroy looked at each other. Fitzroy appeared dazed. "Have they *adopted* me?"

Cliopher took his arm, and turned him gently to continue along the canal. "Yes. I think you'll find they have."

"What an *amazing* thing," Fitzroy declared. And then, as they turned a corner to cross the high bridge with the hanging vines they had so far only gone under, and saw a familiar sail coming down the canal towards them, he added: "How did our boat get back before us?"

~

Their neighbours waved up at them, even as the mast shimmered and skimmed through the stone bridge. It went right between Cliopher's legs, and he shivered at the strange, pins-and-needles sensation.

"That was good magic," Fitzroy said placidly, pleased. "When did you hand over the boat to them?"

"The surge must have carried it to the edge of the city." Fitzroy looked blankly at him, and Cliopher chuckled, took his arm, and explained as they continued on. "The wave made by your island coming up out of the sea."

"Our island. Navanoa."

"*Our* island, yes."

They grinned at each other.

~

There were lights on in their house.

"Those are clever," Fitzroy said happily, perking up as he looked in the window at one. "Set to glow as the daylight goes."

"That is clever," Cliopher agreed, presuming Fitzroy had bought them in his shopping tour of Gorjo City. "You should probably eat something before you go to bed, Fitzroy."

His fanoa made a face. "You're probably right. Kitchen, then?"

He opened the door. "Kitchen."

"Someone's been inside," Fitzroy said, yawning even more widely. He waved vaguely at the sink. "Not the iguana. There's a cup."

There was indeed a cup, carefully turned upside-down to drain.

Fitzroy sagged down onto the bench behind the table, and Cliopher smiled fondly at him as he moved around the kitchen. Even after so short a time as they had lived there it was starting to feel familiar. Homely, even.

Theirs.

Theirs.

He rinsed and filled the kettle and set it on the enchanted cook-top—quicker and cleaner than a fire, admittedly, if less pleasing—and then pondered the pantry. Someone *had* been in: a basket of eggs and a ceramic pot of what turned out to be butter had joined the fruit and vegetables he and Fitzroy had bought at the market. And there were three separate baskets of baked goods—he sniffed in appreciation. Two loaves of hearty bread, a basket of stuffed rolls, and a pineapple upside-down cake.

He brought out all of these.

"What *is* that?" Fitzroy asked, poking gingerly at the cake. "Is that ... pineapple?"

"It's my favourite cake. I wonder who remembered that?" He peered around, but they must have shifted the other chair at some point. Had they taken it upstairs? It was possible. They'd been moving around their mobile furnishings with great abandon.

"Your aunt Oura? She's the baker in your family, isn't she?"

"Could be," Cliopher said, but he had returned to the pantry and discovered there was a glazed clay dish of crab cakes. They were cold, of course, if fully cooked, and he brought them out. "Enya's been here—you remember her, I trust? The chef?"

"The most excellent chef, indeed. I never did let her have my name for that burning fruit dish, did I? Remind me ... later."

"Later," Cliopher agreed quietly, his heart full.

Fitzroy rubbed his face. "Kip, this is a splendid feast but I am about to fall over."

Cliopher considered what he'd eaten, which was one crab cake and half of a stuffed roll, and said, coaxingly, "Can you manage the other half of the roll?"

"Who are you, Conju?" But though he grumbled, Fitzroy did pick up the roll and nibble at it. "It's not that I'm not hungry," he explained after a few small bites. "I'm so tired I can barely move my jaws."

"If you can talk, you can eat," Cliopher said ruthlessly.

"You are *such* a hypocrite. I'm sure you don't eat when you're working."

"That's how I know that if you sleep for most of a day and a half without eating or drinking enough water, you're going to wake up with a horrendous headache."

Fitzroy wrinkled his nose, but obediently drank down the water Cliopher had set in front of him. "Are you going to make me have more?"

"More water, yes." Cliopher reached out and touched him lightly on the hand. "I need you to be in fine form tomorrow," he said, smiling at his fanoa. "Think of the stories we'll have to tell about our newest adventure."

Fitzroy gave him a reluctant smile in return, but his eyes were pleased. He drank the glass of water. "Good enough?"

Cliopher smiled at him. "You made an island today, Fitzroy."

Fitzroy paused for just a moment, his hands on the table. "I did, didn't I?"

"A splendid island. We'll have to go back and have a picnic, and bring back some of the obsidian to make into jewelry."

"What a thought!"

"Go to sleep, Fitzroy. Beloved. I'll tidy up down here."

"Very—well." Fitzroy yawned again as he stood up, swaying slightly. Cliopher followed him outside and watched anxiously as he climbed slowly up the stairs. But he *was* a grown man, and for all the cosseting and service his household had given him, a quite competent one as well. Theoretically.

(Fitzroy had slept without apparent issue on every surface from the vaha's decking to a still-smoking chunk of newly formed rock. He would be able to manage with his piles of cushions.)

Cliopher let out his breath once Fitzroy had gone inside, the upper door on the balcony not banging but swinging quietly shut. "Well," he murmured to himself, and glanced across to the neighbours. The vaha was tied up in its proper place; the two old women had gone indoors, and only their upstairs window was illuminated.

He decided he'd talk with them in the morning, stretched languidly, and had one of the greatest shocks of his life when he turned around and found Ludvic standing there.

CHAPTER SEVENTY-ONE
THE TANA-TAI

For a moment, they simply stared at each other.

Ludvic looked unchanged: solid, sober, responsible. He stood firmly planted, in his civvies—a lightweight linen tunic in a dark brown colour, his Azilinti cape in all its shades of brown and gold slung casually over one shoulder.

"Were you standing out here this whole time?" Cliopher asked finally.

"Sitting." He gestured beside him, where a chair Cliopher hadn't seen before was settled into a comfortable-looking nook under the stairs, with a good view of the courtyard entrance and the dock.

"We came in the front door." Cliopher shook his head and walked forward to embrace his friend. "I'm sorry. I'm tired. It's wonderful to see you. Did you leave as soon as you got my letter?" He tried to count the days. "Has it been long enough?"

Ludvic laughed, quietly, and picked up the chair to take inside. "Only if I'd been prepared to go within ten minutes, the way we did that time to come here. I was about to embark on the sky ship when your letter arrived at the Spire."

Cliopher followed him into the kitchen and sank down on the bench. "Then—how? Who's been gossiping?"

"Paramount Chief Jiano wrote to Chancellor Aioru and me to say you and himself had come."

Ludvic said it simply, but Cliopher, looking at him, saw the way he had shut away his emotions again. "I asked you to come," he said gently.

"I know."

"You were coming anyway?"

Ludvic shifted slightly on his feet, and then set the chair down and sat down backwards in it, his arms folded along its back. "I wanted to see you."

That was a great admission for his friend, and Cliopher smiled at him, rather honoured. "I've missed you," he replied. "Did you get yourself some food? I hope you

—" He stopped and bit his lip, remembering Fitzroy's response to Cliopher *assuming* a few too many things.

But Ludvic was not Fitzroy. "Yes? You hoped I ...?"

"I hope you made yourself at home."

Ludvic's eyes warmed, and his shoulders relaxed slightly. He nodded, just a dip of his chin. That was it: and yet Cliopher felt as flustered and pleased as if that had been a grand declaration.

"You're keeping well, I hope?" Cliopher said. "I hear Conju is still in Kavanduru ... I am told he took my mother to visit with the Grand Duchess."

Ludvic snorted, just a little, and his smile deepened. "I think it was more that your mother took *him* to visit the Grand Duchess, and your sister and niece came to visit. Jiano loans out his sky ship, do you know?"

Cliopher was once more reminded that Ludvic had many hidden depths. He also hadn't failed to notice the deflection. "And how are *you*, Ludvic?"

He shrugged. "Fine. Same as usual. Aioru's doing well ... nothing big since you left for him to deal with, fortunately. It's only been six weeks for us. I've been working on security for the Jubilee, now that it's all but certain the Red Company will be in attendance. You've been busy?" He made a vague gesture which probably encompassed all the changes wrought by Cliopher's adventures across Sky Ocean and on either side. "Earning your own legend?"

"I've been doing my best."

"Good. He'll like that."

He was always Fitzroy. Cliopher regarded Ludvic carefully. "Are you going to tell him?"

Ludvic glanced down at his hands, the gold smudges gleaming in the kitchen's light. But he had already made his decision, at some point in the weeks since Cliopher had left, in the hours and days since he'd received Jiano's letter that they were there in Gorjo City. "Will you stay? When I tell him."

"Of course," Cliopher replied gravely, and he echoed Bertie's phrasing with a certain ironic appreciation for how much easier he found it to say the words than to accept them. "Any time."

~

They cleaned up the kitchen—or rather, Ludvic cleaned up the kitchen, putting away the food and washing the dishes with economical, assured movements. Cliopher watched him, unable to quite bring himself to move. His entire body felt limp as a jellyfish on land. "We only arrived a few days ago," he explained. "We haven't really figured out ... *living* here."

"Lots of time for that," Ludvic said.

"I suppose so. I hope so."

"Head all right?"

Cliopher realized he had pressed his knuckles to his temple. "Yes—no—I don't know. It was feeling healed ... He made an island today, and the magic ..."

"An island?" Ludvic considered for a moment. "Is that in your stories?" Cliopher blushed, and Ludvic laughed almost silently. "It *is*, isn't it? Will you tell me?"

"It's a long story ..."

"You called him *beloved*," Ludvic said quietly. "I heard you. You've loved him for a long time, Cliopher, but you did not call him that before you left."

They had spoken of Cliopher's anger and hurt that Fitzroy had not given him his name.

Cliopher shook his head, and that did hurt. He winced. "We have a word," he said quietly. "Fanoa ... it means the greatest of friends. Like Elonoa'a and Aurelius Magnus were said to be ... though we met them, Fitzroy and I, and we learned they had a different meaning ..."

He told the story, trying to be precise, economical with his words as Ludvic was with his, and barely noticed when Ludvic pushed over a plate of food. He ate a few bites reluctantly, not sure how to say he was entirely lacking in appetite—but Ludvic was regarding him with such entreaty and expectation—and spoke about the sea-witch and the albatross, the island with his heart in its depths, the endlessly long stair up to that cold welcome to the House of the Sun.

Ludvic understood that persistence, and he understood, too, in a way perhaps no one else had or could have, just what Cliopher meant by his negotiations.

Even Fitzroy had appreciated the *story* of it most. Ludvic understood the sacrifices Cliopher had made.

And he understood, in a way Cliopher did not think Fitzroy could, how hard it had been for Cliopher to find his way to equality.

"Thank you," Cliopher said hoarsely, when Ludvic passed him a cup of steaming water with lemon and honey in it.

"You're not the only one who will wake up with a headache if you don't eat or drink before bed," Ludvic observed, his craggy face suddenly lighting up. "You take better care of others than yourself."

Cliopher grimaced. "That's probably true."

"Probably?"

He laughed. "You know me too well, Ludvic." He sipped the drink, grateful for the comfort of the honey on his throat. Ludvic was companionably silent, easy to sit with, to enjoy simply *being* with. Rhodin or Conju or Fitzroy would all have kept talking, and it would have been entertaining and fun, but this silence was restful, too.

Ludvic used his finger to pick up various crumbs on the table. "Your family kept coming by today," he said. "They brought things ... I sent most everything upstairs, unless it was food."

"Shall we go upstairs? It's more comfortable. Theoretically. Fitzroy bought cushions, if he didn't take them all for his bed. He bought the strangest assortment of things—all necessities, he claimed."

Ludvic snorted a tiny laugh as he stood. Cliopher brought his cup with him, and as they climbed up the stair, he explained about their ridiculous efforts to get the annual stipend, and felt it a great victory when his friend laughed. "No, really, that's what happened. Then I fell asleep and he went out shopping by *himself*."

"Not entirely by himself, given all your relatives," Ludvic pointed out as they went inside. "Though some of the ones who came by today just wanted to give you things."

Cliopher let the door swing shut behind him and stared at the items now spilling out of the sitting room and into the dining room.

"There were a *lot* of cousins by today," Ludvic said gently.

There must have been. There were chairs—actual chairs, with finely curved backs and seats made of ruddy brazilwood—and a beautiful ebony table—and mats of every quality from the most utilitarian to the sort that must have been made by the greatest weavers in the city. There were baskets, and wooden bowls, and a whole stack of firewood in an elaborate wrought-iron and bronze stand. There seemed to be clothes, and there were more cushions, and there were no less than three bookcases, and ...

"There's so much," Cliopher said, walking forward. The fire-pot of daylight illuminated the space with its comforting, warm light. It sat on a new table beside the brazier, which had gone out. There was another item on the table: a bilum made of fibres dyed midnight and fire-red and bronze.

The bag was empty, bar a small pouch of fine tinder. It was just the size for a pair of striking stones. For Cliopher's pair, when he was able to bring together the tanaea he'd been given by Tion of Mae Irión and the tovo he would collect from the Ring.

"Your great-uncle came by with that," Ludvic said, coming up beside him. He was such a comforting presence, a warm, muscular bulk filling the corner of Cliopher's vision. "He said ..." He paused, as if concentrating to get the words exactly right. "He said *Ask Kip what tana-tai means.* Yes, that was it."

Cliopher stroked the bag, which was beautiful, newly made.

"And so?" Ludvic nudged him gently. "What does tana-tai mean, Cliopher? Kip?"

"I like it when you call me Cliopher."

"Is that what you prefer?"

He hesitated a moment. "You are family, so you may certainly call me Kip, the name my family uses," he said, and glanced at Ludvic, who was regarding him with a very stern expression. "But I like hearing my full name in your voice, too." He moved over and sat down in the soft embrace of a well-cushioned armchair.

Ludvic removed a precarious stack of baskets from a second, matching, chair, and drew it to a companionable distance away. "Cliopher. Kip." He tilted his head, as if tasting their various flavours, then smiled and changed the subject. "The tanà is your cultural role, is it not? The keeper of the fire."

"The tana-tai is the eldest tanà, the senior one," Cliopher explained. "There are equivalents for the other lore-keepers. The fena-tai is the senior fenà, and so on."

"*Tai* means *senior*, then?"

"It has several meanings," Cliopher replied automatically, and then slowed down as he heard his own words. "It means ... *first*, but in terms of origin or source, rather than rank."

"Because it is not rank here, but status."

"Yes." Cliopher frowned down at the bag in his lap. His tunic was covered in small smuts from the island-raising. The bilum felt good in his hands, the fibres smooth, tightly woven. "*Ta* is the root for *fire*. The Islander language is ... compounding, I guess you could say. Words radiate out from the seed-meaning. *Tana* means fire, and *tanà* is the fire-keeper, and then there are different kinds of fire ... and the dances

... and then all the metaphorical meanings, too. *Tai* means *first* because it is the word for the first fire. The one the third son of Vonou'a—" He stopped. "The fire that Samayo Atēatamai brought home from the House of the Sun, the first fire, is called the *tai*."

They both looked over at the fire-pot sitting next to the brazier, the polished coral glowing with the internal radiance welling out of it.

"Is that also a tai, then?" Ludvic asked after a silence.

Cliopher took in a deep, shuddering breath. The room smelled good—there must be perfumes or dried flowers mixed into the items around them, or perhaps there were candles or incense—he could smell tiarë and jasmine and the lingering chocolate-scent of tui flowers. "I suppose it is," he said softly.

They sat there for a moment, very quiet. Not even the crackle of a fire, nor the constant lap of waves, nor the breeze in the sail or the palms.

After a moment he became aware of a deep, sustained sort of drone, and frowned.

"It's himself. Snoring," Ludvic supplied, looking amused. "He must have got himself into a funny position."

"We'd been sleeping down here," Cliopher said hesitantly, gesturing around the room.

"No furniture," Ludvic agreed. "A fire." He smiled. "Company."

Cliopher nodded, breathless. "We weren't ... we're not lovers, Ludvic."

"You said that was a difference between you and himself and Elonoa'a and Aurelius Magnus."

Ludvic made it seem so much *easier* than anyone else. "Yes," Cliopher whispered.

"And now, after a great work of magic, he's gone upstairs to sleep. To the solarium."

"Yes." Cliopher brushed trembling fingers down his tunic. "Ludvic ... I ... He's been trapped in towers ..."

"He's *chosen* to sleep there tonight," Ludvic said with certainty. "You can join him, if you like?"

Cliopher was exhausted, but he had revived enough from the food to be able to talk at least a little longer ... and he had *missed* Ludvic, too. He did not want to leave this conversation, not yet. He wanted to keep it burning ... let their conversations strike sparks from each other, homely ones, happy ones ... He frowned, catching the tail end of a thought, a fish darting through his mind.

"Thought of something else *tana-tai* means?"

He looked up at his friend sitting there, fully at ease, and smiled reluctantly. "How do you know me so well?"

Ludvic shrugged. "Watched you, too, you know. Listened."

"And now it's time for questions," Cliopher said almost under his breath. The thing he'd always been so uncomfortable with, after all the times he'd been told to *be patient*, to *look first! Listen first! Questions later!*

At some point he'd come to think that it was never *later*, and the questions would always be unwelcome.

Which was absurd, now that he'd phrased it like that. But it was true: and how many things would have been different if only he'd been willing, if only he'd *dared*, to ask the questions?

"I remember, long ago, my uncle Lazo saying he'd never be tana-tai, because he had not gone for the tanaea," Cliopher said, half to Ludvic and half to himself. "I was curious, but I didn't ask ... thought it wasn't the time to ask ..."

Ludvic was silent, empathetic, encouraging.

"Do you remember that Tion of Mae Irión gave me a stone? A striking stone? He told me that there used to be one man, one canoe, who would come to the island where the fire-striking stones were found. One man, with the red-coral efela he saw me wearing ..." Cliopher's hand went up to his efetana. "Buru Tovo went sailing, across the Wide Seas."

"He found the striking stone."

"Yes."

"You've gone sailing across the Wide Seas," Ludvic said.

"I didn't go *for* the tanaea," Cliopher said, but that wasn't true, either, was it? He had not gone to search for it—it had never occurred to him to search for it—he had never *asked* if he should, or could, go searching for it—but he had shaped his whole life with the hope he would one day be the tana-tai at home.

"The tanà shows the people who they are. That's what people say."

That was the responsibility that had always waited for him, when he finally gave up on the wider world and came home. That intense, intolerable pressure to be the exemplar, when he could not consider himself the true exemplar—not when Buru Tovo was the example that went before him, Buru Tovo and Uncle Lazo.

The traditional Islander, the tana-tai who had not handled money until his ninetieth year ... and the city Islander, who had made for himself a humble, ordinary, pleasant life within the expectations and constraints of being a rural nobody in the far hinterland of the Empire, and yet was also, in his quiet, competent way, a trained lore-holder ...

And then there was Cliopher, the one who had left.

The one who had declared he would go see if this emperor was worth standing beside, as Elonoa'a had stood beside Aurelius Magnus. (And he had been; he was.) The one who had declared he could run the government better than the proud ministers and administrators of Astandalas, because he had the *Lays* and the *Lays* were full of wisdom. (And they were; and he had.) The one who had told everyone who would listen that he would sail to the House of the Sun, as the third son of Vonou'a had before him, and bring home a new fire for the islands.

A new tai for the islands; a new fire for the hearth of the world.

"I am the one who left," he said, gripping the bag tightly. He imagined the stones that would go into it, one day soon: the tovo, which could come from almost any beach around the Ring, but which Cliopher would collect from his island, from his great-uncle's stretch of the beach; and the tanaea he had been given by a man out of history, because he had not lost his culture to the empire, and the Last Emperor of Astandalas had recognized an efela of the Ke'e Lulai when he saw one.

Cliopher had looked at Alun and Nala and their daughters, all the Islanders who had come to his own version of the Singing of the Waters, and thought: *what it means to be an Islander must also include this.*

And he had looked at Clio paddling his coracle in the mill-pond in the magical forest of his foremothers, with his mother's blue eyes and his father's black hair and golden skin, in his mouth the *Lays* and questions about the saltiness of the sea and what a breaking wave looked like—

And that, too, was what an Islander was.

He was an Islander. Because he had left—and come home—and left again—and everywhere he had gone he had taken his culture with him. He had taught people words and pronunciations, he had lived by the lessons of the *Lays*, he had tried—he had tried *so hard*—to be the tanà for everyone he had met. The world had given him all its most complicated problems, and he had patiently tried to untangle them.

Patiently. Well—sometimes.

Sometimes impatiently, sometimes furiously, sometimes despairingly, sometimes wrongly.

Sometimes he had made more problems than he had solved. Sometimes he had given up, quietly, in the privacy of his rooms, sobbing for the futility of his work, for the impossibility of it, for the fact that he would never be done climbing that endless cold and narrow stair, and the basket of mud that was the world would never be any lighter upon his shoulders.

(And when he had at last climbed out of the narrow spiral, what had he found but that endless long straight stair, with temptations on every side? And the basket that was even heavier, digging into his shoulders, pulling him relentlessly back.)

(And then that last harrowing stair across the open face of the heights, the fall ever further below him, trying not to lose his nerve so close to the end—)

He had given up, he had railed and raged, he had broken things, he had written furious letters to Basil, he had broken pens and inkpots, he had broken *systems* ... he had wrecked himself on so many reefs, weathered so many storms, limped through so many broken moments.

He had dreamed his whole life of a fanoa, of *his* fanoa, and at last he had reached him, and been met as an equal.

He had stood before his ancestors, the heroes of his people, and they had thought him the judgement of posterity. He had bowed himself before them, and they had lifted him up.

They had built him a ship, and taught him to navigate, given him the legends and the truths of their legends, and in turn he had shown them—told them—taught them—what it meant to be an Islander.

What did it mean to be an Islander, if Cliopher Mdang of Tahivoa, Viceroy of Zunidh and tanà of the Ring, was not one?

"What does it mean to be tana-tai, Cliopher?" Ludvic asked quietly.

"It means you take what you have learned here, within the Ring," Cliopher said, "and you cross the world to find the tanaea and learn what it can mean. You bring them together to light a new fire. The tanà shows the Islanders who they are," he said, and he knew he was right—his whole life had led to this moment—it *had* to have led here—"and the tana-tai shows them who they can be."

Uncle Lazo was a great man in his way, but humble, unassuming, his external social rank far lower than his status in the community. He had his barbershop and he tended the fires of the city, and people came to him with their knots to untangle and their problems to be heard.

Buru Tovo travelled—he walked the Ring, visiting village and island, lighting fires, teaching all who came to him how to light their own. He lived the *Lays*, diving down into the waters off the reef, bringing golden pearls into the light of day. He lived as their ancestors had for dozens of generations, his heart quietly married to the Son of Laughter, by each word and each action showing the people that they had not lost that ancient knowledge and wisdom, that they still could live in the old ways.

And then there was Cliopher, who had refused to stop until he had entered not only into the history of the outsiders, not only into the *Lays* of the Islanders, but all the way into legend.

He thought of the island raised out of the sea for him, the shells he and Fitzroy had brought back from the depths of the sea, the sun shining through the translucent curve of that high obsidian wave, striking fiery rainbows from some hidden layer within the stone.

He had not stopped until he and Fitzroy had entered into *myth*.

He looked around the room, the items people had brought. His family, yes, and undoubtedly others. "Fitzroy didn't order all this," he said. Not that Cliopher would have minded if he had—not after Fitzroy raised *an island* for him—he might have minded yesterday, if it had all shown up then—but it hadn't.

"No," said Ludvic, who did not seem at all fazed by Cliopher's long silence and tumultuous heart. "I didn't get the impression that he had."

Buru Tovo had not handled money until he had collected the annual stipend to pay for the sea train so he could visit Cliopher in Solaara. He had not *needed* to, but that was only partly due to spending the majority of his time in the Outer Ring and its traditionally non-monetary economy. When he was at home on Loaloa Buru Tovo did not need money, because he had usage rights for the reef and parts of the island, and he had his coconut trees and breadfruit and fishing grounds, and he had a share in the yam and taro crops as well.

But Buru Tovo spent a fair amount of time in the city, where bartering was still practiced but not as predominant. Yet he didn't need money in Gorjo City either, because ... because he was the tanà, the tana-tai.

"It's the custom that you give to the tana-tai in return for all that he does," Cliopher said, hating that his voice was still uncertain.

"They want to give back," Ludvic said quietly, gently.

"Yes," said Cliopher, his hands closing once more around the empty bag in his lap, which would one day soon hold those symbols of fire and community and the bringing-together of all the things Cliopher had tried so hard to fulfill separately.

"I met Masseo Umrit," he went on, because he had to say something else—his heart was full as a wave about to crash upon a beach, and he needed something to hold onto. "I liked him. He's a good man, Ludvic. You can ... you can let yourself know him."

Ludvic chuckled softly. "Always another fire to light, eh, Cliopher?"

CHAPTER SEVENTY-TWO
TRUTHS

Cliopher woke early, to the sound of voices, laughter, a snatch of music, the scent of good things.

He sat up, amazed at the softness of sleeping on cushions, the smooth cotton sheet. Beside him, Fitzroy was still asleep, burrowed between his own cushions, one hand reaching out.

One bed had been delivered, the day before, but he'd told Ludvic to take it; Cliopher had not wanted to leave Fitzroy to sleep alone, not in the tower.

It was very early, the sky still rosy with the dawn, brushed with fine feathery clouds just the colours of the feathers he had been given by the Wind That Rises At Dawn. Cliopher brushed back his hair with his hands, smiling at the memory of the wind smiling at him.

The windows were open wide, and though the wind was gentle—the fishing floats were chiming softly—he could hear the sounds of the market in Zaviya Square drifting up.

He stood, stretched, and went downstairs to the sitting room. It looked onto the courtyard, so he walked through to the back of the suite he had half-decided would be his. There he could look down at the stalls being set up. The vendors were yawning, if apparently cheerful for all that. Someone had a small cart with a fire in it, and he was brewing coffee ... and someone else had a cart with fried pastries, the cinnamon and vanilla wafting up to his nose even a storey above the ground.

Without further thought Cliopher shrugged into one of the silk dressing gowns Fitzroy had decreed were necessary purchases, and opened the balcony door.

Before he got to the bottom of the stairs, he discovered that Ludvic—fully dressed, his hair still damp from a bath—had already been out and come back, for he came out of the kitchen with a clay pitcher of coffee in one hand and a paper bag of pastries in the other.

"Oh you glory," Cliopher breathed, and moved aside for him to come past. "I'll find mugs—"

"There's some up there," Ludvic replied over his shoulder, so Cliopher hastily returned to open the door and clear off a space for him to put down his refreshments. There were mugs, elegant porcelain things that could equally easily have been Fitzroy's choices or some gift. "There was no coffee in Sky Ocean," he informed his friend solemnly. "Nor tea. Nor chocolate."

"Not *my* idea of the realm of the gods," Ludvic replied, with barely a smile. He looked around. "Do you want to sit in here? Or we could take the chairs out to the balcony ..."

For a moment, Cliopher was paralyzed with the memory of that *wish* he'd had, ages ago: to be able to sit on his balcony with a friend, having their coffee in the morning. "Yes," he said, trying not to snuffle even as tears welled up. "Please."

"You bring the coffee, then," Ludvic said, and picked up the two armchairs as if they were made of nothing more than basketwork.

It was grand, sitting on the balcony. The air was lambent, with a crystalline quality that seemed as if it would turn to gold at any moment. The bywater was very calm, reflecting houses and bridge and the vaha with eerie perfection. Little birds were busy in the plants Saya Oyinaa and the rukà had in pots outside their door, and several rolypoly finches came almost immediately up to investigate their new neighbours.

Cliopher drank his coffee, and ate the pastries, and felt as if he had never been happy before.

He looked at Ludvic, smiling; Ludvic smiled back, but his eyes were dark and sombre.

Time to ask questions, Cliopher reminded himself. Make the space for Ludvic to unburden himself, if he wished. "What are you worrying about?"

"I didn't tell him ... my secret," Ludvic whispered miserably. "I should have, shouldn't I?"

"He didn't tell *you*, either," Cliopher pointed out. "I told him what you told me, of how you came to join the Guard, because he was worried ... he *is* worried, still, I think ... that you will be upset to have spent your life serving an emperor who didn't want to be one."

"It was an honour to stand beside him," Ludvic replied fiercely. He struck his chair with his hand, and the finches scattered. "There is *nothing* he needs to feel concerned about. He fulfilled each and every duty that came to him—more than honourably fulfilled, as he says in his poem. What could anyone do but respect and admire that?"

"Indeed," Cliopher replied, sipping his coffee.

Ludvic frowned at him, and then relaxed, chuckling ironically. "What a pair we are, eh? You can barely accept praise for the things you have worked very hard to achieve, and I can hardly—" He stopped, and looked down at his coffee. "You think he'll be glad to hear my story?"

"He's going to be *delighted* to hear it. I promise you, Ludvic. He's ... himself, you know. You know—I *know* you know—that his Radiancy was a ... certain face. So was the dashing renegade and rebel poet. That's part of him, but it was never all there was of him, and neither is his Radiancy."

"Of course not," Ludvic said simply. "He is like you. Changing course according to the conditions, but always aimed in the direction of his heart's desire."

Cliopher caught his breath at that spear-like clarity. "I ... I know I have been like that," he said, admitted even, for had he not been seeking after that white shell this whole time? He had gone to Astandalas in the first place because of that story—

"He has, too," Ludvic said. "*You* know that. It was in your essay about his poetry. We have always known his decency and his brilliance and his kindness. And," Ludvic added, with an almost mischievous smile, "also his sense of humour."

Cliopher laughed, and then he heard a sound, and he looked up to see that Fitzroy was standing at the open door. He had heard quite a bit of the conversation, he must have; he was just barely not weeping, his eyes shining and his hand over his mouth.

He didn't think—he simply reacted. He stood up, and reached for Fitzroy's arm, to welcome him, bring him into their company. Fitzroy resisted a little before stepping delicately across the threshold of the doorway.

Ludvic cleared his throat and shuffled his feet together, and then he stood up and very carefully did not salute.

It had probably been equally as obvious when Cliopher had very carefully *not bowed* on seeing Fitzroy for the first time.

But he hadn't, and Ludvic didn't, and Fitzroy stood there, trembling in Cliopher's hand.

"Ludvic," he said, his voice dipping and wavering like the first note of a song.

"Fitzroy," said Ludvic, and stepped forward to embrace him; very gently, moving slowly, so neither of them spooked.

Cliopher quietly let go of Fitzroy, letting his hand brush against his fanoa's back as he went around them to enter the sitting room. He found one of the wicker chairs, and a third cup from the set, and he brought them back outside. Fitzroy had bowed his head to Ludvic's broad shoulder, and from the quivering in his shoulders was either weeping or laughing.

Both, it became clear, when he released the guard and stepped back. "You knew the whole time," he said. "I can't believe ..." He trailed off, and then he said, firmly, "Thank you, Ludvic."

Ludvic nodded, deliberate and steady, and waited for Fitzroy to sit down before retaking his own seat. Cliopher passed Fitzroy the coffee, and refreshed Ludvic's and his own cups.

"I'm surprised to see you here," Fitzroy said, his voice valiantly light. "I trust nothing is awry?"

"I came to see you. Both of you. Not because of anything. I wanted to see you," Ludvic replied, nodding at Cliopher before focusing his attention on Fitzroy. Only the way he had closed his hands into fists indicated any of the tension Cliopher was quite certain he felt.

Fitzroy smiled radiantly, and it occurred to Cliopher with one of those shocks that no one had simply come *to visit* Fitzroy in ... decades. People came for court, or ceremonies, or because he summoned them; to do research in the libraries, or to seek an audience and have a problem solved. They did not come just for ... him.

Ludvic had never been much of one for small talk. He hesitated, very still and focused, and then he said, the words falling solidly into their little pool of interested silence, "I had something I wished to tell you. Fitzroy."

The birds down in the courtyard were singing; the sun had come up enough to peek through layers of buildings, and the light was filling the courtyard with as much golden lambency as Cliopher had imagined it might be able to hold. The streamer of feathers on the tip of the vaha's mast glowed scarlet with the intensity of the light.

Fitzroy said, "I will gladly listen to anything you say, Ludvic."

His voice was warm, welcoming, curious: and his eyes were bright, his face serene, his posture attentive. If he were concerned what Ludvic might tell him—and Cliopher thought he probably was—he showed no hint of it.

It was good that Fitzroy was starting to find some middle ground between his Radiancy and Fitzroy Angursell the Poet, a way of being that was neither impenetrably serene nor forever on the cusp of manic.

"My people do not name the dead," Ludvic said baldly, the same opening he had used when telling this story to Cliopher. (And how many times had he said it in his mind, imagined the conversation, worked out how to say it?)

"I know," said Fitzroy softly. A flash of curiosity, quickly suppressed, ran across his face and was replaced by focused attentiveness, as if Ludvic were the only person in the world.

Ludvic frowned briefly at his hands, glanced at Cliopher—who nodded encouragingly—and then gazed levelly at Fitzroy. "I have told you how my mother raised me."

"Yes," said Fitzroy, even more softly.

"When I was sixteen, a man, the elders told me to leave the village. Before I did, my mother told me my father's name." A pause. "I had thought him put to death according to the law, because he and my mother ... conceived me outside of marriage and before my mother was an adult according to the law."

Fitzroy went immensely, intensely still, his eyes sharp.

"You have heard this story," Ludvic said, lifting his eyes. Cliopher did not know what to name the expression in Ludvic's face, save that it was deep. Perhaps it was the outcropping of a great reef of submerged desire, or hope, for the father he had never known.

"I have heard a similar one," Fitzroy replied, perfectly without emotion.

Ludvic hesitated, then firmed his mouth. "It is the same one, I expect. My mother told me that although in the minds of the villagers the law had been obeyed, and my father was dead to them, he had not been cast over the cliffs for the sharks, but had instead been exiled."

Fitzroy exhaled a controlled breath; breathed in again, on that count that both Cliopher and Ludvic knew was one of the few ways his Radiancy had ever shown that his inner thoughts and emotions might be affecting him.

"Will you do me the honour of telling me his name?" Fitzroy asked.

"You know it," Ludvic said uneasily. "Masseo ... Umrit means *no-name*, in our language." A pause; and now Fitzroy had closed his eyes, some shadow crossing his face. "He made it a great one. That name. Him and you."

"All this time," Fitzroy whispered, leaning forward, examining Ludvic's face with hungry eyes. "All this time—and I didn't *see*! And yet you look so like him—Cliopher, did you see it? Did you know?" He laughed shortly, but wildly. "Of course you did! You were sounding Masseo out so carefully, I thought it was because of how much you and Pali rubbed each other the wrong way, but it wasn't that at all, was it? You wanted to be sure—"

He turned to Ludvic, and leaned forward in his seat to grab him by the hands. "Ludvic. Ludvic. My dear Ludvic. Masseo is going to be—I am so—" He laughed, and tried to smile, and then let go of Ludvic so he could cover his face. "I am overcome."

Ludvic looked across at Cliopher, his solid face breaking apart in confusion as he hesitantly drew his hands back. "What do I say?"

He had hardly ever seen Fitzroy break down, Cliopher realized numbly: and never with happiness. "What do you want to say?" he said out loud, and mouthed *uncle* when he was sure Fitzroy was not looking.

Ludvic blenched, then seemed to take heart. "I stood beside you gladly," he said to Fitzroy. "It was ... perhaps it was wrong of me, but I ... I always thought ... in my culture, it is a good thing, to stand beside your ... uncle."

Fitzroy peeked between his fingers, then put them down on the table as if for support; the tears were very close to the surface. He gave Ludvic a smile of tender, tentative enquiry. "As if I were your father's brother. As if we were truly ..." He didn't finish, or perhaps couldn't.

But Cliopher heard the unspoken word, and so did Ludvic.

"Yes," he said, hardly any more loudly. "As if we were."

"All this time?" Fitzroy said, dashing the tears out of his eyes with his hand. "All this time?"

"Always," Ludvic said, but his hands were trembling, and he looked as if he wanted to do something else with them but didn't know what.

Fitzroy reached out to take Ludvic's hands again, and both of them grew still and intent.

Cliopher decided he had probably provided a sufficiency of moral support, and quietly got up. He squeezed Ludvic's shoulder, brushed his hand over Fitzroy's hair, and went downstairs to the bathhouse, where he and the iguana had a somewhat contentious negotiation over who got to use the shower.

≈

After he had thoroughly investigated and experimented with Fitzroy's collection of toiletries (which included many lotions and unguents he had never heard of, and which were surely not *necessary* by any stretch of the imagination—though they did, he admitted, smell very nice—and most of them felt good on his skin), he felt he had probably given them enough time to talk privately.

It would probably take both of them months, if not years, to figure out their new relation, but—well, there *were* going to be months and years in which to do so, weren't there? Fitzroy might go adventuring with the Red Company, but then again, so might Ludvic—so might *Cliopher*—and anyway, the Red Company might all end up coming to visit Fitzroy in Gorjo City, too.

It *was* one of the most beautiful places in all the Nine Worlds.

He went out and considered the house again. His house—*their* house—already looking much more lived-in, loved, with a towel hanging over the balcony railing and the chairs sitting there, and—

And the potted shrub now standing beside the kitchen door.

He walked across the courtyard to investigate. It was a tiarë shrub, glossy-leaved and with a few blossoms scattered about its branches. He dipped his face and breathed in the fine, sweet scent. He loved frangipani but there was something so *Islander* about tiarë.

The kitchen door beside him opened, and his cousin Enya popped her head out. "Kip! Good *morning!*"

"Good morning, Enya," he replied. "Did you bring this?"

She glanced down at the pot and shrugged. "No, it was being delivered when I arrived. Good gracious, Kip, you look splendid. Nora *said*, but it's not as if she's spent much time with you. Is it true? Did you really go sailing across Sky Ocean with your lord, who is really Fitzroy Angursell?"

He grinned at her. "I did. We did. My—" He hesitated for only a moment, as the image of the great wave of the island rose up in his mind's eye, fire flashing against the blue sky. His grin widened. "My fanoa and I."

Enya uttered a piercing cry, clapped her hands together, and then flung herself around his neck. "Oh, Kip! Finally! Oh, *congratulations!*" She kissed him and then started to dust him off. "Dear me, I'm sorry, I've got flour all over you—I was just making you a few things—you don't know how to cook, really, do you?"

"Not appreciably, no," he agreed. "Didn't you bring the crab cakes earlier? They tasted like yours."

"Oh, that was nothing, they were already made." She flapped her hand at him. "Come in, come in, do you want coffee? I like your friend Ludvic, by the way, *what* shoulders." She poured him a cup of coffee, which he accepted (though it was his third—and he was still rather unused to the stimulant—he resolved to worry about that later), and gestured him to sit down on the bench. "Let me tell you, Kip, I am so, so glad to hear you actually call him fanoa."

"You're not going to tell me I've got my head too far into the *Lays?*" he asked dryly.

"Don't you sound just like Uncle Cliopher!" Enya patted a circle of dough with deft fingers. She seemed to be making some sort of tart—well, Cliopher was not going to complain whatever she made. "Don't be silly, Kip. For one thing, you've *always* had your head too far in the *Lays*, and look at you! Bringing back fire from the Sun!—can I see it, by the way?"

"Of course. It's upstairs."

"Incredible." She dumped a bowl full of something into the tart case and smoothed it out with a wooden spoon. "Galen and I are *so* glad you've finally acknowledged your fanoa. Everyone's always told us it's old-fashioned, you know—

'no one does that any more'—'don't be like Kip and go off chasing viaus'—whoops!" She giggled. "But they do say that, you know."

He was not surprised, not at all. "I do."

She sobered. "You would, wouldn't you. They've told you often enough."

"You, too," he said.

"You never let anyone stop you, did you? I've always admired—When you talked at the opening of the restaurant about how I'd fulfilled my dream—" She stopped, a little choked up, and busied herself with the tart, creating a lattice out of leftover pastry scraps and brushing them with some sort of wash. She put it in the oven, nodded at something else that was already baking, and fiddled with the vents. "I love this oven. So old-fashioned but *such* good work. Imported, of course ... no one does this kind of ironwork here, let alone the enchantments."

Cliopher sipped at his coffee and wondered just how long it would take him to be able to handle such flitting conversations again.

Fitzroy could flit from subject to subject, but Cliopher knew the way his mind worked, and after their voyage together he also knew most of his fanoa's preoccupations and musical and poetic influences.

Enya's words were bubbling, burbling over, swift as her hands about her vocation. She set several bowls into the sink, wiped down the table, and began to peel an orange with a small paring knife. "The thing is, Kip," she said, "I remember you talking about how you would be fanoa with the emperor one day, and if *I* remember that ..." She grinned at him. "But then you never *said*. Not even after the viceroyship! We were sure you would announce it then, but you didn't, and it's not exactly the sort of thing ... it's like a marriage, isn't it? In the *Lays* it's always *acknowledged*. There's always that public element. A partnership."

"Yes, I suppose so," he agreed weakly. But perhaps Fitzroy would like a ... well, not a wedding, but a ... a party, yes. Cliopher could handle a party.

It would have to be a *big* party, with the number of Mdangs, and of course then there was the Red Company, and the rest of the imperial household, and Cliopher's friends ... and perhaps there were others amongst the Imperial Guard ...

It might be quite fun, actually. When they were retired, and everyone could come.

"You see, Galen and I have always thought of ourselves as fanoa. Two halves—and a business partnership. Everyone said we couldn't be, really, because we're related, but I think that's silly, don't you? It's allowed to change the meaning, isn't it? You have."

"Changed the meaning of fanoa?"

"Have you?"

He opened his mouth, and then paused, and he grinned sheepishly at her. "No. Or not intentionally. I did learn that Auri and El—Elonoa'a and Aurelius Magnus, that is—used fanoa because in their day they couldn't marry each other."

Enya's eyes went very wide. "How did you learn *that*?"

"I met them."

"Goodness." She looked down at her hands, and absently ate several pieces of her orange. Still chewing, she said, "*Goodness*," even more emphatically.

He laughed. "I have a lot of stories to share."

"Kip, you're ridiculous. I know you know this, but it has to be said." Enya shook her head. "I do love you. Especially how ridiculous you are. Anyway, that wasn't what I meant—I meant how you've always been all 'The *Lays* tell us who we are and how we go forward but we have to pick our own destination' and 'Of course I can go off and become the head of the government and still be an Islander' and 'What do you *mean* I've forgotten how to be traditional, look at me doing the fire dance in the Palace' and oh!, now there's also 'You know what, I'll just *sail* to the House of the Sun and bring back fire,' because eradicating poverty and letting the whole world have the room to create whatever they wanted wasn't enough. Things like that."

He flushed, grinning. "Well ..."

"So you and—Fitzroy Angursell, *really*, Kip, you should have *seen* the look on Nora's face when she came for dessert at ours and told us what had happened—I *cooked* for him! And then you never told me his name, so it wasn't till the viceroyship ceremony that I even found out it was for the *Last Emperor* and he liked my cooking."

"I'm sorry," Cliopher said, grasping hold of that. "He'd ordered me not to say—"

"And you weren't fanoa then, were you?" she said shrewdly. "Just his secretary." She snorted. "Head of the government. His *hands*, if I remember the title correctly ..."

"The Hands of the Emperor, yes."

"And somehow you resisted *all* the terrible innuendoes and never even smirked. You're disgustingly sincere. You always have been." She shook her head and reached across the table to pat him with a floury hand. "Such a role model. So now, you and your fanoa, Fitzroy Angursell, who is *also* the emperor of Astandalas—really, Kip, you're disgusting and ridiculous and honestly, no *wonder* you never came home, you got to tell everyone what they ought to do *and* you got him—"

"Enya."

She ignored his reproof. "Anyway, if you can be your own sort of fanoa, and 'Auri and El'—cannot *believe* you have a nickname for Elonoa'a, that is *impossible*—anyway, if Elonoa'a and Aurelius Magnus can be their own sort of fanoa, then so can Galen and I."

"Yes," he said, holding on to that certainty.

"Yes," she replied, half-mockingly, half-sincerely. "We can set a new fashion. I bet more people will follow Galen and me, it's easier to run a restaurant than the whole world."

Cliopher chuckled, and Enya wrinkled her nose at him, obviously pleased at this idea. She then jumped up, opened the oven, pulled out the tart and a tray of what appeared to be fairly elaborate miniature cakes, admonished him to let them *cool* before he ate any of them, told him long-sufferingly that if he touched molten chocolate like that he was destined to be burned, wasn't he?—and had he been that foolish in Sky Ocean, or had he just levelled a withering glare at the Sun and—

And at that point both of them were laughing and she cried, "Oh, I am going to be *late*! Keep being ridiculous, Kip! Galen will kill me!" And she ran out the door, leaving Cliopher remembering how Enya had always best revealed her true emotions with her food.

She had come to his house before opening her own restaurant simply to cook exquisitely beautiful delicacies for him, and that was before he'd mentioned the word *fanoa*.

He was still sitting there several minutes later when Fitzroy and Ludvic came down the stairs—one almost as swift as Enya, the other much more measured in pace —and fell upon the food as if nether of them had seen anything like it before.

Ludvic did pause and lean over Cliopher's shoulder to say quietly, "Thank you."

And Fitzroy, when Ludvic had turned to wash his hands at the sink, gave him a dazzling smile and said, "My heart is singing, Kip! If only—"

He stopped there and turned his smile to Ludvic, who returned it hesitantly, shyly, and the conversation moved on, but Cliopher felt the flicker of an idea, and he cupped the two halves of his heart around the spark to shelter and cherish it.

He had given the world the space and safety to create. He would do the same for his friend, his fanoa, his Fitzroy. One day it would not be *if only*.

CHAPTER SEVENTY-THREE
RECOMPENSE

After breakfast, they spent several hours sorting through the piles of items upstairs, much interrupted by visitors who had, so they said, heard that Cousin Kip and his lord—oh, his *fanoa*?—who was actually Fitzroy Angursell had come home from their adventures, and yes, they knew they were supposed to be leaving Kip alone while they were 'mending their sails', but they'd seen the vaha, its sails were perfectly usable.

Cliopher was not sure how to respond to this; Fitzroy found it at once hilarious and baffling.

"Where are they all *coming* from?" Fitzroy whispered to Cliopher as yet another person arrived at the door with some small token of their—or, in this case, their parents'—esteem.

Fitzroy's eyes were brilliant with amusement as Cliopher, ignoring this impossible-to-answer question, greeted the young emissary. He smiled down at the girl. "What can I do for you?"

"Mama says you're to have this, and welcome home," the child said. She was perhaps ten, gap-toothed and sweet-faced, and thrust an empty terracotta plant-pot at him. "She says she knows you're not staying for long right now, so she'll give you the plant that goes in it later."

"Thank you, and thank your mother," Cliopher replied, accepting the pot gravely.

"Donu *says*," the girl went on, peering curiously at Fitzroy, "that you met the Sea-Witch."

"I did," Cliopher agreed.

The girl transferred her attention to him with a frown. "Did she have long, long fingernails?"

Cliopher tried to suppress the shudder that ran through his body at the memory.

"She did. And she had glittering black eyes like beetles, and she wore a dress made out of seaweed."

"Hmm," said the girl. "Donu says people who have gone to the sky come back strange."

Fitzroy suppressed a snort. Cliopher said, "What do you think?"

"I think," she said frankly, "that everyone says you were a little strange before. But they also say you made everything better, so I guess it's okay to be strange. Goodbye!" She skipped off before he could say anything further.

"And who was that? Or Donu?" Ludvic asked, since Fitzroy had given in to his mirth.

"I have no idea," Cliopher replied, and set the terracotta pot down beside the door. "It's a nice pot, at least."

"It is."

He glanced around the courtyard, then turned to Ludvic. "Have you seen the two women who live next door?"

"Said hello when they were going out," Ludvic replied. "Haven't seen them come back."

Cliopher hummed. "I'll have to catch them later ... I want to thank them for returning our vaha."

"They seem to have made a grand parade around the city," Fitzroy said, recovering his poise. "Given that *everyone* now knows the sails are mended."

"I suppose I'll have to thank them for that, too," he responded dryly. He regarded the stairs unenthusiastically, and then had a very clear thought. "We don't have to keep going right now," he said, marvelling. "If we don't want to, that is."

Fitzroy's eyebrow winged up. "Do *you* not want to keep unpacking, Kip?"

"Well ..." He shrugged, and began to smile. "No. It's a beautiful day and I'd much prefer going for a walk."

"Easier to avoid talking to people that way, too," Ludvic said, with a suspiciously straight face.

Fitzroy laughed richly. "I know—why don't we go ask someone about those shells, Kip? And what else should be on our efanoa. Please come with us, Ludvic— we'd like the company."

"Yes," Cliopher said, meaning it.

Ludvic smiled very slightly. "Glad to, in that case."

Mardo Walea was alone in his shop, examining a pile of warokainë shells, when they arrived.

The shop looked as it always had: the walls covered with subtly beautiful tapacloth hangings, so the great arrays of efela mounted on them were shown to their full advantage. The bank of waist-high cabinets still ran around three of the walls, their many drawers holding all the raw materials of the efela-merchant's trade.

Mardo himself was wearing a simple cotton tunic and trews in the Vangavayen style, the neck open to show off the complex patterns of his own efela. Cliopher took a deep breath, relaxing in the calm, easy atmosphere of the place. He'd slowly moved from the front wall to the back over the years of his life, as his wealth and knowledge grew and he was able to attain to more impressive efela.

The efà set down his jeweller's loupe and regarded the three of them with some amusement. He nodded politely at Ludvic and Fitzroy before focusing on Cliopher. "I had been wondering when you might show up. You've been given a couple of efela since the efela nai, eh? A few of great name, even."

Cliopher reached up to grasp the third of his efela, the one with the pearls and the sundrop cowrie and the sea-witch's hidden garnet, before he recalled the one Elonoa'a had given him to pass on to Jiano.

He dropped his hand, but Mardo had noticed. He said, with something approaching resignation, "And where did *that* one come from, Kip, given that your family sent me your efela when they thought you'd died?"

They would have sent them home—all those markers of Cliopher's life—to make the funerary efela, the ones that would be displayed and then handed on to his heirs. (Whoever that would be ... Cliopher had not instructed any apprentices as tanà, and his nephew Gaudy held the Vawen dances, not those of the Mdangs ...)

"I was given it," Cliopher said slowly. "Like Eranui and the Five Shells ..." He told the story, and then, with a glance at Fitzroy, added, "I woke up with it when I came back to myself ... here."

Mardo pursed his lips, before chuckling. "You never do anything by halves, do you? So Vou'a gave you an efela ... And that was after Mau'alanio'ina came to you— it's in my keeping, as well, by the way—and I saw you hand Izurunayë over to our new paramount chief."

"I applaud your efforts at keeping a straight face," Fitzroy said, grinning at Mardo. "Tell him about the name the Grandmother gave your efela, Kip."

"We didn't come for that," Cliopher protested, his face burning despite everything.

"Come, now, Kip, surely you're not going to deny me the full tale of *all* your legendary efela?"

Put like that, of course he wasn't. And—he had never had to downplay his achievements before Mardo Walea, who had always been fair when Cliopher told him his deeds and asked for efela to represent them.

"The Grandmother, the Woman Who Lives in the Deeps of the Sea, called it Kiofa'a," he said, and unclasped the efela so Mardo could look at it. The efà picked it up reverently as Cliopher explained a bit of his interactions with the Grandmother, frowning as he heard the garnet rattling. "That's from the Sea-Witch," Cliopher explained, and then he had to tell that story.

Ludvic listened with great interest, and Fitzroy wandered around looking at the efela on the walls, smiling occasionally when Cliopher looked up to catch his eye.

"Well," Mardo said at the end. "We'll have to talk about this at much greater length, I can see." He nodded, stroking his chin, and handed Cliopher his efela back. "What a story, Kip. And that wasn't even why you came in?"

"No," Fitzroy said, returning to the table. "The other day, Kip and I went to go see what might lie under that new star, the one he hung in the sky, and since there wasn't an island there I raised one for him ..."

"As you do," Mardo said, his lips twitching.

Fitzroy bestowed one of his most beautiful smiles on him. "Just so. I understand there is, or was, a specific tradition for efanoa. Cliopher and I have decided we would like to follow that tradition—"

"Have you now," said Mardo, grinning outright now, when Fitzroy paused.

"Just so. Before I raised the island, which we have called Navanoa—"

"A perfect name."

"We thought so, thank you."

Mardo laughed. "Before you raised Navanoa, yes?"

"We had a strange and marvellous experience at the bottom of the sea, where we found these shells," Fitzroy said, and set his half on the table, scarlet interior down. "A pair, which we took as being appropriate for our efanoa."

"Just so," Mardo replied, obviously enjoying the banter. "I assume Kip has told you that fanoa has the foundational meaning of a common, ordinary, white shell?"

"A cowrie, perhaps, or indeed a clamshell," Fitzroy agreed.

Mardo picked up the shell, running his finger gently along the rippling layers, and then he turned it over so the gold-flashing scarlet caught the light. "*Oh*," he said, and did not say anything for quite some time.

∼

"It seems appropriate," Ludvic said phlegmatically, "that you would manage to find, or be given, the shell of an extinct kind of mollusc to be representative of your love for each other."

"I'm going to spin threads of starlight from your new star to string them on," Fitzroy declared.

"Is that a new skill?" Ludvic asked politely, and Fitzroy spun a glad, splendid story for him.

Cliopher could not say anything. He walked between his friends, Fitzroy on his right, Ludvic on his left, smiling at relatives and friends and strangers as they passed them.

He recalled that journey, so long ago now, when he had walked from Kavanduru to Astandalas, entirely alone. Homesick, lonely, afraid—and eager, too, for what lay ahead, trying to hold true to his ke'ea.

There had been a moment, crossing the border between Zunidh and Ysthar, when he had turned his head and seen the silver line of a distant, foreign sea.

He had not left the road to follow its calling, not then.

And yet—

And yet here he was, somehow, with that horizon encircling him, all its possibilities suddenly able to be discovered.

∼

They bought flying-fish sandwiches from a little booth not far from their house for lunch, and regretted only getting one each when they'd finished them before arriving home.

"We can go out later for a snack," Fitzroy suggested. "Do a bit more sorting first."

He was clearly taking great joy in setting up the house. Cliopher found himself pleased by that discovery. He would have thought he'd like it more, but was finding it somewhat overwhelming. Ludvic's presence was a great help.

There were letters waiting for them on the kitchen table, where Cliopher had gone in to fetch a jug of water. The iguana was also there, reclining full-length on the table with its tail on the letters and several pieces of fruit in front of it.

"Well, My Lord," Cliopher said, "may I take those, please?"

"That's the *iguana*!" Fitzroy called from outside.

Cliopher laughed. "I know! It's in here!" He tugged the letters out from under its tail—the iguana did not seem particularly bothered by this—and took them upstairs along with his jug. "We have mail," he explained. "The iguana was guarding it for us."

Ludvic snickered softly. (He had, so he'd mentioned earlier, already made the iguana's acquaintance.) Fitzroy turned the letter Cliopher gave him over in his hand, his face still, quiet. "I wonder who this is from," he murmured. "Who knows we're here?"

Cliopher looked at his own missives, recognizing their hands easily. "My mother ... my sister ... Conju ..."

"Mine's from Conju as well," Ludvic said.

Fitzroy glanced at theirs, and he went forcibly still. "So is mine. I hadn't ... I didn't recognize Conju's hand ..."

"I don't imagine he writes formal notes to you very often," Cliopher replied, glad all over again that he could still make Fitzroy smile.

~

Vinyë's letter was straightforward and enjoyable: she was pleased at her visit to Old Damara, slyly delighted in how she had surely surprised him with her friendship with 'Melissa,' rapturous about travelling to an entirely new part of the world, and that landlocked. Pleased, too, about how their mother's adventure was going.

Our mother has had the most amazing holiday with Conju, Vinyë wrote after describing the Summer Palace where they were staying. *They have grown very close ... it is lovely to see her so relaxed and happy, and I think it has been good for Conju as well. He always seemed rather high-strung before, I must say. I think he's enjoyed being able to share all these lovely things with Mama, and help her to feel beautiful too. She's been telling me about all the things she's tried and how she reckons you should have been listening to Conju a great deal more about how to take care of yourself ...*

Conju agreed with Vinyë on that front; though Cliopher had long known that his friend thought him almost ascetic.

He wasn't—he had *liked* experimenting with all the unguents and lotions Fitzroy had bought—it just didn't really occur to him to get them for himself. But he had come to enjoy having well-tailored clothing ... and it had to be said he very much did like having other people responsible for maintaining the cleanliness and order in his household.

He made a note to himself to look at hiring a housekeeper of some form, since with the possible exception of Ludvic it was unlikely any of the other people living in Saya Dorn's old house would be inclined to *clean*.

Then he read Conju's letter.

Dear Cliopher,

I thank you for your letter. What adventures you have been having—and you sly thing, dropping such dramatic pronouncements as 'my hair has grown out by a good foot' into the middle of your metaphysical vision-quest or whatever it was—I hope you are taking excellent care of it. Go talk to your uncle Lazo, he understands hair, he will know what you need to put in it to keep it looking its best.

NOTE WELL: This is NOT the same as what He will need, his hair will be a completely different texture to yours, do not let your uncle go NEAR His hair, I have been discussing the matter with many skilled aestheticians and I have written to give Him my advice.

You may thank me, by the way, for heading off the imminent arrival of your mother, sister, niece, and the Grand Duchess and her household. When they heard you and He had returned to Gorjo City they were all for returning to greet you and give you a full Islander welcome, but I pointed out that He had not finished his quest—or so I presumed from your letter, and while I understand why you were perhaps a trifle incoherent—One would not wish to say, hysterical—

(On which note: what does 'fanoa' mean? It could possibly be a misspelling of fayna, but I am positive that you would not DARE to propose the idea you and HE are fayna now, however intense your relationship has always been.

I know you are something of an iconoclast, Cliopher, but there is iconoclasm and then there is (if you were anyone else I would stop there out of a sense of decorum, i.e. '—well, you know!'—since anyone who knew the meaning of fayna could, or at least, ought to be considered a man of culture and refinement—but you do like things to be said outright)—there is iconoclasm and then there is fucking the icon. Part of me profoundly hopes that I am wrong about this and this 'fanoa' thing is some Islander concept I've never heard of, but then there is another part of me that acknowledges (what have you people done to me) that it would probably do him a world of good to get done and also that you'd be the best person to do it, by which I mean him. Of course we cannot let that Domina Black come near him, I'm sure you'll agree with me.)

—Given your Grand Adventure and weeks or months without any writing utensils at all, you must have been beside yourself, nevertheless your letter was not to your usual standards of clarity and concision at all—and therefore, as I told your family, you are probably not finished with your quest and will not be staying long at all. After strenuous argument I was able to persuade them that it would be better to wait on such a grand visit until you had officially retired.

Do not make a liar of me. You have a full four months before you need to return to the Palace, and there is much to be done but not by you before He comes back with a full head of hair and, no doubt, a head full of music and previously illegal poetry. Do ensure he also comes back with an heir, though I will say that from all I hear, that mage Tanaea—the Mother of the Mountains' assistant, and good friends with Say' Aioru, according to all the gossip—is doing a lovely job. They have been tinkering discreetly, but very effectively. You know how I've always told you and Him that it's the little details that matter. It's wonderful to see young people with such a solid grasp of the fundamentals.

So if you spend all your time visiting with gods and romping with renegades, you will probably not destroy your life's work. Probably. Before He left Rhodin gave even odds of one of you burning everything down in a fit of pique but that seemed low to me. —Neither of you would want to destroy the Post service, at the very least.

Now, I assume you will want at least a little gossip, so that you are not entirely lost when you return home. I begin, naturally, with Prince Rufus, who has rocked all of Amboloyan society by announcing he is finally elevating his eldest son to an advisory position and granting him minor executive powers ...

It took Cliopher a moment to remember what *fayna* meant; and then he recalled Fitzroy telling him about how the Shaian word for male lovers had emerged after the days of Aurelius Magnus, and must have been a borrowing from the Islander term Aurelius had used.

He rolled his eyes fondly at how clearly Conju's voice and mannerisms came through in his writing, inwardly squirming a little at the dig about him *stating things outright*, indeed. About a word Cliopher had refused to let himself even think for decades.

(He missed Conju terribly, but he had to admit he was glad it was Ludvic here with them, right now.)

The letter from his mother was long—very long, he found as he unfolded page after page, glued together accordion-style for some unfathomable reason—and turned out to be a diary-like account of her travels with Conju.

He found himself laughing and crying at different points, and more than once shocked by the sharpness of her observations; and he found himself picking up his pen at the end and writing immediately to her with the suggestion she think about publishing it as a kind of travel memoir.

～

Ludvic said his letter was what he had expected, and looked satisfied saying so. Although Cliopher was very curious, he forbore pressing for details.

Fitzroy, however, had holed himself up in the solarium and would not come down when called.

Eventually Cliopher went up, only to discover that he had turned himself into a crow and was sitting on the windowsill staring at the city spread out below him.

"I suppose," said Cliopher casually, leaning against the wall beside him, one hand on the windowsill, "that you don't want to talk about it?"

The crow ruffled its feathers and resolutely did not return to human form.

Cliopher smiled sympathetically. Judging by his own letter, Conju had quite possibly attempted to disguise—or possibly demonstrate—all his emotions by an extended discussion of haircare. "We're here if—when—you want us," he said.

"Ludvic and I were thinking we'd go out for a walk and find something to eat, if you'd like to join us? In about an hour."

The crow ruffled its feathers again, then sidled along the windowsill until he brushed up against Cliopher's hand. His feathers were very soft and warm, but he did not stay long: in one sharp movement he opened his wings and was gone out the window.

~

Ludvic was in the sitting room, sorting through yet another pile of baskets, when Cliopher came back down. "Well?"

Cliopher shrugged. "He turned into a crow and flew away, but I think he'll probably join us when we go out."

Ludvic tilted his head. "He turned into a crow?"

And so Cliopher got to explain that, too. At least insofar as he himself understood the situation, which was barely.

"Hmm," said Ludvic thoughtfully, spreading out a set of wooden game-pieces on his lap. "Pikabe said there was a crow following you before the landslide."

"It wasn't *him*."

"No, I shouldn't think so. Pikabe seemed to think it was one of his gods."

Cliopher sat down on a stout wooden chest. He didn't remember the lead-up to the landslide very well. But there was something, some vague impression, of a feather —a long black feather, like the one he'd traded for the mirimiri of Ani ...

"Why would one of Pikabe's gods be following *me*? Though I suppose Pikabe was there."

"Pikabe's from the Voribo." Ludvic smiled slightly at Cliopher's incomprehension—the name was distantly familiar, but he couldn't bring it immediately to mind. "They're the folk who live north of Solaara. Between the Escarpment and the Fens."

Cliopher did remember those strange events surrounding his Radiancy's departure—the ruckus at the Imperial Necropolis, the burning of the Fens—but he'd not heard any sort of mention of a crow-god.

"Did he think it was connected to the burning of the Fens? I didn't have anything to do with that."

Ludvic tipped the game-pieces back into their basket. "Not you, no. Pikabe said he'd told his village elders about the events on Lesuia—the Moon coming down, your encounter with your god in the market—"

"Did *everyone* realize that was what that was?"

Ludvic laughed. "How could we not?"

Cliopher smiled reluctantly, knowing by now that he deserved the teasing for thinking that encounter with Vou'a had been anything as private as he had originally taken it for.

Ludvic had a great laugh, rolling up and breaking like one of the deep-water swells coming in to land. Cliopher enjoyed hearing it as well as seeing Ludvic's amusement in his eyes.

"Pikabe reckons the gods are moving because of Himself, the end of an age, that sort of thing. It's probably true. He says that Crow, his god, is a trickster, but he treats his people well."

"He lost his arm in that landslide."

"His arm, but not his life," Ludvic replied quietly. "And you received a gift, didn't you?"

Cliopher nodded, smiling wryly, and touched the efela. "Along with the concussion."

"The gods repay their debts," Ludvic said. "That is what my mother told me."

"Well spoken," said a dry, unexpected voice, and Cliopher stood up hastily to see that the Son of Laughter had entered the room.

His mind raced through the stories in the *Lays*, and then he stopped himself consciously, for he had not invited the god within and yet here he was—and they were kin by marriage, after all.

"Buru Vou'a, come and be welcome beside our fire," Cliopher said therefore, bowing over his hands in respect.

Ludvic, who had also stood, bowed equally politely before clearing off a third chair of the items piled upon it. "May we offer you food? Water? Coffee?"

"Words and deeds of welcome," the Son of Laughter said, his eyes crinkled with an amusement Cliopher did not fully understand, but he hopped upon the chair with every evidence of comfort. "Not everyone is so cunning as you, Kip Mdang of Tahivoa. Nor so polite as your friend! What name do you have, hmm? What island? What dances?"

Ludvic saluted sharply. "My name is Ludvic Omo. My island was Woodlark in the Azilint. We do not have your dances, but the head of my carving is Odongai."

Vou'a tilted his head. "My condolences for the loss of your island. May you find a solid place for your feet, a hearth to warm your soul, a safe resting-place for your heart."

"Thank you," said Ludvic, very solemnly, and gestured around him in one smooth, easy motion. "Thanks to my friend, I have."

Cliopher swallowed hard against the dignity of his sorrow, the depth of his surety, the knowledge that he had been able to offer this. (The gift that his offer had been accepted, that Ludvic was finding *home*.)

"Yes," Vou'a said, his eyes glittering as he turned to Cliopher. "You have an unusual talent, Kip Mdang, even for a tanà—even for a tana-tai. You promised me once you would bring a new fire to the hearth of the world, which was a fine promise, indeed! And yet you have brought it. A new tai." The god's regard was heavy; weighted. "And more than that, haven't you? A new star in the sky ... a new fire at the hearth ... a new *island* ... and something lost long ago restored. Your fanoa spoke of recompense. What then do I give you, I wonder?"

Ludvic had accepted the gift Cliopher had offered him. Fitzroy had accepted the gift Cliopher had offered him. Cliopher had been working hard to accept the gifts his family laid at his hearth.

He lifted his chin, his heart thundering, but he had no idea what to say.

Vou'a could not give him what he wanted.

The Son of Laughter could not give him the stanzas in the *Lays*—those words had to come from his people. And they would, for he had taken all that his people were and could be and he had *lived* that truth, walked into legends for them, and finally come home to claim the deeds he had done.

The god of mysteries could not make his family love him—nor did he need to, for they did. They always had. And those who had gone before him sailed in that great flotilla down the Wake of the stars in the sky, rejoicing in the deeds that were done and yet to be done.

Cliopher was the only one who could claim his status. This was not court: he would not be showered with honours he did not lay claim to.

"What do you want, Kip Mdang?" Vou'a asked him.

(There had been other encounters with the god, his Buru Tovo's friend, in Cliopher's life. *Answer him!* Buru Tovo had told him over and over again. *Is this where you stop?*)

He had whispered a secret into the two halves of his heart, and tucked the ember into the resultant shell as a gift for Ani.

His heart was thundering at this unexpected offer, the unanswerable question. The god waited, patient as the shadow in the depths of a cave, as the land holding out its shore to the sea, as the mystery that could never be plumbed.

He stood there, ready for a negotiation that he did not know the terms of reference for.

—And there was a shadow flitting across the room, and a whisper and rustle of wings, and a black crow dove through the wind-eye above the brazier and shimmered into a somewhat windswept Fitzroy, his eyes bright and fully focused.

"Ah, you've come!" Vou'a said, just a little too quickly. "I was just giving my thanks to your fanoa here, for the gift he gave me. Tovo raised him well, eh? Such a good boy, so kind and generous to his elders ..."

He glanced expectantly at Cliopher, but Cliopher could not pay attention to him, not with the feral gleam in his fanoa's eye.

Fitzroy regarded the god guilelessly. "Were you hoping I wouldn't notice your arrival? The house called me, and this is not a negotiation for Cliopher alone." He nodded at Vou'a, at Ludvic, and came to stand beside Cliopher.

"Ah," said the Son of Laughter, grinning. "You have something to say?"

Fitzroy glanced at Cliopher, who simply stared back at him, wordless. His fanoa smiled and then turned back to the god, intent and serious and as alive as the moment before he set his hand to his harp. Cliopher's found himself lifting his hand to the efela at his neck, his hand settling around the obsidian pendant, the smooth curve of the efevoa.

Fitzroy put his hand on Cliopher's shoulder, his touch warm. Comforting. Ludvic's face was as calm and unruffled as it ever was on guard, but his eyes were soft.

"I am a velio, I know," Fitzroy Angursell, the last Emperor of Astandalas, said to the Islander god, in the Islander language, "and yet I have studied your ways as best I can, for love of this man, my friend, my stalwart counsellor, my fanoa. And one of the things I have learned is that for the Ke'e Lulai it is one's obligation to choose how you respond to a challenge-song made to you."

Cliopher sucked in a hard breath, not so much at this challenge thrown in the face of the god, the Son of Laughter, his Buru Tovo's friend (lover, husband, life companion), but for what it said about himself.

"Ah," said Vou'a, his face wrinkling as he grinned at Fitzroy. "You have listened well." The god looked at Cliopher. "Have *you*?"

Look first. Listen first. Questions later.

For so long Cliopher had hesitated at that third part of the instructions. He had asked questions—so many questions—so *many* questions—until his family cried at him to *stop—be quiet—would you sit still and* listen *for once—*

He had learned to sit still, to be quiet, to be patient, to *listen*.

They had complained he had lost his fire.

But he had not shown them that the embers burned fierce as ever, safe in the hearth of his heart, lighting fire after fire in the wide world until at last the flames, passed hand over hand, reached his family in the Ring.

Look first. Listen first. Questions later.

Cliopher had learned so well to look, to listen, that he had rarely needed to ask the questions: the answers he sought were presented to him, the gossip and the news, and the problems he had spent his life trying to fix.

To the challenge-song offered him by the very existence of the *Lays*, he had replied with his entire life. He had thought that was clear enough, claimed loudly enough, *obvious*.

And yet: at court the unspoken display of clothes and jewels and ornaments was legible to those who knew the court customs, and Cliopher, for all he had spent his life in that court, still stumbled over the nuances.

Why had he ever thought his family, outspoken and direct as they were, would be able to read the silent markers of rank and accomplishment? *That* was not the way of the *Lays*.

He had known that, crossing Sky Ocean: he had lifted his chin, an Islander from the modern day, before Elonoa'a and Tupaia and the legendary crew of the *He'eanka*. He had shown the sea-witch and the Grandmother and the very Sun himself who he was, who his people were, what they could be.

Fitzroy's hand gripped his shoulder gently, returning him to his physical reality, the god standing before him as if he were any other person. Cliopher took in a deep, quiet breath, centring himself as he had before so many committees and court challenges, shifting his position so he stood straight and proud, balanced on his feet, his eyes level and his expression giving nothing away.

The air smelled of the faint incense Ludvic had lit, and the friendly wood crackling in the brazier, and a faint briny, fresh scent that seemed to hover in the air around the Son of Laughter.

Brine. Sea-water and fresh air: from the god who had taken the mirimiri and disappeared in a flash of light and thunder without another word.

Look first. Listen first. Questions later.

Cliopher glanced up at Fitzroy, and then back at Vou'a. "From the depths of my heart I brought a secret for you to take as a gift to your fanoa. In return you took news and the gift of a new skill to mine. From the House of the Sun I brought your fanoa's lost mirimiri for you to return to her. As my fanoa has mentioned, it is thus your turn to reply. What would you suggest I ask for?"

"One for a token, and two for a promise," the god said. "And what did they say, in the House of the Sun, when you negotiated so splendidly?"

Cliopher smiled. "The Sun cried that it had been a long time since the Grandmother last took a favourite, and the Grandmother whispered in my ear that I was surely one of yours."

Vou'a laughed, his kookaburra cackle. "You *are* one of mine, Kip Mdang of Loaloa! What a thing to be, the rising tana-tai who brought home a new tai! The descendant who told the Ancestors who they are! The one who left—and who came back!"

"You have not answered the challenge," Fitzroy murmured.

The Son of Laughter laughed again, the sound bouncing oddly in the room. "You, little mage, little sunling, my *dear* little one, my tirului—" Cliopher shifted, and the god cackled. "Too much? Still, it's all true. I would gladly adopt you as one of mine, fanoa of my husband's grand-nephew, but you are well claimed." He tilted his head, watching as Fitzroy went very still. "Ah, that is news to you, is it? Well, well, even Kip Mdang cannot know everything, can he?"

Fitzroy shook his head once, his face completely serene.

"Yes, yes," Vou'a said. "Enough stalling, eh? Ey ana, as Tovo likes to say. Ey ana. Here we are, a challenge sung loud as the sunrise across the face of the sky. One token was I given, and one have I returned. Two for a promise ... and the promise *I* was given is that a mistake need not remain eternally; that sometimes the remedy is found by another."

"And so?" Cliopher said, feeling very daring, but aware of the steps of this dance.

"Ey ana, I thought you had learned patience! A gift for my fanoa, and one to yours. And a remedy for an ancient, insuperable loss for my fanoa ... so what can I return to yours?" He grinned, having clearly thought of something, and looked up at Fitzroy. Cliopher felt a very sharp shudder want to crawl up his spine; he was suddenly very aware that the seemingly innocuous-looking old man in front of him was a powerful and capricious god.

"An unimaginably great good was done for me," Vou'a murmured. "In return, a fivefold gift for you, Fitzroy Angursell of Navanoa." He held up his hand, fingers spread out. "One: Three visions of your fanoa when you needed them most, fuel to keep your heart-fire burning. Two: Three visits from friends of mine when you have most needed a mystery, riddles to keep your mind alert to the challenge-song singing for *you*. Three: when the time is right, an introduction to and help with your godfather, who is another friend of mine."

He hesitated for a moment, clearly revelling in their attention, their shocked amazement, before grinning roguishly.

Fitzroy's hand was tight on Cliopher's shoulder, seeking support rather than giving it now.

"Fourth and fifth," the Son of Laughter said, "I speak for my fanoa and myself when I offer a gift and a boon and the ear of the Sea and the Land to the two of you."

He clapped his hands together and gave Fitzroy an arch glance. "Good enough for you?"

But it was not Fitzroy who answered, but Ludvic.

He cleared his throat, and the Son of Laughter looked sharply at him. "Yes, witch's son of a lost land?"

Ludvic's eyes flashed at this epithet, but he otherwise spoke as evenly as ever. "Tell me, Son of Laughter: one of the names of the godfather of Fitzroy Angursell—is it Crow?"

That surprised Vou's as sharply as Cliopher's presentation of the mirimiri of Ani. He drew his breath in with a hiss, and then laughed his kookaburra laugh again. "Oh, you are a sly one! You can be one of mine too, if you like, if no one has adopted you yet?"

"I am part of the household of your kinsman," Ludvic said sturdily.

"So you are," said Vou'a. "So you are. Ey ana! A sly one and a clever man indeed. And good shoulders, too, as Tovo described to me." He gave Ludvic a gleeful once-over, which the guard endured with merely a raised eyebrow and a small smile. "Now, witch's son, I am bound by a promise not to name a certain name until all the conditions are met, if you take my meaning." He grinned. "Nonetheless, I can and will and do say that certain parties will be very pleased indeed at how things are progressing!"

Vou'a winked at them, twirled on his foot, and disappeared into a shadow.

"Crow?" Fitzroy said weakly, sitting down, as if the god's disappearance had stolen all the air out of the room.

Cliopher took a breath, for he hadn't: the air felt full of effervescence, like the mineral taste of the cold, clear water in the depths of a cave. He sat down in one of the arm-chairs they'd put near the fire, opposite Fitzroy, who had put his chin on his hand and was staring at the fire-pot of day on the table in front of him.

"He's a trickster god of Eastern Dair," Ludvic replied, still standing at ease between them. "We have stories down as far as my islands. I've heard he was supposed to have some sort of connection with Harbut Zalarin, the one whose son was the first emperor."

Cliopher blinked. "I've never heard that story."

"You wouldn't have," Ludvic replied imperturbably. "Not for everyone's ears, you know. But this is a matter for ..." He hesitated, and then he smiled radiantly at them both. "For family."

"Family," said Fitzroy, even more faintly, and then: "Crow?"

"Crow," agreed Ludvic. "He's been dropping feathers like clues."

"Some of Vou'a's gifts have already happened," Fitzroy said, frowning. "The visions ... I told you, Kip, of the one with the boat at night ..."

"Perhaps you didn't recognize it as Kip," Ludvic suggested.

Fitzroy frowned more deeply, turning inwards. "I've had a few flashes other times ... but he said it was when I particularly needed to be heartened ..." He drifted off, and stared at the floor, before raising his head and staring somewhat blankly at them. "When we were on holiday, on Navikiani, I told you of a dream, do you remember? That was a dream from deep in my ... the time after the Fall ... I was dreaming I was lost." He caught his breath. His eyes were bleak. "It was bad," he whispered. "I almost let go ... and then I dreamed of a hall, a secret door, and inside it: the harp and the book ... *my* book ... and in the corner of my eye, there was someone standing there, someone I trusted, someone I knew was absolutely *beloved* to me."

Cliopher's heart twisted. "You survived that, Fitzroy. You're not lost there."

"No," Fitzroy said. He took a deep breath, one of the ones on a long, gentle count, until he was a little more composed. "And the third ... then ... the third was long ago. When I first heard *Aurora* was banned—I pretended it was all to the good, that it was fitting, that it was even *desirable*, but I—" He smiled crookedly at them. "I loved that poem. I was so proud of it. And then it was banned."

Cliopher could not take it, and moved over so he could kiss Fitzroy's forehead. "It was always my favourite," he murmured.

"All that humming," Fitzroy said, laughing weakly. "I guessed."

Cliopher knelt beside him, one hand on Fitzroy's bare knee below his long tunic. Fitzroy looked down at the floor, and then he said slowly, "When I heard it was banned, there was a night where I wondered if—if I would ever do anything that was *real*, that was *worthy*. That was true. And I had a vision, a dream, of someone—a boy with bandaged hands, opening *Aurora* and—and—" He caught his breath, as if he were barely a moment away from sobbing.

"And loving it," said Cliopher, swallowing hard. And then he held out his hands, his palms upright, and showed the very fine, pale white scars that ran across the base of his fingers. He gazed steadily at Fitzroy. Perhaps he might not have remembered this, if Au'aua had not asked him that silent question about his efela ko. "The day I collected the obsidian," he said, touching the pendant with one hand. "I found a beautiful round piece, like a ball. Got almost back to where Buru Tovo and Uncle Lazo were waiting for me when I dropped it."

Fitzroy hissed. "What then?"

"It broke. Quite in half. I cut my hands, picking it up to carry to the boat. I was devastated. Thought I'd ruined everything," Cliopher replied, remembering Buru Tovo's friend—Vou'a, of course (of course)—asking him if that was where he stopped.

(Telling him that there were many things that came in halves, broken or otherwise.)

"I came to visit Saya Dorn and she gave me a book her friend in Astandalas had sent her." He felt his face soften into a smile. "A brand new book, just out. First printing."

"*Aurora*," Ludvic said, since Fitzroy appeared to be speechless.

"*Aurora*," Cliopher agreed.

"You weren't wearing Islander clothes—in the vision. I only remembered the bandaged hands ... but it was a tunic ..."

"It was known to happen from time to time."

Fitzroy closed his eyes; when he opened them they were dry, but full of magic. "What happened to that copy? Do you still have it?"

"Alas, no," Cliopher said regretfully. "After I'd read it enough times to memorize it, I shared it around the city—it was the only copy, I think, that made it out here—and one day it never came back."

Ludvic sighed. "What a pity!"

"I know! I'm sure my teenage annotations would be *fascinating*."

Fitzroy covered his mouth with his hands in that Rhodin-like gesture again.

Cliopher gave him a slightly suspicious glance. "What is it?"

"The copy in Navikiani—it was full of notes," Fitzroy said, dropping his hand to reveal a brilliant smile, all his glumbles forgotten. "Surely it wasn't yours?"

"Surely not indeed! That would be an astonishing, incredible piece of—"

"Serendipity?" Fitzroy said, grinning. "As if one of us were a wild mage?"

"Or were touched by the gods," Ludvic murmured placidly.

Cliopher huffed. "Well, if you'd ever shared it with anyone, I could have told you."

"I didn't share it with anyone because I was *reading* all the notes," Fitzroy replied with dignity. "Well, that settles that, Kip—we *must* go back to Basil's inn as soon as possible, we need to confirm whether it was your copy. And then," he added with relish, making Cliopher's heart swoop and soar and in general act very intemperate indeed, "and then we can talk about your interpretations and why almost all of them were wrong."

"I might have different ones now," Cliopher pointed out.

Fitzroy gave him a burning, gloriously amused look, the sort that had made everyone fall in love with him. But Cliopher was the one he had chosen back.

"Obviously, the ones you wrote in your exhortation about the poet laureate were the more *correct*. But the ones from when you were a teenager are much funnier."

CHAPTER SEVENTY-FOUR
DAWNINGS

The day after Vou'a came to bring recompense, Cliopher woke up very early, before dawn.

He lay there for a few minutes, listening to Ludvic's steady breathing, Fitzroy's soft snores. They had all gotten a bit tipsy, the night before, on rum that someone had sent over (all these gifts, with no senders' names, no way to return thanks; Ludvic and Fitzroy kept assuring him these gifts were return thanks already, he did not need to do anything besides graciously accept them and, potentially, give on; i.e. the rum) and ended up falling asleep in Fitzroy's solarium sharing stories.

Eventually, Cliopher thought, they would become old news, a part of things, no longer notable.

He could see the new star, *his* new star, glowing near the western horizon, not yet set, and smiled. Eventually. But probably not yet.

He went downstairs without waking his friends, dressed in fresh clothing (one thing to be said for leaving Fitzroy to buy the necessities was the acquisition of several outfits more than Cliopher would probably have bought; they had yet to need to do laundry), and then decided to go for a walk. He could have gone for a sail—when he looked reflexively at the vaha, he discovered that someone (Cora, it must be) had brought over his old vaha, the one he had made with his own hands, his little *Tuitanata*.

He went to look at it first, examining the care with which Cora and her students had restored it, his heart singing with a strange, welling joy. It was small next to the vaha Hiru and Pinyë and the others had made for him, nowhere near so elegant or so beautiful ... but it was *his*.

He patted the prow, with its clumsy decorative carving, and promised the *Tui-*

tanata he would sail her soon. Then he turned, let himself out the front gate of the courtyard, and went out for an amble.

The city was quiet, sleepy. People were awake, of course—fishers readying their boats for a dawn sailing, home-makers getting ready for the day, a few early shop-keepers setting up—but although they exchanged smiles and quiet greetings, no one was much inclined to chatting.

It was cool, the air sweet, full of night-time fragrances. Cliopher wandered aimlessly, admiring newly painted houses, newly planted pots, newly added public art. Everywhere there was the evidence of tiny little improvements, and there were so many more little art and craft studios and store-fronts than he remembered.

It took him probably too long to realize that the fact they could exist in such quantities was due, at a fundamental level, to the secure foundation his annual stipend had provided. Gorjo City had not had an appreciable degree of real poverty, since people always had the option of returning to the islands of the Ring and living traditionally, so the effects had not been anywhere near so dramatic as in some parts of the world. Nonetheless, the effects were there, and becoming more and more visible by the week.

He remembered the thriving Esa'a of the *other place*, and compared it to the increasing vibrancy of his Gorjo City, and he was proud.

Cliopher had provided the foundation for this, footings for the pilings of the floating city. But it was his people who had chosen to build their dreams up into reali-ties. He had not suggested someone take that dank corner between two buildings and turn it into a shady garden, overhung with ferns and a mosaic depicting a pair of striking blue coconut crabs, a little bench set there for comfort.

He sat there for a moment, because it was there, that bench, and looked out across the boardwalk to a view he recognized after a few minutes was of a wedge of Tahivoa lagoon. The street-lights ran along the edge of the lagoon, illuminating someone who was preparing a traditional vaha off to one side; right next to Uncle Lazo's barber shop.

Cliopher made his way through an alley short-cut he'd forgotten he knew about and emerged a few wharves down from where, yes, his Buru Tovo was preparing to set sail.

Buru Tovo did not appear particularly surprised to see Cliopher emerging out of the dim pre-dawn. He looked up when Cliopher stopped on the wharf, nodded once, and returned to checking his sail and lines. Cliopher sat down, legs swinging, and watched him move with the economy and grace of a long lifetime of practice.

"You coming, then?" Buru Tovo asked finally.

Cliopher smiled widely at him, undid the mooring line, and stepped aboard. Buru Tovo grunted, and it was just as it had been all those days of Cliopher's youth. But better.

~

"Are you going fishing?" he asked after a few moments, when Buru Tovo handed him an oar and directed him to paddle.

"Was going to visit you first," his great-uncle said, adjusting the sail to catch a faint breath of wind. His old canoe skimmed across the still waters of the lagoon, almost as much a part of the old man as his legs or his hands. "Then ... out sailing."

Cliopher caught his breath as he saw the faraway look in Buru Tovo's eyes. "You're not ..." He stumbled over his words as his great-uncle looked at him in faint challenge, but he was not the young Kip who had needed to learn to be silent (*look first! Listen first!*), nor the older Cliopher who had needed to learn when it was the time to ask questions. "Are you planning on coming back?" he asked quietly. "Or is it ..."

Buru Tovo's face creased with quiet laughter. "No, no. I want to go sailing Sky Ocean, visit the House of the Sun and claim the guest-right you won for us there, but not yet." He fingered the kookaburra feathers braided into his hair. "My husband's taking me to meet his fanoa. Heard there's a new island for them to dance together on."

Cliopher met his eyes, and saw the wonder he felt shining there also in his great-uncle's. He smiled, looking down at the small eddies coiling and uncoiling in the wake of his paddle. "Is he?"

"Ey ana," Buru Tovo said. "It wasn't possible before, not if I ever wanted to come back, but it is now." He nodded, and settled back comfortably, one hand on the tiller, the other on the sail's rope, guiding the boat with deft touches. There was enough wind here to catch the sail, and Cliopher drew in the paddle. The water fell off it in silver droplets.

"I'll have to go one day, you know," Buru Tovo said, circling the vaha in the middle of the lagoon so he could go down the canal towards Cliopher's house from a better angle. "Won't live forever. One day I'll sail with the Ancestors."

"I know," Cliopher said, his throat closing. "I will miss you."

"Not gone yet, boy."

He grinned and blinked back the tears. "I know. I love you, Buru Tovo."

His great-uncle grunted, and jerked his chin in the direction of the golden star just visible between the buildings. "Given a name to that star, then, have you? The island, I'm told, your poet named."

"Navanoa," Cliopher whispered. "The island's name is Navanoa."

"And the star?"

"I didn't know I ..." He shook his head. "I didn't think about naming it. There's precedent in the *Lays* for naming a new island ... but a star?"

Even as he said that, he knew it wasn't quite true. The other Kip of that other place had not ferreted out the history of 'Gorjo', but Cliopher had. Buru Tovo cocked his head, gently releasing the sail so the vaha turned into the small bywater leading to Cliopher's courtyard. His vaha was smaller than the one from Sky Ocean, its mast just able to fit under the arch of the bridge. "Thought of something, have you, boy?"

"The last Gathering of the Ships was held under a new star, the daylight star, Kori'iho," he said, which was how it was described in the *Lays*. "They started to call the location of the meeting after the star. The first Astandalan governors wrote it as Korijo first, later Gorjo. You can see the shifting spelling if you look through the old tax records."

Not that anyone other than Cliopher had ever looked at those tax records, in their huge parchment rolls deep in the back rooms of the Imperial Archives. But Cliopher had.

"Koriho's still a star in the sky," Buru Tovo observed. "Only at night now, mind." He drew his canoe to a smooth berthing next to Cliopher's vaha. "That new star of yours shone in the day for a good few weeks, before you came home."

Cliopher rubbed his hand over his face, just once. "No one said."

"Lots of other things to talk about first, boy." Buru Tovo shrugged. "You don't need to name it. They'll keep on calling it Kip's star if you don't."

"No!"

Buru Tovo cackled in a way very reminiscent of the Son of Laughter. "No? Then you'd best head them off. Those Who Name The Stars are getting very antsy. If you don't talk to them before you go off again yourself, you'll lose your moment."

"It's a light on the prow of the *He'eanka* ..."

"That name's already taken. Come on, boy, you've always been a clever one."

Because the tests were never done, were they? There was always another challenge, another choice to keep on or turn back, another ke'ea to follow or a ke'e to rest a while under—

Cliopher took a breath, remembering that star-island, the legendary star-farers, Aurelius who was so like, and so unlike, his distant descendant Fitzroy, Elonoa'a who had thought his people had dismissed him for loving another man.

Elonoa'a had followed Aurelius, all the way across that impossible Sky Ocean. Cliopher did not think that Auri would mind the symbolism of following El's star towards the hope of healing.

"It's not *my* place to name a star," Cliopher said. "But if anyone would like to have my *opinion*, Elonoa'a isn't taken, except by Aurelius." He smiled at his great-uncle. "It's a worthy name for the star at the prow of his parahë, if the Nga lore-keepers agree."

Buru Tovo only nodded once, but Cliopher could see the old man was pleased. Very pleased, perhaps. "Two celestial fanoa for the fanoa down below."

"Two lovers, husbands if they could have been," Cliopher reminded him. "They made fanoa mean what they needed it to." He smiled, looking up at the windows of Fitzroy's solarium, which were catching the faint peachy and lavender and dove-grey tints of dawn. "Just as we will."

"You've got it bad, boy," Buru Tovo said; Cliopher grinned at him and shrugged, for of course it was true. "Go on then, make us some coffee before I go out to meet the sea."

"I'll do better than that," Cliopher said, focusing down on him and turning the challenge gently back. "I shall give you a flame of the Sun to take with you in your fire-pot, Buru Tovo."

～

Buru Tovo went off after his coffee, a fragment of the indivisible light of the Sun in his old clay fire-pot. Fitzroy came down, grumbling about the early hour and the devastating scent of fresh coffee, while Cliopher was carefully transferring some of the eternal not-embers from the coral fire-pot Auri and Tupaia had given him.

"Elonoa'a is a great name for that star," he agreed, and then: "Oh, are we giving gifts? Then Buru Tovo, let me tell you something you will enjoy."

Buru Tovo immediately perked up. "My ears are ready."

Fitzroy leaned over and whispered into his ear something that made the old man cackle so hard that Cliopher became worried he might pass on to the Ancestors from it.

"No, no, that is the best thing," Buru Tovo declared, wiping his eyes. "A star, an island, a new fire, and a delightful secret. What gifts you have brought me!" He waggled his finger at Cliopher, though any sternness was much reduced by his quivering shoulders. "Now all you need is an apprentice of your own, Kip Mdang! And a woman to keep you hopping, men really aren't the same. And I should know."

"You don't have a man," Cliopher objected. "You have a god."

"I had my sister and your mother, don't I? Don't need to be married to have a matriarch. Hope you know what you're getting into, poet-mage."

Fitzroy gave Cliopher a sly, delighted smile. "A family, Buru Tovo. And a beautiful culture to share."

"Don't need to give up your own to share ours," Buru Tovo said decisively. "Our seas are wide enough. Speaking of—better go or I'll be late."

Cliopher accompanied him down to his vaha, and embraced him before he pushed off again. "Fair winds and fair seas, and an island full of all you need when you are ready to land, Buru Tovo."

The old Islander words, the ones El had spoken to him, fell into the air with strange and lovely significance.

"I go with Vou'a to meet Ani, that they may do the dance that once brought life to the first islands, boy," Buru Tovo said, patting him on the shoulder and then giving him the ancient Islander greeting, forehead to forehead. "I haven't handed everything over to you yet, Kip. We still have to walk the Ring together one more time. After the greater festival."

"Yes," said Cliopher, and let him go. "Give my love to your husband and his fanoa."

"Getting uppity are you, now?" But Buru Tovo was visibly touched and greatly pleased, and he busied himself with heading off.

Cliopher watched him out of sight past the bridge, waving when his great-uncle turned once to wave at him. There wouldn't be that many more years of the old man's company, but there would be some.

And then, Cliopher thought, that great night-time vision of the Wake rising brilliantly in his mind, and then there would be the endless glorious sail across Sky Ocean with the Ancestors.

A motion caught his attention, and he turned his head to see that his neighbours had emerged onto their patio. They waved, and he went over to them.

"Coffee?" Saya Oyinaa asked, offering him a cup.

"Thank you," he said, accepting it, and then hesitated. "I wished to thank you for collecting our vaha." He smiled sheepishly at the two old women. "I hadn't secured it sufficiently to keep it safe through the surge raised by a new island."

Rukà Siana was old—older than Uncle Lazo, if not so old as Buru Tovo—and had curling silver hair halfway down her back and very deep-set eyes. She and Cliopher had barely traded a dozen words in his lifetime.

"A new island," rukà Siana said, "and a new star in the sky. Have you named it?"

"The island's name is Navanoa," Cliopher replied, extremely glad for Buru Tovo's advice. "The star hangs at the prow of the ship *He'eanka*, and thus I had thought that Elonoa'a would be a fitting name for it, if those Who Name the Stars wish for my thoughts on the matter."

The two women laughed, one light and breathless, the other rough and deep.

Saya Oyinaa said, "We were glad to bring the vaha back. Sails beautifully."

"It has served me—us—well."

"All the way to the House of the Sun and back," rukà Siana said, and nodded at her wife.

Tiru Oyinaa nodded back. "We were thinking, Kip Mdang, that even though it's not a matter of 'finders keepers'—your vaha *is* very distinctive, after all—there's still a certain question of ... recompense."

"Is that so?" Cliopher asked, his attention prickling.

"Indeed," Saya Oyinaa murmured, offering him a plate of pastries they had presumably brought out for their breakfast. "You have *two* vaha, after all, if I'm not mistaken. Or so I have heard that other one there, the one the university folk have been using for demonstrations, is yours. Do you, then, really need *both*?"

Cliopher looked at them, his mind racing. That was the beginning of a challenge —but what did they intend for him to ask for in reply?

(What did *he* want, anyway? *Did* he need two vaha? What place did all this suggest for him and his community? Would Fitzroy want one?—that, at least, he had an answer for ...)

"Well," he said slowly, "I confess I'm intrigued enough to hear you out."

Saya Oyinaa grinned; her wife leaned forward. Cliopher settled himself down for a serious round of bargaining.

∾

Fitzroy raised a very his Radiancy eyebrow at him. "What do you mean, you *lost*?"

Cliopher shuffled his feet, trying not to blush. Why were they in the kitchen, anyway? It wasn't meal-time and even the iguana was absent. "Only the boat."

Fitzroy hesitated a moment; Ludvic laughed almost soundlessly and said, "What did you win?"

"I don't think that's relevant," Cliopher replied loftily. "What does it *mean* to win? On a philosophical level—"

"Did I hear someone mention philosophy?" a voice cried, followed shortly by Ghilly. She grinned at them. "I brought you some of the books I was talking about, Kip. But please, am I interrupting?"

"Cliopher has just been telling us how he managed to lose the boat in the negotiation he just had with the neighbours," Fitzroy explained.

Ghilly considered this for a moment. "What did he win?"

"That's where the philosophy came in."

Cliopher decided he could make tea—they'd found a small box of it in amongst all of the other *necessities*—and accordingly busied himself with the kettle and tap.

"Hmm, there *are* some interesting philosophies of war that have to do with winning and defeat," Ghilly said thoughtfully. "Have you ever read Assonge, Fitzroy?"

"I have, but I prefer Fithiray—a much more humane conception of ethical responsibility, I have found. Assonge is somewhat more utilitarian than I appreciate ..." He trailed off and gave her a charming smile. "Not to mention she deliberately misconstrued the situation with the Customs House in Ulstin-le-Grand to make a point, and then, when I published a rebuttal containing several publicly verifiable *facts*, called me a flibbertigibbet with intellectual pretensions."

Ghilly stared at him. "You're *Fitzroy Angursell*."

Fitzroy nodded gravely. "I am."

"Goodness." She set the books she was still holding down on the table. "Goodness. That means you're even better-read than Kip." Her eyes were calculating. "And —do you like talking about philosophy? Because Kip's the only one, and he's hardly read anything in *years*, you know—"

"Too busy, I expect," Fitzroy replied, with a faint, glimmering smile. "Ghilly, I've also been busy and haven't read nearly as much of late as I'd like to, either. But I do— I used to like talking about philosophy very much." He glanced at Ludvic. "And poetry, too."

Ghilly pounced on this. "But you're almost retired, aren't you? I'd stopped too, when I was working, but since I've retired—and we were sailing around the world— Bertie was working on his monograph and Toucan paints, so I *read*—oh, this is good. This is very good. Because I bet you—oh! You're *also* the lord emperor, aren't you?"

"Alas, yes."

"No, no, that's perfect, because you know about *magic*. Kip's never read any philosophy of magic, he always used to say 'why do I need to know about magic, I have the *Lays*', but he's also the man who said 'just don't think about time,'and *really*, Fitzroy, he can't get his own way all the time, can he?"

"I understand," Fitzroy said even more gravely, "that it's bad for the character."

Cliopher snorted at this emergence of the old, familiar, fiery Ghilly, the Ghilly *he'd* once fallen in love with—the Ghilly he was still friends with, all these years later —and both Fitzroy and Ghilly turned to look at him.

"I interrupted," Ghilly said. "Kip was being recalcitrant and I interrupted your efforts to make him state something outright, I do apologize. Let's go back a few steps. Kip, you say you lost your boat in the negotiations with your neighbours."

"He has a very odd idea of what it means to *lose* in negotiation," Ludvic observed. "I have noticed this."

"It's true," Fitzroy said. "Lord Mdang!"

Cliopher had turned back to the stove, and he jumped in response to the sharp tone. "My lord!"

"And where is the iguana? Better yet: where is your answer?" Fitzroy demanded. "What did you receive in exchange from the neighbours in return for the boat the very Ancestors, the star-farers of the *He'eanka*, made for you?"

Cliopher *did* blush. "Their house."

CHAPTER SEVENTY-FIVE
THE SPARK

Cousin Louya showed up one afternoon and spent half an hour lounging with the iguana without announcing her presence. Cliopher had been arguing amicably with Ludvic about the placement of various items of furniture in the upper suites; when they came out into the sitting room, they discovered that Fitzroy had been watching Louya with fascination.

Cliopher decided not to say anything, and went down to greet his cousin.

She was laying flat on her back on the courtyard stones, the iguana stretched out in the sun beside her. "Cousin Louya," he greeted her.

"Cousin Kip," she replied dreamily.

He stared at her, but she didn't move, not even to open her eyes. Her eccentric clothing—a mishmash of family patterns and garments from other cultures—spilled around her, bright and busy as a coral reef.

"Thank you, Louya," he said, "for your advice regarding sea turtles. I gave them the honour I could, and was well recompensed for it."

"The shamans have asked me if I want to train with them," Louya murmured. "Can I have this iguana? If I'm to be a seer I could have a familiar, couldn't I?"

"You could," he agreed. "You'll have to ask Fitzroy and Ludvic—and My Lord, of course," he added, when the iguana opened one eye to regard him with its alien reptilian stare. "I understand it's quite attached to the house."

Louya hummed, and then flapped her hand at him. "Well, go on, then, Kip, don't stand there interrupting our conversation. I'm sure you have plenty of other things you could be doing."

～

Everyone came: Cliopher's aunts and uncles, his cousins and second cousins and *third* cousins, his friends and their relatives, all the lore-keepers, various people who were simply curious about the fire Kip Mdang had brought back from the House of the Sun.

And a journalist from *The Ring o'News*, who had realized he had the story of the century and who was deeply disgruntled when Fitzroy Angursell refused to give him any *proof*.

("The *Csiven Flyer* won't listen to me if I don't have *proof* you're really also Fitzroy Angursell!" he said. "Are you *sure?*"

"Very sure," Fitzroy replied, every inch the emperor. "Would it help if I promised not to tell any *other* newspapers before you get the chance to publish?")

There were so many people that Cliopher ended up spending most of his time in the courtyard, holding audiences. Fitzroy and Ludvic both seemed greatly pleased to keep themselves out of the way upstairs, and not at all sympathetic to Cliopher's inability to keep the conversations to under a quarter-hour.

"Island time, you know," Fitzroy said to Ludvic, who nodded. "Off you go, Kip, there's your uncle Lazo. At least you like *him*. We'll bring you coffee later. Keep you fortified."

~

The torrent of visitors slowed after a couple of days, leaving in their wake an increasing readiness to set off again.

They discussed their plans, lounging in the mostly-organized sitting room one evening. It was still more bare than any of them liked, since the main decorative feature was the many baskets they had been given, but they now had comfortable chairs and a teapot Fitzroy had unearthed in some dusty corner of an old trading store.

"It seems the most practical option would be for us all to take the sky ship to the garrison in north Amboloyo," Ludvic said, spinning a globe of the world they'd been given. "You could go through the gate to Alinor when it next opens, I could then continue on to Solaara. Might stop and see if Conju's ready to return while I'm about it."

The globe did not show the silver lines of the sky ship routes, but Fitzroy knew where he'd placed the Lights that anchored their magics, and they all knew the approximate stops. Cliopher knew that the sky ship routes from Gorjo City went to Jilkano, Solaara, and Lorosh, so to get to Amboloyo would probably mean a slow traverse between Lorosh and Kavanduru.

Not that it would be anywhere near as slow as ocean sailing. He considered the globe, but that *was* the practical, logical, workable option.

Fitzroy gave him a speculative glance. "You look less than enthusiastic, Cliopher."

Cliopher gave him a small, embarrassed smile, and said nothing.

"No," Ludvic said, looking vastly amused. "It's not adventurous enough, is it? For either of you."

"All these years in which Kip valiantly pretended to be reasonable," Fitzroy said, shaking his head, but he was grinning. "His true colours coming out at last."

"That set-down of Lord Lior should have given us all the clues we needed," Ludvic agreed. "Am I right in assuming you want to rejoin your friends and continue with your quest, Fitzroy? Since, as we have discussed, neither of you need to come back to Solaara until you do have your chosen heir. And even then—"

"Yes, yes, Tanaea does indeed sound splendid." Fitzroy shifted in his chair. "Even if she's the right person, I don't think I can handle returning yet, Ludvic."

"I know," he said very simply.

"And there are—I wasn't lying when I sent you the letter—I had a dream, a *vision*, of someone who must be related, in the tower of Harbut Zalarin on Colhélhé —and there's—" He stopped. Cliopher had not told anyone, not even Ludvic, about the Sun's message to his penultimate descendant, so Ludvic merely regarded him with steady, patient curiosity. Fitzroy heaved a sigh and gestured vaguely in the air. "The Sun told Kip that I have a daughter by the Moon, Ludvic."

"Ah."

That was all Ludvic said, but he leaned forward and placed his hand on Fitzroy's knee. "Of course you want to find her."

"I don't know if she has power—though how could she not, a daughter of the Moon?—or how old she is or—or what her name is—or—or *anything*, Ludvic." Fitzroy's voice caught, and he gestured more wildly. "I don't know *anything* about her. I didn't even know she *existed* until Kip told me." He took a deep breath, his eyes bright, distressed. "She might not have any of the qualities necessary to being a lady magus. She might not *want* to be one. I don't know if I *want* to have a daughter follow after me like that. Kip's worked so hard to dismantle the power and inheritance structures of Astandalas—to hand over the title to my own next of kin would undermine everything Kip's done—everything *we've* done. And it would be *bad poetry*, Ludvic!"

Ludvic captured one of Fitzroy's flailing hands.

Fitzroy looked down, at the way his hand fit into the golden smudges with which he'd marked Ludvic, back when he'd had a heart attack and Ludvic had knelt to save his life, no matter the cost to himself. The grief and guilt flickered in his eyes.

Ludvic met his gaze solemnly, and without saying anything, lifted Fitzroy's hand and pressed it gently to his lips. Fitzroy stilled, regarding him with distraught eyes, and gradually subsided. "There," Ludvic said quietly. "Of course you want to find her. You don't need a *reason*."

"I'm supposed to be looking for my heir, and everyone keeps telling me she's already happily ensconced at the Palace," Fitzroy muttered.

"You can keep looking, even if Tanaea is the one you eventually find. No one's expecting you back for a few more months yet. I promise you we're all doing well. The world is thriving without you."

"Just what every head of state wants to hear, eh, Kip?" Fitzroy muttered, but he was already smiling, and he squeezed Ludvic's hand tightly.

Cliopher watched him carefully, and decided a small prod might be in order to help him regain his equilibrium. "What should we do, then?" Cliopher challenged, softening his tone with a cheerful, engaging smile. "Fitzroy Angursell, the great adventurer: what do we do?"

"To have an adventure?" Fitzroy leaned back in his chair, squeezing Ludvic's hand briefly before he let go. "Well—" He grinned. "My usual advice is to go look for something else entirely."

Ludvic laughed once, sharply. Cliopher considered the tone with which this was said, which was both highly amused and, he was fairly sure, quite earnest, and he said: "Very well, then. Shall we imagine options?"

"I've already gone looking for the Three Mirrors of Harbut Zalarin *and* the long-lost diamond of Gaesion—the Star of the North, you know, Ludvic—or rather, the diamond named after it. But I found those ... rather more quickly than I anticipated," he added, frowning slightly.

"Perhaps something more metaphysical?" Ludvic suggested, but Fitzroy made a face. Ludvic added placidly, "Perhaps not, you've always preferred to express the concrete and permit the metaphorical meanings to be the brilliant surface or hidden depths of your poetry, haven't you?"

Cliopher blinked as any number of things he'd loved about Fitzroy's poetry came into sharp focus by that one statement. Fitzroy himself seemed torn between being very pleased and somewhat despondent with respect to the mention of his poetry, and Cliopher felt his unresolved constellation of ideas come into relation. "That's it," he said. "Let's start with your poetry."

"For the book that was left behind at Basil's inn?" Ludvic said, then shook his head immediately. "No. I know." His voice was sympathetic. "You've not written anything new, have you?"

Fitzroy clearly did not want to answer, but although he dropped his gaze to the pen he was rolling between his fingers, he did not otherwise respond. They both waited him out, and finally he said, "No. I haven't."

Cliopher didn't say anything, and neither did Ludvic. Ludvic put another piece of wood on the fire, as he was closer, and Cliopher carefully nudged his foot against Fitzroy's.

"It's been so long," Fitzroy said, slowly, softly. "I keep feeling the ... spark, but I can't—it won't *catch*. I'll have what I think is a new melody, a few notes—a few words—and it used to be that I could take those and spin out a poem, a song, as easy as ... as breathing, they just *came*. Now it's like ... grasping for a handful of water, a fistful of air."

Cliopher glanced at Ludvic, who was listening closely. "You're a poet, Ludvic. How do you write?" he asked.

Ludvic lifted his shoulders up and down in what was not quite a shrug. "I am very slow," he said. "I must go over the idea in my mind many times before the words come. Once they are set then I can write them down, but it is mostly in my mind first."

"I'm glad you had something to occupy your mind while guarding me," Fitzroy said. "The gods know I wanted to be writing poetry most of the time."

"I was paying attention to the surroundings," Ludvic replied reproachfully. "But when exercising, practicing, that is when I think."

Fitzroy turned expectantly to Cliopher. "Well, then? What brilliant solution do you have for this?" He snapped his fingers, and a shimmer of magic washed through the room. "Magic I can do for the wishing! That used to be the hard work," he murmured, looking at the light gathering, hovering above his palm. "Is that where all my poetry went?"

Cliopher regarded him, but his earlier ideas were coalescing. He turned to Ludvic. "Will you clear a space? Fifteen paces should do it, I reckon."

Ludvic nodded once, unsurprised, unperturbed. "Indeed."

"What are you doing?" Fitzroy said suspiciously, but Ludvic got up to clear one side of the room, shifting a few pieces of furniture (and the omnipresent baskets) out of the way, while Cliopher hurried to the beautiful desk Vinyë had given him. He collected his favourite of the new pens, the gleaming peacock-coloured ink, a sheaf of paper with a pleasing texture, the wooden board he'd set up as a makeshift lap-desk for writing letters, and returned to the sitting room.

Fitzroy's glance went to his writing materials, and then the open space Ludvic had cleared. "Kip," he said, strangulated.

"Fitzroy," said Cliopher, and then, with a challenge in his voice, "My lord."

"That's the *iguana*," Fitzroy returned immediately, closing his hand so the magic winked out. He didn't stand up. "Kip. Kip. *Cliopher*. I don't have a poem in my mind right now."

"Don't you?" Cliopher sang the notes of the melody Fitzroy had been humming when they went to create Navanoa.

"You and your challenge-songs," he grumbled. "That isn't ..."

"Finished?" Cliopher asked innocently, and set up his materials.

Ludvic went over to him and held out his hand until Fitzroy, still grumbling, took it and let him pull him upright. Ludvic positioned him at one end of the open space, and moved Fitzroy's chair out of the way. Fitzroy sighed. "It's not going to work," he said warningly. "I'm out of practice and there's no poetry and it's—*fine*, Ludvic, I'll start pacing—why do you think that will make me feel full of inspiration, Kip? All those years of me dictating the most egregiously boring pronouncements!"

"They weren't egregiously boring," Cliopher declared.

"Yes, but you like censuses. And policies. Legal documents. Grandiloquent imperial pronouncements." Yet Fitzroy had settled into his familiar rhythm of pacing, his stride sure, unhurried, steady.

Cliopher hummed *Aurora* softly, picking a section that consciously, deliberately, exactly matched his fanoa's gait.

The steady four-fold measure had been a flexible tool in Fitzroy's hands, swooping from the broadest comedy up to the highest peaks of beauty; he had played with pattern and rhyme, with variations on the metre—*Aurora* had whole passages of limericks, of clerihews, of doggerel verse, even of prose—all in service to the humour and dignity and fundamental decency of the story of the princess who had been caught in a tower and learned how to free herself with the help of her friends.

"Kip," said Fitzroy, "what are you even writing? I'm not *saying* anything!"

Cliopher was writing *Aurora* from memory, his pen moving easily, steadily, the words flowing from his pen, the beat of Fitzroy's footsteps steady, certain, familiar, beloved.

Aurora, the greatest poem of an age. The copy Saya Dorn had given Cliopher in this very house had been a gift to him; a gift he had given to the community; a gift that had eventually come around to a vision Vou'a gave to Fitzroy, his fanoa; a book Fitzroy had found in a secret cabinet, reminding him of who he was—who he had been—who he could return to being.

"Kip, it's not—you *know* I can't just say 'Oh yes, I am Fitzroy Angursell the Poet, please disregard the entirety of my career as Emperor of Astandalas, it was a temporary aberration under the influence of a family curse, I promise it won't happen again."

"We've made certain it won't happen again," Cliopher agreed.

"You have, at least! Kip Mdang, who told his cousin at the age of fifteen he could run the world better than any emperor—should I be chagrinned that you were right?"

"You were the one who appointed me to my positions."

"I liked you—you looked at me. Then Ludvic did, and Conju, and I started to come back to myself, though of course—of course—not all the way. What a fire you lit, Kip."

The words were falling into a rhythm, not quite metrical, but Fitzroy's hands were starting to move in his familiar expansive gestures, and Cliopher was writing down every word he said, waiting, watching with the steadfast attention of all the years of his service. Ludvic had faded, as the guards knew how to fade, into the background, a calm and sturdy sense of safety, security, strength.

"What do I tell everyone?" Fitzroy said, flinging his hands out as he wheeled at the end of his line and turned back towards Cliopher. "Do I tell the lords of my court that I have spent the entirety of my time playing elaborate games as I watched them at their own—allocating them points or demerits depending on their skill at dancing, at courtship, at espionage? Do I say that I spent half my time making up dirty limericks about them?"

"Did you, my lord?" Cliopher asked demurely.

Demurely, but the challenge was there.

Fitzroy retorted, with magnificent disdain: "There once was a wizard called Dorn, whom no one around here dared scorn, for her familiar companion was *eerily* reptilian—in fact, the only iguana in town!"

Cliopher diligently kept a straight face. Fitzroy glared at him. "Don't you dare immortalize that, Cliopher Mdang. That is probably the worst poetic effort I have ever countenanced. I can hear Jullanar sharpening her editorial pens now."

"I'm sure she'll appreciate the opportunity," he said, quite as placidly as Ludvic, meeting Fitzroy's gaze with as much guilelessness as he could demonstrate while he wrote down their words.

"Show-off!" Fitzroy paced up and down, his steps a little choppier, faster, his eyes flashing, and then he said, "Damn you and your challenge-songs! What do you want of me? A dozen terrible limericks?"

"As you wish, my lord."

"Do you see an iguana? Or worse, Prince Rufus? Now there's an apt subject for a limerick. *The Amboloyan Prince, Rufus*—hmm—*a hero of kicking up a fuss— pompous, dull, boring—we're forever imploring: MUST his speeches be always superfluous?*"

And he was off, up and down the room, his voice rising and falling as he spun words out of nothing, his steps keeping pace with the jaunty rhythm of the limericks, his hands darting through the air as he sought the correct phrase, the perfect rhyme.

Prince Rufus (hero of what might just be Cliopher's new favourite poem) was followed by the rest of the seventeen princes of the provinces of Zunidh, all the way down to *Not a prince but a paramount chief.*

Fitzroy finished the last limerick triumphantly, a gleam in his eye—a challenge as visible as Cliopher's—but Cliopher was focused on his writing, and he refused to laugh.

Fitzroy paused with his weight on the balls of his feet, as if he were about to turn a pirouette and become a crow—or as if he were about to suddenly announce the greatest work of magic since Aurelius Magnus bound his empire into peace.

But it was not magic that was running through Fitzroy's veins now, or only that common, ordinary, splendid magic of words—imagery and rhyme and rhythm—and the disciplined imagination of a great poet who had forced himself to close the door of his heart to protect his soul.

Cliopher looked straight back at his fanoa with a silent *well? Is this where you stop?*

Fitzroy narrowed his eyes, and they held there, perfectly still. Intent. The challenge reverberating in the air between them: the tinder burning brightly. It needed more and larger pieces of wood to burn a proper blaze.

Cliopher knew this man before him better than anyone else in all the Nine Worlds.

He heard a creaking noise, as if someone were coming up the stairs outside, and he registered that Ludvic had moved over to the door, but Fitzroy did not look away, and Cliopher refused to let a distraction defeat him. Ludvic would deal with whatever it was.

"It's like that, is it?" Fitzroy said, in a very low, very imperial-sounding voice, his magic slowly welling up into the room, limning everything with a sense of buzzing urgency, of burgeoning life, of the sudden possibility that everything might come alive and become something new.

"Is it?" Cliopher replied, equally quietly, equally intensely.

They held each other's gazes: the great mage with his golden eyes full of magic, and Cliopher who was an ordinary man but who had looked full upon the face of the Sun and not been blinded.

The air was heavy, heady, full of the scent of fire, of the frankincense Ludvic had burned to clear out the corners, of the lingering fragrance of the jasmine-scented tea they'd been drinking earlier. Cliopher breathed it in, drawing the air deep into his lungs, filling himself with that life, that magic, that challenge.

He had gone to the House of the Sun and brought home a new fire for the world. He had hung a new star in the sky. Perhaps he did not write new music himself, had never found a poem come springing to his mind or his tongue or his hand, had never painted a picture, never shaped a sculpture, never grown a garden.

He had planted the tui tree that grew in the gardens of the Palace, and he had created a world where there was time for food and friends and family and art.

There was so much more art in the world because of him, because of the *room* he had made in people's lives by the stipend, because he had lit the fire that provided them with warmth and shelter and encouragement and food for their hearts.

He held the spark Fitzroy had struck, and he held Fitzroy's eyes.

Fitzroy was glittering and magnificent and every inch an emperor, a folk hero, a *legend.* His voice could have seduced the Moon or half the Nine Worlds into following him. "What, my lord Mdang? An island wasn't enough for you?"

Moving slowly, ceremoniously, each movement weighted with significance, Cliopher set aside the pages of limericks in favour of a blank sheet, and he dipped his pen in the peacock ink, and he waited.

The thunderstorm-heaviness in the air intensified; above them there was a jangle as if the wind had blown through the glass floats in the solarium. The same gust whipped through the room, scattering the limericks and sending a spray of sparks up out of the brazier.

Very deliberately, Cliopher smiled.

Fitzroy uttered one of those words of magic, which made the air ring like the inside of a struck bell, and without moving a step he growled out a line of poetry.

"Hear, O ye children of the sun and of the wind, of the emperor Aurelius called Magnus and his fanoa from across the sea: sing with me of their deeds of magic and daring, their high-hearted courage, their love that crested the very sky, and weep, all you lovers of beauty, for what glory once was in the world."

Oh, thought Cliopher, very clearly: *There it is.*

His pen sang across the paper as a lifetime of repressed poetry came flowing out.

Oh yes, this was it indeed.

∾

The introductory stanza was high tragedy: Cliopher was not at all expecting for Fitzroy to wave his hand in the air, declare there would have to be some historical research, make a turn into romantic comedy, and then swerve straight into erotica.

He managed to keep a straight face through a dozen increasingly hilarious innuendos, supposedly the first conversation between Aurelius and Elonoa'a, until Fitzroy dropped euphemism and began outright description.

Cliopher tried, he really did, but when Fitzroy started to compare the dimensions of El's prick to various kinds of bananas he could not help himself, and sniggered.

Fitzroy raised his eyebrow, but his entire demeanour was full of triumph. "You disagree with the plantain? Trust me."

"To know what is most poetically appealing?"

"That too, of course," Fitzroy replied very serenely.

Cliopher set down his pen. "You cannot mean that the way that sounds. And I cannot believe you're really going to write an erotic scene about them."

"Of course not, Kip," Fitzroy said, his face all guileless innocence. "What do you take me for? I respect both Auri and El far too much to do them such a disservice as that."

"What is this, then?" Cliopher asked, gesturing at the scene. "Were you just trying to make me laugh? Should I take that out?"

"No, no, you mistake me!" Fitzroy's voice was full of barely suppressed mirth. "I am not writing an erotic *scene*. This is going to be an *epic*, Kip. With all the details."

Cliopher stared disbelievingly at him. "You're going to make up an erotic epic about Elonoa'a and Aurelius Magnus."

Fitzroy grinned slyly. "Oh, I'm not making it *up*. I had plenty of time while you were off on your quest to solicit all their stories."

At that moment someone behind him laughed.

Cliopher swung around to see that Aya had come in and had clearly been trying very hard to keep quiet while Fitzroy was composing, but she had lost the battle with her composure when Cliopher lost his. "Please," Aya said, tears streaming down her face, "*please* go on."

"That was Auri," Fitzroy said, and Cliopher rolled his eyes.

But he couldn't keep up even a pretence at severity, not when Fitzroy's whole bearing was relaxed, joyous, *happy*. "You're going to make me scribe the whole thing, aren't you?"

"You did volunteer," his fanoa replied gleefully. "But we are being poor hosts. What can we do for you, Aya?"

"Nothing," Aya said, "*nothing* could be better hospitality than hearing you declaim your new erotic epic about Aurelius Magnus and Elonoa'a. Your *new* poem!" Her eyes were shining, and despite her laughter she was clearly very sincere. "I knew you were Fitzroy Angursell," she added, greatly satisfied. "I *knew* it. And you so carefully didn't deny it."

Cliopher looked down at his pen, cleaning the nib to hide his fading blushes. Aya *had* declared her suspicion—realization, indeed—out loud, to Fitzroy, in Cliopher's presence, and Fitzroy *had* responded with amusement and very circuitous words, and Cliopher had *still* not seen the truth.

"It was all I could do not to fall upon your neck in gratitude," Fitzroy said, with a light tone. "Which would have been a poor reward to you, given the taboos still in effect in the time. However—welcome! Come in!"

"I don't want to interrupt if you're writing—well, I have already, haven't I?" Aya laughed. "My apologies. I was so excited when I got back from Lesuia and Jiano told me you'd come from an adventure to Sky Ocean." She gave a bright, sparkling look at both of them. "The stories are all true, aren't they?"

"Not sure about all of them," Cliopher murmured. "But some of them, yes."

"Don't listen to him," Fitzroy ordered. "Come sit down, Aya."

"With pleasure." She sat down in Ludvic's empty seat. Cliopher gathered together his writing materials and the precious pages of Fitzroy Angursell's first new poetry in decades. Aya was a writer, a novelist, Jiano's wife—Cliopher's own second cousin once removed. He was glad she'd been the one to hear that first glorious outpouring of poetry.

"—No. I was going to ask about Sky Ocean and your poetry, but I must know: did you actually *measure* Elonoa'a's penis?"

"I believe in being as accurate as is poetically appropriate," Fitzroy replied very seriously. "I know you agree—your mysteries are full of excellent detail."

She coloured happily. "All the better for slipping in the misdirections, right? Something *you* know. I can't believe how you hid in plain sight. Perfect."

Fitzroy shrugged, smiling a little wryly. "So yes. I'll probably change it to a more impressive poetic simile—perhaps the pillars of the House of the Sun, eh, Kip?—but I wanted to be sure I'd be accurate. Auri and I had a fun afternoon collecting various bananas to compare."

Aya nodded enthusiastically. "And it was really the length of a plantain, Kip? I mean, are we talking *proper* plantains or, like, a dwarf variety—"

"I was not involved in measuring *anyone's* penis," Cliopher exclaimed in exasperation, which was the point where Ludvic finally broke down into laughter.

~

Fitzroy was unsurprisingly in a high-flying mood, which Cliopher observed with a full heart.

Aya was much better at raunchy repartee than Cliopher had ever been. She and Fitzroy were trading increasingly ridiculous yarns; Aya was cackling wildly and Fitzroy had started to do accents. Ludvic caught Cliopher's eye, and they met near the door. "Shall we get some refreshments?" the guard whispered, just Aya said, "Oh, have you never heard the one about the pearl diver and the fisherman?"

"Is it about Buru Tovo? Because I have a story that probably tops it!"

"Let's go," said Cliopher to Ludvic, and they escaped downstairs, grinning and laughing at each other.

CHAPTER SEVENTY-SIX
AWAY

Toucan and Ghilly came by before Aya left, bearing with them a great pot of fish stew and fresh bread.

"We're not that incapable of cooking," Cliopher said when they arrived.

"We're better," Ghilly replied, taking the tureen over to the dumbwaiter. "Or at least Toucan is—argh!"

This was because the iguana was reclining on the shelf inside the dumbwaiter. It had apparently been asleep, and lifted its head with an extremely jaundiced expression that reminded Cliopher of the Albatross in Sky Ocean.

"Perhaps," Toucan said, "we could just carry the pot upstairs."

"Probably a good idea," Ghilly said. "What did you say you'd named it, Kip? My Lord?" She giggled and did a small curtsy to the iguana, which flicked its tongue out at them. Ludvic silently took the tureen of soup so she could close the dumbwaiter door.

Cliopher opened the outside door for him, just in time for a gust of laughter to reach them.

"Who is that?" Ghilly asked, tilting her head. "I'm sure I've heard that laugh before ..."

"Aya inDovo Delanis is here. With Fitzroy. They're talking about techniques for writing sex scenes," Cliopher said.

"Oh, I can't possibly miss that!" Ghilly said. "Give me the bread, Toucan, you and Kip can bring up the dishes." She darted lightly up the stairs, followed by the phlegmatic Ludvic carrying the pot in one hand.

A glad cry met them, and something Cliopher could not decipher but knew was Fitzroy in full joyous flight.

"Oh, I like him so much," Toucan confessed as they collected the requisite cutlery and dishes. "I knew you loved him—it's been obvious from your letters for *so* long, your great unrequited adoration—don't look like that, you were not nearly as cagey about that as you probably thought you were." Toucan regarded him with a deeply fond smile. Cliopher tried to bear it, rather than turning immediately to the pantry to hide his face. "When we finally understood it was the Lord Emperor we were all ... worried, I guess? Because he *wasn't* Aurelius Magnus, was he?"

"I'm not providing comparative measurements," Cliopher said desperately. "You can get your own banana scale."

"I beg your pardon?" Toucan said. "I am fascinated by what could possibly have led to that response."

Cliopher felt himself go red; Ludvic sniggered. He turned to the pantry, looking for the butter. "Don't ask. Just—don't. Will you grab those bowls, please? Thanks."

"No worries." Toucan set the bowls on a tray, though his expression suggested he might well ask Fitzroy for clarification when Cliopher was out of the room. (So long as Cliopher *was* out of the room.) "So, Kip, we didn't come just to eat the food we brought with us."

"Mm-hmm."

"So beautifully noncommittal! I am so glad I got to see you being *properly* Lord Mdang, by the way, when we came to that open court and you didn't know we were there. It was splendid."

"It feels a long time ago," Cliopher replied honestly, wondering if they even owned five spoons. Well—so long as *someone* didn't mind using a coffee-spoon ... "I'm so glad Fitzroy doesn't want to go back to Solaara yet ... nor does Ludvic or Aioru or anyone think we need to."

"Good! We did want to ask. Ghilly and I, that is. Whether you were going back to Alinor and—and Basil?"

Cliopher nodded. "That's the plan, though we haven't figured out quite *how*. The most logical way is to go with Ludvic on the sky ship to the same place where Rhodin and I crossed over ..."

"Oh goodness no, no, never go the same way *twice*," Toucan exclaimed.

"Have you a better idea?"

"I do, as it happens. Much better." Toucan grinned at him. "But it comes with a price."

Cliopher regarded him warily. "Oh yes?"

"Nothing terrible, don't worry. It's just that you mentioned the concept of faravia ... and Ghilly and I are feeling somewhat overwhelmed by coming back after our journey, so we were thinking of maybe going to the Epalos for a bit ... and then I remembered there was a story my grandfather's told once or twice, about how there's a cave on one of the islands that leads ... somewhere."

"Somewhere."

"Somewhere," Toucan agreed, grinning.

"And the price?"

"Well, it's a cave sacred to the Nevans, so ... we want to come with you."

Cliopher regarded his friend in amazement. "You do? Come on an adventure? With us?"

"I've spent a long time, this last year, wishing I'd been brave enough to visit you in Astandalas, in Solaara, to see all the places I always wanted to see," Toucan said, his voice determined; he seemed tense, as if he felt a need to defend himself, make the argument. "I decided I wasn't going to hold back any more. Ghilly's in agreement. We want to spend time with you—get to know your fanoa better—and I want to see Basil again, Kip. I really do."

"You don't have to justify yourself to me," Cliopher said, and reached out to embrace Toucan. "I'd love to have you and Ghilly come. Bertie, too?"

"No, he and Cora are sorting themselves out. He's agreed to sail us across to the Epalos, whenever we're ready."

Cliopher looked down at the trays, and then up at Toucan, who was smiling radiantly, relieved, almost excited. "He's spontaneous, you know. Might want to leave immediately."

"That's what Bertie said," Toucan agreed. "Kip's come home to himself, *and* Fitzroy Angursell, he said. So we made sure we were all packed before we came over here. Bertie will come by after supper. Just in case."

It took Cliopher and Fitzroy less than two hours to be ready to go, and that included both eating supper, cleaning up the dishes, and saying their farewells to Ludvic and Aya.

"I'll tell your family where you went," Aya said. "They'll listen to me. Probably."

Ludvic nodded phlegmatically. "I'll shut up the house. Make sure the iguana isn't stuck inside the pantry."

"Or the dumbwaiter," Ghilly murmured.

"Do we need to feed the iguana?" Cliopher asked.

"I don't see why," Fitzroy called down from the solarium, where it sounded as if he were throwing things around with abandon. He stuck his head down the stairwell so his voice would be clearer. "We weren't feeding it before we came, and all it's wanted has been to steal our fruit and prevent our full access to the bathing facilities."

"A grave crime," Aya said.

"You have no idea," Cliopher replied, sighing, and winked at her. The twice-daily battles Fitzroy had with the iguana over the bath were one of his favourite things about living in the house.

(The iguana had refused to go with Louya, and did not seem particularly interested in either Ludvic or Cliopher, which Ludvic hypothesized was due to Fitzroy's magic. The question of whether Rhodin, who had a minor gift at magic, would be equally beset had given them all much anticipatory amusement.)

"What about the house next door?" Ludvic asked. "Do we have to do anything about that?"

Aya looked immediately interested, and so Cliopher had to explain how he'd traded his vaha from Sky Ocean for the neighbours' house.

"And why would you do that?" Aya asked.

"They were quite convincing about the point that I didn't really need *two* vaha," he said, and then, when Aya simply regarded him with an expression that she probably gave her children (and which reminded him that she'd been one of those secretly teaching Fitzroy Islander without *telling him*), he added, "And they've agreed to let Cora and the Nevans and anyone else who's interested look at the construction."

"That explains your *choice* of which boat to trade, but not why you wanted their house."

"They were quite insistent that that was the terms of exchange. I'm not sure they were particularly thrilled at the number of visitors we've already had, not to mention our likely future ... houseguests."

Aya tilted her head, and started to smirk. "Kip Mdang, did you acquire a house so the Red Company could live next door?"

"I'd better get the rest of my things together," he claimed, and hastened out of the room before the full eruptions of laughter from Aya and Ghilly (traitor as she was) could get too loud.

Cliopher did not actually have very many things he wanted to take with him: the new notebook, two pens, a bottle of ink, a couple of books to read, a tin of tea, several new tunics to go with his trews, a comb, and the box in which he'd been accumulating small gifts for Basil, Sara, and Clio. He'd added some excellent coffee in for Rhodin, who'd been somewhat disparaging of the brews available on Alinor.

Ludvic followed him into the room with Vinyë's desk, where they could be assured of a certain degree of privacy, and he asked Cliopher, hesitantly, quietly, to tell Rhodin about Masseo.

Ludvic also gave his permission for both Cliopher and Fitzroy to tell Masseo about *him*, if his father should ask for stories of this son he had never known.

"Is there anything you want me to avoid saying?" Cliopher asked, thinking of how difficult it had been for his friend to tell him of the lonely, difficult path that led ultimately to here.

"I trust you," Ludvic said, very simply. "And *him*."

"Fitzroy," Cliopher murmured, gently teasing.

Ludvic smiled. "Fitzroy."

~

In the two days it took them to sail to the Epalos, Fitzroy dictated several more pages of spectacularly filthy poetry at Cliopher, played his harp at the request of Ghilly and Toucan, persuaded Cliopher to join him in singing a few of the songs they had learned from the crew of the *He'eanka*, and informed Cliopher that no matter how splendid all that fresh air and sublime simplicity of the vaha had been, there was something to be said for coffee.

"And bathing facilities," Cliopher agreed. It was the second morning, and he had to admit it had been splendid sleeping safe in the knowledge that Bertie was in charge of the boat and its sails.

"Fruit," Fitzroy added. "And beer."

Cliopher could take or leave the beer, but he was enjoying the game. "Company."

Fitzroy tilted his head. "Beds."

"Fresh water."

"And writing materials."

They were still grinning at each other when Toucan came yawning into the kitchen, where they were admiring the bubbling percolator and the aroma of fine, freshly ground Vangavayen beans. Toucan ran his hand through his hair, making it stand up, and said, cautiously, "Am I awake enough to know why you're grinning like that? It's not more poetry, is it? Should I fetch Ghilly?"

(Ghilly was utterly fascinated by both the process of dictation and the resultant verse. More than once, the day before, she'd expressed amazement at the idea that she could *watch*—or rather listen—to what would undoubtedly become a famous poem coming into existence.

"It's like watching a seed grow, or a flame," she said, and then her face softened as she glanced at Cliopher, who undoubtedly looked almost as choked-up as he felt at that description. "It's wonderful, Kip.")

"No, no," Fitzroy said. "We were just comparing the decadent conditions of this yacht to the traditional vaha."

"I am so grateful not to be eating *only* fish and coconuts," Cliopher said heartily.

"That's not fair, Kip, we had an extravagant stash of fermented breadfruit."

"And taro, dried mango, and sago."

"Not that we actually ate much of the sago."

"Ugh," Toucan said, and took out his cup. "I think I like a more luxurious form of travel, myself."

They poured themselves their coffee, doctored it with sugar and cream to their satisfactions (and that was another great luxury—fresh cream!), and took themselves onto the deck. The sails luffed pleasantly, and Ghilly, whose turn it was on watch, waved from the wheel.

"It's varied, adventuring," Fitzroy said, leaning against the railing and smiling down at the pod of dolphins that had emerged to accompany their progress. He hummed a few bars, from a song Cliopher half-knew. It was all so beautiful, the fresh, clear air of the morning, the distant humps of the nearest islands of the Epalos group already visible, the dawn wind playing with his hair. "Food, and beds, and conditions generally, I mean. Sometimes you're sleeping outside, and sometimes you're the guest of a great lord."

He grinned at Cliopher. "And sometimes you're the guest of a great lord *and* you're sleeping outside."

"I'm only a great lord because you insisted," Cliopher replied.

"One of the greatest joys of my life was the expression on your face when I asked you if you wanted to be Duke of Ikiano and you refused with language that would make a sailor blush."

Cliopher rolled his eyes. "And *have* you managed to make Bertie blush yet?"

"Eventually," Fitzroy replied complacently, and sipped his coffee. "We both learned a few new words after you went to bed."

⁓

The island Toucan's grandfather had told him of was one of the small uninhabited islands tucked away to the northwest of the group. Bertie sailed them at a safe distance from Ve'ea, the central hub of the Epalos and the largest community after Gorjo City in the Ring.

"Would we find ourselves embroiled in Mdangs?" Fitzroy asked curiously, looking at the white buildings climbing up the slopes of the harbour at Ve'ea.

"No, it's my relatives we're avoiding this time," Toucan said, chuckling. "Just keeping things simple. Do you need anything?" he added abruptly. "I've got to help Bertie with the course. We've got another hour, hour and a half, maybe, then it's finding the cave and seeing where it actually goes."

"I'll be able to assist with that," Fitzroy assured him, and Toucan nodded and went aft.

Cliopher settled down more comfortably in the long chair under the shade awning. "This is incredible," he said softly. "I'd dreamed ..."

Fitzroy gave him a quick glance, then slumped back dramatically in his own lounger; but Cliopher could see the small smile on his face. "So had I."

"What do we say, when we come back to your friends?"

"What do you want to say, to Rhodin and Basil?"

Cliopher considered. "The truth, I suppose. That's what I said in my letter ... if it arrived."

"So little faith in the postal system," Fitzroy murmured, his smile growing. He stretched out, one hand brushing lightly against Cliopher's shoulder as he brought his hands behind his head. He was wearing one of his new tunics, a rich violet cotton, the colour almost luminous against his skin. His eyes were half-lidded.

Cliopher wriggled his toes. "This really *is* much more comfortable, isn't it?"

"No need to prove anything to *me*," Fitzroy murmured. He sounded half-asleep. "Nor anyone."

"No," Cliopher said, as simply as Ludvic, as solidly, as certain of himself as he had ever been of his ke'ea. His islands burned in his heart: Loaloa that had always been his (and never, for all that, quite been *home*), Navanoa that was nothing yet but bare rock and possibility ... and Gorjo City that was no island at all, but nevertheless his. "No, I don't."

"What we do need to do," Fitzroy said thoughtfully, "is start our efanoa."

"We need a cord of some form," Cliopher said softly.

"I've been working on it." Fitzroy dropped his hand down to the side of his chair, where he'd set his small bag of necessities. Cliopher watched as he drew out something that looked like nothing so much as a handful of thundercloud, complete with lightning.

"Yes?" Cliopher found it hard to take his eyes from the mass, even as Fitzroy seemed to be resolving it into separate strands. The only thing he had ever seen that seemed anything like its simultaneous nearness and distance had been the Sun's great flame.

"These are the shadows and starlight I have been spinning, the way Vou'a taught me," Fitzroy said.

"They're magnificent," Cliopher said honestly. The threads coiled in Fitzroy's hands like the shining, shimmering strings for his harp. "I wonder if you could string your harp with them, too?"

Fitzroy laughed. "*These* are earmarked for our efanoa, Kip, but now that you say it ... A harp strung with starlight and shadow sounds very fine, doesn't it?"

"Superb," Cliopher replied. He reached out, and was surprised that he *could* touch the strands. They felt like a shadow across his skin, but the dark threads moved when he tugged them.

Fitzroy gently pulled apart the mass to show a glimmering golden coil in the centre. "These are spun from your star, as the light came through the glass fishing floats ..."

He must have awoken while Cliopher slept ... Perhaps, Cliopher thought, it was the soft, regular thrum of Fitzroy's spindle that had allowed him to sleep so deeply and well, on those piles of cushions in the solarium.

"We could braid them," Cliopher said, brushing his fingertips very lightly over the silvery-gold threads. It was easy to imagine how beautiful they would be against Fitzroy's dark skin, the white and scarlet shell in the hollow at the base of his throat.

"Yes. Or perhaps there's a way to twine them?" Fitzroy frowned. "I feel as if there's something called plying that might be what we want ..."

"I never got that far with spinning." He grinned and gestured at Toucan, who was standing near the bow of the ship with Ghilly, pointing at something in the water. "You could ask the nearest Nevan."

Fitzroy tsked fondly at him. "Since the string is *my* contribution, I'll ask my own lore-keeper, if you don't mind? Jullanar will know."

Now Cliopher could look up at him, and smile at the shy delight, the mild anxiety, in his fanoa's expression. "This is wonderful, Fitzroy. And of course we can ask Jullanar's help. She's part of your family, your culture ... our lives."

Fitzroy's eyes were brilliant, and he dropped the strands of shadows and starlight into his lap, so he could reach out, apparently unable to stop himself, and take Cliopher's hands in his.

Cliopher's hands were warm, and Fitzroy's were cool, as if he'd dipped them into the water. "Look at us," Fitzroy said softly. "How far we've come together, Cliopher."

"All the way to the sky and back."

Fitzroy lifted his hands and pressed his lips to the back of Cliopher's knuckles. "All the way home."

～

Bertie's yacht had too deep a draft—or the island too shallow a slope—to get very close to shore, so they lowered his small canoe and used it to ferry themselves and their belongings to shore. Toucan and Ghilly had sizeable rucksacks, and Ghilly had excavated a walking stick from some cunningly hidden closet on the boat.

"I don't need to be playing the hero," she told Cliopher defiantly, who had in fact been admiring her forethought, and told her so. "Oh!—Well, that too!" She grinned. "We're really going on an adventure with the *real* Fitzroy Angursell!"

"We are," Cliopher replied, laughing.

"I'll see you for the Jubilee, if not before, then," Bertie rumbled, and embraced them one by one in turn. He didn't hesitate before engulfing Fitzroy, but Cliopher saw by the working of his eyebrows as he turned away that he had not been quite so sanguine as he'd appeared.

"Fair winds and gentle seas, Bertie," Cliopher said, the words those Elonoa'a had told him. "Thank you for the lift."

"Any time, I told you," Bertie replied, harrumphing, and climbed into the rowboat so he could return to his yacht.

They watched him until he'd used the pulley to hoist the canoe back into place, and then, as he moved to reset the sails and prepare to return home, they turned to the jungle.

"I suggest we go this way," Fitzroy said, from where he'd been conferring with Toucan. "There are two caves, but there is a Border that way."

None of them could dispute that certainty, but Cliopher, at least, felt a shiver run up his back. Fitzroy seemed entirely serene and unconcerned, but then, this was the sort of situation he clearly revelled in.

There was a narrow path that started between two huge breadfruit trees. Toucan led the way, Fitzroy behind him with Ghilly and Cliopher bringing up the rear. Ghilly was grinning with an excitement delightful to see, and Cliopher hummed softly to himself as he enjoyed walking through the familiar jungle.

After about half an hour they came to a steep hill, where a waterfall plunged down into a deep, crystal-clear pool. The place was ethereally beautiful, overhung with flowers, vines, the huge, beautiful leaves of half a dozen shrubs, colourful butterflies with iridescent blue or purple or golden-green wings fluttering in clouds, long-tongued honeyeaters chuckling as they dipped from blossom to blossom.

"Oh, let's rest here a minute," Ghilly said. "If that's allowed, Toucan?"

"Yes, so long as we don't go in the pool," Toucan said. "We can drink the water in the cascade, but the pool itself is sacred."

"And the cave?" Fitzroy murmured; his eyes were luminous, and his attention was clearly on the magic. "We're close. I can feel the Border ..." He took in a deep, deep breath, as if he were tasting the air. "Alinor and ... Colhélhé, conceivably, tangled together. Well done, Toucan."

"I know where the opening is," Toucan said, looking extremely pleased with himself.

They drank from the cascade out of their cupped hands, laughing as the spray cooled their hot faces and sprayed their dusty feet. There were a few insects buzzing around, but Fitzroy absently waved them off; being a mage, the insects *stayed* waved off.

Now that was a luxury. Rhodin had had to apply himself with much more effort to keep the flies off them when they'd been riding through Fiellan.

It was good to think they would be reunited with Rhodin soon. *And* Basil. Cliopher watched as Fitzroy and Toucan discussed the best way to get to the Border quietly, while Ghilly had taken a short walk.

Cliopher stirred and investigated the basket of provisions they'd brought, using the metal knife he'd acquired in Gorjo City to cut a few banana leaves into appropriately-sized platters. Picnic foods: stuffed hand-pies, dumplings, fruit, smoked fish. They had enough for a day or two; Fitzroy had said, airily, that they would undoubtedly find *something* after that.

Ghilly returned with a tiarë flower tucked behind her ear and another for each of them. "There's a thicket of them over there," she said, handing the flowers out. "There, Fitzroy, that's a proper Islander look."

"Proper for Tisiamo," Toucan murmured, but he was smiling. "No, Fitzroy, you put it behind your left ear if you're single—your right if you're taken."

Fitzroy gave Cliopher a very brilliant look and carefully moved the flower to his right ear.

Cliopher felt a wash of some nameless emotion—some indescribable wonder, some intense humility, some astonishing gratitude, some sort of awe. He blinked hard, unable to prevent the smile, the dawning joy, from showing on his face.

"Don't hurt yourself," Toucan whispered. "He'll still be there tomorrow."

~

While Toucan was making a small offering to the sacred pool, Fitzroy held his harp in one hand and played an unfamiliar rippling passage.

"Do I need to take notes?" Cliopher asked him quietly.

Fitzroy beamed at him. "No! It's starting to flow, Kip."

"I am happy to take dictation for as long as you want me to."

"And I am glad for it," he assured him, before his smile turned almost sly. "Although I can imagine that there might be parts of my new epic I'd like to keep a surprise ..."

Given the lovingly explicit passages Fitzroy had seen fit to dictate for the very opening of the poem, Cliopher wasn't sure he wanted to know what, exactly, his fanoa meant. "I am sure I'll enjoy it whenever I read it," he said.

"Are you coming?" Toucan called; beside him, Ghilly was giggling.

Cliopher realized he and Fitzroy were standing very close together, and he rolled his eyes at her before following after.

The path wound behind several dwarf bananas with brilliant blue flowers, their huge leaves disguising a rocky outcropping with a narrow passage between the boulders. The island was a raised coral atoll with extrusions of some much-folded sedimentary rock; this part seemed to be limestone, though Cliopher did not know enough about geology to be able to tell any more than that.

A few steps away from the entrance the narrow passage opened up into a kind of atrium: they stood at the edge of a deep grotto, open to the sky above them and full of ferns and other shade-loving plants. Toucan stopped them before they entered the atrium.

"This is a sacred place," he said quietly. "I obtained permission from the elders to bring you through, but please don't stray off the path or touch anything. Fitzroy, is the Border down there?"

Fitzroy's eyes were gleaming more brightly than the dim light would seem to permit. Magic, Cliopher thought, his heart beginning to beat a little faster at the thought. It was not that he was unfamiliar with magic, or even with Fitzroy's magic ... but it was always exciting to see it at work.

"Yes," Fitzroy murmured. "Not *very* far, but down there, somewhere."

"Very good," Toucan said. "Usually we would light a torch, but I was told ..." He shook his head. "Will you trust me? There is a section that the uninitiated should not see. I know the way, if you'll trust me to guide you through the dark. Then when I say, Fitzroy can light the way with magic."

"Of course," Fitzroy said.

"This first part, down the hill, you can keep your eyes open," Toucan instructed, and led them down a steep path that zigzagged into the bowl of the grotto. At the bottom there was a pool, very still and very clear, with what seemed to be dozens of nautilus shells laying on its bottom.

"Don't stop," said Toucan, ushering them past the pool, past columns of hewn coral, others of black basalt, and Cliopher, following behind him, felt as if he'd turned a corner in a familiar house and discovered a door he'd never seen before.

The path led them into another cave, this one more of a tunnel, with a level, sandy floor. The light did not reach far: Cliopher was reminded irresistibly of the cave on Vou'a's island.

"It's level and straight," Toucan assured them. "Nothing to fall into. I've been through this part before."

"A relief," Fitzroy murmured.

"Perhaps we could hold hands?" Ghilly suggested. She grimaced. "I don't really like caves."

"They're not my favourite either," Fitzroy said, and moved his harp over his shoulder so he could reach out for Cliopher on one side and Ghilly on the other. Ghilly gave Toucan her walking stick and took his other hand, and thus, with the scent of tiarē in a cloud around them, disguising any hint of stone or water or rust or rot, they went into the dark.

It could not have been more than a quarter-hour later when Toucan stopped and told Fitzroy he could raise a light.

Cliopher had listened intently as their footsteps echoed: first through an enclosed passage, then they had entered some sort of great cavern, then a series of smaller chambers, and now they were in a space that sounded quite large, if not as large as the first cavern.

Fitzroy hummed a soft note, and a faint, warm light began to shine from nowhere in particular. It stayed dim and faint for a considerable time, long enough for their eyes to adjust and see they stood in what looked almost like the Sea-Witch's corn-filled hall.

The pillars here were not wood nor carved by hands: they were great conical stalactites and stalagmites reaching towards each other from ceiling and floor, the white limestone forming bead by bead at their tips.

"This is as far as I have ever come," Toucan said in a hushed voice. "We know of the door that leads ... *somewhere*, there are old stories of people who have gone—and a few who have *come*—this way, but no one for many years."

Fitzroy let his light strengthen, and he turned around, face intent, head tilted, looking or listening for something only he could sense.

"How interesting," he murmured. "There is a sense—very distant—of something that is *almost* Voonra ... there must be a fold of the Borderlands muffling it." He gestured vaguely to the left, downhill, and then turned more resolutely to the right, uphill, from where a soft draught was blowing. "This way there is Alinor and perhaps a way to Colhélhé, if one found the right key. I can guide us."

"Where on Alinor will we end up?" Ghilly asked, her eyes wide; she had tucked herself against Toucan's side, so her husband could put his arm around her shoulder for comfort. "It's good to have the light," she said, more to herself. "Toucan, you'll be able to find your way home? If we come this way back?"

"If," Toucan murmured, but he turned to the cavern mouth behind them and considered it for a moment. "There are other openings here, yes," he said. "Perhaps— a symbol?"

"The Nevan family symbol," Cliopher suggested.

Toucan nodded, and fumbled in his bag until he could pull out a small pouch that turned out to contain some art supplies. "I have this fantastic ochre from— where was it, Ghilly? Amboloyo?"

"You got it in Boloyo City but I think it came from Northern Dair or Mgunai or somewhere like that."

"That's right, inland Mgunai." Toucan unfolded a rag from a length of a deep red ochre. He considered a moment, then drew the inverted vee and curving third line of the Nevan's symbol. "You know," he said, adding two straight lines across the bottom with a flourish, "I'd never realized just how *much* this is clearly a traditional sail until I saw your vaha, Kip."

"It's the whole vaha," Cliopher said, realization dawning, as he pointed to the two lines. "There are the keels. It's just very stylized." The Nevans Tied The Sails—and wove them, too, very often; the fenà spun everything from threads to fishing lines to anchor ropes.

"Clear enough for any Islander coming this way, at least," Toucan said, and tucked away the ochre again. "And now for the Shaian method."

"That's me," said Fitzroy, and led them unhesitatingly through the stalagmites.

They were not long in that cave, insofar as Cliopher could tell the time. Not even long enough for him to get bored enough to hum the *Lays* (or *Aurora*); by the time he felt confident in keeping his footing on the wet, uneven surface, Fitzroy had turned to a side passage and suggested to Toucan that he draw a unicorn with his ochre to indicate it led to Alinor.

Toucan's unicorn looked rather more like a rhinoceros from the Imperial Menagerie in Solaara than it did a horse, but Fitzroy shrugged and said it would probably do the trick for any lost souls coming through these caves in the Borderlands between worlds.

The passage to Alinor was narrower, but no narrower than a corridor in a house, and Fitzroy's warm magic was very helpful. It was comforting to reflect that if the stones shifted he could probably prevent a landslide.

Before Cliopher could work himself up about the possibility of a landslide blocking them forevermore in the cave system, the passage ended.

"It's a door," Ghilly said blankly.

"So it is," Fitzroy replied, his voice full of bright interest. "A wooden door. With a handle and everything." He reached out and depressed the latch; the door swung silently open. "And not even locked."

They all pressed through, curiosity far stronger than any sense of discretion or danger.

It could have opened onto anything—a prison or a palace, a roof or a forest or a barn—but what it opened upon was a cellar.

And not just any cellar. Cliopher took five steps past an array of ancient, dusty barrels, and then even above the scent of the tiarë he could smell honey.

"It's Basil's inn," he said. "I'm sure of it."

"No way," Toucan said flatly. "How does that even work?"

"Wild magic serendipity," Fitzroy said happily. "Ask your wife, we've been talking about all the theories I know, none of which can possibly be correct! Do you hear something?"

They all went obediently silent, and clearly heard the sound of a door opening—distant music and the sound of voices and laughter poured through—and then feet thumping loudly down stairs on the other side of the room, hidden behind the stack of barrels.

"That sounds like Clio," Cliopher said, and walked forward to where his nephew was squatting in the area where Basil had taken Cliopher once, frowning down at the floor.

"Looking for something?" Cliopher asked casually, leaning on a support column.

"Dad left his keys somewhere, so Mum's sending me *everywhere* to look for them and I'm missing the party—" Clio stopped looking under the sink and looked slowly and suspiciously up. "Uncle Kip?"

CHAPTER SEVENTY-SEVEN
COMING HOME

They found the keys—or rather Ghilly did; she said she'd always had the knack of seeing the very obvious, since they were sitting in plain view beside the barrel of ginger wine—and Clio excitedly gave them a very confused synopsis of the past month since Fitzroy and Cliopher had disappeared on their adventure.

"And now it's harvest-tide so we're having a grand festival in the village," he concluded. "Everyone's out on the green. There's dancing. Do you need a room first?" he added as they went up the stairs. "Uncle Kip and, er, Dad said I shouldn't call you Uncle Fitzroy but you are, aren't you? More or less?"

Fitzroy, visibly choked up, nodded speechlessly.

Clio nodded with complete unconcern for upending someone's world. "Great. *I* thought so. Anyway, your rooms are as you left them, well, not exactly, because we did go in and dust and stuff, but your things are all there if you want to get changed or anything—"

Never one to miss a bathing opportunity, Fitzroy agreed readily. Cliopher laughed, but he felt dusty and grimy after their passage through the caves, and so they parted ways at the stairs, Clio to take Toucan and Ghilly to a room, Fitzroy and Cliopher to theirs.

"That was remarkably convenient," Cliopher said to Fitzroy. "Did you know that passage was there?"

"I knew Zunidh was somewhere nearby," Fitzroy replied with a shrug and a smile. "You did, too—you pointed straight to that door when I asked you where your island was, you know."

"Home," said Cliopher, smiling. "I'll see you out there?"

"Flower behind my ear and all. Promise." Fitzroy nodded and went into his room, and Cliopher turned to his. At least no one could see him smiling like a lovesick teenager.

(He'd never been a lovesick teenager. He'd only mooned over Fitzroy Angursell's poetry and the love Elonoa'a bore for Aurelius Magnus, and sworn that one day he would have a fanoa of his own. And—inconceivable fact—he *did*.)

His oboe was tidily in its case, and the bed was made. Before he could wish for it, Clio bustled back in with a fresh ewer of warm water. "I told Mum you're here, Uncle Kip! Dad's out on the green and most everyone else is dancing or eating, but I saw Auntie Jullanar and she knew something was up."

"That's great," Cliopher replied, meaning it.

Clio hesitated, mooching around the window and fiddling with the curtain. "Uncle Kip, I've been thinking. While you were gone."

Cliopher looked at him, decided that his nephew mostly wanted a listening but not too obviously expectant ear, and therefore moved around the room, looking for the clothes he'd left there. If there were a party down in the green—and if he and Fitzroy were announcing they were fanoa—(and both of those things were true)—well. Perhaps it *was* a good thing that Féonie and Franzel and Conju had insisted he bring half court costume with him. Just in case.

The garments had been cunningly wrapped in tissue paper around a small case that turned out to contain jewellery. Cliopher set the bundle on the bed. "Go on, Clio," he said casually, keeping his body relaxed, open, slightly turned towards his nephew in unspoken encouragement.

"Well ... I was thinking how I really liked learning the *Lays* from you," Clio began.

Cliopher hummed, the tissue paper rustling as he unfolded each delicate layer. The familiar fragrance of the orange-blossom water rinse they used at the Palace wafted up, and he felt a momentary prickle of tears for the thought of the care with which Féonie and the rest of his household there had treated him.

"And I've always liked hearing the stories from Dad about you, and your dreams, and ..." Clio trailed off, scuffling a bit with his feet on the carpet. Cliopher nodded and separated the garments.

Half court costume involved a long tunic, quite closely fitting, with one or sometimes two layers of robes above it, and—at least for someone of Cliopher's rank—also a mantle overtop.

"That's beautiful, Uncle Kip," Clio said, leaving his intense examination of the curtain to come look at the clothes. "Are you changing into that for the party?"

"I thought I might, yes."

His nephew nodded, reaching out to stroke the mantle. "What kind of fabric is this?"

"That's ahalo cloth, from the Vangavaye-ve. The fringe is foamwork." Cliopher grinned at him. "It's a bit extravagant but that's what happens when you end up acting head of state. Traditionally paramount chiefs might wear it, or very respected lore-keepers."

Clio tilted his head, very like his mother, and then he straightened his shoulders and faced Cliopher squarely. "Uncle Kip, I have been thinking while you were gone," he said again, as if it were a rehearsed speech, "and I would very much like to sit at your feet and learn to be tanà."

Cliopher set down the tunic. "Would you now?" he replied softly.
"I would."

Buru Tovo had grunted and said, "We'll see," when the twelve-year-old Kip had asked him the same. He'd taught Cliopher—taught him well—but he'd left it to Cliopher to learn the lesson that he needed to step back, look at the wider picture, figure out what he was *really* being taught.

Cliopher had tried that, with a few of his earlier secretaries and other underlings, as he gained people in his offices and departments and ministries. It had been so very much easier to *teach* them how to step back, look at the wider picture, figure out what else was going on. He'd learned, too, that people generally liked to know what they were learning and why, and tended to learn better if they were told; those who were stubborn enough to persevere without that were rare.

There were many things he had learned from his Buru Tovo, and one of them was that Cliopher was not the tanà he was, and would not be that kind of tana-tai, either.

He left the superlative court costume on the bed and embraced Clio formally, forehead to forehead, and then, standing back, kissed him on the forehead as well. "I would be honoured to have you sit at my feet, Clio el Mdang White," he said.

His nephew gave him a wide smile, hugged him tightly around the middle, whispered, "Thank you! I won't disappoint you, you'll see!" into his chest, and then darted out of the room calling "Mum! Mum! Mum! He said *yes!*"

Clio thus missed the sight of Cliopher having to wipe away his own tears, but that was all right. He would undoubtedly see Cliopher overwhelmed again soon enough.

～

The half court costume consisted of brilliant white muslin for the long tunic, with embroidery in the Mdang family designs on the cuffs and hems and up the long front of the garment. Over it Cliopher put on two robes of diaphanous silk: royal blue set with white seed pearls in the tigers and waves pattern that Féonie had devised to be his court design, with electrum and sapphire fastenings holding the robe closed. Above the royal blue he wore an open gold-shot bronze silk with golden pearls and bronze and blue embroidery once more in the Mdang patterns.

The mantle was ahalo cloth in glowing scarlet with a faint shifting shimmer of white-gold and orange-bronze, just the colour of a flaring ember.

His cousin Clia, who was an assessor in the ahalo cloth warehouse, had sent the bolt to him specifically, to be used, she said, 'For some grand costume where you can thumb your nose at everyone'—and *that* had been long before she could have had any knowledge of Fitzroy's true identity!

Unless, he thought as he did up the electrum fastenings of the lower robe, Aya had talked about her suspicions, and his family had somehow managed to avoid passing that juicy gossip on to him. He would have thought that impossible, but they *had* managed to keep Bertie and Ghilly and Toucan's voyage from him, so they could keep a secret if properly motivated.

Regardless, here was the scarlet, just the colour for the Red Company and for the first shell on his efanoa, strung on a narrow braid of golden starlight until they could ask Jullanar for further instruction.

Féonie had made him a pair of dress boots in the old Astandalan style to wear with the garment should he need to be out in, as she put it, inclement conditions. The boots were of a supple leather, dyed deep blue to match the robe.

He brushed his hair, tucked the feathers behind his ear, replaced the tiarë flower behind the *other* ear, and took a deep breath.

He didn't have any more than a hand mirror in his bedroom, but even though his garments did not sit *quite* perfectly—he had put on muscle in his shoulders and back after all that time sailing—the ahalo cloth mantle would hide that, and he was sure he looked good.

He set the mirror down on the desk under the window, beside the brush, beside his lovely, perfect writing case, and gripped the back of the chair.

His heart was fluttering in his throat. Basil knew what it meant to him, what this would mean to him, for Cliopher to come downstairs with the tiarë behind his right ear, another efela around his neck, the light of Sky Ocean still clinging, just a little, to him.

Before he could work himself up, there came a quiet knock on his door. "Come in," he called, turning from the desk, though he stopped halfway through the motion when Fitzroy came in.

His fanoa had also changed into finery: a silver-spangled blue velvet outfit that must have been the one he'd worn so precipitously landing in Masseo's village to answer that postulant nun's prayers and be taken for Aurelius Magnus come again.

The silver-gold ribbon of starlight and the red and white shell looked just as striking against his throat as Cliopher could possibly have imagined. And his eyes ... oh, his eyes were burning-brilliant, just the colour of the heart of the flame of the Sun in Cliopher's fire-pot.

"Fitzroy," he said unsteadily, gripping the chair.

"Kip." Fitzroy looked him up and down, frankly appreciative, and let the door swing shut behind him as he came into the middle of the room. "Cliopher Lord Mdang, Viceroy of Zunidh and tana-tai of the Wide Seas Islanders."

"Your fanoa," said Cliopher, drunk on the tiarë blossom behind Fitzroy's ear, the feel of the garments against his skin, the cool air, the joy in his heart.

"What did you say yes to Clio about?"

"He asked to sit at my feet. Learn to be the next tanà."

"Ah!" Fitzroy smiled, the brilliance in his face tempered with the softness of affection, of love. "I'm very happy for you."

"Yes. I am too. We're here and ... he's here, and Basil's here, and *your* friends are here, and so are Toucan and Ghilly and Sara and Rhodin, and Ludvic—and Conju is happy for us, too."

Fitzroy laughed lowly. "He is certainly very enthusiastic about our hair."

"Yes."

"I didn't just come in to see if you were ready," Fitzroy said, after a moment. He was fiddling with his signet ring, and looked, for a moment, very like Clio with the curtain fringe. "I had a thought."

But Fitzroy was not Clio. Cliopher did not need to pretend he was only half-listening so he wouldn't spook. Cliopher could smile, and look him straight in the eye, and wait with patience and joyful anticipation.

"I have been thinking," Fitzroy said, "that even with my adding the threads to our efanoa, it is still very much an Islander custom." He paused; Cliopher nodded. "And so," he went on, "I have been thinking what could be part of *my* culture, to show ... perhaps not exactly the same thing, because we do not have a concept for fanoa ..." He trailed off, and then smiled, almost smirked. "Not *yet*, that is. We shall see the effect of my epic about Auri and El."

"Fayna is a Shaian word," Cliopher pointed out.

"I'll be sure to clarify the manifold and various meanings of fanoa," Fitzroy replied lightly. He bounced slightly on his feet, and then came over the remaining few steps to stand right in front of Cliopher. He put his right hand on Cliopher's, still gripping the chair back. "Kip, Cliopher, my dear friend, my fanoa ... the other half of my heart, my mirror and my match, my right hand ..." He smiled. "You are all these things and more, and I want nothing more than to share the rest of my life with you, unless it be to tell everyone else about how wonderful you are."

Cliopher laughed, because otherwise he would cry, and he knew Féonie would be very sad if he let his tears spot his superlative clothes.

"None of that," Fitzroy chided him gently. "I've got handkerchiefs galore—Jullanar's influence, you know." He grinned and produced one, though he did not hand it over immediately. "But first: Kip Mdang, I would like you to have this, as a token of my esteem, a promise of my affection, an affirmation of my readiness to follow your star wherever you wander with it, an acknowledgement of my willingness to raise an island for you whenever you need one, and ..." Fitzroy took a deep breath. "And a statement of something I have never quite dared say in its full simplicity before, which is that I love you."

Before Cliopher could say anything—before Cliopher could *do* anything—Fitzroy tugged off his signet ring and placed it on the palm of Cliopher's hand.

Cliopher looked at his fanoa. "That's the Imperial Seal," he said, but even without looking down he had closed his hand around the ring. It was warm in his hand from Fitzroy's body-heat, his inner fire.

"It is," said Fitzroy. "And you know very well that there is not another person in all the Nine Worlds and the lands beyond whom I would trust with it."

"I don't know what to say," Cliopher said, knowing his face and his heart were both open as the proverbial shell on the beach.

Now Fitzroy smiled, a curving, splendid smile, a Fitzroy Angursell smile. "'Thank you' will be quite sufficient, my dear Kip. Seeing as you've already done all the hard work of taking down the empire and creating a home for me."

~

They went down together. The signet ring felt odd on Cliopher's right hand; the gold kept catching his eye. There were candles in each of the inn's many windows, reflecting on the glass and the polished fittings inside, and the old building seemed to be full of its own ghostly, friendly merriment in echo of the party beyond its doors.

Sara was sitting on the bench outside the door, well-wrapped in her shawls. She smiled with immense fondness when they reached her. "There you are, Kip, Fitzroy," she said, quite as if they had not been unexpectedly gone a month. "Don't you both look *splendid*. How are you?"

"We have tales from here to the House of the Sun and back to tell you," Cliopher said.

Fitzroy nudged him with his elbow. "Look at that! You *are* capable of making dramatic pronouncements to people you love as well as those you dislike."

"I've been learning from the master," Cliopher replied, and Sara laughed.

She breathed in deeply, inhaling the fragrance of the tiarë flowers as Cliopher bent over to embrace her shoulders; the scent seemed to agree with her, for when he straightened, a bit of healthy colour had come into her cheeks. "I look forward to hearing everything, when things have quieted after the festival. Everyone's out on the green, as you can see."

The green was full of garlands and candle-lanterns and fireflies and music. Great bonfires burned at each end, and there were tables along the sides of the common space filled with food and drink. A dozen musicians—including but not limited to the locals Cliopher had played with that summer—played on a small raised stage just down from the inn, and couples and groups dressed in their best were dancing with great enthusiasm. The music was catchy: traditional tunes from the region, some of them familiar from the summer, some not.

Cliopher picked out people he knew: there was Rhodin, dancing with Sardeet Avramapul, both of them in full finery, Rhodin dashing in black and dark green, Sardeet glorious as the white birds of the dawn in silver-chased white. Basil was at the table where his mead must be on offer, talking with two young men in what looked like some form of Alinorel court dress—the young Viscount and his friend, quite possibly—and there was Masseo, talking with the St-Noire blacksmith—

"There's Pali and Jullanar," Fitzroy said, pointing across the green to where the two women were standing beside a bonfire, watching the dancers. Pali was in her indigo robes, a sky-blue belt at her waist, her long hair loose to her waist.

Jullanar was wearing something that looked a deep red in the firelight, her hair catching gold and bronze lights. "Don't they look splendid," Fitzroy murmured fondly, seeming quite content to stand beside Cliopher and watch.

They stood there for several minutes, breathing in the air, the sounds, the full glory of being there, together, certain of their places. Cliopher kept an eye on his and Fitzroy's friends, and saw the moment when Pali and Jullanar caught sight of them: one elbowed the other, and both looked across the green. Jullanar waved; Pali folded her arms so her indigo robes flared around her.

"Shall we go to them?" Fitzroy asked.

Cliopher regarded him, and a beautiful thought took root in his mind. "It's a fair ke'ea, across that sea of dancers," he said, half a jest, half a challenge. "Shall we set our course in the local style, and dance across?"

"It's been a long, long time," Fitzroy said. "And I don't know the steps of these dances."

"Neither do I." He held out his hand to his friend, his fanoa, his beloved.

Fitzroy paused, and one eyebrow rose up in his most imperial gesture. "Not that that's ever stopped either of us, has it, my lord Mdang?"

"Indeed not," replied Cliopher, grinning as he saw Sara trying valiantly not to laugh at them. He winked at her. "We can make fools of ourselves together."

"Is it my turn to take the lead on that, or yours?" Fitzroy asked solicitously, and while Cliopher was still laughing, tugged him down the stairs to the green, into a space that conveniently—one might even say serendipitously—opened up for them.

EPILOGUE
THE CHILDREN OF THE SUN

Every morning, the temples set along the easternmost wall of the city of Yedoen let loose thousands of white doves to greet the rising sun and wheel in their multitudes across the vast bazaar for which the city was famous. Yedoen was the greatest trading city of Colhélhé, and the dawn flights of doves were the signal for the stalls to open, the bells to ring, the people to stir.

Today Cliopher had woken very early, his sleep disturbed by a strange, lovely dream of sailing with the Ancestors through a morning sky. He rose from bed to open the shuttered windows so he might look out over the city.

For the first time in a week, it was clear: the unfamiliar stars of Colhélhé were pale specks in a sky almost as teal as the shell of Ani's tear. Cliopher gazed down at the sleepy city, observing the small trickle of people making their way into the warren of streets and squares that contained (or at least supported) the great bazaar.

He knew from the short time they had already spent in the guest-house that no one would stir before dawn, except perhaps for Pali, who sometimes practiced her exercises before anyone else was awake.

Cliopher had come to a kind of truce with her, but it was definitely easier for both of them to be polite after breakfast.

He dressed in simple, good clothing—not so fancy he immediately looked a worthwhile mark, nor so poor that Fitzroy or Rhodin would chide him for his excessive humility—and tucked his wallet into the inside pocket of his trews, well-hidden by the tunic and open robe (if accessible through a clever slit in the tunic), in case he found some delight to add to the breakfast table.

And then he made his way from the Old Town in the northern quarter of the city, where they were staying, to the eastern wall, so he could watch the birds be released from their towers.

～

The doves were much smaller than the white birds of the dawn, but they were beautiful, their shadows tinted lavender and blue as they wheeled against the brightening sky. Cliopher admired the elaborately carved wooden grilles that covered the stone dovecotes. Each grille opened with a long string that led back to the temple precincts: they opened simultaneously, to the sound of a bell sonorously tolling the moment the sun crossed the horizon, and after the birds exploded out of their roosts in a great rush and flash of wings, the grilles clattered shut one after another.

The birds would return at sundown, he'd been told, entering their towers from another direction, each pair—they mated for life—returning to their same roost.

Cliopher climbed up a stairwell to walk along the ramparts, nodding politely at the temple guards standing watch out to sea. They were clearly there mostly for decoration, and he wondered what strange and wonderful thoughts might be passing through their minds as they looked out at the silver line of the horizon, the smudges of distant islands, the bright sails of trading ships forever coming and going from the great port of the city, which lay below the eastern temples.

The wall was only in good repair along the harbour face of the city—the houses and buildings had long since spilled outside on the inland side—and after following it north as far as he could, Cliopher descended a stair and picked one of the crooked alleys leading in roughly the right direction.

This one took him through a street of fabric vendors—thousands of bolts of coloured cotton, printed in hundreds of colours and patterns—and then opened onto the splendid square in front of the Yedoense palace of government. There was a fine fountain there, depicting fish-tailed horses—hippocampi, Fitzroy had told him—and a splendid enamelled-bronze sea dragon coiling through the water.

There were dozens of cafés along the square, and Cliopher had been slowly working his way through each of their morning's offerings. Today he went into one called 'The Silver Swan'—though the sign was certainly made of tin, and very lovely it was, too—and ordered a coffee and sweet roll for himself to enjoy on the square, and a larger package of pastries to take back to the guest-house.

Cliopher took his coffee and orange-cardamom roll to an empty table, nodding amicably to his neighbours as he sat down. It had to be admitted that the people-watching in Yedoen was fantastic.

It was said that you could find anything in the grand bazaar of Yedoen, and the Red Company had visited several times: Fitzroy and the others had regaled them with stories of their treasure-hunts in the winding streets and covered arcades.

Rhodin had taken the tales as a challenge, of course, and had been extremely happy poking for the greatest rarities he could imagine—although there had not, as of yet, been any rumour of the Merrions or their dinosaur soulmates, he and Sardeet had found many other curios and wonders to bring back to their guest-house.

Cliopher, for his part, was enjoying people-watching and exploring the book-sellers and stationers. He had already spent far too much money on new pens and inks and half a dozen notebooks. But then again Fitzroy's occasional bursts of dictation were occupying many of the pages, and Cliopher had started to take his own notes (in prose, of course) of their travels. If he ever did write a memoir—and he was coming more and more around to the idea—he would not want to ignore the adventures he had this side of his long career.

The orange-cardamom roll was excellent, better than the coffee this morning. Cliopher made a mental note of them both, ranking them against the other cafés on the square, and relaxed in his chair as a small flight of doves circled overhead and then landed on the edge of the fountain.

What a thing it was, questing with the Red Company!

Rich, rolling laughter—almost familiar, save that it was clearly feminine—drew his attention to the table a couple over from his. Two women sat there, laughing freely at whatever one had just said, faces tilted back out of the sun so he could see their profiles.

Cliopher's breath caught.

The two women looked to be about the same age—early thirties, perhaps—though the air was crackling with power around them, and if Cliopher had not spent a great deal of time with a certain great mage he would have been seriously wondering if they were divine.

But he *had* spent that great deal of time around a certain great mage.

And—these two women—were they sisters, perhaps? Or cousins? They shared a striking similarity of feature, though one was much darker-skinned than the other, and their hair was a familiar cloud of tight curls, though one wore her hair in a much sleeker and more structured style than the other.

And their eyes ... even in the shadow of their umbrella, he knew that limpid, liquid gold, the sheen of magic and the brilliance of intellect and humour.

He forced himself to finish his roll, his coffee, let them subside from their laughter. Then he wiped his mouth and brushed off any stray crumbs, and stood up, glad he'd chosen to wear that perfectly unexceptional finery Féonie had made for him.

He walked the few steps over to them, holding himself solidly in himself, and smiled easily at them. "Excuse me for the interruption, sayeva," he said politely, consciously choosing the court phrasing, his own accent. "I hope I do not offend, but may I ask your names?"

The darker-skinned one, with the more exuberant hair, gave him a candid smile. "Gladly, sir!" Her accent was educated Alinorel—he'd heard several exactly like it during his sojourn at Basil's inn. His interest sharpened even further. "I'm Domina Aurelia Anyra, Professor of Magic at the University of Tara."

She did not say more than that, but then she didn't need to: Tara was the most famous university in all the former empire of Astandalas, and to be a full professor there, at her age, was an achievement to be admired.

Cliopher bowed politely in the court style, perhaps hewing a little more closely to equal-to-equal than the Master of Etiquette would have considered appropriate. But then Cliopher and the Master of Etiquette had rarely seen eye-to-eye. The professor inclined her head back with equal courtesy. Cliopher turned to the other woman, who was regarding him with rather more suspicion.

Her skin had a curiously luminous effect, as if the bronze tone—rather like Rhodin's, he thought—was gently lit from within. Her hair was in many shapely wedges that framed her face perfectly, an effect which Cliopher knew from watching Fitzroy about his ablutions required a considerable amount of effort to achieve.

"For my part," she said, her voice rich and cultured, though her accent was almost entirely unfamiliar (could it possibly be Ystharian? The only person Cliopher could compare it to was the Lord of Ysthar—), "I am called Circe of Aiaia. Who are you, sir?"

Circe of Aiaia, who had challenged the Lord of Ysthar to the Great Game Aurieleteer, the victory-prize that world's crown, and very nearly won.

Cliopher bowed again, equal-to-equal, and then he smiled at them both. "I am Cliopher Mdang of Loaloa," he said simply. "I am the Viceroy of Zunidh."

The two women looked at each other, and then back at him, with expressions of surprise, surmise, curiosity—oh, he knew that curve of Circe's smile, that flicker of Aurelia's—*Aurelia's!*—eyebrows, that glint in their golden eyes.

And then Aurelia Anyra, Professor of Magic, said delicately, "And why did you come to our table, Lord Mdang? I have heard rumours that your lord was, shall we say, travelling ..."

He smiled at them, perfectly at ease, the white doves wheeling against the blue sky, the golden buildings, the limpid morning ear.

"Yes," he said, offering them the gift of the truth, of the wild surmise in his own heart, the match of the growing interest in theirs. Oh, what a gift to offer to his fanoa! Not one, but *two* clear relations! "I'm in the company of someone who would very much like to meet you both."

They looked at each other, the two magi, and then Circe nodded and the professor said, "I think both of us would like that very much, sir."

"Cliopher, please," he replied. "I imagine we'll be seeing a great deal of each other from now on."

Acknowledgments

With the greatest of thanks to Alexandra Rowland, for their splendid editorial work and manifold other assistance, including a certain limerick and a splendid phrase about iconoclasm they kindly permitted me to use.

Thanks also to Jessica Guarneri for her thorough copyediting and incredible turnaround times, especially with all my changing deadlines.

(Any remaining typos and infelicities are, of course, my own.)

Author's Note

At the Feet of the Sun is the second full novel (and what a long one!) in the Lays of the Hearth-Fire. There will eventually be a third (*Common and Ordinary Goods* is the provisional title), but not for a few years.

In the meantime, look for more of Cliopher and Fitzroy's adventures in the Red Company Reformed books—*The Resplendent Jullanar of the Sea* and *The Questing of Artorin Damara* (both forthcoming) are the next in line.

If you haven't discovered them already, you may well enjoy reading the novellas *Petty Treasons* (his Radiancy's perspective on Cliopher becoming his secretary), *Portrait of a Wide Seas Islander* (Buru Tovo's perspective on his journey to visit Cliopher in Solaara during the course of *The Hands of the Emperor*), and *Those Who Hold the Fire*, which expands on the young Kip's efforts to obtain the obsidian for his efela ko.

No matter how long a book is, there are always things that have to be left out from the final version. *At the Feet of the Sun* is no different; there are several bonus chapters from the perspective of the amnesiac Kip available to those who join my newsletter or the Discord server HOTE Support Group.

Thank you for reading!

— Victoria Goddard

For the newsletter: https://landing.mailerlite.com/webforms/landing/u8j8y4
For the Discord: https://discord.com/invite/bbXMcqehPs
For general news and announcements: www.victoriagoddard.ca

Milton Keynes UK
Ingram Content Group UK Ltd.
UKHW011332070324
439104UK00002B/498